Praise for *The Salt Line*

"You have created a vast world. You have created a number of worlds. And for two weeks I have been passing through your worlds and on almost every page new vistas are revealed. Vistas and sounds and smells and tastes as well as threads leading from one world to another page by page. This vast book contains some lofty peaks the likes of which I do not know many ... A glorious and mighty book. In a few weeks time I shall return to read it ... and I shall restrain myself from commencing a rereading right away ... In the meanwhile thank you for this wonder."
– Amos Oz

"Few novels such as this have been written in literature in general and in Hebrew literature in particular ... The Salt Line is a novel that gives the reader a jolt, both intellectual and emotional. Its importance lies in its attempts to observe and understand the functioning of human agency in general and Jewish-Israeli human agency in particular."
– The Brenner Prize Committee

"A monumental masterpiece ... The novel's powerful, mature narrative voice produces a flowing read that one follows with unbroken interest ... Captivating and engrossing ... [Shimoni displays] marvelous skill for telling a story, with power, intensity and rare virtuosity." – *Haaretz*

"A magnificent work which harks back both to the dimensions of the genre of the novel when it was at its peak, and to the aspiration to embrace an entire period, and to tell a story. The story is complex ... The talent is awesome ... The virtuosity Shimoni has required of himself is impressive ... It seems that he is conversant with all of the literary ploys that are at the disposal of a writer of prose." – *Iton 77*

"Colorful, rich in imagination and in precisely what it will take to transport you into another world... What will almost certainly capture your hearts will be the way in which the author describes, as if in a movie script, situations that are close to the cinematic." – *Hitrashmut*

"This is a book I shall not forget. With patience, acuity and fine discernment, a great canvas of life is spread out in this novel ... The great narrative achievement also contains great ideas. This is a book that asks what human beings have been given by religions and ideologies that have decayed, and what there is in them that cannot decay. It is a book about the passions of the body and the soul that burn within people; engendering beliefs and journeys and torments and stories."
– Prof. Nissim Calderon

"I read The Salt Line with infinite enjoyment. This is a book whose inventiveness is boundless ... The Salt Line is a rare masterpiece."
– Prof. Miki Gluzman

"A festival for book-lovers ... A special festival for Hebrew-Israeli culture ... Shimoni writes with supreme precision and polish, with a sophisticated technique and complex and credible psychology, and after doing impressive research. This text breathes, it lives and sustains itself ... Superbly written." – *Yedioth Ahronoth*

"Shimoni's ability to shape linguistic constructions are almost never seen in contemporary literature ... [He] expresses profound philosophical and social contents in a rigid and austere narrative framework ... Shimoni is a wizard at description and he uses this talent in The Salt Line to express ideas, and not to preach ... Shimoni succeeds in enthusing, exciting and enthralling us, and to make us want to take the trek together with him." – *Ynet*

YOUVAL SHIMONI

THE SALT LINE

Translated by Michael Sharp

CROWSNEST BOOKS

Crowsnest Books
www.crowsnestbooks.com

Distributed by the University of Toronto Press

This is a work of fiction. All the names, characters, businesses, places,
events and incidents in this book are either the product of the author's
imagination or used in a fictitious manner, and any similarity to actual
persons, living or dead, or actual events, is purely coincidental.

Cataloguing data available from Library and Archives Canada

ISBN 9780921332909 (paperback)
ISBN 9780921332916 (ebook)

Printed and bound in Canada

For Ayelet

The author is grateful to the Oxford Centre for Hebrew Studies
and to Literarisches Colloquium Berlin for residencies which
contributed greatly to the completion of this novel.

Contents

Part One   10

Part Two   177

Part Three   471

Part Four   707

Part One

1

A gamin lean and gloomy, a tiny Russian in a desert town where his mother's hats fail to amaze, a remote trading town in which the commotion of passing caravans is cut by muezzins' calls and the ringing of Chinese gongs and the groans of wandering winds. His clothes are worn out and dirty, and he walks on the roof of the inn between low wicker tables and wicker stools and gathers up all sorts of leftovers and puts them in his pockets, and with the very same agility pours the remnants of drink from bottles and glasses into a small squashed metal flask that he removed from its hiding place in his trousers (remnants of arak or vodka or chang, his mother won't notice the difference after a few sips anyhow), gathering up and pouring and quietly singing a song into whose Russian melody undulations steal, slow and soft like the humps of the camels he saw on the way.

But here, at the foot of this inn, there are only donkeys: grey and dusty, grazing on grass grown by a sewage ditch at the far end of the courtyard, and from the heights of the roof he throws some of his leftovers to them after burying the flask back into his trousers between the elastic and his belly. Far above him is a vast sky whose tranquility remains undisturbed other than by grains of dust, and from time to time a crow or a vulture.

"They don't want any!" the boy says, disappointed after a while, and throws another fistful of crumbs from the roof to the donkeys and puts down a few melon peels whose fruit has all been eaten. "Donkeys," he calls out to them from the roof, "Donkeys, don-keys!" And looks at them as they continue to feed on the grass. It's noon now. Hot, very hot and very dry, and no breeze stirs the scorched air.

"What d'you think, that they're birds?" a voice asks him from the far side of the roof (the speaker asks with effort, and not with the deep voice which will be attributed to him a few decades later in another country thousands of kilometers away). "Birds eat crumbs, but donkeys – no."

He speaks to the boy from his stool. He isn't sitting on it but rather his back is supported by it, and his legs are spread out in front of him on the roof layered with sand carried by the wind. The soles of his feet are bare and filthy; not only is drinking the water of this Kashgar dangerous but also when it comes into contact with cracked dry skin.

"You're a donkey yourself," the boy says to him.

The man deliberates a while at the far side of the roof, and for a moment the big toes of his bare feet rub against their neighboring toes. "That really is what I am," he says, "take a look at my ears, Sasha!" And right away behind each one of them he places two equally dusty fingers and wobbles them for a moment, and since the boy is not yet convinced, he raises the pairs of fingers to his temples and stands them up, a ridiculous image on a roof as desolate as the desert that surrounds the town.

The boy scrutinizes the man's face and the ears he's grown for himself. He hasn't decided yet how to respond to him: whether he's just-saying-so, or he's just-pretending, or whether he's just someone who his mother won't remain the girlfriend of for even a week. They first saw one another on a train between Tashkent and Andijan on one of the stopovers, but it was only at the inn in Kashgar that the man befriended his mother.

Again he draws close to the edge of the roof that has no railing despite its bone crushing height, and from there watches the donkeys feeding on the grass on the fringe of the open sewerage ditch.

"Maybe if you give them something to drink," the man says from behind, "they'd get an appetite," but the boy doesn't turn his head to him. He kneels down and rests on the palms of his hands and brings them close to the edge of the roof and leans forward.

"Give them from your bottle, Sasha, the one you hid in your trousers."

The boy bends his head farther from the edge of the roof toward the space below it. "In the end there'll be nothing left for you!" he calls to the donkeys in his high-pitched voice. "And what'll you eat tomorrow, don't you think about that?" His tangled dusty hair bobs slightly as he nods his head at them; for a long time a comb hasn't been passed through it.

"Maybe if you'd give them a little to drink -" the man says to him.

"But it's my mother's bottle! And they don't drink that, you're just saying that!"

"Haven't you ever seen them drunk? A drunk donkey is even funnier than a drunk bear, but then of course you've also never seen a bear."

"Of course I have! It was with a gypsy who played a drum for it and then the bear -"

"But you haven't seen one drunk."

"You're drunk yourself!"

The man moves his lower back nearer to the stool supporting him and again leans his elbows on the sand covering the roof. "I wish I was," he says. "Should I tell you what I am? I haven't even told your mother yet."

"Mother's in the room," Sasha says.

"Mother's in the room," the man concurs. "Generally most of the time she's in bed. Your mother must have spent half her life in bed."

Though he doesn't understand exactly what he means, the tone of his voice bothers him more than the words, Sasha turns an angry face at him. "Don't speak about her like that!"

"I only said that she likes being in bed," the man answers. "I wonder how she managed on the train without a bed, after all, you didn't have a cabin on the train did you?"

"You also didn't have one!"

"But I didn't need one. Do you know what I really need, Sasha?"

"I don't want to talk to you! I don't like the way you talk!"

"What do you know about the way one should talk?" the man answers. "You haven't seen anything in your life yet."

"I've seen lots of things! Lots!"

"Yes?" the man says doubtfully. "Like what?"

Sasha strains his mind; he's seen so many things lately that its now hard to choose one of them: for two whole weeks they travelled on the train, and in its windows landscapes changed from coniferous forests to forests of foliage and from fields to arid planes and to deserts, from marble unwalled cities to cities of mud fortified by mud walls, and no station resembled the one before it.

"A camel," he answers after a while, "a camel with two humps! We saw it from the window from close and it had something in its mouth and it was eating and you could see its yellow teeth -"

"Yes, but that camel wasn't drunk!"

"No," Sasha admitted in a quiet voice.

"So you won't get to see a drunk camel, but maybe a drunk donkey if you just take out your mother's bottle."

Sasha hesitates.

"You're a bright boy, Sasha," the man says to appease him. "One day when you're big your mother will be proud of you, if only she gets out of bed. Not that you're not big, but when you get bigger what do you want to be, someone who feeds donkeys?

Sasha ponders and picks his nose and finds something there and examines it between two fingers. "A fireman," he answers a moment later and flicks off what he removed from his nostril with his middle finger.

"A fire-man," the man slowly repeats the word. "In the middle of the desert we've got ourselves a little Petersburgian who wants to be a fireman."

"I'm not little!"

"I mean as a Petersburgian," the man says to him. "After all, in St. Petersburg there are people so tall that they have to be careful not to bump into the streetlamps, surely you still remember that, Sasha?"

No, Sasha doesn't remember at all.

"And do you remember the people who fly?"

No, Sasha also doesn't remember them; there's no such thing as people who fly!

"Once," the man gathers his knees to his chest, widening two strips in the sand, "I saw someone who flew so fast that even the birds couldn't catch up with him."

"You're just saying that!"

"I even saw horses flying! Not donkeys, but horses flying with their carriages."

"You're just saying that, Mother also doesn't believe anything you say!"

The man (only in the eyes of the boy is he "the man"; actually he's not yet twenty-three; and by the close of the twentieth century he will be called "grandfather," despite that he will never be seen by his grandson nor by his son, and the longings of the son will permeate an entire dynasty) keeps silent and sifts a fistful of sand between his fingers until his hand empties out.

"It seems to me, Sasha, that Mother will still be putting up with me at least until she gets someone new in my place," he says and again spreads his legs, returning them to the strips which he widened on the layer of sand covering the roof. His left leg doesn't return exactly to its place and he moves it a little, as if it's very necessary to be precise here. "A fireman, Sasha? There's a fireman sitting next to me, but he doesn't see the fire one meter away from him, because he only cares about the stupid donkeys. Who'll let you be a fireman if right here next to you there's a terrible fire and you do nothing about it?"

Sasha turns his head to him, and his eyes follow the large hand which is lifted and circles round and round over the desert to show him where the fire is; on and on the hand circles the parched landscape until it completes an arc and returns to the gaunt body whose back is still leaned against the stool, and taps the sunken chest, as if to say: the fire is here, here, right here – inside.

"I knew you were lying!" Sasha throws a fistful of sand from the roof.

"Why don't you give them some sand?" the man says. "Not that it'll help them to fly, donkeys don't fly. And d'you know why? Because they don't get hitched to carriages. There are only donkeys inside the carriages, sitting and scratching their beards." His eyes, which all this while have been half closed from the glare of the sun and the grains of sand, open. "Just be careful, Sasha, not to bend too far, it's one thing not to want to talk to me, and another to fall off the roof."

"I won't fall!"

"Don't break the donkey's backs, they've got enough trouble with mites." And as if having heard his words, the donkeys shake their tails to drive away the mites surrounding them, and the light of the sun clasps the miniscule wings. "And you too, Sasha, don't get your back broken like that – one *phfft* and it's had it, together with the nape of your neck. Do you know what a nape is?"

He raises his hand to the back of his neck and feels it with the tips of his fingers from top to bottom and back. "It's where you fastened the chain for Mother yesterday when she leaned forward, d'you remember that she asked you? That's where it is. One *phfft* and it's had it."

When Sasha turns to him, he sees the fingers of the man letting go of his neck and falling to the sides of his body again and from there to the layer of sand covering the roof, a layer which will thicken on and on as long as the desert continues to dispatch its grains of sand toward the roofs of the city that have invaded its domain.

"That's what it's like with women," the man says, "chains, necklaces, pendants. And men, they're only given a noose, and they don't even need to look for someone to fasten it for them, for that there's a special person wearing a special hat. Maybe that's what you'll be when you're big?"

While Sasha is weighing up his words and trying to fathom their meaning, a bird glides in the sky above and they only notice it when its shadow flutters on the edge of the roof and vanishes.

"A fireman's helmet is very nice," the man says. "I'm not saying it isn't, but how about a hat that covers the whole face? Only the eyes can be seen like this," and slowly he raises the palm of his hands and covers his face with them on both sides of his nose and spreads his fingers slightly to allow two vertical slits for eyes.

"Cuckoo," he says to Sasha. "Cuckoo! Don't you want a hat like this?"

"I don't want anything from you and Mother also doesn't! Soon she'll wake up and tell you to take your things and go!"

From under his dusty eyelashes for a moment the eyes of the man seek the bird that passed by, a crow whose cawing already wanes in the distance, as if it urged its shadow not to lag behind and then gave up on it. "But where can I go to?" the man says and with his eyebrows indicates the vast desert surrounding Kashgar.

A wagon approaches on the path to the inn and its canopy sways to the weary rhythm of its horses, and Sasha gets up and walks the length of the roof's edge to watch them from the southern side.

"Just be careful not to fall," the man calls out to him, "so that you too don't start dancing in the air for us like the one they put a noose on. Imagine your mother waking up at last and finding out you've suddenly decided to dance in the air."

"Yesterday," Sasha says to him from the side of the roof, "Mother danced with somebody else, not with you!"

The horses stop at the back entrance of the inn, and the ascending column of dust they raised passes over them as the wagoner jumps from his bench to the sand.

"She danced with that soldier," Sasha says and watches the wagoner, who lingers next to the left wheel.

"Exactly which soldier are you talking about, Sasha?"

"That soldier with the moustache!"

"The-soldier-with-the-moustache," the man says slowly from his stool. "A soldier with a moustache, and hasn't that wagoner down there got a moustache?"

"No," Sasha answers.

"Take a good look," the man says from his place.

"He hasn't got one!"

"Maybe if you lean over a bit more," the man says, "you can see better, it's hard to see a moustache from so high up."

"He hasn't got one!" Sasha says, "He hasn't!

"So he hasn't got one," the man says, "you don't have to get mad about a moustache, Sasha. That crow also didn't have a moustache and that didn't bother it at all. Did you see how its shadow raced across the roof?"

Sasha nods his head.

"Well, that's what you do when you want to fly, you race across the roof." The man presses his back slightly backward against the stool, and when it's blocked by the wicker table, an empty bottle shakes. "You race until you work up speed and then lift your arms and go like this in the air," and he raises and lowers his arms spread out to the sides.

"It was just its shadow! Just its shadow and not itself!"

"Doesn't it do the same thing on the ground? Race until it works up speed?"

Beneath them the wagoner is trying to extract from the tip of his finger a fine splinter which is stuck in it.

"When you flew a kite, Sasha," the man says, "isn't that how you made it fly? Racing with it until it works up speed and lifts up into the air?"

"I don't want to talk to you!"

"No, then no. If that's the case I'll fly by myself, I don't need cowards with me."

The man leans his elbow on the seat of the stool whose wickerwork is worn down and unravelling, and that way lifts himself up and stands on his feet. "You think I wasn't scared that I'd fall? Sure, I was, very scared! But if you think too much, you don't run fast enough in order to fly," and with his hand he indicates all the places one can fly to from the roof of this inn – in the north and in the south, in the east and in the west, all the four winds of the sky which from here do not seem much different from each other, not in their expanse nor in their desolation.

"*Hzzz!*" the wagoner in the courtyard says to one of the horses, and the horse again turns his head forward.

The two of them are watching him from the roof, the man and the boy, and Sasha memorizes that call: *hzzz!*

"That's also not the way to fly back to St. Petersburg," the man says, "if by any chance you want to fly home."

"I don't want to go home!"

From the back entrance of the inn a stocky woman comes out and places the finger of the wagoner in her hand and examines it until she finds the end of the splinter stuck there, perhaps from the wheel spoke, and removes it between her fingernails.

"Do you want to race me, Sasha? Who gets to the edge faster?" And with a motion of the hand the man invites the boy to draw near him, to come even closer, nothing to be afraid of; and to stand still next to him, yes just like that.

A long, wide, sandy stretch of roof is now spread out in front of the two of them, up to the end there are no tables and stools, and all is clear for a race, and beyond the roof all the vast space is absolutely clear, there are two ends to it, the one distant, beyond the horizon, and the other near, just two floors below them.

The two of them are now standing at the southern edge of the roof, the man in cheap cotton dusty clothes, and the boy in his worn-out Russian clothes, and below them, on the path leading to the inn, another wagon now approaches.

"Let's see who can fly higher," the man says to the little head next to his hip, "me or you or the crow. It tried and succeeded, so why shouldn't we?"

He shakes his legs again, once the right and once the left. Sasha also shakes his little legs and their shadows quiver on the roof. "So I'll start to count now: one, two," – from the corner of his eye he studies Sasha's face and his stance, in case he'll drop out of this race to the end of the roof and onward, or the contrary, he'll suddenly begin to run before starting time – "and thr-ee-" – for a moment he delays, the legs of the two of them are taut, and before the number is completed he lowers his gaze toward a wagon entering the courtyard.

"Let's wait a bit," he says. The wagon's horses lessen their speed and the dust they raise lessens too. "If a bird isn't concentrated, do you know where it can find itself Sasha?"

"I once saw a baby dove and it didn't know how to fly yet and it hardly had any feathers and suddenly it fell down from the window –"

"The windowsill," the man says.

"Then its mother flew down to it and afterward tried to touch it with her beak and it moved a little but only because of the beak, then she touched it again on the tummy –"

"Like this?" the man suddenly leans over Sasha and bends his head down to the small belly and rubs it with his bony nose until he becomes ticklish and giggles, and the sounds form a fine fragile path into the hot dusty air.

"But you didn't see donkeys from your window," the man says. "Baby doves, but definitely not donkeys! And your mother surely didn't stay in bed there all the time. Didn't she take you for walks? Straight out of bed and off to Nevsky Avenue? And to the Fontanka? And next to the Semyonovsky Bridge?"

Sasha fixes his eyes at him; the last name is unfamiliar to him.

"Semyonovsky," the man says, "where all the bad people end up."

Below the two of them, with hurried speech and agitated hand movements the second wagoner is describing some incident which occurred a short while ago before they reached here from one of the far-off alleyways.

"Do you know, Sasha, what they do to them after putting a noose around the neck? They tickle their tummies! And then they simply take one false step and fall down below – one *phfft* and they've had it!"

"You're just saying that!" Sasha becomes angry, but before completing his statement he moves slightly and draws a step away from the man.

"What's wrong, Sasha?" the man also moves from his spot. "I'm only asking you to do it for me."

"Too bad Mother got to know you! Right away when we saw you on the train I told her not to speak to -"

"Your mother," the man interrupts him, "with all she'd drunk, would have even spoken to the donkeys."

"Don't speak about Mother like that!"

"And if I do, will you push me down below? What more do I have to tell you about your mother, maybe the way everyone looked at her on the train? And what songs the soldiers sang to her, and when everyone around heard -"

"Shut up!" Sasha shouts, "Shut up! Shut up!" and covers his ears with the small palms of his hand.

> "She entered the inn,"

the man sings,

> "and the innkeeper said to her -"

"Shut up! shut up!" Sasha shouts and fastens his hands to his ears,

> "I'll host you in my inn
> And you'll host me in yours -"

Sasha removes his hands from his ears and raises his fingers to the corner of his eyes, first to his right eye and then to his left and wipes them on his trousers. "They didn't really mean it! The soldiers were just having fun!"

"Yes, just having fun," the man replied. "And not only the soldiers, the travelling salesman also, what a nerve he had, what was he thinking to himself, that your mother could be bought with creams?"

Over his ears Sasha's thin fingers are again curved into small fists until their knuckles turn white.

"He should have been flung from the train," the man continued, "one *phfft*! It could have been easy for you, when he stood there in the passageway with the open door. It's just that you, Sasha, d'you know what you are? A coward!"

Sasha moves his palms slightly away from his ears and turns his head toward the man and looks at him again, not at his face but rather at his body positioned precisely at the edge of the roof.

"Just a tiny push," the man says. "Any child could do it!" And he draws closer to the edge of the roof, and his toes are already in the space beyond it.

Below them in the courtyard a foreign name is being repeated over and over, and from the derisive tone of the words accompanying it, it's apparent there is also a reference to that person's mother and father and their ancestors. Grains of sand continue to mount upon the wagon, and on the canopy of the second one, whose stitches have begun to unravel, two patches wave in the wind like small wings.

"Just look at the difference between the wagons here and the ones in St. Petersburg!" the man says. "And that's without mentioning the coaches and the carriages and the horses - don't you miss the coaches and the carriages of St. Petersburg, Sasha? And the Neva, God, what beautiful bridges the Neva's got!" He looks down, and in the sewage ditch at the bottom the murky water continues to flow, slow and thick from its foulness. "That's their Neva, Sasha."

As if it's listening to them, one of the donkeys sticks up a long ear and then shakes it in order to get rid of the flies which were bothering it and brays.

"Hee-haw," the man says on the roof, "hee-haw, hee-haw! And how does a horse go?" He stretches out the palm of his hand into the air to examine the breeze passing through, and instantly grains of sand which the wind dropped gather in it. "Not just any horse, the horse of a carriage with decorations and curtains, have you ever seen one like that?"

"Of course, I've have! I've seen lots of times!"

"A minister's carriage," the man says, "not just any carriage."

"We once even saw the Tsar's carriage! We saw it from far away because they wouldn't let us come near, there were lots of people around and you could hardly stand and everyone ran to see it from close and to kiss its shadow, Mother also wanted to."

"Why shouldn't Mother kiss the shadow? After all, she has to kiss somebody." Sasha glances at him with suspicion.

"To see a carriage, Sasha," the man says, "not from below but rather from above, like from here. That way you can see all the dirt because they only clean around it and not on top. The sides were so polished you would have thought it had been licked by a tongue."

"Once..." Sasha hesitated for a moment, "Mother took something out of my eye like that with her tongue so that it wouldn't prick and her tongue tickled me a bit when she did it, so I laughed and suddenly it came out."

"Listen here," the man says, "what your mother only knows to do with her tongue! I mean when she's awake, and she's not too drunk. And when she's not in the mood. And when she's not too hot and not too cold. And when there's nobody more promising around. For instance, that travelling salesman with his suitcase of creams."

"She -"

"It's not important," the man says, "don't tell me. What I don't know is like it never happened."

"She put her arms around him," Sasha said. "She thought that I didn't see but I did!"

"Don't tell me about it," the man says, "didn't you understand me?"

Sasha hesitantly moves away from him one step and then another toward the straw stools and the low wicker tables. On the table near him, whose wickerwork the sand has already patched together, an empty bottle sparkles in the sun.

"And that carriage," the man says, "d'you know what happened to it? Its roof flew right off together with all its dirt, and the sides also flew off, and the wheels came loose, and from the top you could see one of them rolling to the other side of the street, as if it had never been attached at all! And the horses weren't completely finished off yet. The minister, yes, but it took time for the horses to die. One still lifted its head and bared its teeth; they were so yellow!"

"You're making it up!" Sasha becomes angry.

"I only wish I was making it up."

The wind passes through their hair, rumpling it and mingling with more grains into it.

"And the minister's head, d'you know what happened to it?"

Sasha's eyes stare at him and a spark flickers on his tender stalk-like neck, a reflection from the bottle in front of him.

"First, while he was still in the carriage the minister tried to raise his arm, he thought he could stop everything with his arm, as if they had only thrown something rotten at him, like as if I would throw something at you now" – his gaze strays for a moment on the roof until it arrives at the wicker table – "let's say this bottle, wouldn't you raise your arm?"

The soles of his feet take another step and sink their heels into the sand. Step by step he advances from the edge of the roof toward the boy, to the low wicker table and to the bottle placed in its center, and Sasha draws back from him and his little legs bump into the stool behind them and suddenly cave in and seat him there against his will as if in a brace.

"Wouldn't you lift your arm so that a piece wouldn't suddenly get into your eye? Well, that's what the minister did," the man grabs the bottle, "he lifted his arm. And one of the horses suddenly began to rise up on its back legs with its horseshoes in the air, as if it'll stop the bomb that way, and a moment later you already couldn't see a thing, only smoke. And there was also the smell of sulfur like you smell arak here. Can't you smell the arak?"

Sasha's eyes are fixed on the bottle which sparkles in the sun.

"And you could hear the horses," the man says and advances another step toward Sasha. "You couldn't hear the minister, but you could hear the horses whinnying." The palm of his right hand sways at the side of his body back and forth and the bottle sways with it, and the remnants of arak move inside it and turn white-hot in the sun.

"Hee-hee, hee-hee. And the bomb," he says in a moment, "how does a bomb go?" He hoists his arm backward with the bottle and its shimmering glass clasped in it and holds it for a moment, hung in the air.

The boy's eyes are fixed on the mouth of the bottle tilted downward and dribbling the remains of the drink onto the sand, and when the bottle is raised forward and hits the edge of the table, a dull thud rises from the wicker.

"And how does a table go?" the man says. He is still standing in the same spot and the wind rustles around him as he raises the bottle to the level of his eye and inspects it to see whether it's cracked. "There wasn't one window that wasn't broken, and there was a little boy, maybe your age, who even made faces at me from his window before that, but afterward I didn't see him anymore."

"Once," Sasha says from his stool, "I was pricked by a pin and it hurt terribly and lots lot of blood came out my finger, so Mother –"

"Listen everyone," the man says. "Sasha cut his finger!"

"It pricked me!" Sasha says, "The pin in her hat pricked me and lots and lots blood came out my finger so Mother –"

"From a hatpin!" the man says. "Which hat was it Sasha, the one with the feathers?"

Sasha looks at him with suspicion. "With the flowers," he answers a moment later.

"With the flowers!" The man drags a stool from his right and sits upon it opposite Sasha, and between them stands the wicker table and the bottle once again in its center. "Isn't that the hat from the train?"

Sasha tries to remember.

"The soldiers were so impressed by her hat! They all started to sing together."

"Shut up!" Sasha shouts, "Shut up!"

"The whole compartment," the man said, "everyone there started to sing to her: *She entered the inn –*"

"Shut up," Sasha says again, before he carries on singing, but his voice becomes weak and his eyes are cast down to the wicker table and the bottle in its center.

"D'you know what I'd do in your place, Sasha? One push from the roof and I won't be here anymore to make you angry. I'd go straight to heaven or to hell, you either go up or down. Didn't Mother tell you about hell?"

Sasha doesn't answer.

"It's even hotter there than here! And on the beds there they stretch all those who are too short and shorten all those who are too long. And d'you know what they do to someone exactly the right size?"

No, Sasha doesn't know.

"They let someone like that dream his dreams, because there's no greater punishment than that, and when he wakes up in the morning they make him see all that he dreamed around him. Let's say, Sasha, that he dreamed about – what makes you scared the most?"

"That the train will crash," Sasha immediately answers. He's forgotten his decision not to answer, and now his bright eyes don't see the roof and the surrounding expanse, but rather other sights. "The train was speeding fast and suddenly another train was coming and all of a sudden there was a big bang and I was scared that –"

With a brisk movement the man grabs the bottle and forcefully strikes the roof with it, on the solid hardness beneath the sand, and this time the bottle shatters. Only the glass neck remains clasped in his hand, and the glass bottom lies on the sand and spikes protrude from its rim.

"From Minsk to Pinsk," the man says, "asailorsoughttoseeksixsheep."

"What?" Sasha says.

"Then in hell you would've woken up inside the train," the man said to him, "and opposite, the second train would come, straight toward you at the fastest speed. FromMinsktoPinskasailorsoughttoseeksixsheep. Can you say that?"

"From Minsk to Pinsk?" Sasha asks and his eyes are still fixed on the glass spikes.

"It doesn't matter," the man says. "The fire made by two trains crashing is nothing compared to the fire of hell."

For a moment, he looks around him and the boy's eyes follow his gaze as if onward from there, in the distance, enormous flames will be seen bursting from the cracks of the earth or from the grains of sand, flames that fuse the expanse of sand with the horizon and the rim of the sky which in a few moments will catch ablaze to the height of its dome.

"Relax," he says to Sasha. "The fire of hell is deep enough."

Sasha considers his words gravely; being high up of the roof calms him. And as if swapping a secret with someone his own age he turns to the man and asks him what he's the most scared of. "The very most," Sasha says to him.

"Of you, Sasha!" the man answers. "That you don't push me off the roof!"

He spins the broken neck of the bottle on the table like the needle of a compass or like a frantic second hand of a watch. "FromMinsktoPinsk," he says, "once I could say it so fast, even faster than the train, even faster than blocks of ice in a stream at the start of spring. Have you ever seen blocks of ice in a stream? Once a goat stood on one like that, it was still tied to its staff, and how did it go? Come on, Sasha, how does a goat go?"

Sasha looks at him.

"Meh-meh-meh?" he chuckles suddenly.

"From all the noise of the river and the ice," the man says, "you couldn't hear the goat at all. And on the opposite bank a few children stood with a giant branch, and what did they do? They pushed it into the water!"

But why? First only Sasha's eyes ask and afterward his voice as well.

"Because they were bad children!" The man spins the neck of the bottle on the wicker table again. "That's what it's like when you're bad. And not that I was any better than them." He stops the broken bottle and places the palm of his hand on its spikes as if to check whether its weight is ample for them to be stuck into his flesh. "Have you ever been bad, Sasha?"

"I once lied to Mother, she came to ask me if I -"

"Really bad," the man interrupts him, "so bad that you couldn't understand how people in the street don't cross over to the other side."

"She gave me money to buy something and I didn't buy what she said because I wanted something else and afterward I told her that I lost it on the way and I -"

"Wow, you're so bad, Sasha!" the man says to him and examines the hollows made by the glass spikes in his palm.

"And I cried but not really, only so she'd think that I was sorry that I lost it, and then she kissed me and hugged me so tight and after that I really did cry with tears and everything because she hugged me like that -"

"Then maybe you won't get to heaven," the man says. "No-no, we're through with heaven."

Again he places the palm of his hand on the spikes of the broken glass and secures them to it and closes his eyes and concentrates on the sharpening pain in his flesh.

"You're bleeding!"

"And how does blood go?" And with the same decisive movement with which he brought his palm close to the glass spikes the man now bends down to the sand and lifts up the base of the broken bottle and rises and brings it close to his face, to his eyebrow and his nose and the hollow of his cheek – the longest glass spike he directs toward the slope of the cheek and the shortest to the bridge of the nose, until the thick greenish bottom conceals his eye, but he doesn't yet fix any glass spike to his flesh.

"Wipe it," Sasha says, because drops of blood are flowing from the palm of the man's hand down the slope of his arm.

"*Tiff-tiff,*" the man says, "that's how blood goes." Through the glass bottom of the bottle he looks at the boy, and the thick base covers his eye like a kind of eyepatch for whose need the deed has not yet been done, and that deed will be done by itself, by its spikes.

"In the end you won't be able to see anything! It'll get in your eye and you won't be able to see anything and -"

"So I won't see," the man answers, but moves the broken bottle slightly away from the eye whose brow has been injured, and places it on the wicker table. His tongue slants toward the corner of his mouth and licks the blood which has flowed to it, and above his split eyebrow a fresh drop of blood immediately appears.

At the sight of the dripping blood Sasha says "I once saw a bear. A gypsy was drumming on his drum so that the bear would dance -"

"A bear," the man says. "Sasha once saw a bear! Isn't that the bear you spoke about before?"

"The gypsy was drumming on his drum but the bear didn't want to dance so the gypsy hit it with a whip and the bear lifted its foot a little, but it had a sore there with flies so straight away it put it back down and the gypsy hit it again, so I put my hands over my eyes - -"

The man sticks his tongue out to lick the blood, "what was he singing to his bear? Was he singing about honey?"

"He was drumming!" Sasha answers, "Drumming, not singing! He was drumming on his drum, don't you understand? He gave it sugar but it didn't help. The bear licked his hand and straight after that he beat his drum but the bear -"

"He should have given it honey," the man said, "not sugar, honey! Don't you know bears like honey, Sasha?"

"And afterward a boy passed a hat around to the people, but nobody wanted to give him money because the bear wouldn't dance, so the gypsy -"

"Blood and honey," the man says.

"So the gypsy hit it with his whip," Sasha says, "right on his foot with the sore! He hit it hard and the bear lifted it a bit and he hit it again and I couldn't watch so I -"

"You put your hands over your eyes," the man says. "Isn't that what you did so that you wouldn't see anything? So why don't you also do that now, Sasha."

Slowly and ponderously he rises from the stool and pushes it back and turns to the stools alongside and advances and passes one and bumps into another and continues on and shoves another one aside with his leg and moves ahead on his way to the edge of the roof, and the bare soles of his feet make footprints in the layer of sand and the wind hastens to blur them.

Sasha, after watching him for a while, gets up and hurries after him and takes hold of his hand – they've known each for a whole week and the man didn't always annoy him like that (he's yet to annoy many more people in another country decades later, at the close of the century) – and hangs on to it and is dragged behind him for a meter or two and is dropped and then takes hold of his foot and doesn't let go even when the man shouts at him to let go. With his slender hands, Sasha grasps the man's knee, his shin, his ankle, and is dragged behind him a meter and another meter and another meter between the stools on the sand covering the roof, on and on he's dragged like that close to the edge, where beyond lies the wide-open space to the courtyard of the inn down below and straight ahead to the entire empty vast expanse.

"So now I'll dance," the man says, "just like your bear.

2

Leh, 1904

In the fluctuating light that floating clouds dimmed and inflamed and whose hues varied from moment to moment, Dr. McKenzie returned his gaze to the small window and was glad that none of the patients or their many relatives were to be seen in the room: the shadows of the clouds draped the houses that were piled up on each other in the distance, houses that were in what was called the capital city only because the villages in the vicinity were smaller, and his fondness for the place was aroused again, despite its remoteness: it was not the roof of the world like the mountain range surrounding it, but rather a god-forsaken hole that only people who had lost their way and missionaries came to live in by choice, arriving fully conscious and not on a stretcher.

The slopes again changed their shades: a new cloud covered the sun, larger than its predecessor, and the golden light waned and afterward turned mauve together with the slopes, and the shadow of the cloud, murky with dust, was cast over the entire small town. In the main street perhaps beasts of burden were still progressing on their way to unload their goods, tea and salt, silk and velvet, wool and peaches and pots and cauldrons and opium, but he was more interested in what wasn't being peddled.

From the corridor now rose the familiar smell of cooked food, surely tsampa, and though he had no desire at all for barley porridge, he was not angered by this violation of the rules, because the rules had still not been written on any signpost or wall, and anyway only a few would know how to read them. In his first years here he was sometimes still taken aghast by the sights of this hospital, which had been erected with good intent and staggering ignorance, but gradually he became used to it, and not infrequently instead of becoming angry he was amused, and even wondered if in some other place in the world, on this continent or another from which he came, he would have been amused like that during his work, even for a few moments.

The large signpost that detailed the characteristics of leprosy one after another – 1) Leprosy is a disease caused by bacteria. 2) Most people have a natural resistance to leprosy bacteria. 3) Leprosy in not transmitted by heredity. 4) Leprosy in all its stages is curable. – had not yet been placed at the side of the path in the year in which that injured man had been brought to the hospital on an improvised stretcher carried by four coolies; more than half a century would pass until then, and on the semi-wall in the entrance to the building, instructions for visitors had still not been written. They would be written only at the end of that year, and from time to time the doctor would try them out in his head, correcting and adding and removing in order that they be clear enough when finally written: 1) Spitting is forbidden. 2) The spitting of Chutki Pan Masala on the walls or on the floor is forbidden. 3) Please use the spittoons and garbage tins. 4) Visiting the hospital in a state of intoxication is strictly forbidden. 5) It is forbidden to donate gifts or money to hospital staff in the event of the birth of a male son, or the recovery from a serious illness, or in order to bypass those waiting in line. Before these instructions are to be written, there will be a need to fill the cracks in the wall and to get rid of the lizards who inhabit them and to whitewash it all afresh, and for that too no small amount of time will be required.

To the first instructions, which had been turning over in his head for some while, he now added, because the smell of smoke also irritated the nostrils of the injured man in his passed-out state: 6) The lighting of fires in the corridor and the cooking or frying of tsampa is strictly forbidden!

For a moment, above the pale face of the injured man, a thin anguished face in which the eyes are sunk and its beard unkempt, he ponders if it would be advisable to append to the list of prohibitions one more: the use of magic lanterns in the confines of the hospital is strictly forbidden. Yes, the thought passed through his head, despite that in the whole of Leh there was but one such apparatus, and only an oil lamp projected the pictures.

Once again he moved the toes of the injured man up and down, slowly and gently; the big toe was generally the first designated for amputation. Afterward the gangrene spreads to the other toes, and advances from them to the fleshy padding of the soles, and in severe cases continues on to the heels and from there climbs toward the shins. To deteriorate to that stage, ice and snow are not necessary, accumulative dampness and temperatures close to zero and continued neglect would be enough. After the loss of sensation in the fingers, and the loss of the will and ability to remove boots, plus the fear of seeing what will be revealed inside them, the gangrene acquires optimal conditions.

Its development is covert, and time passes until the extent of it is clear; not infrequently it spreads to the thighs, and when they are amputated their owner becomes a shadow of his former self that someone else transports from place to place, if he doesn't have the strength to drag himself by his hands (usually the hands are less damaged) or he drives himself on a board with wheels.

The injured man hadn't yet been awakened by the tumult rising from the corridors and from the sick wards, despite the large crowd there, men, women, and children, and against the instructions which the doctor formed in his mind, they did not hesitate to eat Chutki, to spit pan masala on the floor and walls, to ignore the spittoons, to visit the sick in a state of intoxication, to give tips to the medical staff to advance them in the queues: five rupees or ten, or blocks of yak butter spotted with flies.

With the sick came relatives and with them sacks and pouches full of rattling housewares and food for the coming period and some bundles of firewood. Fires were lit at the end of the corridors – the first time he saw a fire here he could not believe his eyes, but that is natural here no less than the murmurings of the witch doctor – and pots and cauldrons bubbled over them. Milk was churned in dripping cloth pouches, and ropes were stretched from wall to wall and chunks of meat were hung from them to dry, and to all these he adjusted and no longer tried to oppose.

The town, which only had one street worthy of its name, took pride mainly in the palace of King Namgyal that looked like a poor imitation of the Potala in Tibet despite having been built before it and all the remains of its glory having been long lost: all the carvings of the large gate have been eroded by the lashing of the rains and the interchangeable sun and snow, if they have not yet been nibbled on by voracious woodworms; and in the empty halls the frescos have faded, the colorful hangings with the devas and demons illustrated on them have become tattered. The giant statues of Buddha have become filthy from the soot of the wicks, and in the royal library grains of dust and moths vie with each other for the remains of decaying pages whose bindings have come apart.

So meager was the palace that for the coronation ceremony of King Namgyal the guests were asked to bring their own chairs with them, and when it was over the hosts hurried to thank them for this contribution before it would be taken from them. Afterward, the royal family gathered again in the single room that was heated in the palace, and Princess Detchin played with the gift she had received – a squeaking doll. To her mother, the queen, the missionary and his wife gave a small flask of hair oil, and the commissioner and his wife garnered the affection of the king with a magic lantern capable of projecting sights of London, Paris, and Rome onto the fading frescos. In return they were given by the servants four loaves of bread baked in the fire oven of the palace, each one wrapped in wrinkled newspaper.

But above the palace was a glorious sky whose clouds, mauve and gold and black, were colored by the transformations of the weather and the light, and at the rim of the sky the highest mountains in the world surrounded the valley and the palace that overlooked the capital city, and each night the snow on the peaks conquered another part of the slopes with its whiteness.

In the journal of his travels, after having visited the graves of his predecessors, intrepid explorers like himself (and more than a few such journals the doctor had read for the purpose of his plan), the Swedish explorer Hedin waxed poetic thus: "A yellow-reddish light falls on the gravestones and on the poplar trunks, and the mountain wind blows reminding the leaves of the hubris of all things. However soon in the commissioner's home bottles of champagne will be opened at the farewell dinner given for another crusader whose wanderings were not yet over in the wilderness of central Asia."

Who that crusader written about there was, the doctor did not remember, and perhaps Hedin was writing about himself. Either way, each and every year, in the few months during which the mountain passages thawed, some fame craving geologist or archeologist would land up in Leh, a zoologist seeking a new species of animal to be named after him, a botanist for the self-same reason pursuing a plant that no one had ever seen, or a bird watcher seeking a bird that does not fly in European skies, and in the small European colony even one guest was enough to change its entire daily routine. And the plans of the guests would also change: those who came from Western universities as well, whose budgets funded their research, on their arrival to this remote hole of Leh their aims were less clear than they had been, and not infrequently, within a few months and despite their plans, something inside them to which the doctor was unable to attach a name unraveled, regardless that the doctor himself was well acquainted with that sense of unravelling.

So isolated was this place, that at times it seemed to be a world unto itself with its own laws, its gods and idols and demons and its monks who knew how to interpret each whim of these creatures with the confidence with which the doctor diagnosed an easily identifiable illness (only a few were easily identified; with all the others he felt his way until they disappeared or worsened until there was no doubt as to what they were).

Among the guests staying here were arrogant people in whose eyes the Ladakhi were not far removed in their development from apes, and there were others who after a month in Leh, sometimes even less, already began inserting into their speech, by necessity or not, a word in Ladakhi, and many adopted the local greeting and insisted on that "joolay" as on a magic password which will open up the secrets of the East to them. Even a formidable explorer such as Hedin, after a few discoveries that bought him everlasting fame, frequently used joolay.

There was a time, at least until the summer of ninety-seven, when McKenzie himself dreamed of everlasting fame which he would win on discovering a miracle drug for some incurable disease (though for animals and not for humans); and afterward his dreams narrowed to the discovery of the disease itself, which at least would be named after him, and in the end he was far from that as well. Even his distinguished teacher, John Alfred White, failed to achieve that. Indeed, all those diseases had existed in the world for thousands of years before he was born into it in a small village in the county of Oxfordshire, and the thought that he, Ed McKenzie, would eliminate their viruses from the world was highly presumptuous no less than some of his other hopes which were felled that summer.

He therefore felt no sorrow on hearing about others who were forced to relin-

quish their hopes, if because of their rude awakenings or if because of their fellow-
men, for instance that explorer, a fellow countryman, to whom it became clear that
all the ancient scrolls he had unearthed had been recently faked, or the boastful
Frenchman whose escapades were mocked at the modest balls of the commissioner's wife: how he had been whipped by his captors , how they dragged him in the
water between the jaws of crocodiles ("Nikotzeh-nikotzeh," he said to his captors
in their language after each lashing or snapping of the jaws, meaning: "Everything's
okay"), and how they placed a white-hot metal rod close to his eyes, and only the
memory of his loved one which caused his eyes to tear saved him from blindness.

The memory of a loved one, McKenzie knew, did not save one from anything.

"Nikotzeh-nikotzeh," he now said softly without believing in it, and opposite
him the injured man still hadn't opened his eyes.

He had seen more than a few wounded men here, the dying and the dead too,
and more than he pitied this injured man he was curious to know to what purpose
he had come all the way here. But it was now superseded by a different curiosity,
the one he had been concerned with the entire past year.

From the small window facing north, the greyish cloud could still be seen veiling
the alleys of the bazaar with its shadow, and the caravan must have been already
unloading most of its cargo there under the watchful eye of the caravan-bashi.
Isa knows how to keep an eye on dozens of his animals while at the same time on
dozens of coolies, on the merchandise being unloaded, and also on the merchants
of the bazaar who try to undervalue its worth.

If three months ago he had been surprised by the doctor's request, his amazement was not evident in his face. He was indeed asked for something which did
not belong to his field of expertise – not disinfectant substances, nor bandages, nor
pain relievers – nevertheless it doesn't seem that his request puzzles Isa any more
than all sorts of other requests, and perhaps over the years he's already become
used to the strange requests of the Europeans.

"I'll try and get it for you," he said then, and this cautious statement was
enough for the doctor; it was many more times trustworthy than the immediate
response from his aide, Rasul, who without hesitation would promise anything
desired by those who approached him, from shells used as wind instruments to
elixirs with the power to restore male potency or to mend a broken heart.

He hadn't yet tried the shells – some time would pass until he would request
them to be bought for him – but one evening on one of the local festivals he tested
a few flasks of the elixirs in the bazaar, and in his heart he was thankful for the
narrow alley on which he could totter along from wall to wall without falling, and
also reminded himself that there was no point in repairing the one or the other:
after all, both those organs, the one in his chest and the one between his legs, won't
be put to future use. He could perhaps return to Rome one day, and also stay at
that hotel again next to the Via Veneto, and perhaps even be given their room

again with the small balcony facing the alley, but on that railing there – stone railing stained with pigeon droppings – the one who leaned with him at the time will never lean again.

"I'm cold," she said to him then, "hold me," and the two of them entered the room. A dozen red roses on the verge of wilting stooped from the vase which stood in the center of the small table, and when Kate bent forward to smell them (a few of them were already balding, and red petals were scattered on the table), he could see her rounded breasts in the décolletage of her blouse.

3

"Don't pay me now, pay me only if I get what you want," is what Isa said before his caravan went on its way. With these people of the East it's indeed preferable not to keep the price open for last minute bargaining, but he relied on Isa not to take advantage of his weakness – the weakness of someone wishing very much for something he doesn't have, and even if he does obtain it there's no guarantee it will fulfill its purpose.

The entire length of the western slopes now turned gold, except for their rifts whose depths darkened, but the gilding was temporary, dependent on the whims of the clouds and the wind. And the wind spun the clouds and unraveled them, passed over the prayer flags of the monasteries setting them in motion in order to carry their verses to the heavens (for that's what they believed here).

With a skillful gentleness he now held the soles of the injured man and massaged them again. He transferred his hand from the little toes to the big toes and moved each one up and down, and whilst doing so he again sensed the flaccidity of the skin which had softened and the chill of the flesh that brought to mind the touch of a drowned man drawn out of the water.

When the man was brought here and unloaded from the stretcher and the coolies sent outside, he had to carefully peel away the filthy bandages which were wrapped around his legs, and because of the stench he breathed through his mouth. The soles which were exposed were swollen and filthy, and even under the filth the change in color could be discerned, but they did not yet have the shade that necessitates immediate amputation.

The nails of the small toes were ingrown, and between the toes here and there were signs of a fungal infection, an ailment that actually had life in it with no fatal danger lurking. Organs do not fall off from fungal infection, amputation is also not required, no one suffering from it arouses pity like the cripples stricken with frostbite or leprosy, and if not pity – since the heart had hardened even before he reached here – at least a revulsion so acute you want to get rid of them at any cost.

In Rome and in Naples the filth of the beggars was enough to intimidate Kate. "Let them ask, but quietly," she said, "if they would only ask quietly and not pester one, I would give them." She wanted to school them, just as she wanted to school slack porters and sluggish waiters or the hotel receptionist; she had no doubt the receptionist had winked at the two of them when he gave them the key to their room, despite that on the first day, when they arrived with their suitcases, the wink flattered her. The next times it annoyed her so much that she considered complaining in writing to the Baedeker publishing house, who with such negligence recommended a hotel as dubious as this and for which they are paying good money (it was McKenzie who paid, and not with his money but rather from the monies he borrowed for the purpose of this trip which was intended to mend a few unmendable matters). It was not at all clear whether the clerk blinked for some other reason; McKenzie was of the opinion that he was suffering from some allergy, perhaps to the pollen of the yellow flowers blossoming in the hotel garden.

While still fastidiously examining the frostbite of the injured man's big toes, Kate came to mind again, from the small soles of her feet with blisters from walking the streets of Rome to the brown belt which she bought in order to emphasize her waist to the new hairstyle that she adopted there for herself. "When in Rome do as the Romans do," she said to him, and within a few days adopted a few more behaviors, but the beggars of Rome she detested and also feared as if not only was their filth and stench contagious but also their deformities; the empty orb of a street cat's eye is not as threatening as that of a blind man ("Bella donna, bella donna," one such had called out to her in the hoarse voice of his drunkenness, exactly the way young healthy Italian men called out to her with bravado, despite having only one eye and one hand with which to grasp the edge of her coat).

"One bothers you in the street and one winks at you in the hotel!" she complained as they went up in the elevator and the blinking receptionist remained behind them. "He also winked at the Germans, I saw it." At nights through the walls of their room the groaning of that couple could be heard; and towards the end of one night, half-awake in the diminishing darkness, he saw her sitting up in bed and placing her ear to the wall.

When the injured man was offloaded here with his travelling trunk, it was said of the Russian – Rasul had said with his usual conclusiveness – that apparently he had decided to die and had they remained one more week on the way, he would have been left to the crows. The coolie stretcher bearers murmured something in Bihari and departed, but Rasul did not cease to prattle on. "Rasul he see Phelingpa from all the world and he be okay with everyone, but this man right away you see he not okay!" Because he was sick of his prattling the way he was sometimes sick of this whole continent (at moments like these he wanted to return to England, until he reminded himself that it wasn't possible), he asked him just how exactly does one see something like that: yes, please explain to him, after all, it's never too late to learn.

Right away the caravan-bashi's assistant caught on that he was being mocked, and an expression of insult spread across his face. "Rasul understand people," he answered, "and a man whose head messed up, only blind man not see it!"

It transpired that he had seen the Russian for the first time a month before that, and if anyone in the world had any doubt that that Russian wasn't quite right in the head, then there, in Kashgar, he had already done some odd things: he stood on the roof of the inn with some small boy, what exactly he was doing with him isn't clear, and after that he threw a bottle from the roof straight at the head of the commander of the guards just in order to help Tenzin, they could have indeed killed him there and then on the spot.

And it's not that Rasul didn't like him, he did like him (and he immediately lifted his right hand and took an oath); Rasul he has big love for people, and people they also have big love for Rasul; and also he doesn't care that he helped Tenzin, and if Rasul has enemies its only Tenzin, but in the end who bring him here to the hospital together with his trunk, did Tenzin bring him? No, Rasul bring him!

And he also didn't think at all (again he took an oath on his breast) that maybe he'll be given something here for that, not true, not true, not true. Even if doctor force his hand open and put something in it, let's say ten or twenty rupees, Rasul will say to doctor straight away: no thanks, Doctor, you don't have to, I didn't do it for that! Also not for thirty. Rasul he just always like to help people, and all the people they like Rasul, yes even that Russian: in the end who did the Russian stay with?

"With Rasul," he himself answered his question and turned his gaze toward the corridor; perhaps his eyes were searching for the girl who passed there previously carrying on her arms a bundle of twigs for heating, and in his usual way he tried his luck with her as well.

A moment later the injured man opened his eyes to a narrow slit and stared at the two of them from the depths to which he had been consigned. A few reddish gleams flickered in the passage on the part of the wall that could be seen from the entrance of the room, and flakes of soot flew around there from the fire beneath the pot, and it seemed that the injured man was shuttering his eyes from them.

As if the caravan-bashi from the bazaar had heard them, at the entrance of the room two coolies appeared who were sent to return the improvised stretcher to him together with his talkative assistant. With his black fingers one of the coolies placed the tent poles together and sloppily wrapped around them the canvas upon which the injured man had been carried, and the other turned to Rasul and informed him in broken Ladakhi: "Isa say you come right now, right now."

This new insult, of a contemptible coolie telling him what to do, even if in the name of their commander, was insufferable, and a moment passed until Rasul regained his composure and turned to the other coolie. The first one still retained some of the authority of the caravan-bashi, but his partner, who had been sloppy in folding the stretcher, was ordered to immediately open it up outside and shake it out as should be done, and only afterward to fold it up again – but not before Rasul sees how it was cleaned. On repeating his instructions his self-confidence returned to him, and since the doctor was still bent over the bed of the injured man, before leaving he said to him in a loud voice:

"Maybe girl come again, and doctor say to her Rasul he come again?"

"Maybe," answered the doctor.

The room emptied and in it there remained only the doctor and the Russian and the crows.

Dr. McKenzie did not see them and only discerned a movement which passed over the Russian's eyelids, but apparently (this he understood after some time) they were flying inside there, black as the soot flakes: ascending, gliding, circling in the air, and he, since he had seen nothing but the movement of the eyelids and no other change in the injured man's condition was noticeable, approached the window facing the courtyard and opened it to call to Rasul, who was hectoring the coolies cleaning the stretcher.

His arms were folded behind his back and his feet stood apart, a stance he copied from Isa, he supervised their doings and every so often bent down and berated them. "That look clean to you?" he said as he bent down. "That clean?" He passed his finger over the canvas in order to sweep up a shred of dirt, inserted his small finger into the hollow of one of the poles, as he had once seen a sergeant do with the soldier's rifles (there were barracks on the way to Changspa, and every morning soldiers stood there for inspection).

"Rasul," the doctor called again. "Please remind Isa about what I asked him for." Unhurriedly, Rasul turned his head toward him.

"He'll know what it is," said the doctor.

"Rasul not ask what doctor want from Isa," Rasul answered with insult on his face, "but Rasul tell Isa."

"Rasul," the doctor said to him from the window in order to placate him a little.

"Rasul he ask nothing," the Ladakhi answered with head downcast. "Because if someone not trust Rasul, he not trust and Rasul he not ask."

"Rasul," the doctor fibbed, "who can I trust in this damned place if not you?"

Farther on from there a large cloud cast its shadow over the town from the north to the south, from the monastery of the yellow mitered monks to the bazaar. The doctor did not see the caravan from where he stood, but it was not difficult to guess that while the merchandise was being unloaded, one or another of the animals lifts its tail and empties its bowels without a shred of respect for the cargo and the long way it travelled, and that clouds of flies rush there, and competing with them for the booty are pigs covered in dry crusts of sludge.

About this the doctor used to say to his few guests: "You wanted exotica? Here's exotica for you," but he already knew that by the time they would return to their homelands they would have forgotten all the clouds of flies and the filth of the pigs, they would forget the sewage floating in open ditches, and they'll describe all they've here with glorifying words that they themselves heard before their journeys; and he knew as well that he himself will probably never leave this place – a damned place, one of the utmost remoteness, but it was his place, and he most likely will end his days here.

When the caravan drew near to the bazaar at the end of its long journey, the dusty dogs lying at the sides of the road must surely have got up and barked with their hoarse throats; no yak burdened with merchandise instilled any fear in them, and certainly no pony, and only two-humped camels aroused a measure of respect in them. In the caravan's cargo, inside crates and sacks and bags, were bricks of tea and rolls of silk from China, sacks of salt from the lakes of Chang Tang, rolls of brocade and binoculars from Russia, rolls of felt from Yarkand, shawls from Kashmir, dried apricots from Baltistan, copper utensils from Srinagar, knives and forks from England, well-thumbed nude photographs of Parisian prostitutes, opium bricks from Shanghai, blocks of hashish from Kulu.

Hashish he had already tried, in Kulu itself; opium he hadn't yet tried; and prostitutes he had had experience with, not Parisian ones, but those in Brindisi and in Bombay who had caused him more than enough harm. In any event, he was not wanting that merchandise.

Opposite his window, on one of the apricot branches, a magpie sounded its call looking very grand with its tail elongated like a trail and with its white and black feathers, differing greatly from the usual darkness of crows' feathers. *Chap-chap*, it called again from its branch, *chap-chap*, and its long tail moved up and down.

Does not the crow also contain some inherent divine secret? After all, here on this sub-continent they worshipped not only cows and cobras but also monkeys and mice, and in fact, what not? The doctor had come such a long way from his previous life, from the years in which he still attended church, and having spent so much time among semi-pagans and total pagans, there was almost no difference in his eyes between one god and another, the same fears and yearnings had given rise to all of them.

Chap-chap, the magpie called again, *chap-chap*.

In this small European colony, between sips of tea served at Ann's, it was related recently that in a church in Dharamsala the priest ordered a new statue of the Crucified one, and in complete earnestness the local artist suggested adding more arms to Jesus like Shiva had, and on each hand the hole of a nail; and here in Leh they believed in a Buddha that will one day return to the world for the people and redeem them from their suffering like the Crucified one. Only the believers in Ganesh remained content, and more often than not the doctor preferred the smiling face of that god with the elephant head to the tormented face of the one for whom he had been baptized in the same church in which his father's fathers had been baptized. He had not brought him redemption, only exile.

He returned to gaze in the window: again the colors of the clouds had changed, and on the slopes the shadows had deepened, cast by the large rocks depleted of their strength to continue rolling down.

4

All sorts of adventurers and explorers came to Leh motivated by curiosity or the will to make a name for themselves, while others were motivated by a sense of remoteness, seeking a place far enough where they could put roots down, and to which of these the injured man belonged it was not possible to know.

His heartbeats were not promising. As to his state of mind, the doctor only knew what Rasul had told him, but among all those coming to Leh, who do so with a completely lucid mind? He himself certainly did not belong to the lucid of mind when he arrived here, and after all, the definition of lucidity of mind changes from place to place, as the gods change and also as the rules of morality change – things that Dr. McKenzie would not have conceived of doing on a different continent and which even his unfortunate luck did not lead him to do there, he was undeterred from here in Leh.

He now treated all the rogues which he saw here with forgiveness, only if their roguery did not cause anyone's death: crossing that boundary was forbidden. But in his eyes it was not terrible when they deceived customers about the quality of the merchandise if those customers could afford to pay, or when they used trickery in some dubious miracle that found enough fools who believed it. Had he himself not been aided by trickery in his veterinarian days? For example, with sublimated iodine and turpentine that caused crimson smoke to rise from wounds, thus persuading the farmers of the effectiveness of the treatment? Perhaps the chemical reaction helped the penetration of the iodine and perhaps not; either way, it looked marvelous.

The plan that he and Tenzin hatched, each for his own reasons, also did not seem terrible in his eyes, even if there was no beneficial intent in them. Tenzin's father had become a broken man by the end of the century, and he, a well-loved veterinarian, against his will had become a wanderer and left on a long exile, it's no wonder that they both wished for vengeance.

When he placed the tips of his fingers to the side of the neck of the injured man, he felt his heartbeats and counted them again. They were now also frequent, at once sharp and fragile. Could he cure him? Local witch doctors crushed and ground grasses and stones and stirred the mixture in water and kneaded it and chanted all sorts of mantras, and their patients were cured; and fortune-tellers revealed clients their fates by the stars of the sky or the formation that grains of wheat created on the skin of a drum. One only had to believe in the meaning given to them, and he was unable to give that kind of meaning to any suffering person, least of all his own suffering.

At the commissioner's wife's evening teas they mocked the witch doctors, but frequently they were more helpful than his medicines because people trusted in them and were still doubtful about him; only his operating instruments impressed them because they gleamed like the instruments of a ritual. In England he cut open the stomachs of dogs who had accidentally swallowed rubber balls, inserted his hands beyond the elbows inside the genitalia and anuses of cows and mares, on the caravan in which he came here he let the blood of a pony who had developed hoof tissue induration and only then did they begin to appreciate him a little (until then it seemed to each and every one that his only advantage was the whiteness of his skin), and last summer in the villages he performed cataract operations on dozens of villagers, and with more than half of them, despite not having any previous experience, had been successful.

When he became established here it seemed as if his suffering had vanished, but lately it reappeared. In his room in Changspa not only did the yearning lift his hand with the glass it was holding and fling it against the wall or the floor or to the twilight outside; there was anger in him as well. Not for one moment did he forget the money he had borrowed, the promises he had made to the farmers and for whom ("It's better this way," he heard her voice again from beyond the mountain peaks). With a sharpness that was painful, he recalled her instability and her unpredictability, her resentment toward London and her longing for London, her attempts at domesticity in the village and her disappointment from the village and from herself for not succeeding in making a home in it, her desire to stand out in every place at all times and her withering the moment she felt she wasn't desirable, in her husband's eyes or the eyes of total strangers, Britons or Italians – all this had no explanation, neither did his love for her despite it all; no explanation and no cure, and no operation could remove it.

For his operations in the village, he needed to be helped by recommendations from Rasul, who disclosed that the doctor had operated even on the Queen and now she sees like a baby; in vain he tried to explain to him that babies actually cannot see well. And even though the royal operation ended in success and the cataract was removed, he preferred not to be reminded of it. There are acts which do not end the moment they seem to have ended, and their manifest beginnings also have concealed roots. When the Queen was hospitalized, she was accompanied by her whole entourage, and none of them enraged him more than the King himself, who every evening would come to visit carrying the magic lantern which he received as a gift from the commissioner, and in order to put the Queen comfortably to sleep he would install the oil lamp of the apparatus and would project sites of London, Paris, and Rome on the opposite wall: the Big Ben tower could be seen there and the river Thames and Trafalgar Square – yes-yes, right inside this miserable hospital – Parisian boulevards and the Arc de Triomphe; the ruins of the Colosseum in Rome and fountains and marble statues; and the doctor wondered every evening if by chance he and Kate had also been photographed among the passersby in the piazzas.

Perhaps they were blurred there and were included in the crowds or in the shadows of the buildings, nevertheless they had been there, if in fact these photographs had been taken then: a man and a woman in their attempt to repair the first year of their marriage, she a glamorous Londoner – that's how he saw her in the beginning – and he a cumbersome villager, she has a new hairdo and beneath her arm an expensive leather handbag which she bought in the morning, and he has coins in his wallet which he's saving for stamps; and not far off from there, on the opposite sidewalk, among the passersby, with confident steps and without haste, his ruination advances. Yes, without difficulty he could imagine the one he did not wish to see there, as with any panoramic photograph of a city which on sight one could assume that at least in one of its streets some crime is taking place, and which only due to the distance has evaded the camera's lens.

Until not many years ago he still used to say to his alternating assistants that he would give a year of his life in order to know what the unconscious hallucinate about at moments like these from the depths of their souls, but it's been many a day since he's said that to anyone, and the interior of the soul seems something better not to become involved with. Throughout recent times he behaved like a practical man: examined the facts he gathered, made calculations of profit and loss, made advantageous connections – connections like those he had with Tenzin and with the caravan-bashi – for the long term and from considerations which he tended not to share with anyone. How long was that term? Very long, Rome was the place of its inception.

He could have raised that damn Italian to the heavens in crimson pillars of smoke, yes, it could have been a glorious spectacle. Or, at the very least, he would have placed him next to him during some especially repulsive operation, for instance the time when in Begbroke he operated on the colonel's cow which had swallowed a metal wire. How sure of himself the colonel had been at the beginning of the operation ("Doctor, I've already seen some tough things in my life"), and how stooped he had seemed by its end, after the stomach suddenly burst out when, on one of his attempts to push it back in, it suddenly squirted a murky jet which had found itself an outlet; after which the colonel looked as dark as a Tamil.

Unwillingly he saw the Italian again walking parallel to him and Kate on the opposite sidewalk of the Via Veneto, and he wasn't even one of those oily-haired Italian men whose chief occupation was flirting with female tourists; this Italian had an understanding of sculpture, and paintings, and all sorts of other antiquities, and not only Italian ones. He also took pains to say, without being asked, in which antiquities he specialized, and mentioned the name of the Asian desert where they had been discovered, and at the time that name meant nothing to McKenzie; in his eyes, deserts were associated only with Africa, and under no circumstances was it conceivable the day would come when he would live one caravan convoy away from those regions.

For that man, the professor, one characteristic hue was enough to identify each and every single painter with the same skill with which he, the veterinarian – he was then still a veterinarian – diagnosed an animal disease from one of its symptoms, for instance, lead poisoning from the foaming of the mouth of calves after eating strips of old paint. This man was a researcher of ancient scripts and not a researcher of art, but he gave them a detailed lecture on Michelangelo's David, abounding with comparisons, and speaking especially at length about his loins. "Not only did your Victoria attach a fig leaf to him," he said about the copy which was sent to the Queen, "but also some of our popes," and for a moment it seemed he was directing his words on matters of modesty and shame also to McKenzie's shame.

A few meters away from them, a small shoeshine boy was bent over his box, and when the German tourist placed her pudgy hand on his head, the boy was entranced by her touch like a puppy, whereas Kate distorted her face; she was wary of his lice and the sleep in the corners of his eyes. She did have affection for the blind eyes of marble statues as did she for the muscular bodies, and every time her gaze lingered on them, he would stand up straight demonstratively, as if he was up for renewed appraisal from the very comparison with the statue. Actually, David didn't impress him at all, despite its stature – he had seen a copy of it in London, exactly a year before their trip – that David stood like a model with his sling, and not like someone intending to hurl a stone at a giant and subdue an entire army with it; and if his innocuousness wasn't enough, he had a tiny John Thomas. Some of the statues in Rome had similar ones, and the German tourist directed his wife's attention to one such, and Kate also blushed.

Those two Germans, neighbors on the other side of the wall in their hotel ("a pair of animals" is what they called them), they kept meeting by chance at all sorts of places that tourists habitually visit; he was therefore also not surprised to see that man again in the Vatican halls or in some piazza, drawing back a step or two from a painting with narrowed eyes, or slowly encircling a statue in order to become acquainted with it from all angles. "That one's a professional," Kate said of him, "you can see it right away." She had enough integrity to admit that in every museum she first looked at the copper plaques next to the frame (only in the churches she didn't hesitate to also look at what hadn't been pointed out in the guide; there it was not important what others said, but rather what her heart said).

After detailing all the virtues of Bernini's David, as opposed to Michelange-lo's, without any hesitation he began talking about the saint which Bernini had sculptured, a saint whose facial expression on the moment of union with the Lord resembled the expression of a woman achieving a climax: the head was slanted backward, the lips parted, the tongue stuck out to the side, the eyes rolled from pleasure. "You simply have to see it," said that man of short stature, of scant forelock, the erudite, the nuisance, the expert on sculpture and on painting and on antiquities and what not, as if he had already been appointed their host, and for a moment it seemed his words had been especially directed at McKenzie, who the entire previous night had tried to bring such an expression to his wife's face.

In the vase in their room the roses shed more red petals onto the small table (the chambermaid didn't bother replacing them); their stems stooped farther, and with them his organ withered.

5

Of all the crows flying around there in ever growing circles – a movement passed beneath the lids of shed eyelashes – the doctor did not see even one, and in time will also not see; he'll only hear about them and about their circling. Time after time they flew around there inside, ten black crows or more.

The sky was a pellucid light blue and a few feathery clouds floated in it, and for a moment, while the doctor was still crouching over him, the Russian imagined seeing all ten of them ascending and gliding and soaring up and up and his bleeding intestines suspended from their beaks and swinging to and fro in the air.

Then the quiver passing over his eyelids ceased, and from above him the doctor sensed that he was slipping through his hands again, down and down he drew away from him, and the gap between his breaths widened and their rhythm changed.

Dyah gamat kuni
Sang ha bashinmag

The song had been sung in another region, but the caravan didn't remain there. Someone in the center of it cried out sonorously, and all the others answered him from one end of the caravan to the other until all their voices mingled in the wind. Dozens of animals trudged along, from ponies to two-humped camels, and the Russian – that's what they called the injured man there: the Russian – was carried on a stretcher improvised from two tent poles and its canvas, and the coolies cursed in Bihari all his father's fathers, because a week after their departure from Kashgar they were already required to carry him on their shoulders.

The mountain is high, the valley is low,
Am I mistaken, my friend?
Shout your answer.
The gods are eternal, we are impermanent,
Am I mistaken, my friend?

A few crows circled above him – at first two, afterward three and a day later there were already six – they circled and conducted vociferous consultations in the sky, and for a moment it seemed that he understood their words, and if not all of them then at least his name which was mentioned over and over in the sky.

Five days earlier the caravan crossed a stream that only due to the force of its flow its water did not freeze between the white banks, and the crows were not yet flying in the sky, not a dozen nor half a dozen. The horse on which Poliakov rode – that was his real name, his two other names already have no use – stumbled on a pothole on the floor of the stream and threw him into the water, and after they drew him out shivering and dripping they changed his clothing like a baby and placed him on the back of one of the coolies, from where he was transferred to the back of one of the ponies, and before that they had told him it would actually be better not to ride; to walk, yes, on foot, because there's no better way to restore body heat. If he wants to live, they said to him, he has to keep moving.

On this pony, the new one, worrying signs became evident even before they reached the middle of the ascent: blood dripped from its nostrils, and its stomach bloated and hardened, and it was clear that it was stricken with altitude sickness. Its rider, a native of the plains (in the province of his birth in southern Russia there were but a few low hills visible beyond the bend in the river), was unaffected by the altitude, as if the attack on his feet had been enough, while his pony had been conquered by it. "He brings bad luck to everyone, that Russian," said the coolies around him, and he thought (he did not understand their language, but the tone sufficed): yes, it's true, my bad luck will be enough for the lot of you.

In the middle of the ascent, the pony beneath him collapsed as if its legs had folded from the weight of its distended stomach, and he got down from its back and stood next to it and had no sensation in his legs, and a moment later the pony tried to rise and again collapsed and fell on its side, and in the sky – for the first time his gaze was then lifted to it – a few crows were preparing for their meal.

With a gentle motion of the thumbs, the doctor raised the injured man's eyelids and peered into the whites of his eyes and the opacity of the pupils and let the eyelids drop. The injured man sunk back into his swoon, his facial features were clenched, and it seemed as if he was trying, silent as he was, to toss his head from right to left in order to express his outrage at the sights he was seeing. His features articulated defiance, but with the same suddenness with which they had been clenched they also unraveled, and instantly all expression was wiped from his face.

What the thing was that the Russian so refused to come to terms with, McKenzie did not know, nor toward what his defiance was aimed: toward the people of the caravan which he had joined, that they not abandon him in the mountain snow, or toward him, McKenzie, that he not amputate his toes; or perhaps the Russian was defiant of utterly different things that had occurred in the place from where he came, somewhere in the expanse of the enormous country which had never aroused curiosity in the doctor. In fact, the county of his birth was enough for McKenzie. Indeed, had what happened not have happened he would never have left Oxfordshire.

6

Two days after the breads wrapped in newspaper, a tiny prayer drum also arrived at the home of the Harpers, and as a sign of thanks they sent to the palace a few giant turnips which they grew in their garden, and Tenzin remarked that Mrs. Harper was a good woman, not like the commissioner's wife, who at the most would have given the queen the holes in her records – the ones that were played over and over on summer nights, and then the straying sounds of a piano spread through the darkness of the Leh valley. Until then the valley had been accustomed only to the monk's oboes and horns and shells, whose deep sounds seemed to be directed not to the heavenly gods but rather to the dense earth. That was where the doctor intended to hide the components of his plan as well, at least the shells, in the depth of the earth or the sands, provided that Isa will obtain all the necessities for him.

If he does not obtain them, at least he will not tell anyone about the strange requests he asked of him; he could trust him completely, him and also Tenzin, his partner in the crazy plan, and only of Rasul the doctor had his doubts – Rasul was a great chatterbox, a flatterer, and an incurable boaster. Indeed, Tenzin also defined himself according to his attitude towards the Sahibs, but the one aimed to please them, while the other, Tenzin, did not forgive them for denouncing his father as a traitor and a liar, and his grudge was directed not only to his father's commanders in Dehradun but to all their British fellow countrymen, and not only to them but also to the French and the Germans and the Italians since they too were light skinned like the British, and no less than them the Russians for not finally getting rid of the British, and for every pale faced Phelingpa who arrived at Leh he had but one wish in his heart: get the hell out. "This is not the place for any of you, Doctor," he reminded the doctor more than once, deviating from his reticence. "It's also not yours. A man should live where he was born and die there also."

"But I like this place," McKenzie would reply, because he had already become attached to this remoteness and didn't see himself living in any other place, least of all the county of his birth. In his eyes, it was better to encounter some giant dzo in the morning, lying majestically in a harvested field whose sheaves seem to be intended for its belly, and not to meet some two-legged acquaintance who raises his hat to you only to murmur behind your back something that was better unheard. And the Oxfordshire farmers did have something to murmur about behind his back and something to point out, and after the implementation of his plan they'd have a lot more.

Certainly not much remained of all their fondness and esteem, even that damned summer, and in time they're sure to enter him into the small mythology of the village alongside a few characters whose memory has been kept from generation to generation, and not thanks to exceptional qualities; for instance, alongside the one whose barn burnt down in the middle of his mother's funeral and whose flock was also then stolen. Who was he there, in those village tales? Perhaps the-poor-man-whose-wife-left-him-in-Rome, or the-thief-who-escaped-with-their-money-and-in-the-end-drowned-together-with-it (that was what Kate said so that she could remarry).

Should he return there he would seem to them a ghost, and they would have no joy in finding out that he's still alive. Until his undoing because of Kate, he was thought of as the most decent of men: he refused to comply with anyone who tried to deceive insurance companies claiming that his cow died from a lightning bolt (signs of singeing could indeed be seen on it, but so too could candle wax next to the singed part), he pointed out to a lord that the pedigree of his new horse had been faked and was undeterred by his anger; and as to the matter of the sublimation of iodine and the turpentine, his one single trick, the farmers viewed it with fondness and even insisted on it and demanded it. "First of all, get some red smoke out of her, Doctor," they would say of their injured cow, "so we can see it working," and he brought forth puffs of red smoke from the wounds and quite often healed them too.

In his years here, the doctor had seen more than a few soles of feet and palms of hands with that bluish hue, and also saw how with the correct treatment they heal from week to week. On no account should they be dipped in hot water: what is needed is a gradual heating, and massage too can be very effective, and talking as well, yes, if only this injured man would be so kind as to wake up and not cling to his swoon, and if only the doctor not be distracted by some other matter, and certainly not by something unrelated to the health of the patients.

A tin sound could be heard from the corridor; perhaps at last they were dragging the emptied pot of tsampa outside in order to wash it in the ditch water. Despite the instruction he formed in his head (Dragging pots in the corridors is strictly forbidden), he was already accustomed to these sounds just as he was accustomed to multi-limbed and multi-eyed deities and to this remoteness, which in time became his remoteness. Were it not for one issue, he would have said that if he had decided at the time to exile himself here and stay on for years, it's perhaps not such a terrible exile, but in actual fact he was like a sentenced man forced to hear from afar about the success of his rival, owing to whom he had distanced himself from the company of people – hearing about his high standing, about his fame, about the honor bestowed upon him; how successful Magnani is, how erudite Magnani is, how sharp Magnani is, how witty Magnani is, and not what a son of a bitch he is, and worst of all, to hear about the woman who chose to live her life with that Magnani.

All these past years, in which he often recalled Kate's shortcomings, which each time were more pointed, he continued to miss each and every shortcoming of hers and wished to avenge that man. Such is how things evolve in their deceptive ways: the acclaimed researcher who so impressed her with the stories of his journeys, in the end stuck to his podium, while he, McKenzie, a village veterinarian of no importance sailed and journeyed to Leh; and does not treat cows and horses here, nor yaks and camels, but humans: these Ladakhi, at whose sight she would most definitely have turned her nose up, and Europeans too, but should Magnani arrive here, he would indeed not lift a finger for him.

The injured man opposite him groaned again. On the bed his face was distorted, and for a while it seemed that at any moment he would release himself from his state of deadlock: his head shifted from side to side, and his arms and legs moved as well, as if his defiance had spread to the tips of his toes, or as if they had at last thawed out. "No?" said McKenzie to him. "What, no?" And in his same frame of mind thought: when you wake up just don't tell me, in Russian or Urdu or Jewish or any other language, that you arrived here because your wife ran away from you, because that I won't believe.

Then his head quietened from its tossing, and the doctor looked again at the wounds on the thighs and shins and at the organ sticking out of his torn underpants, a circumcised organ (he had seen ones like it with the Muslims who were brought here, but this injured man definitely was not a Muslim). A thought came to mind, and right away another joined it: what would Magnani have said about that? Is it not so that in front of the statue of Moses he ridiculed Michelangelo, who had made a mistake, no less than the mistake he had made with the statue of David: to the prophet he gave horns and to the king a foreskin.

A passing Ladakhi peeked in from the corridor and in his hand a large cup with steam rising from it, and for a moment it seemed that the injured man's nostrils widened slightly and sniffed the air, but his breathing remained as feeble as it had been.

"Drik, drik," said the doctor, because the Ladakhi was still peeking in from the corridor.

That word was good for everything or almost everything; about what can't you say "enough"? Perhaps about love; that needs other words, but here they won't be needed.

He does not have a great gift for languages, and for the plan which he has formulated with Tenzin he'll definitely need help in that matter; he knew that already in the reasonably early stages, but he did not imagine that he would receive it from one of his patients.

7

For a few moments, from the place in which Poliakov was left lying, the white peaks surrounding him resembled foaming waves whose motion was halted at the apex of its momentum, and the tiny figures seen on the face of them – all the people of the caravan drawing away from him – are not progressing toward any destination, but rather are struggling like him to float and to breathe with what remains of their strength, and they are like survivors of a wrecked ship with no visible flotsam on which to grasp.

The horses also struggled to float: icicles hung from their nostrils until becoming detached and dropping, and new icicles were formed there while others extended from their eyes as well; and there would have been ice in the moustaches and beards of all those who had moustaches and beards, had they not covered their faces and left only a narrow slit for the eyes.

His vision had also been preserved, but only in order to behold his sentence in all its stages: from the convergence of the crows from the ends of the sky through the circling of their flight to their swooping deep down and the poking and the extracting. It was a terrible sentence, but he had no doubt that the punishment fitted his deeds. And with complete acceptance he waited for it to be executed, whether by any god or whether by the power of a simple symmetry, whose beginning was in Russia, in the river and in the village and in Minsk and in St. Petersburg.

More than once or twice above the mountainous path a black crow could be seen rising into the air with an eyeball in its beak, the eye of a pony or a yak who had collapsed on the path or rolled down the slope, held between the two parts of the beak and sparkling on its way up high, and it seems that with an extracted eye such as that he himself will view his body laid on the ground, and from the other, which still remained in its socket, he'll watch the crows, until it too will be extracted. All at once he heard the flapping of black wings in the sky and the beating of his heart between his ribs on the land, a mountainous land whose name he did not know nor its location (he only knew that it was south of Kashgar, and north of Ladakh), and anyway it was of no importance, and not only because it had all turned white.

Years before that, he had been encircled by the white of the flat land from where he came and to where he will not return, and the goat (it was a goat there and not a pony) did not carry any load on its back, nor was it ridden. The goat floated on its island of ice on and on downstream, and the boys, three from a neighboring village and with them his brother, Izu, ran parallel to it on the right bank, that only the week before had begun to thaw.

And the island of ice whose diameter was only one meter was being swept in the water and a pole was stuck in its center and tied to it was a worn-out rope that with one pull would come loose, and at the end of the rope was that goat whose owner was perhaps still searching for it; and no crows were yet circling above it, only the children were lying in waiting.

And why was he reminded of it now, its chin tuft and its bleating and the stumps of its horns (they will be last to be seen, until they're also swallowed by the water)? Not because of the boy, Sasha, in Kashgar, to whom not long ago he had told all about that, but rather because had it not been for the goat perhaps all the rest would not have happened: the barrel, the deep waters, the carriage, the gun.

But now, in his swoon, he is only thinking: goat. Goat, goat, goat.

On and on it floated downstream and at first they accompanied it only with their gazes and afterward with their legs as well and now they are already running and chasing it as fast as they can and with all the rage which it aroused in them, the boys of a Russian village whose name nobody in the capital had heard of. "It must have come to fuck the nanny goats here," says the tall one with a dirty fur cap on his head. "Here it'll fuck only fish," answers the chubby one with golden down on his chin, and the older brother and his young brother, Izu, are also eager to observe everything and are not lagging behind.

At the bend of the river the white island and its white sailor are halted by a tree trunk that had collapsed when the thawing bank crumbled, and now they can all make their assumptions: maybe the goat will gnaw the remnants of the rope and try to walk from its white island onto the trunk and reach dry land that way; and maybe it will stay on that island until the ice melts and it sinks with it ("It won't sink, it'll swim, they swim like dogs!"); and maybe it will get caught up in those branches and be strangled in them ("It's lived long enough, that old one, it's completely white").

From the north, new chunks of ice are already arriving in torrents, more and more islands and sandbanks are glistening in that May sun: in the center of one of them a circle of soot is inscribed and in it the remains of a charred tree trunk, and on another the furrows of wagon wheels, and on a third, whiter than its predecessors and slower than them, stands a dwarfish snowman, from the center of its face a carrot sticks out with which to sniff the air in amazement at this land that renounces its whiteness with such ease.

"You call that a snowman?" the tall boy jeers. "Everyone must be dwarfs where he comes from."

"They shrink from the cold," explains the one whose face is covered in

pimples, and the tall one (Stas is his name; and that's what he'll be called years later,
when they'll be holding sledgehammers and planks and pitchforks and goads in
their hands) wonders how the goats manage to fuck at all in that cold of the north.

"It floated here just for that," says the third one, "just so that its balls thaw out."

They laugh, and the two brothers laugh with them, although the joke was not
meant for their ears: initially the elder laughed – Ilya is his name, Ilya Poliakov;
he's not yet called Sergei Gomolyov, or Grisha Ivanov – and then his little brother,
Izu, joins in, he who imitates him in everything and still believes that there's nothing in the world to prevent him from doing anything he wants to do, should he so
wish it.

With bewilderment and sadness the goat bleats on its island of ice in order that
from one of the banks a hand or a branch will be reached out to it to be grasped
or that a rope will be thrown for it to be pulled to dry land – that's what it seems
they are doing, throwing and missing and gathering up the dripping rope from the
water and running onward on the bank and hurling it again and missing again – so
it seemed, but their intention was different. And the goat is not granted a reprieve
as would be customary for a man who falls unharmed from the gallows, and they
aim the waterlogged noose at its neck, not to pull it from the water but rather to
strangle it ("But why did they do that?" Sasha asked on the roof); and they all run
parallel to it and hurl the rope again to the center of the river, to the bank of ice
swept there, hurling and missing, and the agile among them have already hastened
to the next bend in the river and in their hands a long branch, not because they
believe that it will get caught up in that branch and that way they'll succeed in pulling it to the bank, but just to stop it from making that effortless motion right in
front of their eyes, moving only its chin tuft, a smooth constant continuous motion
which mocks not only their efforts but also the entire land of ice being churned
around it.

"A goat like that," says the panting chubby one, "could easily fuck a whole
flock, one minute for each nanny goat."

"But those are the fastest," says the tall one and turns his gaze at the two brothers – the elder one and his brother, Izu – "because half of it's cut off." And only now
the boys laugh, and their eyes stray to the elder one and his little brother as if the
defect imposed upon them in their infancy will be revealed through the material
of their tattered trousers.

They throw fistfuls of mud saturated with ice water at the goat, but it evades
them all with the white island on whose deck it stands and bleats in that high-
pitched sound, protesting and puzzled, and the agile among them already reach
the next bend in the river and find another large many-branched bough that broke
off in the last storm, and they lift it and balance it, thus like a giant pitchfork it
will obstruct that sailor floating along in front of them, and at the bend in the
river where the water gushes, its bleating is discernable only by the quivering of its

defiant white chin tuft. On and on it sails with that constant motion and suddenly even urinates in order to add to the water surrounding it or to show the pursuers its attitude toward them: it will piss if it wants to, it will bleat if it wants to, it will quiver its chin tuft if it wants to, even in front of the large bough which they have difficulty lifting up, and they shout to each other not to let go and spur each other on to aim the fork of the branches at the white neck in order to capture it or choke it or decapitate it or at least to finally stop its journey.

Maybe it comes from Siberia, where not only bears turn white, but also the night and even bonfires that freeze over (so an uncle of one of them said, a soldier), and it sails on its ice deck with an uplifted neck and bewildered eyes whose long white lashes blink one last time before it's pushed into the water and disappears in it, and after a very long moment it reappears farther on from there, its anterior shuddering, and it lifts its white head with great exertion and concentration with a kind of genteel strain, as if its only worry is not getting the tip of its chin tuft wet again. Its ears are pulled back and its nostrils are flared and it struggles with all its might to identify a fragile evasive sound, not their laughter, and to smell a distant fading scent, not that of the bough that hits it and is raised again, but a different scent whose origin is the land from where it came or another to where it is going.

The bleating heard now, slight and soft, is coming from the mouth of the little brother, Izu, who is pulling at the elder with his hand over and over to do something, after all he is the older brother: he should stop the boys, threaten them, shout and hit them and block them and that giant bough which they are all now lifting again and the whole of it drips before hitting the goat again, one last hit at it and its whiteness that still sticks out while straining the neck and nostrils, and it seems that the goat is even trying to breathe through the horn stumps, those two stumps that are seen last and whose ends appear for a brief moment from within the cloud of blood spreading in the water.

8

"Male nudity was not something he didn't like," Magnani said then.

Without any difficulty the doctor's thoughts wandered from the damaged bluish body to white lofty marble statues, perfect from head to toe, perfect, yes, even if over the years a hand or a foot or a nose or a John Thomas broke off. It was the last thing he was supposed to think about in the hospital, nevertheless that's what he thought about. Who is master of his thoughts? How the Italian started to explain to them, as if they had requested it, that Michelangelo did not sculpt the leaf, he actually chose to leave his hero in his nakedness.

While they were looking at the statue – not the statue of David but rather the statue of Moses, who was reasonably clad – he drew near to them as if fortuitously and introduced himself. And they in their stupidity responded. Is this your first time in Rome? Yes. English? Yes. Well then they should know that whoever really wants to become acquainted with a sculptor of genius should preferably take leave of Michelangelo and also forgo his innocuous David or Donatello's (quite by chance, he said, he had heard they were intending to travel to Florence), and instead go to see Bernini's David in the Villa Borghese: there you see rage! There you see decisiveness; there you see how the entire body is taut for hurling the stone at the giant! Bernini, they must have heard of Bernini? And about the Baroque period?

At this point McKenzie ceased to listen, but Kate took in every word. Against his will he again pondered upon their last night in the hotel: upon their almost royal four poster bed and the hollows that the headboard knobs made in the wall by being tossed about by all the couples who had been there previously.

And indeed there had been other nights, more than a few, and only in the latter part of that year, the first year of their marriage, when she was sick of village life, did those nights become less frequent. But she had hoped that they would simply get on the train and all would change, or the moment they got off in Rome all would change, or the moment they entered the hotel, and it did not happen that way. Time was required, and she had no time. Reconciliation was required, but she no longer had the strength for reconciliation. Adapting anew to a man you had loved was required, familiarizing anew to a body you had been familiar with, and she no longer wanted habit; here she wanted her emotions to be stirred up, to be awoken ("I want to feel my body again," she said, "I'm still a young woman, Ed"), to be tossed about in that bed the way her predecessors had been tossed about.

The expression on her face he knew he would remember all his life: there was no amazement in it, not even sorrow for him or for her. It disclosed a grudge, there was no mistaking it, like on the face of someone who suddenly discovers he has been deviously sold defective merchandise at an exorbitant price, and after giving the person who had cheated him an opportunity for atonement, it turns out he's irremediable.

Afterward she turned toward the wall – the German's wall – and when their voices began to be heard again, she covered her head with a pillow. She then lay on her stomach, careful not to touch McKenzie with her elbow or her knee, and from his side of the bed he saw strands of dark hair sticking out from beneath the white edges of the pillow, futilely sweaty. A section of the shoulder which he had previously kissed was still exposed, and he could also see the roundness of the hips that he had kissed as well, but the fullness of her buttocks was hidden under the sheet that she pulled up to her waist, and he saw only the quiver that passed through them after she moved her hand there.

"You simply have got to!" said the man opposite the statue of Moses. "Without Bernini it's as if you haven't visited Italy at all." And when Kate asked him why he was here if he finds Michelangelo so inferior, he replied: "To strengthen my opinion," and because Kate was silent, he added that only the past week he had returned to Rome from a long trip to the East, and from a certain aspect he now also feels like a tourist here, however in his own city: an odd feeling and not without interest.

From where exactly had he returned? Kate asked. If they want, he replied, he'll gladly tell them all about it, there are some pleasant cafés in the vicinity, and there's no shortage of trattorias here. But McKenzie glanced at his watch (how was he to know that he himself would traverse similar distances and to the very same areas), raised an eyebrow, and reminded Kate that they were being expected. The sole people they knew in the whole of Rome other than the winking hotel clerk were the German couple, and of all things they could both be heard close by, haggling with the little shoeshine boy who placed his work tools at their feet.

"Perhaps some other time?" said the Italian politely. "Yes, some other time," he replied to him, and at the time did not imagine how many times their paths would cross (the man really did decide to behave like a tourist in his city for the whole of the first week of his return, visiting all the sites that tourists visit and with the same edition of Baedeker and the same schedule), until those paths changed completely: McKenzie left Rome during the day, and afterward, when there was no point staying in Rome, moved south to Brindisi, and as for Kate, what she then did was better left unknown.

And who the hell did she go off with – that thought was very worst of all, there was no antidote against it – with some pale character who was no better looking than McKenzie and no more robust than him, the kind of erudite researcher who would sentence her to a humdrum life no less that than that to which she had been sentenced in Oxfordshire, even if the illnesses of animals had been exchanged by the ills of disintegrating paper of all sorts of ancient manuscripts (prior to her decision there had been a few more nights, and each worse than the ones before it, when she found a perfect excuse).

"And to have to sleep with chickens?" she asked him the first time he proposed marriage to her; then, cautiously, he tried to raise the possibility of her coming to live in the village. "The whole time I'll be forced to think where those beautiful hands of yours have been shoved into." And nevertheless, to his complete surprise, some months later she agreed to marry him and also declared she had decided to learn to love his profession, his animals, the open fields, and the serenity of small villages where the only events that take place are those that church bells announce with their ringing – a birth or a death, nothing important took place between them – and perhaps she really meant it at the time.

In Rome, during all the last years, her life must have been narrowed to erudite arguments between the colleagues of that man and insignificant quarrels on all sorts of dry matters; nevertheless, he had no difficulty imagining her as a professor's wife, enthusing with complete seriousness over some ridiculous discovery like that heap recently uncovered on one of the excavations in the Taklamakan desert that was nothing but refuse whose contents had been preserved by dryness and gave off a thousand year old stench. That finding was joked about in Leh for an entire summer, and there were those who wondered if those crazy explorers would even rummage through a heap of excrement with equal enthusiasm, just to find out how the digestive system operated a thousand years go. The ladies turned their noses up on hearing that jest. Jokes about the hygiene habits of the Ladakhi usually did amuse them, starting with their annual bathing – at least that's what they were told – to their custom of licking their plates at the end of a meal, and including the baby diapers that they padded, believe it or not, with the crumbs of dry goat excrement (whose ability to absorb matter is actually excellent; McKenzie never noticed any signs of irritation or infection with their babies as often occurred with European babies; and unlike throughout India, only few failed to make it to maturity).

The thought of what kind of a mother Kate would have been crossed his mind, and even when he heard that she had become a mother he found it difficult to conceive of her ever changing a baby's diaper or getting her hands soiled with its secretions, or washing, cradling and singing to it or telling it a story, although she did like to listen to all sorts of tales; it was not hard to picture her on a plush armchair in an old multi-corniced Roman building surrounded by bambini shrieking and running around, and Magnani's mother or his sisters or his housekeeper or all of them together caring for the children in her place: diapering them, feeding them, dressing them, cradling them, and getting rid of her cigarette smoke with waving hands – a slim cigarette with a long elegant holder – her lipstick was not only imprinted on the mouthpiece but also on his heart.

Even in the village she didn't relinquish the cigarette holder, as a sort of last remnant of her life in London; and one night, which even now he can't forget, she told him about some old colored rag that absorbed her mouth odors and accompanied her throughout her childhood and was dearer to her than any toy. The thought of her kneeling in prayer every night on her tiny knees before going to sleep (she did that too), caused a pang in his heart.

Stories circulated around the village about Brown's wife, for instance, who was seen leaving the barn in a state of total disarray a moment after Archer's nephew had come out of there; and also about old William's eldest son who hasn't been seen around because his wife left him with the children; and there were other stories with a different ring to them: Archer's nephew enlisted in the army and was sent to India and ever since has been spoken of with respect, and everyone noticed how Brown's wife took care of her husband after the accident, and gradually all was forgotten, yes; but to return, not from a neighboring village but from Italy, and alone? And that, after everyone had told him that the wedding had been a mistake for which he would pay dearly?

For a long time – summers and winters and years – the doctor found no remedy other than alcohol, but for the past few months he had gone to sleep with a clear head, and before nodding off he even read one of the books borrowed from Mrs. Harper and didn't let go of it until his eyes closed. An age-old memory sprung to mind in the mornings on seeing the dropped book at the foot of the bed: how his mother would come to his bed at night and gently take some illustrated book from his hand and bend toward his forehead and kiss him, and he wouldn't open his eyes until her lips touched his mouth. "You sleep like an angel," she would say. For a while McKenzie did resemble an angel and there were mornings when she bent over him as he slept on his stomach and kissed his prominent shoulder blades and said: "What have you got there, Eddie, wings?" And with the very gentlest of motions she would then lift him up as if he floated from his bed.

"Yes, we have a pair of wings there," he heard her say even when he would stand at the bend of the path leading to Changspa and urinate into the darkness. That was his favorite spot for urinating on the way home, and when he stood there the dark valley brought to mind in its odd way one of the local legends – providing he was drunk enough and from the alcohol fumes the words of Callahan from *The Simla News* rose – that told of a giant bird whose feet had imprinted this valley and whose wingspan spread from horizon to horizon.

Had he drunk a little more, perhaps he would have also heard the clap of the enormous wings, but his legs led him back to his room in Changspa, and many times he didn't bother to get undressed. He just removed his shoes and immediately flopped onto the bed and covered himself to the top of his head. Yes, he, the doctor, who used to reprimand the locals about their hygiene habits and demanded of them to heed their personal hygiene often slept in his clothes. It was the chang that caused this, or the loneliness, or the cold, or the memory.

There were more than a few ludicrous tales associated with English birds in his native county, a few of them competed in their asininity with those of Ladakh ("One for sorrow," they used to sing about the magpies of Oxfordshire, "two for mirth, three a funeral, and four for birth, you must not miss!"), but the kind of nonsense that will be incorporated in his plan would have been inconceivable to him in England. The learned folk there were of a different ilk, they would have made do with the Bodleian library in Oxford, and not one of them would have been tempted to cross an ocean and ride a pony or camels for weeks just to get his hands on some disintegrating document whose language was as vague as hieroglyphics (and furthermore, that was the way he wanted it: that in the whole world there would be not one soul capable of deciphering it in its entirety, and especially not that Italian).

As to the learned folk of Oxford, their only adventures took place in the evening hours in the confines of their pub, "Molly's Inn", and he once heard one of them say to Molly as she leaned over their table in all her ampleness: "Molly, I would give up my bronze bust for yours." Yes, on one hand dry scholarliness, and on the other all sorts of salty insinuations like those of that Italian who spoke of the pleasuring of Bernini's saint.

On their first morning there, after two full days with many goings on, from a few pleasant moments to the worst of quarrels, he heard her bathing for hours in the washroom, and in the large four poster bed emptied of her body, he pictured her nakedness, wetted, soaped, washed, and instantly the erection he lost the night before returned to him. There was an air of bitterness between them: all the air of Rome was tainted by the air of their country which they had carried with them on the train. At evening time Kate wanted to strew her clothing around the small room and he tried to restore some order, to which she said he didn't know how to enjoy himself, that he had never been able to let go a little, that at long last she's out of the depression she had suffered from in the village and now he's making her depressed again. She wanted to order room service in bed, and he said they didn't have enough money for such luxuries, to which she called him a miser, someone who doesn't know how to indulge his wife; he said that no one in the village had been on a trip like this, to which she replied that was exactly his problem, the village was his standard for everything in the world.

He listened to the sounds of her in the bath: she sloshed about in the water, the soap slipped from her hand and she felt around for it, and afterward something could be heard that was perhaps the sound of hair being washed. He could have entered the washroom while her eyes were shut beneath the foam, but he stayed in bed and listened: she started to softly sing some Italian song that they had both heard in one of the trattorias, a song whose every verse started and ended with "amore mio".

Only when she had finished her doings did he enter the washroom, and she then passed him by in silence, wrapped in the broad hotel towel, and another towel wound around her head like a turban; who would have conceived that the day would come when he would live in the homeland of turban wearers? In the bath he had heard her say, "I'm going down to eat," and with an unforgivable delay he asked whether she didn't want him to order something to the room: something small or even a full breakfast.

"It's a waste of money, isn't it?" she answered quietly, and instantly his organ became limp.

Afterward, when he went down to eat, she hurried to finish her meal, and after going up to the room she hurried out onto the balcony, and when he went out to the balcony she hurried back into the room, each time her eyes avoiding his eyes; it seemed that at any moment she would go to cleanse herself from his gaze as well.

The Muslims (the thought now popped into his head, faced with the circumcised genitals of the injured man), when left with no water around are permitted to purify themselves with sand. That's what he once read, or perhaps heard on some evening in the commissioner's house from Hedin in person. A great learned man was Hedin, as well as a great adventurer, and McKenzie wondered for a moment whether such an attribute could also be applied to that son of a bitch Magnani whose total adventurousness perhaps only amounted to robbing someone else's wife. Yes, he thought to himself, it is possible, after all when they met him for the first time he had just returned from a year's travelling in the deserts of Asia.

With sand, he pondered again about Muslims and deserts, and for a moment he could see Kate sloshing about not in the bath water of an Italian hotel, a bath supported by lions paws whose white base had surrendered to a simple dripping tap, but rather in one of the dunes of Taklamakan, and bright grains of sand dot her naked body and cling to her pubic hair.

Sand rained down from the heavens there in the desert (so related the local legends whose origins are in the ruins buried there) and covered everything under it. Dozens of small settlements were buried with all their buildings and inhabitants, and for a brief and very pleasing moment, in his mind's eye he could see an enormous capital city such as Rome being covered in sand as well and disappearing beneath the mass of its grains: the Colosseum filling up with sand to its galleries, the triumphal arch surrendering to the sand and being swallowed by it, their hotel buried in sand to its roof and above.

He still remembered how they entered the small hotel that had managed to maintain a modicum of its splendor, and with what pleasure he wrote their common name in the guest book, Mr. and Mrs. McKenzie, and how the clerk explained to them in his singsong voice, that it's a special room kept for young couples. Perhaps he winked at them, perhaps just blinked, perhaps neither. Either way McKenzie recoiled from his gaze. Due to the clerk's age, it seemed like the look of a pervert, one who peeps at the goings on of young couples.

"It's so hot here," Kate said, and the elevator operator, as old as the reception clerk, carried their suitcases up the stairs, while they were jolted in the rattling elevator cage. Despite the heat she pressed close to him, and between floors they saw the elevator operator moving farther away up the stairs whose carpet had faded. Had they known what they would know later, perhaps they would have left their suitcases on the ground floor of the entrance, and certainly wouldn't have given the elevator operator such a generous tip at the doorway to their room. At the time, they still thought that they were standing on the threshold of paradise.

Right away Kate approached the window. Below, between the branches of a tree whose type they were unfamiliar with, a street corner could be seen with a clothes shop on one side and a trattoria with a café next to it on the other; the branches of another tree obscured another shop. The din of the streets reached the room, the rattling of the carriages, the tumult of the passersby, a distant voice of a singer.

"Buona sera, Italia," Kate said to the street, as day began to dim and its lamps were lighted although darkness hadn't completely fallen. Afterward, overjoyed as he had not seen her for a very long time, she lay on the bed, arms spread out, removed one shoe with the other and let them drop to the floor and said to him: "Come, amore mio," but he felt the whole street was watching them: the passersby from the sidewalks, the café dwellers from their tables.

She reached out a hand from the bed, and he, instead of coming and lying down next to her and at least cuddling a bit, drew her toward him so that she'd get up. This hotel room in which they could actually do whatever they wished instilled a vague faintheartedness in him, as if they were a bride and groom from the previous century and this the first time they would be united together; though it was worth remembering, even then: what her London lovers knew he would never learn.

9

"Tell your brother to jump in and fetch it, jump, jump," they turned to him, the elder. "D'you want us to make you jump?"

Izu's shoulders shook and his hiccupping between sobs filled the boys with mirth. One of them, the chubby one, even imitated him. Until that moment the little brother believed there was nothing in the world he would be prevented from doing; the older brother, who defended him at home each time their mother found fault with him just because he had inherited too many of their father's features; now disappointed him irreparably. "It didn't stand a chance anyway," he tried telling Izu before that, and in the river no trace remained of the goat's blood.

"They're good in the water," the tall one says looking at the river down whose slope chunks of ice are rushing to their unknown destination. "One of them once split the whole sea into two!"

"And also turned water into blood," says his friend, "let's say about from the bridge to the dam everything was red." And now those three boys and the older and younger brothers all try to picture the Berezina turning red all the way up to the small wooden dam at the slope of the stream where the felled trunks stop before they are tied together into rafts and sent onward.

"He also turned all the fishes into snakes," the boy whose face was covered in pimples continues and throws a twig into the river with his right hand.

"So what?" says the tall one. "Jesus turned one fish into a thousand fishes, into two thousand!" And the ears of his fur cap shake for a moment as if confirming his words. "And made a thousand cakes from bread," he continues and they now contemplate that wonder, until the aroma of a million cakes baking almost rises in the air between the spray of water and the pieces of ice.

"That same one of theirs," says the pimpled boy, "also drowned their enemies, together with all their chariots and cannons. It was a long time ago, before Jesus was born."

And now they are debating – without paying notice to the elder and his little brother Izu – if there had been chariots at all, or if those ancient soldiers still used stones and snowballs filled with stones, or sticks and slingshots, or bows and arrows or knives, like the one the chubby boy got from his uncle the soldier; only now were they reminded of that knife, despite that it certainly could have been of use to them in their war on the goat.

"There must've been knives!" says the first one. "Didn't they have knives?"

From the edge of the water the tall boy turns his head to them. "Kolya," he says to the chubby boy, "you could've tied your knife to the branch and it would've made a -" he does not know the word "harpoon" and says "javelin" instead, but Kolya isn't keen on endangering his knife in the river, he only got it two days ago.

From its sheath he slowly draws the small knife that for all the past days has not been separated from him, looks at it for a moment, aims and throws it, and the blade glistens in the sun or in the dazzle of the ice as it's lifted up and hurled and sticks into the branch, causing the handle to quiver for a long while.

"That's easy," says the tall boy. "Let's see you hit something moving!"

The chubby boy weighs his words and looks at the knife; he doesn't want to throw it into the water.

"Not into the water," says the tall boy. "At the barrel. Let's see you hit the barrel."

He draws close to the branch and extracts the knife from it and with the edge of the blade cleans his nail the full length of the dirty tip.

When he finishes the knife remains in his hand, and he begins to walk toward the village and doesn't look back; he has no doubt the others will follow, also the two brothers that are led by their backs being pushed and their behinds being kicked.

The pushes are too soft to flatten them and the kicks too soft to injure them, and not because they are being spared by the boys, but rather to keep them in one piece for the new amusement that will replace the previous one: not only will the knife take part in it but the barrel as well. "There're too many people here," says the tall boy and leads them onward. Step by step they advance, five children and a knife.

The game they will be playing they've played more than once: one takes the part of the Tsar, a few act as soldiers of the guard and a few as terrorists attempting to assassinate him. It's a game far more compelling than catch or hide and seek or cops and robbers.

Izu is not watching him anymore nor is he crying. It seems as if something within him has been broken and he no longer expects anything of his older brother, nothing; after all he's also being led onward by being pushed. These are still moderate pushes: step by step they advance, the five of them and the knife, and the roar of the river fades behind them, and the goat with his cloud of blood has already been forgotten when the inn appears in front of them.

The windows on both sides of the entrance are cloudy from vapor, and when the heavy door opens, a soldier with the collar of his uniform open bursts forth and hops to a wooden post used for tying up the horses so that he can piss, and he lingers there until he is shouted at from behind: "It's your turn, Boris," and he turns around and goes back inside.

They now bend the heads of the two brothers whose god turned a whole river to blood – his head and the head of his little brother Izu – they bend them with firm fingers reaching from the neck to the forehead and sneak them into the back yard through a breach between the boards of the fence, and in this yard is a large pile of garbage in which a pig rummages and next to it a chicken, and in another corner a washerwoman crouches over her washing. Her large behind rests on her heels, her knees are spread apart on either side of the tub, and the dress sagging between them is completely wet. On her right a large pot is steaming on clay bricks between which flames flicker, and when they blaze in the wind their shade of yellow stands out against the murkiness of the mud and the greyness of the sky.

"You can light a cigarette between their legs," says the tall boy knowingly, not about the washerwoman but rather about women such as the one the soldiers in the inn are going up to and he and his friends sneak another look at the washerwoman's knees before lifting their eyes to the second floor of the inn, as if it would be possible to see the fire being lit that way through the vapor covering the windowpanes.

The tall boy had already found a barrel cast off in the far end of the yard, and in a hunched walk he hurries over there and begins to roll it on the ground. The knife he took possession of is now embedded in his pocket and only the handle sticks out from it. One of the windows of the second floor are opened, and from the duskiness of the room, part of a naked body flashes, round and quivering, until a large hairy hand reaches out to it, and afterward the window is slammed with the vapor still covering its pane. "Oh Boris, oh Boris," the hoarse voice of a woman says and falls silent.

"Oh Boris, Boris, Boris," the boy with the pimples groans and moves his pelvis back and forth in a copulating motion opposite the window, and the tall boy continues to roll the barrel, and its rolling – if the washerwoman took any notice – seemed to be part of the general happenings of the yard: the rummaging of a pig, the hopping of a chicken, the bubbling of a pot, the rolling of a barrel. Only in the boys' eyes was a carriage embodied in it. True, one of the spokes was broken, but when it will be set down the slope its speed will be no less than that of the Tsar's carriage.

10

He actually did prepare well for the trip: he read the guidebook over and over throughout the hours of their journey in the train travelling south and crossing the length of France, until Kate became annoyed and said to him: "Take a look outside, Ed, instead of burying your head in the guidebook the whole time." He occasionally glanced outside. In his eyes, the rural landscape couldn't compete with that of Oxfordshire, and anyway he did not like cities, and in a moment or two he returned to Baedeker and memorized all sorts of details with which to impress Kate after they crossed the Italian border (*The earliest remains of prehistoric men discovered in Italy are from the Paleolithic era and date approximately from 20,000 B.C. More developed cultures appeared between 3,000 to 1,800 B.C., and worth noting among them are the Ligurians who settled in the area called Liguria today, the Sikeloi who settled in the Lazio region and in southern Italy, and the Sards who developed a shepherd culture in Sardinia* – "which is why Sardinia is called Sardinia," he intended to eruditely inform her).

"For God's sake, Ed," she said in the compartment, "take a look at the scenery outside, aren't you sick of the guide?"

He left his finger between the pages and saw a wheat field at whose edge two cows were grazing, and it was not difficult for her to guess what was going through his head.

"You must be missing Oxfordshire," she said, "are you, Ed? If it was up to you, you would have let me sink into a depression which I would never have got out of. Thank God for this trip."

When she moved in with him, she gave up the plays of London, the concerts, the exhibitions, the parties, the wandering through Soho alleys in a merry group and all the love affairs she had had until renouncing that lifestyle and deciding to raise a family. He had heard about three of her lovers: an actor of anticipated greatness, particularly in roles as a lover; a banker, a family man who in her company became as foolish as a boy; a major of whom much was expected in India and Africa. After a short while she understood that none of them would make her his wife: not the actor into whose group she tried to be accepted, not the major who it seems preferred his regiment companions to her, and certainly not the banker. There was a time when she imagined manipulating the three of them and arousing jealousy between them, until she realized that none of them viewed her as a potential life partner.

In France, on their way to Italy, they saw couples kissing for so long they could have started at one station and finished at the next; and in Italy they saw the bottom pinchers, not in particular the bottoms of their wives; and he still remembered the dark tunnel in one of the Alpine passes, when it seemed to him that the passenger sitting opposite them placed his knee close to Kate's, but when their compartment became light again their fellow traveler seemed as calm as before and was buried in his newspaper. *Corriere della Serra* was the name of the newspaper and McKenzie thought that each time he would come across its title the anxiety of the tunnel would rise in him and did not yet know that it would be replaced by far worse anxieties.

After hundreds of kilometers or more, when the passenger with the newspaper eventually got off, he wanted to ask Kate if in fact that man had touched her in the tunnel, but he didn't ask, and a joke he had heard one night in the pub still resounded in his head about a soldier and a nun travelling in a train, the soldier hasn't been home for a month and the nun has been in a convent for ten years.

He remembered the station exit for the masses of people scampering and flocks of porters swooping down on them, and one in particular who was more daring than the others and spoke only to Kate and explained to her in a singsong voice that for a bella donna like her he's prepared to make a special price (perhaps only doubling it instead of trebling it). He still remembered how the next day they ordered spaghetti bolognaise and chianti in the trattoria: the wine was neither good nor bad, the spaghetti was too long, and only a few bits of meat were sprinkled in it resembling lice in hair. He thought that they were being cheated and that they deserved a real portion of meat and not just a pinch of these crumbs, but when he called the waiter, he made no hurry to attend their table. On finally arriving he began to explain something in an irritating inflection, until he gave up and made some vague gesture with his hand toward McKenzie and departed. A quarter of an hour later he brought a clay bowl with a few more crumbs of meat, cold and unseasoned, and the spaghetti too had turned cold, at least his had; Kate had finished hers, and all the while she ate she didn't cease looking at the passersby and not for one moment did it seem she intended to help him, on the contrary, it seemed she was ashamed of him for making such a fuss over nothing.

Afterward – she added a coin to the tip which he left – she wanted to carry on walking the streets for a while, and he wanted to go up to their room; he suddenly saw the room as a place of refuge, there at least he couldn't be cheated. A row instantly erupted between them, and in the end he surrendered to Kate and trudged after her alongside shop windows whose clothing displays she enthused over whereas he saw their own reflection in the glass and just how unsuited they were to each other. He had no doubt that her London friends would have suggested she go in and choose some flattering item of clothing, from a dress with a generous décolletage to a pair of garters.

By the time they returned to the hotel, the clerk had been replaced, and the person sitting behind the counter, a tall fellow whose black hair most probably had been combed with his long fingers, looked like a student who intended on taking advantage of the night for his studies. A thick book was open in front of him, and when he was so kind as to reach out the key to their room he didn't bother to check whether they were really the ones who had rented the room, and right away he buried himself back into his book. That way all sorts of complete strangers could have asked him for the key, but Kate, instead of being worried about that, was actually amused.

"Imagine us going into the room and finding two other people in bed," she said, and he did not think it funny. Had she done such things in London, joining other couples? Her theater friends were certainly capable of anything, and the two who visited her in his clinic at the start of their acquaintance showed great interest in the morphine he kept in his cupboard. "Wasted on the cows," they said. For their part, the cows could be operated on without any anesthetic, just so the two of them could get a little high. In vain McKenzie tried to explain to them why it was necessary to anesthetize a foal whose leg was out of joint, or a cow into whose behind a whole thermometer had been swallowed during an examination. That picture of him and the cow amused them a lot, and it seemed that without any difficulty they could imagine how his arm was inserted into the depths of its anus up to the elbow.

Here instead of cows there were yaks and dzos, and the Ladakhi treated them by themselves without morphine or ether, without alcohol nitrates, without camphor solutions, without Chlorodyne, Formalin, Sal Ammoniac, Hexamine, sulfur acetate, white liniment, mercury perchlorate – he still remembered the labels on the bottles which he left behind him, and a few of them would have been useful here as well, in this mission hospital.

To the patients who recovered in spite of the lack of medicines, it was customary to say here what was said to prisoners whose term of sentence had come to an end: farewell and hope not to meet again, skiyot le drik. Will he be saying that to this injured man? He can't tell. Perhaps in his own country that will be said to him one day as well, should he return there when all this is over –after all he'll be giving the village an even worse name. "We trusted you doctor," they'll say to him, "and look what came out of that. Skiyot le drik."

The Swedish explorer, Hedin ("Our Sven," the commissioner's wife called him each time she updated her guests about his adventures), was the first to go out to the Taklamakan desert to map the area between the Yarkand and Hotan rivers, and the commissioner's wife had high hopes for this journey. "Our Sven will find antiques for our garden as well, right Sven?" she said to Hedin, although he explained to her and her guests that antiques were not intended to serve as garden decorations but rather for the enrichment of human knowledge. "That's exactly what I meant," Ann replied.

How would Kate have behaved had she found herself at one of the commissioner's wife's evening teas? McKenzie had no doubt that in Rome, on finding herself an erudite man of renown and marrying him ("Magnani married a beautiful English widow," one of the explorers who reached here related) she became a respectable lady of society – it was her great dream, greater even than that of the theater – who hosts not only explorers in her parlor but also poets and actors and writers and artists and members of the nobility, and her ex-husband, if he still pops up in her memory sometimes, will at the most be the butt of jokes. "You wouldn't believe what he spoke to me about in the evenings," she would perhaps say in her Roman parlor. "Foot and mouth disease! I wanted to invite people over, for us to talk to, to laugh with, and he…" And she really did want to invite people over, but there wasn't anyone to invite: the villagers didn't like her, and after half a year during which she tried to find favor with them and put down roots (decorating his home with all sorts of items she bought in London, learning to embroider, tending the garden, making a small vegetable patch; one has to admit: there really was nothing she didn't try) she gave it all up, and when her old friends came to visit she would listen to their stories like legends from a distant land in which eras ago she too had lived, until she went into exile.

To her mind she certainly was worthy of a better fate than that: her suitors, while they still wooed her, would send bouquets of red roses and long letters and notes and poems of love, as opposed to McKenzie, who at the end of the first month of their acquaintance gave her, and without any hesitation, a pair of canaries and a pair of parrots, and in complete earnestness explained to her that if she observes them every morning, in time she'll get to know each bird so well that she'll be able to give each one of them a name. "You have no idea what satisfaction there is in learning to identify them," he said to her in his stupidity. It was written in the newspapers that the Russian Tsar, who just that month had come on a visit to London, calls to his wife all over the palace with their private whistle that imitates canary song, and he thought to himself: why's that acceptable in Russia and not here?

"Your canaries, Ed," she said to him after just two days, "are silent from depression," and he was forced to take them and the parrots back (in actual fact they frightened her, she told him afterward; even then she feared in the village she would feel like them, a prisoner in a cage, but she really and truly had hoped to build her future in the village). Nevertheless, to everyone's surprise, she consented to him and married him in a ceremony the likes of which it was said was yet unseen in the village – she consented to what seemed like a caprice but was in fact a desperate decision of hers to raise a family with someone who at least wouldn't disappoint her like all his predecessors had; his sticking to a daily routine seemed at the time his greatest asset.

On Hedin's first journey – he was now more comfortable thinking about him – the water in the goatskin bags ran out, and his men were so debilitated they didn't know if thirst had disrupted their minds or the liquids which they had drunk to quench it (alcohol from the primus stove and camel urine). When a white heron flew above the caravan, it was only Hedin who was resolute enough to crawl in the sand for many hours to the place where it had landed, and when he reached there on his last legs he found a clear waterhole and thus he and his people were saved. It was hard for McKenzie to imagine the Italian leading a delegation like that into the Taklamakan desert, but in truth he was not well acquainted with the Italian. What kind of acquaintance is that which amounts to no more than a few random conversations next to some Roman statues? Nevertheless, it transpired that those conversations were enough for Kate to make her decision, even if combined those conversations added up to just over an hour (at least that's what he thought at the time).

And perhaps – it's best to admit to it – everything actually started to become shaky sometime back. There had been that first night and there had been that morning during which Kate bustled with energy. It seemed she had decided that if her newlywed husband had spoiled the night, she should at least be compensated for it in the morning by the hotel staff, as if her husband was their responsibility, like breakfast or the linen of the giant bed with the copper headboard ("It looks like this bed's been through a lot," she said a few moments after they entered the room and unloaded their suitcases and hung their clothes in the cupboard. They also stood side by side opposite the mirror in order to check how they looked together: Signor and Signora McKenzie). The next evening when they returned from their stroll through the city and the same night clerk appeared on the other side of the counter with the same thick book open in front of him. In the elevator she asked: "Did you see what he was studying?" And said the name of a philosopher that McKenzie had never heard of and that one of her London friends, a philosophy student, idolized. "I think that's nice," she said, "taking advantage of the night for studying. Though I'm sure he gets disturbed a lot, that's to say by women." He did not like that statement either.

He approached the window and closed it and pulled both sections of the curtain over the pane. She became angry. "Why are you closing it? At long last you can see some life here and not the gloomy village." He felt personally insulted by the insult of the county of his birth.

"I used to wake up there in the morning," she said, "and look out the window and think, it's so quiet here that all that's needed are flowers to be brought and placed on my grave. What reason did I have for getting up at all?"

And again he felt the insult of the fields and the meadows and the avenues of trees planted hundreds of years ago at the side of the paths. "We can always travel into London once in a while," he said, and from the expression on her face realized he had answered poorly. "Why shouldn't it be the other way round," she replied, "that we travel to the village once in a while?"

To that he answered (still standing next to the window, and the curtain slightly dimming the streetlights) that they had already spoken about the matter more than once, about his clinic, about his obligation to the farmers, and that he really doesn't see any reason to re-open the whole argument here and now.

"If not now, when?" she replied. "Before it's too late. What did we make this trip for Ed, if not to try and save our marriage? Ed, I do love you, but how can we go on like this. Please open the window a bit more please, so we can see something of the street."

"A bit more will bother me," he replied.

Afterward they faced each other with angered frowns. She went to the wash-room; he lay on the bed in his clothes and heard her taking a long shower. For a moment it seemed as if the wallpaper flowers were spinning around his head. Perhaps it was caused by the chianti they had drunk in the restaurant, perhaps by the crumbs of meat added to his spaghetti, or perhaps it was his anger. His right hand, restless, felt around the drawer next to the headboard and took out a page with rules of conduct in the event of a fire, a forgotten coin, a wrinkled map of Rome, a Bible not much different from those which the mission distributed to the Ladakhi in order to convert all their Bodhisattvas to one tormented Jesus.

When she emerged from the shower dressed in a bathrobe which she brought with her and not the hotel's toweling robe, he wondered if it wasn't another crit-icism, perhaps about the quality of the hotel that he had chosen for them; her London friends would have rented a room in a hotel of far better quality even if just for a weekend break. True, they had all disappointed her, but perhaps she was reminded of the good times she had had there.

When she parted both sections of the curtain to the right and left, the night-time street was once again revealed with masses of sparkling lights from the stores, from the cafés, from the trattorias.

"Don't let yourself be seen like that," he said from the bed and watched her leaning on the railing. Only her back could be seen, but the curve of her breasts surging toward the street from the opening of the robe was almost perceptible to him, and how the passersby lifted their gazes to it.

A few moments passed until she turned around to him ("You'll catch a cold like that," he said). Even standing up straight the opening of the robe was wide and very revealing, not only on top but also on the bottom, exposing her legs and more than a bit of thigh. They too could be seen from the street, firm and glowing and when she walked forward, the inside of the moving thigh shone, first the right and then the left, and he thought: she intends to go out to the corridor like that, she intends to go down to the street like that, she intends to sit like that in the trattoria and order more spaghetti and chianti for herself.

"Did you find any treasure?" she asked when her gaze fell to the open bedside drawer.

"Just a Bible," he replied and with the tip of his finger pushed the drawer back closed.

She paused for a moment on the way from the window to the bed, next to one of the shoes that she let drop from her feet and on whose heel a leaf had been skewered, and as she continued to walk he could smell the scent of soap and her perfume. He reached his hand out to her, the rustic hand of an animal doctor.

"Forget about it," she said. "Why don't you read something from the Bible like they do in your village?"

She sat on the other side of the bed and leaned forward toward the soles of her feet and began to massage her toes from the small to the big ones, and he said something banal about the quality of Italian shoes. Yes, that's what he had to say to her, to which she replied from her bent down position: "They're also good at spaghetti," and again he feared she was mocking him. For his part, he had long forgotten about that spaghetti. ("Bolognaise!" he waved the menu at the waiter. "Bolognaise!" As if Bolognaise was the name of the chunk of meat he had been deprived of.)

He straightened up slightly on the bed and leaned back on his elbows and saw the curves of her breasts revealed in the opening of the dressing gown almost to the nipples and asked if she wanted to make up. "To make up over what?" she answered from her bent position, the big toe of her right foot was mainly what was bothering her. "If you'd ever seen me really quarreling you wouldn't have wanted to marry me at all."

She crossed over to the left big toe.

Again he tried to pull her toward him, and again she refused. Her arm shook off his fingers even before he could take hold of her, and while doing so her shoulder was revealed: rounded and soft and totally unattainable.

"What did we come here for?" he asked.

"We came to see Rome," she replied, "the piazzas and the fountains and the museums; is the Uffizi here or in Venice?"

"In Florence," he answered.

"So we'll go to Florence as well," she said, "we'll go everywhere, to Naples and to Capri and to Amalfi as well, isn't that what everyone does here?"

And then he did something that he'd rather not remember: he tried to reach out a rustic hand to her again; no, not to reach out to her, to take hold of her. Perhaps desire overpowered him, and worse than that, perhaps he believed that was the way to overpower her, not only her body but her heart too; that way she'd realize he's not one of her spineless London friends, the ones who delight in stories about shoving hands into the anuses of cows.

Somehow they rolled onto the floor: once more he reached out his hand to her shoulder, she tried to get up and he was dragged behind her causing her to fall beside him. For a moment the two of them were stretched out on the carpet, he in his clothes and shoes and she in her silk dressing gown which opened further, and still he would not desist. "Let go of me!" she shouted, and when he grasped the left side of her dressing gown and she again tried to escape his grip, her belt became undone and all her full-bodied inviting nakedness was revealed, a nakedness that no Italian had yet touched.

"Let go of me!" she shouted. "Let go of me!" And because he feared her shouting would alarm someone, he placed the palm of his right hand over her mouth to silence her, and with his left hand undid his trousers in order to release what was asking to be released from there and thrust it between her legs, and futilely kept on ramming into her. The more hampered he was, the more insistent he became and pressed down further on her mouth to crush it with her head tossing in refusal, until he felt her chin slipping beneath the palm of his hand and her teeth sinking into his flesh, and all at once he collapsed.

At first it was as if that event had just been a lovers' quarrel that a good night's sleep would wipe out; they were still trying to find a compromise between her will and his will: she wanted to enjoy all the benefits of the city, while he was repelled by its tumult and all the museums and the churches. In the Villa Borghese, for instance, she was swallowed by the exhibition halls while he preferred to stroll in the garden outside. "It's a good idea, Ed." she said as they left. "Instead of arguing, let's give each other some freedom, I'll go to museums and churches and do my shopping, and you go wherever you want, that way we'll miss each a bit until the evening. Friends of mine did that in Madrid." She had friends who travelled to all sorts of places in the world, and at the beginning they still came and were astonished to observe the changes she had undergone, until the novelty wore off and their visits lessened. One of her childhood friends who still came told her she was looking washed out and glared at him accusingly.

The next day she already began to behave like her friends in Madrid: she went to the Barberini palace while he strolled along the Tiber enjoying himself as he had not done all the previous days, and at night they each fell asleep on their side of the bed; the following day she went to see the Corsini palace and he went to the Villa d'Este just to stroll through the gardens; she went to the Capitol and he went to the hills of Castelli Romani. Afterward he wanted to travel to Lake Bolsena ("the largest volcanic lake in Italy" it was written in the guide), and when he tried to interest her in the lake, because he was already feeling her absence and it seemed as if that violent night had been erased, she refused. "Let's meet tonight," she said. He went to see the lake and its surrounding hills as well as the meadows in which sheep were grazing, and she went from Santa Maria della Vittoria to Santa Maria Maggiore to Santa Maria del Popolo to Santa Cecilia in Trastevere, and lingered in them not only due to their sanctity and the beauty of the icons (nowhere was the gauntness of the ascetic Lord better represented, and she, with all her fondness for enjoyment, believed in him with all her heart). In one of them, she must have met the Italian again, this time by herself, and after lecturing her on all the statues and icons there, perhaps he suggested she dine with him in a nearby restaurant. He must have asked her where she intended going the following day, and the day after; and if she was tired perhaps he suggested resting a while in his office in the university which by pure chance was fairly close by, and there she could even see some of the findings he brought back from his last journey to the desert. No, not the Sahara, there are other deserts in the world besides the Sahara.

Hedin, the first of those who went out to Taklamakan, spurred his men on to advance farther and allowed them no laxity: one of them who left a hoe at the excavation site the previous day was sent back to fetch it, and on his return to the caravan strayed from his path and encountered the remains of the wall of a house that had filled up with sand and whose ancient inhabitants had shriveled like mummies. Afterward, at the depth of two meters, an avenue of poplars was discovered and orchards whose treetop nests were filled with sand. And it was told – yes, stories like these circulate here – about a bow that had been buried with the archer who was drawing it, and that the moment the sand was removed from above, the arrow that had waited a thousand years was finally shot.

All that and even the most preposterous things were related at the evening teas of the commissioner's wife and added some color to the humdrum routine of Leh. But one must, the doctor knew with absolute certainty, strive for the golden mean and always be precise. It's one thing if this injured man opens his mouth and speaks about a mountain demon which was revealed to him on the way with its thousand eyes and teeth, and another thing completely if he tells about a storm which uncovered ancient corpses in the snow that had preserved them.

But it was not corpses he was intending to bury, objects were enough for him, and he won't be burying them in the snow. For hundreds of years, the inhabitants of the area had been deterred from digging there, they had been so frightened by tales of the fate of those who had tried to get their hands on what had been swallowed by the desert. One who succeeded in extricating even a single gold ring from the sand – it was told – after taking a few steps sank and was swallowed by the same sand. And so, at night, with a clarity granted to vision only by alcohol, McKenzie saw Kate: reaching out an avaricious hand to the sand and digging and pulling out a sparkling gold ring and placing it on her finger (the one she received from him she didn't like), and after a few steps – steps in which her buttocks wiggle and attract the eyes of nomads from all corners of the desert – she sinks into the sand with the ring.

Every good fraud, from faking the pedigree of a thoroughbred horse to faking a lightening wound on a cow, requires a germ of truth, and from the start he and

Tenzin planned to base themselves upon undisputed facts: ruins that had already been discovered in the desert, sites that were already marked on maps, findings that had already been exhibited in museums. And should they add to them, (and he himself won't be doing that; after all, he didn't intend going out to those areas), they would only be things that had a foundation, like someone who forges the painting of an acclaimed artist not on a clean slate but rather on top of an ancient picture painted by someone unknown from which its vintage will be attained.

It seems he had to traverse thousands of kilometers and reach this hole of holes, Leh, in order to fathom how to avenge the Italian: not with a duel; that had long passed from the world, not with a fistfight, he and Magnani had little to do with boxing (he himself hadn't boxed other than in his youth and then only once), but rather with the bait of some forged finding, the kind that would attract a curious and fame hungry explorer from Rome to here. He would harbor no regrets, even if in complete contradiction to the Hippocratic Oath, were the Italian to lose his way in the desert, as had almost happened to Hedin. He did not plan anything towards that taking place: in his eyes it would be enough, at least for the time being, that the Italian fail with some dubious discovery, as Hernell had failed with the manuscripts he bought in the markets of Kashgar and Yarkand. You're lucky, he mused, that Stein and Hedin had already left here, lucky that only the minor explorers remained here like Hernell who was notoriously gullible. No wonder he was tempted by everything they flogged. If the Italian would only be as gullible as him, their plan would work.

Yes, one slip would certainly be enough to cause the Italian not only to fall from his position at the university but also from the heights of his self-assuredness which so impressed Kate. "True, he doesn't have muscles from dealing with horses and cows, but he's got charisma!" she said about him on the evening of the second day, and he wondered if that quality, charisma, which is usually attributed to leaders, is not in fact the flip side of the absence of hesitation and doubt. He had no lack of both hesitation and doubt. Unfortunately, the one thing that was worthy of doubting – his marriage – he had not doubted at all.

11

Every now and then a prod is needed and when they dawdle, they are spurred on from behind.

Izu is crying above the barrel being pushed. Mud sticks to his hair and murky tears flow down his cheeks and his nose is running as well, and while pushing he wipes it with the back of his hand and doesn't return his gaze to his older brother.

"You mad at your brother for letting you push like this?" A stalk of grass is stuck between the lips of the tall boy, with a knife he decapitates stalks of couch grass which sprouted between patches of snow and weren't trampled by the rolling barrel, and without dropping the stalk from his mouth he begins to sing in a voice deeper than his natural voice and tries to get the tune right.

"Stalks of graaain," he sings, "don't be angry with us, flour is made from yooou."

He bends down again and decapitates a few stalks, as if their tops had grains of wheat in them and he had a sickle in his hand.

"Tell your little brother," he says to the elder one – despite that he's not behaving like an elder brother at all – "to shut up because he's giving us a hole in the head." He looks at the little brother with scorn, even though Izu's crying is quiet and halted.

"What's wrong, little chick? You have to sing when you're harvesting," And he sings the harvester's song close to his ear, and with the polished knife blade he scrapes and carefully removes a small lump of mud that was stuck to the hair of the child's temple and slowly wipes the blade on his bloated, soft, baby-like cheek.

"Stalks of graaain," Izu's voice can be heard, faint and hesitant.

"Don't be angry with us," the tall boy says to him.

"Don't be angry with us," Izu sings.

"He could have been in a choir," says the pimply boy. "I swear he could have been in a choir."

The older brother instead of answering, bends toward the barrel and pushes it onward. On their left and on their right the ground is patched with muddy snow and here and there a tree trickles the remnants of its whiteness; there's already a hint of forest from those trees, and its proximity doesn't instill fear despite there being more than enough reasons to fear it.

"What's the matter, you in some kind of hurry?" the tall boy calls out. The knife blade is held between two fingers and aimed at its target with one narrowed eye, and the hand already moves backward to accumulate momentum, and the knife is flung forward and hits the boards of the barrel between the brothers' hands and falls to the ground. For a moment they all watch it as if the blade was guilty of having missed, until the older brother bends down and reaches toward the handle. In a flash, even before he could grab it, his head is banged against the barrel and hits its boards with a dull thud, and a filthy felt boot is forcibly placed on his hand that is still feeling around for the knife and sinks it into the mud. He had been pushed by force and now his hand is being tread on, and all this is just a preface to what they intend to do in a few moments and in a few years' time.

On and on the barrel is pushed toward the wooded hill, toward the track deforested for felled trunks to be rolled down to the river. It's a wide track no steeper than the path levelled by their feet, but much longer than it and therefore capable of lengthening the amusement: on both sides of it one could play hide and seek behind the trees, and one could hide acorns there and stones or snowballs or a bomb or a knife, one could rush out from there and hurl them at whoever was passing by on the path: a Tsar in his carriage or a boy in a barrel.

"Is it tough for you, little chick?" the tall boy asks and now as well there is no compassion in his voice. "On the way down it will be easier, and we'll make your brother a king as well."

"We'll make a kinnng of yooou -" the pimply boy sings.

"And d'you know what we'll make you?" asks the tall boy. "A general!" For a moment he doesn't remember if the commander of the Tsar's guard was in fact a general or if he was just a polkovnik, but it doesn't make much difference.

"We'll make yooou a gen-e-ral -" the pimply boy sings.

"Enough of that, Petya," the tall boy says to him. "Aren't you tired of that by now?"

"But why, Boris, why should I be tired, I'm never tired. Oh Boris, oh Boris, Boris, Boris."

The tall boy chuckles for a while, and the two brothers slow down on the incline of the path. It seems as if the barrel is getting heavier from moment to moment, and the forest appears as one solid mass except for the felled trunks that are separated from their community of trees. Most of the mud that had covered the barrel has already been shed, and with each roll on the incline of the path, the gap left by the missing spoke is revealed, and the interior of the barrel is also revealed and appears to be black; perhaps it contained liquor once and perhaps wine, but now it seems that only darkness fills it.

"Won't the knife squeeze through there?" asks the tall boy when faced with the gap, black and deep. And he bounces the knife in the palm of his hand. They advance with the barrel on the incline of the path, and in a moment through the rustling of the dripping treetops the name of the leader of the Tsar's assassins is sounded, Zhelyabov, the one who placed the men on the street corners and had a dagger in his pocket with which he intended to complete the task should the bombs fail – they heard about that in the village, albeit a long time after the assassination.

"Okay, you be Zhelyabov," the pimply boy said. Now, as the incline becomes slightly more moderate, his only struggle is to decide who he'll be in the game: a Cossack or a terrorist, whichever, only not that coward Rysakov, who after being struck two or three times already began to inform on all of them. "Let him be Rysakov!" he signals with his eyebrow to the chubby boy who every once in a while continues to kick the barrel between the two boys as they push it.

The barrel, with a less strenuous motion, has reached the landing where a few dozen felled trunks await being rolled down on their way to the sawmill or to the river whose roar is very dim and faint from here – here it's the land of the trees, as there it's the land of the water.

"So, little chick, you want your brother to be a king?" (The king, Alexander II, sat in a carriage to which two pairs of horses were harnessed, and its wheels waited to be come loose from their axles and roll freely on the paving stones, twenty-four years before the wheels of the Minister's chariot will do likewise.)

Izu doesn't answer. He stares only for a moment at his older brother's eyes, still amazed by his impotence, and immediately diverts his gaze from him, and only then he (I'm the elder, he reminds himself) bends toward the opening of the barrel and takes a quick look inside and another look at the boys, and before any of them says a word and before he surrenders to his fear, he crouches down and shrinks himself into the opening.

Inside the small space of the barrel the world grows even larger: the forest trees tower upward to the skies, and the three boys gain added height, and even his small brother, Izu, is now taller than him (almost as tall as he will be years later, when he'll hurl all that had been stored up in his heart at him, and not only about what happened in the river and in the forest but also about what happened in the backyard of their home).

"D'you think I'm scared?" he says and puts his head inside as well and curls up completely, and after a moment he already tries to roll the barrel from inside by tossing his shrunken body around, but the barrel is stopped by some small stone.

"Izu," he calls to his brother from inside, "Izu," he calls again, "roll it, d'you hear me? Roll it downhill."

Izu remains on his spot, dirtied with mud from his shoes to his head. He doesn't know whether to consent to his request or not: if he consents, it will seem an implicit forgiveness of the older brother's having forsaken the goat, but the consequences of this forgiveness are dangerous; and if he doesn't consent because of his anger toward him, the older brother will remain without any punishment. He's incapable of formulating these thoughts, but because of them he remains hesitant.

"Izu," a voice is heard again from inside the barrel, "roll it already!"

"Aren't you gonna roll your brother, Izu?" says the boy with the pimples. "Your brother's asking you to, he wants to be a king!" And again they try to tempt Izu to participate in their game: they'll make him commander of the guard, a polkovnik or a general, whatever he chooses.

"Izu," the voice from inside the barrel calls out – and how determined and self-assured it was - "roll it, d'you hear me? Roll it downhill!"

"Just don't say afterward that we forced you," says the tall boy.

"Anyway, you won't hit it," the older brother answers from inside.

"If I don't," answers the tall boy, "I'll get it inside myself,"

"And you'll give me the knife too."

"If I don't score a hit. If."

Izu looks at the tall boy and at the barrel with his brother inside it.

"Won't you roll your brother, Izu?" says the pimply boy.

Izu doesn't budge from his spot. More than anything he wants to be home again, even if his mother won't be all that happy he's returned, and especially now, when their father has left on one of his journeys and she can forget the sight of his face for a while.

"What's wrong, little chick?" says the tall boy. "Have you stopped doing everything your brothers tells you to?"

"Maybe he should run in front of the barrel," the pimply boy suggests – that's the way the commander of the guard raced in front of the Tsar's chariot – but the tall one tells him he should roll the barrel by himself, and not too fast, so it won't dodge the blade.

"You're a big hero, you are," says the voice from inside the barrel, which is now, despite its boards and spokes, like a living being, turtle-like – that's how it seems to Izu seeking his big brother's eyes swallowed by the darkness of the barrel.

"Go stand there," the tall one says to his friends and indicates a nearby spot that also has tree trunks to hide behind. "And you, you'll be Rysakov," he says to the chubby one.

"We'll make you Ry-saaa-kov -"

He sings and for a moment takes pleasure in the sound rolling from the top of the hill to its slope, overpowering the rustling of the dripping treetops and the roar of the river.

Everyone scorned the assassin who opened his mouth and informed; and if that wasn't enough, he made a mess in his pants on the gallows before they hanged him. That too was related in the newspaper edition that landed up in their village where it was kept for years with its stains and wrinkles.

The tall boy is already moving down the slope and the chubby one is following him, and the two of them turn from the edge of the path to the trees on both sides, and the roar of the river reaches them, affirming its existence here as well: more and more chunks and fragments of ice are swept in its current, an enormous white fleet that is perhaps close to declaring its surrender to the spring.

After a moment it's already impossible to discern the boys within the trees.

"Roll it already!" a voice says from inside the barrel, his voice.

"Should I roll it?" the pimply one again asks the trees on the slope.

"Roll it," the trees answer, and the pimply one complies: he places his foot on the barrel and rocks it toward the stone which halts it, he increases the force of his pushing and the barrel skips over it, and after that there's nothing any longer to stop it other than the two dirty hands that halt it for a moment.

"On with it, Tsar!" the pimply one shouts to the trees on the slope and lets go.

There is no longer anything to stop the barrel on its way down.

A fistful of acorns are thrown from the left at the darkness of the opening but they all hit the boards, and Izu's eyes are glued to the right of the path whose trees are one dark solid mass through which it's impossible to see any trunks or a blade and not even the one who is planning to hurl the knife at the barrel.

The barrel continues to roll down the slope, and with each roll the gap that the missing spoke left is revealed. And from the right of the path, from the land of the forest, the knife is suddenly cast; it doesn't dazzle at all in its flight and its thrust is not heard while cutting the air, and the blade is indistinguishable from the handle as it's hurled toward the barrel and reaches it and hits its boards and ricochets from them.

"Grab it, Kolya, try again," the pimply boy shouts from the top of the path to the chubby boy, and he bursts forth from the darkness of the trees on the left and bends down and picks up the knife that the barrel left behind and runs down the slope as fast as he can.

"Not from there," he hears from the top of the path, "try from your side!"

The chubby boy runs on the slope.

"Now," shouts the pimply boy.

Close to him, at about waist level, Izu covers his eyes, but between his little fingers, which spread open by themselves, he can see the knife cast again and flying again and reaching the barrel and hitting it, but not its opening.

"Grab it, Stas, it's on your side," the pimply boy shouts.

From the right of the path a fur cap bursts forth and bends down to the knife that the barrel left behind, and from the left the chubby boys runs and in his hand a broken branch he found among the trees.

"What are you waiting for," he hears from the top of the path. "Throw it!"

All at once they are cast, the knife and the branch, and the barrel is diverted from its progress like someone blind and rolls to the edge of the path and slams into a tree trunk.

"Ilya!" Izu cries out from the crest of the hill (the first time he's called him by his name), and the barrel hesitates for a moment whether to remain in its place or continue down the slope.

From the top of the hill and from the slope of the path the others watch the halted barrel. The roar of the river is dim and faint, more and more chunks of ice are swept away in it, smaller than the ones before them, and in contrast, the boards of the barrel remain united into one entity. There was no knowing whether or not it still had any life in it, until its captive and its king bursts out stumbling in his movements like a baby. He gets up on his feet slowly and takes a step toward the path and another two or three slow steps up the slope after which he stops and stumbles and falls.

"Ilya!" Izu calls out to him; his voice is very frail.

After a moment the knife can be seen clasped in his hand, and immediately they all pounce on him and in an instant knock him to the ground. The tall one rides on his back and with his right-hand clutches him by the neck, the pimply boy rides on his leg holding him down, and the chubby boy pulls the knife from his hand.

"Leave him alone, leave him alone!" Izu shouts and tries to pull the pimply boy off his leg and gets shaken off the way one shakes off a dog clinging to a trouser leg. And from there, sobbing, Izu crawls to the chubby one and tries to grab hold of his leg, his thigh, his ankle (yes, just like Sasha will hold on to his leg on the roof of the inn in Kashgar), and again he's shaken off and falls on his back like an overturned beetle. "What's with you, Izu?" says the tall boy who is still sitting on the back of the older brother. "D'you want us to put you inside there?"

Izu continues to cry; his tears slide down his cheeks, and his nostrils fill up.

"We'll make a king of you, Izu," he cajoles him, "king of the chicks."

Slowly and with effort he gets up (hetheolderbrotherhetheolderbrother) from the muddy ground: his face is filthy, his clothes too, and he is slightly bent due to the last beatings or due to the barrel. "I'll get in," he says to the boys, "leave my brother alone." He still had courage in him.

This time – when they kicked the barrel again – it travelled faster than before, the fastest a barrel could possibly roll down a slope, and the boys no longer cared whether it would be damaged by the knife or by the river water at its end. Fistfuls of acorns beat on the boards of the barrel, stones thundered, again and again the knife blade sought its mark, and right away they ran and picked it up and cast it again. This time no branch diverted the barrel from its course and it continued on the track that the felled trunks had levelled by their rolling to the river, a track wide enough for more than a few barrels.

Roll after roll it turned, and the gap of the missing spoke could no longer be seen, and anyway it's not the knife that will penetrate through it, but the water of the river.

With each and every roll he was tossed between the boards encircling him and his shoulders were pressed against the rounded panel and his head spun: one moment he saw the blue grey of the sky, one moment the white of the treetops, one moment the brown of the earth, everything was interchanged and blurred until he shut his eyes and waited to make contact with the water.

"They're good with water," someone said far above him.

"Maybe it'll split in two and he'll pass through the middle?"

"He'll turn the fish into snakes!"

"He'll turn it into blood," said the tall boy, who had already removed his fur cap; it was getting warm.

For the final ten meters, at the end of which the barrel will reach the water, they didn't say a word, and when it finally fell into the river – with a great crash creating ever widening circular ripples – they stood tense straining their eyes to see whether it floats or sinks and whether he manages to get out of it, and a moment later they began running down the slope so that heaven forbid they wouldn't miss anything: how the water splits into two, how it turns red, and how snakes erupt from it or just swirl around. A few desperate bubbles will rise and from moment to moment will fade until all is calm.

From the crash alone (like the explosion of a bomb which at that time he hadn't yet heard or seen) his hands and shoulders and the rest of him were ejected from the barrel, but he was immediately surrounded by water, its chill and murkiness and the chunks of ice floating on it, all conspiring to draw every bit of air from him as if fingers were inserted through his nostrils and throat into his lungs. What did the boys see from where they stood? Perhaps a small dwindling whirlpool.

"Ilya, Ilya," his brother called out anxiously from the slope of the hill, "Ilya!" and the light fractured by the ice, and the air through which the light passes also called to him, as did the river bed; and the chill of the water pounded his face and his body, penetrating his clothes and hardening them, turning them to stone over his twitching arms and legs – the way the legs of the men hanged on the gallows in Semyonovsky Square will twitch and convulse – on their way to the river bed that is no firmer than the water and where one also sinks and the feet are dragged down and down.

There is no one to share with him the bubbles of the fish that rise and burst around him nor his own bubbles which are entangled in the twisted roots and fragments of reeds and branches and between swarms of leeches and seaweed and something nameless and devoid of an outline which is perhaps the force of the current, its transparent muscles and its grip and countless transparent fingers which disentangle him from the river bed and the thicket growing on it and sweep him upward and upward and upward to the white ceiling which his head hits against and is pushed away and hits again and searches for a breach or a crack that will allow him to lift his nostrils above the water even if everything below is freezing: his mouth with his chattering teeth, his chin, neck, chest, belly and legs, let them all freeze providing that those two nostrils remain and a modicum of that good air.

They didn't spur him on by shouting "let's see if you can, let's see if you can" in order for him to split the water for them or to walk on it, and their curiosity is the same as it was when the goat was pushed into the water, and all they want to find out is just how long his twitching will last. He advances beneath the sky of floating chunks, jerking and thrashing and pulling himself by the white jags above him and moving forward half alive, half dead with the aid of exhausted fingers stiff from the cold until he'll see the sky above, that grey fluffiness which does not hit one but in its indifference lets him twitch on and on from there to the opposite bank. There were no crows above him, not two nor twelve, there were only boys on their bank.

"Did you see him?" In the end, they left him alone the way a hanging man whose rope has ruptured is left, and only observed him from their bank as he grabbed onto the unearthed roots and pulled himself toward the firm brown earth, to its muddy bedding where he could spread himself out with open limbs and smell all its scents and wait for his breath to return. He did not wait for Izu, but Izu came: he slipped away from the boys with little steps onto the bridge and crossed it and came down from the bridge to the other bank and drew close to him with much fear and crying bitterly, because he thought he was dead.

Izu sobbed over him and gently wiped his scratches. His little face leaned over him and called out to him to get up, again and again, until he got up. Izu had already forgotten about the goat and was not yet angry with him for the coming years; he had not yet been irredeemably disappointed by him and had not yet elucidated all his failings to him: as a brother, as a son, as a human being.

12

Suitable paper and ink will be found sooner or later, if not on this caravan, then on the following one; but then too the main thing will be missing. What exactly will be written on the paper with the ink (real ink and not soot mixed with water) and in what language, about that the doctor still had no hint of an idea. Prescriptions were the only writing tasks that his profession required, and if there ever had been a time when he still dreamed about publishing a scientific paper that would bring him fame, he had been absolved of that dream as he had from all others.

Every detail had to be heeded, that was a basic condition, and on this matter he could be substantially aided by the experience of the swindler who had made a fool of Hernell – both in his successes and in his failures – since all in all Mohan Lal had succeeded well, and it's probable he would have continued to do so for many years had he not been exposed.

There had never been a lack of swindlers and dubious storytellers in these parts, seven hundred years ago as well: the acclaimed Marco Polo told in his diary (the doctor had read a number of travel diaries in the past year) about a giant bird who could lift an elephant in its claws, and about the wizards of Tibet who could move the clouds in order to lend shade to the palace in summer and water its gardens in winter. It was said in the small European colony that should those wizards come here they would do well to first make sure that there were enough chairs for guests in the palace of Namgyal. Marco Polo in his time was also condemned as a fraud, and more important than anything was that their own fabrication, in order to succeed, not be exposed ahead of time; in due course, yes, but before then – no.

"Doctor, if we prepare everything properly, nothing will cause us to fail," Tenzin had said to him a month earlier, on seeing the concern in his face. For the first time in years, McKenzie was in a state of mind that could certainly be defined as excited, and for the first time in years he was adamant not to fail.

How I loved her, he suddenly thought, and was surprised by its arising and being worded in his mind in the past tense, and how I hate him. Beyond those mountain ridges, the highest of the world's mountains, and beyond the sea, was the sun-drenched Italian peninsula and the island from where he came, a foggy island whose low clouds hide the sun and even in summer drizzle a fine chilly rain. In winter, had the two of them continued to live together, they would have lit the fireplace and roasted chestnuts, and outside the cold would turn the fields grey until the sun rose, and they would cover themselves with one blanket, he and Kate and all their wrinkles (he also wanted to see her past her prime, becoming lined together with him), and they wouldn't be cold even should the fire be extinguished, and he wouldn't answer the calls of any farmer, no matter how urgent.

At times the yearning was so strong he thought he would perhaps join one of the caravans going to Bombay and from there take the first ship to England, even if it was a cargo ship and he would be forced to scrub the decks. After all, on such a whim he had sailed from Brindisi. Every day he went from his hotel to the port wearing the same clothes (only half a suitcase had been left by whoever had burglarized it at the train station in Rome, and anyway he didn't feel like changing them) and found a sense of peace in the commotion of the porters and travelers and sailors making their way to the ships anchored there, or going from the ships to the gates of the port, and every day one of those ships sailed to some destination. His envy of the travelers was still only abstract – *if it was just possible* – until by the end of the week it had been substituted with a practical statement: in actual fact why not.

He still had money, the whole amount that had been designated for their journey minus what they had both spent and what he had used for the train ticket from Rome and the hotel in Brindisi and the bars he went to at night, where in one of them, more dingy and stifling than the others, an English sailor said to him: "Listen to me, Doctor, if you're looking for something to do, go to India, they're looking for people like you." Griffin (that was the sailor's name, and his friend was Evans), was referring to his qualifications as a veterinarian of which the army was in need, but he didn't sail to India to join the cavalry, and not only because he had already sunk irredeemably low – that is to say, not only because of that – but also in defiance of everyone who knew him until then as a dedicated and responsible veterinarian, whose single shortcoming was his blindness concerning the woman he had chosen, and to show them he was up to doing other things; and in defiance of his wife as well, in whose eyes he was incapable of digressing in any way from the routine of his life and surprising her by some bold move, despite having surprised everyone else by marrying her. And this act that was in no way acceptable, was also in defiance of himself; yes, he was still a young man at the time.

Until then the idea of sailing, any sailing, seemed completely unrealistic, exactly like that mythical sea that in a few years' time Tenzin would suggest incorporating into their plan. At the time they were drinking from a jug of chang served to them in a small restaurant in an alley off the street of the bazaar, and in token of their friendship, that evening Tenzin revealed the secrets of hunting flies to him – he instructed, explained, and trained him; a hunter of lions or snow leopards couldn't have done it more seriously.

"You have to aim not at the place where they are now," he said to him, "but to where they'll be in one moment. Now you try."

McKenzie tried and missed.

"Where they'll be in one moment!" Tenzin said to him again. "Not two moments – just one!"

McKenzie tried again, and this time hit so hard that the plate of momo shook and one of the dumplings fell to the floor.

"Now a few of them will definitely be coming here," Tenzin said to him, "so at least aim for one of them the right way and kill it. Don't think of it as a fly, Doctor, but as a person, the person you hate most in all the world. Think that it's your Italian."

McKenzie waited for one to land again and tried again with much effort and when he succeeded – the fly was completely squashed on his palm – the diners from the three other tables looked at him, and one of them said something to his neighbor that Tenzin was hesitant to translate.

"What did they say?" asked McKenzie.

He evaded answering.

"What did they say?" asked McKenzie again.

"They're stupid," replied Tenzin, "don't take any notice of them."

"What did they say?"

Tenzin was still hesitant. "It's just that we say," he answered after a moment and then lingered again, "someone who kills a fly that way is someone who's only a hero among flies."

"You're not telling me the truth," he was already well enough acquainted with his new friend to know he was hiding something from him. "Tell me what they said."

"That someone who lifts his hand against a fly that way, isn't capable of lifting it against a man."

"Tell me exactly what they said!" he wouldn't give up, but Tenzin refused to answer. They had clearly noticed a long while ago here in Leh that he doesn't live with a woman: not a European nor a local, not even with one of the women of Yarkand who join the summer caravans and who couple, as they say, between the humps of the double-humped Bactrian camels. And even had they not known what transpired between him and Dianne Barnes, they certainly knew that he rejected the girls whose fathers sent them to him as a token of appreciation for their having been cured.

"They're stupid," Tenzin said, "take no notice of them," He filled McKenzie's glass and drank with him, and after another glass or two it seemed to McKenzie that together with the drink he had also swallowed one of the flies that had drowned in it, and he didn't care.

"People also spoke about my father," Tenzin said to him, "for years they spoke about him that way."

Although he spoke about his father in the past tense, the way one does about the dead, McKenzie could not have asked for a greater sign of friendship: he, a complete stranger, a lazy feeble Phelingpa, to be compared with such ease to a highly accomplished scout? Perhaps Tenzin had also seen in him the mark of defeat that had been etched in his father, but his father's defeat had come only after he had completed his mission and his superior commanders refused to believe that he had accomplished it, whereas he, McKenzie, had no mission until this one.

"What did they say about him?" he asked.

Tenzin scratched his neck,

"What did they say?" McKenzie asked again. It was the chang that instilled courage in him, this drink was light and fizzy and no less agreeable than English beer.

Tenzin lifted his hand and squashed the fly on the table. "They said that anyone who tells such stories about himself" – he removed the tiny carcass with his third finger – "has got a small linga." McKenzie already knew what a linga was; the last time his was pleasured was in a hotel in Bombay. They were being watched again from the other tables, and at the one in front of them an old man chewed with his gums like the motion of a camel's jaw; that anyway, was what it seemed to the doctor.

"Okay, then we've all got small lingas," he gave a sort of chuckle which right away was substituted by a burp, and instead of being embarrassed and apologizing, he was proud of it as if in that way he'd become one of the locals.

Tenzin's father went disguised as a monk on a mission for the intelligence headquarters in Dehradun to map the hilly region of Tibet, and after terrible ordeals, when he finally completed his assignment, the ones who had dispatched him regarded the maps he created as fruits of his imagination and draftsmanship talents and not as genuine measurements of the terrain. "But I was there!" he said to them. "I was there!" And he repeated that in the long corridors of the headquarters building and again in the flag quadrangle of the Scottish company of riflemen who were marching in the shade there, and repeated it to the rickshaw-walas, the porters, the beggars, the bazaar merchants, and his persistence was no less than that of McKenzie in Rome, when he left the empty room and spoke to the chambermaid, the elevator boy, the reception clerk, the doorman.

So great was the scout's heartbreak that he lost the will to live: he withdrew into his sewing alcove in the bazaar as if into a lap, and when McKenzie passed through the alley, he sometimes saw him stooped in the darkness of the alcove silently cursing the thread, the needle, and his eyes which had become dull. It was not a cataract; it was something rooted in the soul, similar to that of his own upon arriving here: it had been defeated.

"Doctor," Tenzin said to him when only the two of them remained in the restaurant (even the old man chewing the cud got up and left), "we'll succeed and nobody will find us out, not even Stein," They were particularly fearful of Stein who had exposed previous forgeries.

"Stein's also got a small linga," McKenzie chuckled and burped again.

13

Perhaps, at the end of a long recess (eight years had passed since McKenzie had come here), a new member of the club-of-the-defeated-of-Leh had arrived.

For a moment the man shifted himself on his bed: he moved his head, his shoulders, his right hand, but still clung to his swoon.

At least I'm through with that club the doctor said to himself, I've got other plans now.

And perhaps even Henry, a senior member of the club-of-the-defeated, will also recover, should the renovation of his new home satisfy Ann and be more impressive than that of his colleague in Kashgar. As for Harper, he was perhaps the only one who came to Leh in the prime of his powers or of his belief in his powers, at least in his capacity of missionary, despite having scant influence over the Ladakhi. They were more at ease with their own deities, and no wonder: one who sits on a lotus and smiles is certainly a lot more heartwarming than one tormented on a cross, and were not the believers in Buddha here promised he would return in the future to save them? Who for heaven's sake, the doctor pondered, wouldn't want to believe in a god that would return to save him one day, from the clouds in the sky or the peaks of the mountains or the depths of the sea.

The plan of his and Tenzin's focused on the sea ("So what if there isn't one here?" Tenzin said, "One always dreams about what isn't there"), and on all those who stare fixedly at the heavens hoping to be saved. He once said to him: "That's how people behave, Doctor, tell them there's gold in the clouds and they'll come with buckets and wait. If the cloud moves, they'll move with it, and if it disappears, they'll wait for it to return. Do you believe in anything, Doctor?"

He shook his head from side to side.

"Once," said Tenzin, "I was also a believer, I believed in you people, you were my gods."

Then, for the first time, the man of the caravans spoke about his father and his superiors from Dehradun who dispatched him.

"He almost died for them on the way," he said, "and when he returned home, we hardly recognized him. He was a completely broken man, and that, Doctor, is something even you couldn't treat."

"There are many things I can't treat," McKenzie replied.

"When he reached Dehradun from Lhasa they told him to go home, they said Leh is a lot nearer than Lhasa. And do you know what he did, Doctor? He started walking, but before that he still had had something to stay alive for – not for his family, Doctor, for your people and your maps – and after that he had no reason to live. You must know about that, Doctor, from the hospital, someone who hasn't got anything to live for doesn't live."

He nodded. For a long while he too had had nothing to live for, and only of late had he found a satisfactory reason, even if no good would come of it.

"I was ten years old when he left, and when he returned I couldn't believe it was really him. He slept for over two days, and each time Mother came to look at him she'd start to cry. I was the only one who didn't feel anything. Have you ever felt that your heart was empty, Doctor?"

He nodded; after all, more than once or twice during the past eight years he had felt that way.

"When he woke up, Mother said to him, your little son is afraid of you and the big one hardly recognizes you; was everything you did for the British worth it? Only when evening fell did he undress himself of his rags and take them outside and burn them, he almost jumped into the fire himself, and even then I didn't pity him, Doctor, because he favored your people over us."

Every morning they saw him at home made them sorry he had returned. But one morning he went to the bazaar to give the tailor some old clothes to take in for him and for or the entire day sat with him in his alcove and watched how he mended and sewed. There was no need to measure thousands of kilometers, only hips and shoulders, and when he wanted to close up shop he asked him to teach him his profession, the way he had previously learned the art of mapping, only to be later branded a liar.

"But one day, Doctor," Tenzin said, "before you even begin to understand what's happened, we won't be needing the lot of you anymore. Not your medicines, not your Jesus, and certainly not your maps or your telling us what to do."

"If that's what you think of us," said the doctor, "why help me?"

"We've got a common goal," Tenzin answered. "But your Italian doesn't interest me; to hell with Magnani."

Sure to hell with him, thought the doctor.

"People here know these places from the day they were born, without any map, and you come and plant your flags on the mountains here, but without our guides you would've got lost. The day will come, Doctor, when the people will rise up and get rid of you; they already got rid of you in Kabul and it will happen here too, maybe it will happen sooner in Kashgar."

The doctor had never been to Kashgar and will probably never make his way that far north.

"That's where I come from," Tenzin continued, "and I almost didn't make it out of there alive. If it hadn't been for the injured man that we brought to you, the

Russians there would have caught up with me on their horses, they were already close." It transpired that Tenzin stood in their way, and because he refused to move aside, the guards of the Russian consul were enraged and began chasing after him through the alleyways. "Have you ever felt you were being hunted down, Doctor? One moment more and the horses' hooves would have been on top of me, and only at the last moment they stopped. Their commander's head was hit by a bottle from the roof, and do you know who threw it? Your injured man."

It was hard to imagine this injured man, who was brought here frostbitten and unconscious, picking a fight with the commander of the guards of the Russian consul in Kashgar, but it was also hard to doubt Tenzin's words; he didn't tend to exaggerate

It was impossible to know if the bottle had been thrown accidentally or intentionally and from where exactly it had been hurled. At the time the Russian was half drunk, and it's a wonder he didn't fall off the roof or down the steps together with the bottle. "Had he fallen," Tenzin said, "he wouldn't be lying here with you."

For a moment he pictured the man standing with the empty bottle on the roof of the remote inn, and around and below him the vast expanse of sand – such was the landscape of Kashgar, according to the map and to what people described – and had his imagination been slightly more developed and not as dull as that of a veterinarian, perhaps he would have succeeded in also picturing the cavalry-men surrounding Tenzin and how a bottle was flung at their commander from the height of the second floor; but he hadn't yet reached that stage.

"Joolay!" cried a loud joyous voice from outside, and only now did the doctor consider the long period of time the tumult of the hospital had slipped away from his ears. Silence wasn't commonplace, true, there were times when he could doze off, shutting his eyes and allowing the heaviness of his lids to overpower him, but the silence that prevailed around him now wouldn't have been possible had the attention of the sick and their visitors not been drawn to something taking place on the other side of the building.

He looked at the injured man a while longer, at the long fingernails of his hand (about the state of their cleanliness his mother would have said one could have grown potatoes under them, and who ever heard of a sweet little angel who grew potatoes under their fingernails?), and since it seemed that he had no intention of waking up in the coming minutes, or dying during that time, he got up from his chair and left the room.

The pot of tsampa had already disappeared from the end of the corridor, but the embers on which it had been heated remained, and above those embers hovered the smell of a cooked meal, murky with smoke. From the back entrance the apricot tree could be seen with slits in its trunk made by the ropes of the horses which had been tethered to it, and beneath a cloud of flies a small brown heap that had been deposited by a pony could be seen just before Rasul spurred it on to gallop back to the bazaar on its short legs.

Outside on the section of the yard that had been levelled to facilitate the new wing, for whose construction the money never arrived, were three children, Bihari according to the color of their skin: a girl approximately twelve years old whose face was made up like an adult and two boys who were apparently her little brothers. Beneath the nose of the smaller of them, a snotty path glistened in the dust which covered his face. Their sister marked out a rhythm for them with tiny cymbals, and on 7the hard ground the two of them performed somersaults: the elder one held his brother between his legs and with each somersault the pain in his little face was apparent, he barely held back from crying.

A few years ago, McKenzie would have interceded: he wouldn't have permitted such cruelty toward a child, despite that it was perhaps the only way for those three to make their livelihood or that of their family, but now he just stood and watched: the elder one had already let go of his grip, and the small one, after standing on his feet and wiping his eyes, approached the filthy sack that stood beside them and took a sooty pot out from it, and without delay sat on the ground and turned the pot over and began to drum on its base according to the sister's rhythm. She glided to the center of the circle of spectators and began to dance, moving her hands slowly with a snakelike motion which began in her shoulders and ended at her fingertips, she swayed her bony pelvis slowly and animated her made-up face as well, while her seven-year-old brother went round the spectators with a begging bowl held in his hand.

They were being watched by patients waiting for cataract operations and by others whose eyes had been operated on and were covered by a patch, alongside were some intestinal patients from a nearby village, a young man with crutches whose foot had been amputated, and two old men.

When the bowl returned empty, the girl peered into it and mumbled something, and the seven-year-old pushed his little brother away from the pot and sat down and began to drum in place of him. It was a more vigorous drumming than before, and the girl enlarged her movements as she drew closer and closer to the spectators. Her lean arms became more and more flexible and below her very short almost unfilled blouse her dark belly curved in and rounded out, and her head moved from side to side, from the strings of colored glass beads around her neck up to her oiled hair, while her eyes remained fixed forward gazing at one particular spectator and moving on to another.

When she noticed the doctor, she began to advance toward him with the same dance movements, and he immediately took a step backward while she continued to wiggle her meager pelvis at him. The spectators now looked at McKenzie and waited to see what he would do: he was the director of the hospital, but above all he was a Phelingpa, and at that moment that's all he was, a Phelingpa whose behavior was odd and endlessly amusing. He withdrew backward, but by then the girl was standing opposite him, her head at the level of his chest and her fingers almost touching him, and since he was left with no choice, he sighed and took out his wallet and extracted a worn out one rupee note and extended it to her little brother, but before he approached with his clay bowl, the girl brought her head nearer and with her eyes glued to McKenzie she stuck out her reddened lips and caught the note between them.

Her brother's drumming now became more unconstrained: at times he beat on the pot with his fingers, with his nails, with the palms of his hand with his small fists; sometimes he drummed on the sides, sometimes on the base, changing the resonance of the pot and its sounds. But the girl, with somewhat stale dance movements, drew close to her little brother, and her made-up eyes hinted to the center of the circle.

He joined her unwillingly and began to imitate her movements to the best of his ability, and after blurting out something to him in Bihari he began to move his small pelvis in a motion that, had it not been for his smallness and his wretchedness, could have been construed as being of a sexual nature: he thrust his little pelvis back and forth in his worn out trousers in the midst of the dusty air through which his sister weaved and he seemed even more despondent than he had been while doing somersaults with his big brother.

"Drik, drik," said one of the Ladakhi's, enough, enough; and his neighbor had something to add about those Bihari who would do better to return from whence they had come.

Harper would have used "He who casts the first stone" as a quotation, but in fact that is exactly what happened. The doctor didn't manage to see who the culprit was, but after the first one was cast and hit the side of the pot and another struck the little drummer's shoulder, a groan escaped from his lips and he rose and fled with his little brother and their sack. The big sister was in no hurry. Walking backward, she withdrew step by step in the wake of her brothers, and her made-up eyes glared at the small audience, as if saying to them: you wouldn't dare! And not a stone was thrown.

Did her red lips utter something as she passed by McKenzie? No, it's unlikely she said what he imagined he heard, but he had heard similar words in the hotel in Bombay where he had tried to find consolation after what had taken place in Italy. Afterward, while his patients returned to the building erected for them by the mission, he watched from the path and already obliterated all that he had seen or heard. He shaded his eyes with the palm of his hand and strained to see if Rasul and his pony were at the edge of the path, on their way here from the bazaar in order to inform him of the caravan-bashi's answer:

Yes, doctor, I've got them for you.

Yes, doctor, the first as well as the second, both of them.

And then, with the paper and the ink in their possession, he and Tenzin could order all the rest of the items as well: the mother-of-pearl, the shells, the salt, the anchors (they had come to mind only a month before, but quickly became the most important of all the items), and once they have them and the paper is filled with everything that needs to be written on it, the caravan could finally leave on its way.

What exactly will be written and in what language they didn't yet know, for the time being they only had the basic the idea, but it was enough for them to decide what objects they would require. When he looked at the incline of the path again, for a moment he imagined seeing – yes, even in the imagination of a veterinarian whose dreams at night are completely earthy – not the blurred silhouette of a rider on his horse, diffused and faint the way it appears though a haze, but rather the tip of a ship's mast quivering from the heat, whose puffed sails will soon be revealed as it advances closer, and as it grows larger, the pointed prow of the ship will also be revealed with its prominent wooden statue (how familiar was the face of the woman carved there).

14

In one of the ruins buried in the Taklamakan – where the caravan would be heading – the shrunken corpse of a man was discovered and in his hand a small wicker bat that he waved as the sand instantaneously flooded his house, as if that would stop the grains like flies; so it was told, and small wonder flies appear in the tale. On summer days their number increased to such an extent one might wonder how out of all the countless Indian deities, flies hadn't attained their own temple, since it often seemed they were the masters of the world and that no living creature had yet been created capable of defeating them, not a human, not a tiger, not an elephant. Animal species and kingdoms would pass from the world, but the flies, will last forever.

There were also a tale about a magic oud that was discovered there. The moment the sand was removed from above its strings one could hear sounds that had waited a thousand years to be heard, sounds that the one who played them – so it was told – every woman in the world would fine irresistible, and possibly even today would. Perhaps, the doctor reflected, if I had only learned that song things would have been different. There was a somewhat silly paradox: had he known the song, maybe Kate wouldn't have left him; but in order to hear the song, he would have had to come to this place.

In the small European colony of Leh all these tales were subject to jest, but he had learned to respect them, and not because they were true, on the contrary, because they were enjoyable enough for one to simply succumb to them. And they were certainly more fascinating than the learned analyses Stein made about his heap of junk: not only did he take measurements precise to the centimeter, but he also made a detailed inventory of the rotting contents, a list no less punctilious than the inventories of British army stores. There were payment slips for mercenaries, forms for lost military equipment, protocols from court marshals concerning various types of negligence and graver acts (someone was tried for bestiality with a cow), a ruling over an altercation that broke out between soldiers and shepherds (it was ruled that the shepherds compensate the regiment with eight fat sheep of the commander's choice). Soldiers' letters were also found: their wives on the other side of the kingdom wrote about the first words their children had spoken, about their height marked on the doorframe at the beginning of each month; and their husbands, in letters that hadn't been sent, told about the routine of the barracks, about their horses, their yearning, their love.

"My darling," one wrote, "I'm sitting now in the watchtower and writing by candlelight, I thought of you the whole evening, and do you know what I especially thought about?" In Leh, after having deciphered all the parts of the body of the Chinese woman with the pet names given to them, they said it was no wonder the Chinese had been defeated. As if the sand itself had been an army whose regiments of grains had been made to charge, and that had the Chinese been more alert while on guard in the turrets of the wall instead of being occupied by lustful thoughts, they would have succeeded in skewering the grains on their arrows.

My darling, the doctor reflected, I'm standing a foot away from the hospital where I landed up, a hospital for human beings and not for animals, and thinking only of you. And do you know exactly what I'm thinking of? That night in Rome when you turned your back to me, your shoulders, your hips, your bottom. My God, Kate, you never gave me a chance.

Because he was again thinking about his rival, he kicked a small stone lying opposite the tip of his shoe and missed and kicked again, and this time the stone flew a meter or two. On the path leading to the bazaar the two children could still be seen walking away with their sack, their sister behind them. The patients and their visitors had already returned to the building, all except the Ladakhi who had spoken to him previously. He stood a small distance away from him, and only when the second kick succeeded and the stone landed did the Ladakhi advance another step but was hesitant when he saw the expression on his face.

"What is it you want?" the doctor asked him. He spoke to him in English, and the Ladakhi, although only understanding the tone, paused.

"What is it you want?" asked McKenzie again.

The man pointed to his throat and McKenzie signaled to him to open his mouth and stick his tongue out which the Ladakhi did right away.

McKenzie glanced at the tongue: it indeed had a yellowish covering, likely the residue of food that hadn't been washed down, but nothing worrying could been seen on it or the throat.

He asked the Ladakhi to say *ah* and then to make the *ah* longer, *aaaaaah.* That request was also complied with but at the end the man pointed to McKenzie's throat with an insistence that caused the doctor to wonder if something had indeed happened to his throat.

He lifted his hand and touched his neck: it was in one piece, though unshaven. Shaving was a tiresome business, and he often pondered if it wouldn't be better to grow a beard, and if not now, perhaps after their plan is completed.

Only when the Ladakhi directed his eyebrows to the open corner window did the doctor hear a murmuring rise from the room, a soft murmuring in Russian or in some other language, and since it was a good sign that the injured man was beginning to recover, he settled for a brief nod at the Ladakhi and allowed himself to remain outside a moment longer – maybe Rasul on his pony will soon be seen around the bend. True, he would be without the requested ink and paper, whose need he was totally unaware of, but at least he would have the caravan-bashi's answer concerning their matter.

But the path remained as vacant as it had been.

15

"Do you want the birds to eat you up? Is that what you want?"

"Do you want to die? Aren't you ashamed of yourself?"

No, he was not ashamed.

All the long way from Kashgar to Leh the high peaks seemed to be floating above the caravan as if they belonged to the sky and not the earth, and the crows who could only be heard in the air, hadn't yet tried to land and cross from their domain to that of the land, but he was already waiting for them.

Afterward, Poliakov's eyelids became heavy with the covering of frost on his lashes, and when he opened his eyes after an immeasurably long time, he saw the animals chewing the remains of the feed from the sacks tied to their muzzles. One had collapsed with its burden and still tried to get up once or twice but eventually remained crouched on its front knees and would most probably be frozen like that. After a period of time, the caravan-bashi shouted all sorts of words in their language or in the language of the high mountains that observe everything, and the coolies lifted up the improvised stretcher on which he had been laid, He was already lighter than its poles and lighter than the filthy furs that covered him as if they could save his feet from freezing. By then death itself had begun to lick him from the tips of his toes.

But the caravan-bashi refused to give up on him there, not in the mornings when he stood before the caravan and wearing the coat one of the Sahibs had given him, and not in the evenings when he would sit among the unloaded crates of merchandise were arranged around him and hear about the state of their animals like a warlord whose regimental commanders come to report on the mood of their soldiers before a decisive battle – their war was against those mountains and their chill.

The feet had already been taken by the mountains, completely conquered by their icy chill, but Tenzin refused to give up on him and for hours rubbed the soles of his numb feet like a savage trying to kindle a fire with moist twigs. From the stretcher he wondered how they were not fed up with him and didn't abandon him by the side of the path, in the snow. When they reached the pass and prayed and inserted the colored rags into the mound of stones that had been erected there (the mountain demon had a taste for colored cloth), he thought it would be better they cast him into the chasm, and that way the storm would weaken and subside.

Wasn't that what was done? He saw the chasm as an enormous gaping jaw into which horses and mules and yaks had already been swallowed, and in the stupor of his consciousness he tried to recall the name of the city Jonah prophesized about after having been spewed out by the whale, but it wouldn't come to memory. It certainly wasn't Leh. How on earth could anyone live in a place called Leh?

The doctor looked at his face.

The Russian's eyelids quivered, and it seemed as if any moment he would open his eyes and talk. He'd ask where he was or for water, and McKenzie wouldn't understand a word, but wouldn't find it difficult to decipher what it was he wanted.

His eyes opened slightly: at first only the whites could be seen, then the irises were revealed, brown and blurred. Then his mouth opened as well: his cracked lips detached themselves from each other and a dull sound escaped from between them, a sound that hinted at no word, just from a throat that had been blocked for many days and was now being opened.

"Water?" the doctor asked the injured man in English and brought a glass of water that had been placed beside him close to his mouth. He gently lifted his head and tilted the glass to his lips, but the injured man made no effort to sip the water. With a skillful motion the doctor placed the corner of a wet towel on his lips and moistened them and again tried to make him sip, but the water drizzled onto his chin and from there to his neck and the sheet under him.

"You have to drink," he said to him, and the brown eyes held him for a moment and let go. Like a parent trying to coax a child to drink, the doctor tilted the glass to his own lips in order to show how he drinks from it and how tasty the water is, and afterward he drew the glass near to the lying man again and slowly filled his mouth with water and waited for the throat to imbibe it. A slight swallowing motion could be seen, but most of the water drizzled once more onto his chin and his neck and the sheet.

The Russian's eyes looked at him, but they had an extinguished look and it was evident that any moment he was liable to sink back into his swoon.

McKenzie almost gave him the local greeting since they wouldn't understand each other's languages anyway, and he only knew two words in Russian, spasiba and dasvedanya but didn't recall their meaning.

"Here," the doctor indicated to the walls of the room with his hand, "is a hospital," but the injured man continued to stare at him through the slits of his eyes and didn't respond, not with his voice nor with any facial movement.

"Doctor," he pointed to himself, directing his finger at his chest, and hoped that at least that word is familiar to the Russian and would be understood through what remained of his swoon. "And here is Leh," he indicated to the window and to the small houses of the capital that again were covered by the shadow of a cloud.

That name, Leh, the injured man must have known; after all, it was the destination of the caravan he had joined; and indeed that's how he himself arrived here years ago, in a caravan whose men would have preferred making their way without him; but he came from the south and not from the north, dry and not wet, and fully conscious. No, he thought after a moment, by no means could it be said that I was completely lucid.

"You fell from your horse on the way," and he walked two fingers over his knee to show how he had slipped into the stream, and the injured man's eyes were held by the movement of his fingers as if they also signified the pony he had been on and the chill of the snow's waters and the incline of the slope. Afterward, his eyes closed again and didn't open even when a quiver passed through them.

On the way, when the stretcher bearers spoke to him, every now and then they added some derogatory nickname in their language, and it was easy to discern the contempt in the tone of their voices, because they would have preferred carrying crates and sacks rather than him. But even without their fear of the caravan-bashi, they wouldn't have dropped him on one of the slopes – he was as filthy as they were, but beneath the dirt his skin was white and he was a master by birth, as if in Russia he had dozens of tenants in the village on the banks of the Berezina, and in Petersburg hordes of male and female servants.

To prevent him falling, he was tied to the stretcher and bound as if in a madhouse, but instead of walls against which to hit his head until he bled, there were only white slopes in the distance. "Is that what you want?" Tenzin asked the same question as the caravan-bashi's, "To give in to them?" And with a movement of his head indicated to the crows circling in the sky, "In Kashgar you didn't give up like that," he reminded him, but even that place, his last abode, was already fading from memory with its mud walls and winding alleyways. "There you fought like a man," he reminded him, "like a Gurkha." Tenzin hadn't one good word to say about the fighting ability of his Ladakhi nation. He spoke as if the Russian had been holding a weapon in his hand and not an empty bottle, and his heroism not narrowed to the throwing of that bottle at the man who had attacked him.

He as yet didn't know his name was Tenzin and knew nothing about the caravan, its people, animals, merchandise and destination, and also not about the slopes or the stream into which he would fall. He only saw the band of bodyguards chasing after the Indian with an arrogant gallop like the guards of the Tsar or the guards of the minister whose name he'd rather not recall. His behavior in Kashgar was unlike his behavior in Petersburg: he didn't recoil and withdraw, he wasn't stricken by cowardice, and he didn't let them attack the man who stood in their way. He didn't allow them to trample him with their horses' hooves or strike him or kick him in the ribs, in the stomach, in the head (in Petersburg the head was banged against the road), he simply aimed the bottle at the first one of them and hit him, and thus Tenzin escaped from their hands.

"It was the bottle that fought, not me," he replied from the stretcher when he still had enough strength to reply and didn't add: I was motivated by guilt. "The bot-tle," he repeated, enunciating each syllable so as to be better heard, but the Indian insisted on repaying him by helping him regain his strength, as if no aim was worthier than that. The thin glum man of the caravan continued tirelessly to rub the soles of the feet of someone who didn't want his body returned to the living.

"Leh," said the Englishman.

He had already introduced himself and described his role, but Poliakov wanted no doctor at his side; the man stood above his bed as he himself had stood two months earlier above Levin's bed, and Levin also had no desire for the company that had been forced upon him. It was not a glass of water that he placed close to him but rather a revolver.

Every day on his way here – thousands of kilometers from Petersburg – one more animal dropped dead, and the crows, though there was enough meat for all of them, quarreled over the choice bits. Every night the icicles extended from the nostrils of the animals, and if at night they themselves lamented their lives ebbing away, icicles would extend from the corners of their eyes as well. Every morning the sun rising in the east was reflected in the depth of all those moist eyes, and it rose slowly in shades of blood, until it was removed together with the eyes and sparkled between the two parts of the beak like a stolen earring.

"The soldiers would have beaten you to death there," Tenzin said to reminded him again how he had endangered himself for him, "if they hadn't found out you were from their country."

They had let him off fairly lightly on discovering he was Russian (at first one of them whipped him, in place of his friend who had been stunned by the bottle), they let him go as if like them he was a Cossack and had got drunk the way they get drunk. They also didn't insist that he pay his respects to the man whose protection was their duty, the Tsar's representative in this remote province, but urged their horses on and galloped off to accompany the consul who was sitting in his carriage behind shuttered curtains like that minister in his carriage; but beneath the wheels of the carriage there were no paving stones, only sandy potholes and clouds of dust waiting to fly away.

Had it not been for that incident he wouldn't have joined the caravan. Perhaps he would have remained on the roof of the inn between the wicker stools and the low tables, and perhaps, right before the eyes of the boy, he would have run to the edge of the roof without stopping there, but the boy held on to him and managed to stop him, not by his meager weight – he could have easily have been shaken off – but by his pleading, the way his younger brother, Izu, had also cried out to him after he had been rolled in the barrel.

"You have to drink," the doctor said to him.

Afterward, he joined the caravan, and for a while it seemed to him that he might reach some place distant enough where he could forget all the previous places he had been in, until he fell into the stream.

Tenzin continued to rub and massage the soles of his feet, and when he became tired, he opened his coat and placed the cold soles close to his stomach to thaw them out, and he knew should he feel some sensation, it would be the warmth of the Indian's chest and his slender ribs, and perhaps he would count them instead of what he had been counting.

The other Indian looked at them from the path, and when he approached the Sahibs' tent, their small dog barked at him, to which the Indian replied: Not nice not like Rasul! Everyone like Rasul, who not like Rasul? Only dog not like Rasul!" But when a movement was heard in the tent he relented and said: "Good dog, Dushi, good dog. Who best dog? Dushi best dog," and the terrier bared his small teeth and growled.

For a moment from the stretcher he imagined smelling the tea, rising pungent and sweet from the sooty kettle swaying from the hand of the Indian, until its scent was replaced by the stench of carcasses, and that too he only imagined smelling – the cold froze each animal in its place and preserved it in the position in which it had died: one kneeling on its anterior, another lying on its side, and one of the ponies that rolled down the slope remained upside down on its back, its four legs sticking up to the sky.

"Who's the best dog?" said Tenzin, his eyes still facing the entrance of the tent where his fellow countryman had been swallowed up. "Rasul is the best dog, there's nothing he wouldn't do for the Sahibs." He also mocked the Sahibs – he had no doubt that from the capital of Ladakh they would hasten southwards to the balls held in Simla just to boast of all sorts of adventures that had never taken place.

In the east the sphere of the sun had already risen above the summits, slow and pale and hesitant as if it was still possible to relent and fall back into the chasm. With vigorous steps unhindered by the snow, the caravan-bashi passed them, and when he reached the coolies and the animals, the loading was at its peak: one group lifted the crates and sacks breathing heavily and bound and buckled them up, while the other was tied up against their will and groaned and neighed or emptied their bowels. The crates were loaded, the chests, bags and sacks; and the-man-of-fire (that's what the Sahibs called him, to recompense him for his foul-smelling occupation) gathered their droppings into a sack to be used for heating, and after they were cleared away the snow still emitted a vapor.

"Rasul, for long time he no more work with shit!" said Rasul as he tethered the sooty kettle to the handle of the kitchen utensils crate, and before he drew away Tenzin was already imitating him and said: "And why is that? Because now Rasul he lick it straight from Sahib's ass." Tenzin tied that numb body to the stretcher skillfully and tightened the ropes as on previous mornings, and he, while still bound up, asked Tenzin in a mixture of languages that they used (some Russian, some English, some broken French) not to make it too tight: in any case, it would be no disaster should he fall off.

"But you won't fall off!" Tenzin answered him. And since he saw where his eyes were directed to, he told him to stop looking at the sky, and that the crows weren't there because of him. "In Kashgar," he reminded him again, "you weren't afraid of anything," but even in the blustery wind the hollowness of his words was clear; he knew that the white man hadn't endangered himself for his sake.

"The way the bottle hit his head! He fell from his horse like a sack!"

It was an exaggeration: while the Indian was being whipped, the Russian was coming down the outer staircase (the boy left the roof before him), and it was the height and his fuzzy head from cheap alcohol that had activated his hand; he suddenly became a big hero, a man of men, until the whip of the second caval-ryman was lifted and wrapped around his leg and pulled him from the stairs. He was dragged like that all the way down to the sand, from where the Indian had already got up and fled, and in a moment he himself would have been trampled by the horses' hooves and squashed underfoot there, if the mother of the boy hadn't shouted from the window of the inn: "Leave him alone!" And when she told them where he had come from, the whip stopped in midair.

"Ruski?" the soldier asked him, and he nodded to him from the sand, as if he really was a Ruski and not a Zhid[1]. And afterward, much puzzled, the soldier asked him from his horse why he had helped some miserable Indian, and instead of answering, he lifted his hand from the sand with the bottleneck to explain what had activated it. After all, Ruskis understand very well what alcohol does to one.

"Vodka?" the Englishman tried, perhaps he would at least recall that word, and now too he didn't answer. He wanted one thing: to get rid of the sight of the Englishman.

Afterward, after everything had been loaded, they left on their way again (what day was it? He already couldn't remember), and once again they travelled along the mountainous path, ascending and descending, they and their animals and his stretcher, and when the caravan stopped to prepare for the night, he observed them the way he had observed his travelling train companions on the long jour-ney from Petersburg to Andijan: hundreds of travelers changed over there, and one could look at each one of them not to etch their features in one's memory, but rather to erase their predecessors features with them, and to know that the face of that traveler will also never be seen again, just as the landscapes in the window will also not be seen again. At first the pine forests were replaced by thickets of foliage and they too dwindled, and afterward the trees along the way also thinned out, and wheat fields replaced rye fields and they too dwindled and were replaced by

---

1   A derogatory form of the word, "Jew."

the bushes of the plane, and after them nothing could be seen anymore. The dust that arose in the compartment penetrated the eyes and the nostrils and the throat, its grains almost as cunning as those snowflakes.

Afterward, all the other sights returned, as clear as the crows' beaks: the minister's carriage a moment before and a moment after the blast – he deserved to die, neither his friends nor he himself had any doubt about that, some of the horrific acts the minister had allowed to happen were committed right in front of his eyes – and the window through which he saw Maximov lying on the sidewalk, and the jail cell where he was incarcerated for two weeks and then released for no reason ("We don't need you to be here, you can be of help to us on the outside, let's hope what happened to Maximov doesn't happen to you"), and afterward there were other things he didn't wish to recall: whether they had happened before or whether they had happened later, it would have been better had they not happened at all.

16

Brindisi was full of seagulls.

They could be seen everywhere, even in his hotel one stood on the windowsill, and at night their shrieking could be heard from the direction of the port. Not a word was written about them in Baedeker, nor about Brindisi, but McKenzie had arrived there in the middle of that damn summer of ninety-seven, and not because he was deliberating whether to fill sacks with their feathers.

That wasn't how he had planned the trip, but he didn't want to be reminded of that anymore; not about the maps of Europe he bought months before, not about timetables, not about pocket dictionaries, not about conversation manuals. He arrived in the port of Brindisi with only the conversation manual, and on the day he sailed – after finally deciding where to sail to – he was almost late for the ship, because the night before he had got drunk in the hotel, a hotel where no married couple stayed. One of the women who stood on the sidewalk opposite the entrance turned to him when he returned from the bar and asked him "howdyoodo?" with a pouting of the lips that brought to mind entirely other matters.

On the deck of the ship, he still recalled how afterward she stood opposite the dirty window of his hotel and opened it with a shove and spat a fulsome thick globule outside, a woman neither young nor pretty, who remained dressed all the while he busied himself with her. She dealt skillfully with his trouser buttons and he wondered what she would find there, and when she discovered what she discovered, he silently cursed the whims of his body which had come to life in her honor.

On the ship as well, he still remembered her spitting into the street; he stood leaning on the rear railing, watching the trail the ship drew behind it, and below him, on the sea water, the foam seemed white yellow like sperm. What was the word she said as she spat? It must have been some comment about the taste. Here, in the mission hospital, a midwife who had worked some years before then knew how to predict the sex of the fetus by licking its mother's sheet. Yes, he had witnessed wonders such as that here, and every time it turned out she was right, she smiled calmly the way she also smiled at the goat that was suddenly seen passing through the corridor (that too happened here) or at the aunt of a patient who in the morning came out from under his bed after having slept the night there (that too happened here).

Imagine, he said to the Russian in English without actually using his voice, that someone is sleeping under your bed. And worse than that, imagine that your bed becomes empty, and the one who had been lying there left you only a note on the nightstand. Imagine that, on a bunk in a ship's cabin, all the way from Brindisi to Bombay, you can still feel her body like someone who's had a limb amputated and still continues to feel it. But then perhaps that's something you're going to feel, he said to him; the pain of an amputation.

"Vodka?" he asked him again and brought the cup close to his lips and carefully poured the water into his mouth and saw his throat swallowing. "All Russians love Vodka," he said, but the Russian didn't react.

You and I, out of all the places in the world we had to come here, and it seems to me that you too won't be leaving so soon.

And just don't tell me you were also left a note on a nightstand when you went to the post office, though you don't much look like someone who likes going to the post office. God only knows what you do like and what caused you to flee here.

"Drink, drink," he said once more in English, despite his lack of any reaction and his eyes remaining closed.

In the waiting room of the mud building in front, more than a few people had gathered during the last hour waiting for him to examine them, people the Silk Road had brought here on one of the caravans with this or that cargo, from spices to wool to opium. It was given a lovely name, "the Silk Road", despite silk being only one of the commodities that was passed along it, and in his eyes there was no longer any exoticism associated with it. "Star of the Seas" was also a becoming name for a ship. providing you could see it through the fog of alcohol as you run toward it in order not to be late, but there was nothing in that name that indicated Stella Maris, not its passengers, nor he himself.

"Are you sure you don't want to drink?" he asked again, and this time also was not answered.

"Well, then not," he said and returned the cup to the table.

Through the porthole of the ship – he stared through it for hours during the first days when he still kept to his cabin – the foam at the top of the waves seemed to be ignited into a white fire, and after some years, when he sat with Tenzin in a small restaurant next to the bazaar, for a while it seemed that its whiteness was vital to their plan no less than the whiteness of the salt or the shells and the seaweed, after all, it too leaves its mark on the shore; but they renounced that as well, just as they had renounced the whiteness of the seagulls' feathers.

For many hours on the warm nights, he stayed awake on deck, and the sea shone with a myriad of microscopic creatures, and when the moon was full, a trail of its shine spread across the surface of the water. Not far from him, couples stood and cuddled, and he could hear their murmurings, whisperings, stifled laughter, sometimes even a groan. During the warm hours of the day, he would stand alone toward the stern, and it sometimes seemed to him that if he'd stand silently enough and reach out the brandy in a gesture of invitation, seagulls would land on the railing on his right and on his left the way pigeons land in San Marco Square to peck at breadcrumbs (that too was recommended by Baedeker) and one of them, braver than the rest, would even dare to have a taste. He didn't call out to them, it hadn't yet come to that, but he whistled and clicked his tongue at them the way he used to whistle and click his tongue at dogs and at horses or at the parrots and canaries he bought for Kate.

No seagull was tempted, not by alcohol nor by the palm of his hand, and a particularly impertinent one even made a dropping on his shoulder. He sat down at the stern of the ship, leaned his back against the railing and spread his legs out in front of him, and the passersby skipped over them and didn't take the trouble to move farther off so that their talking about him would be swallowed by the wind (that he was a doctor they all knew, but they raised all sorts of speculations as to the reasons for his journey: they said he had got medicines mixed up, embezzled money from the hospital where he worked, stole wallets from patients he had anesthetized, shamelessly felt up his young female patients, and that he had even forgotten a pair of scissors in the stomach of someone he had operated on; and with all that, for some reason they saw him as a doctor for humans and not for animals. The worst of the rumors was his preying on women, as if to increase his pain they added: "he in fact had a beautiful wife," and in that they had of course hit on the truth).

Sitting there he was already drinking straight from the bottle, and the seagull that landed on the railing moved its tail once or twice and made a dropping on his shoulder. It was annoying. It was insulting. It was yet another humiliation. Right away he cursed the seagull and its mother, but in a moment or two was already talking to it, perhaps aloud and perhaps only with his lips, and he said to it: come on, move your tail, do it once more, why not. My wife shat on me, so why shouldn't you.

The doctor turned his gaze from the bed in front of him to the corridor – the patient previously seen passing through there had returned, and in addition to him he had to examine the old man whose testicles had swollen like melons (when he walked he carried them in both his hands), and the boy whose cuts had festered (his father had tried to insert his medicine into cuts he made in his flesh), and there was a monk who had grown a breast like an old wet nurse, and one who wished to turn his skin white like the skin of the Sahibs, and another who insisted on receiving medication to stop the growth of his stubble because he believed it was robbing him of his potency. Those were the easy cases; time would deal with the difficult ones. It would cure or put an end to them.

They all sat patiently in the waiting room, each wearing the headdress of his nation or tribe or religion: the Ladakhi with hats whose brims curled above the ears, the Balti with black hats, the Yarkandi with green hats lined with fur, the

Muslim women with veils, the Punjabis and the Sikhs with turbans, and none were bitter or grumpy in the manner of Europeans in waiting rooms. For the most part they accepted their illnesses with complete equanimity, the way animals learn to adjust to their illnesses or even being maimed, or like others who accept their approaching death.

Not all of them, true, not all of them. There was Burgess's reddish cow – for some reason that came to mind, perhaps because it happened on the day Kate and her friends arrived from London – who the moment its infected udder was touched, kicked him above the knee causing him to hop around on one foot for a few minutes, and when he returned to it he was kicked again and flung against the wall of the barn where he doubled up in pain. He almost wept from anger but was determined to return to the cow and treat it, and still it kicked him, not because it had become accustomed to the infection, but because it couldn't bear any further pain, and with each kick Burgess chuckled and made no attempt to stifle his laughter, though he very much wanted his animal to be treated, after all, it was his most beloved cow.

The cows of Oxfordshire were almost as beloved as members of the family, but in no way as holy as the cows of India. The only one that approached a degree of holiness, at least in the eyes of its mistress, was Mrs. Adams' spaniel, but he didn't want to be reminded of that dog or its mistress – it too was a memory he could do without. Would he have chosen Margery Adams under different circumstances and made her his wife instead of Kate? No, it somehow had been decreed that one afternoon Kate would arrive from London with her friends, and her violet scarf would wave in the wind, and he would fall in love with her like a young boy.

17

"No?" said the doctor. "No what?"

The injured man didn't answer.

Speak already, he said to him though not aloud; if you've got something to say, say it. Before that he had wet the corner of the towel and moistened his forehead and he seemed slightly calmer, but in a moment began to toss his head in a movement of stubborn almost despondent objection.

I kept things inside for eight years and do you know what happened as a result?

The Russian didn't answer.

What happened is that I'm about to do something I may regret for the rest of my life. Did you ever regret anything?

The Russian (he had used a number of different names after joining the Socialist Revolutionaries) actually had quite a lot to tell, should he return to consciousness and decide to answer.

For a day and a half he lay in his clothes in a cheap Petersburg hotel and didn't get up. He had fulfilled his mission, without which the assassination wouldn't have been carried out, but that small mission was enough to bring about his breakdown. Through the smashed window of the hotel, a summer breeze blew even when the sky turned dim and darkened. When he thought about the man left lying three floors below him, one of his partners in the minister's assassination who had been caught by the police, or about his father who had been left lying the yard of their home – and he often thought about both of them – he decided not to allow fear to crush him, even when the police and soldiers and detectives would burst into his room. He lay on the stained mattress and the fragments of glass spread on it and couldn't tell whether the moaning and groaning he could hear was coming from the next room or from the back of his mind. The heavy breathing rose toward him from all the rooms of the hotel, and in his frenzied dreams sometimes all the women - the bony, the fat, the young, the old - were replaced by the girl he had left in Minsk – he knew her as Masha, but in truth she was named Miriam – but not all of her was replaced in them, just part of a curve or her eyes or not even that, just the tiny drops of sweat above her upper lip. But in the dream, Masha with lipstick smeared on her lips and her eyelashes blackened, demands her money in advance and haggles like a merchant, and afterward exaggerates her groans to increase her payment or to give pleasure also to anyone who might be listening and peeking from the other side of the wall (the wall had a hole in it, as every room had, and had anyone taken the trouble to peek through it they would have seen a man lying on his bed in his sweaty clothes, silent as a corpse, his hand still holding the crumpled handkerchief he waved yesterday on the street corner down below, to signal to the bomb throwers when to throw them).

For hours on end he lay there in the hotel waiting for them to break down the door and couldn't understand what was keeping the detectives. From his window on the third floor he not only saw the assassination, but also how the soldiers of the guard caught Maximov afterward and how they beat and kicked him and knocked him down on the paving stones a few meters from the crater the bomb had caused and how his head hit the road and his mouth gaped and his eyes turned toward the clear sky from which the smoke is already beginning to dissipate, or toward this window of Room 312.

He lay like that for two and a half days, though the total amount of time had become blurred, until they broke down the door of his room.by kicking it in with their revolvers drawn. All the detectives and policemen and soldiers were certain he would shoot at them or try to blow them up together with himself; but the only weapon he had on him was that handkerchief. They were really disappointed. All at once the room was filled with people: more detectives and more policemen and more soldiers as well as a prostitute with her client. They stood around his bed and looked at him as if he was the commander of operations or his deputy, or at least a bomb engineer and not just a handkerchief waver.

That, after all, had been his entire role: some wave from platforms to a loved one in the window of a receding train until the sound of its horn fades away, and some wave from the pier at stern of a sailing ship. He waved from a hotel window to the street corner below him in order to signal the approaching carriage (at the time only the beating of the hooves could be heard, *clip-clop*), a grand carriage with a trio of horses harnessed to it, the driver dressed in a uniform with a peaked cap on his head, a minister's carriage: *clip-clop*.

He had once been a minister, when his body was still whole and his organs weren't spread all over together with pieces of the carriage, and his right hand still protecting his face, as if it was possible to halt the bomb and its explosive device with a manicured hand – a hand that had permitted ruffians to rampage, and did nothing to hinder them: the ripped cushions, the shattered furniture, the welling pool of blood, everything he saw from his hiding place in the attic through the slit between the damaged slates.

When he joined Vera's group, all that was expected of him was to be a lookout, in this case from the third floor of the hotel. They knew nothing about his true conduct in the village; on the contrary, they thought he had handled himself heroically. He was instructed to book into the hotel under an assumed name and identity ("No more Poliakov," they told him) and to memorize his name and profession and his assumed history so that he could repeat it even if woken up in the middle of the night. He was ordered to watch the street from his room and at the right moment to wave at the bomb throwers standing below, just to wave; and he was expected to remain silent, and not to give anyone away even if beaten, threatened, or made promises.

"Will you talk or won't you talk?" Duchin asked. "That's all we want to know; can we trust you or not?"

"Answer him," Vera said.

"You can trust me," he replied.

The policemen uprooted him from his hotel bed that was strewn with fragments of glass, and as he stood there in silence, one of them punched him in the stomach and he doubled up, the second one straighten him only for him to receive another punch and be pistol-whipped in the face. After that they had handcuffed him and pushed him along the corridor. The women stood with their clients and watched him, lipstick smeared around their mouths and makeup around their eyes, while they thrust him forward, receiving a hit here and a kick there, and still clutching that handkerchief which became heavier from moment to moment, as if he was no longer himself, Ilya Poliakov, but rather someone who is going to pay with his life for them and the handkerchief is his cross. The thought passed his mind that instead of nails they'll pierce him with the glass fragments of the smashed window, and not only in the palms of his hands and his feet but also in his chest and stomach and eyes and temples.

But he didn't do it for them, it was rather for himself – he was no saint, what had he to do with sainthood? And the whole group were also far from saints, even if self-sacrifice was of the highest value in their eyes, at least in Vera's eyes (Duchin mocked her: "Just don't be in such a hurry to sacrifice yourself, Vera Alexandrovna, it would be better to use some discretion instead").

The policemen pushed him along the corridor, and at the stairs one of them, Igor was his name, pondered whether to kick him from behind and roll him all the way down, but his colleague reminded him they had been told to bring him in one piece. One of the onlookers shouted: "Don't break his neck, otherwise there won't be anything left for the hangman." They led him down from floor to floor whose doors opened one after another, and through the cracks he was peered at by large eyes and small red, pink, and brown nipples, and only at the final staircase Igor couldn't restrain himself any longer and kicked him down it.

At the bottom they picked him up with one pull of the handcuff chains that almost ripped his arm from his shoulder and led him outside to a carriage whose curtains were shuttered. And as he rode in it (the driver didn't have an official uniform, or a peaked cap, only a tattered coat patched at the elbows exactly like those worn by the counterfeit drivers of the revolutionaries), he thought about all the men responsible for previous assassinations, it was well worth learning from their readiness to die in the struggle for the nation's liberation. He thought too of the masses who stood on the sidewalk and watched those men all the way to the square. He also thought of the drums beaten there, and about the black wooden placards waving here and there together with those holding them. There were five placards and on each one written in large white letters was: **the king's murderer, the king's murderer,** five times **the king's murderer.**

But he hadn't killed any king or a minister of the king and not even the carriage driver of the minister, and should they hang a placard on him at the very most it would say: the handkerchief waver.

If he had killed anyone, he hadn't killed him from the hotel room but rather hundreds of kilometers from there, not at a street junction of the grand capital but in a neglected village yard. He had not done it with a bomb or with his hands, but with his eyes: he killed him with their pupils. There are those who kill with their hands and those who kill with their pupils, it's enough for them to watch from afar and do nothing. A woman there was forced to eliminate the print of her baby's mouth from the palm of her hand, while he, Poliakov had to eliminate those sights from his eyes, because the-eye-is-the-lamp-of-the-body, isn't that what they say? "And if your eye is unclouded, your whole body will be full of light," the son of their god said to the crowds that gathered around him. "But if your eye is evil, your whole body will be full of darkness," he said even before he knew he would be crucified, "and if your right eye causes you to stumble, gouge it out and throw it away. It is better for you to lose one part of your body than for your whole body to be thrown into hell."

But the sentenced men were not crucified, they were hung, and Duchin told him about it in all its gory details in order to test his determination: how their heads are covered with hoods, how each one is placed on a stool, how a rope is wrapped around the neck, how the stool is kicked, how they flutter in the air and how afterward the rope is cut and the body drops and hits the platform and is then dragged to a black coffin where quicklime is poured onto the body, the face, the eyes. The body and eyes are darkened by the whiteness of the quicklime.

But those eyes, which have no light and no innocence, he saw punctured and rolling like marbles on the ground – the ground of the yard of his home not the platform of the gallows – and all the sights they had seen rolled with them: quilt feathers swirling in the air, pieces of furniture hurled from windows, slates extracted from roofs, fragments of glass that had once been windows, dismembered body parts which the blind dog strays among while covered in a stained prayer shawl and the shed feathers stick to it as well.

They were all white, they had not been blackened yet.

18

The doctor had only heard a little about the goings on there: a few rumors reached Leh about revolutionaries who are trying to put an end to the Tsar's rule and the monarchy in general, and perhaps they had already killed one of the Tsars, but this Russian didn't look like a revolutionary. Younghusband also didn't look like an adventurer yet nevertheless was one, and Lord Curzon didn't look like a lord when he was treated in the hospital here – there is no heroism in nakedness, and certainly not when one is defecating like a baby due to having drunk contaminated water.

Since he was thinking about water, he moistened the lips of the Russian once more and wiped his forehead and his temples as well as his eyelids devoid of lashes –perhaps they were shed after the ice had formed a crust over them. Only the dead were preserved by the snow, but the crazy plan he had formulated with Tenzin will be executed in a desert that possesses the same powers of preservation. Hedin and Stein had already obtained much information about the area; different as they were from each other they complemented one another,. In one aspect they were similar, neither one had raised a family – they had saved themselves from what he had learned the hard way - what it's like to have horns.

When those popped up in his nightmares, they didn't grow from his head like that statue of Moses, but were stuck into his belly or his loins, not the horns of a calf or a bull but rather the horns of a Minotaur, about which Magnani also had something to say during that short week. That was the division of roles between them: he, McKenzie, would lecture about the digestive system and the genitalia of bulls, and Magnani would relate all sorts of ancient Greek legends. How ridiculous he must have sounded when among the extolled marble statues that had all lost an arm or a leg, he insisted on telling them about a stud bull that had broken a leg and found difficulty mounting the cows, or about a five-legged calf, or about the universal-cattle-cure (the one that on its vial stated it was beneficial for coughing, lung infections, dysentery, milk fever, infected udders, intestinal cramps, calving difficulties and reproductive difficulties and for itching), which perhaps would have also cured hybrid creatures such as these. Magnani smiled politely and began telling about the maze at whose end the Minotaur lay in waiting and about a certain Greek (that's what he called him, "a certain Greek," as if McKenzie wouldn't remember his name anyway) who tied himself to a pair of wings in order to escape from there, and Kate lapped it up like a child being told a bedtime story, and not only due to the pleasantness of his voice. There was a sort of contradiction to her: on one hand the clear-headedness that had empowered her to decide to marry him, and on the other hand an old yearning for all that was beyond the reality of her life, including the stories of saints and all sorts of fool's tales. And now, after eight years had passed, hadn't the time come to tell such a tale to Magnani?

At the annual dinner of the Geographical Society, Stein showed a surprising sense of humor when he returned to Hedin a wooden folding measuring stick that had been forgotten in one of the ruins, the way a surgeon would return the scissors that a fellow doctor had left in the stomach of the patient. That story too was told more than once on winter evenings in Leh, and the commissioner's new adjutant said in Stein's heavy accent (in truth, Stein wasn't German): "Pleez, Herr Haydin, your measuring shtick!"

Was not McKenzie also imitated behind his back? It's likely that he was. Anyway, when they began ridiculing Stein and what he had been occupied with for over a year, McKenzie listened attentively. He wasn't interested in the rags that had been discovered or the fragments of documents, and most certainly not in one-thousand-year-old pumpkin peels, but the scripts that were concealed in the ancient refuse interested him greatly; all his curiosity was focused on them, and their stench was completely forgotten.

At the time, beside himself and Henry's new adjutant, Ann was also hosting the missionary and his wife, and Dianne, Henry's secretary – that's how he saw her at the time and definitely didn't envisage a common future for them – as well as a merchant who was passing through Leh on his way south. Dianne, who every weekend would dissolve yet another nearby mountain peak in translucent water-color shades, asked the merchant if by any chance he had happened to see the frescos that had been taken from the desert. Hadn't that caravan with the frescoes passed through Kashgar at exactly that time? (Yes, murals were also discovered in the ruins, and the researchers also took those to museums in Europe, after they had been hewn out with the layer of wall bearing them.) It gave Dianne an agree-able sensation to think of herself and as a link in a long chain of artists, profes-sional or amateur, whose origin were the cave artists.

"What could possibly have been drawn there?" the merchant replied. "No doubt some god with ten hands and ten eyes." And whether that god was portrayed there or not, it was done on a layer of mud mixed with cow dung, The merchant ridiculed the men of the caravan who took pains to pack and transport over thou-sands of kilometers - if the ladies will pardon him for a moment - painted shit.

The ladies blushed and pardoned. Oh, how the ladies of Leh love to blush and pardon!

After more than a decade here, the doctor found nothing wrong gods who had many hands and eyes, after all, some tales from the Bible and the New Testament were no less preposterous. In any event, Ann's guests were more interested in the latest gossip than in the deeds of gods, and if for some reason one of the usual house guests was absent, all the rest would speak about them to their hearts content; without malice but with considerable amusement (Dianne and Giles for instance, has anyone heard what's going on between them? "That Giles," Henry said about his adjutant, "doesn't seem to me to be interested in women at all").

Did they not gossip like that behind McKenzie's back? For a long time they had tried to make a match between him and Dianne, and it was probable they gossiped about him no less than the passengers on the ship to Bombay, but because all the people of Leh had their weaknesses, and each one of them knew that no one comes here without being forced to do so, they were somewhat forgiving of each other's weaknesses, if only because none of them wanted their own not to be forgiven. They were many and had to be banished all the way here.

For a moment (the window facing Leh remained as empty as it had been, and there still was no sign of anyone waking up) he tried to picture Dianne, not the familiar image of her, solemn even when painting, but rather an unkempt Dianne, but didn't succeed. It was utterly inconceivable that she could take the place of Kate.

"Ed," Ann said to him on one of the first days of spring, "I'm sure you'll both find common ground and that Dianne will make you an excellent wife, after all, you're also not that young. You've both been living alone for such a long time, so what could be more right?" Afterward she found a pretext for them to meet, and Henry helped along: why doesn't he and Dianne write a detailed letter together to the treasurer of the district (Henry knew that treasurer from Lucknow; he barely knew the multiplication table, the old fart), and Dianne with her fine command of the language could draw up a list of all the hospital's needs for the coming year.

It was the first evening that he had spent alone with a woman since the evenings in the hotel in Bombay, and they sat in her room with the draft of the letter and conversed and drank tea, and after she filled his cup she was careful to return the kettle exactly to the center of the napkin. A lace cloth was also laid on the nightstand, and on it a vase of flowers whose stems were cut exactly the same length; her books were arranged on the shelf alphabetically and in a perfectly straight line and not a speck of dust could be seen on them - it was doubtful they had been read by her. For so long everyone had tried to make a match between them, until this evening arrived when she apparently decided to take the advice given to her in order not to become an old maid.

Dianne told him many things after they had drawn up their letter to the treasurer ("Henry says he's an old fart," he wanted to say to her in order to shock her, but didn't). She spoke about her family that she misses terribly – they're all in England and she hasn't seen them for ages. Doesn't he miss anyone? She told him about all the places she landed up in with Henry as secretary and bureau director, there wasn't a place that Henry didn't take her along with him, and how her secretarial work fills up her day and how much satisfaction there is at times, in the knowledge that even her small self was making a modest contribution to the Raj and the British Empire. It was only here, perhaps owing to all these mountains and the snow in winter, that she sometimes feel so lonely she –

In mid-sentence her small hand rose to her eye in order to wipe the corner with a handkerchief on which her initials were embroidered, and when the hand returned to the table, tightly closed, he reached out his hand and covered her small fist and the handkerchief together. Right away he saw her shoulders beginning to tremble and her face twitching like that of a child and didn't know what to do. He never knew how to conduct himself with a crying woman. A moment passed before he got up from his chair and hesitantly gave her a friendly hug. She seemed alarmed by his touch, but when he began to disengage himself she clung to him like a child to its father or its older brother and afterward like a woman to the man she had never possessed. He froze. Had he taken one more small step, things might have taken place in her room at that hour of night, but he hastened to mention an urgent call at the hospital, one of his patients was apparently hovering between life and death – it didn't sound too bad, that hovering between life and death – and before he had even finished the sentence her grip on him had become limp and her grip on herself had weakened. As he left the room he saw her drooping in her chair and facing the window in which the silhouettes of the poplars merged with the black of the slopes and the night.

Whether a moment later, in one fell swoop, she yanked the tablecloth with the napkins and the kettle and the cups, he couldn't know; perhaps she removed everything slowly in a routine manner, and also tightened the tablecloth afresh and arranged the lace napkin in the center once more. The following day she took sick leave, probably the first she had ever allowed herself. On the evening of the same day, when he arrived at the commissioner's house for a visit, Ann said to him: "In God's name, Ed, what did you say to her? Is that how we can count on you?" Henry led him to the passage and said: "Really, Ed, she's travelled hundreds of miles with us, the poor girl, and we've never seen her in such a state, what did you do to her?"

In the passage of the commissioner's house he wondered why those who desired him he had no desire for – the Adams widow and Dianne the virgin – and afterward he wondered what would have happened had be behaved differently and after a while found out she had been infected by the souvenir he brought from Bombay; he, the doctor, on the back of his pony, had transported the Neisseria Gonorrhoeae bacteria to Ladakh like the exotic animals that were transported to Chinese emperors (he did not yet know whether he was completely cured).

Had it not been for Kate, he would not have gone to prostitutes, not in Brindisi nor in Bombay, but for one month they were his women, different as they were from everything he knew. There had been one month, enchanting and deceptive, in which he and Kate were attracted to each other because of their differences, and it took a while before she began to criticize him about his conservatism and his occupation and having never done anything out of the ordinary, even not during his years of study in London, at an age when one can still do crazy things – after all, in the village the farmers run his life, them and the illnesses of their animals. She chose not to ridicule him about his church going Sundays, unlike her friends. Not only were the Holy Scriptures heard there, but also what was new with the neighbors: did the cow give birth? Does the boy still wet his bed? For a while that simple camaraderie to her preferable to the cynicism of those London friends, and only when she had lost hope were their voices echoed in hers. "They warned me!" she said and her voice trembled, but she did not pack a suitcase, as he sometimes feared she would – that one day when he returns he'll find that she's disappeared.

"Maybe give me one of your medicines," she said having not yet calmed down. "If it helps animals, it might also help me." She learned the names of the medicines one night in the clinic, and not because she had begun to take an interest in veterinary science but because she wanted to find an occupation for herself during the long hours. And why shouldn't she replace his sick assistant, like an understudy filling the star's place and being discovered as having talent. Within a few minutes she learned to roll all the names off her tongue, and later took pride repeating them in the ears of her friends the way one boasts of exotic names from a safari in Africa: lead acetate, white liniment, mercury perchlorate.

"Mmmercurry Per-chlllorate," her London friends giggled in his ear and more than anything were amused by the universal cattle cure. It sounded like a religious term owing to its totality (in Kate's ears not in a derogatory sense), and the ridiculous name made them think also of a universal-sheep-cure or universal-human-cure, something to replace alcohol or sex.

Aunt Elizabeth, who had met her friends three or four times, said that with their upturned noses it's a wonder the rain doesn't enter their insides, and of her they said that she should be put in a museum just as she is: with that mummified hairdo and those high collars and that pious expression on her face, God, how did she bare children, from the Holy Spirit? On the last Sunday of September they went to church and sat in the last row and giggled all through Reverend Stewart's sermon, and at the end, in spite of Kate's attempts to stop them, gave a lengthy ovation as if requesting an encore in a concert hall.

A month later the priest said to him: "Are you sure you're making the right decision, Ed?" And he replied: "Yes, she's not like them. I could see that from the start. She herself wants to move here." The priest looked at him and at the carriages drawing away – her crimson scarf waved there – and a moment passed before he said, "I just hope with all my heart you're doing the right thing, Ed."

"Better now," she wrote to McKenzie in the letter she left him, "before everything gets too complicated. Right now at the beginning before we have children." That's what she wrote, as if children could have been born from nights such as that first night in Rome or the one when he forced himself on her.

She added: "A year has passed since we were married, Ed, and it hasn't been a good one, not for me and not for you, it's better that we don't lie to ourselves."

He didn't lie. He was surprised. He had gone to post a letter and wasn't expecting this.

He had left the hotel and walked to the post office. "You don't need me for buying stamps," she said, although before that she had intended to buy something from the shop on the corner. There was a long queue in the post office and after a long while, when at last his turn came, someone popped up in front of him and McKenzie tried to protest in English.

"Non comprende," said the obnoxious man who bypassed him, "non comprende Inglese," Those words made McKenzie even angrier, because it was clear everyone around understood his meaning perfectly. When the clerk began to attend to man, McKenzie fumed. He was after another night of little sleep: he had lain tense in bed aware of the sounds coming from the other side of the wall from the German couple, and also aware of every rustle made by Kate beneath the sheet, though they both pretended to be asleep.

In the post office, because the clerk had given his place to someone else – he even moistened his thumb with his lower lip and stuck the stamps for the man – McKenzie let out a curse in his finest English concerning the man and his mother. He didn't raise his voice but could be easily heard and it wasn't difficult to guess its meaning, and the man turned around and punched him, instantly seating McKenzie on the floor. Someone bent over him with a glass of water. "Aqua," they said to him, "aqua," as if to extinguish the fire in him; and he really did feel his face was burning.

After he recovered (someone reached out to him the pen that had fallen from his pocket, and another his glasses that by some miracle were not broken) he stood in the queue again, and the clerk then hinted with his hand for him to approach and those in line made way for him. On the other side of the counter the clerk spun his finger next to his temple indicating that one mustn't get involved with crazy people. "Pazzo," the clerk said, "pazzo."

"Si," replied to him.

When he left the post office it seemed as if hours had passed since arriving there: passersby filled the sidewalks, people sat at cafés and trattorias, and the greyness of the post office changed into a clear day with all the colors of the street. For some reason the incident in the post office induced a sense of calm over him, as if to teach him a lesson: problems indeed arise but ultimately will be solved and the good in man overcomes the bad. On the postcard he wrote:

Dear Aunt
As you can see, we are wandering around and taking in all the delightful
treasures of Rome.
It's a magnificent city, and with all due respect, London simply cannot
hold a candle to it.

Yours,
Ed and Kate

In this mood he walked back to the hotel. It seemed that the pedestrians were
smiling at him, or perhaps they were smiley by nature. On one of the balconies
someone was singing in a loud voice, and below him a boy rolled a hoop on the
sidewalk; a blind man tapped his white cane, a woman walked two wooly dogs
whose species McKenzie did not recognize. Above the roofs the sky was a clear
light blue never seen in England, and one could easily consider the idea of journeying to other cities – Venice, Naples – journeys that would erase this miserable
first week as if it had never happened.

He walked back to the hotel feeling optimistic. The receptionist smiled at
him and McKenzie returned his smile and went up the stairs. The carpet covering
them was somewhat worn and the wooden banister wobbled beneath his hand,
but all that seemed to him to be part of the journey. He had no doubt that in years
to come he and Kate would recall this hotel with affection: its frayed carpet, its
wobbling banister, the reception clerk, perhaps even the four-poster bed.

He thought should he find her in the room – when he left she was reading
Baedeker and marking a map of Rome – he would finally do the deed that hadn't
been done on the first night, it would be done with delight and not by coercion;
perhaps now they both would desire it. He knocked lightly on the door of their
room (207 – that number would be cursed forever and ever), and when she didn't
answer, he thought she had dozed off and opened the door. The bed was empty,
and not only the bed: the entire room seemed empty. His suitcase was still in its
place, but her suitcase was gone; all the new pairs of shoes that had been previously
arranged at the foot of the bed were gone, the new scarves she had hung on the
corners of the mirror were gone, her new hats were gone, her shawl, the stocking
he almost tread on when he left for the post office. Her toiletries were gone from
the bathroom, but the scent of her perfume remained in the air; she must have
sprinkled quite a lot on herself before leaving.

But he still didn't understand she had left, he was just surprised by the emptiness the way someone whose house has been burglarized would be, until he found
the letter laid on the nightstand. Only then, on the sight of the white page with the
ornamentation in its margins – he himself had chosen that notepaper in a lovely
stationary shop – he began to understand the unthinkable had happened. And
right away he said to himself: perhaps she just moved to another room? After all,

she did complain about the room their neighbors on the other side of the wall, especially about the neighbors. And in a moment the chambermaid will come in and help him move his things as well, she simply had first helped Kate with her suitcases.

"Dear Ed," was written at the top of the letter. "By the time you read this letter I won't be here."

For a moment these words had the ring of a suicide note, but he wasn't truly afraid of that, even when she had complained about her depression in the village.

I beseech you Ed not to try and find me and to try to understand why I did this. It's better we part like two adults who tried something for a while and didn't succeed very well. We're still young and each of us can go our own way. Do you think it would be better for us to live together for years just because you were lent you the money for this trip, and to have children that we don't' really want and to torment each other for the rest of our lives? That way would also ruin our children's lives, after all, I came from a home like that. One thing I do know, now it's still early enough. And now that we're actually here and not in your village, we can make a decision calmly. You have no idea what an effort it is for me to write this letter, and how much I've thought about you and how it's tearing me up inside.

Tomorrow (that is to say, today, as far as you are concerned) I'll find a suitable time for collecting my things; that seems to me the best way. It's not cowardice, Ed. Sometimes it's better to avoid unnecessary conflicts that are of no value. I think if I were to say all this to you face to face it would be much more hurtful: not only for you, but for me as well.

I wanted to raise a family with you, Ed. In the village, not in London. But for a whole year I tried to make friends with everyone there and they simply didn't give me a chance. They though me arrogant, that only clothes interest me, that I don't know how to make a home for a man and would never know; they said that I spent the whole day in bed. In the end they were right about that, because what did I have to get up for? There were days when I simply didn't know why I bathe and comb my hair and eat, and you noticed nothing of that; the cows interested you more.

I had high hopes for this journey, I thought it would be our opportunity to start afresh. But here, rather than everything working out, nothing turned out the way we wanted — admit it, Ed, we never had a week like this even in our worst times, and I don't only mean that night, I mean in general. So I'm decid-ing for both of us, because it seems the rightest thing to do. It's not easy, but to carry on as before would be worse (in fact she had found a place to sleep and had probably telegraphed her banker friend to transfer money to Italy for her sustenance in the event of Magnani delaying). *I'm sure you will recover and find yourself another woman; after all, you were an eligible bachelor, and perhaps because of that the women of the village couldn't bear me. I'm sure,*

Ed, you'll make an exemplary father; I can clearly picture you with a child on your shoulders, or explaining with great patience about all the animals, and taking it for walks through the fields the way you used to take me - first week to Kensington, the second to Spring Hill, the third to Yarnton and the fourth to Chadlington, and afterward all of them over again - not that there wasn't something pleasant about returning to familiar things, there was, at least in the beginning.

He had taken her on those walks for her to become as enamored with the county of his birth as he was. He had never made so much effort with a woman before. None of the women he had known could compare to her, not in the radiance she showed when happy, and not in how she withered when offended. During the hour he was missing from the hotel, she took with her only the clothes that she had bought in Rome, because she had made a firm decision, both despondent and calculating at once; to put an end to their marriage– she decided to shed it from her like a lizard skin.

He had seen one like that, scaly and wrinkled, in a crack of the hospital wall, lifting its head and lowering it, as if praying while at the same time peeking at him with two large round eyes darting here and there (perhaps the drumming of the children had woken it).

He looked again at the incline of the path through the window. There was no trace of the three children. What was it he wanted? To see Rasul returning from the bazaar with the answer to his request? He wasn't expecting him to be carrying paper and ink with him or that all the other objects had been loaded into his saddle pouches; objects all connected with the sea.

"We'll get everything," Tenzin said to him, "besides that, when people want to believe in something, nothing bothers them, not even when something's missing, not even the truth."

In the corner of the corridor – it took a while for his eyes to adjust to the dimness after the harsh light outside – new twigs could be seen under the pot that had been restored to its place and would not doubt be used for the evening meal. Soot covered the surrounding walls up to the height of a man, and on the opposite wall a round face was etched into that soot, not much different to the faces European children would outline with a finger on a windowpane after having blown their breath upon it: two dots for the eyes, a very short line for the nose, a concave line for the mouth.

"We'll get everything and he'll swallow the bait," Tenzin said. From all aspects the deed was criminal, but many European standards have no validity here: the women of Ladakh married a few brothers without shame, and in Kashmir men married a few women without shame, and throughout India young widows were still burnt together with their husband's bodies. Other tenets of faith predominate here as well; the European idea of being born again and of eternity was replaced here by the complete antithesis, the idea of becoming nothing – in fact, it seemed here in the East there was no greater punishment for man than to be born again.

And indeed it is a punishment, he reflected opposite the face of the injured man, in which no feature moved, a punishment and not a prize. Who in hell would want to go through all this again?

19

Forty steps was the necessary distance for preventing a chain of unplanned explosions – it was the only detail they shared with him in the briefings and Poliakov was filled with pride it had been revealed to him. Apart from that he knew nothing about the bombs; they never showed him one. Never! (He repeated that to his interrogators who didn't believe him.)

The sight of the street afterward was horrific: in an instant its appearance had changed, and when the smoke dispersed everything in the crater the blast created could be seen, the little that was left of the carriage and its passengers. People were running around, and on the bridge of the Obvodny Canal a trio of dappled horses with shorn manes were dragging two wheels behind them.

From the window of Room 312 the bicycle of the roving detective could be seen on the other side of the crater: it was completely bent and one wheel was still spinning in the air. Its rider sat open-legged on the ground, his right hand pressed to his stomach and blood dripping through his fingers, and when the other detectives, whose carriage hadn't been damaged, came up to him, he tried to get up but failed. He pointed to Maximov; and tried to say something. One of the detectives bent down to listen to him while his partner approached Maximov who was lying in a peculiar position. His face was striped with trickling blood and a crimson puddle was forming alongside his stomach.

"Who else was with you?" the detective asked but Maximov didn't reply or move.

"Who else was with you?" the detective again asked – no, not asked, shouted, his voice could be heard up to the third floor.

Horses were neighing on the bridge. The one on the left had collapsed and the other two were struggling futilely to drag him.

"Who the hell else was with you?" the detective shouted and kicked Maximov in the elbow; his eyes were clear against their sooty backdrop, wide open and decidedly sparkling, and for a moment it seemed that they were turned toward the hotel – at the window of Room 312 – but perhaps he was looking at the sky. The smoke had already been dispelled from there but the smell of sulfur still remained, heavy and seeping into the depths of the lungs.

"Someone must have helped him!" a voice was heard from the street where curious bystanders had gathered, and a woman taking her dachshund for a walk pulled him by his leash away from some unidentifiable object he was sniffing on the sidewalk. She asked what had happened and they answered her and the dachshund bared its teeth.

"Who else was with you?" the detective shouted again, ignoring the small crowd. The blood continued to spread on the sidewalk. From the greenness of Maximov's eyes that had become clouded and surrounded by soot, the glare of the sky or the hotel window was reflected: for a moment it seemed that the silhouette of the man watching everything three floors up was doubled, and when he withdrew from the window back to the dimness of the room, he heard the fragments of glass ground beneath the soles of his shoes. The thought passed through his mind that if one of them pierced his foot a shout would escape from his mouth and Maximov would at least know he was also suffering.

"How does your sweetheart write?" he asked him a month ago in the apartment that served as a hiding place, while faking letters for him in the event of his suitcase being searched. He replied that she doesn't write, didn't write and never will write, and in that Maximov found an apparent similarity in their situations. "They break one's heart just by being so beautiful and so delicate," he complained in a whining voice. Vera was doubtful about that since the flower seller Arkady had fallen in love with not long ago - after his previous thousand affairs – was neither beautiful nor delicate. He sometimes reminded Poliakov of his jokester friends from the yeshiva[2], though rather than his barbs being aimed at some tyrannical teacher they were aimed at the Tsar in person. He especially liked to mock the security arrangements of the palace, mimicking him double checking that the doors were bolted, searching for assassins behind the curtain and looking under the bed to check if any bombs were there. He mocked himself even more, while writing fake letters he said no woman had written to him nor ever would, and he well understood them.

"Who else was with you?" the detective repeatedly asked. His partner returned to the carriage and stood on the rider's platform to survey the length of the street. Their colleague still sat on the road and held his stomach and the spinning front wheel of his bicycle had already begun to slow down.

"Who else was with you?"

That was their system; to repeat every question ten, twenty, thirty times, until you're exhausted and answer.

"Who else was with you?"

The detective grasped Maximov's sooty face between his thumb and forefinger, and right away the thumb was covered in streaming blood; he must have pressed one of the pieces of metal that were stuck in his face.

Maximov groaned.

From the first floor of the hotel the voice of a woman was heard talking to the

---

2   An Orthodox Jewish institution for study.

crowd below her, perhaps she disengaged herself from a client and approached the window to watch the goings on. "Have pity on him," she called to the detectives, "the guy's half dead!" Only her elbows leaning on the windowsill could be seen, and below her it seemed as if the entire street was covered in bits of broken glass, just as in Bykhov the ground had been covered by feathers from torn quilts; as if the yard had turned white from snow, and afterward turned red and muddy and stank. That sight, together with all the voices and smells associated with it, he had tried to banish from his head and for a considerable time had succeeded.

"I saw him looking up there!" said a shopgirl who had come out of a nearby clothing store. "And after that he threw the bomb. There was definitely someone else!" It transpired that just as she was cleaning the display window from the inside (she still held a crumpled rag in her hand) she saw Maximov gaze up at one of the top floors of the hotel – which floor she doesn't exactly know, but a floor high up, of that she's certain.

Three floors above the street, in the room from which he should have fled immediately after the explosions, he withdrew from the window back into the dimness of the interior, and again fragments of glass were ground beneath his shoes. For a moment, it brought to mind the sound of snow being flattened, but it was summer then, the middle of July, and his whole body was sweating, and not only from the heat.

"But who was travelling in that carriage?" asked the woman with the puppy, and they told her the Russian Minister of the Interior's name, and the puppy barked.

There were already two dozen or more people on the sidewalk and they surrounded the detective and the injured man in a crowded tightening circle. There were men, women, as well a boy of ten or eleven.

The detective stuck a clenched fist into a wound on Maximov's midriff and the shout that escaped from him silenced the horses on the bridge: one of them stood there on his hind legs and neighed, perhaps it was trying to free itself from the harness tied to the horse that had collapsed, and farther on from there, at the point where the bridge joins the road, for a moment a familiar tall upright figure could be seen, perhaps Volodya, under whose clandestine supervision the mission had been executed and who had made sure each one of them was in his appointed place. He had a new disguise, but his walk hadn't changed, a watch chain shimmered from his waist. In the middle of the road, sitting next to the bicycle, the detective groaned. His colleague was still surveying the length of the road when he shouted to other detective to ask Maximov about the minister's servant who today of all days wasn't travelling with him.

"Did the servant help you?" He stuck his fist into the bleeding wound and once more turned it, and the sooty head moved from side to side. From the injured pelvis the blood had found itself a pathway between the paving stones and the fragments of glass.

His bed was also covered with fragments of glass, and he hadn't allowed himself to drop onto it and let them pierce his body. Gomolyov was the name given to him, Sergei Gomolyov, very Russian sounding like Ivanov before it. In his suitcase, between his clothes, were fake love letters that Maximov had written for him, this time in a slanting handwriting (how I miss you, Seryozha, there's not a day I don't think of you, not a night, when will you return?), and on one of the stamps below the post office seal, a pair of red lips was imprinted. He remembered the words of the letters well, they filled him with much pleasure and much pain, because if the girl he really had left had written to him, she would have had just one wish: go to hell; and it was his opinion too that it was a fitting place for him.

When he looked outside he saw how they were dragging Maximov along the road to the sidewalk in front of the hotel – they dragged him by the armpits, and a crimson trail was drawn after him on the paving stones – he also saw the soldiers blocking the curious onlookers from congregating again. The detectives that had come with them, spread out for the length of the street. They were not only surveying the passersby and the haberdashery and cigarette peddlers, but also the entrances of the buildings, and there was no doubt that with systematic searching they would also reach the hotel and examine it closely floor by floor; nevertheless he didn't budge from his spot.

"Why don't you ask at the hotel?" the shopgirl called out from the opposite sidewalk. "He must have been helped from there! The whores who work there would do anything for money?!"

"And I suppose you work for free?" someone answered.

From his window he turned his eyes to the crater in the road: whoever rose out from there must have wanted to get a close look at the pieces of the carriage whose side panels were smashed along with the man who sat between them – the most powerful of all the ministers of Russia and the one who allowed rioters to rampage and the police to ignore them. A few meters away from the debris of the panels, the head of the minister could be seen through the velvet curtain of his carriage; no features could be made out, not those of the minister or anyone else.

"So?" they said to the man who came out of the crater. "Did they dig a tunnel or not?" Earlier the assumption had been raised that a mine had been detonated under the carriage from a tunnel that had been dug under the road, as had happened some twenty years before when the Tsar was assassinated. It had been dug from inside some nearby store – perhaps a grocery or a cheese store.

They asked the shopgirl if it had been dug from her place and recalled how when Tsar Alexander the Second was assassinated, a gentleman was being shaved in a nearby barber shop and was killed when the barber's hand suddenly slipped from the noise of the blast or the shock wave. He died before the Tsar who lingered for a few hours before departing this world.

An argument broke out whether Tsar Alexander died right away or later that night. It seemed there was nothing more important to them than the hour of Tsar

Alexander's death twenty-three years ago, as if one of the most senior of the ministers hadn't just been killed.

Maximov's groaning rose, louder than it had been, and the two detectives who dragged him got up and wiped their hands on a tree trunk. One of them picked up something from the sidewalk, and crimson handprints could be seen on the tree trunk. The smoke had completely dispersed, and only the smell of sulfur lingered in the air: heavy, foul-smelling, refusing to dissipate.

When Poliakov bent over farther from the smashed window the glass fragments were sharp against his neck, but he stuck his head out and looked at Maximov's face: it was sooty from the neck to the hairline, his lips split and his eyebrows singed, but when his eyes opened they were green and clear, and from of the road it seemed that with their expiring strength they clung to the man above them – him. A bird flew above the roof of the building opposite him and also looked down for a moment and pointed to him with its left wing as if to say: the one you are looking for is hiding here, here, what are you waiting for?

Down below they showed Maximov a tiny tin soldier in a white-red uniform ("Some kid must have lost it," the voice of his neighbor in the hotel could be heard), they swung it in front of his eyes whose lashes and brows were singed. "There was at least one other man with you," they said to him. "Do you think we're playing games with you?"

From the end of the street a two-wheeled cab with a pair of horses harnessed to it drew near and stopped at the crater, and a chubby gentleman in a jacket and a brimmed hat and clutching a briefcase in his hand nimbly got down from it, it must have been the doctor who had been summoned to verify the death. His cabdriver went down with him to the crater and uncovered the torn body (it had been an easy death as a matter of fact, more painless than all sorts of other deaths): he removed pieces of the side panels and tatters of upholstery from above it, and only when the last of them were removed, the doctor approached and what remained of the minister writing down his findings in a notebook.

"Maybe he should also examine the driver of the cart?" a woman in a straw hat called out to them. "Doesn't he also at least deserve that?" And those around her agreed with her because it was just like the gentleman being shaved when the Tsar was assassinated. That poor cart-driver went to work in the morning, and in the afternoon was gathered together in pieces, Lord help us!

"Can I get a towel here?" asked one of the two detectives that were bent over Maximov and turned his head to the boy at the entrance of the hotel, the one who brought cigarettes and candy to the prostitutes.

His colleague was kneeling on the sidewalk in a crouched position, and between his knees Maximov's head was eclipsed, dark as the head of a black man.

The detective still held the tin soldier in his right hand, as if to prove his claim that another man had been involved and when he wasn't answered he threw the toy into the air and caught it, again and again, until he let it fall in its white-red uniform straight onto the sooty face beneath him, and Maximov groaned.

"There was at least one other man here," said the detective, "just tell us who it was and where he is now."

"It's for your own good," said his partner.

From the entrance of the hotel the boy came out in rags that one of the women had patched together for him and reached out a tatty towel to the first detective who then wiped the blood from his hands. "We can ask for another towel and bandage you up but give us one small reason for doing that."

"Or calling the doctor for you," said the second, "he's still here, he could treat you."

Maximov was silent.

On the edge of the crater the doctor reached out his hand to the cabdriver and took his square leather briefcase and returned his notebook to one of its compartments, and from his jacket pocket he took out a white handkerchief and wiped his forehead.

"He can sew you up," the first one said. "Look how much you're bleeding."

But Arkady couldn't see: both his eyes were closed and his mouth was clenched between the detective's two knees. This time he didn't even groan when the detective threw the tin soldier into the air again and let it fall. This time it hit close to the left eye, and when it closed from the pain he bore his teeth in an arrested cry.

"Oops," said the detective.

Not far away, in the middle of the road, the stretcher bearers drew close to the crater and descended into it, and a moment or two later one of them cursed when he reached the remains of a body. Apparently he was no less refined than Poliakov who had medals been bestowed for refinement his entire chest would have had been covered in them.

Afterward the stretcher bearers were seen rising out of the crater with their load, and farther on the doctor's cabdriver whipped the horses and the coach went on its way. The receding rhythmic beat of the hooves reached the hotel, unlike the beat of his heart it was regular and suddenly slowing down.

Two men who looked like detectives caught a young man in a beret and the uniform of a railway worker just like Maximov's uniform, and the coach bypassed them on their right. The young man struggled with his captors: he tried to extricate himself with all his might, he kicked and cursed and wriggled and freed one arm and for a moment it seemed like he would succeed in getting away, until they overcame him when one of them struck the back of his neck with the butt of his revolver – perhaps a Browning like the one that Poliakov had been refused.

"Your friend's been caught," the detective said to the sooty head, "now we won't need you to tell us anything. You can remain silent as much as you want, to your death."

At the end of the street the railway worker was thrown to the ground, and his captors held down his shoulders and his kicking legs. A shout was heard from there, and more than pain and anger it was one of dismay, like a toddler who suddenly discovers how unjust the world into which he's been born is; but the voice was the voice of an adult trying to free himself from his captors. "Let me go!" he shouted. "What do you want from me?" The block of people who faced him as one solid mass, said that the man who escaped wore a peaked cap and not a beret and was wearing ordinary clothes and not those of a railway worker; and the shopgirl also stood her ground and repeated her story, but her voice was no longer heard in the tumult of the crowd. There was a noticeable movement toward the captured man, and the soldiers restrained the curious onlookers like a small herd: with subdued force applied to those in front gradually reaching those at the back.

"I should have been home an hour ago," the dog owner complained, was it her fault that just then she went for a walk? "Be thankful you didn't go to the barber," said a voice from the crowd and right away chuckling could be heard. Someone who didn't hear the joke wanted to know what they were laughing at. He was told and a spirit of good cheer prevailed.

Beyond the bridge, the church bell chimed four times, and afterward the clock struck one. A whole hour had passed since the assassination, and from the hotel room that hour seemed like a full day, a year, an era: before which he had been a different man. Two months ago he had been a different man and not only by changing his name and place of birth and parents and fiancé and her letters (I'm sitting opposite the window and rain is falling, is it falling where you are? It's beautiful and sad when the sky weeps, but I'm not weeping, Grisha, I'm waiting for you and won't stop waiting).

"He's dressed just like you," the detective said - three floors below Poliakov - to Maximov's bleeding face, "the beret and uniform of a railway worker. You don't even have to tell us where you got it from, he'll tell us everything. Your friend will tell us everything he knows.

Maximov was silent.

"You've already missed out on the doctor, but we can still take you to a hospital. Don't you want a doctor to treat you? A doctor could save you."

"Maybe he prefers a nurse," said the second detective.

"There's not much he could do with a nurse."

Afterward they dragged the railway worker along the road. The policemen held him by his ankles and pulled him as his head hit the paving stones over and over. They dragged him so that the two of them could look into each other's faces, the captured terrorist and the railway worker suspected of helping him, only because he was dressed in the same uniform. The sound of his head hitting the paving stones could be heard up to the hotel window. In spite of this, Poliakov didn't budge from his spot: he didn't call the policemen and admit to his guilt, he didn't try to distract their attention, he didn't lift a finger. The dimness of the room protected him, and from the street his window was certainly no different from all the other windows that had been smashed; and besides, he was already skilled at observing things from afar.

Had he not been created in His image as someone whose entire function in the world amounted observing from afar?

He had been created in His image, he thought, and in a moment the transparent, smoky likeness of the hidden god was substituted by the face of the man who had fathered him.

20

"Tateh," he said, "Tateh," and it seemed to the doctor that was what the injured man called his mother, and not only due to the pleading tone of his voice but also to the similarity of the name of the organ for suckling – do not all languages have a common origin, at least most of them? And the moment the Russian became silent, his thoughts wandered to that soft, warm part of the body.

He thought about her. Not his mother who had suckled him for a very long time ("I told you that's would happen!" his father said to her years later), not Kate on the balcony of the hotel in Rome, but the prostitute in Brindisi; that word was doubled when she asked if he'd like to have another go between her breasts and pushed them against each other forming a crevice because he looked so miserable to her.

"Scusi," he said at the time, as if it might seem an insult that his potency was not being renewed, and she said: "Va bene," no matter, precisely according to the conversation manual.

The Russian's hand moved on the bed, perhaps it intended to hold on to something, but only his fingers were raised slightly and then dropped.

The doctor lifted up his wrist and measured his pulse again: its rhythm had quickened, but not to the extent that arouses concern. Had he not counted sheep before that? No, he had been tense and anxious, whatever he had been counting must have been threatening.

His aunt (again he rapidly crossed an entire ocean) also didn't like sheep, neither dogs, cats, horses and cows, and had it been up to her, she would have preferred he treat only winged creatures, and let all the rest drop dead, sheep too, despite that they didn't *moo* very loudly but bleated quietly.

Perhaps her conscience was bothered (a sealed letter from a law office in Oxford informed him of the small inheritance he had received), that she hadn't done enough to stop him, after all, old people have more than enough time on their hands for pangs of conscience, even if they hadn't been guilty of anything. Had she not opposed his marriage vigorously enough? She had even taken the trouble to find all sorts of corroborating signs and symbols in the flight of the birds she saw from her kitchen window.

He used to hide in her garden behind one of the stone gnomes and peek out and call to her from there. "Cuckoo! cuckoo!" and hide again, and the aunt would pretend to be surprised and say: "Where's Eddie? I can't see Eddie! Has anyone here seen Eddie?" She said at least gnomes don't mess up the lawn the way dogs do. She was disgusted not only by mongrels whose mothers mated in the fields with dozens of males, but also by well-behaved pedigreed thoroughbreds that he himself examined and verified. Yes, that was what they faked in the country of his birth, horse and dog pedigrees, and McKenzie knew just how to expose frauds like that.

Who knew then that in the end he would specialize not only in faking documents, but also faking the places where they were hidden? It might sound preposterous and absurd, but he was completely lucid, as was Tenzin, and what they had planned from the beginning of summer now seemed operable. It's one thing to go to the ocean with a bucket in order to transfer its waves beyond the mountain range, like the Chinese man who relied on his offspring to carry on that work, and quite another to concentrate on one wave and what remained of it. The first is preposterous, the second feasible.

Out of all the objects that would be necessary for their plan, it seemed the shells would easiest to obtain, because they arrived here with the Silk Road caravans, being used by monks for ceremonies in all the monasteries of Leh. Lucky, he thought, there's nothing in the world that holds within it the sight of the sea the way that shells preserve its sound.

"You can hear anything that way," Rasul once said to him, "Rasul he hear his womans like that" – he then touched the lips of the shell lying on the doctor's table as a paperweight – "that way he know what be born!"

"But how?" For a moment McKenzie wondered if a shell hadn't been used like a stethoscope, the way a glass is placed on a wall in order to hear what's being said on the other side.

Uncharacteristically, Rasul became embarrassed and fell silent and a blush spread over his dark brown skin. The doctor still didn't understand. "From the stomach?" he asked.

"Not from the stomach," Rasul answered, and because the doctor looked at him and waited for an explanation, he overcame his embarrassment and extended his right arm and spread two fingers apart and brought the finger of his left hand close to that exposed gap and said: "From there."

The doctor, after fully understanding him, allowed himself to cast doubt on the method. He had heard about the licking of pregnant women's sheets, but even the Amchi with all his tricks wasn't assisted by it.

"Rasul understand womans better than Amchi!" Rasul said with resentment, and because McKenzie continued to be doubtful, he rounded the forefinger to the thumb on his right hand and tried to convince him with an explanation no one could contest. "After all, the opening of woman (Rasul used a different word) is where you go for where baby lie, Rasul he got good ears! Not only hear, he sing to it."

For a moment, against his will, McKenzie could clearly see a smooth and soft belly with a head bent over the lower part and tilting its ear to the naked privates, or singing or placing its lips there to kiss it: not the entanglement of Rasul's hair, but rather a head with scant hair in whose center there's a bald patch like the that of a monk. On some nights that image returned to him in the darkness in his room: the Italian bending forward with his small bald patch between Kate's legs, and talking talks to the fetus growing inside her, lecturing it about the world it will be going out into and preparing it for life with the two of them in Rome.

On the third page of the letter she left on the nightstand in the hotel, she wrote about the two trips that had determined their future. She wrote about something he had known for a long time; how she came to be in his village. Her friends had taken a wrong turn and only by chance arrived there. That's how you and I met - she wrote - you gazed at me with that certain look while treating a horse, and I noticed you had good hands and a big heart, and also that you wanted me in a way that they had long not wanted, and that's something, Ed, I will never forget. What else will I remember of you? Many things. Not only our Sunday outings, but also your embarrassed look the first time you asked me to dance; I waited a whole month for that, and you could hardly believe my consent. I also remember the excitement of your body at the time, I haven't forgotten that.

After that, she wrote about the trip to Italy and the effort she had made, how she had tried and failed time after time. How they met Magnani in the museum by chance and how he impressed her with his knowledge. It would have ended there, she wrote, after all, that's what it's like on trips, one chats for a while and goes one's way. But two things happened (the word three was erased). What the first one was, he knew immediately: the night he had tried to force himself on her.

I was hurt by that, she wrote, and I thought if that's what I do to you, turn you into a mean and violent man, then really what's the point of going on. And the following day, when I met him by chance in the church (you must be saying: that hypocrite with her churches!) and he suggested we walk together for a while, I thought to myself, why shouldn't I walk around Rome with a true Roman, and what's more, a university professor. I thought I could learn about the city from him and in that way so would you, you would learn by being a little jealous — you would learn that you had to make a little more effort for me, Ed McKenzie.

Here he stopped reading, and not only because his sight had become blurred: he stopped because he thought he would cause himself further pain if he continued. What was the use, the facts were clear: his wife had left him. Time passed until he read what the second thing was that changed her plans. One of the times she had been with him in a restaurant, Magnani got up to speak to an acquaintance from the university, and an English woman from a nearby table turned to her and they chatted for a while, as sometimes happens abroad when meeting people from one's homeland. The woman was alone. Her late husband had apparently left her enough money to stay in an expensive hotel and also to continue paying for her room when she travelled to other places – Capri, for instance, to where she intended to travel the following week. She had noticed Kate talking to Magnani and was sure she had come to Rome alone and found herself an intelligent, well-educated Italian. When she heard she was married she said: "See what fate does to one!" She told her that fate had taken her husband life in an accident and that she had mistakenly thought her life was over. Fate could also change Kate's life in an instant if it had introduced her to the Italian here. It has a way of creating an opening for whoever is brave enough to pass through it.

She apparently did not think of passing through it until the third thing happened. What it was exactly, he didn't know. She had chosen to point out only two things, and the next entire five lines of the letter had been erased so that it was impossible to identify even one letter. Perhaps she had written about a different kind of meeting with Magnani, and perhaps only about her new friend who had proved to her how hopeless her marriage to the country veterinarian was. Perhaps the woman had offered her hotel room to her for the week she wouldn't be staying in it, and that way, even if Magnani would hesitate, she wouldn't be left without a place to stay.

In the next paragraph, for some reason, she chose to tell how in fact Magnani doesn't surpass him in anything, on the contrary, Ed surpassed him in almost every aspect, Ed is committed and industrious and loyal whereas Magnani is boastful and needs many women despite beauty not being one of his virtues, The professor doesn't even live alone but with his mother and sisters (yes, the whole building belongs to them). In this part of the letter she suddenly recalled another point to McKenzie's credit, but instead of consoling him, he found the compliment hurtful: And I'm not sure he would be able to bring a horse to the ground the way you can. I didn't forget that, you see, I was so impressed by it at the time. That was the first time I wanted you; all my friends suddenly seemed so childish, and I wanted you to bring me to the in a field like that, not to let me move. Just look at how all that got turned on its head here. There was no consolation in all these words of encouragement she had taken the trouble to write; when all was said and done, she had chosen the Italian.

We have our whole lives ahead of us, Ed, she wrote at the end, and it would be a pity to give up everything for something whose chances do not seem particularly promising. That, Ed, has to be admitted.

After he finished reading, he stayed where he was and stared at the pages; for a moment it seemed to him her voice could be heard speaking to him from those pages, until he crumpled the paper into a small ball and then crumpled it further. For a while he continued to sit like that at the edge of the bed. Through the glass door of the small balcony and the lace curtain that covered it, the building opposite could be seen, and in one of the windows an old woman was sprinkling water from a can onto a plant on the sill. When she finished, she put down the can and looked down at the street. Even from a distance, she appeared extremely wrinkled, and her eyes, if not dulled by cataracts, could not have been sharp; nevertheless, it seemed to McKenzie that she was studying him and the letter in his hand. His fingers clasped the paper even tighter.

When he got up from the bed a few moments later and went out onto the balcony like someone who decides to display his disgrace for all to see and to show the world he has the strength to withstand it, the old woman was no longer to be seen in the window. Perhaps, he thought, she had a heart attack that caused her to fall and she's twitching on the floor and there's no one to hear her. That's the way it is, each to their own calamities.

He leaned on the railing and looked at the street below him: pedestrians passed by on the sidewalk, carriages travelled on the road, the boy he had previously seen rolling a hoop was now rolling it in the opposite direction; and when he passed beneath the balcony, he called out to him: "Bambino! Bambino!" but the boy didn't lift his head. He called to him again, as if he'd find some errand for him and in the end everything would return to as it had been before: Kate's suitcase, her shoes, her scarf, the dropped stocking, the toiletry bag. The boy disappeared around the corner of the street.

Afterward he went out to the corridor and looked for the plump chambermaid, but only her wagon stood at its end with a bucket and a few rags on it. It seemed to him if he were to succeed in finding the chambermaid and ask her a few questions, all would become clear: exactly just what had happened, if anything had happened at all.

"Signora!" he called, "Signora!" but there was no answer. From where he was, he surveyed the two rows of doors and began to walk very slowly toward one that seemed to be slightly ajar. He thought perhaps the chambermaid was cleaning the room despite that it wasn't logical she'd be doing it without her wagon. Even before reaching the door, he heard sounds from inside, and through the narrow crack left by the door, something could be seen which seemed like sweaty skin in an up and down motion. His feet were fixed to the spot and he listened to the sounds until they became silent, and only then he plucked up courage and peeked inside: it wasn't Kate, nor the plump chambermaid. He managed only to see part of the foot and sole of a woman's leg foot before she disappeared into the washroom, whilst doing so stepping on a pair of man's underpants that had been thrown on the carpet. The man stood opposite the window and from his back it seemed he was gazing down at the street as he himself had previously done, until the movement of the man's hand was revealed to him; he held the curtain in his right hand and wiped his loins with it.

He returned to his room which seemed just as empty as it had seemed when he left it. It was a disheartening emptiness like the that of a house whose owner has become impoverished and whose objects have been confiscated, and only the pale rectangles left by the pictures on the wall testify that someone is living there. But after a few moments, he discovered the comb she had left in the washroom, perhaps because a few of its teeth were broken, and on the edge of the basin was an empty perfume vial whose scent had been preserved in it. The smell of her hair lingered on the comb, and he managed to move it away before the bile in his throat gushed to the sink.

Afterward he approached the bed and lifted up the crumpled pages of her letter and opened them again: had a few letters been smudged by tears, perhaps he would have been somewhat forgiving; or the opposite if he had seen those tears as some kind of deceitful trick. The Baedeker she had been reading when he went to the post office he found on the bed. It opened almost by itself on the page she had been reading, the chapter about Rome, and the remains of the map that had been torn from it could still be seen.

So Carlo hadn't see fit to come and fetch her, he pondered and gloated; he was reminded how deficient her sense of direction was and hoped she'd lose her way through the streets of Rome but didn't believe that would happen any more than he believed the shred of information he would receive from the hotel receptionist. In spite of that, he went down to the ground floor, and since two tourist couples were standing in front of the counter with their suitcases and the receptionist was dealing with them, he went to the porter standing outside to ask him if by any chance he had seen someone. "Una donna," he said to the porter and tried to describe to him what Kate looked like: he made signs with both hands of a wavy movement drawn from his head to his shoulders to show him the length of Kate's hair, and right away a big grin spread on the porter's face, he even winked at him; there was no mistaking the movement he made: he also raised his arms and made a wavy movement, but in front of his chest to show the large the breasts of the donna he meant.

"No, no, non comprende," McKenzie said to him, and from the discouraging sound in his voice, the porter bent a finger to bring down the price.

Toward evening, in the dimness of his room – he didn't bother to illuminate it – he sat on the edge of the bed and paged back and forth through the Baedeker she was kind enough to have left. He sat there completely naked after having washed himself in the bathroom and dried himself with her towel. The guidebook heaped high praise on the museums of Florence, the palaces of Venice, the views of Naples, and other places that the tourist should under no circumstances miss out on. The delightful treasures of the Occident were written about there, places of antiquity where one could easily imagine the people of those glorious eras walking and talking; landscapes that could not be bettered by any in the whole of Europe;

and the hearts of the local people and the extent of their hospitality that every tourist would derive pleasure from.

"Take note," it was written in Baedeker, "even someone who is not by nature an art lover will find himself wonderstruck when faced with the glorious works hung here -"

He turned the page with a sharp movement as if later in the paragraph her Carlo might be mentioned and perhaps there would be quotes from parts of his speech delivered opposite a marble torso sculpture or one with a broken nose or a John Thomas. He immediately wished those defects and more upon Carlo: that his arm be amputated, his leg cut off, his nose broken as well as his thing.

He sat like that on their bed until night fell in all its darkness, and when he turned on the light he saw the reflection of the room's interior on the glass door of the balcony and his own reflection: a naked man whose wide shoulders were sunken. No horns grew from his head, but there was no need for them: his defeat was apparent in his shoulders, his back, his face. For a moment, he felt like one of the animals he treated when they were already too feeble to object to the instruments that he inserted into their bodies: forceps for giving birth, syringes, fleams, ropes for neutering.

A light came on in the window of the building opposite him and a pigeon could be seen standing on the windowsill, and instead of viewing the street, it turned its small head toward the room on the other side of the pane. A moment later the window was opened, and he saw the old woman who had watered the plant that morning. Her mouth was slightly open, perhaps she was making a noise with her voice for the pigeon, and a moment later she began to crumble the piece of bread in her hand.

He had difficulty falling asleep that night. The ghostly image of Kate lay on the bed and turned its back to him as on the three previous nights, and at exactly eleven o'clock the German couple on the other side of the wall began their love making session, and the creaking of the bed could be clearly heard, the woman's groans, the bellowing of the man. When sleep finally descended upon McKenzie, in his dream he saw the way from Begbroke to Oxford and the marsh on the left and the ducks flying from after each shot of the hunters: one after the other they fell to the ground, and a fat one dropped on his head and by the time he managed to get it off him a pack of the Lord's greyhounds came running. All at once they surrounded him, pounced on him and took hold of his clothing; all except a red dog that clung to his leg and copulated with it.

He could have used one of their return tickets (her ticket he'd give back or sell or give away or throw the damn thing away), but he didn't want to return, and certainly not continue the route he had planned for them both before the honeymoon. Since he didn't yet know what to do, he went down to the dining room and found himself a vacant table. "Buongiorno, buongiorno," those seated at the nearby tables said to each other, and only his table no one approached – perhaps his calamity could be seen in his face.

When he returned to his floor, he saw the plump chambermaid in the corridor pushing her wagon in front of her, and his legs began to run towards her even before he had time to think. When he tried to explain his request, she pointed to the doors came before his room. She was probably trying to explain to that she'll come after she cleans those rooms.

"No, no, non comprende," he said to her, "la donna -" again he tried to describe Kate's hair with a wavy movement from his head to his shoulders, and in front of her watery eyes, in which not a spark of understanding could be discerned, he almost added the movement the porter had made, but didn't. The chambermaid looked at him for a moment from above her wagon and began to walk heavily toward his room, her large buttocks swaying in front of him beneath the knots of her white apron. She opened the door to the room with one of the keys from her bunch, glanced inside it and immediately returned her gaze toward McKenzie.

"La donna," he said, answering her silent question.

The chambermaid entered and peeked into the washroom as well; she looked at the basin and the bath, until she detected McKenzie behind her in the mirror and recoiled. From the flow of speech that burst forth from her mouth he understood only the words "famiglia" and "bambini" and her fear of him. He withdrew to the entrance of the washroom.

"No, no, non comprende," he said to her and tried to calm her, but her fear only grew. In all her fatness, she hurried to pass him and went out to the corridor, heavy as a cargo ship, and when the sound of the slammed door echoed, he was worried that she might summon the reception clerk, the hotel owner, the polizia, and whoever else, until he heard the door opening alongside the place she had left her wagon.

He sat down again on the edge of the bed, exhausted as if he hadn't slept the whole night. In the opposite window he again saw the old woman, again watering the plant. The old woman had her pigeons and her plant, while he was left with nothing.

21

The face of the railway worker expressed terror, as well as enmity for the man who was the cause of his being beaten. In a cracked and trembling voice, because he was very young, he swore on his mother's life that he had no connection to what had happened here and he had never seen that man, the terrorist, in all his life. He almost wept at the feet of the detectives, being so young and so innocent, but Poliakov didn't budge from his window.

Maximov also tried to say something, perhaps to verify the words of the worker so that the detectives would at least leave him alone or perhaps to distract them in some other manner. Perhaps – it was also possible – to direct them toward the person who had really helped him and who is now standing and watching them from the hotel window. But the words he tried to speak were swallowed; and his eyes, that for a moment opened and sparkled were fixed on the tin soldier that was being thrown above him again, until they were fixed not on the soldier or the sky toward which it was being thrown, but on the window of Room 312. This time there was no doubt that Arkady had spotted the figure in the dimness of the window and that he identified him.

Something at once vague and clear passed between them and crossed the distance of three floors: not the assassination, but the letters and notes that Arkady had written in the name of his fictitious fiancées, so that they would give the false impression of real life to his suitcase, lying between his clothes and underwear. Through the hotel window, it seemed for a moment they had flown off and were soaring through the street above the injured man – and not the tin soldier.

"Write to him as they would have written to you," Vera instructed him with an amused look, "all the saleswomen and servants that you've ever fallen in love with. Every other day" – she turned to Poliakov – "Arkady comes back with some new love from his lookouts, sometimes it's a flower seller, sometimes a servant, some-times a thirteen-year-old girl that he swears he'll wait for until she grows up. My own niece, Arkady! Aren't you ashamed of yourself?"

From the depths of the street, his eyes, whose greenness had become clouded, opened and strained. Their pupils were fixed on him. Alongside Arkady, the worker who had been dragged from the other end of the street was still trying to appeal to the detectives holding him, and the dismay that had been heard in his shouts had been replaced by something else, at once despondent and insistent, as if in those few moments he had grown up. One of his eyes was swollen, his cheeks were scratched, his right ear was bleeding.

"So just what were you doing here?" asked his captors.

He began some detailed and confused story about the shift he had swapped with a friend from work, because today is a special day for him –

"Sure, it's special," they said to him and kicked him in the ribs.

He tried to convince them that he hadn't done anything, and in a pleading and strangled voice asked the detectives how they could blame him for this thing, after all he's someone who every time the Tsar's carriage passes kissed its shadow for luck. It's only because they don't know him, he said, that they can think such things about him. If they'd just go to his workplace and ask around about him a bit -

"We'll go and ask."

They'd tell them what kind of a person he is and how everyone likes him and what a good worker he is –

"And nevertheless, what were you doing here, instead of being at work?"

Again he tried to explain, and parts of his prolonged explanation could be heard up to the third floor: about the woman cleaner at the railway station, who he wanted to buy a birthday present for; no, not in this street, everything's too expensive here, he just wanted to take a look here, he'll get it made somewhere else from cheaper material, in the area where he lives. His child Vanka needs a mother, everyone tells him that, because his mother... a long time ago, that winter... his voice choked and high above him a bird chirped. Yes they all tell him Vanka needs a mother, like all children do, and he once saw how well Marina gets on with children, , how she looked after that boy who got lost in the station, exactly the same age as Vanka. And tomorrow is her birthday, so he thought that –

Again, his voice broke. His battered cheek was turned to the sidewalk and a tear furrowed a path in the dust that covered his cheek.

"Can't you see he hasn't done anything?" someone from the crowd gathered opposite called out, and on the sidewalk at the foot of the hotel it seemed that Maximov was trying to move his hand from the crimson puddle toward the worker, but the moment he noticed it, he pushed it away as if a snake was crawling toward him.

"Why don't you believe me?" he asked. "Why?"

Someone in the crowd mentioned the peaked cap of the man who had fled, a peaked cap not a beret; and once again the voice of the shopgirl was heard: she swore on everything she held dear that she saw that worker pass by the front of her display window. He stopped for a while and even made her laugh at the time, because what would someone like that have to do with the kind of clothing sold in their shop.

"So you also saw him from your display window?" the same voice that had annoyed her previously asked from the crowd. "When do you manage to do any work?"

But the shopgirl insisted: she had seen both of them, but that there was no connection between them. The first, the one who was wounded, wasn't at all interested in her display window, nothing interested him other than the parcel he was holding, he didn't even notice she was cleaning the windowpane from the other side, he only lifted up his head and looked up at the hotel.

"Were you expecting him to look at you instead?"

Laughter burst out and the shopgirl forgave the insult. "Someone definitely helped him from there," she said again; so they should leave the railway worker alone and let him go home to his child who's waiting for him. "Let him go!" she shouted at the detectives. "Can't you see he's just a child himself?"

Once again, the tin soldier was thrown into the air. When its momentum ran out it turned over and dropped determinedly toward the sooty, bloodied face.

"So who did help you?" the detectives turned again to Arkady. "Who? Someone must have signaled to you from somewhere that the carriage was getting close."

Arkady remained silent.

"Was he standing on the other sidewalk? Maybe on the corner?"

It seemed that while the head was tossing on the sidewalk, the eyes were still fixed on a point high up above them, on the third floor.

"On the corner?" the detectives asked. "Was he standing on that corner?"

Slowly and with much effort, Arkady moved his head: centimeter by centimeter he brought his bleeding chin close to his chest upon which his torn shirt had turned red.

"Who?" they said to him. "Who was standing there?"

Arkady mumbling something: his cracked lips opened slightly and the detective who bent over him tried to understand bits of the syllables that escaped from his mouth, mixed with bloody phlegm. "The flower?" he said. "The flower seller? Did anyone here see a flower seller?"

Arkady tried to nod again and more vigorously.

"Flow," he said and tried again "er," And after amassing more air in his lungs said: "Seller, seller!" And the last syllable he emitted as if he had dug it out from the depths of his innards.

"Was a flower seller standing there?" asked the detective who was leaning against the trunk of a linden tree, addressing his question to the crowd on the opposite sidewalk.

An argument broke out: if she had been standing on the corner or not.

"She hasn't been here for a week!" the voice of the shopgirl rose again. "And not long ago she told me she's going to move to another street because everyone here's stingy!"

"She told you all that from the display window?" they teased her again.

The detective kneeling over Arkady moved his head closer to his bleeding lips: and again they opened and again a few syllables escaped from them, as if Arkady was stricken by the urgency to tell something of great importance before his strength runs out.

"She wasn't what?" said the detective. "What wasn't she? She wasn't working together with you?"

Arkady moved his head slowly.

"She only gave the signal?" said the detective.

Now Arkady's voice strengthened and many syllables suddenly rushed from his mouth. The detective tilted his head and placed his right ear close to him.

"He said," the detective said, "that she... that she what? That he, that he... bought.... flowers from her... that he said to her.... that... the flowers... are a prize for someone? Not a prize, a surprise... that the flowers are a surprise for someone."

"But she wasn't standing there today!" the shopgirl insisted again. "She hasn't been here for at least two weeks!"

"Before you said one week," they said to her.

"And then, when... when the carriage came near" – the detective continued to translate the syllables one after another and join them until they resembled words – "he asked her... to do what? To give a signal... for him to throw... the bunch... at the carriage? From where he was standing. He didn't want... to be seen ahead of time – " The detective moved his head closer to the mumbling lips in order to hear better.

"He said to her... that his girl" – the detective continued to decipher the disrupted choked syllables – "sitting there... that he wants a prize... not a prize, to surprise... to surprise her like that... with flowers."

"He still had the nerve!" said the detective who was leaning on the trunk of the linden tree, and again a short argument broke out: no flowers could be seen on the road, not even one, but then things many times bigger had also disappeared in the blast: for example, some of the coachman and the minister's limbs. On the other hand, how could anyone mistake the minister's coach for an ordinary coach?

"What was she selling there, orchids?" someone asked from the crowd.

"Flow- flow-" Arkady mumbled again, and this time his voice was heard without the mediation of the detective, and his eyes suddenly opened wide as if to gaze at their blossoming and not at the smashed window; but he was looking there, at Room 312, at the men who stood and watched everything without doing a thing.

"But she wasn't there today!" the shopgirl said. "In the end, the person who really helped him will get up and go, that's if that criminal's still in the hotel."

Because the detective leaning on the trunk of the linden tree insisted on clarifying with Maximov why of all places he stood here to wait with his parcel, he began to slowly spit out a new story from the depths of his bleeding throat: one syllable after another, For a moment it seemed they were combining forces in a joint effort, the injured terrorist and the man interrogating him: one raising a shaky syllable from his throat and one releasing it into the street air. The passersby were still being delayed between two junctions as the soldiers scoured the street from store to store and from building entrance to building entrance. How long would it take before they reach the hotel? Poliakov didn't know. He only knew that it wouldn't be long; and in spite of that, he didn't budge.

When the syllables had been deciphered, it transpired (to those who believed it; the shopgirl did not believe a word) that, the terrorist and his girl had met on the bridge across the Obvodny Canal last autumn. Arkady, was going in one direction at the time and she was just then coming from the other direction. Aglava was her name. "And tha… that –" he mumbled on, "and that…" another moment passed; Maximov's chin reddened, as did his neck.

At the time it seemed that the railway worker was also listening to the story, and perhaps in these words he momentarily found an echo to his story, the real one. They were lying on the same bed, the stained sidewalk, the worker who was caught and beaten through no fault of his own and the terrorist whose blood convicted him right from the moment of the blast.

Syllable after syllable was spat from Arkady's throat in order to fabricate a story about the flower seller who apparently had helped him, despite her not knowing what she was doing: she, and not the man watching him from the hotel window. It would have been enough for him to turn his eyes toward him from the sidewalk, but he chose not to.

"You'd better start speaking to the point," the detectives said to him. "We can still get you to hospital in time. Who's going to believe your nonsense?"

Arkady was silent.

"Look they said to him, "there's a carriage waiting, by some miracle it remained intact. A journey of a few minutes and we're there." No damage had been done to it though it was traveling right behind the minister's carriage, only Ptizin's bicycle had been between them ("Come to think of it where is Ptizin?" They suddenly remembered their colleague; and on the third floor he wondered if Ptizin, might be searching for him now, and still he did not budge). "Ten minutes and you're in hospital. Even less if we go fast."

They promised Arkady the best doctors would examine him, and nurses would look after him. Before long they'll stop the bleeding; God, there's so much blood pouring out, it's hard to believe that so much blood could come out of one person.

Arkady didn't open his mouth, nor his eyes. But through the eyelids and the blood, his pupils were focused on one thing, very far and very near, miniscule and mammoth, and are fixed on it with all their expiring strength.

"Mer-" he suddenly said , "mer-" and again was silent and struggled to gather air to his chest that rose and fell with the tatters of his shirt and with his remaining strength. "Cey," he mumbled with a determination that was waning as his blood spread over the paving stones, "and from the hotel window it sounded as if he was shouting "Have mercy," loudly from the depths of the street and with crashing syllables but it was only a delusion: Poliakov spoke a different language, and no one begged his mercy, no one could rely on him for that.

22

"Water?"

"Whiskey?"

"Vodka?"

"Vermouth?"

"Wine?"

Just when he had given up and approached the window he heard the sound of a movement behind him, and when he turned round he saw the Russian rising from the bed with effort, leaning on his right elbow and trying to get up, but not like someone waking from a sleep or a swoon, rather like someone carrying out his actions while still incognizant. His eyes were open, but it seemed as if he didn't notice him or anything else in the room. With an effort he put one foot down from the bed onto the floor, a bare swollen cracked foot the color of hypothermia, and fell back; and again tried to rise and again fell, and rather than give up he made another try.

His mouth opened and his cracked lips mumbled something that sounded like a Russian name, and the doctor wondered if it was his name and he was introducing himself to him, though he wasn't looking at him but into the window, and before he could approach him, the Russian collapsed again and his chest rose and fell on the bed with such a vigorous motion that the doctor feared he might have cracked a rib. Only then did he approach him.

"Dr. McKenzie," he introduced himself, but the Russian had already lost consciousness again.

"Why shouldn't you sleep a while?" he said to him. "It's the best medicine." The ropes of the bed barely sunk from the weight of his body, it had become so thin on the journey, or perhaps had been thin from the start. The trunk he had brought with him was easily slipped under those ropes, though in any proper hospital it would have been banished with its filth.

In the empty hotel room in Rome, McKenzie stared at the ceiling: on the other side of it was a bed, and beyond the ceiling above it another bed and on top of that another one, and all of them occupied by couples busy with their morning love-making, and each bed made its own creaking sound.

He began to pack. He folded the first clothes carefully but soon tired of it and stuck everything that came to hand into the suitcase, and only after he closed it by stamping on it with his foot, he remembered to go to the washroom and take his toiletry bag and the vial of perfume and the comb with the broken teeth. He opened the suitcase again and stuck them into it as well. He then straightened and folded the pages of the crumpled letter and put into his jacket pocket (Dear Ed - he still managed to see the words, again).

At the train station – he first had to settle the account with the reception clerk and then pass by the porter and see him wink and be assisted by him anyway to have his suitcase placed on one of the carriages waiting in front of the hotel – he got lost for a moment in the tumult. Hordes of people were leaving, and even greater hordes were entering, dozens of porters were carrying suitcases and travelling trunks and round hat box in and out. Merchants were proclaiming their wares, a locomotive horn cut through the tumult, and when it faded it was replaced by the *clickety-clack* of trains travelling. The belches of smoke emitted from the locomotive's chimney hovered beneath the high ceiling of the station like a flock of clouds that would soon rain down, but at the time it was summer, the summer of 1897, and he still didn't know where he'd be travelling to.

He had to be helped by a porter, and even before he managed to look for one, two were already standing in front of him and handling his suitcases, each pulling in a different direction. It seemed that any minute the handle would come apart. "Basta!" he shouted (he already knew that word too), and they both looked at him. McKenzie had no doubt that the porter on the left was the one who had carried his and Kate's suitcases on their arrival in Rome. The porter looked back at him. "E la donna?" McKenzie read in his eyes and instructed the other porter to carry his suitcase.

At the ticket office – for a few moments he debated between Ancona and Brindisi and in the end chose Brindisi because it was farther away – the bald man who sat there biting into a sandwich asked him: "Uno, duo?" McKenzie wasn't sure whether he meant the number of tickets or whether a return ticket but it made little difference. Uno. A one-way ticket for one person.

The locomotive honked again and discharged its smoke. The dials of the large hanging clock showed that there was no need to hurry, but it was an unnecessary reminder: he had no reason in the world to hurry. In his eyes, the minutes and hours were of no importance, only what had ended that summer was of any significance, a scorching summer even in the eyes of the Italians. In every direction around him people could be seen licking ice cream, even the adults, and when he discovered where the roving stall was (a small hand cart on whose sides colorful balls were drawn that resembled balloons more than ice cream) he ordered the porter to come with him. A few people were waiting there, and when his turn eventually came, he deliberated between the flavors like a child. "Strawberry," he finally said, the word he read on one of the small signs, each stuck into a mound of a different color. "Strawberry, only strawberry." He felt that should the strawberry flavor be pleasant to his palate; the entire journey would be agreeable.

While the vendor filled his cone, he saw a family approaching the stall: a man and a woman and their two children, a boy and a girl were being pulled by the parent's hands to hurry them up, and suddenly they were released from their grip and lunged toward the stall and pondered the ice cream flavors as he had previously done. While they were deciding – neither the brother nor the sister wanted strawberry, they both wanted vanilla and another flavor with a melodious name that McKenzie couldn't understand – he saw a man with a beret approaching from behind and pushing his way toward the stall. As he bent toward the ice creams he stealthily put his hand into the father's pocket. He was nimble and the wallet was fished out in an instant.

McKenzie continued to lick his ice cream very slowly. It was hard to sense the flavor of strawberry in that frozen pinkish saccharine glob in the cone, but he carried on licking like a child, until the pickpocket ambled away, and a moment or two later was already swallowed by the crowd, searching for a new victim.

Good luck, a voice in McKenzie's head said, may you have good hunting. And the same voice said to his own victims: you pickpocketed my wife, so may all your wallets be pickpocketed, may your suitcases also be pickpocketed and your trunks and your fat children, you deserve it.

All the while the porter stood next to him and looked at the ice cream on the stall with yearning eyes. It seemed he would have very gladly accepted a small advance payment in the form of ice cream, but McKenzie took enjoyment in seeing him like that. In his eyes all Italians had become one specific Italian: young or old, men or women, it was even completely clear to him what the children would be doing in their adulthood. He had no desire to sit in their company in the café he saw across platform number one, nor in the restaurant at the other end of the hall, and when the porter asked to where ("Where, mister?" he asked. "Where to go?") he indicated to platform number nine, despite that there was still no train standing there.

Newspaper sellers proclaimed their headlines, peanut vendors their peanuts, cake vendors their cakes. Someone shouted: "Alfredo! Alfredo!" And from afar the shrieking bark of a small dog could be heard. New clouds of smoke, denser, replaced their predecessors which had unraveled beneath the high roof, and only the masses remained as they were: a mixed multitude of people scurrying here and there, and just for a moment he was jealous of them, all having some purpose; at the time it seemed it didn't matter what it was, merely that there should be one.

But he was soon silently saying to himself and to them: all those purposes of yours, not matter what they are, are all hanging by a thread, go home and what will you find there? A letter on a nightstand, and you'll regret the moment you began to read it, open the window and you'll see the neighbor opposite laughing at you with a toothless mouth.

Only when a frightened puppy suddenly burst forth between the people's legs, its leash tagging along behind it, did he vaguely remember there were other things in his life besides Kate, things he had been aware of a long time before he knew there existed a woman like that in the world, one he would fall in love with, court, propose marriage to one winter night in the local pub (and of that she said: "Really, Ed, couldn't you have found a slightly more romantic place?"), and again, a month later in a new restaurant in Oxford, and a month and three weeks later in Mr. Winterbottom's field on a wonderful spring Sunday morning, after he succeeded in persuading her to go for a walk with him in an area that also had a glorious history: right here, on this very spot, King Charles the first galloped as he escaped from Cromwell, and if you listen for a moment you can hear the beating of the hooves. They sat on a log of wood lying there, and she surrendered to the rays of sunlight that filtered through the clouds and lit up the edge of the field. Perhaps at the time she thought what was good for a king would be good for her as well; and perhaps because she was ambitious, she thought one day they would also speak of her in these words: right here, she had lived between this year and that year, until her star rose in the skies - any sky that could contain her radiance. No, when she came to him, she had already surrendered her dreams; after all, he himself was part of that surrender.

The dachshund ran toward him as if in some mysterious way it knew what his occupation was. Out of the masses coming and going and waiting for trains, it ran on its short legs straight to him, perhaps something of the scent of the dogs he had treated reached its nose, or the horses, or cows, or sheep, perhaps even the scent of Mrs. Adam's spaniel. Between dozens of pairs of legs this dachshund ran with its leash trailing behind it, and only by chance no one stepped on it. Its elongated face was headed straight for McKenzie.

The spaniel had a collar padded with velvet. It also had its own leather-bound diary, and a few weeks after he came into the world, Mrs. Adams began making entries in it and using his own name, the way mothers do for their babies. For instance, she wrote: "Today I learned not to make wee wee in the house and got a prize for it - a biscuit." That too was some sort of fake, though its intention – unlike his and Tenzin's plan – was well-intentioned.

Also written there was: "Today Mrs. Adams spoke with the neighbor a while and said to her: 'Believe me, Mrs. Hawthorne, the love one receives from a dog, even children don't give!'" She also wrote: "My whole life has changed thanks to Puponi; without him God knows what would have become of me." Or: "Today Mrs. Adams forgot to shut the bathroom door -"

McKenzie remembered that page well, its beginning and what followed, because on his next visit he saw that the name of Puponi's mistress had changed in the diary from "Mrs. Adams" to her first name. He read the diary that remained open on the armrest of the chair. If he had been summoned for no special reason, he thought, at least let him be somewhat amused. Written there, in the same rounded handwriting, was, "In the evening, Margaret set the table for both of us and also laid a white tablecloth and lit candles and placed a few cushions on the chair for me so that my head would reach the table and also tied a napkin on me. She even poured some wine for me in my bowl, but it wasn't tasty at all! 'Margaret,' I said to her, 'all that wine isn't good for you, better you stop!' but she didn't stop, she drank and drank and laughed for no reason, which wasn't funny at all, it was sad."

When Mrs. Adams saw that her hints were to no avail, the wording in the diary became even more explicit. She had no doubt that he had read the open pages, but he still didn't imagine how all this would play out; at the time he was blind, as he would be blind in his marriage. For instance, it was written there a few months later: "Today Margaret didn't even open the shutters in the morning, she just turned her head to the wall." Or: "Last night Margaret cried in bed again and also wouldn't allow me to get up onto it. 'Go away!' she shouted, 'What do you think you are, Puponi, a human being? There are some things you can't do!' And I knew she was right: to drink and to eat is important and also to go for a walk, but most important of all is to be loved, and without that one doesn't want to get out of bed at all because there's no one to do it for and one doesn't want to eat and drink because there's no one to do it for and there's only one thing that I'll regret and that's that my Puponi -"

The dachshund, after escaping from the masses coming and going and waiting at the train station in Rome, reached McKenzie's shoes and sniffed them. "Alfredo!" a woman's screeching voice was heard from the crowd filling the station. He bent down to the dog and patted it with his ice cream stained hand, and it lifted its face toward him and licked his fingers. "Good dog," he said to it in English, "good dog." "Alfredo!" the woman's voice was heard again from afar. "Mister, where to go?" asked the porter.

For a moment longer, McKenzie surrendered to the touch of the dachshund's rough tongue, but then from the dog's owner suddenly appeared and accused him – him of all people! – of stealing it. It seemed to the owner, a well-to-do man according to his dress, that McKenzie was intending to put the pedigreed dog into his suitcase (it turned out that it had a grand pedigree) and that way sneak it out into to the streets of Rome or worse still, onto one of the trains standing there. Perhaps the suspicion arose in him due to the apparent closeness between McKenzie and the dog, or perhaps his unkempt appearance was enough: disheveled hair, unshaven, his shirt stained with the moist pink blotches that the ice cream drippings had left.

It was the porter who saved him from the dog's owners and masters. ("Alfredo mio!" she said to it as she bent down to kiss it on its nose. "Alfredo caro!") After having paid the porter his wage and adding a generous tip, he stood on the platform and looked at the iron tracks extending from the station to the horizon, and the dwindling small cloud of smoke of the receding locomotive, and the rushing of another drawing near to the station, and the commotion of those getting on and off on the nearby platforms. Though all of that was happening just a few meters away from him, it was another world, a world in which everyone has a destination to reach and family members and friends waiting for them there and worrying if they're late. Perhaps the Russian once stood like that at the station from where he left, if not fled for his life. For a while he stood among the hordes of Italians and looked around him; he, the veterinarian of Oxford County, a man esteemed and loved until this journey, didn't know where he was going to.

When he became tired, he sat down on an empty luggage cart and leaned his back against the iron railing at its rear. And an hour later – he knew in advance that he would have to wait a long while, but it was preferable to waiting in the hotel – he pulled his suitcase and lifted it up onto the cart as well and stood it between the iron rail and his back. He then folded his jacket and inserted it between his lower back and the suitcase and spread his legs. Before dozing off, he still managed to see that on a few of the nearby platforms there were others doing the same.

When he awoke, the day was beginning to turn into evening. He had missed his train: his sleep had been so deep that he hadn't heard it coming and going. One thing astonished him; that no one had tried to wake him. Perhaps the porters found other carts, and perhaps they were put off by his appearance. He could have got up and gone to a nearby hotel – there was no shortage of hotels in the vicinity of the station – but such an action seemed complicated and beyond his capability; he hadn't eaten the whole day, and that surely must have weakened him. He still had the sweet taste of ice cream in his mouth, and when he touched his face, he felt the stubble that had sprouted on his cheeks and his chin.

Trains with dozens of carriages entered and left the station one by one, masses of people got off them and masses got on, while he remained on his cart. He had already begun to plan how he would sleep the night there and wait for tomorrow's train; this bed seemed desirable to a hotel's four poster.

He nodded off again. Perhaps another train stopped opposite his platform and perhaps not, he couldn't tell; anyway, all the surrounding sounds had become blurred into such a dim, continuous, ongoing tumult that he found it difficult to believe other sounds could reach him or that there was a silence in which only his breathing could be heard. In his nap, the dachshund appeared to him panting as it ran, and afterward it licked his hand and his face with its small rough tongue, and right away was replaced by a rat sinking its teeth into his cheeks.

He awoke in dread; a piece of newspaper that the wind had blown was stuck to his face. The station wasn't as full as it had previously been and the tumult had lessened, and on the platform on his left, to his surprise, he saw the pickpocket. Like him, he was sitting on a luggage cart, and on the top of the suitcase that was standing there – perhaps his own, perhaps also stolen by him – and emptying a few wallets, and after transferring all the notes to his pocket he threw the wallets onto the tracks and a train entering ran over them. Then, before the carriage doors were opened, the man noticed him looking at him. He showed no suspicion at all, perhaps in his eyes he was a homeless drunk, a nobody of no harm to him, and possibly a colleague of his profession.

He thought he would remember that night in the station for many years to come, but actually began to forget it that very same year. It might have been completely forgotten had it not risen in his memory during one of his first years here, when he had a sudden yearning for England and entertained the thought of moving south before the snow cuts Leh off from the world. But that night in the train station of Rome, he sat on the luggage cart having made a resolute decision never to return to England. Had the Russian also made a decision like that about his country?

He saw the station emptying. The café, the restaurant, and finally the snack bar extinguished their lights. The stand owners covered them with tattered sheets and moved them on their small wheels to some place at the rear of the station, and the small clouds of smoke that the locomotives had discharged vanished. In the entire large hall and its platforms, only a few homeless drunks could be seen and a woman who was drinking with a wildly bearded man from a large bottle of Chianti. After it was emptied, it was thrown onto the tracks, and when it shattered, they cheered. The man got up and stood on the edge of the platform where for a moment he fumbled with his trousers and began to urinate onto the tracks, and the woman also got up and without any shame squatted on the edge of the platform and did the same. The trickling could be heard clearly in the silence that had fallen on the station. It was the woman who first noticed McKenzie, and while squatting called something out to him, and when he didn't answer, she called out again. He pointed to his ears to show that he couldn't hear her from where he was, and when she shouted in a louder and coarser voice, he made a gesture of helplessness with his hand to illustrate that he doesn't understand a word. She rose from her squatting position, smoothed her dress down with her hand and began to advance slowly toward him with her drinking companion. They both staggered but were stable enough to continue, and a few moments later, when they discovered his suitcase on the luggage cart, they looked at each other and also at him and asked: "Tourista? Tourista?"

"Si," he replied.

"Franchese? Ingelese? Americano?"

"Inglese," he answered.

They reached the second bottle of Chianti out to him. It was almost empty, and when he brought it close to his lips the smell of their mouths rose to his nostrils, but he allowed the drink to go down his throat, and when he returned the bottle to them, they signaled to him to carry on drinking. "Tutto, Inglese," they said to him, "tutto," and he drank the entire bottle.

With complete naturalness, the man sat down next to him at the rear of the luggage cart, and the woman sat at the front facing them both. A moment or two later, without asking permission, he pulled McKenzie's suitcase from his back and leaned against it in place of him. Now only his folded jacket remained for his aching back, and he added another fold to it. Then the woman pointed to his jacket, signaling that she wanted it, and pointed to her lower back, and McKenzie passed it to her. "Grazia, Inglese," she said to him.

She stuck the jacket behind her back and gathered up her knees and pulled the edge of her dress over them, but her calves remained exposed, and part of her thighs were revealed. When McKenzie's gaze wandered there, she uttered the same call that she had previously sounded; and this time, because it was not shouted but spoken from the distance of a few feet, there was no sound of defiance in it. What exactly she had said he didn't understand. Instead of answering, he turned his head to the tracks.

In a short while the man began to nap, and it seemed that the woman too had become tired, because she pulled the jacket out from her lower back and unfolded it and spread it on the boards, and without any embarrassment sprawled herself out there. The soles of her bare feet were inserted between McKenzie and the man sitting next to him. In doing so, her dress was farther raised, and more of her thighs were revealed. Between the railway sleepers, a few mice were scurrying, perhaps searching for food leftovers that must have been plentiful; some of them seemed reasonably plump.

That position was still uncomfortable for the woman, and with complete naturalness she lifted her exposed calves and placed them on McKenzie's thighs. For a moment or two, they rested there crossed, but then she began moving them and her bare soles began to feel his loins with the kneading motion of suckling kittens. When she looked directly at him with eyes containing remnants of makeup, she again said the words she had called out to him before. "Si?" she asked him. "No," McKenzie answered, but allowed her to continue, and in spite of his wish he felt his organ stiffening beneath the sole of her foot.

"Si! Si!" she said to him.

"No," he replied again still not moving from his spot.

"Si! Si!" she said. "Si!"

When they both returned to the cart, its floor seemed to have been completely painted with the colors of his clothes which had all been hastily removed from the suitcase. Perhaps they weren't to the man's taste, or his measurements were unsuitable; one way or another, most of the clothing had been left and the suitcase as well, lying alongside the cart with its lid open.

With two eager hands, the very same hands that previously had roved McKenzie's body and loins, the woman began to rummage through the clothing: she foraged, shifted, turned over, pushed and sniffed, until she discovered Kate's vial of perfume and examined it from all its sides and began to twist the lid open; perhaps she had a suddenly yearning for this small indulgence stronger than she had for any of the clothing. "No!" McKenzie said to her, despite that the vial was almost completely empty, and gave her another money note, added to those he had given her in the shelter of the stall.

After dozing off in the cart on a bed of his clothes he saw the dachshund, Alfredo, in his dream, dashing toward him again with its leash trailing behind it, but by the time it reached his outstretched hand, its elongated face had been replaced by the golden-brown head of Mrs. Adams' spaniel. It stood on its hind legs and placed its front paws not on the luggage cart but rather on the edge of a bath, and from there began to lick white foam bubbles from the shoulder of its mistress who was sitting silently in the water that had turned red.

On her last night, she wrote a summary of the day in her spaniel's diary, and McKenzie ripped out that page and tore it up into bits so that no one would see what was written there. It was a far simpler deed than the one he was planning now: tearing was all it took. no writing was necessary. He was not proud of that affair, though many praised him for taking care of the spaniel until a suitable home was found for it. He was even more ashamed of his behavior when he learned that to some extent Kate's interest in him had its roots in that incident. "I heard that she did it because of you," she said to him one night, and it was clear she was impressed. Who at the time could have known that she herself would consider desperate thoughts such as those, and specifically because she would be living together with him – until she found an opening.

23

That image would be clear at the end of the century, and only in a dream: the porter ascending the steps with his load. His steps cannot be heard, although he is large-framed and muscular, but instead there is the sound of a copper lock being struck on the side of the trunk with each step and the rattling of the bones inside it. It was not a filthy travelling trunk being carried there, scratched by the long journey from Leh through Kashgar to Minsk and Petersburg and Bykhov and from there to Odessa and from Odessa to Jaffa, but rather a small brown colored coffin: and inside it, despite it not being large enough, tossing between the panels and the convex lid (in the dream it was curved) a yellow skeleton that after years is being returned to its home. Afterward the dream shifts to the interior of the apartment, and the trunk is laid there in the guestroom, and its lid is opened from inside: it's gradually lifted, and the one doing the lifting releases himself and rises up out of the small coffin like a sleeping man rising up from a bunk on a train after a long journey – it is his father who abandoned him in Russia and has never seen him – and after he straightens up, bony and dusty, he transports his bones from room to room in the apartment; stopping opposite a copper jug or an ivory statuette, a picture or a window that the old man's mother refuses to open in the dream as well, and from the passage his father enters the washroom and in the basin washes the bones of his palms into whose joints grains of dust have seeped.

A few moments later (in the dream it is the blink of an eye), after glancing in the mirror, he goes out to the balcony and looks at the street from the deep holes of his eyes (the old man in the dream has no doubt they are the holes of the eyes of his disappeared father), and the wind passes through his skull and between his ribs and whistles, and sparrows fly off the tree in the yard as if they had been shot at by the sounds it makes. Gleaming from the wind his father returns to the living room with slow steps and slowly seats his exposed pelvis on the chair and places a slender yellowish leg over the other with a rattling and a squeaking. Without astonishment and without sorrow the old man-boy looks at him in the dream, without longing and without bitterness, because his disappeared father had been dead from the first moment he heard about him, dead with no uncertainty about his death, so dead that it seemed that he had been born dead and died dead, as if from between the legs of the woman who gave birth to him in the village on the banks of the Berezina he had emerged with these bones.

The mother of the old man – only now she appears in the dream – goes to the kitchen and fills a glass with tap water and returns to the living room, and without checking where the trunk had been unloaded she reaches out the glass to the porter and says to him, "tfadal"[3] (in the dream, for some reason the porter is an Arab), and the boy, Nachman, sees how her eyes follow the brown Adam's apple of the porter and the glistening trickle from his lips to his chin, and how her look darkens when she notices a scratch on one of his fingers – they are brown and long as they grasp the transparency of the glass and the water, and blood is sprouting from one of them; apparently it was scratched by a piece of wood jutting out from the spot where a burglar had tried to break into the trunk. And right away the old man sees his mother hastening back to the passage, a picture of agility and action – she, her arms, her breasts, and her thighs that with each step reveal a pale section netted with bluish veins between the flaps of her dressing gown.

In the dream, whose colors have not faded and are sharp and full of life, the porter places the empty glass on the low round table in the guestroom, and on the side a fingerprint can clearly be seen turning red from blood. He picks up the glass again and turns his head toward the pictures on the wall, first to the one on his right and then on his left, and then turns his black shining eyes on the boy Nachman, and in broken Hebrew asks him, "Your mother she draw that?" And Nachman shakes his head. "Your father?" the porter asks, and Nachman shakes his head again. "Where your father?" the porter asks. "Your father in his work?" And for a moment Nachman considers what to answer. He's not even sure of his father's name: Ilya or Eliyahu. Afterward, his mother returns with cotton wool and a vial of iodine in her hands, and she stops the porter from wiping his scratch on his trousers and stands opposite him in a dressing gown, a woman of thirty who had been abandoned in Russia with child, by the old man's father whose belongings the porter carried on his back.

In the dream, the porter is somewhat embarrassed by the woman and by the boy watching them both, but she reaches her hand out to the glass and from above it gently pulls the long brown finger with the sprouting drop of blood and releases the glass from his large palm and places it on the table.

The afternoon light comes from the balcony with the chirping of sparrows, and Nachman's mother – her head lower than the porter's chin and her breasts slanting from the gown toward his sweaty stomach – slowly and carefully passes a small cloud of cotton wool over the brown finger turning it red, and wipes the length of the finger with gentle up and down movements, and the porter allows her to carry this out in silence, and his large Adam's apple also moves up and down and the pungent smell of sweat and of something else as yet unnamed in the dream reaches the balcony and the awakening in her.

The old man is roused from his dream with a feeling of nausea and goes to the bathroom to drink a glass of water The glass is standing on the ledge of the basin

---

3   Arabic for "be my guest."

as on every night and in it are his dentures. He has to remove them and fills the glass with clean water, and after he drinks from it with small sips, he returns the dentures to it. After the second and final departure of his wife he can leave them like that, there is no one else in the apartment to be disgusted by the sight of them, but he finds no joy in this, only sorrow over all those who have abandoned him: his wife who went off with another man, his father who he never knew, and his son who went travelling in search of that father's trail and perhaps is just running away like him.

24

Rasul and his pony still cannot be seen on the path. Grains of dust rose up there and small pillars of mist twirled in the distance and McKenzie still waited. He waited with great patience for almost three months.

Lately, the trade in looted antiquities had flourished so greatly that even the exposure of Mohan Lal's forgeries hasn't harmed the business. Those who had been enticed by him cursed the day they met him, but all the others were as eager as before to discover findings that would make them wealthy or bring them fame, merchants or explorers or high-level officials, and in Kashgar the consuls of Russia and Britain unashamedly competed with each other over the collection of antiquities they had amassed there. There was no shortage of antiquities in the markets of Kashgar and Urumqi and other places on the way, so Isa said, and as someone who had led more than a few caravans, he knew more than a little about that; he said that besides wool and salt in the markets it was also possible to find ancient manuscripts whose discoverers knew their worth was greater than their weight in gold.

The doctor was waiting for paper and as yet didn't know exactly what would be written on it. What would Henry have said had he known about his plan? He would no doubt have been surprised, despite that some of the doctors who had landed up here – doctors from any field, from medicine to ornithology – preferred to occupy themselves with other matters. One of them, a veterinarian like himself, took an interest in the goats here and dreamed of exporting their renowned wool and establishing an industry of shawl making in England; another tried his hand at espionage for the intelligence people in Dehradun. They had extremely sharp minds could certainly have been of considerable help here, had the doctor shared his plan with them.

They deserved respect for their daring and their stratagems – some of which was incorporated in the plan – but Henry claimed that one who is accustomed to lying to his enemies ends up lying to his friends as well in order to farther himself, while honest and loyal people like himself are sent to remote places where the only way to improve conditions is to invest money there that had originally been designated for other purposes.

In its agreeable parts the plan brought to mind the splendid carriage destined for the ruler of Afghanistan ("the Trojan carriage," it had been called), a carriage with four horses whose heads had red tassels, was sailed down the river on an

enormous raft. From the banks of the Ganges it must have looked like the carriage
of one of the gods, but in that way its course was charted all the way to the capital
of Afghanistan in case the British might decide to invade there. It was also said that
for the entire length of its route it was accompanied by vast swarms of fish whose
scales were eternally gilded by its radiance.

It's your good fortune, Doctor, he said to himself, they don't worship flies here.
Had they also been sanctified; how would you have passed the long nights in the
room until you were tired enough to fall asleep?

The seashells – they had been added to the list immediately after the paper and
the ink – he had already seen in the hands of monks during his first week here,
and the other objects he became familiar with over the following years: the mast
for instance, and more precisely, the fertility pole that every new year dozens of
people struggle to place upright with the use of ropes tied to its top ("Like Rasul's
thingamajig," Rasul said of its appearance), and in the eyes of a foreigner for a few
moments it could also appear like the mast of a giant ship whose deck is sunk in
the ground. That's how he had once hoped to see the ship on which he had sailed
from Brindisi: sunken above its deck in the earth from the depths and fish floating
above the tip of its mast.

And there were the sea fossils found in the area – they too had been considered in one of the early stages – and there was the monotonous song of many
verses heard ad nauseam in religious ceremonies here:

> Where did the land of the people flourish, oh, daughter of Sali?
> The land of the people was created first on the waters of the lake, oh, daugh-
> ter of Sali.
> And what sank and floated on the lake, oh, daughter of Sali?
> Dust sank and floated on the lake, oh, daughter of Sali.

It went on and on like that: on the treetop that grew from the dust, a bird
landed; the bird brought a worm in its beak, and from those two all other living
beings were created, all of whose beginnings was the dust on the water, and it was
on that water that their plan had been based; but to himself, after he returned
alone to his room where only flies awaited to be hunted by him, he thought: from
a worm you came, Ed, and to a worm you shall return. Yes, he had learned more
than a little about digestive systems in his veterinarian studies, from the tiniest
ones of hamsters to the double intestines of cows, but the most important digestive system of them all he had learned nothing, despite that all the others would
be digested into it.

And who will eat them all, oh, daughter of Sali?

There were a number of similarities between all the gods and their deeds, even if the settings around them had changed, and about this matter he had heard quite a lot from Magnani. Even in India, he said, they tell of a flood and about one who survived it; Manu was his name, and this Manu once found a small fish and raised it in a cup and from there transferred it to a jug and to a barrel and to a lake and to the sea, and at the time of the flood that giant fish towed Manu's boat and thus he was saved.

"That's a nice story," Kate said.

And in a distant desert like the one from which he came only a week ago, Magnani said, a flood of water had been replaced by a flood of sand, but on the same principle: mankind had sinned and the gods had punished. "That is to say, if you believe in them," he said and pointed a dwarfish finger upward. "Anyway, the Jews didn't invent anything new."

The gods were summoned by seashells or ram's horns or by the clear voices of children (Oxfordshire had a glorious choir), and no doubt will continue to be summoned in the coming centuries as well, here and in Italy and in England, and it was on that unfounded expectation that their plan was based. Who does not wait in vain? Christians and Jews, Muslims and Buddhists, they all expect even more than someone who has lost a loved one. For the implementation of his plan, he already knew, no less than fifteen beasts of burden would be needed to carry the equipment (the matter of the anchors would need further clarification; he had absolutely no idea what their weight was), but provisions for the way would be required, and they would need their own beasts of burden; horse grooms or camel drivers or coolies would have to be paid, and he had already calculated that all the savings bequeathed to him by his aunt in England would be enough, and he wouldn't even have to sell her house in order for this work of forgery to succeed.

Yes, he, the doctor of sound mind had decided to carry out, even if not with his own hands, the forgery of an apparently ancient manuscript, which he as yet had no idea what would be written in it. At the start of his planning he even wondered if something meaningful had to be written there at all – would it not be enough to take all sorts of letters from here and there and mix them all up? And would not the explorers see in them the results of the cross-cultural contact between the caravans that travelled the Silk Road and the settlements where they stopped? He had already forgotten most of Magnani's lecture in Rome, forgotten also all the anecdotes that Callahan related on his visit here; maybe the process was called syncretism or synrectum or some other name, what the hell did it matter. In any event, one day in his room, opposite the darkening slope, he thought a forgery of that kind would be a somewhat technical and boring act, and he was already fed up with being bored. He wanted to be amused a bit, at least that's what he told himself – wasn't that allowed?

And there would be no reason to be sorry if Magnani were to swallow the bait and endure some hardships on the way, not even if he get lost in the desert. But instead of the doctor envisaging a whitening skeleton and a dune piling up

on it like on a dried wooden stump, for a moment he envisaged Kate safe and
sound dressed in widow's weeds that even further accentuated the pureness of her
skin, and she's standing in the hotel room in Rome examining her reflection in the
mirror, wearing a delicate black veil through which her eyes shone, and a black
brassiere and black garters, and in that attire she goes out onto the small balcony
and leans on the railing and flutters her eyelids at all the passersby on the street
below he. And with this image in mind, he wasn't sure whose memory it betrayed
more: the memory of Magnani or the memory of he himself.

His aunt repeatedly warned him, and again and again he refused
to listen, and last spring, the late spring of Leh, he was somehow
located by the law office of "Barnum and Barnum" acting as her
emissary – perhaps someone had spoken of him on their return to
England – and in a letter stamped with a red wax seal he was notified
of a small inheritance he had received (it is with deep regret that
we inform you of the death of our client, Mrs. Elizabeth Ackford,
of advanced age, in her home at 19 Graves Road, hereafter "the
property"): some savings and the house whose appearance, much to
his surprise he still remembers, the well-tended lawn whose edges
were straightened as if by a ruler, the garden gnomes with lichen in
their beards, the polished glass door of the dinner service cupboard,
the carved sideboard with its curled handles, the enormous jar from
which in his childhood he would take sweets (hereafter "the property").

Even worse than the ill omens his aunt perceived on the eve of his marriage
– for instance a trio of red breasted birds on their way to the cemetery – was the
look on Kate's face. "It's not the look of a woman in love," she claimed. At the time,
he thought it was simply her provincial aversion to Londoners plus all her super-
stitions, and here years later he himself is occupied with all sorts of omens and
legends, since they are no less necessary to their plan than its physical objects.
Who are he and Tenzin like now? Someone who can perhaps get his hands on a
bottle of water from the Jordan River, but his congregation hasn't yet heard about
the son of God who immersed himself in that water and sanctified it; or someone
who could display a hair from the prophet's beard, but no one has yet heard of
that prophet and his prophecies; or someone who could display for all to see the
branch of a tree in whose shade a tormented prince reached enlightenment, but no
one has yet heard of that prince and about his enlightenment. What would Jesus,
Mohammed, and Buddha have been without the stories that gave birth to them?

What would remove that wife snatcher from his podium in Rome? More than
anything, the explorers were attracted by all sorts of remote cultures that they
longed to expose, and what is more suited to concealment and exposure than the
sands of the desert? Much had been told about Taklamakan – not only about the

all-engulfing flood of sand, but also about the women who attracted the nomads to drink from the juice of their privates (they would surely have turned their backs on him), and of one who wanted to hear to the song of the dunes so badly that he ordered his men to plug their ears with wax and tie him to the hump of a camel, but the camels also became dizzy by the singing and one by one were swallowed with their riders in the sands.

Up until the last year the barrenness hadn't aroused any interest in him, and even now arid landscapes cast a depression over him. In his eyes, the valley of Leh was preferable beyond compare; in time he had learned to love it no less than he had the county of his birth years before. He loved its fields, the fruit trees that succeeded to grow on the edges of the arid slopes of the Himalayas, the towering poplars that delineate the gardens of the homes, the tended flowerbeds– from such beds a turnip was picked in the morning for the hungry cow, his neighbor, and from his window every morning the landlord's young brother could be seen going out to the yard and pulling one up and standing upright and staring for a moment at the slope and the line of snow, and also getting rid of all that had accumulated in the depths of his nostrils during the night. He examined his findings at length, as if they were tiny crystal balls in which his entire future was written and he would show no embarrassment should he discover McKenzie watching him from his window; after all, there were tales told here about a beetle of the nostrils on whose wings the soul is carried when they fly from the nose, and of rafts made of excrement upon which battalions of mice sail toward the enemy army to gnaw at the strings of their bows. It often seemed here that disgust was a European concept.

These weren't bad tales, but he was in need of a different one, just as Homer at first had been in need of an altercation with the gods in the sky. Had his hero not also sailed from his land and almost drowned?

The ocean raged even more than the Aegean Sea: the waves stormed and the ship rocked and collided with them, and more than a few virtuous ladies and gentlemen turned pale and vomited; and those that somehow still managed to hold on glared at McKenzie as if he was to blame for their situation, and should he be so kind as to disappear from their sight, the sea would become calm and leave them be. Jump, the passengers of the ship said to him with their eyes, jump so that we don't see you anymore; jump together with your bottle.

He himself actually did not vomit then, as if the ship's turbulence balanced his private turbulence. Giant waves crashed onto the stern and everything became wet and slippery and it wouldn't have taken much to slip into the sea; it would have been enough to let go of the railing for a moment, and with the next lurch of the ship he would be flung and beaten or swept away by the crashing wave. He had no doubt that he would not walk on the water.

Not to jump wasn't that simple. Sometimes more courage is required not to do something, and especially if you have absolutely no idea what awaits at the end of the way. When he decided to return to his cabin – not letting go of the railing even for a moment – he also decided that from now on he would return to being a responsible adult, that is to say, he would stop being the ship's fool; and first of all, he would stop drinking, brandy or wine or whatever contained even one percent of alcohol. He lifted up his arm and hurled the bottle into the sea. For a moment he saw it floating on the water and right away it disappeared.

Afterward in his cabin, he washed his upper body in the wash basin, shaved and changed clothes. Shaving was the most difficult, and twice he injured himself, but he was also grateful for the blood that oozed from his face until it was blotted with a small piece of paper. When he entered the dining room with his new look, all the passengers who had previously scorned him gazed at him, still fearing that in an instant everything would be upset: as he drew near, it seemed as if they were flaring their nostrils in order to hunt out the smell of alcohol he probably had attempted to camouflage with aftershave, scrutinizing his appearance and his bearing and waiting for the moment he would slip up again.

Perhaps they would have left him alone had there been someone else on the ship to fulfill the role of fool, but since there was no other candidate, they firmly insisted that he continue to fulfill it. They lay in waiting when he accidentally dropped a fork, exchanged looks with each other when a button on his shirt was missing, chuckled when his drink went down the wrong way and he coughed ("He's simply not used to drinking water"). To the very last day he felt like an outcast: true, they didn't get up from the table when he sat down next to them, they just wrinkled their noses, but if he arrived early and sat there first, no one would join him.

Afterward, a new issue arose: someone accused him of daring to stare at his pubescent daughter, some Lucy or Susie or whatever-her-name-was, and repeated it over and over, despite it being a complete lie. If any of them had seen Kate just once, they wouldn't have imagined it possible to swap her for some rosy cheeked cupcake, not even when she once approached him while he was leaning on the stern railing and asked him why he was sad. "I'm not sad," he replied to her, and the matter was closed. And in truth, it wasn't sadness he was feeling at the time; he was through with sadness. A sort of emptiness remained in his stomach, and when he thought about it, that emptiness didn't seem like the emptiness those in mourning speak of, but rather like that which a cow feels after a calf has emerged from her – as if he had given birth to something now: to his new life. He felt certain about that.

If cows truly felt that way, he did not know. Usually, he would grab the leg of the calf and pull it out, and afterward the cow would look satisfied and regretful and tired, all at the same time. It was a completely different matter when there were complications with the calving, and from all the exertion the cow continues to push the whole uterus out - go and try placing that back inside. It can last for hours, and what is the strength of a man opposed to the strength of an obstinate cow, even an ordinary unsacred English cow.

He still well remembers the bay of Bombay on the day of his arrival: the incredible commotion of hundreds of small fishing boats and rafts and dinghies scurrying between the steam ships, the slime floating on the water, the line of ramshackle rickshaws waiting on the platform and the rickshaw-walas in their dirty clothes quarreling over customers, and the thin coolie who in the end led him between the hordes of merchants and between two sacred cows, one that was chewing the cud and one that was defecating. At the sight of the bustling port he thought he had done well in choosing to sail here; that such a commotion and such squalor would wipe away all the remnants of Rome, that a filthy mob such as this would banish all the pomp of the passersby of the Via Veneto, and there was nothing like a ridiculous statue of an Indian god with a paunch and a trunk being served offerings of rice stained with curry, to wipe from memory those extolled marble statues whose models it was hard to imagine eating something – they were so perfect.

The statue of that god with the elephant head they fed, gave drink to, wafted incense over, and the coolie that led McKenzie pointed to it and said: "Ganesh! Ganesh!" and probably expected a generous tip for fulfilling the role of tourist guide as well. Afterward, when they had moved farther away and McKenzie turned his head back for the last time, the bay with all its vessels was confined between two rows of buildings and became small and was pushed to the end of the street. The hand of British architects was apparent in the large public buildings, and at the familiar sight of their staircases he knew it would be better to distance himself from Bombay with all its reminders of England, and at the time he still didn't know of a place called Ladakh and its capital Leh – only by chance would he hear about it on the train – and that there, in the Moravian mission hospital, he would find his workplace.

He could have remained in that hotel in Bombay to which the rickshaw-wala took him (lodging cost just pennies) and carried on living there for months on end with all sorts of outcasts like himself; Europeans whose bodies had been destroyed by some illness that spread from the intestines or the loins or the heart. He himself, despondent as he was at the time, took care from the start to guard against illness: he ate only cooked vegetables and drank only boiled water, and allowed the women of the hotel to pleasure him only one way, and only on condition they not look at him during the act: the eyes they fixed on him from their kneeling position were dark and shining, sad or joyous or indifferent or totally bored, and only when they promised "no looking sir" did he allow them to begin; on no account were they to look at him. On one of the bobbing heads he held, he saw lice crawling. His eyes were transfixed by them. It seemed it was necessary to reach a low point such as that in order to set out on a new path; no, that isn't the truth, after all, it hadn't been enough for him and there were other things he had done. One morning while urinating he felt a burning sensation and recalled what was written in the textbooks about *Neisseria gonorrhoeae* (*Do not mistake* – his mind was reminded of the small consolation – Neisseria gonorrhoeae for Treponema pallidum, the cause of syphilis).

After treating himself to the extent it was possible and almost becoming used to the burning, there were the train carriages: for hours on end he travelled on trains that did not at all resemble their European counterparts, not even in the hooting of the locomotive; throngs of people were squashed into the carriage with their chickens their children and their packages; the chickens crowed and the children cried and sometimes vomited or defecated, and at every station bands of merchants lunged toward the windows and entrances selling everything imaginable, from sweet tea in small disposable clay cups to portions of lentils and rice wrapped in banana leaves spicy to the point of tears, and his organ still dribbled. And through the dusty windows the vast country could be seen with its endless plains that for hours and days contained nothing for the eye to behold: not bell towers, not farmhouses, not a hill, not a forest; only here and there were dusty palm trees whose tops had turned white, or a team of bony buffalos ploughing and tilling the soil whose furrows will be filled with dust even before they finish the job.

In the carriage, room was made for the fat Brahmins, for the Sadhus smeared with ash, for lepers without fingers and noses, and his own organ still dribbled. Yogis sat in the lotus position and didn't move with each tossing of the train; pickpockets picked pockets – somewhere between Bombay and Delhi his watch disappeared – and at the stations gaunt porters waited to carry sacks of flour and rice on their heads, or travelling trunks reinforced by iron, or towers of suitcases tied with ropes.

Even without his watch the time passed: the sun set and rose in the windows, and with each evening it seemed he had gone farther away from Rome, but a moment later he knew that he hadn't really gone far and that perhaps he would never be able to sever himself from her.

25

"He wants to be Poliakov the Second," his mother would ridicule him, "no less."

Poliakov the First, famous throughout Russia, was a train magnate whose fortune was first made from trading in trees, and in every possible way his father tried to find some blood connection to him through distant cousins of cousins, until he gave up and made do with their common name and common fondness for trees. "He wants to be a big man," said his mother, "first he should be a man."

Standing at the rear of the yard, she mumbled to herself seeing him through the window, sitting there with sunken shoulders at the dinner table and a bottle only half emptied in front of him, because he wasn't even capable of drowning his defeat with alcohol: after the second glass he already wasn't able to pour for himself or lift the bottle to his mouth.

He returned from all his business trips full of plans just as he had been when setting out, but not a ruble richer, and each time he would try to endear himself to them with trifles he bought on the way and anecdotes he had heard, either about crooks and robbers or all sorts of dubious miracles (a talisman placed on the stomach drew out all its sickness and caused it to swell up like a watermelon). All that couldn't compare to the accomplishments of the Petersburg and Moscow rich who had started out just as he had, with forest trees: they turned the trees into railway sleepers and purchased entire railway lines – Poliakov the First bought the Moscow-Kiev line – and established villages and towns along the way. They became so wealthy that even the Tsar himself borrowed money from them. Yes, that's what happens when one becomes wealthy: money attracts money, and not only money, but respect as well ("Maybe you should leave something for the Tsar, Shloime," his mother said as his father helped himself to the remains of the soup from the sooty pot).

In winter, on nights that he slept at home, he would get onto the bunk above the heater and spread himself on it in his clothes and his boots, and a few moments later his snoring could be heard, more thunderous than his voice during the day ("We missed that so much, didn't we, Ilya?" his mother would say to him), and when his snoring began to vibrate, all the tumult of his dreams while asleep and while awake became apparent: vast forests were felled between his eyelids, rafts of their logs were sailed on the slope of the river with all the hopes he hung on them, until they crashed on the waterfalls. Those waterfalls of Ekaterinoslav seemed liked the end of the world, more distant than the mountains of darkness, and all the cities beyond them just an unsubstantiated rumor. Who could have known then that he, his son, would one day reach the loveliest and damnedest of Russian cities, and instead of strolling through its avenues and squares or across its bridges, he would deal in terror? Who could have known he would move far away from there as well?

He could still remembered going with him the first time to watch the men tying the tree trunks together on the river ("Just keep him away from the water, Shloime, after all, you don't know how to swim"): and when they were bound to the rafts on the river to be sailed to the awaiting sawmills, one could already foresee the railway sleepers that would be made from them, as well as the masts and the wagon shafts, but the gallows couldn't yet be foreseen.

There were hundreds growing in the forest, thousands, tens of thousands, they would be enough for the tens of thousands of informers and for all those that would kill them and for their children and their children's children, but Ilya won't become the father of a child, despite perhaps having left one behind in Minsk ("No, don't do that," Masha begged, "please Ilya, no, I asked you not to"). There it was sown and continued to grow while he was on his way from Minsk to Petersburg, and from Petersburg to Andijan and from Andijan to Kashgar and from Kashgar to Leh, because what connection does he have with children, and why should they have to grow up in a world in which such terrible deeds are done, some by his own hand.

For a few moments he could see the inside of that womb (the womb of Masha-Miriam, who has a childlike belly and innocent eyes and love in her heart, and for whom? Out of all the people in the world it had to be him), between its moist walls, not a fetus wrapped in membranes but some sort of tiny man whose face is mature and hard like his own face and whose beard is tangled like his own beard and he's already dressed and patches are sewn on the elbows of his sleeves like on his own elbows and his shoes are worn out like his own shoes, and before he emerges from the womb into the world he peeks through the slit between the thighs and deliberates whether to leave.

And why should he leave, if perhaps like him one day he'll be sent to kill?

There was so much he saw and so much he experienced the year he left his village. He slept outdoors, went hungry, took any work he found: he gathered chicken eggs in the corners of yards or finished them off with a blow, the neck stretched like a rubber band in his left hand and wrung with his right; he herded cows (that was relatively easy), gathered food leftovers for pigs or picked beetroot leaves for them that were tasty to him as well (he saw no impurity in pigs, only a common fate). On a summer's afternoon he led them to foul-smelling mire waters to wallow, and when they were slaughtered, he blocked his ears not to hear their screams, but in the city ate their flesh; his entire daily wage was often no more than half a loaf of bread and a few slices of sausage. That was during the good times when he found work; in the bad he identified with the pigs.

One day someone called to him to come and unload a burdened wagon, and to his displeasure, it seemed he was returning to his father's trees – unloading trunks from wagons that came from sawmills or from riverbanks. "You work too slow," they said to him at the time of payment and sent him off, and afterward he worked in a cigarette factory and was fired because he couldn't keep up with the pace; he offered to work as a porter in storehouses and in the market and reconciled himself to the disparaging looks he was given, he loaded sacks of potatoes on his back and almost collapsed, until he found a livelihood suited to his muscles and became apprenticed to a house painter and learned to scrub pieces of loose whitewash from walls and to caulk cracks and to walk on a ladder in the room without spilling the bucket. Between jobs he slept any place he could find: in barns on a bed of straw, on hard benches in public parks and in the entrances of churches as well, and on cold nights he searched in stairwells for walls on whose other side were heaters or at least people's voices. Yes, worse even than the cold and the hunger and the weakness was the loneliness, there was nothing more painful than walking through a street where all the windows of the buildings were lighted and the sound of song and music could be heard as well as sporadic bursts of laughter, and from one end to another there wasn't a living soul, just him and his steps.

"If you believe you can do something, you'll succeed," his mother used to say to him in his childhood, but she didn't foresee any of this in her fortune telling bowl, in the islands of oil floating on the water; she didn't foresee the stench of the third class railway carriages, not the forlornness of the house of Torah study, not the alarming size of the capital city, and not his small room and his nights there; not these expanses, not these mountains.

Two months ago he was transferring stacks of underground pamphlets in a suitcase with a secret panel, and before that, until joining the group, he only carried old newspapers in it, those he padded his clothes and shoes with against the cold, and in order to keep warm he stamped his feet and jumped on the spot and rubbed hands and did push-ups. He did everything he could to keep warm, everything he didn't do on the way to Kashgar; there was no refuge from the hunger, the body made its demands and there was no silencing it. Everything had to be done to satisfy it: asking for bread left in bakeries at the end of the day, searching for rotting vegetables in the market, after all, it takes time for the remnants to turn into refuse, and a little rot in fruit can even add to its sweetness. He also went to the back of restaurants, to peek into garbage cans. He did everything a mother would do for her baby, but his baby was not the one that continued to grow in the womb in Minsk but the gaping hollow in his stomach; there were days when he felt a large hollow in his stomach, and more than once, as if forgetting from where he came, he sneaked into church courtyards where wakes were held; he, the Jew, entered there, passed through the gates of the church, and only the first time hesitated with each step he took; he reminded himself what his father would have had to say about it, and stopped ("Tateh," said a familiar voice inside him, his own voice when he was still a child); and thought what the rabbi of the yeshiva would have had to say about it, and stopped, and what his few friends would have had to say about it, and stopped again lest the earth open its mouth wide and swallow him; no, not the earth, his father. He won't shout or hit him, but would stoop and shrink himself, because if he would ever know about this, it would be a blow from which one doesn't recover (that's what he thought then before he had really been struck by a blow).

And once, on a wintry Sunday, when the cold and the hollow in his stomach had already swallowed all his thoughts and only loaves of bread appeared before his eyes, rising from moment to moment, he entered a church during the mass. It was a Sunday, and he approached the candles and the icons and found a place on one of the benches and sat down and waited his turn to receive holy bread, for the foul taste of hunger to banished; and when he opened his mouth for the priest like the beak of a fledgling, he almost chirped from all the hunger, until the priest reached out the flesh of the Crucified One with a delicate well-manicured hand and fed him with it – it was thin as a biscuit, without taste and without volume – and he thought, perhaps now the earth will open its mouth wide and swallow me, I'll be struck by lightning, but he wasn't swallowed or struck (and in his memory the head of his father stooped between his shoulders even further).

He never stole, never, not even when he saw some gentlemen with a bulging wallet, and one had only to reach one's hand out. On days like that, the splendor of a carriage was enough to drive him crazy – its quartet of horses were indeed better nourished than him – he was even driven crazy by the pomp of the buildings, by the cornices that had no use, by the ornate banisters of the entrance steps, by a pleasing melody heard from within. All the Nevsky and Moravsky display windows were superfluous, since the buildings themselves were enough to drive him crazy with their doormen in admiral's uniform standing in the entrances as if at the gates of Paradise wearing extraneous epaulets and peaked caps, and the chandeliers in the windows and their clusters of blinding lights and the deafening sounds of a piano coming from there. Just as Vladimir had written so pertinently in the pamphlets he had distributed before he had been given a handkerchief to wave with and later a revolver to kill with. "We will destroy them in houses should they try to hide in houses, we shall destroy them in courtyards should they flee into courtyards, we shall destroy them in city alleys should they flee there, we shall destroy them in the avenues and the streets of the Metropolis, we shall destroy them on bridges, we shall destroy them in squares, we shall destroy them in villages." That's what he wrote, "in villages," but in Bykhov the village of his birth, the hooligans were given free rein to run riot in every house they entered, his house too; and in the yard of the house, not far from his father's wagon, his corpse lay on the ground, beaten and unconscious, and who remained by his side? Only the village fool.

26

First they thought about the struggle between the god of the sea and the god of the land. In the small restaurant next to the bazaar, above plates of momo McKenzie and Tenzin spoke of the tale about the temple that sunk again and again in the sands, because beneath it was the sea that the god of the ocean had placed there. Some such folly.

It was a preposterous enough tale, but not fascinating enough, because it was linked to just one temple and not to the entire country, and the explorers needed something far more complex to attract their attention. Because the more complicated the matter before them, the more their curiosity grows; and McKenzie was thinking mainly about the curiosity of one man in particular.

Last summer two Canadian mountain climbers arrived in Leh intending to climb one of the Himalayan peaks after having already climbed the Andes, and among other things told how the Indians wait for their ancient gods to return from the land to which they had sailed (why exactly those gods had left them, he didn't remember). At the time the story didn't arouse any interest in the doctor, nor the Canadians' intention to add another mountain to their list of conquests. For him it was enough to view the mountain from his room window.

Had it not been for the seashells which the Indians used to listen to their gods on their return – they would stand on the shore with the seashells in their hands – perhaps the crazy tale wouldn't have come to mind then, and certainly not last August; but since there were seashells in Leh, and Callahan had come to visit at the time, the idea popped up, and from that moment it refused to go away. Yes, he, Edward McKenzie, suddenly found himself thinking about the mass of illiterate Indians standing in a long line on the shores of Mexico or Chile or Guatemala, wherever, and blowing into the seashells like the monks do here. It seemed that the details of the story he had heard had become mixed up in his mind with what was custom here: those Indians didn't blow into the shells but rather listened to them, their total desire being to hear the gods returning; their voices or the sound of the oars or the sails. He did not remember from where they returned– in any event not it wasn't from the clouds but from some distant shore, at least as distant as the port of Brindisi from the port of Bombay. And perhaps the gods too got drunk on the way like he had.

Here in Leh alcohol helped him think. It had a burning taste and was throat

scorching and gut searing, but effective for renouncing moral mores and liberat-
ing the mind. Somewhere in the desert, close to the ruins buried there – between
Tavek-kel and Loulan – as often happens, relics of a similar faith would be found, a
faith no less preposterous and silly, whose believers also waited hundreds of years
for their gods to return on ships. Here they had some sort of enlightenment, he
or Tenzin, because the idea was also accompanied by a sort of blurred and dusky
vision. Alcohol doesn't cause such visions to arise; neither does hashish, perhaps
only opium, but he hadn't tried that yet.

Instead of just the ships of the gods returning – three, seven, a whole fleet, or
just a few dinghies – the entire sea with all its waves would return with them, the
same sea that had retreated with them hundreds of years ago and since then its bed
had turned into desert. In actual fact, he and Tenzin hadn't invented anything, the
matter had already been related in the tale of the dispute between the god of the
ocean and the god of the land and was even somewhat supported by the words of
geologists who had found sea fossils in the environs of Leh. How the sea evolves
into the desert, McKenzie could envisage for a few moments even without drug-
ging himself, despite that no ground known to him had ever dried up that way:
how the exposed bed begins to crack and split open, and how in the place where
fish and seaweed had once been, sand is now caught up in a whirlwind.

Gods sailing away in ships and returning in them seemed no less or no more
fanciful that the Crucified One, it was precisely as preposterous as someone
who allowed himself to be nailed to the cross for the sake of mankind and then
returned from his grave with the nail holes. He had weaned himself off the belief
in Christ during the time of his studies. There had been a moment that can he still
recall accurately, despite the moment itself having nothing unusual about it: he
was sitting during mass and gazing at the statue of the crucified Lord which the
candle flames illuminated and cast shadows over, and he thought: men created it,
humans, and not only the statue but also the one who was sculpted there; and his
veterinarian studies and Darwin were not required, it was preceded by an inner
understanding, a sort of lucidity of the mind and of the heart, until the new folly,
their plan, replaced all that had come before it. All the millions of years of evolu-
tion have still not succeeded in exempting the human race from folly.

While even one detail of the plan was yet to be finalized, he was already imagining
Magnani informing Kate one evening in their Roman apartment (it was probably
an ancient multi-corniced building; and was probably filled with leather bound
books and all sorts of souvenirs from his travels, the most indecent ones were actually kept in the bedroom) that he had to leave on a journey in a few months' time
and under no circumstances can it be postponed. "Kate, my dear," he would say,
or "Kate, my honeypie." Or he would call her by some Italian delicacy, tiramisu for
example, "If I don't leave right away, others will get there before me." And afterward he heard her, perhaps in their guestroom beneath the magnificent chandelier

that he inherited from his ancestors, trying to understand what was so important there that required a two-month journey, and in such haste. So what if they
found some ancient piece of paper in the desert – it had waited a thousand years
there, couldn't it wait a bit more? And he could hear Magnani trying to explain the
importance of the discovery to her with great enthusiasm, and how imperative it
was that he himself deals with everything. Perhaps he spoke with the same enthusiasm that McKenzie had once expressed when explaining the accoutrements used
in his clinic (Kate was horrified by the sight of them, she said that they looked
like torture devices from the Middle Ages: testicle clippers, horn clippers, calving
ropes; it had been the first time he tried to share the secrets of his profession with
her).

In his imagination he also heard Magnani suggesting to her that they corre-
spond for the entire duration of his absence; the post reaches the desert via the
caravans even if it takes two or three months, and a kind word can work wonders
- a a compassionate letter, not like the one she left on the nightstand in the hotel.
She would describe what she did the whole day, how much she yearns for him and
how much he is missed by all; she would write that the large apartment is too quiet
and that sleeping alone makes her sad (that's what she had said to him in Begbroke
on nights when he had been summoned to farmer's dairies), and how she has to
undress alone in their bedroom, and what she takes off first and what afterward
and how she lets everything fall to the floor (a sight McKenzie remembered well:
how she let all her clothing pile up around her legs) and walks to the bathroom
completely naked and sits there in the water and very slowly passes the sponge
over her face and neck and breasts, and how she wipes all those places dry very
slowly and returns to the bedroom and lies down alone on the large bed - lies on
Carlo's side.

An extraordinary idea was needed to attract him here, and it took many stages
until it was consolidated, and if one of them had been lacking perhaps they
wouldn't have continued to develop their plan. First of all, it became clear how
easily Mohan Lal had operated; someone that one shouldn't even buy an egg
from according to Tenzin, (years before the forgery business, Mohan Lal had a
fortune-telling chicken; and then transferred to forging signatures and from them
to ancient relics, and after he heard about the prices ancient scrolls fetched in the
markets of Kashgar and Yarkand, he transferred to them, at first the shreds that
had been discovered in caves, and afterward to manufacturing them). For two
months their small colony was in an uproar: the ladies took pity on Hernell who
had been enticed by him and whose standing was instantly shaken, and typically,
Henry gloated, and only Harper continued to stand by him and blamed everything on the converted Jew, Stein, who in his pedantic way was trying to atone for
the acts of another converted Jew who for a million pounds had offered the British Museum a parchment on which apparently was an earlier version of the Ten

Commandments. Then there had been that evening at the commissioner's home, when Ann had invited Callahan, and not only did he add details about Mohan Lal's scam, but also explained how easily more explorers could be ensnared.

It was a pleasant summer evening and they were sitting on the western veranda, and the roving reporter, on whom all their eyes were fixed, detailed for them what the fraud would require, component by component and the quantities, as a woman would in giving details of a cake recipe: a few tales about the gods, a touch of the golden age, a rupee's worth of etiology, mix them all together and heat slightly and what do you get? The stuff that religions feed off. Callahan was pleased with himself, and right away rewarded himself with another biscuit and was careful not to direct his gaze at Harper, since the missionary had already been offended by him the previous evening.

"If it's mountains you've got here," said Callahan, "then tell how these mountains were created and rose to such an exaggerated height that even the coolies can hardly breathe here." (Before that he had complained bitterly about their indolence and their stupidity; "One might as well be talking to a pony," he said.)

Harper was horrified: Is that how he speaks about his religion? Without his wife at his side – she still hadn't returned from her birdwatching trip – he was doubly sensitive about the honoring of Christianity, and Callahan, who had still not renounced all standards of courtesy, hastened to say that that was not the intention of his words, absolutely not; after all, even in his eyes, Christianity surpasses all the nonsensical beliefs that prevail here and had written quite a lot about it in *The Simla News*.

A week later Mrs. Harper returned from her trip around Lake Tsomoriri and together with a few exquisite water bird feathers she also brought with her two or three folk tales whose central focus was water, tales she had heard from nomads on the way – an intrepid group of people in her eyes, and a gang of ignorant savages according to Tenzin who had accompanied her.

That was actually how the whole idea was sown and began to grow; first and foremost, it needed to be based in the soul. It would have better had there not been such a thing at all, and McKenzie would certainly have preferred to have got rid of his years ago, but since it had come into being and was a fixture, it served as a basis for all the rest. At times, for instance in the evenings in his room, when the dark slope could be seen in his window, steep and arid up to the line of the snow, he could almost see the newspaper headlines in front of him, first *The Simla News* and afterward *The Bombay News* and *the Calcutta News* and *The Delhi News* and not only them but also throughout Europe – in *The Times* and *Le Monde* and *Corriere Della Sera* – headlines proclaiming in giant letters the downfall of another explorer, "A pitiful downfall that unfortunately calls into question all his previous discoveries" (that was what had been written about Hernell). "Pitiful", of course, only in the eyes of the fallen one, while he, McKenzie, would be filled with joy.

Ann poured more tea and dished out more biscuits. Henry watched her dancing attendance around Callahan and wondered when he would cease with his learned explanations and finally tell something that he, Henry, could learn from, even if just by a hint, about what was being discussed in Simla in the matter of his promotion, but the reporter preferred the ladies: from the way they gazed at him it seemed they had never heard analyses such as these from explorers who had stayed here, and more than a few explorers and senior officers of renown and high level government officials had been guests on Ann's veranda; but Callahan had the advantage of being a newspaper man and they hoped he would mention them favorably in one of the forthcoming editions and probably imagined how in *The Simla News* he would report the wonderful evening he had spent in their company, so that in Simla how they would know it was possible to host cultural evenings no less grand than those held in the lounges of London.

"And so," Callahan polished off another biscuit in two bites, "it's enough to tell of some ancestors who were once able to climb every mountain in the vicinity until they sinned and were punished, and ever since no one can climb them anymore." He looked extremely pleased with himself, and after he wet his throat with some tea in order to smooth the way for another biscuit, he again complained about the coolies: it was simply atrocious, they climbed so slowly, in his stupidity, one of them let a crate of cigars fall from the middle of the slope and he was forced to watch it roll down to the river and drown, that is to say the crate, pity the coolie didn't drown in its place. Afterward, to please his host, he was so kind as to volunteer an interesting news item to Henry, though not in the matter of his promotion but at least in the matter of the non-promotion of others.

Since they had moved onto corridor gossip, he didn't continue to develop that recipe which he must have heard in one of the lounges of Simla, and the following morning, as McKenzie gazed through his window at the mountains surrounding the valley, he tried to visualize in his dull imagination those ancestors slowly climbing toward the mountain top, and at least one ancestor for whom no peak was high enough; but the slopes remained empty and no divine voice from the heavens echoed through the valley. Only his neighbor the cow could be heard mooing in anticipation of its turnip.

No holiness could be seen in that animal then, nor when it was taken out to pasture, but it was certainly more esteemed than the monkeys hopping through the temples in Simla or than the holy rats of Bikaner. It was no wonder that in the first stages of the plan (yes, that's what it was called, "the plan"), they were still debating whether to place at its heart, instead of cows or seashells and anchors, a holy fish whose remains would be found not far from the remains of the manuscripts. Naturally, the skeleton of a whale would be desirable – if they could obtain such a thing – half buried in the sand and through whose ribs caravans of camels would pass. If for every sip of chang or for every fly they brushed off their plates they would have obtained one centimeter of a whale, they would have left the restaurant with its tail, at the very least.

There was no shortage of strange yarns here, And the silk caravans brought with them more and more tales from the markets of Kashgar and Urumqi, but the source of the idea for the whale was actually Venetian, many years before Kate's Roman. There was no end to what Marco Polo described, at least in the Indian version of his diary: of a caravan of ostriches and zebras that was led to the palace of the Emperor of China, of seventy-seven dwarfs that were sent to him in a box, and of another caravan that chose to bring with it a whale whose enormous aquarium hundreds of camels dragged even after all the water had been evaporated by the sun, and only its enormous skeleton reached the palace with vultures were flying between its ribs.

"I tell him thousand times" – Rasul said about Hernell – "Sahib, it all lies, this new paper, maybe one month, Mohan Lal he write on it how sand bury hundred city in one day." It had been part of the local folklore concerning the Taklamakan desert, until Hedin arrived and dug in the sand, and it transpired the story apparently had a basis in reality, though the cause was not a sudden sandstorm, but rather the slow process of desertification; and after Hedin other explorers came, Hungarian, French, and German; and after them Magnani would come.

Come, Carlo darling, come, said the doctor, the way Kate must surely have called to him at night in bed.

He himself perhaps wouldn't have reached here had it not been for one Mr. Green, an official who had returned from a survey he had been sent on in the north. By chance he heard him in the railway station canteen on the way to Pathankot, complaining about those who sent him and about Ladakh and its capital Leh.

"What neglect!" he said. "What a backwater!" Green thought he had seen everything in India, and it had become clear to him, not only was the south backward but the north as well. It's simply unbelievable, he said, even if there actually isn't real poverty there and food isn't lacking. All that, he said, is even more intolerable if one remembers that not far from there is Kashmir with all the comfort one can buy for a few rupees. God, what a dream of a holiday one could spend there on the banks of the lake in Srinagar.

In Ladakh, it turned out, they hadn't heard of the invention of the wheel and therefore there are no roads or paved pathways; at the most there are narrow trails, and those too are not made by man but rather by animal's hooves; and no tourist in his right mind goes there on purpose, one can count on one hand the number of Europeans who come there on a planned visit, and where did they house him? With his ineffectual assistant assigned to him for the survey, one who was so kind as to vacate a room for him with a large window one meter away from the family dairy – not even a meter, less than that! – and every morning he had to awake to the mooing of a cow and sometimes at night as well if the cow was having some bad dream, then it wasn't a *moo*, it was a *mooooooo*. Just to make up all the hours of sleep, he needs a month's holiday now, and they won't even give him a week, and what will he tell them, that he almost hadn't slept because of a cow and its mooing?

In the railway station canteen theirs was a conversation between two strangers who won't be seeing each other again, and when he was asked by Mr. Green (that was his name, Green, and when he introduced himself, McKenzie wanted to answer: nice to meet you; Smith, and be as inconspicuous as he was there, but he hadn't yet come to that) McKenzie could have replied anything about where he had come from and where he was going to, since they anyway would never see each other again. He hesitated for a moment and Mr. Green scrutinized him with his small eyes.

"You're new here," he said to him a moment later, "you haven't even been in India for a month. Am I mistaken?"

"No."

"And you're still young, not even thirty. Am I mistaken?"

"No, you're not mistaken."

"Then just be sure to be careful, young man," Mr. Green said to him, "if you don't want to end up like me and in twenty years' time and have to travel to every forsaken hole for some unnecessary survey that you've been sent to make there. There's no shortage of backwaters like that here, believe me."

But he specifically chose to travel to Ladakh and its capital Leh. He thought then it was possible to get there by train and didn't know the hardships he would endure until arriving. On the way he heard further aspersions from two wool merchants and a cavalry officer who for some reason had chosen to spend his holiday there: how for nine months of the year the snow cuts the area off from the world, how no one leaves their houses, and when summer eventually arrives, there's nothing to do.

Neighborhoods of miserable huts could be seen on the outskirts of Bombay and Delhi, and swollen-bellied children played alongside open sewerage ditches among starving pigs and crows who hadn't found enough garbage to rummage through, and here and there a statue of Ganesh could be seen and in front of its trunk an offering of rice the color of curry (and in the south – so he heard – there were statues of the king of the monkeys, Hanuman), and he already knew than that even if here in India there were animals he had never treated such as elephants and monkeys and camels, animals every veterinarian worthy of his name would see as a challenge, he would never treat animals anymore.

From Delhi he travelled north, and one day the plains began to arch and steepen and become covered by forest, and it seemed that at last he was travelling somewhere and not just getting away from somewhere else, even though what that place was he didn't know. And what he would do there he also didn't know, and only of one thing was he certain, that he would continue travelling on and on until he felt he had distanced himself sufficiently and wouldn't let all these Indians (they all stared at him and bothered him with questions) dishearten him, because under no circumstances did he want to go back: how could he go back, how would he explain were he to go back?

The yellowy, dusty horizon was replaced by moist mists, and cannabis plants grew wildly between the houses of Kullu, sometimes the height of a man and more, and with the asceticism he had sentenced himself to, he found little consolation at night in the blessed blur of the drug. He had tried ganja and charas, and without any conscience, on the contrary, he regretted not having become acquainted with this excellent medicine months before (it was also beneficial to babies: when suffering diarrhea attacks, their parents would burn ganja in front of their rectums and within a short while the diarrhea would cease).

At the time, nobody knew what his occupation was or if he had any occupation; to the people of Kullu he must have seemed like one of those lost whites that weren't good enough for the army or administration or commerce and not even for family life, but the little money he had and the awe of British rule was enough for them to call him "Sahib" even when he was completely groggy from the cannabis. He passed the entire monsoon season in Kullu and felt that he was becoming moldy like the walls of his room, and only when the rain ended did he begin to find out from the merchants how to go northward to Ladakh and to Leh.

After two weeks during which he almost stopped smoking (only in the evenings was he tempted to do so), he found a place on a pony caravan that transported fabrics woven in the villages of the valley and ganja and charas to the north. Again and again, he was warned that if he wasn't used to the altitudes of the mountains on the way he could become ill from the thinness of the air and even die, but he paid no attention to these warmings. "But Sahib, there's no air," they repeatedly told him, and even illustrated to him with exaggerated gestures shortness of breath, dizziness, the ground caving in. To himself and to them he answered without any hesitation: what will be will be, and he had no change of mind that the farther he distances himself from Europe the better, whether he ascends the heights of the mountains or descends to the bottom of a pit, or whether he goes up in smoke like their dead. He had once attended that ceremony in Kullu, and for the first time smelled the scent of a human body roasting in fire, a heavy almost choking smell even though they tried to cover it up with all sorts of incense.

In the valley and throughout India they had been celebrating the mighty victory of the god Rama, after smoking what he had smoked, he went to listen to some soothsayers to whom all sorts of curiosities and wonders were revealed in all sorts of ways, from the puzzle of wheat grains strewn on the skin of a drum to the letters that a chicken took out of envelopes that were arranged in front of it – that's how he first learned about Mohan Lal and at the time didn't yet know that the coming years would bring them much closer together. The thought that one day he would be involved in forgery was no less preposterous than the thought that he would be the owner of a fortune-telling chicken or would run a hospital.

"One time people they do everything," Tenzin imitated Rasul's inarticulateness, though they refrained from sharing their secret with him, "even they lift yak into air, if they want lift it. Doctor want sometime lift yak in air?" They were sitting in a small restaurant next to the bazaar and had already drunk more than a little alcohol.

McKenzie shook his head.

"One time people they climb even Chomolungma to the top, but when they finish Chomolungma they look for mountain more high, and when they no find, you know what they do, Doctor?"

Again, he shook his head. Chomolungma was the Tibetan name for the highest of the world's mountains – he only knew that.

"They want see bottom of the sea."

Both were well sated and very relaxed, and all the problems of the lack of hospital equipment were forgotten, all the cataract operations he would have to do the following day. The chang had already done its work, and only for a moment was he afraid that when he'd sober up nothing of this would be remembered; indeed, alcohol never made you forget anything, not even when you wanted it to with all your might.

The continuation of the tale progressed by itself: the gods were furious with mankind ("Isn't it enough you were given mountains? Isn't it enough you were given snow? Now you want the sea as well? Now you won't have either of them!"), and in other words, more refined, if only someone could be found to write them: the gods decreed that mankind would no longer ascend to the mountain peaks and would no longer walk on the bottom of the sea – the heights would not be for man, nor would the depths – and not being content with that, they added a further punishment, many more times terrible than the previous one.

What would the roving reporter of *The Simla News* have had to say about that? It's reasonable to presume he would have been satisfied. Years before he had seen him in Kullu being swept with the masses rushing to the bank of the river on the festival of the gods; for the first time he saw gods on their journey and also saw the force of the impassioned masses. In amazement and with trepidation, he observed them and remained where he was until they all returned from the river. He had difficulty spotting Callahan among them. despite his size

The gods were then carried one after the other on their palanquins to the tent of the most senior of them in order to bow to him (they must have been laid before this god or inclined toward him), and from there the palanquin bearers began their way back to their villages. One by one they left the Valley of Kullu, while McKenzie contemplated his journey which would commence the following day; his mind was not yet occupied by gods whose wanderings traversed worlds.

Seven years later, when the reporter happened to arrive in Leh and saw that McKenzie had attained rank among the small European community ("The last thing I would have thought about you is that you were a doctor"), he told him more about that festival and how he was almost trampled when he ran to the bank of the river with the celebrating masses. Only by a miracle he got out of there alive, that's what he told, and what was most amazing was that the damned chicken had predicted it a day before, it was written in the letter it took out with its beak: that the following day he would be saved from certain death.

"And you've also survived well," the reporter said to the doctor and looked at him closely with his small eyes whose lids were almost as bloated as his double chin.

"I get along," McKenzie answered him, and didn't tell about the hours he spends alone in his room, not about his nightmares in which a painfully familiar woman does the deed with another man, not about the celibacy he sentenced himself to ever since Bombay, and not about his fear that with every urination his organ would drop off like the noses of lepers.

"I don't at all remember you saying you were a doctor," said the reporter of *The Simla News*.

"I didn't," he answered him.

He had seemed to Callahan the same as he had seemed to the people of Kullu, a weird European, one who could drop dead among strangers and no one of his family would know he was dead or where he was buried.

"It could still happen," he said quietly.

For a moment the reporter scrutinized his eyes, seeing in them what he saw he decided to hearten him with exaggerated compliments, as if McKenzie himself had established the hospital on his own initiative and with his own hands, for people who up until then had made do with spells and amulets. "One thing you haven't told me, Doctor," he said afterward, "is if on the way you caught altitude sickness or not." And to that he answered with one word, though it deserved elaboration: altitude sickness was a bad business, without doubt, but there are things many times worse, and not only the sickness he was infected with in Bombay and of which he still hadn't been completely cured.

On his last evening in Kullu, after having packed his few belongings, he sat opposite the window that overlooks the valley and smoked his chillum as was the local custom and wondered if in a different place he would not have tried a stronger drug than this, opium for example, a drug that promises a complete daze and sheer memory loss, and in his heart thought it a blessing that only cannabis grew here. The smoke rose up, twirled and unraveled, thickening and sweetening the air, but he didn't open the window; Callahan's words came to mind about the flowering fields of opium on the Thailand-Burma border and he fell asleep sitting in his chair. He would definitely have missed the caravan had it not been for the children of the landlord invading his room early in the morning, chasing each other in their game and running around the small room as if he had already left, and if not he himself, his authority seemed to have left there. He was suddenly struck by hesitation; perhaps it would be better to heed all the warnings he had received?

But a moment later, when in his window the clouds began to rise from the tops of the cedars in the valley, he said to himself aloud: "What will be will be," and got up and stretched and went out and walked with his bundle for a half an hour or more toward the northern exit of the town, and there saw dozens of ponies of the caravan all loaded up and their grooms tightening the final bindings of the trunks and boxes and sacks. They greeted him and showed him the pony allotted to him, a creature of short stature as were all his species but sturdy and with eyes that sought kindness, and on seeing him he decided from that moment on the pony's name would be Leon. For two weeks Leon was his first friend in India, and he didn't need to hurry him up or steer him, because the pony knew every centimeter and learned to recognize his changing moods and suited his strides to them. When they settled down for the night, he would give Leon a sugar cube and feel his warm rough tongue licking the palm of his hand. He couldn't conceive of a more pleasant sensation, there or anywhere else.

The landscape changed almost every day (that's how it must have changed in the eyes of the Russian as well, despite that he had arrived in Leh from the north): the cedar forests became sparse, and the mountains, whose summits became higher and higher, turned rocky and the remains of muddy snow could be seen on them. From behind, below the winding path, the villages drew away and became smaller, and every morning beyond the edge of the path a layer of dense cloud could be seen like a fluffy floor on which no one would be injured should they roll from the slope and fall onto it. Soon the villages could no longer be seen, and the nights got colder and colder, though it was summer then – the altitude not only exhausted the cedars but the blazing of the sun as well. Every night the animals were stood in a circle in order to block the wind with their bodies, and all the people of the caravan slept in their clothes one next to another covered with pungent smelling sheep fur. They all knew his name and between themselves must have wondered why he had no servant or his own tent, but they continued to call him Sahib and every evening offered him their foods not forget ting to warn him about the spiciness after having stopped warning him about the thinning of the air.

Behind his back he wasn't called Sahib but was probably given some uncomplimentary nickname, until one of the ponies became afflicted by hoof tissue induration, and when he succeeded in curing it their attitude toward him changed, as if he had accomplished a double conjuring act: one on the pony, who walked again and carried a load, and the other on him himself, who returned to be viewed in their eyes as a genuine Sahib (all in all, he had only let a little blood from the poor pony; and he not only punctured a small hole in its neck vein but also put a stick in its mouth to bite on so that the movement of the jaws would intensify the blood flow; and all that without anesthesia, not for the pony or its master, who it seemed was also on the point of fainting). After the pony was healed Isa invited him to his campfire the way a captain of a ship invites an honorable passenger to sit at his table, but most of the hours of the day he spent in the company of the pony Leon and was content with that. They were still far from Leh, and on the back of the pony, with its measured stride, he almost didn't sense the thinning oxygen. Only when he got down from it and walked alongside it in order to loosen his bones, he found he became tired within a few moments despite not carrying anything on his back.

He had already learned a song that the coolies sang on the ascent and joined in the chorus with them and had also learned the customary cry they called out to the gods on the peaks across from the piles of stones their predecessors had formed there. "Kiki soso yahr gyalo!" they would all call out to the white peaks and the valleys at their feet, whether those valleys were visible or hidden in the clouds. "The gods shall prevail; the demons shall know defeat!" And when he called out together with them, he no longer contemplated his own demons. Only at night they sometimes returned to slip into his dreams, and on one occasion they were doing the deed right there inside the circle of the sleeping men, beneath the stinking sheep furs that rose and fell with their bodies, and when he awoke in dread he saw the sky above him and its stars close enough to touch, but through the snoring around him he could still hear the moans and groans.

The whole of the next day he was groggy, and Leon the pony, who sensed it, made a special effort to moderate his strides and every once in a while tilted his large head and peeked at him with a gloomy eye seeking kindness. But the moment he fell asleep on its back and was tossed to the rhythm of its hooves, he was immediately back on the deck of the ship, standing at its stern and reaching out a bottle to the seagulls; and when he lost his balance, Leon the pony couldn't help him. There was a small snow-water mountain brook there and to his luck he was only slight wet, and when he found himself sitting in the shallow water he came to his senses and hastened to get out and remove his boots on the bank and dry the soles of his feet and change socks. Afterward, he dried his boots above the small fire the coolies had kindled, and in that way also dried the ends of his trousers and his behind – all actions the Russian hadn't taken before he was brought here to the hospital.

He entered Leh on the right-hand side of the caravan-bashi's, and it was already being said of him, in the spirit of exaggeration that prevailed here, the doctor had the power to cure every animal from a pony to a yak, despite never having even seen a yak's tail until then. Two weeks later, Harper came to him with his unusual offer and utterly convinced there was nothing improper about it:

"You've studied medicine haven't you? You took anatomy didn't you? That's enough for us, doctor."

At that hour, for the first time he gave thought to the injured man, perhaps owing to the apparent similarity there was between the two of them, both having been strangers on their caravans, although there was almost a difference of a decade between those caravans.

Russian, aren't you interested in what you caravan is unloading? He asked him silently and didn't wait for an answer.

27

The street of the bazaar couldn't be seen from the window, nor the small alley that emerged from it where the restaurant that both he and Tenzin were fond of stood.

"Bamboo stalks?" McKenzie asked. The bamboo wasn't his idea.

Before that, an intermediary stage had been added: before the gods left on their ships – blowing wind in the sails or harnessing the whales or a flock of clouds to the ships – they punish the generation of sinners who refused to relinquish their desire to see the bottom of the sea and to that purpose went to pick bamboo stalks. As in many other tales, mankind ignores the warning given by gods: everyone picked a long bamboo stalk for himself so that they could breathe from the bottom of the sea, and they all entered the water (perhaps those stalks originated from some Chinese tale that came with one of the silk caravans, in almost all of them there were bamboo stalks and kites made from them; or perhaps it resulted from the vast amount of chang that they had consumed).

"Only their children they wait for them when go far into waves" - Tenzin continued to mock Rasul's mode of speech, but there was also sorrow in him, and had it not been for that he wouldn't have incorporated him in this deed of revenge. The children only saw the tips of the bamboos while deep down in the sea their parents examined the seabed. "They saw all the fish there and all the crabs and all the seashells and all the… what else is there, Doctor?"

"*Treponema pallidum*," McKenzie answered without thinking, but perhaps would have answered that even had he thought for a while; after all, there isn't any light in those depths, so all the creatures living there must seem – pallid.

"And the men they say, we not come back until we not see lowest place in sea! We be on top of Chomolungma, so we be also be at bottom of sea! And they go in more and more, they walk with the fishes there."

"Between the fish and the *Treponema*," McKenzie said again to be accurate, and reflected on those depths, their extent and their darkness and their creatures that no light beam bathes - *Treponema pallidum*.

That way, in the tale they had concocted, the people continued to move through the depths, in complete contradiction to the warnings of the gods, confident in their powers to do as they please. "They be stupid," said Tenzin, "and in end, when bamboos no stick out anymore, water fill them from top to bottom and the people they breathe no more and they all drown."

McKenzie lifted his glass. "Terrible," he said and took a sip. The story sounded excellent.

Through the bead curtain, a pig could be seen cumbersomely trotting through the alley, and a group of children ran after it, stoning its fat body with clumps of mud, and inside the restaurant they drank to the memory of that generation of giants that had drowned. The diners around them worked their chopsticks with amazing agility, they drank, talked and looked at the entrance. The dusty dog lying there didn't open its eyes until an ascetic pilgrim passed through the alley, walking slowly and prostrating to the ground along the route of his predecessors, intending to absolve himself of all the sins of previous incarnations.

Had he stood at the stern of the ship with a bamboo stalk in his hand instead of a bottle of brandy – the thought suddenly passed through his head – what then? Perhaps he would have dived down with it to the seabed, and stepped through the depths, all the way back to the port from where he had sailed, and mounted the platform with the bamboo and walked to the train station with the bamboo and travelled to Rome with the bamboo, and at the train station he would mount a carriage with the bamboo and travel to the Via Veneto and their hotel and would go up the stairs with the bamboo and open the door of their room and beat her repeatedly with the bamboo, had he only found her in the room.

The gods in the tale that they had concocted were not greatly merciful; on the contrary. They came to the children that remained alone and told them their parents would never come out of the sea (that was Tenzin's addition) and that no doubt they themselves would one day pick bamboo stalks in order to see the fish down below.

The fish and the *Treponema*, McKenzie said to himself again. *Treponema pallidum*.

The gods were so enraged that they said: what do we need mankind for? They're always doing stupid things, so now we return to our own place! And before they sailed on their way that mortals are prevented from crossing, they gathered all the children on the shore and told them of the punishment decreed on mankind from now on: they would never lift a yak into the air with one hand, they would not lift a pony, they would even find it difficult to lift themselves. Instead of bamboo they would have a stick, because they would find it difficult even to walk on the ground.

"And that's how the gods they leave in their boats," Tenzin swallowed a burp – the burp was entirely his, not borrowed from Rasul – "and when they go, all the sea go with them, all its waves they go rolling after them."

"Like a carpet," McKenzie said. It was a captivating idea: the sea rolling that way with all its fish gathered up, and it would never be possible to sail back to the place you had left.

Where did such ideas come to a caravan man from? (It should be admitted: at least half of them came from Tenzin.) It wasn't hard to guess: from the caravans. So many stories were told at night around the campfires. After all, there was no greater warmth than that induced by those yarns and no greater light than the light they contained.

That tale of theirs had a continuation, and its continuation was no less vital to their plan than the first part (and there was still no one to put it into writing, and the language it was to be written in was wanting). At its heart were the children who had been orphaned and had returned to their homes alone and had to learn to do everything by themselves: to hunt animals and birds, and to fish, and to light a fire. "They were alone," Tenzin said, "and every day they go to shore, even that no one come."

Again, the Rasulian tone took control over him – the ridicule concealed the sadness.

And in the same mocking tone, he told how the children shouted as loud as they could, called out with all their meager might to their mothers and fathers, until they became hoarse and lost their voices. "And all the time they not stop waiting, you wait sometime like that Doctor?"

McKenzie didn't hasten to reply.

"Me yes," said Tenzin, "I waited four years. Almost half my life at the time."

"Now I'm waiting," McKenzie said, as if his anticipation was a few months old and hadn't continued since that summer of ninety-seven.

"And I not wait," said Tenzin. "But those children they yes, they stupid."

With the help of the alcohol, further detail was quickly added: all thousand children stood on the sand in the place where the waves of the sea reached before it disappeared with the ships of the gods. They stood on the salt line, supporting each other and gazed at the empty horizon, and with all their might called out: come back, come back!

"Were they calling the sea?" asked the doctor.

"The sea."

Their expectation was clear: if the sea returned, its ships would return too. "But no one answer them," Tenzin said, "and no one come back." He was silent for a while; his thoughts wandered.

Year by year the orphans grew up alone, and when they became adults and had their own children, they thought – this continuation was necessary – perhaps the gods hadn't heard them because their land was far away, and if they go to them now, at least to the place where the sun sets, perhaps then they'll hear them from there. Luckily (no, it wasn't luck, their tale developed as it did for a purpose), that thought wasn't realized. Those children now had children of their own and they pleaded with them not to leave them, until they gave up their plan.

"They got wise," Tenzin said.

Opposite the restaurant entrance, a bony chicken could be seen trying to fly, and the dog opened one sleepy eye and didn't take the trouble get up; a moment later that same pig hurtled through the alley from the opposite direction, its entire back stained with the mud the children had thrown at it, and the moaning sound it made was almost human. At the tables around them, dumplings were bitten into, glasses that were emptied were filled again, and the noodles were removed from their bowls with chopsticks and nimbly raised to hungry mouths; a sight that made the need for a knife and fork superfluous.

"And only one time a year," Tenzin returned to his previous tone, "they all of them come together again." In a long line they assemble at the place where the sea had once reached and stand side by side, and together they all call out to the sea to return. They stand with the anchors and with the mother-of-pearl and with the salt, and place the seashells next to their ears in order to hear the sea in its return.

A sight like that is worthy of being engraved in the memory, it was even more imaginative than the one the two Canadian mountain climbers had seen in Guatemala or in Mexico or in Chile: there they stood on the edge of the sea and waited for the ships of the gods to return, while here they waited on the edge of the desert not only for those ships but for the sea itself; and even took the trouble to scatter salt in the place that had been the water line, and they unloaded sacks of seashells and mother-of-pearl and stuck anchors into the sand (only recently were they added to the list; a man-made object was necessary, one that by no means whatsoever could seem accidental).

The logic seemed clear even through the mists of alcohol: if the sea knew that all its objects were there, perhaps it would gather up its waves and return, and with it the ships of the gods and the gods themselves. That – more or less – was the tale, no worse than the tales millions of people believe in throughout the world, and one that they decided to put to paper in an alphabet they would somehow concoct. All the objects needed for the fraud they intended to transfer hundreds of kilometers to the east and bury between Tavek-kel and Loulan and then wait for the right time to arouse the curiosity of European explorers, especially that of a particular Italian. They would await the gullible in the sand, covered and hidden like Hedin's and Stein's ruins. It wasn't a cargo too large or too expensive but one a small caravan would be able to carry. Their budget was limited, unlike Henry's flexible budgets, and had Aunt Elizabeth not remembered him in her will, the entire project would have remained beyond the realms of thought.

Aunt Elizabeth said a familiar voice inside him, the voice of his forgotten childhood. On no account could she have conceived of her nephew faking documents in India, and not documents concerning horses lacking pedigrees but gods, at least in the eyes of their believers; all the innocent and the gullible and the wretched from here to Rome – all the desperate, all those clutching at straws, all those who deceive themselves and cling to their deceptions, all the dreamers, all the visionaries, all those forever expecting ships to return with their sailors and the entire sea they had sailed on and which had disappeared together with them.

"That's how it is when people yearn for something," Tenzin said. "Have you ever yearned like that, Doctor?"

The doctor put his glass down. "Yes," he replied. "And I'm still yearning."

Part Two

1

Tel Aviv 1994

"Lady, do I look like a yo-yo to you?" The porter said to her from the entrance – a Jewish porter and not an Arab, like the one that will appear in the old man's dream after the passing of more than seven decades – because she cried out to him inside the apartment that, for her part, he could take the trunk back to the person who sent it, whoever he was; and the old man, who at the time was eleven years old, drew a bit closer. From the end of the passage, he looked at the porter and the iron plated trunk on his shoulder, a sturdy hairy shoulder; a grey undershirt exposed its muscles and the outburst of sweaty armpit hair that was tangled and wild and looked like a wig stuck there. A moment later, his mother came out of the guest room with vigorous steps that seethed with loathing, wholly intending to answer the porter's question in her own fashion, that is to say: yes, that-is-exactly-what-you-look-like-to-me, like a yo-yo, so go back down the way you came up and don't leave this thing here. Chuck-it-to-the-four-winds! But her eyes, which looked the porter over, lingered as if against her will over the curves of his interwoven muscles and on the ends of the black hair on his shoulders and on the drops of sweat that glistened on his forehead and on his temples and on the armpit hairs as well.

On the right hand wall of their passage, whose whiteness is even murkier than the whiteness of the other walls of the apartment, hung a round mirror in an engraved wooden frame, and next to it stood a wooden hanger on which only two coats could be seen even in winter, one large and one small, and above that was the head of a stuffed stag whose horns branched out toward the ceiling, and the cracks there must have been made by the stag ramming against it at night like a prisoner in solitary confinement (there had been a very distant time when the old man had thought that).

His mother didn't want the trunk in the apartment. Even before she saw its boards and its iron plating and even before she smelled its scent, she recoiled from it, even before the porter's heavy steps could heard on the stairs, even before his horse in front of the building neighed. She found horses repugnant, owing to their neighing and the beating of their hooves or owing to the tossing of their carts which in Russia were called brichkas and in India were called arabas – but that's something she doesn't know; only her grandson will know that in due course – or owing to the brown heaps they leave behind them in the street that attract clouds of flies. But more than anything, she found repugnant what that thin horse brought on its cart (she was notified about it in a registered letter signed by some English doctor whose name she didn't read to the end), she found repugnant the travelling trunk fastened by bands of rusted iron, and her repugnance began before the trunk travelled even one kilometer on its long way from Leh to Kashgar, and before its boards were pissed on by dogs that sniffed it on each of the stations through which it passed. Perhaps there weren't any dogs at the start of the way, in the remote place where her husband died, that is to say, no dog other than him.

More than once she had said: "That dog" or "That bastard," and when the old man asked her who she was talking about, she would become silent and send him to play in the yard for a while, and he would obey and walk to the end of the passage and open the door and go down the steps, and on his left, at the height of his head, was the thin black stripe delineating the part of the wall painted with oil paint against dirtying children like himself and like those who beat him up when he was smaller.

The old man had once been a child who was sent to play in the yard, who collected colored marbles and climbed trees, and afterward became a youth who shaved the first fluff from his chin and fell in love with a girl and wooed her shyly, and afterward became a student and a substitute teacher at a high school, and afterward a soldier proud of his uniform and his rank, sending letters and postcards to his mother from every place the Jewish Brigade landed up in, and despite that she only read them cursorily, she kept them all; after all they were the only letter she ever received.

She didn't like the woman he chose for himself after the war and would look at her grandson – who when she sent the porter on his way was not yet even a passing thought – in amazement and with reservation, and she still wondered how an hour one night at the beginning of the twentieth century could have caused all these continuations to take place in time, continuations that contain a future concealed from the eye and out of the reach of her imagination. She was especially put off by the dogs her grandson raised and loathed them not for their fleas but for their constant efforts to please their masters; after all, the path of her life had been determined by one night in Russia, a night in which she had sacrificed all the coming years in order to please a man she loved, and even before the rising of the sun, she realized they had been sacrificed in vain.

She was forced to raise her son alone, and before that she was forced to leave the only two places she had ever known and which she had never intended to sever herself from, and to emigrate to a new country of which she knew almost nothing. She had to ignore all the rumors that trailed after her and also hurt her son, when the neighbors' children were big enough and hateful enough to fling what they heard from their parents at him. All that happened in the backyard of the building where she sent him to play, while she lay on the bed in her room with slices of cool lemon placed on her forehead to relieve her headache and dozed off like that not only with the shutters and her ears closed, but also with a closed heart. She wanted her son to finally know the harm that had been done to her; and know the life she had been sentenced to and therefore he as well, not because she was evil by nature – she had been innocent until that night in Minsk at the beginning of the twentieth century – but because by then she had lost all faith in humankind, completely and irremediably.

But at that noon hour – a warm humid summer hour at the beginning of the second decade of the twentieth century – the old man saw his mother pressed up against the passage wall, a woman in her thirties whose hairdo is unraveled and her fists clenched in the pockets of her stained dressing gown, and instead of walking to the door and shoving the porter aside (chuck-it-to-the-four-winds!) or retreating to the far end of the passage and at least avoiding any unnecessary contact with him, she stays in her place and allows the porter to pass between her and the wall, and the trunk and the shoulder almost touch her, and the pungent smell of male sweat emitted from the gaping armpit rubs up against her from her nose to her ankles.

The old man stayed where he was: before then he had watched the street and had seen the porter's cart stop in front of their building, and not for a moment did he consider that the trunk would be brought up to them; and afterward he ran to the door and opened it to a crack in order to see to which apartment it was being brought; and when the steps neared their floor, he closed it silently, and when knocks were heard on their door, he hurried out onto the balcony again, and only now returns from it and his trouser pockets are swollen with apricot pits[4] that he's been gathering from the beginning of summer.

In the small kitchen at the end of the passage (a primus stove was lit there with a large pot on it, and dishes and cups had been heaped up in the washbasin for two days already; the old man still remembers that detail) he saw her offer the porter a glass of water after hastily checking its cleanliness and wiping it again with the flap of the dressing gown. She treated her dressing gown the way she treated the dishes and was in no hurry to wash it, but the old man loved the smells it gave off, those that the material absorbed from her cooking, those that were added to it on the balcony when she finally watered her plants and picked the leaves that had dried up, and those that were emitted by her body – those were dearer to him than the rest.

When the glass was emptied, he saw his mother fill it again, and how she watched the porter empty it again in two or three gulps that trickled water onto the stubble of his chin and onto his neck. Afterward, he saw his mother offer the porter in a slightly cracked voice a small kitchen towel to wipe himself with ("Take it, take it," she said, "don't be shy"), and he also saw the hesitation of the porter

---

4   Used in children's games.

("Wouldn't it be a shame, Ma'am?") and noticed the look he gave her while passing the towel over his chin and his forehead (he stood in the middle of the small
kitchen and seemed very concerned not to make any extraneous movement). On
finding confirmation in her eyes, he passed the towel over the black hair ends
on his shoulders, and the glistening drops of sweat were also wiped away. After
another hesitation he passed the towel over his armpits and their sweaty hair, first
the left and then the right, and when he lifted his arms, the smell emitted from
there became more pungent and his muscles bulged and hardened.

Only then did the porter sense that he was being watched from the kitchen
entrance (perhaps the old man made some movement, possibly intentionally. in
order that his mother finally remove her eyes from the porter's arms), and instead
of becoming annoyed it seemed he was suddenly embarrassed, grown up as he
was, because he immediately crumpled the towel in his large palms and in a low
bashful voice said: "What a pity I've ruined your towel, Ma'am."

His voice cracked and was slightly hoarse, as if the sweat had drawn the mois-
ture from his throat, and he didn't seem much heartened when she assured him
in a casual tone: "It's not terrible, it can be easily washed," nor when she replaced
strands of unruly hair behind her ear and said to him: "Anyway, I only do washing
for him and me," and then pointed to her son only with a fleeting movement of her
eyebrow; at the time old man, was no more than the motion of a plucked eyebrow.
For a moment the porter looked at her and then at her son and became even more
uneasy when she said to him with a sudden boldness and in much haste: "It's no
problem really, your undershirt -" but then she lowered her eyes and began to
twiddle the edge of her dressing gown belt between two fingers, and for a moment
the old man feared that she was about to open it. Afterward, only the sound of the
pot and the flame beneath it could be heard, and the sudden desire arose in the old
man for everything to catch fire with a giant flame.

Grown up and ill at ease, the porter remained standing in the middle of the
small kitchen, the crumpled kitchen towel soaked with sweat between the palms of
his large hands. His undershirt, a faded workman's undershirt, darkened further as
the sweat stains spread from his arm pits to the large sweat stain around his navel,
and his scent became sharp and more pungent than it had been. A scent like that
the old man had never smelled: it was a solid and dark smell and didn't come from
the pores of the skin, or from the armpits of the porter or his navel, but from the
deepest depths that the boy was unable to imagine, a space between the male and
the female.

In the corner of the passage, the trunk still stood with its rusted lock and sealed
with a layer of filth, and for a moment it looked like a faded treasure chest from
pirate stories on whose treasure some terrible curse has been cast, and all who lay
a hand on it will become impoverished or lose their hand, and those are just some
of the lesser troubles that await them (perhaps the flame will emerge from there

and destroy everything, the old man thought: the passage and the kitchen and the whole building, until it reaches the porter's cart and destroys that too).

At the rear of the kitchen, bubbling sounds rose from the large pot standing on the primus stove: large bubbles swelled and burst and reappeared and swelled and burst again in the thick fluid (perhaps vegetable soup, perhaps borscht, he had already forgotten that detail; and anyway, the old man liked all her dishes), but the scent of the porter, pungent and spreading, overcame the entire smell of the dish being cooked there. When the porter gave a quick glance at the pot, whose lid the steam shifted, the old man's mother tensed as if it was her he was studying: through the steam, with a moist look marked by black eyebrows in whose thickness drops of sweat also sprouted, and new droplets were already being formed on his forehead and his temples, and they too are odorless in comparison to his other scent, the dark scent from the depths of the male.

But the porter no longer looked at her, nor at the pot. He returned the lid to its place with a dim sound of cymbals, and thick drippings flowed from its edges, and he dropped the towel onto the tablecloth that had old stains dotted by grains of sugar and salt and breadcrumbs and two flies walked between them. Afterward, the porter again passed between the old man's mother and the wall: grown up and silent, he moved forward between her face and her breasts and her stomach and her thighs and the wall, and it seemed that with all his might he kept even his scent from rubbing against her body. And after he went out – on the way he kicked the trunk and pressed it closer to the wall, and on leaving hastily touched the dusty mezuzah[5] - it remained in the place where it was unloaded: at the end of the passage, alongside the entrance to the washroom with its light musty smell, left there like silt spewed by a stray tidal wave before retreating and returning to the sea.

For a moment the old man's mother stood still, twiddling the dressing gown belt between her fingers, and then, the old man was still watching her, she went out onto the balcony and leaned on the railing and looked down at the porter leaving the entrance of the building and walking to his cart parked at the sidewalk. His back was also sweaty, from his hairy shoulder blades to his hips, and with a heavy springing step he mounted its platform and sat down and held the reins between his spread apart legs. A thin horse was harnessed to the cart and with its tail it whipped the flies that were bothering its posterior and right away began to move, but the porter after glancing back, causing the old man's mother to flee from the railing to the rear of the balcony, grabbed the whip that lay at his feet and lifted it up into the air and whipped the horse again and again and again, and the horse whinnied and exposed its large yellow teeth.

---

5   A piece of parchment in a decorative case fixed to a doorpost and inscribed with Hebrew verses from the Torah. It is customary for observant Jews to kiss it by touching their mouths and then the mezuzah, on entering and leaving by the doorpost.

That same hot dry summer evening, the old man saw his mother standing and surveying herself in the large mirror of the clothes cupboard: with the tip of her fingers she felt the corners of her eyes and stretched them, and afterward pursed her lips from which tiny wrinkles branched, and placed the palms of her hands beneath the bra cups curving from the slip and lifted them slightly, until she noticed his gaze inside the mirror and suddenly shouted at him to get out of the room in a voice he had never heard come out of her and which continued come out of her the next day and all the days that followed.

The whole of that week the old man's mother did strange things she had never done or will do again: from Mr. Shtub's pharmacy she bought a new hairbrush and new hairpins and cosmetic soap as well as bath salts, and the next night shut herself up in the bathroom, and through the crack left by the door the old man saw her sitting in the bath water with closed eyes and encircled by the flames of Sabbath candles that she placed around her, and on her face an expression that he didn't know whether was of great suffering or great pleasure or both at the same time, and wasn't afraid but instead wished a large flame would erupt and consume her.

That whole week every morning she went to the square where porters waited for clients, sitting in their carts one behind the other with their ropes and their sacks and their clouds of flies. Perhaps that was how, years before in St. Petersburg, she had walked to the corner of Moravskaya Street and Nevsky Avenue to the brichkas parked there, and at the time it wasn't transportation she was seeking, or a cart driver, but rather for one who perhaps had disguised himself as a cart driver solely to get away from her and her swelling belly.

Every morning she went to that square, coiffed and fragrant and with a vigor the old man had never seen in her before ("Get out of here!" she shouted at him every time he tried to peek into her room), until on the fifth day from his cart one of the porters said to her in a voice rough from cigarette smoke: "Lady, there's really nothing for you here, go back home to your son." And another lying down chuckled, "He's not keen on you lady, don't you get it?" And a third whose gaze lingered on her from the height of his platform added: "Lady, he's got a twenty-year-old girl, they just got engaged, the girl's a rose, believe me a rose, but if she hears about you, she won't think twice about sticking her thorns into your face." And his friend who had chuckled from the worn-out blanket padding his cart said: "What does she know about things like that? She might think your joking." That last remark finally got her moving and sent her back home, with her hair once again unraveled, because the new hairpins she had bought she ripped from her hair and threw to the ground one after the other on the way, and not because she believed someone would bother to find his way to her home by following them.

In the passage the trunk no longer stood in the place where it had been left. At first it was pushed by the small hands of the old man and with all the weight of his small body, afterward it was dragged with those hands onto the threadbare carpet and onto the decorated floor tiles and onto tufts of dust that had gathered on the threshold of the balcony, and afterward it was dragged onto the balcony itself, a frontal balcony from whose rear wall plaster has peeled and from whose ceiling the whitewash has swelled and almost all its pot plants have wilted and its railing is so corroded that the rust has already left it in search of other prey. And there, in the corner of the balcony, on the day the old man brought a screwdriver and hammer from his room, he tried with all his childish strength to break the hanging lock: blow after blow he struck the lock and suddenly the screwdriver was deflected and hit his thigh and blood poured from it and he had to stop it with a rag before he could begin to rummage through the trunk, first with his fingers and afterward with his arm whose entire length was swallowed by it- a small soft grop-ing hand that has long sunk and become lost beneath the wrinkled skin and the shriveled flesh of a ninety-year-old.

The old man drums with his fingers for a moment, and Amnon looks at them: brown stains spread over the skin and it seems it has been freckled by the sun from the other world, the one that sometimes weighs down his wrinkled eyelids even in the middle of a conversation and suddenly causes his mouth to gape open with the thirst of a desperate fish and his head to slowly fall to his chest, until some random sound awakens him: a car horn in the street, a door slamming in the stairwell, the sound of music from a neighboring apartment, the stirring of his son who gets up from where he was sitting, because, like his mother before him, he's sick of this apartment where he passed his childhood and the only place where some vestige of it remains.

"I have to be going," he then said to his father.

2

England, 1994

It's a village which doesn't even have a village idiot, and nobody gets senselessly drunk in its only pub. The travels of these villagers are brief, only seldom do they go to London and when they do they return the same day, its tumult being too much for them. Until the man he's come to meet here returns from his vacation and might agree to talk with him, they'll no doubt continue to make jokes about Amnon behind his back: about his accent that garbles their language, about the backpack he carries with him like a boy, about his shirt which gives off the smell of curry, but he didn't start his journey into order to find favor with anyone.

What exactly he'll discover here, he doesn't know, but even evading an answer is a statement; that he learned in his glory years at the newspaper. Don't investigative journalists who cross continents have backpacks like these? No they don't; after all in his good years he also used a small trolley case that he took with him to Buenos Aires, to Marseilles, to Delhi, to Kiev, to London; at the time his air flights, hotels, living expenses and whatnot were paid for ("Everything except female escorts," Kramer had described it, "at your age, I wasn't even given bus tickets").

A month before his journey he bought the backpack in a large camping equipment store, and for a moment amused himself with the thought that the young people who filled the place, all of whom were recently out of the army, must have seen him as an adventurer who on his travels had replaced many backpacks, but none of them paid any attention to him. Twenty or more young people were sitting in a circle around someone who had returned from the East and was telling them the places worth visiting – from tropical beaches whose only danger was a coconut falling on your head to mountain temples through which monkeys scurried – and he looked them and wondered how many of them would reach those places and how many would pass them up and return before the end of the way, as he had done at their age. And the thought passed through his mind between the shelves of sleeping bags and the shelves of shoes, that the most grueling and most dangerous path isn't the one that lasts a month on a mountain slope in Nepal ("Sleeping bags and shoes are most important," the guide said to them. "So invest in a good sleeping bag and good shoes, you guys."), but rather the one you go through toward an awakening.

While the young people around him continued to jot down the recommendations given to them, he wondered how many of them, when they reach his age, would return like him to this store knowing perhaps they're wasting their time, and that now in their adulthood their mistake will be irreparable; but nevertheless, like him they'll be resolute in their decision to make that mistake – they'll leave their wives and children and their old parents and take off. At the cash register, he asked for his backpack to be wrapped because he didn't want to wear it on his back in the street among the passersby, and in the taxi that stopped, the driver glanced at him through the rearview mirror and said: "For your son? I could tell right away. I know what they're like, the moment they finish the army they want to get out of here. This country's screwed up, believe me."

The sleeping bag he bought was packed inside the backpack, small and light and resistant to water and cold. The salesman in the store praised the perfect insulation and also the zipper that never gets stuck. To the aluminum frame of his first backpack he added a binding strap which he dismantled from an armored vehicle to be able to attach a sleeping bag to its base, and that backpack travelled with him to Holland and Italy and Spain and France and even to Norway and the high cliff that overlooks the North Sea. The sun that set opposite him was yellow and wintry and didn't complete its path toward the horizon but stopped close to the sea and lingered there as if recoiling from the chill of the water, and then it began to slowly return backward. He got into his battered van and hoped its engine would hold out for a bit longer, and when it started he thought he would never forget the sight of the midnight sun, but in fact he doesn't remember it other than from a postcard be bought on the way with the ten stages of the sun's path going back and forth. He didn't bother to send or keep it: what for?

For a while he stored the backpack and the sleeping bag with a few other belongings in the dusty apartment he began showing to agents that summer, and after each visit of the agents and their clients he would take the backpack out of its hiding place and examine all the zippers like a boy, one after the other from large to small ("Believe me," said the salesman in the store, "a zipper can ruin a trip.").

"How pathetic," the woman he had left would surely have said had she seen him standing like that, a forty-four-year-old man with a young person's backpack, but she never saw him like that, not then and not even on the day he left their home. A taxi driver honked his horn outside, and she didn't bother to turn around; the driver honked again, and she covered her head with a blanket and he went out with the backpack. Udi was asleep in his room, and on one of the slats of the shutters two blue and red striped socks were laid to dry, and beneath the windowsill a golden candy wrapping that had been thrown outside could be seen, and he imagined hearing his light snoring but didn't draw close to the window to peek in. The dog slept in his kennel on the other side of the building; he was a great sleeper, Albie, and on nights when he wanted to take him out for a walk to calm himself from some quarrel, he had to knock on the side of the kennel for him to be so kind as to get up and come out.

He felt no sorrow about leaving the street of their home with its potholes and garbage bins (the road that was promised them hadn't been paved, nor will it be paved), and a dim memory arose: the sight of airport asphalt runways with heavy and low December asphalt skies above them, and that gloomy greyness is breached only for a moment by a convoy of suitcases being transported on rail carts to the plane under his watchful eye. He was still a young man at the time, and his job was to search for suspicious objects in the terminal of Orly Sud. He thought if he saved enough money from that job he'd fly to South America and sail on the Amazon and travel south to Tierra del Fuego. Over twenty years have passed since then and he won't get to do that. During his glory years at the newspaper, he was only sent to capital cities, but in a short while it seems he'll be travelling to a truly remote place – after raising a family and breaking it up, the remoteness of a place where a person can disappear without leaving behind a trace now captivates him.

"Is it nice there?" she asks him over the phone.

In the house he rented in this English village according to her recommendation, but also to her resentment (five years earlier she had holidayed in an area close by with her family in summer, when she still had a real family), on arriving he saw a green ladder standing in the entrance next to an apple tree, and he still hasn't used it, not even once. The house where she had holidayed also had a tree and a ladder like that but her two sons preferred climbing it without the ladder ("And what's more in short pants!" She had told him in great detail exactly where they had been scratched and how she treated them; she had treated him in much the same way at the beginning of their acquaintance).

"It's nice here," he replies, and doesn't wish to say more than that. It seems to him he's not obliged to account for himself to anyone, not even to the few people who loved him.

In the plane on the his way here, his breath condensed on the round window and was only dispelled when he drew his face away, and the thought crossed his mind – down below, the buildings of Tel Aviv became small and the shoreline became distant – that if suddenly some stray seagull or crane flew into one of the engines on the edge of the wing and caused it to malfunction and the plane dropped with all its passengers even before crossing the Mediterranean Sea, he, Amnon, had already done a lot for this flight, He had broken away from his previous that no longer interested him. He had made the announcement in the kitchen, had seen her face seemingly fall apart, heard the bubbling of the oil in the frying pan and her cracked voice, saw Udi coming in thin as a strip of pasta – she used to call him "macaroni" and wrap him in a hug – and asking what happened. For a brief moment, through the round window, the stray crane was replaced by a stork with a chubby solemn faced baby carried in a bundle held by its beak. They looked

at each other through the windshield, one looking at his past and one at his future
– he, Amnon, was that baby being swung in the air.

"Do you feel at home there?" she asks. Twice a week she makes sure to call him in
order to remind him what he's left during this time out he's taken for himself (that's
what she called it, in those empty words). It's clear to her that if he continues travelling the way he planned to, there's no knowing whether he'll return.

"Time out?" she said to him after her son fell asleep. "Is this some sort of
basketball game?" She cuttingly reminded him of his age. So where does he have
the time for a timeout, she said, and where exactly does the money come from,
after all, he hasn't become rich from his job. That detail she knew full well: after all,
they met at his workplace. She now asks if he's met anyone; an abandoned woman
wouldn't talk that way, not about such trifles, but she's careful not to be on the
attack.

He replies with an evasive answer and doesn't mention the pub and the waitress there, or the horse who approaches the boards of the fence every morning
when he passes by, or the dogs that stop to sniff at his trousers on the path of their
afternoon route that winds around the small cemetery north of the estate (he had
already read every name on the gravestones; the man he's looking for isn't buried
there), nor pub dogs.

When she asks him if he misses her a little, her voice fills the mouthpiece,
and then the line is filled with his silence. In his bad hours, he sometimes wonders
whether the organ for missing someone hasn't atrophied like any other organ not
put to use; in truth, he never nourished it enough: not with photographs, not with
letters, nor with anything else intended to clutch at the passing time. What one
remembers, one remembers, and what is doomed to be forgotten will be forgotten.
Perhaps a limit had been set for the Poliakovs and his father had used up the entire
share meant for all of them.

He'll be staying in this village for just a month and then will continue on his
way. He let his apartment in Tel Aviv at a loss; he was too quickly enticed by the
agents who disparaged everything in it, from the floor tiles to the damp ceiling,
but the sum he received was also enough to sustain him on his travels for years, if
that indeed is his wish.

Travelling for years, he thinks. And that juvenile thought excites him specifically for its youthful preposterousness, because he doesn't know what those years
will be like, or how many there will be; perhaps there won't be any. Everything he
knew in advance bored him to tears.

In the pub he befriended mainly the dogs in the yard, before he went in to drink
and after he left. Between entering and leaving he slowly drank a glass of white
wine and stared at the pub dwellers, or at the television screen, or at the page of
a newspaper stained with the prints of glasses. He read about a slip of the tongue

made by the heir to the throne, about the latest partner of a pop starlet, about Manchester United's recent acquisition, about a demonstration of fox hunters whose activities had been curbed with some restricting order; in protest the hunters even fired into the air and a duck fell from the sky into the courtyard of a school (*A DINNER FROM HEAVEN* was the headline in the local press). Their last war had taken place a few years ago on a distant island in the southern hemisphere, and now shooting ducks makes the headlines. Instead of amusing him, the thought of the innocent duck actually nauseates him. It's an old nausea, more than ten years old, whose origin is the shores of Lebanon.

Around him the pub dwellers contentedly down one half-liter glass after another while he is still on his first and last half glass of white wine. Not only in that do they differ from him: they were born here in this village and with certainty will grow old and die here like their father's fathers, while there's no knowing where he'll land up and for how long. This fog, not that of England, but of his coming years, is agreeable to him even if it ends badly.

3

St. Petersburg, 1904

"Did you talk to them?" Duchin said across the table. "Did you open your mouth? Did you squeal?"

When by surprise Poliakov released from the secret police headquarters and all the other prisoners remained in custody, his colleagues looked askance at him: suspicious, begrudging.

"No," he replied. "No."

"Look me in the eye," said Duchin.

He looked him in the eye.

"Is that how you looked them in the eye?"

"Yes," he replied.

"In the eyes of both the interrogators there?"

"Yes," he replied.

"Perdischenko's and Telegin's?"

"Yes," he replied again.

"And also that policeman's, what's his name, the one from the village?"

"Antip."

"Did you look him in the eye?"

"Yes."

"So why don't I believe you?" said Duchin. "Why?"

"Because you don't believe anyone, Duchin," said Vera.

Beyond his back, in the window on whose handle hung the umbrella which served as an all-clear signal to all those coming here, the building across the road was lit up with its windowpanes ablaze from the rays of sun that crept through the clouds, and Duchin's large smooth bald plate also changed color.

"I believe you, Vera." he answered from his table.

"I'm glad to hear that."

"I also believe Volodya," said Duchin.

"And for that we're both grateful."

"And I also believe" – Duchin ignored her cutting tone – "in the shared future that awaits you and Volodya despite that I myself had other dreams about that matter, as you know."

"You're not going to start all that again, Duchin."

"No," he replied.

He raised his doubts he was harboring: the unexpected releasing of Poliakov and the fact that none of the other prisoners were released; and all that taking place after the many unpleasant things revealed about Poliakov's personality in the past, not to mention that he had been enlisted against all the rules.

Duchin began to ask him detailed questions about all the stages of the interrogation: exactly what were they trying to find out, exactly what did he answer, and if he kept silent as he claimed, exactly how did he keep silent: like someone confessing or like someone denying or like someone who hadn't been there at all? There's a big difference.

In the matter of the bombs for example, it was obvious they had asked about them, exactly what did he answer? What did he say when he was asked who prepared them and who transferred them and how did they do it. And if he kept silent, exactly what had they understood from his silence?

"Did you tell about the apartment?" he asked him afterward. "Where it is, in what street, what the number of the building is, on what floor, what name is written on the door?"

"No," he replied, "I didn't tell them."

"And how Vera Alexandrovna brought you here, did you also tell them about that? Without consulting anyone?"

"No," he said again.

From the entrance of the inner room, Vera looked at both of them for a moment longer before turning around with the newspaper she was holding, and the door creaked behind her before it was slammed.

"Aren't you tired yet, Duchin?" her voice became dim from the other side of the closed door, and from her room, cupboard doors, and drawers, were heard being opened and shut one after the other.

"Duchin turned to him again. "Did you tell them about the signals that were agreed upon? Not a thing? Not about the umbrella behind me or the rug in the entrance?"

"No," he replied.

"Not about the bicycle chain down below?"

"No," he replied.

"So why don't I believe you?" Duchin said again, and beyond his back the windows of the building opposite dimmed when the clouds merged and Duchin's baldness with them.

"Maybe because you made your mind up about him the first time you saw him," Vera said from the inner room. "That's why."

"No," said Duchin. "He himself showed us the person he is when a few meters away from him a man was almost beaten to death. It wouldn't have taken much to finish Maximov off right there, what did he do?"

"We've already been through all that," said Vera. "After all, you wouldn't agree to give him a weapon would you? No!" She stood in the entrance of the room wearing a maid's uniform, and her hairdo had been altered for her to place a headband around it, but she looked as lovely as before, and even in her anger she enjoyed being looked at.

To all her attempts to defend him (she twice mentioned to Duchin how resourceful he had been the morning she had been disguised as a beggar woman and her cover was almost blown, even though he didn't know her at the time, he rescued her from the hands of the detectives. She also brought up the assassination again saying that he had carried out his mission: he stood at the window of the third floor of the hotel and signaled to Maximov when the minister's carriage was approaching; and if he did lose his head afterwards, he hadn't harmed anyone), Duchin replied: "You can't be sure of that, Vera Alexandrovna. The facts speak for themselves."

He specified these facts: Poliakov was released from custody at ten in the morning and by seven that evening on Sadovaya Street the detectives had already arrested two lookouts who were so well disguised even their own mothers wouldn't have recognized them. "I might not have proof," he said, "but I've got a healthy logic."

He turned to Poliakov and asked him if at least this time, in the matter of Levin, they could depend on him not to lose his head; he could make amends for the harm he had done. He should get out there as quickly as possible and not lie there for a day and a half without moving until the police catch him.

"Which is what you did," he reminded him.

Since it was Vera who first brought him to the apartment used as a hideout, and who has often been reprimanded for her rash behavior on that day, she tried to defend him. She was an assertive woman, the complete opposite of the girl he had known in the provincial town who didn't know how to stand up for herself.

"It could have happened to anyone!" said Vera. "For God's sake, Duchin, it was his first time! And with all the sympathy I have for Maximov -"

"With-all-sympathy-I-have-for-Maximov?" Duchin said slowly from the other side of the table and reminded her exactly what the detectives did to Maximov in the middle of the street, right below the hotel window, and how her dear protégé saw everything from his window and didn't lift a finger.

Instead of answering directly, she reminded Duchin that the man he's calling her protégé had experienced things many times worse, things that to their good fortune they've never had to experience, referring to his last visit to his village. She still thought the resourcefulness that he had shown when they first met on the street corner (he directed the detectives in the opposite direction) was an example of his capabilities but didn't know what was behind that resourcefulness: no wonder he himself was also amazed by it.

The first time he saw her she was sitting on the sidewalk in her beggar's rags, a baby in her lap and a begging bowl in front of her, the eyes of her filthy face eyes looking straight ahead past all the pedestrians, and when he stopped and bent down, taking pity for her – it arose from some place – he noticed that her baby was nothing but a bundle of rags. Right away she grabbed his wrist and hushed him by pursing her lips; it resembled a kiss, and a long extinguished and forgotten desire arose in him.

Not far from them, at the side of the road, a vacant carriage was parked with its horse eagerly chewing stalks of straw from a worn-out bag. The coachman glanced at them from his platform, and Poliakov didn't know he too was in disguise and had no interest in passengers. The coachman then watched the ministry building entrance; nothing out of the ordinary could be seen there, but his eyes were fixed on the people passing through it, so that the moment the man they were both waiting for – the coachman on his carriage and she from the sidewalk – comes out, the carriage would leave and follow him (they had bicycle riders for that purpose; and newspaper sellers and shoeshine boys, as well as and fake drunks and fake prostitutes just as the Okhrana[6] had of their own; but at the time, the streets seemed perfectly normal: the drunks were drunk, their peddlers were peddling, the prostitutes were prostituting themselves – arousing desire or pity, provided those looking at them still had desire or pity or any other emotion in them).

In the tavern they went to after the detectives were far away, among the tumult of the drinkers and the tobacco smoke and the smells of vodka and cabbage and farts, she asked him his name and where he lived and where he had come here from and why. He mumbled something about the village and his parents' home and what had happened there and led to her to believe he and his mother hadn't shut themselves up in the attic by choice, but that the rioters had locked them up to prevent them from disturbing their actions in the yard. He told only a little in the tavern, and someone next to them burped and another hiccupped and a third farted, and even through the languid twirling of smoke and the dirt that had carefully been applied to her skin, her face was feminine and beautiful, and she looked at him with such pity that even if for a moment he thought of being more honest about what he was telling her and admit to his weakness at the time – no, not weakness, far worse than weakness – he didn't do it. All the while, her baby lay in her lap with its head close to her breast as if by habit despite its raggedness having already been exposed; and when one of the drunks offered her a substitute ("I'll make you a real baby, honey"), she answered him without hesitation that if the baby resembled him no one would give her so much as one kopek. She wasn't bothered by the chuckles that erupted around her, on the contrary, it was clear that she enjoyed being looked at, even by bleary and purulent eyes.

In the din of the drunks around them, a din intermingled with all the smells of the tavern, she asked him if the Jews had been harassed before that, and inquired about the faith, as if it was also his faith. Do they believe in the same god as every-

---

6   An organization set up in 1881 in Russia to suppress revolutionary activities.

one else she asked, but not in his son? (She had already heard something about that from a friend but wanted to hear more.) And what about a messiah, she asked, has theirs already come or not?

"He hasn't come, nor will he come," he answered her. "Your baby's more real than he is."

And what does he believe in, she asked; after all, he has to believe in something, there's no such thing as a person who doesn't believing in anything, someone who doesn't believe in anything isn't really alive.

On her right, between the legs of the next table, a large cockroach could be seen scurrying and a shoe reached out toward it and missed, and Poliakov pondered a while and said: "In nothing."

"Don't you believe in yourself?" There was only one answer she was willing to accept and began to speak fervently about the ability of man to bring about enormous changes just by the force of his faith. She mentioned that in the village he came from -   Bykhov? - wherever - since he had succeeded to survive, he must have believed in something. No one could have fought like that without faith. And in Minsk too, where he went afterward there was no shortage of brave comrades; one of Tsar Nicholas assassinators came from there, a young woman who actually was one of his people.

Because he was silent, she thought he had been persuaded by her arguments, and he didn't bother denying it. In the corner of the room the cockroach could be seen again, outside the range of the threatening shoe, confirming that the danger had passed; and perhaps it was a different cockroach.

From their table he looked around; there were too many faces there, and all their expressions were alike and familiar to him ad nauseum. On their right, the drunk who had previously addressed her passed by again and his gaze roved unashamedly over her breasts. "Vodka for babies," he said, and when he grinned his front teeth were revealed, crooked and yellow. "Like your mother's," Vera replied and surveyed his grinning face from the sleep in his eyes to the ends of the hair of his chin. "She must have given you real vodka, not milk," and from the end of their table someone hit him with a small lump of bread, thereby declaring his defeat, and when the bread fell to the ground the cockroach hurried toward it with its protruding feelers quivering.

They looked her over as well and perhaps were thinking of saying something but gave up the idea, fearing her sharp tongue, and the pleasure from the standing she had attained among them in such a short time could be discerned on her face, and not only because she wanted to fight on their behalf so that they wouldn't have to drown their sorrows in alcohol. At the time, he saw in her the satisfaction of a woman conscious of her power over men, until one of the other women sitting there noticed her hand stroking the doll's rags and saw that the filth had missed her nails. "That one's got the nails of a lady," she said, and despite a triumphant reply delivered from a nearby table ("She doesn't stick her fingers where you stick yours"), they both got up and left.

Two streets away from the tavern and about a half an hour's walk from the street corner where she had watched the ministry building, Vera stopped in front of the entrance to a small hotel and told him to wait there until she came out. He was completely open to this chance adventure after a night in which he was forced to hurriedly flee from his room like everyone who doesn't have a resident permit, and for hours on end he roamed the streets.

If he gets very very bored, she said to him at the entrance, he can count the people coming and going; there's no shortage of traffic despite the hotel being small, every moment someone's going in and coming out. It's that kind of hotel.

He had been through a long exhausting night, and after she went in he leaned against the wall of the hotel and felt his shoulders becoming limp and his eyelids closing and the sounds becoming dim, until he suddenly heard a laughing voice calling to him from one of the windows above. For a moment he wondered if the beggar disguise had been replaced by a different one, but the woman in the window was completely real. "You don't have to sleep standing up," she said to him from her window with lips that were too red, "come up and sleep with me, honey."

A moment later Vera came out of the hotel in the simple and clean clothes of a governess, and straight away intertwined her arm with his thus declaring owner-ship over him, as if it had always been their custom to meet like that on the side-walks of Petersburg. Like a fiancé whose jealousy has been aroused she drew him away from the hotel and its windows, and as they walked, he was reminded of a different touch in a different city and tried in vain to drive that memory from his mind: there he hadn't been viewed as a potential colleague – the girl that he had become acquainted with saw him as a boyfriend, and then a lover, and then a life partner, and then a husband and a father. In order to begin that process, she one night entrusted her demure delicate body to him, as if by that ensuring that he wouldn't leave her the following day; he would leave only because at the end of the tracks the world at large awaited ("That's where the world is," his mother used to say to him in the village and point to the horizon, "go there, Ilya, and forget this place as quick as you can.").

No, an insistent voice now said at the back of his mind, no. During one short visit to his village – he nonetheless did return there once – he learned everything it was possible to learn about the world and about himself as well; it was a terrible lesson.

With the same speed with which Vera had adopted the voice of a fiancé, she later became serious, but before then told him there had been a time when she was forced to use that disguise as well: no, not that of a governess, those are actually comfortable, but that of the woman from the hotel. Yes, the one with the purple dressing gown revealing her breasts; you think I didn't see how you looked at her? Just don't lie now!

It transpired that on one of her previous lookouts she walked along the right sidewalk of Panteleimonovskaya back and forth for half the night, and it was so cold that at times she wished someone would stop and put their arms around her, no matter who. "Really," she said, "in the end *I* would have paid *them*."

She was the complete opposite of the girl from Minsk – Masha had no disguise, not that of a beggar or a governess and certainly not a prostitute, and she had no daring; actually that wasn't true, she did have, daring and courage, a lot of courage; after all, without that courage she wouldn't have consented to him and hence endanger her future. Though she had no disguises or a baby made of rags, she might have a real breathing baby of her own, if she hasn't already gone to one of those women who take deal with things like that. They do it with a long knitting needle, and what a terrible sight it was, a needle being inserted between the legs and probing and pricking here and there the way a stick is inserted into a snake pit, but he continued to envisage it in his mind and also knew who the father of the snake and its killer was.

Against his will, for a moment longer he thought about her - she belonged to his cursed people, and not only was he sick of that people and their religion but also of the area allotted to them like lepers whose illness was their faith – and wondered what would become of her if she didn't get help from one of those women: she would first be banished from her uncle's house and afterward from Minsk; and even if they spare the baby, perhaps she herself will return to her village or travel on from there to other places, perhaps even to Petersburg. Maybe in the end she'll come to a hotel like this and call to passersby from its window, dressed in a completely open purple dressing gown.

"D'you think I didn't see your eyes popping out?" Vera said pulling him like a jealous fiancé.

They passed a bridge and turned right and then left and went into an alley and came out into a large street, and after about a half an hour's walk from that hotel Vera lifted her head to one of the upper floors of the building on the other side of the road, and at the time he didn't yet know she was looking at the window on the right for a black umbrella hung there signaling that the area was clear of detectives. Before that she had turned serious at the sight of a real couple that passed them on the main street: an old man and woman who clasped each other like two wrinkled toddlers before crossing the road. A horse neighed in front of them, and the coachman cursed the father's fathers of his horse or those of the old man delaying him.

"Look at them," she motioned to them with her eyebrow – the old couple began to cross the road with hesitant steps – "take a good look, because with us there's little chance of getting old." On the way she had already suggested he join her and her friends, and since he agreed, she felt it necessary to put the record straight.

"Who wants to get old anyway," he answered. In the middle of the road, between its two lanes, the old people froze on the spot, terrified by the galloping of the carriage horses. They stood there hand in hand, like a brother and sister whose mother has sent them to buy something at the shops without realizing the danger she's placed them in.

"No one's going to ask you whether you want to or not," said Vera, "they'll just put the rope around your neck and kick the bench."

"The bench?" he didn't understand.

She explained to him: they stand the condemned man on a bench, and the hangman or the hangman's assistant kicks it.

Later, in the apartment used as a hiding place (apart from the umbrella in the window and the bicycle chain in the stairwell there were other signals: a fold in the doormat of the apartment and two cigarette stubs squashed beneath it), further details were added to that picture by Duchin: how every time the condemned man at the gallows was too thin, the hangman put his arms around his shoulders to add weight to him and didn't let go until his neck was broken. "The neck bones pop," said Duchin. "And someone like you, Poliakov, who doesn't weigh a lot, they'll only be too happy to hug. Maybe you should know that before you decide with such ease to join us. What have you got to say, Poliakov?"

That was how he was enlisted. Afterward they gave him underground printed manifestos to transfer hidden between the secret panels of suitcases, and for too long a time that was all that he did; and later they gave him a silk handkerchief to wave to the assassins of the minister from the window of the room they had booked for him in the hotel, and afterward he lay down in that hotel for thirty-six hours until he was caught by the police and the soldiers and the detectives and whoever else, and later he was released under puzzling circumstances, arousing suspicion; yes, in him as well; if he was in their place, he would also have been suspicious.

4

Throughout his childhood years, the old man's mother didn't tell him anything about his father, and that way he could imagine him as he pleased, enlarging and glorifying him like some kind of lofty entity which years ago, before starting to search traces of it in Russian newspapers from the beginning of the twentieth century, he had searched in the books of his childhood and particularly those of Jules Verne. Later, he grew up and learned a little from history books about the years during which his father had been a young man, and was able to anchor him at the beginning of the first Russian revolution; and at the same time, since his absence couldn't be filled by words, he sought clues of his father in his own city, Tel Aviv, at rallies and celebrations and processions where speeches were made by the heads of pre-state Israel who had immigrated from Russia. Other children rode for hours on their father's shoulders, and he his mother carried in her arms until she tired, and afterward, when he was put down, he had to make his way through the crowd until someone stopped him with the reprimand: "Where d'you think you're going, boy?"

He, the old man, was that boy.

"One-two, one-two," the feeble microphone and the capricious loudspeaker were tested on stage, and something always went wrong. Either and the sound didn't work or was it replaced with a continuous high-pitched tone (were there really already microphones then? Suddenly, he's not sure about that); and a glass of water was placed on the speaker's table or a bottle of soda whose bubbles rose and faded away and from the speaker's pocket a wrinkled handkerchief would always be extracted to wipe a sweaty forehead.

But stories were told about those speakers, dwarfing all these trifles, and the old man heard them far above him between all sorts of sounds and smells that were emitted from sweaty armpits and irritable stomachs. Sometimes opposing stories were related, gossip as well as slander, but there were some about whom there was no dispute. For instance, it was agreed by everyone that in Russia, years before the first Hebrew power station had been established, its future founder, Pinchas Rutenberg, had been a dangerous terrorist; and it was said that in the famous mass procession to the Winter Palace in the month of January in the year 1905 it was Rutenberg who with his own hands had saved Father Gapon from the shots of the police and the soldiers; and he too who executed that priest a year later for betraying his comrades. True, it was difficult to conceive of those deeds on seeing the speaker, but it was an appealing contradiction.

Perhaps the old man's father had also marched there – after all, he was living in Petersburg at the time – among the thronging crowd of demonstrators. Had he marched in that procession from the workers' quarter to the Winter Palace in the freezing cold of January? (Small clouds of vapor floated from the mouths of the demonstrators and froze in the air, and the folds of their flags were as hard as tin). Were his father's tracks also imprinted there? And were bullets also shot at him? ("There he is," his father said to Rutenberg and pointed to the priest who marched at the head, "first his beard has to be cut off so that he won't be recognized!" Bullets whistle all around and bodies drop and horses' hooves trample the reddening snow making it even more filthy.)

Not only did he connect that episode to the father who had disappeared, he tried to imbue in him all that had been missing in his life the way parents strive for their children to achieve all they themselves didn't achieve in their own lives; and each time he spoke about him with his son, it seemed he was testing not only if it sounded feasible to him, but also whether it would possibly arouse pity in him, the ninety-year-old orphan who had been abandoned before he was born, an orphan who had been deprived of even the simple information that in some place he had a father who knew of his existence – who remembered that he had a boy like that, a youth like that, a man like that, an old man like that.

Somewhere, from a city of white nights whose river freezes over in winter, and after it from a valley whose surrounding mountain peaks are covered in eternal snow, for a while it seemed his father was watching over him, and in a soft voice that crosses continents and years he'll talk to him, and perhaps even reach out a sturdy and scarred hand and caress his white head; or pinch the old man's wrinkled cheek with the same fingers that had pulled the trigger of a revolver and assembled the mechanism of a bomb. It seemed for a while that there, in that distance between the winter capital of Russia and the tiny mountainous capital of an Indian principality, real life was being lived, and what he read about in newspapers from the time (during the first hour and forty minutes, when the Emperor returned from overseeing the legion on guard, villains assassinated him by casting two exploding balls beneath His Excellency's carriage) occupied him more than a pipe bomb in Tel Aviv or a stray shell in Gaza alleys. In that way, he linked all the events of his era which could add glamor to his father, and consequently to himself as well. Like a jigsaw puzzle of many pieces with one missing piece, even if never found, when put together one could at least make out his silhouette.

"As far as I'm concerned, it could all burn," his mother said as if she had belatedly read the thought that had previously passed through his mind, "the trunk and everything in it; only why wasn't it burned there together with him?"

The old man had to struggle with her not to throw those belongings into the garbage can, despite it being a fitting place if only due to their stench; and a few decades later he had to defend the memory of them to his wife Ada, because after he was fired from the university and all his great plans had been replaced by having to proofread trifles for a newspaper, it was only in the past that the promise of a different life could be found, a life better than the one he was living, a life of pomp and glory. Not even a trace of that could be seen on the television news, not a hint of the intense and spectacular life every man could live if only he could pluck up the courage. A life happening between the red snow and the gold of exploding carriages seemed to him a life worth living, but he wasn't living it. And even if some of his father's actions went wrong, they had vision as well as cunning and daring, attributes he constantly sought in his father, because he himself didn't have vision, or cunning or daring.

And so he became accustomed to the triviality of the dreary job he found after being fired, deeming himself unworthy of anything better; and at the same time far beyond them remained the hint of mighty deeds he himself will never do, because he lacks his father's unique qualities, qualities that could rescue a man from a dreary routine whose destination is chillingly clear: the pit into which the black stretcher will be emptied, the earth that will be poured into it over the body rolled in, the convoys of ants that will arrive, the maggots.

Showing no respect, the freeloaders from the burial society will come in their black faded clothes and roll him, Nachman, into the pit, and after they lay the heavy concrete slabs on top of him the way they had placed them on top of Ada, and fill the pit with earth the way her pit had been filled, they'll leave there in their black dusty vehicle, and at the next traffic junction they'll stop at a kiosk to buy a hard-boiled egg or tuna sandwich, and between bites they'll complain about the lack of pickled cucumbers in it or about the weight of the deceased.

He has a paunch, and lately he wonders if his son isn't also growing one like it; and if the woman he's taken up with during the past years isn't the cause of it – she's no spring chicken but someone with experience who certainly knows how to feed a family; first she fed it, then she broke it up, and then she eyed his son at one of his workplaces; he was always changing the places where he worked and where he lived. Out of all the women in the world he had to choose her, someone who from the start it was clear would be problematic. There's was no knowing how out of all the possible similarities to his grandfather, he chose defiance toward the institution of the family.

And when finally he came to his senses, four years later, he decided, instead of finding himself another woman and raising a real family, to travel without bothering to tell him exactly where and for what and for how long. The old man again had been abandoned, for the third time in his life, and in his heart bore a grudge. Nevertheless, when the emptiness of his apartment became unbearable, he envied his son for the freedom he had granted himself by getting up and travelling.

5

The guestroom here has a fire, and three comfortable chairs with armrests wide enough to put a cup of tea on them, and there's a small sofa whose cushions are soft, and heavy curtains beyond which are lace curtains beyond which is a double windowpane beyond which a small garden can be seen, beyond which sprawl enormous meadows whose ends are hidden from the eye. The motor highway cannot be seen from here but should a window be opened it can be heard. In the bedroom on the second floor there are handsome convenient nightstands and cupboards and covers that are pleasant to the touch are spread on the bed like the ones she bought for the house they rented together (in complete contrast to the bedding in the apartment where he lived before that. On her first visit there, she removed the tattered covering and sniffed the sheet beneath it, searching for traces of her predecessors).

A very large wooden desk stands in the study and under different circumstances, had he conducted his life differently or had he been a different person, he could have sat at that desk and written weekly articles for a newspaper about the embarrassing affairs of the royal family or quoted exclusive leaks from 10 Downing Street, or been our-correspondent-in-the-county-of-Oxfordshire and reported on the shooting of ducks, or the priest's last sermon, or the end of the bell-ringing course or the donation toward renovating the church that recently celebrated its nine-hundredth birthday. It's an incomprehensible number to him: he comes from a country whose buildings last only a few decades until higher ones are built in their place, and before meeting her, he changed his abode every year or two without missing the one he had left. At the beginning a van was enough for his belongings, afterward a small truck was needed, and when they moved to the house he rented with her, her belongings alone required a huge lorry, and now, at the end of this process, he makes do with a backpack. Only a small section of wall remains from his people's temple, and even during the time when the temple stood firmly, an ark with handles was kept in its holy of holies ever ready to be transported on its wanderings. His grandfather had wandered: he left his county and homeland and

the house of his father and the woman he had made pregnant and went to a different country to which no god directed him and where he chose to live and to die.

"Not even a little?" she asks about his missing them.

Giving up hope from his silence, she asks him to describe the view from his
window, and when he scrimps on that too she enquires about the rooms of the
house and asks him to describe them as well; that way she can picture him there,
He doesn't respond. It was from her that he had heard about this region, long
before he knew that in one of the villages here lived a man who could be of help
him; if you could call the information that he sought to hear from him help; information perhaps better left unspoken.

Over the phone he said to her: "The house is okay."

And when in her gentle voice she asks about the view, he replies: "The view's
also okay," and before she requests details, he curtly says: "The nearest house is a
kilometer away."

"You haven't got neighbors here either," she says, and it's impossible to know
whether she meant to compliment him on his choice – after all, he couldn't bear
neighbors – or to hurt herself. For a year he had lived in his grandmother's apartment which had been vacated by its occupants until he got sick of the neighbors,
while she objected to the city and to the building and to the apartment itself and to
his staying so far away from her; at the time they didn't know the distance would
be the cause of their deciding to live together and finding themselves a house with
some land. His realty agent pointed out that the layers of stickers on the post boxes
were enough to indicate that in a building like this, where most of the tenants rent,
one can't expect good neighborly relations or good general maintenance ("A prestigious apartment it's not," he said, "and you need the money. If someone is willing
to pay a higher price for it only God and Ninette know," – the agency was called
Ninette Properties – "but I've got a buyer who'll pay up without any fuss, and he'll
turn this hole of yours into a peach of a home.").

The English house was equipped with every conceivable electric device, and
it took a while for him to succeed in coping with all those implements, none of
which he had in his apartment in Tel Aviv. That apartment didn't even have a guestroom worthy of its name and no furniture worth mentioning ("An apartment for
slackers," she said on her first visit there, and didn't need her expertise in design
to state that; the neglect was apparent everywhere. There was much lacking in the
apartment; things that month after month he put off buying. But he didn't rent a
house with her because of the things he lacked, nor did he go off travelling because
now he had them). Until her divorce proceedings were finalized, they had to sneak
a look at the street through the shades to ensure no one was following them, and
for the most part only saw the neighbor's truck with its store of glass bricks in
which the sunlight was hoarded. "When we live together," she said one of those

times, "we'll make ourselves a window with glass bricks like that, okay?" There was one similar in her home (he visited there only once) and described how the light passes through the glass bricks and how in the afternoon hours the bedroom is painted in shades of the setting sun, the bed too. She often spoke about her home: about the yard and all the plants around it, about the large kitchen window facing a weeping willow – according to her she had planned the kitchen with that beautiful tree in mind, and about the Persian cat that he already knows (he took it down from a treetop during the first week of their acquaintance, and had only seen the house briefly), Puma, who greets her when she comes home. She also told him about the kneading motions the cat made, how it moved its front legs while being stroked exactly the way it did to his mother when still a suckling kitten. "Like this," she said and demonstrated with her hands on his stomach, "one day he'll do it to you too." She already visualized the time he would come to her home and not just for an hour: swinging with her on the swing in the yard, mowing the lawn while she watered the plants, sitting in the kitchen opposite the weeping willow in the window, going into the bedroom with her and being painted with her in the light passing through the glass brick window.

She had no doubt that, at the end of the long divorce proceedings, they would all live together there, he and her and her son and the cat – there was no dog yet – and that he would give up his apartment in Tel Aviv. In the end they chose a settlement between Tel Aviv and her moshav7, and she filled the house they rented with her furniture and her plants and her little son and a cat and a dog that she brought from a birthing on a neighboring kibbutz, and in an enclosure in the yard rabbits multiplied, and he and her son, Udi, prepared slanted boards for them to climb toward the apple tree, and the sight of them between the branches was so strange that visitors couldn't believe their eyes (at the time, visitors still came calling; their quarrels hadn't yet began to erupt in their presence).

During the first months in the apartment in Tel Aviv they made love only once a week under cover of a closed shutter and music to drown out their sounds; those were their worries at the time, not to be seen, not to be heard. For a lengthy period, they were worried about possible bugging being carried out by private detectives that her recalcitrant husband had perhaps sent to spy on them, the kind of detectives one sees in the movies: the type that sit for hours in a car with a flask of coffee getting cold, and at the right moment burst in with cameras flashing, if they had not unknowingly been photographed before then. After all, cameras have become so tiny they can be floated into the intestines; that's what his father told him they did with his intestines, without even a hint of censure as to why he had not accompanied him to that examination and why he had forgotten to enquire about the results. Perhaps he had already given up on him, and not only as one who might continue his grandfather's mischief, but also as a son.

Close to a hundred years after his grandfather disappeared, and after the newspaper had stopped financing his trips, his adventurousness had narrowed to

---

7   A co-operative settlement.

a love affair with a woman separated from her husband, a mother of two boys (the eldest chose to live with his father); an affair that demanded the strictest rules like the ones for spies in enemy country - he sometimes joked with her - and the rules became part of the routine of their meetings: she never parked her car alongside his house, they never touched each other in public, never kissed in public, never embraced in public. "Our love will live only in shadow," she said, "is that what you want?" For a while it lived in light until it withered.

"Is the bath comfortable there?" she asks him through the earpiece as if she and he had no greater worry than the measurement of the bath or the workings of the taps, as if he hadn't made that declaration in the kitchen and they hadn't had a terrible row whose details are best forgotten. She still remembered the shower-head in Tel Aviv that he hadn't bothered to fix, one of the many malfunctions he hadn't dealt with in the small apartment. Despite having no place allotted to her, from month to month more and more small articles of hers could be seen there, as if in that way preparing him for the day the two of them would live together. In the bathroom that hadn't changed much since the days his grandmother bathed herself there, vials of perfume were added to the small cupboard, creams, sprays, lotions, make-up removers. A second toothbrush was added to the glass on the sill of the basin, expensive cosmetic soap replaced his everyday soap. On the phone now, she still recalls the trickle of the shower and the narrow bath of their rented house ("It's exactly the size of my hips!" she complained while they still hesitated between choosing that house and another in the vicinity. "If I sit in it, I won't be able to get up, and you do like my hips, don't you?").

Here, in the English house, the bath isn't comfortable: the gas water heater is slow, the flow feeble, the air cold. If he were to see the curves of her body before him in the bath or the motion with which she raised her pelvis to him or turn her behind to him or bend toward his loins, he wouldn't have reached the climax as he would have in his youth. Only at a late-night hour, under the coziness of a duvet, does his organ awaken like a nocturnal animal in its den. In the evening, he closes the curtains almost completely: the sight of the meadows casts a pall over him and the space left for them between the sections of the curtain allows him to adjust to them in the morning, until what has remained of the dark dissolves from the sky and the ground and a new day is born for him to continue his research; after all, he has a purpose. In his job he had been dealing with trifles worthy only of the back page of a provincial newspaper, whereas this investigation will be spread over two continents, just as in the good days that will never return and which from the outset were nothing but a delusion; there was something he needed to deal with in all his investigations, whether in London, Buenos Aires, or Kiev, and he avoided it in all of them.

A short while after sunrise the dogs bark, and this week, the third, it seems he can already recognize some of them by their sounds. In the afternoon when he walks

along the path congenial to their owners - encircling the estate and the small cemetery and turning northwards – the dogs sniff at his trousers (perhaps the scent of
his dog is still preserved in them), and their owners greet him with a friendly nod
of the head. They already know who he's come to meet here, for whom he's come
all the way from his country, a small distance compared to the one he's yet to cross.

The dog of the man who left on holiday is being walked by one of his grandsons, and the moment his leash is let go of, he begins to sprint joyously, and only
after a hundred meters or more turns back to ensure his little master is still there.
If that grandson resembles the man he's come to meet – a man whose age is the
same as his father – perhaps he's also redheaded or at least was so in his youth,
before such and such decades; but McKenzie's appearance is in fact not important,
and what he'll have to say won't make any difference by now, good or bad. At the
most, a week after speaking to him he'll travel onward from here, even if he won't
he doesn't find out anything more about his destination.

The only open space that his dogs knew when he was a child was the public
park next to their home, and from the balcony he used to watch his father walking
them there and stopping and waiting for them to relieve themselves with endless
patience. Who could compete with his father for patience? After all, he waited
years for the man who had fathered him, despite not be able to know that he had
fathered him at all, and he continued to wait for his wife, Ada, even after she left
home twice; until his last breath, he waited for her.

"And the kitchen," she asks as if he was a gourmet cook, "how's the kitchen? Have
you got everything you need?" She finds difficulty imagining him in that English
kitchen that has an oven, microwave, toaster, dishwasher. The kitchen of the house
they rented together was equipped with all those, but in the apartment in Tel Aviv
they had to make do with omelets and salad, and once in a while she would bring
baked goods from her home especially for him, as if she didn't have a flourishing
career and is solely a housewife. At the time he consented to many things, but still
not to the most fundamental of them all, the possibility of them living together in
one house.

"The kitchen's fine," he answers and doesn't tell her about the frozen dinners
he buys from the local supermarket and in that way is accustoming his palate to
foods of the land to which he'll be travelling, foods whose spices require more than
a brief adjustment. In her voice he hears the regret about him and her and their
life together that's been abandoned, after all, for a while – not a year, not two years,
almost four years – it seemed they had established a family. "I could have made us
all sorts of tasty things," she says, "don't you sometimes miss my cakes?" For one
of his birthdays, she baked him a tiramisu cake from a recipe she received from a
good friend, and within an hour they polished off more than half of it, and for her
sons she bakes chocolate cake that they can devour in an hour, and sometimes for
that cake alone her eldest son is prepared to forget his anger toward her for a while
and come and visit. "I do miss them," he replies and afterward hears her content

silence, her pensive silence, her hurt silence: how is it that only in this matter he's prepared to admit to his longing; surely she isn't the sum total of her dishes. So what if they quarreled, so what if he made his declaration in the kitchen? Many couples make declarations and reconcile and quarrel again and reconcile again, that's the way of the world.

Afterward, she asks if he at least is taking care to eat healthy food (the way she used to ask her eldest son when his father decided to console himself with some young thing) and not all sorts of prepared supermarket meals, and without any hesitation he replied: "Yes," only for the first week he didn't lie to her about that. Since then the Indian cashier smiles at him at the sight of the frozen meals he buys, meals on which a red-hot chili pepper tree designates the degree of its spiciness and every week he adds another pepper tree. In order not to bother with washing dishes, he eats his meals straight from the baking dish, and if someone were to peek in from outside, they would see that he barely uses a knife. But no one passes through the driveway of the house, not in the morning, not in the afternoon, and not in the evening, which is just fine.

How does his old father eat now that he's alone? He wonders for a moment, against his will; after all, he had abandoned him as well; his father sits in the kitchen opposite Ada's empty chair and eats straight from the tin, or in the cafeteria of the municipal library among high school students who came to do homework, and there are no meadows like these outside and no ducks and bell ringers and queens and no crown princes. Such is the paradox: in order to clarify what happened to the man who deserted his father even before his birth, if indeed he is travelling for that purpose, his father is being deserted again in his old age. In truth, there's no paradox here:, more than the chronicles of that grandfather, more than the deeds he did or didn't do in Russia, more than all his heroic acts or failures, he's curious about the course he took from there and from everyone he left behind there, and even more than the course he's curious about that remote place where he disappeared; perhaps it still has the power to make people disappear.

In his youth, before the trip he made in the van, during the short term when he had been a junior security guard and still knew nothing about the drudgery and crooked practices of intelligence organizations, he often amused himself with the thought that one day he'll be summoned by telephone or by a letter on which the sender's details aren't specified, to some office with an innocuous name, and after filling out a few questionnaires with many clauses and a long interview that someone will observe from the other side of a one-way glass pane, he'll be offered a false identity, a different name and a different profession and a different life, and there in that office all the identifying signs that link him to the place from where he came vanish, even his childhood memories will be all replaced by others. However, he was never summoned to that office, not by telephone nor by letter, and instead one day got himself involved in the unnecessary tailing of a man throughout the French terminal who for some reason seemed to him suspicious.

He also recalled the film of some Italian director in which a man, Jack Nicholson played the character, receives the identity of another man – he gets his passport and his airline ticket and arrives at a desert town on the border of the Sahara Desert to a small hotel in which a room had been booked for him, and there on a dusty single bed, beneath a slow clattering ceiling fan, he waits day after day, not knowing for what. And that waiting, even should it prove a terrible disappointment in the end, now seems incomparably better than all that's familiar and known, providing everything that he needs to clarify will be clarified in it.

When he returned from that trip in the van, he thought his parents wouldn't recognize him – his hair had grown long and his beard had grown wild – only the dog, Linda, would identify him and jump on him and lick his face, but the dog had become old and had difficulty getting up for him. He lingered for a moment in the entrance and looked at his parents; it seemed they were not at all happy he had returned. A week passed before they told him about their divorce, and afterward he rented an old house outside the city, and from a rickety armchair he would see through the window how night falls on a loquat tree and how all its leaves and branches meld together into a black silhouette that is gradually swallowed by the dark and found great serenity in its being consumed. It was no less pleasing than travelling into the night, when the road is paved only in light beams, and if for a moment they are extinguished – he had done that more than once– its entire length would disappear, as if it had never been paved. Years later they also had a tree like that in the yard of the house they rented together, as well as two mango trees and one lychee tree and a giant Ficus in whose branches he built a wooden balcony of sorts for Udi to look out from, and at times the cat would join him there, and Albi would bark at them or howl with jealousy from below. It was a sight he thought he'd never see, a boy on a platform of planks and two animals competing for his love. There were other sights he never would have conceived seeing and being part of, but nevertheless got up and left on his travels. He has a pretext, and not even a bad one, but what has that to do with the truth?

The dog of the man he's come to meet here – McKenzie Jr. – is young like their dog; at least its behavior is not that of an adult dog: on the path it runs and jumps with puppy-like joy, hurrying to bring back the branch his little red-headed master had thrown him, and sometimes it would be overcome by a playful rebelliousness and continue to hold the branch in its mouth and shake it even when his master tries to remove it from between its teeth. Had McKenzie Jr. got him into that habit? It doesn't matter, and what he'll find from this McKenzie also won't change anything, even should he show him documents and pictures. What benefit would documents and pictures be to the dead or their descendants? At the most, some marginal details would be added and wouldn't shed light on the essence. Nevertheless, he would wait here until McKenzie returns from his holiday. He is not pressed for time: he's already cut himself off from one place and no one is expecting him in another.

"Don't you get bored there?" she asks him. "After all, you aren't doing anything."

"I'm resting," he replied to her.

"It's important to rest," she says, "very important. After all, you've been working so hard. God, how hard you've been working." She's not only teasing him
about the newspaper he worked for until his travels – a negligible local paper, not
like the national newspaper he had worked on before that – but also about the
circumstances of their meeting; they had met there in the filthy corridor on the top
floor, and each time he makes her angry (there are conversations in which almost
every word that comes out of his mouth makes her angry, if only because it's being
uttered from another country) the love between them is instantly obliterated. If
her love won't be reciprocated, she'll prick and hurt him as much as she can: who
ever heard of a man of his age, in his mid-forties, taking a backpack and travelling
off like a soldier just out the army and leaving behind the small family they had
established; true, without a wedding ceremony, and the son is not his son, and the
house is rented, but that's what they were; a family.

"Doesn't your local paper need a roving reporter there?" she asks, not waiting
for an answer.

That little newspaper to which he irreparably exiled himself, never over-
stepped itself: dreary updates from council meetings, personnel replacements of
the community center board, the plodding local soccer team in one of the bottom
leagues. Often, despite having supposedly come to terms with his professional
decline, he reminded himself that in his glory years he had had more than enough
publicity, something not many journalists achieve, and if he had fallen, at least
he had from where to fall. Now, he was only envious of reporters on the monthly
travel journal because their trips are financed by the newspaper, the way his investigations had been years before. One of them travelled on the Trans-Siberian train
from Moscow to Vladivostok, and another climbed the seven highest peaks in the
world, and one investigated the medicinal plants of the Indians in rain forests, and
what was he doing at that time? He was writing about corruption in the municipal water company and the collapse of the sewerage system; he imagined seeing
it flooding the main street one night - even without a drop of alcohol in his blood
– and in it were swarms of dead silvery fish huddled together like the ones he had
seen in Lebanon, sparkling in the shit rising from the manholes.

"Not here," he answers softly, possibly to her, possibly to himself, "but maybe
they'll need one in the place I'm going to." He answered her almost voicelessly
and distanced the mouthpiece from him; he doesn't wish to hurt her further. He's
already hurt her more than enough, despite him not being a basically bad person;
that's what he'd like to think, and there are moments in which he succeeds in that.

Such is the tally: a beloved woman and a child (true, not his child, but the two
of them had already bonded); an elderly father whose years are numbered, and one
dead person. All those he'll be leaving behind him.

6

One day when his mother wasn't home he decided to break into the trunk. In his short pants whose pockets bulge with marbles he knelt down and inserted the tip of a screwdriver into the lock and struck its head with a hammer, a weak muscled but very determined boy of eleven, he struck and struck as if that way he'd break open not only the filthy trunk but also its owner's heart, but the lock wouldn't respond. Then Nachman inserted the screwdriver again and continued to strike it, and for a moment he wondered how no one heard the blows: not his mother, who had gone to Moshavot Square as on all the previous days to search for the porter who had brought the trunk, or their neighbors. And after a brief rest he quickened the strikes and with one of them the base of the lock came apart with the lock, and the screwdriver in its momentum slanted down toward his exposed thigh. The old man hadn't felt pain like that since the summer when he was beaten up by the big children in the yard, and until his crying erupted, he just looked at the blood flowing down his thigh. Sounds rose from the street: pedestrians stepping on the sidewalk, a car blowing its horn. a bicycle rider cursing and from one of the buildings on the other side of the road a woman shouted: "Moshe, Moshe, if you don't come straight away, Daddy's gonna come down." Only then did he come to his senses and he lifted the lid of the broken trunk and looked inside it, and from the heap of tatters inside he pulled out a piece of material with holes in it and pressed it to his thigh in order to stop the bleeding (that's what he had heard should be done) and continued to sit cramped on the floor of the balcony and in that way tried to stop the shooting pain.

He sat in his short pants and his improvised bandage on the balcony for a long time, and the sun began to set at the end of the street. For a moment it seemed that it would land on the slope of Allenby Street and not in the sea beyond it, until it found its way to the waves and lit up the edges of the sky. He then got up from the floor and approached the trunk again and with eager stained hands began to rummage through it, as if between the disintegrating articles or beneath them, he would find the thing that he had been deprived of all these years, or evidence of its existence – the love he had been denied even before he was born – perhaps he would find some justification or explanation; and if not, at least something that would permit loathing his father from now onward and banishing him at last from his mind and from his heart.

Years later he tried to convince himself that his father went on his way without knowing about his fatherhood, but instead of that consoling him, the thought hurt, because then his entire existence in the world seemed random and meaningless, a chance meeting of sperm and egg. He wasn't a son whose parents planned on bringing into the world and raising with love. but a case of statistics in which his existence could have been prevented by one tiny change, after all, he had studied some statistics while still an academic whose future was before him. To his good fortune the war broke out, creating an opportunity for him to forget his hurt, and despite his lack of experience and his age – he was reaching forty and in his regiment was nicknamed "the old man" - he could start to do daring deeds like his father had in his time, as if for that very purpose the world war had broken out.

Two or more weeks passed until he found someone to translate the letter that was in that trunk for him. None of the shopkeepers in their street knew English; Dr. Shtub the pharmacist probably knew, but he didn't want to ask him, and when the tall teacher coming out of the high school gate consented and took the letter from his hand and brought it close to his glasses, his whole being tensed.

"Where did you get this from, boy?" the teacher looked at him suspiciously.

"I found it in the street," he replied.

"Just like that, without the articles?" the teacher asked.

"Articles?"

"It says here something about articles," the teacher said. The old man didn't know that *(Articles of your loved one are included)*. "It says that this letter was sent with that man's articles. Weren't there any articles with the letter?"

"Articles?" the old man said again,

"Articles," the teacher replied. "Was the letter already opened, or did you open it?"

"I opened it," the old man said and immediately regretted his reply.

"In the middle of the street? You stood in the middle of the street, with everyone around and opened it?"

"There wasn't anybody!" he answered, and in truth there was no one next to him when he opened it; there were several people in the street, but not on the balcony of his home.

"There are always people in the street," the teacher said. "My young friend, the days are gone when there were just sand dunes and camels here. What time was it when there was no one around?"

The old man hesitated for a moment, but afterward lied to him without difficulty.

"In the morning?" the teacher said with surprise. "In the morning! You found this letter in the morning in the middle of the street and there weren't any people around and you opened it. It doesn't look like a letter that someone picked up in the street."

"It was inside a packet!" the old man hurried to reply. "So I took it out and then I opened it."

The tall the teacher bent down to him. "Look me in the eye, my friend," he said, "look me in the eye and tell me again that you found it in the street in a packet."

Nachman lifted his head and looked into the eyes of the teacher: they appeared large through the big lenses of his spectacles, blue and round and protruding, and didn't lower his gaze.

"Listen here my young friend," the teacher said, "I haven't yet decided whether to believe you or not. Should I believe you?" He wasn't convinced by the answer he received, or by the innocent look on the boy's face, but rather by glancing at his watch: the recess was nearing its end. The girls skipping rope or huddling in the shade of a tree, the boys playing football, the teachers smoking at the back of the yard, were all about to return to their classrooms; and the teacher, who had been on his way out, now changed his mind.

"Okay, my friend, what's written here is that that man has a..... some import- ant matters to organize before he can return home. And he's very apologetic about it" – the teacher raised his glasses slightly and brought the letter closer to him, as if to see the writing better – "yes, he apologizes greatly and sends everyone his love, and especially to his children. He sends them many kisses, but much to his sorrow, he cannot return to them in the near future."

"And can he next year?"

Again, the teacher bends toward him and it seems that his eyes are larger and protrude even more through the thick lenses of his spectacles and any minute will burst through them. "My young friend, where exactly did you say you found it? And just don't tell me again 'in the street,' because we've got a lot of streets here."

"Next to Moshavot Square," Nachman hastened to answer him, "where the cart drivers stand with their carts and horses and then the wind blew the packet and I stopped it with my foot and I felt something inside it, so I took it out and it was the letter, and the packet blew away in the wind."

With a doubtful look, the teacher examined the envelope, first its front and then it's back and turned it over again.

"There's no address here," he said, "no name and no address. And also, no stamps. Doesn't that seem a bit odd to you, my young friend? To me it does. But on the other hand, if you think about it (he said those words silently), who says you always have to know everything, sometimes it's better not to know (that too he said to himself, and his face became long). Anyway, my friend, one thing I can tell you: problems like the ones this man's got sometimes can take a long time to sort out, if you can call it that."

The old man didn't understand; his whole face stated that, and the teacher looked at him for a moment longer.

"Until the problems solve themselves," the teacher explained, and the bell rang. Some of the girls gave their skipping ropes one last turn while others swapped one last secret among themselves, and the boys gave the ball one last kick and the teachers took one last drag of their cigarettes, but only years later, after the old man went to that high school and begun to learn English there, did it become clear to him what exactly was written in the four lines of the letter. He had guessed it years before then, but on one Tuesday at the beginning of the spring, those words were joined together to form one statement, chillingly clear, and unlike many other statements, there was no fear it would be forgotten. Everything else would be forgotten – his childhood, his youth, all the years at the university and the Brigade and the *Davar* newspaper would be forgotten – but not that statement.

After all, his brain is developing more and more holes in it from year to year, and not only are more sights and sounds in which an entire life is stored slipping from his memory with every step he takes, but even while asleep in bed – even then the sieve of his memory continues to unload its burden, and things that he remembered in the evening, he finds difficult to recall the next morning. Often, especially when on the brink of sleep or when awakening, it seemed that a slope was forming in his cognitive mind; the abyss of oblivion toward which man advances is firstly inside his own head, before the head and its owner are cast together into the other abyss. And even now there are moments when he feels some gate hadn't noticed before is opening near to him, and he's being prodded in the back, and the direction is completely clear.

Only his father – Ilya-Eliyahu Poliakov – apparently continued to maintain his eternal youth in all the remote places he reached: sharp-witted, brave as Rutenberg and enterprising as Zhelyabov, many of whose histories Nachman has already completely forgotten (his visits to doctors who examined his memory were futile, they read him lists of words with a measured beat and asked him to repeat them from the end to the beginning, and by the third word he had already become confused; all the methods he read about of great men who had astounding memories were futile: Darius the Babylonian – or was it Cyrus? – knew all the soldiers of his army by name, and Seneca could repeat hundreds of lines of poetry from the end to the beginning, while he, Nachman, now finds difficulty remembering whether it was Seneca the elder or his son), but what the high school teacher hid from him he hadn't forgotten nor will he ever forget:

Enclosed are the articles of your dear one, whose death we sadly were obliged to declare

Signed: Dr. Edward McKenzie
Moravian Mission Hospital in Leh, Ladakh, India

7

Petersburg, 1904

The interrogators had a clear aim when they cast suspicion on him.

"Look," they said to him, "we're thinking of releasing you, the weather outside is so lovely, maybe even tomorrow we'll release you. But you know what your comrades will think Poliakov; that if we released you so easily you must have given us something in return." And right away, in that office that resided not in a damp dungeon but on the airy second floor and didn't resemble an interrogation room at all, they once again mentioned the previous assassination attempt which hadn't been carried out. They went into minute details that somehow had become known to them, and which he heard for the first time from them:

1. Poliakov – with two bombs, on the landing of the Fontanka River.

2. Borishansky – with two bombs, in the fishermen's alley.

3. Maximov – with one bomb in the cart, opposite the side wing of the police station.

4. Matsivsky – on the other side of the road, in order to give everyone a signal with the hat ("With a hat, Poliakov," they said to him, "there wasn't a handkerchief in that plan").

5. Kalyaev – with two bombs on the Tsepnoy Bridge, on a lookout over the Panteleimonovskaya and maintaining eye contact with number one and number three.

"You all signaled from the sidewalk," they said, "Matsivsky with his hat. There wasn't any hotel in that plan, no handkerchief. So why should we believe you that all of a sudden everything gets changed in the second plan?"

"Just put yourself in our place, Poliakov," they said, "for one and a half days you shut yourself up in a miserable hotel, lying in the small room on a filthy mattress opposite a broken window, and all that only so we wouldn't catch you with a handkerchief?" He should put himself in their place for a moment, they said, because they could easily put themselves in his, and even understand him, absolutely. A young man who from a remote village comes to the capital, and all at once the wide world opens up before him; who wouldn't be enchanted by this place; it's an enchanting city.

Beneath a strip of faded light blue sky in the window overlooking the inner courtyard of the secret police headquarters, a dozen or so windows of the opposite wing could be seen, and behind those windows perhaps many like him sat in front of pairs of interrogators; in offices and not in dungeons, and there were no instruments of torture other than words.

When he was brought inside (a policeman in uniform brought him in and took advantage on the way to punch him as he walked, and every once in a while gave him a sudden push that almost made him fall; sometimes with an added curse, and sometimes in complete silence when only the sound of their steps could be heard) the two who were waiting for them were deep in conversation, and the elder, to whose chin a little silver grey beard added bulk, said to his colleague with calm decisiveness: "This will end badly."

From his large table he didn't turn his gaze to them as they entered, and the young interrogator, who was leaning his shoulder against the wall next to the window, said: "But why should it end badly, why d'you always make everything so black?"

"When you reach my age, Kostia," said the elder, "perhaps you'll understand a few things you don't quite understand now."

To that, the young man answered right away: "I'm pretty sure when you were my age and someone said something like that to you, you also didn't want to listen to them." That reply brought a slight smile to the elder's face. But when the young man continued and said: "From your smile I can see I was right, so now it's my turn not to listen." The older man's face turned serious as if it had been hinted that in some other matters too, he was past his prime.

The policeman still stood firmly at attention. Both hands were pressed to his sides, almost innocent looking had it not been for the knuckles that had reddened after punching Poliakov on the way from his cell. He wasn't a strong man, but his blows were well directed and timed for when they were swallowed by the shadows of the vestibule pillars ("Why don't you try to escape?" he suggested to him then. "Just try and see what I'll do to you").

The policeman looked sideways at the books in the bookcase: perhaps trying to read their names, and perhaps he was just impressed by the leather binding and the gold lettering. When the bearded man spoke again and said to the young man: "Nevertheless, Kostia, there's no law that says everyone has to repeat the same mistakes," apparently the policeman had caught an itch, because he was vigorously rubbing his right ankle with his left through his boots without moving from his place.

"That's probably something you were also told then." the young man said and continued observing the inner courtyard from the window.

The elder man seemed pensive, but perhaps that too was part of their act, because in a short while, after having released the policeman by raising an eyebrow, he turned from him and from his colleague to Poliakov and said to him, as if sharing his thoughts with him: "There are those who insist on making mistakes even when they know it's a mistake, and there are those learn from the mistakes of others. Now you decide how you intend to conduct your life Poliakov."

His colleague approached the door and locked it after the policeman left and took the key out of the keyhole.

"He won't escape," said the elder man.

"For safety's sake," said the young man. "There are some things I've learnt from other people's mistakes."

"He won't escape," said the elder man again. "There's no danger of that. And do you know why? Because he's not someone who's capable of escaping; right, Poliakov? You aren't capable of anything, except lying in bed for a day and a half."

"And waving a handkerchief," said the young man.

They then instructed him to sit in one of the armchairs in the sitting room area. The elder man – Perdischenko was his name, Oleg Timopievich Perdischenko – sat in another armchair, and the young man relaxed on the small sofa and stretched his legs out in front of him. A rug covered the floor, and its pattern and colors had become indistinct.

He was no longer called Gumilyov according to the documents found on his clothing (in which he was given a different place of birth, a city not a village; though in the same province of his birth, so that he could describe it if need be. Different family members, who all lived there, were given to him as was a profession, a travelling salesman for Shereshevsky's cigarette factory which he was familiar with having worked there for a month). With those documents on him he might have lasted a long time, had he not done what he did; that is to say what he didn't do: after all, he had remained in the hotel until his room was broken into.

At first the detectives suspected someone else staying at the hotel on the floor below him, lacking documents and sturdier than him, who by chance had been seen in the window at exactly the moment of the assassination waving his hand at an acquaintance he saw on the street. After they beat up him up for an entire day, he was prepared to admit to everything, not only to his connection with the bomb throwers but also with their ancestors' ancestors, he also admitted to his part in assassinations that had taken place before he was born including that of Tsar Alexander and the three governors. Later the detectives returned to the hotel hoping not to find anything there, at the most some clue belonging to someone already far away, but when they broke into Poliakov's room, they discovered him on the bed surrounded by fragments of glass, lying in his clothes and his shoes and his sweat and gazing at the ceiling: to help him sleep, he counted the flowers on the wallpaper; for a day and a half he counted them from right to left and left to right, from top to bottom and bottom to top, and for the few moments when he succeeded to sleep they appeared in his nightmare-filled slumber with the twisting of their roots and earth tightening around him.

"I hope you're comfortable here with us," said the elder interrogator, and the younger, who still took the trouble to appear courteous, apologized for the state of the upholstery whose time had come for a replacement.

"Yes," the elder agreed sadly with his colleague. "Maybe with the next renovations our turn will finally come."

"You also said that the last time," the young man reminded him, "and with those exact words. Do you still believe all those promises?"

"Of course I do!" the elder let his gaze linger a moment longer on his colleague's face, unsure if he meant only to spin out their game with their suspect or if some barb had been aimed at him. He had given Telegin that exact same look on the previous day of interrogation each time a statement like that was made, but right away would return the conversation to its course. In that roundabout manner they had already succeeded to extract one incriminating fact from Poliakov that he wasn't supposed to reveal, despite that at the time he was captured, the handkerchief was still in the palm of his hand.

"Yes," he had admitted to them the previous day, instead of keeping silent as demanded (Duchin had demanded): yes, he was the one who signaled from his window to the bomb throwers that the carriage was approaching. He could have said nothing, as he had been instructed ("Don't even let a sound out!"), but in his stupidity or his fatigue or both – no, not stupidity or fatigue, but from fear – he opened his mouth and spoke; he had been afraid to the point of trembling.

In the sitting room area, the likes of which are not found in any interrogation cellar, they said to him that if he doesn't talk and confess, he'll be accused of something much worse; not for waving a handkerchief, to hell with the handkerchief, but for throwing one of the bombs; from the very same window. And right away they found some witness who apparently saw him do it, not from the street but from the next room: there's no shortage of peepholes in the thin walls of that hotel and someone had just peeped through it; he thought he'd see a prostitute with a client or some adulterous couple, and instead he saw Poliakov. They then made up a new detail in the interrogation report – it was the young man who made it up, and with astonishing quickness – according to which there was a clear mark on the roof of the carriage created by the blow of a heavy object that had been thrown from above: at least from the second floor, and more probably from the third, his floor, despite the roof having flown off from the bomb.

"You understand, Poliakov," Telegin said to him, we actually found the roof of the carriage intact. It was far from the crater, but completely intact. You can see exactly where the first bomb fell on it and from what angle but it didn't explode the way you thought it would. They went into detail about the plan to throw a bomb from the hotel window, and it seemed that any moment they'd be praising the idea – it sounded so practical and effective coming from them.

They then repeated and all the details they expected him to reveal to them: his instructions, after all, he must have received them from somewhere: from where exactly, in an apartment? Where was that apartment, in what district, in what street, on what floor, in whose name was it rented, what did they see from the window; and if he hadn't been instructed inside an apartment but rather in the street, which street was it, what was its name? And if not in the street but rather in a public park, which one, what was its name? There's no such thing as I don't remember, he must remember something: what kind of trees grew there? What were their names, and what did they look like? And was there a fountain there? Did it have statues? What were they of?

The hotel room had to be booked in advance so that it wouldn't be occupied on the designated day: who booked it, who paid, and where was the money from? And how did he reach the hotel – by foot or by carriage? And if by carriage, did a real cart driver transport him or one of their fake ones? They already known about their smart cart drivers who carry out surveillance while driving ("Maybe you practiced with one of them before," said the young interrogator, "as if it was the minister's carriage? Didn't you throw all sorts of things onto it from above?" The substitute bombs, he thought, could have been a pumpkin or a watermelon and he reminded his colleague of a report made by one of their predecessors who waxed lyrical in his description of two bullet injuries found on a corpse. One, he wrote, was the size of a cherry pit while the other it was the size of a plum, to which Perdischenko replied: "Not all reports, have to be as dry as yours Konstantin Niko-laevich."

They've also got waiters and shoeshine boys and newspaper sellers and flower sellers and peddlers and beggars with babies made of rags and whatnot, they know everything. Little birds whispered in their ears. In the end, they all open their mouths and talk: in a tavern over a glass of vodka without knowing they are being listened to or here in this room.

Yes, they sat on this very armchair and squealed.

It was a very spacious room, furnished grandly two decades ago, when enough money from the department's budget was still being allocated for that purpose and not transferred for special expenses as in recent times. In the sitting room area, opposite the two armchairs, stood a small sofa – it could be seen even between eyelids swollen from fist blows and lack of sleep. The upholstery must have been thick and dark in its early days, and the wallpaper of a different shade during the years when Poliakov wasn't at all aware that an office like this and a department like this existed and when the capital was still no more than an unsubstantiated rumor and revolutionaries just vague images on the pages of a newspaper.

The left wall and half the wall around the door were covered in high book-cases, and behind the polished glass panels of their doors stood all the volumes of the encyclopedia and the finest Russian literature as well as new and daring works one wouldn't expect to see there but were displayed there unhidden from the eye.

"You probably all read that garbage," they said to him as if he was a great reader of books. "You and those comrades of yours." They could understand a village boy coming to the big city and suddenly finding people to talk to, all sorts of students and workers with all sorts of exciting ideas and believing that just as he would be prepared to do anything for them, they too would do anything for him. That sentiment had a certain magic to it, shall we call it a common destiny? Camaraderie?

"Gangs of pickpockets also feel that way," said Telegin and crossed his legs and inspected the upper of his right shoe, a polished shoe made of choice leather.

"We can understand how they trusted you. Who wouldn't have put their trust in you after what you'd been through: a man goes to his village on a visit and gets caught up in an event like that. Who wouldn't have feelings of revenge? Such a man would be prepared to do anything; not to drink, not to eat, not to think about what he's getting involved in. Maybe you didn't even know the danger your comrades were putting you in. How many of them were there in the apartment, five, six, eight?

Inside the office that was also used as an interrogation room, they began quoting all sorts of details from the second assassination plot as well, the one that had been carried out and in which he was a participant, He knew nothing of those details and didn't know whether they were true or had been fabricated on the spot to further confuse him. They spoke of another bomb thrower, and about the two men disguised as cart drivers; after all, without them the bombs would not have reached their destination. But more than that pair, the interrogators were interested in the two at the top. First of all, the commander of the operation, the planner and leader, and then were man who prepared the bombs without whom the assassination wouldn't have been carried out. "Who was it, Poliakov?" they asked. "Where did they get the materials from and where did they assemble them? There are limits to our patience, Poliakov."

Seated comfortably, they told him exactly what was planned to be done with the surplus bombs, the ones that wouldn't be put to use and were too dangerous to keep. He then learnt (before that he knew nothing about it, so strong was the compartmentalization) that two contingency plans had been prepared for the surplus bombs: one in the case of failure and the other in the case of success.

In great detail they described what his comrades had planned in order to prevent unnecessary danger, especially after the work accident that had occurred to one of them in another hotel in another district; in a respectable hotel - work accidents can happen to anyone and not only in hotels. "How can one forget what happened there, in the Bristol Hotel?" they said to him, as if he also had some connection to that hotel and the bombing that demolished more than half a floor. They began telling him in great detail about the plan to sink them (he himself had experienced being sunk but had never heard about the sinking that they spoke of), a plan whose purpose was to conceal the surplus bombs.

"Yes, to sink them in water," they said to him, "where else could they be sunk other than in water?" They then added further details: one bomb was planned to be thrown into the lake of the village Volynkin, the second into the lake of the Peterhof monastery, and the third into the estuary of the Neva. "Not a bad plan," said the elder interrogator, "simple and very effective, if only that Sikorsky of yours hadn't become confused from fear. You wouldn't believe what people sometimes do out of fear."

"He'll soon believe it," said the young interrogator.

It transpired that instead of going to the park and renting a boat and throwing the bomb into the estuary of the Neva, Sikorsky (or whoever it was; he had never heard that name until they said it) wanted to get rid of it on the way. "He asked one of the boat owners to take him instead of sailing there alone," said Perdischenko, "and after a short while had he threw the bag into the water just a meter away from the boat owner, he also offered him a bribe not to tell us about it."

"He gave him a bribe to be exact," said Telegin, "not offered – gave. Ten rubles. Not that it helped anything."

In the same tranquil tone, Perdischenko added more details. The boat owner didn't exactly see what had been thrown, because at that moment he was looking at the bank, but clearly heard a heavy object falling into the water and understood that it was the bag. He asked Sikorsky if his wallet was in the bag that had fallen into water and if he had the money to pay, because some people who had sailed with him remembered too late that they didn't have any money.

"I'll have the money," Sikorsky answered him, and the boat owner wondered what had been in the bag that was thrown: books? Maybe he finished his exams and wanted to get rid of them, what a waste. Maybe there were love letters in there? Things like love letters, said the boat owner, it's better to burn, he's talking from experience; it's the only way you can get rid of them completely, so that they won't hurt anymore. "Letters?" Sikorsky said to him and grinned. "There was a letter to the minister."

The following day the boat owner heard about the assassination and right away put two and two together and went to the police; he remembered exactly where he had let the passenger off, what he looked like and what he was wearing, and that same evening Sikorsky was caught and didn't try to resist at all, the big hero. He was brought here to secret police headquarters, and very little work was required of them. He was one their easiest clients.

"Your Maximov didn't utter a word," said the elder interrogator. But this one? He simply didn't stop talking."

He had been like a mute three floors below him, a mute while being mistreated and bleeding on the sidewalk; no damning detail passed his lips, all it would have taken were for his captors to raise their heads to the window. Poliakov already realized he would carry Maximov's steadfast stubborn silence in his heart as if it had been carved in stone.

"We heard quite a bit from him," said the young interrogator. "Not only about the pogrom he had witnessed, after all he's a Jew, like you, but also quite a few names. Lots of names. Your name too."

"You've already seen something of our methods," said the elder and hinted about what could have been seen from the hotel window after the assassination: how the three detectives caught the injured Maximov and all they did to him afterward, they showed no mercy; and how there was a moment when Maximov could still have been helped by a doctor, the one who came to examine the minister although it was already clear he had been killed in the blast, and instead of treating Maximov they did the opposite, They too have methods like that for people who refuse to talk.

"The bombs," the young interrogator said to him, "who prepared them and where? And where were the materials from and who assembled them and how exactly were they transferred? And where did you receive your instructions, whatever they were?"

They added a veiled threat: work accidents can happen anywhere, even in this room.

8

Tel Aviv, 1994

Hordes of young people were walking in the street or sitting in cafés, and when he looked up at the apartment of his childhood from the sidewalk, only the balcony walls that had been painted pink could be seen, and on the washing line small colored panties swayed. A fancy café had been opened on the ground floor in place of Mr. and Mrs. Shtub's pharmacy, and one evening when the old man peeked inside, it seemed to him that all those seated there turned their heads toward him over cups of coffee and cappuccino and saw him as an intruder (it was only in the newspaper archive that no one paid any attention to him, as if he himself has faded and yellowed too), and for a moment he wanted to say to everyone from the entrance: "I was here before all of you! I used to bring Mother her tablets from here!" His mother had pills of all sorts of colors and sizes, every medicine and the ailment it was assigned to alleviate, some that the doctor diagnosed and others that he found no trace of despite her vehement protestations. Migraines in particular bothered her: when they struck she would lie down in her bedroom and ask the old man not to make any noise, and he always complied. He would go out to that balcony and view the street: not far from there stood the *Davar* newspaper building and beyond its walls were giant printing presses and typewriters whose thousands of key levers rise and fall, and he didn't yet know then the day would come when his mother would push a tea cart in the corridors there, and years later, exactly a month after the university notified him he no longer was of use to the faculty, he himself would work there, and for years would be stuck in a minor position to which no one ascribed any importance. From the height of the balcony, whose railing he barely reached, he longed to do daring deeds like his father.

A pristine silence always prevailed in Shtub's pharmacy and when the pharmacist addressed him from above the counter, it was always politely as if he were a grown man of short stature: "What can I do for you?" and he would reach out his small hand and give him a note in his mother's handwriting or some prescription one of the doctors had written and wait a long and delightful while until the medicines were brought. Sometimes one of the neighbors also waited there for her medicines, sometimes a passerby from the street would come in, sometimes there were adolescent boys hanging about in corners and waiting for all the others to leave. He didn't know how old they were, but they were no longer boys, and they looked at him as they would at a baby or a midget.

When he would return to the apartment, his mother would ask him from the end of the passage, from her room, from her sunken bed: "Did they have it?" and most times he would answer: "Yes." She would then ask him to bring her a cup of tea with the medicine and he would go to the small kitchen (he could still remember the gurgling of the tap there and the murkiness of the drizzle released from it, the folded newspaper inserted beneath the short leg of the table, the zigzag of the crack in the marble work counter; only one thing he didn't remember, whether it was their first or second kitchen: what he had seen in the second apartment is best forgotten). "Put some lemon in it for me," his mother would remember to ask when the slice was already floating on the tea – from year to year he cut them thinner and more transparent – and he would bring her the tea and place it on the chair next to her bed and take care not to look at any small portion of her nakedness that sprouted from under the pique blanket.

One day in the afternoon, as he left the pharmacy with the medicines that he received for his mother in his hand, one of the boys walked out after him. "You taking that for your mother?" he asked. "Yes," answered the old man (at the time he was wearing short pants whose pockets bulged with apricot pits, and around his neck the apartment key hung threaded on a piece of underwear elastic).

"What's wrong with her," asked the boy.

"Migrown," answered the old man.

"Migrown?" said the boy, and on his left and right his friends snickered.

"So that's what the pills are for?" asked the boy. "For her migrown?"

"Yes," answered the old man, and all the apricot pits suddenly became heavy in his pocket.

"You're a good son," said the boy. "How many pills have you got there?"

"I dunno," answered the old man, and with his little fingers felt the pills in the small paper packet.

"So read what's written there," said the boy. "Don't you know how to read?" and pulled the packet from his hand and read: twenty-one pills, three twice a day.

"That's what she takes?" he asked after he opened the packet and took out a large white pill. "I swear it's like swallowing an apricot pit. Have you ever swallowed an apricot pit?"

"No," answered the old man; he once swallowed a piece of candy, though not on purpose; one moment it was in his mouth, and suddenly it somehow slipped down his throat and got lost inside him.

"If you do an apricot tree will grow inside your stomach!" said the boy. "A tree with lots of apricots and with roots in your legs."

"It's not true!" said the old man. For a moment he thought that maybe they were just trying to make him laugh because where would the branches and fruit come out of, his mouth?

"So, swallow one now," said the boy. "Whad'ya prefer, a pit or this?"

The old man made a motion of refusal with his head and lifted his eyes to his mother's bedroom window: the shutters were half closed, and between the slats an opaque dimness could be seen, and beneath it lay his mother on her bed, her ears plugged with cotton wool.

"So, whad'ya prefer?" asked the boy again. "We haven't got any more time to waste on you." He put his hand into the old man's left pocket and seized a fistful of pits from it and dropped them on the ground except for one that he left in the palm of his hand, and in the other he held one of the pills.

The old man shook his head in refusal, and the boy made a fist over what he held in his palm and then mixed them in the air so that the old man would point to one of them without knowing exactly what he was pointing at. "Choose," he said.

"In the end he'll go and call his father!" another boy said, a sheepish youth whose upper lip was darkened with down.

"How can he call him?" said the first one. "He hasn't got a father, right?"

The old man hesitated, and from inside his sandal his big toe felt the ground of the courtyard that in summer became dry and hard. "He's a board," he said after a while, and glanced at the bedroom: the shutters were still half closed, and the spaces between its slats appeared as opaque as charcoal.

"That's what your mother told you? That your father's a board?"

"He is a board!" the old man insisted. "He's in America!" America was entirely his own invention; his mother spoke only of overseas and wasn't prepared to say another word about it: not where his father was nor what he was doing there.

"In America?" said another boy, freckled and red-faced. "How nice for you, he'll bring you lots and lots of presents from there."

"Yes," replied the old man, but wasn't sure that was how it would be. The pits in his pockets became heavier despite that half of them had been looted.

"So, ask him for a toy train," said the freckled one, "that's the best present there is. One with an engine and passenger coaches. Ten coaches. They've got them in every store in America."

"And also a bridge," said another boy, curly-haired, "the rails come with a bridge. Without that, they're just ordinary rails."

"Orright," said the old man, and again his big toe felt the ground of the yard from inside his sandal.

"D'you want us to write him a letter for you? We can ask him for the train."

"But he hasn't really got a father!" said the first one. "Don't you get it? His father isn't in America, he's never even seen him!"

The others reflected on what they heard, weighing the new information, and the curly-haired one pointed his sandal at one of the apricot pits and kicked and missed it.

"Are you an orphan?" asked the freckled boy. He asked his question with a matter-of-fact curiosity; in the same voice he would ask how many uncles or cousins the old man had; or which football team he supported: Maccabi or HaPoel.

"My father's a board!" the old man said again to them and to himself; and the bedroom shutters above were half closed as before, and the poplar leaves hid their silvery colors. "Orphan" was a word from books, like "stepmother" or "princes and princesses" or "happily ever after."

"A board?" the boys laughed again.

"Show us one letter he sent to you!" said the first boy. "Maybe then we'll believe you. Or a postcard. A postcard's also okay. As long as it's got a stamp."

"Have you got stamps?" asked the second one.

The old man hesitated.

"You haven't got any stamps!" the boy declared. "Right? You haven't even got one! And d'you know where your father really is? Should we tell you?"

Just then Mrs. Shtub came out of the back entrance of the pharmacy and shook the dustpan in her hand, and a little dust was shed from it.

"What are you doing here, children?" she asked.

"Playing with apricot pits," answered the curly-haired one.

"This is a pharmacy not a playground," said Mrs. Shtub. "And you" – she turned to the old man – "Your mother's waiting for her medicine, aren't you ashamed of yourself?" What did you give it to this hoodlum for? Take it" – with a brisk motion she plucked the packet from the first boy's hand and returned it to the old man - "hurry home upstairs. And give it to your mother, she should only be healthy."

"Yes," said the old man. He began to cross the yard, and on his right and his left he saw the pits that had been looted from him strewn like precious stones that if not gathered immediately will be lost forever. As he began to go up the stairwell, cooking smells from the top floor descended toward him, and right away saliva filled his mouth to the teeth. There was no one in the stairwell, and he bent over the railing and spat toward the floor below and a transparent thread extended from his bottom lip like a spider web. For a moment it seemed to him that he heard voices from the direction of the pharmacy, and immediately the fear rose in him that Mrs. Shtub would come from there and call him a "hoodlum" too, but no one entered the stairwell and only his steps could be heard in it.

"My father's in America!" he said to the dim space. "In America! America! America!"

From one of the upper floors, perhaps from where the cooking smells spread, a door slammed, and the silence returned, but it was tenuous.

"And he'll bring me a train with ten coaches!"

On his right, from his sandals to his head, he was accompanied by the greenish murkiness of the wall that was delineated by a thin black line. At times the old man would stand against the wall on the landing in order to check his height;

that line was a lot firmer and more exact than the dotted lines his mother's pencil marked in the entrance to the kitchen.

He hadn't grown. It seemed he'd even become shorter.

"My father is in America!" he said to himself again.

In the apartment, when he opened the front door, he right away heard his mother calling out to him: "Did they have it?" And right away he answered: "Yes."

"Then make me a cup of tea to have with it," she asked, and he went to the kitchen and prepared a cup of tea for her and was proud that he could do something that was usually done only by adults or children much older than him. He liked to see, the how the fire comes out from the small holes like a genie imprisoned in a bottle, and how all the colors coalesce into one flame; and he liked to hear how the water rages in the kettle and how it grumbles and bubbles, and each time was amazed at the speed with which it calmed the moment the fire beneath it was extinguished.

But this time he didn't enjoying making the tea at all, and when the water bubbled, he defiantly said to the kettle and to the entire kitchen: "My father went away and he'll bring me..." Before he completed the sentence, his hand reached out to extinguish the fire, and the steam that continued to rise up wasn't emitted from the locomotive chimney of a multi-coach train but rather from the sprout of a kettle.

"Can you manage?" his mother asked him from the end of the passage.

He carefully carried the cup of tea to her in a glass saucer in which he also placed the small packet of pills. In the entrance of the bedroom, he stopped for a moment until his eyes adjusted to the dimness and his nostrils to its smells, the smell of sweat and of unbrushed teeth and another that he couldn't identify; and across form him, between the slats of the shutters, strips of sky and the foliage of poplars could be seen.

"Is father a board?" he asked, and still didn't put the glass down on the chair. From the armrest the brassiere let its cups hang one after the other toward the wooden seat, toward the prints that the previous cups of tea had left (it wasn't the apartment on Shenkin Street, but the one before it he wished to forget; there he had seen the man open her brassiere and remove it).

His mother gazed at some point floating in the space of the room beneath the ceiling and the pieces of whitewash. Her eyes were swollen: perhaps from sleep, perhaps from an infection, perhaps from something else.

"Where's my father?" he said, and his hand shook and the cup wobbled in the saucer and the surface of the tea slanted toward the glass edge with the slice of lemon that floated on it.

"Why are you asking all of a sudden now?" his mother moved beneath the pique blanket with the smell of her sweat and with the smell of her teeth and with the other smell.

"Tell me!" he insisted. "Tell me!

"He's abroad," she acceded to him.

"And will he bring me presents?" He hadn't yet put down the cup on the chair or her pills, he held on to them a moment longer in his small hand as some sort of collateral.

"Yes," she said but didn't look into his eyes, "he'll bring you presents."

"A train!" the old man insisted. "Will he bring me a train?"

"A train?" said his mother and turned on her side and faced the wall, and above the edge of the thin blanket he saw her naked shoulder with the scar from a smallpox inoculation.

"He liked trains," she said to the wall. "I don't know about other things, but trains he liked." Another sound was heard suddenly from between her face and the wall, a sharp fragmented sound, and he didn't know whether it was crying or laughter.

"Yes, he liked trains a lot, he was willing to travel for weeks on them just so that he wouldn't... just so that wouldn't..." And again, that sound was heard,

"FromMinsktoPinskasailor," said his mother to the wall, "soughttoseeksix-sheep."

"What?" said the old man.

"It's a kind of sentence," said his mother. "FromMinsktoPinsk. It's like you say PeterPiperpickedapeckofpickledpeppers."

That's how she distracted his thoughts for a while, she was very skilled at that, provided she found enough strength while lying in bed (in a different way she had distracted his thoughts from that other man, their landlord, and from what he did to her; "Do you want us to carry on living here?" she said to him at the time. "Well, that's the price."). But a year later, during the following summer, he saw those same boys in the pharmacy: some had dark down on their upper lips while others boasted shaving scratches or a greasy forelock, and they no longer bothered whispering in the corner but spoke in deep voices next to the counter as well, and they didn't wait for the pharmacy to empty before asking for the thing that they had come for.

The old man had also grown that year: he already knew not to say "migrown" but rather "migraine" and knew that his father wasn't in America but in Russia, and that you could travel there for weeks by train, and the apricot pits that had been in his pockets were replaced by small and large marbles in whose transparency shards were imprisoned as colorful as the feathers of tiny parrots captured in amber.

He was sent to buy his mother cough syrup, not because she was coughing but because she found an old prescription under her bed that hadn't been used. And a moment after he left the pharmacy – "tell her to be well," said Mr. and Mrs. Shtub – the boys had already encircled him from all sides, as if to continue what they had begun the previous summer.

"For your mother?" asked the first, who boasted a new prominent Adam's apple.

"Yes," answered the old man.

"What's that, syrup?"

"Yes."

"Has your mother got a cough?"

The old man hesitated for a moment because couldn't recall hearing her cough lately.

"Yes," he replied.

"How many times a day d'you have to take that?" asked the boy. And even before the old man managed to look at the label, the bottle was pulled from his hand and afterward he himself was pulled by the arm and dragged to the court-yard; and there they immediately surrounded him on all sides, and the small bottle was passed from hand to hand and each one in turn sniffed it and made a face.

"Does your mother swallow this?" asked the first one and right away spat out a thick glob and his large Adam's apple moved.

"If she swallows that, she can swallow anything," said the curly-haired boy and the others snickered. "Sure, there's nothing you mother won't swallow." Their giggling was replaced by laughing, and the freckled boy held his stomach from laughter.

"What did they tell her she's got?" asked the first. "What did the doctor say?" This time he spat in order to get rid of the taste of the syrup.

"I don't know," answered the old man. His eyes were lowered to the ground of the yard. A lone apricot pit could be seen next to the path to the garbage cans, perhaps one of those that were looted from him last summer, and at the sight of it, it seemed that all the marbles in his pockets had swelled up and had become heavy as rocks.

"Weren't you there when he examined her?"

"No," answered the old man; he looked at the pit again, and it seemed that any moment the marbles will tear his pockets.

"D'you know what the doctor did with his stethespoke? What he examined with it? He listened to her lungs, that's what he did. And d'you know where the lungs are? Right here, where her tits are!"

His friends snickered, and one of them, with a long clearing of his throat, gathered a small dense lump of phlegm and tried to hit the spot of his previous spitting. Tiny bubbles burst there, until that spit too was absorbed in the ground of the yard.

"And before that? Before that he told her to get undressed 'cos with clothes on you can't hear anything. You can hear a pregnant woman's baby like that. You can know if it sounds like a boy or a girl. Maybe your mother's pregnant?" The boy looked at the window.

For a while they were all silent, perhaps in the silence of the afternoon they were trying to picture that sight, a few meters away from her bedroom window. The wall of the building gleamed, and the shadow of the poplar tree that stretched out at its foot became progressively smaller, as if it too would soon be absorbed by the ground of the yard.

"He put his stethespoke like this -" said the boy, and with an agile movement he suddenly placed the base of the small bottle close to the old man's chest under his shirt which he lifted up with one pull, and the touch of the glass was cold and sticky. "Like this," said the boy again, "and then he says to her, say ah. Come on, say it," he spurred him on and added to the pressure. "Say it, you idiot, what are you waiting for!"

The old man raised his voice under the pressure of the small bottle, but the bedroom shutters didn't open and no movement could be seen there. Because she was in the habit of sleeping with her ears plugged with cotton wool, it seemed that in order for his voice to reach her his little legs would have to cross a vast cotton field whose whiteness spread from horizon to horizon, but it wasn't cotton that in a moment his back was against, but the hard ground of the yard upon on which he had been thrown, and from his forehead to his ankles he was pricked by small stones. And way far above him, tall as giants, the boys stood and snickered.

"It's done lying down," said the first, as if explaining that act and the others that are yet to be done.

There were some things the old man would rather not remember. It wasn't the passing years that helped them to be forgotten but his own objection to retain their memory. That forgetfulness, unlike all the others, he blessed. Perhaps they forced him to drink the cough syrup against his will – one held his mouth open, forcing the jaws asunder to the point of being torn apart, and one poured; and another one sat on his stomach and another on his thighs, and one imitated the sound of the syrup, glug-glug,– and perhaps they turned the old man on his stomach, and in order to listen to its hidden contents and to discover what he had eaten for lunch they rolled down his trousers and placed the small bottle on his bottom. That remembrance was unbearable; it was inconceivable that some boy would bend toward his bottom and listen to it, but nonetheless it arose; perhaps to conceal a different remembrance, even more unbearable.

He blessed that forgetfulness but the sights that followed he nevertheless remembered well:

How they all stand over him, and a snicker lengthens as it passes from one to the next, and with one voice they say to him from high above, beneath the gleaming sun: "Bastard, bastard, bastard son of a bitch."

How his fingers feel the hard ground, until he takes a fistful of dust and tries to fling it at the boys, but even before the grains reach halfway the wind grabs them and they're flung back at him.

The boys burst themselves from laughter and the freckled one doubled up, held his stomach and said, "Any minute I'm going to shit in my pants."

"Do it on him," the curly-haired boy suggested

They then came closer to him. "Call your father," they said, "he'll come help you?" And they touched him with the tips of their sandals the way one touches the body of a small animal found run over on the road, completely flattened.

"Bastard, bastard," they said to him, son of a thousand whores."

He tried to say something to them but was choked whether by the dust the wind flung at him or whether by the crying that rose up inside him. "I, I -" he tried to say and fell silent.

"You're what?" they said to him. "You're a bastard, that's what you are, bastard-bastard soneofabitch sonofathousandandwhores." and pushed him with the tips of their sandals.

"So, call your father," they said to him, "call him to come save you."

"He'll come from all the way from America," they said to him.

"He'll bring you presents." they said to him.

"A toy train," said the freckled one, "with an engine and ten coaches."

All that while the old man's small hands felt the ground of the yard like an overturned beetle moving its legs in order to roll back over, and because his body had been moved from where it was by their sandals, his fingers now reached the fragments of the bottle, first the base that had become detached when it fell from their hands and hit a stone – what exactly happened before that he doesn't remember – and then toward the neck of the bottle that remained with a curve of serrated glass and the nauseatingly sweet smell of the syrup.

This time the wind didn't grab anything from his hand or divert anything from its path to be flung back at him; and in the silence of the afternoon, into its sweaty steaming sluggishness, the shattering scream of the boy suddenly burst out. The old man hit the freckled boy, and not because he aimed specifically at him but rather because he was standing opposite him where the broken piece of glass completed its path into his freckled face; and between the fingers of the boy that were lifted and pressed to his eyes too late, blood flowed and didn't stop.

Then, for one last moment of the sluggishness that had been upset, there was no one in the yard other than the old man and the boy. But in addition to the cats hiding in the garbage cans, were all the marbles that had been scattered from the old man's pockets when he was thrown to the ground. In the afternoon sun those marbles sparkled on the ground of the yard like extracted eyeballs happy to be freed from their sockets.

Then Mrs. Shtub came out of the pharmacy.

Then Mr. Shtub came out.

Then many people could be seen in the rear windows of the building, on the first second and third floors, and only his mother's head couldn't be seen among them: she was still asleep in her room.

After a short while Mrs. Shtub took him up to their apartment: she pushed him in front of her on the stairs or dragged him by the arm and almost ripped it from its place, or first pushed and then dragged (only the whiteness of the coat he still remembered clearly) and she rang the bell and pounded on the door, and his mother didn't get up.

Then the pharmacist pulled the key that was hung around his neck – "give it to me, you little hoodlum," she said– and opened the door, and in the entrance made a face at the stale air and pushed the old man way from her, toward all the smells that were compressed in the passage. "Away with you, little hoodlum," she said and raised her voice so that it would be heard at the other end of the passage, in his mother's bedroom, whose door left a narrow gap from where the dimness seeped out.

"That's what comes from raising a boy without a father!" the pharmacist called out to the end of the passage, and because there was no answer, she continued: "That's where all your illnesses come from, only from that!" And those sounds, being repeated from one end of the passage to the other, when joined together were saying to the old man the very same things the boys in the yard had hurled at him: bastard bastard, bastardsonofabitch sonofathousandwhores, and coming from the mouth of the pharmacist they sounded even worse.

At that same hour the pharmacist's husband closed the pharmacy and accompanied the boy in an ambulance to hospital and the sound of the siren in all its intensity didn't equal the scream that had been heard in the yard. Even when the sounds of the ambulance waned at the end of the street and faded from the nearby streets as well, it seemed as if the scream was still coming from the backyard; and even a day later it was still hinted at by the marbles scattered there, marbles that no boy came to take, not openly or furtively, and they all remained wide-eyed day and night, and every morning shed tears of dew or dog urine.

A week or a month or two later – that detail also slipped his memory – they said the boy's eye would heal, and that stitches were enough. And when he was released from hospital all sorts of rumors circulated through the streets about what had happened in the yard at the time and also what had happened before that, which the old man prefers not to remember.

For a very long while, at once silent and deafening – his mother had already removed the cotton wool plugs from her ears, and on the chair next to her bed they also looked like extracted eyeballs with yellowish irises - the old man's mother looked into his eyes. Rays of sun passing through the slats of the shutters illuminated him with grains of dust whirling around him. There was no anger in her gaze about him having injured the boy perhaps to the point of blindness, nor even of a mother's love for her son who had suffered an injury the nature of which she didn't know and that had been grave enough to warrant such an act. Tousle-haired and sweaty she looked straight into his eye as if they were windows – he had once been told they're the windows of the soul – and through them she saw something better left unseen. She didn't look at him as a son and not even as a stranger, but rather as a man nauseatingly familiar, a man loved and hated who had succeeded to infiltrate into her home a few years ago in disguise, and had it not been for that disguise which up to that moment seemed perfect, she would never have let him in.

With a motion that couldn't be opposed, she spun him around inside the rays of light let in through the shutters, and in a voice was still thick with sleep said: "Are you like him?" She shook him by the shoulders to get an answer, and the old man knew she was speaking of his father.

"Show me your hands," she said to him, "show me the one you threw the bottle with."

Slowly and hesitantly, he reached out his right hand, and she immediately pulled it toward her with a violent motion even greater than that of the pharmacist and began to examine his fingers and the flesh and the grooves of his palm, like a palm-reader. Afterward, she turned it over and meticulously examined the other side as well, from the base of the hand to the fingernails that in his infancy she used to bite gently with her teeth, and then examined the left hand the same way, and here too she didn't find what she was searching for, the giveaway sign: if not a mark of Cain, at least a callous or a scar that until now had escaped her eyes and one perhaps like his father had; no, not in America, but from Minsk to Pinsk.

"Is that what's going to become of you?" she asked him. "Is there a little murderer hiding behind all this?" And even before he could reply she lifted up his right hand, not by force but with a surprising gentleness, and pressed his palm against her cheek and the small lines the cushion had imprinted, and she closed her eyes and concentrated entirely on the touch of his hand and after a few moments pulled it down the slope of her face and farther on from there, and the old man then felt her heart pounding, until she dropped his hand the way one drops vermin.

"You never can know," she said silently to herself. "Never." And then she opened her eyes, and the old man saw the sleep left in the corners and also the immense fatigue that filled them, fatigue that no sleep could ease, not daytime or nighttime sleep. "Now go," she said to him, "go so that I don't see you for a while."

The old man went out to the balcony and viewed the street.

Three rusty iron bars had been installed above the stone railing to make it higher, and the old man's head didn't reach beyond the third bar, and from between them it seemed that from the street down below, the sidewalks, the shops, the road and cars travelling on it, everyone was looking at him – all the passersby, the artisans from their alcoves, the cart drivers from their carts, the drivers from their cars ("automobiles" they were called then, and there were few) – and with their eyes fixed on him they're all saying: murderer-murderer or Bastard or bastardmurderer or bastasrdbastardsonofabitch sonofathousandwhores.

At the very most, he took someone's eye out (that's how the act was formulated in his mind), and he was proud that he had fought back against the big boys and had driven them away and said to himself, "They deserve it." There was no way of knowing exactly what harm his father had done in Russia that his mother should give him that name, or why she distorted her mouth when she spoke of him, not only her lips but also her voice from the depths of her throat and her chest.

After some time, perhaps at the end of that summer or the following one – he had forgotten that too– he asked her about it. They were in the bedroom, and dust could be seen everywhere, even on the chair next to her bed where the imprints of teacups differed one from the other only by the thickness of the layers of that dust, and the smell of her sleep were also mixed with a faint smell of lavender from the sachet pressed beneath the pillow, the sourness of armpit sweat and other hidden places with additional body odors that he didn't yet know of, and they were as dense and heavy as the residue of dreams that turned fetid.

"Why did you say that about father?" he asked her.

"What?"

He reminded her and she immediately denied it. "Did I say that?"

He reminded her when it was and she fell silent. Afterward she tried to explain that she didn't mean it, she was just very angry at the time and very alarmed. When people are angry and alarmed they say all sorts of things and not everything should be taken at face value.

"So how it should be taken?" he insisted. "How?"

"Your father - " she began and fell silent. Her eyes were still swollen from sleep, and for a moment, when they became clearer, the old man waited for her to maybe reach out her hand to him now, not to examine his hand one finger after another but to stroke his head as other mothers would their children. But she just closed her eyes and banished the sight of the room in which she had suddenly awakened and perhaps also some other sight that emerged from somewhere and attached itself to the sight of the room just as the grains of dust had done.

After some time – he doesn't remember how old he was at the time; everything had taken place in the very same room – she told him in a voice rusty with sleep that his father was a revolutionary; someone that makes revolutions in his country so that things will change, meaning everyone's lives, that's to say for the better, for health, wealth, and whatnot. He was a revolutionary.

And revolutionaries aren't murderers, no, it wouldn't be accurate to call them that, but it does sometimes happen that they kill people. Yes, like soldiers kill, and you wouldn't call them murderers. Just don't ask her what the difference is, and anyway all that happened in another country far far away that she doesn't want to remember. What's the point of remembering? There's only pain in those memories, nothing but pain. And when Nachman was born, his father wasn't with them at the time, he was far away, God, how far away he was. In another country.

What do you mean how did he go, he went by train; he just got on a train and went; on the eight ten train. There were trains at ten ten and twelve ten and two ten, but it was urgent for his father to travel on the eight ten train. Not the eight, the eight ten.

"From-Minsk-to-Pinsk-a-sailor – a hollow hoarse laugh rolled from her mouth – sought-to-seek-six-sheep, fromMinsktoPinskasailorsoughttoseeksix-sheep. Let him try saying that very fast, the fastest he can, instead of bothering her and concerning himself with things that aren't suited to a boy his age.

"But where was he?" the old man insisted. "Where?"

"I told you," she replied. "In another country, in another city."

"But where?" he insisted, "What city?"

She said the name that was unlike any he knew, and the sounds of the foreign name floated for a moment in the space of the room, rounded and glowing, until they fell and were lost and couldn't be differentiated from the noises of the street: the honking cars, the calls of the rag-and-bone man and the tapping of his horse's shoes, a guttural curse, the wind passing through the poplar leaves.

"But why did he go away, why didn't he stay with us!" insisted the old man. "Why?"

"Why?" said his mother. "Why? What does it matter why, you hadn't even come into the world when he went away, you were here - "

She pointed to her belly above the pique blanket that covered her, with its old stains of sweat and tea, and the thought of her belly and of himself inside it confounded the old man even more.

"Did he stay in a hotel there?" he asked. He was already prepared to forgive his father for running out on them if he had stayed in a posh hotel, the kind with cars parked at its entrance that tourists wearing fancy clothes get out of and servants in uniform carry their suitcases inside, twenty suitcases for each one (in all his days he never saw a hotel like that, not then or afterward, it existed entirely in his imagination).

"A hotel?" said his mother. She suspended each syllable in her mouth as if examining the suitability of their taste for swallowing – they were bitter, and again she distorted her mouth.

"You could call it a hotel," she said after a moment or two, "if you absolutely insist on it. Not that rooms were rented there for more than an hour, but you could still call it a hotel. If you absolutely must, call it a hotel."

"Just for an hour?" He didn't understand how they slept there for just one hour.

"I didn't say they slept," said his mother. "Did I say they slept?"

He asked her if they rested there.

"Rested?" said his mother. "It wouldn't be accurate to call it that."

"So, what then?" he became angry. "What did they do there? What?"

"What did they do?" said his mother. "It's a place that men and women go to…. to spend some time together."

"An hour," said the old man. "Just an hour?"

"About an hour," answered his mother. "Sometimes even less. Sometimes it's over in even half that time, sometimes even in a few minutes, it's just that after that -" she fell silent.

"After that, what?" asked the old man. "After that, what?"

"After that it remains with you your whole life. It doesn't leave you after that."

The old man tried to understand; he looked at his mother with inquiring clear eyes, not yet befogged by cataracts.

"It just doesn't leave you," said his mother, "it's already there. And from the moment it's there, it starts to grow, day by day. You can actually feel it growing there, and see how, every day. It's simply there, it's taken his place, by then you can't ignore it and can't be gotten rid of, you can never ever get rid of it."

Averting his inquiring look she turned her eyes first to the ceiling and to the damp stain in its center and then to the darkness beneath her eyelids.

"It takes you over," she said with closed eyes. "And it grows. Like a tumor. And when at last it comes out, you're scared to look at it, you're scared to see what came out. God, it's scary."

"What's scary?" asked the old man. "Tell me!!"

"It's scary," answered his mother. "It's yours, even though you didn't ask for it, and you don't know how to raise it, even if your uncle gives you money just so you'll make yourself scarce. It's yours, but it's not yours alone. It resembles you in many ways, but there are all kinds of other things. It came out of your body, but not only from there. And that's scary. And then gradually, without noticing it at all, and without meaning to, it's maybe the last thing you thought would happen, it starts to get your love. Gradually, and without asking you if you want to or not, and without knowing anything about you. It starts getting your love, day by day, in every possible way.

"Later, you already forget how it all started. Not that it's simple, but you forget. And it carries on growing, the whole time, even at night. And you hardly sleep at night, you want to make sure that it's sleeping, that all's well with it, that it has good dreams, not like your own, that it doesn't wake up from them in the middle of the night the way you wake up. That it's not all sweaty like you, that it doesn't scratch itself. You watch it while it sleeps, many times a night, and see how it sleeps in such peace, with such confidence that you'll look after it, that you won't let anyone in the world do it wrong, as if you weren't almost as weak as it. Because what does it know about you, nothing, and what does it know about the world, nothing. And what do you know? Nothing.

"So you stand next to its bed and listen to its breaths in the dark in complete silence, hear how they become calm until it falls asleep. And later, in the middle of the night, you come again to check if it's breathing, its breaths are so quiet that sometimes it's scary. You touch it to see that it's alive, that it won't leave you. It's something that came out of you, out of your body.

"Then, almost without one noticing, it starts to grow, too fast, it's already diffi-cult to hold it in your hands, and sometimes it doesn't want you to hold it. It becomes an independent little man with his own desires and likes that you know nothing about. And there are all kinds of things that make him angry, and you don't understand where they come from; such anger in such a small body which came out of you, out of your very own body. There had been someone with you, but then he came out of you.

"You even make pencil marks on the doorpost see how he's grown, and so that he can also see. And he's so proud of that, there almost isn't a morning that he doesn't measure himself there against the doorpost to check if he didn't grow another bit in the night. He places his little hand on his head or some book, some-times even cheating a little, but not from being bad. Why should there be any badness in him? After all, he came out of you, out of your body.

"And all the while, he keeps on growing. You can already see how one day he'll be taller than you, how one day you'll seem small next to him, how he'll protect you then. Or the contrary, he'll leave; it could happen, you already know that. In the meanwhile, his clothes become too small for him, the shirts and the pants, the shoes, you keep on having to buy him new things with money you don't have. And somehow you manage, it doesn't matter how, and you say to yourself: it could also be worse. Really. A lot worse if you remember how it all began. It's not something you want to remember but can suddenly pop up even when you don't want it to.

"You're never at peace, the only peace one has is in the grave. And there's no lack of reasons to be afraid. You're afraid every time he leaves home, it doesn't matter where he's going, and when he's at home you're afraid if you don't hear his voice for a while something might have happened to him. And when nothing happens to him, you fear what will be when you find he's changed; there's that age when everything changes. All sorts of little habits appear that you suddenly iden-tify, even just something small in his speech. and only you know where it comes from. And that's without him ever having seen him, not even once, and also you never having seen him again. There were only rumors: all kinds of rumors, from various places; rumors better left unheard. How he was here and how he was there, how he did this and how he did that -"

"Who?" asked the old man. "Who?"

"Who?" said his mother. She opened her eyes and focused on the damp stains of the ceiling. "The one who made you."

She closed her eyes and the old man saw how her chest rises and falls beneath the pique blanket.

"It only takes a few minutes," she said, "not an hour, nor half an hour. An entire life in a few minutes. And after that, one can up and leave, there's no short-age of trains. every hour or two, it only depends where to. For him it was urgent to get the eight o'clock train, had there been one at seven he would have gone at seven."

From where he was, very close to the bed, and in the midst of the smells encompassing it, the old man reflected for a moment on what she had said, and out of all the questions that could have arisen in his mind, he asked how many coaches that train had – it was extremely important to him to know how many coaches the train had.

"How many coaches?" said his mother. "What does it matter how many, God, all the coaches can go to hell together with him. Twenty, thirty? What does it matter, it only matters that he sat himself down there. Probably in the last coach, so he could as far away as possible even before the train left the station."

She said that with closed eyes, either because she was trying to picture him sitting in the last coach or because she feared what she would see if she opened them, and the old man saw how shrunken her eyelids were and how the rows of eyelashes were fastened together. But that train intrigued him, and he asked his mother if later on it travelled over a bridge. What was being conjured up in his mind at the time? A long bridge on tall pillars or arches with a gushing river or a chasm beneath it, and a train and all its coaches hurtling above was something he only saw a few decades later in Italy.

"A bridge?" said his mother. "If there was one, it's a pity the train didn't fall off it."

And when she saw the old man's eyes opening wide, she reached out a hand from under the pique blanket toward his head, and the sour smell of sweat suddenly burst from the depths of her armpit that then seemed dim as a cave. She placed the palm of her hand on his head, but she didn't have enough strength or desire or love to caress him. After a while, her hand became heavy and he wanted only for her to take it back. Her hand was removed from his head even before he asked.

"What does it matter?" she said again. "All of that happened in another country. And here in Israel for a while it seemed that one can get by somehow, what does it matter how, at least as far as the big things are concerned. So, it doesn't matter how all this started, heredity doesn't matter at all, it only matters how one raises a child. How you yourself raised him. How you used to stand next to his bed every night to see if he's sleeping, to check that he's covered, to listen to his breaths, to smell him, to wipe some saliva from his mouth, from his cheek, to kiss his eyelids, his eyelashes, his forehead. Until you're woken one day at three in the afternoon and told that your son took someone's eye out."

"I didn't take it out!" cried the old man. (Two months previously the boy was released from hospital; his eye had recovered completely, and he was even proud of the small scar that was left below it.)

"But that's what they told me," his mother said, "and that you weren't very sorry about it, on the contrary, you were even glad. And that you're a little hoodlum; those were the words Shtub used, she enjoyed saying all that and that it was all because you're being raised without a father. But the truth is the complete opposite; if God forbid you become a hoodlum one day, it'll only be because of him and what he was."

"He was a revutionary!" the old man proclaimed. He didn't want his mother to say another word about his father, good or bad.

"Alright," said his mother, "alright, so he was a revutionary, if you insist. And he stayed in a hotel and travelled over a bridge, why not. Whatever you want. Twenty coaches or thirty, even forty, whatever you want. Now just go so that I don't see you for a while."

9

England, 1994

"What's with you and churches?" she asked Amnon. "Have you suddenly become religious?

Instead of answering her questions or mentioning his articles from India about the religious riots that erupted there (after all, they weren't acquainted at the time), he tells her about the church leaflet whose sheets are handed out for free: about Reverend Carter's column, about the seasonal bazaar whose proceeds will go toward renovating the roof of the nine-hundred-year-old church, the recommended walk of the month: everyone passing through Mr. Winterbottom's field in an easterly direction will be promised - even before arriving at the avenue of linden trees - that if they just listen closely they will hear the hooves of King Charles the First's horse in his flight from Cromwell. The Zulu News leaflet is also handed out in the church, and its focal point is an article about the choir of the provincial diocese of Durban in South Africa that recently recorded a medley of a dozen psalms, among them *Sanctus Holy-Holy, Inhliziyo kaJesu, Jesu Mhlengi Wethu (Jesus, Our Lord Save Us)*. Recordings can be ordered at the post office.

She asks him if that's really all he has to tell her about; those dumb leaflets that he found in the church.

She asks him if he's all of a sudden he's attracted by Africa, because that's something she's never heard from him yet, about India yes, about Africa no, what connection could he have with Africa. It would make sense for her; after all, she spent three years there when she was little.

On his first trip to India, he was sent to cover the riots that broke out in Bhagalpur between the Muslims and the Hindus. "Put the emphasis on the similarity between them and us," the editor said (Barkai particularly liked to say "put the emphasis" or "with special emphasis on -") and he reminded him of that same year when both those crazy countries gained independence from the British, and the wars concerning the division of the land that broke out in both of them, and the insane willingness of religious extremists both here and there to fight to the death because of some ancient myth – the Hindus claimed the large mosque of Ayodhya was built on the ruins of an ancient temple to the god Rama. It happened three years before the riots broke out in Ayodhya itself, but the Bhagalpur riots were enough to justify an article: in the conflict that erupted between the Hindus and the Muslims, more than a thousand people were killed, and the editor expected him to mainly emphasize the Islamic violence.

"With special emphasis," he said, "on how people are prepared to kill each other there. Imagine that here the Dome of the Rock is destroyed only so that the Temple can be built in its place. And not that it won't happen one day, in the end it'll happen, lucky I won't be here. Oh, how'll you'll all miss me." (The editor defined himself as moderately right-wing, someone that believes that with wisdom and good sense everything can be achieved, and that there was no need for the insane violence of the religious extremists or for the cancer eating away at his body.)

He didn't travel to Bhagalpur nor to Ayodhya, nor to the ancient red mosque of Delhi, neither did he make appointments with people who could perhaps clarify matters to his readers regarding the religious conflict. Instead, he made do with some sweeping descriptions and a predictably superficial analysis, and to that he added some color –that's what they called it at the newspaper - with a few shocking facts that hadn't been published in the Israeli press: children who were beheaded, others who were flung from roofs; a woman whose breasts were slashed, and another, Bunni Begum was her name, who was found with her legs cut off at the bottom of an empty pool with sixty-one mutilated bodies around her – all Muslim. For that information it was enough to read a few articles in newspapers he found in Delhi, where details were also given of the slogans the Hindus chanted on their processions: "Hindi, Hindu, Hindustan, Mullah Bhago Pakistan!" - India for the Hindus, Mullahs go to Pakistan – and "Babur ki auladon, bhago Pakistan ya kabristan!" - children of Babur, run to Pakistan or to the graveyard" – and the similarity between the Hebrew and Hindu words, kabristan and kevarot – written kebarot, brought to mind the similarity between auladon and yeladim, meaning children, and for a moment he regretted not having completed his university studies.

Instead of travelling to Bhagalpur – a journey of more than twelve hours on a packed train – he made do with interviews he supposedly held with a few public officials and with people in the street and did all of that on his last day in Delhi. Before that he waited in his hotel for the weather to improve, because he wanted to fly to the north in order to try and understand something about his grandfather, as if the very place itself he died in could elucidate his life. Only in the second half of the week, after becoming fed up with the weather in the north, did he bother to find out when trains leave for Bhagalpur and bought a ticket and went to a popular cheap restaurant to listen to the locals, and that night suffered an upset stomach. For two and a half days he stuffed himself with pink and yellow and red pills given to him in a dubious pharmacy and was too dazed to get out of bed, and only one thing concerned him, the fear of not being in control of his sphincter and debasing himself like a baby or aged invalid, as perhaps might happen to his old father one day. He only recovered the day before his flight to Israel and did the one thing he could with the little time at his disposal, he sat and wrote about Bhagalpur based on what he managed to gather from the newspapers he found. And so his article was peopled with "a school pupil caught up in the eye of the storm," "a woman from a poor area whose two brothers were found at the bottom of the pool," "a worker whose family lives in a mixed neighborhood," "a local newspaper reporter and the first to cover the riots," "a Cambridge graduate who chose to return to the city of his birth and live there," and also Ratna Bey, 65, a flower seller from Bhagalpur, who asked: "Who can I sell flowers to like this, when everyone here is killing each other? What are the flowers blooming for at all?"

He had no difficulty describing her, despite never having seen her: bent and wrinkled like his grandmother who lived her whole life without a husband, white yellowish hair that hadn't been washed for weeks, clouded eyes netted with blood vessels – as his grandmother's eyes were – and the toothless mouth whose lips are drawn inward and emit the smell of rotting gums and bad digestion (smells he too remembers from childhood), and her bunches of flowers are held in a scrawny and trembling hand like his grandmother's hand washing him on evenings his parents left him with her; he thought of her then; the memory of the man who abandoned her is what attracted him to the north.

Over the phone Naomi quietly asks him, surpassing her anger, whether it's not yet clear to him that there's only one thing in life that's really important, and that everything else can go to hell – all the articles that he wrote and will write and also all the houses she designed and will design. All in all, she says, they weren't so bad together. Families are like that, you quarrel and you make up, and you don't suddenly throw it all away. When she herself decided what she decided concerning her husband, it didn't take one day. And his own mother delayed breaking up her family and waited for him to grow up. But he's like that grandfather of his, who started it all.

Silence fills the distance between the two mouthpieces, and for a moment he recalls the place she was sitting in – the alcove of the window facing the garden – he can trace the path of the telephone wire from the house to the seashore and into the sea where it lies on the seabed and the fish pass over it or float above it like the ones he saw from the promenade in Sidon.

On the other end of the line, he hears the cat purring quietly; while they were speaking perhaps it rubbed up against her and she responded by stroking its back which arched at the touch. "Puma!" he heard her voice again, apparently it had unintentionally scratched her. "Don't scratch me, scratch him!"

Then, as if the cat was appointed to arbitrate between them, he justifies himself by saying that he went away to think about everything a bit more, and as the cat purrs again, the lie is clearly convenient to both of them.

The smell of curry that spread through all the rooms is difficult to get rid of, and every time Miss Baker comes to clean the house, she makes a face and hastens to open all the windows despite the chill outside. On the first day, she explained step by step how to operate the washing machine, They both bent over the drum and his gaze momentarily wandered toward the lower part of her neck and farther on from there, and she was quick to straighten up. "You've got the manual," she said to him, "take a look at it."

Perhaps she thought he was flirting with her, and perhaps she didn't know any single men who were forced to do their own washing. When he lived in Tel Aviv he didn't have a washing machine, for half a year his stereo was out of order, and there was a time he was even too lazy to replace the burnt-out bulb in the kitchen; instead, every night he transferred the nightstand lamp from his bedroom to the table, and after that too burned out, he ate to the light of old Hanukkah candles that were lean and quick to melt. He pressed their tallow to the Formica surface that had been damaged from the days his grandmother had lived there, possibly from a burning pot that had been put down without a base for it.

One winter evening so long ago it's hard to imagine it ever had been, during an electricity stoppage that went on for a long while and that he wished would never end, his father told him about Edison's inventions by the light of a candle and about the night of his funeral when all the lights in the United States were extinguished for one minute – it must have been a stirring sight, that total pitch-dark, the sight of a giant country turning black, thousands of unlit streets from Maine to Alabama and all the buildings and the farms that were swallowed in the blackout, a sight worthy of being remembered had Amnon's mother not been absent at the time. Look how that came to mind here in the English village; a man gets up and leaves his country and his life there, and it seems to trail after him.

That week when his mother became fed up with her obligations as a mother and a homemaker and a wife, his father substituted for her as a bedtime storyteller, He didn't try to evoke a sweetness in his voice, and not only because he didn't read him tales for tots; how could any sweetness be evoked when Ada was absent and it was unclear whether she would be returning. Amnon the boy listened: sometimes fascinated by the colorful illustrations (his father read to him from one of the volumes of the illustrated encyclopedia for children), sometimes bored and wondering what his mother was doing now and where. It was painful to think about her in a world where he has no place.

His father added details to what was written in the encyclopedia, things he remembered from the time when his future at the university seemed certain, all sorts of trivia that he had immersed himself in before his sorrow over Ada overpowered him, and he would expound on them until Amnon's eyelids closed. The colorful illustrations would infiltrate his sleep with the voice explaining them, and sometimes they would turn into a convoluted dream in which his absent mother would appear and fade away. A wind billowed the sails of three-masted ships:

Columbus's *Santa Maria*, Darwin's *Beagle*, and the *Bounty*. In a small room in Padua, Galileo turned his telescope toward the night sky, and in the depths of the darkness the moons surrounding Jupiter and the rings that encompass Saturn revealed themselves. His father didn't say a word about Galileo's renowned courage, because he knew the correct version of his speech before the Inquisition, a speech that was entirely, contrary to what laymen think, a surrender to the religious extremists and not one of defiance. No doubt he found consolation and strength in the fact that a lauded genius like Galileo had succumbed to his weakness.

Years later, during one of the religious riots in India, the Hindu masses demanded that a young Muslim deny his faith and praise one of their gods, and when the young man refused and replied that it would be better to die, they poured oil over him and set him alight ("He died for the sanctification of the name of Allah," was how he phrased it in a paragraph dealing with the riots of Gujarat, and had no doubt the editor would cut it out). Those were the riots which preceded the riots of Bhagalpur by twenty years, and some of their details interested the editor: a Hindu policeman who had inadvertently caused the Koran to fall from a hand driven cart that was obstructing the traffic on the road was attacked by Muslims; and a Muslim policeman who caused a copy of the Ramayana to fall incited the anger of the Hindus; and added to all that was the act that took place thousands of kilometers from there, in Jerusalem, when an Australian Evangelist who sought to hasten the coming of the Messiah, set the Al-Aqsa mosque alight, and when the news reached India it further exacerbated the riots ("from the Middle East to the Far East," he wrote, despite that India was not really in the Far East).

How far all that seemed from the English village and its serenity, from the ancient church and psalms sung in Africa: *Sanctus Holy-Holy*.

His father had been in Africa with his regiment until the Jewish Brigade was sent to Europe. The landscapes of the western desert, which at first captivated him, couldn't compete with the landscapes of Europe in his eyes. There was no mosque in Cairo or Alexandria whose glory could compare with the churches of Rome, and he also found beauty in small country churches that his regiment encountered. What would this village have seemed like to him? He certainly would have appreciated the small church and its bell tower and also the fields and meadows, as far as the eye can see, with no electricity poles to spoil the view and no patches of exposed earth, certainly not of sand. He often he gazes at them from the windows of the house, as if there was some promise in their spreading out before him, but in telephone conversations with his father he tended to be brief.

"It's nice here," he says to him but doesn't go into detail; after all, he won't be staying here long. The man he's come to meet – had it not been for his father he wouldn't have known of his existence, but nevertheless he doesn't mention him in their conversation, lest he awaken false hopes in him – will surely be returning here soon. And after he hears what he's seeking to hear from McKenzie Jr., he'll continue on his way, and he doesn't elaborate on that over the phone; what would be the point? His father was principally concerned with the acts of his grandfather in Russia and attributed wondrous deeds to him, but one might wonder about the basis of those deeds, even with the realization that Communism had failed. He harbors the same doubt toward any act an individual makes for the good of a group of millions of people or an idea whose essence is too abstract – flags that are brandished and whose poles are far too easily stuck into the bellies of others.

There was a time when he too felt a common destiny with a large group, and twice did deeds that were supposed to have been for the benefit of a large mass of people, once in the war and once on the newspaper, and he regrets both times, which were very different from each other. The benefits of that war were dubious and its motives even more so, and the series of articles in his newspaper were also of no benefit, because the opposition they aroused strengthened his critics. He should ask himself whether those deeds were really done for the general public or out of his own needs: after all, he saw in the war an opportunity to experience something dangerous and more exciting than any anything that could happen on his travels – yes, he had been a great fool, and not only owing to his youth – and in the articles he wrote after the war criticizing those in charge of the country's security, it was not them he was concerned about, nor was it the publicity the articles would bring; it was easier to attack a large system than to look straight into the mirror.

A person would do better to focus on his own lot, that's what he thought afterward, and to make a serious effort to do good; it would be more than enough if everyone behaved that way. And that too of course was a juvenile thought; after all, many would prefer to be swallowed up in the general public and draw their strength from it. And to be perfectly straight, which would be fitting in this decade of his life - half of which has already passed – it would be easy for someone who is concerned only with his own private lot to look away from the injustices perpetrated outside of it. Isn't that what he's been doing all the last years? Often justice seems like a kind of blanket which is too narrow and too short and which will always leave some limbs uncovered, and due to its shortness people will die. To be honest and accurate, he said to himself: there wasn't one centimeter of justice in what you did in the war.

In this decade of his life, it seems to him that if he forgoes things he hasn't done up till now, he'll perhaps never get to do them, and in contrast, the deeds he's already done – the ones really worthy of being called deeds – seem so marginal that it's not clear why they required all the decades that had passed if their duration amounts to just a few hours or days. If they were to be grouped together, they wouldn't be older than an infant. It seems there are things in which he does take after his father, for instance longing for a different life, better and more fitting than his or at least more exciting. In his heart of hearts, his old father yearned for blood and fire and pillars of smoke like those that enveloped his unknown father and for the era in which he lived; while he, a month after leaving his home, made do with a bar waitress. She wasn't pretty, but maybe she'll be the one to erase the memory of the woman he left, and if not her maybe someone else further along in the trip – the memory of her and her son, and the animals they raised; and of an evening after the news bulletin, when she mimicked some Chinese minister so perfectly that Udi began to hiccough from all the laughter; and evenings when her elder son joined them and tested them with his eyes to decide whether they were deserving of his trust and in the end found them so and even agreed to play a jazz piece for them with his own improvisations; and how in time he and the boy found a few subjects of common interest, and how pleased she was about the effort he made for him which included reading some of Dicken's novels; and how every morning he would wait with her small son at the end of the street for the school bus, and Albie would sit at their feet and ignore the cavorting of the neighbor's little dog. How impermanent it all was.

Had she heard him now, she would have said that if he wants to end up like his grandfather, then that's what he deserves, to disappear beyond the mountains of darkness (a term his grandmother used and which she had heard from him), and just as well they didn't have a child together; but there's one thing she doesn't understand, especially at night when she goes to sleep alone, without a hug and without a zsheezsha (what they called what they did before the act itself), why she wasted four years on him. She said that to him on their last night before the morning on which she didn't bother getting up and parting from him.

He put on his backpack, and she didn't look at him; he came to the entrance of the room, and she didn't turn her head; he opened the front door of the house and lingered for a moment, perhaps Albie would come running joyously with his tail wagging and his tongue out, but he was fast asleep in his kennel on the other side of the house. He went out the garden gate to the taxi, and for a moment thought the driver was the same one who picked him up after buying the backpack, but it wasn't. "There's no place like Anatolia," that driver had said to him, "take it from me, it's paradise. You get there and you don't want to come back, where does it say your whole life has to be in the pits? In the Torah?").

"What did you say those Zulu psalms were called," she said over the phone, despite having been irritated by that previous conversation.

"*Sanctus Holy-Holy, Inhliziyo kaJesu,*" he replied. "*Jesu Mhlengi Wethu.*"

"*Jesu Mhlengi Wethu?*" Not wanting him to remember only her anger and her grievances, she tries to make him laugh; she knows how to do that, the way no one before her managed to. She can do a perfect Parisian accent without knowing more than five words of French, speak Japanese like a Samurai without knowing a word (she learned nothing from the Thai laborers recruited to work on her father's farming settlement other than to guard her cat, so that it wouldn't be eaten). Now she's trying her hand at Zulu.

"*Jesu Mhlengi Wethu,*" he confirms.

"I would go to Africa," she says; a safari sounds much more interesting to her than this trip of his, and she hasn't been there for a long time. Does he remember her telling him she spent three years there in her childhood? And does he remember – she must have told him – how her father, the big hero, would return with some carcass of something on the engine bonnet, and then they'd see him skinning it in the yard. He replied that of course he remembers. But if he really did remember things – she says – he wouldn't have left her like that.

He remembers that Land Rover from her stories, the giant tortoise that lived in their yard, the baboon that once swing from the ceiling lamp, the dog Nohiri, the goldfish Sir Stanley. Sometimes the image of her as a child rose in his imagination, riding on a tortoise, reaching out a banana to a baboon, but he doesn't repeat all that. What for?

She told him about Africa right from the start of their acquaintance, stories very different to those Kramer reported in the newspaper, but from the moment the idea of traveling came to him, Africa was a place not to be mentioned, a place only good for memories, like that backwater in the East, Leh. Her governess, Matutu, and the servant, Jobu, the monkey and the parrot, the tortoise and the goldfish, the Alsatian, the unending expanses (her father, on mission from the Israel Defense Forces trained black soldiers and not on his own accord like Kramer's hero), the dusty Land Rover on whose windows she would draw with her finger; all those were relegated to the back of the memory and covered in dust. One sight however did remain; the dog Nohiri, running after them the day they travelled to the airport. She watched it through the back window of the Land Rover and saw the distance between them growing from moment to moment and Nohiri becoming smaller and smaller, and her barking fading, until she was enveloped in an enormous cloud of dust.

"I hate partings," she had said more than once to him, "can't you understand that?"

In her adolescence she refused to look at the hundreds of slides her father had taken in Africa. When they were projected onto the wall, they'd be accompanied by his jokes which amused no one but him and that was the least of her allegations against him. "That one hasn't been to the dentist for a long time," he said at the sight of an elephant that had lost one of its tusks, or "those black women haven't heard about bras," or "that sergeant will go far, from the parade ground straight to the palace"; or "that dog was so loyal" (Nohiri could be seen lying on the threshold of their home and with a half closed eye watching her and her tortoise, Charlie, who was grazing on leaves large as the palm of a hand).

She had a scar on her forehead from those years in Africa – a horse did it to her. It was there that he first kissed her before moving down to her eyes and her nose and her mouth and also farther on from there. When she was three her father sat her on the horse belonging to the Colonel, his companion on hunting trips and on visits to bars in the capital (he would remain loyal to the ruler in the coup, and later the ambitious sergeant would liquidate him without a qualm(, and in a moment of absentmindedness, when he was probably making one of his wise-cracks to find favor with the Colonel, she fell off the horse; the scar was caused by hitting the ground or perhaps by the horseshoe.

For a while he pictures that small child: sitting on the horse and trying to touch its mane, patting her dog Nohiri, and saying all sorts of endearing things to her that in years to come she would say to Albie; travelling in her youth to an aunt in Brooklyn and in a dark stairwell some Jimmy or other helping her to discover her body; and an architecture student presenting her final paper in front of a stern group of lecturers and being complimented, unlike her colleagues, and announc-ing to her father her decision to divorce her husband, a successful software engi-neer and a devoted father to his children. "You think only of yourself," her father said bluntly, "you'll scar your children for life!" She fell silent and wanted to point to what had been engraved on her forehead when she was younger than her chil-dren, but she knew he probably was right and that the scar on a forehead was pref-erable.

There wasn't one word about a safari in the Zulu News, he said to her, the leaflet placed at the church door together with the local one. Psalms, yes, and a few words about old Gogo who departed this world and whose memory will remain with us forever, but nothing about a safari. But there was a short article about –

She interrupted him; she's fed-up listening to nonsense which has nothing to do with their lives. And as for a safari, the only thing that would tempt her to go on one would be the chance to throw him from the jeep to some hungry lion. And for a start she's throwing out all his belongings.

He replied that he had no doubt she was capable of doing that. He can remem-ber the time they were sitting in a restaurant by the beach, when she removed the napkin from the fork in which it was wrapped and placed the teeth of the fork against the palm of his hand pressed them down firmly and said that was what she would do to him if he tried to get away from her.

Nonetheless he had got up and left; he has a purpose, even if a flimsy one, and he has the funds, even if not for a long time. One of the editions of the travel maga-zine whose reporters he envied was devoted to the region to which he had chosen to travel,. not Africa but rather central Asia. Smiling people could be seen with a peculiar headdress whose edges where curled, and two-humped hairy camels, and heavily furred yaks, and a creature called a dzo that looked like a cross between a yak and a cow. There was a photograph of a cave for seclusion in which monks shut themselves until reaching enlightenment or until their deaths, and a dish called tsampa was mentioned and a drink called chang, a kind of light beer, and despite not particularly liking beer; he thought he would taste the chang and drink it in gallons (he had got drunk with Naomi only once and had said some unnecessary things he wouldn't have dreamed of saying when sober, but the worst thing he ever said to her he said when perfectly clearheaded). Perhaps the chang will fill him with delight, why the hell not, at the very least he would become a bot dazed, and maybe that would be enough. He sometimes thought that about that when yet another fruitless day came to an end here, and night fell on the English house and its environs, and in all its darkness only a lit window in the distance could be seen, small and unreachable like the entrance to an Indian cave on a mountain slope. He was not expecting to reach enlightenment on this journey to the east, nor an awakening; he was more than enough awake.

The man he's come to meet is indeed connected to his grandfather, but he hadn't got up and left for his grandfather – a dead man with no trace left of him is not reason enough. And a dead child? The question came to mind and was immediately banished. And anyway, McKenzie Jr. wasn't in the village now. People here work hard for a living, they said of themselves, whereas McKenzie Jr. had lately begun to travel all over the place like a young man, they said in the pub, adding that in fact he wasn't born here at all, and he was used to traveling from childhood. His father was a veterinarian, and their grandfathers still fondly remember his magic touch with sick animals, until he unfortunately abandoned his home and profession and travelled to the ends of the earth, and there, in a backwater he for some reason chose to live in somewhere in India, his son was born. Only sometime later his son was sent here to school and afterward studied in London before returning to the village, and for years he treated the offspring of the animals his father had tended, until deciding to leave and travel in Europe; if he's so happy there, they said, maybe he should move there instead of complaining the whole time about how everything here is going downhill (the new highway also disturbs them, but unlike him, they don't have much hope for the Green's initiative to cover it with earth; they're reasonable people, you can't bring back the past,: not the large swathe of land expropriated for the road, not the Indian sub-continent, not Africa and all the colonies).

Only at night did the dim noise of the cars on the highway hidden from the eye abate, and on the way back from the pub it's mainly dogs one hears from both sides of the old and damaged road: first the pub's dogs, then all the others. There's no garden without a dog or two and every time he goes walking there's always one to bark at him. The road is completely dark and its potholes are filled with rainwater, and on cold nights the puddles are veiled with a covering of thin ice. His foot becomes overtaken by a childish motion causing him to place his shoe on that covering and cracking it and quickly pulling it away from the rising puddle; but in Tel Aviv the puddles were never frozen, and he did something else to them;

furrowing a canal with his shoe that lead the water from one puddle to another and joining them into a lake.

"Is snow falling there yet?" she asks over the phone. In her eyes a whole season has passed since he left.

"No," he replies.

"We could have been lying down and watching it through the window."

She had arranged it so the pines could be seen through the window from their bed, like a crowded audience watching them. They would watch the rain, and on more than one occasion she complained that the architect should have doubled the size of window; then they could really have felt they were in the midst of a grove.

"But it's not falling," he replied and doesn't mention the frozen puddles or the joy in cracking them.

"Here it's still hot," she says and starts to describe the late sirocco that suddenly descended on them; and above it all (her anger toward him is momentarily forgotten, she's bothered about a household mishap), the air conditioner in the living room is out of order and she has to go around the house half-naked.

He wonders if that's really what happened, or if she's trying to remind him of her nakedness, and immediately right in front of his eyes, in the English room, he sees her nakedness, white and abundant and soft and smooth and warm and inviting.

"Maybe the air conditioner just needs gas," he said over the phone, but she interrupts him. Every word of his makes her angry now and it would be better for him to keep silent.

She too is silent, and from the other end of the line he hears her breaths or imagines hearing them. A dog barks, and then another, and others join in; the entire village dog choir.

"Can you hear them?" he says. "The dogs." He means well, alluding to the dog they both loved.

"I can hear the biggest dog of them all," she replies.

The choir persists for a while until the dogs become tired.

"Maybe they were waiting for you to join in," she says. "Your friends."

On the day they met each other, she had come to deliver a notice about her cat that had gone missing, and at the time he told her he was a dog person, and those words reverberate between them now.

10

St. Petersburg, 1904

"If it was up to me, you would have been out of here long ago, Poliakov. Understand?"

It was perfectly understandable, and had he been in Duchin's place he would have behaved exactly like him: he would have sent someone who is of no use unceremoniously to hell or home, if there was any difference between them at all.

In the case of Levin, Duchin apparently had specific information: one of the workers from the Putilov plant heard him at a secretly convened meeting making statements completely at odds from those he was sent to make in order to incite the workers, and it transpired that Levin, who could set hearts alight, whose speeches probably caused dozens or hundreds of people to join the revolutionaries camp, was in the habit of speaking in two tongues, he could speak about the very same things in different ways according to his objective at that specific time; and from that it could be deduced that he incited the workers to join the revolutionaries camp, for them to be handed over to the secret police afterward.

That worker from the Putilov plant, Mitya was his name, who according to Duchin you could trust with your eyes closed, said that Levin he had a chameleon's tongue, and knew how to spin everyone around it. "If he told people the sun is extinguished in the sea," Mitya said, "they'd believe him." He continued reporting what he had heard Levin say in one place and what he had heard in another: here he praised the Tsar and the Tsarina, there he criticized them harshly and called for their ousting; here he praised the leader of the Narodniks, there he spoke highly of his persecutors; the very same fact was stated according to his objective at that precise moment: to glorify the regime or to incite against it, in that way discovering where his audience's sympathies leaned." He also wrote down everyone's names," said the worker, and Duchin mentioned that in the apartment used as a hideout, "everyone gave them to him without fearing. Had he spoken to them a little more, they would all have brought axes." The axes were those mentioned in the manifestos that were secretly distributed in factories and became tattered from all the hands they passed through. *The day is approaching when the flag of our future shall be hoisted,* was written there in Volodya's refined language, *it shall be*

hoisted skywards no more to be lowered. Thereupon shall we all march toward the
Winter Palace and topple its gates and break it and eradicate all its inhabitants, and
should they cowardly flee from us, we shall clutch our axes as one and fall upon them.
They shall not know any mercy! And the follow passage incited the audience even
further: *We shall destroy them in the squares, should the villains dare to be encoun-*
tered there, we shall destroy them in houses should they try to hide in houses, destroy
them in the alleys of cities, destroy them in the avenues and streets of the metropolis,
destroy them on bridges, destroy them in villages.

    "We shall destroy them!" the crowd would answer. "Weshalldestroythem!"
cried the factory workers who remained for the meeting after hours of work
between their machines and mounds of filthy rags and heaps of metal chips, and
the bedding could be seen for the length of the walls for those who will be sleep
there and screens of worn-out blankets to conceal the couples in their private
moments.

    "Weshalldestoythem!" the crowd cried against the followers of the Tsar, in
other factories they cried out against the revolutionaries, and all had been incited
by the same eloquent Levin.

Vera stood in the entrance of the side room and watched the two of them,

    "It shouldn't be at all complicated," said Duchin while crushing with his pencil
remnants of burnt paper on which the address had been written and crumbling
them into an ashtray. "A regular building in a quiet neighborhood, first floor,
windows facing the street, they aren't closed yet at this time of the season. When
you get there it'll be almost empty, it isn't the time when the building becomes full,
or the street. A small street, more an alley than a street. Tell him, Vera, you've been
there."

    He looked at her for a moment but didn't wait for her to confirm his words.
With a precise exhalation he blew off the piece of burnt paper that fell on his desk:
he bent over the desk and blew, and from the entrance of the side room the woman
called Vera applauded: a refined applause, the tips of her fingers hitting the base of
the palm, like a spectator in an expensive reserved theater box.

    "Or maybe it's also too complicated for you?" Duchin said and his small
shrewd eyes peered not at him but at Vera, as if requesting her to form an opinion
on the matter.

    "No, it's not complicated," she answered in place of him. She placed her hands
on her hips and her dress became arched and slanted to the floor, a wooden floor
unpolished and unwept since the apartment had been rented with its few pieces of
furniture. "He'll do it. You'll do it, right?" She turned to him with the same voice
in which she had spoken to him the first time he saw her, on the corner of Moravskaya Street and Nevsky Avenue, two months ago. They had been two very long
months in which he had done things that he'd never have believed he'd do, but
that's what he also thought about the prior two months.

"Yes," he replied to her, "I'll do it."

"You won't get all softheaded at the last moment?" She asked, not taking her eyes off him, and that's exactly how she had looked at him from the street corner where she sat and begged, and in her lap a tiny baby very well wrapped and very silent; she looked straight at him until he could no longer withstand her gaze and placed a coin in the bowl in front of her.

"No," he answered her. "I won't get softheaded."

Duchin balanced his pencil on one of the indentations of the ashtray and turned his large bald head toward him, and in a moderate voice told him that generally speaking he has all the patience in the world, while she, Vera Alexandrovna is short of patience, but this time the tables have been turned.

"Right now his fuse is short," Vera said from the entrance.

"And all of a sudden she's got a sense of humor," Duchin said.

Behind Duchin's back on the handle of the large window facing the main street, a black umbrella hung signaling the state of the safe haven; and in the entrance of the building a bicycle was tethered to the railing of the staircase with a long chain; the short chain had a different function.

Duchin suddenly asked him if he knew how to sharpen pencils.

"Do you at least know how to do that?" he asked him, and before Poliakov had time to consider the question he threw the pencil that had been laid on the ashtray at him. He then took a large pocketknife out of the desk drawer and also threw it at him and when he caught it – he caught it nimbly with one hand. There were other things he had learnt to do in the forest when still a boy and never imagined he would come to this damned city one day – he turned his bald head away from him and in that same moderate voice said to the entrance of the side room: "He actually knows how to catch a knife. Now let's see if he knows how to use it." And the open desk drawer, after been placed on its tracks again, was slammed shut.

"Will he do it with a knife?" said the doubtful voice from the other side of the wall.

"What do you want him to do it with, Vera Alexandrovna?" said Duchin. "Pencils are sharpened with a knife."

Since he hadn't yet been invited to sit down, he sharpened the pencil standing: one by one he spattered wooden chips from the darkening tip into the wastepaper basket, as if his not only was his ability for sharpening pencils being tested but for doing other things as well. The basket was filled to the brim and a few letters appeared here and there on a piece of paper, and seeing them, the thought passed through his mind that if someone like Levin had wanted to take revenge on these two, and all the others, he could have found a way, a way they themselves taught him; to empty out this waste paper basket and deliver some of its contents to secret police headquarters; and if not straight to there, at least to one of the junior detectives who were not difficult to recognize from a distance. Even he had already learned to identify them; he had learned many things here these past two months, things it would have been better never to have learned.

Vera reached out to him the two keys of the bicycle chain as well as a rolled-up newspaper, the one he himself had brought with him, and he immediately sensed that a weight had been added to it: the weight of an object wrapped in newspaper in order not to be seen, and certainly not from one of the windows on the opposite side of the road.

"We'll miss it," Duchin said, looking at them from the other side of the desk.

"It won't be missed," said Vera. "He's not going anywhere with it, you're not going anywhere, right? Only to replace the long chain with the short one. It's a fine time, Duchin, when I have to remind you about the rules."

"I wasn't talking about the bicycle," said Duchin.

"No," said Vera, "but we won't miss that either. Tomorrow evening he'll bring it back here, you'll bring it back, right?" And again she looked directly at Poliakov.

"Yes," he answered her, "I'll bring it back." When he tightened his grip on the newspaper, he felt the shape of the object wrapped in it from the curve of the butt to the tip of the barrel. The cylinder bulged in the middle and arched the paper above it like a pregnant belly.

The old hand in the window opposite him went back and forth, illuminated by the light of the oil lamp. The charcoal iron was being driven over a shirt back and forth in a slow and careful motion with all the time and patience in the world, and from where he stood he also saw the clay bowl in which the old woman dipped her fingers in order to spray the shirt with water; he also saw the table on which she was ironing – a wooden dining room table whose surface can be seen worn down and jagged around the folded blanket placed upon it. Three chairs stood around the table, and the fourth was moved back so that the old lady could stand there and iron. Should the garment continue to wrinkle she would probably show little resentment about having to repeat the action over and over, just as she would show little resentment about the washing she has to do or sewing on a button or darning or hanging clothes up to dry. She harbors no fear of the darkness on the other side of the window from which he observes her.

He peered at her from the street whose entire length was lit up by gas lamps except by one near the window (it had been shattered by one accurate hit a short while before then). Back and forth the hand continued to move over the material it was ironing, a gaunt and wrinkled hand even from a distance, but the iron was driven effortlessly with the charcoals in it, and neither their blackness nor their heat could be seen.

"There's nothing simpler than that," Duchin said in the safe house, "it could be over in a minute. You can do it all with the pistol from the street without wasting time. Just shoot and do it."

The iron was being driven again, and still he didn't remove himself from the fence where the smell of urine rose; he remained entirely immersed in the darkness beneath the broken gas lamp. As if in some dream-like state, he imagined hearing the noise of the flame rising from the wick, thought it would be impossible for him to actually hear it or even the gurgling of the oil in the container. Had it not been for the beating in his chest and between his temples perhaps he would have heard what the old woman was softly singing above the garment she was ironing, but the beating wouldn't subside: not in the chest nor between the temples.

In the depths of the window, the old woman's lips were moving, and her hand let go of the iron and reached out sideward and dipped the fingertips in a bowl of water and was raised and shook transparent drops onto the garment. And right away the iron moved again with the fire hoarded in its coals, a miniature hell hidden there like the one hidden in the earth and driven through space with it.

The old woman was ageless and all her femininity had withered. She now began to iron the other sleeve: that of a man of his height and his age; and if the similarity in size and age wasn't enough, they had both been given the same damned god at birth – "The irony of fate," Duchin said, "but why should only Christians kill Christians?" - a god whose believers don't even pronounce the letters of his name out of fear, because even their sanctity can become a curse (Jehovah-Jehovah-Jehovah-Jehovah, he took pleasure in repeating the name, and knew he wouldn't be punished for it). To his father, he was the god of a distant remote land, or the god of the earth being transported by a stubborn hand back and forth in space, to no particular purpose.

He hasn't believed in that hand for a long while, and in general, there are very few things he's continued to believe in over this past year, and least of all in himself; there was already abundant evidence for his existence not being worthy of being believed in. The people who sent him to this address he still believed in, but in this small alley, opposite the windows of the apartment and the silence, he is stricken with doubt whether the owner of the shirt being ironed is indeed there in the back room, as they said he would be in the briefing and is waiting there for him to come; and the purpose of his coming is to silence him for once and for all.

"What did he do? Nothing other than opening his mouth," Duchin said. "Maybe that's something you know about Poliakov? He had the same interrogators as you did, that nice couple, and they also released him. And then he still goes to work like before, meets with people like before, and his mother still prepares his food like before and washes and irons for him so that he's well-dressed the next time he goes to inform, maybe that's the only difference between the two of you?"

"How can you compare them at all?" Vera said.

Duchin didn't answer, but the expression on his face said that no answer was necessary. "Give me back my knife if you're not going to be using it," he said.

And with the same skill with which he threw it from his desk, he caught it quickly in spite of the weight of his arms. In an instant, the knife was returned to the drawer.

The black umbrella hanging behind him swung slightly after he hit it with his elbow, and Poliakov looked at it and pondered whether someone perhaps watching them from some building on the other side of the road might understand it as a signal.

Fragments of glass from the shattered streetlamp were strewn over the sidewalk, and one of them was ground beneath his shoe as he drew closer to the side window. The stone that had been thrown at the lamp still lay on the sidewalk, but he won't be needing any stone. Another piece of glass cracked under his foot, and in the first window the old woman was still moving the charcoal iron back and forth. As he came closer he could see the shadow of her hand which the oil lamp made dance on the wall; the hand was stable but its shadow trembled, as if it alone was effected by old age, and Levin's father could now be seen in profile, asleep as before and a thread of saliva dripping from the corner of his mouth and glistening in the light of the oil lamp. He wasn't snoring and must have been breathing through his open mouth.

"Our best speechmaker," Duchin said of Levin; and what else did he say about him? Not only that he opened his mouth and squealed right away, but worse than that, that the whole arrest was probably staged ("Even Stanislavsky," Duchin said, "could have learned something from them"); and either way, there's only one punishment for actions like that. From his desk he briefly described how things must have developed: how Levin was brought to secret police headquarters to Perdischenko's office, and how Perdischenko and his aid, Telegin, induced him to talk and scared him ("Isn't that something you know about, Poliakov?"), and perhaps he had co-operated with them before that. Had they themselves bothered to find out a little more who and what this Levin was before accepting him into the organization, had they checked some of the details he gave, they certainly wouldn't have relied on the address he gave with such ease, the kind of address that only now, when they have to send someone urgently to it ("You," Duchin said), do they find out where he really lived:

Not in Tsarsky-Gorodok. Not squashed together with a few other workers in a filthy apartment with smells of alcohol and sour cabbage and farts and piss and vomit and with cracks in the walls teeming with cockroaches, but rather in the center of the city. True, he's not the only one who lives there without a permit ("You Jews always succeed to get by in the end," Duchin said, "and I say that with appraisal, not God forbid with criticism"), and everyone knows that for a few rubles the concierges turn a blind eye, but to live in the neighborhood that they live in and in such comfort? A room for the parents and room for himself? Where exactly does all the money come from? True, Levin's father in his time supplied all sorts of things to the army and even became quite rich from it, but all that was in a small provincial town, and since then his father's been through more than a little trouble; and now Levin brings his parents to the big city, a city where he himself is just a guest, and not even legal, and puts them up and supports them, a truly model son, but where exactly did the money come from, down the chimney?

The owner of the apartment who was also the concierge, when still healthy, had previously lived alone and an added income would certainly do him no harm, but to take them in like that, so assured it would all go smoothly? "And there's no mistaking the look of them," Duchin said. "Maybe in your case some foreign blood got mixed in, but with them you can see it from the first minute." And look how, in spite of everything, no one in the world bothered the Levins, they're so complacent that they don't even bother hiding during the police raids ("While you run around," Duchin said, "sometimes wandering the streets for whole nights. They don't").

"Does he even know how to use a pistol?" he asked from his desk and the doubt could be heard in every syllable.

"He learned how to," Vera answered from the entrance of the side room, "Volodya taught him."

"What would we do without Volodya?" said Duchin.

11

"And so it was discovered that within the hollow spheres that the evil ones maliciously manufactured there were two pipes made from burnished copper , and the mouths of both of them were covered by corkwood stoppers, and a glass tube penetrates and descends into them from the rim to the bottom of the pipe, and on it another wrapping of rubber material is wound, and is filled completely with sulphuric acid (schwefelsäure), and on its opening is a cotton wool fuse dipped in salt and sugar, and from that fuse another two fuses joined to their other side branch out and reach the small capsule (kapsel) full of pyroxylin with nitroglycerine and the noisy mercury." On the yellow of the page (it was the science section of the newspaper *Ha-Tsfira*) in the neon light of the municipal library and the bustle of its visitors, a blurred thumbprint that was a hundred years old or more could be made out, and perhaps the paper had been spotted with old age like the hand turning its page - the hand of a ninety year old man to whom most scientific innovations remain foreign, from the locomotive to the atom, those intended to be beneficial and those intended to be harmful.

And at the time one of those pipes are broken, it was written there, the sulphuric acid makes contact with the chemical compound of the salt and fire is born. Only then will the capsule crack open with a loud sound and its fragments will fly in all directions, and until the force of gravity summons them back to earth, they will have managed to sow destruction in every place that they strike."

The power of bombs and shells was revealed to Nachman while serving in the Jewish Brigade combat regiment, and especially in one battle in Northern Italy. He had mistakenly been complimented on his actions there, as if bravery had been in them and not terror. It's better not to remember what was done to his comrade by a shell, in complete contradiction to the force of gravity, no flowery language can soften that, nor is it likely to soften the sights his son saw in Lebanon. His wife Ada didn't require a bomb or a shell, it all occurred between her temples, where the force of gravity worked well: the moment the edema in her head was arrested, the skin collapsed in the place where the dome of the skull had been sawn in an operation, and her head resembled a deflated ball, a twin to the silver balloon that somehow had wandered to the ceiling above her bed. One of her neighbors was apparently celebrating a birthday, or members of her family were celebrating while she lay unconscious like Ada, and the inscription "congratulations" floated above her with three exclamation marks, until the gas ran out. Even then his son wasn't around; the force of gravity didn't work on him, nor the force of the command to honor one's parents.

His son promised to phone him at least once a week, and a week has passed and not a call. The old man always feared not reaching the telephone in time, and always rushed to it to snare its ringing before it disappeared, and afterward he would pant into the mouthpiece for a few moments until his breathing became calm. "In the end, you'll give yourself an attack like that," Ada said to him when she was still living at home, and it seemed she was mainly worried about the possibility of being forced to take care of him; and one cranky young woman who was mistakenly looking for some Kobi and didn't identify herself by name, ranted at him while he was still gathering his breath: "Are you breathing at me, you pervert, go breathe at your mother, not me." Nachman was more amazed than insulted by the woman's rudeness, it was as if not only did electrical devices change from year to year, but also the souls of the people who use them. He lamented the days when people still took the trouble to write each other letters and didn't make do with phone calls in which everything and nothing was said, it was as if everyone had lost all shame. Had letters still been written their envelopes would no doubt have been transparent so that the things they had to say could be seen by all: love, longing, passion ("I can't wait to have it on with him," someone sitting behind him on the bus said, and Nachman didn't immediately grasp what that was about).

A year after he left his village in the south of Russia, his father also carried letters of love, passion and longing among his clothing in his suitcase (albeit fictitious and fake from their first line to the postage seal), letters the likes of which no Mossad agent would carry today. He liked comparing his father to the people of the Mossad in his old age. He didn't see him only as a terrorist or a revolutionary, but as a sort of daredevil secret agent, though after watching one of the James Bond films, he was disappointed. He saw a lot of elaborate toys there, and stunt after stunt, but beyond that – nothing. He found it difficult to picture his father equipped with all sorts of sophisticated gadgets that did the job in place of him, and certainly didn't see him flirting with every beautiful woman in the vicinity or relishing a martini. After all, his father was a serious man, of that the old man had no doubt, and only his behavior concerning his first born, and perhaps only son remained mystifying and unforgivable.

Instead of a small multipurpose briefcase, his father had a trunk reinforced by iron, battered and scratched and reeking of dog urine; and in place of a pen that shoots, he probably used a pistol or his hands (even the sight of hands tightening around a neck didn't arouse horror in the old man; he had no doubt his actions were justified), and in place of an expensive car armed with missiles he had his feet. The old man himself had been a good walker in his youth, and if that was the case, his father must have been many times more so; and perhaps out of all his father's virtues he had inherited nothing other than his capacity for walking, at least in his youth. He now found walking difficult, but insisted on not being aided by a stick, as if it was some devious invention whose main purpose was to expose it owner's slackness.

It sometimes seemed to Nachman that owing to the comfort enabled by modern devices, people using them have become lax and have sunk into pleasant and paralyzing slackness and are therefore no longer capable of performing truly great deeds. The slackness extends to everyone, army generals as well, who more and more seem to resemble senior executives: balding, paunchy, over eloquent in their speech; and even Mossad agents, whose daring the whole world had once been in awe of and feared, had recently been exposed time and again in their slackness and have behaved like total amateurs: caught bugging the embassy in Cyprus, forgetting fake passports in a public telephone booth in London, and when arrested without any struggle, waited like weaklings for representatives of the foreign office to rescue them. It seemed to him that only his father dared to travel thousands of kilometers throughout Asia under countless false identities and carry out tremendous deeds without any support of an army or intelligence organization, and certainly not of a government office. In his childhood and in his youth, he associated him with the marvels of tales he heard, and in his adulthood, in the years that he was an academic and had become more moderate, he found other areas of interest, but in his old age his old yearning for marvelous tales resurfaced, and this time without any constraint.

Was his father not, for instance – yes it was easy to imagine it above the yellowing newspaper sheets in the municipal library – one of the instigators of the daring plan to smuggle dynamite into Russia via the North Sea? John Crampton was the name of the ship designated for that, but in no newspaper or history book was it mentioned who besides Rutenberg had dealt with the shipment. And perhaps he was also one of the planners of the flying machine that would shower bombs on the Winter Palace. At the time, that machine on whose development the Italian inventor Bucello had worked, hadn't yet been named, airplane or airship; in the skies of Russia only hot air balloons flew, dependent on the grace of the winds but overcoming the might of gravitational power

In his youth, the old man had no doubt that his father had participated in those deeds, and even one of them would have been enough to glorify his image and in that way somewhat fill his absence (his absence was the only thing he experienced up to the fifth decade of his life, and that was certainly enough). In his adolescence, all previous emotions had been replaced by insult, and he tried to wipe from his mind any vestige of his father and fill that absence in all sorts of other ways, and for many years even succeeded in doing so, until he became old; then all those expectations again rose up in his heart, groundless as they were. All at once his past wish was renewed in all its force: if he were not to return, at least he would be a model figure, head and shoulders above everyone else, a man that only owing to secrecy newspapers and history books had omitted to mention his part in daring assassinations, in amazing prison escapes, in purchasing ammunitions ships, in approaching the Italian Bucello (his plan had failed like the previous one – no bombs were showered from the sky on the Tsar's Winter Palace, no dynamite reached the shores of Russia on a ship via the North Sea).

Only in one period of his life did the old man carry out actions of real meaning, when he serving in the Jewish Brigade (he enlisted at a relatively old age; he stopped his studies in order to fight together with the young, against the man who had risen up against his nation to destroy it), and especially during one night of battle in northern Italy, when the British were finally so kind as to let the brigade fight. Those hours in which he himself was placed between life and death, he wouldn't have forgone for any fortune – that's what he would say years later, but it had been a bad and unnecessary battle and its end was bad as well: Rosenstein had been instantaneously cut in half when a shell exploded, and afterward he had to carry half of his bleeding body (if not for that it would certainly have been difficult to carry) to the farmhouse where the medic treated the injured. "He's no more alive than the legs you left there," the medic said to him when he dumped his load in front of him, "now go wash yourself." Next to the wall was a kind of trough made from an empty fuel barrel cut in half lengthwise, and a moment later its water turned red from blood. Only after he had washed himself a little the old man looked at Rosenstein again – he had been his number two machine gun man, the one who delivered the chain of bullets – and wondered if he was still alive when he lifted him out of the crater, and if Rosenstein had tried to tell him something on the way and he had missed his last words. "Wash yourself well," the medic shouted at him, "so that you don't catch anything that he might have caught from the whores of Rome."

He had carried his machine gun partner in his arms though a minefield without knowing that the field had been mined, therefore it's hard to attribute great courage to him, (at the time he feared more than anything the reaction of his company comrades were they to know he had abandoned Rosenstein), but that contact with death was also a contact with life, because he had never felt so alive as in those moments. For a while he looked at Rosenstein from the edge of the crater, until the sound of the explosions subsided a little and the smell of gunpowder dispersed slightly, and only then he descended into it and dragged him by the armpits minus his two legs that had disappeared. In vain he looked for the company signal operator in order to call for help on his two-way radio; from all sides, on the right and on the left, in front and behind, not a living soul could be seen. Afterward, in that stillness after the bombing, twenty or thirty meters to the north of the crater he saw the silhouette of a giant cow and thought that where it stood there must been no mines. It looked fat and its jaws moved right and left and chewed an ear of corn, and when the first rounds were fired the tracer bullets darted in its large brown eyes and suddenly mooing could heard. At the time there was no more pleasing sound than the mooing of a fat cow in a field. The company signal operator was left lying a few meters away from it, as silent as his two-way radio, and the old man (that's what they already called him then in the brigade) deliberated for a moment whether to lay down his load there and flee, after all, no one had seen him except for the cow who mooed again. When the silence returned, he looked at the battered two-way radio and pondered for a moment whether he might succeed in bringing it to life but feared that if he'd lay Rosenstein down he wouldn't lift up him again and carried on walking.

That walk between two hills in Northern Italy wasn't measured by time: perhaps it lasted an hour, perhaps a few hours. Only his bleeding load was clear to him, and as the blood ran out of it so did its weight increase. Rosenstein had never been heavier than during that hour, not even when he carried a machine gun on his body with its ammunition (the pictures of naked women he kept in his belt didn't add any actual weight). There was no point thinking about the two-way radio, but in Nachman's head messages were being formulated to the commander of the platoon, the commander of the company, the commander of the regiment, and even the commander of the brigade, Brigadier Benjamin, and in these he repeatedly reported, according to the rules of speech used over the two-way radio, the injury of his number two.

In that way he reached what was left of a farmhouse that was being used as an improvised hospital and reported Rosenstein's injury to the medic, as if his condition was visible the moment he laid him down. "I have an injured matchstick," he said as was customary to say on the two-way radio.

"You have a dead person," the medic said to him. He said it almost cheerfully, as if notifying someone that a son had been born to him.

12

England, 1994

This is how they met:

Four years before his trip to the English village, she came to the bureau of the local newspaper where he worked ever since he had been fired from the national newspaper and went up to the wrong floor. In the corridor, whose walls hadn't been whitewashed for years and whose plants were filled with cigarette stubs, she bumped into Amnon while he was holding a cup of coffee that he had taken from the vending machine after hitting its side. He was already skilled in that: two and a half years after his major downfall, he adapted to almost everything. The plastic cup swayed in his hand and some coffee spilled on his clothing; she apologized. A stain spread over the front of his trousers and she took out a moistened baby's towelette from her purse and gave it to him and he tried to remove the stain with it; that's how they met. The arts reporter came out of a nearby room, on whose door hung a poster of a band from some small town whose players were photographed crossing a faded crosswalk the way the Beatles crossed Abbey Road. He looked at both of them for a moment and asked Amnon if that was the way he usually behaved, rubbing himself like that in public places, and if it didn't bother the lady here.

"It doesn't bother me," she replied.

She had an obedient Persian cat who usually didn't run away, but two days ago it disappeared for some reason and hadn't returned. The notice she wanted published with his picture, described its thick grey fur, its green eyes, its dense tail, its intelligence: it comes when its name is called, it runs out to greet her when she arrives home in her car and raises up its glorious tail, and in order to pee it lifts that tail with the coquettish motion of an English lady lifting her tiny finger while holding a teacup.

But he didn't know all that at the time, he didn't know that even here in England he wouldn't see English ladies like that, other than in television period dramas with a lot of girdles and a lot of muslin. In the local pub, when a few old ladies gathered one evening to celebrate a birthday, none of them lifted their tiny fingers, and the period drama that was being shown in the background they watched with only half an eye and didn't complain when someone switched the channel to watch a football match. One even reveled in the handsomeness of the center half, another longingly remembered George Best's hairstyle. "Georgie, Georgie," she said, "where are you Georgie?"

In the building of the local newspaper all of that was still only within the realms of chance; it was still only about her cat that had disappeared and the reward offered to the trustworthy finder.

"Every morning he comes to me in bed and waits for me to stroke him," she said to him next to the vending machine, "and if I'm still asleep, he starts to howl for me to get up." She had been looking for the graphic artist who was dealing with the notice, and while wiping his trousers with a moistened towelette, he wondered if she had said "to me in bed" or "to us," and at the time didn't foresee mornings when that cat, Puma, would come to their bed, and after it their dog would also come running so that it wouldn't be deprived of being petted, and she would calm it with words of endearment as if she was making peace between her sons.

When the arts reporter returned from the toilet, he lingered awhile next to them. He had often wondered how Amnon managed to reconcile his fate in this penal colony an obscure local newspaper whose readers didn't number even one percent of the readers of the national newspaper he had worked on, and for most of them briefly paging through it on the way garbage bin was enough. "I'm stuck here," he would say, "but you know what it's like to be there!" - "there" was the daily national newspaper, the dream of every journalist on a local paper and especially the younger ones. The arts reporter had tried by every means possible to get there, whether by repeated applications to the editor or by connections to close associates of the deputy editor and the night editors, and in desperation also by the aid of all sorts of scoops whose sources he adamantly refused to reveal, if indeed they had a source other than himself.

He said he would also be prepared to wail at her like that every morning next to her bed to be caressed, without thinking twice, because there was no one to caress him now that Shira had left him.

When he drew away from them, she asked him who that was, and Amnon hesitated whether to throw the moistened towelette into the pot plant on his right, a withered philodendron with a small cardboard sign stuck in its soil proclaiming **I am not an ashtray** with three exclamation marks written with a red felt-tipped pen: (at the national newspaper they had well-tended Bonsai trees) and dozens of cigarette butts smoked to the filter were piled up there as well as a few olive pits and two candy wrappings. That's how they met, in that depressing setting time had brought him to and where he had let it bring him to. Four years after that meeting, when he announced his intention of leaving, standing in the house that they rented together, she saw that depressing setting as bad omen, not just an incidental background to their meeting but a view of their future.

In the corridor of the fifth floor, she was amazed that this local newspaper (she only read the personals page (had an arts reporter. What did he have to write about here, the new show at the community center?

She lived in one of the most prosperous settlements in the area, a well-tended co-operative settlement that with time had become a prestigious suburb of a small city, but if she could have, she would have moved to the big city where her and her partner's office was, without a huge garden and trees and three levels she herself had designed for a large and happy family, and that now only one of them was in use. The cat that had disappeared, Puma, enjoyed the quiet: every morning, after receiving its dose of caresses, it would retire from the company of humans and cuddle up into some alcove it found for itself: an empty shoe box, a shopping bag left on the floor, a briefcase not returned to its place, an open chest drawer. It would get up onto the windowsill in her eldest son's room and wait for him to return from school and was once found inside the clothes cupboard of the little one, lying on the shelf of folded sweaters like the princess on her seven mattresses.

The cat vanished two days before she came to the local newspaper building where Amnon directed her to the personals floor, and when they went out of the corridor into the stairwell and its smells – cigarette smoke and the stench of urine and pest control spray, smells that never existed in the building of the national newspaper – he changed his mind and offered to accompany her. He heard his voice with surprise; for a very long time he hadn't addressed a woman that way; the timing was odd being after a sleepless night and not one of debauchery. He had been unable to fall asleep as happened every year on that date. "Anniversary night," he called it to himself, and usually didn't tend to talk to anyone the morning after, and least of all to flirt with women. The smell he gave off in the morning wasn't from cigarettes or urine or pest control spray; it was the smell of death, despite that no one smelt it but himself.

Anyway, he said to her, he had to fetch some article of his from the proof reader, and hoped she wouldn't ask what the article was about; two hours before her coming he – who before the age of thirty had made a name for himself with some global investigations – had completed a brief article about the oversights of the local water company and the outrageous accounts it sent the residents (the biblical paraphrase he chose for a headline "Therefore with joy shall ye draw money" like the dull subject matter, was accepted without objection).

In the dimness of the stairwell, with a hint of the pleasing scent of her perfume, she asked him whether he's been here a long time.

"Too long," he replied.

She looked at him and waited for an explanation, and it seemed that she too was in no hurry to return to her activities: not urgent work, not some errand, not anyone who's waiting for her (at the time, her son was in a flying model aircraft class).

To her question he answered that's this job at this local paper is what he has for the moment and knows that moment had gone on for a very long time and that maybe it's better not to try and foresee how much longer it will last.

"And what about you?" he asked on the landing between the floors. "Have you been here long?"

The last time he approached a woman, one hot and humid evening in Tel Aviv, he was surprised when the response was positive, but he'd rather wipe that from his memory, starting with the small café to the waitress's small ground floor apartment where he was awoken the next morning by the noise of the garbage truck right on the other side of the wall. The window was open and didn't even have a curtain, and the white-hot light that burst in was unkind to both of them, as well as to the deed that had been done in the night.

She replied that she had been in the building for ten minutes, which is to say nine minutes too many, and she's already stopped counting how long she's lived in the area. To tell the truth, she said, sometimes she's a little jealous of her cat Puma who can simply pick up its feet and disappear.

"Puma, Puma," she suddenly said in a different voice, soft and gentle, "have you claimed your independence?" She glanced at the picture she had prepared for the notice, in which the cat could be seen in all its glory: with its brushed grey fur, its thick lifted tail, its slanted eyes, and its whiskers (only its wailing wasn't preserved there, and which he would hear for the coming three and a half years, until his leaving). For a moment, the fear arose in her that perhaps the hairs of its whiskers might not be visible on the paper used for the newspaper, but the cat's appearance was so special that she had no doubt it would be identified, if only that deserter, that traitor would be so kind as to return home. As if the idea of disappearing had never crossed her own mind. But she can't disappear, she works.

"If you also vanish," he said to her, "maybe they'll make a notice about you." And perhaps he had said "we'll make," he doesn't remember anymore exactly what he said there on the dirty landing in the stairwell. He could still feel his sleepless night throughout his entire body he: in the heaviness of his limbs, his headache, his weary eyelids, in the discomfort he sensed in his chest; the promenade with all its hotels whose walls were punched with holes from shrapnel, and farther on from it was the sea with all the fish floating on its surface, and only the boy Ali could no longer be seen.

In the dimness of the stairwell, she returned his gaze, still holding the small box of moistened towelettes in her hand when she quietly asked what he for instance would have written on a notice if she really had picked up her feet and fled; after all he's a journalist, it would be nothing for him to word something like that. Yes, it was absurd: a man and a woman standing in a filthy stairwell wording a disappearance notice, but that's exactly what happened on a cloudy day at the end of May on the stairs of the local newspaper, in the midst of smells of cigarette smoke and urine and pest control spray. It even seemed more ridiculous now, from the English house, because the one who sought to disappear and had already taken the first step to that end, turned out to be him himself.

The cavity of the stairwell amplified her voice slightly as she spoke, and somewhere below them, on the second or third floor, a door was opened and creaked. "Chaimon!" someone very irritable shouted from inside. "Chaimon, if you don't come back in an hour, I swear it'll be the end of you!" Afterward a door was slammed, and steps could be heard descending the staircase and leaving, and the stairwell became silent.

Leaning against the wall, he began to word the notice in complete seriousness, the way he did with the trifles he published in the newspaper. There was just a little light in the stairwell, and every once in a while, he needed to confirm an unclear detail of her appearance, and apart from that he almost wrote without hesitation; he was so full of confidence at the time, a flirt, as if everything he had tried in vain to blur with alcohol the night before had been completely erased. "A woman in her thirties," he said, "of medium height and build, last seen between the fifth and sixth floors of an office building in a commercial center. Her hair brown, her forehead high. Her eyes" – he deliberated – "brown, her lips" – again he delayed – "fleshy." It was absurd, yes, but that's exactly what happened; from a notice about a cat, they were bound to each other for four whole years, and it often seemed it would last forever.

"Are my lips fleshy?" The description surprised her a bit; for a moment she pursed them as if their thickness would be reduced that way.

"Anyway, they're not thin," he replied, and again a door was opened on one of the lower floors; someone was emptying something out over the railing, perhaps an ashtray (on the floor of the parking lot, hundreds of butts had piled up, and the arts reporter said after a weekend in Rome that it was their Fontana di Trevi, only instead of lira they throw Marlboro and Time[8]).

She asked Amnon to continue, and in the dimness of the stairwell he continued. He, who for a very long time hadn't flirted with a woman – with that waitress almost no talking was required – mentioned the color of her blouse (black), but didn't mention how well it suited her figure, he also didn't mention the scar on her forehead, because she might be embarrassed by it; he mentioned the slacks she was wearing (jeans), but not the fullness of her thighs. He mentioned the color of her sandals (light brown) and their smallness (from the night he had passed in Tel Aviv, he could still remember the waitress's shoes that had fallen and were overturned by the side of the bed, the squashed fruit of a Ficus tree had stuck to the soles of one of them, and the boxer shorts he saw in the corner of the room, and then disgust mounted in him as it had the only time in his life he had paid a woman, in Hamburg, in the St. Pauli quarter, when he was still a young man and not travelling on a mission from the newspaper).

"A reward will be given to the trustworthy finder," he completed the notice he

---

8 A popular Israeli cigarette brand.

and was very pleased with himself, as if until a few years ago he hadn't been occupied with mysteries many times larger which required ongoing investigations and trips and flights and thousand-word articles.

A door opened on the fifth floor, and the female proofreader came out into the stairwell, and from a distance he saw the headline upside down, **Therefore with joy shall ye draw money**, as well as the secondary headline that the editor had added, **from the pockets of residents**. The editor was fond of wordplay (his former editor preferred quoting high level sources he heard in private conversations), and he then reconciled himself to his style and no longer tried to protest; all his protests, small and large, came to an end when he moved here.

"No more mistakes?" he asked the proofreader.

Through angular spectacles with curly ornamentation on the bridge of the nose, the proofreader scrutinized them both and asked about the money reward they had mentioned, because she likes rewards a lot and the salary here is nothing special, so just tell what she has to look for.

"The lady's cat," Amnon replied; only then did he notice that he didn't know her name.

Afterward they sat in a café in the square in front of the local newspaper building, far enough from the fast-food restaurant where the reporters used to eat lunch ("Shawarma Empire under David's Management – Free Salad"). It was noontime, and the softening sunlight only slightly improved the neglected square and its shops: here and there the colors in the dusty display windows were refined, but a few shadows became extremely elongated, making the disfigured paving stones of the square seem even more sunken, and the weeds that grew between them taller. The owner of the café served them, and when she returned to the counter, the cat owner asked him what he had done with his life before devoting it to local water company fraud – that can't be what's he's done all his life? He didn't come across as someone like that, she said (she hadn't read his articles; she'd never heard his name). For a moment he was flattered by her words and immediately thought: what difference does it make what I did, I'm here now.

At the time it seemed to him that she distinguished him from the dreariness that surrounded them (other things could also be seen in the twilight: spider webs quivered in the corners of the ceiling, a gecko lay in waiting in another corner, and on the sign opposite them, "Levi Properties," someone had written with a red felt tipped marker *Levi Robberies*), and he sipped the coffee and heard himself say that he had done all sorts of things with his life but avoided going into detail, as if in his past there hadn't only been some successful articles that had engaged his readers for a while, but all sorts of mysterious activities whose time hadn't yet come to air.

"It sounds intriguing." she said and continued to drink her tea in small, measured sips; perhaps all that while she had been thinking of her lost cat.

"And now I'm here," he said, "our reporter on drainage matters."

"Drainage is important," she said, "very important. What would we do without it?"

The arts reporter passed them by again with a dripping portion of shawarma in his hand, and he nimbly drew it away from his clothing before he took a large bite into the pita bread and closed his eyes for a moment and examined the taste like a wine taster deciphering the year of its harvest. He then half opened them and tilted his head slightly as if to concentrate better. "Well, it's not cat meat," he said and continued to chew even as he spoke, "definitely not grey Persian. Can I join you?"

"We're just leaving," she answered. "Bon appétit."

But they didn't leave, they stayed there. The owner asked if they didn't want any cake; today's came out really well, cheesecake, it hadn't sunk like the time before. The arts reporter walked off, but his statement about the cat remained after him, and her face saddened. Her biggest fear, she said, was that the cat had been run over, and that horrific scene passed through her mind the whole of the last two days: how she'd be walking in the street or driving and would suddenly see Puma spread on the road, his grey fur run over and his insides spilled out, and more and more cars passing over what remained of him.

She again praised his temperament: his smartness, his patience; how Puma, could cuddle up in any place, how in summer he sprawls out on his back with his legs apart into order to cool his body on the floor, how he lets her young son, Udi, do anything with him he likes, without complaint. She mentioned children for the first time; perhaps in that way trying to find out if Amnon, also had children.

Since he didn't know how she'd react to his ongoing bachelorhood, he preferred to speak about his childhood and about the dog he had had then, a shaggy mongrel after whose death he didn't want any other pet: not a dog, not a hamster, not a budgie, nothing that would one day die. He decided then it was better not to become attached to anything that in the end will cause sorrow, whether from death or from parting (the tears he wept over that dog he hasn't wept since, not when his mother left home, not even when she died in Ichilov Hospital on a wintery Saturday night, and not even over the death he could have prevented and hadn't prevented in Lebanon).

"For an entire month she lay dying," he said about the dog four decades after it was buried in the orchard next to their home, as if it was the worst death he had ever witnessed in his life. "At the time I didn't know at all yet what death was."

She sipped her tea and looked at him. For a long time no woman had looked at him that way; he must have seemed to her like an overgrown baby, and perhaps it was the contrast between his occupation with its glamorous image and that childishness that aroused her curiosity.

"And you've lived alone ever since?" she asked and already understood something about him.

That's how they met.

After two or three days the cat was found: someone saw it in a treetop, it had
apparently fled there from a dog; a long ladder was brought from her neighbor's
house, and on their way down the cat managed to scratch his face. After the scratch
had healed – she had gently applied iodine to it in her bathroom – it seemed that
at their age, no longer young, they had suddenly found comfort in each other
thanks to a grey Persian treetop loving cat. She came to him in place of women he
happened upon whose names he forgot after a week or a month, and he came to
her in place of a loving husband, a senior in a high-tech company, well-liked by his
colleagues and those under him and devoted to her to the point of dreariness ("I
could already tell how it'll be when we're in an old aged home," she said about him),
but time passed: the days, the weeks, the months. At first they were content with
her weekly visit to him, it was enough: the hiding, the stolen hours, their refraining from being seen together, the caution they took with telephone calls until the
divorce came through; there was excitement in all that. "I could have worked for
the Mossad," she once said about the secret life she lived throughout that period,
and he deliberated whether to tell her what his investigations had uncovered in the
years he worked for the daily newspaper: how unglamorous that organization was
when examined beyond its aura, how flimsy that aura was (he well remembered
what an ex-senior official had said to him about living under an assumed identity
while neglecting his real family, about the twisted excitement of danger, and how
the state was considered above all, just like with the darkest regimes).

   In the middle of winter their adventure began to lose its luster, the excitement
had become blunted. At their age, it shouldn't have come as a surprise, but nonetheless, when faced with each other's weaknesses, they seemed to them like terrible
defects which had been hidden deceitfully and which shouldn't be glossed over,
until they were they find their right place in the entire composite whose outlines
hadn't changed, the composite that was a loved person: far from perfection and
sometimes insufferable, but still loved in all his defects. More love was required for
that, and it seemed they were advancing another step on the path whose continuation seemed certain. But afterward, from week to week and from month to month,
that too passed.

   "Do you think you can keep me up in the air like that?" she said to him, She
wouldn't agree to meeting him just once a week, she wanted to know there was
someone waiting for her every day and every night, and don't tell her that he's a
lone wolf - a lone wolf's mattress doesn't look like his.

   When she tried to arouse his jealousy with compliments she received on the
train or from drivers at traffic lights ("Are you selling? Men asked about her Fiat
only in order to hear her voice) or from her clients ("You've made such a beautiful home for us, it's a pity I'm already married"), but he showed no signs of jealousy. Feeling   insulted she'd ask: how come he doesn't become angry, how come
he never compliments her, how come he's not summoned into action in order to
protect their love? She liked the way she looked and took good care of herself, she

also enjoyed her work and derived great satisfaction from it, and her little son brought a glow to her face every time he embraced her, and her cat was also bound to her as if she had given birth to it, and for all these reasons she was, for the most, calm and very much at ease; it was only Amnon who managed to disrupt her serenity with his repeated refusal to be jealous, to talk about the future, to show he wasn't indifferent.

"You don't really want me," she said to him at the beginning of the summer, "deep inside that's what I feel. God, why did I fight for you? I could have had a dozen like you long ago."

"I don't doubt that," he replied, making her even angrier.

During the Monday and Thursday phone calls, all the trivia he collected here sounded of no importance to her, and all his answers more ridiculous than those of an adolescent. "How pathetic," she remarked about the journey he intends to undertake, as if he was soldier just out of the army and not a man over forty, a wiped-out journalist who instead of trying to fight for his future, picks up and leaves.

She still hadn't completely given up on him, perhaps more than anything it was important to prove to herself that she has the power to change him until he becomes worthy of the price she paid for him; she left her home on the moshav for him and separated her children from their friends, and in the eyes of her elder son, that action doubled her guilt: not only had she banished her son's father to a small apartment in the city, but she had also given up the house, and for whom, for a man who in no aspect was superior to his own father; and what's worse, by that deed she had also given up on her eldest son as well, and that was something he couldn't understand: after all, she's his mother, how could she have forgotten him like that for this man, Amnon? He could have identified with the elder son – he also still has anger towards his mother, despite that she's already dead – but didn't.

He still remembers her telephone conversations with her children during the first weeks, when she'd check that they had returned safely from school, that they found the meals she had prepared for them; that they know how long to put them in the microwave. All those questions she used to ask while naked and still sweaty, but totally practical from her mussed hair to the soles of her bare feet; standing in the passage – not in the bedroom – and explaining to her elder son how to warm up frozen pizza for him and his brother or the spaghetti that she had prepared for them with chicken wings in teriyaki sauce. Above, her face was attentive to the earpiece that was almost all swallowed by her hair, and below, her nakedness was moist and still imprinted with the wrinkles of the sheet. He was continually amazed how quickly she managed to move from one world to another.

For a moment her curves flicker in front of him, even though her age and her births are evident in them. Her face has remained beautiful and her smile hasn't yet furrowed the skin at the sides of her mouth. Without difficulty he could see those curves arching over the sheets in the meager light coming through the slats of the shutters or sparkling opposite him like when she used to shower in the bathtub with him; that's how they washed themselves in the apartment in Tel Aviv, standing in the bathtub: the showerhead barely drizzled, the hot water ran out too fast, the bottom of the basin was sullied from the dripping tap, and with every visit the small cupboard above the basin filled up with more and more of her toiletries, and in the house they rented her small son's toothbrush was added and with it children's toothpaste, striped in red and white and tasty as candy.

After knowing him for four years it's hard for her to imagine him crossing long distances like those he crossed in his youth or in the years he worked for the national newspaper; it's hard for her to imagine him buying an airline or train ticket, renting rooms in a hotel, finding his way through foreign cities between millions of people, trying to express himself in their language, inquiring, bargaining, insisting (her work requires her to contend daily with hard-nosed engineers, dissenting municipality officials, vengeful neighbors, husbands who want things this way and their wives who want them another way, house renovators who can never be completely relied upon; even the one she brought from Sakhnin[9] and had been so enthusiastic about, had begun to be neglectful, and because he's an Arab she couldn't get annoyed with him; once again it turned out that her judgement had been faulty).

She also tells him about her children so that he won't forget them, despite that they aren't his and that he only really knows the little one. When she and him first became acquainted, when they learned about each other mainly through what their bodies taught them, she would play him the messages the children left her so that he'd get used to their voices, and also described them to him; the elder is independent and defiant, hard on himself and on others, the little one is soft and pampered, a compromiser, a quarrel stopper, a teacher's pet. She breastfed him until the age of three, and in the bedroom, there were moments you could sense the movement with which she offered her breast to a longing mouth, smaller than his own, a blind mouth who knew her body in all its hidden depths.

Since he remains silent and the silence lengthens – outside the crickets' chirping in the fields can be heard, and inside the earpiece there's a sound of a distant police car siren or an ambulance– she becomes angry again. Had it at least been a work trip, she says, but that's not why he went. Why did he go? Because he was sick of his small family, his daily routine, his country that he had twice fought for and twice had failed, and those two failures still trail behind him. He was a great fool at the time, like his grandfather during the time when he thought he would be part of the great deeds that would change the face of history – history has a face of stone, on which everything has been engraved, from good to bad, and each feature is engraved in blood.

---

9   A large Arab town in northern Israel.

He didn't even ask her – she says – he simply faced her with a fact, and of all places in the kitchen: the cat lay on the marble counter to cool its body, far enough from the electric kettle, and withered lettuce leaves that she had left for the rabbits lay on the windowsill. He took them outside because he preferred to be in the enclosure: he wouldn't hear any criticism from the rabbits about how he's wasting his life.

When she saw him from the window bending over a new burrow that the rabbit had dug – a man in the fifth decade of his life, in tatty jeans and a sweaty shirt, who in his time knew how to get Scotland Yard detectives to talk about matters of security and Argentinian businessmen about matters of espionage and Russian stage actors about the matter of a murdered prime minister, and now his relationship with animals was better than his relationship with people – she said: "She's got sense, she'll do everything to escape from the enclosure," and he replied: "But she can't cross an ocean." Only at a late-night hour she asked him what he meant exactly.

They went through a bad summer, there wasn't a defect they didn't find in each other during its languid, dreary course, there almost wasn't anything that they didn't argue about, from what television programs to watch to the degree that fans or air conditions should be turned on and the frequency of watering the garden.

"Answer me," she said, "tell me what you meant."

After he explained, she moved to the edge of the bed, and when he tried to lay his hand on her she shook it off with a movement of the shoulder. In the dark, the rattling of the fan could be heard again. Each time it reached the end of its path something grated there, and through that sound and the sound of her silence facing the wall, for a moment you could hear, as if by some kind of sorcery, the crashing of one of her plants that fell from the hands of one of the workers when she moved here and the crying of her son separated from his older brother and all his friends; and also the silence of both their isolated years in this community where no one had made use of her talents, and you could also hear all the other men she could have lived with and who could have promised her and her sons a solid future, a real family, a home.

In the morning they didn't speak to each other, and her small son, groggy from sleep as with every morning, didn't notice anything. He dream was interrupted just as he was awoken: in it the rabbit had escaped from its enclosure and Albie was chasing after it like crazy through the yard, until the rabbit climbed to the top of the jacaranda tree like a cat, and a ladder has to be brought to take it down.

"You'll miss the bus!!" she shouted at the boy; that dream reminded her too much of the circumstances of their meeting.

13

Petersburg, 1904

From the darkness of the small street, Poliakov's hand reached out towards the curtain. With the tip of the barrel he touched the lace and moved the curtain to the right with its white perforated peacocks and imagined hearing a soft rhythmic snoring coming from the warm dimness of the room.

The breath was so soft it seemed for a moment there was no one in the room: that somehow Levin had deceived them again, or perhaps the lookouts had been mistaken; or he had been too hasty to execute a plan that was not yet ripe; things sometimes had gone that way and ended in failure. And why was he hasty now? There was more than one answer to that.

The dark inside was thick and didn't lighten even when he bent farther over the windowsill and heard the rhythmic calm breathing of a man. In his room Levin breathed as much as he liked, with serenity and with complacency, he also inhaled the scent of the man watching him, a scent that would disappear in the end the way his other marks of identity disappeared: his name, his beard, his sidelocks, his name that went from Ilya to Sergei, his beard that was replaced by a smooth chin and smooth cheeks, and his shorn sidelocks that sometimes his fingers still rose up to curl. Perhaps Levin's hand rises like that, and if wakes up and doesn't struggle – if the pistol is pointed in time – perhaps he'll open his mouth and pray to the same god that they both deserted.

From the windowsill, he looked at the bed as if the outline and facial features of the sleeping body would explain how a man could be sound asleep with a baby-like serenity after the deeds he had done, all of them many times worse that those he himself had perpetrated the past month. What preceded the past month is best forgotten, and sometimes he even succeeded in doing that until night falls (the night was a world unto itself with its own laws; the moment his eyelids were shut the space around him was replaced by a different space; the small room was replaced by a house not in a city but in the country, and the darkness of the Petersburg sky was replaced by a clear spring day in the village, and the silence was filled with the voices of the cheering masses and the rattling of their weapons: pitchforks sledgehammers, axes, shepherds' goads, and his mother was next to him, breathing heavily, and his father was laid down in the yard with his chest exposed, and it wasn't possible to see whether the chest rose and fell).

You know something, Levin, he said to him silently, not only did I make my beard and sidelocks disappear, I made an entire house and village and river and forest disappear. I made my father and my mother disappear and my little brother and also a woman who loved me. Shlomo and Hannah and Izu and Miriam; I made them all disappear, so what's that in comparison to making a smell disappear? The smell of his breath rose to his nose, the stench of a rotting tooth, he felt its stabbing as the rot made its way: inward to the tooth and the space of the skull or outward to the mouth and the space of the world.

Only a blurred silhouette could be made out inside the dark rectangle of the bed, and despite that he still hadn't moved from the spot where he stood, it seemed to Poliakov that instead of getting rid of each other he and the sleeping man are actually becoming closer to each other, and not only on the strength of the deeds that each in his time had done without knowing the existence of the other – as if they had been competing who could be the more despicable – but also on the strength of the deed that will bind them together in a short while with one bullet.

The thought rose and faded and his head became empty, and again there was the aggravating pain in one of the molars on the left side of his mouth: something or someone was drilling into the lower jaw and from the jaw into the skull, and he cursed silently and right away looked to his right and to his left to make sure no one had heard him, and there was no one there: the children he had sent away still hadn't returned. Perhaps they were still trying to fulfill the task he set for them, or perhaps they had already found something else to occupy themselves with.

In the dark yard, enveloped by the stench of urine he almost stopped sensing, neither the light of the oil lamp from the first window nor the light of the streetlamp around the corner reached him. He had spared it and had instructed the hoodlums not to smash it, despite them being eager to do so ("He can take it out in a second," they proudly said of their sharpshooter). They had no doubts as to their power, as if their weapons weren't stones but rather this pistol, this heavy sweaty Browning whose butt was so comfortable to grasp.

Between the eyes, he thought, but knew he it wouldn't be done that way.

Are you comfortable? He silently asked the sleeping man from the window. Is your mattress soft enough? Is the pillow soft? Even the Tsar doesn't sleep that well. He then thought, what if he has a cat and it starts howling and wakes him. He hasn't got a dog, a dog would have barked long ago, but what if he has a cat; Duchin mentioned he liked talking about cats.

Levin and his audience were fond of the story about the shop and the cat that sat in its entrance no less than the story about the Tsar's assassination ("He knows how hold an audience," the trusted worker from the Politov plant told Duchin):

how from the back of the shop a long tunnel had been dug to the middle of the road in order to plant a mine and detonate it when the imperial carriage passes, and how earth was removed from it night after night in empty barrels; and how the diggers were almost caught when a sanitation committee headed by a general paid a visit, and how they were all saved by Vaska the cat - the general had in fact turned up his nose at the smell of the whey, but because he liked cats and the cat rubbed against his leg, he bent down to stroke it and forwent continuing the investigation.

That story would usually raise a smile on the faces of Levin's audience and even get laughs, but right away Levin would become serious and move on to one of the prison stories, and who wasn't impressed by them. Poliakov had also been impressed on hearing them from Volodya and Maximov, and how different they were from all the stories told about the righteous in Bykhov and in Khalitsa and in Minsk, and about all sorts of well-known people of dubious repute whose miracles were mere trickery whose goal was the dropping of coins into their pockets: how in a small dark cell in Petropavlovsk Fortress, the man who invented bombs made drawings demonstrating how to build a flying machine, and not for himself to escape in, but so that his successors would be able to cast bombs onto the Winter Palace from it; and in another cell, someone passed the time left until his hanging by drawing a map of Russia on the wall: the borders were outlined by the soot of the oil lamp, the rivers and lakes were colored in blue paint that he scraped from the door of his cell, and the ground – the entire ground of that vast land – was painted in the blood that he let from his body which turned brown when dry; it had previously been red, unlike the blood of their masters, blood that one day will be let onto the walls of the palaces.

But now Levin said nothing, he slept. His chest rose and fell in the darkness, and his eyelids remained shut.

To another audience Levin didn't speak of revolutionaries and their bravery, but about the one whose throne they sought to overthrow, Tsar Alexander (they were well known stories that existed in various versions): how on the day of the assassination his ministers tried to persuade him not attend the parade inspection at the artillery school, but he refused; and how on the that very day he intended to inform his close associates that he had decided to grant all his subjects a constitution; and how he awoke early in the morning and went for a walk in the palace garden with his children, because in the whole of Russia there was no better father (so Levin told his audience, while Maximov in the safe house said: "The biggest bastards can be angels to their families"); and how he went to pray in the church as on every morning, because he never forgot whose subject he was; and how he returned to his study in the palace in order to sign documents there, among them the draft of the constitution he intended to bestow upon his nation - "For you," Levin said to his audience, "for each and every one of you!"

Once again they tried to persuade the Tsar not to attend the parade inspection, and again he refused. "I will not shut myself up in the palace," he said, "my nation is not in the palace," (about that Duchin said: "The stupidity of the house of Romanov alone will bring us victory") and they pleaded with him to at least change his travel route, but none of that did any good. The Tsar, it's well known, insisted on taking a guard of a dozen Cossack horsemen with him, who didn't prevent the assassination. Levin related all those details to his other audience but kept silent in fitting places to deepen their attentiveness and to sip some water from a glass. He told how the Tsar had insisted on returning to the crater created by the first bombing, and how a student dressed in a light overcoat and carrying a satchel stood opposite him, and how the satchel was opened and from it a bomb was taken out and thrown at the Tsar. "In cold blood," said Levin, "just like throwing a stone at someone" ("Courageously, without blinking," Vladimir said in the safe house when they were not discussing their plan but rather the one that preceded it by a quarter of a century).

Dozens of people were injured in the explosion, and the Tsar, despite being critically injured, didn't ask to be given precedence over the others. He spoke softly to those surrounding him, his voice almost inaudible, but resolute as always. "If I am sentenced to die," he said, "I shall die in my bed" ("That's what was written in the newspaper," Maximov said, "but he probably swore like a muzhik").

On your bed, Levin, Poliakov said to him from the other side of the window, on your bed.

Another piece of glass shattered beneath his shoe, and in the other window the old woman was still moving the iron backward and forward, but he wouldn't be needing an iron: not to hit him with, not to press to Levin's face or stomach. One small bullet will be enough with the easy movement his finger will make on the trigger, one movement: backward. The previous night the thought amazed him how that movement sends a few grams of lead into space, and had it not been for their speed they would be worthless, and that's what will stick them into Levin's chest or his temple, thereby halting all the systems that activate the body, the way a grain of sand inserts itself into the complex mechanism of a clock. That's what he thought about the previous night in his room opposite his window through which he could have easily thrown his pistol, had he decided to get rid of it; and also thought about it in his bed when he lay the pistol on the pillow like an ornament on velvet (the way jewelry was displayed in Nevsky Prospekt); and later too, when he slipped it beneath the pillow, and felt the cylinder through it like a swollen belly pregnant with death and more death and more death and more death and more death and more death.

He took the pistol out from there and pointed it at the ceiling, at one of the damp stains; and to the one next to it; and the one after it. And then he aimed it at the window facing the street and switched to the length of the wall and from it to the wall opposite his bed and from there to the wall next to it, until he completed a half circle and returned to aim at his bed and at the pillow and at his head and felt the chill of the metal drilling into his temple. A thought then passed through him that if he were to shoot – if he were to press the trigger with that easy movement – his amputee neighbor will probably pound on the wall with his fist; after all, that's what he did every time a noise irritated him. If after a day or two a stench rose from his body, whose limbs are all intact but whose chest is empty, he will most probably be rolled up with the mattress and thrown into the street the way garbage or broken furniture is disposed of.

The barrel was still aimed at his temple, until he detached it from there, and lying on his back as before, he peered into the dimness of the barrel and tried to see some spark there, the glint of the tip of the bullet or the blazing of the eye of what lurked there like at the bottom of a well.

I see you're having sweet dreams, Levin, he said silently from outside the window – it was slightly open and the fold of the curtain billowed toward the street – he was envious of the sleep he was enjoying.

Sweet dreams, he said softly, begrudgingly, because they were the opposite of his. All the black coffins could be seen clearly in his dreams, the entire convoy floating on the water: he didn't see them on the platform of the gallows, arranged at the back with their lids open waiting for the sentenced men, but rather on the river of his village, floating with their dead down the Berezina instead of trunk rafts, and crows stand on them and their beaks peck and make holes in them all the way to the rapids, and at the same time he hears the knocking from the bank and from inside.

In the dark, a step away from the window, it suddenly seems to him that he senses the smell of Levin's breath in the night air, a sourish heavy and nauseating smell of food that hadn't been washed down and digested, and through it, too sharp to bear, was the smell of a rotting tooth like the one in his mouth: the rot had found itself a hold in a hole there, a breach through which to infiltrate into the body and fill it, or a way out from inside the body. There was more than enough rot in there.

In the dark left by the shattered streetlamp, he swallowed his saliva and felt it go down his throat, but right away it returned to his mouth and he spat out a thick globule into the darkness where his spit was swallowed and turned black. Had his illness been different, he thought, one that destroys the lungs – tuberculosis for example, what's wrong with tuberculosis – perhaps he would have put Levin to death like that: by spitting. But it wasn't the lungs inside him that were ill it was the soul.

14

Six-year-old Amy Robbins said: "It was a brilliant performance of Hansel and Gretel," while Anabel Blatcher, six and a half, had her doubts: "All in all, it was a glorious show, I'm not saying it wasn't, but there were moments that were terribly frightening!" Jeffrey Blair, five, took an interest in the pieces of candy that Hansel and Gretel strew on their way to the forest and asked who got them at the end of the show. Even in the pub there were some copies of the Church leaflet, and the show put on by the pupils of the William Fletcher School was mentioned in it, and a few of the youngsters who had seen it were quoted like veteran theater critics.

Not even one word was written about the man Amnon had come to meet (he travelled to England solely for that reason; for his future journeys he would have other reasons).

The first inquiry into the matter was made by his father during the years of the Second World War on one of the days of calm, when he served in the Jewish Brigade. With the help of the battalion adjutant, a lieutenant of Indian extraction who had connections with the division headquarters, he inquired where the possessions that his father left behind had been sent from, and that's how he discovered who the doctor was who sent them: from the Moravian Mission Hospital in Leh to Kashgar, and from Kashgar to Petersburg, and from there to Minsk, and from Minsk through Odessa to Palestine. Through his connections the adjutant managed to find out that this doctor had family relatives and even obtained the address of McKenzie Jr. who had been sent to school in England, For a while it seemed that from this address in an English village whose name his father had never heard of, he would find the answer to every question.

In the year of 1943, the Jewish Brigade was in Egypt and hadn't yet participated in any battle, but Nachman, though he wanted very much to fight and for that purpose had left his studies at the university, didn't only have the Germans in mind but also the very act of enlisting in a great struggle worthy to sacrifice one's life for – hadn't his father done so before he disappeared? – and no less than he was interested in the Nile and the pyramids or Field Marshall Rommel, he was interested in the Ganges and the Indus and the Brahmaputra. A thin bespecta-

cled Jewish man older than all his companions in the company, he cultivated his
connections with the adjutancy for the sake of his own private war, where the one
who had been cruel to him had also been the object of his yearning from childhood. From roll call to roll call, he not only thought about the world war taking
place on three continents, but also about his own old war that he renewed after
all the years his intellect had been dedicated to his studies, a war whose single
possible victory would be finding an answer to the question why his father had
travelled to where he had travelled and why he had abandoned his mother and
him. Instead of the pyramids and the sphinxes perhaps he might have preferred
a meager shrine without any sarcophagi coated in gold but a small grey urn, and
instead of the harbor neighborhood of Alexandria with all its brothels and bead
curtains rustling in their entrances – a sun drenched pier in the Bombay harbor
where dozens of porters compete with each other for the luggage of those arriving, or a railway platform covered in sand, the one at the end of the Trans-Caspian
line. While the Egyptian sun beat down on his head perhaps he was thinking about
Indian monsoons that he didn't exactly know about and was mistaken in thinking
their showers brought relief.

Instead of Bombay, his battalion was sent to Italy, and at the end of a battle
between two hills of no importance something changed in him. Under the ruptured
ceiling of a farmhouse that had been turned into a hospital where the shouts of its
injured were carried straight to heaven, for a while he stopped thinking about the
time before his birth and about the man who had fathered him, and until the end
of the war his dream of crossing continents was replaced by the simple desire to
live, and when in Rome he wanted to be pleasured by the woman whose pictures
Rosenstein had carried in his belt.

Amnon can't remember why he told him that,. Perhaps he sought to warn
him about adventures with dubious women, for instance with a mother of two
who preferred her own good to that of her children, in that she had left their father
for him. With the same recklessness – his father was trying to hint to him, despite
for years having refrained from giving him advice – she was liable one day to also
leave him and go off with another man. Apparently that was the purpose of his
words that Friday, when he told him what he had got up to in Rome, and at the
time didn't say a word about his wife Ada who had turned her back on him ten
years before that. He left no trace of her in the apartment and even refused to utter
her name until she was hospitalized in Ichilov and could no longer turn her back,
or swallow, or open her eyes, or breathe.

In the end, it was Amnon who left. Before the trip he feared the McKenzie he
was looking might have already died (and if so, would he return? No-no), but in
the small cemetery north of the estate he found no tombstone with his name on it,
and in the local post office they told him it was too cold for McKenzie Jr. here in
winter: after all, he wasn't born here. The father had travelled across half the world,

and the son, in his old age, seemed to be sick of veterinary medicine and suddenly suffered an attack of travel fever, as if the angel of death doesn't reach everywhere.

At first, he didn't intend to talk to strangers about his mission – he wasn't even sure how he would broach the subject with McKenzie Jr. – but he nevertheless inquired about where he had gone off to, and even hazarded a guess. His guess surprised them. "What's he got to look for there?" the post office clerk answered him. "It's the last place on earth he would travel to, after all, his whole life long he's cursed his father for having had him there." The clerk's amazement was such that right away he shared it with those waiting in line. "We've got enough Indians here, haven't we Mrs. Irons?"

The old lady replied that actually in their village the situation was relatively okay, but in London it's shocking, everywhere you look you see Indians, Pakistanis, Chinese and what not, all colors and all types, and because of that she no longer likes travelling to London to visit her daughter.

The clerk asked after Rosie who he remembers as the little girl who barely reached his counter and would stand on the tips of her toes to ask for a stamp. Her manners showed everyone what a good upbringing she had received at home.

The queue advanced slowly and it seemed that everyone was taking an interest in Amnon: what was his connection with McKenzie Jr.? Maybe he had reached his own country on all those journeys of his. That was their way of asking delicately where he came from, but he had no desire to reveal that here, not where he lived there, not his occupation or any other detail, small or large, about his previous life; the same crazy desire for a new identity resurfaced. How juvenile it was, how irresponsible, how impossible; and still, the less they knew about him here, the better. It would have been better had he known as little about himself as they did, but he had already learned many things about himself which would be impossible for him to forget. What if the facts he found out about his grandfather turned out to be something he'd rather not have known about? Find out first, he thought, and only then you'll know if you made a mistake.

All in all the son's a completely different story from his father, they said in the pub. He always seemed a very responsible person, that is until he went on pension. What was his greatest adventure? Besides being sent from India to England as a child – and quite rightly so, to avoid the mudslinging his father was subjected to – was flying to Turkey with a herd of cows. The filth of the cows was preferable to the mess his father had got himself into.

McKenzie Jr. flew the forty cows that the farmers Bill Baker and Noel White had sold to some Turks. Is there anyone here who doesn't remember the great Bill Baker? I mean, of the older folk. Over giant glasses of Guinness the told how before Bill Baker's and Noel White's cows were loaded, the entire plane was filled with hay because that's what McKenzie Jr. requested. It was a cargo plane, and the cows were lined up for the entire length on both sides like inside a giant cowshed. They were Jersey cows and couldn't care less that they were flying in the air, as long as they had something to chew on. So even though they'd never flown before then, they all felt at home, at least in the beginning, The doctor had travelled a little as a boy, but that was on a ship not an airplane, where would there have been airplanes then? His father had once got into trouble over some business with ships ("Not ships, boats," someone corrected), and then the son got himself into trouble with an airplane. That's how it goes, and some things are better left unknown.

About the things Amnon had got himself into trouble with; it's also better not to elaborate on: even the woman he left behind in his country didn't know anything about them until that Saturday she stayed in his apartment with her small son, and what he had told her then over the phone, she now flings at him mercilessly; in fact isn't that – yes, it's become clear to her – the real essence of him?

Against his will, he recalls it all, and then pushes the entire matter away. Even while it was happening he turned his back and returned to the shore at the foot of the bombed promenade (another bomb fell into the sea and brought masses of fish to the surface) to the uniform he left there with his army boots; the one for whom he had gone into the water could no longer be seen beneath the swarm of dead fish. In the English pub, thousands of kilometers from there and over a decade ago, his eyes seek something to hang on to: one of the speaker's faces, the curves of the waitress's body, the surface of the counter with the prints of glasses, the glint of the beer taps, the row of bottles with their labels. Over these past years he's become an expert in pushing away anything that's liable to darken his spirit (one can develop the skill this requires), but in the last telephone conversations Naomi no longer spares him: she's already sick of the role of the submissive woman waiting for her man, as well as the role of the strong woman who lets him travel until he has pangs of longing. If she doesn't have the power to make him return, she'll at least hurt him as much as possible; after all, she knows his weak spots.

Everyone had already heard the purpose of his coming to their village; rumors here, as in all small places, spread fast. He no longer aroused their curiosity, any more than their curiosity was aroused by the national news which seemed far away from the village and had little to do with it, as if Britain was still an empire and the news is happening far away over the sea, or as if they themselves were living in distant colony whose charm has faded. In the church leaflet (taking a glance at the local press was a habit he maintained from his years as an investigating reporter. He had visited England a few years ago for an investigation he was carrying out at the time) a bazaar opening in a month's time was written about, and afterward a list of funerals appeared:

11 August – Jonathan Kilroy of 23 Spenser Way
14 August – Alan Ernest Hawkins of 42 Martin Way
19 August – Eileen Robins of 29 Jerome Way

(McKenzie wasn't listed there, neither son nor father.)

A story also appeared with a moral that was somehow related to fish, and for a while it seemed fish had been trailing behind him for years, everywhere he went; and if not from childhood, at least from that damned beach whose name and sights and smells are better forgotten. The story was posted in the church leaflet for its lesson and not for the sights it described. The distance from the village to the sea is vast, and only in comparison to the place he intended travelling to would it seem near, because that place in the east is thousands of kilometers away from any beach; but that wasn't the reason he was travelling there, though perhaps it was reason enough.

A young man strolling on the beach at sunset saw an old man lifting starfish from the sand and throwing them back into the sea. When he reached him, he asked him what he was doing.

"Starfish will die if they remain on the beach in the afternoon sun," replied the old man.

"But the beach extends for many miles and there are millions of starfish on it," claimed the young man, "how will your efforts make any difference?"

The old man looked at the starfish that was in his hand and returned it to the sea. "It will make a lot of difference to that starfish," he replied.

And that tale too, with its simplistic moral ("Childish," he would have said were it not for the context), became connected in his mind with that beach and his actions among the fish floating there.

The plane they hired wasn't new – the pub dwellers said – and owing to what it was used for, no one took care of it the way they should have. There cow dung in it was so old, you wouldn't have seen it in even the most ancient cowsheds; the plane was a genuine jalopy, but they only discovered that after it had taken off. Anyone who knows this story shouldn't listen, but there's one person here who seems interested in it. What does it matter why, maybe he also has ideas of moving his herd someplace.

"Have you got a herd?" they asked him and he shook his head.

"Well, maybe one day you will have."

But to where he's going, he'll be travelling alone: without a herd and without a dog and without the one who brought the dog into their home one Friday afternoon and said: "Meet Albie." He'll travel alone to Delhi, and from Delhi to Pathankot by train and from there to Dharamsala or Manali and from there two and half days by bus or Sikh lorry to that place called Leh. He had already found out most of the details: the travel routes, the length of the journeys, the prices, how many months the way was covered by snow and when it began to thaw. In the end, in the mountainous valley of Leh, in the Moravian Mission Hospital or one of the slopes around it – slopes where only the mountain peaks were always covered in snow and whose ground was arid in the summer months, almost desert-like – or in some other place whose existence he isn't aware of, he'll perhaps find traces of his grandfather and perhaps not; and perhaps his own trace will be lost there the way his grandfather's were. There was magic in those two words, "lost trace," despite that a disappearance such as that would be unfeasible in an era when few things remain truly lost. Maybe that was the case in previous eras as well: certainly not everything disappeared, there were lists of the dead, lists of the sick; people who remembered things, people who heard things from their parents or grand-parents. Leh is a small place and must have been even smaller then, besides the Ladakhi it was mainly the British who lived there, and how could a young Russian who landed up there not be engraved in the memory. They didn't know about his Jewishness, but his Russianness was certainly evident from his appearance and from his accent, even if he called himself by a different name. What was he doing there? How did he support himself? Had he severed ties with all his previous contacts and made a home in Leh? Was he riddled with regret? Did McKenzie Sr. know him even before he became a corpse?

Matters such as these did not make the church leaflet. After the large advertise-ment for Parson's Candles (Parson's Candles do not blacken with soot!) he read in an ecological column advising gardeners not to over-garden: Allow the field grass to grow and the ivy as well, thereby providing the insects with cover. Mankind is only a small part of the wondrous wealth of Creation, and should you open a small window in your gardens to the Lord's imagination, you'll never be sorry for it!

Every corner of the garden of the house he rented here is well tended: once a week the gardener comes to look after it and even gathers the apples that have fallen, should he see him in the window he greets him with a nod. If the gardener wonders to what he's doing here, he doesn't express it. With a small wheelbarrow he clears the fallen leaves, the rotting apples, the weeds he's uprooted: he doesn't agree with the advice in the church leaflet; perhaps he's never paged through it.

Did McKenzie Jr. read it? They didn't say a word about that in the pub (instead they said: "In any event, the doctor only knew about ships, and as for Bill Baker and Noel it was the first time they'd ever been on a plane").

Angry, weary, insulted, no longer expecting to being told other things, she said to him: "And that's what you've got to tell me? That nonsense from the pub?"

She was already fed up with those banalities by which he evaded her ques-tions, and one question in particular, one that wasn't asked again, despite that she stills finds is hard to believe all the years she had invested in him were in vain (she had never been defeated in her wars, she once told him: not when fought over men or over professional matters; after all, it's the struggle that gives things meaning).

"Pity you didn't go with them," she said, "maybe they're planning some flight with donkeys?" There's no jocularity in her voice. Her sense of humor is better than that; no other woman knew how to make him laugh like she could, but now she's totally serious. Or maybe a flight with fish? She hadn't forgotten what he had told her about the vast swarm opposite the beach in Sidon and the boy Ali; for that she would have filled the whole plane with water from the nose to the tail, despite that those fish were all dead.

At the end of meals in cafés she used to polish the knife with a paper napkin and turn the side of the blade to her face to serve as a mirror and check if any crumb had been left between her pearly teeth; when she saw one, she'd sweep it away with her tongue in front of the knife mirror. "What are you laughing about?" she said the first time he saw her doing that. "There're a lot more things one can do with a knife," and aimed the blade at him. There was a threat in that movement as well as a certain beauty and recklessness, unlike their petty quarrels all the past summer in the presence of her little son's anxious eyes.

The times when she erupted and shouted at him he would tell her she's acting like a crazy woman, to which she'd reply, without any offence, it seems he had never lived with a real woman, someone with temperament and not someone lovey-dovey twenty-four hours a day. To live with, she said, not just to fuck and leave, to live with one woman in one apartment with all the anger and the reconciliations that go with it. It's something they don't write about in newspapers, but no frontpage headline is more important than that, nor all his highly praised investigations, and what remained of them? Nothing. And if he thinks for one moment he can have one foot outside and fly off to another continent, he's mistaken and it would be better if he doesn't come back; yes, he can disappear from her life completely, from her and her children who's she's sorry got to know him at all. She's right, of course: he had done to them what his grandfather had done to his father and what his mother had done to him. On the phone she said: "If you don't come back by the end of the lease, I'm throwing everything of yours out. Into the street or into the rabbit enclosure."

Their history had been concisely recorded in that rabbit enclosure at the end of the yard: the day he brought her son the first two rabbits in a cardboard vegetable box where they lived for a week, and the day he built a cage for them large enough for Udi to stand up in; and how together they built a small wooden house where the rabbits could sleep at night; and how the first birthing went, how many died at birth and how many during the first week and how many survived and grew and gave birth; and how he and Udi fenced in a section of the yard around the cage so that they could have themselves an area to wander around in for an hour a day (they were coaxed back to the enclosure with the bait of lettuce); and how they started to leave them in that area at nighttime as well, and how they dug burrows where they gave birth to more rabbits. Udi's absentmindedness was also recorded in that rabbit enclosure and Amnon's resulting anger (for the most part he forgave him and filled up the water and food in his place), and her attitude to the rabbits as well, from her joy in their fluffy, quivering kits to her revulsion towards them in their adulthood ("That ugly one," she said about the rabbit whose fur had turned completely dark when she became pregnant), but each time they gathered together to receive lettuce leaves or carrots from her hands, she would melt – they were to her almost as lovable as the cat and the dog when they vied for her affection.

The morning after his announcement, she weighed the electric kettle in her hand and for a moment it seemed she was capable of making dangerous usage of both the kettle and the boiling water, but she returned the kettle to its base and faced the stuck sliding window whose sill outside had turned white from the droppings of pigeons whose cooing could be heard.

She listened to them. They sound agitated and angry and must have been shouting at each other.

"Why fix the window if you're leaving anyway?" she said.

She held the kettle again and filled one of the two Denby cups to the rim as the steam rose. She didn't fill his cup; she just lifted it up and checked the rim that had been damaged from one of the times he had washed it.

"Why did I buy them for you at all?" she said. "Even a disposable cup is wasted on you."

She then drew close to him with the steaming cup in her right hand and looked into his eyes, and he didn't know what she intended doing until he felt the touch of her left hand, at first cursorily and then gently and then lingering and making longer movements. "You see," she said after a while, "my friend here doesn't want to go away."

From the window of the English house, in the dark field he imagined seeing the magician who will be booked for Udi's birthday (a young man who had lived in Japan for years and knew all sorts of Samurai exercises) and how the glint of his giant sword will be raised above his apprentice, how the watermelon laid on his stomach will split and be replaced by a melon, and the melon by an apple, and the apple by a plum, and the plum by a grape, and the grape by a raisin, and after the raisin there's nothing more. The sword is already raised and glints again in the darkness beyond the window with his reflection in it, and since there's nothing beneath the sword, it will slice the stomach itself, to the back and to the spine.

"I'm talking to you!" she says over the phone. "And you're not even listening!"

She's making one last attempt only for her children; after all, she'll recover, of that she has no doubt, but why scar them again?

In order to prove he had been listening to her, he repeated word for word everything she had told him, from the birthday with the magician to camping by the Kinneret[10] (how on the first night Udi enjoyed himself so much he hardly found the time to talk to her, but on the second night he was already homesick: "Home, if still remember what that is), and his words angered her again. "It didn't interest you at all," she says, "you were probably thinking about something else."

Through the window he sees his own head placed on the apprentice's stomach in the darkness of the English field, the head which is reflected in the windowpane and its face that of a stranger, laid there in order to separate the blade from the stomach, until that image was driven from his eyes. Look, all his body parts are intact: from his ear pressed close to the telephone receiver to the soles of his feet.

One of his own birthdays and his first camping experience popped into his head he says – as if it's a conversation from the early days of their acquaintance whose end is unclear – and that's why he didn't answer right away; he is angered by her reaction to that memory which rose from some forgotten place and has been carried inside him for almost four decades. He tells her about tents made from blankets joined to each other with knots tied around stones and tied to oak trunks with resin dropping from their trunks,. That's exactly what he was thinking about, he says to her and is insistent: the camp and the tents made from blankets; and any moment he might start explaining to her how knots are tied around stones; after all, she had never been in a youth movement, but she was fed up with his explanations.

"God," she says, "I'm talking to you about home, and you're talking to me about tents."

His stories from the pub about the vet who flew with a herd of cows tire her like the stories of the trips he made in his youth. She had often made gibes about them even before he expressed his desire to travel again: didn't he buy a van? And didn't drive to the north of Norway with it, to Nordkapp? How thrilling, how come his name wasn't mentioned together with Amundsen and Nansen; and wasn't there one who died on the way, what was he called, Scott? Her elder son was interested in things like that. And didn't he live before or after that in Paris for a while? Ah, gay Paree, funny how no one there in the city of lights taught him to kiss properly; and didn't he search for suspicious objects at the airport there? And didn't he once even follow someone suspicious for a while? How exciting! What's Entebbe in comparison to the Paris airport – her ex-husband had been on the Entebbe raid, true, not with the main combat force, but he had been there. She had rightly made gibes at all those, but it didn't deter him.

He's familiar with her anger and understands it from all the previous times he's infuriated her: after all, she gave him her best years, a woman's last chance to open a new chapter in her life – only his mother, Ada, managed to do that at a late age – and she had lost more than a few clients thanks to him when she agreed to

---

10 The Sea of Galilee.

live so far from the city, among all the sloppy people who live here, and that's the way he repays her? "How didn't I see what was clear to everyone except me," she says sadly; it was as clear as the diagnosis of a terminal disease: Amnon isn't someone you can raise a family with, he couldn't even raise himself.

What had he really done with his life? Opposite the third or fourth house he had lived in, one that he rented for a year on a settlement in the Sharon region, lived a man who at the time seemed to him to be very old, though probably not any older than his father is now. And one morning, when he left the house, the old man turned to him from the threshold of his house, leaning on his walker, and in a cracked and somewhat astonished voice said to him, as if continuing some conversation he had been holding in his head: "It passes so quickly!" And he gestured to the small street and the dusty summer sky that had begun to heat up above him. "Life passes by so quickly," he said again, and sounded like someone coming out of a cinema and talking about the film he's just seen, a film that hadn't fulfilled all the expectations pinned on it, and even if some had been fulfilled it was hurrying to finish.

For the entire last decade that saying had been reverberating in his head and was flung from temple to temple; under no circumstances should it be left to prey on his mind and discourage him, every means against it was valid, even falsehoods, provided he could convince himself of them. He tried: weren't there years in his life when he had accomplished things? At a young age – not yet thirty-three –he had been sent to London, instead of using the local reporter, to investigate the assassination of Ambassador Argov, after which the Lebanon War broke out (at the time it was convenient for him to focus on the ambassador); he had even been sent to India to cover the religious riots; and to Buenos Aires to investigate how their national spy had built his cover story; he also flew to Russia to investigate an assassination of the Russian prime minister Stolypin at the beginning of the twentieth century which had apparently been carried out in league with the security services. That damn article was the beginning of his downfall. It's not always easy to locate the moment when everything starts going downhill, but it started then.

It was meant to be the crowning glory of a series of his articles on security matters. He had often been helped by using secret services retirees as sources, but this time he not only aroused the anger of his colleagues, but of the paper's readers as well. He raised the question: could what had happened there happen in Israel? "It could never happen here," he was told. Many readers expressed a similar opinion in letters they wrote to the editor, resenting the very comparison and wondering how the newspaper had sent him to Russia just for some apparent scoop based on a shaky premise from the beginning of the century, and a shadow was cast over all his previous articles: someone who sees conspiracies everywhere would be better off in therapy and not in the weekly supplement. They may have had a point there: he had grown up in a house where life was based on falsehoods – the ones told by his father about his father and the ones told by his mother to his father – how could he not think that everyone in the world deceives everyone else.

"Amnon, Amnon, what have you got yourself into?" his colleagues and friends said, and Kramer shouted at him: "Weren't you warned to be careful and not get into a mess like me?" But he had insisted on carrying on. Amnon, Amnon, he said to himself after checking which points were accurate and which had he bent a little for his needs. But it was too late, a retraction was no longer possible.

"Take a lesson from what happened to me," Kramer used to say to him, and he hadn't listened closely enough. In Africa, Kramer had joined the renegade deputy commander of an elite unit and sailed with him down the Zambesi or the Congo, and on their journey to a remote airfield on the edge of the jungle he felt like Conrad on the boat sailing to Kurtz, although his Kurtz was standing by his side on the deck and sniping at waterfowl. The landscapes they passed by Kramer described in poetic outpourings, and those who knew Africa well claimed his sins of inaccuracy were plentiful and one should doubt the rest of the details he submitted. Later, all sorts of rumors about the commander reached Israel: it was said he had been helped by his soldiers to smuggle diamonds; that he had forced them not only to learn the unit anthem by heart but also to have its symbol tattooed on their flesh.

When they tired of his African stories, they'd say to Kramer, "Why don't you go back to Kampala?"; or Kinshasa, or Kasese (some particularly liked saying: "Go back to Kasese, Kramer"). While to Amnon in his downfall they said: "Why don't you go back to Kiev."

"God," she says over the phone again – he's trying to explain to her about tying knots around stones – "you really do deserve to end your life in a tent."

From here one can't see the saplings that they planted together in the yard of their home and which have already become trees; from here one can't see the deck from the gate to the front door he built with his own hands; one can't see the puppy she brought to their new home and is already a large dog whose affection they vie for the way parents would a son (when they stood at the end of the yard and called him, he'd start to bound in one direction and halfway would stop and turn his gaze in frustration at the one he left behind). HhHe has no intention of withdrawing from the crazy desire that sprung up in him like in his youth, to travel thousands of kilometers by himself, and that's even without the appended pretext; responsible reasoning is not a supreme value when it's so annihilating.

"It's a chance that won't come again," he said to her about the house he managed to find in the area he wanted to travel to, and more precisely, where he could begin his inquiry into the missing details concerning his grandfather; after all, she herself had told him how beautiful the area is, how peaceful, how different from their country. She had even showed him photographs she had taken there during the holiday she had spent there with her family: her boys in an apple tree, her husband reaching out a sugar cube to a dappled horse, herself crumbling bread from the edge of a boat to three ducks.

He left in autumn to travel to this English village surrounded by vast fields, and in the mornings the sheep sleeping in them look like cocoons of mist, until they rise to their feet and all turn in one direction. Every morning on his way to the grocery store a grey horse stained with scales of mud comes rollicking towards him from the fence and draws near to the boards for him to scratch its forehead. Its eyelashes are dense and long, the sleep in the corners of its eyes almost human, and when it rolls back its lips, long yellowish teeth are revealed.

"Good morning," he says to the horse quietly, "did you sleep well?" He's already given it a name he saw in the church leaflet: Jonathan Kilroy; and some-times he asks it, when there's no one around, what it dreamed last night. His own dreams he prefers not to remember.

15

"Can you imagine? A train that looks exactly like his own magnificent train and just as expensive, and yet he doesn't travel in it?" Levin had spoken about the strict safeguarding of Tsar Nikolai and told how on every outing of his from the palace, dozens of guards and soldiers surround him, and on each journey he takes by train, sentries are stationed at every junction of the tracks; and so great was the concern over the imperial train, that a twin train was added, just to confuse the assassins. It was a fine trick, no less than their own tricks: true, they didn't have twin carriages, but in order to confuse their enemies in the secret police they disguised themselves as coachmen, newspaper sellers, shoe shiners.

Before Poliakov was enlisted to assassinate the minister, he had been a successful beggar for a whole month. At first, they thought of adding a patch to one eye, but the fear arose that it might impair his sight (he had been assigned to reconnoiter the entrance of a building on Panteleymonovskaya Street). In the evening in his room, he looked into the fragment of mirror whose surface was peeling. Every morning the peeling would add boils to his face. He wanted to see what he would look like with an eyepatch: it made him look scary – not like a beggar, not even like a pirate. His eye was blacker than black in the mirror, and at night in his sleep he saw a familiar figure that only momentarily was himself, a figure whose eye sockets were empty, and its bleeding face was bent toward the ground and its fingers groped the earth of the yard, and not far from it a dog was licking an extracted eyeball, until it slipped away with the gait of a thief, like one who's grabbed a chicken drumstick from the table.

He was a successful beggar, but the others were more effective; perhaps not the coachmen who in order not to arouse suspicion with lengthy their parking, every once in a while were forced to transport a chance passenger; but those that were disguised as vendors could walk back and forth with their wares, and it was them who obtained the most information: not only all the details of the minister's daily schedule, but also what his horses and carriage looked like and how a bicycle rider accompanied him from behind: one always rode a few meters from the left back wheel, armed with a pistol, and from the time the information became known, bicycle riders ceased to look like bicycle riders; and how much more so every train whose many carriages could have been those of the imperial train's twin or the original all its glory.

"Can you imagine," Levin would say to his other audience, "how much a train like that costs?"

It was a surprising question, and in order to elicit an answer from his listeners, ("He knows how to twist everyone around with his words," Duchin said about him) he led them through relatively familiar things: not an entire train but just the velvet that lined the seats, or the silk from which the curtains were made, or the carpets and the crystal chandeliers. No wonder they listened to Levin; who wouldn't listen to stories about that wonder train that even has a grand piano whose feet are screwed to the floor of the carriage?

How much do you think all that costs, Levin would ask his listeners, young and old workers, complete imbeciles and semi-imbeciles, turners, welders and stevedores, and only in the Politov plants was there one who listened to him addressing a different gathering and saying things in complete contrast.

"A million?" someone said, and right away the sum was doubled and trebled by people around him, as if they were participating in a public auction whose winner would receive the entire imperial train, the original or its twin.

"And that's just one train," Levin would then say, "now times it by two and you'll see that many families could live on that for all their lives."

When he addressed his other audience, all that would change: the significance of the security instructions, the role of the imperial train, even the Tsar's character. Levin would then specifically emphasize the distorted insufferable situation, when a bunch of reckless people dare to brazenly disturb the Tsar's tranquility, and with it the tranquility of all Russia.

"Shall we let them threaten him like that?" he would ask.

"We'll hang them!" someone planted in the crowd would respond. Before those listeners a completely different Tsar was described: not a despotic spendthrift and tyrant, but a compassionate ruler who makes do with little, a devoted family man who every evening reads bedtime stories to his children; and man so in love with the Tsarina and she so in love with him that she still blushes when he whistles their secret signal in the paths of the garden. That picture was heartwarming: how the mighty Tsar of Russia whistles to his wife like a young boy, and how the Tsarina blushes like a maiden.

"A man like that," Levin would say about him to his other audience, "compassionate, merciful and loving, despite the enormous power he wields; can we allow a few lawbreakers to ruin his state of mind?"

In front of this audience that was not much different from the previous one, the descriptions of imperial luxuries changed completely: a spendthrift emperor was not portrayed but rather the contrary, a man almost ascetic, and the meaning of the double imperial train had also changed: it was not meant to protect the Tsar but his family. He's not one to spare himself, and there's no father that loves his children more, not for nothing he's known as the father of all Russians and not only of his son and daughters. What man in the world, Levin asked those listeners, would let all that be destroyed? What man, and for what damn reason? Just because of a few lawbreakers, a gang of violent criminals whose time to twitch in the air had come?

"Hang them!" Levin's audience would answer him. "Hang them! Hang them!" They then uttered a full-throated cry as if they were gathered not in a factory among silent machines but in a square among assembled masses whose tumult is interrupted only by the beating of drums and the swinging of a rope.

Duchin had witnessed the execution of Zhelyabov and his comrades after the assassination of Tsar Alexander; but even someone who had never seen a hanging had no difficulty in imagining its details: the noose wrapped around the neck, the choking throat or the breaking of the neck, the legs twitching in the air, the tongue protruding.

"That was something Levin feared," Duchin said, "just like you. With ease you could have swapped places with each other."

Without batting an eyelid, he looked straight at Duchin and promised he would carry out the deed as required; he would go to Levin and kill him. And afterward he heard Vera reminding everyone how he had been through some things many times worse, things she wouldn't wish on anyone, and he had managed to come out unharmed.

"Unharmed," Duchin said, "but that's not the point, Vera Alexandrovna, coming out unharmed."

He still didn't trust him.

You piece of dirt, Poliakov said softly to the sleeping man, you son of a bitch.

Before that he had seen Levin's mother with his own eyes in the first window and saw in her only devotion to her son, while with his mother one could never be sure how she would behave. On nights when his father didn't sleep at home and he would creep into her bed and her warmth, he wasn't sure whether she push him out, and if he stayed and woke up there, she would look at him in the morning with her brown eyes that were quick to light up, and say to him: "Just don't grow up, Ilya, do you hear? Don't become like him!" And when he did grow up, she said: "But you'll do other things, promise me Ilya!" He promised without knowing what he was promising; he only perceived the plea in her voice as well as the threat and knew that unlike his father, she always carried out her threats.

Levin's chest rose up and down, calmly, complacently, blind to what was to come.

I can see your ribs rising and falling Levin, he said softly to him. Doesn't your mother give you enough to eat? But those ribs were well padded, and there was no doubt Levin ate his meals in an orderly fashion.

There was a smell of flatulence in the air, slight but reasonably evident, and it fanned Poliakov's animosity further. You spoiled brat, he said softly to him, and against his will he thought of his own mother and the dishes she cooked, and about the room in their house in the village which served as a kitchen and the children's room as well as a guest room. His mother never allowed his father to doze off next to her the way Levin's mother allowed his father sitting on the kitchen chair. His mother would immediately start bothering his father not to close his eyes and fall asleep, not to sink into a sleep and start to snore in her ear – "one would think you've been doing such a lot, Shloime, that you deserve to sleep," she would say to him – that he shouldn't think the sin of his marrying her has been forgiven, nor the sin of his failed dream of vast wealth that even the Tsar would envy ("The Tsar doesn't like people snoring," she would say to him and shake him).

They sent me to kill you, Levin, he said to him with a sealed mouth, and I'll kill you here on this bed with a pistol or with a pillow so that only a slight smell will be dispersed. What did you eat, you son of a bitch? You eat and eat and my tooth aches after eating just bread with bread, does that seem fair to you?

I'll kill you, Levin, he said softly, with this pistol or with my hands, we're yet to see which is more convenient, because the people you turned in also had a father and a mother; but he wasn't thinking about them now, not about all the others and their parents, but about his own parents who could never be together in one room in such tranquility as this. "Did the Tsar ask after me, did he send regards?" His mother would needle his father and ask him if the next time he meets with the Tsar, that's to say after his meetings with the dukes and princes, would he be so kind as to send her regards. And also s to the Tsarina, yes, from the bottom of her heart. And also the Tsarevich. Perhaps the Tsarevich will come here to play with Ilya? They can climb trees together. After all, if he can't all those trees, at least let them climb them. "Have you finished?" his father asked.

"No," she replied. "And regards to the sisters of the Tsarevich as well," and her hands don't cease the work they're doing. "Such beauties," she said, "so delicate, perhaps a match for Ilya can be arranged with one of them, the way a match was arranged for me and you? Without knowing until the last moment who they'll be spending the rest of their lives with until death."

She didn't notice that he was watching them nor was she looking at his father; only at the beetroot she's chopping with violent rhythmic movements. She was completely submerged in that beetroot and in her animosity which began beneath the wedding canopy and which grew from year to year and only abated when his father was away on his journeys, She would be quick to conceal any sign he left behind: not only his plate and glass in the kitchen (right away she pushed them to the corner of the cupboard), but also the wheel prints of the cart in the yard; they were swept and scrubbed with a broom made of twigs as if in that way the cart, and the one sitting in it in the distance, would also be wiped away. There was more than a hint in that of things to come, but their son was too young then to under-stand that.

"Are you finished?" his father asked again.

"Why, are you in a hurry to go someplace?" she asked. "Maybe some general's waiting for you?"

"Someone else in my place," said his father, "would long ago -" but he didn't complete the sentence and just looked at her while she continued to chop the beet-root with the same violent rhythmic movements and the same merciless deter-mination she would display during the pogroms, and the last time he would visit their village.

"Would have already what?" said his mother.

"Would have silenced you long ago."

"If only there *was* someone else here! And you" – she turned to him when she remembered him being there – "go and give the peels to the geese. And don't go too far, maybe the Tsarevich will really come to play with you, wouldn't you like to play with her, Ilya?" And right away she returned to chopping the beetroot, and the rhythmic beating of the knife could be heard every time it hit the wooden board.

"Why do you turn him against me? Come, Ilya," his father said to him, "come to Daddy, I haven't seen you for a whole month." But he recoiled and released himself from both of them and went out to the yard into the twilight falling there, holding fistfuls of peels in his small palms: they were moist and cool and pleasing to the touch. At the end of the yard the geese could be seen gilded by the sunset and gathered together like a large flowering, until they saw him and separated from each other and began to hop towards him, elegant and ridiculous and gaggling.

In the next room the iron was still moving and the wrinkles in the material were being smoothed by its weight and its heat. The coals inside it and must have red hot. Coals can be beautiful especially when you see them at night, have you ever seen coals at night, Levin? (On and on they moved down the Berezina River on rafts sailing south, and their fire rose into the darkness from the crates were filled with earth.) You bastard, he said to him, why didn't you stick a piece of coal up your ass to block it.

Or in the holes of the eyes, the empty sockets, to see what you had done. But he felt the burning in his own eyes, sharp and painful: perhaps tears sprouted there in the dark, not brought on by this dead person, Levin, who wasn't dead yet, but by the dead before him in Petersburg and in Minsk and in Bykhov. Coals in the eyes, he said softly to Levin, maybe that way you'll light up in the dark like an animal in the forest. And coals in the mouth as well, to burn your tongue: after all, you were one of us.

He suddenly began speaking to him in the plural, as if he himself had been one of that group he had got to know only a few months ago and only by chance.

He had never really been one of them, even in the assassination,. Whereas Levin had been part of the group, a skilled speaker who knew how to incite his audience to any purpose, a friend to Duchin and Volodya and Vera, and not just for two months but for years (until the day he entered the headquarters of Okhrana: he was driven there in the special carriage whose curtains were closed without even a slit between them, or went through the gate on his own initiative and crossed the inner courtyard that was surrounded by the three department buildings; without hesitation or a policeman prodding him, he went up the wide steps padded by a crimson carpet fastened to them with brass rods; step by step; went up or was taken up to the second floor, and walked or was led through the long corridor whose floor was polished to the point of causing a glare and stopped opposite the door before the last, on whose brass plate engraved in curly letters was the name Perdischenko).

16

"Your friends just used you, Poliakov, and when they were finished, they threw you away, for example, how d'you think we came to that hotel, just by chance?" That's what they said to him in person on the other side of that door, the one before the last. "That we were we just strolling down the street going from house to house? No, a little bird whispered in our ear. Not whispered, squealed to us very loudly: you'll find who you're looking for in the Alexander Hotel. On the third floor, at the end of the corridor on the right, in Room 312."

And perhaps he added, whoever he was, if indeed there had been anyone (Levin hadn't been let in on the secret of the assassination): the man you're looking for won't do anything when you get there. He'll just be lying on the filthy bed and listen to the moaning on the other side of the wall. And on the floor of the room there'll be fragments of glass scattered from the smashed window, and they'll be scattered on the bed as well, and he won't have the strength or the will to get rid of them; on the contrary, he wouldn't care if they were to be stuck into his body.

"And not that we were especially looking for you," Perdischenko continued. "Forgive me for saying so, Poliakov, but you're just small fry. But nevertheless there are two or three things that you know. I always say that to everyone who joins our department: gentlemen, never disregard anyone, because even small fry know something about the sea. You must have met two or three people, and you must have heard about another two or three from them, it's better not to keep things inside."

Afterward, in a surprisingly friendly tone, he said that's something he doesn't only say here, but also to his family. "I tell my daughters," Perdischenko said, "get it all out, my darlings. Get it out when you're angry, Daddy will still love you. Get it out so that you don't, heaven forbid, become bitter and bad tempered like a lady we all know. I say it with humor, Poliakov, we all love their dear mother very much. Shutting herself up in her room for an hour is enough to make us miss her like crazy."

It was the third or fifth day of the interrogation, and at the time he wasn't sure whether he had talked in his sleep and divulged some name in the course of another interrogation he was undergoing in his nightmares, no less palpable than this real one, and whether in the end he would awake from that one to another interrogation, identical to it in everything. For five days and five nights he didn't have one proper uninterrupted sleep and found it difficult to discern between the sights outside of his eyelids to those inside them: the very same room waited for him inside when he closed his eyes, the same room Levin will be interrogated in, and the same Perdischenko and Telegin in it waiting for him to break.

"Almost every night after the girls have gone to sleep, my lady says about friends like yours, Oleg, I don't like your profession, you yes; you know that, but not your profession. And I'm also a little scared, because someone who spends all his time with scum – not you, Poliakov, heaven forbid I meant you; after all, she doesn't know you exist and also won't know – is liable to catch something from them. My lady worries about me, and she's speaking from love."

He looked at him again and examined his face that was only slightly bruised at the time.

"Love," said Perdischenko, "love. That thing people are prepared to give everything for – love and not some idea." With his right hand, between the forefinger and the thumb, he smoothed his small beard and looked at the man he was interrogating; he had a blackened right eye, and a scab was forming on a wound on his forehead, but his nose was intact and all his teeth were still in place ("Leave them for the meantime, Antip," they had said to the policeman).

"Have you got anything really dear to you Poliakov? Not an idea. A person, one loved soul? Do you know what love is at all? No one does crazy deeds like the ones you people do if there's at least one person in the world dear to their hearts. One person, Poliakov, not everyone – when everyone is dear to someone, no one really is Do you have someone like that? Someone who you would be prepared to do everything for?"

Perdischenko raised his glasses onto the bridge of his nose in order to see better. "I thought as much," he said a moment later, and turned his head to the window and for a while looked through it, first to the inner courtyard and the buildings surrounding it and then to the sky above them. "Nice weather today," he said, "a really nice summer day. Not too cold, not too warm. Nice. And you could go outside from here as if nothing had happened."

The hours lengthened and spun around their axis, and the questions that had been asked at the start were asked again. The bombs: who had prepared them and where, in what place were they stored and in what way were they transferred, in exactly whose cart: Volodya's? "The tall handsome fellow, impressive even when he's dressed like a cart driver. Were they transferred in his cart?"

For some reason the only one they hadn't asked anything about was Duchin; they asked about all the others, but not him. They knew Volodya was a student and that Vera came from a wealthy family, and Maximov they knew had chosen to sacrifice himself by not turning in the one watching him from the hotel room, looking down at the street from his window.

Later they said they understood him completely and that had they been in his shoes they would behaved just like him, who wouldn't be filled with tremendous desire to take revenge on those who had mistreated his family?

"The helplessness," said Perdischenko, "they must have been holding you firmly and not letting you move a finger." They didn't even let you turn your head away," said Telegin, "they wanted you to see everything to the end."

The elder and the younger interrogator looked at him with understanding, and Poliakov gave a slight nod, almost undiscernible, he nodded despite that no one was holding him at the time, only his mother, and he could easily have shaken her off her and gone down from the attic to the yard and try to do something, the way he could have gone down from the hotel room to the street and try to help Maximov.

One of them said that helplessness reminded him of another helplessness, the one he would experience in the Semyonovsky Square when the rope would swing there.

"Sergeant!" Perdischenko called out to the locked door. "Are you still there?"

"Yes, sir," answered the policeman on the other side.

"Konstantin Nokolaevich, would you please open it for him?"

Telegin approached to open the door and Perdischenko remained standing next to the bookcase.

The policeman entered and clicked his heels.

"Antip Yepanchin," the policeman stated his name.

"We know you well, Antip," Perdischenko said to him fondly and asked him about his family; has the little one recovered? Has his temperature come down? Well, that's the main thing; the worst is behind us and the boy's on the way to recovery. In the end he'll be a tough guy like his father. "You're a tough guy, Antip, aren't you?"

"Be careful your fists don't connect with anyone by accident. Do you ever raise a hand against the wife?"

Antip was insulted to the depths of his soul: never in his life had he raised a hand against Katya, never! Others maybe do that, but not him! His insult was visible in the corner of his mouth, and for a moment he looked like a defenseless child against which an adult has laid a false accusation,

"Okay, okay, you're like a pair of doves," Telegin said to appease him, but Perdischenko sought to put the facts straight: actually cranes are known for their devotion not doves.

"Do you have a sweetheart like that?" they addressed Poliakov (she was in Minsk, but he had got up and left her). He shook his head.

"Never had anyone? Not even that phony beggar woman?"

Again he shook his head.

"She's called Vera, isn't she?" Telegin said.

"But then that's not her real name," said Perdischenko, "and we would be happy if you would be so kind as to tell us what her real name is."

He really didn't know if their names – Vera, Volodya, Duchin – were their actual names or just made up. After all, when he smuggled pamphlets he was called Sergei Gomolyov or Grisha Ivanov, and for a while they all called him Seryozha and later Sasha, and at the time his real name and his real life had been completely forgotten.

"What's her real name?" they asked him again. "First name, surname, what's her father's name?"

They didn't believe him that he didn't know. A moment later they signaled to the policeman with the movement of an eyebrow. He approached and grabbed him and lifted him out of the armchair with one hand and grasped his shoulder to stabilize him and with the other delivered a punch to the stomach and doubled him up.

"What's her real name?" they asked.

Again they signaled to the policeman, and again he grabbed him and stuck his fist into the exact spot where it had previously been punched. Now the blow hurt even more and some moments passed until the place where the pain was felt could be defined – deep down in the stomach. Perhaps some inner organ had been crushed, the spleen or the gall bladder or another organ – not his heart, after all he has no heart - maybe the intestines, he definitely has intestines, he knew their sounds well from the hours of hunger or the times he filled his stomach with cheap soup that continued to bubble inside.

A few days before that, in the hotel where he was captured, he heard a woman from the other side of the wall saying that the greatest closeness between a man and a woman is when they're lying together on a bed and hear stomach noises and don't know whose they are. "Instead of them pretending how much they love me, I'd much rather just lie quietly next to my man and not know whose stomach is speaking."

That had happened the day after the assassination, when he still lay in his clothes on the sunken bed in the drafty room and pieces of the windowpane were ground under him with every moment his body made, and time after time he cursed those pieces of glass for not having pierced his flesh. Between his sweaty temples a hazy picture rose of some saints of theirs he had seen in one of the halls of the Hermitage, Saint Christopher or Saint Sebastian or some other saint who hadn't been crucified but was bound to a wooden post with dozens of arrows stuck into him. For a moment, he saw his own body with dozens of glass shards stuck into his flesh, until a client left the neighbor's room, and when the door was slammed a woman shouted after him: "Cheapskate!" But a moment later she was already singing softly to herself.

Two months before that, in the provincial town whose entire size was like one neighborhood of Petersburg, he had become friendly with a respectable young woman, a salesgirl in a department store, younger than him and better than him; Miriam was her name but he called her Masha, and in her gentle hesitant way she began to fall in love with him or with whoever she imagined seeing in him, so great was her longing to have a sweetheart. And one evening, when her uncle and all his family had gone to a wedding and had given the servants leave until morning, he came to visit her and for the first time saw her small room, so orderly that the first thing he felt like doing was to put in into a state of disarray, from the flowers on the embroidered tablecloth to the buttons on her dress, but he's wasn't being questioned about her here.

"Her real name," his interrogators said to him, "first name, surname, name of her father, and where she comes from."

Again they signaled to the policeman with the movement of an eyebrow, and again he forcefully lifted him to his feet and stuck his fist into his stomach exactly into the spot where it had been previously punched: in the spleen or the gall bladder or the intestines; and doubled him up, depleted of air and deaf to the sounds emitted by his own throat, until the pain eased a bit.

"The real name," they said to him again, "of your sweetheart. The phony beggar woman."

They reminded him that he had gone with her to the hotel and had waited below until she changed out of her beggar's rags, and that afterward they had both walked onto the bridge leading to the neighboring quarter – yes, for the entire length of that route someone was watching them, until they disappeared from his eyes because of two carriages that suddenly kept close to each other.

"Where did you go from the bridge?" they asked him. "Where exactly: the name of the street, the number of the building, the floor number, what name was written on the door?"

Consequently, he was reminded of another bridge, not of stone but of wood, not the rickety one of his village that every spring was shaken by blocks of thawing ice that struck its pillars, but the sturdy one of the provincial town; and how he and Masha stood on it one evening, leaning on the railing and watching the boats sailing beneath them, and the couples sitting in them being rocked and caught in the circle of lamplight on their way toward the dark.

And should he and Masha have a baby, she would sing a lullaby to it, a soothing song with a lilting melody. But he didn't want to reflect on that, not on a baby nor its parents, not on his own father and mother, nor on their village and the river there and the small wooden bridge, nor what floated beneath it with the crows pecking at it all the way to the cascades.

"Where did you go," said Perdischenko, "what street, what building, what floor? We'll keep on asking you that, Poliakov, until you answer."

And since he didn't answer, the policeman punched him again, aiming his fist at the place where it hit the previous times. Before that it seemed to him that all sensation had been dulled, but the pain sharpened and churned inside him.

The interrogators were referring to Vera, but his thoughts wandered again from bridge to bridge, from woman to woman: from a stone bridge to a wooden bridge, from the one who wasn't ashamed to disguise herself as a beggar or a prostitute to the one who was shocked to the core on seeing a drunk woman lift up her tatters.

"They're like animals," Masha said after a while, and with every statement of hers the sight they had just seen came alive in his mind and stimulated him even more: the masculine hand swallowed in the rolled-up dress and feeling its way inside it, the exposed knees, the soiled white of the thighs.

She already knew then he would be leaving the following morning; for a whole week he reminded her of his intention, at least in that matter he had acted fairly. She tried to persuade him to stay, and he refused; it seemed to him that moving to the capital was no more difficult that moving from Bykhov to Kalitsa and from Kalitsa to Minsk. In vain she tried to describe life in Petersburg in gloomy colors as she had heard in the department store from whoever who had been there, a huge noisy and cramped city, its streets thronging with the masses. "Here everything's so small and quiet," she said, "look how quiet is, just the two of us in the street, no one but of us."

"The two of us and those drunks," he replied.

She stopped beneath a streetlamp and he stopped too.

"Did we have to see a thing like that on our last night," she said softly.

"Yes," he replied.

"Three drunks."

"Yes," he concurred but wanted to be accurate and say: two men and a woman but didn't.

She asked him quietly why he insisted on leaving so early in the morning; he can go if that's what he's decided, but why so early in the morning? If he'd only wait a few more hours tomorrow, she could part with him properly.

He replied that partings were better made brief, and that even when he left his village he didn't prolong the ceremony, on the contrary. And when she asked if he would write to her, he already knew he wouldn't, not a letter, not a postcard, not a note. And indeed, he didn't write; not a letter, not a postcard, not a note, and also didn't not stop over when passing through her town, not on his way to the village, nor on his return, despite that she was the only one who perhaps could have consoled him over what he had seen there.

Afterward, they reminded him again what they already knew: the five months of tailing that had been required of him and his friends to find out the schedule of the Tsar and his routes, months in which they learned to identify his carriage even from a distance of a hundred meters (the trio of dappled horses with cropped manes whose reins were set with silver nails for ornamentation; the blue uniform of the coachman and the shape of his beard; the servant who sat alongside him in a uniform no less grand; and also the deep blue shade of the carriage, the gold decorations on its edges; the thinness of the wheel spokes; and the old lamps – the minister was jealous of the Grand Duke's acetylene lamps and intended to replace his own as well).

They also reminded him how they had planned their actions according to the hours of the minister's leaving and the hours of his return ("A man of regular habit, the minister") and his route when to travelled to the Tsar to deliver his weekly report; after all, the hotel had been chosen according to that. And really – they said – why take the risk of just standing in the street, between all the passersby, if a hotel could be found that overlooked everything from above? That was what Konstantin Nikolaevich himself used to do, yes, even if now it seems he's only occupied with his shoes (he was still looking at their tips, first the right and afterward the left). "We would have behaved like you," Perdischenko said to him again and added that it wasn't hard to identify with him: a young man coming from some backwater to the big city, and of course feeling cut off from home affects him.

"He was cut off from his chickens and his cows, Oleg Timofeyevich," said the young interrogator and continued to gaze at the tips of his shoes. "And when the train started moving, he probably didn't know what was moving, the window or the fields."

Perdischenko was then reminded of his daughters who had also reacted that way the first time they travelled by train; they didn't know if the train or platform was moving.

"Did the sound of the horn scare you?" asked Telegin.

He then asked if he had been frightened by the smoke of the locomotive – in his village they only burn cow dung, isn't that so? – and did he know how to relieve himself and wasn't frightened by the gaping hole in the floor of the toilet booth and the tracks flying below. It was Telegin who asked about that, whereas the elder interrogator in his usual manner disapproved of any statement of his colleague that contained any trace of crudity. They also wondered if he had anything to show the conductor when he came to check the tickets: the elder thought he might have kept the ticket thinking it was some kind of money note not to be thrown away, that's how it is with village folk, while the young man said: "Village folk might not understand that Oleg Timofeyevich, but Jews – yes."

His colleague didn't like generalizations of that sort: true, there are more than a few Jews who deal only with money, but not all of them are sly and moneylenders. Some are and some aren't. Just as there are good Russians and bad Russians, sly and stupid, heroes and cowards. Just as that man who died from his bomb in the lake hadn't been a moneylender or sly. Anyway, everyone here's grateful to the fisherman who raised it in the net and to the Klotilin Fishery Company. True, there had been more than a little complacency there, as if it wasn't possible the bomb could explode again.

Speaking of fisherman, the elder interrogator was reminded of the little illustrated book he used to read to his daughters every night before bedtime and the question the little one had once asked him – it was the well-known story about the fisherman's wife and the three wishes – why beg the stingy fish the whole time instead of just asking it to turn herself into a fish and that way she'd get everything she wanted. "Isn't she smart?" Perdischenko asked.

Telegin seemed pensive: he undid a shoelace and tied it again, despite that the two loops had previously been exactly equal to each other. "But Oleg Timofeyev-ich," he said, "that way she herself would have ended up in someone's net." And right away he also raised the assumption: perhaps that fish itself had once been a fisherman's wife.

They returned to the business of Poliakov's Jewishness and asked him if eating fish was permitted or were some allowed and others not. Doesn't he miss home cooking? And his sweetheart – maybe he had a sweetheart in the village, and if he didn't, he might yet still have – did she cook him everything she had learned from her mother? What a pity he's giving up all that, and for no reason. It would be enough for him to answer two or three questions for them to give him a train ticket to anywhere he wanted, they would even inform his sweetheart that he's returning. She'd wait for him on the platform waving a handkerchief, that's what handkerchiefs are for. How could such a nice innocent boy not have a sweetheart?

But he had got up and left her.

17

And this is how they met:

He saw her in her uncle's department store when he came to buy a pair of socks, and because of his color blindness he was hesitant in choosing between one pair and other and when he asked her their colors, she thought he was teasing her. A boy the height of her waist stood by her side and looked at him through thick glasses. One of his nostrils was running and she bent down to wipe his nose, but he hit the handkerchief and wiped his nose on his sleeve. "Don't touch me!" he screamed and stamped his foot. He then tugged at the folds of her dress and because she didn't immediately respond to him he ran out to the street and before she could catch him jumped into a puddle and trampled and trod in it splashing all around., Afterward he pointed his muddy sole to the edge of her dress and threatened that if she doesn't take him to the fair right away ("You promised me!" he screamed) he would dirty it.

A few heads were turned towards him, but the other shop assistants, who knew their boss's youngest child well, continued to offer their customers materials and clothes.

When he asked her why she allowed him to behave in that way, something in her face became undone until she fastened her lips together; perhaps she was embarrassed by the mere fact of his addressing her in a matter not concerned with the shop.

"Because I need a place to stay," she replied, and asked him if in his opinion that was a good enough reason.

Two weeks before that he had come to Bykhov from Minsk and had already found work in the storeroom of the train station and for the time being he doesn't care where he sleeps at night. That's what he said to her, but nonetheless she asked where's he's living – after all, he doesn't sleep in the street. He gave the name of his lodgings, a hostel for wagon drivers; and that on his way here he had slept in places far worse.

And does he intend staying there for the rest of his life? Until he's old and grey?

Those words until he's old and grey made him laugh; he didn't go so far as to look beyond the week or the month.

"Why you talking to him!" the boy shouted and again tugged at the folds of her dress, and then her belt and then her hand, and when she tried to calm him down by laying her hand on his head he shook it off and took a step back. "Why you talking to him!" He threatened to tell his mother and again she tried to reach out a calming hand to him, and with an astonishingly swift movement he lifted his bespectacled face and stuck his little teeth into her hand.

"You should be ashamed of yourself!" he shouted at the boy. "Are you a dog?" A fuming voice burst out from his throat. He had never shouted at his brother Izu that way; on the contrary, it was Izu who had shouted at him, out of disappointment.

Only one shop assistant looked at him as did one customer, the others continued with their own business. The boy looked him over quietly through his thick spectacles, and when his one nostril ran again, he let it take its course towards his mouth, and didn't so much as glance at the handkerchief extended to him. "Nobody's gonna sell you anything!" he screamed. "I'll tell them not to sell you anything!" and his pinkish tongue stuck out beyond his upper lip and licked it. "Tell him, Miriam. why don't you tell him! Miriam Shmiriam, Miriam, Shmiriam!"

For a whole month, he tried to persuade her to take an evening walk with him in a distant quarter where no one would know them and where they couldn't bump into her uncle and his sons: not only the little ten year old screamer, but also his two older brothers who harassed her in all sorts of other ways, their poor family relative who needed a roof over her head and the few rubles they paid her after deducting from her wages the price of the objects she had broken. They had in fact been broken by the little boy who was almost as wicked as the eldest son (above all, she recalled the night he hung from a branch opposite her window and peeked into her room while she was undressing to go to bed).

In the end, she agreed to leave the limits of the neighborhood only because the uncle and his family had gone to a wedding in a distant town. On the way, he already took hold of her hand and she didn't protest, and occasionally while walking, the sides of their bodies brushed up against each other. They heard the sound of the river even before going onto the bridge, and when they leaned on the railing the sound separated into its components: the trickling of the water, the splashing of an oar, a choked laugh, murmurings, and at times a joyous shriek rose towards them. The reflection of the gas lamp that lit up the platform. flickered on the face of the water.

A small boat passed under the bridge, and the bundled-up entity in the darkness didn't come apart before their watching eyes, and for a moment it seemed that one could hear the rustling of cloth, the smacking of lips, a groan. Perhaps that was the right time to draw his face close to her and kiss her, but he hesitated; even in that distant quarter he felt afraid, and the uncle's house now seemed a more suitable place, though suitable for what exactly he wasn't sure. And perhaps even there, in the uncle's house, in her tidy well-kept room, he wouldn't have done any act that might disrupt its order, had they not seen the three drunks beneath them on the landing: a woman of undetermined age and two men, not young, whose arms intertwined with hers on both sides.

When the first one suddenly collapsed and pulled with woman down with him, his friend remained standing on his feet to the best of his ability until he too sat down. From the bridge, hidden from the eyes of the three, they saw the woman shake off the grip of the drunk who had fallen, but she didn't get up and only dragged herself on her large behind until she managed to lean her back against the lamppost. The drunk that had fallen began to move slowly in the darkness: he crawled like a large lizard, until his hand appeared in the circle of the lamp light and felt its way towards the woman, first to her worn out shoe and then to her ankle that was exposed up to the slope of the shin. With a clumsy movement, he pushed his hand under the material and went deeper into it farther and farther between her legs, and she relaxed. tilting head back and spreading her knees slightly, and the dress was stretched between them and hid the hand finding its way beneath the material. A trickling sound could again be heard, perhaps the trickling of the river water being swallowed into the mouth of a bottle floating on its surface, until it's filled and sinks to the depths; and another sound could be heard, a hoarse choked sound that rose from the woman or from the drunk or from both of them together.

Then – this also happened – the second drunk bent towards the décolletage of her dress and sunk his head into the softness of the flesh that was exposed there, and the woman reached out her hand to his neck. For a moment, it seemed she would pull him by his hair and thrust him off of her, but slowly and tenderly she moved her hand over his tangled hair that was stuck together by filth, combing his hair with her fingers while he bent towards her and suckled. Her eyes were closed and all her facial features were concentrated on the acts being done to her.

"Mommy," said the drunk, "mommy, mommy," and didn't lift his face from her.

On the bridge, a few meters away from the three, Masha turned her head away. He remained where he stood.

"I'm going now," she said.

Only then did he let go of the railing, and for a half an hour or more only the beating of their steps could be heard on the bridge and on the road they passed through and on the sidewalk after it and then another road and another sidewalk.

"Like animals," she said.

"Yes," he answered, but didn't think that; all the way she was careful the sides of their bodies didn't brush up against each other.

From the next street corner, a few meters away from them, the uncle's house could be seen: large, dark and silent. Only in one of the small windows on the first floor a dim light shone through a curtain, and when he asked her if they had left someone at home, perhaps one of the servants, she said that the servants had been given leave until tomorrow; and that she had left the oil lamp in her room lit so that she wouldn't have to return to a dark house.

And before that, she had even cleaned that oil lamp: she washed the glass from the soot, trimmed the burnt tip of the wick, filled up the container. Some of the oil had spilled and she had to wipe it up, and for a moment the thought then passed through her that were she not to wipe it up perhaps a fire would break out there, and for some reason it didn't seem a frightening thought to her.

Let it all burn, she thought for a moment; yes, that was the kind of mood he had put her in. She told him she had never spoken with anyone like that and reminded him that he too had said he'd never spoken to anyone like that, so why is he suddenly going away, and what's more on the first morning train.

He didn't hear the whimper; he only saw her shoulder quivering when she turned her face from him. And when he lifted his hand to her shoulder, she shook it off as if a loathsome bug had landed on her.

"Go," she said to the sidewalk, "if you want to go so much then go." Her head, with its braided plaits, turned to the wall of the corner building that had been stained by dirt sprayed from the wheels of passing carts.

He lifted his hand to her shoulder, and this time she didn't recoil and didn't move from where she stood, and he felt the warmth of her body through the material of her dress. The material was delicate, he felt that too.

"Let it all burn," she said again, and he asked her not to talk that way, why say such a thing. In God's name that's not the way to talk.

She asked what it had to do with God.

A movement of her eyelashes swept the tears that had sprouted between them, and she looked at the window that was no higher than the fork in the lower branches of the oak tree growing opposite it. A lace curtain covered the window-pane and had flowers woven in it; through their petals the lit oil lamp could be seen in the room. It must have been placed on the table.

"Let it all burn," she said, "and let them not get a thing from the insurance company, they'll have to sleep on the landing like those drunks."

Then the whimper turned into a laugh, but a moment later the laugh was choked and turned back into a whimper, and she sniffled once and once more and wiped her nose with the back of her hand like a little girl.

"Do you see that branch?" she said and sniffled again. "He climbed up to it and hung there like a monkey." It happened after the eldest boy hid the key to her door and she began to block the keyhole with paper and to obstruct the door handle with the back rest of a chair placed under it. At night he would rattle it until giving up and spitting out some despicable curse from the other side of the door that she wouldn't repeat.

"Like a monkey," she said again and entertained the thought that if she had only had a bit more sense that night, sense and courage, she could have poured a little oil onto the branch, out of the window, and set the branch alight to burn together with the one who had climbed up to peek at her.

Again, the whimper turned into a cry-like laugh, and it too died out.

But she only has courage in words, she said, and sometimes not even that; perhaps in her small town she seemed courageous, her father must think who knows what she's doing here, and probably ready to rend his clothing[11] if she goes with whoever she wants without asking his permission, and on each visit there she has to pretend she's content on her new path, content, content, content.

He suggested waiting outside until she comes out and tells him that there's no one there. She opened the two locks with two keys and left the door slightly ajar, and he saw her drawing away into the entrance hall and passing through the dark parlor. There was no one in the street, no cart passed. He could have entered after her without anyone noticing, but remained standing where he was, and his gaze wandered to the branch of the oak and explored the brackets upon which the eldest son had climbed to the fork in the lower branches. He then spotted the writing and the drawing that had recently been engraved there with a pocketknife or a nail; they were as despicable as the curse the eldest son spat out from the other side of her door, and the words drew an image in his mind that mustn't be contemplated, one far more accurate than that engraved on the trunk.

When he entered the house, he saw a piano with a vase of flowers on it in the parlor and on its right sofas. The wide steps at the end of the entrance hall were covered by a carpet runner, and the fabric was worn down in the center of every step, where it had been stepped on many times. When she went up in front of him, he looked at her ankles, the movement of her buttocks, her narrow hips, the roundness of her shoulders; and also saw the writing and drawing on the trunk of the oak tree almost tangible with the act described in them.

When she opened the door, her small room could be seen illuminated by the light of the oil lamp, and it had a warm congenial appearance, he found the small table with the embroidered cloth a pleasing sight. There were two shelves on which her few clothes were folded, and a bed, a girl's bed, on whose cover flowers were embroidered like those woven in the curtain.

"Sit," she said, moving the chair and drawing it slightly away from the table.

He sat on the chair, she sat on the bed; they had never been in such close proximity.

He then told her about the forests – those that he missed in the city – about their treetops that join to each other, and how his father used to evaluate the worth of entire forests according to the amount of railway sleepers that could be manufactured from them, and about the sound a treetop makes when it falls; and he also told her about the rafts that sail on the river at night, and how the men at the back of them kindled small bonfires sailing their flames between the darkness of the sky

---

11 An ancient Jewish custom expressing mourning, grief, and loss.

and the darkness of the water to all the places he had not yet been; and he also told of the cascades which in his childhood seemed to be at the end of the world, until he learned that the world was many times larger and not only Pinsk and Minsk were in it but Kiev and Moscow and Petersburg and other countries and continents beyond the ocean that he would never see were he to remain in his village.

"I've been to China." she suddenly said, and again a cry-like laugh was emitted from her throat, until it was choked and replaced by a whimper. "I've also been to Africa and Venice as well. She then bent down and stretched her hand out under the bed and felt around for a moment and from her case took out a photograph album, the kind sold in the department store, an album with copper foil on its cover and black pages.

She straightened up, leaned her back against the pillow again and began to page through the album: most of the pages remained black and empty, and only on the first ones a few photographs could be seen with white serrated edges pressed by the corners into cardboard angular holders black like the page. "Here I am in China," she said, "on the wall, can you see?" The local photographer's store had a backdrop with a hole cut in its center for a head to be stuck through. Her head could be seen with a flat wicker hat on it while she stands on a wall no higher than a cemetery wall. "And here I'm in Moscow," she said, "can you see?" On another painted backdrop with a hole in it, her head could be seen wearing a papakha in front of the gates of the Kremlin with its golden onion-like domes above here like a cluster of conical hats. "That was at the end of my first month here," she said, "when I was still happy to be here."

"The Chinese hat suits you," he said; the flat wicker hat could still be seen in the album open on her right knee.

"Don't I look silly in it?"

He said that she didn't, not at all! She looked sweet in it, sweet and naughty.

She found it funny that someone should think of her as naughty; even as a child she hadn't been naughty, she had been serious, but never naughty! Yes, from the age of ten she had already become a little mother to her sisters, and while he was playing in the forests with his friends she had to watch over her sisters and take care of them.

"But you are naughty here!" he insisted.

She said that the Chinese hat was skew and no one had taken the trouble to tell her, not the photographer nor his assistant. One could forgive the photographer who disappeared under his black cloak, but why didn't the assistant say something?

"Why should he say something," he replied, "the hat really does suit you."

She asked him if he really meant it, and he said yes. He also said he was sure that if she didn't have some naughtiness in her, despite all her protests, she wouldn't have been photographed like that at all. On the outside she seems so serious, but inside there has to be something naughty in her! Where else had she been photographed, he asked.

She showed him and had already turned the album slightly towards him: in one photograph she stuck her head out in the middle of a painted jungle, and for some reason wearing a Turkish fez, All around her were lively monkeys and elephants whose trunks twisted upwards and some striped animal that perhaps was a giraffe or just a long necked zebra; in another she sailed on one of the canals of Venice in a gondola beneath an arched wooden bridge (Venice in the picture very much resembled Petersburg, and the gondola's bow twisted upwards like the elephant trunk in the previous picture).

"Don't the Italians have a hat?" he asked, because in that picture her head was bare.

"Apparently not," she replied. "If they had, he would have given me one. He or his assistant."

It turned out that in the photographer's shop there was a hanger where all those hats hung: the red fez with the tassel, the Chinese wicker hat, a balding papakha, and an Indian turban with a peacock feather whose designated backdrop had been ruined when acid developer had accidentally been spilled onto it.

"That turban also would have suited you," he said.

She asked how he knew, and he said that he could picture her in a turban.

"Can you really?"

He placed the tips of his fingers on the page of the album opened on her knee, outlining a kind of turban with the fingernail of his thumb above the photographed head and adding ornamentation, and suddenly she changed her seating position, as if all at once the weight of his thumb had grown to the weight of an animal foot with unsheathed claws. But he didn't remove his thumb, he fluttered it over the photographed cheek, her cheek, perhaps removing a grain of dust from there, perhaps caressing it.

In the picture on the other side of the page, the photographer and his assistant had given her a white umbrella with abundant tassels falling from its edges, and the handle, on whose tip the head of a parrot was carved, she rested coquettishly on her shoulder as if any minute she would spin it and charm men with the dizzying tassels. He wondered how the photographer and his assistant had posed her at the back of the shop; corrected her posture, changed the angle of the hand; he also wondered what passersby might have seen from the street.

She answered him, and when he asked if she hadn't been concerned about remaining alone with the photographer and his assistant for more than an hour, she asked what had she to be concerned about: everyone had good things to say about that photographer, one has to make an appointment a week in advance, sometimes even two weeks.

"Nevertheless," he said, "two men and a woman."

"You're still thinking about that!" she said.

He turned another page, and while doing so, as if unintentionally, the back of his hand light brushed against her stomach next to the side of the album and through the fabric of her dress he felt the warmth of her body and how she shrank at his touch and restrained her breath as silent as a small animal playing dead in order not to be attacked. He turned his chair towards her, raising a squeak from the wooden floor that thundered through the empty house.

The album had many pages, but only first ones contained photographs: from China, Venice, Africa, Paris, Moscow, from the deck of a Trans-Atlantic ship (the waves twisted upwards like the elephant trunk and the gondola bow). By then he had already moved to sit next to her on the bed. She didn't protest.

With the next page that he turned, the back of his hand brushed against her stomach once more: the back of his hand fluttered up and down over the frozen, tense, dead stomach. And with the next page – Big Ben was drawn there, high as an oak tree – he let the his hand linger a moment longer until the page was turned; the one after was already empty and black, he lifted the back of his hand above the edge of the page and in that way touched the lower part of her chest, lingering for a moment; it was warm and soft and he felt the movement of the diaphragm. With the next page, black and empty like the one before, he raised the back of his hand farther and through the delicate fabric rubbed the breast once and once more and once more; and then he heard her breathing.

She asked him to stop: for God's sake, stop, they shouldn't have come here at all, from the moment they walked in she knew she had made a terrible mistake, so please stop. But the album was still open on her knees and the hand he withdrew was placed on the blackness of the empty pages with all its weight, and she didn't try to remove the album and the hand on it: perhaps she was paralyzed by his touch, perhaps her belief in certain restrictions had weakened, and perhaps this way she hoped to bind him to her and ensure he wouldn't leave.

She asked him to let her be but he stayed where he was. He should leave her alone, she had already explained to him that she only has courage in words, and not always even that. She would never travel to all those places, Africa and China and Venice and Paris and London, nor to America and not even to the Land of Israel, not in her wildest dreams would she dare to go near there. Maybe he would, because his dreams are those of a boy and not of an adult man. Just leave her alone now, don't touch her like that, stop.

Leave her alone and go away, she said but didn't remove his hand, if that's what he wants then leave. As far as she's concerned he can sleep on the train and live on the train, if that's what he wants, but what's he got to do in Petersburg – she spoke to the black album page as is if it had been appointed to mediate between them – what will he live on there, what will he eat and where will he live? They won't let him stay there, they'll banish him right away or arrest him, that's what will happen in the end. To them, he's just a zhid; he's only Ilya to her. She said that in a soft voice and her body said it too, and for a moment he hesitated and almost pulled away, but his hand was already roaming over her.

To the questions she asked in that frail voice, not to him but to the black album page lying on her knee like a shield, he replied that he intends to find work in Petersburg; you can always find some chance work, just as he had found in the villages and towns on the way here, no job is unacceptable in his eyes, he had found work here on that first day they met.

"It's a pity we met," she said and asked to be left alone, not do what he's doing now, to stop.

"It's not a pity," he replied to her, "it's good that we met."

She peered into his eyes to see if he meant what he had said, and the album fell from her knees and she made no attempt to pick it up. "It's late," she said as if the time would thrust him off of her, "do you know what the time is?" He didn't know. He took out his watch from his pocket and looked at the dial. It was so late that he hesitated to say the time; in fact, their being here together at an hour like this had long passed the limit from which there was no return.

"Show me," she said and pulled the watch towards her, "show me the time." She loosened her grip on the watch and its chain stretched; it was warm, not from the touch of his hand but from the depths of his trouser pocket, and when a crimson glow spread over her face he knew exactly why she was blushing. She glanced briefly at the watch and dropped it in his palm the way one rids oneself of a contaminated object, a dead mouse.

When she spoke, she addressed her words to the floor, to the gondola in the photograph or the gondolier or the bridge painted above them. "How will you find a place to sleep there," she said, "without knowing anyone? How will you know where to go, Ilya."

He'll find somewhere, he replied, and continued doing what he had been doing before and she no longer pushed his hand away. And if by chance he doesn't find, he said, he'll sleep outdoors in some public park as he had done more than once, he had slept in barns, in public parks, in stairwells. So he'll sleep on a park bench or one in the train station, what's wrong with a bench. I'll be a bit hard, not like this mattress sinking under their behinds.

He fell silent and sensed the slight movement of her thigh when a muscle clenched there, but she didn't move it away from his leg nor did she move his hands away.

Beyond the window the branches of the oak creaked, and perhaps the voice of some nocturnal bird was sounded there, a bird concealed by the darkness. Her eyes turned to the window.

"Has your cousin by any chance been there again?" he asked, and without hesitation supported himself with her knee when he got up from the bed and approached the window and moved the curtain aside and looked out until his eyes became adjusted to the darkness. The foliage of the oak quivered in the wind, but only leaves were borne by that branch opposite him and it had only been shaken by their movement.

She didn't change her seating position but replaced the album on her knees as some sort of protection. Her back still leaned against the pillow, and through the material of her dress and her undergarments were the softness of her stomach and the roundness of her breasts.

He bent down next to the table and looked at the oil lamp and straightened out a tiny wrinkle in the cloth. His gaze then wandered over the two shelves and the wooden box with sewing implements like his mother's, and the box where she kept letters she received from her family, and the drawing that must have been done by one of her sisters: a large heart surrounded by flowers. She followed his gaze from the sunken bed.

The little one drew that, she said, the one she loves the most and misses the most, what she wouldn't give to see her now and kiss her. Everything she saves here, even if it's not much, she sends home, they need it more than she does. Yes, she had also left her home like him, but not like the crazy plans he had; God knows where they come to him from. "We're allowed to be here," she said, "this is our place! They can't get rid of us, Ilya," and moved the open album slightly with her right hand until its spine rested between her thighs with a side on each thigh, on the right the gondola and on the left the tower of Pisa no higher than a streetlamp.

If they boot him out of Petersburg, then so what; let them if that's what they decided.; that way it'll only give him more reason to travel on and see more places. The world is big, gigantic, Russia's big, Russia's gigantic; you can travel through it by train for weeks from one end to the other and still not see everything, so why the hell should he agree to stay in the small corner allotted to their race like a community of lepers? He's no leper.

She looked at him and some thought undid the features of her face and changed her expression, until she regathered them. "Neither am I a leper," she said.

Only after studying her face and the sound of her defiant voice that lingered in the air, he returned to sit on the bed, and again the mattress sunk and brought their behinds, their thighs and the sides of their bodies close together. He shut the album, and when he lifted his hand he felt her soft breath trembling beneath it, as quiet and delicate and the breath of a bird, until he bent toward her chest following his hand and rested his head there like the drunk they saw from the bridge and pressed his lips to the material of her dress until he felt or imagined he felt her nipple stiffen, and with his head pressed close like that he smelt the scent of lavender.

Then she lifted her small hand and moved it toward his head where she inserted her fingers into the hair at the forehead. They were inserted firmly rather than and grasped his head, not to pull him off from her but to press his entire head to her breast, as if he had become her baby. Once again the branches of the oak outside creaked, its foliage rustled; a night wind was making its way towards a distant destination, shrouded by the dark.

Mommy, he almost said to her, the way the drunk under the bridge had said, but didn't.

He was being her son, her infant, until he moved on to other things. Then she fell silent like an animal playing dead, and asked him not to do that, begged him not to do that, because it wasn't nice, stop that stop stop under no circumstances should dare to do that and that as well and especially not that. And when she became tired of objecting or for another reason she hadn't yet admitted to himself, she asked only that he put out the oil lamp: put it out, please put it out; and when it was done, she let him do all those acts to her, and not because he had exhausted her, but because she hoped it would bind him to her despite that he had sworn to her nothing in the word would bind him: not a family, not a woman, not guilt.

On the very same night and on the following days and nights in other places – as if the soul has some boundary that when breached, allows everything inside it to burst out since there are no boundaries after it – he blamed himself for other things, even more grave, where it was not unborn fetuses that died, but adults who gave birth and would have given more births, and the burden of the things he blamed himself for was lighter than he had assumed. Only at night they sometimes rose up between his eyelids and filled them, until they were penetrated by the nightmares of his neighbor on the other side of the wall, and he would then wait for them to also drown his own nightmares among mines exploding in the Sea of Japan, and at least the lesser ones: the rustling of the material, her curves on the bed covering that had been rumpled; the tiny sounds that she made under him until becoming silent again; her soft continuous crying noticeable only by the quivering of her shoulders; her eyes that were fixed on him when he got up from her and the surrendering and defeated motion with which she turned to the wall.

18

"Isn't your sweetheart waiting?" Telegin asked.

Beyond the locked door the steps of the policeman could be heard pacing from one end of the corridor to the other, and from the inner courtyard the gate-keeper could be heard arguing with someone wanting to enter: perhaps a peddler offering his wares to the people of Okhrana.

"If you want to see what's going on there," Telegin gestured with his eyebrows toward the window, "take a look, Poliakov. It doesn't bother us, really. Does it bother you, Oleg Timofeyevich?"

"No," replied Perdischenko, but he seemed pensive.

Telegin put his leg down from the small sofa and folded the newspaper that had been spread under his shoes and squashed it into a ball and flung it accurately into the wastepaper basket. His colleague complimented him on his throw. What young bachelors can allow themselves to do at home - practicing throwing into a wastepaper basket - no family man can do; not throwing things nor all sorts of trysts with Gypsy singers in the middle of the night.

"Nor busying yourself with bombs in the middle of the night," Telegin replied and rose to his feet and smoothed his trousers down with his hand and checked his reflection in the windowpane. "While family men celebrate birthdays, Poliakov is busy with bombs."

They still didn't believe he had no connection to the bombs and all he had done was wave the handkerchief at men who threw them. "You must have seen or heard something," they said, "you're not blind or deaf."

For a while it seemed they had been dividing roles between themselves in the course of the conversation: Perdischenko spoke about birthdays and Telegin about the day of death, and both toward the same purpose, to break him; one telling how he celebrated with his loving family and the other about his dubious entertainment on the very same night, in a hotel where a bomb accidentally exploded in one of its rooms. "Did you have any connection to that?" Telegin asked. "He was celebrating a birthday at the time, what were you celebrating?"

It transpired that Perdischenko had turned fifty: a golden jubilee. "Most defi-nitely an age when one can begin to see old age approaching," Perdischenko said, as if he had no better conversation companion to share his thoughts with other than the man he was interrogating. "But then you, Poliakov, won't even reach thirty."

Telegin gave an unnecessary explanation; mentioning Semyonovsky Square and how far one could go there, actually how high: above all the masses who'll come to watch the hanging and the only thing higher will be angels floating in the sky. The angels reminded his elder colleague of the birthday his daughters celebrated for him: Irena and Nina, who were angels themselves even if they didn't have wings.

They had decided to prepare a surprise birthday for him, he said, and everyone in the house made a conscious effort to keep it secret, they even made old Marfa swear she wouldn't utter a word. "In our house there really is no reason for concern," he said, "not about treachery or informing or of being followed. On the contrary, everyone was keen to keep the secret. But one day I see everyone blushing the moment I walk in, and Marfa falls dead silent every time I come near, she had a had a sour look on her face and I managed to hear a few words. It wasn't that I was making any special effort to find out what they were preparing for me, but nonetheless I heard. Do you understand what I'm getting at, Poliakov? After all you aren't stupid. You just act stupidly."

"Do you people celebrate birthdays?" Telegin asked (the last time the square was mentioned they spoke about the phase after the hanging; "you'll get a coffin," they promised him as if announcing a prize and not a punishment, and asked about the curious custom in this matter, and if wasn't somehow connected to the way they welcome babies into the world; when they're born the organ with which children are made is cut, and when they die their bodies are thrown straight into a pit, without any coffin, with a kind of primitiveness inconceivable to any cultured nation).

Poliakov found difficulty remembering the last time his birthday had been celebrated. In a different era, he had so much wanted a pocketknife – that he remembered – and what was it he had to make do with in the end? It was easier remembering when his brother Izu's was celebrated, and more painful, because at the time he still behaved like an older brother.

When Perdischenko returned home one day – so he related – not that he didn't knock on the door, he did, but the girls didn't hear, and on entering the room he saw a book of songs on the piano he hadn't previously seen, and also spotted their handwriting on it. The girls immediately shut the book, but he began to understand something: the little ones were preparing a song for him specially for his birthday. There was only one thing he couldn't understand – that's what he said, as if they had gathered here to discuss the family rituals of his home – why such a lovely idea seemed unfit to Marfa; something that was evident from all the wrinkles of her frown. "After all, she's not stupid," he said, "she just sometimes acts stupidly. Though unlike you people, no one dies from her stupidity."

He took a long sip of the tea, and it was clear it was pleasing to his palate.

With that, a sign was given to Telegin to read from the report that Perdischenko wrote on the night he celebrated his birthday, in his orderly cursive handwriting, describing the bombing that had taken place in the Bristol Hotel – a respectable hotel actually – and not that anyone's blaming Poliakov for that, after all, he had been in another hotel, the one they caught him in, but perhaps he at least knows the name of the man who was killed?

"No," he said; he had never been in that hotel and hadn't heard about the bombing there.

"Look, Poliakov," Telegin said to him, "we're not saying that you're responsible for what happened there, we're only asking the name of the man who was there; we can't hurt him any more than he hurt himself."

That anonymous person in the Bristol Hotel, it transpired, for some reason died half-naked. Yes, he dismantled the bomb in his underpants, perhaps he was hot; it's scary just to think about it! He also died in those underpants, and more precisely, in what was left of them and of him. With your people there seems to be some connection between bombs and hotels, anyhow, perhaps that way he could remember what happens when a bomb explodes in a person's hands? At least in the beginning that anonymous person still had hands.

And not only was his room damaged, the rooms around it were also badly damaged, as was the corridor and the hotel restaurant below. The floor of the adjoining room was covered in fragments of furniture – that's what was written further on in the report – a chest of five drawers and a table were destroyed, two pillows were rent apart, a chair was smashed, and at the foot of the double bed shreds of blankets and sheets were found. "In addition," Telegin continued, "parts of objects were found that didn't belong to the hotel. And do you know what they belonged to Poliakov?"

He didn't know, and right away they told him: to the detonating device of a bomb weighing two or three kilograms that had been prepared for being thrown from a distance, and it's not hard to imagine the kind of damage that would have been caused had it exploded inside the carriage of a high-level personage.

"And doesn't all this mean anything to you, Poliakov?" Telegin asked.

"No," he answered.

"Didn't you see or hear anything?"

"No," he answered again.

"Interesting," said Perdischenko. "Most interesting, because unlike you, even when I did everything I could not to know about something – something completely innocuous – I nonetheless got to know quite a bit about it. But go on please, Konstantin Nikolaevich."

His colleague needed no urging, and no detail was omitted: not the cracks discovered in the section of the wall between the two windows, not the fragments of the table and chair that were found on the other side of the road near the iron gates of St. Isaac Cathedral, not the two amputated fingers: the fourth and the fifth fingers. "The bomb," Telegin said, "was apparently placed on the table, right below the window, and an accident occurred and it exploded before its time. Those fingers flew twenty-one meters though the air."

Perdischenko sipped the tea again. "Girls in their innocence," he said when he put the cup down, "cannot conceive at all that such things happen; what possible connection could they have to acts like that?" And again, as it is for that purpose they had gathered here, he returned to his birthday and his two daughters. "Wouldn't you like to be a father one day, Poliakov?"

He didn't answer.

"Let me tell you," Perdischenko said, "there's no greater happiness, and especially at my age. Children remind one of something that's completely disappeared from one's own life, something one's already forgotten the name of. Innocence, Poliakov, innocence. The way they look at you is enough, watching them sleep is enough, how much trust they put in the world, as if you and your bastard friends didn't exist at all. That peace and calm when they dream; what connection could they have to awful deeds? Anyone who sees them then cannot but help ask himself how all that one day gets lost. And I'll tell you how, Poliakov: because of people like you."

Once again a dim commotion could be heard from the courtyard, and Telegin looked out there.

"Innocent children," Perdischenko continued, "can't conceive that terrible things are being done in the world like the ones you and your friends are doing. How could they conceive that on the third floor of a hotel a man stands and gives the signal to someone waiting below with a bomb in his hand. Let's say, Poliakov, that's all you did."

He sipped his tea, ignoring his assistant who was rustling through his pages.

"Unlike you Poliakov, I picked up things here and there without even making an effort." One day he returned home and heard a sound he had never yet heard coming from the girls' room: it seems they had decided to add a flute to the piano, and the lady playing it, a woman of about forty, he later saw coming out of the music room with a long case under her arm, and since then she's been presenting herself in the house twice a week.

And last week – Perdischenko continued – in a neighborhood he doesn't usually visit from his carriage he by chance saw that lady walking on the sidewalk with her case, taking small steps and entering a building. "Take note, Poliakov," he said, "I wasn't trying to find out anything, but that's how I suddenly found out where she lived. Maybe you also found something out by chance, without actually being involved in it?

"After all, things like that happen," he went on, "and no wonder. It's not hard to notice a woman in the street with a long flute case. But it also wasn't hard to notice your friends." And right away he gave details: his friends might not have had flute cases, but they did have round boxes, more than one or two. "Didn't you put them in hat boxes? I'm talking about the bombs, Poliakov, only about the bombs." And he also knew where those hats had been bought – a little bird told him about that – in what neighborhood in what street at what number. "They didn't keep their mouths shut, your friends, and they also told what you did with the hats that were inside there, you yourself, Poliakov."

He didn't answer because he wasn't sure if it was true or a trap they were setting him, and because he remained silent the other interrogator went back to reading his report. If he won't tell them about the bombs, they'll tell him – maybe that way he'll remember something – and as the description became drier so the details sounded more threatening.

"Next to the eastern wall," Telegin read out, "bits of the cupboard and the table were found, a heap of wooden chips and a curtain that had become detached due to the shock wave. Remains of clothing were also found: shreds of a shirt, one sweater sleeve, as well as a pair of trousers intact. Forty centimeters from the pieces of the cupboard the body of an unidentified man was found. The neck was ripped from the throat to the nape, and the face was severely damaged by shrapnel and from burns and was turned approximately a hundred and eighty degrees backward as if on an axis. That body was found spread out on its back without its upper or lower limbs. What do you have to say to that, Poliakov?"

He didn't reply.

"At the end of the examination these conclusions could be reached: inasmuch as most of the damage caused to room number twenty six was in the western section close to the window that faced St. Isaac's Cathedral and in the place where the table stood, and inasmuch as most of the damage caused to the corpse was found to be on the upper body and especially at the ends of upper limbs, one could conclude that at the moment of the explosion the chest area of the corpse and its stomach were very close to the bomb which it seems had been placed on the table next to the western window and exploded owing to some fault, and from the force of the explosion that anonymous person had been flung toward the opposite wall and remained lying thirty centimeters away from it. One can reasonably assume that in such circumstances the death had been immediate. Do you understand that, Poliakov?"

All that happened on the second or third or sixth day of the investigation; their number had become hazy. On one of their mornings or evenings Perdischenko related, as if there was nothing more important, how he heard for the first time the song his daughters had prepared for him, a song that didn't stop at his present birthday, but continued to the following ones ("We happily await your coming old age / like angels in a fairy tale," and the next verse continued from his old age onward: "Our lives were a secret, and our deaths were shrouded in a veil"), and again he mentioned the bomb that was drawn out of the lake.

It seems what had happened to that bomb once happened to Perdischenko's neighbor's shoe: for a whole week his shoe had been considered drowned because it had fallen off while he was fishing and his neighbor already pronounced it dead, until one day, quite by chance, it was caught in the hook of his rod and rescued. And the bomb, after being rescued from the net among dozens of twitching fish, was transported in a wheelbarrow to Klotilin's office, and dried itself off there in comfort until the police arrived.

A thought like that could come to mind now: that right here, in this pleasant office, sits a man who claims not to understand bombs, and opposite him sit two interrogators who find it a little difficult to believe him, and what would happen for instance, if they shut this man, ignorant in matters of bombs, in a room with a bomb – it would be greatly worth his while to dismantle it, because he couldn't be sure the bomb wasn't about to explode. Why shouldn't they try a little experiment to find out without any doubt whether he knows how to work with bombs or not. It's one of the two: if he knows, he'll succeed in dismantling it; and if not, it will simply explode in his hands, and that way his innocence will be proved: there'll be some benefit in it for him.

No, they won't be doing it here. Of course, not here. Even if there's someone here who thinks the time has come to replace the furniture. How about outside the city? In some empty warehouse no one comes to. Or an empty hut of a rail-road guard? Like the one where twenty-five years ago they tried to dig a tunnel to the tracks to blow up the Tsar's train with a mine? Something that could be a reminder to us all that even then, in the legendary era of the Narodniks, there was no shortage of squealers. In the end everyone was caught, everyone without exception twitched in the air like the fish in Klotilin's nets.

Sometime later, a few minutes or more, when his cup of tea had been emptied, Perdischenko raised something new to ponder, something linguistic: why use such a negative term, "squealing," when in fact they were speaking of wise people who for wise reasons chose to co-operate with the secret police, some for money and others for their lives, and who's to judge them? Who can judge a man who in order to stay alive agrees to hand over those who sent him to his death with such ease, while they themselves, his senders, evaded the rope? One could certainly identify with such anger.

Even Perdischenko, on his fiftieth birthday, when thoughts arose not only about his age but also about death itself, found a kind of anger rising in him. The girls had sung about it innocently, of course, those dear ones, and there's nothing dearer to him in the world than them. The guilt lay on their teacher, and with all the sympathy he had for old maids he wouldn't be sorry if her flute were to explode in her hands or in her mouth.

How was it worded in the report about the Bristol Hotel? "Without upper limbs, and the face was turned approximately a hundred and eighty degrees backward as if on an axis." Konstantin Nikolaevich even had taken the trouble to measure exactly how many centimeters separated what was left of the anonymous man and the eastern wall.

"The western," Telegin corrected, "the eastern faces Voznesensky Prospekt."

And since the wall with the window had been mentioned, and since the man being interrogated still refrained from talking – this time he made a firm decision to lapse into cowardice the way he had in the village and in the hotel – Telegin again raised his old suggestion:

If he had been occupied only with a handkerchief, why shouldn't they finally get to see how he waved it from the window of his hotel. The Excelsior, not The Bristol.

"Why don't you show us," said Telegin. "Go to the window and demonstrate for us."

19

Tel Aviv, 1994

My dearest son, my soul's beloved

I pray you have grown splendidly and are diligent in your studies and are a loving son to your mother. For many a year have I have longed for the moment to be in your company, and oft have despaired and with much striving have rallied and reminded myself – he, the old man, reminded his father to recall the flowery language of the newspaper sheets of *Hamelitz*[12] - may I not forget that which should never be forgotten, because on the day I deny you and my love for you, there shall be reason to live. Therefore should you diligently hearken to my deeds at the ends of the earth, know you my son my thoughts were only of you, and the deeds were done for you to be proud of me.

Your loving and eternally longing father

Or this:

My son, joy of my heart, site of my longing

And so on.

In his childhood and youth the old man imagined reading missives from his father all composed with flowery language in the spirit of the times, He occupied himself vigorously in the wording of the letters that had somehow made their way to him – wrapped around the leg of a carrier pigeon, plugged in a bottle tossed between waves, reached out to him by the dark hand of a messenger wearing a turban – all kinds of ways other than the way he real letter had reached him, the single one whose contents were better immediately forgotten. And there were other letters he imagined in his adulthood and his old age, written not by his father but rather by his two other abandoners, his wife and his son, but those were less painful.

From a small village on the banks of the Berezina, his father arrived in Petersburg and from there landed up in the east by circuitous means, and from there on one summer's day in the second decade of the twentieth century his last possessions arrived with that brief letter. At the time, the old man had to struggle with his mother not to throw those possessions into the garbage bin, despite it being a suitable place for them if only for their stench. He became a boy and a youth and

---

12 A Hebrew language newspaper published in Russia between 1880 – 1904.

a man, a sergeant in the Brigade and a doctoral student at the Hebrew University and a proof-reader on the *Davar* newspaper, and once again he had to protect those possessions, at least the memory of them, from his wife Ada.

He once read in the motoring section of the newspaper about a vehicle with a front-wheel drive and Japanese jeeps whose departure angle on harsh terrain was seventeen degrees; and that term, departure angle, whose meaning in matters of cars he didn't know, made his heart tremble. How is that angle measured, beyond which the jeep apparently overturns and all its wheels leave the earth? His mother obstinately refused to speak about the man who had departed from her, and the rare times he was mentioned in a conversation it with a faceless and voiceless "he," "he" loved and hated, a place to long for and to loathe. "He" who should be forgotten she had been sentenced to remember, a scoundrel who sowed the seed of the fetus in her stomach and let her give birth to it alone in the small town among small-minded people and sail alone with that child all the way from Odessa and raise him God knows how after the money she received from her uncle ran out.

A fair amount of time passed until he also knew how she managed; he discovered, quite unintentionally, how she paid rent to her landlords (she hadn't yet started working as a tea lady at the *Davar* newspaper). Only by chance he heard them while walking on tiptoes in the passage, silent as a tiger.

"You're still a young woman," Mr. Hirschson said to her in the living room (perhaps not in those exact words), "and you've got a sweet little boy that you're bringing up alone, and that certainly can't be easy. After all, you're earning pennies, and besides, a boy, every boy, needs a father (he, the old man was that boy, a boy and not a tiger), even if only from a financial point of view. There's not a boy in the world, Miriam – I hope you don't mind me calling you by your first name - that doesn't need a roof over his head, not one. Now, if you lived alone, Miriam, you could still have allowed yourself to move from place to place, I'm not saying that's not possible, but to do all that with a small boy? It's just wouldn't be moral or responsible to put him through that, to ruin his life that way."

Then Mr. Hirschson fell silent for a moment, and the old man wondered why his life would be ruined just by moving from apartment to apartment – the thought of which actually excited him – but before he could reflect on it Mr. Hirschson continued to speak.

"What am I suggesting to you, Miriam, to steal? To murder? After all, I'm not a criminal, and quite a few people in this city even think of me as a respectable man. And here you are, Miriam, a beautiful young woman; all the troubles you've been through haven't succeeded to destroy your beauty. You're permitted to blush, Miriam. Like any beautiful young woman, you must have your needs, and I don't mean only board and lodging. And I too, Miriam, have my own needs, even if I am a few years older than you." (He was at least three decades older than her.) "It's nothing to be ashamed of, Miriam, and certainly no crime, so if there's some point where our needs can meet, why shouldn't they meet? What do you say to that, is it so terrible?"

Mr. Hirschson was silent for a moment, perhaps he intertwined his fingers on his paunch or relaxed in his armchair, and the old man shrunk further in the passage; he was standing behind the coat hanger, hidden by the coat and the blush that must have been spreading over his face, despite not even understanding half of what was said.

"It's certainly no crime, Mr. Hirschson continued, "and the alternative, Miriam, is many times worse, and very very discouraging. Surely you can guess what that is? The alternative is very simple and would be a pity to have to mention it, why spoil the pleasant atmosphere between us that way. But at the worst, Miriam, if God forbid we get to that and it's well worth your while we don't get to that, then I myself will bring that porter here, the one you chased after – yes, the tenants in the building still talk about that – but only for him to take all you and your boy's things and throw them to the four winds. Think about it, Miriam."

His mother didn't reply. She stayed where she was even when Mr. Hirschson got up from the armchair to examine a crack in the wall; he drew his head as well as his finger close to it, and with the tip of his fingernail peeled a sliver of whitewash to check how deep the crack was, and only then she replied: "I need to think it over a little, Hirschson, give me time."

"But of course, Miriam," answered Mr. Hirschson right away, "I didn't mean that you couldn't think it over a little. Your son must be returning from school any minute, and you're doing all this only for him. He's so sweet. But if for example we decide on tomorrow, for example between ten and eleven when the boy isn't home, you'll have enough time to think about it at night, and we'll both have enough time to ourselves in the morning. What do you say, Miriam? I think it's a fair proposal. And until then there'll be no porter or anything else, and that's even though I pass by their square quite a lot."

The next day – a Monday, and that's one of the details he'll never forget, even if his memory degenerates further – he came back from school early, and again entered the apartment stealthily with his satchel on his back (he told the teacher he wasn't feeling well). He heard nothing in the stairwell, but when he crept into the passage he heard strange noises coming from the living room and peeked in there: his mother's head could be seen at the height of Mr. Hirschson's waist, and for a moment it looked like she might be cutting off a cotton thread with her teeth after having sewed a button on his trousers, and Mr. Hirschson's closed eyes could be seen and beads of sweat on his bald head and his open mouth salivating, and then what was going in and out of his mother's head could also be seen and it wasn't a cotton thread, and Mr. Hirschson gave a large bellow and forcefully fastened her head to him. A moment later – a very long moment, in which it wasn't clear if he hadn't choked her, and maybe it would have been better had he choked her (that's what the old man, thought, years later when he understood) – his mother got up and rushed to the toilet and vomited, and from his armchair Mr. Hirschson listened to the sounds coming from there just before getting up he said: "It's not poison, Miriam, you know, even the opposite," and with emboldened steps went out to the stairwell, doing up the buttons of his trousers, and the old man withdrew to the small kitchen that faced the courtyard.

"What are you looking at me like that for?" she said to Nachman when she came out of the toilet and saw him waiting for her. "It's all because of you. If it hadn't been for you, this wouldn't have happened at all!" That's what she angrily said to him and went into the bedroom and slammed the door behind her. She probably got on to her bed and closed her eyes the way she did every time the awaiting day didn't seem worth facing. He stood a moment longer behind the closed door and listened; afterward he went to the guestroom and looked at the armchair Mr. Hirschson had sat in, as if he might still find some button or bit of thread, and from there he returned to the passage and opened the toilet door to peek at the bowl breathing only through his mouth and not crossing the doorway in case the bowl had overflowed.

"What happened, sweetie?" he imagined hearing her calling him from the other side of the closed bedroom door and calling him again in a softer voice, but no word was said, no syllable. The same silence prevailed in her room as on the day he was beaten up by the boys in the yard – the silence of sleep or the silence of deep objection.

"Is your father in America? They mocked him on another occasion (there was no shortage of occasions).

"He's aboard!" he replied and didn't have the faintest idea where he was.

"D'you want us to tell you where he really is?"

He didn't want them to but they told him. He blocked his ears too late.

"Your father's underground!" they said.

A column of ants was advancing towards his feet and he lifted one foot and stamped on them; a snail was grasping a crabgrass leaf and he smashed its shell with the sole of his shoe; and on the way home he still managed to throw a stone at a cat with a chewed tail but missed. Afterward he went up to his mother and asked her about it, and this time she didn't hasten to look away as she usually did, and after a long moment she satisfied his curiosity and said: "Your father? Your father's in heaven watching over you," and there was a time he believed that: his absent father floated in heaven beyond the clouds during the day and the stars at night and watched over him from there. It was a consoling thought: the clouds and the stars were much closer than America, you could see them with your eyes.

That consolation she herself undermined that very same month, when tired of hearing him repeat what she had said every moment he was struck by fear or loneliness, whether because no friend ever came to play or whether because she herself ignored him. "Even if your father was in heaven," she said angrily one night, "he would have run to the farthest end just so that he wouldn't have to see us" And when she turned her face away from him, he saw her shoulders quivering and heard her breathing and understood that she was crying and hated her. "It's not true! It's not true!" he shouted to the back of her neck. "It's not true!" But when he ran out to the balcony and looked at the sky, a sky of day's end, and strained his eyes, a glowing figure, almost blinding, could be seen at its reddening edges fleeing on its way beyond the horizon.

In the middle of the coming winter, one of the girls in his class who lost her father, spoke about him in a certain way. Then came the heavenly era which didn't last long, no more than two months, when that saying of hers ("My father's in heaven!") which he repeated to anyone who was prepared to listen, especially to himself, began to outrage his mother. "Heaven?" she said. "Heaven? You know what, you might just be right, because any place that you and I weren't in was heaven to him. But now he's dead."

The father of the girl from his class died, the ants on which he stamped died, the snail that he squashed; the neighbor's dog that was run over died, the flies he stalked with his hand died, the bugs he threw a shoe at, the chick that fell from its nest died, the cows that were carved up at the butcher died, the horse that suddenly fell in the street died, all the people whose names appeared in black frames[13] died, and only their letters still continued to flutter for a while until the paper was ripped up by the wind.

How does someone die who had never been seen alive? An entire life was missing for it to come to a close, but gradually, until the end of that year, he became accustomed to the idea that his father is not in America or in heaven or in paradise; he's underground, even if it's not exactly clear where that ground is, and certainly not in this country. It could be anywhere other than this country.

When Ada left him she continued living in the same city, and he was careful to avoid that area in order not to add to his suffering. It was possible they could meet by chance on other streets of the city, but they never did. Perhaps she went everywhere in her new husband's car. He probably took her flying to all the places she wanted to visit which Nachman had refused to do ("what's wrong with here?" he would say).

Only once he consented and they travelled abroad to Rome, a trip she had longed for – she wanted to see the piazzas and the fountains and the museums, but he extended their tour to include the battlegrounds of the Brigade – and from there they continued on to Belgium and Holland. He had already been through the length and breadth of Italy in the war, and before then had also travelled to many other places. He had been in the western desert and Cairo and Alexandria and had beheld many sights throughout that period including the pyramids, the Sphinx, the Colosseum, the Arc de Triomphe, windmills and dams. He also saw

---

13 A custom of posting a black framed notice reporting a recent death.

bombs exploding, rounds of tracer bullets in a night sky, wounded men, men with amputated limbs and the dead; he also saw old prostitutes riddled with syphilis, and children pimping their older sisters for a packet of American cigarettes, and Jewish survivors gaunt as skeletons and so fragile he feared to embrace them, lest they fall to pieces in his arms.

The war had been horrific, the deeds committed terrible, but at its close, after he travelled to Amsterdam with his regiment, he felt at long last, toward the end of the fourth decade of his life, he had become a man worthy of his father. The years he served in the Brigade had been the fullest and most important of his life, so too had been the year he consented to Ada's wish and took her to all those places. They left Amnon with his uncle, and every two or three days sent him a postcard which they'd write together: on the back of the Colosseum, or the back of windmill or of a Dutch village girl in clogs. On one postcard he explained to his son about gladiators, in another about the wind that sets a millstone weighing a ton in motion, and Ada would add: "Nony, look after yourself, we miss you." Once she wrote: "Nony, you won't believe what your father almost did today" – the old man wanted to balance on the railing of the bridge as he had done for a bet taken with a friend in the Brigade, and on no account would Ada agree to it.

That night, in a one-star hotel whose neon sign cast flashes of light into the room, he watched her undoing her braid and spreading it over her back and asked her to leave it that way, at least until the end of the trip. Why? She asked him in Italian, "Perché?" and he said – what was it he said? The neon sign flashed and emitted a buzzing sound from the exposed fluorescent bar whose glass covering was broken. "Because you are at your most lovely that way," he replied.

Time had passed: in the bomb craters grass had come up and wheat grew, bell towers whose tops had been lopped off measured time once again, monks pulled the bell ropes again. He remembered not only the man he had carried on his back up the side of a hill and down a slope to the battalion aid station, but also a monk with a crazed look in his eyes who wandered the streets of Rome prophesying with a burning wrath reminiscent of Biblical prophets, and when he heard that they were Jewish soldiers he became terrified as if they themselves had murdered the son of his God, if not with a hammer and nails then with their rifles (in winter they carried them upside down so that the rain wouldn't get into the barrel; "don't let flowers grow there," the sergeant used to say). It was summer, and the oiled barrels glistened in the sun, perhaps they appeared to the monk like a lance that pierced the son of his God. He cursed their mothers and their father's fathers and saliva dribbled down his chin, and suddenly he burst into tears and wiped his eyes with his fists like a child.

He didn't even bother to get off the bus when he took Ada to see the battlegrounds. After travelling for two hours suddenly those two hills could be seen on his left, both covered with wheat, and that covering was enough to turn his stomach – most painful to him was the wind passing through the ears of corn - and when he stuck his head out of the window he saw the driver looking at him in the side mirror and cursing him for dirtying the side of the bus. "It's alright, Nachman, it's alright," Ada said to him when he put his head back inside she wiped his mouth with her handkerchief like a little boy.

From Italy they travelled to Holland, where his regiment had reached at the end of the war. Though they didn't fight there at all, it was in Amsterdam that he finally felt he had become a man worthy of his father: he had participated in a great war, a world war, and unlike him he had been on the winning side. He might not have committed acts of bravery and didn't win any medals, but he had fulfilled his role in a proper fashion, and even the major praised him in front of the whole company for rescuing the body of his comrade from the battlefield. Amsterdam captivated him more than any other city he had visited, and not because of its cordial citizens, but rather its water canals. Those of the Russian winter capital may have been longer and wider, and on bridges like these, or longer and wider ones, his father had walked, and on the water beneath them blocks of ice floated on their way to the North Sea; and perhaps his father had sat there disguised as a beggar and watched the minister's carriage pass by in order to ascertain the most suitable time for the assassination.

At the time he sent a postcard to his mother by military post and wrote about the resemblance she would find between these canals and those of the city of her birth, Leningrad or St. Petersburg, or Peterburg, and in the reply he received two months later, she wrote that he was mistaken: she came from a tiny provincial city, not Petersburg or Petrograd or Leningrad; other people lived there, not her; his father had lived there for a while until he fled to the four winds and changed Petersburg for some hole that's hardly marked on the map; fled like a mouse and died like a mouse, and good riddance.

He insisted on seeing pomp and grandeur in the past, a tempestuousness and strength of spirit of which there is not even a trace in the present. Whereas the past had held the promise of a different life which one could live, if only one could find the courage to live it; and there was some consolation in the thought that somewhere an alternative life existed, if not within the reach of one's hand then within the reach of one's yearning. It was only when he was abandoned in his old age that he found no consolation in abandonment: some of Ada's clothes still remained in the cupboard, the imprint of her head could be seen on the pillow with two or three long black hairs whose roots were white, and her fingerprints were still evident in the disarray of objects strewn throughout the apartment wherever she wanted to or was tired of.

She had already left him once, when she was still young: she went away for a week with a travel bag in her hand, and he didn't know whether she had gone with a good friend to a resort in Safed, as she had said, or whether she had gone off with another man. That whole week he looked after Amnon by himself: took care that he ate, brushed his teeth, washed, changed clothing, that he not be sad before bedtime and not wonder too much about his mother's disappearance. At night the old man would lie alone on the wide bed and see her in the darkness of the room as he had seen her on the trip they made in the footsteps of the Brigade, in a light dress and her loose hair waving, attracting the gaze of men.

Five days later he found a card from her in the postbox, it was photograph of the Safed resort surrounded by trees, but whoever had been sitting there with her didn't appear in that photograph. On the back, written in her agitated handwriting she wrote: My dear Mano, how I miss you both! It's lovely here, you can see for yourself from the photograph, but I miss you and Nony and all the mess that I left behind. You most probably have already put everything in its place the way you like to do. It's been good to get away for a while, Nachman, but mainly to learn what's really important in life — and that's you and Nony. You do forgive me, Nachman, don't you?

"Your mother simply decided that she needs a new life," he said to their child when she tired of him the second time. He said it in the driest tones of his voice, and their son was amazed that at their age they were still capable of such whims. They must already have seemed old in his eyes, and even before that he must have found it hard to think of them as having needs and desires and passions.

In the corner of the living room, on the small carpet, not far from the large backpack their son had unloaded there with the flight labels still on it, lay the old pointer that already had difficulty lifting its head even to eat, and from time to time the three of them looked at its lusterless eyes and the feeble wagging of its tail that barely lifted off the carpet and right away dropped onto it again. It looked at them with blurry half-closed eyes and at the time seemed like a living symbol of its owners' situation: their marriage was dying.

After her second and final leaving, he refused to speak about her, not a word, and after he imposed new order throughout the apartment no trace was left of her, and only the silence of the rooms where every object stood in its rightful place sometimes recalled the complete opposite, the turmoil that had previously filled them. Yes, no normal woman would do a thing like that and certainly not at her age, but that was exactly what she had done. Before leaving the second time said she'd had enough, and he still didn't understand of what; she said she wasn't prepared to be buried alive with him, and he still didn't understand what life she felt she was missing: coffee houses? Films? Plays? They weren't life itself, mere diversions.

In life — as he sees it — real acts are done that change fates and are far from any kind of diversion, but he hadn't accomplished any such acts and nor had his son. Now, for instance, out of all the places in the world his son had chosen to take a vacation, he chose an English village where someone lives who might know something about the man who fathered him. His son who purely by chance found a house there said the place was charming and that the landscape had a calming effect, and that he has no intention of becoming involved in all that; "all that" meaning his grandfather, meaning their family, meaning their very existence in the world. No, his son showed no curiosity about his ancestors, not about their deaths, the adversities of their old age or their loneliness – that's how Nachman more and more feels lately: old and lonely.

Hello Dad, he could have written to him, I'm staying here in this English village surrounded by fields and meadows, and outside it's raining, but inside the house I'm renting is warm and pleasant, and I'm sorry that you aren't here with me. After all, you now have no one in the world to talk to, not even a dog! What a mistake I made, Dad, when I thought it was better that you don't get a new dog. There's no one in the world who doesn't need a living being next to him in order not to go crazy from loneliness.

When Ada left and took with her the only diversion he had allowed himself in his life then, Sigmund, the puppy, for a while it seemed its absence was more painful to him than her absence; at least that's what he said to himself. But on that day and the following days and the following years he still remembered in great detail the years they had been alone, without dogs and without children: their first meeting in the Atara café in Jerusalem in the summer of 1948, and how the curly haired waiter had looked at them; and how captivated he had been by her vitality and zest for life and her enthusiasm over all sorts of trifles that up until then he hadn't given any thought to; and their lodgings in an abandoned Arab house whose owners they complete forgot about after a month, and the deep alcove where they could sit together at night and talk, and not only talk (he told her about everything he saw in the war and exaggerated only a bit, so that she'd respect him a little more: he didn't take credit for any dead Germans, but had rescued his company from a minefield when he volunteered to walk ahead of them); and the mulberry tree from whose branches the neighbor's children came to pick leaves for their silk-worms, and how she said: "When we have a child, Mano, you'll explain to it how they make the silk" (no doubts had yet been cast on his academic capabilities); and the summer they travelled to Italy and Holland; and the hour his son was born, an early morning hour of a stormy winter day, and how he taught him to read and write before first grade ("We'll send him straight off to university," she said). And in spite of everything, the week she left he hung on to the dog and was prepared to fight for it the way one fights for the custody of a child in a court of law. If his own father had wanted him that way, an entire life wouldn't have passed without them seeing each other even once.

Just a week from the day of her second and final leaving, a week when he tidied up and returned everything to its place (a whole day was required to clean the fridge: remnants of congealed shriveled egg yolk in small bowls forgotten in its depths, tomato halves kept for salad flowering with a downy mold, and cucumbers that had rotted and stuck to the bottom of the drawer like naked snails until they were scraped off with a spatula), he already began to miss the disarray that trailed after her from room to room, and against his rules he even allowed the objects remain slightly out of place. At the time, he still didn't admit to that yearning, and only asked his son, who mediated between him and Ada, that the dog be returned to him, not for his own sake but for that of the dog who was used to the public park. In the apartment she had moved to – he didn't want to know who she was living with there, and only wished for her to slip down the stairs or have a heart attack or a stroke – Sigmund must be missing his bushes and trees.

After the dog was returned to him with a new leash attached to its old collar, he never mentioned a word about Ada, not in name nor in deed. And once again the two of them strolled through the paths of the park in step with each other, an old man and his dog who with time had learned to temper his capering, and only when they returned to the apartment and opened the door, he with his key and the dog with his paws, he sensed Sigmund's disappointment at the emptiness of the apartment and its stillness: the objects had become silent, it seemed they were only in tune with themselves when constantly moved around.

There had been times – he can still remember them – when he would wake her in the middle of the night by touching her back and her shoulders and her behind, and without looking at each other they did the deed between a state of sleep and being awake and without exchanging a word. The old man had once had passions and desires, and Ada would respond to him with great enjoyment and was only careful nothing should be heard on the other side of the wall. With eyes that had not yet dulled he would look at her nakedness in the morning, and his gaze would rest on beautiful women in the street and on magazine covers on display at kiosks, and every time he brought home a copy of *This World*[14] she would be annoyed by his lingering looks at the women photographed in it. Years later, she still remembered the nude model both of whose names, Tsiona Tuchterman, were repulsive to her ears and seemed equivalent to her two large breasts almost completely bared other than for the small black line that had been drawn over the nipples. "Go to Tsiona," she would say to him every time she didn't want him to come near to her, "Tsiona will give you what you want." And who did she go to? He didn't know nor did he want to know. He was told she had been seen in one of the neighborhoods close by and that she had apparently moved there, and he avoided going near it, he was told she was looking wonderful, and his heart soured; he was told – after a very long time – that she had stopped coloring her hair and his sprits lifted somewhat, that she was finally admitting to her age.

My dear Mano, my heart's own
      In my stupidity I thought that I was still a young woman who can do whatever she wants in life and found out that I couldn't. Finding that out wasn't

---

14 A popular weekly magazine renowned for its permissiveness.

easy, but it's better to admit to a mistake than be stuck with it forever. "Forever", Nachman, what a ridiculous word that is at our age! I miss home, I can't say it more simply. I miss your seriousness, your thoroughness, your Germanic pedantry, I miss the living room we furnished after a thousand and one arguments; you no doubt haven't changed anything there, that's if you haven't found something the neighbors put outside. I know you more than a little, Nachman: until something isn't completely broken, throwing it out isn't permitted. I also miss the little notes you stuck on all the spices whose labels had peeled off, I even miss all the terrible quarrels we had over matters of order and cleanliness.

So what do you think of this possibly: you tell me how messy I am and how you can't find anything in the house because of me, and I'll try to be a bit more orderly, I promise, but not too much, after all, weren't those contrasts between us what attracted us to each other from the start? How unsuited we seemed to that curly haired waiter in the Atara café who by now must be an old man. What is this practical joke that one moment we were a young boy and girl and a moment later we're without hair and without teeth and barely walking? Take me back, Nachman, I'm asking you, after all you're capable of taking an old armchair off the street that the neighbors threw out when they got tired of the upholstery, so now I'm a kind of armchair like that: I'm not wanted here anymore, Nachman.

All that was never written nor ever will be.

20

"It's almost an hour late," said Vera. They were still waiting for Vladimir, and he they had told to wait in the entrance hall and hadn't yet sent him to Levin. From the sound of her steps on the other side of the door, she could be heard approaching the window; she must have been watching the street again.

"Sometimes it can take a little while," Duchin replied and reminded her that their enemies also had a few professionals, not just one or two, and they certainly don't lack the means. "If only we had a tenth of what they've got."

"But in the end we'll beat them," Vera answered, "we'll beat them!" And despite her decisiveness, she sounded like a little girl trying to cheer herself up with something which if not repeated over and over, perhaps would be proven to be beyond her powers.

"Of course, we'll beat them."

They fell silent. "What I want," she began to say.

"Is for Volodya to return already," Duchin said.

"You're also allowed to be a bit worried, Duchin."

"I'm not worried about Volodya, He also doesn't need me to worry about him."

"Are you mocking him again?"

"No," said Duchin, "I'm not mocking Volodya. If there's anyone in the world that I don't mock, it's Volodya." After all – he said – there's no one who can shake off someone following him better than Volodya, so he won't return here before he's absolutely sure that the coast is clear.

Vera didn't say anything, perhaps her question was being asked by her eyes alone.

"Yes," Duchin replied even before she gave her question the chance to be asked, "of course, I'm also thinking of that possibility. After all, their people are everywhere, only you, Vera, for some reason still insist on ignoring all rules of caution."

"Why don't you scold me for a change, Duchin?"

Perhaps she was standing in front of his desk: a young woman of average height whose curves were filled out, whose braid, even after being shortened fell to the middle of her back; and opposite her, behind the big desk, a bald man whose small shrewd eyes didn't avoid her gaze, and who's still doubtful as to the trustworthiness of the newly joined young man after being surprisingly released from the Okhrana headquarters (he waited in the entrance hall for the decision not only in the matter of Levin but also his own).

"If Volodya doesn't scold you," said Duchin, "who am I to scold you?"

"And do you know why he doesn't do that, Duchin? Why he, with all his caution, never scolds me like you do? Because he knows that sometimes one has to take a chance, one has no choice. History moves too slowly and sometimes one has to give it a push, and if the whole time one thinks only how not to get caught, in the end nothing gets done because of all the caution!"

"I've yet to see anyone who got hanged, Vera Alexandrovna, from being too cautious. But the contrary – yes."

"And I," said Vera, "haven't yet seen anyone that gets something done without waiving the rules of caution a bit."

With much patience and in a quiet voice, Duchin reminded her that he hadn't always been on this side of the table, that he had measured more than a few streets on foot quite a while before she joined them, yes, before she even took one step on the sidewalk; he had enlisted in the organization a good few years before-

"I was still a child," she interrupted his words, "I've already heard that, Duchin, I've heard it a thousand times, aren't you tired of reminding me?"

"No," he answered and insisted on being accurate: she, Vera, hadn't been a child then. Actually, she hadn't been born then, the thought hadn't yet popped into the minds of her mother or father; even if they weren't thinking about all their vast possessions and they weren't yet thinking about her at all. He spoke slowly, with restraint, like someone explaining something to a slow-witted person or a child.

"So I wasn't a child," she answered him. "I wasn't anything at the time. It was just you Duchin with all your heroic friends, and just don't mention them once more now. Not that they weren't heroes, the Narodnovolets, but it's a different era now! Or maybe they weren't cautious enough for you?"

"Yes," he replied, "they certainly could have been more cautious. What you said before about history you took from them, Zhelyabov said it, and his end was not wasn't something decreed by fate.

"His end," she said, "will be the end of all of us sooner or later."

"And wouldn't it be better, Vera Alexandrovna, that it be later, and that we still manage to get some things done?" He didn't wait for her reply, and she didn't intend giving one. "If we all behaved according to your whims, we would all have been in jail a long time ago, waiting for them to take us out of there to one place only, the square. And they wouldn't even ask you, Vera, where you prefer, Petropavlovsk or Shlisselburg. We'd arrive straight at the square, to swing from the rope."

"But there'll be others to replace us!" She said. "That's something Zhelyabov also said, if we fall, others will come after us. What we don't manage to do, others better than us will do. There's not a day when someone new doesn't join us, there are hundreds, if not thousands, and let's not lose our nation because of all the post-ponements and indecision. The people don't have time for these delays of yours Duchin."

"The people," said Duchin, "so once again we come to the people." He now insisted on clarifying just exactly who she means by these "people" of hers. "Explain to me please, Vera Alexandrovna, once and for all what you mean by the people: the workers? the farmers? The coachmen? The drunks? Which of them?"

"All of them," she replied.

"The rabble also?"

"Yes," she answered, "them too, after all no one is born that way, rabble! That Duchin also isn't something decreed by fate, and who are you to call them that. How can you sit in your chair and call them rabble?"

"Some wise men said -"

"Just don't quote them to me again!"

"Give freedom to a child -"

"They were patronizing," Vera said.

"- and it will destroy it, freedom to a people means lawlessness," Duchin plac-idly completed the sentence. "They deserve rights, of course, under no circum-stance should they be exploited, but don't make them out to be saints! I saw them then," he continued quietly, "you weren't born yet, but I was there in the square. Thousands were there and thousands were standing on the route, just to see Zhely-abov being hung in the square. Twenty-three years have passed, Vera, and I haven't forgotten how those people of yours behaved at the time."

On the other side of the door, the two of them were talking about a different people, not Poliakov's people, but aren't all peoples bad to the same extent? He had also read Herzen, and despite having to be helped by a dictionary he was capti-vated by his marvelous way with words – "saving a nation is the greatest tyranny of all, it means sacrificing the freedom of individuals for some great abstraction, some monster concocted by metaphysics or religion" – wasn't that statement valid too as far as Jews are concerned? With them even life itself was sacrificed for that and not only freedom, whether they wanted it or not. Hadn't his father died in the yard of their home?

He wasn't supposed to be listening to them, but these past months he had become used to eavesdropping on everything everywhere, so quite naturally he eaves-dropped on them as well. He was being watched by the deer head above the lintel of the closed door, hanging there with cobwebs spun between its long horns where a fat spider moved lightly above the sparkling eyes, as if assessing the strength of its web.

Is it easy to walk like that? He asked it softly, and until they finish debating his case and decide if he's capable of carrying out the act or not – if he can go to Levin and silence him – he wondered if the spider didn't get tired of all the spinning and hunting, and another thought entered his mind, nonsensical but refusing to go away, that perhaps the deer had only been born in order for the fat spider to hunt flies between its horns, and this whole building had only been built for its horns; and this whole giant city, the beautiful damned city, had only been founded in order for him to be sent from this building at 31 Zhukovsky Street to an alley in one of the other quarters to kill a man, if they indeed assign him that task (he wanted it: there was no other way to prove his loyalty to them, there was no other way to cause all the previous deaths to be forgotten – only by this, if he can cause a death to be forgotten by a death).

In the end, there wasn't enough time for them to weigh things up and decide, but everything culminated here – in this alley where he now stands opposite Levin's window, with him lying on his bed and sleeping, God knows how, a deep sleep. You sleep like an angel, he said to him softly, like an angel, though he didn't believe in the existence of angels. And in the depths of his head, not far from the place where his drilling toothache wound up, a few dozen angels momentarily appeared like a flash, wings plucked and hanging by their legs on hooks like slaughtered chickens in a butchery, and in an enormous shop, the back of which is the horizon, sat their master, that Jehovah into whose religion he had been born, and the apron on his paunch filthy with blood. Vengeful and begrudging, cruel and zealous, the complete opposite of his son who stands on church gables summer and winter, spring and autumn. And a thought sprung up that here he himself comes now to this sleeping man like that vengeful god in which he doesn't believe, coming to Levin to kill him while his parents are in the next room.

Behind him was the empty alley and around it this entire adored and abhorred city that he came to with high hopes and crossed vast distances to reach, and now he stands in this quarter opposite the window and in his hand this pistol called a Browning, funny name, Browning. And perhaps he'll do it with his hands, he'll pull the pillow from under his head and place it over his face and smother and smother and smother and smother and smother the way he sometimes wanted to smother himself.

For instance, when he came out of the secret police headquarters, isn't that what he wanted to do? But then, after a few meters he just stopped and placed his head against the wall of a building; and knocked it against it, over and over and over and the skin became chafed and torn and his forehead began to bleed and he knocked it again.

21

"You be careful of those friends of yours," they said to him at the Okhrana, "they already forgot you once at the hotel, and they'll do it again."

From the inner courtyard of the Okhrana building the sound of an acute and agitated neighing of a horse was heard, and after it the voice of the coachman pleading again with it: he promised the horse an entire sack of feed if it moves its old ass and that wagon, it was carrying only a few pieces of wood, and after all, it once hauled sacks of coal and rocks.

"Why you begging it like that?" the gatekeeper shouted. "That way it'll never move. It only understands a whip. Haven't you got a whip?"

The coachman didn't reply. Again, he spoke softly to his horse and only a dim murmuring came from him towards the room.

"Does what's going on outside interest you more than us, Poliakov?" Telegin asked and informed him that his behavior was very impolite, but if he's more interested in what's going on outside, then please, go to the window, the way he had previously suggested, and take a good look at the coachman and the horse, because he won't get to see many more horses in his life.

"With a whip!" the gatekeeper shouted again, and his hoarse voice rose from the courtyard to the window of their floor. "What have you got a whip for, Grandpa?"

"In the end he'll move," answered the coachman. "I know him, he just wants to be spoken to a little bit."

"That's what you call a little bit, Grandpa? What do you think this is here, Grandpa -" for a moment the gatekeeper deliberated how to define the kind of place where people talk to horses, but the suitable definition evaded him. "A circus?" he shouted when he eventually found the definition. "D'you think it's a circus here, Grandpa? The secret police is here, not a circus."

Telegin approached the window and looked at the courtyard and what was happening there, and when he opened his mouth to speak his colleague preceded him and with a quiet and weary voice said that he knew exactly what Telegin was about to say: that once again they've been passed over, no? That now they're replacing furniture for someone else and not them, wasn't that what he was about to say to him?

"And I can also tell you whose they're replacing," said Telegin, "it's not hard to guess, that bootlicker, Ardalianovitch. Who if not Ardalianovitch?"

On hearing that name, Perdischenko's eyebrows shrunk, but he quickly regained his composure and reminded his colleague that Ardalianovitch is also a relative of Rogozin from the budget department: under no circumstances should that be forgotten, so no wonder they're replacing his furniture first?

"A distant relative of Rogozin," Telegin specified, "just a cousin of a cousin, or not even that."

Again he watched the inner courtyard and studied the cart and its load: a table, two armchairs and a small sofa that were tied to each other and to the sides of the cart.

"However, one has to admit," he said and still didn't turn his head towards the room, "that Ardalianovitch had quite a few successes lately. And do you know why, Oleg? I'll tell you exactly why, because he's tougher with the ones he interrogates, he doesn't let them off easily. He would have locked up this character long ago with the bomb in some old warehouse and left him there until he confesses."

For a moment, the courtyard was silent. Perhaps the gatekeeper turned to deal with some other matter, and perhaps the coachman returned to placate his horse by scratching its forehead or with a sugar cube. After a while and a horse's neigh was heard and another after it, and the moment the second one quietened, the voice of the gatekeeper rose again more disparaging than it had been.

"You call yourself a coachman, Grandpa? Look for another job! They once brought one here who you could see right away wasn't a real coachman. He came with a cart and didn't even hold the reins properly. Turns out he was a terrorist. Maybe you're also a terrorist, Grandpa?"

Now the horse decided to stir from its spot: the wheels moved, the cart creaked, the pieces of furniture bumped into each other.

Telegin's head, which protruded from the window, came back inside and turned to his colleague. "They're in much better condition than our furniture, Oleg, come see for yourself. The upholstery is still completely intact, there isn't even one stain on it!"

In the courtyard, the wagon rattled here and there when the shaft was pulled and the horse responded to the placating words of its owner, and Perdischenko came to watch it from the window. A thought possibly entered his mind in the matter of the furniture removal. Instead of being thrown out or sold for pennies it could be put to good use in a place not at all far away, but even before he put his thought into words, Telegin preceded him saying to him: "Don't even think of it, Oleg Timofeyevich!"

The cart passed through the gate, and when it slammed with a metallic sound, Perdischenko removed himself from the window. Anyone who thinks – he said – that he has any intention of giving in to Rogozin or to anyone else, anyone who thinks he's someone who gives in will find out sooner or later he's making a big mistake. "I don't give in to anyone," he said to Telegin, "and I won't give in to you as well my friend." He turned to Poliakov, and afterward approached the armchair and sat down in it and tilted the cup which was empty; he studied the remnants of the tea, or the shine reflected at the base.

"And speaking of fake coachman," – he again placed the cup on the right armrest – "we'll get back to the bombs later; you must have seen fake coachmen, it's a disguise you all like."

"No," replied Poliakov.

"Did you never see any of your dear friends disguised as a coachman?"

"No."

"Not even two months ago next to the sidewalk opposite the Ministry building?"

"No," he replied again (that's what he had been ordered by Duchin: deny everything and don't give any details, because every superfluous word will implicate him further).

"Strange," said Perdischenko. "Konstantin Nikolaevich and I know that you arrived there early in the morning after a night you didn't spend at home. You were seen there, opposite the Ministry building. In your home - no, but there - yes."

"To be accurate, that's no home," said Telegin. "it's a hole. Only cockroaches have a home there, behind the wallpaper."

On one of the previous days of investigation (their number had become hazy, to the point where he wasn't sure how long he had been detained there, weeks or months) they described the wallpaper of his room to him, its faded flowers, the smell of damp that rose from the places where it was peeling, his bed with the sunken mattress that only a trunk pushed under it prevented from sinking further, the bundle of pamphlets they found in the secret bottom of that trunk, subversive pamphlets from the months when all his role comprised of transferring pamphlets. Since they had mentioned his room, they began speaking about his neighbor on the other side of the wall, the amputated soldier whose leg was left behind in the Sea of Japan; they were amazed by that coincidence; on one side of the wall a man who was prepared to sacrifice his leg and even his life for Russia, and on the other side someone who wanted to bring destruction upon it.

Destruction, yes. After all, that's what all his and his dear friends' actions are aiming for,. but who will be destroyed? That's something we're yet to see.

I – another voice in his head began to say, dimmer than the previous one; and fell silent right away.

Yes, what about you? All the other voices answered him, what about you?

I want, it replied like the ones before, I very much want yes very very much – this desire of his he announced in an extremely loud voice, not a whisper – to live yes to live. But not to live like this, said another voice, not like this: it would be better to die than to live like this, it would be better to be blown up in some abandoned warehouse, it would be better to be thrown from this window, to be lead to Semyonovsky Square, to be hung.

It would be better, he thought: because once, long ago, eras ago, he had wanted to be a good person, yes, there had been a time like that. He had wanted to be a good person or at least not a bad one, and certainly not a murderer or an accomplice to a murder, and not even someone who permits a murder to take place. They all came to mind, and not only to mind but to his whole being, his helplessness in the attic, his helplessness in the hotel, and also his helplessness when he sank in the river of his village in spring under the ceiling of felled logs and ice.

I want, the same forgotten voice said in his head, but then they were leading him to the window: not to an abandoned warehouse with a bomb that had been drawn up into the net of the Klotilin Company, but only to the window of their office with the handkerchief that they gave him: Antip led him, for that he had been called again from the corridor.

"Why don't you finally show us how you waved the handkerchief? Telegin said to him. "Perhaps we'll be convinced, you never know."

The policeman held his neck and led him, bending his head as if he would first be demanded to lick the sill, and whilst doing so examined the hardness of his neck: he felt around with his large fingers and pressed and crushed it, he felt the nape and pressed there as well until he uttered a groan.

"Just be careful, Antip," Perdischenko requested alongside the bookcase, "not too much force. We're still hoping for him to talk."

"Only you're still hoping, Oleg," said Telegin.

The sounds from the courtyard hadn't yet risen toward Poliakov: not the beating of the small stones that the gatekeeper threw at the trunk of the oak tree in the corner of the courtyard, not the curses he uttered with each miss, not the indignant chirping of a bird hidden from the eye.

Only the voices of his interrogators were heard and the voice of the policeman; and his voices were also heard, those that reached their ears and those that remained inside his skull. I wanted, I wanted to live, he tried to justify himself, I wanted to travel, I wanted to see more places, I wanted to get to know more people and women, I also wanted women, and because Masha came to mind, he saw her face again as it appeared the moment before she turned to the wall and curled up like a fetus, and he saw their fetus quivering its hands and its tiny feet and a knitting needle stuck into its soft belly.

A putrid drop, he said, and wasn't saying it about the baby. Know from where you came –; and did not complete the sentence, because he didn't believe that somewhere in the world or above the world there was some entity before whom he will have to give an account of himself.

Know from where you came, he said. From a putrid drop, and where you are going, to a place of dust, maggots, and worms.[15]

---

15 A quote from *Ethics of the Fathers*, ethical teachings from ancient Rabbinic texts.

"Why don't you show us at last how you waved?" Telegin said to him.

Then the policeman opened the window and sounds rising from the court-yard could be heard, crystal and clear. The cursing of the gatekeeper and the beating of hooves from the road beyond the gate and in the distance the chiming of a bell. All around the city bustled and wasn't silent for a moment.

"Why don't you kiss the window," Telegin said to him, "don't all of you kiss windows?"

"They don't come in through the windows," his colleague remarked.

"But they can leave through them," answered Telegin.

The blow he was delivered was so strong – the policeman flung his head against the sill – that the wings window shook from the force of it, and only when the sound quietened down was the policeman signaled to let go of him (Perdischenko signaled with the raising of an eyebrow, and Telegin said: "Really, that's all we need, Oleg, for the windowpane to break. It will take a year for Rogozin to be so kind as to approve a new one for us.").

And since they were in no hurry at all – it was the fifth or sixth day of the interrogation and it seemed they could continue that way for another fifty or sixty days – they began to converse at ease about windowpanes and the glazier who made an agreement with the hoodlums of the quarter, they'll do the breaking and he'll do the fixing.

Antip then bent his head further down until his entire upper body was outside the window, and far below him the gatekeeper stopped throwing stones and lifted his head toward him: perhaps he'd seen sights like that more than once or twice, and it clearly interested him more that aiming stones at a tree trunk.

Inside the room, the two of them continued to ask him questions. They lifted their voices slightly to be heard outside over the sound of the wind rustling the leaves of an oak tree. They asked him about the bombs for the thousandth time, and the secret apartment, and the names of his partners.

The windowsill pressed against his stomach and the courtyard seemed both very near and very far, and the section of wall beneath the sill could be seen with its murky traces of rain and melting snow.

"Names," they said to him, and bent him over further.

Now his testicles were pressed against the sill, and a thought arose with the pain that sliced through him: let them be squashed, let them be squashed.

"Names," they said to him, "names."

In order to make clear to him the danger he's incurring if he perseveres in his silence, Perdischenko's cup of tea was brought and placed on the sill: first it was only tilted in order for the remnants of the sediment to be poured out from it and in that way demonstrate the path from the sill to the paving stones, afterward it was thrown in the wake of the sediment and smashed to pieces far below him.

"Names," they said.

Because he didn't answer, he was shaken again and pushed against the exterior wall, against the marks of rain and snow, and the handkerchief dropped from the opened palm of his hand. But right away they pulled him back into the room, and not in order to let him alone, on the contrary: the moment his legs stood on the floor, the policeman bent toward his shins and hugged them the way a man would hug a woman's hips, but only to lift him up towards the sill and stick him farther out of the window, until his entire body would be outside or until the policeman would be ordered to let go and drop him into the courtyard following the handkerchief that swung to and fro in the air until it landed not far from the cup.

"Names," they said to him, "names."

Held by the ankles and his whole body outside, the paving stones drew nearer and the sound of the wind became stronger and it seemed that the weeds growing from the crack in the wall had become longer; and the gatekeeper's face lifted toward him from below suddenly looked funny, perhaps out of curiosity, perhaps out of a malicious joy, perhaps out of compassion.

"Names," they said to him again.

At first, they held him by the ankles with his face to the wall, and an ant there seemed as large as an animal in a forest whose trees are those weeds sprouting from the wall. They then turned him around in the air being shaken and hit until his back was against the wall and his face toward them.

From the windowsill, the old interrogator and the young interrogator observed him from both sides of Antip the policeman and it seemed to him that any moment, before ordering the policeman to drop him into the courtyard, they would draw their cheeks in and gather saliva and spit into his face together, and a thought passed through him: let them spit, why not, I deserve to be spat on. And if they tell the policeman to let me fall, I deserve that as well, to fall and shatter like that cup of which only fragments remain. I'll soon be joining those fragments next to the handkerchief.

Those fragments far down below him seemed silent and serene. A moment before, they contained tea that had been drunk in small sips, but they didn't seem to be suffering now: they seemed serene and tranquil, and he too will be serene and tranquil down there, yes, an unsurpassable serenity and tranquility.

"Names," they said to him from the windowsill, "names."

It wasn't a tear that flowed down his face, but his saliva flowing upside-down, brimming from the corner of his mouth to his eye to his forehead to his hair.

"Names," they said again from the windowsill, and the policeman gave him another shaking that would once more hit his head against the section of the wall below the sill.

But then, instead of ordering the policeman to deliver another blow mightier than all the ones before or to drop him down to shatter in the courtyard, they ordered him to pull him back into the room. They had given up on him and told the policeman to wait a while.

Perdischenko returned to the bookcase, and Telegin to the seating area where he sat down on the small sofa, put his feet up on the pillow, and this time without taking the trouble to spread newspaper beneath them. The policeman, before going out to the corridor, lifted his right hand, but only to check the stitching that had split in his armpit.

"By now it makes no difference if you talked or not," his interrogators said to him, the older or the younger or both together, "it has no significance," and in order to make sure he understood, they explained: they have no anger toward him, on the contrary, and instead of avenging him for his silence, they actually intend to release him. Yes, why's he amazed? Instead of soiling their hands with his blood, they'll give him back the few possessions of his they had confiscated, bid him farewell, and let him go wherever he pleases, and even wave their handkerchiefs at him as he walks away. Only one handkerchief, the other fell to the courtyard.

"We'll open the door for you," they said to him, "you can go back to your friends, and what do you think they'll do, receive you with open arms? What do you imagine they'll be thinking; that you had some tea with us?"

Battered and dusty he stood at the window with drops of blood still flowing from his head to the nape of his neck and between his shoulder blades, when they suggested to him, with great courtesy, whether he would so kind as to answer some questions, since his friends anyway won't believe he hadn't spoken here, why keep quiet?

He should use his head now and decide for himself what's better: the false blame of his friends, which could lead to cruel revenge (they have only one punishment for informants), or a confession of his true guilt before cultured people who are willing to listen to him, a confession that will release him to a new life; should he so want he can return to that group of his and be as friendly as he wants with them – he'll never be asked to return here, to secret police headquarters. they won't hold their meetings with him here but rather in one of the restaurants on Nevsky Avenue – and if he prefers to travel, he can go anywhere he wants from here, and this time with all the necessary documents. Yes, Mother Russia is vast, with endless open spaces, and with iron tracks covering the length and breadth of it, he can travel through them all and with a sum of money in his pocket given to him for that purpose. What does he think?

From the open window, whose sill is stained with blood, the rattling of the laden cart and the rhythmic beating of the hooves could be heard, and this time the coachman didn't need goading calls or lashes of the whip. Telegin turned his head to the window and his colleague approached to glance down at the courtyard.

"His furniture?" Telegin asked, like one who already knows the answer.

In the window, Perdischenko's shoulders were slightly hunched.

Telegin clicked his tongue and mumbled something that included the name Rogozin, and his colleague nodded.

"Rogozin's got it in for you," said Telegin. "and after you had been such fast friends!"

Perdischenko turned to the room to set the record straight: Rogozin had never been his friend, far from it, at the very most he was once a neighbor on his floor; and besides that, not replacing furniture doesn't mean having it in for one, after all its just furniture, and he's doing just fine with this sofa, Konstantin Nikolaevich, and if the upholstery is a little tatty, he would do well to ask himself whether he didn't have some part in that, he and his shoes.

Telegin also sought to set the record straight: after all, the upholstery had become tatty years ago, and only then did he permit himself to put his feet up there. His feet and not his shoes; since he always spreads newspaper underneath, lucky the Petersburg journalists are so productive.

"Antip!" Perdischenko called to the door and to the corridor on the other side of it, and right away it opened and Antip entered.

"Yes, sir," said the policeman and clicked his heels.

"Take him to the hospital now," said Perdischenko. "Let them examine him and treat him. It's very important that a doctor see him, and not just some nurse. Afterward bring him back here and give him new clothes from the storeroom. I want him to look like a new man when he leaves here. Understood?"

"Yes, sir," answered the policeman.

"And no more beating and punching."

"Yes sir," said the policeman.

"Look me in the eyes, Antip."

Antip raised his eyes.

"Now go."

He was transported in a carriage and not in a prisoners' cart, and in the hospital he allowed them to feel his ribs, to tap on his back, to open his mouth wide with a wooden stick and examine his tongue, to peer into his pupils, to undress him, to clothe him, and when he was returned to the secret police headquarters, his interrogators said: "You look like a groom," and Telegin even got up from the couch to fix the stiff collar he received from the secret police quartermaster store.

"There's no way your friends will think you didn't talk," he said to him, and when he saw a spot on his shoulder, he gently removed it with his third finger. "Who would believe you didn't? In their place we also wouldn't believe you." But the one sole consolation they said, is that all this won't last long, because their account with him will soon be settled by his friends.

"They'll believe me," he said, because he valued and respected those friends of his, more than he had ever valued and respected anyone, not even his parents: not his father, whose deeds were of no benefit to anyone (no, responded a voice from the back of his head or his chest, no; all that had changed on that last day, have you forgotten? Already?), and not his mother, even though he valued and respected and loved her (no, a voice was heard again from the back of his head or his chest, no; all that had changed on that last day, have you forgotten. Already?).

"They'll believe me," he said again, because his friends had already once believed him about something that wasn't true. They had no doubt that at the time of the pogroms he had heroically opposed the rioters and fearlessly protected his parents (but you'll never lie again, the voice at the back of his head or his chest said now, under no circumstances will you give in to fear again promise me promise that you won't give in. Once long ago you wanted to be a good person and not a coward nor an accomplice to a murder nor someone who allows it to take place right in front of his eyes, and, after all, it wasn't only your father who had been killed that way, have you forgotten? Already?).

They'll believe me, he thought, because he trusted their judgment and valued and respected them for their fervor, their determination, and their purity of heart. He believed they would be prepared to die for a great ideal. an ideal intended for all humanity and not just their own people. They'll believe me, he thought, because if they had already once believed him purely out of their affection for him, they'll certainly believe him now when he tells them he honestly didn't expose any of them to his interrogators.

They'll believe him, he thought; after all, he hadn't let them down: they gave him pamphlets to transfer from one place to another and he transferred them, they asked him to signal to the bomb throwers when the carriage draws near and he waved from the hotel window at exactly the right moment; it was only afterward that he let them down, when he became stuck to the hotel bed like a squashed worm.

But I've changed since then, a voice said from the back of his head, I've changed. And he believed that from now on he'd behave the way he had once wanted to behave, before becoming corrupted; he'd behave like the person he hoped to be, the person he wanted to be! A voice from somewhere at the back of his head and his chest said, the person I wanted to be!

They trusted him now as well, they relied on him enough to place a loaded pistol in his hand with six bullets not meant for a tree trunk or a bottle for target practice nor for his own temple, in no way his own temple, but rather for the man whose treachery was unquestionable– that's what Duchin said – for Levin.

In a moment, I'll point it at you Levin and press the trigger, he said softly to him.

The Adam's apple of the sleeping man moved back and forth, back and forth, and his chest rose and sank, rose and sank.

22

Tel Aviv, 1994

There had been a time when it seemed to Nachman that a completely revolutionary idea had come into his head, true, only in the academic field, but an idea that could advance research and perhaps even change the face of it from its very foundation, just as his father had aspired to change the face of society. He had had great dreams in his youth, and in fact had been destined for them from infancy; after all, his mother had named him Nachman[16] as if he would have the power to console her over the disappearance of his father, but he hadn't succeeded in that, not even slightly. Their surname, Poliakov – his mother borrowed for herself so that he wouldn't be considered a bastard – in his youth, he had Hebraized to Poleg, and he was called Mr. Poleg at conferences and university seminars ("And now Mr. Poleg will lecture on -"), when they still predicted a shining future for him and at least a promised tenure.

After the war, in his second period of study, for a few years he had been the protégé of a renowned professor who was proud of his students who had been former servicemen of the Haganah,[17] the Palmach[18] and the Jewish Brigade. The professor had been a brilliant scholar in his time, and when his brainpower faded, he was so kind as to sign his name and degree to articles his better students had written, one of them being Nachman. At some point his relationship with Nachman soured for no apparent reason – perhaps one of his colleagues slandered him to the professor - and he then halted his advancement. His downfall was swift, in any event that's what it seemed like from the distance of years: in the faculty he was suddenly urged to find a respectable publishing house for his dissertation, and in unequivocal language it was made clear to him that his entire professional future depended on it. It was humiliating, it was insulting, it was simply despicable, and when a few students came to him and said that they'd be terribly sorry if he left, that's to say if the rumor is correct ("We can't understand what everyone here wants of you") their encouragement hurt him no less than the rumor.

---

16 Hebrew for "consoler."

17 A Jewish paramilitary organization active during the British Mandate of Palestine (1921–48).

18 An elite fighting force of the Haganah.

He was surrounded by bad people and was fed up with all their intrigues. In fact, they had already given up on him in the faculty: the number of courses he was allotted had been reduced, the colleague who moved into his room had his name written above his on the door, his post-box had been moved away to an unsuitable place, and afterward disappeared completely. "We'll keep your mail with us," he was told by the secretary's office, and was forced to have to ask them for his post and each time suffer their impatience; that was the greatest humiliation of them all, standing in front of their desks and watch them hastily turning over the pile of brown envelopes, in vain. Not even one student attended his tutorials.

There had been a lecturer in the faculty who after being fired returned home and went into the kitchen and took out a nylon garbage bag from a drawer, put it over his head, tied its ends under his chin and chocked himself to death. Such a practical thought never entered Nachman's mind, and such a death was contemptible in his eyes; in contrast, even the death of the Brigade soldier, Rosenstein, whose leg had been blown to the four winds seemed a worthy one, and even more so the deaths of the heroes of the Russian Revolution (in the beginning he wanted to focus on them, and the renowned professor diverted him from his beloved revolutionaries - who on the gallows had been martyrs without a god - specifically the allegiance to a god that had never ceased to exist among the Russian people and who had undergone all sorts of metamorphoses in some strange cults. He was urged to find some common patterns there, and in that task, much to his ruination, he sank).

He decided to find work that wasn't too difficult and where he could receive tenure and not have to endure unnecessary friction with all sorts of enemies. He didn't completely give up old dreams, and for a considerable time still told himself that should his resolve return to him, and at least his diligence, nothing would disturb him, even his new place of work, to occupy his nights with academic work outside of the university and its intrigues and perhaps complete it. For some moments, he saw himself finishing his research even if it required years, and in his mind's eye he also saw how astonished all his past colleagues from the faculty would be, and first and foremost the extolled professor.

The green lawns of the campus were replaced by the sidewalks of Shenkin Street, the podium and the board with its chalks were replaced by the crowded proof reading table of the *Davar* newspaper; in place of all-embracing theories (he didn't make do with the common patterns he found in Russia), he was required to occupy himself with petty details, erasing unnecessary letters and excess brackets, moving incorrect full stops and commas to their fitting place, and to do all that alongside his colleagues who used the same table. Nonetheless, within less than a year he had been drawn into the work of proofreading almost as deeply as he had been drawn into the mythical patterns he had been researching and was without doubt the best of the *Davar* proof-readers and the most senior from the perspective of his knowledge and even found great peace of mind weeding out what he found necessary from the paper. He read all the publications of the Academy of the Hebrew Language and articles on linguistics and made rules of his own more logical than those of the Academy. For a few years, he was called "our Doctor" in the department or "our walking encyclopedia," until one extremely hot summer – at least that's what it seems like from the distance of years; the sirocco being the cause – they began to tire of his corrections, and then, since the oppressive heat affected him too, he decided to take action. The revolutionary academic idea awoke in him again (it wasn't ignited, it just awoke; with him great all-embracing ignitions didn't occur), and one day, when Ada wasn't home, he took down two cardboard boxes from the storage area where his research papers had been put away. He once believed he had found a common pattern in the basic stories of the great religions – he had come a long way from Russian cults – and that the perception of time found in that pattern is what decided their attitude toward death and marked the differences between the religions; that seemed to be the most significant point, their attitude toward the void from which man comes and to which he departs, and in the boxes were the hundreds of pages he had written until reaching the conclusion that Frazer the Scot, and Eliade the Romanian and Cassirer the German, and especially Levi-Strauss the Frenchman, who had gone farther than all his predecessors, hadn't left enough room for those coming after them, and certainly not for someone who didn't have a command of so many languages like they had, and hadn't read so many books like they had, and wasn't familiar with dozens of gods from a number of pantheons as if they were neighbors in the building. On the following nights, after Ada had gone to sleep, he shut himself up in the small study (the back balcony that had been closed off with blocks) and read all his cards and pages again and tried to examine them once more from a new angle, a surprising one that hadn't yet been used by anyone before him, not even the French structuralist who based his patterns on the beliefs of savages. At twilight, on one sirocco day, dressed only in an undershirt and nevertheless sweating, he came to an understanding. It was a painful understanding, and at the time he saw only one positive thing: that there was no one at home. His son had gone to a friend, and Ada, God only knows where she had disappeared to every day during those hours.

He packed all his papers and cards and took the cardboard boxes one by one to the empty lot opposite the house, a lot that was filled with wood sorrel in winter and chrysanthemums in spring, and now consisted of thornbushes as tall as his son. All the spring flowers among them had withered and died, the chrysanthemums too whose pollen, when they still stood upright, would dot Linda's black coat and cause her to let out such a human-like sneeze that he would say "bless you" to her even when there were people around.

He could have thrown the pages straight into the dumpster or buried them in the ground like he did their first dog, but he chose to burn them. At the time he was dressed in khaki shorts and a loose undershirt and all he needed to carry out his operation was one small box of "Nur" matches here in the clearing on the small lot of thorn bushes. Not all the matches caught alight: some were moist, others broke in two by the movement of his hasty hand. Panic overtook him, lest he regret the act before it was completed. He had never carried out such a decisive deed; in the few battles in which the Jewish Brigade participated, he had been one of hundreds of soldiers, but here on the lot he stood alone. None of his university colleagues could have conceived that his research would end this way: while they hadn't held him in much esteem, they certainly didn't foresee an end like this.

The sirocco sky darkened above, and yellow sparks floated up and disappeared, and the torn bits of black paper that flew around no longer resembled the pages that he had filled with blue ink in his small handwriting. Four floors above him, on the other side of the road, the crumbling of the pages to ashes couldn't be seen, but from time to time, when the flames rose, from the balcony his face could be seen lit with a ruddy hue, the fire glinting in his glasses and beads of sweat pouring down his forehead. He allowed the sweat to slide over his face and continued to watch the flames grasping the pages of his research on the perception of time at the root of the great religions. The pages burnt well as if they had waited years just for this moment.

"Are you out of your mind?" One of the neighbors from the next building shouted, and Nachman bent down toward the cardboard box and took another bundle of pages from it and cast it into the flames – there was joy in it as well as danger, and he recoiled when the flames mounted again.

"Be careful the thorn bushes don't catch alight!" another neighbor shouted to him from one of the lower floors, and from a nearby window some wise guy asked him if he hadn't finished burning leavened bread[19] or had he got a bit confused with the date. "There's going to be a big fire here!" a neighbor below him added with fear in her voice, an old woman in a faded dressing gown buttoned up to the neck. "It's all dry thorn bushes here!"

Without looking at them, he bent down again and took more pages from the cardboard box and served them up to the fire as well, like a man feeding a beast of prey without taking caution his hand doesn't get bitten along with the chunk of flesh he's offering. "Daddy, Daddy," his son called to him from the balcony, because he only now saw him, and the pointer Linda barked, but he did not respond to either of them.

It was supper time, and all those who had watched him from their windows had already turned from there to sit down to eat ("He's just burning junk," one of them said about his research and all the years he had put into it, years about which Ada had said from the very beginning: "They're just leading you by the nose, Nachman, and in the end what? Are you going to start looking for a job when you're past the age of fifty?"). The falling night let the flames turn its edges

---

19 A Jewish custom carried out before the Passover festival.

red, and in the spreading ruddy darkness the fire and its sparks flying above the thorn bushes could be descried, until it demolished all the pages.

When it became completely dark, he went back up to the apartment, lighter than he had been, not only from weight of his boxes but also from the weight of the illusory dream he had nurtured, one that was fitting for someone else to dream and realize, someone in whom a real fervor pulses and doesn't perish. His face was sooty, the hair of his legs was singed to the knee. Linda the pointer came to sniff him, and Ada, who had returned from one of her outings and had eaten alone in the kitchen, looked at him as he passed his hand over the dog's head with a kind of automated petting. The dog sensed its rigidity and didn't respond.

Ada threw a kitchen towel to him for him to wipe his face with, and he let it drop to the floor and didn't sit down on the chair at the head of the table but rather went to the small back balcony and from there to the bathroom. In the white light reflected by the bathroom tiles, he stood opposite the basin and removed his glasses and examined his face in the mirror: in the place where his glasses had been two light rectangles remained moist with sweat, and in their center were two eyes only slightly familiar from some ancient era. For a long time, he stood and looked into his eyes in the mirror that way, he didn't even turn on the tap to wash his hands, and when his son tried to get his attention, he ignored him.

"Daddy, Daddy," said his son, and he continued to look into the mirror: the face of a savage could be seen there because of the soot on his cheeks and forehead and chin, or the face of someone who threw a bomb which had made him sooty, and for a moment he found his reflection pleasing, until he looked directly into his eyes: no savagery could be seen in them. A long while passed before he asked his son, without turning his head to him from the mirror, if he could see what he sees there.

"Where?" His son asked.

"In the mirror," he answered him, "Don't you see the mirror?" The entire bathroom had become that mirror, all his years up to that moment.

Then, surprisingly, Ada went out to the small kitchen balcony, passing the brooms, the squeegees and cartons of toilet paper, dressed in faded house clothes that he preferred to all her pretty dresses, and for the first time in his life, his son saw her hug him in front of his eyes. She hugged Nachman from the back the way she used to hug him in their first home in Jerusalem while he washed dishes in the kitchen sink, and afterward she put her chin on his shoulder the way she used put it then and for a moment gazed at both their reflections in the mirror, but he recoiled from her touch and moved aside and sat down heavily on the edge of the bath and examined what was left of the hair on his shins. The dog drew near him, and he ignored it.

"Why blame her?" Ada said.

"No one's to blame," he replied.

The hair ends were singed and he slowly passed the palm of his hand from his knee to the ankle. Between the edge of his short khaki pants and the inner thigh, a wrinkled testicle sprouted from his loose underpants, dangling, and Ada said something to him in some sort of private language of theirs that had been long forgotten. He uttered a weary chuckle he spaced his leg out farther.

"We won't be having any more, anyway," he said. That's it, it's over." That's how he also belatedly answered her previous question.

They used to lie in the double bed at night like two strangers and hear each other's breathing and each other's snoring, until they fell asleep. How he longed to hear those sounds years later, after she left him and went off with another man, and more so when she lay in hospital in the special care wing and that man had already been laid to rest; but by then a tube was attached to her throat and she was being aided by a respirator, and other tubes were attached to other places and he didn't want to know what they were conveying, because the body that a few decades before he had fondled and caressed and impregnated, had been reduced to something only numbers changing on a screen testified to still containing life. He also pondered for some moments what would happen if one of the tubes were accidentally disconnected or if he would do it with his own hand but stayed where he was; he had good reason to do it, and it would have been easy to do – no nurse was around, and his son was in another country.

He looked left and right, he listened; no steps were heard in the corridor, and all her neighbors in the ward were sunk like her in comas from which they wouldn't awaken. Only the Filipina caregiver who watched over a tiny old lady was awake and singing a lullaby to her like every evening, as if she wasn't asleep anyway, singing in her soft gentle voice as if she was her child, and gradually, against his will, his eyes also closed.

23

Petersburg, 1904

"You won't want anyone else after that, Anushka," the drunk suddenly said departing from the melody, and when he tried to return to its notes from the bench in the square, it was like someone trying to catch a train that had already left the station and if he doesn't run he won't reach.

"There's your people," Duchin said.

Vera fell silent for a moment as if she hadn't heard his words, until the refrain was heard again. "Yes, he's also my people," she said, "and I'm not ashamed of him."

"You, Vera Alexandrovna, aren't ashamed of anything."

From behind the large desk, he looked at her eyes that turned away from him and at the clenched mouth and the swallowing movement that passed down her throat and disclosed her worry.

"He's on his way," he said to her profile that was riveted to the windowpane and the street beyond it. "He'll come, Vera."

"Can't you even say his name?"

"Vladimir will come," he said, "he might a little late, but in the end he always comes. They could catch me, but not him. Don't you trust Volya?"

"Of course I trust him, but they're getting smarter all the time."

"Yes," said Duchin. "Unfortunately, they're learning from us, and especially when there are people revealing our methods to them. All kinds of Levins."

She turned to him with a sharp movement and fixed her blue eyes at him.

"Today it's Levin," he said to her, "tomorrow it'll be someone else. Maybe there's already another like that now, and we don't know about him yet."

"No," she replied, "don't speak that way! A lot of good people have joined us and every day more are joining. You're blackening them all."

From the street, the strangulated singing of the drunk rose again: over and over he called out to Anushka in his hoarse voice and promised to let her drink from his wine all night; wine like that, she's never drunk; he'll give her wine straight from his vine.

Duchin spun around in his chair and turned his head to the street below. "Anushka, Anushka," he said softly, perhaps to the windowpane, perhaps to himself, and returned his gaze to the room, to Vera, "listen to what you're missing."

From the street someone let out a curse that included the drunk's mother and grandmother too, and hooves beat on the paving stones and drew away; a church bell chimed dimly over and over. It was three o'clock.

"Anushka," said Duchin, "why ignore a man suffering like that?"

On the other side of the door Poliakov sat and listened to them, despite that he wasn't supposed to be doing so. But the door wasn't properly closed and he was waiting for the decision: will he be sent to silence Levin or not, will they trust him and his hand with the pistol, or doubt him due to his mystifying release from custody?

Months before that, when they were still undecided in the matter of his enlistment, the three of them were in the apartment, and in order to appraise his determination they described to him in great detail the masses that would gather to watch him, the black cart in which he would be transported from the jail to the square, the black coffin that would be waiting for him at the back of the platform of the gallows and its bottom padded by whitewash. "That's what awaits you at the end of this journey," Duchin said, "and are you sure, Poliakov, that that's what you want?"

He nodded. He didn't care if that's how all these months end: on the gallows. He had already seen greater horrors, some of which he had been party to.

"There'll be no pardon for you," Duchin said, but he still wasn't frightened; a while would pass until his fears would return and compensate themselves generously for all the time they had been suppressed. Since he had seen sights many times harsher in his village, it wasn't difficult for him so see these: the black cart, the black coffin padded with whitewash, the drummers, the infuriatingly beautiful clear spring day – on such a day, the Tsar's assassins were executed, and Duchin had witnessed it in his childhood – all the ninety thousand people that crammed the sidewalks leading to the square ("Didn't you say eighty thousand the last time?" Vera said).

Stools were placed on the platform ("Didn't you say a bench the last time?" Vera said); each noose and its stool beneath it. Duchin even heard two people gambling then as to how many minutes each sentenced man would stay alive.

When they asked him to go out and wait in the entrance hall (they were deliberating about his enlistment at the time; Levin's name hadn't come up at all), he didn't hear them for a while, until their voices were raised in an argument. He wasn't supposed to be listening but nevertheless listened – was it his fault that the door didn't prevent it?

"So they went up on to the gallows and it's a horrible death," Vera said, "but someone who thinks only of that all the time, Duchin -"

"Will never be able to hold his head up," Volodya completed in his quiet voice.

"That, Volodya," said Duchin, "we can put into one of our next pamphlets."

Their words became blurred again; only the name of the square could be heard, and after it the names the sentenced men's leader and his girlfriend were heard, and Duchin said: "There's no shame in learning from others' experiences, Vera."

"It's a new century, Duchin! And if I had seen everything you spoke about, I would have been filled with such anger that I would have done something – anger and not hesitation!"

"Not hesitation," he answered softly. "Learning from experience isn't something to be ashamed of Vera Alexandrovna."

"Learning?" she said, "I could have learned things at university and I didn't. I gave up learning for what's really important. Volodya gave up his family, left a wife and a child. We didn't come here to learn, Duchin, we came to take action; remind him, Volodya."

"Let him finish talking," Volodya said, "and leave my family out of it."

A while later he went out to the entrance hall, glanced at Poliakov, and went back to the room and left the decision to Duchin whether or not to let him join their ranks.

His eyes rested on the door, and above the lintel, the head of the deer stared at him with its glass eyes, and for a while his attention was distracted because the pierced eyes of the dog rose in his memory: out of all the atrocities he had witnessed in the village, that one, the slightest of them, appeared and arose: not the woman who tried to scrub the imprint of the baby's mouth from the palm of her hand – she tried with a brush, with an iron horse comb, with a file, with a knife – not what the rioters inflicted on the tailor, the glazier, the baker – with a hammer, with a fragment of glass, with dough – nor what was inflicted on his father without any accessories other than one coin.

"Carry on being cautious, Duchin," Vera said from the other side of the door, "be cautious, be cautious, be cautious. And if you think that that's not enough, be a little more cautious, and one day, when they lead us to the gallows because we weren't cautious enough but actually did something, you can come and watch."

"The gallows are not a decree of fate," he said to her.

"Maybe they are," she replied.

"Only if one isn't cautious."

"Come and watch us," she said to him again, "stand in the crowd and watch us on the platform and on the stools and say to yourself: You see, they weren't cautious. I told her to think twice and three times, and she didn't listen to me. And just don't tell me again about how everything was before I was born."

"Do you think there wasn't anything in the world before you were born, Vera?"

"Sure there was! Everything was there before I was born! The Neva and the Tsars. The Tsars were always there, but when I die, Duchin, they won't be there anymore -" A fervor could be heard in her voice, as if Russian palaces with smoke rising from them had become visible, burning chariots, tens of thousands of blazing red flags raised by the masses.

"You express yourself so beautifully," said Duchin, "with such a winning inner conviction and with such eloquence. Yours or Vladimir's, what difference does it make whose."

"Does Vladimir bother you that much?" The wasn't any wonderment in her voice but rather sorrow.

"On the contrary; we're all brothers on the same path, and perhaps we'll come to the same end. I was just impressed by the wording, Vera Alexandrovna."

"What difference does the wording make! The content is important, not the wording. And not even the content, the actions!"

"Just be careful, Vera, I'm asking you, don't break the windowpane. It might be a beautiful day outside, but it would be a pity for the window. And also a pity for your nose, Vera. Who wouldn't be sorry for that cute nose if something God forbid happened to it?"

"I wouldn't be sorry, not even if something worse happened! If I get caught, Duchin, it'll be because I listened to my heart– the heart, not the head!"

"Ah," said Duchin softly, "so we've come to the heart." He began to open the desk drawer and it got stuck on its tracks. He struggled with it for a moment and finally took out what he was looking for: a pocket watch whose chain had become entangled with something.

"The heart is quite a complex thing," he said, "more complex than a watch, even more than a bomb, Vera, because we know exactly what's inside, we put it there ourselves, we assembled it, but with the heart – no. All sorts of things go in, all sorts of things go out, and everything there changes all the time."

"Maybe with you, Duchin, it changes all the time."

"And not with you, Vera?"

She didn't reply.

"Of course it changes," he said to her. "It changes without one noticing. It seems that someone here has already forgotten what she once felt about a few people we both know well."

"Someone hasn't forgotten!" she answered him. "And anyway, we don't have time for this talk!"

"Time," said Duchin slowly, "is something we actually do have. Maybe just not the desire. We once had the desire, but then it left. And we know full well, Vera, where it went and to who. Why did it go there? Not because Vladimir is younger and more handsome, not that he's not younger and more handsome, he is, but the desire went only because it seemed to us that Vladimir knows everything and is totally sure of everything he does, while Duchin with all his doubt -"

"You, Duchin," she interrupted him, "I never desired."

A silence fell, and Duchin played with the cover of his watch, opening and closing it with a beating sound.

"I needed someone then," she said to him, "just by chance you happened to be there."

"By chance?" The watch was moved to the edge of the desk.

"I used you," she said. "If it hadn't been you it would have been somebody else. Just by chance it was you."

"You used me," he said softly. "And I," he continued quietly as if talking to himself, "For some reason I actually remember a few other things."

"I'm not interested in hearing about them!"

"Completely different, and not just one or two things. We lived together in one room, Vera, not for a night, or a week, for a whole month."

"Because we had to!" she said. "Didn't you yourself say we had to live together."

"Yes," he said to her, "we really did have to. Otherwise they wouldn't have rented the apartment to us. And without the apartment -"

"And you took advantage of the fact that I was new and young and hardly understood anything?"

"And that you were so beautiful?" he said to her and paused for a moment. "God how beautiful you are, Vera."

"Don't say that to me," she said. "I asked you not to say that!"

"I remember you quite liking hearing that, you even asked me to tell you exactly how beautiful you are, and just where you are beautiful. You were even standing right next to this window. Although this dress wasn't -"

"Once," she let slip, "once. It was a long time ago and time passes, Duchin, maybe you should look at that watch of yours, what else is it for?"

They fell silent, a silence Poliakov heard from the entrance hall. The sofa he was sitting on must have been left by the owner of the apartment for the tenants together with the rest of the furniture, but it's doubtful whether the folded bedsheets on the edge had been spread over them at the time, two sheets and a blanket. They emitted a slight smell of sweat, Duchin's sweat that had been banished to the entrance hall, as well as a slight smell of socks (one sock sprouted from under the sofa), as if they had been preparing him – even before it had been decided to send him to silence Levin, even before it had been decided to enlist him – for the smells he would smell in Levin's room, were he to enter it.

The eyelids of the sleeping man couldn't be seen from the dark alley, but his facial features revealed themselves within the darkness: his high forehead, whether from wisdom or whether he was already beginning to bald, his eyebrows that were neither thick nor thin; the sharp nose whose large nostrils widened and narrowed, his mouth, so adept to making speeches for all purposes – so Duchin said –a thread of saliva could be seen drooling from the corner of it like his old father in the kitchen, and one could imagine his Adam's apple moving back and forth along the neck. The silhouette of a chair stood next to Levin's bed, and on the armrest some clothing could be made out, perhaps a shirt, and on the seat was a glass of vodka or water, probably water ("No alcohol, no tobacco, no women," Duchin had said of him), and when the eyes adjusted to the darkness in the room – he was still standing outside and looking in – it seemed that the glass was only half full. Perhaps Levin had awoken between dreams and sipped from the glass the way he sipped when making a speech.

The stench of urine emanated from the ground of the yard and became thicker, but it seemed Levin didn't sense it; his large nostrils widened and narrowed, widened and narrowed, and with the air inhaled into them perhaps came the smell of the man standing opposite his window, and will it be exterminated together with him? No, he had to banish that thought instantly from his head the way he banished some other thoughts from it, at least in the daytime. Nighttime was a different matter: then they struck the temples from the inside like the sledgehammers of the rioters on the doors of the houses or became sharp like the nails that were stuck into the tailor's nostrils. Only the tongue wasn't connected to all that: the tongue became longer and swelled and filled the entire cavity of the mouth until it sprouted between the lips and was then pulled out with terrible force and stretched to the roots and placed against an anvil as cool as ice, and instantly an axe was lifted to it and instantly it fell ("Did you talk there or didn't you talk?" Duchin said. "We only want to know if you opened your mouth or not").

He feet were stuck to their spot the way they had been stuck months before to the attic in his village, and the way they had been stuck in the hotel to the bed strewn with fragments of glass, and his right hand became heavy with the pistol it held: the elbow leaning on the sill, and the hand inserted into the dark room with the Browning and its six bullets, one of which was enough.

You piece of dirt, he said silently to the sleeping man, but didn't move from his spot.

"From outside," Duchin had instructed him in the secret apartment after the knife had been replaced with a pistol, "don't waste one unnecessary moment," and in the end they didn't have enough time to decide whether he would be sent to kill Levin. But without further hesitation – he had hesitated more than enough times, and each time an innocent man had been hurt – he leaned his free hand on the windowsill and lifted his right foot toward it and hoisted his body up raising hand with the pistol grasped in it on his way inside, to the darkness.

24

"It might actually be a good idea," Vera said, "a drunk is even better than a beggar, because no one stops to give him money and block the view." And then, as if casually discussing disguises for those tailing and for the lookouts and not waiting for Volodya to decide about Levin's punishment, Duchin said that too much attention would be drawn to someone disguised that way, especially if he sang terribly out of tune to some lost Anushka like the one here.

Down in the street, someone cursed a cart driver whose horses strayed from their path, and Vera tensed on the spot and listened.

"It's not Volya," Duchin said to her. "Can't you already identify Volya's voice?"

"No, it's not him," she said. "But the cart driver dropped him off before at the corner of the street. He made three rounds with him until he decided that the coast was clear. I can identify Volya's walk even among a thousand people."

Their voices could be heard through the door, and Duchin raised the query: why in hell did Vladimir get off here, so close to the secret apartment, if he fears being tailed? Someone as cautious as Volya wouldn't put himself in any unnecessary danger; he's not only endangering himself that way, but also the apartment and them – "and especially you, Vera, it's totally illogical!"

"Then it seems he's not worried," she answered and said he wasn't walking or looking in their direction, he was just someone walking in the street. "But it's him," she said, "even from a distance like this, I can identify him."

As if in answer to her words, the singing of the drunk rose again from the street, intermittently loud and soft. Perhaps he had been awoken by the din of the street, or by thirst, or had been struck once more by the longing for his sweetheart. "Come night and bring Anush-ka to me," he sang, much out of tune and with a desperate ardor, "come, Anushka, and heal me."

"Poliakov!" Duchin called out. It seems a decision had been made in his matter.

But he was in no rush to reply: he lingered for a moment so that they wouldn't think he'd been listening to them, and in truth he hadn't been listening every single moment; he only got up once and approached the door and kneeled and peeped through the keyhole, and immediately withdrew, knowing it was something one shouldn't do. He had already done more than enough things one shouldn't do, in Bykhov and in Kalitsa and in Minsk and in Petersburg and where not.

"Poliakov!" Duchin called again.

"Yes," he answered and opened the door and remained standing in the entrance.

Maybe he was intending to send him on some errand concerning Vladimir, or just get him out the apartment; one way or another, at almost the very same moment brisk steps were heard coming up the stairs and stopping a while in front of the door, where a key was turned in the lock, once and one again, and then a door opened and more steps were heard followed by a sneeze.

Vladimir stood in the entrance, his cheeks cleanly shaved – his full thick beard had been reduced to a goatee in the French style – and his forehead and temples were sweaty, and it seemed despite all the experience he had in evading those tailing him, the last hour hadn't been easy for him. He wiped his forehead with the back of his hand and gazed at all those present, from Vera to Duchin and from Duchin to him, probably wondering about his presence there.

"This time they were close," he said and wiped his temples with the palm of his hand and pulled his sweaty hair back. His smart European clothes were wrinkled, and when Vera approached and hugged him her head reached his shoulder, while the other side of the desk Duchin watched them both.

"We were worried about you, Volya!" she said to his chest. "God, how worried we were!" She lifted her eyes to him, and then her hand as well, and with a white handkerchief whose corners bore her embroidered initials, wiped his forehead.

"She really was worried about you," said Duchin. "Unlike her, Volya, I wasn't worried. I was certain you'd arrive safely."

Vladimir looked at him for a moment, perhaps trying to study his eyes through the thick lenses. "They were close this time," he said, not with complaint but noting an unpleasant fact not to be ignored. "They're improving all the time, and now those bastards are sticking to their goal no less than us." With a gentle yet firm movement, he let go of Vera and crossed to the window and observed the street from the space between the curtain and the windowpane.

Without turning his head towards the room, in a quiet restrained voice he began to tell about the two men who followed him on foot for the entire length of Sadovaya Street and almost making no effort to hide themselves, and also about another who followed him afterward, alone, with skill that would put even them to shame: not keeping too close to him, not standing out from the crowd; stopping at times, letting people pass him by, sticking to his mission. And then he was also replaced, this time by two men in a carriage. "They've got new carriages now," he said facing the street, "and they're even more careful. On leaving the quarter it was replaced by another so that I wouldn't start to become suspicious." He passed hand over his neck beneath his starched collar and loosened it, clearly uncomfortable in his clothes and the goatee trimmed in the French style.

"Two on foot and one more in the carriage?" Duchin asked.

"Three on foot and two carriages," replied Vladimir.

"My God, Duchin," said Vera, "maybe wait a while with those questions?"

She offered Vladimir something to drink and he refused. "You're all sweaty," she said to him. "Just look at yourself! Did you go the whole way on foot?"

"Of course on foot," he answered. "I haven't got wings yet, and just as well I haven't, where would I hide them."

The only way you can only be swallowed up in a crowd is on foot. He arrived as fast as he could to the market and mixed in with the buyers; sure, it was a little difficult in these clothes, but there were a lot of people there, and it was easy to get lost among them. Only after an hour – he said – only when absolutely certain no one was following him, he got onto a carriage and came here, unescorted.

Vera's hands were lifted to his neck and began to gently massage it and with the pressing of her thumbs she relaxed his muscles while Duchin looked on from the other side of the desk.

"And I still did a few rounds here as well to be sure the coast was clear," said Vladimir, "that's how much the bastards have improved."

"You made three rounds," Vera said, "I saw you from the window."

"You saw me?" He was worried: if she identified him, why shouldn't others.

"But I didn't know that it was you," she reassured him. "I identified you only by your walk, and who besides me knows you like that? Volya, I felt such relief the moment I saw you,."

The two of them stood a moment longer like that, illuminated by the light filtering through the curtain.

"What's really worrying," said Vladimir, "is that they caught on to me while still on Sadovaya." No one followed him from here, the secret apartment, he's sure of that; and also on the way back he wasn't followed; but on Sadovaya they suddenly appeared a few meters from him, as if they had known in advance he was supposed to arrive there, on the corner of Sadovaya and Inzhenernaya.

Duchin said it still doesn't prove anything and remarked that the secret police had people in all sorts of places in the city, and definitely in those areas; the detectives had probably been waiting there on a regular shift and simply identified him the moment he arrived. "It could be just an ordinary coincidence," he said.

"Ordinary?" Vladimir still seemed agitated. "They identified me with such ease, with this goatee and these clothes. How did they know I looked like that?" The detectives the Okhrana place on the streets – he said – are nothing special, any child could spot them, but the ones who identified him were professionals, and they weren't waiting there by chance. They were professionals and had it not been for his experience, he wouldn't have spotted them; and worse than that, he would have led them straight here, to the secret apartment.

He turned his gaze to the window, and with the tip of his finger he moved the curtain aside slightly and viewed the street: first right, then left, and finally let his gaze linger on the small square and the drunk lying there.

Vera drew close to him again.

What was he implying by that, she asked and hugged him from behind, inter-twining her hands on his stomach, is he hinting at something?

"I'm not hinting at anything," he replied. And nevertheless, it had seemed to him then – yes, that's what went through his mind – that they knew he was about to come there, and also knew in what disguise he would come, with those clothes and without the full beard, as if they had waited in advance for some French monsieur.

Vladimir's eyes lingered for a while on the drunk in the square.

"He's been here the whole time," Vera replied to his question before it was asked. "At least since we've been here."

To reinforce her words, Duchin said he's been lying around there for two hours already, and there's no reason to be concerned about him. "Vera's absolutely sure he's a good man at heart," he said. "Good like all his people, good and drunk and miserable. Where are you going now, Vera Alexandrovna? We're talking about important things."

But she had already gone into the next room and closed the door behind her, and for a moment the two men listened to the noises being made there, most of which they knew well: a chest drawer was pulled out and slammed shut and after it another, then a dim unidentifiable sound was heard after which the second drawer slammed shut.

"Poliakov," said Duchin.

Only now, as if he suddenly was reminded of his existence and that he was waiting for them to come to a decision over his matter, he turned his eyes to him and ordered him to wait in the entrance hall again until they decide, and it would be better for him that they not be reminded of him then, or any other time.

Vera returned to the room with a square bottle made of thick dark glass in her hand. "Take it," she said to Vladimir, "come on, take it," and reached the bottle out to him, and in the light filtering through the curtain the drink assumed a shade of amber. "French cognac for a French monsieur," she said to him.

"I don't need it."

"Take it," she insisted and stuck the bottle into his hand.

"That's enough," Vladimir said quietly. "We're talking about important things here."

Her hand dropped from insult, and the bottle slanted at the side of her body with the drink shaken inside it. "Ah," she said, "the men are talking about import-ant things," and held the bottle up to the light.

"So then, I'll drink," she said and removed the lid and tilted the bottle towards her lips and eagerly took a sip and another and one more, slightly longer, and her pleasure was evident, not only in the drink but also in the freedom to drink it like a man, straight from the bottle; she who had come from a well-to-do home.

"I really was worried about you, Volya," she said and wiped her mouth with the back of her hand. "Only me; even your wife doesn't worry about you that way."

"Don't mention her," he replied sharply.

"He," she indicated to Duchin, "was sure you'd come in the end. He's always sure, Duchin, he always knows everything. But on the other hand, he's always got doubts about everything, with his doubts he could make -"

Duchin interrupted her. He hasn't got doubts, he said but –

".... mountains collapse," Vera continued.

"But caution," said Duchin. "And what happened to Volya is proof that it's justified."

"Proof?" she said to him. "Maybe you're happy now that it turned out all your warnings were justified? Maybe it would have been better from your point of view had he been caught."

From the other side of the large desk, Duchin studied her face for a long while, and in a soft voice asked her if she meant what she said and if she's not ashamed to bring such an accusation against him.

"No," she said, "I'm not ashamed. You should be ashamed," and looked straight at the seated man.

"He," she turned to Vladimir, "on one hand reassures you you've got no reason to be concerned, and on the other everyone in the world is a liar and a traitor in his eyes. And if they aren't right now, they soon will be. Even if Jesus stood opposite him and let him touch his wounds, he wouldn't believe it was him."

The sunlight that penetrated from the corner of the curtain was refracted by the bottle and the glass glistened.

"Just be careful it doesn't spill on you, Vera," said Duchin from his desk. "After all, it has to be drunk to the full. Isn't that what he said on the cross?"

"Mock me as much as you want, Duchin," she said to him, "but not him, I asked you, didn't I?"

"On the cross," Duchin answered softly, "he nevertheless still had some usefulness, at least according to the story. While with us, Vera Alexandrovna, if one day we stand on the gallows, we won't be of any use."

"Now he'll start telling us again," she said, and her eyes turned to Vladimir, "how he saw them being hanged, isn't that what you were going to say? And what's it all for? Only to show that he knows everything about everything and can quote from everyone, especially Herzen. To hell with Herzen." She looked at Vladimir as he opened another button of his jacket. His gaze still followed the drunk lying in the middle of the square.

"With us, Vera," Duchin said without raising his voice, "in contrast to that story, if there is a Judas Iscariot among us, under no circumstances must we kiss him. He has to be silenced, and there's only one way to do that."

"If there's no choice we'll do it," she replied to him. "We'll send Poliakov, no?"

And indeed in the end he came here with this Browning, almost on his own accord, to this quarter to this room to this Judas Iscariot, Levin.

I won't kiss you, he said to him softly.

On the bench in the small square, the drunk sang a different tune, one that a hundred years before had been sung about Napoleon's soldiers ("Three Frenchmen Crossed the Volga"), and during the last year, following some failures of the fleet, it was adapted for the Japanese ("Three Japs Went Down to the Harbor") and a few traces of the original version still remained:

"They entered an inn
inky pinky parlez-vous"

The interval between the verses he utilized for a deep and purifying clearing of the throat, and afterward spat at the chestnut tree.

Vera's voice could be heard from the other side of the door.

"We aren't them," she said again about the Narodniks that Duchin was praising again.

"You, Vera, are certainly not them."

"Are you mocking me again?"

"No," Duchin replied to her. "No one compares to you, and especially your talent for disguise. You could've been a great actress, what a terrible loss for the Russian theater. Even I fell for it at the time."

"Fell for what?" she said, "I stood the whole night long in the street in the middle of December in the cold, everyone was cold, maybe I drank a bit."

"A bit?"

"Okay, so I drank a lot. And had I not drunk then, nothing would have happened."

"So, something did happen," he said to her. "Before you said it didn't, and now it turns out it did."

"And that's what you're thinking about now? Why don't you say something Volya -"

"It's between you and him," he said after a moment.

"But nothing did happen!" she said, "And you were in Kiev anyway. Two months later, you were still there, and he" – she indicated to Duchin – "taught me things here, gave me lectures. You made a great impression on me then, Duchin, one would have thought that Zhelyabov himself consulted with you before every operation. Who knew you were a boy of twelve at the time?"

"Arithmetic was never your strongest point, Vera Alexandrovna," said Duchin, "not arithmetic, nor calculations."

She pulled Vladimir's hand and he shook her off. "Let him finish talking," he said while still holding the edge of the curtain slightly away from the windowpane and looking down at the street; he was worried as before, though he tried not to show it.

After a while the drunk remembered the start of the next verse:

"Innkeeper, innkeeper, give us your daughter

Parlez-vous"

And a short while later he remembered the rest; not all at once, but a line here and a line there, until they were gathered together into a verse ended by the well-known refrain: the innkeeper refused the Japs, parlez-vous, he said his daughter was too young, parlez-vous, he wouldn't give her to anyone, inky pinky parlez-vous.

They listened to him from the room, as did Poliakov from the entrance hall under the head of the deer. Perhaps the deer was listening too; it was a very old deer and might have heard that song when it still referred to Napoleon's soldiers.

"I'm not young, father
Parlez-vous
I'm not young, father, I've already been humped by the whole village
Inky pinky parlez-vous"

And the last verse he remembered in its entirety: how the Japs went into her room, parlez-vous, but came out of there without their balls, parlez-vous.

There was a moment of silence, perhaps the drunk was searching for a new song to start with and couldn't find one.

"Anushka!" he called out suddenly from his bench, but not according to the notes of any song but rather a call that was addressed to the street, up or down its slope or both together. "Anushka!"

And with the same suddenness with which he began, he fell silent.

"Your people," said Duchin to Vera.

Without letting go of the edge of the curtain concealing him, Vladimir turned to Duchin. "Was he here long before I arrived?" he asked again.

"Yes."

And again the drunk lifted up his voice.

"Your people, Vera Alexandrovna," said Duchin. "The people - singing, drinking and burping. And when you liberate them, if you haven't been hung by then, they won't be going to the Duma but to the tavern."

"But none of them want that!" And she immediately went into detail again as if to a slow-witted person: it's the hunger and poverty that cause that, and the illness, and the disasters. They shouldn't be blamed for that!

"At least be a bit careful with that bottle of yours, Vera," he said to her, "don't spill it by accident. As you well know, alcohol can also instill hope."

"Don't make me out to be a drinker," she answered angrily, "if Volya hadn't been late, I wouldn't have touched it at all. I only took it out the drawer when you still hadn't come, Volya, you'd never been that late before. I was worried about you," she said, "I almost went crazy from worry! While he sat here calmly behind his desk. As far as he was concerned you could come a year later or not at all."

"In a moment, it really will spill on you," Vladimir said to her quietly.

"Let it all spill," she answered and tilted the bottle some more, and when Vladimir held out his hand to her she moved it aside with the bottle, and the drink rose up further in the glass neck and as a result of being shaken stained her dress.

Vera looked at the stain: the front of the dress and its décolletage had been sprayed.

"Now are you happy," she said to them both, "that I really do look like a drunk?"

With two fingers she drew the material of the dress away from her body and began to walk towards the side room and on her way she watered a large, withered plant with cognac before passing the door ajar in front, through which their voices filtered into the entrance hall. It would have been proper not to listen to them, but nonetheless Poliakov had listened; and that was the lesser of things one shouldn't do that he did anyway.

"Don't you care," she said, "if it's ruined or not? You both once did care," she said from her room, and from the street, as if in reply to her words, the drunk let out a long continuous cough, the kind that's entrenched in the throat and the lungs until every bit of phlegm is raised from the very bottom.

"Is he still there?" she asked, "I thought he'd finally gone away."

"You heard him yourself," answered Vladimir from the next room.

"My dress was just over my head," she said, "and it's a little hard to hear some- one with a dress over your head. Did you ever try to hear someone with a dress over your head, Volya? Just try it once." She chuckled; perhaps it was the cognac chuckling from her throat, or perhaps since they were treating her like a drunk, she defiantly tried to sound like one.

"Your dress was just over your head," Vladimir said slowly.

"God, it got so wet! This stain is terrible! It won't come out in the wash, things like that never come out, not blood and not cognac."

"Not blood.... and not cognac," Vladimir repeated her words very slowly.

"Why are you repeating everything I say, Volya?"

"It seems," he said, "that when you want to, you can hear everything. Is there anything disturbing you over your head now?"

"Now I can see him," she answered from her room, and changed her position; perhaps she drew close to the window and also watched the small square and the bench in the shadow of the chestnut tree.

"Why shouldn't the drunk see you like that?" Vladimir said from the next room.

"How could he see me?"

"Just like that," he answered, "the way you are, probably half-naked."

From her room, whose door wasn't completely shut, she asked Vladimir in the cheerful voice she had adopted for the past few minutes, how does he know she's half-naked; on what basis is he saying such a thing; one doesn't just come out with things like that without seeing anything at all. And all the more so not to a woman.

"One thing I can assure you," she said from her room and rustled something, "is that half-naked I'm not."

Some object was moved on Duchin's desk, perhaps the copper ashtray, and outside, in the small square, the drunk again let out that continuous cough entrenched in the depths of the lungs.

"That's a real cough, Volya," said Duchin. "It's not an act. You can relax."

"But I'm not relaxed."

"A cough like that -" Duchin began to say.

"He didn't cough like that before, when he was singing," Vladimir interrupted him, moving the curtain aside a little more and peering at the other side of the street: a carriage was drawing near, and horses' hooves could be heard.

"You've become worse than me," said Duchin, "a person's allowed to get drunk and cough without having any connection to the secret police."

"He's allowed to," Vladimir agreed. "He's certainly allowed to," he said and widened the space between the material and the windowpane.

From the side room, steps could be heard and, after them, a continuous creaking, perhaps of the cupboard door whose hinges weren't oiled. "He must have caught a cold," Vera said from there in her new tone of voice. "He must have spilled vodka over himself and now he's wet all over, poor thing. That's what happens when you aren't careful with it, even when you know you should be, but at the last moment you aren't and it spills." She chuckled to herself again.

"He's allowed to do anything, Duchin," said Vladimir in the next room, "to drink and to spit. But I, Duchin, barely made it here. They were waiting for me halfway, they'd never seen me in these clothes, they'd never seen me without a full beard, and nevertheless they identified me the moment I got there. That can put thoughts into one's head."

In the side room a cupboard draw was slammed, and another was opened. "It just spilled on him," Vera said from there. "Poor thing. he didn't have anything to change into, where would he have. There are those who have and those who have not. I have. Don't you want to help me choose something to wear, Volya?"

Vladimir didn't answer.

"We've already spoken about that," Duchin said to him, "they weren't necessarily waiting for you." In a very patient voice, he explained again that it was part of the regular security arrangement; after all, that was the restaurant that guy usually ate at, the one before didn't like restaurants but this guy does, and even if Vladimir hadn't arrived there, the detectives would have been there. "They were simply placed there," he said, "without any connection to you."

"You didn't mention that before," answered Vladimir. "Doesn't it seem important to you to update me about detectives being there?"

"There are detectives everywhere, it's nothing new. They're all over the city, one has to be careful of them." And besides, Duchin said, wasn't Vladimir supposed to have been swallowed up there between the passersby? Detectives or not, he was supposed to have been swallowed up and to disappear from sight as fast as possible. Maybe he did something that exposed him?

"I was swallowed up," answered Vladimir, "and it was actually easy. There was no shortage of people in the street. And despite all that, they identified me the second I arrived. Who knew about my disguise other than us? Levin didn't know about it."

"Volya," Vera called from her room, "don't you want to help me?"

"They followed me, Duchin," said Vladimir, ignoring her call, "and afterward I had to circle the quarter three times until I was certain the coast was clear. They were after me, Duchin, not anyone else – me. And they all knew exactly how I would look: with these suffocating clothes and without a full beard; just a week ago I looked completely different. I never had hard collars like these."

"So why don't you change Volya?" Vera said from her room. "Come here and change, I'll help you."

"Vera Alexandrovna," said Duchin.

"What?"

"Just what exactly are you trying to do?"

"To get changed," she replied from her room. "What d'you mean, isn't one allowed to change clothes here?

"So, get changed already," said Vladimir.

"And don't you want to help me?" The door of her room creaked a bit as it opened, and the two men looked there until she slammed the door again, and a few moments later came out dressed and combed and without any pretense of drunkenness, as if she had instantly shed all that with the dress she had changed into: the show was over, and again they were faced with a mission that had to be executed in the best possible manner.

"Haven't you finished worrying?" she asked Vladimir. "In the end from all the worry-"

"No Vera," he interrupted her, "I haven't finished worrying."

In her usual voice, the sober one, she suggested that until the police break into the apartment, if there's any reason at all to think they might, they should utilize the time to sum up their new lookout posts: it will certainly be much more productive than worrying. Her lookout posts from her sidewalk, Vladimir's from his platform; and to that they can add, if they insist, Zamyatin's report from the restaurant; Zamyatin had spent more than a few hours there. And may Duchin forgive her now if she's invading his territory; after all, organizing things is his role; why else does he need such a big desk?

"How lovely you are, Vera, when you get started," he said from his desk, and with that looked at Vladimir who was peering outside again, and this time not at the small square but at the building opposite.

So then, Vera said: we know by heart the hours that bastard spends in his bureau, he's also a man of routine habits, (they had a new target that even Polia-

kov knew nothing about, perhaps not a minister but a governor: the success of
the minister's assassination must have encouraged them). And the hours of his
restaurant visits are also known to them, and exactly when he spends time with
his mistress, all that already appeared in the previous reports. His routes are also
known, so what are they waiting for now, the right time?

"Exactly," answered Vladimir. "For the right time."

"But what exactly is the right time? It's never the right time, never! There's
always something that doesn't work out, there's always some hitch. When the hell
is the right time, answer me, when that character dies of old age?"

They were still also deliberating about the question of how come someone had
been waiting for Vladimir next to the restaurant, and so the decision whether to
send him to Levin or not had been postponed. For a while he wanted it badly and
for a while thought: what for, what's the point? Even if all their plans are realized
and the Tsar is deposed and this whole damn country changes its face in a revolution, and not only its face but its entire existence, his life won't turn into a different
life.

"For what?" Vera said from the other side of the door. "Just tell me what the
hell we are waiting for. We've learned all his routes, and we know his whole schedule by heart, just like we knew with the assassination, so for what?"

"For a suitable opportunity," said Duchin in his quiet authoritative voice.
"That's what we're waiting for."

"From your desk? Nothing will happen from here."

Duchin straightened the ashtray with one finger so that its side would be
parallel to the edge of the table – something he enjoyed doing – and Vladimir
looked at his finger and was about to say something.

"Do you know, Vera Alexandrovna," Duchin said, "there was someone with us
once even more hotheaded than you, and even more obstinate than you, and sure
of herself at least as much as you? And she decided that she alone without any help
could assassinate some high ranking official. There was also some personal interest
there, the official had harmed her father in some way, and so Kirilova that's what
her name was, Irena Kirilova – decided she'd do it with her own hands."

"Is it a long story with a short moral that I can already guess?"

"It's a short story without any moral," replied Duchin. He looked at Vladimir
for a moment as if waiting for him to interrupt him.

She didn't have an orderly plan – Duchin continued –Kirilova only knew one
thing, that she wanted to kill that senior official and that no one in the world could
stop her. "He travelled by train a lot and she followed him everywhere, waiting for
the right moment to kill him. She had patience and determination and was no less
obstinate than you, Vera. But there's no good ending to all of this."

"I already understood that."

"She concealed her pistol on her body. It was winter and she hid it under the fur coat. She would pass from carriage to carriage hoping just once to see the senior official without the bodyguards. She didn't want help from anyone and said it was safest to do everything alone. And that's how it was week after week, month after month."

"You said it was a short story,"

"Very short," answered Duchin.

"And without a moral."

"Let him speak," said Vladimir.

"Don't tell me you also fell a bit in love with Kirilova, Duchin," Vera said.

"I admired her," he replied. "None of us had such determination, none of us were as devoted as her. Irena saw everything as her moral obligation, and not as a game the way you do sometimes. An obligation which no matter how many hardships she needed to overcome; she'll fulfill in the end."

"So you did love her," said Vera softly.

Duchin removed his finger from the ashtray. "I -" he said and fell silent.

"Loved," said Vera.

"Are you jealous?" he asked, the sting in his voice creeping back. "Would you prefer, Vera, that there was no one other than you?"

"You never had much admiration for me, Duchin."

"True," he replied. "There wasn't admiration. What there was, it seems to me you know very well."

Again, Vladimir looked at them and this time perhaps his eyes lingered a short while on Vera before he returned his gaze to the window opposite them. "And how was she caught?" he asked. "Why don't you also us how they caught Kirilova?"

"They caught her the moment after she fired the shot," Duchin replied. "By that time she didn't care if she was caught, she was sure she had killed the man, she didn't know that he was only wounded."

"Maybe they were waiting for her?" Vladimir said. "Maybe someone described what she looked like to the guard? She and her fur coat."

"What are you getting at, Volya?" Duchin said.

"Only the three of us knew about my new look. Levin didn't know about it and neither did Poliakov."

"Maybe he heard us," Duchin said, "simply by listening to us from behind the door." And right away he called out, "Poliakov!" And called again in a louder voice.

When he entered, Duchin fixed his gaze on him and indicated with his chin to the chair in front of his desk. "Didn't you hear me the first time?" he asked. "While you were sitting there, couldn't you hear us? Sometimes the door doesn't close properly."

"He wasn't here at the time," Vladimir said. "Only the three of us were here then."

"While you were sitting there," Duchin said again, "couldn't you hear us? We were wondering if you could be believed or not, and do you know what conclusion we came to Poliakov? Maybe by chance that's something you did hear? There's aren't many possibilities here: either we believe you or we don't."

"I didn't tell them anything!" he answered as he had answered all the previous times that he had been asked about his interrogation at the Okhrana.

"We've heard that already. I asked only about the conclusion that we came to."

"I don't know," he answered, and he really didn't know; he actually hadn't managed to hear that; maybe they had decided about him with a nod of the head.

"You-don't-know," Duchin repeated his words slowly. With his third finger, he flicked grains of ash from the edge of the desk, and since his cleaning was still unsatisfactory to him he polished it with the palm of his hand, and for a moment his movement resembled that of the woman polishing her window on the other side of the road, as if it had been coordinated by them – and perhaps it had been coordinated by them; that suspicion hadn't risen at the time – but the woman seemed completely engrossed in her work, and even if she could have observed the window opposite her window, it seemed that she hadn't done so; at least, not at that moment.

"While you were sitting there," Duchin said to him again, "we were speaking here not only about you, but also about an exceptional woman from the previous generation, Irena Kirilova, maybe you've heard of her? A brave woman from a good family who became a revolutionary."

"It seems someone had informed on her," Vladimir said. "Why don't you say it?"

"Maybe you read about her in the paper?" Duchin continued. "After all, didn't newspapers reach your village?"

"Not only newspapers," Vera burst out. "The rioters also reached there, and it was no less terrible, Duchin, than everything you were forced to see. Semyonovsky Square here and trains there, Semyonovsky Square can go to hell together with Kirilova's trains, what's that in comparison to what he was forced to go through?"

"What he told you he went through," replied Duchin. Perhaps he suspected he had lied, and perhaps he would have maligned him even without the suspicion.

"One's allowed to be afraid," she said. "It's no shame to be afraid, Duchin, everyone's allowed. Tell him that Volya, how sometimes you're also afraid and overcome it, explain that to him." Her fingers were still playing with the glass beads of the necklace, an accessory for her housemaid's disguise, until she managed to close the metal clasp and turn it around to the back of the neck.

"Only fools aren't afraid," said Vladimir.

A moment later he tensed: it seemed he had discerned something outside, but it wasn't the square that worried him, nor the street, but the window opposite, the one the woman had polished and then covered with a curtain. A glint could be seen in the corner of the window, a corner like that which Vladimir was peering through; for him his eyes were sufficient, while there – Vladimir had no doubt about it – they were observing them with binoculars; yes; not with spectacles, it wasn't the glint of spectacles or a fragment of a mirror some child was amusing himself with. No-no, there were no children's games going on here.

So, almost on its own accord, and without another word, the regulation for a hasty evacuation was put into action: not everyone together to the street, to whoever might be lurking there, but one to the back exit (Vladimir) and one to the service stairs (Vera) and one to the roof (out of everyone, they sent him to the roof, as if he would be sentenced again and again to such a height), and then each to his own for two whole days, until it would be clarified beyond any doubt that all danger had passed.

He bounded up the stairs to the roof, and there, panting, he advanced crouching until peeking carefully down at the street, and as much as he strained his eyes, he couldn't make out any out of the ordinary activity. The window of the apartment opposite them didn't reveal anything due to the glare of the sun in the pane, and below there were pedestrians as before, alone or in couples, and carriages travelled along the road, slow or fast, together with carts and two-wheelers with pairs or trios or single horses harnessed to them, and in the square the drunk stood opposite the chestnut tree and urinated, and none of his group his could be seen leaving the building, not Volya who left from the back, not Vera who left from the service stairs, nor Duchin, who perhaps went out into the street dressed like Korogin the bicycle importer, and no different in any way from two other gentlemen who then left the entrance of the building.

And what about me, he wanted to ask but didn't have anyone to ask, what the hell about me, and what about that Levin, what had been decided, would he be killed or not, would I shoot him or not. And in the end, he answered himself - on that roof; he spent quite some time on the roof, not as much as he had spent in the attic in his village, but certainly enough – and decided for them.

What do you prefer, Levin, he said to him softly, a hole in the forehead or a hole in the tooth? He thought the forehead might be preferable because pain in the forehead comes to an end.

In the forehead or the temple, he said to him softly, or in your mouth that squealed. That's what Duchin repeatedly said. And whoever has any doubts in the matter, he said, should think what would be better: the danger of killing an innocent man or the danger that many will be arrested the next day and jailed in Petropavlovsk or Shlisselburg until they're hung in the square ("What do you prefer Vera, Levin dead in bed, or Volya hung by a rope?").

Despite the darkness in the room, he tried to discern the movement of the sleeping man's eyelids and wasn't able to, but he knew it didn't prove anything and that it was possible all of Levin's calm was a sham. In your place, he said to him, I wouldn't be so calm, I'd be shitting in my pants, maybe you already have? Isn't mommy going to change you?

His mother, who he hadn't seen for months and will never see again, was fed up with all her obligations as a wife and mother. On the nights his father got into her bed, his hoarse voice could be heard pleading with her and her mocking voice refusing, and afterward there was the sound of frantic struggling and a sob, he couldn't be sure from whose throat it was emitted, and when he understood what his parents were doing there in the dark he wondered if that was the way he had come into the world, with pleading and struggling and sobbing. She didn't sing him lullabies, and most of the tales she told were to country girls, for payment or in exchange for some merchandise. For instance she would tell them with complete earnestness: "Over there, beyond the far hill, there's a wagon approaching with two brown horses harnessed to it. The driver's name is Dmitri and he's scratching his head, God how many lice he's got there!" And it was almost as good as predicting they would find treasure in the yard, the lice never disappointed. Or she would say: "On a train now, from Minsk to Pinsk, five soldiers are sitting, and one gets up and puts his head outside and shouts the name of his sweetheart from all his longing," which was almost as good as predicting to them a loved one will get off at the next station but will never arrive.

To him she said, without looking at patterns of oil floating on water and without exacting a payment: "Between two villages, your dear father is dozing off in a cart. His head is falling onto his chest and his eyes are closing and in a moment he'll begin to snore and saliva will drool from his mouth, but you won't be like him, right? Promise me, Ilya, promise," and placed her hand on his head as if anointing him for a different life.

Your parents are a pair of doves, he said to the sleeping man. And let them only not enter suddenly and accidentally get hurt, it's enough that my parents got hurt.

Hurt? He pondered, you call death hurt?

When the two of them hid in the attic, she didn't have to predict anything from her bowl. He wasn't supposed to be there, but he came on a visit and stayed an extra day. In the city, he had had a sudden longing for the village, and having saved some money in Petersburg, made the journey. When the buildings of the city had completely disappeared, the expanses of this vast country began to spread out on the other side of the window, expanses through which Jews weren't permitted to travel, but always found ways to outwit the prohibition; after all, there was no one in the world who can compete with them for survival, not even the gypsies. Attempts at annihilation had been made on every generation, unsuccessfully, and in that too they found proof of being God's chosen people.

His father believed that; his mother was doubtful. She would say to his him: "Who did he choose, Shloime, you? What has he got to choose you for?" And she would then raise her eyebrows to the sky, despite not believing in God any more than she believed in her husband: there was no gain to be had from either of them.

When his father prayed, he would rock back and forth vigorously, and the

Christian children asked if he also rocked his wife that way, and their parents had more questions to ask. From the roof of their church, their tormented god watched everything around him, and dozens of times a day they made the sign of the cross and blamed the Jews. In the yard – where he wasn't meant to be, and in fact wasn't, he was hiding in the attic – there were some drunks who tried to do that to their neighbor the tailor with their own hands, crucifying him to the door of his house. Time after time, they hit the nail, and time after time missed it, until the palm of the spread-out hand on the door was flattened like a steak.

At first, they were as gentle as seamstresses: a large one gently inserted two long nails into the nostrils of the tailor, and with two filthy thumbs pressed the heads of the nails and pushed them deep into his nostrils further and further inside, until they burst the skin of the nose on both sides close to the eyes, and all his friends cheered. "Carry on, Igor, carry on," they cried, and in the blood flowing from the slope of the burst nostrils, they directed the tips of the nails to the eyes to insert them into the pupils, exactly as they had previously done to the dog (it lumbered here and there in the yard blinded and wailing, its tail between its legs and its body wrapped in a prayer shawl and tripping up in it).

"He chose you, you?" she would say to his father. "Hasn't he got anyone better to choose than you? Is he completely blind?" In fact, perhaps he is, she said, if he let her enter the wedding canopy with him.

"Rather bring me wood for heating instead of occupying yourself with forests," she would say to him, "but even that, you can't!" She herself knew how to split logs with precision, and at times it seemed the beatings of the axe weren't directed at the wood but rather to the life she had been sentenced to.

"This oil floats on water better than all your trees," she said to his father when he returned from one of his journeys and frowned at the village women who had come to hear her tales.

"In my place," he said when they left with the little consolation they received ("the sweet little thing is falling asleep in the train with a finger in her mouth, and in her dream she sees you all"; being in someone else's dream was just as good as having one's fortune told), "someone else would have already -"

"Would have what?" she asked him.

But his father didn't finish the sentence. He took her bowl and emptied it out the window, and in the puddle that was formed outside, the oil glistened in the sun.

"At least that oil floats," she said to him, "not like all your logs. Instead of all those rafts, it would be better to bring me wood for the oven."

She stood next to the window as began to slice the loaf of bread that he had brought.

"That's the most you know how to do – cut bread," she said to him.

He cut slice after slice with the large knife used for meat, though even a quarter of a loaf wouldn't be necessary for the meal. He sliced to the end of the loaf and then cut the last piece into two. Since his mother was still speaking ("You should slice all your business contracts into pieces"), he put his hand next the slices arranged one after the other, and with the back of his pale hand brushed them off the table and without waiting for them to fall he clutched the knife and lifted it into the air – from his chair next to his mother's empty chair he saw his father's eyes becoming enlarged beneath their sparse lashes: they were terrifying – and lowered it not towards her, who was still standing next to the window, but towards her chair and stuck it into the seat. For some moments the handle quivered like a pocketknife after being thrown at a tree trunk or a rolling barrel.

In the yard – years later, the yard he wasn't supposed to be in at all – it all happened without him at first. His father was away on one of his journeys. Sometimes weeks and months passed before it became clear that the forest whose trees he had praised so highly had slipped from his hands into thin air by means of some other nego-tiated business deal. They certainly hadn't been waiting for him throughout the commotion, or after it had completely subsided: when the screaming had ceased and the wailing had died. To the ear of someone approaching from the path-way, the silence was almost completely normal, had the cackling of the geese not been missing from it. The looters had already looted, and the beaters had already beaten, and it seemed even the dead had already been quieted from the torments of their dying.

His father was dozing in the cart at the time and let the horse lead him home, and only awoke when his horse stopped in front of one of the bodies that had been rolled out from the yard, and even then his father still didn't see anything. He gave a sleepy goading call but the horse had smelt the scent of the yard and especially the blood and remained standing in its place in front of the body that had been thrown there – the tailor had been rolled out by being kicked after they failed to nail his hands to the door – and didn't move even when its master shouted at it again. It just bared its teeth, and when its owner lashed out at it with a whip it reared its legs, and only then he saw one of the drunks.

"We have a guest," he called to his friends lying next to him.

And now I'm your guest, Levin.

25

They had all left the fair together two hours before that:

The one walking at their head carried a pink teddy bear he won at the marksmanship stall, and the whole way he tried to seat it on his shoulder like the gypsy had sat his monkey, and also slapped it like him when it refused to obey him; and the one walking by his side held a near empty bottle in his right hand, and after it had been completely emptied he raised it to his eye and looked through it like through a captain's telescope; and behind them all the rest walked not knowing where exactly they were walking to or why, content to depend on those two to find them a greater amusement than all those they had left at the fair (they saw a bearded lady, and a midget of whom it was said was her husband and who she could stick completely between her legs; and a fortune teller predicted in her crystal ball – many-gold-coins-in-the-near-future and also many-beautiful-women-in the-near-future).

That's how they walked, and a few sang some crude song. Here and there, from the side of the way, they picked up a discarded beam or a pitchfork from a haystack or a cattle goad they happened upon or borrowed, promising to return everything. With those beams and pitchforks and cattle goads, their height had grown further, and their throats were parched; throats that had already become one unified throat. They had filled their stomachs with kvass and cheap vodka and added to the gold coins and the whiteness of women's bodies that had been predicted for them was the red of blood, as if hinted by the air itself, though it was as clear as crystal.

When they arrived at the junction there were already dozens of men armed with axes and sledgehammers and iron bars as well as with their herd-like courage and the knowledge no one would stand in their way. For a while they tarried at the junction, all the dozens with all their improvised weapons (the pink teddy bear fell again from the shoulder of the one marching at their head and was lifted up again; and through the empty bottle his deputy surveyed the village houses from their foundations to their chimneys, as if from the twirls of the smoke one could tell to which god they were rising: to the one floating in the sky with his cross or to another hiding behind his clouds), but just then Vasya the fool came near with hops and skips, having been drawn from the field and its flies toward the forest of moving iron bars.

When he reached them, he stopped for a moment in his bare feet and rags and scratched the back of his neck and removed an insect from his hair and squashed it between his fingernails, and then passed his gaping eyes over their faces and their weapons, from pitchfork to sledgehammer and from beam to iron bar and from cattle goad to axe, until he discovered the pink teddy bear, and immediately wanted it and reached out a bony long nailed hand towards it. A moment later the teddy bear was waved in front of his eyes here and there like a slice of sausage in front of a dog, and because he was trying to catch it, they lifted the teddy bear up on a hook for him to jump toward and stretch a hand out to it while the other held his trousers so that they wouldn't fall down. It was all so amusing that they agreed to linger there a little longer.

It was a clear day, and since they hadn't completed their amusements at the fair, they put down the pitchforks and beams and axes and goads and sledgehammers and iron bars and began to throw the teddy bear to one another above the fool's head. "Catch, Vasya, catch," they shouted to him, "jump, Vasya, jump," so that he'd jump higher and his eyes gape wider, half of him joyous that they were playing with him and half of him crying over the pink teddy bear that evaded his hands again and again. And because he was barefoot, they smashed an empty bottle on the ground and then another and a third and fourth so that he'd jump on the broken pieces. "Jump, Vasya, jump." they spurred him on, "Dance, Vasya, dance," and he jumped and danced to prove to them how much he wanted the teddy bear. And even when the red of the blood could be seen, they still didn't agree to give him the pink teddy bear until he show them where the Zhids live here. Some knew a few individual Zhids well, the tailor for example and not only him, but the question was directed at the all the Zhids en bloc.

In his astonishment the fool said in his stuttering wonder "the Zhzhzhzids?" And a moment later turned to the pathway leading to the right, and after a few steps stopped because he remembered that some Zhids also lived to his left and turned there and stopped again and scratched the back of his neck and consulted one of his nostrils too, but his back was already being pushed by a cattle goad to hurry up and find the Zhids for them without delay. They had already wasted enough time on nonsense.

Those who had turned right continued to walk to the right, and those who had turned left continued to walk to the left so that they wouldn't have to make do with what would be left for them. The village was small, and there certainly weren't any rich people in it; at the most, one could take a goose from them or a goat or their daughters' virginity. More time would pass until they would remember the one who could also have sat at the fair and told fortunes.

In the yard – the yard where he wasn't meant to be but had been because he had come from the city on a visit – the rumpus could already be heard rising and growing from the pathway like a murky giant wave surging forward with the sweep of the pitchforks and beams and hooks and axes and iron bars that it will hurl when it crashes. His mother listened to the commotion for a moment and said: "They're coming here, run and tell the neighbors and come back."

He was nineteen then, and for a year had already lived in the big city that she had never visited and never will visit, and nevertheless he obeyed her like a child.

Their neighbor, the tailor, was already standing in the entrance of his house, and behind his back stood the woman he had married a few years before that and with her their child who did not look like her daughter but rather like her little sister. The girl's nose was running, and she held the cloth hand of her doll whose hair was made of remnants of thread. When he told them that the rioters were coming and suggested they block up the door with some furniture, the child also understood something from their voices and the expression on their faces and right away, without uttering a word, wrapped her doll in a piece of fabric she found next to the sewing machine.

When he left there, he heard the bed being moved to the door, and beyond the sharp squeaky sound, the dim commotion of the murky wave surging from the pathway with all its masts could still be heard. A short distance in front of them, like a crab hurrying to escape the edge of the tide, the fool hopped with the pink teddy bear that had finally been given to him, and behind him a zigzag trail of drops of blood. "Dance, Vasya, dance," they shouted at him from behind, or "Jump, Vasya, jump," because he had already become a sort of mascot for them. Even when they prodded him with a cattle goad, it was done amiably, like hurrying a lazy cow but one full of milk.

The thought that passed through their minds at the sight of them was a terrible one, but nonetheless arose and persevered: just as well there were some houses before theirs where they would go before reaching theirs: it was a pure thought in comparison to another that hadn't yet been arisen but already waited in the back of the mind.

"Get inside already!" called his mother and pulled his hand into the house like in his childhood, though he was now taller and stronger than her, and had already seen things she will never see and had done deeds she would not have conceived him capable of doing: first in the nearby town, which in comparison to their village seemed like a city, in a small room stinking of cheap perfume and sweat and sperm, while the next in line waited on the other side of the door; and then in the city which in comparison the town seemed like a village, inside a clean pleasant room whose order was disturbed by his body, and not only was the room disturbed but the life of the young woman who lived in it as well; and then in the glorious damned capital, where one suburb could swallow the entire city, and between them he had travelled in trains with so many carriages the population of several villages could have travelled in them, and the giant country presented its landscapes one after another like a madam of a brothel presenting her prostitutes to a novice client. He had experienced that too, but here in the village, he obeyed his mother.

First they moved the kitchen table with all its gashes and crumbs and glass prints (only the samovar was taken down and placed in the corner of the room), and pushed the chairs between it and the wall including the chair that had been punctured years before by the blade of a knife. They crowded all that together and reinforced it with a sack of potatoes that gave off a smell. Afterward, they closed up the wooden shutters of the window as of readying for a storm, and his mother deliberated whether to let the geese inside. In the end, she decided to leave them as dues for the invaders. Their cackling could still be heard outside, alarmed and annoyed about their being abandoned like that.

He then went up the ladder with his mother to the attic, into the darkness perforated by slender beams of light in which grains of dust were trapped fleeing from the webs woven in the corners.

"The barrel," she said after they had pulled the ladder up, "move the barrel, can you move it?"

He moved the barrel of water kept for extinguishing fires and stood it on top of the small door in the floor. At the time it seemed it would defend them from all harm.

"Jump, Vasya, jump!" those coming on the pathway shouted, or "Dance, Vasya, dance," because the fool was still dancing and skipping and hopping in front of the marchers, and still held the pink teddy bear in his hand and swung it to and fro. Fluff was already sprouting from its split stitches, and the trail of blood left by his dancing soles left was instantaneously blurred by the marchers behind him.

"Now be quiet," said his mother in the attic. "Can you sit still?" She wanted him to be like all the junk was stored there: broken pieces of chairs, a dismantled table a cracked samovar and piles of rags. In his childhood, he used to play there or watch the horizon through a slit, and in his youth he pleasure himself there on a bed of sacks opposite a tattered and stained photograph he won by knife throwing: a naked woman whose nipples were almost erased from all the touching.

"Don't do anything," said his mother, and warned him with her finger as in his childhood. "Do you hear? Sit still until all this passes over," because she anticipated the time after all this, and was preparing him for it, her firstborn who had been caught up here. "Just don't be some hero for me now," she said to him, "I don't know what you've been doing in the city, but here you'll sit still."

He sat still. In the silence of the attic, in the darkness perforated by slender jets of light, they heard the yard gate burst open by a few kicks, and their asking the fool there where to turn, left or right. They then heard them turn not toward their house but that of the tailor (and, at the time, the pink teddy bear swung to and fro in front of them, with the fluff ends sprouting from its stitches and minus one of its button eyes that had been lost on the way).

The then heard them kicking the door, and shoulders striking the door, and sledgehammer blows smashing the door – their neighbors must have placed more furniture between the bed and the wall – and how it was uprooted from its hinges and cast to the ground. And then there was silence.

It was so complete it seemed only the sound of grains of dust flying in the air could be heard, but it lasted only for a moment and right away a shout rose: it was sharp and impossible to know whose throat it had come from, whether that of a man or a woman or a child or a bird or an animal, the only thing they did know was that it burst from the throat of a living being about to lose its life. And he and his mother didn't move and wouldn't move from there even when things many times worse would happen.

Perhaps you'll shout like that, he said silently to Levin, tell me, will you or won't you shout?

Sharp and piercing, a screech lengthened in the fresh air – it was the screech of a child – and in the yard, the geese began to cackle. Thin sunbeams penetrated between the roofing tiles, and though they didn't banish the darkness, in their dim light sights better left unseen were visible: how at once a few dozen men or just a dozen burst into the tailor's house; a dozen were enough as was a sledgehammer that had smashed the door and was already searching for something new to smash and right away found it and smashed that too. There were enough there; the men, the three occupants of the house and the village fool who entered last, after parting from the geese (he cackled at them, and they answered him; "*tiu-tiu*," he called out at them the way the girl had called to them).

In a state of wonder, Vasya stepped on the uprooted door, leaving his bloody footprints there, and when he discovered the girl – small and shrunken even more than she usually was – he waved his pink teddy bear at her in a friendly manner as if she had no more important matters than teddy bears in the pandemonium taking place in her home.

It was a room of four-square meters, and there couldn't have been even one centimeter free of a man armed with a sledgehammer or an iron bar or an axe or a beam or a cattle goad (from the attic, it was hard to imagine how they had even entered there all together, and why they hadn't split up from the beginning into two groups one of which would turn toward a different door, their door). Within a few moments, they tore and ripped everything that was possible to be torn and ripped, and not because they genuinely hoped to find the gold coins the gypsy woman foretold at the fair, but for the sake of destruction alone.

It was all so endlessly delightful; even if the owners hadn't been at home it would have been, but because the tailor and his wife and their daughter were present, it was all the more so. Much better than all the wonders of the fair: than the dancing bear, the drumming monkey, the midget and the bearded lady and the calf with two heads. How pleasant the sound of plates being swept from a shelf by an iron bar must have been, how pleasing to the ears the smashing of bowls being flung, how agreeable the sacks being ripped and spewing their contents, one of potatoes and one of flour that immediately began to rise up into the small space and cramming it even more. It also stuffed the nostrils and caused them to sneeze, one after another, making them all laugh.

"Jump, Vasya, jump," they perhaps shouted to the fool again as they had on the way after smashing their bottles at his feet, hoping his soles would be injured, and this time by fragments of the plates that were covered in flour. All that must have been endlessly funny to them, and since the owners of the house weren't joining in their laughter – not the tailor, not his wife and not the girl – they decided to tickle them with a cattle goad.

It wasn't difficult to assume from the attic what was going on there, and he and his mother could picture it detail by detail without needing words; the voices that came from there were enough: wild, unconstrained and joyous.

Is it their fault that the goad was made for cattle and not for the body of a man? Had the tailor's skin been less delicate, he wouldn't have shrieked that way at all, like a slaughtered animal, shrieking and shrieking until they grabbed him and dragged him by the beard to his sewing machine, a black Singer whose gold lettering was the only gold in the house. In vain, the tailor tried to appeal to them by name – he knew a few of them – in vain, he promised them all new clothes. They found it much more fun to shake his head by the beard up and down to the rhythm of the pedal and to see if the needle could pierce his hand.

The goad was far more effective on the young woman and the child's clothing. It undid an apron from three steps away, tore stitches from two steps away, tore material off from one step away. Afterward, it caused the skin that had been exposed to shudder on the bed when the body was cast onto it, a bed that hadn't managed to block the entrance door when they broke it down. Its punctured quilts didn't spew coins but rather feathers, and the body that had been bared there was lean and bony and shaking, but in their eyes a woman in all senses. The tailor's wife also tried to appeal to them by their names and reminded them of their acquaintance and their common friends and their mothers and sisters, and how much Afansi's daughter loves to play with the doll that the tailor made for her, as he had for his daughter, with this Singer.

When she cried, she resembled her daughter more, but to them she was a women with all her cavities and orifices, and the child was perhaps peeking at her from the corner of the room between her tiny fingers that refused to fasten together over her eyes ("Do they also cut anything of the Zhid women off?" someone asked as they all bent toward the nakedness of the mother; and in the attic, in ear range of them, his mother's face remained sealed).

In the sight of her husband and her daughter and in sight of that fool, Vasya, on whom they had hung the torn attire as if he was a hanger or a scarecrow (even his teddy bear was covered by the corner of a garment, but his only eye stuck out

and watched everything), they forced themselves on her, on her fragile nakedness, one after another after another, and her crying excited them more. Some
took their time and others were quick, some spread her wide and others turned
her over, and the feathers of the unraveled quilts stuck to them all, as if they were
a band of angels.

The first must have been the commander – the one who won the teddy bear at
the fair for his shooting at the marksmanship stall, and years before that, in their
childhood, he had made do with a pocketknife – and then all the others organized themselves. The commander's deputy, the one who on the way had turned
his bottle into a telescope that later was squashed so that Vasya would dance on its
broken fragments, suggested dressing Vasya in the women's clothing they found
there, and in that way replace his tatters – after all, they hadn't been replaced for at
least ten years. And since in the dress torn from the hanger Vasya looked funnier
and also quite maternal ("Have you got milk there, Vasya?"), they suggested he
sit the girl on his knees with her doll, the rag doll she was holding with two slender hands as if should it be taken from her, her last hold on the house would be
severed.

The girl liked to feed the geese and would say to them "*tiu-tiu, tiu-tiu,*" and
reprimand the tall goose if it tried to guzzle the lot, and when the goose would
straighten up its long neck, it was taller than her. She called her rag doll Tita and
was now hugging it with all her might and mumbling: "Tita, Tita, Tita, don't cry,
Tita, everything will be alright Tita."

They suggested that Vasya sit her on his knees and swing her. And maybe
sing her something, some lullaby or the song they sang on the way here – the one
with the innkeeper who invited all her guests to her bed –he could bounce the girl
on his knees up and down, there isn't a child who doesn't like that (so what if the
little one is terrified and clutching her Tita even tighter) and sing to her:

Horsey-horsey
horsey-horsey
galloping-galloping
over fields-over fields

But even before the "fields," a shriek broke out from the small body that wasn't
a child's nor a woman's and not even of a bird's, but that of every living being sensing its life is being taken.

"Don't move," said his mother in the attic, as if he wanted to move from his place
when he heard the voices drawing near and some he even identified despite the
years that had passed since their childhood, and in the darkness he and his mother
were gathered in the corner on a deposit of sacks that he had arranged there in
his childhood and which had also been used by his brother Izu until he left to
study in the yeshiva. All around, from the nearby houses that the rioters had also
broken into with sledgehammers and pitchforks and iron bars and axes and cattle

goads, cheers and cries rose: one of the villagers they came across immediately
had his head sunk in the water trough by them; a woman whose menstruating
disgusted them was dragged by her braids around the yard, and only the quilt
feathers that stuck in her blood took mercy on her; and the baker's head, from
forehead to chin, was thrust into the dough so that his death mask would remain
for his wife; and into the body of the glazier they stuck fragments of glass and cut
off his manhood with a fragment of a mirror and hoisted it onto the cattle goad.
And as for the tailor, after they had finished their deeds with the women (all that
time they made certain that he saw everything, detail by detail), they tried to push
his hand beneath the needle again. Since his flesh was too thick, a boisterous and
eager one of them suggested flattening it with a sledgehammer like a steak, but
another, the inventive deputy, suggested a new amusement: why not replace the
needle with nails?

They dragged him and the uprooted door to the yard (everything could
already be seen from the attic through the slits between the defective roof tiles),
and the tips of the nails were tried first in his nostrils and were stuck there and
burst through the skin close the eyes, and his blood teared. Then a dog that had
fled from one of the nearby yards came into the yard, blinded and crazed from the
prayer shawl trailing behind it and from the small boxes of the phylacteries tied
between its punctured eyes, and they all immediately agreed – even letting go of
the tailor for a moment – one doesn't see a sight like that even at the fair: a dancing
bear, yes, a drumming monkey, yes, but a praying dog? And more so like a Jew?

The dog also wailed and from the attic its wailing sounded completely human.
And from a nearby attic, the Minsk woman who like him had been caught up in
all this by chance hadn't yet been heard. In silence, she huddled up in the attic of
her relatives with her baby until morning and rocked it in her bosom, still believing she had only put it to sleep with the hand that she placed over its mouth. And
where did Poliakov place his hand? He placed it over his heart; and he too didn't
have to make an effort to silence it.

More time passed until the last sounds in the yard died down: some left with
their loot (fabrics, knives and forks, someone's small barrel of something and a
sack of something else; and the sewing machine which the commander and his
deputy had acquired, they dragged it outside to transport it from there), and
others lay the yard drunk from alcohol and from their virility that had been spent
as well as from the blood they had caused to flow. Perhaps they would have continued to doze that way life after a good day's work in the field, had the cart not come
and had the chestnut horse not whinnied, and at the back its master awoke from
his nap and hurried it up in a very familiar voice.

Your father, Levin, is sleeping in the kitchen now – again he spoke silently to the
sleeping man – and do you know where mine is?

"We've got a visitor," one of them called out when the horse reared its legs in front of the tailor's body that had been rolled outside, and with a weary hand he shook his friend lying by his side so that they could begin the party again. The weather was mild: clear and pleasant, and light breezes blew the quilt feathers that hadn't yet sunk in the blood and the mire. But only when he understood a cart had arrived with the visitor, he agreed to arise; and after him another rose and the three of them together, Stas, Petya and Kolya, walked toward the broken-down gate dazed by the alcohol and feeling worn out. They went without their pitchforks and without their iron bars (they were no more armed than the two in the attic), and they certainly wouldn't have got up down had the visitor not suddenly popped up in front of them. But since he had come, they responded to him. The three of them advanced towards the cart and stopped next to it and looked over the man sitting in it.

"He found himself a time to come back," said his mother in the darkness of the attic, "he had to come back just now, the fool." She spoke to his back because his eye was placed close to the slit.

The third one that awoke (Kolya, who in childhood was also plump and whose only virtue had been the pocketknife he received from his uncle the soldier) now struggled to climb onto the spoke of the left wheel of the cart but had difficulty raising his body and it seemed any moment would lose his balance. He grasped the side cumbersomely and barely stabilized himself and looked at the floor of the cart, and right away spat a thick globule and intended to get down from the wheel and go back to lie down – that cart had been disappointing. The other two, Stas, their tall sullen leader, and Petya, who in place of pimples on his cheeks, scars had deepened, urged him not to come down empty handed: if he's already up there, then at least bring the owner of the cart down with him, because who knows what that Zhid kept in his pockets.

That was how his father was caught by the beard and dragged from his seat, and when he tried to hold on to the side, Kolya displaced fingers from there one by one and dragged him down by the beard and dropped him to the ground like a sack of coals. That sound was also heard from the attic, dim and clear at once.

The horse looked back and bared its teeth and sneezed, but they ignored it. And because its owner cried out from pain and lay on the ground, their leader lifted his foot and placed his boot over the protesting mouth. He placed it gently, so that the amusement would not be brief as had unintentionally been the case with the tailor. Years before that, he had placed his foot that way on a barrel in order to roll it down a slope, now he made do with the mouth, and in the continuation of his movement, he wiped his sole on the beard that surrounded the mouth and lowered his boot to the ground and bent down and scrubbed the boot with that rag of hair a head was attached to.

But his deputy – he came out the entrance of the house holding a roll of fabric to bring to his wife – insisted on a real scrubbing. Is that how you scrub? And right away Vasya popped up behind him, still wearing a dress and a coif on his head, the pink teddy bear in his one hand and the tattered rag doll in the other.

He leaned the roll of fabric on the fence and reminded everyone exactly how one should scrub: not with a beard, is that what Zhids grow them for? No, only so they can't be told apart. It must be scrubbed with the tongue. And since the Zhid didn't respond (between the roof tiles he seemed incredibly far and incredibly near and incredibly crushed as well), the deputy placed his sole on the gargling throat. He placed it gently, because he didn't want to kill but rather only to amuse himself for a while longer; and after hinting to the one lying what he'll do to him with that boot if he doesn't obey, he lowered his sole to the ground and let the Zhid weigh his suggestion for a moment or two.

My father, Levin, that was my father.

On the path, the chestnut-yellow-toothed horse looked forward; perhaps its gaze was fixed on the geese cackling in front of the house, and all while it tried to drive away a swarm of annoying flies circling its rear. When the horse's owner recovered slightly, the deputy didn't rush him (that's what he called him to himself in the attic, "the deputy," since he wasn't known to him by name and was probably from one of the neighboring villages), but just asked where he had come from and what he had come for and where exactly was he going: yes, where exactly. And since the man lying on the ground didn't utter a sound, the fool tried to answer in his place. He pointed his pink teddy bear at their house and tried to explain to the deputy that this Zhid is the owner of that house, and before he finished, a few of the rioters who the alcohol hadn't yet completely paralyzed arose and from the tailor's house walked across to the other house, their house, and began to strike the front door, and each strike was more terrible than the one before it.

How do you prefer it, he said silently to the sleeping man, being shot or being strangled?

After all, it was possible to pull the pillow out from under his head and put it over his mouth and press it close, until no further sign of life remained, not a breath, not a twitch, not a jerk. Because even if Levin is really asleep and not just feigning it, he's liable to awaken and struggle like anyone about be killed; why shouldn't he struggle, of course he'll struggle like anyone else. Like anyone else? A voice doubted inside of him. Have you forgotten? Do you forget everything?

Will you struggle? He asked Levin silently.

26

The sounds they made were unmistakable: first, they struck the door with their shoulders, then they kicked it with their boots, and in the end, they hit it with a sledgehammer. They already knew who the owner of the house was. In the darkness of the attic, his mother pressed against him with her whole body, and at the end of the yard, the deputy said again: "Lick," and because he added pressure on the throat with his heel, his father obeyed: he opened his mouth and stuck out his tongue from the filth of the beard and began to lick the tip of the boot that was placed before him.

His mother made him swear not to budge; under no circumstances, she said, should he think of such a thing. "There's nothing you can do," she said to him, "the moment you come out, they'll kill you," and she also held onto his hand, so that he wouldn't go near the entrance to the attic and endanger them both and harm his father more. She might have been right, she might not have been. She clutched his wrist and then his arm, like when he was a boy and wanted to impress her with his muscles. She had expected great things of him: not castles in the air like those of his fathers, but real things, and not in this village or in the town, not even in the provincial city, but in the summer capital and the winter capital and perhaps even in a foreign capital over the ocean.

At the end of the yard, not far from the tailor's body, the rioters drew their boots close to the face of the man who lay there alive, his father. They stood one next to the other and waited for his tongue to lick from each boot splashes of dirt and splashes of blood and here and there a feather that had stuck to all that. And his father – because it was his father who was laid there – was stood on all fours like a dog and licked with his tongue lick after lick, gargling and rasping and coughing and choking. One of them, being merciful, patted his father on the back for him to swallow his phlegm and complete his job, and after he had finished shining their boots, they checked each boot in the sun from tip to heel, and finally when all were satisfied they flattened him to the ground with a kick to his back. For a moment it seemed that they would leave him, but right away it became clear that they didn't intend for him to rest there, but that he continue to lick the ground, their ground, which that insolent man dared to furrow with the wheels of his cart (that is no longer his cart; two of them had already loaded the sewing machine on to the back of it).

"He came from the forest," one of them said, "they even take our trees. And as for his wife, pity anyone who she gossips about."

While they continued to count all the things the Zhids were robbing them of, they let alone the man lying down. He tried to turn on his side like an upside-down beetle and almost succeeded, until they noticed him and flattened him again with a kick in the ribs. He lay there like a squashed beetle, his father.

The memory that arose in the darkness of the attic lingered for a short while, but it was enough to keep him in its place. He saw a muddy carriage way paved by wooden beams and how each time the cart came to the end of one of them, the other end would suddenly rise up; he was still a child at the time. They encircled the small one dessiatin[20] plot of forest and his father counted the trees to estimate the value of the entire forest, and without difficulty calculated the number of railway sleepers that could be made from those trees.

Afterward, they came to small clearing in the forest with a pit in the center and a domed roof over it made of twigs covered with earth. Bluish smoke rose up from it and potatoes were roasting in the small bonfire and his father took two out and gave one to him and one to his brother (the forest ranger had prepared the roast and wasn't there at the time). They were burning hot and looked like coals, but beyond the black of the peel their insides were bright and steamy and soft, and afterward when he and his brother looked at each other they burst out laughing: almost the whole of their faces had been blackened, and their eyes sparkled like those of black men or devils. It was so funny they almost split their stomachs from laughter.

Then his father went to speak to the lumberjacks who he treated with authority, like an owner with his workers, and at the time he felt proud of his father who was obeyed by everyone, and when he went off with them in his cart, he and Izu remained in the clearing. At first, they played catch and ran after each other around the pit whose reel of smoke had already unraveled, and then played hide and seek among the trees and were so engrossed in their game that they didn't notice how the daylight and the trees were darkening and crowding together and from all around they were becoming besieged by the forest. A wind rose from somewhere, and the army of treetops was permeated by a frenzy, and the two of them entered into the pit and waited next to the embers of the fire, huddled like puppies that the forest will come and crush and punish for all the forbidden acts perpetrated on its trees.

After an unlimited period of time and in the boundless dark, their father returned enveloped in the smell of alcohol; he wouldn't let him embrace him as Izu had done. With his small fists he began to strike his chest for having betrayed them by leaving with the lumberjacks to carouse in a tavern, and when his father tried to lift him up and placate him, he kicked his ankles and shins and refused to

---

20 A land measurement used in Tsarist Russia.

be seated like Izu on the cart bench. He climbed up from the spokes of the wheel
and sat at the back and withdrew into himself.

Then the forest ranger arrived, a large wild-bearded man with small sparkling eyes, and when he saw his territory had been invaded, he upbraided him and
poked a pointed finger in his chest as if he intended to puncture it and his father
took a coin out of his pocket and gave it to him.

Night was everywhere and the black of the forest almost couldn't be distinguished from the black of the sky, and the trees marched silently in their wake like a
giant convoy of mourners following them, the dead carried on that cart. They were
surrounded by the forest for a very long time until he and Izu fell asleep, and if later
a dark sky opened wide above the vast field with a multitude of stars twinkling in
its depths, the two of them didn't see them and awoke only when their mother
stood anxiously in the entrance of their house and looked at their faces blackened
and striped with furrows of tears and congealed mucous. Half asleep, they saw her
berating their father and poking her finger into his chest exactly as the ranger had
done before her, but unlike him she couldn't be reconciled and continued to poke
him, because not only has he no sense – she said – he has no heart as well, yes, if
he abandoned his two children in the forest that way; and when he tried to claim
it was for them that he did it (he had paid the lumberjacks to obey him, to demonstrate his authority in the presence of his boys), she separated herself from him
with an expression of revulsion no words can express. Afterward, with unchar-
acteristic patience, she very slowly wiped a moist towel over their faces: once his
face and once Izu's as the soot was faded and was absorbed in the towel, The night
outside also faded, and when they looked into the windowpane their reflections
were clean and beyond them the morning was already rising; he had never seen a
sunrise like that, not before nor after. And where had his father been all that time?
Fast asleep and was snoring.

Through the beams of the attic one of them could be heard saying: "They haven't
got anything; we made all that effort for nothing. They must have escaped through
the window." In their drunkenness perhaps, they had forgotten that it had been
shut and that they had broken it.

In the darkness, his mother pressed up against him more; she was breathing
heavily, and shivers passed through her body. She was no longer his mother but his
daughter or sister that hadn't been born, or just a huddled softness, and he didn't
move. It was unlikely they would forget about the attic; perhaps they were making
their amusement last longer.

"They've got nothing, nothing," someone said beneath them.

And the second one said: "Except for some rotten potatoes and the geese
there."

And the third said: "Maybe the witch makes gold from oil."

And the fourth said: "She's a bigger cheat than the gypsy woman."

And the fifth said: "The gypsy woman's no cheat, everything she said happened in the end."

And the fourth said: "She said we'd find money; did you find any?"

And the fifth said: "She said there'd be women, and there were."

And the first said (hoarser than all of them): "You call a little girl a woman?"

And the fifth replied: "She was good enough for Vasya."

Since they had mentioned the fool, they peered through the broken window and saw him standing at the end of the yard, still in the dress they had put on him and on his head the coif and at his feet the man laid on the earth after he had licked all their boots and the earth they had stepped on.

"Leave here," his mother had said to him a year before that, "and don't come back, there's a whole world out there waiting for you, don't become like him and build castles in the air. Promise me."

He promised.

"Show me your hands," she used to say to him, "these are the hands of someone who gets things done," or: "Show me your forehead," and when she didn't place the palm of her hand on it to check his temperature, she drew her eyes near to it like as if it was window covered with vapor through which his thoughts could be seen.

"I see a journey," she would say with her eyelashes fluttering against his brow, "you can't see what's inside, but I can." She saw railroad tracks in his head, and he believed her, she saw locomotives and thronging stations and trains with dozens of coaches to rescue him from this hole he had been born in. Not only him, but she too. She sent him away from Bykhov like flying a kite on and on to all the far-off places she had been prevented from reaching: he, her first born, was her way of touching the sky.

"They haven't got anything," one of them said.

And another said: "Vasya was the only one who got something, he would never have had the chance to be with a woman!"

They hid from them in the attic, with the barrel of water kept for fires, and the treasure it horded, standing over the door in the floor to stop the rioters should they decide to go up.

But they still hadn't gone up there, not the five who broke into the house nor the others in the yard far down below, which was covered with feathers like thin snow that immediately had become dirty, but then turned red. The blinded dog with the phylacteries tied between his ears stumbled back and forth and howled, and the prayer shawl trailed behind him, making it impossible to gauge what it had once been used for. In front of the ruptured gate the horse stood in exactly the same spot its legs had stopped when it arrived, and in the back of its cart was the sewing machine, and in the sunny afternoon light the gold letters of its make, Singer, sparkled on the black background.

"Do you know him, Vasya?" they asked the fool and pointed to the man laid at their feet, and it wasn't clear whether they thought he might still be afraid to speak against him, or whether they wondered if it was at all possible to identify someone whose face had been so badly damaged. From the attic, the face was recognizable even with all the filth, and even the two hairs of the mole on his cheek could be made out, and one didn't have to see his facial features to know who he was; he was his father.

He was my father, he said silently to Levin, my father!

"Do you know him or don't you?" they asked Vasya again, and the fool consulted one of his nostrils once more and nodded but didn't say anything, not even when he was asked whether it was a worthwhile to search that house. He continued to stand there in his dress and in his coif staring wide-eyed at the man, at his feet and his disfigured facial features, and perhaps he was trying to decipher something evasive that no words he knew defined. He then took his finger out of his nostril, and after pointing to the man laid at his feet he moved his finger towards that house, towards their house, thus hinting to his small audience that if there's some-one who knows whether something is hidden inside, that's the man.

It seemed unbearably clear to his wife and his son – a young man of nine-teen who had already seen something of the world, and a woman whose body had become cumbersome and worn out in the village and only in her gaze some remnant of her beauty remained.

"Have they got something there, Vasya?" asked their leader. "Have they or haven't they?"

"They must have," answered the one next to him. "If not his money, then hers. She charges more than the gypsy woman."

"Have they or haven't they?" their leader said again to the fool and also asked him whether he had swallowed his tongue.

The fool stared at the man at his feet, and then at the man who had given him the pink teddy bear and then at the house at the end of the yard and scratched his neck with a fingernail and scraped something off and inspected it and flicked it into the air with this third finger.

"Have they got something there or not, Vasya?"

"Maybe he's scared of her," one of them raised the assumption (he was called Petya as a boy and was probably still called that), "she might see something bad for him in her bowl".

"She can't see anything," answered their elder, "did she see all this?"

He pointed to the face of the man at his feet with the tip of his boot, and since he had slightly lifted his right boot, he continued the movement and placed it on the man's stomach and pressed so that he'd talk.

In the attic, they had no doubt that he would reveal everything they'd ask him: where their money was, where they themselves were. "He'll sell you and me together," his mother said and her grip on him became tighter.

"Where did you hide it?" asked the leader, but only a vague groan rose from the mouth whose front teeth he had broken with his previous trampling. Perhaps the man wanted to reply to the posed question and satisfy his tormentor and only the state of his mouth made it impossible.

"You've must have hidden it!" said the leader and was answered by a groan.

"How can he talk, Stas, if you're pressing like that on his stomach?" his deputy said cordially. "Let him breathe a little air, have mercy on the man." In his left hand, the deputy held a red apple and peeled it with a pocketknife in a continuous spiral, taking great pains not to break the rind.

"You must have hidden it," their leader said again and lifted his foot slightly away from the stomach, and right away gave another short and painful press with the heel of the boot.

The lying man didn't answer.

"It would be better if you answer us," the deputy said to him like someone giving friendly advice and added another spiral to the apple rind growing beneath the fruit. "Look at your house and tell us where it is so that we won't destroy everything for no reason."

The peeling was completed and he bit into the apple, shaking off the spiral of rind that dropped onto his shoe and saw it sink into the mire.

"If he doesn't want to tell he doesn't have to," one of them said through the smashed window, below the attic and its darkness, and with their heels, his comrades continued to crush the plates they had knocked over with a kind of systematic recklessness

"Why shouldn't he tell?" said their leader. "Of course he'll tell! These people would sell their wives and children for nothing, and here it's his own life." And again, he gave a short press with his heel on the stomach of the lying man, and since only a groan rose from there, he shifted his sole slightly further onto the loins and pressed on them with his heel, and right away the lying man winced, and his hands moved there to try and protect his testicles.

From the window, someone wondered what that Zhid had to hurt there? After all, half of theirs are cut off when they're born.

The commander pressed the sole of his boot into the loins, and with them the tips of the man's fingers, and the groan he uttered was stronger than the previous one; his face was distorted, his eyes teared, but no word came out of his mouth, though two or three would have been enough to stop them; for instance, if he would reveal where the coins – kept for an hour of need – were hidden in the house: in the attic, at the bottom of the barrel of water. The next time the commander pressed the heel of the boot, the groan was so loud that the horse startled and whinnied, and the sewing machine placed at the back of the cart of the cart jolted.

The tip of the boot returned to the stomach and felt around there and was inserted under the edge of the shirt and lifted it and the small prayer shawl slightly above the navel until the ribs were exposed. The man was thin and his skin pallid; his ribs were prominent and rose and fell, rose and fell.

"If that's how the Zhid eats," said someone, "then maybe he really didn't hide anything. The tailor's wife had more flesh on her than him."

"These people don't eat out of stinginess," one of them said, "they'd rather die than spend a kopek." He and his mother peeked through the slits waiting for him to turn them in any moment; it was inevitable and there was they could do.

"They even find coins inside their skeletons," someone said from the window, and there was only one thing they didn't agree on: if the coins were found between the ribs, or in the holes of the eyes or the mouth, that's to say what remained of the mouth. Their leader left his boot on the thin stomach, as if weighing his deeds, and glanced at the cart to make sure the sewing machine was still there.

"If you've had enough, Stas," they called to their leader "let Vasya take over," and someone inside found the fortune telling oil bowl and smashed it with one blow, whether because he knew what it had been used for or whether it was a bowl like any other. None of them had yet lifted their gaze towards the attic; perhaps they feared his mother, and his father was enough for them.

"Dance, Vasya," one of them called from the window, and the fool still hugged the teddy bear he had won and the rag doll he had taken for himself, and its orange woolen threads for the hair quivered in the breeze.

"Dance, Vasya," they called out to him again, "dance on top of him!"

The tip of the commander's boot lingered on his lean stomach a moment longer until he removed it, but the fool wasn't yet sure a space had been made for him there. His wild eyes stared alternately at the ribs rising and falling and at the face of the leader, until Stas indicated he could come and replace him – on that stomach or on those loins or on the ribs or on the neck or on the face or on all of them together.

In his dress and in his coif the fool stood next to the lying man and scratched his neck, deliberating a moment longer, and in the attic his mother said frantically: "Don't move Ilya, they'll kill you the moment you come out," and she reminded him that he still hadn't done anything in his life, he hadn't managed to live at all. "Why in God's name did you come back?" she said to him. "You haven't done anything; you haven't even been with a woman yet!"

I have, he thought, but didn't say anything.

"Dance, Vasya," they called from the window, having given up on finding something inside, "on his stomach and on his ribs," and since he still hesitated, they said the pink teddy bear and his doll want to dance and they can't without Vasya.

"Dance," they called out again, and for a moment his wide-eyed blue eyes gazed at the man lying at his feet. Vasya had never seen such a crazed look in all his days, and nevertheless for some moments it seemed familiar, at first in its stubbornness and then in its plea, the look seemed familiar even though the man was wracked with intense pain.

"Push him, Stas," they called from the window, "maybe Vasya's still scared he'll be angry with him."

"Dance, Vasya," they called to the fool, "let's see how his stomach and ribs take it." They again suggested their commander push Vasya onto the man whose beard was plucked, whose face was completely soiled, whose teeth were shattered, whose ribs were exposed and rose and fell and breathed in all the air of the sky.

In the darkness of the attic, he felt his mother's fingernails and the weight of her body and her breathing: he was her son while at the same time her father and her brother and also her dream of a different life. And before all that, he had been himself, someone who had been overcome by fear, time after time, ever since he had been rolled in the barrel to the river and almost died, because perhaps a person only begins to really fear the moment it becomes clear to him what he's liable to lose.

But the deputy already had a new idea to enhance the amusement: since the Zhid refuses to tell whether there's money in the house or not – the Zhid's suddenly become brave – maybe there really isn't anything in the house. These people aren't big heroes, he would have sold his wife long ago together with the children to stop what they were doing to him.

And if he hasn't got anything, not even one kopeck, then one really has to pity him: imagine that: a Zhid dying here without a thing. A gypsy maybe dies like that but not a Zhid. Let's give him at least a coin so that he can die honorably, a kopek from the ones they found at the tailor's, if he behaves nicely. But just so his friends don't take it afterward – these people are capable of stealing it from him on his way to the grave – they'll put it inside him in a way that no one in the world will find and take. No one.

Two of them were already chuckling from the window as if they had guessed where he intended the fool to insert the coin – in the gentle afternoon light it sparkled between his fingers as he played with it – and the thin body was still recumbent on the ground as before and its exposed ribs rising and falling. His pallid skin was stretched over them like the skin of a drum, and his eyes weren't gaping at anyone one of them, not even at the attic, but at the heavens that were allowing all this.

Only two months later, from the hotel window, he'd also Maximov with the same gaping eyes; and now he's looking at Levin, and what will be done to him, he himself will do.

With a pistol or a pillow? He asked the sleeping man softly.

"Who will find it like that?" said the deputy. "No one." He was shorter than the fool by half a head and his eyes were shrewd and sly, and the coin he was holding he rolled nimbly between his fingers from one to the next until it reached the little finger, causing Vasya's eyes following it to open wider.

"Push it into him," said the deputy and pointed to the ribs, "just push it in between them, in the space, like a money box." He then squatted on his heels and patiently demonstrated to Vasya how to place the edge of the coin in the narrow space between each rib and press on it with the thumb: press it hard, with all his might. No one said it was simple, but Vasya definitely has enough strength for something like that, no?

"Push it into him, Vasya," they now called out from the window, when they understood the prank being played, "push it into him!"

But Vasya remained standing in his spot. He looked at the eyes of the man that sparkled within the grime spread all over his face, and from moment to moment, as the man's powers of comprehension faded, the became more like Vasya's eyes in their bluntness. Only momentarily they cleared and something was being expressed by them, at least the attempt to express something, but it didn't reach his mouth

"Push it into him!" they called from the window again.

They were becoming angry, but Vasya remained standing where he was, hugging the pink teddy bear and the orange haired rag doll to his chest.

Then, with a movement too quick to notice, he was suddenly stood upon the lying man – it was their leader who positioned his foot behind Vasya's ankle and pushed him backward, as they used to do when they were still village boys who played with pocketknives and barrels. In the attic, within the dusty darkness, the lying man's face could be seen twisting from the weight of the body that dropped onto him, and his shoulders could be seen shrinking and how he blocked his groaning.

"Don't you move," said his mother again, "d'you hear?" And since she refused to peek through the roof tiles for even one moment longer, only he remained standing there watching the yard and saw how the deputy handed the coin to Vasya (he was then already on the ground next to the man), how he opened the palm of Vasya's hand by force and placed the thumb and forefinger on the sides of the coin and moved them to the narrow space between two ribs rising and falling.

The man shuddered from the touch of the metal, and the rhythm of this breathing was disrupted.

"Like this," said the deputy and showed Vasya how to press the edge of the coin with his thumb. "Do you see how?" he pressed again, and the man groaned.

"Now you," said the deputy, "let's see you, Vasya."

"Push it in, push it in" they called from the window, one meter below the attic and the barrel placed there on the door with its little hidden treasure.

The coin glinted in the sun – one kopek – until Vasya began to press it, and immediately a groan was heard.

He pressed again, and this time placed the thumb of his left hand and pressed on the right one, the lying man groaned again and seem to shrink: his shins folded into his thighs and his two bony shoulders converged toward each other with his thin arms as if to completely conceal the meager sunken chest, and again he tried to say something very urgent to the fool or to the heavens above, and even before it was expressed, it was swallowed in his bloody saliva.

"Come on, push it in, Vasya, push it into him!" they called from the window. Beneath the windowsill, one of the geese lifted its head from its grain and after it the others followed suite.

"You've got one last chance," the deputy said to the man. "Where did you hide it?"

Next to the wall with the window, the geese began to cackle, first the leader of the flock whose eye might have been spat at, and then the others, until some object was hurled from the window, and they resentfully hopped away from there.

"You've got money, just tell us where," said the deputy, "and we'll let you go. Don't you want to go?" He waited a moment, and the bent to the ground and it seemed he would the pink teddy bear or the orange-haired rag doll, but he just moved them away and picked up a stone, not large, not small: medium-sized.

The geese continued to cackle resentfully, and this time a horse from outside the yard answered them with a neigh, and at the back of the cart the sewing machine moved, and its letters sparkled, as if festive garments had been sewn with it and not clothes for the poor and quilts that will be ripped with knives or the teeth of pitchforks.

"Last chance," said the deputy to the man laid of the ground.

"Push it into him, push it into him," they shouted to Vasya from the window, but for some reason the fool still lingered:, he held the coin in the large palm of his hand above the chest of the lying man, and the coin rose with the ribs beneath it and fell with them, and the man blocked his mouth from the foaming saliva, and his groan was heard only when it infiltrated between his fastened lips.

"Push it with the stone," they shouted at him, and still he lingered in his place. "With the stone!"

"Push it into him or we'll push into you yourself," they shouted from the window. "Do you want us to come and push it into you? Is that what you want?"

The geese continued to cackle, a kind of feverishness had taken hold of them each one of them seemed to be trying to outdo the others, until the pink teddy bear was thrown at them. With one sharp movement, it was thrown by the one who won it at the fair for his marksmanship, and he aimed it at the flock leader, not at its body but at its lean neck, and immediately it and all the rest were dispersed with a vociferous grievance; insulted to the very core of their souls.

"Push it into him with the stone!" they shouted to Vasya from the window.

The stone was neither large nor small, not smooth nor rough; and it was brittle, a stone that if used to hammer a nail into a piece of would be liable to crumble but could be enough for a coin it; provided it's held the way it should be and struck the way it should be: with determination.

"We're coming to push it into you," they called from the window. "Is that what you want?"

The geese cackled again, and from the other end of the yard the orange-haired rag doll was suddenly thrown at them, and Vasya followed its flight wide-eyed until it landed on the back of a tall goose as if wanting to ride it and chuckled for a moment, and then became sad."

"We'll take everything away from you," their leader said to him and hinted with his eyes to the coif that lay on the ground where it had fallen.

"Why take?" said the deputy. "We'll pay him for it, a kopek for the teddy bear and a kopek for the doll."

"Push it into him, Vasya, push it in," they shouted from the window."

The horse shifted in its place opposite the gate, and at the back of the cart the sewing machine shifted as well among the rolls of fabric that had been taken with it.

"With the stone!" they shouted from the window. "With the stone, come on!"

Then the deputy squatted on his heels next to Vasya and grabbed his left hand and opened his fingers and clenched them over the stone one by one, but a moment later changed his mind and switched Vasya's hands – he moved the coin to the left one and the stone to the right, and again directed the coin to the space between the ribs. From his toys thrown next to the wall, Vasya returned his gaze to the head of the man; he looked at his white ribs rising and falling, and for a moment gazed into his eyes: they still sparkled within the grime and the filth, and it seemed he was wanting to tell Vasya something of unrivalled and critical urgency, until a whitish haze passed over them. Perhaps he wanted to remind Vasya how he had sometimes driven him in his cart from village to village, not just letting him hang on at the back like one of the children whose intelligence was on a par to his but seated next to him like his son when they still rode together, but when he opened mouth only a strangled sound accompanied by blood came out of there.

"One small hit is enough, Vasya," they called from the window, "lift the hand and let it drop – one hit and it's in!"

Lying on the ground he had previously licked, perhaps the man was trying to say something concise and simple, something a complete fool would understand, a statement entirely expressing one plea; not to be killed, but again his voice let out a strangled sound from his throat.

"Knock it into him already," they shouted from the window. Once again the geese cackled: first the tall one and then the others; and from the gate, the horse turned its large head and bared its teeth.

"Push it into him already, we're counting up to three Vasya, if you haven't by three -"

Their leader bent down and lifted up the coif from the ground and the fool followed it with his eyes.

"No, don't throw it," said the deputy. "Put it on the Zhid's face so that he won't see his eyes. Maybe that's what's disturbing him, and without the eyes he would have done it long ago."

"We're counting up to three," they said again from the window where a few fragments of glass still remained on the right wing, and when it was slammed against the wall, it shed another fragment to the ground.

"Did you hear them, Vasya?" asked the deputy and waited until the coif was laid over the man's face covering it as much as possible: not only the sparkling eyes but also the gargling mouth within the thinning plucked beard. "If you don't push it in Vasya, in the end they'll come out and do it to you. They mean business."

He explained it to him quietly, mildly, with patience, the way a complicated matter is clarified to a small child, and the fool lifted his head to him, both his hands still placed on the chest of the man: in his right, the stone, and in his left, the coin, and both rising and falling on the man's chest, rising and falling, rising and falling.

"O-ne," they called out from the window.

"Tw-o," they called out.

And in the attic his mother pressed against him more, shrunken and sweaty with fear, and he felt the beating of her heart and the burning smell of her breath when he tried to move the barrel of water above the small door in the floor of the attic and she held on to him with all her might. She was shorter than him and weaker than him, but he stayed in his place.

"Two," they called from the window.

"Th-ree!" They called from the window.

With the large palm of his hand, whose back was covered with golden down and whose fingernails were large and filthy, Vasya began to wipe the mouth of the lying man with a slow movement and lingering as much as he could, round and round his lips, and with the same clumsy and careful slowness, he wiped the forehead with the coif and the two temples and all around his two sparkling eyes, and since the man was still trying to tell Vasya something urgent and critical, something that if not said now would never be said, he lifted his head slightly from the earth and placed his large palm beneath it, but then the others had already come out of the house and grabbed him.

27

Later, after an immeasurable time, the two of them came out of their hiding place, he and his mother – they moved the barrel of water with its small treasure, dropped the ladder and went down it, passed between the pieces of broken furniture and the contents of the sacks that had been ripped open, walked over the flour and buckwheat and sugar – and they couldn't look each other in the eye. Slowly and in silence they went to the end of the yard together, passing the single goose that had survived and the uprooted door, to the place where his father lay: his ribs were exposed, and his mouth and his cheeks and his forehead and the remains of his beard were covered in grime and congealed blood, and his eyes were still fixed on them until his mother shuttered them with her thumbs.

The act was both effective and skillful, as if it hadn't been the first time she had shut eyes that would no longer be opened, and once they were shut the dead man no longer resembled his father. He looked like all the dead, a corpse already hardening and no longer belonging to any family but only to the ants and flies gathering on it; but his closed eyes continued to gaze at him every place he went: in the yard and inside the house and on the bank of the river and on the bridge when he leaned over it, and between the trees of the forest when he went deep inside it, and they gazed at the back of him when he left there and from the mirror in his rented room when he looked into it, and were multiplied in its fragments when he smashed it.

There were days and nights, entire weeks, when he thought he was losing his mind and that his end would be like that of the woman from Minsk who had been caught up there like him and whose baby's mouth had been imprinted in the palm of her right hand, and that small imprint couldn't be wiped away until she cut it out from her palm with a knife.

The pupils have to be cut out, he said to himself: both pupils. And he wondered which pupils he meant, his own or his father's, but he already knew then that even with empty sockets his father would continue to gaze at him.

As they walked on the path between the fields, the treetops on their right and on the their left were pampered by the May sun and light gentle breezes, between them and the chirping of the birds and the buzzing of the flies and the whirring of the gnats, the pitchforks were carried along together with the iron bars and the axes and the sledgehammers and a cattle goad with a male organ hung on it for all to see, for a moment he imagined seeing his own manhood there, from his testicles to the place where in his infancy the covenant of circumcision had been honored though he hadn't been asked if that was his wish. Slowly and silently and without looking at each other, he and his mother moved about the home that had ceased to be a home, and above the yard no feather of the unraveled quilts flew, they had all already sank in the mire.

"I told you not to come back, didn't I tell you?" she said to him and still couldn't look at him. "This isn't a place one comes back to live in, one only dies here." She then looked at his father, after they dragged him towards the house, his body chafing against the earth, and the entire yard was like a sound box that had been created only in order to raise that sound from it: the sound of death. And when they stopped on the threshold and all was silent other than their breaths, they too had become the sound of death.

"Leave, leave and don't ever come back," she said to him, "do you hear? Promise me." And so he left, he and the sights he had seen there and the sounds he had heard there and all the deeds that should have been done and hadn't been done.

She didn't try to read his future in the oil stains; she already saw him moving from Bykhov to Kalitsa, being successful in Minsk as if he had been born there and going on to Petersburg and to Moscow and living there, really living, not the miserable life in the village. She envisioned dozens of stone bridges over the river instead of the small wooden rickety bridge, and streets that were paved from one end to the other in a way that even the houses in the village weren't paved, and avenues better tended than any flowerbed here (they were always put into disarray by the beaks of the chickens and the snouts of the pigs), and churches so high and large and their bells so heavy that ten men were required to swing their clapper – it wasn't his head swinging there, but a copper clapper; his head was still intact and attached to him.

Did you wanted to save your neck, Levin? He softly asked the sleeping man.

Behind his back, through the window from which he had entered, a breeze wafted in from the alley whose lamplight had been smashed (he promised the boy who hits it a kopek; and another kopek to the first one who brings him a live little fish from the river), and he had long completed mapping the room from all the details that had been revealed to him within the darkness: the bed and on it the sleeping man sentenced to die, the small table and chair that had been moved and placed alongside the bed, a glass of water placed there of which half had already been drunk; and a shirt hanging by its epaulet on the armrest of the chair, and Levin's trousers lying on it; and in the next room perhaps his mother had moved on to ironing towels and sheets. All this had gone on for too long.

One day he saw his mother sitting alone at the table after the village girls had departed, and her finger was still wandering around the oil stains in the water of the bowl, and when he asked her what she saw there, she replied: "I see an old woman, a wrinkled bitter old woman. That's what scares me most, the bitterness."

"What does bitter mean?" he asked, because at the time he didn't know what bitterness was, or despair, and she pulled him toward her and said: "Bitter is what I would have been if I didn't have you, come and give me a hug." He hugged her and she laid her chin on his head and pressed a warm soft chest against his face.

"We'll show them," she said to him, "we'll show them, right?"

"What?" he asked.

"What we're worth," she answered and rose from the chair and emptied the bowl from the window and the geese cackled at her.

"I'll make cushions from you if you don't keep quiet," she said to them.

No feather could be made out in the mire when he and his mother dragged his father to the house, and on reaching it they stopped a moment to gather their breaths. The sight of the dead man on the threshold of his house was even more terrible than the sight of him in the yard, and when a white feather swayed somewhere in the air, his mother clutched it in her hand as if it were a bug and squashed it.

"We couldn't do anything," she said to him. "Remember that. They would have killed both of us together with him."

"Why are you silent?" she said. "You don't think they would have killed us? They would have done it in a moment."

"Why are you silent?" she said again.

Afterward, they laid his father on a bed of grains of sugar and buckwheat, and the lone surviving goose hopped after them to the entrance from where it stuck its long neck inside and with its round stupid eyes looked eagerly at the grains strewn on the floor and cackled and hopped inside, while his mother watched. The goose had a long lean neck, and for a moment he thought his mother would reach out her hand and clutch it by its delicate neck and break it, but she let the goose gather grains here and there until it drew near his father's body. "Vulture," she said to it, "have you also turned into a vulture?"

They then raised his father to the bed. His mother held him by the armpits and he the legs, and when they pulled him up and his mother sat for a moment with his dead head in her lap, for a brief instant a painting he had seen in a museum in Petersburg came to mind: Mary bearing her son in her lap, the son of God who had been taken down from the cross and didn't look much younger than her. But his mother hastened to unload her burden and lifted his father's legs onto the bed and straightened them.

"Bring me a bowl of water," she said, "if they left one intact."

From the disorder in the kitchen, he took out a squashed copper pot and filled it with water and brought it to her. She was still sitting on the bed with the dead man, who in life, at least in the latter years, she hadn't permitted to touch her even with his little finger.

His father's forehead was scratched and battered from temple to temple, and above his right eye a large bruised swelled; his gaunt cheeks were soiled and his nose was crushed; his front teeth were broken by the shoe that stamped on his mouth, and the hairs of his beard by which he had been dragged were stuck to each other by the filth and the blood. His mother gazed at all that and began to wipe the dead head with a small towel that she brought.

"We couldn't do anything," she said, "remember that. There was nothing we could do. Why are you silent?"

Slowly she began to wipe the ribs the skin was stretched over, and he looked at the edge of his father's stomach and at the hair ends that were swallowed into his trousers and which began with the organ that had fathered him.

"Nothing," she said again, "nothing in the world. Why are you silent?"

For a moment he wondered where the glazier's wife was – one movement of the hand to his loins had been enough for the rioters and in a second the cattle goad was lifted with its bounty – and where his small son was, because he imagined hearing a fragile crying like the yowling of a kitten. But that voice rose close by, from the quivering body of his mother, until she calmed down.

And where was Vasya? His mind also wandered to him as her crying died down and was replaced by a rhythmic dull metallic sound. He was nowhere to be seen when they left the yard; they both hadn't seen him nor wanted to see him, until they spotted him a few meters from the fence, laid on the ground in an odd position with a tin bucket over his head covering it down to the chin.

It was his voice that was heard now, the metallic dull sound of the bucket as he tried to remove it not with his hand but by knocking his head softly against the fence posts. With what was left of his strength, he rose from where he had collapsed and stumbled to the wall of the house and stood in front of it and hit his head against it over and over, in vain, and battered and stunned and blinded, he began to walk the length of the wall to the entrance of the house.

"You -" said his mother.

He uttered a dull vague sound, the kind made by mutes, but when Ilya drew near to help him, he recoiled and had to be calmed like a child. He stood opposite him and lifted his hands toward the bucket and held the brackets joined to the handle, when there still had been a handle, and slowly tried to move the bucket to the right and to the left, and Vasya groaned.

"Just be careful you don't break his neck," said his mother, "it a delicate thing, a neck."

He then told Vasya to bend down to make it easier for him, and because he didn't understand or couldn't hear, Ilya gently bent his head down, and then his body, so that he'd sit on the ground or kneel and the bucket could be pulled upward.

Vasya responded immediately: he bent beneath his hand like a stalk, whether from weakness or from fear or both.

Legs spread apart, the fool sat on the ground like a marionette whose strings have been severed while Ilya stood above him and held the brackets of the bucket and pulled it upward and this time the it rose and exposed his nose beneath it, all of which had been deformed, and he pulled the bucket further and this time exposed his ears which the edges of the bucket had scratched, and when he pulled it once more to remove it, Vasya lifted his hands and tried to grab the edges of the bucket and stop it. The darkness of the bucket was preferable to him.

28

The old man lifted his finger to his ear and stuck it in deep, and right away heard the scolding voice of his son, a clear and sharp sound even in the newspaper archives of the municipal library, despite his son being in a different country on a different continent. Amnon's comments knew no bounds: they concerned his hygiene habits, the cleanliness of the apartment, the state of the fridge, his clothes, his haircut, the smell of sweat he gave off, as if a smell could distance a son from his father or a father from his son; there are more than enough other reasons for such distancing, and they're capable of creating a distance of thousands of kilometers. His own father had travelled to the end of the trans-Caspian line and continued on from there.

Not that there weren't Russians in those regions during those years – there were more than a few, some were loyal to the Tsar. others his opponents. And naturally there were more than a few Britons who travelled north from India into those regions, even before they tried entering Tibet as individuals or on expeditions as missionaries and merchants and spies; and even some Jews eyed the area, and a few made the journey. Nachman read many books on the subject, almost like the time he had been an academic whose future lay before him. He read how Manya Shohat, in her youth, before emigrating to Palestine and even before she became a Russian terrorist, had actually dreamed of reaching the East; in the jubilee book of one of the Baron's settlements[21] he found mention of a pioneer named Baruch Papirmeister who not only dreamed about those journeys but left his town in Russia and travelled to the East where he lived for years before emigrating to Palestine; but that pioneer certainly hadn't left a pregnant young woman behind as his father had done.

Even if he had been chased by the Tsar's secret police – and about that matter Nachman even in his old age had no doubt – why didn't he make do with destinations closer and easier? His father's journey to the East seemed like a journey of no return, even if his son had been born far away from him and grew up and became an adult and became old. That's how it had been: his father didn't see his first tooth

---

21 Settlements in pre-state Israel that received financial aid from Baron Edmond de Rothschild.

nor the last. Had he also suffered from dental troubles like him? Had some tooth
bothered him during a daring operation? But how could one conceive of an assassin with a cheek swollen from a gum infection or a hole in the tooth.

His false teeth had also been commented on by his son before his journey,
as well as the hair sprouting from his nostrils and the length of his nails and their
cleanliness – he had no doubt his son would be embarrassed to be seen with him
in public, and it had been years since they sat together in a café or a restaurant.
Ever since their tough conversation after the Lebanon War they hadn't done that;
they also didn't go down to the public park next to the house together, the way they
sometimes used to when Sigmund the dog was still alive.

And where was Sigmund now? Under the ground, in the same place the
Pointer and Canaan hound before it had been buried, and where Nachman too
will be buried when his time comes to join his dogs. And the most beloved of
them all – the one that comes to mind now, so good natured and loyal – the black
Pointer that had been with them for thirteen years, from infancy to old age.

In its infirmity it had difficulty getting up from the carpet, the way he and Ada
had difficulty sitting at the same table and watching the same television and sleeping in the same bed (Ada had difficulty!), in vain he tried to strengthen the dog
with words of encouragement. When it could no longer rise, he would support it
from behind to the elevator, and on the ground floor would help it reach the yard
in order to relieve itself, in complete opposition to the regulations of the building he himself helped to compose. Three times a day it was led that way, until the
Saturday when Linda refused to get up. Up till then she would occasionally open
a brown dull eye and make sure all was well with the members of the house, but
on that Saturday, when her momentarily clear eyes turned to them it seemed she
was surveying them for the last time before parting for good. Nachman forgot
about the television newscasts, the prime minister's speech about the future of
the regional conflict was silenced, the regional conflict itself was silenced, and he
asked Amnon if by chance some film remained in the box camera (he sometimes
came out with phrases from the previous generation, as they has been spoken in
his childhood), but when the camera was produced he had misgivings: perhaps
it would be better to wait until morning, until the dog looked better. "Miracles
sometimes happen," he said to his son half-heartedly. "There are people the doctor
who the doctor doesn't give a chance who suddenly get up and start eating." He
inserted his finger beneath the lens of his glasses to the corner of his eye, and when
he took it out it glistened and he wiped it on his trousers.

"I saw you," said Ada, "there's no shame in showing feelings, Nachman."

A few decades would pass until he would repeat that action in front of her
bed in Ichilov hospital, in the special care wing of the internal medicine ward,
and he would be the only one who continued to visit her every morning even on
rainy days and Saturdays, despite her not knowing he was there. Tubes would be
attached to her, and she would be ventilated by a respirator, and the single sign of

life she would show would be a limp handshake ("It's the same with a baby," the doctor would explain, "give them a finger and they press it, it's simply a reflex").

And who will wipe a tear in front of his bed? And who will come to check whether he returns a handshake? Had what happened to Ada not have happened, she probably would have said to her friends without any pangs of conscience: "Lucky I left him in time: that's all I need, to look after him," and if his son continues his journey as planned, he won't have any idea about what's happening in his absence; he'll be flying from country to country and from continent to continent, he'll cross skies and oceans like a young man just out of the army, while he, Nachman, is lowered into the ground. There was a painful symmetry to it: at one far end of his life his father unaware of his birth, and at the near end would be his son unaware of his death.

What has Britain to do with Tibet? That question was posed in faded letters on the yellowing pages of *Hamelitz* in an article whose headline read: The English Expedition in Tibet; and despite that, his father hadn't reached Tibet but a different region, close to it, he read every word and envisaged his father on a backdrop of those landscapes, a tiny figure on is its way up to a snowy summit adorned with clouds. Britain steadfastly seeks to establish its kingdom and to spread its government to the ends of Asia, and Tibet in accordance with its locality is the most supreme fortress in all the world. Around it soar mountain chains, first and foremost the Himalayas, whose heights the clouds fail to scale, and graze on their slopes like weary flocks. The plateau heights of this land reach fourteen and fifteen thousand feet above sea level, and its mountains vary between twenty-four thousand feet to twenty-six thousand feet above sea level, making regular breathing difficult for foreigners. Currently, England is establishing an expedition of military men and with them a regiment of a thousand infantry and two artillery batteries from the mountain force. The leadership of the expedition has been placed in the hands of Commanding Officer Younghusband, to whom the paths of Tibet are as familiar as the palm of his hand, and the English are firmly resolved to have their flag waved in Lhasa, the capital of Tibet, as it is waved throughout their kingdom.

"Look at that old man, Etti -"

"What about him?"

"Wiping his eye like a baby."

"He must have an allergy, everyone's got now."

"Girls," the voice of the librarian could be heard from the lending counter behind a pile of books standing on it, "turn it down or carry on this conversation outside."

"Telling us to 'turn it down!'" said the plump girl crossly. "What does she think we are, a radio?" And nevertheless, for a while they were respectful of Nachman's old age and whispered. He didn't hear them until a muscular young man entered with a ring sparkling in his earlobe and began to look over the spines of the newspaper volumes.

"What a looker," said the plump girl.

Owing to the condition of the old newspaper volumes, it was forbidden to take them to the photocopying machine in the basement of the library, but had it been permitted Nachman wouldn't have made use of it, because he even had difficulty working the electrical appliances in his house after Ada left him. He was regarded the finest of the proofreaders who worked at *Davar* ("Of all time," some joker said, as if of texts had been proofread since prehistoric times), until they tried to teach him to use a computer. Faced with that device, he felt like one of the monks from the Middle Ages who copied entire books with quills, until Guttenberg's invention became widespread and quills became redundant; and with him, in the proofreading room, his pencil became redundant as did the blade of his utility knife with which he scraped off superfluous letters from bromide pages.

Working at the university, he had experienced something similar, and at the newspaper was forced to experience it again, in all its stages; the gaze of his colleagues that evaded his eyes, the hushed chatting behind his back, the broad hints that his place was no longer there and that it would be better he come to his own conclusions. A pretext for his firing had already been sought; over time he had become a nuisance in the eyes of the young reporters and know-all columnists who didn't like their writing style being commented on. "Stick to your job, Nachman," they repeatedly said to him, "Just check if some letter was altered by mistake or some row moved. That's what you're here for, capiche?" At the time everyone on the bureau was saying capiche, because that's what the new editor used to say: capiche.

For more than a few years, they had come to accept his pedantry, whether because they understood its benefit or whether because it was difficult to fire members of the worker's union, but in time, the atmosphere there became more and more reminiscent not only of the university corridors, but also of the rooms in his apartment; there too was someone waiting for him to disappear – Ada – and as for him, he had no intention of doing so. Where would he go? And to whom?

Years before, when they still seemed a small happy family, on one summer day so long gone it seemed from another lifetime, he acceded to his son's pleas and took him to the bureau. His son – what a lovely boy he was then, and so curious – thought that no article is published in the newspaper before it passes under his examining eye because he even corrected the mistakes of the editor-in-chief and his deputy. Outside on the wall of the entrance, giant graffiti appeared in black dripping letters, "Abolish Martial Law!"[22] and under it, some joker had added in

---

22 Martial law was imposed on Arab towns and villages in Israel between 1948-1966.

chalk or a piece of a brick: "Abolish B.G. as well!"[23] and few smears of whitewash concealed previous declarations. In those days the graffiti was tame unlike the slander one sees nowadays on every other wall, because at that time the state was still dear to people's hearts and people had respect for each other, yes, those were different times, times when one could rely on neighbors to inquire about one's wellbeing, to knock on your door in the morning to make sure you had got up, that you hadn't slipped in the bathroom, that you had enough provisions in the refrigerator. There was solidarity among the people then, and there was no time that solidarity was more evident than during times of war.

When he brought his son to the building of the *Davar* bureau, the country was concerned only by the large triangle and the small triangle[24] and the martial law imposed there, and not yet by the Golan Heights and the West Bank and Gaza. A few years would pass until the Six Day War, after which he felt as if all at once the entire nation had become one fearless entity, and his lovely curious son, enthused like him (only Ada expressed doubts and said: "Wait and see the trouble we'll get from those territories"). For all that period, his face glowed, mainly thanks to the bravery many ordinary people like himself suddenly showed; clerks and teachers and gardeners and mechanics who the moment they put their uniforms on were infused with a courage previously unimaginable.

Jokes were made about an Egyptian military policeman issuing speeding tickets to Israeli tanks, or how Lebanon wasn't conquered only because the IDF[25] orchestra was busy with performances at the time. The reporter who was sent to cover the battles on the Golan Heights – a rising star from the news desk who Nachman envied almost as much as he envied the fighters themselves – wrote: "The Golan has never known such revelry and such fury: the flickering of bursting rays, black roses of smoke rising up high in wild celebration, spectacular flights of jets tearing through the skies and showering exploding clusters, and columns of the armored force trampling the ground of the mountain encompassed by smoke from all sides, and all our enemy's outposts succumbing." The words "encompassed" and "succumbing" Nachman had suggested to him in place of "surrounded" and "surrendering" that the reporter had written, and the rising star didn't object.

Eulogies were also printed in the newspaper, and Nachman proofread them with sadness but also with pride, because they were imbued with an uplifting sentiment even when using somber words: "Amiram, we shall not ask why of everyone it had to be you,; we know why: from good seed shall lofty trees flourish, and only if the earth shall be sown by the very best of our young men, like you, Amiram, shall an exemplary country flourish!" The workers of the Mashbir Latzarchan chain store's shoe department – for whom he felt a special closeness since only

---

23 David Ben-Gurion, the first Prime Minister of Israel.

24 Designated geographic areas in central and northern Israel consisting of Arab towns and villages.

25 Israel Defense Forces.

a week before that Ada had taken him there to buy a new pair of shoes at last –
published a notice of condolence to "Dear Mr. Blumenthal and his household," in
which was written: "We are shocked by the tragic death of your son, Shlomo – may
the Lord avenge his blood – on the altar of our homeland, would that you find
consolation in the building and re-establishment of our country. From all your
colleagues at work: Tsilla, Ruti, Fischer, Yehudit P., Yehudit J., and Sarah." Perhaps
it was dear Mr. Blumenthal who had fitted him with his new shoes.

He kept all those old newspapers for years, at first in the living room and
afterward in the balcony cupboard between his son's old toys and all sorts of faulty
electrical appliances, and only after October '73 he decided to get rid of them. As
with the time he got rid of his doctoral thesis, he went down to the empty plot
opposite the building and made a fire, as if only that method was fitting to destroy
all he had believed in and had been let down by (only with Ada he didn't behave
that way), and that evening it wasn't his son who saw him do it, only the dog.
During that war, his son's leg was in plaster, and so he wasn't involved in the fighting, and only a decade later would he experience something in Lebanon of what
Nachman had experienced in the Second World War in Italy. It initially seemed
that once again an entire country was being conquered in a flash, and the joke
from the Six Day War about the IDF orchestra appeared to be right. But a long
time passed before his son was released from special reservist duty and returned
home long-faced and tended not to talk about the war for good or for bad and
answered all the questions he was asked briefly: no, he didn't get the chance to
shoot anyone, not even by mistake, but in contrast he had been shot at – an IDF
airplane had dived towards him and only by chance missed him, he also told him –
in the restaurant where they were sitting, surrounded by the din of families – that
the stench of corpses is something one doesn't forget, and in the end everyone has
the same smell, Arabs and Jews.

A year later, an article was published in which his son raised the question if
Israel hadn't forsaken the life of its ambassador in London in order to find grounds
to invade Lebanon, and in that article and the others that followed also dealing
with shortcomings in the security establishment ("Are we looking after our ambassadors?" "Are we looking after our airplanes?" "Are we looking after our spies?"),
Nachman was so enraged by him, that for many months they hardly exchanged a
word with each other. In fact, only when his son was banished from the national
newspaper to a local newspaper after the final article in the series was published,
the one that angered Nachman more than all the others, did they find a common
language again, a sort of comradeship of dismissed junior employees, from the
university and from journalism. "That's how it is," Nachman said to him at the
time, "the good don't always win," and for the first time in years, he was met with
agreement in his son's eyes.

Out of all the many people who passed by them when they entered the building of the Davar bureau, not even one greeted Nachman; at the most, he received a terse noncommittal nod. The proofreaders' room was at the end of the third floor, close to the toilets whose smell wafted out. The large table comprised of four small tables put together, was generally used by two proofreaders, and on that morning the second proofreader was absent having gone to his nephew's circumcision ceremony. As usual, on the table were cups of coffee with cigarette butts buried in their sediments, half a roll of toilet paper, a glass filled with pencils and pens and felt-tipped markers, and a few empty pages.

He took out two felt-tipped markers from the glass for his son, one blue and one red, and gave him a printed page to draw on its back, and every once in a while, a journalist came in and placed an article on the table. One of them, the crime reporter, said: "Well, Nachman, I see the apple doesn't fall far from the tree," despite that his son was busy drawing a two-winged plane. "Do it quickly," another said, impatiently, "all I need is to get stuck here again because of you, Nachman." It was the political correspondent, a very tall young man with uncombed hair, the editor's latest protégé, and when he went out, the journalist who had come in said it's always like that with rising stars who think a lot of themselves only because of their connections with the editor or someone from the party. "Stars rise and fall," Nachman answered, after all, at university, at least in his first years, he too had been a rising star, and look what came of all that?

His son was trying to make the plane he had drawn grow a third pair of wings, and afterward he also tried to arm it with a frightful machine gun (twenty-five years later he would tell him about the plane that dived towards the small convoy in Lebanon: "Skyhawk or Phantom, what difference does it make, they both kill"), but the cultural reporter who then entered the proofreading room and glanced at the drawing asked if it was a dragonfly. She was not a young woman and with her bleached hair and the deep décolletage of her blouse she bent over the table and said to Nachman: "Is this your son? You look so much alike, it's uncanny! I never imagined you had a son!" After her, the sports reporter entered and asked him what he thought of his headline: "Nett netted again!" (There was a footballer by the name of Nett, a halfback on the Bnei Yehuda or the Shimshon team), and Nachman said: "most admirable," and since the sports reporter waited for another reaction, he said: "really, really admirable," and only then was the reporter satisfied. "I thought over it half of Saturday," he said. "Nett netted again, Nett netted again, it came into my head and wouldn't leave. Believe me, Nachman, you're tops, I don't know what everyone's got against you."

Afterward, his son went to the toilet by himself, and read the writings on the wall, writings that Nachman knew by heart and forgave all the errors. His son sat there until from the other side of the door he heard someone who had come out of the proofreading room, he also heard the tap dripping in the basin. "Did you give it to him?" asked the economics reporter, and his friend probably said, as he usually did: "Now there'll be an hour's delay." "An hour would be good," said the economics reporter, "if only it would be an hour. Believe me, Weiss" (or Katz or Kimchi; Nachman had heard that sentence more than once), "he's so pedantic he would stop to correct 'Abolish the proofreader!' if it was written incorrectly on the outside wall." They must have been surprised by the boy coming out of the inner room; a boy the height of their waists, and under different circumstances he might have lunged at them and butted their stomachs to defend Nachman, if he had had the love for his father in his heart the way his father had for his father, despite the fact that Russian father didn't need his defense at all.

In the afternoon, the second proofreader returned from the circumcision cere-mony, and the economics reporter, who came in to fetch his article, greeted him and asked how it went; God forbid they didn't cut the little one the way they cut articles here. "The whole article was sterilized, almost castrated," he complained about the editor-in-chief, "all the spice was taken out, and why, I'll tell you why, Carmeli, just to suck up to the party members. D'you think it doesn't pay off in the end? Sure, it does."

The second proofreader who had already made himself a cup a coffee (the dirty cups had been returned to the kitchenette after someone complained there were no cups left) said that speaking of castration, did he ever hear the joke about a black man, an Italian, and a Pole sailing in a boat. They sail and sail and sail, and all of a sudden, they see the fin of a shark coming close. What, have they already heard it?

"It's been going around the building for a year," said the economics reporter. But on the other hand, he said, he doesn't mind hearing the joke about the tenor and the whore again. Not long ago he tried to tell it to some colleague from a competing newspaper but messed up the punchline.

"Gentlemen, there's a boy here," they were reminded by Nachman, who up till that moment had remained silent.

"So, he'll learn the facts of life," Katz replied. "D'you know what a tenor is, sonny?"

The boy didn't know and Katz tried to explain to him and demonstrated with a few bits of an Italian aria.

"And d'you know what a whore is?"

"Katz, stop it," Nachman said. "He's isn't even eight years old."

"A whore sonny," the economics reporter continued, "is anyone who's prepared to sell themselves for a bit of money. Take me, for example, what aren't I prepared to do for the ass-licker for him to put my article in. He can chop it up here and chop it up there, the main thing is for him to get it in. Relax, Nachman, I don't intend to corrupt the boy, let time do that and believe me, it will. Wasn't I once a boy? I was a real goody goody and look at me now. A whore."

So passed the day. When they left the building, they were both glad of the dark that fell on the street and hid the graffiti that perhaps had been changed during the last hours according to the suggestion raised in the toilet: abolish the proofreader.

Before that, the page with the drawing of the three-winged plane had been folded diagonally into two and then three and his son made a plane from the page itself and tried to fly it through the window of the proofreading room: the plane first made a dangerous dive across the road; afterward it rose on a stray breeze and took off up to the second floor of the buildings before being swept by the wind above the roofs of the cars towards the slope of the street, on and on to the other side of Allenby Street and perhaps even farther on from there to the sea. It seemed – Nachman was also watching it then – it would stay in the air forever.

That was a long time ago. There was no hint then that his son, after the period of his brief stardom and his articles from various capitals of the world, would be working for a small local newspaper doing a tedious job; there was no hint of the real airplanes he flew in during his stardom, nor of the ones that dived toward his command car in the war on his way to the coast of Sidon; nor was there any hint of the other planes whose tickets he would finance with the payments he would receive from the apartment – Nachman's mother's apartment – and all of them would take him farther away. How would his son know whether he got up in the morning, whether he slipped in the bathroom, whether he had enough provisions in the fridge, whether during the whole long day he found some person to talk to.

29

Suddenly they were three people in the darkness quivering according to the whims of the flame imprisoned in the oil lamp: a mother and her son and him, Poliakov, who had come to kill that son, and God only knows how she had heard something from the kitchen; perhaps it was maternal instinct.

"Who's there? Who's there?"

She stood in the entrance of the room with a sooty oil lamp in her hand, and in its light she saw the one standing opposite her son's bed with a pistol in his hand.

"What are you doing?" she asked, the oil lamp swung in her hand and caused the shadows on the wall to dance. When she lifted it slightly, the shadows were lowered, but still lurched from the right and from the left. "What has he done to you, Mischa, has he done something to you?" She addressed her question from the passage to the bed, and for the time being she hadn't crossed the threshold of the room, a gaunt wrinkled old woman, who from her appearance didn't look like Levin's mother but rather his grandmother. He could have shot Levin and bolted the moment he heard her dragging her feet in the passage, but he didn't do that; there were many things he was supposed to do that he didn't.

"Go away, old lady," he replied to her from his spot not far from the window through which he had entered, and behind him was the street, a small quiet street in a quarter that wasn't one of the worker's quarters of Petersburg; and for that reason as well, suspicion had fallen on Levin.

"Go away, Mother," Levin also said from the bed. He was open-eyed and covered up to his chest, and because of the gun pointed at him he didn't rise even slightly from the bed; the barrel nailed his forehead to the pillow.

"What's he done to you, Mischa?" the old woman asked. "Tell me what he's done!"

Instead of answering her, Levin asked her to go now, yes, to go back to the kitchen now, to Father.

"Did you hear what he said, old lady? Go away from here," Poliakov said to the part of her face the oil lamp lit: a small, wrinkled face whose exact age was unclear.

"You go!" she said to him, and the oil lamp swung in her hand.

Even in the darkness she could see the pistol pointed at her son: the light of the oil lamp caused the barrel of the pistol to gleam and illuminated the right hand holding the butt. "You've got some nerve; this is my house!" she said.

"Do you know what I'm holding in my hand, old lady?" Poliakov asked and lifted the pistol slightly into the air, and the glow of the oil lamp slid down the slope of the barrel to the full cylinder and to the finger bent on the trigger.

"How did you get in here?" she asked as if there was nothing more important that the manner in which he had entered the house.

With a nod he indicated to the window, despite that he was not supposed to answer her at all. He had already heard quite a bit about her and her husband from Duchin; how it was no wonder they had produced a son like that, and it was no wonder that their son had been given the sentence they though fit; the wonder was that it was him, Poliakov, who had been chosen to carry it out, but actually it was no wonder, after all, no one was jumping to undertake that mission.

"Is it money you want?" the old woman asked. He shook his head from side to side.

"We haven't got any money, isn't that right, Borya?" she suddenly shouted back to the kitchen from which she had come; she had left the large table where she was ironing her son's shirt and hurried down the passage with the oil lamp, leaving her husband dozing on a chair with a tranquility he had never seen in his own father.

"Isn't that right, Borya?" she shouted again, and he wasn't sure whether she had heard him and Levin or whether some maternal apprehension suddenly drew her to her son's room. He was the same age as Levin, but his mother was much older that his own mother.

"Your husband's stone deaf," he mentioned to her what Duchin had told him. "How can he hear you?"

"Borya!" the old woman called out again and moved toward him. "Give me that," she said, as if were he not to give her the pistol she would grab it from him with her gaunt shaking hand, standing at the foot of the bed while he stood at its other end. Her movement stopped, and the palm of her wrinkled hand remained hanging in the air a moment longer, and in her left hand she shook the oil lamp and its light flickered.

"Be careful, old lady," he said to her, "you shouldn't play with fire like that." Large shadows danced on the walls.

"Everything will catch on fire here," he said to her, "is that what you want?" And he also asked her whether it wouldn't be a shame for her son; after all, he could get out through the window with his pistol, but her son?

"Don't you talk about my son!" she said. "What do you want from him anyway, what did Mischa do to you?"

What he wants from him, he replied to her, what his friends want, is for her son to pay for what he's done; and not with money, one doesn't pay for everything with money. It would be better if she went back to the kitchen, he said to her, and pointed the pistol at her with a steady hand, not to shoot at her but only to move her away from there.

"I'm not budging from here," she said, and shook the oil lamp again, and with it, the shadows on the walls.

In a chilly voice, he said it would be a pity if something happened to her by accident – she's done nothing, why should she also get hurt?

"But what has Mischa done to you all?" she insisted. "Mischa, have you done something to him?"

"Answer her, Mischa."

"I haven't done anything to him," Levin answered from his bed. "I don't know him at all."

The barrel of the pistol was pressed firmly against his forehead, but his mouth moved ("He's got the tongue of a chameleon," Duchin said), and its smell was heavy, the smell of a person awoken from his sleep; not a night sleep, but Levin was accustomed also to sleeping before he went to speak at meetings ("That way he would arrive fresh," Duchin said, "and could speak for hours").

"Can I give you something?" she suddenly said in a soliciting voice, a tiny old woman who had difficulty holding the oil lamp up in the air for a long time and now had lowered it to the side of her thigh and kept it away from her dress and sweetened her voice like one of the old prostitutes soliciting passersby in the late hours of the night. "I'll give you my necklace," she said, "a gold necklace," and with her free hand tried to remove the chain from her neck, but her trembling fingers had difficulty opening the clasp.

"I don't need your necklace, old lady."

"I'll give you my earrings as well, take the earrings also, take both of them; look what beautiful earrings I've got!"

"I also don't need your earrings."

"I got them from my mother, and she from her mother, they've been in the family for ten generations. They don't make them like that anymore!"

He told her to keep them; that she could take everything with her back to the kitchen. "Isn't your iron waiting for you there?"

While he had watched her through the kitchen window, he saw her moving the coal iron on the table back and forth with a motion that seemingly nothing could stop, not even a shot coming from the next room, but now it was stationary.

"What did you do to them, Mischa?" the old woman said. "What did you do that made them so angry with you? "

"I didn't do anything to them!" he answered in an offended voice, as if he had been falsely accused of something and he was a boy or a youth justifying himself to his parents or teachers. His exposed chest was sweaty though it wasn't at all hot in the room, and the smell of his sweat was heavier even than the smell from his mouth.

From where Poliakov stood, Levin's face was seen upside down, from his high forehead and narrow nose to his mouth. He certainly didn't inherit his lips from his mother: hers were thin while his were fleshy, hers were tightly shut while his tended to open and make speeches; nor was his chin inherited from her, the small double chin must have resulted from her cooking. Yes, the double chin could be seen as well; many things could be distinguished from that angle, and in the past months he had happened to see more than one man from above, in the city or in the village, in Petersburg or in Bykhov, and best not to be reminded of that.

"What did you do to them, Mischa?" the old woman said again. "Answer me!" And since Levin kept silent, he replied in his place and said that her son had spoken too much. Every time Mischa opens his mouth – he said to her – his friends are sent to Petropavlovsk or to Semyonovsky Square: they're taken to prison, or they're hanged.

"They'll take you to prison!" she said to him. "They'll hang you! Entering people's houses with a gun!"

Around the barrel of the pistol, Levin's forehead glistened from sweat, drop by drop it sprouted and grew and slowly spilled towards the bridge of the nose and towards the temples. "Be quiet, Mother," he said, "it really would be better if you leave here." Without moving from the bed, he tried to urge her to leave the room like an invalid urging an insistent visitor not to put himself at risk of contagion for nothing. "Go Mother," he said to her, "go back to the kitchen and stay there with Father."

"Don't you tell me to go!" she said and as if to reinforce her words, she stepped into the room, a little old lady shrunken by all her years who had decided to save her son. From the foot of the bed, she drew near to its side and stopped next to the chair placed there.

"Don't come any closer, old lady," he said to her.

"It's my house! What will you do to me?" and didn't stop.

He moved the pistol to point at her, and in the light of the oil lamp the barrel shone for a moment until only one step remained between them, and the old woman, with the strength she had suddenly found, tried to grab his hand.

Afterward came the fall: that's to say first there was the momentum of his recoiling hand, and there was the moment when the old woman lost her balance, and there was her collapsing to the floor, and there was the chair that overturned when she tried to hold onto it and the glass of water that fell and broke. The oil lamp fell as well, and for one moment the flame increased and in the next was extinguished, and the smell of oil rose from the place of its fall. Another moment passed. He heard her utter a weak groan, and Levin heard as well and tried to turn his head toward her from the bed, until he signaled to him with the barrel of the pistol not to move.

"Mother" said Levin, "did something happen to you, Mother?"

Again, he tried to turn toward her, and again the barrel of the pistol stopped him.

The old woman moaned. Had she broken a bone she surely would have shouted, and she didn't; she just uttered a soft groan which one had to make an effort to hear, but heavy hesitant steps could already clearly be heard drawing near from the passage.

It was the old man, the sounds had apparently penetrated his deafness and his sleep, and he rose from his chair in the kitchen and felt his way down the dark passage toward his son's room. "Mischa, what happened?" he asked and didn't hear the old woman and hadn't yet seen her lying on the floor with the extinguished oil lamp by her side. For some reason, the oil hadn't spilled and caught alight – by a miracle, Poliakov thought: it seems that miracles nevertheless do happen; perhaps the son of God had in fact walked on water, and the sea had parted for us.

"Go away from here, Father," Levin said from his bed and didn't lift his head; the pistol still pressing his head to the pillow.

The old man took another step and struggled to see in the dark. "What happened, Mischa?" he asked again in a voice blurry from sleep. "Where's Mother?" In the darkness, his tall shadow which the years hadn't bent became black, and a moment passed before he distinguished him at the head of his son's bed, and even then didn't address him.

"Who's that man?" he asked Levin.

"Go away, Father, go back to the kitchen."

He was older than her, and obstinacy and determination were apparent in him as well.

"Listen to what your son is saying to you," he advised the old man, and the barrel of the pistol was further fastened to his son's forehead, about two centimeters above the bridge of his nose. Levin had a long narrow nose, the kind that would break easily with the blow of a pistol had he struck him, but he hadn't come for that.

The old woman moaned on the floor. "He wants to kill him, Borya!" she said in a trembling voice. "Don't let him kill him, Borya!" and moaned again; perhaps she had cracked a rib, or perhaps only slightly injured by fragments of glass; it was impossible to know.

"Just don't get any ideas in your head, look what happened to your wife."

They were not things he intended to say, but nevertheless came out of his mouth; and what are words as opposed to his deeds.

"Go away, Father, I'm asking you," Levin said to him again from the bed. "Help Mother up and go back to the kitchen, the two of you."

The old woman tried to lift herself up slightly, perhaps on her knees, perhaps on her belly with the help of her elbows; the sound of the extinguished oil lamp moving on the floor was witness to that, as was some fragment of glass crackling under her, and then she groaned again.

"Don't do yourself any more harm," he said to her from his place at the head of the bed.

"What have you done to her, you hoodlum?" the old man said.

His voice was heard from the spot where the chair previously stood and Poliakov turned the pistol there, and though his movement was made in the dark it stopped the old man in his tracks.

She fell by herself," he said to the old man. "It's your son that does not very nice things, sending his comrades to prison."

"Someone who's bad deserves to go to prison!" the old woman said, and from the height of the legs of the overturned chair, her voice sounded louder that it had sounded when she groaned.

"Look me in the eye, Mischa," the old man said as if their eyes could be seen in the dark, "is it true what he's saying?"

Before Levin could give some false answer, Poliakov reminded the old man that he too was no saint, far from it; he'd already heard more than a few stories about him. "With you," he indicated to him with the pistol, "it seems it runs in the family, from father to son." And right away he pressed the pistol to Levin's forehead again, two to three centimeters above the line of the eyebrows. "Just as well you don't have another child."

"We have got another child!"

Nothing had been mentioned about this in the briefing.

"Mischa's brother, his younger brother... his name's Yevgeny, he'll be coming soon. Any moment."

A lie requires many words, the truth only a few. "Who are you telling stories to?" he said to the old man. "Now he's coming? Right now?"

"He always comes late, always! Isn't it true Yevgeny always comes late?" The old man turned to the old woman who perhaps was nodding her head in the darkness as she tried to lift herself up off the floor again. Perhaps she stood the oil lamp on its base not to spill oil, for its smell to fade into the air.

"Why don't I believe you, old man?" he said to him and ignored the smell of the oil. "Have you got a brother, Mischa? Have you got a younger brother called Yevgeny? You see, old man, Mischa doesn't even know he's got a brother. So now the both of you get out and close the door behind you."

The old man looked at him for a moment longer and bent towards the old woman and tried to hold her by her armpits and lift her. After making much effort to raise her up he succeeded in moving her just slightly and collapsed by her side where he took wheezing breaths from the depths of his lungs, a clump of darkness lying at the foot of his son's bed, and when Levin tried to turn toward him, Poliakov again fastened the barrel of the pistol to his forehead.

"Stay as you are," he said to Levin.

Levin's head returned to its place, but his mouth opened. "Father," he said, "what's he done to you, Father?"

Then, in the darkness that hadn't been disturbed by the light of the streetlamp, the old man tried to bring him down with the pistol: from the floor he pushed him sideways with both hands, and had its force been slightly stronger, Poliakov might have lost his balance and unintentionally pulled the trigger, but he managed to stabilize himself and the pistol in his hand.

"That was unnecessary," he said to the old man when his breath had stabilized as well. He was not only angry with the old man then, but also with himself for being in position he was, just because he hadn't done everything from outside as instructed. "Now take your wife and get out of here," he said and pointed the pistol at them: an old man and an old woman whose son the pistol had been pointed at. At their side, the oil lamp still emitted smells of smoke and oil, but the two showed no sign they intended leaving the room, despite the apparent discomfort of being seated on the floor.

"Why don't you shoot us?" the old woman said. "Come on, shoot! You're a big hero against someone sleeping in his bed and against old people. Why don't you shoot us?" Her weak voice didn't tremble; the old man perhaps held her hand in the dark; even there the closeness between them could be perceived, a closeness he had never been seen between his parents.

"I came for him and not for you."

"Shoot us and leave him alone, shoot us! Mischa's still young, his life has just begun, he only knows how to make speeches; he's never even been with a woman yet! Shoot us, you hoodlum, we're old anyway."

Her voice had become stronger; perhaps she had revived somewhat, perhaps the concern for her son strengthened her.

"I came for your son."

"So shoot then," Levin suddenly said from the bed, "shoot and get it over with, pull the fucking trigger."

"Be quiet Mischa," the old woman said, "that's no way to talk! Don't listen to Mischa, even as a little boy he always talked too much, he was always making speeches."

"Listen to your parents, Mischa," he said to Levin and tightened the barrel of the pistol to his forehead, almost digging into it. For a moment it seemed the sweat of his forehead was rising up the barrel toward his hand but it was his own sweat that dampened the butt and made it so slippery.

"And you, haven't you got parents to listen to?" The old woman asked from the floor. "What would your parents have done if someone came into their house like that?"

"Leave my parents out of it, old lady," he replied to her.

"I'm sure they don't know what you get up to, poor things, I pity them if they should hear how you go into people's houses like that with a gun in your hand."

"They don't need your pity, old lady."

"Your mother should only know," she said from the floor, "going into people's houses like that."

He didn't answer.

"I'm sure she has a kind heart and loved you from the time you were born and took care of you from morning to night, she would have given you the food out of her mouth. And your father too, working all day long so that you'll have something to eat. They certainly wouldn't want to know they produced a son who comes into people's houses to kill them."

"I haven't killed anyone yet," he replied to her.

"How will you go home to them after this and say, 'how are you, Mother, how are you, Father?' and in your heart know that what you've done?"

He didn't answer.

"Just think about them for a while, what would they do if someone suddenly came into their home in the dark with a gun?"

He didn't have to think at all; it had been present in his mind anyway, concrete and burdensome and oppressive, no less than the pain from the tooth drilling a hole into his lower jaw; there was a large hole in the center of the third molar from the left that began at the top of the tooth and ended deed inside the skull.

"If your parents only knew what came out of all their love!"

"Don't talk about them anymore," he shouted, not to defend them but rather himself; after all, there had been no love between them to defend.

"You're a good son," the old woman again tried to appeal to his heart "I knew it right away, defending your father and mother that way. Mischa's also like that, the way he brought us to live with him here in the apartment; many children don't care about their old mothers and fathers at all. But you're not like that, you're a good person, I saw it right away."

"How can you see things like that in the dark, old lady."

"There are things one can also be seen in the dark. You don't need eyes for that, it's enough to feel it in your heart."

"You've got no idea how wrong you are," he replied to her.

"Isn't it true he's a good person, Mischa? Tell him as well, Mischa, come on, tell him."

Her son was silent in the bed. "He's not a good person, Mother," he said in a soft voice a moment later. "He's come here to kill me."

Just as finished talking in that sober reconciled voice, the old man made another attempt: he lifted himself off the floor again, not getting up completely but standing on his knees, putting all his last strength into that movement, and this time the push was vigorous enough to destabilize Poliakov, and when the shot was fired there was no knowing where the barrel was pointing and who the bullet hit. Only after a long moment, an interminably quiet moment, a large piece of plaster dropped from the wall and couldn't be heard hitting the floor, perhaps it fell at the foot of Levin's bed or on the bedsheets.

"Mischa!" the old woman shouted.

A great silence filled the room, and only the old man's breaths could be heard, wheezing one after the other as the darkness thickened swallowing the entire bed from its head to its foot.

"Mischa," the old woman said, "Mischa."

No answer was heard in the dark.

"Are you hurt, Mischa?" the old man asked.

A vague rustling could be heard and after it another, and then hard solid silence.

"I'm okay," the reply came after a long moment, "now both of you really should leave."

Levin's voice was faint. There was no anger in it, and not even fear; only calm reconciliation about the deed that was about to be done.

"Here, take this, you hoodlum," the old woman said from the floor "take everything, just leave Mischa alone!"

Again, she tried to undo the clasp of the chain around her neck, and again had difficulty doing it with her trembling fingers. A wail came from her mouth as she tried to remove the chain that was caught in her hair. "Take it, take it," and she pulled the chain forcefully, "and this as well, take it all." With trembling hands, she removed one earing from the lobe of her left ear, and after it the other, and with a trembling hand inserted them and the chain into his trouser pocket. It's not clear how she reached there: perhaps she drew near on her knees or crawled on her belly with her elbows while he aimed the pistol at her son again. Either way, he found them there the next day, the necklace and the earrings.

"And take this too, you hoodlum!" she said trying remove her wedding ring from her finger, but it stopped at the wrinkles around the knuckles. She tried to maneuver it over them but was defeated by the ring, and once more that thin wail was emitted from her mouth.

"Give him your ring, Borya," she said, "we don't need it anymore, take it off and give it to him."

But the old man also had difficulty removing the ring. On the dark floor of the room, next to the bed of their son whose head was pressed to the pillow by the pistol, the old man tried to turn the ring but it wouldn't budge.

"Try mine, Borya," the old woman said and reached out her hand to him in the dark. He gently turned it a little, pulled at it, tried to stick the edge of his nail beneath the metal and again failed.

"Do you remember how you put it on me, Borya?"

In the dark of the room, from the floor, beside the bed of their son against whose forehead a pistol was being pressed, the old woman began to reminisce as if they had time on their hands: what day it was, what the weather was. "Do you remember Borya? We walked straight out into the rain in our best clothes -" another sob erupted from her throat, and a short while later she fell silent. There was no knowing what had silenced her: perhaps the old man caressed her in the dark, perhaps he hushed her with the clasp of a hand; and perhaps her words weren't meant for her husband but rather to the one pointing the pistol at her son in order to gain more time.

From the bed, out of the corner of his eye, Levin tried to glance at his parents, and had to be reminded of his proper place with the barrel of the pistol; had the barrel been removed from his forehead and had the oil lamp still been alight, the concave imprinted by the pistol in the skin of the forehead would have been visible, but the oil lamp wasn't lit and the barrel wasn't removed from his forehead and would only be removed after being fired.

"We," the old lady continued, "got completely wet in the rain and just then that cart passed by straight through a puddle and dirtied my white dress with mud, and everyone started to shout at the driver, do you remember that, Borya? God, we were so wet, a bucket could have been filled just from wringing out the rain from the edge of my dress!"

"To hell with the rain," the old man said.

He didn't try to get up again, but a movement could be heard from his direction; it could be that he was only moving objects were strewn around him: fragments of glass, the shirt that fell from the back of the chair, the chair itself that had been overturned. The remains of the water from the glass could have been there if they hadn't yet been absorbed by his clothing.

"When Mischa was born," the old woman said, "he had huge blue eyes, and the moment we saw them, we said it must have been from the rain. Do you remember us saying that? Afterward their color changed, they turned brown. And you said it must have been from the mud of that cart. It made me so angry."

A rustling could be heard from where she was; perhaps she shifted herself a little, a woman older than his mother by more than a few years but as lively and as obstinate as her. One couldn't picture her in a white wedding dress or one stained with mud, nor was there time for that: that's not what he had come to the apartment for.

"What cart are you talking about?" the old man said. "Ours was the only cart there!"

From the floor, he mentioned that it had been just the two of them, because all the guests had already left; and that the puddle from the rain had been inside the cart – what a puddle, almost up to the knees, and that's how her dress –

He fell silent, it wasn't clear whether he addressed old anger or that the old woman had made it all up in order to buy time for her son; perhaps Levin had inherited his gift of the gab from her.

Her words had been effective, the fact was: the finger had not yet pulled the trigger, and the cylinder had not revolved more than once. It was a Browning 7.62 millimeter, and five more bullets remained, one of which would be enough for Levin.

"What eyes you had in the beginning, Mischa," the old woman said to the bed, "you can't imagine how blue they were! And someone once said to Father in a joke, Are you sure it's yours?"

"He got his punch," the old man said. "No one makes wisecracks about me."

And again there was rustling, this time coming from the two of them, and the suspicion arose in him that they might be trying to light the oil lamp, not for illumination, but to be thrown at him; they wouldn't even have to hit his hand holding the pistol, it would be enough for his clothing to catch alight to scorch him from head to toe.

Like a memorial candle, the thought passed through his head; and it was clear to him in memory of whom it would burn – certainly not that of Levin.

"Look him in the eyes, Mischa," the old woman said in the dark, "let him see what a pure heart you've got and he'll know you're telling the truth!"

"But he's not telling the truth," he said to the old woman. "He lied to all his comrades. He only told the truth to the police, everything they wanted to know."

"Maybe they hit him," the old woman said from the floor, "those hooligans must have hit him! Mischa never liked being hit. Did they hit you, Mischa?"

"Did they hit you?" he also asked him. "Did they kick you around a bit and slap you and you cracked?"

"I didn't crack!"

"So you told them straight out and they didn't even need to do any slapping."

"I didn't tell anything!" Levin answered.

"Who were you with, Perdischenko on the second floor? Did they send in the tough policeman from the corridor to scare you?"

It seemed that the barrel of the pistol was drenched in the sweat flowing from the forehead, and he placed it firmly in its center again.

"Some hero," the old woman said to him from the floor, "a real big hero!" Coming into the home of old people and thinking that everyone's scared except you."

"Your son," he said to her, "was definitely no big hero."

"Just think if someone had come into your home like that at night! And had made your father and mother take off their wedding rings and beg, think about that! And think how happy they must have been when they got married, and in the end, what came of it?"

"My parents," he replied to her from above her son's bed, "have nothing to do with this."

"And don't you want to start a family?" she said, and her voice strengthened slightly. "To stand next to a woman and put a ring on her finger and kiss her? How can you do a thing like that after this, you won't even be able to hold the ring!"

He didn't answer: not to the first part of what she said nor to the second.

"Every time you look at your hands, you'll be reminded what they did to my boy here, look how Borya's crying in the dark like a child now. Have you no heart at all?"

He couldn't see the old man; perhaps he really was crying softly in the dark, or perhaps it was also part of the old woman's attempt to buy time.

"Think of someone coming through the window into your wife's house holding a gun and saying, 'Your son did something to someone and I have to kill him.' Would you let him do that?"

"I haven't got a son," he said to her, "or a wife."

"A handsome boy like you," the old woman said, "must have some pretty fiancée waiting for him at home! Someone nice and cheerful, and what will she say when she hears what you did to Mischa?" She shifted slightly from her spot and a movement was also heard from the direction of the old man.

He answered the old woman curtly that he had no fiancée, and certainly no son; but for a moment in the darkness, the skin of Levin's forehead changed into skin stretched over a belly, and the pistol was aimed at it and at what was inside it, at the tiny forehead hidden there, the forehead of little Poliakov.

"But you will have!" the old woman said. "Mischa also doesn't have a fiancée yet, but he will have! You're both such young handsome boys, how could you not have. And you'll both also have children, and give your mother and father grandchildren, and one day you'll remember all this, and you won't understand what you were doing here at all!"

"That won't happen," he said to the old lady.

"His brother was also like that, he searched and searched and almost became despondent, but in the end, Yevgeny found someone nice and cheerful -"

"Isn't Yevgeny the younger brother? Aren't you getting confused with your lies?"

"Marriage was an urgent matter to him, and for Mischa it wasn't urgent at all, do you remember, Borya, how urgent it was for Yevgeny?"

The old man didn't say anything; only a rustling could be heard from the direction of the floor and some metallic sound.

"What's your brother's wife's name?" he turned to Levin again from above the bed.

Levin was silent. His mouth could have opened at will, the barrel wasn't pressed to it, but his mouth didn't open; opened at the secret police and now it was sealed.

"Your son doesn't know her," he said to the old woman, "because there is no wife and no brother." And in the dark, where only the silhouettes of the two old people could be made out, the smell of the oil dripping from the base of the oil lamp could be smelled again.

"You're a wise guy," Levin suddenly said to him. "Where did you learn to interrogate people like that, from Perdischenko on the second floor?"

"Shut up," he said to him and deepened the barrel of the pistol into his forehead.

"Who's this Perdischenko?" said the old man. "I never heard you talk about some Perdischenko, Mischa."

"He spoke a lot to him," he replied in place of Levin. "Maybe he didn't tell you about him, but he told him a lot. Tell him how much you told Perdischenko, Mischa."

"If those hooligans hit him," said the old woman, "what could he have done? If they kicked and slapped him like you said, he would have cracked like anyone they did that to. Wouldn't you have?"

"I didn't crack," he replied to her and wasn't supposed to reply at all; he also wasn't supposed to have entered this room, but to do everything from outside, through the window.

"But you were there," Levin suddenly said, "with Perdischenko from the second floor."

Had the forehead been soft, the barrel would have bored into it and reached the middle of the skull, but it was hard, and sweaty.

"You were there," Levin said again, "and they released you even though you didn't talk, so that you'd be suspected by everyone. They did the exact same thing to me."

When he fell silent, the movements of the old people could be heard, together with a fragment of glass that crackled beneath the body of one of them. A faint cursing could also be heard; it was the old man.

"We could easily have swapped roles," Levin said, "and then I would have come to you with this pistol."

The pistol then slid from his forehead to the bridge of his nose and from there was diverted toward his left eyebrow, and right away the eye below it shut. He felt the softness of the eyelid with the tip of the barrel and studied it for a moment.

"Where are you from?" the old man suddenly asked. "You sound like someone from Minsk."

He didn't reply.

"I once knew someone from Minsk," the old man said, "a travelling salesman, do you remember him, Luba? He had good cigarettes and they also didn't cost a lot."

"Maybe he's also coming here," he asked mockingly, "with Yevgeny?"

He didn't fear that but was worried about the children who'll soon be returning from the tasks he assigned them.

"Have you got any brothers and sisters?" the old woman asked. "What will they say when they hear what you've done. Just think of that!"

"I haven't got any," he replied. It wasn't a total lie. After how his brother had shouted at him the way he had – he was in the yeshiva at the time of the pogrom – they no longer spoke.

"Haven't you got anyone in the world?" Compassion could almost be heard in the old woman's voice, as if any moment she would suggest adopting him, she and the old man, and that way Mischa would have a brother instead of that Yevgeny.

"In that case it would've better had they sent me to kill you," Levin said from his bed. "Who would be sorry over you."

It was an unnecessary comment and the barrel of the pistol dug further into his forehead, as if shortening the path of the bullet to the brain, and his finger fastened on the trigger, and he began to pull it backward.

Then children could be heard outside: first the one who had smashed the streetlamp with one accurate stone, and then the others, all of them full of merriment and proud of their accomplishments. They had managed to pull some miserable little fish out of the Neva and brought it to receive the prize they had been promised, two kopeks; perhaps they put the little fish into a hat filled with water and dripping all the way and was now the fish was twitching at the bottom of it; there was no Izu to protect it as he had tried to protect that goat.

"People are coming," the old man said from the floor. "People are coming!"

"Children," he corrected him, but he was worried.

One of the children's voices overpowered the others; they were arguing what they would do with the money: buy a small cake, or perhaps a packet of candy?

"Two kopeks and they're gone," he said to the old man, "one moment and they won't be here; they're just children."

Then, the exact moment they agreed upon a packet of candy, the oil lamp was thrown at him; it was extinguished, and no light penetrated from outside, and in spite of the darkness it didn't miss its target and hit his hand and a shot was fired. That bullet had waited a very long time before leaving on its way – minutes or hours or days – and passed through it in the blink of an eye, and another was fired after it, as if one death wasn't enough.

30

He fled from there at great speed. It was contrary to all the instructions he had received, but that's what he did at the time, run; he didn't know he could run so fast. And when he reached the Neva, he almost threw the pistol into the river, but at the last moment changed his mind, and what luck that he did so.

He sat under the bridge until his breathing calmed and looked at the water and wondered if the children had brought the little fish from there; when he sent them off he didn't know whether there were fish in that area. After a while he got up and began to run along the dock, running its length until the air in his lungs was exhausted and only then did he stop and let his feet lead him at their own pace. It was a long way, and at the entrance to his street he stood on the corner for a moment to make sure that there was no one around that he knew, and then stood in the entrance of his building to make sure the gatekeeper was asleep, and went up the stairs two at a time to the third floor, and before he opened the it he listened for a moment in case someone was lurking inside, but he only saw his bed when he entered and beneath it the travelling trunk, and didn't yet know where to travel to.

When he dragged it outside and opened it, a foul smell arose from within and for a short while obscured the smell of gun powder that had clung to his nostrils ever since the shooting, the way the smell of sulfur had clung to them after the assassination of the minister. He imagined smelling the scent of the Levin's parents as well, at least one of whom had been injured during the struggle with their son before he managed to shoot him – was it his mother? His father? He tried to recall who had groaned and fallen silent and who had uttered the broken cry of old people.

This time, unlike after the assassination of the minister, he decided he would not be delayed for any unnecessary amount of time, and early in the morning would board the first train and not wait for the detectives, or the police, or the soldiers; he had made that mistake once and would not repeat it. Afterward, he lay on the narrow bed and f imagined seeing the children from the alley, pressing their curious faces against the window pane and squashing their noses on it ("Look, look!" one of them said and pointed to what he himself had avoided looking straight at); but unlike Levin's window, his was on the third floor, as far from the street as the distance of the hotel window through which a month ago he had seen the carriage of the minister explode. Mildew stains dotted the ceiling of his room, and when he lay there on his back on the mattress through which tufts of straw sprouted, they resembled continents on a map of the world from which he had been banished, and every morning he had strengthened his body there with push-ups and sit-ups, and not only to overcome the paralyzing cold but also to shake off the remnants of his nightmares.

"Get out of here!" he shouted at the children until their faces faded into the air – one of them suddenly resembled Izu, his brother – and he was still hoping the gatekeeper of the building hadn't see him when he returned, despite that in the dark it would have been impossible to discern the bulge of the pistol in his pocket.

Perhaps under the pillow, the warmth of the metal was still preserved, and the smell of gunpowder still wafted in the air, or he was just imagining it; the smell of cooking drifted toward him, rising from one of the nearby apartments despite the late hour – it was beetroot. With the sensation of hunger, he felt how the hole in his tooth was bothering him again and how the pain seeped into the jaw and from there to the entire skull.

He then pressed the pillow to his cheek the way he had thought he would press the pillow to Levin's face in order to dull the shot or to spare it, and the pain was slightly relieved, as in winter when he pressed the floor with the palm of his hands going up and down doing push-ups to warm himself, thirty, forty, and fifty, and after a short while the chill would attack again. The window of Levin's room had a single pane and didn't block out the cold, nor did it block out the children: again he saw their little faces, squashed and watching him, forfeiting the prize he had promised them with their curiosity, solely to see what was happening inside the room ("Did you kill Father again?" Izu had asked).

How that son a bitch, Levin, had struggled against him. How he grabbed his wrist that held the pistol and both their hands began to move up and down with the movement of a violent dance, how the second shot had accidentally been fired, how in the dark a groan had been heard; from whose throat it had come and what had caused it was impossible to know, the shot itself or just the panic from it, and how dry weeping had been heard afterward, and he was already on his way out, he jumped from the window and pushed the children away and hurtled down the alley.

In the morning, he sat on the edge of his sunken bed and planned his actions: which clothes he would wear to the train station, which route he would take, where he would pawn his pistol in exchange for money (there were two pawn-shops along the route, but only in the second one unnecessary questions wouldn't be asked), what ticket he would request at the booking office, and how when the train arrived he'd go to the last carriage and lie down there and sleep for hours, perhaps days, until the train reached its destination, a destination as far away as possible; the Trans-Siberian line would serve well from that point of view, but he preferred the Trans-Caspian.

But it all went wrong at the pawnshop, and not because of any question he had been asked but because of the paltry amount offered to him for the pistol (his eagerness to get rid of it was too obvious); for a while he stood there perplexed and didn't know what to do – the other pawnshop was more dangerous – but then he felt what had been buried in his pocket when he was still in Levin's room , and without any hesitation, placed it onto the counter: the necklace the old lady had removed from her neck and the earrings she had unfastened from her ears. If she hadn't died, she wouldn't live long without her husband and her son anyway. She had given him jewelry in exchange for bullets, but the bullets had waited too long to be fired.

They had waited for months, years, decades, so he thought afterward when sitting on the train (a night-train of many carriages with dozens or hundreds of windows and through one of them he looked into the dark and at his reflection travelling upon it), perhaps they had waited from the day of his birth – and even before that, long before that, they had waited from the beginning, when he, Ilya Poliakov, had been just a putrid drop like his son – as if everything from the outset had led to it, from the moment his parents had been wedded to each other in Bykhov: that three shots would be fired in Petersburg, that he would abandon his baby in Minsk, that he would desert one of his comrades in the street. As if his whole childhood in the village, his whole youth, his whole adolescence had led to people dying around him, and when finally he would somewhat overcome his fear and shoot a man accused of treachery, he wouldn't even be sure if he man had really been a traitor or not, and he hadn't only shot him.

The locomotive blew a long toot, and no sound was more pleasing than that; the landscapes changed in the carriage window, cedars and firs and oak trees and fields of rye and wheat, and there was no sight more beautiful than that transformation; crowds of people got on, crowds got off, and he remained on his seat and travelled o the end of Russia; but it was not him travelling there on the Trans-Caspian, not him, Ilya Poliakov; the putrid drop was travelling: the drop was tossed in the carriage, the drop saw sunrises and sunsets from its window, the drop was being churned in its tossing and it congealed and gradually changed its appearance, as if in that way its essence would change as well.

31

In any event – they said in the pub – just when that cargo plane was above Yugo-slavia at an altitude of 24,000 feet, and with all the cows in it, one of its engines stopped working!

Yes, that's what happened, Noel panicked and right away began to pray, Bill Baker didn't like it much either but didn't pray, and the doctor, that's to say McKen-zie Jr., just looked at the cows who weren't at all interested in what was happening all around. That how it is with cows. His father had completely forgotten about them long ago; in India he suddenly began to cure people. Or not really cure them, and because of that he got himself into trouble. "By then he was in the grave," someone else remarked.

In any event, only when black oil began to leak from the engine the co-pilot started to worry a bit, and in a moment the engine caught fire from somewhere and began to burn. To burn, yes. God knows how it could be extinguished when they were inside and the engine outside. They couldn't exactly open a window and walk along the wing with a bucket of water, could they? Bill Baker cursed even more than before but suddenly took control of himself and stopped, not want-ing anyone to think that he, Bill Baker the Great, was scared. And he said to the doctor: "Doctor, you certainly never saw anything like this on your way from India when you were a little boy."

And all the while the engine continued to burn right in front of their eyes: not a big fire, true, but all the while it also continued to leak and to spray; God only knows how the whole plane hadn't caught alight yet. And the cows – nothing, they carried on chewing.

"Did they fly cows in India that way?" Bill Baker asked, and the doctor replied that there were no planes there at all, and that he had come to England by ship. After leaving Bombay, right in the middle of the ocean they were caught up in a storm with such giant waves he thought any moment they'd drown; waves the height of buildings and the entire ship rocked, he was all in all a little boy at the time, without a mother and a father by his side, and it was worse than now.

"How could it be worse," Bill Baker said, "in the end you arrived safely, no?"

And now, on the contrary, it looked like the Yugoslavs below will have to gather their pieces or that they'll be completely burnt here like the Indians.

That's how they sat at the tail of the plane and spoke among the cows standing there, and in the circles of the windows they watched the engine continuing to burn. They no longer saw the co-pilot, maybe he had gone in search of a bucket or a fire extinguisher, not that they at all knew how it would be possible to spray outside without breaking a window. And when you break the window of a plane, everyone gets sucked out, even the cows.

"Maybe he's gone to organize a parachute for himself," Bill Baker said, "isn't that what they did in Korea?" Now of all times Noel actually revealed a sense of humor. "Maybe they brought parachutes for the cows as well," he said, after a joke barely ever having passed his lips. From being in such a desperate state, he had managed to make them laugh, and for a moment they saw forty Jersey cows begin to drop with forty parachutes above Yugoslavia, and even then, not stopping to chew.

"As long as they don't shit on the heads of the Yugoslavians," Bill Baker said, "because from a height like that it can kill a person," and again they laughed incessantly, shedding real tears from all the laughter, and as a result didn't see that the engine of the left wing somehow, without anyone noticing, had stopped burning. Not that it had started working, but at least it wasn't burning as before, as if someone had heard their prayers, because at least Noel White had prayed, not the doctor. When they realized this, there was suddenly silence. Previously, they had prepared themselves for their ends, and now it suddenly seemed they might have a chance.

They had already left Yugoslavia by then, and nobody knew exactly where the plane was, until it began to descend. They could see the clouds from the side and not from above, and the plane continued to descend not because the fuel had suddenly run out, as they feared, but because they were already nearing Istanbul. Now the cows seemed also a bit excited. moving here and there and bumping into each other, they even stopped chewing.

"Take it down carefully," Bill Baker shouted to the pilot the way one shouts at a lorry driver from behind, "so that they don't suddenly fall on your head, each one's at least half a ton." Not to mention that a cow falling onto the tower of a mosque, wouldn't be good for the cow or for the mosque. That's how it goes: McKenzie's father saw pagodas ("Not pagodas, the Indians have something else"), but in Istanbul it's mosques.

The temple turrets there are called stupas or chortens – Amnon had already found out about that detail; and on his previous journey to India, he hadn't only heard about them, but also about the caves in the north where monks withdraw for three months and three weeks and three days, or three years and three months or even more, after their entrances are sealed; and at the time the thought arose whether his grandfather had crossed the vast distance from Russia only to be imprisoned in a cave such as that and die in it. And what about you, he asked himself, you who are travelling in his path now?

At the time, he found an excuse to travel to the north from wild idea that came to him, an idea founded in a completely personal matter: to conduct a comparison between monks that withdraw into their caves and between, no more and no less, the prime minister who withdrew into his apartment.[26] He had strongly identified with him in that act after the Lebanon War, despite his views being far from those of Begin, and after all, the ending that he had imagined for his grandfather in a cave in Ladakh emanated from his own guilt, and for all knew his grandfather perhaps hadn't been guilty of anything. He only knew one thing for sure; in the last years of his life his grandfather had lived in a mountainous valley in northernmost India and from there had sent his last belongings in a travelling trunk reeking of dog's urine – his father had mentioned that detail more than once, as if only because of that the trunk didn't remain in the apartment, only because dogs had smelt it and urinated on its boards on its long journey from Leh to Kashgar and from Kashgar to Petersburg and from Petersburg to Minsk and from Minsk to Odessa and from Odessa to Tel Aviv; they had lifted a leg and thereby shown his grandfather what they thought of everything that was dear to him or what the woman he abandoned thought of him.

Over the phone, Naomi says to him: "And that's what interests you, cows on a plane? Udi doesn't stop asking about you, and that's what you've got to tell me?" She talks about her son because she herself has already given up on him, and there's just one more thing she wants; for him to part from the children properly. They at least deserve that.

Three and a half years before that, Udi stood for the first time in the entrance to his apartment, an eight-year-old boy whose freckles reminded him of the way he himself looked in childhood albums, and he could still recall how the boy inspected all the rooms of the apartment. He was very quiet and careful not to be burdensome to both of them, quietly moving his gaze over the dusty bookcases and the table on which prints of glasses and cups could be made out in the dust – he was sharp-eyed like his mother.

"Do you live here alone?" he asked him in amazement. "Without anyone?" He replied in the affirmative.

"And you don't get bored?"

Before he answered him, Udi began to say how bored he gets when he's sick and stays in bed alone at home, or every Wednesday when his mother comes back late from Tel Aviv (it was the day she came to him), and how much he wanted

---

26 Israeli prime minister Menachem Begin withdrew from public life in 1983 and
   remained in his apartment.

someone to be with him at home, other than for the cat, he means. It's not that he doesn't like the cat, he likes Puma a whole lot, but you can't talk to Puma.

They exchanged glances over his head; his loneliness during the long hours he waited for her to return had suddenly been revealed to them.

In the kitchen, he discovered the window beyond which the pigeons cooed outside, and when he came back, he asked Amnon if he didn't want to tame one of them to be a homing pigeon; that way he could send letters to his mother instead of talking on the phone. Again they exchanged glances over his head, and this time Udi noticed it.

Afterward, Udi remembered the promise they'd made to go to the sea on Saturday and asked if it was possible to see the sea from the balcony. But the balcony faced the east, and beyond the rusty railing only the nearby buildings could be seen. It hadn't been swept for months, and a thick layer of dust covered the aluminum ladder that lay there.

A moment later, in the same dreamy voice, Udi asked whether there were goldfish in the sea in Tel Aviv. It transpired he had once had a goldfish named Goldie; it was actually his brother's, but it died. And what that donkey do? He put Goldie in the basin so that he'd find her in the morning when he went to brush his teeth and think that a fish had come out of the tap, and only because the water had suddenly run out, it died. But he immediately saw it was Goldie, even though she no longer looked like Goldie: she didn't move the fins or the gills the way Goldie used to move them, and her eyes looked very odd, not at all like Goldie's eyes, and she didn't shine anymore like Goldie. But it was Goldie, and she was dead.

"Maybe you should go out onto the balcony?" she suggested to her son. "We haven't got a balcony like this." They certainly didn't have a third-floor balcony where they lived, but they also didn't have a rusty railing, pieces of split white-wash peeling from the ceiling, an aluminum ladder lying on the floor whose rungs where stained with sprays of old whitewash. She designed their house herself without compromising on anything (her husband said to her at the time not to save on anything, after all, it's going to be their house for their whole lives).

As curious as an explorer of lands, her son got up and went to the balcony, and at first had to struggle with the glass doors in front of him. They saw him leaning on the rusty railing and looking down at the small street through which only a few cars passed; perhaps he discovered the neighbor from the floor below, the head of the house committee whose voice could be heard each time he directed drivers who had difficulty parking by shouting from his balcony.

"Couldn't you have got some toy for him?" she asked disappointed. "Maybe you would have also got some pleasure from it." But he found no pleasure in this visit, nor curiosity, he would have preferred her to come alone. If she's arranging meetings with her son today, it might be her parents tomorrow and then wanting to get to know his father; as for him, he had no interest in relationships of that sort, not at his age and in his situation. And what connection did he have with children, after all, the last one who came near him came to a bad end.

Eventually they landed – they said in the pub – but they landed the way a tractor lands. And the captain got down walked around his flying jalopy and checked it from all sides, from the tail to the nose and the reverse and from wing to wing, and from his face it was completely clear that didn't like what he sees.

"Listen, Doctor," the captain said, "it seems that you and your friends will have to find some other arrangement for going back, I can't take the responsibility for you," There was no need to say it twice, but right away he said to him: yes-yes, Captain, sure-sure, we understand, Captain, it's okay, Captain, don't feel bad about it. They were sure that they'd find some other arrangement and were already beginning to fantasize about the girls they'd find in Istanbul. "Put Helen out of you mind for a while," Bill Baker said to the doctor, "she won't know. I've heard the Turkish girls know how to roll their stomachs; just by seeing that a man forgets all the girls he knows." The landing had put them all in high spirits.

At first they thought they'd easily get a ticket back, no matter the cost; they hadn't realized that without any cash and with the stink of the cows on them no one would even talk to them. It was a long time ago, who had heard of credit cards? In the end, they somehow reached the city and lost their way in the alleys, encountering many people who didn't know a word of English and certainly didn't see any girl rolling her stomach. They barely ate a thing, it was all too spicy or too sweet, and so they went to sleep hungry in the hotel above the restaurant, three of them in one room with a thousand fleas, and first thing in the morning, after being bitten all night, they went straight to the airport. They wanted one thing only, to return home as quickly as possible. Had a naked girl appeared in front of them rolling her stomach, they wouldn't have changed their minds, they would have said to her: no thanks, and the doctor, even before that, hadn't been keen. Their plane stood in exactly the same place and didn't look any better than it had looked the day before, and the captain was there with the same sour face, and only when he saw them, his expression instantly changed; he couldn't fathom what they were doing there. "This plane might not make it to England," he said, "it's my job; but you?"

"We'll take the responsibility," they said to him.

"I'll have to get you to sign to that," the captain said, and they signed.

McKenzie Jr. also signed. One could have wondered how an educated man, a doctor and son of a doctor, could make such an irresponsible decision; maybe something of his father's stupidity had also been passed onto him: his father had got himself into trouble with a ship ("Not a ship, a boat," someone corrected, and another said: "Only with the bill of ownership"), and the son got himself into trouble with a plane.

Without the cows, the plane seemed even more gigantic than before, but they were really happy to be on it again. Perhaps they trusted that the captain wouldn't have endangered himself like that had he not believed that he'd make it back to England. That's how it is with people, they prefer to believe anything that helps them feel good about themselves. The co-pilots - what they had seen in Korea it's better you don't know - told sick jokes all the way, even on this dud plane they had something to tell for instance the one about the air hostess in the forced landing. How she tells the passengers somewhere above the ocean: ladies and gentlemen, mesdames et messieurs, one of our engines –

"We've all heard it before," they said in the pub, "skip it," because out of all the pub dwellers, Amnon was the only one who hadn't yet heard that joke.

In another week or two, he said to himself, you won't be here: not in this pub, not in this village, not in England. And despite that, it was unclear where exactly he would be and how long his stay would last there, the vagueness didn't dampen his spirits. Get up and leave here, he said to himself again, get up and leave after the meeting with McKenzie Jr., even if he has nothing to tell you, and even if he tells you something better not to know, get up and leave. This journey isn't only in the footsteps of your grandfather, to hell with him and his footsteps, that's if he had left any footsteps behind at all. Leave: get your backpack ready and leave here; it's a nine-hour flight to Delhi, a two-day train journey to Pathankot, and two days by bus or a Sikh truck to Leh. Leave, leave, he said to himself, keep traveling until you cool off inside. She'll probably be even angrier with you and rightly so, and then she'll forget you and rightly so, and she'll also make her children forget you, and there's nothing righter than that; forgetting you as if you had never existed. Only the animals might remember you and, should you one day return, might come to you to be petted, and her children will no longer be children. But you won't be returning, if only because they will have changed, and you will have changed, and who will be returning and to whom?

"Another child in his place," she said on their visit and looked at him on the balcony, "would already have driven us crazy. But look at how he gets along by himself." Udi was still leaning on the railing and looking down at the small street below him or the windows of the next building; in one of them Amnon had once seen a woman shaving her thigh – he only saw the thigh and the hand shaving it, a plump thigh, slightly spread apart, very fair-skinned – until the woman sensed his gaze and the shutter was slammed closed.

After she lay him down on the sofa in the living room and covered him, they heard him yawn, hum to himself, count something, turn over from side to side, get up and go the kitchen and take a glass of water, and she was glad that he felt comfortable in the apartment.

"He didn't go back to bed," she said a moment later, because her ears were attentive to all the noises he made, and he said: "Where else would he go?" and again his hand moved along the path whose twists and turns he was already familiar with and even in total darkness he knew how to find his way around her naked-ness.

She asked if the balcony door was closed, and he mumbled something in a calming tone, and nevertheless got up and checked that the two glass doors of the balcony were closed ("Just put something on," she said, "he doesn't have to see *that*"). He checked that the doors were locked and hid the key in the table drawer. For some reason, he didn't check whether the bolt that fixed the left door to the floor was secured, without that the door could be opened even when it was locked. It was one of the many faults in the apartment whose fixing he postponed from week to week and from month to month.

In the middle of the night, he awoke from a nightmare whose subject matter was forgotten the minute he sat up in bed, and only during the next moments a some of it could be pictured: the balcony could be seen completely dark with the aluminum ladder placed close to the side railing, glowing in the light of the street lamp, and Udi climbs its rungs slowly, going up farther and farther in order see the windows of the next building better or the yard or some other thing, perhaps the sea. He climbs the ladder without any fear and his feet pass the height of the rail-ing, and below him the voice of their neighbor, the head of the house committee, could be heard not shouting at the drivers parking their cars on the sidewalk but rather at Udi, guiding him from below on how to climb farther up until he can see the sea: how to place the small sole of his foot on the aluminum rung, how to hold on to the next rung of the ladder, and how to lift his body up – and right away a thud was heard, and it was that which had wakened Amnon.

Only when the sound was reproduced in his ears did he get up and hurry to the living room. It took a while for his eyes to adjust to the dark. The boy wasn't there.

When he turned toward the balcony, he saw that the left glass door was slightly ajar and he felt his lungs being uprooted from his body. The aluminum ladder was laid on the floor in the exact place it had been laid before, and the rusty railing also looked no different, and that was what brought about his paralysis, because the boy wasn't to be seen there. For a moment, he imagined hearing a vague noise and didn't know whether it was coming from in front or behind him or from the depths of his mind and taking four steps he reached the balcony and stopped on its threshold. He had already once experienced such terror and swore then that under no circumstance would he experience it again: it had happened across from the shores of Sidon.

The boy couldn't be seen on the left or the right. His mouth and throat became dry, exactly as they had become dry then, and moment passed before his feet began to walk toward the railing and didn't stop until he felt the chill of the metal and the roughness of the rust beneath his hands.

All the windows in the building opposite were dark from the first to the last floor, but with its yellow light, the street lamplight also lit the path that led to the backyard and some small object could be seen there, perhaps a toy, and he feared it had dropped from Udi's hand when he stood here leaning on the railing; or that he had dropped it on purpose in order to watch it falling far down below; or that he had thrown it out of anger at having been forced to sleep in a strange apartment where he doesn't even have his own bed, only the sofa in the living room.

Then his eyes began to scan the dark hedge to see whether the boy had fallen onto it, and despite having already experienced terror such as this, it seemed this time it would be much worse, because after all, he hadn't known the other boy. His gaze moved slowly over the bushes by the fence and his eyes stopped at some lump, though it was too small, other than if Udi had sunk between the bushes – with the boy Ali, there had been a moment when only his hand could be seen – until it transpired that there was nothing there other than a shirt or a pair of trousers that had fallen from one of the washing lines.

Also from the side of the railing facing the street, he didn't see anything and turned back to the living room (calling it a living room was a bad joke she had said mockingly). He suddenly thought perhaps he had been in too much of a hurry to come to a conclusion and approached the sofa again and this time didn't make do with his eyes but was aided by his hands. For a blink on an eye, the thought crossed his mind that it was the exact same blindness in which his hands felt around the waters of Sidon beneath the swarm of dead fish, not raising anything other than fleshy seaweed and after it an orange plastic bucket and an orange plastic rake.

When he went out to the balcony again, he knew with dead certainty her son Udi was lying at the edge of the side path at the foot of the first-floor balcony. This time his breath wasn't uprooted but his chest became heavy, and it seemed his breath alone was pulling him to bend farther and farther forward towards the dark void beneath him – perhaps only the washing lines were concealing Udi's small body – until he would join him there on the other side of the railing.

A vague sound caused him to turn his head, it came from the apartment, and he feared that Naomi had awakened and would join him on the balcony and see from there what his eyes had missed: after all, she is his mother.

In the passage, he saw a strip of light spreading from the toilet whose door wasn't properly closed and approached it. Udi could be seen on the other side of the door in his pajamas that covered him with numerous little blue elephants. He stood opposite the basin crying softly at the white tiles, and when he saw him, his crying intensified, and he pointed to the toilet bowl with his little hand. The air freshener spray can lay in its water, it must have fallen when he tried to use it and he was struck with panic because of the damage it would cause the can or the toilet bowl, and more than anything – because of his mother who would be so ashamed of him.

A little boy had never cried in his apartment. It was a soft crying, pent up and inconsolable, as if the deed he had done was irreparable.

"Enough, enough," he consoled him with a calming voice that suddenly rose from his throat, and said that he drops it by mistake at least twice a day, if not three times, and from far away he heard himself saying: "So let's wash hands and go quietly back to sleep, we don't want Mommy to wake up, do we?" He had never spoken like that, in the plural of kindergarten teachers and aunts and nurses in hospitals speaking to their patients.

Afterward, he accompanied Udi to the living room and waited for him to get up on the sofa and cover himself, and when he returned to the bedroom, he saw that Naomi was wide awake.

"You're a good person," she said, "I wasn't sure before, but now I am."

Between his temples, from which drops are sweat were still flowing, a familiar and dull voice replied: I'm-not-a-good-man-I'm-not, because he knew his goodness was a product of his guilt; and not for forgetting to secure the bolt of the door, but a far greater guilt that did not have a good ending.

"And you'll also be a good father," she said to him then, "I didn't know that before, but now I do." And it seemed fitting to reward him for that goodness, but he her touch gave him the chills.

After they fell asleep, a nightmarish dream came to him from other nights, mixed with things he witnessed this night: it wasn't dropped clothing, a shirt or a pair of trousers, he sees far down below him, but the army boots left on the beach and the mounds of sand piled up there, and he's coming out of the water and a huge swarm of dead fish follow behind him like trail, and his hands are empty The orange bucket can be seen again, the one in which dead fish had been brought to their burial, and the orange rake with which their small graves were heaped up; Ali was the name of the boy who had buried them.

He had told her all about it before that,: the mass of silvery fish a stray bomb had raised from the depths and about the boy, and she listened in total silence and remained silent when he finished. Only after a few very long moments, she said: "So what? It happened and it's over, you're a new man now," and through the darkness of the bedroom he studied her eyes to make sure she meant what she said.

Here, in the English house he rented, she says to him over the phone: "God, what a pity I didn't listen to you then."

Although the plane was no longer a shed overhead ("You made a rhyme," the speaker was complimented in the bar), it swayed even more, but they eventually landed safely. Afterward it seemed as if a lucky charm had been placed in their pockets; people said the flight had made them immune like someone surviving a snake bite: lightning missed Bill Baker's barn by a millimeter, a lorry almost hit Noel White and at the last moment swerved and hit someone else, and an irritable horse almost kicked the doctor in the head and only at the last moment he moved aside. People thought they had all become immune. McKenzie Sr. might have died like a dog but owing to that flight his son had grabbed luck by the balls.

YOUVAL SHIMONI

Only after a very long time, they heard what became of that plane in the end and realized that luck has its limits. Someone brought a newspaper from London where it was written that somewhere above the ocean a plane began to lose altitude and dived into the water down to the lowest depths of the ocean and a second later nothing was seen of it. Sheep had been on it, not cows, fifty or sixty sheep, and a month later those sheep were still drifting toward the shore of France, a whole dead flock came out of the sea. The fisherman said even the seaweed have become woolen.

Only the captain and co-pilot no one saw again. That's the way it goes, they thought they would fly cows and sheep in the sky, and in the end, they learned their lesson. Someone who doesn't know his place learns it the hard way in the end – McKenzie Sr. learnt his as well. God only knows the trouble he got into in the end, even the cause of his death is unknown; perhaps he also finished up in the sea.

"Maybe you'll also finish up there," she said over the phone after he stupidly related a few other things he heard in the pub. "You like the sea, don't you?" She's still talking to him: mocking all the nonsense he hears in the pub and the few facts that can be gleaned from them, and nevertheless, despite having changed her approach many times and threatening to get rid of all his stuff, she's still talking to him; he isn't worth it, she'll easily find herself a far better replacement, she meets many successful men in her job, but she still refuses to erase all the last years and to understand how great his stupidity is.

When her anger gets the better of her again she reminds him again about the sea of Sidon: about the long promenade the bomb missed by a few dozen meters, about the beach and what was buried in it, about the waves and what was carried on them. Perhaps in a short while she'll ask whether his Lebanese boy didn't also drift toward the shore of France, with woolen seaweed.

"Wasn't his name Ali?" she asked. And his name was enough to send shivers through him.

"If you find the pub there so interesting," she said. "why don't you become our correspondent about matters of cows and sheep?"

In vain he tries to remind her that the man he wants to meet, Dr. McKenzie Jr. is a veterinarian by profession, and if he knew a few things about him it would make meeting him easier when he finally comes to the pub: it sounds silly, but maybe with the help of the cows and the sheep he'll be able to trace his grandfather's steps.

"Maybe the doctor also understands something about fish," she says. "Maybe he can explain to you what happened to them?" And she did not mean the goldfish that her two children raised and not the one she had in her childhood in Africa, but the fish that he saw floating opposite the demolished promenade, concealing everything in the water. In moments of anger toward him, she uses her most effective weapon, a weapon for which he has no defense – his guilt.

32

Tel Aviv, 1994

There had, for example, been a colonel – what was him name? – who sailed on the River Oxus with an organ being led by a barge, a gift he brought from the Tsar to one of the local rulers just so he could map the way for military purposes; and there was the spy, Grombachevsky, who had crossed long distances on foot for similar reasons; and there was another Russian intelligence man who was sent on a secret mission to the East but was brought back to examine the character of a Petersburgian arms dealer suspected of fanning the riots; and there was an ex-revolutionary, Dmitri Klements, who had become a geographer there.

Why had his grandfather travelled far from Russia to the place from where the English doctor's letter had been sent? Why did he board the Trans-Caspian and not travel in the opposite direction, as was customary? Why didn't he travel to a place where his wife and small child could have joined him, for example Warsaw, Berlin, London, Israel, or to America? These ponderings didn't nullify all the evidence Nachman had discovered in books and newspapers of the time about Russians who made their way to the East; he found no explanation, not in the Tsar loyalists nor their opponents.

In the years of his old age, his heart was drawn to that organ which was sailed on the raft on the river in view of dozens of villagers standing on the banks and watching it (it was carried on and on with a flock of birds above it, and from that day onward they sang the notes it played; at least that's what the locals said). It was that sight which captured his heart, and not the purpose of its sailing, nor all sorts of other intelligence ploys; those were matters his son was drawn to and which fed his articles, helping him to make him a name for himself on the national newspaper, a temporary name made on a flimsy basis. They funded his flights and hotels and travelling expenses, enabling him to produce a few more dubious scoops whose point, in the manner of new journalists, was to debase the state, as if there was another place in the world waiting for the Jews. He son hadn't always been like that, he became like that after the Lebanon War from which he returned remote and crestfallen, and even after a month's rest on the Greek island Ksiathos or Skiathos, he refused to speak about what he had seen in the war. The one and only time they discussed it ended in a bitter quarrel.

Bombs were exploding in the city streets now, just like at the beginning of the century but instead of carriages, buses were being blown up, and one of the explosions could perhaps have been heard here, in the hall of the city library; but they no longer had a mission, nor pomp and glory, only black smoke and blood and the screams of the wounded and the cries of the inflamed mobs, and there was a vast gulf between those cries of "Massacre the Jews!" or "Death to the Arabs!" and the splendor of the revolutionary phrases that sounded almost like poetry (we shall ascend the gallows with no fear or trembling, if it is decreed for us to pay with our lives for the courageous attempt to grant human rights to the people!). Even the lesser figures of that era were infinitely better than the heroes of present times, the ones the two impressionable girls next to Nachman probably had their eyes on: all sorts of singers and football players and top models and top hairdressers whose love affairs featured in articles that fill the weekend newspaper supplements, phrased in cheap and vulgar language ("a hot babe from the Look Modelling Agency was seen in the early hours on the arm of a well-known hunky footballer, and we ask: will he score?"), a chasm exists between them and the heroes of the past, and Nachman, with what's left of his strength, tries in vain to cling to its edge.

And what would Ada do every time she saw him like that? She would step on his toes to stop him from busying himself with all that nonsense and decide once and for all where he's living, in the past or here, with kings and revolutionaries or with her. His past, as time went by, had also become his academic past as a university man, and in vain she tried to persuade him to make use of the knowledge he had accumulated there and write a clear and concise high school textbook and have it published by the small publishing house where she worked. "After all, you like to explain," she said to him, "I use to like the way you explained things to me." It would be only years later, lying in Ichilov Hospital attached to all sorts of tubes and monitors that she would no longer disparage, mock and scorn him; not one bad word would come out of her mouth, and for many long days he would actually wish she would disparage, mock and scorn him, solely to hear her voice again.

When they first met, he was a newly released soldier from the British army who had joined the Haganah and one evening, when two women were required to escort a convoy to Mount Scopus and conceal Luger pistols in their clothing, he went into the Atara café and surveyed all those seated there, until he noticed a long-braided girl sitting alone at a corner table. When he stood opposite her, she didn't hasten to lift her eyes from the book of poetry she was reading, not even when he cleared his throat and asked if she would perhaps consent to take an interest in things other than poetry. She consented.

The next day, the convoy went on its way, and Nachman, who was sent to one of the kibbutzim on the outskirts of Jerusalem on another matter, heard that at the exit of the city the convoy had been fired at and that four people had been wounded, among them one of the woman escorts. He had no doubt at all it was the girl he had enlisted. He tried to find out more details, but no one could tell him who she was and how serious the wound was, and they suggested to him that he simply – simply! – go to the hospital and find out. He went to the Hadassah and Bikur Cholim and Misgav Ladach hospitals, passing from ward to ward, floor by floor, but didn't see her. An image was formed in his mind and led him through the corridors: how he would see her braid dropping down from the white of the sheet and watch her until she awakens, how he would turn to her when the nurse goes out, how he would speak to her, how he would bend to kiss her. After three virtually sleepless nights, he went into the Atara café and saw her sitting at the corner table with the small book open in front of her, as if she hadn't got up from there. It transpired the friend she had brought along had been wounded, and that fortunately it was a light wound, and that she herself had been involved in another shooting; no, she had done the shooting, the escort sitting next her had. Stashek, maybe he knows him? A tall guy with a small scar below his eye? A partisan who had lived in the forests for three years and still kept apples in his pockets. A small smile rose on her face and Nachman felt a pang in his heart.

For a long while after that he used to needle her about her ride with that Stashek and about the shooting. A young Arab waiting at a bus stop gave Stashek a sharp look and moved his hand in a suspicious manner and Stashek decided to get in before him; Nachman didn't ask how the pistol got from her clothes into his hand, but years later that silly song would be heard on the radio about those girls ("Where oh where oh where are they, and where did they hide the Luger"), until the first volume of Yellow Parchment [27] was published and on one of its hundreds of pages he saw the face of that same Stashek among the photographs of the dead: high cheek bones, a small scar below his left eye; his height wasn't apparent from the picture, nor were the apples he kept in his pocket that perhaps had rolled out of them when he was killed in the battle of Latrun. In their first house – one of the houses in the German Colony which after being abandoned by their Arab owners were handed over to released soldiers, and she with her fine taste and deft hands at first turned it into a love-nest and then into a family home – one evening, Nachman saw her sitting next to the table lamp that he made from a copper jug he found in an abandoned house and gazing for a long while at one of the pages of the thick book, and he had no doubt which picture she was looking at. He watched her from the kitchen, and when he thought that any moment she might be liable to draw the page close to her lips, he moved a chair and made a noise with it; perhaps she had already begun to be unfaithful to him, at least in thought. Afterward, they moved to Tel Aviv, and she enjoyed the cafés of Dizengoff Street and the cinemas, and more than anything the beach; she would take her son there and the two of them would return with shells bringing something from the sea into their home. For years, her boss at the publishing house had been wooing her, and at first she

---

27 A publication for the perpetuation of the memory of fallen soldiers.

even told Nachman about it flattered and amused, and afterward she told how miserable her boss was about readers' whims and also about the attitude of his three sons toward him, and in the end she stopped talking about him, refraining from both the good and the bad; and perhaps she really had begun to be unfaithful to Nachman then, and during the afternoon hours when he didn't know where she was, she might have been secluded with her boss in a hotel room opposite the sea (he had no doubt it took place there); he saw her in her petticoat as if right in front of his eyes, and a sea breeze enters from the open window with the sound of beach bats and flutters the petticoat, but she's only comforting his replacement; nothing more than that, only words, like a prostitute who clients come to for a sympathetic ear.

Had she remained with him she probably would have told him that he, who had once been the protégé of a renowned professor, was simply blinded by the past, mixing all sorts of factual fragments he randomly gathered for his own means, because he only had a need for heroes and kings (he recently had begun to take an interest in them as well), inventing a new history as well as a new geography so that the facts don't disturb the falsehoods he's been telling himself about his father. "Your father simply ran away," she repeatedly said to him, "he left your mother with a belly and ruined her whole life. And he ruined ours as well, and yet you still miss him. What are you, a baby?" Yes, that's how he sometimes felt, especially in the latter years, in the apartment that had been emptied of his son and his wife and his dog, in the kitchen where he eats straight from the frying pan or the pot, in the guest room where the television is his only guest, in the double bed from where only his scent emanates, in the slipperiness of the bathroom where he has difficulty getting up, in all those places and in others where he sometimes longed to be hugged, and kissed, and tickled, and be made to laugh; and terrified lest he start acting irrationally, and that soon only fragments of syllables will be emitted from his mouth and saliva will dribble over his chin and he'll have to be fed with a spoon – but by whom exactly?

Ada feared that burden would fall upon her, when she would have to look after him, and in the end it was she who needed him. When he heard from one of the neighbors in the building what had happened to her, he felt a small wave of gloating because she was the one to reach Ichilov Hospital first, and the man who was supposed to look after her, her new husband, has long been in the Kiryat Shaul cemetery (her boss, in charge of the small publishing house). For a moment the wicked urge arose to go to the hospital just to fling these things at her, and for the first visit he took pains to dress in his best clothes and come with his hair combed and face well-shaven to show her how well preserved he was for his age, how sturdy and independent he was, he even had no need of a walking stick (he had heard that for years she had already needed a walker), but when he stood opposite her bed and saw her and how much the face he knew had changed, he collapsed in a chair.

The children of his replacement were angry with her for inheriting the bulk of his money, and it was Nachman who came there every morning, wiped her forehead and her face, and tried to avert his eyes from the terrible stitching in the shaved skin of half her right forehead. During the first days, he still tried to talk to her, because the nurses said it was impossible to know what can be heard in a coma and what cannot; he told her about all the years he had lived alone, about the apartment that had become empty without her, about the bed that had become large, and how much he missed the mess she made and her irritability and even the quarrels and the taunts; he reminded her, without considering the other visitors in the room or the nurses, about the Arab house in which they had lived in Jerusalem in their youth (in her youth, actually: at the time, he was over forty), about the window with the deep alcove and how Amnon's cradle was placed there afterward; he reminded her about their trip to Italy, and how she drove all the young men of Rome crazy with her braid; and how from the first moment he saw her in the Jerusalem café, he knew she'd be his wife, and he was right, even if they had both been through some bad years and several years of separation. He had already blurred one abandonment; that of his father, and he had reacted similarly to her abandonment.

All that while she lay on her back with her eyes closed, and for some moments it seemed she could hear him and for some that her dreams had already reached the twilight zone between this world and what lies beyond it, a zone that had nothing to do with the corrupt members of the Jewish Burial Society,[28] but something entirely different, even pleasant. That's what he thought regarding her and him too when his hour comes, but not regarding his father: not only had his misdeeds become blurred but his death too, and without noticing it, for some moments it seemed his father was shrinking to human proportions.

He continued going to the hospital every morning, and all of them there already knew him as her husband, and each time the nurses would report her situation to him. He found some comfort in that, despite that she herself didn't recognize him or anything else, and she herself was difficult to recognize. From day to day in a progression whose stages were undetectable, the dimples were erased from her cheeks, the muscles of her mouth became limp; a mouth that no longer tried to talk or laugh or cry. The stroke had obliterated the contrast between their temperaments: his moderation opposed to her exuberance; his calm consideration opposed to her feverishness. For years, she had driven her small car here and there, becoming filled with happiness or anger at the same speed, instantly enthusiastic and instantly fed up, dreaming of trips to Paris, Barcelona, and London, while he, after retiring from his job, went no farther than the municipal library, and went no farther there than the periodicals room, and went no farther than the beginning of

---

28 An organization that deals with matters concerning deaths and burials.

the twentieth century (on that route, as on his route to work and back, he would say with a hesitant smile that three kilometers a day, nevertheless, come to almost a thousand a year, and fifty years of that come to fifty thousand kilometers which is almost the length of the equator; and in that way in the end he too will have circled the globe like Magellan).

With the disappearance of her facial expression, all that remained were the narrow tubes on her face that outlined so called features making them identical to all the features of her neighbors in the room, women and men alike. Unseen by all (even by the dedicated nurses), she had moved not only her facial features from her bed to the place she intended going to, but also everything inside her, until all that was left on the bed was an empty hollow shell: and it was that shell that was being ventilated by a respirator, and on which attempts were made to prevent bedsores and choking and temperature rises, and the bedsheets of that shell were changed, despite that nothing any longer pressed on it, nothing pleasant, nor warming nor cooling.

On one of the days of the past month, he thought a miracle had occurred and that she was smiling at him from her bed, the third on the left: he came into the ward and saw her eyes radiating at him, and he had no doubt that she was smiling, and right away he responded to that smile and to her eyes that had at long last opened and whose color had become sharper and dark like the hair that had grown back overnight – it seemed that even her long thick braid could be seen falling from the edge of the bed – until a nurse told him that during the night they had moved Ada to another room, and that the person here was a young woman who had been injured in an accident ("We wanted her near to us," the nurse in charge explained, "she simply still has a chance"). From then on, his visits became less frequent.

"Girls, I won't warn you again," said the librarian.

Again they were looking at the boy with the earring and their eyes accompanied his every movement when he helped Nachman take down previous volumes of the *Hamelitz* newspaper editions from a shelf. He intended to page back more than twenty years before the first revolution when his father had been a young man and had participated in the assassination of ministers at the time, to the years before his birth when the Tsar Alexander the Second had been killed. The Tsar had deserved to die as did his successors, but his start was good and high hopes had been pinned on him, and for all his short life had his father not grown up in the shadow of that assassination? (Or in its light, depending on whose side you are on.) He saw not only his father's revolutionary comrades right before his eyes but found interest also in the one whose seat they were plotting to overthrow and that deserved all their efforts. After all, no one in the world would conceive of assassinating him, Nachman, not with bombs, not with shots, not with daggers.

Between thumb and index finger, with great care, he felt the page of the newspaper: it had become so dry and perforated by the burrowing of moths, that every unnecessary touch shed small pieces with the words that had faded there, and they could barely be read, through the scratched lenses of the glasses: And thus it is! From the North Sea to the Black Sea, and from the River Weichsel to the ends of the land of Siberia, Mother Russia bewails in lament the removal from her head the master and king that to her sons was the source of blessing and a wellspring of salvation. He had not yet read exactly how he had died (he naturally knew the facts, but not in this flowery phrasing), and for that purpose he had to page further through the yellowing pages until details could be made out from the faded letters: On the first day of the month of March at the first hour and forty minutes after noon, on the return of the Emperor from the visitation of the troop on guard, a hollow exploding ball suddenly detonated in front of his carriage, and a mighty thunderous sound rose from the earth and was heard in the surrounding streets, and all the glass panes of the nearby buildings were broken into shards. In this pandemonium the Emperor retained his senses, and on leaving the carriage and seeing two of the troops holding one villain who had thrown the bomb and in his hand the butt of a rifle, the Emperor looked at his face and asked his name, and also urged those positioned around him to summon aid to the wounded. His Majesty made his way toward the side of the street with his escorts behind him, however, he had but taken two or three steps and another villain – yes, that's what the revolutionaries were called here, villains; and in another place they were called scoundrels – drew near and threw another bomb which exploded at his feet, and the Emperor fell wallowing in his blood. For a long time, the king's doctors labored to return him to the living, but all their efforts were to no avail – all the learning of doctors is of no use to a man when his hour comes – and after the passing of two hours they came out and announced with a pained heart that the wounds had been deadly due to heavy hemorrhaging. The Tsar managed to receive a last anointment, and at exactly twenty-nine minutes past the hour of three his earthly life came to a close.

Villain, the thought passed through him, and for a moment he was startled by the word until he became accustomed to it, and he still did not connect that term with the one for whom he was sitting here and reading. A villain. A scoundrel. And afterward he thought that since he had come from his seed, he, who had been born from an injustice done to his mother, could also have been called that, a scoundrel, and from the back of his hazy memory the children from the yard under his mother's window appeared, though it was not a scoundrel that they had called him but rather a bastard son of a whore, son of a thousand whores.

All the efforts of the doctors of Ichilov had also been to no avail; he knew them all, and despite that they all had said the very same thing, he refused to accept their sentence. On the first day, they still declined to speak with him ("What exactly are you to her?"), but afterward he heard a nurse saying: "We should all have such devotion," and he was as flattered as a child. He also wanted to speak with the doctor who had operated on Ada, one Dr. Sigalovich, a skinny and unattractive woman (Ada was a thousand times prettier than her) and saw a man and a woman rise and approached her, and according to the resemblance between them they must have been brother and sister whose mother she had just operated on.

In an unpleasant voice, Dr. Sigalovich told them both the lady had safely come through the difficult operation, a very difficult operation, heavy bleeding had developed which had been very hard to stop. And there had a been a need to saw part of the cranium, she said, and that stage passed successfully, and perhaps all that would help the edema which had developed there, and consequently there could be a certain way out, provided of course it doesn't worsen, so now they must wait. It's a precarious time, she said, not to say critical, it sometimes even takes three days.

"For what?" asked the brother.

"Until it becomes clear what direction it's going," said Dr. Sigalovich.

And for a moment, as in a nightmare, he saw her sawing Ada's head with a small saw in rhythmic movements, back and forth until the sawed section fell, and he shuddered. That's how they used to saw plywood boards in distant handicrafts lessons and make napkin holders from them for example.

A more precise description about what had happened on the day Tsar Alexander the Second died was heard from the head of the Imperial Guard at the trial of the scoundrels: During the passage of the carriage through the street next to Ekaterininsky Canal and on its arrival at the end of the winding street, a hollow exploding ball detonated with a thunderous sound, and horses stood beneath them at the time. I lifted my eyes to look at my surroundings, and behold, a heavy cloud and a shroud of darkness covered the face of the square, and the earth circled and moved under our feet. In a very brief moment, I witnessed that harm has befallen the Emperor's carriage behind me, however His Highness jumped through the carriage door completely unruffled, and his first words were to me asking if the murderer had been apprehended. I lifted my eyes to see among the crowd two troopers from the eighteenth battalion apprehending a young man of few years wearing a kosovorotka[29] and I pleaded with the Emperor to return to his carriage and be seated in it until he be transported to the winter palace. "I shall return to my former strength" the Emperor replied to me, "but I wish to see the murderer." And His Highness faced the young man, and the glowing expression on his face testified to his heart brimming with gratitude and blessing to the Lord above who has been as a shield to him. But at that very moment, there was a striking shattering sound more thunderous than the first, and prostrate on the ground the call

29 A shirt with a skewed collar.

THE SALT LINE

445

of the Emperor came to my ears: "Save me." I lifted my eyes and beheld His Highness, the Emperor, lying on the ground, leaning on one arm and struggling to rise and inhale air. I then gathered my last strength and attempted to raise him to his feet, and a terrible spectacle was revealed to my eyes and shall not depart from them until my final breath: I saw that the Emperor's legs had been severed and flattened from above the knees to the stomach, his footwear and outer garments were no longer on him, and his golden buttons were strewn all around, and much blood flowed from him and formed pools surrounding him, and what transpired afterward, I do not recall, since I fainted and did not revive until the first watch of the morning. For a long while after the battalion commander had concluded his words, lamentations and moaning and woe could be heard from the benches.

A murderer, the thought passed through Nachman, and for a moment he was shocked by it until he also became accustomed to it, and he still did not connect that term explicitly to the man who was worthy of it for similar deeds he did twenty-five years later, a short while after fathering him.

Generations of readers had left their prints on the newspaper, and between the holes made by moths there were hints of the fingers that had thumbed through the pages across the decades from the present to the beginning of the century, fingers that were fat and skinny and rough and tender and sweaty and dry, the kind that also thumb banknotes or cards and others that knew how to press a trigger, throw bombs, place mines on railway tracks, hold a dagger – the fingers of his vanished father from the days he had thumbed through these pages or ones similar in his village, when the paper had still been white and the ink black. For a moment, the old man touched his father's fingerprints as if in that way he was touching him, his vanished father or at least his hand reaching out to him from the depths of the years, but this time he hesitated whether to respond to it.

All around, in place of the scholarly silence of the library, an eruption of chattering could be heard that the librarian found difficult to overpower.

"But I wouldn't do it just like that!" The girl next to him with the light streaks in her hair said. "I have to feel something for the guy! And the eyes are the most important 'cos you can see everything inside. And I also care how tall he is, I have to feel when I'm walking in the street with him nothing bad will happen to me."

"Yes, but when you sleep together" – her friend giggled and folded her stumpy fingers inside the palm of her hand, until they all touched each other– "tall or short doesn't matter anymore!"

Rapid as lightening, the Tsar's two doctors arrived at the palace – were Ada's doctors as hasty as that? – Doctor Kruglyakov, His Majesty's surgeon, and Doctor Marcus, his personal doctor, and with brisk steps they entered the chamber to which his servants had carried him and stooped over him from his right and from his left: the spectacle was awful, no man will forget it to his last day. With skillful fingers they pressed on the artery of the thigh to stem the blood flow, however the Emperor's blood continued to pour as if unobstructed. The doctor of the marksman battalion promptly arrived as well, he had been fortuitously visiting the police building and on hearing the broken cries of the crowd abandoned all his doings and hastened to the palace — hastened, unlike Dr. Sigalovich, from whose point of view Ada had been just one of the many patients whose skulls she had sawed and whose names she would forget on the day of the operation – and in the entrance to the chamber, he lifted his eyes to his colleagues and no tidings were visible in them. A question rose in the eyes of the doctor of the marksman battalion to which no answer was given, and who would be wise and hold the answer apart from He who is seated in a heavenly place.

"Bring me the kit for the amputation and the operation," said Dr. Kruglyakov, after stooping over his king again, "without delay!" The doctor of the marksman battalion immediately hurried back to his house and returned shortly and with him the kit for the amputation and the operation, ready and prepared for its terrible task.

Inside the chamber, to the radiant light of the crystal chandelier, Dr. Kruglyakov bent over the Emperor and placed his ear close to his chest to hear the faint sound of the beating of his heart. A large towel was draped over the right leg of the Tsar and around his knee in order to stem the blood and by applying pressure cause it to flow in the direction of the heart, and around his left thigh a rubber tourniquet was wrapped in order to constrict his breached arteries. In the corridor that led to the chamber, the maids stood embracing each other and raising their voices in lament as Dr. Kruglyakov began his terrible task. With some labor, the glove saturated in blood was removed from the right hand of the Emperor, and beneath it deep burns were revealed and his engagement ring had been squashed and almost entirely swallowed in the flesh of his finger. From the corridor, a wailing sound could be heard, and Doctor Marcus signaled with his hand: hush.

Again the surgeon tilted his ear towards the Emperor's chest and listened to his heart attentively, and a moment or two later it became apparent from the expression on his face that the heartbeats had become clearer than they had been, a motion of swallowing was apparent too and the breathing had deepened. "Praise the Lord," a voice of thanks was heard from the back of the corridor and was hushed. Another injection was administered to the Emperor to rally him, and his forehead and face were wiped with a towel dipped in ice water which shortly turned red from blood. With a firm hand, Doctor Marcus placed an oxygen bag close to the Emperor's mouth and both his cheeks became alternately indrawn and swollen, and for a moment to those present it seemed that the Emperor's breathing was advancing towards stability and that, little by little, it would return to be robust. "Praise the Lord," the voice from the corridor was heard again, and again was hushed. The three doctors stood as one man at the head of the bed and waited to observe the turn of events.

The confessional priest Protopresbyter Bezhnov arrived and conducted the last anointment. The maids who were assembled in the corridor wept silently. For some moments, it still seemed there was hope for the Emperor, but as the anointment ended, Doctor Kruglyakov sensed that the beats were becoming weak. He hurriedly bent his head towards the Emperor's chest to listen to his heart, and the eyes of all those present were lifted to him to perceive the word of God. His breaths were faint, and from them it was apparent they were ebbing towards oblivion. A stillness descended on the chamber from wall to wall, the corridor was silent for its entire length, and silent were the masses waiting in the square in front of the palace. At twenty-nine minutes past three, the breathing completely ceased – Ada died close to midnight, and he heard about it belatedly, after she had already been packed and prepared for delivery – after the passing of some time, the doctors went out toward the palace gate, and in trembling voice announced to the entire large crowd standing in the square that his wounds had been fatal, and that the Tsar, the Imperator, Alexander the Second, liberator of the people and friend to humanity, had passed away. And the people raised their voice in weeping, and they knelt in purified prayer to the one seated in a heavenly place.

He had no difficulty imagining that sight: a square filled with people from end to end, many times larger than the square in front of Arison's inpatient tower, and all kneeling as one and offering a prayer to a low grey winter sky loaded with snow, and all lamenting the coronet of their heads that had been taken from them. Only the voice of the nurse from internal medicine ward number five informed him of Ada's death – it was the pleasant nurse of Yemenite descent who he had persuaded to let him know of any worsening of the situation even though he wasn't a family relative. He got dressed right away and called a taxi, and when the driver heard the destination, he lowered the volume of the radio slightly (some listener was telling the announcer about the dream he had dreamed, and Nachman wondered why people were awake at such an hour and telling their most private dreams even to taxi drivers).

Afterward, there was the familiar route to ward five of internal medicine, to the special care unit: through the first building, past the darkened café and the ATM machine lit up in a bluish light, and onward through the square between the buildings to the inpatient tower, and there, in one of the fancy elevators, to the second floor and left down the long corridor. Again, he had to struggle with the door to open it, and on its other side was the completely dark inner corridor, and only the nurses' station at the end spread some light around it.

He must have looked disheveled and alarmed, because the pleasant sister immediately offered him a glass of water, and when he refused and asked if Ada was still in the room, she nodded her head. Right away he turned to go there, and the nurse hastened to enter before him, and when he reached there, he saw her opening the zipper of the sack lying on the bed, a long dark blue sack, and a face was revealed inside it, an unsightly distorted face, not Ada's face. During the last twenty-four hours the edema had gone down, and the skin had sunk in the place where the cranium had been sawn, and some vague childhood memory surfaced in him of a deflated ball. He drew closer to Ada: he checked her left eyebrow that was higher than the right one, the small birthmark beneath the right ear lobe, and the mole on the side of the neck with the hair that sprouted from it, and even that didn't satisfy him, and he also checked the label attached to the zipper of the sack. Her name was written there with some other family name, and for a moment he wanted to tell the nurse that a terrible mistake had been made and that it must be corrected immediately, until he remembered the facts. The day of the death was also noted on the label, and here too it seemed a mistake had been made, unless she had already died when they phoned him after midnight; that is to say that while he, Nachman, was dreaming his dream (he was walking in a vast field at the start of summer, and a breeze passed though the giant ears of corn and moved them in every direction around him; and it was all very pleasant and very frightening), she had already gone to meet her maker, though she wasn't the only one who would meet him.

The blue sack with its zipper looked like a sleeping bag too thin to protect her from any chill, and certainly not in the bowels of the earth, and for a moment he rested his eyes on her in order to engrave the sight of her in them: she lay there between the folds of the blue sheet, the beautiful woman he had fallen in love with almost fifty years ago, the poetry reader, the convoy escort, the woman who used to be covered with him together under one blanket, the mother of his son who had left him – the girl with the braid he met in the café in Jerusalem, the one he had searched hospitals for, who he had lived with in an abandoned Arab house, who he moved to Tel Aviv with, who bore him a son, who betrayed them both when she went off with another man.

"I'm really very sorry," the nurse said from behind him.

He drew close to Ada again and rolled down the edges of the sack around her head slightly, until the whole forehead was revealed and the stitching that crossed it that had also sunk in the place where a section of the cranium had been removed. Dense white stubble could be seen around the stitching, masculine looking, and on the left half of the head that hadn't been shaved, the white of the roots predominated over the dyed hair, and another silly memory rose in him, how she would return from the hairdresser on Friday mornings with the latest gossip on matters of the neighborhood and on matters of state. The gossip was always supported by personal knowledge, someone waiting for her eyebrows to be plucked knew someone whose cousin had gone out with the nephew of the minister's driver or with the brother of the singer's security guard (they said about her - or about him - that they were having an affair with a married man). When she told him all that, he would be astonished and angry by her sudden stupidity, while she who had been divulging all those bits of gossip mainly to cover up the discomfort her new look had caused her and over which she had taken so much trouble, continued to wait in vain for him to compliment her even if only with one word. What a fool he had been at the time, how stingy with compliments.

When he left the ward after a long while (didn't wait for his son; he would be landing from Athens only the following day), he again passed through the corridor and again pressed for the elevator and again crossed the square between the buildings, and he knew that he wouldn't to pass through this route again until he himself would be brought here. Again, he passed by the ATM machine and its blue light and the dark café, and he collapsed into one of its chairs. All at once, everything he had seen these past months weighed on his back, as if the load of Rosenstein's amputated body that had lessened from year to year ever since he had carried it on his shoulders in the hills of Northern Italy, had been replaced by the weight of the blue sack. Only then he noticed the two silhouettes sitting in the darkness of the café three tables from him and heard their voices.

"And that's what you said to her?" said the silhouette on the right.

"She hardly let me speak! She began saying all sorts of things to me; she said, 'stop telling me stories because it's not gonna help you, Ronnie; just get out of here.' And the girl was with her, stirring her up against me. It gets me down just speaking about it, Zohar. For that I don't mind spending nights here. Just tell me, Zohar, you're still a young guy, not yet twenty, just show me one man who would say no to a woman that comes onto him like that."

"Me," said the silhouette on the left, "no one's come onto me like that yet. First let her come, then we'll see."

"Be careful of that, Zohar, do you get what I'm saying to you? You're a kid, really a kid, you still think life's a picnic. Look at him over there, why d'you think he came here at this hour, for a picnic?"

He did not mean for Nachman to hear and certainly not to answer, but Nachman, despite that his hearing had weakened a lot over the last years, heard; and within the darkness that enveloped all the café tables, he heard his own voice when it answered: "My wife passed away," and he repeated in a louder voice: "My wife passed away," and afterward added her name as well and said: "Ada Poleg passed away," and said exactly when she passed away, a little after midnight, his wife, Ada, and for a moment a thought came to mind that if he hurries to the ward, before the blue sack is vacated from there, perhaps he could correct the name and the date of death on Ada's tag the way he used to correct dates in articles that he proofread.

Afterward, he went by taxi, the same taxi that drove him to the hospital or another in which the same stupid radio program could be heard, and in it the same announcer spoke in the same whispering voice, and only those phoning in had changed. Someone else was telling about the dream he dreamed, and he wasn't listening (he had been walking in a vast field when the nurse phoned, and a breeze passed through ears of corn as tall as cypress trees).

With that sight of the tops of lofty corn ears, he went up to the apartment. On the front door, while struggling with the key, his eyes discerned the scratches their dog had made on the door years ago, when they returned from their walks and wanted to go in – for years he hadn't noticed that, and suddenly he pictured its paw prints. Their dogs had died and returned to dust, but their scratches on the door were preserved like their bites on the legs of chairs from the time they were still puppies, and this discovery suddenly seemed a revelation: a man dies, and the scratches he leaves survive.

On the legs of the chairs, the teeth of the mischievous Canaan were imprinted, and the large-hearted Pointer, and the grumpy Schnauzer. Another dog, a cocker spaniel, had belonged to the Russian crown prince – not long ago he had also read about him – and when Nicholas the second and all his family were executed in the cellar in Siberia, their dog was shot with them. Only the diamonds hidden by the princesses in their girdles were not damaged and the collection of screws that the Tsarevich kept in his pockets and that must have been scattered around his small body like the Tsar's golden buttons.

That information shocked him: to kill a small child like that, with such cruelty? And for what? After all, nothing remained of the Communist Revolution and its dreams. His heart was moved by the little pale Tsarevich who stood in a dark cellar with his pockets bulging with screws the way his own had with apricot pits and marbles, until they were both thrown to the ground, one in Yekaterinburg and the other in the backyard of the building in Shenkin Street, and what the hell for?

Yellowed perforated pages were now before him; numerous burrows had been made in them by moths that stapled pages with the vast expanses of the Russian kingdom to ones with the tiny area of a state, the paint of whose borderlines hadn't yet dried; white expanses of snow to blazing rounded dunes; cathedrals to concrete chimneys of power stations; and daring fighters whose feats were immortalized in history books it to poor wretches like Nachman whose destinies are to be forgotten in the hearts of all. Even her in the hall of the municipal library, his existence had been completely erased, and the two girls, who the librarian previously asked to be quiet, chatted next to him as if he was thin air ("In the end you'll land up like that librarian, Etti, with cobwebs down there!"). The moth – with the twisting of its tiny meek body – had seemingly perforated time itself.

Over and over, emperors, kings, ministers, presidents, and prime ministers were assassinated: in their carriages, in official open limousines, in squares where they made speeches. Rulers were deposed from their thrones and from under them rose others who carried the same name and only the numbers following their surname's changed, or they were replaced by the ones who deposed them who in turn were also overthrown, and in the end the masses again waited in anticipation for someone who had the power to rule. Perhaps out of the weakness of old age, he now tended towards that; the age comes when it's fitting for a man to realize the limitations of his powers. History is blind, as hasty as a young girl and as feebleminded as an incapacitated old woman; only the world is older than her.

"I'd like us to have pretty sheets, red ones, made of satin. And candles all around and a nice smell, like incense. Or maybe to do it in nature, that could also be nice," said the girl with strands of dyed hair, "looking up at the stars above -"

"You'll get ants, Etti," said the plump one. "That's what nature's like, they'll sting your ass."

And what does his son, who hasn't been a boy for a long time, do? He gets up and leaves. The same way he went off to the Lebanon War, and after the war a kind of obsession took hold of him, he searched for hidden intrigues and in every single event, indicating how the lives of men had been regarded as unimportant. They were terrible accusations, conspiracy theories that only a twisted mind could have formulated, but his son claimed – no, not claimed; shouted, became angry and mocked – that anyone who rejected those claims without closely examining the facts was simply afraid to face up to what they were liable to show: that the government had made fools of us and was still doing so; that we tend to be gullible and believe them, and that we prefer to cling to lots of soothing fabrications and not face up to one undermining truth. Was he also inferring that Nachman had chosen to close his eyes throughout most of the years of his marriage? Even when he once saw his rival on the beach chatting with Ada, he chose to believe that it was just a chance encounter and that she would brush him off like any respectable woman would do.

Now his son had gone off to that English village, he had got up and left. And in a short while, a few weeks and at most a few months, he, Nachman, would also be leaving here, yes: he would be found on a bus on the way home, after not having got up from his seat even at the last stop, or he'll be found inside the apartment, on the double bed of which half is vacant, or in the entrance lying in a pool of urine – that's how he had found his mother, in an old dressing gown – the phone would ring and he wouldn't answer, or the doorbell and he wouldn't open, there would be a pounding on the door and he wouldn't hear, it would be kicked in and his body would be shoved forward, dressed in loose underpants and a yellowing undershirt, after trying with his last strength to get up from the floor. Perhaps he would scratch the door with his fingernails like one of the dogs.

Or perhaps he would be found here in the municipal library, in this very hall, his forehead laid on the table on one of the volumes of the perforated newspapers, his mouth open and his false teeth out of place, and a moth feeling its way straight into his open eye.

33

England, 1994

Day gradually turns to night in the sky surrounding the house, and above the tree-tops a gathering of low clouds can be seen from which the rain is hesitant to drizzle. On one of the mornings, a covering of frost could be seen over the lawn and fields, but the snow here is sparse and temporary and the English village is never cut off from its environs the way Leh was for many months of the year.

The man Amnon has come to meet here is probably clinging to life like his father, but their forefathers – McKenzie's and his father's – weren't afraid to endanger themselves, not on their wanderings nor in the remote place they landed up in. For some moments, from a distance, that Himalayan valley seemed like a slot on a roulette wheel into which two-legged balls are rolled in a totally random fashion, but in fact his grandfather and McKenzie Sr. had rolled up there by their own will. What could he hear from McKenzie Jr. that he himself doesn't know? Everything or nothing.

He would have to wait for quite some time south of Leh, until the roads would be uncovered again, and hope that the asphalt wouldn't be washed away down the slopes by melting snow; and even the picture of asphalt chunks being washed away in a turbid torrent and the skeletons of buses rolling down into the depths wasn't deterring, on the contrary: there's was a sense of freedom to it. A hundred years after his grandfather died there it certainly couldn't be considered a dangerous place – many people go there – but perhaps his grandfather hadn't died from the dangers there or from the hardships of the way, but rather from what had motivated him to make that way.

Small wonder the people of this quiet village still remember that during the years their country was still an empire, one of its inhabitants landed up all the way at those mountains; after all, even trifling matters were stored in everyone's common memory, from the crack made in the church bell two hundred years ago to the lightning that struck old Geoff's barn the winter before last. Their fathers had been born here and their father's fathers as well; they had never emigrated from here; they had never fled to another place. Even when Prince Rupert's cavalrymen dashed across here, their father's fathers sat in their houses and watched the horses galloping past.

This had been noted by Reverend Carter in his leaflet (this is where Frog-welldown Lane starts, through which our route passes today. Not far from our pub, over three hundred years ago, Prince Rupert led King Charles' cavalry-men during their forced retreat to the south), and the Reverend also mentioned Franklin the builder and master craftsman as well as the jubilee of the local soccer team, and the wooden plank bridge that its players erected for their community over the small brook next to the pub – a bridge wider than that erected at the other end of the village by the polo team.

There our route will begin, right in front of the lovely home of Mr. and Mrs. Treadwell, the Reverend wrote in his leaflet, the handiwork of our builder and master craftsman (now retired) Mr. Bert Franklin, beloved by all, may he make a speedy recovery from his illness. We shall advance in a northerly direction, on our right the grazing pastures our sheep are so fond of, and on our left the stalks of grain. Let us not forget, my friends, that after the rain the path becomes muddy, so best be equipped with rubber boots (a new shipment has arrived at Mr. Stapleton's shop, and a discount will be given to all who bring our leaflet with them).

Up until the beginning of the twentieth century, only a few white people had reached that region – this he learned when he conducted his investigation before the trip, and with the same thoroughness that characterized him during his good years at the newspaper – and the mark the British had made during their years of rule didn't last long. The black Bentley that had been brought there by circuitous means had no road to travel on, there wasn't even a path wide enough for a cart to pass through (there weren't any carts there; the only wheel that turned was the prayer wheel the Buddhists turned in their temples), and it was stored in one of the King's stables. Mice gnawed the choice leather upholstery, and a family of rats set up home under the scratched rusty engine bonnet, its air horn had been disman-tled and was given to the prince who desired it as well as the winged statuette above the radiator, and exactly a year later it was harnessed to two pairs of sturdy yaks whose coats had been combed with a meticulousness suited to their vehicle (that event too was documented in a number of sources, but in most of them was attributed to a Maharaja and his bulls). Afterward, the wheels with their axles were dismantled, and the engine and all its pistons were uprooted, and for some years the car was carried on palanquin poles by a dozen sturdy coolies. It must have been an awe-inspiring sight: the shell of that Bentley being carried in the air with its headlights extinguished and with the glass panel that separated the driver from the passengers.

His grandfather reached Leh before that, and the hospital the Mission built there even today has little resemblance to an actual hospital. That was one of his fears when he was sent to India by the newspaper: that he would fall ill with some intestinal disease and have to be hospitalized and rely on local doctors. Yes, he,

who had fearlessly interviewed senior members of the Mossad and the General
Security Services and wasn't afraid to cast doubt on truths that endangered the
freedom of anyone who opposed them, dreaded the Indian intestinal parasites,
and the first time that he left the hotel they attacked him and upset his stomach.
At first, he intended going north to Ladakh and not limit himself to the areas of
the riots he had been sent to cover, but the weather forced him to make do with a
conversation in the hotel bar.

"I've already been to Ladakh once," the Canadian said to him after two glasses,
"and I intend going back there next week. No matter what, I'm not coming back
here."

He asked him what exactly he meant: to this hotel or to Delhi?

"To go back anywhere," the Canadian answered and signaled to the barman
by clicking his fingers to pour out again for both of them. Gupta was the barman's
name, and during the next rounds the Canadian enjoyed enunciating his name:
Gupta, fill me up another one, thanks, Gupta, you're tops, Gupta.

It transpired he had already found himself a place in northeast Ladakh, and
when the monk who was dying there leaves this world – "attaining a better reincarnation," the Canadian said without a trace of a joke – he, the Canadian, would take
his place in the cave. Sure, there are many waiting in line, but there's a well-known
way of persuading the heads of the monasteries; he demonstrated his meaning by
rubbing his thumb and forefinger together. At the time, he found it hard to decide
whether the Canadian was being serious: in conversations such as those in hotels
and trains and planes, a man could tell his conversation partner anything, from
a profound truth to a total fabrication, only because it was absolutely clear they
would never meet again.

There's nothing to it, the Canadian said, after all, every dollar is worth a lot
more here, and anyway he won't be needing money again, nor would there be
much left over from what he's planning for himself here tonight, and afterward the
monastery would take care of his needs. "Rice and water," he said, "it's best to limit
oneself to the most basic things."

Sitting with them at the bar were two Indian businessmen, a German and a
Danish tourist; and two young Indian women who looked like escort girls sat at
the far end. There were few more beer drinkers at the tables behind who seemed to
be businessmen, and at one of them a young foppish Indian with an oiled forelock
was making an effort to amuse an older English woman and making sure to fill her
glass each time it was emptied.

"That's why I came here," the Canadian said, "to narrow myself to the most
basic needs. Aren't you drinking? The alcohol here is less harmful than the hotel
water" (drinking the water was forbidden, even accidentally while washing, not
even rinsing out the mouth from toothpaste). "You see those two?" He gestured
with his head at the two women at the end of the bar. "In an hour's time they'll be

coming up with me to the room; I'm spending all the money I've got left on them, except for what I'll be needing for the journey."

At the end of the bar, the two of them were sipping Martinis measuredly in thin stemmed glasses and seemed to be biding their time.

"Maybe after a night with them you won't want to go anymore," he said to the Canadian and was jealous of him.

"On the contrary," the Canadian took a long sip, "I'll get up in the morning with a terrible headache and without knowing at all what happened last night or what I've caught from them. Maybe I'll discover that while I was asleep, they went through my wallet and took everything, even the check book. Not that it matters much, my wife cleaned out the account anyway."

"Is your wife here with you?" Amnon asked. The glass he had drunk on an empty stomach had apparently begun to make him hazy; he felt hot.

"My wife's in Canada," the Canadian replied. "She's a home bird, my wife, doesn't like travelling, prefers to stay at home. Even when she made out with my best friend, they did it in our house. Pour me a little more of your poison, Gupta."

Had his grandfather perhaps granted himself a night like this in Petersburg before going off to Leh? And only then - as if all he had been through hadn't been enough for him - boarded the train and landed up in the East, out of despair or seeking adventure or was it a case of simply fleeing for his life? Amnon would be coming from the south: from Delhi to Pathankot by train (this time he wouldn't be delayed unnecessarily for a day in Delhi), and from there on to Leh – three-four days of exhausting travel on routes that even thinking about them fill the heart with joy: how he'll sit on the roof of a bus with worn out brakes together with Indians and their sacks and see the mountainous landscapes changing from all sides and feeling no more foreign than he had felt in that English village.

The first time he saw McKenzie Jr. on the path in the field he had no doubt it was him: he was walking the lovely Irish Setter in place of the redhead boy who had walked him in his absence. He had waited a long time for this opportunity, and stopped on the path and complimented the dog, on his shiny coat, on his wise eyes, on the way he ran; he already knew that the people of the village greet everyone they encounter on their way, and frequently stop to chat for a while. He once had a dog like that, he lied to McKenzie without hesitation, a wonderful dog, the most wise and loyal of them all (although he never had a dog like that, they had indeed been wise and loyal).

He also complimented the dog's obedience; one short whistle was enough for Jonesy to run to McKenzie and there was no need to throw him some object for him to return panting. His master was glad for that compliment, but it seemed he was beginning to size him up – this stranger who had come to the village. He hadn't yet heard from the pub dwellers all the waitress had said about him.

"I'm on holiday here," he lied to him again and complimented the entire rural area as well, its landscapes and its serenity; it was easy to do that when standing opposite the fields surrounding them both from horizon to horizon.

The Irish Setter turned to a nearby tree and lifted his leg and urinated, after which McKenzie approached the tree and examined the stain that left on the trunk: a slight reddishness could be seen there. Jonesy had already run off following the elusive thread of a scent, ready for action and joyous.

"Poor thing," McKenzie said, "he's urinating blood. You can't tell by looking but he doesn't have long to live and doesn't know it. And he won't know it until his final day, all Jonesy's wisdom stops with that."

Hesitantly, like asking about a beloved family member, he asked him what illness the dog had, and McKenzie said something that sounded like the name of a disease. Amnon looked at the dog who appeared to be completely healthy other than for that reddish stain that he had left on the trunk, but he had found a pretext to talk about his dogs and their ends: how he had taken them on their final days to the vet to be anaesthetized, and how they knew they wouldn't be returning from there (he especially remembered the eyes of the Pointer who even through the murkiness of cataracts appeared to have a great and complete understanding).

"I'm the devil that anaesthetizes them," McKenzie said.

Here he had to express amazement, as if he didn't know that his conversation partner was a veterinarian by profession.

"Someone has to do it," McKenzie said. "I presume butchers also say that but if only there was also someone to help us leave this world without feeling anything."

The dog continued to run on the path in pursuance of the scent and McKenzie followed with vigorous steps. He must have been over eighty and Amnon complimented him.

"Thanks," McKenzie answered. "But I'm like Jonesy."

The second time he saw him was in the pub one evening and he asked if he could join him at his table, and McKenzie, though he was sitting alone, didn't seem particularly happy about it, but was too courteous to refuse.

When he sat down, he didn't waste time on polite conversation and told McKenzie that he had always dreamed of becoming a veterinarian – it was not a complete lie; in his childhood he had really dreamed about that too – but life led him somewhere else. That's how it goes, who doesn't get pushed here and there by life, he said, directing their conversation on to the desired track.

He ordered himself a glass of white wine while McKenzie studied the bubbles rising and bursting in the glass of beer that he was holding. "Yes, that's how it goes in life," he replied, an indifferent reply, "it always pushes one to all sorts of places one hadn't previously thought of." His eyes turned to the side, as if he had had enough of this conversation and these banal statements. "How's Rachel, Tommy?" he asked a tall and very thin man who drew near to their table, and the man called

Tommy replied that thank the Lord, Rachel's fine, absolutely fine: as lovely and happy as ever, and providing milk as before; and even if David still has more than a little to learn until he reaches McKenzie's level, he definitely seems to be on the right path.

From McKenzie's face it was unclear whether he appreciated the compliment paid to him. He sipped his beer and relished the drink; it seemed he had completely forgotten about the young man seated opposite him. The man called Tommy walked away and Amnon put his glass down; the wine hadn't gone to his head yet, despite him not having eaten anything since noon, and he felt clearheaded enough for this conversation. He had a grandfather like that, he said; no, not like Tommy, although Tommy seems very nice, but one that life had sent off to some remote backwater in the East; no one even knows exactly where he's buried.

McKenzie placed his glass on the cardboard coaster. "When you're dead you're dead," he said. He moved the glass so that it stood exactly in the center of the coaster. "Jesus said, and not that I'm a follower of his, let the dead bury their own dead, it's a clever sentence. Our priest always quotes the lesser important things Jesus said, and no wonder, the spring bazaar interests him more than what's really important. The bazaar and Stapleton's boots." He expelled a disparaging exhalation from his thick ruddy nose.

The man called Tommy approached the corner table and stood to chat with those seated there, and Amnon tried to redirect the conversation to its prior track; he said that his father is the same age as McKenzie, but not as robust as him; he said that he fears to think of his father walking a dog of Jonesy's size, not that there are fields where he lives, at most a small public park. His father, he said, lives in the city, but his grandfather was born in a village and died in a village, but thousands of kilometers separated the first from the second. They were separated by mountains and deserts, and much else.

"Did he also have dogs?" McKenzie looked bored; perhaps he feared he'd be asked to diagnose all sorts of symptoms of dogs' diseases from afar.

Before their conversation could go awry again, he said to McKenzie only very little is known about his grandfather who was born in Southern Russia and died in some remote backwater in India. Not a backwater, a valley so high up one could hardly breathe in it, not that he had died from that. Only then did he discern some elusive spark in McKenzie's eyes, but again the man called Tommy passed by and McKenzie turned to him and said: "Just don't neglect her udders, Tommy, you have to take care of that in time."

More people came into the pub, among them the three old ladies who the week before had celebrated one of their birthdays with a chocolate cake and candles and balloons tied to the backs of their chairs. They too greeted McKenzie Jr. and he returned a polite greeting.

On seeing them, Amnon expressed the requisite thought aloud: had they all been born here in the village? And had they always live in it, and will they die here? Generation after generation, how different it is to the situation in his country, where everything is new and people change apartments every ten years. "I presume that you too," he turned to McKenzie, "were born here?"

"You don't presume correctly." McKenzie took a long sip from his beer.

For a moment it seemed the conversation would come to a close with that, but McKenzie put down the glass and said: "I, young man, was born when England was still a world power. I was born when people still said the sun never sets on the British Empire, and what became of it? Hello, Mrs. Haynes, I'm sure David will find what's wrong with Kitty. Everyone here says that he's excellent."

Mrs. Haynes, an old rosy cheeked woman with pinkish shades in her white hair, was slightly offended by his reaction, but cheered up when she was called by the three old ladies to their table. It was probably their regular table, and the remnants of a balloon still dangled from a string tied to a chair.

"They were all born here," McKenzie said. "They lived here, and they'll die here, Mrs. Haynes and all her friends. When I came here, do you think they gave me so much as a welcome? The four of them turned their noses up at the sight of me and had they not needed me years later to take care of their cats and canaries they would have carried on turning their noses up to this day. Cheers, Mrs. Haynes. Perhaps a little beer might help Kitty, should David fail."

Amnon cautiously asked where he had come to England from, and McKenzie lingered a while before answering.

"I came from the end of the empire," McKenzie replied when she drew away. "Not that the empire only had one end. It was like an octopus in its heyday, before everything started to rot. But that end was especially far away, and high as well, the highest. And when there's no oxygen, do you know what happens?"

It wasn't a question.

"What happens is that the head doesn't work properly," McKenzie replied to himself. "What happens is that people do terribly senseless things, what happens is that afterward it's hard to rectify them." He took another sip, longer than all the previous ones, and Amnon waited for him to continue.

"Such terribly senseless things," McKenzie said, "that after them a person sends his son as far away as possible, just so that he won't be hurt by their results."

The son of the greengrocer came into the pub in his shiny leather jacket and right away approached the counter and began chatting with the waitress. She stopped taking an interest in Amnon the day she heard where he came from, and on all the following evenings she didn't even greet him. The wine that he ordered she placed in front of him in silence and refrained from any conversation, as if he alone was guilty of all his country's crimes ("I don't like what you're doing to the Palestinians," she said to him on the first evening), and he, after all, had only been really guilty concerning one of them.

"My grandfather also died in a high place," he said to McKenzie when he saw he wasn't intending to speak further; and told him in his grandfather's case the problem wasn't the lack of oxygen, it might have been better if it had been the problem, but already in Russia his grandfather had behaved strangely.

"In Russia?" McKenzie's eyes wandered over the bar where a few small bowls of peanuts stood, offerings the regulars would receive for free and others would have to pay for.

Amnon explained: his grandfather had been born in Russia but didn't die there. People drift from place to place, sometimes by desire and sometimes not; and just why his grandfather had drifted there isn't clear. The same spark that had previously passed over McKenzie's eyes reappeared.

"God only knows what he did in Russia," Amnon said, "that afterward he had to flee that way, and Buddha only knows what he did in Ladakh."

"Buddha doesn't know anything," McKenzie answered. His gaze, beneath his grey tangled eyebrows, lingered on the greengrocer's son who was bending forward toward the waitress on the other side of the counter and examining the butterfly brooch on her blouse with his fingers. "Neither he nor Jesus knows, nor anyone else, not even our dear priest. Was your grandfather a believer?"

The waitress drew a step back from the counter, and the greengrocer's son, with those same fingers, fished out a peeled peanut from the small bowl in front of him and popped it into his mouth.

"A believer?" said Amnon, and although his conversation partner was perhaps not really interested in these details, he explained that his grandfather was born into a religious Jewish family but had left it together with religion; he left everything, and apparently didn't miss anyone in Russia, and least of all God.

"It's hard to blame him," McKenzie said, "Religion's a fool's consolation. After all, your Jehovah also doesn't know anything. No, Mrs. Haynes, we're not talking about someone you know."

"Blame?" Amnon pondered. In that matter, he said, one can't blame him, but in other matters one could, in more than one or two. From McKenzie's face, a long and slightly flushed face, it wasn't clear whether he had succeeded in piquing his interest, but he continued and said that for some reason his father was sure his grandfather had been an exceptional personality, a hero, a daring leader of a group of revolutionaries, even if there was no proof of that; the older his father gets the more he exalts his father.

McKenzie's eyes wandered to the table of the four old women who were deep in twittering chat and from time to time shot curious glances at their table.

In any event, Amnon said, it seems that in Russia his grandfather had been involved in some problematic matter, he had most likely got into trouble with the law and was forced to flee, and one day he simply boarded a train and reached Ladakh.

"There's no train to Ladakh," McKenzie said dryly, but not like catching out a lie but rather pointing out a fact that is supposedly known to everyone: no train can reach those low oxygen altitudes.

Amnon mentioned that his grandfather came from Russia and not India; from Petersburg, to be precise; and that the Trans-Caspian – had McKenzie by chance perhaps heard of that Russian line? – travels from Petersburg to Andijan, and it's not that far from there, at least in terms of those regions. From Andijan, he said, one can continue to Kashgar, and from Kashgar to Yarkand, and from Yarkand to Leh; not by train, but with one of the convoys that pass there.

"No, Mrs. Haynes," McKenzie said, "it's not in England. There are other places in the world than England. People live there and marry there and give birth to children and send them here by ship, and here all sorts of irritating girls" – he turned suddenly to Amnon – "You didn't meet me in the field purely by accident." His eyes scrutinized him; dark bags hung under them, and his tangled eyebrows shaded them, but his gaze was sharp and piercing.

Amnon admitted to his guilt with a nod of the head. But he really once had wanted to be a vet, he said, and he really does love dogs – throughout the years he had lived alongside one, from childhood and in every place he's ever lived. "I loved them more than all the friends I had," he said, "I was never sorry over a woman the way I was sorry over my dogs when they passed on." It was true, and not a truth to be proud of, and he took a sip of the wine and after it another. "How's Jonesy doing now?"

"Jonesy?" McKenzie replied. "He continues to wag his tail at the angel of death. If only I could do that."

Their third meeting was at McKenzie's house, a two-story cottage surrounded by lawns larger than those that surrounded the house Amnon was renting at the other end of the village. McKenzie opened the door wearing a tattered dressing gown and slippers with squashed heels and gestured him to enter. His grey hair was uncombed, and it seemed that the thick grey hairs on the curves of his ears had become longer.

In the room, past the passage with its hangers and umbrella stand, was a real fireplace; not like the one in the house he rented, where the landlord had placed a Philips electric fireplace in the spot meant for wooden logs. There was also a small sofa and two armchairs and a hand-woven oriental rug, a thin woolen Turkish carpet whose once sharp colors had long faded.

"It's nice here," Amnon said, despite that it was evident from the state of the upholstery of the armchairs and the sofa, and from the dust that covered the shelves and the carpet, an old man lives here by himself. The same smell prevailed here as in his father's apartment, a mixture of body odors and stuffy air and a slight moldiness and meals that had been warmed up too many times.

"But you haven't come here for beauty," McKenzie said. "Sean, come here," he called to a large Persian cat that entered the room with a raised tail, "do you also like cats? Were you ever sorry over a woman the way you over your cats?"

With a silent mincing walk, the cat drew near to Amnon and rubbed up against his leg, and when he bent to it and reached out a hand and stroked it, the cat arched its back and purred.

"Who's ever sorry over women?" McKenzie said. "What good does it do? I had a wife for almost fifty years, Helen was her name, a good woman, no question about that, but for the last forty years we hardly had anything to talk about. Not that it hindered us from putting on a performance for our children and the neighbors and everyone else, we even succeeded in convincing ourselves a large part of the time."

"I lasted just four years," Amnon said. His eyes searched for the Irish Setter, but he only saw the reddish hairs it had shed on the carpet and the sofa; he must have lain on it a lot, and apparently lived peacefully with the cat, like Albie and Puma had lived with them; watching them it often seemed that at least half the mutual antagonism attributed to dogs and cats was an evil plot made up by humans.

"Jonesy's taking a walk." McKenzie answered his unasked question, and with slightly shaky fingers retied the cord of his dressing gown, under which brown faded corduroy trousers could be seen. "My grandson's taken him out so that he won't go crazy here with me. Jonesy won't get to run in the fields for much longer." He turned his head to the window, but through the white lace curtain only fields with linden trees separating them could be made out and the shadow of a large cloud moving over them and darkened them.

"He's a nice fellow, your grandson," said Amnon.

"A loafer!" said McKenzie. "A little loafer! He doesn't take him walking without me paying him for it. That's how everyone is today, money-money-money! Grandpa Charlie give me, Grandpa Charlie buy me. Perhaps it's my good fortune that I won't have to see him becoming even worse as he gets older. Do you want some tea?"

No willingness could be heard in his offer, and Amnon didn't reply.

"You wanted to talk to me about your grandfather, no? So, start talking and let's not waste both of our time. You're a young man and you must have other things to do, and I've already reached the age when there's no more time to waste on all sorts of courtesies. The angel of death" – he fell silent for a moment when the cat jumped onto his lap – "doesn't ask anyone whether he wants to come with him or not. You're scratching me, Sean, stop it."

Amnon looked at the cat who had started to knead McKenzie's stomach with its paws, the way Puma used to do when they were all still living in one house, he and Naomi and her small son and Albie, and in winter his claws would get caught in the sweater and had to be carefully removed and Naomi would become angry about that amusement.

"He won't ask you either, the angel," McKenzie continued. "Even though where you come from everyone's a heroic soldier, no? Defeating everyone."

The cat had become a little more relaxed on McKenzie's stomach and seemed very content there.

"No," Amnon replied, they don't defeat everyone. And besides which, he said, McKenzie isn't going to give the angel of death an easy time.

"Why should he have it easy." McKenzie's hand with its old age spots stopped stroking the cat who lifted its head and fixed scolding eyes at its master. "Once, a long time ago, you haven't heard this yet Sean, he already tried to take me, he almost dropped me from the height of twenty thousand feet when I flew to Turkey with a herd of cows. Cows, Sean, relax, not cats. Only at the last minute he changed his mind and decided to wait a while with me, he dropped the plane a few days later into the sea not far from France. Has he already tried to take you ever?"

Amnon gave another glance at the window: the shadow of the cloud was moving onward, and the linden trees were now captured in its darkness. "Not exactly," he replied.

"People started thinking I was immune," McKenzie said. "First that plane, then there was a nervous horse that almost kicked me in the head, and in the end some aroused bull barely let me out of the cowshed alive, and all in one month. After that, the angel left me for some time and busied himself only with animals I treated. Isn't that so Sean? Do you remember how he almost killed you? What terrible fights I had with him, fair play is not his field, no sir, that angel's a rogue. At times you think you've beaten him and that's it, the bull or the dog have been spared his scythe, but the next morning you discover once again he tricked you in the night. Has he ever tricked you?"

Amnon hesitated again; that matter wasn't supposed to arise, though there were cats and dogs there as well, lots of dogs, and they had a lot of work among the ruins of Tyre and Sidon, work that was well rewarded. "Not exactly," he replied again; after all, it wasn't him the sea at Sidon had tricked.

"It'll happen yet," McKenzie promised him. "He forgets no one, that angel, he's got an excellent memory." The cat in his lap lifted its chin and waited to be scratched there, the way Puma had done. "How old did you say you are?"

"I didn't say," he answered.

When he told his age, McKenzie nodded his large, long head, and passed his fingers through his white hair, thick as the hair of a young man. The angel of death, he said, doesn't care about age, and one can never know which disguise he'll choose for himself, no sir. For instance, when he came to my parents, he came with his scythe inside a tiny mosquito and in that way killed Mother with malaria, and for Father he found another method, he came to him from the genes, and not that Father hadn't given him enough reasons to do it. "He was a veterinarian," McKenzie said, "for this whole region, and in India he suddenly turned into a doctor for humans and even ran a hospital for them, and all that wasn't enough for him, he wanted more. I hope in your life you don't do half the senseless things that he did."

"Maybe I've already done them," Amnon replied.

McKenzie studied his face with a doubtful look, the look of someone who has seen many things in life, too many to accept all sorts of vague answers. "One pays for senseless things," he said. "And you don't look as if you've already started paying for something, certainly not the big payment."

The cat fixed its green eyes on him, and McKenzie passed the tip of his finger between them. On the other hand – he continued - sometimes it takes years, and the payment comes with interest, and meanwhile, for safety's sake, someone else pays, that's how it works. He, for example, landed up here with Mrs. Haynes and her nice friends only because of his father's senseless doings. "You also don't like Mrs. Haynes very much, do you, Sean?"

"Did you come here from India?" Amnon asked, although he knew the answer.

"I came from the moon," said McKenzie. "Straight from the moon. After all, that's why you were looking for me, to ask about the moon, no?" From his lap, the cat fixed its eyes on him so that he'd continue to stroke it, and this time he chose not to respond to its gaze.

"I was sent here as a little boy," he said, "I was on the road, so to speak, for over a month, like a wanderer, and put on a ship in Bombay; a boy of five orphaned by his mother, a boy who hardly knew there was such a thing as the sea, because the biggest thing that he had seen up till then except for the damned mountains was the lake at Tsomoriri. Have you ever heard of Lake Tsomoriri? What have you heard about?"

"About the caves," Amnon said, although he still hadn't intended to talk about that.

"And here," McKenzie continued, "what didn't they make fun of, my accent, my clothes, even the color of my skin, despite that in a few months it had become as white as theirs. What did you say you had heard about?"

"The caves," Amnon repeated. In order to divert the conversation from a gloomy direction, he made some lame joke that connected the Indian reincarnations with the nine lives of cats (the seclusion in the cave was designed to promise a better reincarnation), but it failed to even amuse himself.

McKenzie then rose from his chair and went out of the room, and his squashed slippers were dragged on the wooden floor until they stopped at the back of the house, and a moment later water flowing and cups and glasses clinking could be heard, as well as a curse when some drawer was slammed.

Until his host returned from the kitchen, he pondered exactly what he would say to him; there was a time he had thought of presenting himself as an investigative journalist, and to that purpose had even invented an article whose subject was foreigners who had disappeared in the region from the beginning of the twentieth century – there had been more than few who it seemed had vanished into thin air. At the far end of the house, a cupboard door was opened and slammed shut, probably a kitchen cupboard, and at the same time the cat jumped into his lap and expected him to take the place of its owner for the time being, to which he acceded. He did it with a practiced hand, with the right rhythm and the right strength, and when the cat closed its eyes, he felt the vibration of its purring through its coat and his clothing.

McKenzie entered with a tray in his hands and on it were two teacups and a small jug of milk and a bowl with sugar cubes in it. "Whoever can explain to me," he said, "how all the filth of India doesn't get into the tea leaves is a genius. But there's no tea like theirs."

"You don't like India very much," Amnon said.

"I was sent from there – the milk's not for you, Sean - even before I knew at all what I liked and what I didn't. When my mother died, my father sent me here like a parcel, and if you ask me if I would've gone back there, my answer is: no sir, definitely not; not after everything one sees in London today. I'm not a racist, heaven forbid, but when London starts looking like Bombay, no sir. It's as if I've been sent back there, and once again without being asked. Come here, Sean, give our guest some rest."

With a perfect jump, floating and precise, the cat returned to his master's lap and sprawled out there again as if he had never left him at all.

"I hope I haven't insulted him," Amnon said knowing there was little point trying to appease cats before they make the extent of the insult clear to all and their disdain for their insulters. Afterward, he plucked up the courage and asked McKenzie – that is to say, if it wasn't too impertinent – why in fact he was sent from India to England in his childhood.

"I already told you why," McKenzie replied. "because of senseless things that I myself didn't do but had to pay the price for. Stop it, Sean. Imagine" - this he also said to the cat – "that you kept on hearing all kinds of odd stories about your father; what sort of a life would you have had? Not that he was much of a saint," he turned to Amnon; it turns out that Sean's father was lustful, adulterous and argumentative, an instigator of cat fights, and perhaps Sean would have become like that had he not been castrated at one years old.

What exactly the senseless things were that McKenzie's father was purported to have done in the East, his son couldn't say: perhaps some medical malpractice resulting in a patient's death, a family relative of the local king or a European explorer who had been admitted to the Mission hospital; or perhaps trading in the hospital's medicines such a rumor had reached here; and perhaps it wasn't medicines but something completely different, with far greater profits. Money-money-money, the motive for many things, perhaps his covetous grandson had inherited that lousy quality from him.

"People also spoke of antiquities," McKenzie said, "but people say all sorts of things, and there'll always be someone to believe it. That's how people are, there's no limit to the lies they're prepared to believe in, even if it's only to blacken someone else's name. Not that he was any kind of saint. Was your grandfather treated by him in the hospital?"

Amnon was taken by surprise and hesitated: the short businesslike letter that was attached to his grandfather's possessions had indeed been signed by McKenzie Sr., but whether he had previously treated him or just determined his death, he didn't know.

"I only hope that you don't have any complaints about the treatment," McKenzie continued, "because you won't get even one penny from me, we won't give him anything, will we, Sean? We'll keep it just for us, for us and Jonesy, we'll make Jonesy a lovely tombstone when he leaves the world, and we'll visit him every day. And afterward, come and visit me as well, Sean. You can hunt as many mice for yourself as you want, there's no shortage of them there."

He then asked him the cat's age, it seemed ageless: for a moment it kneaded bellies like a suckling kitten, and the next froze in a regal recumbence like a prehistoric sphinx, and to that McKenzie answered that Sean too, was already not that young, no-no, far from it.

"But," he said, "he wasn't summoned to undergo an urgent examination whose findings were not hard to guess. You weren't summoned, were you Sean?" The cat again appeared very content: his eyes were closed and it seemed that his entire being was concentrated on the pleasure of his owner's touch.

Amnon stirred his tea. A fine smell rose from it, but the cup wasn't too clean – just like the cups in his father's apartment.

"As for me," said McKenzie, "it's definitely my last reincarnation. Sean might have nine lives, but I have one. And there are days when even that's too much, I'm tired." He asked Amnon what else he had heard about those caves, and Amnon, after another sip of tea, chose to tell about the people who come out of them and not about the ones who imprison themselves in them until death (quite a lot had been written about that, and he took the trouble to read everything he could lay his hands on) - they come out half blind or completely blind after their sight had degenerated, with long hair and fingernails, their bodies reeking, and all who receive them on their exit treat them like holy beings.

"I once knew a Canadian," he said, "whose greatest dream was to enter a cave like that."

"Why would a man do such a thing to himself?" McKenzie asked. "You wouldn't go in there, Sean, under no circumstances."

"His wife cheated on him," Amnon replied. "And the last night I saw him in Delhi, he took two escort girls up with him to his room."

"Did you hear that, Sean?" McKenzie said. "That's also something we never did. There were many things we didn't you, but you, Sean, might still do that, why not? My wife Helen," he turned to Amnon, "was a good woman, don't misunderstand me, good and loyal, but in bed she preferred doing crossword puzzles. Did your girlfriend also do crossword puzzles?"

Afterward, he asked if he had children, and Amnon answered his question.

"Then you're as free as a bird," McKenzie said, "be careful of that. Tell him, Sean, what happens to birds that aren't careful."

A shiver passed through the cat's body, as if it had understood the matter in question. "They fly-fly-fly," McKenzie said, "until they crash into a window-pane, and below there's someone with a tail waiting. Have you never crashed into windowpane?" he looked at Amnon.

Amnon waited for him to continue.

"My father," McKenzie said, "also thought himself a free bird, he moved thousands of miles away from England, he also moved from Calcutta and Simla. And what turned out in the end? I turned out a veterinarian like him."

But hadn't his father become a doctor for humans? Amnon pondered,

"Here he was still a veterinarian," McKenzie replied. All his father's instruments remained in the village clinic, exactly as the day he had left them, and after being sent here he used to go in there and play with them. They looked like instruments of torture from the Inquisition, but he played with them like toys, and that father of his seemed to him at the time like Albert Schweitzer and Florence Nightingale rolled up as one, and not just a rogue. "We don't like rogues, do we, Sean? They once tried to sell fake cat food to Sean, tell him what you did then, Sean."

Sean fixed his eyes on him.

"That's all you did?" McKenzie said. "How sanctimonious of you."

The cat blinked with modesty, and when its back was stroked, it raised its behind.

"There was a Russian there, yes, and if it was by any chance your grandfather, there really is no reason to be proud of it. You can tell that to your father, at his age a person should already begin to get along in life not only without a father but without some other things as well."

"I'll tell him."

"And if he's my age," McKenzie continued, "you'd better hurry, my friend. At that age there isn't a person whose plans aren't suddenly spoiled, that's the way it goes. And someone whose plane almost crashes at the age of forty, will surely have something wrong with him discovered in every self-respecting hospital after the age of eighty. We're simply not made to function for such a long time."

He turned his head to the window, and the Irish setter could be seen with the redheaded boy: Jonesy was running joyfully to fetch the branch the boy had thrown for him, and with the branch between his teeth, he looked more joyful than he had been when chasing after it.

"He seems completely healthy," Amnon said.

"As do I," McKenzie replied.

Through the window, the boy released the branch from between the dog's jaws and lifted his arm and threw it again with all his might, and right away the dog leapt after it. This time the branch landed in the field, and the dog was swallowed among the stalks of grain and a moment later only the wagging tail could be seen above them. Amnon tilted the cup to his mouth; inside it he saw a murky line on the porcelain, most likely a tea stain that hadn't been properly rinsed. And nevertheless, he took a sip, the way he did with his father's cups.

Had McKenzie never been interested – he asked when he put the cup down – to return there?

"Where to there?" McKenzie asked, and he answered him.

"I already told you," McKenzie said, "let the dead bury their own dead. Jesus didn't say many things that are wise, but that one is. I never even went back to Turkey, what for? There's only one place I've been going to over the past years and that's France, and not because I like the French, no sir, but there was a family here whose poodle I cured who then invited me to stay at their holiday home in Deauville. Monsieur McKenzie, they said to me, come whenever you like, you saved our Bijou, so our home is yours when its empty. I thought to myself, why not indeed? Go and be on your own for some time, it won't do you any harm. And see something of the sea; after all, you can't see it from here. I also thought that Jonesy would be glad of that, running as much as he wants on the beach and looking for crabs, maybe he'd even enjoy the water. Not Sean, cats don't like being moved from their place, you don't like that, do you, Sean? What would he do without his armchair?"

He stroked the cat who surrendered to the touch of his hand despite the shaking and tilted its head toward it and gradually closed its eyes again.

"And did you go?" Amnon asked.

"I put Jonesy in the car," McKenzie replied, "and all the way he kept his head out of the window the way likes doing. And when we got onto the ferry he went berserk, he had never smelled the scent of the sea, he didn't stop running on the deck and barking at the seagulls, especially when they caught some fish. Only the last winter, when he started urinating blood I stopped taking him, I didn't want him there next to me. I don't mean Jonesy, but rather that scoundrel of scoundrels. It was as if he was saying to me through the dog's urination on all the trees in the area, take note Doctor, I'm getting close to you. You don't want to go for tests, and here I am coming close to you anyway."

He looked at the window: his grandson could again be seen on the path at the edge of the field, and once more he threw the branch far.

"One night, I'll never forget it, I even dreamed about that plane. In the end it fell to the sea, you know, with forty sheep in it, and I dreamed they floated to the shore opposite the house and I had to treat them."

"And did you succeed?" Amnon asked, but his thoughts had wandered from the French shore to a different shore and it wasn't sheep that were floating there.

"In the dream, yes," McKenzie replied. "In the dream I had tremendous success."

He turned his eyes again to the window.

"Being alone does something for one. My wife Helen's been dead for almost ten years, but here in the village you're never really alone, people constantly need me to take care of their animals. And there in Deauville, who do I have to talk to? Then the mind starts working. You gaze at the sea in the window and think that almost forty years ago you could have ended your life in that plane, and you didn't. I was given an extension, at the time it seemed like the greatest gift one could dream of, and what came out of it in the end? Two children and four grandchildren came out of it, cows and sheep and horses and cats that I cured came out of it, as well as those I didn't succeed with, that I was widowed and fairly quickly forgot I had ever been married came out of it, those tests came out of it."

His train of thought was cut off, and his eyes wandered toward the curtain that moved lightly in the breeze.

"When we saw its engine starting to burn, life seemed such a precious thing. One moment it's yours, and the next it can be taken away from you forever, many years before its time. And how I loved Helen then, I loved her like a sixteen-year-old boy! Bill and Noel didn't care about their wives at all, they were already planning what they'd do with the Turkish women, but I did care. I dreamed of the children we would have and how they'd come to us on weekends with the grandchildren. And now what's left of all of that? Sit still, Sean, I wasn't asking you."

A bark was heard from outside, but he didn't turn his head.

"It might have been better to get it all over with then," McKenzie said. "Without all sorts of tests from which nothing can come other than discovering it was in your body from the beginning, in the genes. If you want to take some advice from an old man," he said and didn't wait for an answer, "think twice before you decide on going, even if there had been some crazy person in your family who had made that route. Tell your father that someone who travels so far has little chance of returning. Perhaps at long last he'll come to his senses regarding his father, a moment before he's told, 'sir, we are terribly sorry to have to inform you, sir, that we've found you have such and such.'"

Again a bark could be heard from outside, and they both turned their gazes to the window.

"Do you ever watch flies?" McKenzie asked. "A fly also flies-flies-flies like a bird, certain that it's completely free until it suddenly encounters a windowpane and discovers that it's closed, and from that moment, it cannot stop hitting into the window until it dies. A moment before it still thought it was completely free and happy, but now happiness is over and life is over. So, you tell me what's better, to mistakenly believe you're completely healthy or to hear the truth, that half your body is done for. You see, even when I was on the ship from India it had already begun its work, I didn't feel it yet, but it was already there. That how it is with genes. And when that blind man at the port touched me, I was perhaps already no less ill than him."

"The blind man?" Amnon asked. His host was talking to himself more than talking to him.

"The blind man who wouldn't let us alone," McKenzie said, and with a voice addressing no one specifically, he began to speak about the way from Ladakh to the south with the Indian assigned to bring him safely to Bombay to a certain lady who had promised to watch over him during the sea voyage, a Mrs. Kingsley. How shocked she had been by all the dirt that had accumulated on him during that month on the road – by the smell of him, the state of his clothes, his lice, the length of his fingernails, and all the swear words he had learnt on the way.

Other swear words had been uttered in Bombay, and not that he had heard them coming from Mrs. Kingsley, in her home even the bugs ate with their mouths closed. But a week later, all the way to the port, the rickshaw-walla didn't stop swearing at everyone he encountered, coolies and beggars and cripples and the blind, he was already thinking they'd never reach the ship because of all those who stuck to them. He wasn't yet aware how much he would suffer on the ship, a five-year-old boy without a father and a mother, only with that Mrs. Kingsley. That was how they reached the quay, and for the first time in his life he suddenly saw the sea; not Lake Tsomoriri, but a real sea, an ocean.

"It's something I'll never forget my whole life long," McKenzie said, as his eyes wandered over the expanse of fields beyond the window, "that first time that I saw the sea." How enormous it seemed at the time, and how many ships and boats were there, not less than the rickshaws, but a thousand times bigger, and when they reached their ship, they couldn't see the upper deck from the rickshaw, it was so high, and masses of people leaned on the railing and looked down, and masses more made their way up, families and couples and singles and porters with their luggage, and a moment before they reached the gangway, the blind man began to bother them.

He suddenly reached out his hand for a donation and by accident touched his face, and even before some cry came out of his mouth the blind man said: "What a lovely boy we have here, what a brave boy, a prince not a boy, we have a Maharaja here!" And he began to feel his face with his fingerless hand, until finally a scream came out of his mouth that the entire port heard, the entire bay. His screaming only abated on the deck, but until then he just screamed and screamed, and what did Mrs. Kingsley have to say about that? A boy who swears like an Indian shouldn't wonder that Indians stick to him like that and what's more call him a Maharaja. She repeated that in the cabin every time she took pity on herself for having to watch over him. Just because she owes some favor to Mrs. Harper, does is mean she has to be in the boy's company for the entire voyage, instead, for example, of being invited to the captain's table at meals or to the bridge deck or even to the captain's cabin; who would invite her when she's with a rascal who behaves like some little Indian who grew up on the streets? Who could have guessed she'd be brought someone like this, with no upbringing to speak of and without minimal hygiene habits? The moment she saw the child with that idiotic Indian accompanying him she felt out of sorts.

McKenzie leaned forward slightly, "The moment she saw me she felt out of sorts. Did anyone ever say such a thing to you? And moreover when you're a little boy?" He stroked the cat's head but was not paying attention to his movements, and the cat sensing it, recoiled from his hand.

The Indian alone was enough to make her feel out of sorts – Mrs. Kingsley said – the whole time it's please Mrs. Kingsley, thank you, Mrs. Kingsley, if Mrs. Kingsley want me go I go right away and he know Mrs. Kingsley she look after Charlie like a mother. "Does he call you Charlie?" she asked him in shock, and for the entire voyage, when she wasn't busy vomiting her insides out, he had to hear her complaining about this stupid job she had been saddled with.

She especially complained in the evenings, when she was forced to remain with him in the cabin until he fell asleep, and to stop her from going, he would fight sleep and keep his eyelids open with all his might by various means. "Little rascal," she said when she discovered he was trying to trick her (he held a drawing pin in his hand to stop him dozing off), "if you don't go to sleep right this minute, I don't know what I'll do to you; do you want me to call the captain to tie you to the mast?" That's what Mrs. Kingsley said to him while the first officer waited for her in the corridor and another time, when she was even more irritable, said: "If you annoy me, I'll call that blind man, do you want me to call him?" And from then on, it became her fixed threat.

"That's something I also will never forget," McKenzie said.

From his armchair, his tea having become cold after two sips, he began to elaborate on the things he won't forget besides the sight of the sea: how that hand felt his face up and down and back again, touching the forehead and the eyebrows and the nose and the cheeks and the chin and the mouth and the eyelids, worst of all was when the blind man's finger stumps were so close to the eyes. Sometimes in the middle of the night, he said, especially after the last time he was called to undergo more tests, he wakes up with his pulse racing and sweating all over from fear, because someone is feeling his face a fingerless hand, feeling it up and down and back again. And in the dream the Bombay quay can be seen not far from him, no more than a few meters, and it's totally dark at night, without any torch to shine on it and totally empty except for one large ship. Its horn cannot be heard but it's waiting for him to board, he's the only person on that damned quay and that ship is waiting only for him, and it's not sailing for England.

"Do you know where it's sailing for?"

Amnon nodded his head slowly.

Outside, through the window, the dog could be seen again running joyfully after a flying branch, with a few surviving leaves on it. No ship could be seen there, no quay; only a mass of dead fish floating on the water.

Part Three

1

Leh, 1910

"I had the honor of meeting Schliemann exactly a month before he died," the Italian said when the three of them were still in Italy and the century hadn't yet changed, "and even then, he didn't stop spinning yarns to anyone who would listen. So if it seems to you that I talk too much, it's only because you never heard Schliemann. You have no idea how much he would have talked in my place here."

The Italian really hated me; up to that day he had spoken to me in a mild manner. Perhaps what they saw around them changed his tone - what they saw ad nauseum from McKenzie's point of view – by then he was sick of all the statues and paintings they passed by, as if that was the way to lessen the anguish over their first year of marriage.

"And if there had only been an iota of truth in his stories," the Italian said, "but no! With Schliemann even what seemed like the truth, one would be well advised to doubt, with him it was advisable to always check everything twice."

"You can tell that even from the name," McKenzie said. "What sort of person would call himself Schliemann?"

He didn't exactly remember who Schliemann was, it was the Chianti talking. He already knew then, four days after they arrived in Italy and a decade before the century changed, that even spaghetti with a meager portion of meat could be stomached or doughy lasagna, but the name Schliemann still remained foreign.

"His name was Heinrich," the Italian said, "the name his parents' gave him. Have you heard of his father?"

"What about him," McKenzie said. He had no interest, not in Schliemann nor in his father, and thought the conversation might be terminated with that.

"He was a priest," the Italian said, "a priest who shamelessly stole money from the church fund, so it's no wonder his son turned out like that. But the church fund wasn't enough for his son, he wanted something really big, the biggest and the dearest. That's the kind of person he was, Schliemann. His was a case where the apple fell very far from the tree if you understand my meaning."

McKenzie understood; for a moment his mind wandered to Oxfordshire and to the village, to the apples that fall from the tree in the garden, dropping onto the awning above the kitchen entrance and rolling onward from there; he would frequently wake up at night from the sound of the blow they made – first on the awning and then on the ground. They would often continue to roll to the hedge and only stop there, very very far from the tree.

"He desired treasures," the Italian said among the museum's prized possessions (that's how they were defined in Baedeker: prized possessions). "Nothing less than a treasure would do for him, and he found it under the ground. That's to say, he arranged for it to look as if he had found it. At least half the things Schliemann discovered were not at all from the place where he said they came from, he himself put them there to fit in with the story. That's the way it is: gold without a story is worth less, you wouldn't believe how many carats a good story is worth."

It was the third time they had met the Italian in one of the museums to which the Rome Baedeker sent its readers, instructing them where to stop for a while and what to skip. He had already spoken to them twice before, but this time talked at length.

"I'm not sure how it would have worked on me," Kate said. He wondered about her responding to the conversation – when they walked out of the hotel toward the alley that led to the Via Veneto, it seemed she wasn't going to utter a word, and that's indeed how it was until that moment in the museum; the previous night was still troubling them both.

The Italian scrutinized her with his small eyes and McKenzie didn't like his gaze.

"Schliemann was a sly fox," he said, "and a month before he died, when I met him in Amalfi, he was no less sly. People don't change at the end. Being dead doesn't make him a saint.

"Saint Schliemann," McKenzie attempted to make a lame joke and it was clearly evident the Italian wasn't impressed by his sense of humor or any other attribute he tried showing. His veterinary doctorate was of no use here, nor the hundreds of cases where animals had benefitted from his care, from cows to Siamese cats; in the Italian's company he felt like a country bumpkin.

"In the end," Magnani said, "they really did build that saint a grand mausoleum with the pillars of a temple. He had earned a fortune even before all his discoveries, but that wasn't enough for him. He made money in Holland, in Russia, even in America, and still seemed too little to him. He understood one simple thing very well: gold in California isn't bad, especially if everyone who found a grain of it had to go over to the bank you opened, but gold in Greece, with good story attached to it, is worth much more. You yourselves tell me what sounds better, the gold of some Bill or Tommy or the treasures of King Priam?"

McKenzie couldn't remember who King Priam was though knew the answer the Italian expected to hear, but Kate answered before him. She too had drunk Chianti earlier in the trattoria next to their hotel; that morning they both chose to begin their day with alcohol and the blessed haze it would cast over them and exempt them from talking. Her eyes sparkled, and a blush spread over her delicate skin from her forehead to her neck and perhaps further down from there, over all those areas which on the past nights had remained beyond his reach.

"And then there was also Schliemann's wife," the Italian said. At the time, it seemed he wouldn't cease until he had made dust and ashes of his rival, even if the maggots had already done that in the grand tomb he built for himself in Greece. "The Greek girl he took for a wife straight out of school. He had barely divorced his previous wife when he found Sofia and married her. He arranged the divorce in America, they would never have validated it here. That's how it is when you have money."

Kate hesitated. That fact of Schliemann's marriage to a schoolgirl she found distasteful, and McKenzie was much surprised that she, as opposed to him, the country bumpkin, was hearing about it for the first time in Italy. Hadn't Schliemann been spoken about in London? Hadn't the whole of Europe spoken about him, certainly in all the great capitals, from Rome to London. Naturally not in the village, what have farmers to do with Schliemann? The deepest digging ever done there was by ploughs and gravediggers.

"When Schliemann met her," the Italian said, "he could have been her father, the very least her father! A friend of his, a bishop, made the match. You see, the father steals from the church fund, and afterward the son's friend pairs him up with a schoolgirl. It was a good deal on both sides because she later helped him out a lot. With every lie he palmed off, Sofia said: yes, it's true, I was with him there, in Hisarlik, in Mycenae, everywhere; I helped Heinrich dig with my own hands. Each time Schliemann destroyed something on his way to something else, Sofia was there. Don't you read newspapers in England? Didn't they talk about Schliemann?"

"Only about how famous he was," Kate replied. "Not about those stories. Besides which, in their village" – she indicated to McKenzie by moving an eyebrow – "newspapers don't always arrive."

"O u r village," McKenzie corrected, and the Italian looked at both of them again and it seemed some unpleasant thought was passing through his mind.

"If you think about it a bit," Magnani said, "there's some poetic justice in his death. Not that he deserved to die, I don't mean that, heaven forbid; if people died because of their lies there wouldn't be a living soul left in the world. But to die from an ear infection?"

He had previously talked about the dubious privilege he had had in meeting Schliemann in Amalfi exactly a month before his death; as usual, Schliemann was between journeys, and he too was before a journey, to a different continent and to a place many times farther away, one only few reach, but Schliemann the Great wasn't interested in anything other than his own journeys and the yarns he spun everyone afterward.

"Maybe his ears had become blocked from all his lies," the Italian continued, "and there's a certain justice in that."

"Did he die of an ear infection?" McKenzie asked. The universal cattle remedy came to mind, as if the horizons of his profession had been narrowed to the small gap between the bull's horns, and the Italian was right about what he thought of him. Its qualities were detailed on the label: highly effective against ear infection, lung infection, inflammation of the intestines, urinary tract infection, milk fever, inflammation of the udders – it never disappoints! He recalled Kate's ridiculing the large bottle and its label when she first visited the clinic and he exhibited all his appliances and remedies to her. Hadn't Schliemann behaved toward the Italian just as Kate had behaved toward him? No, she did have some good intentions, like trying to learn the names of the medicines.

"He died in Naples," the Italian said. "Not that the doctors didn't advise him to remain in hospital. But why should the great Schliemann, who had the whole of Troy in his small pocket, let some young doctor tell him what to do. Schliemann, after all, told Agamemnon and Priam what to do; he showed them where exactly to bury their treasures, so what's some young Italian doctor to him who says: Mr. Schliemann, you have pus in your ear; your ear, it could kill you yet if you don't take care of it properly and stay in bed."

"So, he died in Naples," Kate said, "far from his home. It's nevertheless a bit sad, isn't it?"

"To which home exactly are you referring?" Magnani asked. "He had many homes. Wherever he made money he bought himself a house: in Germany, in Holland, in America, in Athens,. And in the end that's where they brought him, to Athens. They built him that mausoleum there with the pillars of a Greek temple, so that in two or three thousand years' time someone might think some ancient king was buried there."

"Schliemann the First," McKenzie again attempted a joke and again the Italian shot him a critical glance after which he again felt like a farm boy whose horizons are those of his cows, and not a doctor of veterinary science. Magnani knew about everything, from sculpture to ancient manuscripts in extinct languages, from Latin to Sanskrit, while he, McKenzie, knew only about animal and had cured many of them, but Magnani discounted his knowledge just like Kate's London friends.

"Not the first, nor the second," the Italian said, "and do you know why?"

They didn't know, and Magnani was happy to oblige. From the first time he saw them, he attached himself to them– not the typical cocky Italian, nor a tourist, but a short middle-aged man, plump, self-satisfied, knowledgeable and conceited, one who bears a grudge against his rivals even after their deaths and flirts with young women with the same determination; a man whose long absence from his country had led him that July week to the commonplace routes all tourists take, from museum to museum, from church to church, from piazza to piazza. Already on their first meeting, he told them he had returned from a long journey, in comparison to which their trip seemed like a stroll to the grocer, and they found out he had excavated a site in the sands of a vast desert that Schliemann didn't even know existed.

"With all due respect" – afterward he spoke about his other colleagues in the same manner: "Hedin, *with all due respect*"; or "Stein, *with all due respect*" names of people McKenzie would have forgotten had he not met them at the commissioner's wife's tea evenings – "in the end nothing will remain of the newspapers that wrote about him, fish will wrapped in them."

That was the first time fish had been linked with the Italian, even if only indirectly; and more time would pass – almost a decade – until mother of pearl and seashells and seaweed and sea salt would play a matter in his matter.

"His discoveries would suffer the same fate as those of Columbus," he said. "Don't think that I have anything against Germans especially. After all, Columbus was one of ours, a son of Genoa, only the charlatanism bothers me."

"Columbus?" McKenzie asked; at least he'd heard of him.

"Columbus thought he saw Indians in America and Chinese in Cuba," the Italian said. "He saw a palm tree and thought it was a coconut, he saw some ordinary bush and thought it was cinnamon, only because he wanted cinnamon to be there. He saw some natives and asked them to take him to Peking, and even when they brought him to some forlorn village with a few huts, Columbus still didn't realize he had mistaken the continent. That's how it is when someone doesn't let any fact confuse him and when he's surrounded by enough fools who believe him. That's how it is with Schliemann – people simply don't yet realize how mistaken he was and how much he misled them."

The people around, tourists like them, continued to move from statue to statue. Only a few took any real interest in statues, and the majority seemed to be obediently following the instructions dictated to them in Baedeker, the way they had done and will continue to do in the recommended churches as well: Santa Maria Maggiore, Santa Maria della Vittoria, Santa Maria del Popolo and Santa Cecilia in Trastevere – those names hadn't been forgotten, nor would they be – that's what he and Kate had also done on all the previous days, despite that there hadn't been much enjoyment in it. A month before the journey, he had begun to brush up on timetables and routes in Baedeker as well as a few useful words in Italian, and ultimately they hadn't been useful, and certainly not in the most important matter of all.

"That's the way it is," the Italian said, "people like to be told stories. And it didn't take long for Schliemann himself to turn into a story, he and his Sofia had become the royal couple of the archeology world. There's no shortage of people far more talented, but they didn't have the stories he attached to his findings."

Was he referring to himself? At the time McKenzie didn't devote much thought to that. He hoped with all his heart that the Italian would cut his talk short and that their ways would part, despite that he and Kate didn't have any place they were longing to go to, and certainly didn't have the tranquility required for just sitting relaxedly in a café. But the Italian went on; for some reason Kate seemed prepared to listen to him prattling on, as if nothing interested her more than disputes between archeologists.

"Stories," the Italian said, "how he had dreamed from childhood of discovering Troy, and how many years he waited before he would finally do that, and how solely for that purpose he made a lot of money, money didn't interest him at all for its own sake. And how all that would never have come into being without the help of one charming Greek girl, and how did he meet her?"

"A friend of his arranged their meeting, that Bishop, no?" Kate answered like a diligent schoolgirl rushing to show the teacher how well she had studied.

"He heard her reciting Homer in class, who else if not Homer? Did you also recite Homer?"

Kate shook her head from side to side and a lock of hair fell onto her forehead adding charm. "Only Shakespeare."

"Imagine you're still at school," the Italian studied her face, "and one day, while you're standing and reciting to the class, the door suddenly opens and a middle-aged man who could be your father enters and listens to you and afterward begins to pay you compliments: on how lovely your voice is, on how precise your accent is, and on your classical features and in the end he tells you in front of the whole class: you will be my wife. You have such a lovely voice and such understanding and such a beautiful wise face, I don't want anyone but you. Will you marry me?"

McKenzie's patience expired and he lost his sense of humor. "She's already married," he wanted to remind Magnani, something which at the time didn't need reminding, but Magnani had already continued.

"Imagine," he said, "that afterward he himself teaches you more that you learnt at school, takes you on trips to all sorts of countries, introduces you to important people, takes you to the best hotels in Europe: the Adlon in Berlin, George V in Paris, the Majestic in Rome. Wouldn't you be grateful for all that?"

Kate deliberated for a moment while McKenzie glared at her. She ignored his gaze.

"Wouldn't you confirm everything that he says he did? Wouldn't you say: yes-yes, he did that and I was there with him when he discovered Agamemnon's mask and Priam's treasure" – it seemed that he was hesitating whether to mention more names – "but perhaps where you come from there aren't things like that."

"We have a horseshoe that fell from King Charles's horse when he fled from Cromwell. They still talk about that horseshoe today in the village," Kate said.

"From what year is the horseshoe?" the Italian asked with serious consideration, and when McKenzie mentioned the year, it was apparent from the look on his face the Italian's opinion of him worsened even further.

"They'll even show you the stone that he sat on," Kate added, "in the field behind the church, and tell you if you sit on it like King Charles and listen carefully, you can hear Cromwell's horses, those are the sort of things they have."

"We have," McKenzie corrected her again, and the Italian looked at them both, and the thought passing through his mind was almost articulated by his eyes.

True, he couldn't know what they had been through the past nights, but after all, a young couple on holiday don't talk that way. Their first holiday had been in Brighton in a small hotel at the end of the promenade where they went on their honeymoon, and the roar of the sea that made Kate so happy bothered McKenzie like the roar of the city, there was no way he could understand the enjoyment people found lying on the beach in complete idleness. After that there had been a very long year in the village during which Kate tried to adjust to the place – she tried to befriend its landscapes, its people, to busy herself with all sorts of housework – but with the lengthening winter and every morning the fields grey with frost to the horizon, her gloom deepened, until one day she declared that if he didn't want her to go mad, he had better take her out of there occasionally. That's how one Saturday morning sitting opposite the fireplace whose flames even seemed grey, the thought cropped up of the Italian sun and the piazzas of Rome.

"It sounds enchanting to me for a girl to recite Shakespeare in class," she said a moment later, "and hear a knock on the door and someone who she's never seen says to her, you'll be my wife. And that she'd travel with him and meet interesting people and live in the most beautiful places; what girl in the world wouldn't be enchanted by that?"

"Where are you staying?" the Italian asked, and Kate mentioned the name of the hotel as well as the name of the small alley coming out of the Via Veneto – what was its name? Much time has passed since then, more than a decade, and a considerable amount of time has passed since the second series of his meetings with the Italian, not in Rome but here in Leh, in this mission hospital.

"What for example did you use to recite in class," Magnani asked, "the sonnets?" It seemed as if he was waiting for her to quote from one of them.

Kate hesitated. She knew Shakespeare's plays well, there had been years when she dreamed of getting a part in one of them, until she realized that her actor friend won't help her in that, even if he had the power to do so. She had awoken from those dreams even before coming to live in the village and didn't even remember one line from the sonnets.

"I'm sure that you would have read them beautifully," the Italian said, cheering her up the way one does a child.

She hesitated and her eyes wandered over the bench in front of them. "At school I was always asked to read at ceremonies and thought one day I would be an actress and the whole of London would come to see me. I still had many great dreams at the time." Was there a quiver in her voice? It was hard to tell in the commotion of the museum.

He feared she'd say there were no ceremonies in their village other than marriages and funerals, but she was silent and sad: her face became drawn and her eyes lost their luster. Their village hadn't yet been mentioned by name, it was one the Italian wouldn't have heard of, nor had anything been said about its bell tower that certainly wasn't ancient enough in Roman terms. Nothing had been spoken about the fields, flat and not hilly like those of Italy and not surrounded by mountain ranges like the those of Leh, the fields surrounding the village were covered with snow only a few days of the year and not for months on end like the fields here.

Yes, the winters here seem endless, and the mountain peaks – the highest of the world's mountains – are perpetually snowbound, and only in summer its slopes are exposed, barren as the ground of a desert, but then the valley blossoms as if it hadn't been covered in a decimating whiteness for nine consecutive months: fields of wheat and oats and alfalfa blossom, apricot and peach trees blossom, poplars and willows blossom, turnips in the gardens of homes blossom.

The ground of the real desert where the Italian dug, isn't even barren; just wandering sands. Beyond those vast mountains and far ahead east of Khotan and north of the Kunlun mountain range, its dunes begin. Rivers of melted snow that ran between them die out, their abundance lost in the sands, and he, McKenzie, hadn't seen even one drop.

Yes, that's how it was: he, who in his youth had sailed from one continent to another without thinking twice, hadn't even gone as far as Khotan, despite having sent the Italian there.

2

It happened this way, if you study everything from the start:

The caravan left on its way at the appointed time, on the day that had been set, at the designated hour; even more punctual than the caravan on which he had yesterday sent little Charles to Bombay and from there to the shores of England and from there to Oxfordshire, the county of his birth, in the hope that no one there would hold his son accountable for his father's deeds.

Tenzin had no difficulty in controlling four camels and eight ponies and five Bihari coolies, and the Russian – he again called him that to himself, the way he had been called before his name was known – helped him to the best of his ability, despite his lack of experience in conducting a desert caravan. In fact, he wasn't supposed to participate in that journey at all nor any other, and had it not been for his insistence he would have remained in Leh in the lodgings Harper arranged for him after his release from hospital. It was the missionary who undertook the problem; straight from the hospital he led him to the place where two weeks earlier he had housed the drugged Russian woman with her son (that's what they called her at the time, "the drugged woman," despite her knowing full well what she was doing).

By then the Russian's body had completely recuperated, and as to his mental stability, Tenzin said he was sure he would recover and conduct himself like a man again, exactly as he had been in Kashgar and in his country before that – the rumor had already circulated that he had been a revolutionary and that his head was wanted in Russia for some daring deeds he had got up to. At about the same time, an incident took place in the bazaar that convinced the doctor of his patient's fitness, and for a while he took it as a blessing, a blessing which in the end turned into a curse.

Two months after that incident, the caravan went on its way, and the doctor remained standing at the side of the track and watched it draw away. He stood alone at the time, and only a street dog, thick furred and dusty like all the dogs of Leh, was so kind as to open a sleepy eye for a moment. The animals' hooves raised dust, a pony neighed, and another answered it, and one of the camels (a Bactrian camel with two humps, as if it had been specially created for carrying anchors) left behind a foaming puddle. Only when the caravan had become small in the distance and had almost disappeared, the Russian boy came running, breathless and panting, and with tearing eyes looked for those leaving, until the doctor showed them to him disappearing around the bend of the track and placed his hand on his lean shoulder so that he wouldn't try to run after them. "Why don't you go back to your mother, Sasha?" he said to him. "She must be worrying about you now," despite that she most probably hadn't noticed at all that he had slipped away from the inn.

The second caravan, the one that little Charles had been sent on yesterday to Bombay, was actually late in leaving, even though Rasul led it and took pains to prove to everyone there was no one more experienced than him for the job. There were many animals and many men on it, and the more there are, the greater the danger they'll be delayed: here a trunk that wasn't properly tied falls, there an unruly pony tries to shake off its load, a camel has an attack of fury and starts to kick. Dozens of people turned out to watch this caravan, the second, and stood on both sides of the track to part from their dear ones: wives from their husbands, children from their fathers, mothers from their daughters; and he, Doctor McKenzie, stood among them and watched little Charles riding with Rasul on his pony held in his arms, and Rasul lifting Charlie's tiny hand for him to wave back, and felt a twinge in his heart.

Afterward, little Charles became engrossed in other matters: for instance, the pony's mane, its injured ear, the cloud of flies circling above it, its blinkers, and also what the pony in front suddenly evacuated from its posterior – a sight that especially captivated little Charles – and Rasul was so eager to please him, that he was even prepared to reveal something to him he usually preferred to conceal: how until fairly recently, before becoming what he is today – and-who-doesn't-know-what-Rasul-is-today; after all, there's no one in Leh who doesn't know what-Rasul-is-today – his job was to gather what came out of the behinds of animals into baskets, for a bonfire to be lit from it afterward. In the end, all food comes out of there, and not only that; it also turns into fire. And where is Rasul today? Little Charles didn't know what to answer: they were still in Leh, but they were on a pony's back on the way to a distant place that he didn't know of; and after all, that had also been said about his mother, Dianne, she went to a distant place and didn't return from there.

"Rasul's with little Charles!" Rasul declared from his place, very proud of the trust the Sahibs had placed in him.

Then McKenzie withdrew slightly backward and was swallowed among the other spectators; it was better they block his view and block the view of him, and that the pain of parting not be lengthened.

There had been no other solution after Dianne's death: only to send little Charles to England to his Aunt Sylvia (a half-aunt in actual fact) and hope that no one in the village of his birth will pester Charles because of him; to send him away and continue to live the same dreary routine that he had lived for years here in Leh until he lost his mind for the second time –there really is no other way to describe his behavior – when he carried out actions that are not to a doctor's credit.

"Not to his credit," is naturally an understatement, because what would you call a man, not specifically a doctor, who decides to marry a woman who everyone other than himself sees how unsuited she is to him, and when he finally sees his mistake, instead of returning home to his previous life he boards a ship and sails to another country? True, he was still a young man then, and young and hasty men are prone to such acts, and at the time, the act wasn't judged by the standards of the village. Luckily for him, Britain was still queen of the seas with colonies here and there, and much time would pass until it would become clear whether Tenzin's prophecies would be fulfilled, according to which it would be reduced to the island it had been in the beginning.

And what would you call a man who had already succeeded in building himself a reasonable life routine in his new abode, established himself and made friends and even improved his standing greatly – from a veterinarian he had become a doctor for humans and was even appointed director of the hospital – and one summer he decided to jeopardize everything, and for what actually?

"Doctor no do with sense," Rasul said to him after the fact. "Rasul he say all the time to him Tenzin bad man and to person who go with him always bad things happen! But doctor think only he got sense in head and Tenzin good man, and in end everyone see who right. And he who not see – he die."

That declaration had more than a pinch of truth in it: there had been more than one funeral after that winter, though not all were caused by the entanglement he had got himself into. Dianne's death for example, had nothing to do with it (malaria mosquitoes didn't fly in from the desert the caravan went through) and it could be said that had it not been for the entanglement he wouldn't have married Dianne, and little Charles wouldn't have come into the world.

That's what he thought when he saw him yesterday, holding the pony's reins with Rasul and already beginning to forget his father who looked on from the side of the track and his mother who watched over him from heaven (that of course is what they told him). And what else would little Charles forget? The two poplars that grew opposite his window and whose shadows scared him at night, and how Dianne would pacify him night after night, and the turnips that the cows loved so much that when they didn't receive them on time they would show their resentment with a long *mooooo*, and the snowman they made together last winter which for nine months stood in its whiteness between the poplars until it began to sweat and diminish; yes, the snowman became shorter and shorter, whereas little Charles grew from measurement to measurement whose lined markings he continues to see on the wall of his room while his son is growing far away.

"Pony like little Charles much!" Rasul said to the boy. "Now pony no like anyone no more, just Charles!" And the boy – his son – didn't look back. Some waved their hands and blew kisses in the air and called out to those who accompanying them, but his son didn't look back. There's nothing more painful than that: seeing your dear ones shrinking in the distance and not waving goodbye because they had already forgotten you.

When the first caravan left on its way five years ago, the one he financed by his own pocket, only a sleepy dog stood next to him at the side of the track (they purposely left at an early hour so that no probing eyes would see them), and before the Russian boy came running and after he sent him back to his mother, he wondered if the caravan would succeed in its crazy mission. Crazy, yes, such was its mission, though for a considerable time is seemed to be succeeding. He hadn't yet learned that success and failure, like love and hate, both about which he knew more than enough from his first marriage, are bound together like Siamese twins.

The caravan travelled onward, the first one, with its strange cargo, the nature of which only two of its men knew, and its direction was northeast and not west, desert and not sea (the sands of the Taklamakan and not the port of Bombay), despite that in its cargo it carried mother of pearl and shells as well as three anchors. At the time he still didn't know the day would come when he would stand again at the edge of Leh and once more watch a caravan preparing to leave, and with desperately longing eyes would see the son that would be born to him being swallowed in it and drawing away and shrinking irrevocably from moment to moment.

"Rasul he look after little Charles like his child," Rasul promised before they left, "until he bring him to Bombay to lady that doctor say." Mrs. Kingsley waited there for the boy; he had never seen her, but she had many recommendations and no other solution was found for little Charles. Through the cloud of dust the animals' hooves raised and through the weeks their journey would last, he could see little Charles holding Mrs. Kingsley's hand – most likely a small hand in a white glove, no less refined than Dianne's hand – and taking small steps with her up the gangway of the ship in Bombay, perhaps even at the same quay where the ship that brought him from Italy had anchored; ascending step by step with his little feet with that Kingsley on the way to the deck that would take him away from India forever and ever, and still he didn't turn his head back.

The sight of little Charles' head from behind was no less heart-rending than his facial features. There was that point in the center of the crown of his head where the hair branched out in all directions, and in the mornings when it stood out like a small cockscomb, Charles insisted on flattening it with water, and in that way often made himself wet from his neck to his waist, and only Dianne could then say to him: "Come to Mother, my chicken," and spread out her hands to him and calm him with a hug. These are things that won't be forgotten even in years to come, little Charles' cockscomb and that hug of Dianne's.

"If doctor want, Rasul take little Charles to his country!" Rasul boasted as was his habit, despite never having been further than Bombay in the west and Ürümqi in the east. "Because Rasul love little Charlie like his child! And Rasul have lot of children, even if not all them know it."

McKenzie has only one child, and now that he's sent him to England he remains alone. Yes, damn Rasul's pony and Mrs. Kingsley's ship and all the waves of the ocean, no less that the malaria mosquitoes that killed Dianne, and no doubt he'll be sorry about his son's going more than he was sorry about hers. The sorrow over the dead, even the most beloved among them becomes blunted with time; the image becomes blurred, it crumbles like their flesh, but when someone continues to live far away and grows up there, their absence is constantly present and it intensifies from day to day and is many times more painful. Isn't that how he felt about the one who left him in Italy? Year after year, that bitch Kate continued living there with her Italian, until he drew him here.

3

The anchors that were loaded onto the camels had been dismantled: the wooden parts separate, the central rod with its two arms meant to be moored to the seabed, and the lead casing that holds them, separate, and both were wound and wrapped in woven sacks that concealed their form so that no unnecessary questions be aroused. True, their appearance was reminiscent of primitive ploughs more than anything, but carrying those to the desert too, far from any oasis, would have caused one to wonder.

Griffin and Evans had wrapped them in Bombay with their own hands so that no one would see them (the coolies who stole them from the courtyard of the marine museum had been fired immediately afterward). The task of the packing was of course done before the big argument that erupted between them, an argument that was just one of the bad omens associated with those anchors, and had McKenzie not been a realist by nature, he might have believed a curse had stuck to them concerning their being uprooted from their place and perhaps even before that (they had been discovered in the sea, detached from their ship).

The first of the cursed was a coolie whose foot was squashed on the night they were taken from the courtyard of the marine museum ("taken"; what a gentle word for that act). No one had gauged their weight correctly, and when the third anchor fell from their hands and dropped onto the coolie's foot, his mouth had to be sealed first with the palm of a hand (Griffin had a huge hand) and afterward with a fistful of tattered rupee notes. McKenzie found it difficult to imagine those sights, and not only because of the weakness of a doctor's imagination, an ex-veterinarian: the warm and humid night (so humid that even one's eyelids sweat; he still vaguely remembered that sensation), the marine museum courtyard, the stone anchors shaped like millstones and the iron anchors and the wooden anchors shaped like ploughs scattered there. And the wagon waiting in front of the gate, and the bull harnessed to it meanwhile chewing the cud, and the roar of the sea that sounded as if it too demanded the anchors be transferred into its possession. And Griffin and Evans who domineer the coolies and spur them on with the goading calls of sailors lifting barrels onto a deck; and how the third anchor suddenly falls from the edge of the wagon, when the bull moved from its place, and a shout splits the silence of the night.

McKenzie heard about that only a month later, when Griffin and Evans arrived in Leh with their bounty and demanded the second half of their wages with the addition of unexpected expenses incurred in Bombay, and McKenzie wondered if he hadn't been mistaken by not sending the Russian along to keep an eye on them. While Poliakov had never been in Bombay – he arrived in Leh from the north – his experience in terror operations would certainly have sufficed for such a simple mission (at the time, a number of stories had been told about him in Leh, each one more colorful than the one before, and he didn't confirm or deny them).

McKenzie had never visited the marine museum; he had seen more than enough museums in Italy. It's possible he passed it by on his way from the port of Bombay to the hotel the rickshaw-walla brought him to, but at the time he didn't see anything around him other than hordes of Indians and rickshaws and bulls and maimed beggars; millions seemed to be passing him, some reaching out their hands for a donation. In the shabby hotel he found cobwebs as dense as sheets of cloth and damp stains on the ceiling left by the monsoons as well as other stains on the mattress and not only of sweat; on seeing them he knew that he had reached rock bottom.

But the Russian was needed more for a different matter; and Griffin and Evans, past sailors and present deserters, had informed him they wouldn't need-ing any help. They said even if he asked them to bring him Nelson's cannons they would have brought them ("Had Griffin lived in Nelson's time, he would even have stolen his eyepatch," his partner said); and McKenzie – a respected doctor, the effi-cient – as far as was possible - director of the mission hospital wasn't at all shocked by what they said. It wasn't the first time that he had heard them and had already sized them up in Italy.

He first encountered that pair in Brindisi, eight years before he sent the cara-van into the desert. They were still serving on a ship and were ashore on a short holiday, and in a small port side bar where prostitutes stood in the entrance and sat in corners and received clients on the second floor, they said to him: "Doctor, if you really want to escape, India's the place for you, not Italy. Italy's too small." One of them had even heard that in Bombay they were looking for veterinarians for the cavalry, to which McKenzie replied with complete seriousness that he hadn't had the opportunity of treating elephants and the only elephants he had ever seen were in photographs. Even in his years in India, he only saw statues of elephants – the elephants themselves were widespread mainly in the south, and he had never gone south – and in any event, he had moved here to treat people.

"India," Evans said to him, "is simply another world. The first time we went ashore there, d'you know what happened to Griffin? Tell him, Griffin." The rest of the story had already been forgotten. He later encountered the two of them again in Bombay and then their ways parted, until they one day pitched up in Leh as merchants trying to buy Pashmina wool directly from the goatherds of Chang Tang to save on the broker's fee in Kashmir. "You haven't done too badly your-self, Doctor," they said on seeing him in the hospital, "and who gave you the idea of coming here?" In the end their business venture didn't succeed, and four years after their desertion from the fleet they worked in the service of one of the rajas, training a bunch of his soldiers in drilling exercises with arms.

He met them another time when they were acting as bodyguards for a Frenchman who feared some of his men were intending to rob him and mentioned to McKenzie that should he ever need something one day, even something he considers improbable, he shouldn't hesitate to ask them; because as he can see, they take on anything, even guarding the body of a frog eater. At the time, he didn't imagine the day would come when he'd need wooden anchors (by the same token, he could have been in need of an elephant howdah or a hoop of fire for tigers to jump through), and still didn't know about the marine museum of Bombay and its exhibits: steering wheels worn down by captains' hands, bow statues of women whose breasts stand out against the wind, compasses that led armadas, salt soaked ancient maps, anchors made of stone or wood or iron. A few things had to happen before that, and even after happening, more time would need to pass until arriving at a decision, and still more time until the plan was consolidated, and even more time until it could be tested from a practical point of view. The only thing that couldn't be doubted was the will to carry it out, each one with his own motives: he and the distress the Italian had caused him in Rome, Tenzin, and the distress the British had caused his father here. And what were the motives of the Russian who later joined them? They certainly weren't good ones.

In actual fact, they hadn't thought of being helped by him at all, and had it not been for what took place in the bazaar, they wouldn't have included him in their plan. On that day, he and Tenzin had gone to inquire about prices; they already knew the most important items couldn't be obtained in Leh, but they intended to buy provisions for the men and the animals in the bazaar. There's no knowing exactly how the little Russian boy landed up there, but since his mother didn't bother to watch over him, it's no wonder he strayed so far from the inn; perhaps he had followed the Russian without being noticed by him; they were staying at the same inn and stores were going around about his goings on with the mother ("That's what happens when people from the same country come together," they said at one of the commissioner's wife's tea evenings, meaning a kinship of hearts. "Man whose tsumtsum work," Rasul said in the bazaar about a different organ, "all of him healthy already").

Perhaps Sasha left the inn to watch the dozens of dusty animals who arrived with their loads: Bactrian camels, Tibetan yaks, Kashmir ponies, and Yarkand donkeys. Out of them all, the donkeys were most dear to him - camel humps didn't interest him, nor the long wool of the yaks, nor the sweet little ponies, only the long ears of the donkeys. He gave them all sorts of leftovers he found: pumpkin peels, dry chapatti that would crack between their yellow teeth, a fistful of weeds, and when one of them started to bray, there was no sound more pleasant to his ears. He spoke Russian to them in his high-pitched voice, until the donkey driver came and led them away from there.

He tried to pet a dusty dog lying at the side of the way and perhaps awakened it from a bad dream, or the dog was being pestered by fleas, because the moment it awoke it began to bark and frightened the yak who then started to kick and only by a miracle its hoof missed Sasha.

The Russian appeared out of nowhere, it seems he was on one of his wanderings and heard the commotion and ran to rescue the boy. He often wandered the alleys of Leh ever since his release from hospital, and this time it proved useful.

He would peer into shops, hang around various places and practice a few new words he had learnt, enter one of the monasteries and watch the ceremonies or listen to the slow monotonous chanting of the monks, the kind that would put McKenzie into a deep sleep within moments. Quite often he could be seen sitting with the boy near the chorten on the road to the palace; what they did there together, no one knew. On their chance meetings in the bazaar, the doctor complimented him on his appearance and in his heart of hearts waited for some thanks, but it seemed the Russian preferred that chapter of his life erased, including whoever had been a witness to his weakness.

As with all the guests of Punstok, he found no difficulty fitting in with the routine of the inn: he ate the meals, joined in the nightly card games with chance guests, paged through yellowing newspapers left there; perhaps even enjoyed hearing the latest gossip from Calcutta and Simla if he could understand it. When he arrived, he didn't know one word of English, but foreigners here had little difficulty learning a new language, if they needed it badly enough – that was something McKenzie came to acknowledge, despite that he himself was not among them; he apparently didn't need it that badly. At first they learned to count to ten on their fingers; after that how to say fingers; after that how to say hands and feet, stomach shoulders and head; after that I-you-he-we-you-them, and after that simple verbs, not yet conjugating them, and somehow managing to hold a conversation, even if a faulty one. He himself didn't have to take much trouble; it was his patients who took the trouble to make their situation clear to him by every possible means.

Was that the way Kate learned Italian? That was a sight he had no difficulty imagining, despite the deficient imagination of a veterinarian: how the Italian holds her thin fingers and counts them together with her – uno, due, tre – and how he kisses each finger and suspends his lips there, or worse than that, how he counts his fingers and places each one in her mouth and inserts them deeper; or how he touches her nose and tells her what it's called in Italian (il naso), touches her forehead (la fronte), and her cheek (la guancia), and her chin (il mento), and her lips (again she spreads them apart for his finger); and how he also touches all her other organs from her neck downward, and of them all, McKenzie now remembered only the word the prostitute in Brindisi said to him, definitely not a word found in the dictionary, when she asked him if he didn't want another go, at half price, and this time in her booboo. Does he want? He certainly wanted but his body was already not functioning, and after a few words he remembered from the conversation manual the prostitute mumbled another word possibly meaning "tired" or "exhausted" or something else, more definitive.

Unlike him, the Russian knew more than one language; he knew Russian as well as a little French, and apart from them another language McKenzie couldn't identify, until a missionary in the hospital heard him mumbling a few words in his befuddled consciousness and discovered they were Hebrew. "My dear Ed," he said to him then, "you won't believe it, but at long last an adherent to the Mosaic faith has come to our hospital." Here in this Moravian mission hospital, they had treated Buddhists and Hinduists and Muslims and Sikhs, but no Jew had been hospitalized before him. There had been rumors that Stein was of Jewish descent and that his parents had him baptized as a Christian so that his religion wouldn't hinder him in the future – and he had indeed become a highly praised archaeologist – but he never mentioned his origins.

"It's the language of the Bible, Ed," the missionary said to him excitedly, "just look how far that unfortunate people have drifted!" The fact the Russian had been circumcised had been revealed on the first day of his hospitalization, when the coolies unloaded him from the improvised stretcher, and Rasul assumed maybe seriously, maybe jokingly, that this man, who doesn't believe in Jesus or in Allah, might believe in crows, because the whole way he didn't stop looking at the sky and speaking to them like someone praying.

After he had been released from the hospital and before rumors about his past had begun to circulate, Harper tried to enlist his help not only in the study of the sacred language (he had in his library an English-Hebrew bilingual Bible,) but also in his understanding of the people who spoke it, a people whose entire history, despite their having been chosen by the Lord, had been one scourge after another. To that the Russian had only one thing to say (it wasn't difficult to understand even in the hybrid language he used): "And that's how it will go on." He examined Harper's library with curiosity, and when he saw the small Bible that had stopped a bullet with its prophecies, he said any thick notebook in the owner's pocket would have been stopped the bullet, and it was clear that more than the prophecy which had stopped the bullet, it was its caliber that interested him.

How Poliakov supported himself after the Hebrew lessons he gave ceased, was unknown; it was assumed he had brought a small sum of money from Russia which in this remote place one could live on for months.

By some unlikely coincidence Mohan Lai was then caught (many things that seemed unlikely in Europe were discovered to be a natural part of life here). The forger of manuscripts that were allegedly found in the desert had been seized on some new scheme that promised the villagers a cure for every disease. For each patient he tore a page out of some French book he found in the bazaar and laid the page on the affected area and mumbled something vague which if one believed in one would recover. He would probably have continued doing so until the very last page (it was long dime novel romance), had not two of the patients died within a week, twin brothers, and their father appealed to the amban to pass judgement on him. Mohan Lal had a winning retort he had learned during the years he had lived among Christians. When people came to Jesus to be cured he would tell them it was enough for them to believe in him to be cured. Didn't he say to the blind and the deaf?

This scheme demanded less effort than the one before it, when he had made a living forging ancient manuscripts which he sold for large sums to gullible Europeans; for that he had to smoke and yellow the paper as well as sprinkle sand on it whose origin was allegedly the location where the writings had been found. The entire scroll was filled with a mixture of letters taken from a few languages as well as letters he made up with his partners. Had it not been for that fraud, it would never have entered the doctor's mind to do what he did; true, there were other factors – for example, the two weeks Stein had stayed here, and the visit of Callahan, a reporter from *The Simla News* - but all that was preceded by Mohan Lal's fraud.

The French healing scheme raised the question again of the alphabet required for their plan, and it was in this context the Russian's name first arose, and this time not due to his revolutionary past but due to his Jewishness; but they still didn't seriously consider him, thinking it highly unlikely he could be persuaded to become a scribe. One way or another, more important than the writings were the paper and the anchors.

By then, Harper already had lost interest in him; he could have admired even Ladakhi idol worshipers if they showed the desire to believe in a better world but was discouraged by someone who had no desire or faith and washed his hands off him. He had also refrained from his debates with the doctor ever since the evening they sat in the courtyard of the hospital and McKenzie tried to convince him of the logic found in Darwin's theory.

"I respect you, Doctor," the missionary replied to him, "after all, it was I who brought you here and appointed you director, so I ask you respect me about my faith."

"But I do respect you, Robert," the doctor said, "and I'm grateful to you for the appointment. I respect and appreciate your beliefs and your delightful wife. By the way, how is she?" She had recently returned from her annual birdwatching trip to Lake Tsomoriri.

"Respect and appreciate, but in your opinion we were born from apes."

McKenzie waited a while before he answered. It's wrong to take that as an insult, he said, heaven forbid he insult anyone and certainly not him. "We were all born from them, Robert," he said, "me too. I still have a bone in the back which is the remnant of a tail, and I too have apish thoughts. Perhaps you, Robert, don't have, but I still do, and there's nothing to be done about it.

"And who will redeem us, Ed?" said Harper. "Who will redeem us from that apishness, will an ape?"

In the night sky above them, a sky which in Leh seemed nearer and clearer than in any other place, countless bright stars sparkled many times brighter than those of European skies, and the missionary lifted his eyes to them, as if their appearance was enough to prove the folly of that idea.

"Only time," the doctor replied, "and it takes hundreds of millions of years, Robert. Only time will redeem of us of that, and it has no crown of thorns."

How different to the Christian principal was the plan he had formulated with Tenzin, that crazy plan for whose purpose the caravan was enlisted and equipped and went out to the desert and endured a host of hardships; it had no god who sacrifices himself for the people, not one who was crowned with thorns and nailed to the cross, nor the Jewish god who always conceals himself in the heavens, but rather a band of revengeful gods who instead of remaining with their believers sail into the distance leaving behind a desolate desert.

Mrs. Harper participated in their next meeting, and in between biscuits she told of her experiences at Lake Tsomoriri. Happy as a lark she spoke of its pellucid water, about the cranes and the cormorants flying over and diving into it or drifting on its surface, and she also related some of the tales she heard from the nomads. One told of a vast sea of which the lake is just one of its waves, a hasty arrogant wave that strayed from its path and was sentenced to be imprisoned forever among the mountains. The story almost moved Mrs. Harper to tears: how in that primordial beauty the nomads also saw loneliness.

Stories of wandering waters suited their plan, and fortunately there was no lack of those even in the region they were planning to reach. Those stories hadn't been conceived and related owing to an abundance of water, but because of its fleetingness: rivers were desolated in the middle of their course because thirsty sand demons desired their waters; an oasis was desolated because it directed its gaze at the sun; an angry god punctured the bed of the lake with his staff and emptied it; and in contrast to all those was the story about the baby prince who almost perished from thirst until the ground took pity on him and curved itself in front of him like a breast and suckled him. "Another tender story about the ground there," they said at the commissioner's wife home, and when it was hinted how the villagers fertilize their lands on nights of a full moon, a deep blush spread over the ladies' cheeks, one even stifled a giggle in her glove; and who could have conceived then the day would come when the tenderest of them all, Dianne Barnes, would be the mother of his son.

But little Charlie hadn't been born yet when the first caravan left on its way, and hadn't even been so much as a thought; and there was no childish innocence on that caravan, only the desire for vengeance: for him, against the one who robbed him of his first wife in Rome, and for Tenzin, against those who humiliated his father in Dehradun, and, who did the Russian wish to avenge; there was no clear answer to that, but his motives were certainly not positive, even if they weren't those the commissioner ascribed to him on his arrival (he wasn't the Tsar's enemy, the contrary - a spy on his behalf).

Henry, Henry, the doctor thought, you're the only one who came out of this affair intact: you managed to complete building your magnificent home without anyone in Simla or Calcutta asking exactly from which budget the money had been taken; you recompensed yourself nicely for not being promoted, something they hadn't done, nor will ever do.

This is how it is: Darjeeling had wooded mountains and moderately cool air, Srinagar had its lake and boathouses, but anything north of them was like a penal colony, a forsaken land, and it was feasible that the statements Henry made over and over when his by his chances for promotion were dashed, had filtered into their plan;, it too contained punishments and a decree of banishment– those revengeful gods had banished themselves and left their believers endlessly longing year after year; endlessly, yes, like his own longings for his first wife.

It wasn't hard to picture her surrounded by guests in a Roman salon – that was the difference between her and the commissioner's wife: Ann danced attendance on her guests, while Kate's guests probably danced attendance on her – and she must have had a command of the Italian language by now, despite that throughout their train journey to Rome she refused to even glance at the conversation manual he bought. He memorized sentences from it between stations, and she said: "Really, Ed, if I want something, there'll be someone who'll understand me." She had no doubt about that, and in the end she was right. It seemed it was McKenzie who had made the long journey – he left and sailed from Brindisi to Bombay and crossed oceans – but it was she who had really made a long journey, though at the time she perhaps hadn't even crossed one kilometer in the carriage from the hotel to Magnani's home.

After the yak incident, Tenzin suggested the Russian join their plan: a man like that could certainly be useful to them, he said, even if he he'd never experienced the hardships of a caravan in the desert. For someone who all the policeman of Russia are after, who is feared by the Tsar and his generals (so the ladies heard from someone in Simla, who heard from someone in Dehradun; and Tenzin himself had seen something of that when he first met him), what are trifles like these to him? McKenzie didn't immediately agree; he still remembered how the Russian had behaved in the hospital, how he clung to his swoon to the point where it seemed he really wasn't expecting anything other than the crows to peck at his flesh.

"Are you sure it's a good idea?"

"Only fools are sure," Tenzin replied. "My father was sure of your people, Doctor, and what did he get for it?"

That was a matter better not entered into, and McKenzie was quick to change the topic of conversation. Instead, he tried to reckon the significance of the Russian joining the caravan from a practical point of view, and here again encountered the complicated calculation that had sunk him more than once. Food, equipment, animals, every change in one of these led to a change in another: if every man consumes 1 kilogram of food a day, almost thirty kilograms of food a month is required for each one; and if they use coolies and the trip lasts for a whole month, each coolie could carry only his own food and no more, that is to say, animals would be required for carrying the equipment; but then more animals would be required to carry food for the animals carrying equipment, and more animals for carrying the food for the animals carrying the food for the animals-carrying-equipment, and so on and so forth to infinity. Yes, it was a circular calculation from which Issa had rescued him a month before, but with the Russian joining the caravan he had to recalculate everything. All those calculations – it should be noted – were more bothersome than the awareness the act they were about to commit was illegal.

What would Harper have said had he known what he was busy with? What will he say when the forgery is discovered? (For the time being, in all the years that passed, it hadn't yet been discovered, but more than enough damage had been caused even without that.) At least there was one thing he could be sure of: no one in the mission, not Harper nor one of his colleagues, would be in any hurry to dismiss him from his post at the hospital, because where would they find another lunatic who would agree to go as far north as here just to treat Ladakhis and under such poor conditions. There were no firm grounds for supposing the mission would stop paying his salary, and not turn a blind eye to his extracurricular activity during the time of his temporary insanity, and even if his image would be slightly stained, - there were no spotless white coats here anyway - it would be no more serious than the guilt of some others, for example the stain on the commissioner's new house.

As far as supplies went, nothing was different from previous caravans in the desert: rice, flour, sugar, dried peaches, raisins, potatoes, beans. The main difference lay in small luxuries – Hedin had indulged himself with meat preserves, with condensed milk, with cigars; Stein had even bought Mongolian mushrooms to add flavor to the soup. And of course, equipment that did not belong to supplies was required: saddle bags, ropes, saddlecloth (preferably from Yarkand), horseshoes, hoes, spades, axes, pots and pans and other kitchen utensils (preferably from Baltistan). The Europeans took with them a padded tent as well, but on this caravan, and at least at its start, there weren't meant to be any Europeans – the most senior member was Tenzin, and his abhorrence for Europeans was enough for him not to request such a tent. Only later the Russian joined, but after all, the ladies said he had experienced everything in Russia from the infernal fire of exploding trains to the terrible cold of Siberia, and therefore the doctor didn't feel obliged to provide him with anything other than warm clothing, so that he wouldn't be brought to him again with frostbite and sprawled out like a dead man on an improvised stretcher.

And all that, he thought then, costs a fair amount of money, even if they had managed to avoid being swindled (for example, local water containers that tended to leak). As to the animals, here one had to take special care not to hire ones their owners hoped would soon drop dead, so that they would be compensated by an amount twice their real worth. In diagnosing their state, as an ex-veterinarian, he could of course have been helpful had horses been used, but because only camels and donkeys were used, his role had been narrowed to financing their purchase. What had helped, to his luck (so he thought at the time, no knowing know how bad that luck was) was the inheritance he received from Aunt Elizabeth.

In the end, he paid for a horse for the Russian, and another four camels were bought to carry the anchors that were brought from Bombay, and only when he saw them carried on their humps was he able to picture how they would be buried in the sands of the desert, how they would be covered, how they would be exposed, and imagine how much that coolie in Bombay had suffered after one of those anchors dropped on his foot and squashed it; and that, as stated, was just the first of the troubles. It frequently seemed a curse had fallen on them like on those who dared to move the Pharaoh's treasures from their place; but naturally there was a simple explanation for everything, something completely down-to-earth, just as there had been nothing mysterious about Kate's disappearance in Rome, nor had any curse been cast upon her then husband – there was only his stupidity and his blindness, and afterward his quiet understanding, slowly seeping in, that she was fed up with him.

She apparently preferred a short balding Italian, an untiring chatterbox, an arrogant, patronizing, wife stealer.

4

Perhaps one could try to envisage this picture: a laden wagon harnessed to two bulls or to one, making its way at night through the streets of Bombay, drawing away from the area of the port and the marine museum. And in front and behind the wagon, Griffin and Evans riding their horses as if between them a treasure chest taken from the deep was being led and not just those wooden anchors, not valuable enough to be kept inside the museum and left outside in the neglected courtyard. Perhaps beggars looked at the wagon from the sidewalks on which they slept, perhaps children got up and ran after it and hung on to it and tried to see what was hidden underneath the sheet, until they were driven away by curses or the lash of a whip; perhaps Sadhus accompanied the wagon their eyes sparkling within the ashes spread on their faces and inclined their tridents toward it in the name of Shiva; bored cows continued to chew the cud at one end of their bodies and to defecate at the other end to the flies' enjoyment; and until the streets filled with masses of people and rickshaws and carts and merchant stalls and all their tumult and their smells (those were things that were by no means possible to convey in a letter, not the Indian noise nor the Indian stench; that is to say, had the doctor written to someone, but to whom would he write about that?), until then the wagon continues undisturbed on its way.

Out of all the packed markets of Bombay, rather than envisaging the Zaveri bazaar with all its merchants McKenzie thought about the thieves' market and the antiques alley, where every antique or semi-antique object is on display to be sold, from statuettes of multi-limbed gods to ivory combs with one remaining tooth. "Have you been to Mutton Street, Doctor?" Griffin and Evans asked referring to the antique alley, but during his first month in India he hadn't had any interest in antiques; at the time there was nothing more antique than his marriage.

He also had no interest then in temples and mosques from the previous millennium, nor in the tales associated with them, but in Bombay, beneath Walkeshwar Temple, there was a pool whose water sprung forth and rose when Rama shot an arrow at the ground there and pierced it, the complete opposite of the Khotani story about the lake that was emptied when its bed was punctured; and one of the mosques displayed the coffin of a saint who died in Mecca and was transported to Bombay by the waves of the sea for him to be buried there – perhaps the non-identical twin of the Khotani story of the giant statue of Buddha that floated above the sands of the desert back to its pedestal. There was also an Egyptian god – Horus or Ra, the doctor no longer remembered – whose coffin sailed across the Mediterranean Sea, but he heard about him only from the Italian after he arrived here, and for the first time wasn't angry at Magnani for knowing more than he did.

Perhaps the wagon passed by the hotel where he had stayed when he arrived in India, and looking out at it from its windows were all the girls of the hotel as well as some European women, those from whom he had first learned what alienation is – since they had fallen pregnant to Indian men, they were condemned by the European community, and raised their babies in the hotel and made a living from their bodies, and McKenzie the doctor, a good and kind man, a friend to animals and humans alike, helped them make a living ("And have you been with anyone since then?" Dianne questioned him years later, and even after placating her in this matter, she insisted on clarifying exactly how many he had been with in that hotel, as if he wasn't disgusted by being with a woman who a few moments later was with another man, and he replied: no).

Afterward, the wagon travelled north, to Pathankot and to Manali and to Leh, perhaps even on the very same route that he had crossed on his way here. Onward it travelled carrying three covered anchors, first toward mountains wooded with conifers, maple trees, cedars, and firs (and kindly don't forget the cannabis, he reminded himself, what would you have done all that time without cannabis?), and then toward the arid slopes that slanted higher and higher until reaching that comical capital, Leh, and after it, at the distance of a month's riding, the sands of the desert.

It's quite feasible Griffin and Evans took advantage of the way for a few deals better left unknown and that likely contributed to the fight that broke out between them in Leh – a fight in which he, the doctor, had to intervene and try to separate them from each other. One can pour a bucket of water over fighting dogs and calm them, but those two pushed him aside, and as he fell, he thought: to hell with it, if you want to kill each other so badly, why should I prevent you from that pleasure?

In the end, only Rasul managed to separate them and did it with words of flattery: "Not nice Sahibs fight, only Indians fight like so!" And when Tenzin heard about it, he was quick to imitate him and his linguistic errors: "Better Sahib hit Rasul and not hit other Sahib! Rasul like Sahib hit him!" and similar to the doctor, he also wondered why not to allow those two to kill each other. He had no reverence towards Europeans, and this pair proved to him once again he was right.

In Manali they had to replace the wagon and the bulls for horses, and they must have then discovered that no pony was sturdy enough to carry a ship's heavy anchor on its back, and lacking any other choice, they decided to dismantle the anchors. Their sheet coverings were removed from them, and they were revealed there to inquisitive eyes, and to their good fortune none of the people of Manali had ever seen a ship or an anchor. Before he arrived there the previous decade, they probably had never seen a character like him – that's to say, the way he had been that year – a white man who'd lost his way and was prepared to live in a tiny room whose only furniture was a bare mattress and a chair, and for a whole month he sought answers to his ponderings in twirling cannabis smoke.

Characters like Griffin and Evans had been seen in Manali before then: all sorts of defectors from the East Indian Company or other reckless men trying to earn easy money, but unlike them he wasn't rushing anywhere, and night after night he would sit opposite the window of his room and watch the night fall on the valley and envelope the tops of the cedars, and at the time he had no reason to leave there, not from the room, not from Manali, and not from the darkness of the night. He passed a whole month like that, detached from his surroundings almost like the Russian when he lay unconscious in the hospital – and who knew then that one day he would treat him or people in general – until one day by chance he heard the landlord's two sons talking about a caravan about to go north and realized that he had to make a decision, and twenty-one days later he arrived in Leh and has almost never left its environs ever since, and certainly not for any desert. No-no, not for one moment did he think of joining Tenzin on his journey with the anchors to the desert, despite that being the destination of all the articles he had gathered.

The place for antiquities is the desert; it wasn't for nothing that Hedin and Stein and Pelliot ventured out there before then, (*a Swede, a Hungarian, and a Frenchman go out to the desert,* it sounded like a lame joke), and from the north two Russians had come there, Colonel Przhevalsky and Dmitri Klements, He told Poliakov about them in a small restaurant next to the bazaar, not because he had to bolster his sprit with two fellow countrymen of his who had already made that journey, but because he enjoyed chatting with him.

Poliakov in contrast to him tended not to speak at length and the reference to fellow countrymen didn't impress him at all. "Do you miss your country, Doctor?" he asked him (by then he already knew a few words in English).

McKenzie nodded his head.

"I don't."

"And don't you miss the people there?" McKenzie asked.

"I don't have people there anymore," the Russian replied.

With a skillful movement he captured the fly that landed on the edge of his cup; he had already learned that too. He learned that from McKenzie who had learned it from Tenzin; who would have believed a silly act like that would become a gesture of friendship?

"Everyone's dead already," the Russian continued and shook the squashed fly off the palm of his hand, "and the ones that aren't dead are sorry I'm not dead. Did you ever feel like that?"

The doctor had an answer, but he didn't give it then; they were still not close enough: people had also wished him dead, and not only wished; care had been taken to document his death (Kate's second marriage wouldn't have been possible had a rumor of his death not been circulated and had someone not agreed to swear to it under oath).

"It's not a good feeling," the Russian answered to himself.

"Definitely not," the doctor agreed.

In vain he tried to ask the Russian about the dead he had mentioned: who had they been and how did they die and when? To all those questions he was answered: "The dead are dead, Doctor."

With the dull imagination of a veterinarian, he could have tried to picture chariot horses collapsing and shots flashing, the roar of explosions rolling from a distance, and try to picture this Russian being rescued covered in soot and bleeding, and policemen and detectives and soldiers chasing after him with their pistols drawn (the ladies said someone said they heard from someone that the Russian had assassinated the Tsar's nephew).

"And do you know what else makes a person not feel good?" the Russian asked.

McKenzie waited for him to continue.

"That he has no country. You, Doctor, have two."

McKenzie hesitated: after all, he'd never return to England.

"You, Doctor, only have to choose from the two of them."

Another fly stood on the edge of the cup, and the Russian waited for it to cease moving; that was the moment to quickly bring the palms of the hands close together about a centimeter above the fly, and when it notices them and tries to fly away, the palms are already waiting above in their final closing. That was the secret: not to direct them to the place where the fly is but rather to the place it will be when it flies away.

Is that how duck hunters aim their rifles, a few centimeters in front of the beak? The doctor didn't know, despite that in the county of his birth many go duck hunting on Sundays in the fens (he used to treat their hunting dogs, who quite often twisted a leg in the mud).

"You can also choose your work, Doctor," the Russian went on. "One day you're a vet, one day a doctor, one day a caravan-bashi."

"Tenzin is the caravan-bashi."

He wondered how they would get along with each other, Tenzin and the Russian – a terrorist taking orders from a native, albeit a very wise native, until he recalled they had become friends while still in Kashgar when Poliakov rescued Tenzin from some trouble, just a month before he arrived at his hospital unconscious and frostbitten.

What exactly had happened in Kashgar, he didn't remember: perhaps Poliakov smashed a bottle over the head of a soldier in a skirmish, perhaps he hit him with the bottle from some roof of an inn; he had forgotten the details of the act.

Why Poliakov was on the roof also wasn't clear, nor what the boy, Sasha, was doing there with him. In any event, he reached the hospital delirious.

"You also have a choice," the doctor said to him, "no one's forcing you to join the caravan."

"I want to join."

He couldn't help wondering what motivated him; certainly wasn't the money since he hadn't been promised any more than the paltry sum that would be paid to the Indians, and unlike the rest of the caravans, there would be no findings in the desert, on the contrary, they would be burying the lot. All his attempts to dissuade the Russian from his intentions were in vain; he tried to illustrate all the expected hardships of the way in detail (the sandstorms that darken the sky, the blaze of the sun in the day, the cold of night, the terrible thirst), as if he had experienced them personally and not just heard about them from the mouths of Hedin and Stein at the commissioner's wife's parties between a sip of tea and a bite of a biscuit.

"Why don't you stay here in Leh and rest some more until you've completely recovered?"

"I've rested enough."

"That's still no reason to go out to the desert," he said to him and told him about the scarcity of water and what happens to a thirsty body, starting with the dryness of the mouth and throat, to the nausea and dizziness and the delirium and ending with the throes of death, but the Russian was insistent; he even suggested helping them before the departure.

"And won't you miss the boy?" he asked him. "He's so attached to you."

"He'll get along, I'm not his father."

Sasha was the boy's name, a pet name for Alexander, like the name of some of the Tsars; that's what he explained to McKenzie on another occasion, and when he pronounced the name, his voice became tender.

In Petersburg, the boy's mother had been the mistress of an impoverished aristocrat who promised to make her his wife and estranged himself from her when she fell pregnant, and after him there was a cloth merchant, and after him another merchant, and another, a grocer, and on the train there was always some-one to pay for the rest of the journey in exchange for her services (all that had been heard by Mrs. Harper who decided to help her mend her ways). What the Russian had done with her until she became the property of Sunam Tsering, the most successful merchant of the bazaar, one could only guess, but even afterward he was often seen putting the boy on his shoulders, trying to fly a kite with him. The great terrorist could be seen acting as foolishly as a boy, but if someone smiled at him, his face would immediately become blank.

She received the very best room at the inn (Sunam Tsering paid for it), and every time they wanted the boy gone, the merchant gave him a coin to buy himself candy at the bazaar below. "Mother's sleeping," he would say in his high-pitched voice to all those sitting on the veranda of the inn, so that they would lower their voices and not disturb her, and they would wink at each other. It seemed she had decided she would never be poor nor would she and her son go hungry. "Mother's tired," he would say (probably one of the first phrases he learned in English). He said it with complete seriousness, despite knowing the sounds being made on the other side of the locked door were not of snoring.

The day the Russian rescued him from the yak's hooves, it was only by a miracle he himself didn't receive a fatal kick. "Miracle" is of course a European term; here in India there's only good or bad karma. And how would they describe McKenzie's karma here? At first good, a certified veterinarian at a young age, a flourishing clientele and marriage to a woman from London, up till there everything was well and good, that's to say until the woman from London became fed up with village life.

But his karma was such: he would travel with her from the village to Rome, lose her there, sail to Bombay, reach Leh, turn into a doctor for humans, equip a caravan whose sole purpose was to attract her Italian here, and he himself would be responsible for his safekeeping after his injury – he of all people in the world – and he would also see what happens to his two partners on that caravan, and what happens to the boy, Sasha. And not only did he see, everyone saw.

But for the time being – that's to say, about two months before the departure of the caravan – a fair amount of the required equipment was lacking, and first and foremost the paper (the anchors were already on their way to Leh). With all Issa's experience in leading caravans, in all the markets he passed through he hadn't succeeded in obtaining paper ancient enough for their needs. A rumor reached Leh about one of the cave monks and the ancient paper kept in his cave, more precisely, scrolls that had been written in invisible ink and would be revealed only to the eyes of someone who had attained enlightenment. It was also said that perhaps Sunam Tsering still had in his possession paper like that from the time he collaborated with Mohan Lal on his forgeries. Fortunately, it transpired the rumor was true: there indeed is a monk and there is a cave and there are blank scrolls and Sunam Tsering had obtained paper for his forgeries there, and it was of course possible to write on them even with regular ink, providing the monk would agree to sell them.

At that time, Sunam Tsering was trading in India and left the interpreter that used to accompany him to Russia in Leh, and there was no better opportunity than that to get him to talk. One day, Tenzin tried doing that but failed; the interpreter was too loyal to his master, and all attempts at persuading him to reveal where the ancient paper was kept were unsuccessful. There was no use trying to bribe him, because they couldn't compete with his master's money, nor with the fear he instilled in him. Such was the situation until the Russian entered the picture. When they explained the problem, he said he'd go and persuade the interpreter. How exactly he would do it, he didn't say.

Only months later, when the caravan returned from the desert, the doctor heard how he had persuaded him to accede to them. The Russian explained to the interpreter that since the paper from the cave had been used for a forgery, and the forged item had been sold for much money and mistakenly exhibited in an important museum in Russia, the Russian authorities intended to arrest him and his master the moment they put foot on the sidewalks of Petersburg again, even if their merchandise had narrowed to cashmere shawls. There was only one way to quell the authorities' anger, he said to him, and that is to hand to them over the paper that remained in the cave; in that way, at least, future forgeries would be impossible. Pointing out its exact location would be enough.

When the doctor was told about that months later, he wondered if the Russian hadn't employed additional methods learned while being detained in the cellars of the Russian secret police; it wasn't the ladies who reported that, he heard how he had been imprisoned there for some time from his own mouth and knew that he himself wouldn't have withstood an experience like that for a week, not even for twenty-four hours.

It took place on the night they got drunk together, on the local new year, during the festival in which a procession of monks leaves for the south with drums and trumpets and horns, and their colleagues, in devil's masks, carry statues made from butter to the burning bonfires at the edge of Leh, and with the statues, all the sins and the ills of the city will be tossed into fire. Yes, of all the festivals, they chose to get drunk on this one, the festival of the burning of sins, they sat in the small restaurant next to the bazaar and emptied glass after glass.

"For this, I didn't need to come here," the Russian said when the tumult outside subsided for a moment, "it's also like this with the Jews. Once a year they throw away the sins, how easy." Perhaps they threw them into the water and perhaps the desert, the tumult intensified again and drowned out his words. The deep sounds of the long horns that needed to be held by two men, were heard, sounds in which even after all the years here, McKenzie found little charm; more than anything, they resembled bellowing.

"And nevertheless, why did you come here?" He asked the Russian, and from the expression on his face knew he was in no hurry to reply.

The pungency of the chang they drank is well known to be like that of light beer, but if drunk on an empty stomach, it does its job well, and they both hadn't eaten since the afternoon. "Drik, drik!" They protested politely when their glasses were filled again, and did not really mean it. Again and again, their glasses were filled, and in the mixture of languages being used by them, their drunkenness was slightly less evident than it would have been in regular speech.

Outside, the commotion of the revelers could be heard again; almost all the inhabitants of Leh accompanied the monks on their way to the bonfires that had been lit on the edge of the city, and at their head was Henry in his uniform with all his decorations, and after him the Tehsildar, and the Naib Tehsildar, and the Drukpa and the Naib Drukpa, and a squad of policeman, and the telegraph manager, and the postal manager, and even Mrs. Harper marched there with gusto, much to her husband's chagrin.

"You were being chased, is that why you came here?" It was very important to have that clarified, and the chang loosened his tongue.

Since he wasn't answered, the doctor was helped by his fingers, making them run like a pair of legs across the table between a few crumbs the flies had got hold of, and this time too, the Russian didn't answer.

"I -" McKenzie wanted to revive the conversation and a burp suddenly escaped from his throat, "I came here from Italy," and as if the Russian was showing some interest he continued to talk about Rome. "Rome's a beautiful city, very beautiful, Rome's glorious, to hell with all the Romans." Owing to the alcohol, he was struck by a sort of joviality: his two fingers ceased to be a pair of legs, they were joined together and pointed at the other diners, as if they had all turned into Romans. "Puff-puff," he said like a child, the way they used to aim in the schoolyard at a flock of geese in the sky, "puff-puff."

Poliakov looked at him and at his fingers (about that look, Rasul used to say: "When he look like that, you believe about him everything"), and his face became drawn.

Sometime later – an hour and maybe more – after their cups had been filled two or three times more, they tried to find out exactly where the other had been born. It was complicated: how can you explain what birth is to someone who doesn't understand your language, even if he's completely clearheaded? After a number of attempts, accompanied by miming, it turned out that they had both been born in small villages, far from the capital, and both those villages, the English and the Russian, were in fact not so different from each other: twenty to thirty houses, wheatfields spread out to the horizon, trees, a winding river.

"Nothing ever happens there," said McKenzie, "except weddings and funerals, and my wife comes from London and simply couldn't stand it anymore, so we left." And even though he burped at the very same moment, he heard himself talking like a devoted husband explaining why he and his wife had both decided to move residence.

It was already getting late. At the edge of Leh all the butter statues had already dissolved into the fire, both the large and the small, not much time was needed for that; their devilish facial features softened and melted to the gaze of the onlooking masses, and the butter dribbled and dripped onto the wooden logs being eaten away in the bonfires and roused the flames further. With a bubbling sound, the heads melted with their protruding eyes and their sharp noses, and their fleshy lips smeared with red; their paunches were also softened and melted with their hand-drawn festive garments, and with them the twisted limbs with sex organs, and all the sins that were cast with them fanned the fire even more.

5

The monk ("the gullible goof," as Tenzin called him when he returned from there) was not at all impressed by the modest delegation that reached him. Every morning, the people of the nearby village would lay a small bowl of tsampa and a jug of water on the sill of his hatch and remove the empty small bowl and jug - such was the custom at all the caves of retreat – and if they weren't emptied, they knew that the monk was ill and waited a few days to see whether they would have to break down the wall built at the entrance, or whether he had recuperated in order to continue to be buried alive there.

"A gullible goof," Tenzin said about him even before they went up there, and he warned the Russian that those are the hardest to persuade. With the interpreter it was easier, he said, but it's impossible to threaten someone like that; after all, he had forgone most of his life just to stop being reborn. Harper and his flock wanted to be born again and for eternity, while the Indians wanted to stop the wheel of birth: something McKenzie could identify with. Of course, that's not to say it was fitting to bring an Indian monk close to his death.

The two of them rode to Kaspang on their own, and that whole week the doctor waited for them to return and find out if they had finally obtained the suitable paper. The anchors had already reached Leh, and when he saw them, he was disappointed because they didn't at all resemble anchors as he knew them.

"That's what there was in the museum, Doctor," Griffin and Evans said to him. "There are more ancient ones, just a big stone with a hole for a rope, and you certainly didn't want ones like that. Just pay what's owing to us now together with some minor expenses." And they enumerated them: bribery of the museum guard, money for the coolie whose leg had been squashed, cloth sheets that they bought in Bombay for wrapping the anchors, the compensation they were forced to pay the owner of the pony that collapsed under its load, the gifts they were required to leave in Manali, all that cost money.

"But we agreed on a price," he tried telling them. "You didn't mention any minor expenses."

"Do you want us to take all of it back?"

Something like that hadn't even entered his mind.

Day after day, they had to ascend the mountain slope so that the monk would get used to their voices from the other side of the wall at the entrance to the cave (here they weren't satisfied with a monastery, or a small room or a cell). According to their plan, Tenzin was to tell him that he in his cave is hindering the scrolls from fulfilling their destiny because how could the hidden text on them be revealed to anyone – yes, from their beginning a groundless folly had been associated with them – and there was no response to that claim other than the monotonous mumbling heard the whole while from the other side of the mud bricks.

The following day, they advanced a step farther: when after the one who brought the monk's food had left, they held the small bowl of tsampa and didn't allow the monk to pull it inside. He wasn't a young man, most likely half blind from the darkness of the cave and weak from his asceticism, possibly half-crazed from loneliness; and all those things McKenzie, a doctor by profession, was supposed to have taken into consideration and hadn't, so engulfed was he by his own craziness.

They didn't intend for the monk to starve, but they wanted him to recognize their power. There might have been a moment when the monk tried to gently pull the small bowl inside and discovered it was being blocked, and they didn't even allow him to take the jug of water. He was prevented from opening his mouth and asking them to cease since he had forbidden himself any speech – one word expelled from his mouth would have been enough for him to have to begin anew the count of his years in seclusion. In the end, they left him alone the way a cat leaves a mouse alone until its instinctive tendency is aroused again, but this two-headed cat had been sent by McKenzie himself.

The next morning, the Russian decided to move to a direct attack, at least that's what Tenzin related on their return and ascribed all that took place after that to the Russian. "Tell him," he said to Tenzin, "everyone in the monastery and in the village are already certain he broke his vow and spoke, so why should he insist on keeping the paper?" That method too, it seems, he had learned from his own experiences in Russia – isn't that what his interrogators had said to him?

The next morning, they waited again in front of the hatch until the monk's hand appeared, and when he felt around for his bowl they grabbed it and didn't let go. "Oh, Lama Rinpoche," they said to him, "no one in the world will know whether you gave us the paper, but if you don't give it to us, we'll tell everyone that you did, and for a lot of money!" They also said to him that if he sticks to his vow but causes others to sin by being led to think the vow had been broken – that's what Tenzin said – his own karma would also be harmed; a claim too complex for Western ears, but in this crazy country there are many who are also careful not to accidentally step on a bug, lest their karma be irreparably harmed.

They left him alone for a few hours and when they returned to the hatch and only the empty small bowl of tsampa could be seen, the Russian's patience expired; that, at least, is what Tenzin related on their return. The Russian began to demolish the mud brick wall with a big stone, beating it over and over at the side of the hatch to widen it. Perhaps Tenzin slanted the facts because he had been struck with regret about what they had done to the monk, and perhaps their roles had been divided in advance: one would use persuasion on the monk, and the other would use force. After all, that was how the police behaved in their investigations - that little, even he, the doctor, knew.

"Oh, Lama Rinpoche," Tenzin said to him, "my friend here won't stop until you give him what you've got," And even before he had finished his words, the Russian beat the side of the hatch again, crumbling it further; mud bricks return to their origin with ease. Perhaps it wasn't only the notion of sticking to a task that motivated him, but also his revulsion for anyone who clung to some fictitious holiness. He had made that revulsion evident while still in Leh during a conversation with Harper, when the two graves Kashmir took such pride in were mentioned, In the missionary's eyes they were proof of the locals' willingness to open up to other faiths – the graves of Jesus and Moses, no less, who found no better place than Kashmir to be buried in (the first apparently yearned to walk on Lake Srinagar as well, and the other, who yearned to be buried on a mountain, walked all the way to the Himalayas).

"Moses and Jesus never existed," the Russian said to him at the time.

To the missionary that negation was even worse than what had happened to the biblical stories in Kashmir. "And just what did exist?"

"Evil," the Russian replied. "And from all that evil, people made things up for themselves." His answer angered Harper even more.

After the hatch had been further broken into and the dust had settled a bit, a gaunt old man stooped and bundled up on his mat was revealed in the darkness inside; tresses of his hair fell to the ground and his eyes were shaded by a skeletal hand from the glare that opened up in the wall opposite him. Compassion would have been fitting, but they hadn't been paid for that.

"Oh, Lama Rinpoche," they said to him, "tomorrow when they bring you the food and find that there's an opening here the size of a door, no one will believe that you didn't go outside. And even if they do believe you, we'll take you out ourselves. So, give us what we asked for and we'll go."

When they returned to Leh with their bounty, McKenzie wasn't interest in hearing the details, only the paper interested him. Yes, there was a period in his life when ancient paper and three wooden anchors had been more important to him than anything else in the world, and certainly more than the foolish belief of an Indian monk and what he was prepared to do for it. And what was the end result? He was forced to send his little son to another continent and perhaps never see him again, but then, had it not been for that period, his son wouldn't have been born.

At the time he had already become accustomed to his ascetic lifestyle and rebuffed all the attempts of the commissioner's wife to pair him up with Dianne, and had it not been for what happened – right there in the hospital – he probably wouldn't have changed his attitude. And what in fact did happen? What happened was that the shaman came and drummed on his drum in front of his patients, a sort of stupefying rhythm, and afterward scattered onto the drum grains he brought in a small bag, and according to their formation he gave diagnoses to even the most severe cases whose symptoms baffled the doctor. After the shaman left, he went into the small room he used as an office, sat down in his chair and after a short while took a nap; no, not a nap, a deep sleep fell on him, and a moment later he was already dreaming. The dream was terrifying; a man was plodding in the sand carrying an anchor on his shoulder like a cross. causing him to sink more and more. He only saw him from the back, and in the dream he also plodded through the sand trying touch the man and see his face, and while doing so he also began so sink, up to his knees, up to his waist, up to his neck, up to his nose, up to his eyes, up to his forehead.

When Dianne gently closed the door, it wasn't grains of sand that that filled his eyes, and with a white handkerchief in whose corner her initials were embroidered, she wiped them like a child's eyes (of all people she, the old maid of the British colony in Leh, cared for him like a mother), and he didn't object, having been so terrified by his dream. Outside the chap-chap of a magpie could be heard and the braying of a pony tied to a tree, and when they looked out there, they saw that some lustful equine thoughts were lengthening its organ and Dianne blushed to the base of her neck. Had it not been for the dream and the pony, perhaps they wouldn't have met again for tea, had it not been for these things perhaps little Charles wouldn't have come into the world and certainly wouldn't have been sent off to England.

He thought about his son again: even before they sailed from Bombay, Charles would be nestling against Mrs. Kingsley, no less than he once nestled against Dianne before she fell ill: he'd be sitting on Kingsley's knee, allowing her to stroke his head, ask Kingsley to tell him a bedtime story; perhaps even get into her bed in their cabin, climb down or climb up – most likely up, after all Kingsley wouldn't allow him to sleep on the top bunk – "Charlie," she would say to him, the way they used to say, "what are you doing here?" They weren't angry with him but instead glad he'd come to reconcile and to mediate between their bodies which at the time rarely touched each other.

In the end, their victory was fairly easy. When the monk came to the hatch, they could have taken their bounty from his hand and left without a word, but Tenzin, from outside, held him by his wrists. He didn't hold him forcefully but rather with gentleness, as if trying to learn something that way, something that cannot be learned from words; he related that afterward – wanting to understand from where the monk obtained the power to persevere like that for years. Someone who had been the complete opposite arose in his memory then, the head of the monastery who had ill-treated his father and in whom there had been no asceticism, and certainly no holiness.

"The gullible goof," he called the monk in Leh, but admired his determination and intended to seal the opening that had been made in the wall, even if delayed them. "A day or two won't make any difference to the doctor," he said, "he's used to waiting." They probably made other jokes at his expense; knowing his motivation; a vengeance not worthy of an adult and certainly not a director of a hospital.

Nowadays even the thought arouses a chuckle in the doctor; no, not a chuckle, revulsion and disgust, yes, at himself, but at the time he still wanted to attract Magnani here and degrade him to the point where he couldn't show his face in all Europe, if he indeed would manage to return to Europe and not get lost in the desert. In his mind's eye, he saw him going astray in the sands of the Taklamakan and searching through the terrible terrain stretching from Khotan eastward, plodding in the sand with his pipe and his small paunch and his bald patch poking out and missing even the nearest oasis of all, where they intended to bury his findings; the doctor had no difficulty picturing him dying of thirst or blindly following the heatwave's mirages, even if a retreating or rising sea wasn't revealed to him.

"And all that for a woman?" They must have said on the way and chuckled. Is that the way for a doctor to behave and a mission hospital director at that? And Tenzin perhaps imitated Rasul then and said: "If all the husbands Rasul take their wives they angry like doctor, then desert full of caravans like doctor."

In moments of his drunkenness McKenzie could envision the sight of a sea retreating with its waves rolling backward with their foam and their fish, and the ships drawing away with bloated sails, and at the stern of one of them is a god holding a bottle with which to entice the seagulls, despite that the gods can speak to the gulls in their language.

Dianne used to tell little Charles a story like that about a boy who knew the language of the birds and the animals but didn't want to learn the language of humans. He was a bad pupil and all the teachers were angry with him for not be able to understand anything, and when he was banished from the school, all the birds and the animals came to keep him company and taught him everything there is to know, and in the end he knew more that all the teachers.

"How does a bird go?" Dianne asked Charles, and Charles replied joyfully. "And how does a dog go?" Dianne asked again, and Charles replied, his whole being rejoicing.

"You see?" she said to him. "You also know the language of the birds and the animals, but you'll also be a good pupil and you won't ever be sent out of the class, will you? Tell him, Father."

"You're absolutely right," McKenzie then said.

"And he'll yet be Prime Minister one day," Dianne said in a sudden venture into a future she wouldn't get to see one iota of. "Isn't that so, Father?"

"Of course, he'll be Prime Minister," said McKenzie.

The designated Prime Minister didn't yet know the demands of his role and for a start asked for more chocolate.

"Prime ministers," Dianne said to him, "don't eat so much chocolate; how will they talk to people with chocolate in their mouths and with bad teeth?"

"I want chocolate!" the designated Prime Minister insisted.

That was also something he forgot to note in the letter passed on to Mrs. Kingsley by Rasul: little Charles' fondness for sweet things.

All the positive attributes Tenzin tried to find in the monk in order to delay their leaving the cave they had looted made little impression on the Russian: not his asceticism, not his determination, not his adherence to his faith. Perhaps he also reminded Tenzin what he himself had called that monk – a gullible goof.

"You don't believe in anything," Tenzin said and looked at the cave again. If he doesn't die from strong winds, he said, he'll die from sorrow, and fixing the wall wouldn't be difficult - half a day would do, all it would take is to bring a few mud bricks from the village and block it up; but by the time they returned it was too late.

At the far end of the cave, in the darkness mixed with the light of the sunset coming from outside, the old man could be seen sitting in the same humble lotus position he had sat in all the previous days, but this time they saw him from the back; he had decided to turn his back on all the sights visible through the breach, lest his eyes and his heart and his body be lured there and his vow be broken. A moment passed before his head turned around slightly and his face was revealed in the honeyed light: it had turned red but not from the light of the setting sun. He must have found a piece of brick next to the wall easy enough to pick up, and sharp enough to hit his eyelids with so that they wouldn't be tempted by any of the sights of the outside world: not the setting son, not the glory of the night sky, not the dawn light of tomorrow or all the following days.

"That lunatic," Tenzin said and continued to curse him all the way down the slope; and even in Leh, after they returned and finally delivered him the paper they obtained, he continued to berate him saying how if only that lunatic had waited until morning he would have rebuilt his brick wall for him and nothing bad would have happened to anyone. So what if the doctor would have waited a little longer? No one needs to get hurt for the sake of the doctor's foolishness.

In that, he of course was absolutely correct.

6

He, a doctor obligated by the Hippocratic oath, who had performed dozens of cataract operations and restored eyesight to many, took no interest in the fate of the monk, any more than he took interest in a carcass crows pounce upon. Crows such as those the Russian had counted while in hospital and had invited to feast on his body – always directed their beaks first at the eyes and the testicles.

A month after his release, the two of them sat in a small restaurant next to the bazaar, fairly drunk, when a beautiful eyed Ladakhi girl passed opposite them, and the Russian said something in his language using the word he had repeatedly mumbled in the vagueness of his delirium in hospital: *glaza*, eyes. Since the summer of ninety-seven the doctor knew how to say it in Italian, *occhi*, and more precisely: *occhi magnifici*, because that's what the young men of Rome said to his wife.

What would have happened had Dianne landed up in Rome? She had watery eyes and hair of an indefinite shade, her skin was pale and the contours of her body were vague, yet of all women it was she who in the end became the mother of his son. She would never have disappeared in a foreign city, not from her husband nor her employer. For more than twenty years she had served Henry and Ann with the devotion of a servant, she accompanied them through all their transfers from Mount Abu to Daoli to Madras to Amritsar and to this backwater of backwaters, Leh, but apart from her devotion it was hard for him to find virtues in her; and moreover, that specific virtue, devotion, could be seen to be as dull as the color of her hair or her eyes. He often hoped she would explode the way Kate used to, hurl harsh words at him or turn her back on him in bed and not accede to his solicitations, but she never exploded, never swore, and if he desired her at night she would almost always acquiesce and lie on her back obediently and wait in silent patience for him to do the deed; it was so spiritless that already in their first year he ceased from it.

Only when Charles was born did her find a certain charm in her he hadn't previously noticed: with the boy she became as mischievous as a little girl, and the childishness that suddenly emerged from a faded adult woman who had almost given up on her chances of giving birth sometimes touched him, and he would wonder if in the end it wasn't preferable things had turned out this way, that she should be the one with whom he fathered a child.

Every night she would tell Charles bedtime stories, revealing the imagination she had been endowed with and her ability to extend herself. In her drawings which Ann had lavishly praised in an effort to make her appear more intriguing to him, he found not a shred of imagination, and on weekends when she went out into nature (that's what Dianne called it, "going out to nature"), armed with an easel and brushes and watercolors, she would again and again paint all sorts of seasonal flowers and bits of landscape ad nauseum. The moment her brush touched them they lost their potency, draining all the intensity of the flowering, the glory of the peaks, the green of the valley, the frenzy of changing light.

In the company of little Charles ("sweet Charlie" she used to call him, or "Charlilu" or "Charluli"), she at last was freed of her rigidity; she would tell him not only the well-known stories McKenzie also remembered from his childhood, but others that she made up herself, portraying all the characters, and for the first time he discovered she had other voices apart from the one he knew – the quiet, monotonous, all-accepting voice.

He won't forget, the first time she told Charles about the fisherman's wife and her wishes:

Mandje! Mandje! Timpe Te!
Flounder, flounder, in the sea!
My wife, my wife, Ilsebill,
Wants not, wants not, what I will.

That's what the fisherman standing on the shore and calling to the waves said to the fish each time his wife asked for one of her wishes, and little Charles insisted on knowing the meaning of "what I will."

"She wants things that aren't suited to her way of life." Dianne explained to him.

"What's wayofife?" Charles asked.

"Things not right for her," McKenzie said trying to simplify it for him, "his wife wanted a palace and servants and a carriage, but what does a fisherman's wife need things like that for?" While speaking, he thought what Kate would have said about that in one of her bad moments: that the opposite was true, the first way of life didn't suite her at all: what connection did she have with any village, whether a fisherman's or a famer's village; metropolitan life most certainly suited her. He also knew he was blackening her image to enable him to forget her.

Mandje! Mandje! Timpe Te!

There was one thing the fisherman's wife didn't ask for after replacing the hut with a house and a house with a castle and a castle with a palace: for the fish to replace her husband the fisherman. Kate had done it by her own hand. She simply threw her husband into the sea. All that passed through his mind while Dianne continued the story. Mandje! Mandje! Timpe Te!

Hadn't McKenzie wanted things that were most definitely not suited to his way of life? He wanted to organize a caravan to the desert, endeavoring to make fools of world-renowned explorers; things not at all suited to his way of life. In the end, like the fisherman's wife, he was punished. She woke up in a dilapidated hut and he returned to the routine of this hospital whose buildings are made of mud bricks and whose floors have irremovable grime, and all sorts of witch doctors compete with him and his remedies, and the one solitary important thing had he achieved throughout these past years – his son, Charlie – he had lost.

Glaza, the Russian said in the restaurant and again his gaze followed the Ladakhi girl, *glaza*, just the way he said it while lying in the hospital. He sat in the restaurant with him one more time on the day Tenzin met with his father to try and find out the best way to obtain seashells and where the large monasteries received them from for their ceremonies.

Seashells were not the only thing lacking, but all the rest they planned on getting in Khotan when they arrived there. It was likely seashells would also be on sale in its markets, but one couldn't depend on it. The preparations were not in a sound state, and far from over. Before they could leave they still had to fill the paper with all the nonsense they intended to write on it, and it was still unclear when and how that task, which had been assigned to the Russian, would be carried out. It hadn't originally been planned that he would be the one to do it – what did a Russian terrorist have to do with a job like that? But two months after he left the hospital, it seemed that the ancient language of his people could perhaps be used toward their needs but would have to be somewhat distorted and interspersed characters from other languages or made up by them, in order to pose a challenge to the explorers. It was not a groundless notion: among all the languages of the documents discovered by Stein in his excavations in the desert, Sanskrit, Prakrit, Brahmi, Uyghur, Kharosthi, Tibetan and ancient Farsi (he had prattled on about them at such length that their names had been absorbed in the doctor's memory), some letter written in Farsi but with Hebrew characters had been discovered, and Stein, with his incorrigible prolixity, explained to them that was the way Jews integrated into their new countries while preserving their language. He even took the trouble, as if anyone desired it, to translate the document for them, between sipping tea and eating a biscuit, from its beginning to its end (a Jewish merchant had complained about someone who had cheated him, some banality whose antiquity alone attributed importance to it, and right away someone, most likely Henry's adjutant, said: "He should have got a medal if he managed to cheat a Jew").

"First of all, let him bring the seashells," the Russian said in the restaurant, again postponing the assignment designated to him. They were still waiting for Tenzin to return from his conversation with his father; it was the first time in years he had gone to visit him in his alcove in the market where he mended pairs of trousers and sewed buttons and hems, and it seemed – that's how it appeared to the doctor each time he passed by his small room – that only if some English-man were to be stabbed with each thrust of the needle into the material, would Tenzin's father's soul find rest. The vast Tibetan heights which he had mapped and measured by foot on a mission assigned by his commanders in Dehradun while disguised as a pilgrim, he exchanged for this small room.

At the very same time, a few alleys away, Tenzin stepped carefully over remnants of material and sat down on the low stool in his father's alcove and only the quiet rattling of the sewing machine Kintap set in motion with his foot could be heard.

"Did something of yours get torn?" he asked Tenzin, not stopping his foot. "Did you come for me to mend something?"

"There are things that you can no longer mend."

People passed through the alley and looked inside, and from the next alley came the smell of the naan and the chapatti being baked there.

"You're still angry with me," his father said.

"I'm not angry anymore," Tenzin replied.

The needle of the sewing machine stopped at the edge of the sleeve, and a large fly landed on his father's hand.

"You'll never understand," Kintap shook his hand, and the fly flew away.

More was said between them, and not in hesitant voices, and from the other side of the alley, weavers and cobblers and other tailors must have been looking at them, as well as two children running here and there through the alley.

That Englishman's puppy – the term Tenzin used for his father afterward in the restaurant – wasn't ashamed to tell him again that he simply had believed the commanders ("Simply?" Tenzin said to him, "Simply?"), that without his maps, they couldn't invade Tibet; he had also believed it would all pay off on his return, for him and for all the family, because who would have thought the British would have been so ungrateful? And besides that, his father said, who could have known so much time would pass until he'd return home.

"Four years," Tenzin specified, and didn't accept his father's justification that he had to remain in the monastery until the monks believed he was one of them. Without that, he claimed, he couldn't have fulfilled his mission.

"Your mission," Tenzin said mockingly, "and without thinking twice, you left your wife and children for them?"

Afterward he asked about the seashells, and it transpired that a trade cara-van would be leaving the monastery to sell its harvest in order to fill its coffers, and on its return will bring merchandise for the monastery including seashells needed for ceremonies, their source being a caravan organized by one Kashmiri merchant. There's no need to go to Tibet for them, his father said, it's enough to go to Srinagar and buy them there directly from the Kashmiri. Whatever he's look-ing for – he said and perhaps even believed it at that moment – he can bring him from Srinagar.

"How can you bring me?" Tenzin replied. "Look at yourself, you can hardly get here from home."

They sat without speaking for a while, and the sewing machine fell silent. Opposite them, on the other side of the alley, the weavers continued their labor.

"Do you really think I didn't think about you there?" his father said. "There wasn't a day that I didn't think about all of you, one day you'll understand that."

"Who could understand something like that?" Tenzin replied.

The two children running in the alley reached the alcove and stared at the two of them, and Tenzin banished them with a wave of a hand.

"We were their age when you left," he said about himself and his brother, despite that only his brother was that young at the time, and his father didn't correct him, it seemed that he then understood something.

The two boys in the alley were perhaps little Charles' age now, but at the time he wasn't even yet so much as an idea; Dianne was then just Henry's secretary, the anchors hadn't been buried in the desert, the seashells hadn't been bought, their caravan had not yet left for the desert.

The route of Charles' caravan was far easier, and as it drew further southward from Leh it would come closer and closer to the big cities, first to Delhi and afterward to Bombay, in a kind of painful symmetry: the anchors had been taken from Bombay and transported northward to the desert and were lost there, while little Charles was taken from here and transported southward to the port of Bombay and would get lost there (that is to say, he would set sail, yes, but it was doubtful whether they would ever see each other). Again, in his mind's eye he saw all the dozens of beasts of burden drawing away with their loads, and little Charles bundled up in Rasul's arms and the two of them riding together on one pony.

Somewhere, in the depths of his mind or his chest, the vague memory rose of his father placing him on their old horse in his childhood, a horse that no longer pulled a plough or a cart, but nevertheless his father refused to hand him over to the skinner. "He served me for twenty years," he said, "and now he deserves a little rest. Let Mr. Whitney wait."

Generally, Whitney was accorded much respect by him, and not as a skinner but rather as someone who knows animal anatomy better than any other man in the county. "Whitney has performed more operations than all the veterinarians of Oxfordshire put together," his father used to say. "What he's already forgotten they haven't even begun to learn," and when McKenzie expressed a desire to study veterinarian science, his father showed no enthusiasm. "I need you on the farm," he said to him, "and you'll be in in London." His mother tried in vain to point out the advantages of the respectable profession, a profession that he himself could benefit by on the farm. "Do you think he'll learn in London what I've learned here my whole life with my bare hands?" his father said, and didn't change his views even when he had become a qualified veterinarian, praised by many to his father

"Say what you will," they said to him, "your son didn't waste his time in London, and now he's bearing the fruits."

"What fruits," his father replied, "rushing off to your cowsheds in the middle of the night?"

In his place – they said – they would be happy to know they had a vet at home, what could be better than that? To which he replied he doesn't need a vet at home, he needs another pair of working hands on the farm. He already has a son who helps him, Bill, and he needs another one. Bill's wonderful, there's no one like Bill, but two are needed here. I don't need another pair of women's hands here, he said, "All the serviettes and towels are already folded."

And there was the beloved cow, Dolly, who suffered from a prolapsed uterus (yes, it was she who rose in his memory now, before all the animals of the caravan), and the correct way of treating her was perfectly clear, to administer her an anesthetic and return the fallen uterus to its place and reinforce it with a few stitches, but his father refused to listen. "Constipation, Ed," he said, "the poor thing's constipated! Just give me some linseed oil for her and in two or three days she'll be like new."

She was a good-natured cow whose large brown eyes always shone, but a pink swelling could be seen at the side of her vulva and the uterine neck that didn't seem to worry his father at all, until two days later when the swelling had turned into a large purple lump and had become infected. "Now will you perhaps let me treat Dolly at last?" he asked his father. He had no doubt that if she was not treated promptly her case would deteriorate.

"Are you sure it was linseed oil that you gave me?" his father said.

"She'll yet die," said his mother. "Let him treat her the way he's learned to; Dolly's lived with us for fifteen years and now she'll die just because of your stupidity!"

From her bed of straw, Dolly gazed at them with her large brown eyes whose shine had faded, and only that look of loyal suffering convinced his father; even in that obstinate man something cracked. In silence, he let him administer Dolly an anesthetic and watched him while he washed and disinfected the lump and inserted it back into its place and reinforced it with a few stitches and a rubber band, and only at the end did he see fit to say: "You better not have done her any harm, Ed." And even when she recuperated, he avoided attributing the cure to veterinary science or his son's competence and preferred ascribing it to the workings of time ("Time heals everything," was one of the obstinate old man's favorite sayings).

From all the villages in the vicinity, farmers came to summon McKenzie to attend to their sick animals, but his father insisted on remaining faithful to Whitney and his methods, as if there was more know-how in the slaughterhouse than in all the universities of Europe. And when that retired horse began to die – it was twenty years old by then, and he had no doubt it wouldn't make it to the morning

– his father stuck raw onions into its anus and couldn't understand why the horse didn't react according to his expectations. True, it showed signs of life, but they bore no resemblance to its customary placidness of bygone times.

"Let's see how you'd behave with onions stuck up your arse," he said to his father, and wasn't in time to see the large rough hand lifted and poised to slap him.

There was one more act, the third and decisive one, and Dolly the cow was also at its center, when one morning, about a year after her recovery from the prolapsed uterus, she choked on a potato she had swallowed whole. The potato could be felt from the outside by moving the hand over the esophagus, and foaming blood dripped from her mouth. It seemed that his father, the pupil of Whitney the distinguished scientist, had tried to push the potato down her throat with a broom and by doing so had apparently torn her pharynx, and fluids had gathered, and an edema was formed around the injured spot. The poor thing didn't have a chance, so said his mother as well, but his father wasn't convinced. "Time will heal her," he said, "exactly like the last time." Only the following morning, when she was found lifeless on her bed of straw and two flies standing on her open eyes, was his self-confidence undermined for the first time. "You killed him!" His mother hurled the accusation at him. "Just because you're such an oaf who thinks he knows everything!" And when Whitney came to take her, he and his mother went into the house so as not so see Dolly loaded onto the wagon, and his father, who stayed outside, averted his eyes as well.

This also needs to be stated here: he remembers Dolly better than all the beasts of burden on the caravan, and not only them, also more than the dozens of Ladakhi patients he's treated here, and it's not only because of the quarrels with his father; there's something about the mute helplessness of a suffering animal that touches the heart much more than the sturdiness of its companions and more than the complaints and shouting of people, especially if they had previously preferred their witch doctors.

And this too needs to be admitted: with time the heart becomes coarser and coarser; what had been aroused in him by the first leper he saw in Bombay or all the other deformed people who exhibit their defects for all to see in order to receive a rupee, he would never feel again, and perhaps it was better that way. And after all, not only had he become accustomed to illnesses but also to deaths, and not only them but also to what was done after them, shocking as it might appear to Western eyes. That apparently is what the years do, they blunt every emotion; by now even the desire for revenge has weakened.

He had never watched Whitney skinning an animal or cutting it up, and certainly not when he skinned Dolly; he was too refined at the time, yes-yes, delicate and sensitive, his father had justifiably mocked him. But here in Ladakh, after the long way he had come, he watched the cutting up of human bodies without difficulty – that's what they did to someone when there wasn't enough wood to burn him – and he succeeded in stemming the nausea that arose in him. It was Tenzin who brought him there, and he saw them stretching out and straightening the dead man from his head to the soles of his feet and skinning him with sickening skill and dissecting him into two along the length of the spine from the neck to the testicles and cutting the entire half body into large and small chunks, and thereby only making it easier for the crows that had gathered close by. The head they decapitated with the thrust of a knife and split open the skull with a hammer – he heard that sound reverberating inside his own head – and one of the lhagbas, the oldest among them, took the brain in his hand and turned it around and examined it from all sides. It then transpired that those butchers determined medical diagnoses according to it with the same decisiveness with which Whitney had done.

Ed, Ed, he said to himself, look what a long way you've come since Whitney, and he wasn't alarmed by that, on the contrary: one had to become tough and he had become tough, one had to experience everything and he already knew he would experience everything here, but at the time he couldn't have conceived of this act of fraud that an ex-veterinarian and the son of an ex-spy and an ex-terrorist had teamed up to execute; to bury seashells and anchors in the desert. Yes, it sounded like a bad joke, like one of those lame jokes so well liked by Giles, Henry's adjutant: a banker a general and a nun are flying in a hot-air balloon.

Wouldn't it have been better to continue treating prolapsed uteruses? That certainly was possible, but since then he had already come a long way from which there was no going back: not to the cows, not to their owners, not to his father, not to the young man he had been then.

"Sometimes it's a complex thing, a father and a son," he said about Tenzin in the small restaurant while he and the Russian waited for him – this time they didn't get drunk, everything had to be cared for with the utmost clear-headedness – "it's impossible to know how it will end, but he'll bring the seashells." Again, he tried to get Poliakov to talk, this time by means of father and son relationships, and again he failed. The seashells didn't interest him, nor the anchors, and fathers and sons was a subject he didn't tend to talk about more than he tended to talk about his deeds in Russia. A long noodle dangled from the edge of his plate and attracted a fat fly to it, and when he tried out the new hunting technique he had learned here, it turned out that he still wasn't skillful enough at it.

"You should have waited a little longer," McKenzie said to him the exact words he had heard from Tenzin years before, "you should try only when they don't move at all; the secret is to wait for the right moment."

"Yes, Doctor," he replied to him, as if they were still in the hospital and what connected them to each other was the fear of gangrene in the soles of the feet.

"I learned that from Tenzin," McKenzie said, despite having once told him that, and while the fly that had been spared was deliberating where to land, he wondered aloud why Tenzin was being delayed so long: almost an hour had passed since he had gone to his father, and all that he had to get was the name of one seashell merchant.

The Russian looked at the fly that landed close to his plate again. "Sometimes it's a complex thing, a father and a son," he said, reminding him of his previous statement, and both palms of his hands lifted up, and from the expression on his face it was impossible to know whether he was intending to make a mockery. It seemed that all his efforts were concentrated on the fly again.

Is that not exactly how he felt before his emotions had been blunted, when his own father died? Felt, yes, he still had the ability to feel then. A few months after Dolly's death, on one especially stormy winter evening, before the dinner table dishes were cleared, his father died of cardiac arrest, yes, that's how the obstinate old man died,: not from a certain food nor from the thunder rolling in the sky at the time, and not even from sorrow over his cow. Perhaps he died of sorrow over losing his authority at home, because after the day that Whitney and his sons loaded Dolly onto their wagon, no one listened to him anymore.

But in the church, opposite his coffin – his father lay there in the ancient suit he wore at his wedding – he was struck by a deep sorrow and wouldn't have objected at all if there and then his father opened his mouth stuffed with cotton wool and from the coffin said to him in his rough voice, "Are you sure it was linseed oil that you gave me, Ed?"

"My father died because of a cow," he said to the Russian, as if an opening had been made for conversation, and with the same degree of inaccuracy he could have said at a later time that Dianne had died because of a mosquito or that a crane had killed the boy, Sasha.

This time the Russian succeeded in capturing the fly: he drew his hands close above it exactly in time, and the fly, a moment after flying off from the noodle, was squashed between them.

Dianne's mosquito (a female mosquito, to be precise) had been Anopheles, which wasn't at all difficult to kill if detected in time, but it wouldn't be correct to blame only Anopheles for her death. Above 6500-feet, Anopheles cannot exist, neither males nor females, the air is too thin for their liking, but husbands who cause their wives to lose the will to live, can exist there – and that after all, is what happened to Dianne – husbands who still have the nerve to wonder afterward why their wives aren't trying to overcome their illness. "At least fight for Charlie's sake," he hypocritically said to her all through that terrible November when she was spared no symptom of malaria from a raging fever to vomiting blood, and she no longer wanted to fight for anyone's sake, not even for the sake of her son.

"Every time I look at Charlie," she said, "he reminds me what a mistake I made when I fell in love with you, Ed, and thought that we'd raise a family together. You hadn't yet parted from her at all and nor will you ever; it would have been better had we not been made to meet." In vain, he tried to tell her that little Charles shouldn't be made to suffer because of it – a boy with his whole life before him, what difference does it exactly make what his parents felt for each other before he was born or in his infancy; does he himself know what his own parents felt?

Again, the Russian drew his hands together in the anticipation that a fly would be squashed between them, perhaps the previous one's brother who had come to busy himself with some noodle, and approximately then the Russian boy suddenly appeared in the restaurant, and Poliakov bent toward him and lifted him onto his knee, and the boy's blue eyes gleamed from within his round dirty face. The thing in the world that Sasha wants most, he said (wasn't it to see his father, McKenzie wondered, and wasn't that why he's so attached to him?) is to be a fireman, yes-yes, because the firemen of Petersburg look so fine! In order to explain how important they are to their city, he tried with the few words that he knew in English to praise its sites, each name being more complicated to pronounce – is London also beautiful?

It was hard for the doctor to think of London detached from the one owing to whom he had left England and landed up in the East, but he nodded his head like a loyal patriot, despite knowing already then he would never return to his county – the thought was painful, but he couldn't rid himself of it.

It transpired that the river flowing though Petersburg is called the Neva, and it's from this river that the firemen take water, and when he tried to make the name roll off his tongue (by some vague impulse he tried to pronounce it, as if by mastering these sounds the entire Russian language would open up before him), the boy insisted on teaching him how to pronounce the "nyeh" – "Nyeh! Not niyeh" he said to him in his high-pitched voice and even became angry like a strict teacher and let him alone until he was somewhat more accurate.

Above the boy's disheveled head, his turned his gaze to Poliakov: did he also know from childhood what he wanted to be when he grew up? Surely not a fireman? For a long while they looked at each other, until the boy began to become bored and slid off Poliakov's knees and went out. With small steps he turned toward the bazaar and went to the donkeys standing there with their heads placed in sacks of feed hung around their necks and tried to rouse one of them to bray, but the donkey was apparently occupied with his fodder. "Maybe leave some for the evening?" Sasha suggested to it, the way he had suggested to Poliakov the entire month after his discharge from hospital, and with a small insistent hand he would pull the bottle from his hand, and sometimes also pour the drink onto the ground. It has to be admitted: he owed his recovery to a small boy of six, no less than he owed it to the doctor.

Every morning the boy came to the hospital, and when he was discharged it was he who led him, with the missionary, to the inn. Yes, that Russian let the boy pull him by his hand all the way there, as if in the end a grand hotel awaited and not one of ten tiny rooms that consisted of nothing other than an uncomfortable bed and the smell of damp. It certainly must have been an odd spectacle: the big Phelingpa and the small Phelingpa walking together to Punstok Inn, and the following month the merchants and loafers of Leh enjoyed watching them when Sasha had to coax him to get up from the places where his feet failed him and totter with him to the inn step by step, until he stopped drinking. "Guess what?" the ladies said at the time, as if up till then he drank from sorrow over the Russian people or his friends who had been killed by police shootings. "He's come out of mourning."

Had he himself not undergone a change like that here within a few months? And not just him, others too. That was how this backwater of backwaters, Leh, worked on all the exiles who come here: for a while, weeks or months, all are subject to the shock of their remoteness, but that remoteness itself is what makes it possible in the end for everyone to shake off the burden they've been carrying on their backs – each to his own can of worms – and in a silent pact other circumstances are fabricated concerning what brought them here and what their future plans are, and they support each other's lies. There was a time when Henry still said Leh was just a stepping stone on the way to his promotion ("Kashmir's the place for me," he would say, and Ann dreamed of a window overlooking Lake Srinagar), and according to Harper, it was actually the adherence of the Ladakhi to their old beliefs that promised their adherence to Christianity, Henry's adjutant didn't say why his advancement in Punjab had been hindered (a handsome waiter had been involved in that), and he himself, McKenzie, without any hesitation told how he simply had been fed up with the routine of village life in the county of his birth. Yes, a long time before their plan had been hatched, he preferred a lie to the truth and, already then, he succeeded not too badly in that.

No, it's fitting to be accurate about that too, because that success, he sees today in a completely different light.

Only the mountains here are above all doubt, being higher than the clouds of the sky. Had the Alps been placed alongside them, at the very most they would have served as a footstool.

Only in Dianne's aquarelles were the Himalayas faded as if they had been put through the wash and splitting open at the seams, and those aquarelles could be seen in almost every one of the houses in the small European colony of Leh, because they were hung where they could be seen each time she came to visit. "And what if they're not interested in your paintings?" he once cruelly said to her, because he was angered by her belief that all people are good and do good to each other, and he saw the tears rising in her eyes and wasn't sorry: people are not good, and certainly do not do good to each other, and anyone who mistakenly believes that they are would do well to sober up.

Had he himself not sobered up like that in Rome? And a few years later, when he regarded himself as completely sober, someone arrived here from Italy and added to his sobriety when he related that Magnani had married an English widow whose husband had been killed in Brindisi when he slipped from the pier. It was no less painful than the first matter, perhaps even more so, because it transpired then that his abandonment hadn't been enough for Kate and that she had also completely wiped him out with false testimony in order to remarry; she must have bribed some loafer to testify seen him fall into the water.

Oh yes, it was painful, very painful: it's no trivial matter to hear how one has died. Did that someone, most likely for some paltry bribe, tell how he saw him quivering and sinking in the filthy water of the port? And the bubbles escaping from his mouth until his lungs were filled with water? And if that's how it was, why the hell didn't the son of a bitch try to help him, did he just stand at the side and watch? In his marine nightmares, so very different from the desert ones, he saw himself quivering in the sea and how his clothes saturated with the filthy water of the port impede his movements and pull him deep down by their weight, and how the people standing on the pier (sometimes one person, the son of a bitch, sometimes two, sometimes dozens) watch him with total indifference, their hands in their pockets or folded across their chests. There were nights when that fictitious sight seemed palpable and annihilating, so much so that he found it difficult to extricate himself from it with all his remaining strength to a state of wakefulness where he found himself drenched in sweat and not water, but he wouldn't have been at all surprised to find moist salty seaweed on the sheet beside him ("Don't you want to take seaweed there?" the Russian asked him while they waited for Tenzin, to which he replied that for the time being, the other objects would suffice).

7

At first they thought of preparing two and burying them in the sands of Rawack or Dandan Oilik, but even before they approached the matter, and after having been so insistent that the monk bring both out for them, they decided to make do with one single scroll ("scroll"; the very use of the word arouses disgust now). In the end, it was even decided not to bring it whole but rather just bits of it, since it stands to reason that more time would be required to decipher it in that form and its value would increase and more time would pass until the fraud would be exposed. They didn't have to age the paper, not by adding a brown yellowish hue, not even smoking it by hanging it above a fire, but they still had to concoct an alphabet for it, one that would meet their needs.

By their luck – or their disaster, it depends from what point in time you view it – Harper kept in his library not only copies of the Bible in all languages but also holy manuscripts of other religions ("It's better I should know who I'm up against," he used to say), however, for those he allocated a side bookcase that wasn't protected by a glass front and the books accumulated dust. At first, the doctor heard only about Sanskrit and some of the holy drivel written in it; afterward, from Stein, he also heard about the existence of Prakrit and Brahmi writing, and time passed until he heard about the Syriac and the Kharosthi alphabets, and it turned out that the origin of almost all of them was some Semitic language, Uyghur or Aramaic that was brought here by the Iranian invaders who inhabited India a thousand years before the birth of our Lord.

"If only they had waited a bit more," Harper said, "perhaps they would have spread Christianity that way and saved me work," as if there had been a possibility that the Iranians would exchange their gods for the Crucified One. In truth, only Islam managed to compete with the Eastern religions.

All this information about the languages of the region was no less tedious than the terms McKenzie had to memorize for veterinarian exams, from the names of diseases that were impossible to pronounce (transmissible spongiform encephalopathies) to the names of medicines and their uses (sulfur acetate, white liniment, mercury perchlorate), but it was vital to their plan. They weren't capable of inventing a completely new language or new letters of an existing language (who on earth would do the inventing, an ex-veterinarian or a caravan man?), but they had to put in writing at least a piece of what they had concocted on one night of their drunkenness: gods that drown their presumptuous believers and disappear in their ships, and the sea disappears with them. Such preposterousness, but certainly possible the gullible masses would believe it exactly as they did others, and in this matter they were not mistaken. Five years passed, and the fraud still hadn't been exposed.

It would be best to use an existing alphabet, one of the ancient ones known here, and to change it slightly; it was likely that recognizable roots would be found in the language of the scroll, and that those had developed in the spirit of the people who created that language or the place where it was created (Stein in his time had lectured them about that ad nauseum), and it was important that what would be written would leave enough vague elements for the explorers to decipher; the irate gods and their believers who had angered them (they yearned to conquer peaks, as well as the seabed), and while all the main issues had to be clear, the rest could be clarified in time with the help of the objects that would be buried there, all that the offspring of the drowned had allegedly brought year after year to the shore of the vanished sea in order to cause it and the gods to return – yes-yes, McKenzie busied himself with such drivel; even he finds it difficult to believe that now. But tales many times more preposterous had been told in the region, and in the West too, hundreds of millions of people believed in legends like those according to which they conducted their lives.

One evening, perhaps owing to a chance meeting with Harper, that day, he remembered the language the Russian could help with, the one that the missionary tried to learn in order to read the Bible in its original form. There was no doubt as to its advantages: its antiquity, and the document that had already been discovered in Dandan Oilik, and the Russian's knowledge of the language, but he wasn't keen on the idea. Why had he left Russia, he said, if not to forget the Jews together with their language. His command of the language of the Bible was insufficient, he said, he had never had a command of it the way the doctor had of English or Latin.

"I was a terrible Latin student," McKenzie replied.

"Aren't all the names of the diseases in Latin?" the Russian then asked.

Quite some time passed until he became reconciled to the idea and agreed; and quite amazingly, not only did he consent to the idea but had even found some advantages McKenzie hadn't seen, he would be glad to distort the language for their purposes, he had little fondness for it. Thus McKenzie could have agreed, were they to add statues from the bows of ships to their list of objects, that they be sculpted in Kate's image; so ever entwined were love and hate.

At a late evening hour, at their corner table in the restaurant, the Russian repeated the introductory lesson he had given Harper who at the time still saw him as a teacher of the language of the Holy Scriptures and was still unaware of his heresy. With the tip of his chopstick, he described a letter in the gravy that remained on his plate and said that with this letter the world began, that's to say if the doctor believes what's written in the Bible.

"I'm a Darwinist," McKenzie replied, and didn't know whether in Russia anyone had heard of Darwin.

Afterward, in that thick gravy from which a fly had difficulty extracting its legs, he formed more letters for him and said that those were the letters of God's name and that Jews are forbidden to pronounce them and certainly not the name in full, Jehovah, but he clearly took pleasure enunciating each sound. In the meantime, with great effort the fly succeeded in ascending the side of the plate and Poliakov drew the tip of the chopstick close to it and pushed it back again. "A merciful God he's not," he said.

They still lacked ink, and since they hadn't forgotten the mistake that Mohan Lal had made in that matter, when the ink he used failed the simple test of water, McKenzie enlisted the little pharmaceutical knowledge he had and tried to concoct a solution from his medicines that would have a brown hue and wouldn't dissolve and fade in water. He remembered only very little from the chemistry and pharmacy classes he had taken, and even in the days of his studies that knowledge was used mainly for tricks and not for treatments (for example the stunt with the sublimation of iodine and turpentine; the purple smoke it created was allegedly evidence to the iodine having penetrated the depth of the wound). Night after night he conducted experiments in his room in the hospital, and in the eyes of whoever peeked in at him at the time, he must have looked like someone competing with the Amchi's magic; proof being that during that week he was obeyed more than on all the previous weeks. In the end, he found a suitable compound whose base was also sublimation of iodine, and this solution he brought to Miss P's inn (that's what the Europeans called Punstok) in a small bottle that had previously contained iodine, and it seemed Poliakov was in no hurry to use it.

It was advisable that the caravan leave on its way no later than October and summer was already coming to its end. But they still didn't know what holy drivel intended for the believers would be written on the scroll. And how could they know? They were still deliberating about whether to ask Harper for assistance without of course revealing their purpose. Perhaps they could request he find similar tales for them? But similar to what? Here they would have to go into detail; perhaps he'd could simply find them some tale about the hubris of people and their consequent punishment? Fortunately (so they then thought in their stupidity), even before turning to Harper, the story of the Tower of Babel crossed their minds – more precisely, McKenzie's mind – not from the pages of the Bible, but rather from the church in the village of his birth. The Reverend Stewart had a great fondness for comparisons, and in his sermons for very present event he found a matching event in the Holy Scriptures.

As to their neighbors across the channel, the "frog eaters," the Reverend never had any fondness for them, and in the year that the French iron tower was completed, he was shocked to the very core of his soul – such conceit, the building of a tower so high, and moreover at an event where speakers of all languages are gathered, just like Babel! And how much criminal conceit he found in the numbers printed in the press. Eighteen thousand iron beams weighing more than ten thousand tons! The paint alone used for the tower was more than fifty tons – fifty tons of paint! And more than anything, Stewart was outraged by the number of nails in the tower. "Two and a half million nails!" he quoted from the newspaper in his church sermon, and for a moment, in the bluish light coming from the northern stained-glass window, McKenzie the boy saw them heaped up in the church and filling its space from the heavy carved wooden door to the altar and from the sunken floor tiles to the curvature of the ceiling. "And He," Steward said from his pulpit and lifted his eyes up, "had only three nails on the cross for the gates of heaven to open before him."

The Reverend had no doubt the day was not far off when the French tower would collapse onto its builders, and in his mind's eye he envisaged the engineer Eiffel's scrap iron dismantled down to its last nail. The steeple of their church didn't reach even a tenth of the height of the French tower, but it's been standing firm for a thousand years, and there are nights here, especially around midnight, when the pleasing, deep sound of its bell still rises in McKenzie's yearnings and lingers a while in the air until it fades away.

As to the punishment of drowning, here too they didn't need Harper's advice in the end. He most definitely would have mentioned Jonah the prophet in this context, just as he had mentioned him when Henry and Ann talked about the fakir who buried himself and after forty days was taken out of his grave alive. Even our Lord, Harper said, hadn't been in the grave that long; with him it was three days and nights, just like Jonah in the belly of the whale ("What's a whale got to do with it?" Henry asked Ann angrily; after all, it took place in Amritsar, and if he, Henry, for once has a word of praise for an Indian, it must be with good reason, no?).

"Have you heard about the Red Sea, Doctor?" the Russian asked in the small restaurant next to the bazaar.

McKenzie couldn't recall ever hearing about such a sea.

"The Red Sea," the Russian said again, "where the children of Israel passed through safely and the Egyptians drowned."

"The Egyptians?" McKenzie wondered.

"That's how it is," Poliakov said, "the Jews are never in their own place and are hated everywhere." He drew the tip of the chop stick close to the fly, and this time squashed it.

Another month would pass before the caravan left on its way. All those weeks, they were still finalizing the last items toward the departure, and even when it seemed they were almost ready, more and more problems in need of a solution were discovered. Since the animal feed in Leh was too expensive, at the beginning of August they had to send the beasts of burden to Muglia where there were excellent pastures to satisfy and strengthen them. That same month, the wages of the people were decided, thirty-five rupees a month plus an advance payment for two months to be given to the families in two installments, so that the money wouldn't be wasted by the husbands or the wives. A special grant was also decided upon – fifty rupees – for someone who would prove worthy of it. More rice was bought in Leh, and flour, tsampa and bricks of tea (some of which was designated for barter), horseshoes, hoes, pots, and other cooking utensils. Within a short while it transpired that the bags Tenzin had brought from Srinagar with the sacks of seashells tended to come apart, and they had to order new ones from two tailors in the bazaar; under no circumstance would Tenzin agree the work be given to his father. For the only European on the caravan, Poliakov, preserved meat was bought, powdered milk, butter, and tobacco; in addition, raisins, dried peaches, and apricots were also bought. They intended to purchase the beasts of burden in Khotan; there were a number of Kirkashi traders who rented ponies and donkeys there, and if they opposed sending them to such distant regions, they would certainly agree to sell them for a fitting price. Merchants who had come from there reported that the price of camels had gone up, but in Ladakh only two-humped thick-furred camels could be obtained, while for the desert single-humped camels would be more suitable. Each camel, of either kind, can carry on its back four times more than donkeys and ponies can carry, or two thirds of the weight of one anchor (it was already clear then that the anchors would remain dismantled).

All that while, the doctor waited for Poliakov to finally fill the scroll with the language of his people, but it seemed he had no intention to start and it's doubtful whether he even opened the small bottle of ink he concocted for him. "Couldn't he in the meantime improvise something small in the style of the Bible? Couldn't he at least begin with that?" McKenzie repeatedly asked; insisting on things it would have been better to forgo from the start. Surely he must remember a few things.

"I prefer to forget," Poliakov replied.

But hadn't he been helped by the Bible when he taught Harper some Hebrew and even earned a little from it? Hadn't they compared the translation with the original, verse against verse? That's what he asked, despite it being unclear as how it had been done, after all, Poliakov's knowledge of English had been the very sparce and similarly the missionary's knowledge of Russian.

For a whole month, nothing had been written in his room at the inn, not a word, and quite some time passed until McKenzie discovered what Sasha had discovered on his visit there: the ancient paper remained as blank as it had been. To find that out he had to be summoned to him again as a doctor, and like the time before, it wasn't the Russian who had called him. In the Russian's eyes he was the man who had seen him in his helplessness, someone to whom he owes a debt he can never repay, the debt of his being cured, but also as someone whose single slightly unusual act – his sailing from Europe to India – didn't arouse his respect ("All that for a woman?" he asked him when he understood exactly what all the objects they had gathered had been designated for).

It was Miss P. who sent her boy to summon him, and when he went up to Poliakov's room – until then he had never visited there – he found him soaked in his excretions; there's no other way to describe it. Yes, such is India and such are its contagions, and when they spread though the intestines there isn't a man who could control his sphincter. "It didn't happen to any of my other guests!" Miss. P. repeated, as if someone had attributed the blame to her kitchen, and she expected her boy to confirm her words while he scrubbed the wooden floor of the room from the filth it had absorbed. Afterward, for a week she cooked white rice for Poliakov and gave him weak English tea to drink (even before that he wasn't overly fond of the soupy, buttery Tibetan tea; and who other than the locals drank it willingly?), and the boy continued cleaning after him with all sorts of rags whose murky colors remained even after being washed and hung out to dry. His underpants and clothing were washed over and over as was he himself, as far as was possible, and after finishing his work in the hospital, McKenzie came every day to make sure the medicines he gave him were doing their job, and time and again found proof that one germ was enough to destroy even the bravest of the brave. In that – it's worth noting – there was also some small consolation.

And so the week passed. "It's the second time you see me like this, Doctor," the Russian said when he had recovered somewhat. He lay in his bed, and a light smell of excrement still wafted in the room.

"Aren't you used to being seen like this?"

"And you, Doctor?"

McKenzie wasn't used to it but at least in one period of his life he himself had looked something like that: a shadow of himself. Griffin and Evans had seen him soaked in his own vomit in a small bar in Brindisi, and it took them a while to believe he was a qualified veterinarian and not just an idle Englishman who didn't know how to drink.

"One never gets used to it," replied the Russian, and since the slight stench of excrement rose to McKenzie's nose again, and he still remembered how the Punstok boy had labored to scrub its spray from the floorboards, he was suddenly struck by the fear that the ancient paper hidden beneath them had been ruined.

The Russian looked at him from the hard pillow whose case was tattered, the curly letter P embroidered in its corner almost completely unraveled. "I shit on your scroll, Doctor," he said and in a fit of laughter his body tossed on the thin mattress and on the braided rope under it. "Why shouldn't the gods sail on a sea of shit?" Only his weakness silenced his laughter.

July came and still they waited, despite that Poliakov had completely recuperated from his stomach poisoning. One day they were sitting on the veranda of the inn and Miss P. served them weak English tea as if one of their stomachs still needed to be treated with caution, or perhaps she had simply been lazy to prepare a new batch. From where they sat they could see the bazaar whose tumult was abating at that hour. Below them the spice merchant returned to his shop, and at the other side of the street, opposite the copperware shop, a yak lifted his tail and did what he did, and once again McKenzie's prior fear returned that the scrolls which had been obtained with such effort had been irreparably ruined. In his nightmares (already then his sleep was being disturbed) all the equipment bought for the caravan had been ruined, from the kitchen utensils to the seashells and mother of pearl, and of the three anchors only the lead casing survived after the wooden parts had been burned. The blazing ship anchors was a terrifying sight which appeared in his dreams on more than one night.

The next time they spoke about it, they were walking towards Changspa after Poliakov had agreed to accompany him up to the barracks whose soldiers were then preparing for some parade. All the stones that delimited the parade ground were painted white, the flagpole had been repainted with the regiment colors, the path to the barracks had been swept and levelled, and the soldiers were hurrying each other up. Dozens of short-statured Ladakhi were working on all sorts of nonsense only sergeant majors regard as important, and from a distance they all resembled each other and not only in their height: dark-skinned and dour-faced, poor villagers who had been enlisted for twenty-five years of army service that promised them a living.

It was the hour when the shadows of poplars spread over the path and their trunks create stripes across its width like the rungs of a ladder, but the eyes of the Russian were turned toward the barracks. The soldiers had placed their beds at the edge of the parade ground and stood tautly to attention with their rifles and waited for the sergeant major to inspect them.

"Poor people," said Poliakov, "why don't they don't rebel?"

There was one soldier there who bent down to pick up some object that had fallen from his hand and right away stood up straight, but all the rest didn't budge; they were as frozen as statues. A few crows circled above the refuse that was piled up outside the barracks, and even when one of them dived and took off with a piece of rotten meat in its beak, not one soldier's gaze followed it.

"You would have rebelled," McKenzie said.

"Wouldn't you, Doctor?"

McKenzie pondered for a moment; should anyone take the trouble to survey his life, they would distinguish two periods: in the first, he toed the line and in the second, he crossed it, and by their idiotic plan he could alter the second path of his life; or so he thought at the time. It seemed a new path and a new future were opening up before him, but little did he know in a few years' time he would still be working in that same hospital as if nothing had happened.

"If you had a rifle in your hand, Doctor," Poliakov said when the soldiers presented their rifles to the sergeant major for inspection but didn't complete his question. They were then already very close to the bend in front of the barracks gate.

"Once," McKenzie said, possibly to Poliakov, possibly to himself – and it would have been better he not remember – "many years ago I had to shoot a dying horse. It was the first and last time I did that." He saw the sight clearly as if it was taking place right now: the darkness of the stable lit only by a lantern, and the horse's large teeth shining in the light and one of his large eyes sparkled until he closed it after being shot in the forehead. "He was very ill," he said, and the sound of the shot still echoed in his ears for a moment, "one could see in those eyes of his just how much he was suffering and that he wouldn't last the night, but nevertheless it was difficult."

"But you did it," said Poliakov.

Until that afternoon they had never been outside the limits of Leh, and for the first time they walked that long way together. Beyond the poplars on their right, at the edge of the parade ground, the sergeant major placed the bore of the barrel he was handed close to his eye for inspection and examined it against the light.

"Do you know what he's saying to him now, Doctor?" Poliakov asked.

The sergeant major didn't move his right eye from the barrel of the rifle, his left eye blinked and from the expression on his face it was evident he wasn't satisfied; oh-oh, not at all satisfied.

"Why have you got bears in the barrel, soldier!" Poliakov said and chuckled; and since he didn't know how to say bears in English, he imitated a clumsy bearish walk until McKenzie understood his meaning.

"Here they say elephants," he replied and also tried to make a joke: yes, the soldiers have a whole zoo in their rifles.

That statement amused Poliakov and for the first time during the entire past hour a smile rose on his face. Why don't they buy elephants for the caravan, he said, an elephant could lift the anchor in that thing of his – since he didn't know how to say trunk, he bent his finger the way elephants wrap their trunks around beams at the command of the mahout.

It could have been an interesting sight, a procession of elephants trampling in the sands of the desert and each one wrapping its trunk around the anchor of a ship, but beasts of burden were not their problem at the time, it was that damn scroll on which nothing still hadn't been written; and elephants were mainly in the south, and the only trunk he saw close up was that of Ganesh, the god with an elephant head. All these years in India, he hadn't even seen one mahout at work, and Dianne often said there was no greater wonder than the bond between a giant elephant and its small mahout, something she remembered from the time Henry served in Kerala ("They decorated the elephant in his honor almost like they had for Lord Curzon at King Edward's coronation!"), and McKenzie wondered then why on earth they were trying to pair him up with a gullible secretary, an old maid whose main concern in life was to please and praise her master. Who knew that in a few years' time, on a cloudy summer day at a very early hour, their child would be placed on a pony and would look as small as a mahout on the back of an elephant?

"Have you ever treated elephants, Doctor?" Poliakov asked and he shook his head from side to side.

Here in India, among the rest of its wonders, there were elephant executioners – for some reason he remembered that then, perhaps because the ladies of Leh said the Russian had escaped the gallows – and in executions in front of the Maharaja, the head of the sentenced man was crushed by their feet; it was a chilling thought. And what did the British do about the matter? They allowed it to continue just as they overlooked the burning of widows.

By then the barracks were behind them, and in the distance the first houses of Changspa could be seen, where the doctor had chosen to live despite the long distance to the hospital ("In the end, Doctor, you couldn't part with the cows," Henry said to him the only time he visited). The distance was suitably compensated for by the view from his window, and it aroused in him a love for the house: the steep arid slope, one of the extensions of the highest range in the world, the slope's peak whose whiteness intensified by night and lessened by day, the tender treetops of the poplars beneath it and further down beds of miniature turnips that Dorje picked for the cow's breakfast. In a window measuring three feet, and which was never really clean, the ever-snowy Himalayas and the arid desert and the fertile valley ground could be seen together, as well as the man who took care of his cows ("I'm coming right away!" Dorje would call out to them every morning, answering the long *moooooo* of their hunger).

Beyond the next bend in the path, in the place where a small wooden bridge had been installed over the stream, two women could be seen sitting and doing washing, perhaps a mother and her daughter. Between spread thighs they dipped the washing into the water and then beat it on a large flat stone, turned it over and beat it again. Behind them, on the fence of their house, cakes of excrement stuck there to be dried could be seen with stalks of straw sprouting from them, and far above the roof of the house were the slopes changing their hues and for some moments they seemed to be made from the very same material as the clouds.

Then a shot was heard from the barracks, and for a long moment the sound lingered in the air.

"Maybe someone finally shot the sergeant major," the Russian said.

They looked at the washerwomen as they passed them by: neither of them turned her head toward the barracks. The elder one continued to scrub an obstinate stain vigorously, and the younger sang softly, perhaps a love song or a song to the river god; that's how they sang to the wind when they scattered husks, and to the yak when they ploughed the fields. At that hour the mountain looked airy and lighter than the fields where the wind rippled ears of corn, as if should the wind snatch up a piece of a slope it would be no heavier than a fallen leaf. Oftentimes he would observe those slopes at hours like this from the window of his room, sipping slowly from his glass, lingering like the twilight; and it seemed the mountain was also drinking with him, becoming drunk and hazy with him, and together they'd both drop, McKenzie to his bed and the mountain to the darkness.

"Maybe a bullet was shot by mistake," Poliakov said, "accidents happen, aren't I right, Doctor?"

Yes, accidents also happened in the hospital, but for the most part death was received with acceptance, that's if all the supernatural attributes of the Amchi hadn't been raised against it. "Yes," he replied, and when the Russian asked him if people didn't remember his accidents afterward, and forget all the good things he had done, the doctor felt confident enough to ask him if that's what they had done to him in Russia – reminded him of his mistakes. He was relieved by their proximity to Changspa; it was already clear the Russian would accompany him there.

"It doesn't matter what they remind you, Doctor," Poliakov replied. "It matters what you yourself remember."

Beyond the bend in the path, the house could be seen, roughly plastered and sloppily whitewashed with its window frames painted a reddish brown, and alfalfa drying out on the roof. The window of his room couldn't be seen from the path, but he had lived here so long that this sight was enough to fill him with happiness; albeit a small moderate happiness, not from a sense of ownership, nor from there being a wife waiting for you, a meal she's cooked for you or an embrace for you, and nevertheless his happiness was that of one who has returned to his home.

Then the entrance of the house could be seen, Chondol and Dava's house where he has chosen to live rather than in Leh itself. A large room in the house of his hosts was enough for him, despite that on his salary he could have bought a whole house. In the grounds was a fat goat with udders full of milk chewing grass, and Poliakov hesitated whether to continue; perhaps he wouldn't have gone in had not Chondol's eldest daughter Daychin appeared and greeted them with a warm and shy joolay. Right away she bent down beside the goat and began to skillfully pull its udder over and over, until it sprinkled its milk.

"She's still a child," he said to the Russian when he saw the way he was looking at her.

"We're all still children."

He didn't like that answer. He knew Daychin almost from her infancy, and only after the last winter her body suddenly showed signs of the curves it had produced beneath all her clothing, and one morning he found himself embarrassed by her washing his underpants.

When he directed an inquiring gaze at the Russian, he turned his head and surveyed the expanse surrounding them from the slope of the mountain in the north to the plane spreading southward to the Indus, and from the side of the mountain on which the crumbling palace of King Namgyal stood to the outskirts of the west where the setting sun had passed the horizon line and continued to set, hidden from the eye and still searing – after all, the valley of Leh was so high it still had a long way ahead of it toward the night.

When they came closer and McKenzie pointed out to him the second floor of the house and the window of his room, Poliakov asked him why he had specifically chosen to live here and not near the commissioner's house, like all the English. An explanation was required, and he offered one: these country surroundings, he said, appeal to him more than the city, even if the whole of this comical capital, Leh, was just one overgrown village. Nevertheless, he said, in comparison to the sparsity of houses here it seemed like a metropolis, especially around the bazaar in the season of the large caravans.

"I miss the village a little," he said. "Don't you miss yours?" He already knew Poliakov had come from a village in south of Russia on the bank of a river, but didn't remember the name: Berezina or Bykhov? One of them was a village and the other a river, and forests grew on the riverbank there; that he remembered.

"No," replied Poliakov.

"Nor Petersburg?"

He shook his head from side to side and looked at the girl.

When she finished milking the goat she carried the bucket to the kitchen, and a then came out again and turned toward the turnip beds and bent over and uprooted two of them, and all the while Poliakov followed her with his eyes. Then the mooing of a cow was heard, grumbling and long with all its hunger contained in it, and Daychin gave it a calming call and stepped rapidly to the cowshed with the turnips in her hand.

"She's still a child," McKenzie said again, "and this is not your village."

"I'm here now," Poliakov answered. "And you have a part in that, Doctor."

He immediately became modest; such a humble man was he. After all, he said, it's his duty as doctor to cure his patients.

"You saw me at my worst," Poliakov said to him.

"Every doctor sees his patients like that," he turned modest again.

"And who sees the doctor?"

He had a prepared answer to that, but didn't hurry to say it, and only when the girl entered the cowshed and Poliakov was still looking there, he suggested they go up to his room and having a drink – yes, only the bottle sees the doctor at his worst.

They went to his room by the back stairs, and from the kitchen Chondol could be heard scolding one of her children and then there was a clattering of a pot or a cauldron, and when they entered the room Poliakov looked at the large window with the section of the slope outlined in it up to its snowy summit and drew close to the pane.

"Sit," McKenzie pointed to one of the two chairs, the one he used as a footstool during the hours he sat here alone and gazed outside, becoming blurred from the alcohol while the darkness blurred the mountain. On the windowsill, which was even dustier than the chair, all the carcasses of the flies he had killed on the last

evenings could be seen; every night it was his habit to count his hunting achieve-
ments.

"Even the monk didn't have a view like this," Poliakov said and lingered opposite the window.

While pouring for himself from the bottle he kept for special occasions, he
heard how the monk had been left bleeding in his cave, but this time a calming
statement was added: it's unlikely that the monk pierced his eyes, he just injured
the eyelids with a broken piece of brick – enough to not see the view outside and
not lose his chances of being reborn into a better reincarnation.

"Would you want to start everything again, Doctor?"

No, he didn't want to return to being a boy under any circumstances: he hadn't
forgotten all the misery of childhood, the passing years hadn't gilded them, and he
would also have preferred to erase the third decade of his life. "That monk -" he
began to say, in order to steer the conversation to a track he wanted.

"Don't worry about him."

He must have seen people in Russia with far worse injuries, not from pieces
of brick but from bullets and bomb shrapnel, injuries would lead in one direction.
He gazed at this young man who had experienced things he himself hadn't and
never would experience. He filled his glass once more and took a long sip of gut
burning whisky.

Since they had been talking about reincarnation, he was reminded of what he
heard not long ago at Henry and Ann's about a certain lama who raped a young
village girl only because the head of the monastery's soul was hovering above them
and searching for a new body to be born into – that's how the lama explained
his deed – and had it not been for him, it would have landed up in the body of a
she-ass that was grazing nearby. It was exactly on tales such as these that masses of
gullible people believed in, their plan was based.

In that manner their conversation landed up again about the crazy plan, and
McKenzie found an opportunity to remind the Russian that their caravan couldn't
leave until he would be so kind as to complete what he had offered to do, that's to
say he'd fill the ancient paper with the ancient language of his people.

"It no longer mine," he replied.

Since the alcohol had already taken effect, at least as far as McKenzie was
concerned, and matters of birth had now arisen, he wasn't ashamed to say that his
obstinate father would turn in his grave in Begbroke if he knew what he was up
to now; he would probably have said that once again he was right, and in the end
that's what came from all his veterinarian studies, and that honest farmers would
never do deeds such as those, though they forged lightning strike wounds with
the flame of a candle in order to receive insurance payouts and he was expected
to verify the lie.

When Poliakov asked him if he had seen many such wounds, his mocking
tone was clear; there are those who bend over dead cows in sheds and examine

fake scorch wounds around which candle wax drippings can still be seen, and there are those who bend over the bodies of people in the street whose wounds are genuine and whose source isn't lightning. "The obstinate old man," McKenzie ignored his barbs, "he was the only one in all the vicinity who didn't do that trick." Yes, his righteous father never lied; and he would certainly have viewed their forgery stunt as an eternal disgrace; that's to say – he said – if he had written some word on the paper at all since the last time he saw him at Punstok's inn.

"I haven't written anything yet," Poliakov answered.

There was no point in expressing his anger and so he kept silent. His other partner, Tenzin, had taken part in the planning from its start and there resided in him an acute desire for vengeance as well, albeit not towards the Italian but rather all the Europeans, while for this Russian Jew there was no profit to be gained here. So, after it turned out that not a word had been added to the ancient paper, their conversation turned to Callahan.

The Russian didn't know who he was, and he explained to him; he said that while *The Simla News* wasn't the most important newspaper in India, far from it, one shouldn't underestimate their reporters and what they know, since every summer all the heads of the British rule migrate to Simla to escape the blazing heat of Calcutta; they have a particular fondness for the cool mountain air, and a journalist who wanders along the right corridors and makes profitable connections can hear quite a lot. And in their matter too, Callahan had some beneficial advice that one would have to be a complete idiot not to exploit (a complete idiot or a law-abiding citizen, if there is any difference between the two at all).

"There should be gods," Callahan said when he visited Leh. "What's a story worth without gods?" and he went on in detail: there also must be people who sin and are punished – the greater the sin, the greater the punishment – and most importantly, more than anything, there must also be hope.

"Hope," Poliakov said and took a long sip from his glass. It seems that Callahan's advice didn't speak to him, and when he said that it wasn't easy to put that advice into practice, he didn't mean dipping the quill into the ink he had prepared for him, but what would be written with that ink. He hadn't even written a simple letter, from the day he left his village, not to his mother, not to his brother, not to a woman.

They passed the bottle from hand to hand in the diminishing light, and each time it became lighter and their conversation more leisurely and open despite the drawback of vocabulary. There was a difference of ten years between them, and each one came from a different country, but at that hour, inside the foreignness and remoteness of Leh, a slight closeness was formed between them, and similarities were found. "You also, left everything, Doctor, no?" Poliakov asked and he nodded his head. That's the way a closeness is formed, in stages: first, there is a host that pours, afterward the host feels relaxed enough to pour for himself, and in the end, they drink straight from the bottle one after the other; they hadn't yet reached that stage then, but it seemed they'd be reaching it soon. Since he didn't want to talk much about himself, and at least not about the circumstances of his leaving, he again raised things Callahan had said that could be beneficial to them: yes, Callahan gave good advice after Henry had finished fishing for the bits of gossip he had gathered in the corridors of Simla: irate gods and punished believers and following generations still continuing to hope, isn't that enough to scribble something? At least a few words? Hadn't he, in his past in Russia, not forged anything?

"No," Poliakov replied.

So, what had he done there?

He lifted his hand slowly and stuck out his index finger slowly like a pistol and slowly pointed it outside at the slope and bent his finger slowly like someone pulling a trigger.

"You shot someone," McKenzie said.

Poliakov nodded.

"You shot the Tsar?"

Poliakov shook his head from side to side.

"A general?"

Again, he shook his head.

"So, who did you shoot?"

Poliakov's eyes couldn't be seen in the darkness, only the silhouette of his head and his shoulders could be seen, and they were almost swallowed in the slope. "Someone who had to be shot," he answered and fell silent, and beyond him the mountain was becoming more and more blurred in the dark. The time had come to light the lantern, but the lantern was at the other end of the room and McKenzie didn't get up from his chair.

They drank more. That's the nature of good whiskey, it gets better with every sip, and by then they were already drinking straight from the bottle. The room darkened further and still the lantern wasn't lit. They sat like that for an hour and maybe more, until Dorje's voice was heard beneath them calling the cow; its time for milking had arrived.

Another walk like that from Leh to Changspa was needed in order to get the Russian to finally sit down and begin filling the damned scroll with words (in the end he didn't fill all of it, just a tiny part, but it was enough for their needs). It happened exactly a week later and at the same late afternoon hour.

Once again they left the limits of Leh and walked northward, and again the path was striped by the poplars' shadows, and again they passed the barracks where some parade was being held (perhaps all those parades were preparations towards the parade for a high-ranking commander), and the same sergeant major examined the soldiers rifles with the same strict examination.

"He's still alive," McKenzie said.

"Some people have luck," Poliakov replied.

This time they walked most of the way in silence, and that too is a stage in becoming close: the ability to be relaxedly silent with a fellow man, without taking the trouble to fill every gap in the conversation with words. The air stood still; no breeze moved the ears of corn in the fields. Both their shadows slanted to the right side of the path and lengthened and overran its edge, and in places where it bordered the fields, the silhouettes of their heads climbed the heads of the sheaves.

When they reached the house, they saw Chondol standing in the entrance of her kitchen and throwing out the contents of a soup pot, and Daychin bending down to the beds of turnips and weeding them. The Russian gazed at her, and McKenzie followed his gaze: it was not her hands tearing out the weeds he gazed at, but her pelvis that stuck out behind as she bent down.

Since they lingered for a while and snow was sparkling on the peak in the light of the setting sun, McKenzie said something about snow and it happened that where Poliakov came from a lot of snow fell in winter as well and covered everything: not mountains – there aren't any mountains there – but the village, the fields, the forests, even the river (Berezina was the river's name, yes, and Bykhov that of the village). It wasn't like that in the county of McKenzie's birth, where even if at times small snowflakes were mixed with rain, they never remained on the ground for more than a few hours.

"Everything there is white in winter," the Russian said about the village he had left. Was there a yearning in his voice? He looked at Daychin when she straightened up: through her garments, the curves of her hips could be made out, and the female charm of her movements didn't go unnoticed; it was not yet self-conscious and not applied to attract attention, nonetheless it was unmistakable. He looked through the window and praised the view he found in it and said that if he lived in such an isolated and quiet place like this, perhaps he wouldn't spend so much time outside and would already have done what had been requested of him.

"Maybe I would have finished that fucking scroll," he said, and Daychin peeked at him as he spoke; she lifted her head for a moment and right away went back to weeding: she held the weed as close to the ground as possible and extracted it with its root, and the small heap she made was also painted in the fading light.

While they went up the back stairs to the room (on the way, Chondol offered to bring them tea, and this time he was glad of her offer), he asked Poliakov again why he doesn't use Harper's Bible or at least page through it; no doubt he would find some suitable verses there; they don't need many and Harper would certainly be glad to lend the bilingual copy even if he didn't know exactly what it was required for. More time passed (in the meanwhile tea was served, sweetened, and stirred and let to cool and sipped slowly) until the other idea rose, the one that in the end solved all their problems; or so they thought at the time in their blindness. Instead of the complexities involved in writing a complete scroll ("scroll" - the word alone could cause one shivers), an impossible task for anyone not practiced in it, why don't they make do with fragments of it containing a few key sentences that are likely to arouse curiosity? After all, artifacts such as those had also been discovered.

"That poor monk," Poliakov said, "if he only knew what's going to be done to his holy paper."

It was all still within the realms of just an idea: they had no details as to how the paper would be torn or who would tear it, nor whether the writing should be done first or the paper be torn first. More time passed until the idea of fire was considered; only when the wick of the lantern was lit did they think of it, and then fire was seen as something useful not only for the darkness of the room but also for the white-hot light of the desert. Mohan Lal, their predecessor in matters of forgery had been exposed by the singe marks that revealed the paper had been smoked to evoke an appearance of antiquity, but why the hell not use fire to make the scroll appear it had been burnt and only remnants remained? Oh, how proud McKenzie was of his idea which perhaps sprung from the farmer's lightning fraud. The idea – his very own, genius that he is, idiot that he is – solved a further difficulty: the suspicions against Mohan Lal were reinforced by the fact that no similar findings had been discovered in any previous excavation. Manuscripts in all sorts of languages had been dug up, documents in early and late Brahmi, in Sanskrit and Prakrit and Syriac and even Hebrew-Farsi, but no vestige of the culture reflected in those of Mohan Lal. While by the fragment method – that's what it was called in McKenzie's mind: the fragment method – everything could be explained by the cruel invaders who eradicated the culture that preceded them. Is that not what Stein had explained to them? One nation destroys another or conquers it, and its people are subdued and their temples ravaged.

The question arose of how the jar with the fragments would be preserved in the desert as if there was nothing more important in the world than that nonsense. McKenzie found an answer to that as well – how resourceful, how imaginative, how blind – there will always be some last believer who sticks to his faith and protects it for future generations: a Christian persecuted by a Roman, a Pagan persecuted in Christian lands, or a Jew in any place at any time (Poliakov added that).

How would it be explained that the anchors survived despite the invaders; that question would also have to be very seriously considered. An answer was rapidly found: they are more resistant than paper and wouldn't invoke the wrath of anyone without a scroll giving them some particular meaning.

"You have the mind of a criminal," Poliakov said to him and at that point in his life he had no greater compliment.

But there were further matters that needed clarification. Supposing the first stage of their plan succeeded and their fraud accepted as truth, what would stop the explorers, and first and foremost Magnani himself, from continuing to investigate and uncover the lie too early? That's what they were hoping would happen, for it to be uncovered and devastate Magnani who had been enticed by it. But first of all the bait needs to fulfill its function for sufficient time, and later when the suspicion arises, he will suffer the pain of coming to the most painful understanding – no one easily admits to having been made a fool of.

To Poliakov he said only: "People don't like to admit they've been tricked," and wasn't sure what his conversation partner understood from that. He poured more tea, the break was necessary for both of them, and when the cups were refilled, he saw fit to make some statement about the teapot and its blue decorations – he explained how a porcelain utensil made by Wedgewood came to be in Chondol's hands and what Wedgewood porcelain was, and how Chondol had become accustomed to serving him Darjeeling tea in that Wedgewood pot instead of the Tibetan tea that tasted like soup; yes, the inane chatter of an Englishman from some second-rate joke; all that was lacking was a banal statement about the unstable weather.

"Wedgewood," Poliakov interrupted him. "Tell me, Doctor, did you also drink tea then?"

"When?" McKenzie asked.

"When you were tricked."

Perhaps he was hinting for him to take a bottle of whiskey out from its hiding place like the one they had emptied on his previous visit, but there was no more whiskey, not even on the shelf behind the few books that he laid there.

"I didn't drink anything then," he replied, and he really hadn't drunk anything then: not tea nor whiskey.

Poliakov waited for him to continue, and despite the lack of intention the words came out of McKenzie's mouth on their own accord, as if having waited years for a listener. "I also didn't eat anything," he heard himself saying and told how he wandered around with his suitcase for a whole day without eating and knowing only where he wouldn't be returning to but not where he was heading. All that sudden frankness didn't impress the Russian; he probably had been through weeks like that, months, perhaps even years.

Since he had started talking it was necessary he continue; it was suddenly very important for him to make all this clear to another person, even if he came from a different country and his language was different and he was younger than him by more than ten years. "I was hungry," he said, "the last meal I ate was in the hotel, and when night came all that I had put into my stomach was what I bought at the train station, a little strawberry flavored ice cream."

"Ice cream," the Russian said, "strawberry flavored." He studied his face and from whatever he saw there, his thoughts remained expressed. "Did your wife trick you, Doctor?" he asked without his voice revealing either curiosity, sympathy, or mockery; and who the hell wouldn't mock a husband who grows horns in the middle of a trip to Europe and eats ice cream like a child? "No one dies from that, Doctor."

"And what do they die from?" McKenzie said angrily, and even before he finished he understood that what had come out his mouth was utter nonsense.

Since neither of them was inclined to continue discussing that matter, they spoke of other things – what luck there are things in the world one can turn a conversation to – the Wedgewood teapot had been exhausted, but Harper's Bible still had quite some possibility. That fellow Harper had decided not only to try and learn a little Hebrew with Poliakov's assistance, but also to Christianize him, as if he had already succeeded with the Ladakhis and all that remained was the conversion of this Russian Jew. One Sunday, Poliakov accepted his invitation and attended mass, which even complete atheists like McKenzie attended together with all the members of Leh's small European colony. He went a little out of politeness and a little out of curiosity, sitting down on one of the pews and looking around him ("Is the Russian also here?" someone wondered next to McKenzie, perhaps Henry's adjutant).

Harper seemed happy owing to the occasion itself, because even opposite a small congregation he swelled with satisfaction. That Sunday he was at his best, but it wasn't due to his sermon that McKenzie remembered the day, rather what happened at its end. In the sermon itself, Harper as usual tried to find common ground between things whose connections were flimsy and tenuous and in that he was no small juggler. With astonishing ease he spun winding sermons around *truth* or *innocence* or *grace* or *modesty* and knew how to fish out fitting verses from the Holy Scriptures and weave them together with a few sayings good for all purposes. This time he was concerned with *light*, despite that particular Sunday being a day of heavy rain.

Actually, it wasn't complicated, and certainly not with the opening he chose: "And God said: 'Let there be light.' And there was light" (he then pointed to the window in which a sunbeam was clearing its way between clouds and with perfect timing broke free of them). With some substantial leaps he came to, "The people that walked in darkness have seen a great light," and from there, without any difficulty to the New Testament and quoted a few verses that McKenzie vaguely recalled from the priest's sermons from his childhood and his youth. With a fervor that wasn't evident in face to face conversation, Harper quoted, "The light of the body is the eye: if therefore thine eye be single, thy whole body shall be full of light" (in Begbroke he thought: but the priest's a little bit squint) and "You are the light of the world" – here Harper gazed directly at his small congregation and his eyes passed from person to person from the second row onward; such encouragement was not needed by the row of Europeans.

Without any difficulty after a few quotes, he came to the kingdom of God, for whose coming no mythical era was required and certainly no karmic calculations and reincarnations. "The kingdom of God cometh not with observation: Neither

shall they say, Lo here! or, lo there! for, behold, the kingdom of God is within you."
Harper said to his congregation, "The light is within you."

They looked fairly dark in the faint light filtering through the windows (the clouds outside had gathered together again), and it was good to hear the missionaries' declaration; a dozen Ladakhis heard it, Henry and Ann and Dianne and Giles and Henry's adjutant also heard as well as the Andrews family who came to Leh every summer ("'Within', sweetie - that's inside you tummy," Mrs. Andrews explained to her daughter). Thus, within less than half an hour, the light of creation and been replaced by the light of faith and the light of truth, and from the skies of the primordial world came light into the breast of the true believer and shone from there – "Each and every one of you," Harper said to his small congregation, "is the light of the world!"

Every once in a while, he called in a kind of refrain, "Let us march in the light of the Lord" or just "Let us march in the light" and waited for a reply – "Let us march in the light!" – and he was then answered by the Europeans' row as well. Mrs. Harper answered, Henry answered, Ann answered, Giles answered, Dianne Barnes answered, all the Andrews answered. In order not to insult the missionary, McKenzie moved his lips; the Russian didn't even do that.

They saw Harper turn his gaze towards the symbol of the Moravian Church woven into the tapestry: a fat lamb holding in his front right foot a flag with a cross on it. "The lamb triumphed, let us march in its footprints!" was written there in Latin and English, and that lamb looked so healthy, the sight of it almost made it hard to think about the tormented son of the Lord who had been sacrificed for the sake of all men. That tapestry with the woven script at its edge, "The Moravian Church, Western Himalayas", was one of the only decorations in the small church. On one of the previous festivals, Dianne Barnes had prepared paper cutouts representing scenes of the life of Jesus, but she made them with an unpracticed hand (she fared slightly better with watercolors), and pale spots remained in the places they had fallen from the wall. The altar was simple, as was Harper's pulpit, and no stained glass was set in the windows; when the church was erected, they tried painting its windowpanes a color not meant for glass and the remnants of red and blue brushstrokes could still be seen.

In the corner of the church a wrinkled and crumpled newspaper could be seen, perhaps an old edition of *The Simla News*, with which Harper's assistant had cleaned the windowpanes after having moved one of the pews there and stood on it (the prints of his shoes could be seen there until the congregants sat down). The most festive aspect of the small church was the candles. They swayed in their sticks from the breeze blowing in from the entrance and it seemed their little flames would be plucked and fly off any moment. All that didn't disturb Harper from continuing to deliver his sermon and every now and then insert his refrain, "Let us march in the light of the Lord," and as his voice strengthened so did the response.

The most agreeable part of the service was the Psalms and even Henry's off-key singing and the Ladakhis' pronunciation couldn't completely ruin the vocal harmony of the ladies' voices. With a sense of upliftment, they sang to our Lord that died for them and thanks to whom they were redeemed (so it said in the Psalm, and while they were singing, for some moments it seemed it indeed was so).

Just then one of the candles fell out of its holder from the breeze, and that same breeze transported the wrinkled newspaper from the corner of the church to the candle and set it ablaze. It wasn't immediately noticed; at first it seemed that the candle flame had been extinguished when it fell, but suddenly the paper caught alight, and if that wasn't enough, the breeze caused it to fly onward to the first row of pews, and out of everyone it chose to stop at Dianne Barnes' feet. Dianne shrieked. It seemed that at any moment the edge of her dress would catch fire.

In the small commotion that took place, Henry tried to extinguish the fire with the sole of his shoe, but a few burning torn pieces were scattered around him and someone shouted: "Water, fetch some water! Why is no one fetching some water?" – By then the water was necessary not only for the fire but also for Dianne who had fainted. All that would probably have continued for a while, and possibly with further complications, had the Russian not come from behind and bent down over the burning newspaper and smothered the fire with the worn-out sweater he removed from himself.

By then, Dianne was already stretched out on the floor and the women were trying to revive her, and Henry said: "Doctor, what did we bring you here for?"

McKenzie hesitated for a moment and afterward crouched over her (two months had passed since the visit after which Henry had scolded him: "What did you do to the poor girl, Ed, to make her look like that?"), he raised her eyelid with his thumb and asked the ladies to undo her corset. All the while, the dozen Ladakhis Harper had Christianized were gathered around them, and even if they hadn't been standing there, the church was no place for undoing corsets.

They carried Dianne to a side room, the one in which there was a library of which every book Harper was proud, and the ladies undid the corset and he examined her pulse. She seemed very calm, completely different from the person who had previously been alarmed by the fire and completely different from the person she would become in a few years' time when malaria would force her to take to her bed – then she would be sweaty and feverish and wouldn't want to see anyone, not a servant, not a husband, nor little Charles.

When she opened her eyes and saw McKenzie bent over her, she smiled, and Ann and Mrs. Harper smiled with her as well, and from the entrance to the room Henry said: "In the end someone will thank God for what happened here," to which Harper didn't react. In the church, when they returned and took their seats on the pews, he concluded his sermon and saw fit to praise the Russian refugee, who not only showed great resourcefulness such a short while after being discharged from hospital, but also didn't hesitate to give his only shirt to his fellow man, and thus performed, even if unwittingly, the commandment of our Lord as written in the Gospel according to Matthew such and such chapter such and such verse.

To be precise, he didn't sacrifice his shirt but rather his sweater, and in the coming days Mrs. Harper diligently knitted him a new one, despite that the following day he already bought himself a thick yak wool sweater with money he brought with him or obtained here in exchange for some object he sold. So as not to insult Mrs. Harper he accepted her invitation and came to the missionary's house to have his measurements taken, and at that same visit Harper engaged him in conversation at the end of which he managed to learn one word in Hebrew, light, whose first letter – so he learned – is also the one that starts the Hebrew alphabet. And so the incident hadn't only brought McKenzie and Dianne closer, but also the missionary and the Russian; the one closeness lasted just two weeks while the other four years, and who knew then when and how it would all end.

"He could have learned all the letters," said Mrs. Harper about her husband a week or so later – how proud Harper had been after his first Hebrew lesson, and how determined to continue – "if only he and the Russian hadn't quarreled like that." Even before they arrived at the sixth letter an argument broke out between them on matters of faith, and Harper was so offended at the time that he forwent all the coming lessons; under no circumstance could he agree to such blasphemy being voiced in his own house.

"A dear man," Dianne said about Harper after he married them, but was alarmed by the violence with which he baptized little Charles; it took her quite some time to calm him down. Charlie wet, screamed out of terror, kicking and twitching and crying, and all Dianne's endearments and hugs and kisses were of no use, and only when McKenzie approached and bent over him and tickled his tummy did he calm down. Very fond of tickling he was, little Charlie – was? He still is! – And Mrs. Kingsley should be informed of that matter before Charlie reaches her, but it was hard to believe Kingsley would have any desire to tickle him. With her he'll no doubt learn the meaning of seriousness and all sorts of manners and etiquette, from wiping one's nose with a handkerchief to the proper use of a knife and fork, and by the time the boat reaches England, he'll no doubt have learned to say, "Thank you, Sir," and "Thank you, Madam," at every turn.

When the caravan drew away, he didn't even cry; perhaps all his crying ended the month his mother died or perhaps he didn't grasp where they were riding to and for how long, and perhaps he felt completely secure in the custody of his chaperone ("Rasul he look after Charlie like son!").

How different he was from the Russian boy who at that age was almost completely independent, finding food by his own resources as well as looking after his mother in her drunkenness, befriending strangers on a train and merchants here in the bazaar, bargaining with Miss P. about what they owed the inn (before the end of winter, Sunam Tsering suddenly stopped paying for them), chatting with Mr. and Mrs. Harper, with her about the birds of Lake Tsomoriri and with him about angels (with his fair hair and blue eyes there was no candidate more suited to the role of the angel in the pageant Harper was preparing for the Feast of the Ascension) – a man in miniature who had grown up before his time, and with all the wanderings forced upon him, he had developed an amazing ability to adapt. Yes, that's what McKenzie thought at the time, and who would have conceived the day would come when he would realize that, in that matter too, he had been hopelessly blind. Blindness knows no bounds, and perhaps that is our happiness – the thought often passes through his mind – if man was aware of the number of mistakes he would yet make on the road ahead, how many failures would befall him, how his heart would be hurt, he wouldn't dare take even one step.

8

When Dianne first came to him, three months after she fainted and ten days before the caravan returned from the desert, he didn't take the trouble to act as host, and for a while they made small talk that exempted no one, from Henry and Ann and Stein and Hedin to the Harpers. All topics of conversation had been exhausted and the window darkened, and then Dianne plucked up courage and said she was thirsty, and when he said he would ask Chondol to make tea for them right away, she said that wasn't the kind of drink she meant. They were two single people in this backwater of backwaters, Leh, and after knowing each other for more than ten years they did what people their age do. He didn't even remove the bedspread because he didn't want her to see how dirty the sheets were, and when he awoke, he found her lying next to him with eyes so wide open that for a moment he thought she was dead.

"Hug me, Ed," she asked, almost pleaded, and when he embraced her – the first embrace in all those hours – he sensed how bony her body was and didn't manage to muster up enough desire again, not even when he recalled the naked plumpness of the one who had been his wife until Rome.

He wanted Dianne to leave but knew it would be impossible; it was a late and a white woman wouldn't go on foot from Changspa to Leh alone in the dark. In vain, he tried pretending he was asleep. She lay next to him with eyes wide open and only when he saw how they sparkled, he reached out a hand to her – not towards her body, nor towards her cheek, only towards the small palm of her hand that lay limp on the mattress.

She didn't pull her hand away from him but also didn't respond to it. "Why did I do it?" she said not addressing her words to him. Before he fell asleep, he heard her silently weeping into the pillow, and at the end of the night, when he awoke from a dreamless sleep, he saw her standing opposite the large window completely dressed and looking out between the folds of the curtain, and in the distance the slope had begun to respond to the rising sunlight, gilded from its base to its snowcapped peak which had increased during the night.

When he went down to Chondol to fetch them tea, the Ladakhi woman didn't ask him anything about the second cup, and when she saw them leaving, she didn't say anything other than her usual friendly joolay, while Daychin gazed with curiosity at the white woman he had brought with him.

"Why did I come here?" Dianne said when they left the grounds, and when he tried to tell her that, all things considered, an adult man and woman had spent the night together – no one dies from that nor will *The Simla News* write about it – she burst into tears and her face became distorted like that of an aged child. He didn't know how to apologize or console her or what he would tell Henry and Ann who had probably encouraged her to be daring and take action ("Dianne, dearie," he could hear Ann, "our doctor is somewhat shy, and men like that sometimes need a little help, if you get my meaning").

"A man cannot bring up a child alone," they said after her death, at first behind his back and afterward to his face – Ann took him aside – and it took some for him to be convinced. Before that he was certain it was possible: he could leave little Charles during the hours of the day with Chondol's children and when he returned from the hospital he could play with him, and on weekends he and Charlie would be together all the time; being both mother and father to him wouldn't be difficult – had he not fulfilled both roles when Dianne was ill?

"Just look at the dirty clothes he goes around in," Ann said in a conversation she forced upon him, "Dianne would be horrified to see him like that! When was the last time you combed his hair? When did he wash his hair? Do you know who he looks like now, the Russian boy, what was his name, and you certainly don't want him to end up like him!" It was a hurtful comment, despite being well intended, and one he would not forgive. There was a world of difference between those two boys, the first one's mother was a loose woman who for most of the hours of the day didn't know where her son was, while little Charles had had a pair of loving parents – they at least loved him – and true, he didn't comb his hair twice a day and couldn't remember exactly when he washed his hair, but is love expressed by a comb? Even the hours during which he didn't see him, he knew exactly where he was, and there was no fear he would wander the alleys of Leh like the Russian boy, talking to donkeys or yaks or magpies.

After Dianne died, McKenzie went back to his old room (it was too hard to go on sleeping in the room where the three of them had lived together, a mother and a father and a son who had come to them as a late gift, perhaps too late), and for a whole winter he and little Charles slept in his room on a hard, narrow mattress and he would hear Charles turning over and weeping in his sleep, and all his embraces were of no use. He only wanted Mummy, little Charlie, Mummy! Mummy! He didn't understand why or where she had gone and for how long, and why Mummy hadn't said goodbye to him. Who could explain a thing like that to a child?

"But Daddy's with you," he tried to pacify him, "Daddy's with you and he'll never leave you!" He still believed then that he could raise him alone: that he would find time to play with him in the evenings and on weekends, perhaps not like Dianne, but boy's games; he would tell him bedtime stories, perhaps not like

Dianne, but boy's stories; he would teach him things: arithmetic, reading and writing, perhaps even about animals.

But little Charles wanted Mummy, at night in his sleep and in the morning when he rose, and McKenzie often felt anger and insult that with all his very surprising late love, he cannot fill his son's heart in her place. There was something unfair about it, even maddening. For these past months, when she could no longer bear what was visible in his eyes ("You don't love me anymore, Ed," she said) and didn't want to get out of bed, not even for her son's sake, it was he who looked after him; and even when he fed him or played with him or tried to tell him a story, Charles favored her and like a puppy asking to be stroked would rub his head up against the palm of her hand fallen from the bed. She responded only with a light movement of her hand, and immediately sunk back into her limpness. The malaria, when it erupted again, had no difficulty finishing what one mosquito had begun at Mount Abu.

One Sunday morning the ladies of Leh came to McKenzie to have their say, and at first he was angry at them and their so very polite prying ("We really don't want to interfere, Ed, because it's not our business, but it simply pains our heart to see Charlie like this"), and afterward he listened. It's simply not good, they said, a boy his age growing up without a mother, it's not healthy, it's not right, and moreover in a place like this where only a few years ago we saw what happens to children who grow up like that (not that they're comparing, of course not; after all, the Russian boy actually did have a mother, but her heart was in another place, if that loose woman had a heart at all).

Perhaps in another place, Simla for example or Dehrandun – they said – one could somehow get along, but here, as the doctor himself has maybe already begun to understand, it's not at all simple to raise a child. Yes, close to the center of the country everything is easier, and in cities like Bombay and Calcutta, with all the governesses there and all the childless families that would certainly be happy to have a charming boy like Charlie, there are many more possibilities.

They had heard about the aunts he has in England and the house in the village, and well knew about his obstinacy (why should he give up Charlie, he thought then), so he wasn't surprised by their coming. For a while he even thought they were going to suggest they bring up Charles – were not all the hours Ann invested in planning the new house a small compensation for the loss of her baby in Madras? And wouldn't Mrs. Harper not prefer the company of a charming boy like Charles over all her birds? A knowledge of veterinarian science in not required to understand that people's love for animals quite often replaces some other need.

Within a short while it became clear he had been mistaken. If Ann had expressed such a wish to Henry, he would certainly have said it was out of question at the present, a little boy getting in everyone's way while they're building a new house; and the older the Harper got, the more zealous they were about their hours for resting, and anyway Harper saw himself as father of his whole small congregation.

The ladies had come on that morning to appeal to his heart. Yes, they said, it was absolutely understandable that he doesn't want to send Charlie so far away, to England, but there are other solutions. For example, someone who would come here, a good woman who would love Charlie and he would love her; even if she were not Dianne's equal, she would at least bestow warmth on the boy – a boy needs warmth, they said. After all, had the Russian boy only had a little of that, it would all have ended differently.

And isn't the doctor himself not in need of a little warmth? That's what their eyes said, and for the time being they spoke only of dutiful governesses with references but no less than searching for a governess for Charles, it seemed that they were searching for a new wife to be a mother to his child. It's not simple, they said, they themselves are here only because their husbands had been sent here, and why would someone who could easily find work in Calcutta or Delhi come here? Nevertheless, if the doctor will permit them to explore the matter further, they'll continue do so. In fact, they already have a name or two, they only want to be certain.

Within a short while a third name was added and they continued to explore vigorously, they asked for more references, sent more letters to Bombay and Calcutta by post and by hand via chance guests, but even before the end of summer it was clear that all their efforts had been unsuccessful. No one was prepared to come to this backwater of backwaters.

By then he was already tired of listening to them, and anyway he had already decided to be assisted by his late aunt's good friend in England – he called her a half-aunt – who continued to live on in his aunt's house after her death. It would make it difficult for him to see Charles, very difficult, but wouldn't that difficulty make it easier for Charles when the fraud was revealed here, thousands of kilometers from Begbroke? That's what he decided, despite that the implements had been buried in the desert for over four years and still hadn't been uncovered.

9

In their next conversation he once again urged the Russian to fulfill his role in the plan, and it seems pressed him too far. This language of the Bible he said, is not his language, and not only doesn't he speak it, no one in the world speaks it, not even the Jews, other than a few eccentrics; nor is the religion of the Bible his religion – it had only been when he was born, but no one took the trouble to ask him then, not whether he wishes to be born or what he wants to believe in.

"What do you want to believe in?" he asked him.

Poliakov hesitated and still didn't open the thick volume that had been brought from the church, a copy of an English-Hebrew Bible. "In people," he replied after a while. "And already I don't believe in them either."

Nevertheless, he paged through the tattered Bible and it seemed that despite his reservation he had no difficulty finding words in the pages that would suit the folly they were concocting. Poliakov paged briefly though the thick volume with its tattered leather binding and its title in faded gold letters and that was enough to discover not only words concerning the creation, words many knew by heart ("In the beginning God created the heaven and the earth, and the earth was without form and void, and darkness was upon the face of the deep"), verses that in Poliakov's odd language, when he enunciated them, sounded as if they had been engraved in stone, but also words concerned with arrogance and its end. Already at the start of the book such a character could be found, one that McKenzie still remembered from his village church, when Stewart had compared Paris to Babylon and the builders of one tower to another: "And they said, Go to, let us build us a city and a tower whose top may reach heaven; and let us make us a name, lest we be scattered abroad upon the face of the whole earth" (with what disdain the priest read those boastful words, and McKenzie saw the Frenchies being scattered to the winds when the tower that was built in their land would collapse).

For a moment, the Russian became immersed in the writing; his eyes went back one row and again moved down the page, and his lips murmured something.

"Were you praying?" McKenzie wondered aloud.

"I was cursing," he replied and continued to page.

In the story of the Red Sea which he had no difficulty finding at the beginning of the book – all that was needed was more brief paging forward and more grains of dust flying into the air – there was a verse that could be helpful to them, and its wording was copied word for word into a notebook they had brought: from right to left, in that odd square writing whose letters in their beginning had been engraved with a chisel and a hammer.

In English it was written: "And Moses stretched out his hand over the sea, and the Lord caused the sea to go back by a strong east wind all that night," while in the language of the Jews, after it turned out that a few verses had been omitted from the King James' translation, it was written (McKenzie only caught the sounds and how different they were from English sounds, vayet-moshe-et-ya-do-al-hayam-vayolech) in fewer words and from right to left:

"הברחל סיה תא םשיו הלילה לכ הזע סידק חורב סיה תא הוהי רלויו סיה לע ודי תא השמ טיו",

and the conclusion, suited their matter amazingly well. McKenzie almost burst into cheers of joy then – that's how every liar must feel when reality suddenly complies with him and facts seem to allow themselves to be molded according to his will.

A different and dark ending had been planned for Dandan Oilik, to where the caravan was headed, but it wasn't difficult to suit things to their needs. Isn't that what everyone does? Mold and mold until some mixture is created that one can believe in, and others can be convinced by as well. According to the tale they concocted, the end of the walk in the sea was drowning and not rescue – waves covered those who wished to walk on the seabed – and only afterward the sea withdrew and became dry land, but forevermore (that was the term they intended using more than once: *forevermore*) the hope would remain that the sea would return with the irate gods who had sailed on it. Yes, a folly such as that.

More than an hour passed, and after pickings things from here and there they reached that version, at once successful and cursed, the one that so well convinced whoever was supposed to be convinced. It still had to be written on that damn scroll, and they had to burn or singe all they didn't need and thereby increase the curiosity of the explorers, and especially the curiosity of one particular Italian. And since before everything the words had to be written, and the small room Poliakov had been given at the inn didn't even have a table and the work had been deferred from week to week, McKenzie suggested he do it in his room in Changspa during the hours he was at the hospital – after all he liked the place and enjoyed the walk, didn't he? Nothing would disturb him there other than the cow and her mooing. That's what he said to him, but the fear arose in him that he might try to communicate with Daychin; he didn't like the look he had given her, at the time that look still seemed to be the biggest danger.

It turned it's not that simple to give an almost complete stranger one's room, even for a few hours. That room, where he had lived alone before his marriage and had returned to sleep in after Dianne's death, was and still is a favorite room: meager in its furnishings but prized for its window and the slope was visible in it and with the reminder it contains of the vast distance he's crossed from the country of his birth. There is no more contrary view than that to the flat serene English landscape, and there wasn't a morning here he didn't say to himself on awaking from his sleep: you've come a long way, Ed McKenzie, very long, from which there's no return.

He was certainly motivated by his eagerness to finally complete the deed, and perhaps by his desire for friendship as well. That stranger, a Russian whose life experience was many times greater than his own, despite his young age, aroused his curiosity and specifically because it wasn't love that had motivated his acts in Russia.

"And all this because of a woman?" he wondered after hearing for the first time his plan and its reasons, and then gave as brief a nod as was possible, but the next time McKenzie heard that wonderment, he was covertly annoyed, and when he heard it a third time, he lost his patience and replied: yes, all because of a woman, and said that he, contrary to what he had heard here not long ago, never wanted to believe in all mankind, but just in one woman. To believe in everyone is childish, to believe in one person is perhaps possible. "Did you ever love a woman?" he asked Poliakov, and he didn't make do with that and added whether he only loved pistols and bombs.

"Why should I love pistols and bombs?" Poliakov answered.

For a whole week he came to his room during the hours of the day – a whole month of softening him up had been required, but in the end he was persuaded – and on his return from the hospital he discovered all the little signs Poliakov had left behind him: an ashtray that had been moved slightly, bits of ash, a stain left by the stinking ink he had concocted for him, a window that had been opened or closed, the smell of cheap tobacco (in that way, though in a completely different manner, he would surely discover in coming days the signs that little Charles left in his room before he was sent to Bombay; yes, five years after that fraudulent deed, it was reasonable that he might discover a lost toy in his the room, a glass marble, a broken key, a few rusted screws, perhaps also congealed crumbs that he had removed from his nostrils and stuck to the bottom of the windowsill, and even that congealed mucus would raise a yearning in his heart).

Only on the last day of his being there, when he returned from his work at the hospital, he managed to see Poliakov, not in his room but on the back staircase, leaning on the stone railing and watching Daychin who was standing in the grounds next to the hand pump and filling a bucket of water to wash her hair with. He didn't like that look, and in vain tried to catch his eye. Poliakov was in no hurry to turn to him, even when the girl began to pour water over her head and close her eyes so that it wouldn't seep into them.

"Are you waiting for me or for her?"

"Only for you, Doctor," he replied when the girl finished emptying the bucket.

Weary from ten hours of work in the hospital, McKenzie began to climb the stairs, and on the upper landing, two steps away from Poliakov who was still lean-

ing his back against the stone railing, he stopped. It was dusk and above them the
last flames raged, and in the yard Daychin tilted her head charmingly and began
to comb her wet hair with long continuous strokes, and again he was angered by
the look on Poliakov's face – it was forbidden for any Phelingpa to gaze at a Ladakhi girl.

"Have you ever had a woman?" he then asked him and this time he didn't
intend to desist (being on the threshold of his own home seemed to give him the
right to ask personal questions); and he continued and asked, as if he had already
been answered, if he had parted from her when he fled from whoever was chasing after him in Russia. Poliakov's facial expression said: mind your own business,
Doctor. The handpump was activated again in the grounds and a shower of water
began to fill the bucket once more.

The girl washed her hair a second time; she bent her head, closed her eyes
and poured the water slowly: first over the crown of the head, afterward over the
temples, and finally over the tresses she pulled forward from the edge of the forehead, and only when she finished Poliakov turned to him. "When you parted from
your wife was someone chasing you, Doctor?"

The door creaked, and with the movement of his eyebrows Poliakov indicated
to the room where the table stood with part of the scroll spread over it. "Now what
remains is only to bury everything in the desert," he said (and perhaps only said
"to put" and not "to bury," despite that such a useful word would be worth his
knowing).

The darkness that prevailed in the room made it difficult to discern details,
and they took their time entering. Although the preparations had been almost
completed and nothing remained other than the final stage, McKenzie was having
second thoughts about the Russian joining the caravan. A month before that,
when he told him that he wasn't obliged to be tossed around for hundreds of kilometers and for about two months in both directions, he meant what he said: not
everyone can endure a trip like that.

"Even if it was a year in either direction, Doctor," Poliakov then replied.

According to the Bible, the Jews wandered for forty years in some other desert
fleeing from those Egyptians who drowned in the Red Sea, and compared to that,
what's two months to Dandan Oilik? That, more or less, is what Poliakov answered
then, he had suddenly become an expert on the Bible.

In the grounds, Daychin bent over the bucket and examined her reflection in
its water; it clearly pleased her. When she bent further over the bucket, Poliakov
shifted in his place, as if he was trying to see what was revealed to her eyes from
the top of the staircase.

"She's just a child," he reminded him again, "and I didn't cure you for that."

"You cured me?" Poliakov sounded surprised. "It wasn't thanks to you,
Doctor," and he mentioned the little Russian boy, who, until he began to visit him
in hospital, there had been no change in his condition.

Then the setting sun lit the western window of the room, and from the entrance the table could be seen; most of the damn scroll was still rolled up, and only a small piece of it, the piece they would leave after all the rest would be burnt, was spread out and pressed close to the tabletop by two stones and signs of the square fake writing could be seen on it, and even then McKenzie's curiosity to see exactly what was written wasn't aroused. After all the preparations, after they had obtained by circuitous means most of the items they required, he was in no hurry to read it. Perhaps the end of it all had been hinted to him.

When did they speak about that again? Only after the caravan returned from the journey, and not in his room but rather in the small restaurant next to the bazaar. The journey to the desert had lasted almost four months, and after it, neither Poliakov nor Tenzin nor he himself returned to their daily routine; it seems that is the nature of journeys, their landscapes are irrevocably bound to one's heels (he had only traversed them in his imagination, but that's what had happened to him as well).

Many things began to change in his life, and had they not changed he would not have been standing now and watching the path the second caravan had left on, the one headed for Bombay carrying little Charles on one of its ponies and with him his little wooden cart he used to drag behind him in the grounds and the little boat he used to sail in the watering ditch, and how touching it was to see him navigating his boat and rescuing it with the a branch from some sandbank that had stopped it.

During the last year he played with them less, but McKenzie packed both of them in his trunk so that in every place he would be he would feel at home; he also packed his medal collection, all fakes, the handiwork of Mohan Lal, and also packed Dianne's locket – the one where her mother's picture had been kept – Charlie's grandmother who he had never seen – until it was replaced with Dianne's picture, so that his son could see her in every place he would be from Bombay to Begbroke.

And what did McKenzie do with the picture of the grandmother? Precisely what he did with Dianne's serviettes and her tablecloth holders and also her brushes and paints and her wedding ring (he had also thrown the one before it). It seemed that he had been sentenced to having short-lived relationships with women.

"I don't mind if he plays with that funny cart," Dianne said three years after they were married, "and even with the boat, but you will not bring that kite here!" The kite that had been kept at Mrs. Harper's was completely intact, only its flyer had been hurt, and with the same decisiveness she opposed bringing Sasha's fire extinguishing cart, in her eyes its owner's curse was also attached to it.

"It will not enter our home," she said; *home* was a relatively large room Chondol gave them in addition to his first room, a room spacious enough for a woman and a baby. Was it really home? For the duration of one summer she had pleaded for a home of her own which she could choose according to her taste, and furnish and decorate as she pleased (his salary would certainly allow for that), but in time she gradually gave up those expectations, as if she had said to herself that if that's the house she's been given, and this is the state of cleanliness here – the excrement of the house dwellers was also gathered in order to fertilize the land with it – it would be better not to exhaust herself in a war against the dust or creased clothing or with Chondol's children who had the run of the place; sometimes one of them would slip into their room to hide from his brothers. Yes, that's how it is, sooner or later life slaps you in the face in order that you open your eyes, whether in Leh or whether in Rome.

She already took less and less pains over cleanliness, she was less and less exacting about the serviette triangles that dangled from the sides of the table, she neglected the symmetry of the flower arrangement in the vase and in placing it exactly in the center of the table, and something in her appearance was also remiss: fairly often, strands of rebellious hair could be seen on her forehead or her temples and no attempt was made to restore them to their rightful place, and a loose button or an unraveled stitch could be seen on her clothing. When she fell pregnant, all that was forgiven and nothing could be seen other than her growing belly and the glow in her eyes ("You're looking so lovely, dearie!" Ann said to her, "Henry and I were absolutely sure it would do you only good!"). During the nursing period she still shone until the glow gradually faded and not a vestige remained. One day he looked at her and saw she had aged by ten years.

She still took great pains over little Charles' appearance, washing and combing and dressing him and changing his clothing every time he dirtied it, but she no longer paid attention to her own appearance. "What for?" she said to McKenzie one evening. "You don't look at me anyway." And one winter evening before the snow would mount to the middle of the door the next day, she burst out saying: "Are you still thinking about her? No name was required: it was emblazoned in bright white letters on the black stormy sky.

She already knew things about Kate he preferred her not to know. Two years had passed since the Italian had been tempted by the antiquities he had buried in the desert, but even before that she had heard a fair amount of what happened between them. Lightning flared outside, and thunder rolled like a rockslide, and from the shortening intervals between the flashes and their sound the speed of the approaching storm was evident, and at the time he wasn't thinking about Kate or about Magnani, nor about their children or their apartment in Rome. If the lightning reaches here, he thought with a weary curiosity, what then?

The next roll of thunder sounded as if it would burst their window, but it dissipated beyond the mountain. From her armchair where she sat sloped like him in his, she asked if he still didn't understand everything there was to understand about that affair, to which he had no reply.

He understood everything, but he had difficulty forgetting; nothing remains longer in memory than whatever pains one. It was cold in the room, very cold, and the fire in the hearth didn't help much, and instead of he and Dianne cuddling up together they continued to sit in their armchairs, illuminated by the light of the fire and occasionally the blinding flash of lightning, and beside the bed little Charles' cradle could be seen. He was so drained from crying that he fell asleep in the middle of one of his sobs.

"Why don't you touch me anymore?" Dianne asked, "I'm cold, Ed," but he didn't get up and approach her. "I'm the mother of your child," she said, "you love him, I see that, but he grew in my belly!" She had never spoken like that, but still he remained in his armchair and didn't rise to hug her and say a kind word. She was his too well-paved future, the sentence passed on him, the one given to him like a consolation prize; but he couldn't forget the one who not only abandoned him but was glad about his death (a policeman and a judge verified that).

That matter – his death – he had no difficulty imagining, first in general terms and afterward with a lucidity revealing more and more details despite only a few of them being factual. One of the port drunks saw him going toward the pier and tottering along the length of it, and perhaps the matter would have been summed up and forgotten had a body covered in seaweed not been spewed from the water a week later, bloated and gnawed, and since McKenzie was nowhere to be seen in Brindisi and quite a few of his possessions remained in the hotel, the Carabinieri concluded he was the drowned man. That drunk had left the bar to urinate; he must have been a refined drunk, because he didn't make do with the nearest lamppost or sidewall but walked to the edge of the pier and only there opened the buttons of his trousers, and it was precisely then, according to him, that he saw McKenzie; it's possible he had genuinely seen him on one of the previous days – days when he was still deliberating about whether to board one of the ships anchored in the port and sail to some hell. "Be careful you don't fall in," the drunk shouted and pointed his squirting toward the water. In the darkness of the pier, a few characters who were completing some dubious deal told them to get the hell out of there before they do it themselves, and then someone else was lying on the ground, and he bumped into his leg and stumbled – that's what the drunk related – and a moment later he was already fluttering about in the water.

Hearing that story in Leh, he felt a chill (someone who had come from Rome told it in the commissioner's house as a sort of anecdote that would no doubt cheer him up, being so unfounded), sending shivers throughout his entire body, despite that the water in Italy was probably warm as he fluttered about in it and shouted something that the pisser (he called him "the pisser" to himself and had got used to the idea that the person who had seen him in his final moments was doing that, pissing) didn't understand, either because of his intoxication or because of the foreign language.

Afterward, no doubt other testimonies were added, as frequently happens in such situations: the hotel clerk said from the first moment he saw him the Englishman seemed depressed (and indeed he was depressed), and the barman said no one got to hear that Englishman speak other than the two English sailors, and one of the bar's prostitutes said the Englishman, owing to his depression, simply stopped being a man; nothing she could do helped, she said, and after all the Carabinieri knew well what she was capable of doing to a man.

A report was sent to the embassy in Rome, but not much was done about it; apparently when in Rome the British also did what the Romans did and lost their efficiency. But after two or three months, when the fact of his death had been registered in the appropriate documents, someone right away made very efficient use of it for their own needs: remarrying in a Catholic country was no simple matter and certainly not when you're still married to another. What does a man feel on hearing about his own death and not just from some erroneous rumor stemming from similar names, but one that gives all the details of one's death? Perhaps banknotes had been passed from hand to hand in order to reinforce the lie, and perhaps a celebratory dinner at Magnani's home in the company of his colleagues, or a dinner for two in the restaurant where he had complained about the spaghetti bolognaise.

"Are you thinking about her, Ed?" Dianne asked, and in a flash of lightning little Charles' face could be seen in his cradle, red and swollen from crying and two streams of mucus running down from his nostrils, and at the sight of him he thought: even as a mother you're no better than her, she already has two, and you can't even care for one. It was a cruel thought, yes, but it entered his mind and stayed there.

The following summer, when Dianne suffered an attack of the malaria that had lodged in her blood, she diligently acceded to its symptoms with the same diligence with which she acceded to the commissioner's instructions throughout her years of service with him, and all his pleas for her to fight against the illness were of no use; at least for their son's sake ("And not for yours?" she asked, "Have you already given up on me, Ed?"). The person who looked after their son more than either of them was Daychin, who no longer resembled a maturing child, nor an adolescent, but rather a little woman, Charlie would skip after her in his duck-like gait everywhere she went. "Daytin! Daytin!" he called after her, when it was still difficult for him to pronounce the 'ch' (when he was also asked his own name, he would reply, "Tarly"), but for that Charlie still had to be born, and the caravan to return from the desert, and before that to leave for there.

The Russian indicated with his hand to the piece of ancient paper pressed close to the table with two stones, and the lantern caused shadows to dance and darkened the letters written there. In the end – he said – someone will get hurt on this journey, so the doctor should stop boasting and saying that he cured everyone.

Without hesitation, he replied that no one would get hurt on the journey if everyone behaved wisely.

"Wisely?" It wasn't clear whether Poliakov understood the word or if he was just repeating its sound the way he himself had previously repeated the sounds of vayet-moshe-et-yado. "Doctor, do you really want the Italian to behave wisely?"

With his long-fingered hand, he moved the lantern slightly, allowing the square writing from right to left to be better seen and the drivel that been put down. Perhaps it lit up "bereshit shachnu lechofo shel yam gadol," or perhaps "hava na-apil el pisga sherosha bashamayim."

When the darkness in the window deepened, the faint light of the lantern was enough to raise their reflections on the pane and attract dozens of insects from outside towards it, and Poliakov insisted on asking him: even if you don't mean for it to happen, something always goes wrong, and what will the doctor say then? There was little doubt he spoke from his own experience in Russia.

"What did you say to yourself?"

"There's wasn't time for that," Poliakov looked at the window again: a large nocturnal grey moth crashed against the pane and left the powder of its wings on it, and a moment later, with the same blindness, crashed into it again. "That's what it's like, Doctor, when a bomb explodes." The entire mountain had already been swallowed by the dark, and one couldn't tell whether it had vanished with its snowy summit and with the gods that resided there, like the sea from the tale they had concocted. "And besides that, "he said, "what good would it do to regret?"

It certainly would be a healthy attitude to life, provided one succeeds in maintaining it – what else does one need in life? Having no regrets would be enough. "In the hospital," he said to him, "you didn't sleep well, you tossed and turned in bed, shouted in your sleep. Weren't you having regrets then? Other people count sheep, you counted crows." He had no doubt what those crows were aiming to pounce on.

Then, of all things, Poliakov began relating a confused story from his childhood, not about the bombing of a carriage or a train, but about a poor billy goat that had been swept by the river ("A goat?" McKenzie wanted to be sure), and crows came for its bloated body; yes, that was the tale he told him, one whose evil was directed just at an animal abused by the village children.

And just because of that he had counted crows?

"I was a child at the time," Poliakov replied, as if that was enough to explain all the silly things a person does. And nevertheless, he said that there had been other crows; where aren't there crows, after all, everywhere things die there are crows.

Instead of encouraging him to talk – since an opening had been made for hearing more about his past instead of drawing only on the yarns of the bored women of Leh – he sought to show him that he himself had also seen a fair amount of the evil in people. He strongly felt the need to reveal his experience in that area; after all, evil wasn't a Russian invention. On one of the last days before the caravan went on its way, and without them getting drunk (they only drank tea and didn't add even one drop of cognac), he had the urge to tell Poliakov that he too had once been drowned; and not in a river, worse than that, in the sea, and in the filthy water of a port. And what did it matter if all that had really happened or not? The murderous intention was what was important. It was crucial for him to speak of murderous intentions and all the distress brought about by his wife and her new boyfriend.

"In the Adriatic Sea," he continued, despite Poliakov showing little interest in what he was saying and told to him at unbearable length about that death in the port of Brindisi. He spared no detail: the drunk who left the bar to urinate, the pier from which he apparently had stumbled, his being spewed from the water a week later, bloated and gnawed at to his dear wife's satisfaction (worst of all was the crab that ate his testicles and continued to move its pincers inside his stomach even after he had been drawn out of the water – that was told by the person who brought the rumor to Leh – again and again it cropped up in his nightmares, and he would awaken with his stomach churning and run to the toilet and empty his bowels and was still clutched by the pincers in his stomach).

"Crabs are the worst," the Russian said, and for a moment he couldn't tell whether he was mocking him or had experienced a real drowning.

With a motion of his eyebrows, he indicated to the forgery spread over the table, and in the quivering light of the lantern it seemed the square letters had joined together with all that was written by them, all the details of the preposterous tale designated for the gullible. "And is that why the sea, Doctor?" he asked him, without adding: and for that reason this whole caravan; but that's certainly what he meant.

Yes, it was ludicrous, it was foolish, it was dangerous, it was inconceivable.

Who first brought up the idea? Perhaps he did, perhaps Tenzin, or perhaps both of them in their drunkenness; and if it was him, he certainly didn't bring it up only because of that damn crab, but also because of that wonderfully clear and pleasant Monday he and Kate sailed from Dover to Calais, crossing the English Channel to the shore of France. What high hopes he had held for that journey and how well he had prepared for it and how disappointed he had been. "'La Manche' the French call it," he read to Kate from the guide and owing to two pages he had forgotten to separate from each other, mistakenly thought La Manche was the name of the engineer who had planned it, like Lesseps the Suez Canal and Eiffel the Eiffel tower, and only afterward found out "la manche" meant sleeve in French.

From Kates point of view, La Manche could have been the name of some fish that spawned its eggs there, but being the annoying person he was, he insisted on reading to her all sorts of facts from the guide intended to widen one's knowledge; at least that's what it seemed to him, and he had no doubt that she too would see it that way. Up until the end of the last ice age, Britain and France had been joined to each other! And when the ice thawed, a lake was created, and only after one of its banks collapsed it open up into an ocean! And then this passageway, "the sleeve," was created, isn't that interesting?

"Interesting?" Kate said, "Why not look at the sea, Ed, instead of reading that silly guide? What do I care what happened here in the ice age? Give me your hand and I'll show you what's really important."

He gave her his hand – they were sitting on the lower deck at the time, and none of the passengers were watching them – and she intertwined the fingers of her right hand with his fingers and led them to where she led them.

10

In the sands that spread out to the horizon – curved like them, quivering like them, changing shape like them – a man plods on.

He is bent, and the heavy load on his back sinks him further into the sand with each step. The soles of his feet are sinking, and his ankles can no longer be seen, and grains of sand are rising up around him and around the object on his back, a large heavy object that would be better to get rid of before it's too late, but it's still being carried on his bent back that slants further and further downward. It's not a cross, or a plough, though the object very much resembles a primitive plough – it's an ancient anchor, the bulk of which is made of wood and only its vertical arm and the casing reinforcing it are made of lead. The wood is faded and eaten away, and the lead has long ago lost its color, but the weight of the anchor has been preserved and has perhaps even increased due to the salt absorbed by it in the depths of distant seas.

Griffin and Evans brought anchors exactly like it from Bombay, but in the dream recurring at least two or three times a week – McKenzie doesn't know that; the few things he does know in the dream can be counted on two fingers and that isn't one of them. But with absolute certainty he knows he has to catch up with the man plodding on through the sands before he draws into the distance eastward to the destination he mustn't reach (Catch up with him! Catch up with him! A voice says inside him, perhaps his own voice and perhaps the voice of another).

And despite not having any load on his own back, and in spite of all his efforts, he fails to draw close to the man in front of him by even one step. He treads in his footsteps, and they become deeper with each step, beads of sweat drip on the moist stains left by the sweat of the man carrying the anchor, and even his groans of effort match in rhythm with those that were groaned before him in the air full of dust grains. That's what the wind is busy with, making dust grains fly – that's how it transports the dunes further and further eastward and changes their shapes at its will.

Wait a moment! He wants to shout to the man in front of him, wait a moment! Wait! Wait! But no sound comes from his throat, and with each step the man sinks further in the sands with the anchor on his back. The man is plodding on up to his knees, and when he removes his foot deep hollows are left which the sand sliding into them doesn't fill, and where McKenzie will also step and sink. Again, he shouts to the man to let go of the anchor, to drop it before it's too late; he has no doubt that if the man doesn't do it right away, he will come to a bad and bitter end.

He suddenly knows it's too late. It's already too late and he'll never manage to warn the man, but his legs continue moving on their own accord in the footsteps of his predecessor. They are so deep now, to the extent which it seems the man isn't walking on the sand but stepping through it, and he'll continue to step that way even when the sand covers his waist and his stomach and his chest and his shoulders and his neck and his head, and only the tip of the anchor, the vertical arm made of lead, will protrude above him; yes, that which is actually supposed to sink first, will stick out in the air.

But he isn't sinking alone, that too is now revealed; McKenzie isn't the only one, there are many others walking one after the another with uniform spacing, all are members of the caravan and their animals and all are sinking after him in those endless sands; coolies and horse grooms and camel and donkey drivers with their horses and camels and their donkeys – the entire long line extending behind him; each animal is joined by a ring to the tail of the one in front of it and all are making their way towards the depths of that desert and \the sands. The coolies will sink, the horse grooms will sink, the camel and donkey drivers will sink, the horses and the camels and the donkeys and all the other animals marching there behind will all sink with their burdens or bells or collars if they don't have loads to carry: sheep and cows and horses and pigs and cats and dogs who are also joined head to tail, yes, all the animals he treated in Begbroke when he was still a veterinarian: Ramsay's sheep, Burgess's ruddy cow, the lord's dappled racehorse, Georgie's pigs, Mrs. Wilson's Siamese and the reddish Cocker Spaniel with the fallen tail – is that Mrs. Adams trying to run after it, trying and sinking in the sand and waving her hands and calling to the spaniel to stop?

No, she wasn't running anywhere – he answered himself when he awoke – Mrs. Adams has been in the bath all that time; she hadn't been in it for an hour, or for two or three hours, but had been lying in it for over twenty-four hours before they took her out of the water whose transparency had been lost and colored by her blood. He could have taken her for a wife, or Jenny, the baker's daughter. There had been opportunities like that in his life, and instead of them he had chosen the woman who would in fact destroy his life.

Yes, that's what his life was like now; destroyed – he thought as he awakened a few days after the caravan had left on its way – and there would be no satisfaction for him until he destroys the life of the one who had usurped his place alongside his wife. Yes, that's exactly what he thought for that entire year, fool that he was.

11

They were cooking in room number 1, likewise in room number 5 (in 1 was a man who had a gigantic tumor removed from his leg yesterday, and in 5, if he remembers correctly, an intestinal patient). In room number 2 lies Mrs. Deskyed, which in Ladakhi means "fat and beautiful", and she's not lying on a mattress whose high bed caused her dizziness, but rather on the floor, on a blanket she spread out there ("I'm padded enough," she might have said to him in her language when she spoke to him). In room number 3 is the Kashmiri whose frozen leg they were forced to amputate the week before; the poor man, or the fool, it depends how one looks at it, fell asleep on one of the mountainous Karakoram passes and forgot to remove his wet boots and will never wear boots again. In room number 4, right at the entrance, as if this mission hospital had been established for that purpose, a rope stretching from wall to wall could be seen with strips of meat hanging to dry and which would also absorb the smoke coming from room number 5 (an old man lay there after a cataract operation).

Yes, that's what it was like here, and he had stopped trying to fight all that long ago. It was a losing battle, and first of all he has to alleviate the patients' fear of his examinations and medicines, to make it easier to treat them. True, every country veterinary clinic in England is more sterile than this hospital, but this is Ladakh, and not Oxfordshire, and from what Harper tells of Africa, it could be a lot worse ("Thank God you came here, Doctor," Harper had said to him more than once, "just imagine had you boarded a different ship").

Harper pulled out all the stops when persuading him to move over from treating animals to treating people. He raised all the horrors of Africa before him, just so he'd see that the Ladakhi situation wasn't as bad as it might seem: he described the sweetish smell of black skin that had been shed, the spreading of leprosy patches on the skin and in the depths of the flesh, body parts that fall off one after another – a nose, fingers, hands, toes ("As if a person is being pruned," Harper said; not that there was any lack of lepers in India, but only a few resided in Ladakh and not even one in Leh).

"And the blacks associate everything with their forefathers," he said, "if things are bad it's because they've sinned against their ancestral fathers, and if things are good it's because their ancestral fathers are helping them" – it sounds like the African substitute for karma, and at its base is the same groundless idea that also feeds Western religions: nothing just happens, everything has a reason and a purpose, and there is someone or something that weighs your deeds and passes sentence.

"How can you compare that at all, Ed?" Harper replied when he dared raise that comparison before him. "They are heathens, heathens!" Harper found no similarity between the pagan beliefs and Christianity.

"Believe me," he said to him the day he showed the hospital to him, "it's your good fortune your ship brought you to Bombay and not to Africa, and also your good fortune that in India you continued northward and came to us." That is to say, his good fortune that he didn't get stuck in one of the big cities, Bombay-Delhi-Calcutta, in whose hospitals one surely sees sights far more shocking, though more money had been invested in their buildings; and against that, when dozens of shocking sights appear all at once, do they not make each other lesser? Here in Leh there were only a few, and even then, their effect on the doctor had been somewhat lessened; had that not been the case he wouldn't have been drawn into the crazy plan that had no connection to medicine.

"Here they are still relatively good," Harper said about his new flock (a flock that did not yet know it; only a few had been captivated by the charms of Christianity). "And there, other than trying to cook me, there was nothing I didn't see them doing," and went into detail: from cruel ritual customs to marital relations so unruly even animals in heat were more moderate than them. In the eyes of this opponent of Darwin's theory, they were no better than monkeys.

"Then why, Robert, did you make such an effort to Christianize them?" McKenzie asked. That was on his first visit to him, when it turned out Mrs. Harper had mistakenly sweetened the dumplings instead of adding salt, when trying her hand and making local momo.

"I was young then," Harper replied, "and I prepared to travel anywhere the mission sent me, and I believed with my faith and determination I could succeed in changing their beliefs. I was naïve, Ed, and for more than a year I continued to believe that until I finally understood -" he fell silent.

"What did you understand?" McKenzie asked.

"I understood that to uproot a god from people's hearts, any god, is difficult. Have you ever tried to uproot a great belief from the heart, Doctor?"

Belief no, love yes, McKenzie thought. He had tried for a long time, until he discovered the roots were too deep; it was easier to get rid of couch grass.

"In the meanwhile, I've become more cautious," Harper continued. "Gods with six hands are no better than African gods, but I've realized wherever the mission was too severe, unnecessary opposition was aroused against us."

McKenzie bit into another dumpling; being prepared for their sweetness made them edible. "And what did you do with that understanding?"

"I remained there for another nine years," Harper replied, "and tried to show them the light in every possible way I could, and sometimes, in the difficult moments, it nevertheless seemed only suited to the white man; you speak to them of Christian redemption and they think of their forefathers or of karma, you offer them eternity and they're occupied with previous or future reincarnations."

"You speak and offer, not I," McKenzie said.

"And you'll help to cure them," Harper replied.

"To the best of my ability," McKenzie said, careful not to make promises he couldn't keep. The great promises, he said, he leaves to the mission and the witch-doctors, and Harper immediately became enraged that once again he was linking paganism to Christianity.

A man is born, lives and dies, McKenzie replied, he only believes in that; and even if Darwin was mistaken, there is nothing nor will there be anything beyond death – not another birth in Paradise, and certainly not a thousand – but nowhere in the world are people able to reconcile themselves to that simple premise.

"Perhaps we don't know everything, Doctor?"

"We know enough about death."

And he indeed knew all he had to know then – not about life, but about death.

In the waiting room here, as opposed to the open-air waiting shelters Harper had seen in Africa, where occupants exhibited their afflictions without any garment coverings, the perak headdress of the Ladakhi women could be seen from afar, the black hats of the Balti, the green hats of the Yarkandi, the turbans of the Punjabi; and sitting there were also Patani and wild looking mountain nomads, some of whom had come a longer way than the one traversed by the caravan he sent to the desert. Five years before, when its journey was taking longer than expected, he tried to get information from the patients, and nothing occupied him more at the time. Even if he was required to operate on a member of the royal family, his mind remained on the donkey and camel drivers, the horse grooms, and the coolies he had sent into the desert.

It had taken them two and a half weeks to reach Khotan, their first station, and the merchants who had seen them there needed at least the same amount of time until travelling southwards to Leh and thus even the little news that reached here was more than a month old and had also become slightly garbled on the way: it all sounded too good, almost perfect, as if all the actions of the caravan had succeeded without a hitch, as if it had gone on a pleasure cruise and not an arduous journey into the desert. Though he was pleased to hear these tidings, he was careful not to make light of the hardships that awaited them on the way – they were still at the first station, Khotan, a prosperous city at the edge of the desert, a place to equip themselves and not a place of danger like the coming places that would be truly of the desert.

The first of the reports was from a Kashgari merchant on his way from his hometown to Srinagar who had stationed himself with his caravan in Leh for a week and said that they had all settled into an inn nearby the market, and that already on the following day Tenzin had begun trying to obtain all they were lacking, from beasts of burden to dry beans; he even gave him some recommendations and in exchange Tenzin recommended a few Leh merchants to him. The Kashgari heaped praise on Tenzin for not allowing anyone to hoodwink him, whether with ponies who hated loads or whether with camels fond of fleeing.

There was no lack of ways to cheat; McKenzie knew that too: an external examination of an animal isn't enough; they have to be led here and there many times until it's clear whether they have been properly trained for walking in a caravan and carrying loads. Quite often after their price had already been paid, their sellers would exchange them for others that were defective, and Tenzin, in order that no pony would be exchanged, wasted no time and burnt a sign on their foreheads.

That negotiation with the pony merchants somehow passed without incident, Tenzin had apparently learned some moderation over the past months since being involved in the fracas in Kashgar.

His next purchases he made with Hadj Nasser Shah, the greatest of the Khotan merchants, and purchased from him everything they were lacking except for seashells (the ones they had brought with them from Leh were smashed when their sacks rolled down a slope). Saddle pouches could be found in the market of Khotan for reasonable prices and were better than those made in Srinagar; and three goatskin water bottles were also bought, despite the well-known aftertaste they left in the water. Metal water containers manufactured in Calcutta were unobtainable in the market and in the blacksmith's alley, but they found a container of the same capacity, seventeen gallons, made from oilcans taken apart and welded together. Horseshoes and hoes and axes and pots and cauldrons and pans had been brought from Leh, and in place of the pot that had been battered and bent on the way, a new one was purchased as well as three new saddlecloths in place of the ones that had begun to unravel. They brought with them dried peaches and apricots from Leh, but prunes and raisins were bought in Khotan; their rice and flour was from Leh, but two sacks of fresh bread were bought in Khotan – not with all the other things, of course, but rather at the very last moment, when the seashells were finally purchased.

Hadj Nasser Shah, whose wealth stemmed from the annual caravan to Lhasa, promised to also obtain mother of pearl for them from the dried gorge of Kuruk Darya; and seashells would also be arriving at the market, so he promised, because his supplier would be stopping in Khotan within a few days. In the meanwhile, he tried to sell them a tent padded with wool at half price and an Arctic oven tent which Stein had returned at the end of his last journey, but they decided to make do with sheep fur jackets and the felt socks which Khotan was famous for no less than its jade stones and its grapes (the jade stones were gathered from the Yurung-kash and Karakash gorges, and the grapes were brought from Ujat).

They had to wait until the arrival of that supplier of Hadj Nasser's, the Chinese man who collects shells from the shores of the Indian Ocean, and until then they completed the staffing of the caravan: for the three camels that they bought, Tenzin hired three camel drivers, and also hired two horse grooms for the new ponies bought in Khotan, and a cook, a translator, and most important of all a guide, who two years before that had led Stein to the ruins of Dandan Oilik. Turdi was his name, a name worthy to remember. A fine variety of people had been gathered there: Buddhists, Hindis, Muslims, and even a Jew or an ex-Jew, and during the last days before the departure Tenzin employed a seamer, a carpenter, a leather worker and a blacksmith for the upkeep of all that needed their expertise and their instruments, from sacks to the handles of pots and pans.

And what was Poliakov doing all that while? Since he wasn't able to help much, he wandered through the alleys of Khotan as he had wandered through the alleys of Leh, and out of all the artisans sitting in their small chambers he lingered a while at the carpenter's; not the one Tenzin employed for the upkeep of the equipment crates, but another who specialized in carving furniture, and asked him to make, according to a drawing he had sketched, a miniature fire extinguishing cart with an extending ladder like a wooden ruler of many parts, and wasn't put off by the refusal of the carpenter to deal with trifles. He would have more than enough time, he said, since their journey to the desert would last at least a month.

In all that discussion he had been aided by a translator, Niaz was his name, and it was he who mediated between Tenzin and the Chinese merchant when his caravan finally arrived. On some whim – perhaps his Khotani mistress put him up to it – he offered Tenzin to buy the shells straight from the merchant without the brokerage of Hadj Nasser, and when Hadj heard about it he was enraged. At first, he threatened the Chinese man that he and his caravan would be boycotted throughout the entire area if he tried to evade the brokerage fee owed to him, and afterward threatened Tenzin likewise and also fined him with a doubled commission.

In that way, the price of the seashells whose entire purpose, at least in the first stage, was to be buried in the sands, had been doubled. They were white shells whose clockwise spirals matched the direction of the movements of celestial bodies, choice dakshinavarti and not the inferior vamavarti (those were also found in the Himalaya range, from eras when they were still part of the ocean floor). Hadj Nasser wasn't interested to know for what purpose Tenzin needed them, it was enough for him that no one try again to undermine his standing in the bazaar.

As a result of the fine they had both been given, Tenzin and the Chinese man became friends and Tenzin asked him some questions about his trade. More than anything he was interested in the places the Chinese man had stopped in when travelling through Tibet, particularly the monasteries: perhaps by chance he remembers who he delivered the seashells to; in the Drikung monastery, for example?

The merchant didn't immediately remember that monastery which was quite some distance from Lhasa. He meets so many people on his way, he apologized, how could he remember one specific monk.

"He resembles me," said Tenzin, "only older."

Is he a relative of his?

Tenzin nodded but gave no further details.

Since the description didn't remind the Chinese man of anyone, Tenzin tried to ascertain whether he remembered the head of the monastery whose personal servant his father had been, one who after every night of debauchery would ask his servant to tighten the chain of iron barbs he wore around his neck to add to his self-affliction, and after a night of excessive overeating would insert a finger into his throat and vomit ("The greater the sin, the greater the purification," he was accustomed to tell his monks).

The description reminded the Chinese man of something; he had seen a number of corrupt heads of monasteries on his way, but apparently the head of the Drikung monastery was unrivaled. He remembered his personal servant, who perhaps really did resemble Tenzin somewhat, though he was older than him by at least twenty years.

Did that relative ever ask him – Tenzin continued – to take a letter to someone on the outside or a parcel or at least a note?

By the same token – the Chinese man replied – he could also ask if the head of the monastery's pony had given him something to take to the outside. That family relative was a totally submissive slave.

Tenzin insisted on finding out how many times a year the Chinese man passed Drikung monastery with his caravan, and it transpired at least twice. That is to say, he had passed there at least eight times while his father was living in the monastery and in all those times he hadn't received a parcel from him, not a letter, despite the Chinese man's caravan having gone southward to Leh more than once.

In the meanwhile, Tenzin counted the shells the Chinese man's assistant heaped in front of them, and the spirals that were anti-clockwise he moved aside with the defective ones; quite a few vamavarti had been wrongly placed among the dakshinavarti. "That bastard," he said and didn't mean the Chinese man but rather the man who had ingratiated himself to the British and for them was prepared to clean the head of Drikung monastery's bowl of vomit instead of filling the plates of his children in Leh.

Another cracked seashell was cast aside, and Tenzin tried to gauge how many sacks would be filled with the good shells. Afterward, he deliberated whether it would not be better to put them in crates and pad each one with straw; that seemed a more secure way to move them safely to their destination, a distance of an eleven-day walk, on the back of a pony or the hump of a camel.

Poliakov, who didn't participate in their conversation, took a shell and examined its spirals. He placed it close to his ear, as if in it he would hear the boats of the gods returning with the sea that had departed with them, and from the expression on his face one couldn't tell what he was thinking, not even when he brought it close to his mouth and blew into it and only meager sounds rose from within. The monks in their ceremonies knew how to produce sounds from their shells many times more impressive, and Tenzin made some remark about that.

His people – Poliakov replied – instead of a shell have a horn, not that it had helped them more; in the desert the sea hadn't yet been returned, and no one had listened to them from the sky. He looked at the ceiling of the merchandise storeroom: through the matting spread over the walls thin light blue stripes could be seen, and at the bottom of the side beam a large lizard hung upside-down lurking for insects, and from the place where some matting was missing a sunbeam penetrated and captured grains of dust.

"Do you really not believe in anything?" Tenzin asked.

"Once I believed," Poliakov answered, and the lizard reached his long tongue out and swallowed a flea or a gnat, and the wrinkles on his throat quivered.

McKenzie could imagine their morning of departure from Khotan, because it probably wasn't much different from the morning of the caravan's departure from Leh, despite animals and men having been added to it. It's always the same commotion, even after weeks and months of preparation. The caravan that departed from Khotan wasn't really a large caravan – it bore no comparison to the one little Charles travelled to Bombay on only yesterday – but it's almost impossible for any caravan to have a smooth departure.

He knew that even while it was still departing on the leg of the journey, from Leh northward, and since none of them thought they could conceal its departure, they invented a different aim for it; as if their mission was innocent bartering, wool in exchange for the silk and felt they would buy in Khotan. In the event of someone wondering why McKenzie was there, Hippocrates and his oath were enlisted: he had seemingly come to ensure that the physical condition of the Russian was sturdy enough to endure the hardships of the way, and who could fault him for that?

They left on their journey at an early morning hour, and besides a few family relatives there were no onlookers, and everything was fairly calm, until one of the animals began to behave in an unruly manner. It was a pony whose load was burdensome, whether due to the weight or whether due it not having been tethered properly, and it somehow managed to shake off the load which was then dragged behind it by one of the ropes tied to it thereby maddening the animal. At first, McKenzie didn't see what had fallen, until to his horror he understood it was one of the anchors; not the entire anchor, but great harm would be caused even if only one of the ancient wooden parts were to be broken.

Fortunately, the anchor had been well packed; the wooden arms were wrapped in sacking, and a fall from the height of a pony's back couldn't harm an anchor that had been designated for the depths of the sea. Nonetheless, when the pony began to gallop past the Muslim cemetery and the anchor dragged behind it, the doctor froze on the spot. Angry and alarmed, the pony passed between the tombstones, still dragging the anchor behind it, and in his mind's eye, and to his horror, McKenzie already saw the wooden arms becoming caught on a tombstone and uprooting it or shattering it, and wasn't sure which was worse: a broken anchor or an uprooted tombstone that would cast a curse on their journey; but immediately Tenzin and the horse groom ran there, and combining forces held onto the pony's load and halted it.

Later he discovered the departure from Khotan to the desert was also not without incident and there too one of the animals misbehaved. This time it was one of the three camels Tenzin bought from Hadj Nasser, a bad-tempered fully grown camel with a cockscomb-like tuft of hair on its head. That camel, which could have borne a weight two and half times heavier than that which a pony could bear, would under no circumstance allow two crates of kitchen equipment to be tied to it.

First they tried to make it kneel, but it wouldn't respond, and only when two men managed to bind its rear legs together and a third pulled its tail and Faizul its master pulled the ring in its nose, was it subdued and confined to its place. Still, they hadn't subjugated its spirit and Tenzin wondered then if Hadj Nasser hadn't hoodwinked him with other things.

In the end, the camel gave in, and they succeeded to tie two crates to both sides of its hump, but then its master Faizul began to quarrel with the cook who hadn't tied his utensils properly and their rattling made the camel irritable again. Faizul also raised serious doubts concerning the ability of the Kashgari cook, because a cook who doesn't treat his utensils well –is that how they pack things in Kashgar? – most likely doesn't treat food well, and one can already guess what garbage they'll have to eat on the way.

"I really will feed you garbage," the cook said, and the men who had helped them tie up the camel had to separate them.

At long last they left on their way. The sunrise hour they had planned to leave on had already passed, and a few final joolays and salaams must have been sounded (as they had been on their departure from Leh). The caravan then continued its way through an area of worked land and only after a few hours reached the last borders of the fields where the shade of brown completely disappeared from the ground. The caravan stopped there, and everyone once more checked if the equipment had been properly tied: crates, bags, containers. There is no stage like that, the first one, for discovering defects and correcting them (McKenzie knew that from his journey from Manali to Leh). "Did your utensils get broken?" Faizul asked the cook, as if they were made of glass and porcelain, to which the cook spat out something in his language and Faizul immediately demanded he say it to his face if he's a man and not a female. Before the situation deteriorated any further Tenzin silenced them both, and perhaps the quiet presence of Poliakov was of some help.

At nightfall they stationed themselves between two low hills and when the cargo was unloaded from the animals one could almost hear their sighs of relief. At the end of that day, the first of the journey, one could surmise with some measure of certainty which of them would fulfill their roles satisfactorily in the coming days and which of them wouldn't, which of them would look after the animals well, take care they eat and drink and check for possible injuries from the friction of a rope or a strap fastened too tightly, and which of them wouldn't.

For two hours they sat around a bonfire made from burning Tograk trunks, so dry they caught alight like paper, and the small flames melted the darkness around its edges. The Kashgari cook, surprisingly enough, made a fairly good meal and didn't begrudge Faizul his portion, though perhaps spat in it. Old Turdi, the guide who had led Stein on his caravan to Dandan Oilik and eastward on to Dunhuang, imbibed a good amount of the drink he had distilled at home, and after having his fill demonstrated his vocal prowess. He was hoarse and also sang fairly out of tune, but that song and its many verses – about a rain of sand that buried a hundred cities and villages in one day – needed to be heard before entering the desert. In the fashion of songs and stories, it was filled with flowery pompous phrases at the root of which lay a kernel of truth; in fact, several ruined settlements had been discovered in the sands of the Taklamakan even before Stein reach there, but they hadn't been demolished in a day by a flood of sand but rather by the process of gradual desertification with rivers drying up and by wars that destroyed irrigation ditches, but details such as those aren't worthy of a song or a story.

> "Oh, sand clouds in the sky,"
Turdi sang,
> "Do not shower grains on us too.
> We have not harmed anyone,
> Our hearts are pure."

The beasts of burden and the ones for riding were tethered in a circle within which the men slept wrapped in sheep and goat skins. Someone snored, another farted, a third swore and someone called out in his sleep to his loved one. Poliakov, who found difficulty falling asleep, told Tenzin something about his people in the desert, despite Tenzin showing little interest.

That same night in Leh, hundreds of kilometers south of there, Doctor McKenzie dreamed again about the man and the anchor; he saw him from the back, bent beneath his load and plodding in the sands, and despite that he seemed familiar he didn't know what to call him, and helplessly watched him on his way into the desert, toward the waves of sand that gave the impression of being frozen in their place while in truth didn't cease moving eastward.

In the morning he woke up sweaty, and he wouldn't have been surprised to found grains of sand in his bed, but only a few old stains could be seen there – he hadn't changed his bedsheets for a very long time.

The men of the caravan and their animals must have fallen asleep right away, and when he thought about them, he imagined seeing them huddled up like puppies or each one spread out in some corner or hollow he had found for himself. That's how it had been on his caravan to Manali, where for the entire first week he had been considered something of an oddity, until it was discovered he knew how to cure a pony of hoof problems. Until then he had slept by himself, far from everyone, but that day the caravan-bashi invited him to join his circle, and they no longer called him Phelingpa but Doctor and even Sahib, but he was cautious of this sudden friendliness and preferred the quiet company of his pony, Leon. Every night he would pull it by the halter to some far corner and say to it, sometimes aloud and sometimes only with a look: Me and you, Leon, are going to sleep now, me lying down and you standing, you'll dream about your mare that stayed in Leh and I about mine that stayed in Rome. Yes, he dreamed about her all those nights and not about the women of the hotel in Bombay who were nothing but the acts he did with them on bedsheets so sweaty it seemed they were wet from the large heavy drops of the monsoon.

On the morning of the second day, about half an hour after sunrise, the caravan was already on its way. It was never a simple matter: there was always someone who had difficulty waking up and arising, there was always some faulty binding or some heated argument due to a sleepless night. On the caravan that brought McKenzie to Leh, an iron discipline prevailed thanks to the leadership of Issa, the foremost caravan-bashi who no one dared challenge. How Tenzin controlled his men McKenzie didn't know, but he relied on his experience and his wisdom and also on Poliakov's presence – even the last of the coolies must have been aware of that dangerous Phelingpa, despite his lean appearance; in Russia they had intended to hang him for his actions and for that had come as far as here.

Even if they knew nothing of his misdeeds in Russia, they must have heard something about the Kashgar incident, when a bottle stunned the commander of the Russian consul's Cossack guard, and the story, typically, had been exaggerated: as if he hadn't been standing half-drunk at the head of the staircase of the inn and thrown an empty bottle down below, but rather had fought the Cossack face to face, and when he suddenly drew a knife, Poliakov picked up an empty bottle from the ground and smashed it over his head.

It wasn't a bad story – who had never had the urge to smash a bottle over someone's head? At the time, hadn't McKenzie himself longed to smash a bottle over the Italian's head and castrate him with a glass shard? He could see his testicles inside a broken-necked bottle, floating in their blood like twin fetuses in formalin – but gradually the desire for revenge abated and ended up like this: anchors and seashells and mother of pearl and salt and pieces of parchment ready to be buried in the sands.

They had before them a two day walk along the left bank of the Yurungkash, and during those two days, despite not having entered the real desert, the last mud huts they saw had begun to be forgotten, the laughter of women and children, the trickling of flowing water. All around high dunes of drifted sand could be seen and rushes here and there alongside the bends of the sparse river.

During the months the river was at the peak of its flow, a ferry was necessary to cross it, but now the waters were shallow and many parts of bed with its stones and pebbles were exposed. It was the white jade river; its counterpart in the east, the Karakash, was the black jade river, considered slightly inferior, and there wasn't a man on the caravan who didn't harbor the hope of finding some sparkling stone beneath his feet he could sell on their return and double or even treble his wages. Tenzin strictly forbade taking them – he's paying them a handsome wage, he said, to stop them from being distracted by other matters and not quarrel over stones. But who could pass a small treasure by and not reach out his hand, only because he was promised a few more coins for good behavior on his return? Not for nothing Tenzin feared what always happens when two or more people set their sights on one precious object – an argument, a fight, perhaps even a knife drawn. A group of people alone in the desert (they were still only at its edge, but already had travelled a fair distance from the last settlement) becomes a world unto itself.

After those two days, they reached the southern edge of the Tavakkal oasis, and when their eyes fell on the mud huts of the village, they must have been as happy as at the sight of a city's turrets. It wasn't a large village, and its remoteness made its inhabitants reserved and suspicious. The last caravan they had seen was Stein's and two years had passed since then; they had been hesitant in responding to Stein's attempts to enlist more men for his caravan. At the time they were under the authority of the Amban who had furnished Stein with a signed letter, while Tenzin only had what the doctor instructed him to give in situations like these, the money he inherited from his Aunt Elizabeth, and had she known where it landed up – in a remote village called At-Bashi on the threshold of the desert, for the purpose of buying four more donkeys and for their drivers' wages – she would undoubtedly be rolling in her grave.

The new donkey drivers joined unwillingly and were only persuaded by the lure of money, causing much resentment from the other drivers over the wage difference, despite the agreement that all new members be responsible for their own provisions and clothing and as bring their own hoes with them. That last request didn't surprise them, because with Stein they had been required to dig as well - they dug out what had been buried in the sand, while this time they were required to bury what they had brought with them.

Before they left At-Bashi, the cook tried his luck with one of the young village girls and returned battered. He had a left black eye and one of his front teeth wobbled and it wasn't clear who had beaten him, the father of the girl, her brother, or her fiancée. In any event, when he returned and his bruising was revealed, Faizul showed a sudden fondness toward him and asked whether he hadn't been with a woman since Kashgar, which is to say at least for a month, poor thing, no man should go a month without a woman, but it was clear the cook hadn't been with a woman for a long long time, maybe ever since he was born, because what woman in the world would want to go with a nobody like him?

Again Tenzin had to separate them and this time without Poliakov who wasn't in the vicinity. He had been seen chatting with two At-Bashi boys who were flying a kite whose frame was made from reeds that grow in the oasis. It was a magnificent kite even by city standards, not only in its long twirling tail, but also and mainly for its double frame that enabled it to capture wind currents and maneuver itself in them: at times it soared, at times swooped almost scraping the ground with its belly, and all under the full control of the children who held the string in turn. It transpired this was one of the local skills and those kites played a central role in rituals. Dead souls were carried to heaven on their backs, something they did no less well than Charon's ferry or the Sanzu River Bridge.

When Tenzin saw him stop opposite the two boys sliding down the slope of a dune and flying a colorful kite with one smooth assured movement, he wondered what had attracted him to them, Poliakov told him he knows a boy who would get much pleasure from it. He waited patiently for the children to land their kite and studied the secret of its frame and tail for more than an hour, in the event of it being damaged on the way. It hadn't taken much to convince the children to sell it to him.

It was the second toy he had bought for Sasha on the way and Tenzin wondered if his effort didn't reveal a deeper connection than Poliakov had spoken of – gifts like that a father buys for his son; maybe not all fathers. Sometime later Poliakov told him first met Sasha on the Trans-Caspian train where he had also first seen his mother, in a compartment full of soldiers, on the last part of the way before Osh; he also reminded him that on the day of the incident in Kashgar, moments before the encounter with the soldiers of the guard, he had been standing with Sasha on the roof of the inn and only then had become slightly friendly with him. Before that, Sasha was just the little boy who disturbed him and his mother.

Beyond that, he said nothing, but Tenzin also understood what hadn't been expressed in words. He had been slightly acquainted with the Russian woman in Kashgar before their departure and had seen how little the welfare of her son concerned her. Nor was she particularly bothered by the question who would spend the night with her, not because of her looseness, but rather out of the desperation that caused her not to care what would be done to her or who would do it, provided it would assure her enough alcohol for the following day to help forget the lack of a room and three meals.

"His mother," said Tenzin, "wouldn't have felt it if you brought him with us."

"His mother," replied Poliakov, "wouldn't have felt it even if he had fallen from the roof." That's what he said and didn't know then how close he was to the truth.

Many hours of riding through the monotonous landscape of the sands had taken their toll, and what hadn't been said then would perhaps be said at the end of the day beside the bonfire while waiting for the water in the pot to boil or when they spread themselves out on the sand for a night's sleep. Even an endless expanse of sand can be as intimate as a room when it's outlined by the light of a bonfire or a circle of animals sleeping while standing.

12

The caravan left Tavakkal at an early morning hour and roughly half of the inhabitants of the oasis came to take leave of them – women, children, and other the curious onlookers who envied the wages of the those who had joined but didn't envy them the journey they would make. This time the departure went smoothly: all the equipment had been properly tied, no animals misbehaved, not even the one whose bags concealed jades its owner had gathered in the Yurungkash gorge, despite Tenzin's prohibition.

A woman with abundant beads and bangles blew a kiss in the air to one of the camel drivers, and just then the camel opened its buttocks wide and defecated. The elder of the village also came to part from them, a gaunt old man for whom even a small whirlwind of sand would seemingly be enough to blow into the air, and when he blessed the men of the village who had joined the caravan, they listened in a silence broken only by the neighing of the animals.

The two children from whom Poliakov had bought the kite also came and he showed it to them wrapped in straw and packed in a flat wooden box that he made and they were amazed to see the reed frame they had built packed like a precious object (in exactly the same way Stein had packed parts of walls he had sawn off with frescos on them). Afterward, they shyly asked the name of the boy who would be receiving their kite as a gift, and when Poliakov finally understood their question and replied "Sasha," they repeated the name, tasting its moist, soft syllables in their mouths.

"You could have been friends with Sasha," he said and closed the box and mounted his pony. The hour had come to leave. Had he been clairvoyant, he surely would have left the kite or buried it in the ruins of Dandan Oilik.

They had five days ahead of walking in the sand without any oasis, any shade, any water. On the first day, while they still walked alongside the bank and its green bushes still accompanied them, the animals drank all they could, as if they sensed in the coming days it would be difficult to find water. All around low dunes could be seen no more than three meters high, but the walking was arduous and slow. With each step, the animals and the men's feet sank into the fine sand, and the speed of the camels did not exceed four to five kilometers an hour. At that rate, it was clear that before evening they wouldn't cross more than twenty kilometers, at the most.

At first the briars became sparse and then the tamarisks as well. Here and there a wild poplar still could be seen and a few meager toghrak trees without foliage and their branches blanched by aridity. There were also wilting bushes whose withered roots could be used for burning. Water could still be found at the depth of six feet, (McKenzie knew this from reading Stein's diaries); it was bitter, but with no other water, they'd drink it eagerly. The greater the distance from the river, the greater the saltiness of the water, but that was to be expected – in fact, everything was to be expected: they were taking the exact route that Stein had taken two years previously. Only their purpose had been reversed, to bury and not to dig out.

Toward evening they stationed themselves only twelve kilometers from At-Bashi, but it seemed that dozens of kilometers of sand separated them, infinite and boundless dunes, and when Turdi began to sing his song in his hoarse voice, he was answered by a number of men, some of whom weren't sure of the melody:

> Oh, sand clouds in the sky
> Do not shower grains on us too.
> We have not harmed anyone,
> Our hearts are pure.

There was another song, since clouds here, as is well-known, don't respond to all pleas, and in this song the singers address their towns and villages where the sand has fallen:

> Where have you vanished to, my beautiful city,
> where?
> Where have you vanished to, my beloved home,
> where?
> Where have you vanished to, my beloved?
> You have all been drowned in the sand.

Each song was sadder than the last, but when they were sung in unison opposite the fire, they offered a certain consolation.

Before going to sleep, Tenzin and Poliakov exchanged a few words, and not about a sand flood or water, because the winters in the places where they had been born were snowbound. One spoke of a snow avalanche in the Himalayas under which a caravan could be buried in an instant, and even after dozens of years its men and animals would be found as in the moment the snow had buried them – whoever was yawning was caught in the middle of a yawn, whoever had already fallen asleep was caught in the middle of a dream – and the other spoke about Russia's snows in his broken language: there are no avalanches there, but the rivers freeze over for the length of hundreds of kilometers and turn white like the plains surrounding them (he also told that to the doctor who had never seen the Thames freeze over that way); perhaps he then also told him about the goat that had been swept away on a block of ice.

Perhaps they drank something in order to fall asleep more easily, chang or something really strong, and perhaps not; either way, the following morning at first light they were already prepared for the way. "Have you tied your things well?" They heard Faizul ask the cook, and afterward heard the cook curse.

It was a cold day on which the temperature would not rise above thirty-seven degrees Fahrenheit even when the sun reached its zenith; but there was no wind, and the air was clear and fresh, and in that clarity the dunes could be seen from a distance, curve behind curve alongside curve from horizon to horizon, waves of a vast sand sea whose movements are too slow to discern. How Turdi found his way among them was impossible to know, and quite often he went completely against the direction shown on the compass and was proven right. The contours of the dunes have their own logic, and whoever tries to cross them according to a magnetic needle is liable to trudge in them up to above his knees and sink.

Once Tenzin tried to argue with Turdi over the matter of digging a well, and after that argued with him no more. At the time it seemed to him the animals were thirsty, and therefore he ordered them to stop and dig a well in a place where a few dry bushes could be seen nearby. They still hadn't gone very far from the Yurung-kash gorge, and it was not unreasonable to try and find water at a depth not too great, but Turdi said there was no chance of that: these bushes grow here from time immemorial, even before the river gorge bends eastward, and it would a waste of time and strength, because afterward the men would be exhausted and thirstier.

They dug for hours and battled with the sand that flowed back in (it was mainly the newly joined men from Tavakkal), they widened and deepened the pit, went down into it, and deepened it further, and when from its depths they raised a fistful of dark damp sand Tenzin was exultant and Turdi said nothing. "What do you say, old man?" Tenzin asked him, and the old man didn't reply. "Carry on, carry on," Tenzin urged the diggers on and promised them handsome remuneration the moment water is discovered. Four hours later they reached the depth of six feet, and again had to widen the diameter of the pit into which sand flowed in trickles, in showers, in cascades. Buckets of sand were raised by rope and emptied out, and around the rim of the pit all who had managed to force their way there bent down and waited impatiently to see their reflections in the water. When the diggers reached the depth of nine feet - their heads were already far down below – the sand that they brought up was no longer damp, Tenzin understood he had been mistaken.

Another man might have mocked him, but Turdi only told the camel drivers to give their camels rapeseed oil ("camel tea" is what that stinking drink was called), and the ponies and donkeys received pieces of ice that had been hewn from the Yurungkash gorge while the caravan passed through it and had been

preserved in tin containers wrapped in goat skins. The men also made do with
that, and Tenzin said to Turdi: "What would I do without you?"

Poliakov was not at his best that day: it was evident he was suffering from the aridity of the desert no less than he had suffered from the chill of the mountains on
the way to Leh, but when Tenzin asked him how he was feeling, he made a gesture
of insignificance. A few months before, Tenzin had tended to him on their way to
Leh and enough time had passed since then; if he now decided not to surrender
to any weakness and behave like the man he had been when he first met him, why
should he interfere?

Surrendering to weakness is easy, Tenzin once said to McKenzie, and one
simply has to say no to it and look away.

"You would have made an excellent monk," the doctor said to him at the time;
exactly two days before that Tenzin had returned with Poliakov from their journey
to the cave.

"No," replied Tenzin, "I wouldn't have."

Then McKenzie heard in detail for the first time the part Poliakov had played
in the deed that resulted in the required paper landing up in their hands. The
condition of the monk wasn't clear; after all, he was left bleeding in his cave, either
from his eyes or from his eyelids, and that also seemed like something that would
prey on the doctor's conscience to the grave, like Dianne's death: somewhere in
those mountains, in a cave that was broken into or resealed, that monk is either
alive or not, after having tried to blind himself with a piece of stone in order to
avoid the enticements outside. There are those who inflict a deformity upon themselves in order not to sin, and there are those who without hesitation leave their
fellow man to die. He did not treat his patients in the hospital that way, nor Dianne,
and even the man toward whom all his efforts are directed, Carlo Magnani, was
well cared for in his hospital in the end, despite that McKenzie, wouldn't have been
at all sorry to bury him in the small cemetery behind the church.

"Fine," Poliakov said when asked how he was, despite his skin having become dry
and his lips cracked. He didn't complain about the paucity of water, nor the heat
or the swampy sand, and to those who had heard about his deeds in Russia, his
answer would reinforce the reputation attributed to him, but he didn't always look
or sound that way: in Kashgar it seems he had acted out of drunkenness, and
on his way from there, and in the hospital, he had been delirious, but what that
showed as to the essence of the man, no one could know.

What does he need all this for, McKenzie asked him months before, when he
expressed the wish to help in matters concerning the caravan, and advised him not
to endanger his health again. He won't be the first Phelingpa to venture into the
depths of the desert, there had been geographers and archeologists before him, but

they had aims on which their fame would be built, while he, the Russian, seemingly wouldn't gain anything from this journey.

"Leave the decision to me," he replied and also asked what Tenzin had to gain from it.

"Revenge," McKenzie gave the answer that would have suited himself as well. "And what do you have to gain?"

Poliakov hesitated for a moment. "Have you ever looked death in the eye, Doctor?"

Instead of replying, he asked how that was related to their matter.

"I have."

They then sat down and ate, and Poliakov tried to pick up a few rebellious noodles with his chopsticks. "To one who sees that, Doctor, even once," he continued, "nothing will ever look the same."

His face didn't express defiance, nor sadness, but something else.

"Did you see it in Russia?"

It was a silly question, but still he asked it. Wouldn't one who has seen death once – he said – do everything to not see it again? The thought rose despite that he himself, when staying at the hotel in Bombay, out of which at least one corpse had been taken during his time there, hadn't been careful about the diseases he could have picked up from the drinking water or the food or the women.

"One becomes addicted, Doctor."

"To danger?"

"To that moment when you can either stay alive or die, and not know which will win. You never feel more alive."

McKenzie thought he was mistaken; and woe to him who only on the brink of death feels that he's alive; and told him so, despite that during that crazy year he himself had become rejuvenated and filled with an energy of which there had been no trace during the previous years. When had he ever sensed life in all its vitality? More than a decade before that, in England; and not because that night at the inn above the pub had been so spectacular – not at all – but because he felt there was nothing more important than that motion inside the body of a beloved one, back and forth, back and forth, a motion after which nothing will appear as had appeared up until then. He had been mistaken, of course ("I see that I'll have to teach you a lot," Kate said, the moment after he rose from her and lay on his back, still panting and short of breath, while her breathing remained regular).

"And that's why," he asked Poliakov, "you want to go out to the desert now?" To him it sounded ridiculous, to go out to the desert because of things that had happened in Russia, until he reminded himself that he had travelled to India because of things that had happened in Italy.

"I've never been to the desert," Poliakov answered evasively.

"You haven't been to many places."

"But I will go to the desert."

From day to day the dunes grew, and the temperatures fell. For the most part, the direction of the dunes was from north to south, and even if they changed slightly – for example, from north-west to south-east – their appearance brought to mind waves of a sea that had been sullied by the dust and their motion halted. The spray of their foam were the sand grains blown by the wind and drowning in the depths of its dunes was a possibility and only with great effort the feet of the animals and men were lifted out the sand and with further effort they strived on and on toward the desolate port city.

There were hours when only very little happened, and which were characterized mainly by the response to the monotonous rhythm of the animal beneath one, camel or pony, and at other hours weariness weighed so heavily on the eyelids that thin wooden sticks had to be inserted between them to keep them open. Everyone waited for the respite and its joys – the resting, the drinking, the eating (the Kashgari cook was actually fairly accomplished) – then they would get down from their animals, and the animals would rest as well: the horses and the donkeys standing up, the camels kneeling and spreading their long necks over the sand and only their humps sticking out, and even in their recumbence they would be taller than the ponies. In the chill of the night, it was best to huddle together, animals and men. One even wouldn't recoil from the body heat of someone who had been excessively annoying during the day. All around, as far as the eye could see, there was nothing but the desert and the night.

Perhaps they sang to the sands into which they had travelled deeply, or perhaps they only spoke: there's quite a lot one can say during that time before sleep carries each one off to where it will; a closeness such as that happens to chance passengers on a train who will part ways at the next station, but as for those here, the very next morning when they rise and the caravan departs on its way, they'll only have one destination before them, a cluster of ruins in the desert.

They were surrounded on all sides by expanses of sand that turned black from horizon to horizon, and only a small plot of all that was delineated by the animals sleeping in their circle, within which everyone huddled together. Near to them a donkey braying into the darkness could be heard, and a pony neighing. One of the camels snorted, one protractedly broke wind that seemed to pass through its entire hump. Far above them a black velvet sky could be seen in which a multitude of stars shone; the edges of its dome supported by the silhouettes of the camel dumps – the only feature that could be perceived above the surface of the ground.

Someone, perhaps Faizul, asked his neighbor if to keep warm he had to stink up the air like that camel, and another asked Turdi why tonight, after they had gone further into the desert and were so close to Dandan Oilik, he no longer sang his song to them, and he replied that the song wasn't specifically for that: in summer one sings of snow, in winter of the sun, in the mountains one sings of the sea and in the sea of the mountains, and no one sings about the tip of one's nose, except for old elephants. Tomorrow or the following day – he said – when they reach Dandan

Oilik, they'll probably start to sing about the women they had left at home, and from whom they were so glad to have a little rest, or about their children.

Questions the doctor had refrained from asking, for example if Poliakov had left behind a souvenir in the belly of the woman he had parted from in Russia, Tenzin asked without hesitation: those about to enter the desert with a clear head have already forgone many of their manners anyway. A pot full of coals blazed between the two of them and their orange glow turned grey from moment to moment, and not far off one of the horses neighed again; maybe it picked up the scent of some rodent or desert reptile drawing close to its leg and flinched, and in an instant the other horses joined in the neighing.

"Perhaps it wasn't even born," Poliakov replied. "It would be better not to have another Poliakov in the world."

Leaning on his elbow, Tenzin again picked at the coals and blew on them with and a small flame burned. "And that's why you go to the desert?"

Poliakov lifted himself up slightly and bent his head towards the pot. A pale orange glow lit him as he spat into it, and right away the angry fizzing of the coals could be heard.

It was extremely cold, about fourteen degrees Fahrenheit, and over the mouths of whoever hadn't fallen asleep, little vapor clouds thickened as they spoke. It was the coldest night up to now. In order to prepare tea in the evening they liquefied pieces of ice they took out of the metal containers, and had it not been for the yak butter that had been melted into the water, all sorts of aftertastes of the Yurung-kash would have been evident, perhaps even the scent of the goatskins the containers were wrapped in.

"Maybe it was born and is waiting for you to return?" Tenzin said. "I saw how you bought gifts for the little Russian."

"Sasha," Poliakov said. Perhaps he felt a responsibility for him, despite him not being his son, perhaps he missed him. Who is master over what they miss?

The people of Dandan Oilik – all those they had fabricated for the purpose of the crazy plan – longed for gods that had gone away; so it was written on the pieces of paper they had forged. And all that bother just to execute a plan that would have been better to abandon from its start; yes, while still on one of those evenings he hunted flies in his room and sorted and arranged them, the Delia platura and the Delia flavibasis and the Delia antiqua (at the time he had been engrossed in a scholarly classification and studied the identifying marks of each species of those tiny creatures that even in his years as a veterinarian he had never been required to busy himself with).

He didn't know then that one day he would also study the names of all sorts of anchors as well as the symptoms of dehydration and sunstroke, as if in the hour of need he could determine from afar just how badly the situation had deteriorated, and perhaps salvage it.

Flushed skin, nausea, and rapid pulse are the symptoms of mild dehydration (the body has by then lost two to three liters); dizziness, headaches, nausea and vomiting, shortness of breath, severe dryness of the mouth, cold and pale skin, weakness and difficulty in moving are the symptoms of medium dehydration (the body has by then lost more than four to seven liters); severe disorders of consciousness, delirium and eyesight and hearing disorders are the symptoms of severe dehydration (by then more than eleven percent of body weight has been lost); and symptoms of sunstroke are also liable to develop, that is to say, a sharp rise in body temperature and tissue destruction and convulsions and loss of consciousness. These two progressions are straightforward and completely clear, even a first-year medical student could understand them: the sharp rise in body temperature destroys the tissue, and when the volume of blood is reduced during dehydration, its flow is naturally damaged – at first to secondary organs, so that it continues to flow to the primary ones, and afterward to the primary ones as well: the respiratory system, the brain, the heart.

But he didn't leave with the caravan. He was through with his journeys, and only heard about the caravan from passersby who came to Leh: there were those who saw it on the way to Khotan, there were those who met its men in Khotan itself, and had also seen them in Tavakkal, and afterward, for a very long time, no one saw them.

13

With the sunrise, after a heavy sleep disturbed only toward the end of the night by something as yet unknown, they awoke to a sky not murky from the remains of the darkness but from grains of sand. Gusts of wind howled and swooped on the caravan like a herd of predators the sky had imprisoned, mixing vast clouds of sand and dust – in an instant they came and covered everything and were cast onward and onward, as if entire dunes had been flung into the air, and on their way to their new location dropped grains of sand to cover everything below. It was the karaburan, the black storm, and the further the sun drew away from the horizon and rose higher into the sky, the more its blazing circle was dimmed and reduced. The light was dusky, choked by sand.

Perhaps they would have continued to lie there until the storm passes, each where he had slept – as is sometimes recommended – had it not been for the danger that they could be buried alive that way. They had to get up and shake off the layer of sand thickening and weighing heavily on the body, on objects, on the animals. Only little was revealed to the eye through the shower of the grains, and even that was blurry; only the nearby camel could be seen like a shadow of a shadow in the midst of the waves of a grainy fog, and the chiming of its bell could not be heard as it moved its large head here and there in order to evade the lashings of the sand. It was the youngest camel of them all and hadn't yet experienced such a storm; the others already knelt on the ground and spread their long necks on the sand in the direction of the wind, and one could try and curl up next to their bellies and hope the wind passing over them wouldn't drop its entire load there. After all, that's how dunes are created: around a tree stump, a fallen crate, a bloated carcass. At that hour man and beast were united in their war with the wind and the sand, a war that in order to survive its dangers one had to wait patiently until the storm passes. An hour? Hours? A day? A day and a night? So strong was that storm that it seemed to be blowing from one end of the world to the other with no end to its grains, and that the entire desert had decided to wander to a different place.

Perhaps the legends of Taklamakan told of such a sandstorm, and only fabricated the clouds from which the sand showered down like rain, but at those moments no one was thinking about legends. They were all defending themselves as well as they could against the lashings of the grains that filled the sky, a sky becoming more and more solid from moment to moment, as if in the end it would be a new geological layer conceal the previous one beneath it. The shouts were swallowed by the wind, as were the sounds of the beasts of burden; no neighing, no whinnying, no braying, and only at touching distance could words made by human voices be fathomed. It was impossible to light a fire, impossible to prepare a meal, and whoever tried to chew a piece of naan left over from the night felt grains of sand being ground between his teeth, more than felt the dough.

"Karaburan," shouted Tenzin, because Poliakov hadn't yet experienced a storm like this. The pot of coals that had stood between them in the night was entirely buried in sand, their bundles had also been buried, and only their heads sprouted, covered up to their eyebrows by the blankets and the grains. They lay on their stomachs, the heads in their elbows and their eyes peering ahead reduced to narrow slits.

"Why not be buried alive?" Poliakov said.

Another barrage of grains was hurled at them, and all the shouting of the coolies, the horse grooms, the donkey, and camel drivers was swallowed by the wind.

Tenzin lifted his head slightly and rested his chin on his elbow and strained his eyes to see ahead. The young camel that had insisted on standing, finally understood what his brothers and forefathers had understood in previous storms; it knelt and spread its long neck on the ground in the direction of the wind, and within a few moments its silhouette became blurred.

Tenzin had to shout his question twice in order that it be heard, and for a moment the direction of the wind changed, and from a distance that couldn't be gauged, something could be seen, perhaps a hump or just a mound of sand.

"Because I've been a bad person," Poliakov answered and fell silent; it was hard to elaborate on things, the mouth was instantly filled with grains.

A bag that had come loose from its binding rolled in the wind faster and faster, and from the sound it made it was impossible to guess what was rattling inside it. It seemed that if one of the heavy crates would stand in its way, it too would be blown into the air.

"Who's never been a bad person?" Tenzin said. "And you certainly don't deserve to be buried alive."

"I was bad enough," Poliakov replied and spat out a murky globule that was immediately plucked by the wind.

With those exact words he had replied to McKenzie two months before that, when he asked him if they wouldn't forget his deeds in Russia. "I, Doctor," he said to him then, "didn't ask for money like you (he had already told him about the loans he had taken from the farmers), people were killed because of me."

"People have also died because of me," he replied, and right in front of his eyes he saw not only Mrs. Adams but also all the sick he hadn't cured and perhaps had even worsened their conditions by preventing the Amchi's incantations.

"But you didn't mean for them to die."

"And you did?"

Poliakov then examined the surface of the drink he was swirling in his glass. A small whirlpool was formed in the center and its edges rose and surged.

In the desert, during that morning hour when the sun labored to shine – a distance of two day's walk to their destination – the air was brimming with more and more grains of sand, surge after surge advanced by the wind, and to stop them from penetrating into the lungs, the men had to breathe through a handkerchief or a scarf or the flap of their robes. It would have been better had they got up, but for the time being they remained lying in the place they had slept the night. A layer of sand wrapped them and their possessions and they preferred to wait for calm, for the time when the storm would pass. Some lasted a day, some an entire day and night; the worst lasted three and even five days and only few survived to speak of them.

"If it continues," Tenzin said above his elbow, "we'll try and reach that camel there." He looked ahead, but that-camel-there could no longer be seen, not even a silhouette. Even if its hump protruded above the surface of the ground it would have been covered by sand and distinguishing between their colors would be impossible, a chameleon couldn't be better swallowed in the foliage of a tree. The sand was flung into the face, lashed the eyes, penetrated the nostrils and mouth and infiltrated to the depths of the ears deafened by the wind. At times it roared, at times whistled and howled, and there was no stopping the grains from continuing to charge onward and onward.

Tenzin lifted his arm, shook off the sand a little, returned it to its place and rested his chin on it again and instantly it was covered with sand again as was the curve of his chin. He'll soon have to get up and check on his men and animals, but for the time being he and Poliakov remained in their places. Could they hear each other? The doctor cannot know; he had never experienced a storm like that and the source of all his knowledge is from stories he had heard, either from Hedin and Stein at evening teas at the home of the commissioner's wife or from Tenzin and Poliakov on their return, but those two tended not to go into detail.

"To be buried in sand," Poliakov said, and a few syllables must have been swallowed in the storm, "isn't the worst thing." Perhaps he even took the trouble of going into detail, the way McKenzie had done with him when trying to prevent him from joining the caravan: to die by hanging is many times worse, and to bleed to death for hours is no less terrible, especially when no one tries to help.

Tenzin looked at him with squinting eyes. He had already heard similar things from him on the previous caravan, the one that made its way from Kashgar to Leh, when hurled snowflakes at them and everything around turned white, and within that freezing whiteness Poliakov saw black crows circling above him.

Since the storm showed no signs of abating – it seemed that the entire desert was being tossed in it from Khotan to Dunhuang and all its sands were being transported onward in the air – Poliakov was again reminded, as had often happened in other circumstances, of his forefathers who wandered for years in the desert and half of them dying on the way ("my people" he would say in the same manner as someone else might say "my punishment").

And the ones who came out from that desert alive, he said, didn't even know how to hold onto the land they had finally reached; the Russians knew how, so did the English and the French, every nation had its country, and only that nation was dispersed to the four winds. At a distance of two days from their destination he spoke with Tenzin the way he had once spoken in Leh about his forefathers who generation after generation waited for miracles, just like the people of Dandan Oilik waited for the sea to return. A Russian wouldn't speak that way about his nation and religion, neither would an Englishman or a Frenchman.

Did a longing for England remain in the doctor? He chose not to live there but rather here in this hole of holes, Leh. He bore no grudge against his forefathers or the place from where they came, on the contrary, it didn't take much to arouse his longings: a stone dwarf with lichen in its beard, the large head of a horse bending toward you from the paddock and waiting for his forehead to be scratched, the chiming of church bells on the Sundays of his childhood, the soft light of a winter dusk.

Again, the wind rolled some undistinguished object, and within a few moments it drew away and diminished and disappeared. One had to hope it wasn't one of the items from their plan: it would be ridiculous and infuriating to arrive in Dandan Oilik and find that it couldn't be carried out. It apparently wasn't something heavy: not a sack of salt or seashells and definitely not one of the anchors. For a moment its tracks could still be seen but right away became blurred and disappeared. It seemed the storm would last for at least a day and a night, if not more.

"What animals did they have with them?" Tenzin asked Poliakov about his people in the desert and wasn't particularly impressed to hear about a kind of pillar of sand that went before them and showed the way (right then a whirlwind of sand passed opposite them carrying a few uprooted bushes). He scoffed at the local tales too. Concerning the animals he was only surprised that everyone went by foot, the men, the women, the children, and the elderly.

"They walked until they reached a mountain in the middle of the desert," Poliakov struggled to overpower the wind with his voice as if it was important to tell all this in the middle of a storm: how they all came there and stood at the foot of the mountain and their caravan-bashi ascended to the summit in order to receive orders from their god.

That's what they chose to speak about, or so said Tenzin on their return; two young men two men in a desert, at whose age McKenzie had been busy planning his honeymoon, found nothing else to talk about besides the events concerning a different caravan in a different desert in a different millennium.

In front of them another object rolled in the wind, perhaps one of the coolies' bundles. It came apart, and for a while they gazed at the contents until they were blown further onward and became blurred in the sand; a cracked wooden bowl and spoon and a tattered garment; the bowl rolled on its side like a wheel until it turned upside down and in an instant was buried in the sand.

Afterward, Poliakov said something that all he had previously said led up to. The doctor had heard similar words from him a month before at a very late-night hour when for the first time their plan was being helped by verses from the Bible. "Do you know what's written here?" he asked him, and McKenzie didn't know he was referring to the verses on the stone tablets their leader brought down from the mountain. He remembered the statue of Moses in Rome well with its tangled beard and two small horns, but only vaguely remembered the sermon he had heard in his childhood in the church, though he did remember the vein throbbing in the right temple of the priest when he became impassioned; at the time it seemed to him that God had touched the priest right there and that was his fingerprint. "It's written, 'Thou Shalt Not Murder,' Poliakov said, "and I murdered, it's written, 'Thou Shalt Not Steal,' and I stole, it's written, 'Honor Thy Father and Thy Mother,' and I didn't do that, it's written that lying is forbidden and I lied to everyone. And after all that, do you think he punished me? Did fire come out of the sky and burn me, did the ground swallow me?"

Perhaps your punishment is that it didn't happen, McKenzie then thought.

There had been years when he thought that man lives with the burden of all his guilty deeds: a woman whose suicide you could have prevented but didn't lift a finger for, patients who could have received more effective treatment than all of your medicines and been saved. At times he thought that if there was an entity in the heavens who saw all and judged all, he would have been punished to the full extent of the law a long time ago – dropped off the deck of the ship on which he sailed from Brindisi or run over by the wheels of one of the Indian trains, or see his cock turn black and fall off – but none of that happened. On the contrary: from a country veterinarian he had become a doctor for humans and the director of a hospital, true, a small hospital and not in his country, but his standing had never been firmer; he was one of the respected members of the European colony of Leh. At other times, especially in the evenings when he returned alone to his room, he thought this exile was his punishment. That's how it is, one who continues to live with the burden of his guilt sees everything bad that comes his way as divine retribution – he could have been such a person – while others over the years grow a thick skin like him, simply living life: going to work every morning and even sometimes finding satisfaction in it; eating drinking, and meeting friends, and so it goes day after day in a set routine, maybe degenerate, but fairly comfortable.

No, that isn't accurate: had he lived his life that way, he wouldn't have wasted a whole year on this deranged plan whose beginning was the chatter of a reporter on *The Simla News* and whose end it's best not to think about. Under no circumstances would he have endangered his standing and social connections; he wouldn't have sent a caravan to the desert and endanger its men. In his time he had never experienced the black storm but knew full well about its frequency during this season of the year.

With their first dive into the midst of the storm – not an actual dive of course; they both trudged in the sand walking bent and shielding their faces against the wind with their arms – they intended to reach the camel they had previously seen. They didn't find it right away; some time would be needed for that. Step by step they plodded in the sand to the approximated place, and against the wind Tenzin sounded the calls made to camels on regular days but wasn't answered by any sound other than the roar of the wind. At a short distance the camel was discovered spread out on the sand, and for a moment one couldn't tell whether it was dead or alive, not even from the heat of its body (the body doesn't chill instantaneously), until they saw it breathing – its diaphragm rose and fell and a quiver passed through its skin when they touched it, and it peeked at them through its pale dense eyelashes covered with grains.

It was agitated and alarmed by everything around that had changed and Tenzin had to mumble more sounds before it showed any signs of calming down. "Stay with him," he said to Poliakov and showed him how to curl up close to its ribs, a shelter that would shield and warm at once; even an irritable camel will forget old grudges in a karaburan and this young camel perhaps wanted company. "You have a guest," he said to the camel, but Poliakov refused to remain there and insisted on going with him, and so they plodded ahead in the sand on their way to their men. It seemed that in the storm, the sand beneath their feet had become more crumbled and more like a sinkhole.

For a while they continued to trudge on in the footsteps of each other. The sand was so swampy and the air so thick from the grains flying in it that the delay of one step was enough to make the other person vanish from one's eyes forever in the reddish-brown mist. These dunes were on their own journey; it was like standing below a vast flock of millions of birds migrating from continent to continent and losing one's way in the shower of their feathers, should they be shed; but none of them, not even the Russian, was yet thinking about birds.

When Poliakov came upon one of the crates he almost stumbled and after a short while men's voices could be heard nearby, and one of them who recognized

587 THE SALT LINE

Tenzin's bent silhouette advancing murmured something that wasn't a greeting but rather a curse for him having led them here and how all of this wasn't worth it for thirty rupees a month.

"That's how you look after your crates?" Tenzin asked.

Through the reddish-brown screen that was being woven and unraveled all the while another voice was heard, dim and hoarse, Faizul's voice. "I also told that him that," he said and turned towards a blurred figure sitting a few feet away from him.

"Be careful your mouth doesn't get filled with sand," the Kashgari cook's voice could be heard, also disrupted by gusts of wind, and one couldn't tell whether those two were wrangling or just trading barbs to pass the time.

Tenzin's eyes sought after the other men of the caravan, and again had to plod in the sand and turn his head here and there and wait for a slight abatement of the wind before they were revealed to him: six or seven figures huddled between the donkeys and the ponies, their knees gathered between their arms and their robes covering them like a tent, and another four men pressing close to the camels the way a young camel presses close to its mother. The unloaded crates could be seen, sunk in the sand by a quarter of their height and a thick layer of sand heaped upon their tops; more time was required to detect the bags and bundles and sacks beyond them. One by one, Tenzin counted fourteen sacks of mother-of-pearl, four crates of seashells and twenty-four sacks of salt – they were all there, not one was missing, and had they not been heaped together they would certainly have disappeared. And nevertheless, since large mounds would be heaped upon them by evening, he immediately made two men who were lying down get up and remove the sacks from the sand and place them on top of the crates.

He couldn't see the anchors anywhere, not on his right or left, not in front or behind, and after Poliakov helped him search they still couldn't find them. They had been disassembled in Manali, the body and the arms of the anchor y and the lead casing separately and one hour of the storm would be enough to cover them with sand. For a while they walked back and forth in changing paths to find the anchors with either their eyes or their feet, until Tenzin turned to four of the men from Tavakkal and ordered them to participate in the search.

They got up slowly, grumbling, and shook the sand off them thoroughly as if the wind wasn't continuing to cast grains at them, improved the wrapping of their robes, and those for whom robes weren't enough added some tattered scarf to veil their faces up to the eyes. Tenzin stood them in a line at equidistant spaces and ordered them to move forward together and feel about the sand with their feet until they come across what had been buried in it. Step by step they advanced in a more or less straight line, bent against the wind, but even after going back and forth twice over the area allocated for the search, they only discovered a wooden bowl, perhaps the one that had previously rolled in the wind.

Tenzin then ordered them to take out the digging tools – at least they haven't lost them in their idleness, or have they? – and the man responsible for them, a Khotani who Turdi had recommended (Turdi himself was nowhere to be seen and they said he had gone out to inspect the surroundings and wasn't at all afraid of losing his way in the storm), said the hoes had been unloaded with the crates and the sacks and were lying between them, and nevertheless quite some time passed until they found them. These were hoes with wide blades, effective for digging in sand.

"What are you waiting for?" Tenzin said and urged the others to get up and start working, and unwillingly they took the hoes and organized themselves in a line. They struck the sand, dug a bit, advanced, and dug again. It was frustrating to work that way: as if the grains flung in the wind weren't enough, added to them were those blown in the air from the striking of the hoes. They dug more, advancing step by step, thickening the reddish-brown fog that lashed their faces. Someone swore vigorously in Khotani, another in Urdu, and a third in Ladakhi; they dare swear at Tenzin who they feared but tongue-lashed the hoe and its mother and all its forefathers; the wind was a son of a bitch, and the sand the son of a thousand whores.

When one of the hoes struck the anchor, only a dim sound could be heard and was almost lost in the growling of the wind. Had the iron been struck and had the wind subsided, the sound would have been heard by all, but the body of the anchor was made of wood and sacks were wrapped around it, thus it was mainly the cheering voice of the discoverer that was heard. Perhaps that's the way they had cheered on Hedin's and Stein's expeditions on finding antiquities deep in the sand, but they would have been well advised to postpone that exhilaration for a while. The other half of the anchor was found a few moments later, and not long after that the second anchor was struck nearby, but they still had to search a long time for the third. They must have sworn fiercely at what they called a plough, and if anyone wondered why a plough was needed in the desert, the explanation he would receive was no less preposterous than the truth (that is to say the invented truth, not the real one) – it was once believed, Tenzin said, that if ploughs were to be brought and used here, the sand would turn to earth and become suitable for ploughing. Such an explanation wouldn't faze those who served offerings of curried rice to the statues of their gods every morning, who believed their prophet had risen to heaven on the back of a winged mule whose tail was that of a peacock, or who were certain the prayer verses written on monastery flags are carried in the wind to their addressees in heaven.

At last, the third anchor was found and it too was placed alongside the crates, but Poliakov had added worries. The storm had not yet abated and he insisted on making sure that the reed kite he had bought at the Tavakkal oasis was still intact in its box. Crate after crate was checked (they were only opened slightly to prevent sand entering), until he discovered the flat box containing the Russian boy's kite.

After checking it he heard Tenzin say with this wind the kite will reach the boy before him.

Where was the little Russian boy at the time? He had gone with Mrs. Harper on her birdwatching trip, despite his mother forbidding it. The merchant who paid for her stay at the inn was away from Leh on business and she swore to Sasha they would spend all the time together and that she won't get drunk again and they'll do all sorts of things together; you can't always plan the way things turn out, she explained to him, and one day he'll understand. That Mrs. Harper – she said – the old lady who he's suddenly become so attached to, has never been a mother in her whole life and only knows how to give candy to children and breadcrumbs to birds, but doesn't know how to give her man a child.

When she saw Sasha's eyes, where little trust in her promises could be detected and were mainly sad, she became furious and throughout the inn her voice, trembling with insult, could be heard shouting at him, but before she could lay a hand on her son he slipped out of there. They saw him run out of their room and bound down the steps and continue to run down the street, despite knowing his mother wouldn't chase after him, but find consolation in a bottle or in opium. Afterward they saw Sasha kicking a small stone, causing a dusty dog lying there to get up. He reached out a stalk of couch grass to a donkey and glanced at the sky while at the same time managed to steal candy from a kiosk.

How different little Charles was from him. When the one first breathed the air of Leh, the other was already an irreversible distance away. They were as different as their mothers were from each other: the Russian woman abandoned her son, and the Englishwoman shielded hers to the point of suffocation.

No longer, of course. He's now making his way on a caravan southward to Bombay, riding his pony. And as for Dianne, she only exists now in the silver locket he gave him. She's now buried in the small cemetery next to the church, not only cleansed of sweat but also of her skin and her flesh and her innards and from all the grievances she hurled at him during the last week of her life, after months and years of keeping them bottled up inside.

"Did you have a bad dream, Doctor?" she had asked him years before, and at the time he wasn't sure if it had been a bad or a good dream. A vague notion rose in him when he awoke that the man with his load (an entire anchor was on his back, borne on him like a cross) will sink further and further into the sands, and all his frantic running after him had been in vain; gradually the anchor will sink the man carrying it, as well as the man trying to stop it.

Before putting down a pile of letters and a writing block and envelopes in front of her (she had come voluntarily to finish off some secretarial work) they exchanged courtesies and found themselves a comfortable topic of conversation: Mrs. Harper – how industrious Margaret was, how thorough Margaret was, how Harper should thank God every day for having attained a devoted wife like Marga-

ret; and how marvelous it is that she makes a trip to Lake Tsomoriri every year, after all, she's not a young woman anymore.

"Her birds," Dianne said, "what wouldn't she do for them?"

It was easy for them to speak about Mrs. Harper's birds. A jaybird used to hop after her like a chick after its mother, a magpie used to answer her call and fly to her shoulder, and quite a few Leh folk were more impressed with her talents that they were with her husband and his sermons.

Harper indirectly participated in her trip that summer; not in his own right, but in the task he assigned her, to gather him enough crane feathers for the pageant in which he sought to display Christ's ascension to heaven. He intended to present it at the mission school, and wanted Jesus and his twelve apostles, as well as two angels, to participate in it – all pupils in robes of sheets with cotton wool beards and feathers ("It seems our Robert," said the commissioner's wife, "is a frustrated director"). It was said that Jesus rose to the sky on a cloud, but wings were necessary for the angels, and it was inconceivable that simple chicken feathers would be stuck to them. Mrs. Harper was chiefly interested in the cranes of Lake Tsomoriri, some of whose feathers are shed naturally while others are shed while protecting their eggs from predators, and when Sasha saw them with her, he felt sorry that not only didn't he have a father to protect him, he also didn't even have a mother to embrace him.

Harper still didn't know how Jesus would be carried through the air, even if Dianne would paint a heaven-like backdrop (in the story the angels remained on the ground), and until an idea would arise in his head he allotted the role of Jesus to Sasha thanks to his fair skin and hair, but right away Sasha was prepared to forgo his crown of thorns if in its place he'd receive a pair of wings. "Everyone wants to be Jesus," Harper said with much amazement, "and you want to give up everything for a pair of wings?" He had no doubt the adult Russian had been a bad influence on him, the ex-terrorist with no faith in his heart, because quite often the two of them could be seen flying kites from the slope between the town and the palace. Had not the passion for flying come from there?

The storm abated not long after, as if in order to halt the sand that was being carried by the wind, they had to dig the sand that had already heaped up. That of course is groundless sorcery; no storm, and certainly not the karaburan, can be instantaneously halted, and in the same fashion one could ascribe its ending to that donkey driver who thought he had gone far away enough from his friends, and that under cover of the screen of grains flying in the wind he could kneel down to shit. The cheeky man; suddenly it became clear to him that his posterior was exposed for all to see.

"Look-look," someone shouted, either at the buttocks or at the air that had become clear, and the donkey driver's cursing was no longer muffled by gusts of wind.

Turdi was be seen then, returning from his excursion, all bundled and wrapped up except for two narrow slits left for his eyes. "You've come back, old man?" someone said to him, "We already thought you'd be blown away by the wind."

When the air had completely cleared, the sea of sand appeared as calm as it had been before the storm: the dunes had certainly changed their locations and their forms, but they were so multitudinous from horizon to horizon and as always curved to the south or southwest according to the direction of the wind, making it difficult to distinguish the changes that had taken place during the ten hours of the storm. That's how a sailor must feel after a storm at sea, provided his ship has remained intact.

When Tenzin hurried them all to get up, there were some who rose unwillingly and disagreeably, but the majority were glad the storm had passed and that it was possible to move on: they stood up and shook the sand off themselves, removed the scarves and rags were wrapped around their necks and faces, stamped on the sand in order to rid themselves of the grains in their garments, rubbed their beards with their hands to shed grains from there, and their eyebrows as well. A lazy man, one of the Tavakkal men, questioned the logic of such a short walk – only two hours of light remained – but Tenzin was determined to continue and Turdi supported him and urged the idle on, and the Russian (that's what Poliakov was called by the men of the caravan, as he had been called during his first days in Leh) went around making sure everything was properly loaded and tied up.

"Are you utensils tied up the way they should be?" Faizul's voice could be heard chiding the Kashgari cook again. "We didn't get any food from you, so at least get your things tied up."

The Kashgari cook had a simple suggestion that concerned itself with what Faizul could feed himself with if he's so hungry – no, not with sand, but maybe that donkey driver still has something left in his stomach – and to that Faizul gave an answer that was meant to be witty but became garbled and Tenzin quickly interrupted him. He sent the men from Tavakkal, to fetch their hoes so that they wouldn't suddenly discover in Dandan Oilik they had no hoe to dig with and sent the horse grooms and the donkey and camel drivers to bring their animals additional food before they start the march: some fodder for the donkeys and ponies, rapeseed oil for the camels.

One of the men was occupied for a long time tying up a bag – it was the Khotani who had gathered jade stones in the Yurungkash gorge without permission – and Tenzin, who knew nothing about that, asked him if he intended to continue at that pace. He asked one of the donkey drivers who was scratching his she-ass's forehead if he also scratched his wife like that, and Poliakov supervised the man in charge of the anchors' safekeeping. First he made sure that the order of the dismantled parts had been kept, and afterward that the wrapping of the sack cloth hadn't come loose, and finally that they be well tied to the camel humps. As for the camels, one who had misbehaved was forced to submit by the well-known method: its hind legs were bound, and its ring and tail pulled and thereby made to kneel until its load was tied to it. When all that was finished, only one hour of daylight remained, and the Tavakkal man who had questioned the logic of a short walk raised the notion again, and Tenzin said to him that if he's so afraid of the way ahead why doesn't he stay the night here alone, and when they return to Khotan he can return with them – he or his bones.

They finally departed on their way, and on the surface of the dunes the caravan's twisting column of camels and ponies and donkeys could again be seen, its gait swaying relaxedly as if not long ago a storm had raged here. Every footprint was marked on the virgin sand as if none whatsoever had ever been there from the day the earth had been created, but the fine sand only preserved the hollows they imprinted, without the details, and even they only survived until the next ones arrived.

"Oh, sea of sand,"

From the height of his camel's hump, Turdi opened his mouth and sang in the hoarse voice that grains of sand had make even rougher,

> "How stormy you can be
> and how calm."

"Carry on singing, old man," someone called out from behind, "we missed your songs." And they really had missed them: some sound was necessary to break the vast silence that surrounded them.

> "Oh, sea of sand,
> how angry you can be
> and how serene."

Above them, the sky caught alight from horizon to horizon when the setting sun rubbed up against the margins of its dome, and the shadows of the animals and their riders lengthened on the surface of the honeyed sand that kept its soft tone even when the flames of the sunset raged in the sky with a bloody hue.

Afterward the heavens turned blue and the sand darkened. The shadows of the walking men disappeared, and between the dunes pools of darkness began to form, first at their bases and then further on from there. Two of the Tavakkal men asked if the time hadn't come to stop and station themselves there (no, not asked, grumbled) instead of endangering themselves with a night walk who's end no one could know, and to that Turdi replied that a calm and clear night was forecast, and that's how they would reach Dandan Oilik toward morning.

Quite a few stories had been told about the terrors of the desert on dark nights, whether about the swampy darkness that draws the wanderer into it like the sand, or about the intoxicating sounds that attract one to the depths from where they seem to be coming –the poor man then digs farther and farther thereby digging his own grave. But there were also stories about nights with a full moon whose light's bewitching powers were well-known to all: one of them had a cousin who knew a Yarkandi man who was in love and began walking wide-eyed toward the moon rising over the dunes, until he was blinded by the light and his pupils turned white.

Since loved ones had arisen in the conversation, they began to talk about their wives from whom it was sometimes good to have a rest, but on a night like this what wouldn't they do with them; and a few of the young men amused themselves by imagining the things they would do with the loose women of Khotan on their return; perhaps they compared prices. Someone recommended the one who lived behind the material shop, another the one you could be with for a whole night if you just bring her – what? – he lowered his voice; it was so simple that it's better not everyone hear about it. Afterward they paid tribute to Turdi's wife, who already has eleven grandchildren and in a little while a great grandchild as well.

One of the ponies let out a long bray, and one of the young men whose beard was still sparse and fluffy and who for the most part had listened quietly to the words of those more experienced than him, opened his mouth and spoke. He said – in contrast to them – he would never speak about his wife the way they do, nor about other women either! A woman is a beautiful thing, the most beautiful thing in the world, a woman is a flower, and why make everything dirty like that?

"You're innocent," they replied to him. "When we were your age, we also thought like that."

They spoke about the Yarkandi women who do whatever they want with whomever they want when their husbands are away on a journey, and the husbands don't mind. Not only that; if the husband returns with guests, there's nothing he wouldn't give them, not even his wife.

That detail greatly amazed the Tavakkal men (that's to say, the ones who could hear; one end of the caravan was on the top of the dune and the other end at the bottom of the dune behind it, the one in front still lit by the last of the twilight, and the one at the back already dipped in shadow), for whom prostitutes were something they knew nothing about other than from caravan stories. They also listened with curiosity to the Kashgari cook who told that at the inn where he worked, there was even a Phelingpa woman who did it for money; she had a little boy without a father, and every time she needed privacy she'd banish him outside, and the Russian, yes, Tenzin's friend, used to play with the boy.

"And did he play with her?" someone asked.

Those who previously had been illuminated at the top of the dune were already darkened in the shadows at its base, and those taken out of the shadows were lit by what remained of the dusk, a remnant of a remnant. It seemed that at the next dune, or at the very most the one after it, nothing would be illuminated other than the heads of the camels, and only provided that they are tall enough to be wrapped in the trail of light being gathered together by the setting sun. In the dune behind it, they too will darken in the black of evening falling on the desert.

Anyone who lifted his eyes to the sky would have no difficulty noticing the flickering of the first stars. They seemed hesitant and perhaps were actually the bravest of them all, the ones that clear a path for those coming after them, the ones that appear only under cover of the night prevailing over the world. On such a night one might wonder if caravans are journeying on one of the distant stars, and if the earth with all its sand and mountains is not seen from there as a sparkle in the dark; and having such a thought, one could also see in one's mind's eye expanses of sand and oases and camel caravans on the surface of the stars in the heavens that only the distance, dwarfing everything, conceals from the eyes.

The conqueror of Tibet, the balmy General Younghusband, wrote those kind of lines (a considerable part of his success was due to the maps Tenzin's father had drafted), and to that Henry said, while the wording wasn't bad, one expects other things from a general; it would be better that military men occupy themselves with what's on the ground and not what's in the sky, and especially when their rank was given purely on account of their connections here; that's how it is, who needs ability when you're friendly with Lord Curzon.

They continued to advance beneath the night sky; a medium sized caravan that seemed to have shrunk in the darkness of the desert, until someone declared the appearance of a full moon, like a sailor from the top of a mast declaring a nearby continent – a white-golden shining curve then began to rise from the horizon and gradually ascended and grew, as if a giant eye had opened there, the eye of the night itself, from which nothing would be hidden. At moments like these with a full moon rising over the desert, diluting the darkness with its light, who could not understand how ancient peoples had worshipped it the way they worshipped the sun: it had an awesome splendor, becoming mightier as it mounted the ascent of the sky, scorning the darkness that had previously prevailed.

"Sing something, old man," they shouted to Turdi, "haven't you got songs about the moon?" And they shouted again because he hadn't heard them the first time, but he refused to sing; he gazed straight ahead, and even after they shouted a third time he didn't not bother to reply.

"What's up, old man, have you forgotten your songs?" they asked him, and when he finally answered, uncharacteristically short-tempered and angry, he said he had to concentrate; one who leads a caravan in the desert at night would do better to concentrate on the route and not on songs.

"Don't you know the way with your eyes closed?" they wondered, and to that he replied (and right away turned his head back toward the route) that there's only one place in the world that's possible to reach with closed eyes, and they too will do that, that's to say, reach there with closed eyes.

A silence fell, either due to his meaning or the tone of his voice. The moon, vast and golden and shining, was already floating in the darkness saturated with its light and casting their shadows for a distance. They were blurry shadows and not sharp like the those cast by the sun, but their forms could be perceived on the surface of the sand, and what Turdi had said evoked a ghostly sight: they were bound to the animal's legs but were also being sent toward the depths of the darkness. Under circumstances such as these, how could the memory of one of Hedin's men not arise, someone who every caravan he participated in, carried a shroud rolled up as a turban on his head lest he die in the desert and be buried there. "That idiot, Gupparo," someone said, and Turdi silenced him: better to have a shroud on the head than a cockscomb.

At the other end of the caravan, Tenzin and Poliakov were consulting with each other and preparing for what was to come, that's to say the moment they arrive at the Dandan Oilik ruins and continue on to the next stage of their plan. Someone asked Turdi if he meant to scare them all with his talk and he replied that the time had come for them to take leave of their complacency, because if until now everything had gone right, it was no guarantee as far as things to come were concerned, perhaps even the contrary; after all, something always goes wrong.

At that moment, one of the camels slipped down the slope of the dune with all its load. It seems it had stumbled or sprained its ankle and fallen on its side and continued to slide and roll all the way down with its load whose binding had come loose. It was a camel without a rider, one of those carrying the heaviest equipment. The heaviest of the loads were the parts of the anchor made of lead, and this camel was one of the three that carried them.

"You spoke too soon, old man," someone said to Turdi, "now look what's happened." It was a high dune and within a few moments the camel had gone the distance of sixty feet down the slope and a small cloud of grains enveloped its hump. By the time they reached it (they got off their animals and slid down to the place where it had stopped) the grains raised had already fallen and heavy breathing could be heard, and froth could be seen bubbling on its lips. In its rolling down, perhaps the head had been injured from the load that had become loose and perhaps a snake had bitten it before that, it was impossible to know since no injury was visible, neither on its head nor on its legs.

A camel in such a condition, with all its size, is beyond help. They saw the legs convulse while it lay on its side, stretching the long neck on the sand as if thereby making it easier for the air to reach the lungs, its large eyes peered at them beneath the lashes covering them, and it was clear its days were numbered, maybe its hours. That gaze was one of demise, of someone about to part from the world.

"He was a good camel," someone said, and others also extolled his virtues: he was obedient and good tempered, never kicked or bit, and even during the breeding season it wasn't difficult to control him. They would have stayed at its side longer had not Poliakov and Tenzin arrived there. Space was made for them, and they both bent over the camel and examined it from its head to its hooves; they touched here, felt there, and neither of them found what had injured it, nor was there any point.

When the shot was heard, it seemed that it thundered from one end of the desert to the other and sliced through all the darkness of the sky to its shining eye, despite that it had been aimed at the large head on the ground whose eyelashes were so fair, and its teeth so yellow, and its lips so pink. That head trembled slightly for a moment longer, and the froth on its lips turned red in the moonlight, and Poliakov returned the pistol to his pocket.

"He was a good camel," repeated the man who had praised him before, but Tenzin was already hurrying everyone to unload the remains of the cargo from the dead camel. Time was short, he said, it would be better to reach Dandan Oilik by noon, and for that purpose the camel's cargo had to be transferred to the other animals. They did it unwillingly; perhaps they thought the Russian had been hasty in shooting: one doesn't hasten the dying; better they leave the world at their own pace.

Perhaps the camel was injured when the heavy vertical lead section came loose in its fall (the sackcloth it was wrapped in could only have stopped the bleeding), and now they protested at the weight they were forced to drag up the slope. Its weight is what keeps the anchor on the seabed, and if that wasn't enough, wrapped in that same tattered cloth was also the lead casing that had been dismantled from the wooden arms of the anchor. On the left side of the hump, the camel carried sacks of salt for the purpose of balance, and they had to be untied, and they tried to turn the camel's body on its right side or drag it until the sacks it had squashed in its fall were uncovered. It wasn't yet clear onto which animal they would be loaded, and to their good fortune – McKenzie thought they had become lucky – all that had taken place on the eleventh day of the journey, after half the provisions they had taken for the way had been eaten, and it was possible to transfer the sacks of salt to the animals that were free. The lead parts posed the most difficult problem, and only after a number of attempts a way was found to load them on to one of the other camel's humps, whose crates were then divided between the ponies and the donkeys.

When all that bother was finished, the moon was already very high in the sky whose darkness had somewhat faded; it was diluted not by the light of the moon that had been crowned with a sort of ghostly halo but rather with the light of the nearing day, coming closer and closer not by the changing shifts of time, but rather by the expanse that they're crossing.

Just then, when the entire cargo that had been removed was reloaded and they could depart on their way again, two of the Tavakkal men said they were hungry:

after all, they had been delayed here for quite some time and why not wait a bit longer and eat properly? No one is waiting for them at Dandan Oilik other than a few lizards.

Although they were not popular; like all the Tavakkal men, their suggestion was supported by the Khotanis, and right away everyone was reminded that they hadn't eaten for hours and that their stomachs were rumbling. One even dared to dream aloud about beshbarmak, five-fingered-soup, containing everything of the best, meat and cabbage and carrots and potatoes and rice and onions and peppers and salt, and all so thick that it could be eaten by hand, with five fingers. What he wouldn't give for a bowl of beshbarmak now; all these sacks of salt for one bowl.

"Beshbarmak?" Faizul's mocking voice could be heard. They could dream about it, he said, because at the very most the Kashgari cook will give them naan as dry as tree bark, and they'll probably get camel's tea to drink. They received no tea, but the cook went about the men and from a large bag carried on his shoulder he gave each one a few pieces of crackling naan of which there was no knowing when it had been baked, and more than one of them asked him what the hell he had done with all the good food that had been bought– had he hidden it somewhere? Given it to the animals?

In the meanwhile, the darkness above them was decreasing further, and there were those who then remembered the storm and its end, and more precisely, the moment that naked posterior was revealed to them while kneeling down. That memory seemed now, toward the end of the night, very distant, as if not a few hours had passed since then but rather days and weeks; that's how the karaburan had tossed the enormous hourglass to whose sands they had been subjected.

Since grumblings about the food were still being made, Tenzin promised them that in Dandan Oilik they would eat a dinner fit for kings; yes-yes, the Kashgari cook would show them what he knows how to do. They can even ask this Russian – with a movement of the eyebrow he indicated to Poliakov – who once stayed at the inn where the Kashgari cooked.

"Where the Phelingpa sold herself?" asked one who was aroused by the idea of intercourse with a white woman, and Faizul asked: if the cook had been so successful there, what's he doing here now? But this time he didn't insist on a reply. At this hour of night perhaps he was already tired of his annoyance and perhaps the comradeship felt by everyone who goes on a journey like this into the desert was working on him too. It wasn't only their wages that motivated them, even if they taunted each other from the first day to the last, the urge to wander was what united them all. All sorts of willing or unwilling exiles had gathered in Leh, the only place the doctor really knew, and its remoteness was enough for them, while the natives of Khotan and Kashgar had the desert to go to whenever the routine of their life weighed down upon them.

In his life, the distance the doctor had travelled was more than enough; so he repeated to himself at times, after having turned his back not only on the British Isles but also on the whole of Europe, and he repeated it every time he made excuses to himself as to why he doesn't leave the confines of Leh for a while, even for a few days. He had been innocent then, innocent and foolish; he didn't yet know that a man doesn't have to sail on a ship or mount the back of a horse or a camel in order to be exiled from his home, because for that, the gap between him and his loved ones is enough.

Yes, the forgoing of a morning kiss for Dianne when he left for the hospital was enough, or an evening kiss on his return, or not listening when she told of the trifles of her day: Henry said this Henry said that, and Henry's adjutant sent letters to this one and that, and Ann invited them both for tea on the weekend and the Harpers invited them for Sunday. Only when she was pregnant did she really look feminine, but with those wearisome meticulous details that don't distinguish between the essential and the incidental she told of the changes taking place in her body, and after the birth she related all little Charles' doings the same way: how he burped or smiled or regurgitated or crawled or climbed a heap of pillows like a mountain climber, and how he almost stuck a pea into his nose, how he almost hit his head against the corner of the table. She insisted on breastfeeding, despite that Daychin could have done it in her place (the young Ladakhi who had given birth at the same time, had more than enough milk), and there were evenings when she was too tired to wash herself and collapsed on the bed emitting smells of all kinds of baby excretions, and at times like that he regretted they didn't have more spacious lodgings, that would have allowed them each their own corner.

On his return from the hospital, he would see Charles' nappies hung on the line, washed and still damp, and felt no pleasure on entering the house; to the contrary, it seemed then that the trap in which he had been ensnared was tightening around him, and with Charles growing up, his possibilities of escaping would narrow even more. Yes, in all his stupidity, for the entire first year of Charlie's life he felt that way.

14

They had to encircle a large sand ridge spreading from the northeast to the south-west, and when it was completed the darkness was already decreasing, and the moon diminished and faded into it farther and farther. Before that, they had passed through a deep depression in the land where the animals trudged in the sand that had been heaped up almost to their knees, and here and there stumps of dried-up poplar trees protruded, demanding they be careful not to be hindered by them. One camel had already been lost, but a sprained ankle would be enough to prevent its owner not being able to move on.

When Tenzin was about to order two of his men to gather dry tree trunks, Turdi said to him that those would not be lacking even in Dandan Oilik – this desert had dried out more than enough trees and they all burn wonderfully. They wouldn't have to use smelly animal excrement again, he said, they'll have a real fire there, and the cook, should he desire it, could prepare them a meal fit for kings.

"Beshbarmak for everyone?" Faizul's mocking voice could be heard again.

"Beshbarmak you can eat at home," Turdi replied, and someone piped up how one would think Faizul was used to only the very best, after all, he didn't even have anyone to cook soup for him at home.

This sand ridge they had encircled for a lengthy time was longer and taller than the previous one, more than a hundred meters long and three meters high, more than enough to obscure everything that was behind it. For a while it seemed that the wind had formed it like that solely for them, just to increase their joy when their destination would finally be revealed to their bleary eyes. They were already very close, and perhaps sailors at the end of a voyage feel like them, the moment before land birds could be seen in the sky and the whiteness of seagulls is replaced by the colorfulness of parrots.

In the hazy pre-dawn bluish light, the remains of the ruins seemed more impressive than they would be when seen in full daylight. The lingering morning twilight added a majesty to them of which no trace remained at noon, beneath a beating sun, but for the time being they were fascinated by the sight of pillar stumps protruding from the sand in straight rows, without ceilings and roofs and without the clay walls that had turned to dust. Here and there remnants of a layer of wood could be seen with the remains of the plaster that had once covered them, and from the sand a gnawed window frame protruded, a wooden rafter and pieces of earthenware that must have been exposed and buried countless times in the wanderings of the sand. The floors were buried in sand; as were the courtyards and irrigation ditches, fruit trees, and trees that gave shade. This settlement was approximately two kilometers long and almost one and a half wide (that had already been documented by Stein), and from the place where they stopped only the tips of the treetops protruded from the sand and were as dry as the pillar stumps of the houses. In the depths of the sand there were poplars that had once upon a time demarcated wheat fields or stood on an avenue, and plantations of peaches that had dried up, apricot trees and willows. From year to year and from century to century the sand rose further, and there was nothing mythical about that: at first it heaped up from the bottom of the irrigation ditches and rose and grew higher until they were blocked and the fields began to desiccate; afterward it also covered the bushes that grew on the banks of the ditches and continued to rise and covered the tree trunks as well, and there's no knowing how much time passed until it reached the first fork in the branches – perhaps decades, perhaps centuries – and continued to the second and the third, and stopped only there; for the time being, to all appearances.

One could think of birds being captured in the sand while in flight, as the people of Pompeii were captured in lava, had all that taken place in a moment, in order to punish all the inhabitants of the desert for their sins, but it all took a very long time and there was nothing miraculous about it. The doctor had heard the facts from Stein at one of Ann's evening teas when he explained to everyone how dependent those desert settlements had been on water, and how their chances of survival had been exhausted when two well-known causes came into play: the process of desertification where more and more sand was borne by the wind or the rivers and ditches; and political changes such as wars and changes of government when the central administration becomes destabilized. One year without water is enough to dry out the crops and force the local people to wander onward like tent dwellers.

Yes, it was easy to talk of all that while drinking tea, easy to talk of terrible hunger while chewing on biscuit and even joke about everything afterward; it was just as easy to send a caravan to one of those areas two years later, while McKenzie, carried on his daily routine in Leh, getting up and going to the hospital every morning and returning home towards evening. He already had no need to hunt flies and count them in order to doze off, more than enough things occupied his mind and exhausted him, and quite often he took a nap in the hospital at noon sitting in his chair; but then, uninvited, the man and his anchor rose beneath his eyelids again.

As usual, the man carried his burden on his bent back and with every step sank farther in the sand, and again McKenzie tried to run after him and stop him and from dream to dream drew nearer to him and each time they went deeper into the desert, so deep that even had he succeeded in placing a hand on the man's shoulder (he didn't react to all his calls, perhaps the wind drowned them out), the two of them could no longer return.

The entire anchor was on his back, and such a weight, approximately a hundred and fifty kilograms, even a camel couldn't carry; but the man, who seemed more or less his age and with a similar build to his, didn't seem to be struggling, despite being bent from the load. Had he trod along a levelled path perhaps he would done so in a regular manner, but in the sands of the dream he sunk farther and farther as if unaware of this.

The sound of the wind made his calls to him futile, just as futile as his intention to explain it would be better to dismantle the anchor into separate parts as Griffin and Evans had done when the road the wagons travelled on came to an end. Awaking from those afternoon naps, he sometimes thought of that pair who persuaded him in Brindisi that India was the place for him and that His Majesty's cavalry would be happy to take an expert on horses such as him into its service. Who could have conceived, even in their wildest dreams, he would come all this way from that pier where drunks went to piss?

Tenzin pointed to the sandy area designated for their base, not far from the remains of the central building – the same exposed pillar stumps could be seen there, but spread over a wide area – and before that he consulted with Turdi not only about the needs of the men and the animals, but also the next stages of the plan (that's what they still   call it, *the-plan-the-plan-the-plan*, despite that from moment to moment it was becoming clear just how badly its planning had been).

First of all, they had to water and feed the animals, and they themselves too needed to drink and eat – their stomachs were rumbling again – and all the items they had brought had to be buried in the sands, and the considerations here were more complicated than they had thought. Though they had dedicated quite some time to the preparations, almost five months, it's one thing to make plans in a small restaurant in Leh and quite another when one reaches the destination. They could have brought thirty or forty or fifty sacks of salt, but at the sight of the expanse of sand it was clear all the white grains of salt would be swallowed in it, and who would know that in ancient times a line of sea foam had apparently been formed here. They could also have brought seventy sacks of mother-of-pearl and seashells here, even seven hundred, but even if they didn't become mixed into the sand like the salt, they wouldn't be set apart from it any more than the pieces of clay that are also destined to be swallowed in it. And as for the large heavy anchors that had once served prominent vessels; after being assembled and buried in the sand how could anyone in the world be expected to know of their existence.

They intended to bury the jar containing the pieces of fake scroll in the ruins of the central building, but knew it would be dangerous to pin all their hopes on it – what would happen should it fall into the hands of robbers? Signs or those robbers of antiquities become apparent almost the moment they began digging: here the sawn-off base of a carved cornice was exposed, there a beheaded statue, and not every robber would regret his actions and return all he had taken (that's what they told their men: the objects carried by the robber's animals brought about endless troubles to those who looted them and so they decided to return them to their place).

They didn't mention who had done the looting, whether it had been a learned Phelingpa who forwent his discovery or a local merchant who forwent his profit, but the details of the calamities that befell him, from impoverishment to leprosy, were effective; it seems they all believed the explanation that had been given for their odd task; burying antiquities instead of unearthing them. The real purpose brought about another problem: if everything would be buried in such a way as to be hidden from the eyes and the hands of new avaricious seekers, how in the end will they be revealed to the man for whom they were intended, Carlo Magnani?

McKenzie still remembered when he and Kate first heard him in the museum, where he encircled one of the statues whose nose and whose organ had been truncated and lectured them about the statue and the sculptor in a singsong English with a light Italian accent; and in the next hall, with the same ease of one confident he could overwhelm his conversation partners with his erudition, even in a foreign language, he was already disparaging his great rival Schliemann.

That's how it is, he said, when you have a father who embezzled church funds and a wife who is prepared to lie about anything for you, if you'll just give her the jewels you discovered in the ruins of Agamemnon's palace.

"I also wouldn't have objected to that," Kate said, and McKenzie looked at her, as did Magnani.

"Signora, with your beauty you don't need any jewelry," he said with shameless flirtation, as if he was a young Roman rooster and not a pudgy balding middle-aged man whose chief power was his eloquence.

First, they took care of the animals and gave them water from a container insulated by a wrapping of reeds the camels had begun to gnaw at. Afterward the men drank as well., eagerly gulping down all that was allotted to them and waited for the Kashgari cook to prepare a meal for them: who needs beshbarmak, the main thing is to finally put something into the stomach.

The animals that were free, those who no longer carried loads, they planned to send back to Tavakkal, and as to the others, they were still deliberating about whether to send them the distance of a two day walk to Karya Darya, to drink from its waters and graze on its banks – that's what Stein did when he excavated here – or to adhere to their plan according to which they wouldn't be delayed here for more than two days.

"We won't be here tomorrow," Tenzin said, not heeding Turdi's warning that plans such as those are destined to fail. Tenzin calculated aloud: how long will it take to unload the sacks of salt and mother-of-pearl and crates of seashells? How much time will be needed to empty them and disperse them? A few hours, no more, including digging a ditch, since this was sandy rather than rocky ground. And how much time would be required for burying the anchors? Even if, let's say, an hour would be needed for the unloading from the camels and another for their assembling and another three for digging deep pits and another for covering those pits over; even then it wouldn't take more than half a day. And the small jar wouldn't take more than an hour. What else could delay them?

First, they had to mark the line of foam, – yes, foolishness such as that - the line left by the foam of the waves when there had still been sea here; and more precisely, the line that had apparently been marked by the local priests in their ceremonies, to coax the waves to return with the ships of the gods. To that purpose, Tenzin mounted his pony and with the blade of a hoe marked a long, curved line about one hundred and fifty meters long and ninety meters wide of the eastern border of the settlement. He ascended to the highest point, the base of a ruined stupa whose turret stones had mostly crumbled and were lost, and from there he examined the line with satisfaction. He then instructed the men to start digging and not to be lazy: he demanded a depth and breadth of one and a half meters, because in swampy sand like that, the excavation would be filled with grains sliding from the sides if there wasn't enough space between them.

At the three points the anchors would be buried, they would need to go deeper, but first they were required to reach the initial level, and the labor was taking longer than expected. Because the sand was so soft, it made it harder to remove since it flowed back in. They worked in pairs: one dug with a hoe, and another removed with a spade, and each time about half the amount that was raised flowed back in. Until this stage would be finished – certainly not within an hour or two – Tenzin and Poliakov went to the remains of the central building and in the hands of one of them was the only object they intended burying without anyone watching, and had the dune not separated them from the diggers it wouldn't have been achieved.

In this building, a public building according to its size, when digging deep to the base of the pillars Stein had discovered the remains of frescoes on which local legends were represented, and it was worth considering whether it would be right to bury the jar there. It seemed to them these tales wouldn't interfere with each other: the first ones, the truly ancient ones, dealt with trivialities (silk cocoons the princess smuggled from China in her crown, holy mice that gnawed the strings of the bows of the enemy's army), while their own dealt with the highest of all principles, the gods.

"Have you ever dug like this?" Tenzin asked. He held the spade in his hand and gave Poliakov the hoe with which he had previously marked the line of foam. Instead of answering, Poliakov lifted the hoe above his shoulder and embedded it

into the sand in front of him with great momentum and cursed when the grains
slid back into the pit.

"Not like that – like this," Tenzin showed him. There was no point in using
such great momentum, it was better to sweep the sand away. A sweeping motion
would be more effective.

Owing to the dunes that separated them and the row of the diggers they
couldn't not see if their men were deepening the line he'd drawn for them, but
since Turdi was overseeing the work there, they could be sure that everything
was being carried out as required. The commotion of the diggers only reached
them at moments, when for a while the direction of the wind changed. One time
they heard someone ask Turdi to sing for them, not a sad song, but the kind that
would instill energy in them; and again the direction of the wind changed and they
couldn't tell whether the old man had consented.

Poliakov let out a curse in Russian when the blade of the hoe fell off the pole,
and some time passed until he found a piece of stone with which to affix the blade
again, and right away returned to digging stubbornly to minimal effect. A few
meters from him, Tenzin was digging deep into the opposite side of pit, and that
way they intended to expose a small section in the corner of the hall, between the
bases of two walls. They believed that if the jar would be buried there, when the
time came it could be discovered by a skillful digger, and if properly covered, no
chance passerby would find it.

After a while they swapped their implements and later swapped again. Were
they to take a break, it would probably be for Poliakov's sake rather than Tenzin's.
In his weariness he cursed the sand that was so difficult to remove – one could be
digging in water for that matter – and Tenzin asked him why he was cursing; after
all, no one had forced him to come here. Instead of stopping, Poliakov went into
detail: to hell with the sand and to hell with the one who made the sand.

Tenzin sunk the spade in again and raised it with a skillful movement and did
so a few more times until the base of a ruined wall began to be exposed in the sand:
not a section with a wooden lattice covered in loam, but layers of real wall built
of mud bricks on which the remains of a faded painting could be seen. Perhaps
the princess and her silk cocoons were painted there, or the mice that gnawed the
strings of the bows; it was difficult to discern (the few frescoes that remained had
been sawn away by their predecessors and sent to Europe). What looked like an
eye could have been the faded eye of the princess or the eye of a holy mouse, or
perhaps just a blot.

"Don't you believe in anything?" Tenzin asked.

"No, and definitely not in this."

Despite that he too found nonsense repugnant, Tenzin was suddenly angered
by his partner's scorn for local beliefs, characteristic of most of the foreigners that
came here, and before embedding his spade into the sand again he said there is one
thing he believes in: not princesses or mice, and certainly not in those who come

from Europe to rob their paintings; but that one day they won't be here any longer, all those who don't belong in this place. "All of you," he said to him, the way he had once said to the doctor in Leh, "will one day be gone, and when you look back you won't understand how you were got rid of." The base of the wall was exposed further in its fading peeling colors; what had looked like an eye was indeed only a blot.

"You won't believe how blind you've been," he said. "This half eye has already seen more than all of you."

His heresy had also enraged Harper two months earlier, although for completely different reasons.

"When you look at all this," Harper had said to Poliakov when he was still trying to learn Hebrew from him – they were standing on the veranda and the missionary indicated to the snowy summit and the valley at the foot if it with its fields and trees – "who do you think created it?" According to him, there was only one possible answer, whether the Creator is called by this or that name, whether he's described this way or that; the names and descriptions were just the temporary garments man in his limited understanding made for him.

"I don't know," Poliakov replied, and his gaze lingered for a while on the large cloud that cast its shadow over the fields.

"We were created in his image," Harper reminded him with rebuke, and in order to clarify the meaning of "in his image" he was aided by their reflections in the small glass window in the upper section of the open veranda door. The chubby face of the missionary could be seen there with his shining bald pate and the long strands of hair that he took care to comb over it, and Poliakov's lean, sharp featured, cheerless face.

"In his image?" Poliakov asked, and from the tone of his voice it wasn't difficult to gauge what he meant: if these are what have been created in the God's image, this god can't be all that accomplished. The missionary reminded him that the Lord's forgiveness for those he's created is total and absolute, and in a soft reconciliatory voice and in simple words he said to Poliakov that he should not be blamed for speaking that way; he had been through very difficult things in his life and fundamentally he's a good person.

"I'm not," Poliakov replied. But the missionary still saw in him what he had wanted to see from the start.

The diggers continued to dig. The sand lightened the hair, the beard, the eyebrows and the eyelashes, either by the grains blown by the karaburan winds or by a hoe or a spade. A few months before that, on their way from Kashgar to Leh, the frost had lightened their faces and not by a storm, the vapor of freezing breath before being dispersed in the air was enough.

After a few more blows a dim sound rose from beneath the hoe (a similar sound was just then made by the spade), and Poliakov restrained his hand; a rash blow was liable to strike the floor and damage it. And so the corner of the hall was carefully exposed, approximately half a square meter of an eaten away and crumbling floor, but they had been so absorbed in removing the sand, they didn't pay heed enough if it was indeed a suitable place for their purpose. While the floor had still been covered in sand it appeared to be an excellent place to bury the jar, but after it was exposed, it didn't seem as if holy manuscripts or their remains would have been placed on the floor just like that, even if they had been kept in a jar.

How they solved that problem, McKenzie didn't know. On their return they only said they had found a suitable place, and that the fewer the people who knew about it – the better. Even for him, they said, it would be better not to know unnecessary details; in that way, when everything would be discovered, he could express his amazement with complete naturalness and not need to pretend. And what difference does it make, they said, where exactly they had buried it, the main thing is that Italian find it.

Beyond the dune in the east, about ninety meters from the edge of the settlement, the men of the caravan had already deepened the ditch they had dug according to the line marked by Tenzin. Other than the Khotani crook who had gathered jade stones for himself the day they had walked through the Yurungkash gorge, they all worked vigorously. After the sandstorm it seemed they were all happy to stretch their bones a bit.

"And so, old man, aren't you going to sing anything?" they asked Turdi when they began to delve deep and expected some song to set a rhythm for them, but after he began to sing another one of his doleful songs, they forwent its continuation. Songs like that – they said to him – would be better kept for funerals.

While the jar was being buried, they had almost completed their work, except for the three places that needed extra depth for the anchors, and when they saw Tenzin and Poliakov beyond the dune, they not only expected praise but also a bonus for their efficiency. "Not now," Tenzin said. It was already possible to pour the salt and mother-of-peal and seashells into the ditch, but he wanted to complete all the digging work before that. A bonus, he declared, would only be for the ones who volunteer to dig three pits for the ploughs (what they called the anchors there, as if they had been designated for a totally different ritual), and right away a few sturdy men were found who hadn't been exhausted by the ditch and who were even prepared to compete with each other.

Tenzin ordered for all the animals whose loads were needed for the ditch to be brought and be stood in a long line, and until all that was done, he went with Poliakov to the ruins of the stupa and from there he again surveyed the ditch and the places designated for the anchors: one at each end and one in the middle. But who could guarantee them – the speculation arose, as it had in Leh during the planning stage – that after everything is covered with sand, something of it would be discovered?

They could have brought chains for those anchors, and had they allowed their ends to protrude above the sand, the object they were chained to might be discovered (such a thought also arose in Leh); but no chain would have remained exposed like that for hundreds of years. Moreover, according to the approximated length of the chains and their weight they would have needed another three camels to carry them, one for each chain, and couldn't have borne the financial cost. They had already used all the money allocated for the matter, and McKenzie didn't want to touch the rest of Aunt Elizabeth's savings, and certainly not the house she had bequeathed to him in the county of his birth (Charles had not yet entered the world and he wasn't thinking of him at the time; nevertheless, out of all the decisions he made that year, that was the smartest).

From where they stood, the three diggers could be seen competing with each other, and every once in a while, when the direction of the wind changed, cheers of encouragement could be heard around them. Yes, even in the desert, competitions like this were possible, it's inherent to man's instinct; one could conceive of two dying men betting on the number of people that would accompany each of them to the grave – were not he himself and Magnani like that? He had been half-dead since that summer in Rome and Magnani had been half-dead ever since they hatched their plan.

When the direction of the wind changed it was impossible not to mistake the sound of Faizul's voice: in the name of the Kashgari cook, he promised the one who would complete the pit first a bowl of beshbarmak, and if some of the necessary ingredients were missing for the moment, then the Kashgari would prepare it when he returns home, and his sister will no doubt be much more hospitable, oh-oh, that sister of his knows sure knows how to treat guests.

Right away a fight broke out and others came to separate them, not immediately successfully. One of the peace enforcers received a blow which he returned. This fracas was a sign of things to come. Although it didn't appear to be serious and the trouble ahead didn't start because of it, it still seemed as if this preface was required.

When Tenzin and Poliakov came down from the observation post, twelve donkeys carrying sacks of salt were already standing on the edge of the ditch, seven ponies carrying mother-of-pearl, two carrying crates of seashells (they were chosen for their quiet temperaments) and four camels carrying the anchors. A slight uncertainty began to rise: whether to first bury the anchors and only afterward to unload all the rest, or to work simultaneously. Only after all the cargo was unloaded and it became clear how much effort would still be needed to assemble the anchors, they decided to work simultaneously.

Far away from there in Leh, not a trace of the commotion was heard. For almost a month no actual news reached McKenzie from the caravan, he could only guess very little, and who could have known then the nightmare that visited him in his afternoon naps would be realized.

For more than four months, those anchors had been dismantled, and what had matched before that – the vertical space for the trunk of the anchor, the space of the casing for the arms of the anchor – no longer matched. In the months that had passed, the wood had expanded and shrunk due to the changing hot and cold, and perhaps even the lead hadn't remained as it was. Without a heavy object with which to strike it, and a ten-pound hammer would be advisable, the lead parts couldn't be fixed to their previous places: the vertical section at the edge of the anchor's trunk and the casing on the arms to reinforce them. For a while they tried using the vertical section as a hammer and strike the lead casing that way, as Polia-kov had previously struck the blade of the hoe in order to return it to its place, but it wasn't enough. Then they searched around for large stones, but none could be found in the vicinity. Only expanses of sand could be seen, dunes and more dunes, and it seemed that even a steel ingot would land up crumbling there or be carried by the wind.

"Weren't there any stones where you were before?" Turdi asked and right away the Khotani who had gathered the jade stones volunteered to go to the central building and bring some large stones from there on his horse, but Tenzin stopped him. It was better that no man from the caravan stay there alone for a unnecessary amount of time, and especially that Khotani of whom it was said had his eye set on other things besides the jade stones, and for that reason alone he had joined the caravan.

After the stones were brought (Tenzin and Poliakov brought them in sacks on the donkey's back), the striking of stone on lead could be heard for a while. It was a new sound in the silence of the desert, foreign and disrupting the calm, a sound that continued until the vertical section and the casing had been affixed, and one could only hope that new injuries hadn't been made to the wood, that thin scales hadn't been peeled off it, or that Magnani's eagerness would be great enough to ignore all that.

Would his exuberance be that great? After all, he had sharply criticized Schlie-mann specifically for that, he had mocked his exuberance at Troy resulting in his missing the true remains and continuing to dig to more ancient layers; and after such criticism, would he himself avoid making hasty decisions? McKenzie couldn't be sure. A person can criticize his fellow man – he learned that over the past years – for the very same faults that afflict him, and those crazy months had demon-strated that realization to him in a number of ways: had he not criticized Henry for his squander in building a new house? And Harper for his fanaticism? And Poliakov for his disregard of human lives? And Rasul for his foolishness? While during those months he himself had been no less a squanderer, no less a fanatic, no less a disregarder of human life and certainly no less a great fool. It might be true that their plan had been executed, at least most of it (except for the final stage, the one that seemed the simplest of all), but five years later he sits here in his room in the hospital, the miserable little room he calls his office, and when evening comes he returns to the room of his bachelorhood in Changspa and goes to sleep alone, without Charles and without Dianne, without all the money he invested in the caravan, and without the sweet taste of revenge.

"That's it, old man," declared the one first to finish digging the pit for the anchor at the southern edge of the ditch, and a moment or two later the two others declared that as well. Turdi walked the length of the ditch from one end to the other; to one he remarked that he hadn't made the pit deep enough, to another that he hadn't made his wide enough; only the third had done his work properly.

Only after the three pits had been dug Turdi instructed the men to empty the sacks into the ditch. All the way from Leh they had to take care those sacks don't get damaged (for every tear in the sack they were fined), and now they were at last permitted to get rid of them and must have done so with great enjoyment. It seems that they had all been convinced by the story of the ploughs, and that the salt, mother-of-pearl and seashells had been brought here for the very same reason, and their purpose wasn't the sea but rather rain clouds whose source had been the evaporated sea water – in that way the people of Dandan Oilik had apparently hoped to make themselves safe by their ritual - from both the earth and the sky.

Had it not told been in these parts about an elephant that showered rain from its trunk? Things like that had been related here – from Peshawar in the west to Dunhuang in the east, from Aksu in the north to Leh in the south – and tens of millions of people believed in them, the way in other places it is believed that a mountain can be moved by the power of faith (how Harper loved that verse!) or about a sea that parts into two by the power of a different faith.

The salt was poured from the sacks in cascades of white, and only from one of them it fell in blocks, having become damp. There was no doubt these sacks of salt wouldn't be enough, that all of them together could mark only a white stripe on the bed of the ditch, and nevertheless there was a certain joy in introducing a foreign element into the sand, whether the foam line was intended to attract rain clouds or whether to attract the sea.

Those who emptied the sacks of mother-of-pearl could also enjoy the sound they made in their fall, a gentle sound, pleasurable to the ear. For a moment there arose a small sorrow: those who had brought the mother-of-pearl to Khotan told that in the parched Kuruk Darya gorge there had been an abundance of fish bones, but those, like the anchor chains, they were forced to forgo.

They had to be more careful with seashells, because they were few and precious. They weren't packed in sacks but rather in crates and each one wrapped in straw that was then carefully removed, and the straw was instantly carried off by the wind. They had to wait for Tenzin to decide where exactly to place them, and after consulting with Poliakov he decided to put them between the sand and the ditch bed – in that way they were seemingly waiting for those who would come to blow into them like the wind and thereby call out to the rain clouds or listen to the roar of sea in them, as well as to the ships of the gods in their return.

Then, after the last crate had been unloaded, it was discovered that a few shells were missing, and suspicion immediately fell on the Khotani with a fondness for jade, and he was sent accompanied to the place where the other animals had been tied up and was ordered to show his cargo. When it transpired he had been shrewd enough not to hide the shells in his vessels, Tenzin added a threat: not only a fine, but also all the punishments that had been meted out to those who had removed them from their place, from the lightest to leprosy.

The threat was effective, and when those anchors were laid in their designated spots it seemed for a while that the preparations had come to an end; the anchors had been assembled and all that was left was to drop them into the pits that had been dug for them. But the evil one has been sentenced to is bound to find a path through which to strike, that was a lesson McKenzie had already learned in Italy and should have remembered.

And how could he forget? The moment they alighted from the carriage on to the platform, her eyes widened and sparkled, and with delight he saw how she listened to the lilting sounds of a foreign language. Much quicker than he who wasted most of the hours of the journey from Calais to Rome studying phrases, she learned to say 'buongiorno' and 'buonasera,' and afterward 'quanto costa' and 'chi sono altri colori' and 'e possibile avere uno sconto': 'can I get a discount?' And they always replied 'si, signora,' and something else that he didn't understand other than the pair of words 'bella donna,' and he couldn't imagine at the time what that compliment would lead to.

She didn't get drunk easily, and certainly not on a stomach full of pasta, but when she did get drunk she became almost as loose as a streetwalker; there was a certain an allure to it, and she could be heard in restaurants (a smart one in the main square or a working class one on a side street, to see what the common folk eat) learning from Magnani, at her request, a few juicy swear words in Italian, in a Roman or Neapolitan dialect or both together (after all, Magnani was also an expert on languages), and with what charm they become garbled, much to the amused amazement of the diners.

The Italian word for glass amused her, because she read 'bicchiere' from the menu as 'bitchiereh' instead of 'bickiereh,' and when they left the restaurant she must have been gratified by the 'arrivederci, signora' that the waiters proclaimed with a pleasing lilt as well as the appreciative looks that were directed at her and which flattered Magnani too. She must have been impressed by the respect with which he was treated – 'per favore, Professore'; 'grazie, Professore'; 'arrivederci, Professore' – it was impossible not to compare him to her husband on their first day in Rome when he created a brouhaha over spaghetti bolognaise.

Quicker than him she learned to say: 'scusi, per arrivere a' – excuse me, how do I get to – and more than once she was voluntarily escorted to the next square or to the museum or the church or the restaurant where she had made an appointment to meet Magnani, finding excitement that way before returning to the hotel and sinking back into the desolation of her marriage; being with her veterinarian in the room again would be enough for that. Then Rome would be left outside, and there were just the two of them: a country veterinarian and his London wife, a husband and wife that had gone as far as Rome to try and put their marriage right. On one of the days there he told her about a wounded dog he came across - a carriage had hit it – and she said to him: "You're a good man, Ed, I've always said that." And he knew it wasn't a compliment.

And what was Magnani? A chatterbox and a boaster, a robber of antiquities and of wives, but perhaps – the thought also sometimes arose – he hadn't robbed her from him and hadn't even intended to do so. Not that he didn't enjoy flirting, of course he did, happy to see how charmed she was by his erudition and by the stories of his expeditions and by his witticisms (botany was not on his mind when he spoke about the fig leaves that cover the genitalia of the statues), but perhaps he wasn't expecting all this to develop the way it did; and truthfully, who could conceive that in the middle of a trip to a foreign country a woman would leave her husband and go off with another man?

It was actually possible she had been the instigator, and in Brindisi it wasn't difficult to imagine her asking Magnani for instance – since they're so close to the university, would he mind showing her his office? Surely he has some small collection from his journeys in the East there. On the last day (the last from his point of view, of course, not from theirs) it wasn't hard for him to see her inviting herself there and telling his secretary that she's his guest from England, 'si,' the Professore is waiting for her.

After putting down her suitcase, she closed the door in sight of the secretary and perhaps looked at the statuettes displayed in the glass cabinet, or and took out a cracked statuette from it and sniffed the front and back of it (a year and a half before that she had sniffed McKenzie that way, burying her nose in his armpit); but perhaps – it's also possible – she had already realized then how far her whims had driven her. Quite some time would pass until McKenzie would hear what really happened and how far his imagination had strayed from the truth.

Does not a moment come to every man when it transpires he's not able to impose his will on the world? Perhaps for the first time in her life she then experienced such a moment, and the thought of that gave pleasure to McKenzie: seeing in his mind's eye his unfaithful wife and the professor whose life's course is suddenly shaken, standing in the small office opposite the glass cabinet with his statuettes – if they had been standing there and not on a street corner – and her suitcase still by her side. True, she had somewhere to return to, a hotel room the Englishwoman she met left for her, but she probably preferred confronting Magnani with the fact. If she had asked the Professore about his home, she might have caused him embarrassment – no, he's not married, no-no, but his aged mother and his three sisters live in the house, and it would be a little difficult to explain to them how an Englishwoman had suddenly pitched up with him, even if she hadn't been married (McKenzie provided him with a thousand excuses for his wife to realize how unwanted she was).

In the end, the Professore remembered that one of his colleagues was abroad and that his apartment was empty; while he hadn't left him the keys to the apartment for that purpose he wouldn't be angry to discover it was being used to host a charming Englishwoman in distress. Perhaps the thought passed through Magnani's mind that in the end Kate would land up with his friend and not with him, and in that way this entanglement he had become involved in would unravel itself.

It was a bachelor apartment close to the university and in walking distance of the Tiber (these details McKenzie would later hear from the horse's mouth), and after he led her there in a carriage, extolling the virtues of the apartment for the duration of the ride, he asked the doorman of the building to see to her needs and gave him a handsome advance on the bill. "Don't you want me anymore, Carlo?" she asked as he stood opposite the door, while he, her husband, was still out searching for her.

"Si, si," Magnani replied, but it seemed that more than anything he wanted to return home. She turned to the window; the carriage that had brought her was waiting below, and the coachman whistled some melody to himself.

"Go," she said to Magnani.

What happened afterward was also not difficult to picture: how she sits on her ankles and leans over the suitcase and opens it and begins to peruse the garments folded in it. They were all the possessions she had at the time, her hold on something familiar, and perhaps their touch was consoling. "Haven't you gone yet?" she said to Magnani and rose clutching the dressing gown she had taken out, and she went to the bathroom and opened the taps; more than anything she no doubt wanted to wash away that day from her, at the start of which she had been a man's wife.

Some time passed until she arrived at Magnani's apartment; under no circumstances would she agree to let him into her temporary apartment: she wouldn't open the door for him, didn't answer his ringing and gave the doorman back the flowers he sent. There's no knowing what she did in the apartment. Perhaps for a night or two she slept in the hotel room her English widow friend had left for her.

In order to appease her (that's what she was expecting him to do; while at the same time she sent a telegram to her banker friend requesting him to transfer money to her so that she could return to London should she suffer a disappointment), a greater gesture than the previous ones would be needed: not bouquets of orchids, not French champagne, not a cashmere sweater that had been bought in Kashmir – she had returned them all to the doorman. One morning the carriage waited at the foot of the building, decorated with flowers, and Magnani gave the doorman money to politely and firmly inform her, a week before the time, that the owner of the apartment was about to return. Magnani didn't want to take any risks, and just as well that he did it early; had he delayed for another day, perhaps she would have returned to London and brought her adventure to a close.

For a while she perhaps still amused herself with the thought of staying in the apartment and seeing his friend's reaction on his return, but even she wasn't capable of doing such a thing. She had already learned the price of her whims and an entire week of total isolation in a strange apartment (during the day she wandered the streets, far from the Via Veneto, far from all the museums and churches as well) had been sobering.

After the doorman left – from all he said she picked up mainly the words "none possibile" – she shut the door and again knelt down to her suitcase. There was all the difference in the world packing the suitcase there and packing it in England when it still seemed the trip might rectify their marriage. One after the other she put the items of clothing into the suitcase, underwear, blouses, dresses, belts, stockings, that already gave off the smell of sweat.

What else did she do while staying there? If she thought of him for a few moments, they certainly didn't last long, and she certainly didn't conceive that he, McKenzie, had taken the decisive actions he had taken. It's more likely she believed he was still waiting for her to return: watching the street from the small balcony and standing like that until the lamplighter came, and only afterward returning to their room and climbing onto the bed and waiting for her night after night until a deep sleep fell upon him. How mistaken she had been, how accurate she had been.

When she went down the steps with the doorman in front of her carrying her suitcase to the carriage, she didn't relate to Magnani any more than she did the coachman, but not because she was continuing to trifle with him, rather because she had become weary. She curled up in a corner of the carriage and didn't answer any of the questions Magnani asked her, not even the offer he made, to stop on the way and eat at the restaurant they used to frequent when he was still giving her learned lectures about ancient statues. For the entire journey she looked only through the carriage window, and it's doubtful whether anything she saw was taken in by her eyes. They drove that way until from one of the squares a small dusty dog darted into their pathway and would have been run over by their wheels had the coachman not pulled in the reins, and then a sharp sound burst from her throat, possibly a sob, possibly a laugh.

When they arrived and the carriage stopped, she was in no hurry to rise, she had lost her strength of spirit. "Come," Magnani said to her, "meet my family" – he said it in Italian, since she already knew the word 'famiglia.' Appearing to her first were Magnani's sisters who were waiting in the guest parlor, and it took a moment for her to notice his mother who was sitting in a wheelchair in the corner with a blanket over her knees.

Magnani introduced them to each other; he said her name in full but lied about all the rest; he said she was the wife of an English friend, a colleague who had come to the university of Rome for a year and that a tragedy had occurred; and to leave Mrs. McKenzie alone in an enormous apartment the university had rented for her would be inhumane. They had already heard all that from him before then, but since the whole way to the house Kate had refused to listen to him, he repeated all of it in her presence in Italian combined with English, so that she would know how he had explained her stay with them. Yes, the British ambassador is also dealing with the matter, he said, and for the meanwhile, they after all have more than enough vacant rooms on his mother's floor.

"She'll stay with us," the younger daughter decided, and the older sisters showed no opposition (she ruled them from an early age, Magnani would later say). Magnani still insisted for some reason to convince his mother with what was a complete lie – Katherine's husband had allegedly been buried in a landslide at an archeological excavation – and for that purpose he went to the carved wooden cabinet in which statuettes brought from his expeditions were displayed and took out a terra cotta statuette of a well-endowed curvaceous woman and brought it to his mother ("this was from him," he said to her), and she stared at the statuette. A moment later she lifted the terra cotta figurine to her mouth and kissed it with wrinkled lips and began to sing a lullaby Magnani and his sisters remembered from childhood.

> Fa la ninna, fa la nanna
> Nella braccia della mamma

She sang in her thin voice and carried on cradling the statuette in her arms even when she forgot the continuation of the song.

"She'll break it," said the eldest sister to Magnani.

"It's only a fake," Magnani replied.

15

The seashells, which were as large as the palms of a man's hand curved around a cup, were buried in the sand at half the height between the bed of the ditch and the surface of the ground. They were buried instantly: it was enough to insert them slightly into the side of the ditch, and right away grains of sand slid over them and covered them, and one couldn't tell where in this one-hundred-and fifty-meter-long ditch they were buried. The strip of salt on the ground was mostly covered with mother-of-pearl, but its whiteness was still evident there, despite that more and more grains of sand slid onto it from the sides as well. The anchors, whose assembling had been completed, remained outside, and before the ditch would be blocked up with the sand that had been taken out of it, they had to lower them to the bottom of the pits that had been dug for them at the ends of the ditch and in its center.

Neither Tenzin nor Poliakov knew for certain – how could they be sure of something that had never been tested – whether it would be better to bury all the items until they couldn't be seen at all and thereby risking that they not be found, or to be somewhat negligent in the burying in order to ensure that they wouldn't remain underground forever. The idea arose to give the men a special gratuity of fifty rupees if they held their tongues for a year, enough time for at least one of the items of the fraud to be discovered and for the rumor of the finding to reach Europe and for Magnani to enlist and equip a caravan, but since the secrecy itself was liable spur the men to sell the information as soon as possible to the highest bidder, it was decided to bury the items at a depth not too great nor too small and at a distance not too great nor too small from the border of the settlement, and not to promise any reward but rather to let time take effect: what will be exposed will be exposed, sooner or later.

"What are you waiting for?" said Tenzin. It was a seemingly simple order; a light push of the anchors would have been enough for each one of them to slide to the bottom of the pit that had been dug for it, but that isn't what happened, not with southern anchor anyway. They could have been lowered in two ways: one using the shape of the anchor and allowing its pointed tip to decide its path, and the other being to first slide the heavy end in, the shank encased in lead. Because they had been deliberating over this for some time, the onlookers voiced all sorts of advice, (few pleasures rivalled giving advice from the side), and Faizul's voice could be heard promising the winner all sorts of delicacies in the name of the Kashgari cook. Before that a reward of one day's wages had been promised to the ditch diggers and two days wages to the pit diggers.

"Aren't you tired of that?" someone answered Faizul and suggested that instead of handing out all sorts of prizes to the winners in the name of others, he himself should try to move an anchor as heavy as that; yes, let's see him do it! And after grievances such as those, Faizul had no option and began walking towards the southern pit that was closest to where it stood. One of the Tavakkal men had been intending to slide the anchor from the bed of the ditch to the pit and Faizul called out to delay him.

"Get away from here," the Tavakkal man said to him. "Everyone's already sick of you."

The insult was worse than the previous one: it's one thing when a man of your own standing taunts you and quite another when it's done by someone who in his whole backward life has never been out of the desert and doesn't even know what a city looks like.

"What will you do with the money?" Faizul said to him. "There's nothing to buy where you come from."

So – he continued - let him put the anchor into the pit instead, and from the money he'll get for it he's even prepared to give him a few rupees to buy a bunch of dates or a basket of camel dung for winter. Just don't get them mixed up.

The Tavakkal man's tongue wasn't that quick and so he resorted to his hands (by then Faizul was already standing in the ditch), and when they began to fight and rolled on the bed of mother-of-pearl and salt at the bottom of the ditch, they could no longer be seen by the onlookers. Only a small cloud of dust could be seen as well as the sand sliding from the edges into the ditch; it didn't stop sliding in for one moment.

"In the end, you'll be both remain there," someone shouted at them, and Tenzin threatened that if they didn't stop immediately, he'd cut their wages, but they no longer heard him. On the bed of the ditch, on the mother-of-pearl and the salt that had been emptied onto it for its entire length, they grabbed at each other and struck each other in the face, the stomach, the loins, and choked each other with hands, with elbows, or with a knee. The mother-of-pearl must have pierced their bodies and the salt mixed with sand must have penetrated their eyes and blinded them, and each time they rolled over they drew nearer to the edge of the lower pit, the one designated for the anchor.

Tenzin and Poliakov didn't see any of this from where they stood, and only in retrospect did they fully understand what had happened there. On their return they told McKenzie only the very least of it, but he had no difficulty imagining the rest, and not because he himself was a great wrestler, on the contrary, throughout all the years of his boyhood his father had ridiculed him for being the only one of all the boys in the area who didn't come to blows with anyone – is that the kind of son he's brought up? A sissy? – though he was fairly sturdy, he had no fondness for fighting.

Only years later did he fight with grave seriousness and had even been the aggressor, although he had been incited to it. One of Kate's friends, the one who suggested the idea of medical insurance for the farm animals, was struck with uncontrollable laughter when McKenzie told him he had informed the farmers that at the end of the year he promises to return half the premium if his services hadn't been needed. "Katie, Katie," her friend Stan said, "with him you really won't get further than a cow's rectum."

It didn't happen in Begbroke but rather in London; Kate had dragged him to a play one of her friends was acting in, and after the play they all went to a Soho pub where he drank more than he was used to, and without hesitation suggested to Stan they go out into an alley and settle their differences.

"Are you going to hit me?" Stan asked in amazement. "Katie, tell him not to hit me!" he said in the crying voice of an infant.

"Stop that, Ed," Katie said, "have you gone completely mad?"

"Step outside," McKenzie said to him again.

In a dark alley, despite being a head taller than Stan and heavier than him by a few kilograms, and perhaps because of that, his rival, who it turned out had boxed at boarding school, had the upper hand and agilely circled him again and again and hit him all over, while not one punch of his own hit its mark. "Are you going to hit me?" asked Stan as he danced around him with clenched fists. "Hit me, why don't you hit me?" And in the end, he hit him in the eye and McKenzie collapsed with all his weight onto the paving stones and a smell of urine rose from them.

When the shout was heard one couldn't tell from whose throat it had come. It was terrible, a shout not proceeded by a painful punch or a kick or a fistful of salt flung in the eyes or fingers poked into them, but something worse, and when Poliakov took out his pistol and fired into the air it was already too late. When the sound of the shot faded, silence prevailed, and the onlookers waited in vain for one of them to rise out of the ditch but neither did, as if they had been killed together by the one bullet that had been fired. Tenzin had to approach to see what had happened (he forbade the others to go near), and they watched him trudging through the sand toward the ditch and stopping there. Only then were the two of them visible to him.

In their brawling they had rolled from the bed of the ditch to the pit that had been dug in it, and the sand that slid in from the edge swept with it the anchor that had been placed there, until it was buried in it. Someone whose head is struck by a lead cased shank weighing more than ninety kilograms doesn't stand a chance of surviving. On their way here, when one of the camels had been struck by one like that, the wound couldn't be detected because the shank was still wrapped in sackcloth, but here it was clearly visible: the smashed skull of the Tavakkal man who at the moment of the brawl had pressed the shoulders of his rival to the bottom of the pit thereby separating him from the anchor.

Persistently, with no abatement, the sand continued to slide onto the anchor and onto the two silent bodies beneath it, sticking to the lead and to the blood and to the sweat and to the whitish particles that had been sprayed by the smashed skull. A few moments passed until a sound could be heard, and it then seemed that Faizul moved slightly beneath the body laid upon him with the anchor that had fallen on it, and one couldn't tell whether it was a death rattle or a sign of life.

From there distance where they all stood and watched, Tenzin could be seen delaying for a moment before bending forward: first his head, then his upper body, and finally all of him disappearing into the ditch and pit. Perhaps some of the Tavakkal men sought to follow him and Turdi stopped them, and perhaps it was Poliakov who halted them with his pistol; there was no knowing and anyway was of little importance.

At that time in Leh, McKenzie was sunk in one of his late afternoon naps, and despite his dream being bad, and its continuation even worse, what had really happened was far worse. While he awoke from his nap in the hospital, Faizul was being pulled from the pit by his armpits, and Tenzin, who struggled to raise him to the surface of the ground, battled against the grains sliding in and the collapsing sides. It's possible that he wouldn't have succeeded had Faizul not awoken from his swoon and begun to move his limbs, first one hand and after it another and then his legs as well, and when in end he was taken out and placed on his feet, his face was white from the salt in the ditch (he had been fortunate that broken bits of mother-of-pearl hadn't injured him), and even after wiping his face with the back of his hand its paleness stood out – it was the paleness of death that lightens even the darkest skin.

Faizul didn't say anything when the Tavakkal men drew near the pit, not even when two of them went down to raise their dead friend from it. His whole body shook despite it not being cold, and the cloth over his private parts and his rear end was wet. He was still in shock from the closeness to death, after all, one more roll over would have been enough for his skull to have been smashed. They saw him taking a few uncertain steps and stop and sway and suddenly bend down and vomit. No one approached him, and perhaps he also wasn't expecting anyone to do so.

They had to bury the dead man, and the most convenient possibility was to leave him where he was and heap sand on him – they had intended to fill the length of the ditch anyway and cover everything buried in it – but Tenzin immediately rejected the idea. It had to appear as if it had been done a thousand years ago and more, and what did that have to do with a Tavakkal man who had recently died? The sand and the aridity preserve a corpse, but there's only a little similarity between a shriveled mummy and a bloated dead body.

It would have been better to move the body away, and even if the Tavakkal men weren't thinking of returning the dead man to the oasis where he was born, they wanted to take care of him themselves; he was their friend, and none of the other men on the caravan had even taken the trouble to find out his name. Nonetheless, Tenzin decided not to waste time on that: in these regions many leave their dead to a sky burial. Anyone horrified by the thought of that – and McKenzie certainly had been horrified during his first days here – should better wonder if it is not more contemptible to be eaten by worms.

Poliakov preferred busying himself with his pistol: he loaded another bullet into its cylinder in place of the one he had fired into the air, touched the bore of the barrel with his finger and checked how much soot there was.

It was advisable – Tenzin said to the Tavakkal men – for the entire caravan to leave on its way and that they not wait for the funeral, which by the time it began and ended night would fall. If they moved a short distance away, they would certainly find a suitable place; there was no shortage of sand to cover him with.

"Why shouldn't they bury him the way they want to?" Poliakov asked.

In Tavakkal they kept their own ritual customs and shielded them from strangers, and the Khotani and Kashgari men must certainly have seemed foreign to them no less than the Europeans.

"Because we don't have time," Tenzin replied and instructed the Tavakkal men to load their friend onto his pony and tie him up so that he doesn't fall off.

It was a sight hard to bear: the dead man could have been tied to the saddle lying down or seated, and his hands could have been tied to the reins so that they wouldn't be tossed about, but more important than that was to place a sack over his head and face so that they wouldn't see what the lead casing had done to his face and how it had been slashed, despite that the main injury had been to the neck; it seems that the face had been squashed against Faizul's forehead, when pressed to the bottom of the pit by his shoulders.

Since an eastern wind had stirred again and there was a fear it would blow the sack off, they tied its ends to the dead man's neck, and for a while, until the cloth reddened from his blood, he looked like a sentenced man on the way to the gallows – so it seemed to Poliakov. As to the Tavakkal men, at first they favored tying their friend in a seated position, in their eyes it seemed more proper in his death; after all, they had never seen sentenced men with their hoods.

The afternoon was already coming to its end, and had the dead man been buried in the ditch his fluids would doubtlessly have been absorbed there. Perhaps not only his head had been injured but also his internal organs from the anchor or from Faizul's blows, and in the open air there was an acceleration of the resolute process whereby a living body turns into a corpse, when the only thing going on inside it is the rotting.

Had all that occurred at sea, sharks would have found their way to him by the scent of the blood, but that scent isn't necessary for the desert crows, a hint is enough for them; they quite often gather in the sky above a man who has just begun to die, and it's not his blood or his secretions that attract them, but perhaps (McKenzie had never witnessed it, only heard) the covert smell of the helplessness whose end is death. It was common for vultures to be seen on animals that had collapsed on their knees and not even wait for them to fall to the ground and breathe their last.

First, a crow appeared from somewhere, black and shiny, making a large circle in the sky and after it a second circling, smaller than the first, and after it another, smaller than the previous one, and then casually dived toward its target and landed on the head covered by the sack with a distasteful ease. It stood there for a while like a dove on the head of a statue in a park or square and seemed to be satisfied with the free ride it had found for itself, since the pony hadn't sensed its additional passenger.

A moment later, a second crow joined it, no less black and shiny, it swooped down and also landed on the hooded head; and since the place was narrow for two, it pushed its predecessor away with its beak. The first crow flew off with an angry cry of protest, beat its wings in the air, pondered its actions and dived again and this time landed on the dead man's thigh. Its eyes were now turned toward the stomach, as was its beak. When one of the Tavakkal men bent down from his saddle and took a fistful of sand and threw it at the crow, the wind repelled the sand and the crow remained in its place. With the tip of its large thick sharp beak, it continued to examine the cloth of the dead man's cloak, while the other crow standing on the hooded head examined the sack material in the same way.

At first, they were trial pecks, as if evaluating how much strength would be needed to insert the beak into the cloth and farther, or how many small pecks would unravel it. The first to succeed was the crow on the dead man's head; with the point of the beak it widened the spaces between the sack fibers, and after picking for a moment or two found the most convenient spot where the sack pressed close against the face, that is to say the nose, but the man had a lean nose and the crow was looking for a superior delicacy, and therefore moved its beak higher and knew exactly what it would find there.

Its colleague, sitting on the thigh of the dead man, knew very well what it was looking for. It could have pecked the stomach – while the dead man didn't have a paunch there was nevertheless enough meat there – but it also wanted to begin its feast with a true delicacy, the kind that does not entail the tiring work of ripping chunks off the body. Thus, one beak strived to reach one of the dead man's eyes and the other one of his testicles. They carried out their actions in utter silence, and due to the bend in the route the Tavakkal men couldn't see the harm the crows were inflicting upon their friend. Poliakov and Tenzin also didn't see them, nor the newly joined feasters: two black shiny crows that stood on the dead man's thighs, and a third greyish one that stood on his right shoulder. That crow stood there with a sense of ownership, despite having been a latecomer, and instead of making do with the little tough flesh of the shoulder, it saw it merely as a convenient base and stuck its beak into the sack, and before it reached the cheek another crow had already dived and landed on the left shoulder and pointed its beak at the other cheek.

When the caravan straightened out and the field of vision had opened up again, the first two crows had already flown off with their loot, they flapped their wings, ascended and glided – one of them holding an eyeball between the two parts of its beak, and the other holding a testicle – and before Poliakov aimed his pistol at them, they were already too far off, tiny as a dot.

"Wouldn't it be a waste of bullets?" Tenzin asked.

The first time he saw the pistol, when the wounded camel was put to death by it, he was surprised, because he was certain it had remained with the pawnbroker in Leh, but when it was taken out it seemed it could be put to good use in times of emergency, and this was not such a time.

There were six bullets in the cylinder and only after the fifth Poliakov stopped shooting and was still gazing at the spot in the sky where the crows had disappeared. Perhaps – the thought entered the doctor's mind, although all this wouldn't change anything – on seeing them he was reminded of the ones circling above him in his hallucinations in the hospital and before that on the way to Leh.

"Bury him here," Tenzin said and suggested digging a pit deep enough for the crows to not reach him. Before that, the Tavakkal men tried throwing fistfuls of sand at the crows, but the black birds weren't impressed by that and even when one of the men came out on his horse with a whip raised in his hand to get rid of them, they were quick to land on the man after each lash.

Again the Tavakkal men asked to be allowed to bury their dead according to their own custom, and again Tenzin refused their request. He looked westward toward the sun that was beginning to set, and afterward shot a glance behind at the dead man: six crows were sitting on him and flew off when they were expelled, only to return right away.

When Turdi tried to tell Tenzin it would be better he take his men's feelings into consideration – he uttered the well-known truth, one shouldn't demean the dead, and mentioned one who didn't bury his dead and the earth opened its mouth wide and swallowed him and his dead – Tenzin replied that he wasn't demeaning the dead man, on the contrary, those who insist on postponing his burial were demeaning them.

But that wasn't what they were insisting on, rather on their ceremonies: there were prayers to be said, and incense to be burned, and a kite would be needed to clear the way to heaven for the soul, but Tenzin wouldn't accede to them. Until the darkness that was already deepening around them fell, he wanted to get as far away from Dandan Oilik as possible, and no caravan needs to be delayed because of a corpse, and certainly not one from which a few organs had already been eaten away.

Again, Turdi tried to persuade him to allow the Tavakkal men to conduct their ceremony. One hour would be enough, he said, and anyway it would make no difference to the others – they would say their prayers, fly a kite with the soul of the dead man, if that's what they believe will allow him to reach heaven; after all, the Russian had bought a kite in Tavakkal and they could use it.

"Would you let them?" Tenzin asked him, but the Tavakkal men who heard the offer, hastened to relieve him of his deliberations: a kite like that couldn't carry any soul on its back, because it hadn't been intended for that purpose and also hadn't been made by the right hands. It was said in complete earnestness, and anyone mocking their custom would do well to first clarify whether confining the dead to wooden coffins helps their souls any more.

Since the sun was nearing the horizon and the light was being gathered to it, Tenzin ordered his men to bury the dead man as quickly as possible in the pit they had dug for him, or to leave him as quickly as possible beyond the dune – what exactly he ordered, McKenzie didn't know; he only knew on their return that an argument had broken out between Tenzin and Poliakov, an argument after which they spoke little to each other. When they returned to Leh, no joy could be seen in their faces, not about having put their plan into action nor about their expected wages; and even Leh itself, after months of their absence, couldn't change the expression on their faces. They were solemn and gloomy, contradicting each other's versions not only concerning the argument between them but all sorts of trifles: the depth of the layer of salt in the ditch, the anchor pits, the hole dug for the fake pieces of parchment, and the breadth of the layer of mother-of-pearl, as if those minutiae were of vast importance. No doubt other matters were bound up with their differences, but they specifically argued these matters in his office, as if the doctor himself would come searching for what they had buried in the sands, and not that Italian son of a bitch (that's what he still called him to himself, and at times even aloud: *the Italian son of a bitch*, and some time would pass before he would give up that name).

Perhaps in their argument, Tenzin had mocked Poliakov for his hypocrisy, having defended the Tavakkal men in that way while at the same time finding it hard to part with the kite whose future owner – the little Russian boy – didn't even know of its existence; and Poliakov mocked the hypocrisy of the Ladakhi who always holds himself up as someone who fights the battles of the downtrodden against the white man, and is now behaving towards the Tavakkal men exactly as the British had behaved towards his father. It wasn't difficult to imagine how all that deteriorated, if Tenzin had answered that it might be true that he isn't concerned with the dead, but at least he had never killed anyone.

Poliakov's reputation as a revolutionary, cultivated by the ladies of Leh, still adhered him, but there was just one thing they couldn't understand; why in God's name does he keep company with the loose Russian woman and her son, the little bastard who one can barely distinguish from the Ladakhi children due to all the dirt. "Terrible," they would tut-tut, "not only doesn't the mother know who the father is, she also doesn't know where the boy runs around all day." And indeed, every time she entertained her patron Sunam Tsering in her room at the inn, Sasha was sent out and the door was locked.

"So, how was it with your old lady?" his mother would ask about Mrs. Harper on his return, and also cast a disapproving eye on his bond with Mr. Harper who had taken the trouble to instill the principles of faith in him no less that he had done with the Ladakhi children (after all, it wasn't his fault he had been conceived in the bed of a prostitute), and had even earmarked the central role for him in the pageant he intended mounting for the Feast of the Ascension. Perhaps she had spoken about the two of them not out of meanness but rather out of jealousy and sorrow; her Ladakhi patron was the same age as the missionary and his wife.

All the months the caravan had been in the desert, Harper worked on his pageant, comparing different versions of the story and deliberating which of them to choose, and in the end he decided to take the best of each gospel (about the contradictions contained in the four of them, Callahan once said: "If that happened with us at *The Simla News*, someone would have been fired long ago"): here the women speak of Jesus' grave that had become empty and no one believes them, while there, when Jesus returns and appears, no one believes that he's returned. "Even his disciples!" Harper said, shocked by their little faith, but he already knew who would portray them – all thirteen pupils from the Sunday school – and he didn't deliberate much over their dark skin: the ancient Hebrews must have looked that way, and like them they must have been the children of washerwomen, seamstresses and blacksmiths.

Harper was especially roused by Jesus' conversation with the two passersby who had no notion who he was, and in his mind's eye could already see the gymnasium of the school that had been barracks before Henry agreed to transfer it to the mission, and those two men walking along and talking excitedly about the events of last few days and Jesus joining them (and who seemed more suitable for the part than the Russian boy? Yes, even if the ladies of Leh turn their noses up!) and asking them what they were talking about.

Hadn't he heard what happened in Jerusalem? They are amazed and tell him of the one who had been crucified three days before and whose body disappeared from the grave, and only when Jesus blesses the bread and breaks it do they identify him, and right away he disappears. Night falls – the lanterns will then be extinguished in the hall, or the opposite, candles will be lit on the windowsills and shed light like stars.

They don't know when they'll see him again, and Jesus (one of the Andrews boys will portray him, since Sasha preferred the role of the angel) is already making his way to Jerusalem, and there hears his twelve apostles talking about him as if he hadn't been standing beside them, and when he turns to them, they become alarmed as if they had seen a ghost. "Why are you troubled, and why do doubts rise in your minds?" he says to them, "Look at my hands and my feet. It is I myself! Touch me and see; a ghost does not have flesh and bones!" and only after he asks them for some food and begins to eat are they convinced.

Here Harper chose to combine versions and give Jesus Matthew's version of his words before ascending to the heavens (and in James Andrews' thin and sometimes shrill voice): "Therefore go and make disciples of all nations!" – What verse is more fitting than that to leave its echo in the ears of the Sunday school pupils?

Some time passed until it became evident the children were particularly fond of Jesus' saying, "Touch me and see; a ghost does not have flesh and bones," though not for the right reasons. After one of the rehearsals ended and they all went outside, Harper saw them poking fingers in each other's ribs, tickling each other, giggling, bellowing with laughter, doubling up, and only owing to their innocence forgave them.

All that would have ended without incident had they not begun to run through the small square and had not Gavanath the seamstress's son been tripped up. He lay spread-eagled, flat on his face, and didn't move, like an animal playing dead. Someone – the blacksmith's son and Sasha's colleague in angelhood – kicked him lightly and suggested they undress him and shoving and hitting him they forced him to call out, "Touch me and see, touch me and see," and made him say it also when they felt his girlish breasts and pulled his nipples and pinched his plump behind; it was endlessly funny, but Gavanath wasn't laughing at all. Out of all those hooligans, it was Sasha – despite his forefathers having been baptized Christian – who suggested they make Gavanath bend on all fours and force him to lift his large behind and shake it to and fro (Harper's shock was still evident as he talked about it) while shouting out some word in Russian over and over.

The postman, who then arrived at the church courtyard, saw the minister frozen at his window and the children dispersed in all directions, all except the fat boy whose suppressed crying burst out. So great was Harper's bitter disappointment that he was close to cancelling the entire pageant on the spot. That whole evening as well as the next day he deliberated whether to continue with the preparations ("What do you think, Doctor?" he asked him, who was then not interested in anything other than the caravan he had sent into the desert), and only one thing was clear to him, that no wings be given to one who had sinned and caused others to sin; the other angel, the blacksmith's son, it was still barely possible to forgive, but not the little Russian bastard; nor were all Mrs. Harper's efforts to defend him of any help.

The next rehearsal was cancelled and the following one as well, and only after a week were all the actors assembled for another rehearsal, all except the one who had labored for his role for hours and days making a pair of wings and sticking all the feathers he had gathered from the banks of Lake Tsomoriri to them, and at that evening hour – an hour when the light quickly expires and with it the heat – he remained outside the hall and watched everyone through the window, pressing his eye close to the pane. He was seven years old at the time, a boy of short stature and thin, whose clothes were no less worn out that those of Ladakhi children, and in order to reach the windowsill he placed mud bricks one on top of the other and stood on them with his skinny legs.

It took a while for Harper to notice him and his squashed nose and the gleam is his big eyes. At first, he ignored him and tried to continue the rehearsal as usual, but when everyone turned their heads there it was no longer possible to continue. "You sinner and maker of others to sin!" Harper shouted from inside, and Sasha withdrew his face from the pane. The small tower of bricks he was standing on swayed slightly and him together with it, and the children laughed; a white man, and furthermore a priest, had never afforded them the opportunity to mock a white boy.

"Get down from there!" Harper said. "You bad boy!" But he wasn't a bad boy, and if he hadn't been subjected to the pranks similar to that one, there had been things that he had heard and seen at the inn, each time his mother and her Ladakhi patron banished him from the room and their voices could still be heard through the locked door.

He knew for sure he had done a bad deed, even before Harper said it, but the punishment doled out to him – the deprivation of his wings over which he had taken such pains – weighed many times more than those wings did on his bony shoulders. He was still standing on a few mud bricks whose stability was very shaky and wouldn't go home or anywhere else but continued to watch them. On the dusty windowpane, against which his nose was squashed from outside, tracks began to be formed in the dust, growing larger and lengthening downward, and not from raindrops.

16

When the caravan reached Tavakkal again, on its way to Khotan, the desert oasis could be seen in an unrivaled blossoming. It was afternoon, and the shade of the palm branches didn't extend much further than their thin trunks. A light vapor rose from the spring, no wind blew, and the smell of bonfire smoke stood still in the silent air.

Coming toward them were not only those who had family relatives on the caravan, but all the others as well, men, women, and children, and they soon noticed someone was missing: nine Tavakkal men had left on the caravan and only eight could be seen, and right away it was revealed who was missing. His name was uttered in many mouths and in varying tones of voice, and a while passed until his wife discovered his absence – she had been busy nursing her baby – and even before one of the men approached her to soften the bitter tidings with some explanation, it was evident from her face she was aware not only of his absence but also of the degrading death he had died.

Her infant, who until then had suckled peacefully, began to cry, and she cradled it in her arms and walked to her husband's pony. It lifted its moist muzzle towards her and she ignored the large brown eyes it fixed on her, and with the fingers of her left hand she felt the saddle from its high edges to its concave; she slowly slid her hand up and down the saddle, first with her fingers and then with the back of her hand, and bent over the saddle and breathed in its scent, and only then, when the scent entered her nostrils, did she burst out crying, and a very wrinkled old lady approached her and took the baby from her hands. They saw her – those who were looking there – leaning her forearm on the horse and resting her forehead on it and pressing her face close to the saddle blanket and toward the warm brown body quivering beneath it, the one that had carried her husband up the dunes and down their slopes and had always brought him back home.

Faced with the mourning, the others were hesitant to show their joy over the returning men, but the joy of their bodies couldn't be hidden: the embracing of the men and women who for almost three weeks hadn't touched each other, the children's hugging of their fathers. "Daddy, daddy," they said using uniform wording but in a variety of ways, and even one who didn't know their language could understand. The two rascals from whom Poliakov had bought the kite were also there and perhaps were hoping to do another deal with him, but one of the men drove them away with a tongue-lashing. Kites weren't needed for such matters, but rather to send the soul of the dead man to heaven, despite that he hadn't died here and nor was his body here.

This was customary in Tavakkal for parting from the dead: in China kites had a different use (Callahan had also spoken about that one evening at the commissioner's wife's gathering); the names of newborn babies were written on them to promise them long lives. In Tavakkal, kites were intended for the dead, and the locals didn't make do with one kite but added one for each family member that accompanied the soul of the dead man on its final journey.

It must have been a fine sight, a chain of kites hovering in the air, whether they were arranged in a line one after the other or whether in an arched line, and Poliakov was keen to see it. Tenzin, on the other hand, did not wish to be delayed.

"Give him at least that honor," Poliakov said, while around them the men of the caravan searched for fodder and water for their animals. Poliakov looked ahead: about a dozen men had assembled in the shade of one of the distant palm trees and their voices were mixed together.

The tumult was intensifying and one couldn't tell what was causing it, whether it was a quarrel over fodder or water or the place for tying up the animals or another matter entirely, until Faizul's voice was heard above all the others and he wasn't boasting in his usual manner but was absolutely terrified, begging and pleading for his life – yes, that also happened while McKenzie was napping in his chair in the hospital; worlds could have been created and destroyed between his snores.

Two of the Tavakkal men who wanted to avenge their friend took hold of Faizul, who futilely tried to explain to them that it was not he who killed their friend, it was the plough, one of the three that they took into the desert. It suddenly fell on their friend's head, they were both in the pit and the plough was above, and all the while the sand was falling inside it, then suddenly the plough also fell in with it, that's to say with the sand, and that's how it injured their friend.

Those holding him didn't seem impressed with his explanations; their grip did not loosen.

Yes, they were both in the pit at the time – Faizul said – they had had a slight argument, true, but these things happen, why should he be blamed that just then it decided to fall?

Then one of the Tavakkal men who had been on the caravan intervened, and in a sharp and clear voice said that the whole argument began only because of Faizul: their friend had been working in the ditch at the time, and suddenly this person decided that he wanted to work in place of him and receive the money in place of him, and that's how it all started. And besides, who didn't he argue with? From the first day he never stopped saying all sorts of insulting things to everyone and must have also said something insulting in the ditch.

"Did you say something insulting?" they questioned Faizul.

More men gathered around him, and one shoved him by his chest to another one in the group, and that one shoved him onward. On and on, he was shoved, until the one whose turn it was to catch him allowed him to fall flat on his face, and before he managed to get up, the bare sole of a foot was pressed to his neck.

They then called the woman whose husband had been killed and asked her what she wanted to be done to the one responsible for her husband's death and their baby growing up without a father and she did not ponder much over it.

From where they stood, Tenzin and Poliakov couldn't hear the tumult at its start. When it intensified, they saw about twenty Tavakkal men huddled together in a circle and above their heads a small cloud of grains carried by the wind, and Faizul's voice could be heard shouting for help in a cracked and broken voice, and finally calling out to his mother as well.

When they drew near, he was already sunk in a pit up to his chest, and three Tavakkal men stood around him with spades in their hands filling the pit at a uniform pace. With every lift of their spades, Faizul shut his eyes, and when Tenzin tried to get closer, the Tavakkal men were in no hurry to make way for him. At some distance in front of him, old Turdi was advancing, until someone also stopped him with a firm hand and said: "Don't interfere, old man," and when he tried to shake off the hand gripping him, he was stopped again without any difficulty and told: "We respect you, old man, it's just to stop something bad happening to you by accident."

The ones holding the spades continued their labor: they stuck the spades into the sand, loaded them and threw the sand into the pit that was almost filled to the brim. The sand had already reached Faizul's neck, and when he opened his mouth in order to shout, he choked on the grains that penetrated into his throat.

Tenzin tried in vain to push the man standing in his way. "Don't interfere with this," he was told, and when he tried again someone grabbed him from behind so that he couldn't take even one step or move his hands. Two children, the ones who sold Poliakov the kite, also cleared a path for themselves toward the pit, and others drew close, men and women, young and old. The voices of the few dozen people standing around the pit became blurred and the expressions on their faces were as one, showing little goodness, only anticipation for the moment the sand completely covers the man in it, the way inquisitive onlookers on a beach watch a drowning man whose head is still visible above the water knowing his fate is sealed.

At what moment did Poliakov decide to intervene? Perhaps on hearing Tenzin let out a groan when the man who grabbed him tightened his grip – he had come to his aid from the roof of the inn in Kashgar – and perhaps he intervened during a moment of silence when Faizul's captors continued to heap more sand around and on top of him. The two little rascals glared at Faizul's eyes: his chin was already buried in the sand, and at that pace it seemed within a few moments his mouth and nose would be covered as well. His nostrils breathed in grains, drawing them up from the sand and by then he no longer had the strength to shout at his captors or to those with the power to save him, and perhaps it was his silence that motivated Poliakov to act.

He didn't draw near, nor did he call out to the people assembled there (fifty or sixty or even more) whose skins were made even darker by the shade of the palm branches. Being skilled, he did it from where he stood without any delay. Afterward the silence persisted for a long while – the annihilating silence after a shot – until the dead man's baby burst out crying in the arms of its grandmother. It was immediately joined by other infants who had been carried here by their mothers to witness the sight of a man being swallowed by sand. Only when returned to its mother did its crying lessen, and with the touch of her nipple to its lips the baby fell silent.

Then, as if the paralysis cast by the shot had been removed (no one had been hurt), one of the diggers lifted the spade in his hand, and with measured a momentum, as if nothing had happened, threw the sand loaded on it onto Faizul's head, and right away the other did likewise, and between the palm trees on the left, some as yet unclear activity was also being renewed.

"Don't interfere in this," Poliakov was told, and two men were already coming toward him, but he didn't return the pistol to his belt and instead stabilized it on his arm and aimed and pulled the trigger again, and this time the pistol was aimed at one of the spades and the metallic sound of a bullet hitting the metal was heard. Again, the baby burst out crying and couldn't be pacified until its mother inserted her other breast into its mouth.

Poliakov lifted his voice slightly, despite that those whom he addressed were no farther than thirty paces from him and anyway couldn't understand Russian, but nevertheless understood his meaning. If the Tavakkal had ammunition, it was out of reach.

Above the surface of the sand being played with by the wind, half of Faizul's head could be seen from the nostrils upward, and his eyes, whose lashes were full of grains, were glassy from fear. None of the men of the caravan came to his aid, and when the two little rascals offered to dig around him for money, they were silenced with a reprimand.

"Let him take him out!" one of the men from the caravan said pointing to the Khotani who on their way had gathered jade stones from the Yurungkash gorge; apparently he and Faizul had some joint scheme they had been planning together; at night their neighbors had heard them whispering about it to each other. The Khotani's neck was clasped, and he was led to the pit and when he arrived there and reached out his hand to one of the spades, it was removed.

"Dig with your hands," Tenzin said, "you took the stones with your hands, now dig with your hands."

Then the crying of the baby erupted again and overtook its tiny body, and even when cradled in its mother's arms to and fro it would not be reconciled.

"On your knees," Tenzin said to the Khotani, "and start digging!"

And right then, as he began to dig around Faizul's head with his hands, all eyes were turned from away there. Above the eastern clump of palm trees, close to the treetops, a giant kite lifted up and rose and floated, drawing behind it a dozen long tails surging in the wind – it was the kite for assisting the soul on its way to heaven and was decorated with illustrations of clouds. Behind the palms the forlorn continuous blast of horns was sounded, signaling the ceremony was about to begin, and all who were standing around the pit turned to go there. The widow with her baby also went, and only the Khotani digging with his hands remained (Poliakov ordered him with his pistol to continue his job), and even when the chin and half of the neck of the man buried there was exposed, he didn't utter a sound.

Three horns were again sounded; perhaps one for each family member, or perhaps three players took part in every ceremony. Three young women danced gracefully wearing cloth hats with a sharp peak that brought to mind a bird's beak, and between their sleeves and their hips were triangles of thin material that spread like wings with every lift of the arm. With a light pitter-patter, like the steps of birds, the three of them repeatedly converged and retreated, their hands rising up and down and the material swaying with its pattern of embroidered feathers.

The dancers repeatedly came closer and closer to what had been laid down between them and drew away from it, each time bending their beaks lower down. Three other kites had been placed there, and more pitter-pattering and bending down and tilting the beak and flapping the cloth wings were needed until consent was given – the large medium and small kites began to move and slide over the surface of the sand, their tails twisting and stretching to their full length until they lifted off into the air and soared along the path charted by the first kite. The men pulling the strings from a distance knew their work well, and perhaps the dancers had also waited for a suitable breeze, because it was only after their final bending down, the deepest of them all, that the strings were pulled and stretched, and the kites took off one after the other. They were certainly helped by their sophisticated structure and tails, and perhaps by the clouds painted on them ("And why not?" Callahan would have said. "They're painted on the ceilings of churches, so why not on kites?").

The serene festive flight in a clear pale blue sky must have been an impressive sight, and a Tavakkal man praying to them, waited for his small congregation to repeat the verses he mumbled. All the men of the caravan, even those from communities with different burial customs, turned their gaze to the sky. Perhaps they were thinking of the time a prayer would be said for the raising of their own souls, a moment possibly preceded by a demeaning death as well - after all, no one is immune to such an ending.

The dead man's wife who didn't stop singing softly to her baby also lifted her eyes upward, black eyes whose lashes were long with two teardrops hanging from them, and the further the kites drew away in the sky, the more her voice faded.

When she fell silent, her baby burst into a bitter crying, and in vain she tried to turn its gaze to the heavens. Its round face became distorted, its eyes were flooded, and only the cradling calmed it slightly. When the baby fell silent, it reached out a plump hand to its mother and felt her cheek and her eyes with its tiny fingers, because what was sparkling there seemed more wondrous than all the sights in the sky.

That was not how little Charles would one day react to seeing his mother in pain: he would be filled with fear by the sweat of her fever, the expressions on her face, the words she would utter, the different smells, her ignoring him; she would stop being a mother, and on her wide bed whose sheets were disheveled and sweaty she would just be a woman who discovered husband no longer wanted her and perhaps never had wanted her.

About a month and a half after the caravan left on its way, McKenzie was up to his ears in work. After two relatively quiet weeks, the waiting room was suddenly filled with locals and foreigners who had come from afar, and all the beds were occupied; whether by frostbite patients, or those after cataract operations or with stomach disorders, the usual assortment, and added to them this time was a Dardi nomad who had a giant abscess removed his ear which had been caused by the earrings he adorned himself with (an hour after awakening from the anesthetic, he even asked when he could wear them again), and a woman of prominence who complained about the witchcraft that caused her left foot to trip each time she left her house. She was impervious to the suffering of a man with sicklemia who stared at her and the others with sad blank eyes, since his disease, unlike hers, was incurable.

Afternoon had passed, but day had not yet turned into evening, and the smell of cooking filled the corridors mixed with the smell of smoke and the smell of all sorts of bodily secretions. It wasn't difficult to imagine what was going through Dianne's mind each time she came to do some office work she had volunteered to undertake: for the first minutes she always took care to only breathe through the mouth, until becoming absorbed in some letter to the supervisor of the province or the district about medicines and equipment that were lacking, a letter he had to dictate during those first days but which later would be worded far better by her and written with a penmanship careful not to deviate from the line (the typewriter that has been in his office had been sent to be fixed and for months hadn't been returned).

It was Dianne who suggested that he apply directly to Lord Curzon for the funding of a new wing ("a peacock in a corset" is what Henry called him because of the riding accident that forced the lord to support his spine with a sort of rigid corset), because even if the letter didn't reach him personally, at least the application would be taken care of by one of his senior aides. She didn't share that idea of hers with the commissioner, because in his eyes Curzon was ruled out for any request ever since he had become friendly with his great rival, the balmy General

Younghusband. The commissioner joked about the corset no less than he joked about Stein's irritable bowels or Pelliot's peculiar dishes or about any other oddity found in ones in authority or extolled explorers, oddities that apparently exposed their true natures that weren't worthy of honor: the viceroy wears a corset, the famed archeologist empties his guts five times a day, the noted linguist has a longing for his frogs.

She brought her idea to McKenzie as a kind of gift, and at least as proof that for the first time in her life she was favoring the good of someone else, McKenzie, over that of her employer (and Henry had employed her for almost two decades!). She was always eager to share, whether he wanted it or not, the latest gossip she heard at the commissioner's house that only had any kind of meaning in this backwater of backwaters, Leh: the letter from Calcutta Henry tore to pieces, the new set of furniture Ann ordered from Bombay (the upholstery alone cost a fortune!), Mrs. Harper's latest bird-watching trip (she almost succeeded in persuading Ann to join her).

She also had something to say about Mr. Harper, whether about the pipe he allowed himself to smoke while his wife was away, or about his difficult decisions in directing the pageant he was planning for the Feast of Ascension, and especially after the Russian boy had been banished from the cast in disgrace (that's what Dianne called the group of kids Harper had gathered, "the cast"; and the sheet on which a pale blue sky was painted with white clouds she called "the décor").

"He doesn't yet know how he'll raise Jesus to the sky," she said, "and there's less than a month left!"

McKenzie's face showed an expression of empathy. "Terrible!" he said, and Dianne fixed her eyes on him to ensure he wasn't joking. Time would pass, the whole first part of their marriage, before she would learn to decipher the tones of his voice.

"He was even thinking of getting some assistance from you," she said, and from the look on his face she hastened to add that all that Harper wanted from him was for him to tell him what bush's smoke wouldn't be harmful to the little ones if it would be burned at the side of the stage. "You see," she said, "it's written that Jesus rose to heaven on a cloud; a cloud or smoke, it really makes no difference, as long as they don't suddenly start coughing!"

"Who'll be playing Jesus?" McKenzie asked.

He wasn't surprised to hear that the Andrews' young son had been chosen for the part, but one thing surprised him; how before that Harper had intended the role for the little Russian boy in whom there was no innocence or holiness - how could there be in someone who had grown up like him with a mother like his and without any father? McKenzie didn't much believe in holiness anyway.

He seemed to be interested and so she took the trouble to go into detail about exactly what Harper was planning to do while the bush was burning: when the eyes of the entire audience would be turned to the smoke, little James Andrews would slip backstage and the final lines would be spoken a minute or two later, when a lantern hanging above the stage would cast light, like the light of the son of God who has returned to heaven.

McKenzie listened to her patiently and was mainly concerned with the question of how long the pageant would go on for; events such as these were quite often a bit of a bind because they tended to go on endlessly and one couldn't slip away without insulting someone. Whether they were held in the church or took place at the commissioner's house, one had to sit through to the end still be expected to compliment the participants, even when it was completely clear that your compliments weren't spoken from the heart.

"He also asked if you could tell him the length of the wingspan," Dianne said, "since you once dealt with such things. He wants it to look as natural as possible."

To that, he answered that the only winged animals he treated were canaries and not angels, and almost asked her if on the way here some cherub or seraph hadn't dropped something on her in its flight. It turned out that the little Russian boy's wings had been transferred to the boy who replaced him in angelhood, and that Harper wanted to make sure that they were properly affixed. It also turned out that Sasha hadn't surrendered his wings easily: at first he refused, shouted and cried and held onto them with all his might, and only fearing they'd fall apart after all the hours and days he had spent decorating them, he let go and allowed Harper to take them.

The little Russian was stubborn, and at all the rehearsals after that they saw him peeking through the window from outside; while he didn't ask again to come in, he mouthed the words being said inside and not only those of his part but the others too, despite them not being in his language. One evening, McKenzie saw him returning to the inn, a thin child whose white skin had already become dark from the sun and the dirt, his eyes sparkling in his dusty face. He walked in in front of him with a stoop and took out his frustration on the small stones he came across on the way, kicking them with a childish fury, and didn't calm down even when the merchants in the bazaar offered him something to sweeten his mood a little. The entire past month he had proudly informed each and every one of them about the role Harper had given him and was often seen walking in front of the shops and stalls with a large pair of wings whose edges swept the ground, and in vain they then reminded him of his previous fondness for donkeys. "It's better this way," they said to him after his banishment, "what did you need that weight on your back for?" He wasn't convinced.

How different little Charles was from him! Although it's hard to know, of course, how each of them would have grown up with the other's mother. "Aren't you happy to be with me, Charlilu?" Dianne would ask him when he jealously observed Chondol's children playing in the grounds, and she wouldn't let him alone until he filled all the lines she had drawn on a page with the instruction he color them in.

"He'll yet be an artist!" she declared, as if there was no greater future for a person than that. Throughout her years of secretarial work, it had remained her greatest dream, but Charlilu take care with the lines and only colored them in to satisfy her, and each time he saw she wasn't looking at him he returned to peek at the children in the grounds.

"Why are you crying, sweetie?" she would ask him, "Didn't you get it right? Mummy will help you," and right away she would go back to the page and lead his little fingers in order to complete the drawing: a boy and his mother were portrayed at the entrance of a house, with the father returning from work, and smoke curling from the chimney; it was an English house awakened no interest in Charlie.

Only when she told him about his relatives who lived in England was his curiosity piqued and he wanted to know more. His grandfather – her father – was described like a character from some legend, the owner of a huge hotel, at least as big as King Namgyal's palace or the Imperial Hotel in Bombay. As a matter of fact, he was a lessee of a small wayside inn, consisting of a pub and five small rooms, one of which was used by the waitress each time she entertained one of her regular clients (so Dianne related one evening, when she at long last lost some of her embarrassment). Even Dianne's young brother, the black sheep of the Barnes family, she described in her stories as a figure to be admired, a daring adventurer like Hedin and Stein and Younghusband rolled into one, although he wandered from place to place only because the authorities were looking for him (it should be noted here: he was a small-time crook, all in all, and minor in comparison to the fraud in the desert).

When Charlie was finally allowed to go down into the grounds, Dianne stood at the top of the stairs to watch over him, despite that Chondol's children accepted him warmly: when they played "the wolf and the lamb" they took pity on him and the wolf didn't devour him, and when they played "hide and seek" they pretended they didn't see him even when half his body was visible behind a bush. But when Chondol called them to come inside the house and help her fan the fire in the oven, an act that was forbidden to him, he watched them sadly until they disappeared into the house, and when they went out of the grounds to the stream, he observed with longing eyes how they would skip small stones on the water or build bridges and dams like those the adults made in the irrigation ditches in the fields. Sadly, he had to make do with a puddle next to the pump in the grounds, and from it he trailed tiny ditches with the tip of a twig.

"You are not to leave the grounds!" Dianne said to him. "Their mother might not care, but I do!"

In the autumn, Chondol's children and their friends took baskets out into the fields and paths and slopes to gather the droppings of horses and donkeys and yaks to be used for heating in winter; they also gathered fallen leaves to be used for frying barley before grinding it. While he wasn't forbidden to gather leaves, what boy in the world could compare the enjoyment of picking up a dry leaf to picking up a fresh dropping or a lump of excrement?

"Their mothers don't give a damn!" she said, despite that no mothers could be more devoted to their children than the Ladakhi women who carry their babies with them for months on end, and who on no account could understand how European women leave their babies in the care of a nanny and allow them to spend most of the day in a cradle.

There had been a time – it should also be noted here – when McKenzie was glad to find her waiting for him every evening on his return from the hospital: his bachelor room had been decorated and adorned, and scents of cleanliness were in the air; the table was set (before then a table cloth have never been spread on it) and the dishes she cooked in Chondol's kitchen laid upon it, two or three portions of the basic fare she had learned to prepare in her father's pub though some of the ingredients were lacking (what, for example, is shepherd's pie without mincemeat and potatoes?) and some local dishes she had learned on her travels with Henry and Ann throughout India, changing the spices here and there. The two of them used to eat and chat pleasantly the way couples are supposed to: he would tell her about the daily hospital routine and about all sorts of unusual events (she was particularly interested in the illnesses of the royal family), and she would tell him about the goings on in the commissioner's bureau, and for a while they found joy in those trifles.

After less than two months her belly began to swell, and she would place his hand on it and ask over and over: "Can you feel him?" (She had no doubt it would be a boy) and when he finally felt movement there, he was more excited he was expecting to be. Her pregnancy was a good period: her lifeless, lusterless face seemed, perhaps for the first time in her life, radiant and glowing, her small breasts were filled, and she had never looked more feminine and desirable. It was after the birth, which had been fairly easy, that their relationship began to falter: their lodgings being outside the limits of Leh just because he preferred the country landscape proved to be unwise, and the extra room that Chondol had allotted them was not of much help. All Ann's suggestions for him to come and live among the Europeans of Leh, he rejected year after year. He was unexcited by all the socializing and the seasonal tumult of caravans he found insufferable. The thought that he, McKenzie, would one day raise a family didn't seem feasible at the time.

Dianne and he and the baby were a three quarter of an hour walk and a quarter of an hour ride from Leh, and there was no European woman in the vicinity who could help her in a time of need, someone to advise her or even just to chat with. Charlie was a screaming baby, whether because her milk wasn't palatable to him, or whether he sensed her lack of experience and her fear. McKenzie didn't instill confidence in her and that period of his life – parenthood – suddenly seemed like a sentence.

Beyond the highest of the world's ranges and beyond the valleys and the high

regions and the plains and the Indian Ocean, was his first wife, and in his stupidity he hadn't forgotten her yet. In the routine of nursing and burping and infant
maladies and waking up at night and nappy changes (under no circumstances
would Dianne agree to use the absorbent powder from goat droppings the Ladakhi women relied on), he still saw in his mind's eye – an eye that had not matured
nor yet learned its lesson – Kate - riding in an open carriage, inclining her body
back in Mr. Winterbottom's field, slowly undressing in the Roman hotel room.

Time would pass until he could conceive that perhaps the years had wrought
changes in her as well: she had become a married woman again, and in all those
years she hadn't abandoned her second husband, Magnani; she had also become
a mother, two bambini had been born to them, a girl and a boy, and she had
apparently raised them well, that's how they appeared in the picture he found in
Magnani's wallet when he was brought to the hospital after his trip to the desert,
about a year after Tenzin and Poliakov had returned from there. The moment
he remained alone with him in the room (the coolies who had carried Magnani
had left) he began to rummage through his possessions; not the large ones, they
remained with the caravan's equipment being unloaded in the bazaar, but the small
things. How instructive the information one finds in a man's wallet is.

In the partition for coins he also found, apart from a few Indian rupees and
one Afghan coin, an Italian liretta, with the portrait of the king stamped on it –
what was his name, he'll remember in a minute – which was enough for him to
recall his last night in Rome when he slept in his clothes on a suitcase cart; and the
two drunks who latched onto him in the train station with their bottles, and the
woman who led him behind one of the stalls; and the burgled suitcase where the
remnants of Kate's perfume were left as well as the letter she wrote before fleeing
("Dear Ed, when you read these words"); all that was portrayed in one liretta, no
less tangible than the depiction of Vittorio Emanuele the First.

And also in the wallet – a shabby leather wallet with some unravelling stitches
– were two folded notes; in the first were perhaps chapter headings for an article
Magnani intended to write about his discovery or the start of a letter to Kate in
Italian (the thought was unbearable), and in the second note, the tattered one, a
few words were written one beneath the other, perhaps items of equipment for the
caravan or just a forgotten shopping list for a Roman grocery. That thought was
easier to banish –Professor Magnani and his wife must have had a housekeeper
and servants; there was also a folded candy wrapping in the wallet (perhaps kept
for their daughter who collected such things) and a Chinese stamp with a torn off
piece of an envelope (perhaps kept for their son).

What memory would remain for little Charles of him, his father? He would
probably remember all the things that caused the ladies of Leh to decide he wasn't
fit to raise him by himself: for example, their meals together (he was sick of the
Ladakhi dishes and would prepare all sorts of omelets in Chondol's frying pan
and take the pan up to the room), perhaps the time he gave him French liqueur

to taste, just so that he clarify without any hindrance who he loved more, him or his mother. Charley hiccupped. "Who?" he insisted, "Tell me who," And Charlie answered and hiccupped again and burst out crying, and McKenzie himself too, for the first time since his wife's death, cried.

Even at the funeral, he didn't cry. As if watching what was happening to someone else he saw the coffin was being carried to the small cemetery, and through a kind of mist – not a thin veil of tears, no tear was shed from his eyes – he saw the ones who had come to console him, all the members of the small European colony of Leh as well as a few Ladakhis, and everyone had one thing to say (at least that's what it sounded like): you have to be strong, Ed, for Charlie sake; and more than anything, he wanted to be left alone.

On the way to the grave, he looked at the tombstones on either side as if simply strolling there and took pains to read what was engraved on them the way one reads the writings alongside paintings in a museum. Engraved on the tombstone of the gossipy Belgian geologist who had died of severe blood poisoning, was: "May his quest for knowledge be a guiding light to all," and on the large tombstone on which the depiction of a cavalier and his horse had been handsomely embossed, a tombstone that had been erected in memory of one of Henry's predecessor's in the service, a list of all the colonel's postings was engraved, like a letter of recommendation whose addressee is the earth, in Gujarat, Punjab and Himachal Pradesh, and at the end was engraved: "This tombstone was erected in his memory by his loving wife, Mary-Louise, and not far is the day when the two shall be reunited for eternity." While those accompanying him were advancing to the open grave his eyes sought the tombstone of that Mary-Louise, without success. Instead, his gaze came across the tiny tombstone of one James Bridges, an infant who parted from this world at only three months of age, and next to the tombstone stood that of his loving and grieving mother who passed away only a week after his death. "This monument was erected by his father and her mourning husband who prays for the resurrection of the dead," was engraved beneath one of the statues of angels - a tiny one for the baby and a large one for its mother, his wings gathered while she shields him with hers - and McKenzie wondered if sorrow alone had killed her.

There were already those who notice his gaze was wandering here and there and came to support him as if he had been struck with dizziness and any moment would faint. At the head of the small procession walked Henry and Ann, who knew Dianne better than he did; for two decades she had been with them every place Henry had been stationed. Ann, in a new black dress with a wide-brimmed hat and a black veil (not an unusual sight in London or Calcutta, but certainly unusual here), wept – a genuine weeping, from the depths of her soul, perhaps she suddenly realized just how much she would miss that quiet companion of hers, whose dullness served as a background that highlighted her ladyship. Afterward, onto the coffin she dropped a choice pashmina scarf she had bought for Dianne in the winter and hadn't managed to give it to her or at the last moment had decided to keep for herself.

Henry, in a formal voice with the required accentuations as if previously rehearsed, placed his right hand on his chest and declared that never had he nor the British Empire a more devoted secretary, and perhaps at the same time wondered who would be sent as a replacement, if indeed anyone would be sent and that in Calcutta it wouldn't be said he should be so kind as to make do with his adjutant, who is probably idle most of the time. But Henry was also sorry about her death: from where he stood, McKenzie saw him lift a finger to the corner of his eye as the coffin was lowered into the pit, and it was moist and sparkling when he lowered it.

They had shared a common past, many times longer than his with her: she was twenty when she started to work for Henry, and together with Ann he accompanied her through all her difficulties in adjusting to the monsoons, the Indian heat, the Indian food, the tumult; the two of them also accompanied her through her engagement to a promising young officer, and during her heartbreak when he favored another over her ("The fool," Ann said to console her, "he doesn't know what he's missing!"). They also encouraged her to volunteer taking on all sorts of secretarial tasks that had accumulated on the doctor's desk at the hospital – perhaps in that way he would discover her virtues.

Harper, some of whose obligations concerning the church were also placed into Dianne's hands, read from the page in his hand, after making certain that everyone was listening. In a pleasant voice the missionary asked the lord to gather to him this pure unblemished soul, with only benevolence and readiness to be of solace to all mankind. "She was so delighted with the son that you gave her," Harper said, "and all who witnessed her in her happiness saw the greatness of your grace of which one should never despair." About the malaria that had again struck her not a word was spoken, he only made a gesture of helplessness with his left hand and said: "Like a bud she blossomed and wilted and was gathered to your name."

Mrs. Harper didn't wait for him to fold his page, nor did she read from any page; she spoke directly to the grave from the depths of her heart: "You were always so quiet, Dianne my sweet, and so modest and refined! So so refined!" She then burst into tears, and only when she had calmed down somewhat did she speak in a choked voice about Dianne's great hobby, painting, and how beautiful all the landscapes of Leh appeared in her works, perhaps more beautiful than they were in reality. "I promised I would take you with me to the lake to paint the birds there, and never managed to! Forgive me, my dear, forgive me!" Again she sobbed, her whole small body shook from crying, while not a tear fell from her husband's eyes.

"One can see all her refinement there!" Mrs. Harper said about Dianne's paintings, and all those who had received a painting as a gift from her nodded their heads, despite it being doubtful they would keep them, no longer having to fear insulting her.

Someone mentioned Dianne's singing in church – the purity of her voice that was so suited to the purity of her soul and the purity of her paintings – and McKenzie then thought: purity, purity, purity; from all that purity there was nothing left in her, and at the same moment he regretted the thought. Then, from the sorrow that suddenly rose in him, he imagined seeing her through the lid of the coffin and the earth that was heaped upon it: laid there with her hands crossed, hands that for the whole week had struggled with the sheets soaked with her sweat; her serene face, her smooth forehead and her eyes closed, eyes he had closed with his own hands and which before that had gaped like her mouth shouting at him in a broken voice for the last time: "You don't love me, Ed, you never did!"

Then, as in his dreams from a few years ago, at the heart of which was the man plodding through the sands of the desert with the anchor on his upper back (when at last the man's head was turned to him, he found himself looking at his own face, and instantly they both began to sink into the sand), for a moment through the earth of the grave and the lid of the coffin he saw himself; and more precisely, not really himself, not his own face, but the face of the man who had been identified in Brindisi as Ed McKenzie, a drunk who had stumbled on the pier, and it had been most convenient for his wife and Magnani to think that he, an English veterinarian and an abandoned husband, had parted from this world in that way.

It had not happened instantly, of course: only when Kate became pregnant and a quick marriage was necessary, the need arose to legally annul her previous marriage, an act almost impossible in Catholic Italy. It wasn't hard to presume the details: first they must have tried to check whether he had returned to England, they spoke to some lawyer in Oxford about dealing with the matter, and when it was discovered he hadn't returned from the honeymoon and that no one in Begbroke knew where he was, an inquiry was set up in Italy; first of all in the hotel (someone there, a chambermaid or the lift operator, perhaps remembered that he had left the next day), and that's how it had been engraved in their memories: ("the Englishman whose wife fled from him"), and afterward they checked with the embassy and with the police.

It was improbable someone would have remembered him at the train station in Rome, but it was possible that in Brindisi he might have left some possession of his behind – after all, he had sailed from there blind drunk and barely managed to pack – a paper or a document or even his pen with his name engraved on it, and since he was a foreign subject, the matter had been reported to the embassy; that was apparently how his disappearance had been determined, but it still had to be connected to the drowned body that was floating in the port of Brindisi a week a later, and a case file in which a British citizen was involved wasn't easily closed.

Further persuasion must have been required. The local police commander had to be persuaded it was in his interests not to miss the opportunity of solving the case and win praise, perhaps some money changed hands. And how convenient it was for Magnani and Kate to believe he had drowned, otherwise they would be in constant fear of his returning, and what would a Catholic who discovers he's wedded a married woman do? And so the identification was verified, as if it was possible to identify a body with any certainty after an entire week in the water.

Had the drunk been buried? And before that, had the body waited for months between blocks of ice in the mortuary? McKenzie did not know; Brindisi was a hot city, but the Italians had all sorts of embalming methods that had been developed in the monasteries, though it was hard to imagine they would have been used on an anonymous drunk; perhaps the body had been exhumed from a grave and reburied. Either way, it wasn't hard to picture the first burial ceremony: the simplest of wooden coffins, without attendants, just a priest and his assistant and a few loafers, and without any tombstone except for a simple wooden cross made of two boards nailed to each other. Perhaps someone had complained of the stench; or perhaps they said it was lucky that man had filled himself with alcohol before jumping into the water, without which he would have stunk more. About the second burial ceremony, if it had taken place, he didn't want to think.

If those participants had afterward gone into one of the bars, perhaps it would have been the same bar where he had sat with Griffin and Evans when they suggested to him to travel with them to India and to forget all his troubles there, and to make a good living in the cavalry. He was a young man at the time, downtrodden and drunk, and thought to himself: why not. His claimants were waiting for him in Begbroke, and his aunts were there, and also the priest who at least twice had tried to warn him about the marriage.

The three of them sat in that bar, and one of the women tried to make advances at him.

"Our doctor's a little tired, Gina," Evans said to her, "he's facing a tough decision."

"Gina will help him with that," said Gina.

"The doctor will order you something to drink," Griffin said, "right, Doctor? And us as well," and made sure McKenzie also drank another glass; and another one; and one more; and one last one. It seemed there was nothing more important to them than persuading him to board the ship and sail the next day; perhaps they really were shocked by the frame of mind he was in – he didn't care, he said to them, if when he went out to piss he'd accidentally drop into the water from the edge of the pier – and perhaps they bet among themselves whether they'd succeed to convince him or not.

"You're still young, Doctor," they said to him and praised the Indian women and their suppleness and told him about the lustful Ajanta statues and about holy marble phalluses upon which barren Indian women sat in order to become pregnant, and at the time India seemed to him a vast continent filled with lust, a continent where a man need not fear for his wife, since no one there stuck with one woman anyway.

He was still young then, utterly despondent and totally groggy from alcohol, and apparently they really had bet on his sailing, maybe with the owner of the bar and had therefore taken the trouble to accompany him to the hotel at the end of that night and help him pack his possessions, and the next day lead him to the ships gangway.

"Aren't you boarding?" he wondered then.

"We've got a few more errands," they replied.

Only after the ship had sailed did he realize they had remained on the shore and more than two months passed before his chance encounter with them in Bombay where he learned they had been involved in some smuggling in Brindisi. When he met them in Bombay they were dealing in ivory, and a while passed until he was reminded of them again and knew that if there was anyone in India who could obtain ancient anchors for him at a bargain price, it was them ("What happened, Doctor, have you started treating the fish in the sea?" they asked him).

Since then, death had also become associated with those damn anchors, the death of the Tavakkal man and very nearly Faizul's death, and the kites that were flown in the oasis for raising the soul of the dead man must have already crashed in their fall and been covered by sand as well. There's more than enough sand in the desert to cover a flock of kites, armadas of holy ships, legions of cuckolded husbands.

And so it was, in a small bar in Brindisi his future had been decided; and not only his future, but all those who would be involved in the matter: his two partners in the lunatic plan and all the other participants, and also the little Russian boy who too would be harmed by it, and also his second wife who was not yet his wife, and his son who was not even yet in the realms of a thought.

17

Like all the oases of the Tarim Basin, the Khotan oasis was shrouded by dust, at least that's how it appeared from a distance, but after close to a month in the desert, it was perceived by them as a metropolis. "One can already smell home," someone said. More than one or two men still fixed their gaze on the bed of the gorge, trying to discern the sparkle of jade stones, until Tenzin assembled them all and reiterated his previous prohibition, perhaps adding another threat.

At a distance of a few hours away from Khotan there were already those who from the backs of their horses and donkeys and camels were already imagining the foods they would eat when they arrived, the drinks they would drink, the mattress they would spread out on and not get up from for an entire week; and like a company of soldiers returning from an exercise or a battle, they mainly imagined what they would do with the women there. There wasn't a man, including the doctor, who hadn't heard what the Khotani women were capable of.

Afterward someone asked old Turdi if he had anything to say on the matter of women, and in general, what's happened to him lately that he's been keeping so quiet; and Turdi, after hesitating for a moment, replied that only young roosters and fools speak that way, those from whom no chicken has yet laid an egg. "You too were once like us, no?" the young men said to him, and Turdi was silent. For the first time of this whole expedition, he looked really old, as if while his experience had been required, he had found enough strength in him, and now that the expedition was coming to its end, there was no longer any point in fighting his weariness.

"How did that song go that you sung about the sea of sand?" Tenzin asked in order to lift his spirits a little. "It was nice the way you sang it and how everyone listened to you," but Turdi didn't respond to the compliment.

Then Tenzin tried to cheer his spirits with his family who must be waiting for his return and watching the east daily from their windows to see the caravan coming out of the desert, and all of them will certainly come to welcome him: his wife, who was so different from the loose women of Khotan, all his sons and grandchildren would be there – his six sons and eleven grandsons – but all that didn't change his mood.

Clouds of city flies no less determined than desert flies latched themselves to the rears of the animals, and Turdi's horse neighed in anger as well, and he stroked its neck until it calmed down. After a while he mumbled something perhaps to the horse, perhaps to himself, and only one word could be heard clearly, the word "ploughs", and when Tenzin asked him what he said, he answered him: "You brought a curse with them," and hurried the pony up when it lingered next to a bush to tear off a small branch and its leaves. "A curse," Turdi said again. Again, he spurred the pony on with his cracked heels, and the small horse began to walk with the branch being chewed between its teeth. Turdi wondered about something else: not only why bring ploughs to a desert, but why had they specifically taken him with them – being already an old man.

"What would we have done without you?" Tenzin replied, and even that compliment didn't improve Turdi's mood.

Then the first houses of Khotan could be seen in the distance, and the pillars of dust the animals raised with their feet were surely visible from there, and curious onlookers quickly gathered between the houses. Vapors of heat spiraled upwards and dissolved the outlines, making it difficult to tell how many people were waiting for them, but there was little doubt that every moment more were joining.

"Your whole family must be here," Tenzin said to the old man to lift his spirits, "just look how many have come, old man!" He indicated to the west with his hand and Turdi strained his eyes.

Even if his sons had come – he replied in a listless voice – all they're really interested in is the money he'll be getting at the end of the journey; they're as greedy as the one who took the jade stones.

"But they love and respect you!" Tenzin insisted, and to reinforce his words he reminded him how they all came to part with him on their leaving, he saw it with his own eyes.

Then Turdi made a vague gesture with his arm; perhaps the few who loved him and those who just pretended to love him passed through his mind, and the balance made him more dejected (it wasn't a question of numbers; who knew that better than McKenzie; what meaning is there in the love of many, if the one you are interested in doesn't return their love).

In the distance a few stray dogs began to bark; they may have barked before then but only now could be heard. And the market idiot, who wore seven hats on his head like the seven stone hats worn on the heads of the condemned (that was how they were executed in Khotan: not by stretching the neck with a rope but by being compressed by stone), came joyfully toward them, all smiles in which the black spaces between his teeth were exposed. Ever since being sentenced to death, he had lost his mind – the neck vertebrae hadn't snapped, but he had lost his mind – and Turdi's face became darker at the sight of him, as if he wasn't someone who had been saved from death, but its harbinger. What he had been sentenced for, no one remembers for certain, but he stuck to his hats as if all his strength was in them, like someone who has been immunized by snake poison.

Now he came joyously towards them, capering and dancing around them.

He probably had welcomed previous caravans in that manner, but this time the old man recoiled at the sight of him. "He comes here every day to wait for you," said one of the loafers, "and keeps asking, when is Turdi coming?" He must have thought he'd make him happy and earn a coin that way, but what happened afterward wasn't clear: it was told that a gust of wind blew the hat off the fool's head and landed it right on the old man's head; however, it was more feasible that the wind, even if it had it blown the hat off, hadn't placed it exactly on his head, and the fear of that happening had been enough to upset his balance; either way, he was led home for his wife to take care of him, and not due to the hat hitting him but rather to his seventy-year-old exhaustion.

During the days that Turdi rested at home Tenzin and Poliakov dealt with matters of the caravan and deliberated mainly on how right it would be to bargain over the prices of the animals and the equipment they intended to sell and which had been bought only for the needs of Dandan Oilik and would be of no use Leh. They could have decided not to leave Khotan until a worthy buyer was found, but delaying in Khotan cost money, possibly resulting in more of a loss than a profit.

Those deliberations must have begun on the way, and some investigation into the matter had been carried out as they walked down the main street, along whose entire length, like the street of the bazaar in Leh (so those who came to Leh from the north told; McKenzie had never been to Khotan), were lined with dozens of shops and stalls and there was great commotion of buyers and sellers and the whinnying and braying and snorting of horses and donkeys and camels; but Khotan is many times larger than Leh (that's what those who came said), and many more caravans pass through it.

They must have enjoyed walking down the long street where from both sides cakes dripping with sugar were offered to them, kebab on a skewer and shash-lik, date juice here and pomegranate juice there. Through the opening of a large hall women carpet weavers could be seen immersed in their work, and in a shop nearby rolls of silk and brocade were being sold (those materials also reached Leh), and at the entrances of food shops dozens of spices of all sorts were displayed in all their colors, and the smell of cinnamon and ginger and cloves was mixed with the smells of baking and frying and the excrement of animals and the urine of dogs. In the darkness of butcher shops, as in Leh, the carcasses of skinned goats were hung by their feet on hooks, and the infiltrating rays of sunlight shed light on the redness of exposed meat and the whiteness of fat or ribs. The bakers stood over clay ovens in which fire burned as if in pits, and every once in a while one of them bent down to stick another roll of dough to its side; ice cream vendors led their handcarts from one end of the street to the other and to the thirsty they served small lumps of ice yellowish from the yolk that had been mixed in them – Leh didn't have that – and for those coming from the blazing desert sun there surely was no delicacy more refreshing than that, even if mixed with dust.

Hundreds of kilometers south of there, in his room in the hospital, it wasn't hard for McKenzie to imagine the questions all sorts of inquisitive people asked the men of the caravan he had sent, and perhaps in their place he too would have asked the same questions. As to the answers, if the name of the place it had come from, Dandan Oilik, was mentioned (a place not far in terms of caravans, many of which traverse more than eight hundred kilometers on their routes), perhaps the interest lessened or perhaps actually increased, because what in hell's name is there to search for in that backwater that has no treasures. Then the lie they had embraced rose again: they were sent there on a mission for one of the Sahibs who had decided to return to the desert some antiquities that had brought a curse upon him. Maybe that story had been heard before and they had only been asked if the curse had not harmed them as well. And indeed it had, but they did not as yet know how much.

A month before that, when they had come from Leh, the men of the caravan had taken lodgings at an inn south of Khotan and had difficulty sleeping because of the flea bites, and in the one they had now chosen they were hoping for other company at night. For the time being they were in the dining hall (a few tables of rough wood stood with benches on either side, and on the tables were glass and plate stains and all sorts of old stains that generations of flies had examined), and a thickset woman dished out chow mein to the diners from a bowl, and when their plates were emptied, Poliakov hoped the beds would also be to their satisfaction, because there was nothing that he wanted more now than to sleep.

Didn't he ever want to be with a Khotani woman? Tenzin asked, and Poliakov didn't answer or maybe made a gesture of scorn with his hand, and Tenzin became angry. An argument broke out between them that they half-heartedly admitted to when they returned to Leh, but they refused to talk about its circumstances; he once assumed its start had been there (What, the women here aren't any good for you? Tenzin might have said: are only girls with yellow hair good for you?) and later assumed it had been at a different point in the chain of events that ended with little Charles shipped to another continent to save him being hurt when the fraud would be exposed with the one who had planned it.

By pure luck, someone to take care of Charlie was found, the woman who had helped his aunt in her last years and had lived in her house, and according to her will, despite the house being left to him, could continue living there until her dying day. Without much difficulty, the ladies of Leh managed to persuade her in their letters how important it was that a woman raise little Charles, because men, as we all know, will always have more pressing matters than sewing on a button or combing hair or wiping a nose.

He wondered if Charles would be protected there from the consequences of the fraud's discovery. The rumor of the finding in the desert would reach Italy and later the rumor of the fakery, and the two would also reach England, in London

and in Begbroke, even if it took months. Perhaps at first they would find it difficult to understand what their veterinarian had to do with such matters, but they
would soon say: one who starts with a small fraud ends up with a large one, and to
reinforce their words they would also mention Palmer's young son, the one who
began by copying in exams and ended up by faking horse pedigrees. And who had
exposed those frauds?

McKenzie! Yes-yes, in the end it seems he had learned something from it, and
not for the good. That's how it is in life, every man is faced with good and bad and
has to choose which path to take.

Palmer's son was sent to prison, but in those regions of Asia acts of crookery
many times bigger didn't end with imprisonment (even the one who succeeded in
fooling Hernel, an erudite man of even greater repute than Magnani, was let off
with a few whippings; and no man would whip McKenzie). At the very most they
would gossip a bit, he thought, whisper behind his back, exactly the way they now
gossip and whisper behind Henry's back, and after not long, a year at the most, it
would all be forgotten as was customary in this backwater of backwaters in which
there isn't one man without a can of worms that brought upon his self-exile here.
That's what he thought at the stage of the planning, and afterward, during the
months the caravan was on its way, ceased to occupy himself with the matter.

And what would Harper say when he heard about it? Far more than the act of
fraud, he would probably be enraged by the scorn shown toward people's beliefs.
"One who doesn't believe in anything has an empty heart," he said angrily to Poliakov after the argument the ended his visits to his home in order to learn the holy
language. "Not you, Doctor, I know what's happened to your heart, it's broken, but
in every break like that there's still a lot of love!"

"But I don't believe in anything, Robert," he said then.

"That's what you say, Ed," Harper replied, "and I for one, if you'll permit me,
don't really believe you're like that. There's no way you could convince me that
you've never prayed your wife would return to you or that you'll return to her. And
who did you pray to then?"

"There had been a time like that," McKenzie admitted, "but it's over."

"It's never over," Harper said, and he was more right than he imagined.

When Tenzin went up to the second floor with one of the women, Poliakov
remained alone, and those sitting there looked at him with curiosity. When they
tried to engage him in conversation, he pointed at a bowl of pulao in front of him
or shrugged his shoulders to make it clear he didn't understand what they were
saying, and perhaps one of the women came and sat on his knee to let the warmth
of her body remind him what a real man should hunger for besides pulao, if such
coarseness was customary not only in portside bars (the women of the hotel in
Bombay, McKenzie recalled, showed some tenderness and even some childish

innocence when they said to him: "Sad not good, Doctor, why sad? Let me make you happy!).

When Tenzin returned from having done what he had done on the second floor, he asked Poliakov if in the meantime he hadn't changed his mind about the local women, and if he had something else in his trousers besides the pistol. He must have been a bit drunk – for the first time in all the past months he allowed himself that freedom – and despite Poliakov not understanding every word of his, it wasn't difficult to understand his meaning.

"You haven't," Tenzin said. "And what are all of you without your weapons? Nothing." And with a startlingly quick movement he reached out his right arm to the pistol stuck in Poliakov's trouser belt and Poliakov grabbed his hand at the wrist and stopped it.

"Go to sleep," he said to him and got up and stood opposite him, "tomorrow we'll forget all this."

"But why should we forget?" Tenzin replied and tried a movement in a counter direction and right away was blocked again. The alcohol weakened him, perhaps also the pleasures he had taken in the room above them.

"Tell them what you did in Russia," Tenzin said, "let them know what you did there -" He was still being held by the wrist, and Poliakov inclined the hand backward and Tenzin together with it.

"Why don't you tell them what you did in the cave?" – with his body inclined he struggled to turn his head towards the table on their right – "Just to steal everything that a holy monk had!" Sitting there were Muslims, Buddhists, Animists, and all of them honored monks, no matter who their Gods were.

"Tell them how you threatened him," Tenzin said, "what you said to him -"

"You were with me," Poliakov replied and still grasped his wrist.

"He aimed a pistol at him," Tenzin continued and half his body was already inclined backward, "and he said to him, if you don't do what tell you, then I'll -" At that very moment he somehow moved his left hand, and when Poliakov tried to block him, they both lost their balance and began rolling on the ground, one holding the pistol and the other trying to pull it from his hand, and above them the onlookers were already betting who would win.

Then the landlady came out of the kitchen and looked at the brawling – a bench they had bumped into had been overturned, and as it fell one of them sitting on it pulled a bowl away from it and its broken pieces were scattered in all directions – and someone suggested to her throwing water over the two, the way one does with dogs, but the shot preceded her.

For a moment it wasn't clear what had been hit, until a trickling sound was heard from the barrel that stood in the corner of the hall and the thin drizzle that burst from a small hole could be seen. It only contained water and its stream moistened the earthen floor, coloring the two men rolling on it, and then pistol was lifted from the muddy ground and when a second shot was discharged all gazes were lifted to the ceiling.

It was a loam ceiling mixed with animal excrement and straw which the bullet punctured with no difficulty and pieces of whitewash and loam fell onto the table below. Up there was the room Tenzin had previously gone to, the room of one of the two prostitutes of the inn and a long moment passed before she was seen at the top of the flight of stairs, curvaceous and staggering slightly.

"What happened to you, honey?" the innkeeper called out to her in a fearful voice. "Is everything alright?"

Of small stature, almost a dwarf, she drew near the edge of the landing, her face uncharacteristically pale; she wore the faded dress of a European woman and a hat from whose veil only torn bits remained. With trembling fingers she undid the buttons of her dress until the corset was revealed – it must have been bought at some market where the old clothes of European women land up, and perhaps it was Tenzin who had brought it to her on one of his visits, because that's how he liked her to do the act with him. She also undid the laces of the corset and the injury of the bullet that hit her body was revealed - at the side of the waist a shallow scratch could be seen, but at the sight of blood she staggered again.

"I told you all those clothes will bring you back luck!" the innkeeper said and climbed up the stairs to her, and before she reached the top she turned back and said to the two that they were the cause of all this and it would be better she not see them for a while; they should either go to sleep find themselves another inn.

The top of a poplar tree could be seen from the window of the room they went up to, and roofs with alfalfa spread on them for drying (that's how the roofs of Leh also looked). Tenzin spread himself out on his bed in his muddy clothes; the alcohol, the fracas and the hardships of the journey overpowered him, plus the pleasure he had taken, and after a moment or two he already began to snore. Poliakov approached the bowl standing in the alcove of the window and wearily immersed his face in it and when he lifted his head he saw the mud spreading through the water and making it murky. Then from the entrance he called out to the boy who served as a room attendant but to no reply.

Mud continued to drop from his trousers hung on the backrest of the chair when he got onto the bed in his wet underpants whose whiteness had been sullied. His gaze was held by the webs in the corners of the ceiling – and in which Indian hotel aren't there any? A quiver passed through them, and a breeze also ruffled the cloth sheet hung in the entrance (in Bombay there had been a door, and the girls used to knock and enter).

Afterward he rose from the bed and walked to the chair and from the trouser pocket he took out the pistol and cleaned the butt from sprays of mud before calling the boy again. Without his bare footsteps being heard, the sheet was pulled aside, and the boy entered, dark and thin, his thick lips almost like those of a black man, and at the sight of the pistol he stopped in his tracks. The barrel pointed towards the bowl in the window alcove, and the boy went there and removed it, and with the same silent gait he returned with clean water in it, and only after looking here and there and no longer seeing the pistol – it had already been inserted beneath the rolled-up blanket that was used as a pillow – he calmed down, and his behavior then changed (stories like these were also related about Khotan). A sycophantic smile rose on his face, and he showed the clean towel he had brought with him and said something to which Poliakov shook his head from side to side. He also did that when the boy showed the bowl with the same inviting smile, and when he drew close to him with the towel he had wet with its water.

"Get out," Poliakov said, but the boy, eager to offer his services, started to explain something to him, pleading and coaxing and smiling, and when Poliakov understood what he meant by pouting his thick lips he reached out his hand to the folded blanket and took the pistol from its folds and the boy fled outside.

"I suppose he's also no good for you." Tenzin's voice was then heard.

What passed between them from that day on until they returned to Leh, there's no knowing for certain, but back in Leh, it was evident there had been no reconciliation on the way. In order to avoid unnecessary quarreling, they decided to divide their final tasks: Tenzin would deal with selling off the surplus animals and Poliakov with the equipment, but since they had accepted Hadj Nasser's offer to buy everything from them in one transaction, the matter didn't take long, and no splitting was required. Hadj Nasser still tried to hoodwink them a little, and instead of paying the full amount he suggested giving his part in merchandise, but Tenzin objected. They prefer money, he said.

"Who doesn't?" Hadj Nasser replied. He was sitting on a stool and his hands rested on his paunch as on a cushion as he passed prayer beads through his fingers, and from the cage hanging in the entrance the large parrot confined there watched him.

"That's what we agreed to," Tenzin insisted and didn't hesitate to tell Hadj Nasser that if they don't receive the sum in full, they'd sell the animals and the equipment separately and that there's more than one merchant already waiting for that.

"The Chinaman?" Hadj Nasser replied scornfully and continued to pass the beads through his fingers. His eyes turned to the wicker cage because the parrot opened its curved beak and chirped something; for some reason, it sounded like the name of the Chinese man, Lu-Chi, and the merchant silenced it with a click of his fingers. And nonetheless he ordered his son-in-law to bring them the full amount and counted the notes one by one in front of their eyes; just before the last one he stopped and declared it would be their caravan's contribution toward the renovation of the sacred tomb of Maheb the Holy and they certainly wouldn't want to insult anyone here by refusing. Again the parrot chirped something which this

time sounded like cursing, perhaps in Urdu or Uyghur, and Hadj Nasser said to
the parrot: "You too!"

After the deal was concluded, Poliakov went to the carpenter from whom he
had ordered a miniature fire cart for Sasha, with a tiny barrel the size of a tin can
and a folding ladder that could be extended from the back of it to knee height.
He still hoped the gift would please the boy despite that Sasha was occupied by a
completely different matter at the time (he had already given up the role Harper
had taken from him in the pageant but found it difficult to give up the wings).
Only when the carpenter showed his handicraft, proud of having done something
he had never done before, the first doubts were raised in Poliakov: it looked like
a toy suitable for a child of three or four and not for a seven-year-old boy and he
wondered if Sasha might be insulted rather than pleased. It seemed that the kite
would be a better gift; he hadn't forgotten about Sasha's fondness for heights.

"No good?" asked the carpenter.

"Very good," Poliakov replied, but on seeing the small children running
outside he wondered if it wouldn't be better to give them this toy, even if they had
never heard of a fire cart or firemen.

At that blazing afternoon hour, from his window above the tops of the poplars, old
Turdi saw the caravan of kites coming to accompany him, a glorious festive caravan from which no color was lacking: at the head, above the sacred tomb of the
holy one, floated the kite that showed the soul the way, crimson red and its dozen
orange tails as long as the street of the bazaar, and in the white-hot sky behind
it a continuous colorful caravan could be seen, and the number of its kites was
greater than the number of the family members gathered around his bed, and he
thanked them all – at least that's what he thought he was doing, though no sound
was uttered from his cracked lips as he looked at the window – for taking the trouble to come and accompany him on this day, a day on which the air was still, to
the point where the sides of the lungs stick to each other as if they had swallowed
sand, and hot to the point of being scalded and there is not even the smallest bit
of shadow for shelter. And how could there be shadow in this vast sky opening up
wide for him?

Yes, there's no point denying it: the doctor was accountable for this dead man
as well.

18

"Charles!" he can hear Mrs. Kingsley calling to his son on the deck, "Charles! Come here! Come here at once, Charles!" Charles, and not little Charlie, and definitely not Charlilu, as Dianne had called him. "Charles McKenzie, if you do not present yourself here at once, I will be forced to punish you!" Mrs. Kingsley could be heard warning him, "I'll count to ten, Charles, and if by then you are not standing here in front of me, I don't want to think how I'll be forced to punish you -"

Her strictness was clear, and perhaps all that had taken place while still in her apartment in Bombay. Charles had only seen that much furniture in Henry's new abode, but he had never played hide and seek there, and Ann used to walk after him from room to room making sure he didn't break or tear anything or leave his fingerprints. That old maid Mrs. Kingsley was also fearful for her possessions; but Charlie's a good and obedient boy who at the most will explore the apartment's hiding places just a little.

The Russian boy, in whose time Charlie hadn't been born, would certainly have run wild there: jumping on beds and sofas, opening all the drawers, going into the pantry and checking out every item there, perhaps even tasting them; but Charlie, at the height of his freedom – during the months following Dianne's death, when all house rules had been abandoned – never misbehaved. Even before Mrs. Kingsley's counting reached ten, he most likely would be standing before her; he hadn't meant to annoy her at all, and she might pay him some heavenly compliment, mentioning his mother watching from above and being pleased he's well-behaved.

Only on the ship, after boarding, Charlie might give himself free rein, because he had never experienced such a thing. Hand in hand, they'll ascend the gangway from the quay to the deck, with many porters going up and down and rushing in all directions, the frenzy a complete contrast to the mildness of the caravan; and how amazed Charlie will be by the size of the ship! How impressed he'll be at the port by the number of passengers and porters and sailors! And more than anything he'll be impressed by the size of the sea; in the whole of Leh and its environs there's no river wide enough according to which one could imagine an expanse of water that stretches from horizon to horizon.

"Charles!" Mrs. Kingsley calls out to him, "Charles!" or: "Charles McKenzie, if you think I intend chasing after you throughout this ship, you're quite mistaken."

One of the sailors who had left a son or a nephew in England would perhaps offer him to show him the boiler room – large boilers like the ones there he surely had never seen! – But Mrs. Kingsley would refuse all his pleadings. What if something should happen to him? Who would they come complaining to, only to her!

McKenzie had never seen the boiler room of a ship, and even if on the Stella Maris on the way to Bombay one of the sailors had offered to show him that kingdom within a kingdom, he wouldn't have consented. Only one thing interested him at the time; to get away from Italy as quickly as possible, whether by the power of boilers or sails or oars or by a large wave that would sink the ship down into the depths.

"Charles!" he can hear Mrs. Kingsley calling his son in that unknown but very real future (real almost to the point of crying) when Charles would already be on his way to another country. "Charles!" she calls out to him again, but in a different tone, if the captain invited them to sit at his table – it would be the boy that catches his eye, and not this dried up old maid – and before that she would no doubt rehearse Charles about the correct knife and fork to use so that he wouldn't embarrass her and his dear mother watching everything from above.

She would perhaps find a companion on the ship to chat with, to gossip with about the other passengers, about the captain, about some common acquaintances in Bombay, and Charles would then get away and explore the length and breadth of the deck with the same cautious daring with which he explored Chondol's grounds the first time he went down there by himself. Dianne watched him from the top of the outdoor staircase and McKenzie said: "Leave him, he'll manage. If he falls and gets a bump, he won't die from it." And she became annoyed. Each time he was injured, she would kiss the wounded place and suckle the pain from it, and sometimes his moans were exaggerated just to win more and more kisses, until from things Chondol's children said he understood he should stop that and grow up. "Stop it, Mummy!" he would say afterward, but his body still surrendered to her mouth and embraces.

On the ship's deck (which must have been at least as large as the deck of the Stella Maris, with life boats on both sides covered with a tarpaulin, and couples leaning on the railing here and there), Charlie would no doubt go to the bow and view the vast expanses the ship was intended to cross, and perhaps he would spread his arms out to the sides like the figurehead on an ancient ship and the wind would ruffle his hair like McKenzie used to ruffle it with his fingers. On becoming bored, he would go to the stern, and if he had sailed like him on the Stella Maris, and if time hadn't erased things far greater and much more important, perhaps he would have discovered his fingerprints on the railing from when he held on there with all his might not to be swept away off the deck; perhaps he would sense what had suddenly become clear to him, specifically because he had almost been swept into the sea: that he must live.

"If Mummy could see you," Mrs. Kingsley would reprimand him if she found him there, "it would make her very very upset!" But in Charles' eyes Mummy was already a vague entity, loved and frightening at the same time, someone who had been so concerned about him and had prohibited him from so many things, someone he had trusted more than he trusted his father, but also someone who in her weakness had broken down and cried like a baby; someone who had declared her love for him at least once every hour but who had also shouted at his father: "So why did we have him at all?" And she meant him, Charlie. No, it wasn't love she was expressing then but another emotion, a frightening one, and she didn't want Charlie to come and wipe her sweat with a small towel or wave a Chinese fan for her. "Go away from here, Charlie," she would say, "go and find something else to do. Mummy's not feeling well."

So very little was required for her to be forgotten from McKenzie's heart: a week after her funeral, no, not a week, less than that, the vestiges of the order she had imposed had been wiped out, even her odor barely remained. For three days, Daychin scrubbed the room, and from time to time burst into tears; she who had tended to her throughout all the last weeks and in whose arms she had died; in that way declaring she didn't want to do so in her husband's arms.

Even before she had become ill, the order of the house had gone awry, and in her illness had become more disordered, but then, while lying in their bed, all that seemed secondary to her illness and the questions it raised: when would another wave of fever come (the respite between the waves lasted forty-eight hours), and how many of the symptoms would appear with it: only high temperature and chills or headaches and nausea as well? Only nausea or vomiting as well? Only vomiting or diarrhea as well? And how much would she burn with fever, and how much would she suffer, and how much would she give up and surrender? And would she again say things to him she would never have dared to say when she was healthy?

You're still thinking about her, aren't you, Ed?" she said. And when her husband arrived here, it only became worse. "God, what a fool I've been!" In her bed, her back and neck supported by pillows, she permitted herself to say things she had never said, everything that had been blocked up inside her all the while she till nursed some hopes for their marriage.

"How I hate you, Ed McKenzie," she said and burst out crying, and in vain he reminded her that the boy could hear everything. "Let him hear," she replied. "Let him know the kind of father he's got." And he sent little Charles out to play with Chondol's children, despite the grounds being empty.

A short while passed until he began to get rid of everything she left behind, and not only the odors of her illness (in the end the scrubbing and the incense got rid of them; but the incense, from the moment it became associated with her illness, became no less nauseating), and the rest of her things, but also the objects that had been put in order: serviettes and embroidered tablecloths which in better days had been spread on the table diagonally so that the triangles of their corners would fall from the center of each side, a teapot and a Wedgewood tea set, salt cellars and sugar bowls and whatnot. He also got rid of her paintings, aquarelles in which the peaks were blurred with some kind of a misty substance, and even King Namyagal's dilapidated palace at dusk seemed weightless, almost nebulous.

She had given her paints to Chondol's children (who three years before had received Sasha's fire cart and kite), and on one afternoon they managed to exhaust all the pleasure that could been gained from them. He sometimes saw two of her paintbrushes in Daychin's hair bun – she refused to accept Dianne's few pieces jewelry from him but adorned herself with those two paintbrushes as if they were jewelry.

What remained after a few months? The stories she told Charles that were inscribed in his memory. Every night he would ask him to tell him one in place of her, for instance, about the weathercock that turned around on the roof of her house in England, or about the garden with stone dwarfs (he had no difficulty telling that one; his Aunt Elizabeth also had a garden like that), or about her father's inn, or about the water birds that fly above the fen and the hunters that hunt them on Sundays – one once fell on a woman's head and remained there the whole day like a hat!

There was a fen in Begbroke and there were also hunters there and he had no difficulty telling Charlie about that too. At times these were things that made him feel close to her: their pasts held a few common landscapes, views of hills and fields and fens, as well as the sound of shots and the commotion of hunting dogs barking.

Her loyalty to Henry and Ann also remained; in any event, that's how it was preserved in their memories: there was never a time that Ann mentioned her name without adding "poor" before it and saying a few words about her life that had been cut short, and just when she had succeeded in raising a model family with such a charming child. Henry would verify her words with a nod and again say what an excellent secretary she had been, one that cannot be replaced, though in truth for most of the hours of the day she had been idle.

And her grave also remained. An outstanding location had been set aside for the cemetery; the dead always get the best views, and one could sit on a stone bench there in perfect solitude, because all the other graves, whether government personnel who had died here or of explorers who had been killed on their travels, no one came to visit.

The Ladakhi sit for forty days opposite their dead or their images and read all kinds of instructions to them from the Bardo Thodol on how to find a way to their next reincarnation, but McKenzie hastened to bury Dianne and never sat opposite her grave and spoke to her, as one quite often sees in cemeteries (his Aunt Elizabeth, for instance, used to talk that way to Uncle William whose infidelities were all forgotten). He never spoke to her aloud or to himself about how their son was growing up, he didn't quote any clever remarks he had made: and certainly didn't speak of his fears for the day it would be revealed to all that he had been involved in an act of fraud like some crook. Even during the toughest days, when Magnani returned to Italy and it seemed that within a month at the very most, someone would surface and prove it was a forgery, he didn't tell her about it and certainly not to her tombstone.

"You'll only be glad when I'm gone, Ed," she said to him more than once during her last months, "nothing will bother you any more from thinking about that harlot, and at least don't pretend that you care for me! Come to Mummy, Charlie."

"You shouldn't speak like that when he's around," McKenzie said her, although Charlie wasn't daunted by those words but rather by the illness that relayed them from her mouth, and to that she replied: "But that's what she was, wasn't she? And it's not terrible if Charlie learns a bit about life, not so, Charlie? It's just a pity I didn't learn in time. Come, Charlie, I'll tell you a story now." It wasn't the first time that she had told him a story, but this story was different, it was about them. The smell of vomit was in the room, stronger than all the smells of sweat and the smells of incense that Daychin had lit, and his son, with his sensitive nose, didn't stop sneezing.

"Once upon a time there was…. a princess," she began, and the strands of her hair were spread in all directions over the pillow, "who didn't have a mother or a father, she only had a brother far far away and the only thing that brought a little happiness to life was when she -" – for a moment she fell silent and her eyes wandered over the walls on which her paintings were hung – "embroidered. Yes, everything possible, and everyone said to her, princess, why do you embroider so much, princesses don't have to embroider at all! And deep in her heart she knew that only one thing would bring her happiness…" Her gaze misted over and Daychin wiped her forehead with a moist towel, until her eyes cleared again. "But no prince came to her, not even one! And she continued to embroider, more serviettes and more tablecloths and more curtains, can you imagine that, Charlie?" With a moist sweaty hand, she pulled him to her, and he recoiled – the smell of quinine was also heavy in the room – and a moment passed until he let her embrace him.

"Until one day, a lone prince came to the kingdom, you listen too, Ed" (at the time he was standing opposite the window and looking out: the sight behind him was too harsh, and though the window was open, he imagined seeing the reflections of his wife and son on the slopes opposite him, and they too were saturated with the sweat of the fever). "And the princess thought, why shouldn't the two of them live together?"

Her voice trembled and Daychin leaned over her and wiped beads of sweat from her forehead. "That's how it is, Charlie, things one waits such a long time for finally come in the end! It's just that bad things sometimes come even when you don't wait for them, and good things in the end sometimes reveal themselves not to be good at all." She fell silent and pressed Charlie even closer to her meager chest, and when she felt chills, their son felt them as well.

"So they married and there was such happiness at their wedding, you can't imagine how joyous it was! It was the most beautiful wedding that had ever been here, that's what everyone said. It was beautiful, wasn't it, Ed?"

He nodded slowly without turning to her, and in the eyes of someone looking in from the outside – had someone been standing there – it could have appeared as if he was nodding his approval to the mountain to darken; it was already dusk.

"And everyone came to tell her how wonderful she looked, even Mrs. Andrews who hardly knew her! But later that night, tell him, Ed, how much I disappointed you." She fell silent and in the stillness a magpie could be heard; Charlie's voice could also be heard mumbling something. He was already beginning to become bored and she kissed him on the forehead and the moment she released him he wiped his forehead with the back of his hand.

"What does he need to hear all this for?" McKenzie said.

"What for?" she replied from their bed. "So that he'll know what kind of a father he's got," and her eyes drilled into his back when she returned to speak in a voice that was both feverish and fragile, fervent and frail to the point of expiration. "Let him know what his father was really thinking, and about whom."

Then Charlie lifted his head from her chest and listened to the sounds coming from the grounds – that's what he always did at such moments, like a prisoner to whose ears a sound comes from the outside world. Chondol's children filled the grounds with their commotion.

"Do you see, sweet Charlie?" She asked, suddenly lucid. "The prince once had a princess in a different land, and when she threw him out, instead of forgetting her, the opposite happened. Take heed, Charlie, a person remembers best the ones who hurt him."

"Isn't that enough?" This time he turned from the window to the room, to her and to their son and to Daychin who stood by the bed, ready to help with whatever was required. "Why does he have to hear all this?"

"He doesn't understand a thing," she replied as if to soothe him, and a moment later continued without any wish to soothe. "But one day he'll understand, won't you, Charlie? It was simply a prince who didn't know what was good for him -" She lifted herself slightly off the bed; her back was propped up by pillows, and it was evident how much Charlie wanted her to release him and allow him to go out into the grounds – his gaze kept wandering to the door as if he could see all the games he was missing through it. "And oddest of all, Charlie, was that the new princess had also become like that! Just because he dreamed about someone else, she wanted him even more, and by then even you weren't enough for her -" Her voice broke and she reached out the palm of her hand to him and waited to stroke him like a puppy, the way she used a year before then, but he recoiled from her touch and her hand remained hung in the air. Again, she reached out an emaciated sweaty hand, and this time he unwillingly acceded as she stroked him with the tips of her thin white fingers whose grasp on him was already a measure of their grasp on life. "And for that reason," her cracked voice quivered, "the illness came upon her."

"It came from mosquitos," McKenzie said.

Dianne tried to grin, but that grin looked like a spasm. "Do you think it sat quietly in the blood all these years," she said, "and only broke out now, Ed?"

He had already been told about two previous outbreaks, both from which she had come out well, and he reminded her of them; and when she answered that neither of them was as severe as this, he tried to hearten her by saying that over the years her body had become strong and that no mosquito could overpower her, not even a thousand mosquitos. "You also have something to fight for," he reminded her, "and someone," and made an effort to cheer her spirit which throughout the previous years, while there still had been some point to it, he had disregarded.

She was still hugging Charlie, and a breast was exposed from the opening of her stained nightgown, meager and pale and imprinted by the wrinkles of the cloth, and the smell of quinine in all its sharpness could be smelled again. Strands of her moist hair were still disheveled over the pillow whose whiteness had been sullied; every morning Daychin combed it as if they were be going out for a stroll, and now it looked as if a comb had never been through it. She was silent and her forehead was burning: new beads of sweat sprouted over its entire breadth and also sparkled on her eyebrows, sliding from there and being captured in the lashes. Only a thin slit was open between them, and what was visible in her pupils was a small and faint blaze, like that of coals which a last flame has roused.

Her eyes closed; her grip became limp. "Mummy's a little tired, Charlie," she then said.

A chill passed through her, and after it another; they could be seen passing through her shoulders and her facial features and even her eyelashes. A murky bubble of saliva burst from her mouth and Daychin leaned over her and wiped her lips and mumbled something in Ladakhi that must have been words of comfort. Another bubble sprouted from her mouth, it swelled and became larger and larger, until it burst.

19

At her funeral (another week passed until her body consented to the will of the soul and surrendered to the malaria) a statement was naturally made about the heavens from which she'd watch over her son, and afterward the sound of earth hitting the coffin could be heard, and it would have been fitting if on hearing that sound a quiver would pass through her husband and the father of their son – it would have been fitting for McKenzie to shed a tear, to choke up, to try and stop the one who is taking his wife from him, and at the very least to tear his hair out, but none of that happened. Only late at night, when he put Charles to sleep in their bed (Daychin not only changed the bedclothes but also the mattress), he saw her surrounded by earth on all sides and woke up startled in the dark room; its darkness was dense and heavy and as stifling as a grave, until he suddenly felt the warmth of Charlie's little body at his side.

Afterward he lay awake for a long while and couldn't fall asleep; thousands of tons of earth lay on the coffin that had been left in the grave, and until they would crush the lid with their weight, their grains trickled into it – first he saw one land on her cheek and waited for Dianne to get rid of it with her hand like one gets rid of a fly, and right away another landed, and another, and another, and soon her whole face was spotted with grains and the purity of her skin gradually disappeared beneath them.

Eight months after her death, during which quite a lot had happened (not like the abundance of events during the year the caravan went out to the desert), what remained was surely only bones and remnants of flesh. That's how it is, everything is doomed to decompose, whether beneath the earth or above it: flesh and bones, love and marriage, whatnot.

The body of the drunk that fell from the pier in Brindisi also decomposed, and perhaps Kate, in person, came to identify it, and without so much as blinking saw in his gnawed face the face of the husband who had kissed her when there had still been love between them, and the stomach that was ripped by crab claws, the one that had bumped into her stomach or her buttocks on their good nights. More than her infidelity, the thought was hard to bear: how his wife had come to identify the remains of his body only so that she could remarry.

The day will come when there will be no remnant of the status he enjoyed here, when the fraud is revealed and his part in it is discovered and it transpires he had acted like the lowest crook.

Another two weeks passed terribly slowly during which time he didn't know anything about his caravan, neither good nor bad. In fact, for over two months he had no idea whether their mission had succeeded or not. No wonder he was unable to fall asleep at night and in the afternoon would suddenly doze off in the hospital, and that too was disturbed by the horrors of the desert.

"I'm worried about them," he said to Dianne when she came to help him with secretarial work and couldn't understand what he had to do with a caravan that had left for Khotan over two months ago. And since he had to invent something, he began a convoluted explanation about an item that Tenzin was supposed to be bringing him from the Khotan markets. "What item?" "Something small for the hospital." "Equipment?" "No, medicine." "Are there medicines in Khotan you don't have here? He became tongue-tied and to untangle himself from the confusion, said (much to his complete surprise; before that he would never have conceived of saying such a thing) regretfully there were patients who didn't have much faith in European medicines, and would only agree to take them if they receive the Amchi's potions in addition. In fact, it was at that very moment that he first decided to use that method to persuade those who refused medicines; instead of struggling against the Amchi and his cronies, to be helped by them.

"I can't believe you would do such a thing," she said, despite understanding the logic of the matter, and especially when he justified it by what he had once heard from Harper about his mission to Africa: the more he and his colleagues tried to fight the local beliefs, the more the natives continued to practice them in secret, and since that was the case, why destroy forces in a hopeless war and arouse antagonism instead of searching for a way to their hearts.

"Harper did that?" Dianne was amazed.

"No," McKenzie replied, "but had he done so he would have had more success."

That same day the caravan left Khotan going southward, and two weeks passed until it reached the outskirts of Leh. Since it was not a large caravan, only a few people in the street of the bazaar raised their eyes at it and then looked away. Only one observer continued to watch tensely from one of the roofs – the little Russian boy who was expecting their return. A few times a day he would go onto the roof of Punstok's inn and gaze at the horizon or do other things there, prompting McKenzie to ask him to inform him of the caravan's arrival and promising a small reward in return. During those months, Sasha had learned to assert himself in his dealings with those older than him and had become as shrewd as the locals – a comment made in the commissioner's wife's parlor; the little Russian bastard has become as bad as an Indian – and so wouldn't make do with a vague promise. In exchange for the information he demanded money and set the amount at two annas.

Many great expectations often end with some unglamorous occurrence: years of veterinarian studies can end with a brown cascade bursting from the intestines of a sick cow; a great love that fills one's entire world can end in an empty hotel room. And in the same way, no drums or trumpets were heard when the caravan returned to Leh, just some braying, but in the eyes of one who waited for it, the pillars of dust that preceded it and told of its coming were enough. Sasha was on the roof of the inn at the time, not only as a lookout but to continue his secret occupation only few knew about, one that began the week after Harper dismissed him from his role in the pageant.

He had a new pair of wings with him, though they couldn't compare to the previous ones in size or splendor; after all, not only eagles fly in the sky. The blacksmith made the skeleton of those wings from iron wire and prepared a base for them that fitted the boy's shoulder blades. He reduced the dimensions, because it wasn't clear where he would find enough feathers to cover them with this time. "Come to me at the end of day," he said to Sasha as he had the last time, "when there's no one about." And at the end of the day not only did he affix the wings to their base, but even placed them on the lean body with his own hands, feeling his bony shoulder blades and making certain they don't hurt him - but why should they hurt him, Sasha's already a little man and the wings don't hurt, right? The blacksmith's a big man and nothing ever hurts him, look at the muscles he has, Sasha, here and here and also here.

The tailor, Tenzin's father, who Sasha had asked to sew each wing a cloth covering on which feathers would be stuck (as he had done the previous time), also told him to wait until the end of the day when there was no one around, but he wasn't afraid of him, not then and not now; without knowing anything about the hardships he had endured in Tibet and Dehrandun, the tailor seemed like someone even children have no need to fear. He wanted some kind of payment, not something equal in worth to money, like the blacksmith wanted, but real money; a small amount, and wasn't prepared to forgo it. "You have to learn that everything in life has a price," the tailor said to him, "and don't ever expect favors from anyone. One day you'll even thank me for it." And nevertheless, Sasha managed to persuade him to wait until the end of the week – the doctor had promised to pay him two annas when he informed him that the caravan had arrived.

On the roof of the inn that no one went up to other than him, he sorted the feathers he had managed to gather on his wanderings in Leh and its surroundings. They were the simplest of feathers, dirty from the ground or the filth of the bazaar and some were even defective – very different from the splendid feathers that had been brought from Lake Tsomoriri. The right wing had been completely covered, though only with a thin meager layer, while the other was still bare like the wing of a fledgling. He carefully fitted the pair of wings onto his thin, modest shoulder blades, and when the wind blew on the roof it made a light rustling sound in his ears that didn't at all resemble the rustling of the previous ones, but nonetheless was a pleasant sound.

At the same hour, the air in the hospital was already heavy and stifling, and McKenzie returned from a round in the sickrooms. He saw the fingerless man seating his small son on his knees, stroking the boy's head and rubbing his puffed cheek with his stumps (here they lost fingers only from the cold and not from leprosy), and also saw the Kashmiri woman whose legs had been left withered and dangling by Heine-Medin disease, and God only knows how she reached Leh. The sicklemia patient was also there, sitting and staring around him with his eyes bulging like those of a frog, as if in that way he might better see the world from which he was parting.

He left the malaria patients for last, and not because it was a disease that in general wasn't fatal (only the African strain, the falciparum, was fatal, but one could somehow live with the Indian strain, that is to say someone who wanted to recover and live). None of the patients could say how they contracted the disease whose spreaders can't reach these heights and whose source only lately had become clear; it had been termed "bad air" in the Middle Ages owing to the air of the swamps that seemingly caused it.

Yes – he should be concerning himself with just one thing, but other things kept cropping up and among them one of the dreams of his youth – a man could make a name for himself from diseases, not only from antiquities but from illnesses too, terrible as they might be. Had he, for instance, focused on malaria and occupied himself only with that, he might have preceded others in discovering its source; it was actually during those years that researchers made a name for themselves on three continents that way. The parasites in the infected blood cells were discovered by a Frenchman, and then came a Cuban who raised the proposition that mosquitos transfer them from person to person (who knew there were doctors in Cuba?), but only eight years ago – when McKenzie was already here in India – it was finally proven in Calcutta that the damn mosquitos were the source of it all; not Ross in Africa with falciparum; but here in the Indian sub-continent, in a Calcutta hospital. And what was McKenzie occupied with at the time? They hadn't yet begun their crazy plan and the idea hadn't yet risen, but he was probably handing out all sorts of placebos to all sorts of bothersome people in order to be rid of them; and had he been involved in research with the same zealous determination he later showed, he might even have found a cure for Dianne.

A few moments after he came out of the last sickroom, the Russian boy arrived, flushed from running and so excited by his message he forgot to translate it into words he had learned here. In fluent Russian he informed him that the caravan had arrived, and though McKenzie only knew two words in Russian, dasvedanya and spasiba, he understood his tidings.

Had it not been for his job (after all, he didn't shirk all his responsibility!), he would have left the hospital instantly and gone to the bazaar to meet the caravan on its arrival, but he remained for two whole hours, gnawed by the speculation whether all that had to be buried had indeed been buried in the sands.

Sasha received his wages and hurried out, and later could be seen going farther up the path and the doctor had no doubt where he was going. In fact – it transpired a while later – he first went to pay the tailor and only then ran to wait for the caravan. It was a fairly hot day in May (there was no mistaking the date, not even five years later: it happened the day before the Feast of the Ascension), and the thawing of the snow on the mountains had already begun.

At the foot of the mountains and in all the low-lying areas, the streams and the irrigation ditches were filled, and Mrs. Harper's birds, flock after flock, had returned from the places where they had wintered, and among the familiar sounds of the sparrows and crows and doves that even in winter didn't stop, one could hear the joyous sounds of the returning men. At the edge of the fields, the first flowers were already in bloom: primroses and irises, buttercups and anemones and belladonnas (the name of that flower still aroused disgust in McKenzie and not because of its toxicity; it was what the young men of Rome called Kate even when she was walking with him). At four and a half thousand meters perhaps a blue carpet of forget-me-nots could already be seen and orchids which also blossom at that time, and other flowers whose names McKenzie didn't know, but Dianne, who knew each one by name, used to pick bouquets of them and the loveliest ones she would press between pages of a thick book (time would pass until he'd find them between pages of his books).

Sasha looked into the distance: flowers didn't interest him, his gaze was attracted by the pillars of dust the animals raised, and he waited until one by other their riders could be seen. Perhaps he was whistling to himself or trying to imitate the hoopoe sounds that were being made by the bird of that name.

It was easy to spot the very moment the caravan arrived at the outskirts of Leh: the joyous running, Poliakov lifting him up onto his pony's back with a sturdy hand (the way, five years later, Rasul would lift little Charles, and that swinging motion did not promise good things) and riding with him into Leh. He must have told him his presents, the fire cart and the kite, and Sasha like any boy hearing about gifts he's about to receive, couldn't wait. He gazed at the sacks on either side of the saddle with longing eyes.

"Let's first get there," Poliakov said to him, and instead of allaying his curiosity as he should have done, he asked him about his mother, and Sasha replied unwillingly, "She's sleeping."

"When isn't you mother in bed," said Poliakov.

A few months ago the boy would have protected his mother, even if he wasn't exactly sure from what, but this time he made no attempt, and not only because the gifts were foremost in his mind. He spent long hours alone on the roof without her noticing his absence, and what did she know about what he had been up to lately? Even if he did tell her about his role in the Feast of Ascension festival, he certainly didn't mention he had been dismissed from it and ostracized. As to his presents, he realized the cargo would first have to be unloaded from the animals who would then been fed and watered - and the men too. Poliakov patted his stomach with an open fingered hand to show how empty it was.

The boy stayed with them while they tended to the animals. Afterward he went with Poliakov to the small restaurant in the nearby alley, and while he waited for his meal the boy fixed his gaze on him expecting to hear more about his presents – what colors were the fire cart and the kite? How long was the ladder? How high does the kite fly? But Poliakov kept silent, his thoughts were focused on a different matter.

Tenzin supervised the final stages of the unloading. It was at moments like these at the end of a mission that people tended to be negligent, and mishaps were liable to happen, and especially when they had to answer the questions of inquisitive people who gathered around them: where exactly had they been? In the desert, but where in the desert? And what had they brought from there and what had they sold there? Tenzin was miserly in his answers, and when someone said one would think he wasn't just the doctor's assistant but the doctor himself and at the very least a Sahib, he pretended not to hear.

In the restaurant, Sasha turned his head towards the kitchen. Something was being fried and the smell of burning wafted from there, and after sniffing with his little nose he asked how big the fire cart was; this big? His spread his arms out to indicate the size, but Poliakov brought them closer to each other – like this – much to Sasha's disappointment. "That's like for little children!" he complained. He was clearly insulted.

In order to cheer him up, Poliakov began to describe all the qualities of the kite: how it could be maneuvered in the air, how it could ascend in a moment and then dive and lift off again right away and spin both its tails in the air. It made the wrinkle that had been formed between the boy's eyebrows vanish, but he was in no hurry to get up. It seemed to Sasha that the chow-mein noodles Poliakov was eating would last forever.

Afterward, Poliakov drank, and Sasha watched the glass and his Adam's apple going up and down until the glass was emptied and then immediately refilled, and only when nothing was left in the jug, did they leave. When they reached the place where the equipment was being unloaded, they found Tenzin counting the trunks and the sacks and the bags that were arranged in five large piles whose height was greater than the stature of a man, and when he finished, he said that the doctor was waiting for them – as indeed he was, in the hospital. He had one last pile to count, he said, and then they'll be off to the doctor.

"I'll just give the boy his present," Poliakov said and looked at the five large piles, but it was difficult for him to locate his boxes, and when he began moving one here and one there, Tenzin said it would be better to wait until the men return; they had gone to eat with his permission. Poliakov sought his boxes for another moment but the dust that covered everything made it difficult to distinguish between them.

Another boy would have stomped his foot and burst out crying, perhaps even beat his little fists against someone who had disappointed him like that, but Sasha neither stomped, cried or beat his fists, despite having fixed his large eyes on Poliakov in wait of some magic that would reveal his presents. It seems during these months he had learned to accept disappointments like an adult.

The three of them turned towards the route that led to the hospital and Poliakov put him on his pony with the reins in hands. The pony paid no attention to the little horseman and walked in accordance with the pony in front of it. Some of the merchants sitting in the entrances to their shops watched them and asked Sasha if he had decided at last to exchange his wings for a horse, but he answered no one.

When they arrived at the hospital, Poliakov put him down on the ground and Sasha went to corner of the yard. That May had enjoyed beautiful days, and the treetop of the apricots growing there was already spotted with fruit. Sasha reached out his hand to one of the lower branches and jumped to try and reach the fruit. When Poliakov and Tenzin went towards the building they saw him beginning to climb the tree, and a moment before entering Poliakov told him to be careful, because the fire cart and kite were waiting for him.

McKenzie remembered that moment when the two of them entered his office well: they were so dusty he could just barely distinguish between them, the dark native and the white man; that is the nature of journey to form the nomad in their image.

"Hello, Doctor," they said, and he indicated with his eyebrow to close the door behind them.

The moment they sat down opposite him he could smell their scent, a mixture of sweat and bonfire smoke and horses, but the journey wafted from everyone who came here from a distance.

"Everything's been taken care of," Tenzin said.

He looked at them both and waited for them to go into detail: what does everything mean? After all, a man never achieves everything he desires.

"Everything's in the sand, Doctor. The anchors, the seashells, the mother-of-pearl, the salt; they're all in the sand."

He asked about the pieces of ancient parchment, an odd fear rose in him that a suitable place hadn't been found for them.

"They're also in the sand."

"As well as a dead man who's also in the sand," Poliakov said. He then heard for the first time about the fight that had broken out in the desert, and how one of the anchors had slid from the side of the pit and hit one of the men. It must have been a horrific sight: for a moment the nightmare that had visited him all the past months came to mind, but in it someone sank in the sands and was swallowed by them: no skull was smashed, no blood flowed, no shout was uttered: the sand swallowed the man walking in it in total silence

When he asked them if they had done anything to stop the fight, Poliakov said he had fired in the air, but it was too late. No sorrow could be seen in his face, only weariness. And what was McKenzie's face expressing at the time? He wanted it to express deep shock – it was impossible to imagine the terrible fact of a man being killed because of their plan! – but in secret he had hoped such would be Magnani's fate. And who could know that exactly a year later, after all the objects had been raised from the sand, Magnani would survive and be saved by the very last person one would have expected to act that way.

Since his face expressed shock, Tenzin explained that one of the men he had hired before leaving for the desert, Faizul by name, had constantly argued with everyone; there's one like that on every caravan, he said, and had they not been assigned the task of burying anchors in the desert, it could have ended as it usually did with a black eye and a few bruises;, one doesn't get killed that quickly by fists.

It's not a question for a doctor to ask, and certainly not a director of a hospital, and ever more so of a mission hospital, and nonetheless he asked what they had done with the body and waited for an answer, as if he was a murderer whose partners in crime had been requested to conceal evidence. But there had been no murder there, just an accident, and even if there had been violence prior to it, he hadn't been the perpetrator. In thought, yes, he doesn't deny that; he often envisaged Magnani swallowed in the sands and dying of thirst on the top of a dune or being preyed upon by the beaks of vultures. It was a heartwarming sight: with absolutely clearly he saw how they pecked at his temples until reaching the brain, the brain of a learned man who knew how to deliver a lecture detailing the differences between Michelangelo's David and Donatello's David and Bernini's David.

"The body's also in the ground," Tenzin answered briefly as Poliakov had done before him. "Just like the anchor."

Then the gazes of the three of them were turned to the window: Sasha was riding on one of the branches of the apricot tree and reaching his hand out to its fruit and Poliakov called to him something that sounded like a warning or a reprimand.

"Let's hope the little Russian doesn't get a bellyache," Tenzin scoffed.

The little Russian took a bite from the fruit and spat it out and dropped it from his hand, and then reached out his hand again to a pair of apricots at the end of the branch.

"Leave him alone," McKenzie said to Poliakov when he intended to call out to him again, "he knows how to look after himself."

Then from his cloak, Tenzin took out the ragged pages on which he had listed all the expenses and income from the journey, he carefully unfolded them and began to read: how much the animals they bought in Khotan cost, how much they sold them for, how much the food cost, how much the extra kitchen equipment cost, how much they paid the Tavakkal men who they hired on the way. The hush money, meant for ensuring no one talk about what had been buried in Dandan Oilik, he gave back and explained that after some deliberation they came to the conclusion that the attempt to silence them was liable to hasten the discovery, and it would be better to let things take their course, to let time take effect.

How conceited they were at the time, the two of them and McKenzie, and how naïve.

It seemed then that if they had successfully completed the first stage of their plan, the difficult stage, they were certain to succeed in the next stages as well, and that the gods themselves – at least the angry gods of Dandan Oilik – would stand by them; not only would something of what they had buried in the desert be exposed when the time came (that did happen) and the rumor reach Europe (that also happened, by way of Leh and Kashgar and Calcutta and Petersburg), and not only would Magnani lead a caravan to Dandan Oilik and discover all that had been buried in the sands (that also happened), but that even the final stage of their plan would be realized, the very purpose of it all.

That is not what happened, in any event not during the five years that had passed. For the time being, according to all the experts, Magnani had made a discovery of unparalleled importance, the most important of the last decade, if not more, and the man who should have been harshly punished had actually won fame. Yes, that's how it is: out of all Magnani's colleagues and mousey university rivals (and McKenzie knew some examples of that species from his homeland; nothing impressed them less than his veterinary doctorate) no one declared it was a case of fraud. On the contrary, it seemed that all those shrewd wise men enlisted to verify the authenticity of the fake findings: the pieces of scroll, the antiquity of the paper and ink and the writing and its contents, and the wooden anchors, from their form reminiscent of a plough to the lead casing binding them. All those wise academics – he had come across that in England as well – gain no greater satisfaction than sinking their false teeth into someone's portion, solely to be able to write articles about them with a thousand and one footnotes (there was a pub in Oxford where those types drank and debated all sorts of silly trifles at length, but when they became drunk they belched like wagon drivers).

Since the fraud hadn't yet been exposed and in the meantime had only brought Magnani honor, it turned out that McKenzie – whose beautiful, adored, exhilarating, adulterous, contemptible wife had been robbed by that Italian – had in fact strengthened his rival even more. Yes, wondrous are the ways of God, Harper would have said, and not only about the glory he had bestowed upon his archenemy with his own hands, but also his saving him; wondrous are the ways of God and wondrous are the medicines his creatures have developed. Magnani had returned from the desert a shadow of his former self and had almost pegged out on the way and in the hospital as well, and who treated him here like one of the royal family? And who seethed with anger? And who behaved not only like a disciple of Hippocrates but like a disciple of Jesus? He, McKenzie, yes: no man had ever turned the other cheek with greater readiness than he had done.

He hastily went through the columns of numbers Tenzin gave him. Every expense was written there in an amazingly orderly handwriting and it wasn't difficult to check the calculations despite the paper being tattered. There was no mistake there, at least not in the calculations he checked, and he had no doubt that the others were also precise. Tenzin was a trustworthy man, a model caravan-bashi and if in his heart he harbored something against Sahibs in general and the British in particular, he didn't intend to express it in that way.

"You see, Doctor," he said quietly, "we bought nothing unnecessary."

When he complimented him on that, it made him happy; with all the grudges he bore against Sahibs he took pride in having led the caravan to the desert in proper fashion, and as to the Indian sub-continent, he had a far-reaching vision no lesser than the return of the vanished sea: the return of rule to the Indians.

The only things out of the ordinary that had been bought, Tenzin said, were the presents for the Russian boy, but those hadn't been bought from the caravan's budget.

For some reason, as if he hadn't eagerly waited for them for more than two months, McKenzie saw fit to inquire about those presents. Of matters many times more important he still had not inquired, for example further questions about the man who had been killed by the anchor: not whether he had family, a wife and children, nor how they had reacted when they learned he had died. When he heard about the fire cart and about the kite, he still didn't know –neither did Tenzin or Poliakov– of what little use those toys would be to Sasha.

He hadn't yet heard anything about his little wings, while they had already heard about them on their arrival, at first from the merchants who provoked Sasha in the bazaar and afterward from the boy who on the back of the pony told Polia-kov he would fly with them to the sea, yes; these wings were better than the ones before even if they were small. He told Tenzin who had sewn them and when he heard that his father had demanded payment his face darkened. About the black-smith and his muscles, Sasha told them nothing.

It wasn't hard to see him through the window as he climbed to a higher branch than the previous one. Poliakov called to him again in Russian, warning him again about unripe fruit or about falling, and also said how sorry the presents he had brought would be if he couldn't play with them.

"I will play will them!" Sasha replied from his branch. He was riding it like a horseman as no longer holding on to anything.

Only when they returned their gazes from the grounds to the room, the really important matters were discussed (that, at least, was how it seemed to them). McKenzie had invested a fair amount of money on this caravan and a fair amount of hope, and if he wished to make certain all the effort hadn't been in vain, who could criticize him?

He had become something of a pest and a pedant, lingering over every detail; had he paid the same heed to the stock of medicines and bandages in the hospital, he would certainly have raised its level for the benefit of his patients, but he had forgotten all about them. Where had everything been buried, he asked, and they told him in detail: where exactly had the clay jug been placed (in the site of the remains of the ruins), and where had all the rest been buried (in the ditch that was dug west of there), and pits were dug for the anchors that took up more space, and in the southern pit the accident occurred.

And besides that, he asked ("that" was how he termed the death of a man as if an insignificant nuisance had been spoken about, and who knew then there would be further deaths, one of which would take place within the walls of his house, on his bed), had there been other problems? He was mainly concerned about unnecessary questions that could be asked by the men of the caravan, for instance by that problematic character, what was his name? Faizul? Is he liable to cause problems?

"There can always be problems, Doctor," Tenzin replied and again mentioned that in order for everything they had buried to be discovered one day and the rumor of it to reach Europe, it would be better for things not to be kept totally secret.

Then, when they no were longer paying attention to the boy crawling along his branch (he occasionally returned to the previous fork in the branches in order to choose a new one to crawl along), he also wondered whether someone who came to Dandan Oilik in the future, for example the Italian, would see there was something there other than the ruins. To that they replied that anyone who came there would first start digging in the area of the ruins, and that was how the bait they had buried there would be exposed ("It's in a good place, Doctor," they said to him, "not too high and not too deep").

But how could anyone know – he continued to ask, while some of his patients waited for him in the corridor and others waited in their beds – that they also had to dig three hundred feet away from there and search for some ditch with mother-of-pearl and anchors? He remembered the place well from the photographs of Stein who had already excavated twice there and had shown the photographs at one of the commissioner's wife's evening teas: besides the remnants of those pillars and a few dry stumps of wild poplar trees, nothing interrupted the monotony of the sands, and why the hell would anyone start digging there specifically?

It transpired they had marked the place: at three points along the ditch that had been refilled with sand, they heaped up a pile of stones, two at the ends and another in the middle. No, not just regular stones, there are no regular stones in the desert because the sand covers them as well, but those taken from the ruins.

And won't the sand cover those piles of stones? He continued to question them as if there was nothing more important in the world than the fate of piles of stones. Yes, in years to come, the sand will cover them, they answered him, of course it will, that's how dunes are formed, but they're expecting ("Isn't that what you wanted, Doctor?") that within a year the gullible Italian would arrive here.

Then Sasha began swaying on the branch he was sitting on; at first just a slight almost unnoticeable movement, and afterward his head could be seen going up and down in the window when he increased the momentum like a rider spurring on his horse or his donkey, but he made no sound and no joy could be seen in his face, only determination or apprehension, perhaps he was testing the strength and flexibility of the branch, and when Poliakov shouted to him to stop, it swayed a few moments more.

Morning and night, ever since their leaving for the desert, McKenzie had waited for news from them, and who the hell could criticize him for not taking an interest in the Russian boy? Sasha advanced along the branch, pressing close to it with his small body like a lizard, and his right arm reached towards some apricots at its end, even though they were greener than the previous ones.

Just then the door opened, and an unfamiliar head peeked in, perhaps a patient or a family member, and with a short wave of the hand, McKenzie showed him the way out. Perhaps a man was standing there, or a woman, or an old man, or an old woman, maybe the elderly woman who had tried to approach him before that and had come to try her luck again.

"When will you finally learn to knock on the door?" he let slip out and waited for the door to close.

"We don't even know how to knock on a door," Tenzin said, "isn't that what you were thinking, Doctor?"

None of the three of them were looking outside, and even if they had looked they wouldn't have seen Sasha; he had climbed onto another branch and was higher than the window frame, possibly already close to the treetop.

20

The hospital corridor was empty when he accompanied them outside. "Go and rest a while now," he said to them with the generosity of a patron who first of all makes sure his men have carried out their job properly. Afterward he returned to the office and remembered that he hadn't seen the boy for a while, and when he looked at the treetop and didn't see him, he assumed he had climbed down and found himself another activity.

The bottle of French cognac he had belatedly taken out for them ("You give opium to the Chinese and alcohol to us?" Tenzin said) still stood on his table and he deliberated for a moment whether to drink the little that was left in it. The label had become slightly detached from the glass, and he tried to pull its corner off between two fingernails the way the Indians delouse themselves, until through the window he saw Poliakov from the back. He saw him only for a moment, and right away he bent down and vanished from his eyes. Another moment passed and he heard him speaking in Russian, flustered and anxious – half the label was already peeled off – and another moment passed without seeing or hearing him, until he rose up and appeared again in the window. He was carrying Sasha in his arms, covered in dust and as silent as a corpse, and he continued talking to him in a feverish, pleading Russian. "Sasha, Sasha," he called and slapped his cheeks lightly, the right and the left. The boy was completely still in his arms, his limbs limp as an abandoned marionette.

A few moments passed, and McKenzie still didn't go out of his office toward the two of them – the small amount cognac he had drunk on an empty stomach must have made him a little hazy, and the label was still held between his finger-nails as if it mustn't be let go of until it was completely peeled off – and the boy still didn't open his eyes. His face wasn't calm, not like a face that has found refuge in a swoon or in death.

"Sasha, Sasha," Poliakov called to him again.

A few more moments passed and when his eyes finally opened one couldn't tell whether he had fallen from the tree and lost consciousness and perhaps received an injury not visible to the eye, or whether he was just spread out on the ground pretending to be dead to see how his adult friend would react (no thud had been heard from the room). His face appeared tightly contracted, but that might for his prank not to be discovered. Perhaps he lay there on his back or on his stomach waiting for someone to notice his absence, to be concerned about him, to go searching for him, to call out his name, to lift him up. He had to wait for quite some time while they were occupied with their matters, and when Poliakov drew near to him perhaps he shut his eyes and held his breath. It would have been fitting for McKenzie to go out to the two of them, for the director of the Moravian hospital to let go of the cognac and the damn label and examine the boy as any doctor who honors his profession, but still he busied himself with the label, and by the time his head had cleared and he pulled himself together, he saw Sasha open his eyes and giggle.

Poliakov still hadn't put him down from his arms, and when the boy released himself from his grip his small back could be seen, dusty from the ground he had been lying on while pretending to be dead. A few of the green apricots he had thrown from the treetop were strewn at his feet, and he kicked one of them and it flew into the air for a moment and landed. He could have been signaling to Poliakov the way to Leh, where his presents awaited.

The three of them returned to the town while he tidied his desk a little (he was waiting for Dianne to come and type another letter for the district supervisor). They parted at the entrance to the bazaar and Tenzin turned toward the tailor's alley.

His father's neighbors, tailors for generations, heard heated voices in his small room, shouting, cursing (some of which was directed at the distant past when his father had left home, and some the recent past, when he tried to teach the Russian boy a lesson he himself had only learnt in his adulthood: not to expect favors from anyone), and this time too they didn't interfere. After Tenzin left there, one of them deliberated whether to go to their neighbor and check on his welfare, but soon heard the rhythmic rattling of his sewing machine.

Where Tenzin went from there no one knows, and time would pass, almost a week, until his destination would become clear even to himself. Leh had become a kind of crossroads for them from which each one would go his own way, and only McKenzie, who had instigated it all, remained in his place.

It was afternoon, and the tumult of the bazaar had slightly subsided. The hungry had gone to eat and the tired to rest. The merchants no longer called out throatily and the fervor of those bargaining weakened; even the donkeys didn't bray other than obligatorily, and only their tails swayed vigorously to banish the flies from their behinds. Poliakov and the boy continued on the way to the inn.

"Will you give them to me now?" Sasha asked about his presents, and Poliakov nodded his head and cheered him up – who else would he give the cart and kite to if not to Sasha? – but on reaching the grounds of the inn his boxes weren't in the place they were supposed to be. Apparently, the men of the caravan were in no hurry to return after the break allowed to them.

Sasha, very disappointed, turned his head away to hide his eyes. Perhaps he was already imagining how they would go up onto the roof of the inn and fly the kite from there, how he would run with him on the roof from one end to the other until the kite takes off and its two tails spread out behind it, and if the string was long enough, he would fly it to the sea of Petersburg, yes, even beyond the Admiralty Tower, and there's no tower higher than that in the whole world.

Poliakov lay a hand on his shoulder, and when the boy tried to shake it off, he said to him that since the box hadn't been brought to them, they would go and bring it themselves. That promise, made in a trusted and calm voice, delighted Sasha, but Poliakov was in no hurry. First of all – he said, and the boy was already holding his hand – he must go and say hello to Sasha's mother.

"Mother's sleeping!" Sasha said.

Poliakov might have asked him if she was alone right now, and maybe he preferred to find that out for himself. When he asked Sasha if he wanted to come with him, the boy shook his head: no, he didn't.

It transpired that Sunam Tsering had left that morning on a caravan to Delhi and would be away for at least three months, and that he hadn't paid for the last month – so said Punstok, who was well aware not only the debts of her guests but also their occupations and nocturnal habits.

Poliakov seemed pensive for the moment and asked if she could give something to the boy to eat, and she, who liked and pitied Sasha, hurried to the kitchen and brought the dumplings that he was fond of. When she returned, Sasha was already no longer there.

Poliakov went up to the second floor, and for a moment thought he heard someone climbing the stairs behind him, perhaps one of Punstok's children who helped with the cleaning. He heard a noise again and again ignored it, and when he reached the landing he turned to the left, toward the corner room. The room Sunam Tsering had chosen for his white mistress was the best room of the inn and Poliakov lingered for a moment opposite the door before knocking twice. The door was shut with a small hook, and in the space that remained between it and its frame nothing could be seen.

He pushed the door, displacing the hook and entered. The room was in darkness. The window on the opposite wall was covered entirely by wicker slats and thin lines of sunny light striped the room, and whirling grains of dust hovered in them with the spirals of smoke that swirled from the bed. It was a very large bed, made according to a special order, and on it Sasha's mother could be seen spread diagonally on her stomach, her full length also striped by lines of light and shade. They curved over her buttocks and thighs, of which only one was covered by a silk sheet, and gradually the profile of her face could be made out, its features blurred by the languid smoke: the black that outlined her eye had dissolved and her lipstick strayed past the borders of her lips between which a long thin opium pipe mouthpiece was inserted. She leaned on her right elbow and the swirls of smoke rose slowly from the small, compressed nugget at the bottom of the pipe, they wove through the air, intwining and unravelling, the intoxicating scent spreading through the room. When the eyes became adjusted to the darkness, the precious objects with which Sunam Tsering surrounded his Duniasha (he called her by her Russian pet name) could be seen: carved chests of drawers and wooden and terra-cotta statuettes and small rugs and a decorative copper tray with an oil lamp to heat the opium and a giant mirror in which the entire room was reflected, as well as the boy who stood behind Poliakov calling out: "Mother's sleeping! Mother's sleeping!"

"Go outside and play for a while?" Poliakov said. "Your mother wants to be alone."

Sasha stayed where he was a moment longer and since his mother didn't turn her head to him and his adult friend was waiting for him to go, he turned around and left. Duniasha didn't change her position: she lay on her stomach and was completely absorbed by the nugget of opium in her pipe, even when Poliakov closed the door and returned the hook to its place. Whether she mumbled some-thing or remained silent, there was nothing that interested her less than what was happening around her.

"I'm back," Poliakov said. "I'm back, Duniasha, aren't you glad?"

No answer was heard and not another word was said, but after a while, famil-iar sounds could be heard from the other side of the door, and the one eavesdrop-ping there detached himself and drew away so as not hear their end. Those sounds revolted Sasha more than anything.

From the ground floor, an immeasurable distance away, Punstok's voice could be heard calling him to come and taste the dumplings she had prepared specially for him, and though he was very hungry he didn't answer her. One of their neigh-bors on the floor, a lively Kashmiri merchant, passed him and began to descend the stairs, and the cleaning girl asked Sasha where he was going and if he didn't want to accompany her to the rooms she was working in. Perhaps they would find something someone had forgotten. But he shook his head and appeared to be very busy. With small steps he went to end of the small corridor where the ladder to the roof stood and waited for the girl to go into one of the rooms, but she stopped in her place. "Won't you come with me, Sasha?" she asked him again. She waited a moment longer for him to answer but in the end lost hope, as he began to climb the ladder.

"I saw you," the girl called after him, "what's there for you to do on the roof?" Instead of answering her, he grabbed the rung above his head with his right hand and with effort raised his right leg another rung and after that the left as well; the rungs were suited to the legs of an adult, but nonetheless he continued ascend-ing. The girl went on her way along the corridor. There were three doors, and she stopped at the corner door and listened to the sounds coming from there; she was still young, but already knew what they were.

Before he went out onto the roof, from the height of the ladder he looked down at the corridor and saw her standing opposite the door and trying to peek between the gap that it left. He then moved up another rung with effort.

The sun had already passed its zenith, but still blazed like a white-hot ball and no shade of orange could be seen in it. On two rugs Punstok had spread on the roof, apricots and peaches were being dried, one rug for each fruit, and he took a peach, tasted it and grimaced and threw it in a large arc to the street. After that he cautiously approached the edge of the roof and bent down, perhaps to see if he had hit one of the passersby. He remained bent like that a moment longer at the edge of the roof, and had someone seen him then, he would have seen him drawing in his lips and cheeks and dangling a string of saliva from his contracted mouth lengthening and glowing in the sun. He was fascinated by it in its path from the roof downward, until it was cut off by the wind.

"Sasha, Sasha!" Punstok's voice could be heard as she stood two floors below him at the entrance to the inn, watching the street, and he pressed close to the roof so that she wouldn't spot him should she lift her head.

He then turned to the place where he had hidden his wings. A pile of junk covered with a faded sheet of cloth stood in the corner of the roof with the wings hidden there, protected by the armrest of a dismantled chair. They were small wings, less than half the size of the previous ones which Harpers ordered to be passed on to his replacement in the pageant, but even had he placed the first ones onto his shoulder blades the outcome would have been no different.

He looked at them again. How miserable they seemed in comparison to the ones before: one was completely bald, just a cloth stretched over the iron wire frame, and a few unsightly feathers covered the other one, but he placed them onto his shoulder blades, lifting up his small pointy elbows to that purpose. The blacksmith had fitted them to his measurements, and if he recalled his touch it perhaps gave him the shivers or perhaps he was already beyond that, because his eyes were facing onward from there. In order for the wings to maintain their shape, two iron wires had been added between them to stabilize them ("Look how much care I'm taking for you," the blacksmith said), one on the chest and the other on the back.

When he moved forward the small wings quivered on his shoulder blades, and one of the feathers that had not been well stuck was shed but he did not notice it. At the edge of the roof he kneeled down and looked at the street: the Kashmiri merchant came out of the entrance of the cloth store, and the salesman called after him and lowered the price further; behind the Tibetan restaurant a boy of his age knelt and washed the dishes in the ditch water; and an old man who had a rolled-up carpet on his shoulder passed from shop to shop, and before each one spread out his carpet. A donkey let out an irritated bray, and Sasha didn't even look at it. Two Yarkandi merchants drew near to the inn and chatted in a language he wouldn't try to learn anymore.

A magpie flew above the street, and when his gaze accompanied it, the roofs of the buildings of the nearby alleys were revealed to him with rugs spread out on them, and beyond the last roofs were the arid slopes of the mountains. The monastery of the Gelugpa order could be seen with its white dusty walls and tattered prayer flags waving in the wind, and from there the dim sound of the large horns could be heard, so deep it seemed to be rising from the insides of the mountain. For a moment he listened to them and then let his gaze sail farther on from there toward the other slopes. Snow could be seen only at the heights of the peaks, and in vain his eyes sought the mountainous pass through which he and his mother had come from Kashgar an immeasurable amount of time ago.

Beyond those mountains were the real and vast cities with roads and sidewalks and parks and squares and marble statues and chariots and rivers with bridges and churches and steeples and above them a sky that refused to darken in summer, and when would awaken from his sleep there, he would see his mother staring outside with glassy eyes and would wait for her to blink in order to know that she wasn't dead. There and here in Leh they subsisted by the grace of men whose smell stayed on the sheets and on her; her beloved warm pleasant smell absorbed their smells. "I'm doing it for you, Sasha," she frequently said to him when she sent him outside, but after the man had gone, most times she didn't even want to open her eyes and he learned to leave her to herself. There were many things he learned; too many.

The iron wire that was stretched over his chest to stabilize the wings pressed slightly and he tried to make room for it with his thumb – the way a man sentenced to death did to prevent the rope scratching his neck. "Sasha, Sasha!" Punstok's voice could be heard again below him, and that worrying call made him move from his spot.

He lay at the edge of the roof, at the corner above their room and tried to listen: those sounds could no longer be heard. From behind, the pile of junk was lit by a diagonal light that lengthened the shadows of the chair legs with the sheet that covered them, and he noticed the small feather that had been shed from his right wing when he got up, but he didn't pick it up.

"Sasha, Sasha!" Punstok called again to the street, and this time he responded to her call. He went to the opening of the roof he had shut before, looked down for a moment and turned back, and from the rear end of the roof he began to run forward with the two small wings being tossed around on his back. He ran on and on, past the rug of the peaches and the rug of the apricots, over the rooms of the inn and their lodgers, he ran and his small wings continued to sway on his back and shed more feathers, and his shadow ran in front of him faster than him and reached the end of the roof before him and the space beyond it.

In the corner room, had they looked through the window, they would have seen his wings coming apart in the air, but only the thud attracted their attention. Until then his mother stared at the swirls of opium smoke, and Poliakov closed his eyes and fell asleep; and even the thud, because it had been so small, almost went unheard.

There wasn't a soul who didn't talk about it throughout the weeks that followed: how Punstok ran to the bleeding body, her hands dropping the bowl she was holding; how the merchants gathered round, abandoning their shops; how heads popped out of the windows of the inn, numbed or drowsy or drunk or drugged, and among them the heads of his mother and Poliakov. It was told how the sound that came out of the Russian woman's throat could be heard in the distant monastery, while of Poliakov it was told how not a sound was uttered from his mouth, not a shout, not even the boy's name. What was written on his face then was still imprinted on it when he reached the hospital carrying Sasha in his arms.

"Can you save him, Doctor?" he asked, and they both knew that not Jesus nor Jehovah of the Jews could save him, nor the Buddha, and certainly not the gods of the vanished sea. Dianne, who had arrived a few moments before, also saw Poliakov entering with the boy in his arms; he was only bleeding slightly from his nose, and his eyes were wide open, their shine as deceptive as the shine of glass. Poliakov put him gently down on the table, between the typewriter and the pile of old letters, the way one puts down a tender and fragile day-old infant. "Do something, Doctor!" he urged him, "Do something!" Dianne remained seated, pale as a sheet. It had been a very busy day in the hospital and all sorts of inquisitive people gathered there, and a woman, the aunt of the sicklemia patient, began to murmur some prayer, no longer directed at his recovery but rather at his next reincarnation. His eyelids didn't move, his chest was still, the drop of blood that fell from his nose had already congealed. "Why don't do something?" Poliakov asked, and in the light coming from the window the table looked like an altar.

21

Death, in its way, not only works on the body it has taken but on everything around it, and this time it marked the end of an era with an unequaled acuteness. Within a week, Poliakov left Leh as did Tenzin before him, but their ways split from each other: one turned to the mountains, and the other, a week after having clashed with his father, rode to Dehrandun and paid no attention to the sentry at the gate or to anyone else who tried to stop him. He tied his horse to a tree whose trunk had been whitewashed up to its top and wasn't frightened by all the officers he ran into and entered the colonel's bureau with a vigorous step and fearlessly told him what he thought about the way his father had been exploited and alienated. The colonel listened to him patiently for a while, until he had had enough of his insolence and ordered him to leave, and since Tenzin had further things to hurl at him and the intelligence wing and the British army and the entire empire, the colonel signaled to his adjutant with his finger. "Your father volunteered for his mission," he said to Tenzin, "no one forced him."

When two military policemen entered, Tenzin didn't allow them to lay a hand on him, and before another two had been summoned, he had already ripped the maps together with their arrows and flags from the wall they had been spread on and tore them to shreds. "Go and make new maps of everything," he said to the colonel, as if copies hadn't been made.

In Leh it was told he was waiting for his court case, and that they'd no doubt be severe with him in order that no Indian ever think to be insolent again, fifty years after the Sepoy Mutiny. "The impertinence," Henry said about him, "it will do him no harm to cool down in jail a bit."

Exactly a month later, Henry and Ann held a housewarming for their new home when the last furniture arrived from Simla, and to placate the locals they again invited the Lama who prior to building had come with his brass mirror to capture in it all the spirits that might bother the builders; now that the building had been completed, the spirits could be released into the world from the box in which they had been imprisoned.

They didn't hear about Poliakov that whole year, until a caravan that had passed the Kaspang monastery arrived in Leh and one of its men said that their Russian had one day arrived at the monastery, and after he asked about the monk in retreat and heard he had passed on to a better reincarnation, he said he would

679

ride to the cave and stay there for a while. Perhaps he went to sit in the spot where
the monk had sat to reflect on all the deeds he done from the moment of his birth
as well as previous reincarnations; a monk like that could recall the field he had
ploughed in a reincarnation as a farmer, the javelin he had raised up in his reincarnation as a warrior, his horns when he had been a yak, the motion of his wings
when he had been a butterfly, and it's also possible for these reincarnations to be
enclosed in your life and your body, and then you will reflect upon the horns of the
young man you had been (they had grown instantly in Rome) or the claws of the
man you had turned into here. A man could reflect upon his deeds from morning
to night, and after that reflect upon his reflections of his deeds, and after that to
also reflect upon his reflections of his reflections of his deeds, and so on to infinity. It can be done in a sealed cave, and it can also be done in a hospital; McKenzie
himself, had more than enough time to reflect upon the events of that year, even
if mud brick walls hadn't prevented him from going out and no Russian pistol was
obtainable. What has a doctor to do with pistols? One mistaken diagnosis would
be enough and even that wouldn't be necessary, it would be enough not to return
love to one who had been expecting it.

Stories like that have a way of reaching Leh belatedly, and when they do reach
there it's impossible to know which of their details are factual and which are fabricated, the advantage of the latter being their appeal to the imagination. On more
than one night, he saw the Russian before his eyes, sitting in the cave on the stone
that had been used by his predecessor or pacing from wall to wall like a prisoner in
his cell or increasing his pushups daily, as if, were he to separate himself from the
ground one more time – he would be redeemed. What would the doctor have done
instead? There was no knowing. He certainly wouldn't have concentrated, like his
predecessors, on a grain of dust floating in the air; only someone who has reached
a supreme degree of concentration can follow one grain among all the others, like
someone who identifies his dear one among thousands of people.

If Poliakov hadn't called out to the god of his people at that hour, he also
certainly hadn't called out to that god's adversaries, and certainly not to the gods of
the vanished sea (that could have been interesting; the doctor's thoughts suddenly
wandered to *The Simla News* reporter Callahan who had begotten that idea: yes,
what would you say to that, Callahan, if in the darkness of the cave the masts of
their ships would suddenly have been revealed?). Perhaps – such a thought could
arise in the mind – he called out to the woman he had impregnated and left in
one of the Russian towns. No doubt the doctor would have called out to a woman.

What he had done there (from all the versions the doctor had heard, he chose
to believe this one), was a thing he himself never could have done: to taste the
taste of the metal and to feel its chill, to press the teeth against it, to push the
barrel farther and farther into the depths of the mouth and to know what the bullet
would do to the skull, to the brain. Not that he himself didn't deserve punishment
for his guilt, he certainly had enough of that: Mrs. Adams in England, a Kashmiri

man here and at least four people from Leh, who in a different hospital and under the care of a different doctor – a real doctor – would definitely have survived; and above all there was Dianne and her illnesses; after all, he hadn't cured her, not of the malaria and not of the hunger for love, for which he himself was the reason. Nonetheless, it never entered his mind to kill himself. What good would that do?

Could anyone be lonelier than a man in a cave on a long night that will only end with the flash of a shot? Without a living soul next to him, not even moving shadows, perhaps only the shadows of his past. Had McKenzie been a man of conscience like the Russian, perhaps his temples would have cracked open on their own accord even without the help of a bullet, but conscience was also invented by man and in itself is not an entity in the world, no anatomical atlas illustrates it. When does the hand lift the pistol – if that indeed did happen – to the mouth? When do the lips open to the barrel as to the lips of a sweetheart? When does the sweaty finger begin to slowly pull the trigger? A wave of nausea suddenly rose in the doctor with that thought, like when a finger or a wooden spatula is inserted deep into the mouth, since every touch of the soft part of the palate arouses the vomiting reflex. Perhaps Poliakov had inserted the barrel only as far as the bony part and then for a moment checked which of them was harder, his palate or the metal or the shadows of his past: Russian dukes and ministers and generals and added to them a shadow of the recent past, the smallest and blackest of them all.

The one who brought Poliakov's box to Leh months later, said that the shot that had been fired there still echoes between the walls of the cave, and another monk related the same years later, but it's reasonable to assume that if indeed he had fired a shot, no one heard it: at the time, all the people of the monastery were immersed in one of their ceremonies, and the sounds of the horns must have drowned out every sound other than the voice of the mountain delivering its words through them – dim, deep, lingering.

It would naturally have been better had he left a parting letter, and at least a note explaining why he did what he did (we demand a letter from the parting one, give us a letter! But would it indeed have been helpful?). And if he had shut himself up there to atone, as in time they said, perhaps it would have been enough for him to note those who he had killed, of whom so little was known about here; but he left nothing behind other than his sooty fingerprints on one of the walls of the cave or his footprints on the slope on his way down to the depths (such a version was also heard, according to which he had rolled down with his pony or had galloped it down there).

The Sunday after that, to an audience of no more than twenty pair of mostly European ears, Harper quoted in church a verse from the New Testament dealing with children and the punishment to whoever hurts them – "It were better for him that a millstone were hanged about his neck, and he cast into the sea, than that he should offend one of these little ones" – while there was no sea in the cave, one could sink to one's death in its darkness. "The bullet of a pistol," Harper said, "can be heavy no less than a millstone."

The women of Leh were more interested in the fact that Mrs. Harper had stopped speaking to her husband than who was to blame for the death of the little Russian bastard. She refused to accept his explanations and wore black as if in mourning for a family member, and all her birds, from swallows to majestic cranes, failed to raise a smile on her face. "Did you see that?" they whispered on leaving the church. "They didn't exchange a word!" What had first been kept a secret was soon known to all and caused some disagreement: there were those who supported Mrs. Harper in her small protest, and there were those who claimed she wasn't fulling her duty as the missionary's wife, because wives of public personalities had an obligation to the public and shouldn't harm their husbands. Ann, for instance, felt that way, finding an opportunity to praise herself on her total loyalty to Henry even if he was at times somewhat annoying.

Henry said: "There's no need to make an issue about one less Russian."

22

Explorers on their way to some discovery are prepared to endanger themselves: not only Italian archeologists who go out into the desert, but also doctors who carry out all sorts of medical experiments on their own bodies, though McKenzie, of course, couldn't be counted among them. One could appreciate those researchers for their courage and readiness to sacrifice themselves for the sake of medical science, and one could also scoff at their limitless craving for honor. Yes, they could be ridiculed even if there was some substance to their discoveries, unlike the case of Magnani (he had come from Rome for the very purpose of satisfying that craving for honor; and germs attacked his intestines).

By some sort of coincidence, three such explorers and researchers had gathered here, even if not in body: there was Magnani, whose journey to the desert had gone surprisingly well with his caravan fulfilling its mission in the best possible manner though he himself arrived in Leh in very poor condition – McKenzie found himself gloating, yes, why deny it – and besides him, the Japanese researcher Kiyoshi Shiga and the American, Daniel Salmon, were here at least in spirit, and if not in person, their faithful representatives were here; the intestinal bacteria named after them. Kiyoshi Shiga (is that a name for a researcher - Kiyoshi Shiga? And moreover, one who had been highly praised for his discovery) had won world fame before turning thirty for his in-depth research into feces, yes, that was where the bacteria he discovered multiplied; and the American, Salmon – who was even a veterinarian! – lent his name to the bacteria found in not much better a place, the intestines of a pig. World fame awaited them there, in human feces and the intestines of a pig, and when Magnani was brought to the hospital (like Poliakov before him also on a stretcher, though not an improvised one, he had taken care to equip himself with a real stretcher in Kashgar), it wasn't clear which of the acclaimed bacteria, the Shigella or the Salmonella, had decided to attack his intestine.

One thing was clear, he was defecating his guts out, and if he didn't recover soon, Harper would have to compose another eulogy approximately a year after the one he composed for the Russian ("This orphan is therefore now joined to our Lord in Heaven for eternity," he said and Duniasha listened without understanding, not even when he mentioned the Virgin Mary and said that in heaven the boy would finally have a mother who would love him with no bounds. She wept bitterly throughout the entire ceremony and walking at the head of the small procession she seemed totally unaware of those following her. When she saw the small grave that had been dug behind the church she tried to throw herself into it and only at the last moment was stopped, and one of the ladies said: "Now she remembers? Now?").

One couldn't tell exactly what had attacked Magnani; at first the symptoms of the bacteria are fairly similar: temperature, spasmodic stomach pains, watery diarrhea that becomes mucosal and bloody. That's how he was brought to the hospital, on a stretcher soiled by his excretions and reeking to the point where the coolies carrying him deserved to be pitied, besides for his heaviness (he still seemed fairly rotund, despite all the weight he had lost, and it was clear that in Rome with Kate he hadn't known hunger for one moment) and Rasul bossed them around exactly as he had done at the time Poliakov had been brought here. Like a sergeant major putting his soldiers through their paces with an "atten-shun" he ordered them to put the stretcher down from their shoulders and didn't let them alone until they scrubbed it and not a trace of the turmoil his intestines had wrought upon it was left. Every now and then he went out into the backyard to check on their work as if in preparation towards a parade for the commander of the division.

Each time McKenzie went out, and actually even when Rasul stood with him in the room, the wretchedness of his sick rival was enough for the thought to rise in his mind (and who in his place wouldn't have thought it?): where is all your acclaimed erudition now, Magnani, in your underpants? (They were soiled; his clothes didn't have to be removed to know that.) And where, Magnani, is your acclaimed prick, the one that fathered two children for Kate, has it also become dirty with shit? Yes, that's what he thought at the time, and show me a man who was never glad of his rival's misfortune; but all that didn't last very long.

Until the coolies finished scrubbing the stretcher, Rasul updated him about the successes of the caravan he had been in charge of: it took them only two weeks from Kashgar to Dandan Oilik! And they only were delayed in Khotan for one day! (In the months prior to that, all sorts of odd antiquities landed up in in its markets: mother-of-pearl and seashells and also what was possibly a plough and or an anchor, and it was that which attracted Magnani from Rome, the moment he heard about it.)

Magnani relied on him for everything, Rasul said, everything! More than once or twice he had told him: "Rasul, you more than my right hand, you my two hands together and also my head, what I do without Rasul!" Outside the coolies poured another bucket of water on the stretcher and squatted on their heels and began to scrub it with a rag.

"Everything he need," Rasul continued, and Magnani was laid before them, passed out from the heat and the loss of fluids, "Rasul he get for him, even things he not get for himself! Nothing Rasul not get. If Magnani go to Cartny and Perfovsky (McCartney was the British delegate in Kashgar, and Petrovsky the Russian delegate, and in exchange for their assisting the caravan they expected to enlarge the collections of antiquities they had amassed there), Rasul he go to market and ask, and who you think Doctor get more?"

"Rasul, for certain Rasul," McKenzie answered in his idiom, and Rasul peered at him for a moment to ensure that he wasn't mocking him.

It had been over a year since a white man had been hospitalized, and this time he knew he wouldn't be sorry should the cure fail: if the patient didn't awaken from his swoon, if he didn't regain the fluids he had lost, the fat, the scent of his aftershave which Kate added to his virtues ("Take a lesson from him, Ed," she said, "a man doesn't have to stink of cows"). The man who had robbed him of his wife lay before him, and from his entire all-embracing erudition and wit and daring – unlike him, he hadn't sent others to the desert in his place – all that remained was the stench.

"He say to me, Rasul, if not for you, we all get lost and don't find anything in the end, we not find one anchor there! He say to me, if not for you, Rasul, we die without water, and if not for you -" the continuation of the sentence slipped his mind and McKenzie came to his aid: "If not for you we die without food." Once again, Rasul peered at him, questioning his sincerity, but McKenzie had already ordered him to undress Magnani and to clean him up. He still didn't know for sure whether his feces were bloody or not, and that was the major difference between regular upset European intestines that aren't accustomed to eastern foods, and a real illness, from Salmonella poisoning to dysentery and typhus of the stomach.

Yes, it could have been perfect revenge, seeing his rival pouring his soul out of his rectum, not silently but with flatulence or a burst of diarrhea, but he made sure that they clean him and give him fluids and begin to carefully feed him white rice and rusks, until his stomach calmed down slightly and didn't purge everything that was put in it.

Whether Shigella or Salmonella had made Magnani ill couldn't be determined even on the day of his discharge, and the patient, from the moment he had slightly recuperated didn't hesitate to debate the issue with him. It transpired that before leaving on the expedition he had not only heard about Salmon but also about Kiyoshi Shiga and knew he had made his discovery at a young age and that Salmon had been so kind as to lend his name to the bacteria one of his assistants had discovered.

"I made sure to be updated while still in Europe," Magnani said from his bed in which he already sat up. "I prefer to know what I'm heading for. Don't you, Doctor?" Even then he still didn't recognize him: he had lost his glasses in the desert and the beard McKenzie had grown that year altered his appearance, and anyway from the start Magnani hadn't taken the trouble to etch his face into his memory.

McKenzie nodded, though wondered if indeed it was worth knowing in advance everything that is revealed in time.

Until Magnani's discharge from the hospital there had been a while when his recovery was far from a certainty, and for two whole days he looked just like the dying patient in the next ward, and seeing him then he thought – and without any sorrow – how he would dispatch a matter-of-fact letter to Italy briefly informing of his untimely death: it had been said of McKenzie that he drowned in the port of Brindisi, and what would be said of Magnani? That he drowned in his own excretions.

"Come va?" McKenzie asked him when he was brought to him on the stretcher, how are you, and he was sure Magnani wouldn't recognize him even if he recovered and had spectacles made, and not only because of his beard, but because of his status here: not a confused tourist and cuckolded husband, but a hospital director, one of the notable people of the place.

Magnani made no reply, he hadn't heard him at all.

According to the hour of the day, he made sure to say to him buon giorno or buon pomeriggio or buona sera or buona notte, despite that morning, noon, evening or night couldn't have been good from Magnani's point of view; and there was another sentence he could have said to him, had he practiced it beforehand, a longer sentence, with a few multisyllabic words: finalmente ci incontriamo, we meet at last, the way Magnani said to him and Kate each time they met by chance or not by chance in some museum or church, as if they were old acquaintances who only needed to be brought up to date about some detail from the past twenty-four hours, and not the whole lifetime they had led in different countries.

Although it seemed to him that the smidgen of Italian he had learned on the train had long flown from his head, he discovered that he remembered quite a few of the phrases he had memorized for the hotel receptionist in Rome: how he would ask for a camera libere, a vacant room, and hope the clerk wouldn't reply: "tutto occupato"; and how he would emphasize he meant letto matrimoniale, a double bed, and not letto singolo, a single bed; he also prepared himself for the moment they would enter their room and he would approach the window and declare in amazement: "che panorama stupendo!" But in the end the thrilling view was reduced to a Roman apartment block and an elderly woman who watered her plants every evening.

That damned summer he was so proud of the few sentences he had learned and the intonation he thought he had mastered, fool that he was, deaf and blind; and Magnani then told them how exciting it was to return to Rome after all the months he had spent in the East, and how he had decided to come as a tourist seeing the city for the first time, just like a charming British couple.

McKenzie then quickly paged through the English-Italian conversation manual; there was a sentence there that fitted this occasion, "Ho gradito molto la tua compagnia!" I've enjoyed your company very much, but Magnani patiently explained to him it was customary to say that at the end of a meeting and not at the start, while at least two enjoyable hours still awaited them here, and when they leave the museum he would be happy to invite them to a fine restaurant. Statues are very important, yes, but even Michelangelo ate in order to have the strength to carve marble. By the way, do they know how he used to sculpt at night?

"Mangiare," McKenzie said in order to display his knowledge. "Si, mangiare," Magnani replied and gave a short lecture on the advantages of the Italian for eating, a tuneful lingering word, as opposed to the English word that was as sharp as a knife: in Italy one enjoys one's food, taking time to savor it, while in England in one syllable everything is swallowed. What pleasure Kate found in his words and was even more delighted when he compared the Italian "amore" with its English parallel, also monosyllabic and in a hurry to finish.

Kate found pleasure in everything he said: in the continuation of the story about Michelangelo (he sculpted at night wearing a cap aided by a candle fixed to its peak with wax), in the stories about Caravaggio's fights or Leonardo's fading colors, and McKenzie even suggested that in following days she visit what interests her and he what interests him, nature; he still hadn't grasped what interested her most, more than all the museums and churches in Rome – a different man who would give her a different life.

Magnani lay helpless before him in the hospital, and he, the cuckolded husband, a British exile who would never return to his country, made sure his patient was taken care of, given food and drink and washed; he himself tended to him with his own hands, and not because the love of mankind had suddenly been awakened in him but because only Magnani could tell him about Kate: was she content or not? Had she changed in Italy the way he had changed here? And is she still as beautiful as she was, or had the years and the births taken their toll? Had something of her wildness remained, her vivacity, her whimsy, or had the years and the births and perhaps the foreign country toned her down? And did Magnani pleasure her on Roman nights more than he had succeeded in his time – yes, he wanted to ask that as well – and how the hell had he succeeded in persuading her to become a mother? (He heard about the two children born to them a few years ago.) It was hard to forget her fears in that matter: the swollen stomach, the thickening of the body, the physical and emotional enslavement involved in rearing a baby, the responsibility for a small helpless creature toward which she might perhaps not feel anything.

When he saw Magnani was recovering slightly, he found an excuse to ask him in the incidental manner of a doctor chatting to his patient: "E bambini?" He skipped the prior necessary question concerning the matter of marriage, and Magnani, not wondering at all, hastened to answer: "Due," and the two fingers he lifted seemed like a V for victory. He also hastened to proudly state the names of his children, Claudia is the eldest, and a real little mother to her brother, and during the months when Kate couldn't take care of her new baby – yes, there had been months like that – little Claudia looked after Nino; his wife had a few problems at the time, no, not physiological ones. It happens to many women, does the doctor have a wife?

It took a moment for McKenzie to reply, after swallowing his saliva, "No, I don't."

It happens fairly often, Magnani said. Women become struck by depression and not only after the first birth when they realize their youth has ended and how demanding motherhood is. What luck the women of the Magnani family stood by her, no baby could have received better care.

He chatted in eloquent English and McKenzie listened to every word. His wife, Magnani said, barely got out of bed at the time, she found no reason to open her eyes in the morning if the first thing she saw was her baby. When the first was born, they didn't yet understand exactly what was happening because there could have been other explanations, and besides, Claudia resembled Katie very much, and when she saw her for the first time, that's to say when she already agreed to see her, she was pleased to discover the resemblance. It was actually the second birth that was more complicated, and not because Nino wasn't lovable, but because he resembled himself, Magnani, a lot – and she didn't much like that. They went through tough times, but who doesn't, the doctor also must have.

By then he had recovered completely and could be discharged from the hospital, but McKenzie refrained from doing that because of things he wanted to hear from him. How had their conversation come to be about the children? Magnani held a notebook in his hand whose pages were filled with notes from Dandan Oilik, and here and there a hasty sketch could be seen of the site or one of the findings: an anchor or a seashell or the stump of a pillar, and while McKenzie pressed a stethoscope to his chest, the notebook opened on a page where one of the children in Italy had doodled a house with a tiled roof and a smiling sun above it. For a moment he thought of pretending innocence and asking if a house like that had been found in Dandan Oilik but decided to ask outright about his children.

The baby, Magnani said, is in fact what connected his Englishwoman to Italy. Had it not been for her, he wasn't at all sure Katie would have stayed with him. And because of that he had allowed it to happen that night if the doctor gets his meaning.

McKenzie looked at him: if Katie had tired of him and wanted to go back, it was perhaps that she missed her London friends who from a distance could be perceived as being able to offer her a different life; she certainly didn't miss him, her ex-husband. Either way, the thought of this Italian and Kate in one bed, perhaps an elegant four poster that had been passed from generation to generation of Magnanis, was too hard to bare, and there was only one way it could be subdued, by flooding the two of them in runny feces, from the foot of the bed to it headboard and from the surface of the mattress down to it depths, but he had already missed the opportunity.

Yes, he wanted guarantees, Magnani continued, and who in his place wouldn't? A man whose wife comes to him after doing such a thing to her husband; how could he not want guarantees?

"What did she do to her husband?" he asked in the most indifferent voice he could effect.

"She simply left him in Rome," Magnani replied, and still didn't identify him, not by his face nor his voice nor his pain.

"Simply?" McKenzie said.

"From her point of view, it was simple. The husband was certainly not happy about it."

McKenzie busied himself with the stethoscope: he meticulously examined its one side and then the other and polished them both with his sleeve.

"A woman coming to a man like that," Magnani continued, "how could he not have fears? Even if one could understand her a little because her husband left her alone for whole days, in their village as well as in Rome. He simply preferred nature; he was a veterinarian."

"It seems your bacteria was discovered by a veterinarian," McKenzie said without looking at him. "Don't make little of veterinarians."

"God forbid!" Magnani replied. "But even if you aren't mistaken in the diagnosis, the bacteria wasn't discovered by Salmon but by one of his assistants."

He then chatted a little about Kiyoshi Shiga, as if a moment ago they hadn't touched on his broken heart and the woman who had broken it. He said it was unlikely Magnani's intestines had been infected by that bacteria (the stool test was inconclusive), and they discussed Shiga's slow promotion after that amazing discovery in his youth. That's how it is, Magnani said, there are those who dig in the sands of the desert and arrive at distant eras, and there are those that dig in excrement or pig's intestines and stay there.

"Have you ever treated pigs, Doctor?" He was almost waiting to be asked that question by him, as if his true identity had already been revealed to him through the beard and through the quiver in his voice, but instead Magnani began to tell him about his first visit to India and how he had once stayed in the house of a farmer and the moment after evacuated his bowels in some kind of area fenced off by palm branches, he saw the snout of a pig poking in and eating what he had left behind him. "Do you see, Doctor," he said, "a person eats a pig that eats his excrement, so what in fact is he being served on a plate?"

Because of that story – he said – his wife refuses to visit India, despite that in Bombay and in Calcutta there are some truly splendid hotels, no less than the Adlon in Berlin, or the George V in Paris, or the Excelsior in Madrid. Yes, he's already taken her to all those places, he's fortunate that his forefathers were successful merchants. Nevertheless, he didn't try to persuade her to come with him to India because Katie is someone who knows very well what she wants, and someone who doesn't understand that in time, like her first husband, understands it when it's already too late.

Yes, it wasn't exactly a perfect marriage; that much seemed clear from the first moment he saw them (they first met standing opposite a Greek statue lacking upper limbs and amputated and castrated, perhaps also decapitated). It was immediately evident that her husband preferred to get away outdoors, and that his wife, on the other hand, wanted to stay. She circled each statue twice, not that anything remained in front, if the doctor gets his meaning; that's the first thing that breaks on statues. It seemed she was comparing each statue to her husband the comparison wasn't in his favor and the entire trip to Italy wouldn't change her mind.

"Did you meet in other places in Italy?" McKenzie asked politely.

"She didn't want to travel to other places in Italy with him," Magnani replied. "It seemed she couldn't stand him any longer."

McKenzie swallowed his saliva, and it burned his throat. "And you saw all that in the museum?" This time his question and his amazement were absolutely genuine.

Magnani nodded. Yes, it was not difficult to see that; and so it happened in the end Katie simply faced him with a fact. He had been waiting for her in the trattoria next to the museum when she suddenly got down from the carriage, and to his astonishment, with her suitcase as well, he simply couldn't believe his eyes: it's one thing to flirt with a woman, even a married one, and quite another when she suddenly comes to you with all her clothing! She hadn't shut the suitcase properly and when the coachman put it on the sidewalk, half the clothing spilled out. And what could one say then, "Welcome to Rome"?

"And what did you really say?" McKenzie asked politely.

He only helped her gather the clothing and didn't call a waiter to help because he wanted to think to himself quietly for a moment and first of all to understand, and when he asked her what had happened, she said, don't you see?

"What would you have done in my place?" he asked and with the candor two strangers on a train allow themselves, he told how he deliberated what to do with that Englishwoman who didn't seem to know how to separate fantasy from reality, between what was just a little harmless game and real life. Should he send her back to her husband? Say, listen sweetie, I think you've gone a bit overboard, perhaps that's really what he should have said. He could have sent her to some other hotel and tell her to rest there a while and afterward they'd think about what to do next, after all, one doesn't do things like this hastily.

"Definitely not hastily," McKenzie said and looked for something nearby to busy himself with.

"It's one thing," Magnani repeated, "to flirt with a tourist, even in the presence of her husband, and another thing completely to take her into your home with a suitcase!" And especially, he went on, when surrounded by the women of the Magnani family – they've inhabited an entire building for generations, and maybe

Katie thought he had some charming attic on the Via Veneto or opposite the Villa Borghese. That's why he put her up in the small apartment of one of his colleagues who was then on an excavation outside of Italy, and quite some time passed until he understood there was no going back from this act she had done. Days passed, God knows what she did all those hours alone in the apartment, until the date arrived for her and her husband to return to England, it came and went. And not that she was enjoying herself in that apartment, it didn't even have a good view but she said: I'd rather climb the walls here than go back to the village.

McKenzie began to clean his stethoscope afresh; it suddenly seemed very dirty.

"And what could one do then?" Magnani said. "A woman in a foreign country without anyone, and there was no denying he was a significant part of it." Yes, he then understood he was deeply involved; a man has to take responsibility in situations like that. In an opera it would be enough to sing an aria but in life actions are required. And so he brought her his family at the end of the month, they were all still living together at the time, his sisters were still unmarried and his mother was still alive.

He turned around on the hospital bed to puff up the pillow supporting his back; he seemed completely healthy and had asked to be discharged two days before then in order to organize a caravan to take his findings to Bombay and from there to Europe. McKenzie refused on the grounds of him needing more rest.

He reached out another pillow to him to also insert behind his back and waited for him to go on; he wanted to hear what he had to say to the very end and not leave any detail unclear, painful as it may be. It was better to be aware of everything, he thought, as if all those who say it's better to know than not to are right.

For her moving to him – Magnani squashed the pillow – he had to invent a little lie and said she was the wife of an English colleague who had died suddenly in Italy, and that he felt a moral obligation to help her. After a shock like that it's difficult to return home, she didn't have any family relatives there and everything would remind her of her husband's absence, whereas by staying here, the heat of the sun and the beauty of Rome and above all the warm-heartedness of the Italian people would all help her recover. Yes, it was a fairly lame explanation – wouldn't everything here remind her of the death of her husband? And what exactly had he died from and where was he buried and why didn't she ever go to visit the grave? Those were very good questions and not much time passed before his young sister started asking them. "Do you have sisters, Doctor?"

"Sisters?" McKenzie was surprised by the question.

"Brothers or sisters?"

"A brother," he replied and for a moment, and for the first time in years, he calculated in his head the age of his father's favorite, Bill ("Look at Bill," his father used to say, "Bill works, Bill knows how to work and loves to work, and you?").

The Magnanis – Magnani said – are a very close-knit family. His young sister winked at him, and the elder ones were glad to host an English tourist and danced attendance on her and swapped clothes with her, but it wasn't at all easy for her. At times he would return from the university and not know whether he would find her there, and also wasn't sure whether he would be sorry to find she had gone. It was complicated for her; Katie came to terms with the gap between fantasy and reality the hard way, when most people come to terms with it much earlier. Had it not been for his young sister, she might have got up one morning and gone to the British embassy and asked to be helped to go back, not to her husband, only to London.

"Naturally not to her husband," McKenzie said quietly.

But his sister – Magnani continued – had begun to introduce her to her friends and took her to all sorts of places in Rome he didn't even know existed, showed her how beautiful and interesting Rome was even without museums. To hell with museums, his sister said, we're here to live! By then he began to worry, he didn't like her running around at all hours and with all sorts of bohemian characters. But when she sensed his concern, she specifically carried on. That's how it is with women, no? The doctor must know what he's talking about.

McKenzie nodded.

And not long after, Magnani said, it already wasn't important how she had come to them, it was only important where all this was leading. By then, his sisters had already decided to make a match between them, what better solution was there for her widowhood and his bachelorhood? And anyway, his sisters said, her late husband would no doubt be happy seeing from heaven his wife in good hands.

McKenzie turned to the open window. No breeze entered through it, and it seemed that the air outside was standing still, though its movement could be clearly seen in the leaves of the apricot tree.

And had that husband really – he began to ask, and his voice cracked and right away he cleared his throat – died?

He then heard from Magnani about his drowning in the port of Brindisi and how the body had been identified. Owing to some identifying object he had forgotten in the hotel – the English-Italian conversation manual – a combination of circumstances made the mistaken identity possible; the desire of the local police inspector to close the case played a part, as did the desire of the British consul to be rid of the affair, after it transpired the missing person hadn't shown any signs of life in his own country.

"It was impossible to know for certain if it really was him or not," Magnani said, "but no one saw him anymore. And if it wasn't him, he had simply evaporated into thin air."

McKenzie looked through the window for a long time: an uprooted bush was rolling up the path, and on one of the curves it veered to the side and dust rose there. For a moment it vanished from his eyes, perhaps it bumped into a stone and was blocked by it and right away was again carried onward by the wind. It was the fitting moment to turn to Magnani and say to him: I did not evaporate into the air, here I am in front of you, but he had not had everything buried in the desert just to expose himself to him now.

"Did you not feel any guilt?" he asked without turning his head to Magnani.

"Guilt?"

Magnani was surprised: Katie had instigated it all, and after all he didn't have to lie to her husband! A love affair in the presence of the husband is a complicated matter, and one really does have to lie every step of the way, but when he's no longer around? And he certainly had had no part in his death, in his drowning or whatever it had been, only the alcohol he had drunk in some bar in the port had been guilty.

"The alcohol," McKenzie said after him very slowly and each syllable fell apart in his mouth as he tried to recall what he had drunk in that bar, and from all the drinks he had mixed he remembered only the Cinzano and how bitter the taste of vomit was afterward. "Was her husband a drinker?"

"He didn't look like one," Magnani replied, "but even someone who doesn't drink can go crazy one day and drink until he doesn't even remember his own name. Haven't you come across cases like that?"

He then turned to him from the window; had Magnani still been as ill as he was on the day he had been brought to the hospital, he would have stopped the treatment instantly, not given him medicine, not given him food and water, let him defecate his guts to death. But it had already been decided he would be discharged the following day.

He busied himself with the stethoscope again and thought of the moment this stethoscope would be placed close to the cool chest and hear no beat; how pleasant the silence would be to his ears.

"One doesn't drink like that from happiness," he said to his patient, and Magnani looked at him for a moment; for the first time it seemed some notion was awakening in him about their conversation and also about his conversation partner, or the man he was beginning to make out through the beard and the years.

On the hospital bed, he pulled the edge of the blanket up to his navel and farther up to his chest and then up to his neck, and to his chin. "It was she who came to me," he reminded him in a weak voice and seemed then as vulnerable as he had been when he had been carried on the stretcher, "not I to her," and it wasn't clear if his words were addressed to the doctor treating him, the director of the Moravian mission hospital in Leh, or to the veterinarian tourist he had met in Rome the previous decade, despite that that man – young and innocent – had long passed from this world.

23

"The honorable Mr. Callahan," he began to write and erased it and rewrote: "Dear Jim," and erased it again and wrote, "To the roving reporter of *The Simla News*, Mr. James Callahan," and was sorry Dianne wasn't here to write his letters for him, the way she had done up to their wedding and a few months after it, until little Charles was born. And this letter was actually connected with her more than all the letters she had written then: all sorts of orders for medicine and equipment or requests for budget increases.

"My dear Callahan," he chose for this opening, "I hope you still remember your visit to us a few years ago," but how could the roving reporter of *The Simla News* remember one unimportant visit, if since then he must have visited dozens or hundreds of places and met dozens and hundreds of people, and only in the eyes of the inhabitants of the European colony of Leh had that visit been special, because for the first time someone had thought their backwater of backwaters worthy of an article.

How Ann had danced attendance on him, hoping he would write not only about Leh and not only mention Henry in the article, but also her and her parlor that is no lesser than the parlors of Simla, and how the ladies of Leh also hoped they would be mentioned for their charm and grace; how they flattered him, really wooed him, despite that he was a fat, arrogant and fairly repulsive man. Even the tobacco in his pipe had a loathsome smell.

"Dear Sir," he wrote, "I don't know if you still remember your visit to us in Leh a few years ago, but the edition in which your article was printed has been kept in more than one home. A few pleasant evenings were passed by you, my dear sir, in our company and by us in your company. The commissioner's wife hosted you with all the required etiquette, perhaps you'll recall her" – after all, she hadn't stopped smiling at Callahan, solely that he'd mention her fondly – "and perhaps you were no less impressed with her husband. You must have noticed with what restraint he listened to your assessment in the matter of his promotion, a not especially encouraging assessment, it should be said, and in time one that was proven right" (but how nonsensical to think he'd remember that matter; after all, wherever he went his hosts must have tried to extract from him all sorts of pieces of gossip he had come across in the corridors of power).

"Perhaps, Sir, you will recall the woman who in time would become my wife,

Henry's secretary, Dianne Barnes, the quiet unassuming girl who suggested typing your article for you so that you could be free that last evening for more enjoyable matters. Perhaps engraved in your memory, dear reporter (Callahan, you son of a bitch, he wanted to write but didn't), is Henry's adjutant who amused you by imitating Lord Curzon's walk (it was clear Curzon was no favorite of yours) or the accent of the archeologist who for an entire summer rummaged through a pile of thousand-year-old garbage. 'Garbedge' he called it, and you burst out laughing and asked him to repeat that twice too" (that laugh made all his fat shake and also sprayed slivers of saliva in all directions, and the ladies, out of their great estimation for the reporter, abstained from wiping their cheeks lest he be insulted). "You almost choked with laughter, Sir, until Henry came and patted you on the back. He must have enjoyed that at the time, showing he still had strength in his hand, after the woeful future you foresaw for him.

"Perhaps you will also remember, Sir, our devoted missionary, Father Harper, whose views at the time of your visit with us had not yet become completely extreme, and at the start of the evening the two of you could still hold a pleasant theological discussion. You must remember that when he tired of the reasoning of your arguments, we both got up and went out to the veranda and chatted there. And it is precisely on that matter that I turn to you."

Damn it, Callahan, he said to himself, even if you don't remember anything of all that, you should know that you ruined my life then. No, he hastened to correct himself; it had already been ruined once in Italy, but because of you, Callahan, it was ruined again.

"'His Jesus,'" you said about Harper at the exact moment we went outside, 'is no more real than Buddha or Padmasambhava. With him, the shroud and the nails were preserved, and with them the teeth and the hair.' About that, of course, you were right: had all the teeth of Buddha been gathered from all the temples in which they were preserved, they could have gnawed an adult elephant to the bone. About all Harper's circuitous arguments, according to which it was out of the question that the Holy Scriptures are mistaken, you said that all that was required was some kind of innocent faith and a few appropriate artifacts with tales affixed to them. You listened to our missionary in discomfort when he spoke with tremendous fervor about the landscapes of the Holy Land that had been given to the Jews when they had still been worthy of it, landscapes that ever since his visit there, on his way from Africa to the East, he had not ceased yearning for. You heard him tell with delight how he had visited the valley in which Jesus had been crucified, and his empty grave in Jerusalem, and the desert in which he had to contend with the devil, and the lake in the Galilee where according to what was written, he had walked on the water.

"And so, Doctor,' you said to me on the veranda, 'all that Holy Land is an untended, backward, ugly place, with people that are untended, backward, ugly.

And as to that lake, there are a thousand more impressive lakes here and in Europe, and needless to say I did not see any footprints on the water there.'

"You again said that what was needed was all in all a good tale and asked whether I didn't sometimes tell tales to patients in order to give them a little hope – 'hope, Doctor,' you said, 'is the most important part of healing!' – and I replied that with the few Ladakhi words known to me it was difficult to tell tales, and anyway they listen to the witchdoctors more than they listen to me.

"I offered you more tea, and instead of thanking me you complained about the meager hospitality, and when I promised that we'd finish off a bottle together afterward, you warned me that quite a lot had already been put into your stomach. And indeed, quite a lot had been put in there (I heard, by the way, that you are no longer a roving reporter, that these past years you seat yourself comfortably in Simla and young reporters get sent in your place, and that your belly is developing nicely).

"Before we had even drunk one drop, without any show of manners you asked whether I was married. It would have been more reasonable had you asked me if I'd already found a new wife, because I had told you about Kate in Manali, but since you hadn't remembered, I answered that I live alone – I simply skipped my first wife as if she had never existed, and the second, Dianne Barnes, wasn't yet my wife.

"You said in that case no one will disturb us drinking and told me how your ex-wife one day said to you: 'Jim, it's either me or the bottle,' and that you simply poured yourself another glass. You quite enjoyed repeating that on the veranda, the 'Jim, it's either me or the bottle,' and it didn't seem as if you were joking. In Manali I heard other things about her from you, but just as you didn't remember anything of what I told you there, you also didn't remember what you told me. Our entire meeting there had been meaningless to you, and even now, when this letter reaches you, perhaps you'll ask yourself who the hell is this nuisance.

"This nuisance, Callahan, is the one whose life has been ruined again, owing to you.

"God only knows how we both landed up in the same places at the same time, the first time in Manali when I still didn't know what I would do in India, and the second time in Leh, when I had already been appointed director of the hospital. How surprised you were to find me here as one of the honorable members of the colony! It took you some time to recognize me, but there's no need to apologize; after you another old acquaintance of mine was here and up until the very last moment, I wasn't sure whether he recognized me or not, and it's in the matter of him that I turn to you. But let's not put the cart before the horse.

"'Your missionary,' you said to me on the veranda of the commissioner's house (you were surprised about being argued with, and moreover in such a remote place such as ours), 'has no doubts at all, everything written in the Bible is true as far as he's concerned.' It's his privilege to think that, you said, but with the same senseless confidence people say, 'They wrote about it in the paper,' or 'I read it in the paper,' or 'It was written in the paper that -' as if everything in the paper was true, and you of all know the measure of truth that appears there. 'And I'll let you in on a secret, Doctor,' you said, 'it's not only like that with *The Simla News*, but also with the *Calcutta News* and the *Bombay News*, and even the *Times of London*. Not long ago they published a new version of the Ten Commandments in it from some fake parchment, and immediately printed an apology afterward. And if in another thousand years something remains of all those newspapers, people might still think that the stone tablets were genuine, or that Curzon and Kitchener really did refute the rumors of the conflict between them.

"'Is there conflict between them?' I asked you, despite that we in Leh are not interested in the intrigues of the high-ranking, and you replied that those kinds of news items aren't printed in the paper other than as a means to conceal the very opposite, and that those two, Lord Curzon and General Kitchener, if it was up to them, would long ago have sent each other to hell or to England, but the newspaper readers believe everything. You asked whether I was a man of faith, and I again replied to you, exactly as I had in Manali, that ever since I had heard of Darwin, I found it difficult to believe in the Creation.

"'Welcome to the heretics club,' you said with a kind of patronizing pleasantness, and perhaps you said: the monkey's club, or both of them, I no longer remember. You said it was the right club to be in, even if it was a little hard to picture someone like you – you spoke of yourself with surprising humor – a not especially thin journalist, hopping from branch to branch on the treetops.

"'What could I have said to him?' you pretended innocence when we spoke again of Harper, but I heard you with my own ears say there are so many contradictions in the Holy Scriptures that no court in the world could succeed in determining what happened at the crucifixion and after it, and that sort of coverage is what one calls tendentious coverage, and similarly, despite the vast difference, Lord Curzon's coronation ceremony had been written about – yes, with all the differences that exist between a crown of thorns and a crown of gold. You also said that every ancient nail discovered could be said to have once been stuck into the cross, and that if an oar were to be found in the desert, it could be said with the greatest of ease there had once been a sea there.

"It was quite pleasant on the veranda, and you continued to speak of the tendency in people to believe every bit of nonsense as long as they benefit from it – Hernel gets world fame for the forgery he believed in, Harper gets the next world. You said that people who want to believe in something will find a thousand and one reasons to justify that belief, and not only in a God, in a person close to them as well. 'Would you like to hear bad things about a person close to you, Doctor?' you asked me, because you didn't remember anything of what I had told you in Manali (no one in Rome came to tell me bad things, I discovered them myself).

"But now, on this June evening, I am mainly thinking about what my son will hear about me in a short while. Yes, a son was born to me five years ago, to me and Dianne Barnes who I mentioned before and who is no longer with us. You roamed the length of India for your newspaper, and here in Leh a family was established and even lasted a few years: a father and a mother and a child, how simple. You should know that there had been a time when that little family seemed to me the most important thing in the world, the only thing worth fighting for, but yesterday morning, a few hours before the great heat began, I parted from my son. We parted, Callahan, and not for a month or two. I sent him to England and for many long years, so that he can live his life there peacefully. And in fact, only because of weighing these thoughts about Charles I still don't know whether this letter will be sent to you or not.

"'No one,' you said to me on the veranda, 'wants to hear bad things even if they are true, and everyone wants hear good things even if they are complete lies.' You weren't telling me anything new with that, a man is after all capable of lying to himself as well and not seeing what is clear to all, and who knows that better than I. You then began to tell again of Curzon's coronation ceremony, and how you described to the readers the city of magnificent tents that had been erected for King Edward, and the beautiful elephant howdahs, and the jewelry of the women and the Maharajahs, that if sold, no Indian would remain hungry from Leh to Trivandrum (that's what you said to me, but you didn't write a word about that in the paper).

"A ceremony like that – you said – had never been seen in India, and who wanted to hear about hungry or dying Indians or about the border troubles. A coronation is beautiful, death is ugly. And besides which, you said, because you were still absorbed by your argument with Harper, a lie one repeats many times turns to truth in the end. 'Take Curzon for example,' you said, 'today he's a demigod, but while studying at Balliol do you know what they said about him?' You said that had you quoted even a small bit about that in the paper they would have fired you quicker than that lecturer who fell in love with him at Balliol.

"You spoke about the great famine that erupted a year after the coronation (to our good fortune, it didn't reach the north), when people dug into the earth with fingernails just to find some edible root, and in the newspaper you only wrote how worried Curzon was and how he didn't sleep at night. 'Sometimes criticism is a luxury,' you calmly explained and reminded me that I too need to fill my belly, and that had it not been for that basic need I certainly wouldn't have agreed to manage a hospital without even having minimal training for it.

"I replied (inaccurately, as you will soon see) that I at least make an effort to fulfill my role as well as possible, while you give up your assigned role beforehand, and then it was your turn to become angry and you asked who decided that journalists have a responsibility to the truth or that there is one truth and not many. Between being a knight for truth and living – so you said – you choose the healthy option. You were not ashamed to tell me that all through the great famine you had a small Indian girl who at night you could believe loved you. 'That's how it is,' you said, 'there's truth and there's life, and everyone decides on which side to live.'

"In the small restaurant next to the bazaar they kept a bottle for me, and we both sat in the corner, and you didn't stop talking. By the time you had filled yourself with alcohol, not much remained of the outward appearance you presented to all at the commissioner's house, of the man who is accustomed to drinking with high-ranking government officials. You were already looking quite shabby, and I was no longer fond of you. Imagine, Callahan, how I feel about you now.

"With the same boastful tone you told how the series of your articles about Indian paganism had won great acclaim in its time, and that after it you didn't hesitate – nor did you hesitate to tell me about it – to write about the Sati ceremony in which you had apparently participated, and also about the ceremony of Kali worshippers at whose climax a six year old boy had been sacrificed, and all who read those articles could have thought that you, Callahan, with all your fat, managed to hide behind some tree with your typewriter. You didn't hesitate to describe what they did to the boy's tender neck, and his plaintive look that you won't forget to your last day. No one doubted your words, and when the remains of a bonfire were found in a forest, there wasn't a shadow of a doubt what it had been used for.

"'A piece of an oar in the desert,' you said again when the bottle was almost emptied, 'no more than that. That would be enough for people to believe that there once had been a sea there.' You couldn't have imagined what that saying would instigate, or perhaps you could imagine it and therefore said it."

No, he didn't say it maliciously; after all, Leh and its people didn't occupy his mind the day after his visit. And it would also not be correct to say that immediately after the visit the crazy plan was born. Had other people not joined, had it not been for Tenzin's deep grudge against white people and had a Russian refugee not arrived here by chance, it wouldn't have come into being. And who would have believed it would be so successful; successful to the point of failure – after all, in the end the fraud was intended to be exposed, and that is not what happened.

"My dear Callahan," he writes and moves his hand away from the ink stain left by the pen, "I know you are no longer a roving reporter, but I am offering you one last expedition, and what will be discovered on it will be read the world over. All the governmental gossip from the corridors of Simla and Calcutta you supply your readers with, reaches London at the very most, while what I am offering you now will reverberate throughout all the great capitals.

"So gird your thick loins and go on your way again (or send a few young reporters in your place). Start in Bombay: first check with the marine museum what happened to the anchors that had been placed in the courtyard up until five years ago, someone must remember them. And if that's not enough, you can also check where the paper for the scroll came from (reams of words were writ-

ten about that after the discovery, thousands more than had been written on it
itself). You didn't visit many monasteries when you came to us, and you can now
rectify that matter: inquire at that Kaspang monastery about a monk who blinded
himself, and if that also isn't enough, Callahan, go northwards to Khotan, you or
you reporters– yes, right on the border of the desert, a trip like that certainly won't
harm your figure. In the bazaar look for one Chinese merchant there, Lu-chi is his
name, and he too will tell you some interesting things about the seashells he sold
six months ago. And I'll let you in on more details known to me, Callahan, and
when you publish them in the newspaper there won't be anyone who can claim
it's a journalistic fabrication – the fabrication won't in the newspaper, it'll be in
the world of science: in all the acclaimed universities of Europe, in all the journals
that wrote about it, in the geographical society that awarded him a medal for the
discovery, and I am of course referring to the Italian, Carlo Magnani.

"I suggest another journey to you, should you need it, and this time go southward to Calcutta. Imprisoned in the jail there is the man who was my right hand
in the organization of all that, Tenzin is his name. You'll find him in the wing of
the very worst criminals, just because he dared to be insolent towards a few intelligence officers in Dehrandun. It's possible that due to his attitude towards the
British he'll refuse to talk with you and tell you about the caravan that he led to
Dandan Oilik in the autumn of 1905, but you can make do with a question about
the anchors and the paper. It would have been good had I been able to also send
you to the Russian who helped us, but to my regret he's no longer with us, and no,
not because of me, I did not fail to cure him. By the way, you are under no obligation to also mention me in the article. If you have a drop of conscience, perhaps
you won't want to leave this hospital without a director. When all is said and done,
a mediocre director like me is better than nothing.

"Tenzin could tell you how we wrote down a few passages to be used as a skeleton for the tale that has no doubt reached your ears, and God only knows how
it didn't sound familiar to you. You said that a piece of oar in the desert would
be enough, but we didn't make do with that. And we succeeded, Callahan, we
succeeded! – We succeeded so well that until today no one has yet exposed our
fraud, no one has come forward and said that the findings had been buried in the
sand no more than a year. All the last years I was hoping that at least you would
be suspicious, that you would remember our conversation on the veranda of the
commissioner's house, but it seems you were already completely immersed in your
new role. All sorts of dull articles about government seniors might give you more
power and influence now, but the response to the article concerning what was
discovered in the desert will exceed everything that you are familiar with.

"It won't be hard, Callahan, you'll only profit by it. You don't have to be highly
educated (neither of us studied at Balliol) to understand that all the news you are
busy with doesn't last even for a week, while this is about things that don't disappear from one day to the next. We will both disappear in the end, but these things

will continue to be spoken about even when not a grain remains of either of us. To be practical, Callahan," - he speeds the pen up and is careful it doesn't drip – "I suggest you begin with the anchors, because that was the most important finding at the first stage. The mother-of-pearl can still be somehow connected to some arid desert gorge, Kuruk Darya for example, but even if a few barges had sailed there from bank to bank, they certainly didn't have anchors like that. Admit it, Callahan – and hell, why shouldn't you show some generosity – it's a slightly more thrilling idea than your idea of an oar."

Around those anchors arose the pleasing assumption of an ancient rite whose ceremonies were conducted in the place where the ancient settlement of Dandan Oilik still remains standing; and afterward the assumption expanded to an entire theory at whose center is an ancient civilization from the first years of the Common Era, and when the excavations were completed, a decisive ruling was stated that it concerned an unknown religion whose believers lived at the oasis. At the time, McKenzie thought his plan had succeeded – in his foolishness that's what he was hoping for. During one excavation period (the autumn of 1906, and in the winter he married Dianne), the entire length of ditch that joined the anchor pits was uncovered, and the mother-of-pearl, the shells and the salt that was laid on its bed were found; to great surprise they had been preserved there in the formation in which they had been laid down, apparently many hundreds of years ago. And when the pieces of the fake scroll were uncovered in the ruins of the central building, the full picture had apparently been completed. Magnani was photographed as a victor, holding up the clay vase in which the torn pieces had been buried.

The letters that were discovered on the pieces of scroll didn't present special difficulties; there was no lack of people who knew Semitic languages at Rome University, and when the writing was deciphered, the preposterous tale that had been concocted in Leh rose from its contents, and at its center was the sea that had covered those regions until it disappeared; and from the writing also rose the foolish expectation of the locals that the sea will return with their gods that had punished them for their arrogance, an expectation that in the newspaper of Calcutta earned the headline "The Pining of the Ancestors," nice word, pining, the doctor thought when he read that, and wondered what would become of his own pining that had been no less disappointed.

As to Magnani, he didn't stop speaking about the ancestors and their pining in interviews he gave to daily newspapers and in articles he published in scientific journals containing numerous footnotes – those journals arrived in Leh after much delay, but when they did arrive the doctor derived much pleasure from them. Not for a moment did he conceive that no one in the world would challenge the authenticity of the findings.

Only in the matter of the inhabitants of the ancient settlement and the number of years it had been inhabited was opinion divided, but not in the matter of the religion that prevailed there, and shortly researchers of religions found all sorts of syncretic connections (that's how it was defined; and it took a while for the doctor to understand the matter in question) between the unfounded tale that had been concocted in Leh and the basic stories of other religions. He, an ex-veterinarian, read for example the words of some learned men (two Oxford doctors as well as one professor emeritus) who said that even if the wrath of the gods mentioned in the scroll derives from the biblical god's character and the written letters of his believers landed up here, the story of the sailing, contrary to that, has definite Hellenistic roots or Etruscan or even Phoenician (McKenzie had never heard of the Etruscans nor the Phoenicians), because the Hebrews, with all their well-known love for commerce, were not known to be seafarers. "Their noses endowed them with the sense of smell for business," wrote the emeritus, "but they never sailed ships." In articles containing many words and footnotes, the start of the Messianic expectation at the end of the first millennium before the Common Era was mentioned in connection to the pining of the ancestors – that always confused McKenzie: is the end of the millennium before the Common Era one thousand or is it zero? - An expectation whose expression is found is various cultures, including the late Buddhist Theravada or Hinayana or Mahayana schools.

"Messianic expectation," he chuckled when he read that. And after all, one doesn't fall in love with a messiah, doesn't kiss him, doesn't make love to him in Mr. Winterbottom's field, doesn't marry a messiah in a village church whose bell tower is in urgent need of renovation, doesn't travel with him on a second honeymoon with money loaned from farmers, doesn't allow him to meet a garrulous erudite Italian in a museum, doesn't allow him to flee to him one morning even before the chambermaid had made up the room (that fact sometimes seems of great significance: had Kate at least waited for the chambermaid to arrive, perhaps everything could have been avoided), doesn't allow him afterward to give birth to two children, a girl and a boy.

"Denounce him, Callahan," he writes in a firm decisive hand, "for the sake of the scientific world: that the man has been making a fool of the archeological community for over four years, and you and your journalist colleagues have substantially helped in that. And even if he's completely convinced the discovery is genuine, the truth still has to be exposed."

Expose him, he's thinking, and destroy him: that he not be mentioned in scientific journals other than in disgrace; that he not be invited anywhere to lecture on his findings, that the geographical society demand the return of the gold medal it awarded to him, that his position at the university be taken from him. Destroy him, Callahan – he thinks but does not write – destroy him in a way that the man will be ashamed to walk the streets of Rome, to sit in any piazza, to enter any church or museum. Do it, Callahan – he silently puts him under oath – so that he'll be ashamed to gaze directly at his wife and tell her what's in store for them: no more the salon for entertaining the high society of Rome, no more the holidays in the most expensive hotels in Europe, because from now on he'll be ashamed to entertain guests and ashamed to write his name in a guest book. And she too will be ashamed: it will then be ignominious to be Signora Magnani and think everyone pities her, or worse than that, are angry with her, because how is it possible that she didn't know anything about all that.

He had frequently pictured them in their home: an old building that belonged to the Magnanis for generations and on the walls of its rooms portraits of the family forefathers, and in all that large building, when the children go for a walk with the governess, there would be just those two, the husband and the wife and the calamity that had befallen them. "Have no mercy," he writes to Callahan, "expose the fraud and denounce him!"

A grudge will most surely be borne since she won't forgive Magnani for their downfall: is that what she left the village for, to be ostracized in the Italian capital? And he can see their children as well, the son and the daughter, who can't understand why Father and Mother are sad and angry, why all their classmates make up insulting names for them and won't speak to them; after all, they've done nothing bad to them. "No, Callahan, I have no mercy," he writes. No one had mercy for his son when he was separated from his whole world yesterday morning.

Be accurate, Doctor, he tells himself: no one did anything bad to him, the ladies of Leh suggested sending Charlie to England only out of concern for his future; it was impossible to be a hospital director and a doctor and a father and a mother all at once. They had been so shocked on their last visit and had been so right: it would be better for Charlie to grow up in England with that half aunt in peace and quiet, eat nourishing meals, wear clean and ironed clothing, have his hair combed three times a day, be bathed every evening. There he wouldn't chew his fingernails, pick his nose, gnaw on pencils. He would study at a proper school with children of his own age and perhaps even have a few of the teachers that McKenzie had had, and at break time he could play with well-mannered English children, washed and combed and ironed instead of Chondol's little savages.

As to well-mannered English children – his thought follows the train it began – when the rumor about what he had instigated here would arrived there in the end everything will be known), all the fine manners they had learned will be forgotten and they'll react exactly like any other child, that is to say, with cruelty. They'll mock Charlie, make up insulting nicknames for him, boycott him and the mothers will no doubt encourage them. "The apple never falls far from the tree," they will say as if it had been written in the stars that little Charles would also one day be revealed as a fraud. Little Charles would be miserable, ridiculed and isolated just like that boy, what was his name, whose father had been convicted for embezzlement at the time – they pushed him into the puddle, threw acorns at him, spread carpenter's glue on his seat, put cow dung into his satchel (McKenzie had been responsible for the last misdeed).

Forgive me, Charlie, he said to himself, forgive me in advance. There are periods in one's life one has to go through and be strengthened by them and continue onward fortified, that's the nature of the world. Isn't that so? Right away he questions himself; were you strengthened and did you continue onward?

Forgive me, Charlie, he says again; after all, children forget easily: one day you quarrel and fight and swear you'll never speak to each other, and the next day everything is forgotten. Is it, indeed? He questions himself again. The boy whose father had been convicted for embezzlement – Art Winslop, he remembered his full name now – was boycotted with his entire family and they all left the village in summer; their possessions were loaded onto a wagon toward the end of the night, his satchel as well, and before the light of dawn they were gone). But nevertheless, there is a difference, he answers himself, because he, McKenzie, hadn't misappropriated the school's funds, he had only made a fool of the man who stole his wife.

"Son of a fraud," he could hear the children calling Charlie, and Charlie crying terribly and running to that half aunt to protect him, and how could she, in her old age, protect anyone, and moreover from a band of revengeful children. On the day of his arrival everyone would ask where his parents were, and they would hear their parents talking about his father the veterinarian who had the nerve to send him to the village as if nothing had happened.

"If only he at least had a brother," Dianne once said.

Their door had been open and little Charles could be seen outside, leaning on the railing and watching the children playing in the grounds.

"Look how he's grown, Ed, imagine how happy he'd be if he had a brother."

He looked at Charlie's ruffled hair and was glad he hadn't let her cut it. "So why don't you let him play with the children in the grounds?"

"Because him I can still keep by my side," she replied. Perhaps she was directing her words at him, her husband, and perhaps she already foresaw the day Charlie would be sent to England, and worse, the day all his friends would ostracize him.

"It's not a complicated mission, Callahan," he continues writing. It seems to him now that under no circumstances should the discovery be stalled for even one moment longer – it's been delayed for over four years, and as with every waiting period the last moments are the longest of all. But he's not urging and pressing only Callahan like that, but himself as well: a sort of crazy notion rises in him suddenly that if everything is revealed in the coming month, perhaps it will be over before little Charles reaches England, and thus the scandal will pass him by. But that's not how things go: a sensation such as this doesn't disappear from one day to the next.

I would be happy, Charlie, if all this hadn't happened, he says to himself, but Daddy had a dispute with a bad man who took a precious thing from him, the most precious thing that he had ever had, the most precious and the most beloved, the woman who could have been your mother. That's not precise, of course; after all, a different child would have been born to him and Kate, but it seems that he's avenging Charlie and not himself.

"And if you hear all sorts of bad things about me," he writes to him (his small figure has already concealed all Callahan's fat, and the addressee of that page has been changed), "remember that Daddy loves you very much and will always love you, and that none of us would want to be judged only by his mistakes." That saying which isn't suitable for the ears of a child he then tries out on the page meant for the reporter of *The Simla News*, and already it's not clear whether the page will be sent and to whom it will be sent.

"Daddy's not a bad man nor a fraud, Charlie. There were a few people that I perhaps deceived a little, but not without reason! I want you to know I don't stop thinking about you every moment, day and night, and that I'll always remember even the smallest things associated with you. Not only how nicely you rode the horse when we parted, like a real cavalier, but how you used to gnaw on pencils at home like the hamster you once had, do you remember him? And how you'd pick your nose with a reflective gaze as if all the secrets of the Creation could be discovered there, yes, even that. And how you would pee in an arc on the wall of the cowshed and try to draw something – you have no idea, Charlie, how I'd like to see all that again. Mummy painted with watercolors, and you did it your own way.

"I've already prepared two large maps in my room to see where you are every day of the way, first from here to Bombay and then from Bombay to England, because there's nothing more important now than knowing where you are and how you are feeling and what you are seeing around you: after all, it's such a very long way! And if you are comfortable on the pony, and if you aren't sick of Rasul's chatter, and if you don't forget to wear a cap, and if the flies aren't bothering you. And if when they come you still remember how to catch them, with two hands, Charlie, not with one, and if you are careful not to lose your balance. Has your behind been chafed from all the riding? I know the distance you are crossing every day, and I can mark it on the map with one of the pencils you left at home and your teeth imprints can still be seen on it, as if I hadn't told you a thousand times it's not healthy. Now I'm actually glad that you didn't listen – when I put it in my mouth, I can still feel the teeth imprints on it, funny, isn't it? Funny and also sad, very sad." It's also sad that the letter he's writing now on hospital paper won't be sent.

"After you reach Bombay, I'll also mark the route of the ship on the map of the world, I'll pin a small paper boat to it like the ones Mummy used to make for you, and I'll move it every day and that way accompany you on the ocean as well. Don't be afraid, Charlie, should there be high waves and the ship rocks, always remember that I'm watching over you from here, just as Mummy is from heaven, and not only her, all the angels with her as well. There's lots of room for them in heaven, and even if you don't see them, always remember that they're there, behind the clouds. You can hear their wings at night even while asleep if everything around is quiet.

"When you reach England at the beginning of September, rain will most likely be falling, the kind you've never seen – thin rain that never stops which I hope you'll like. I don't have a map of England yet, but I'll get one from Henry and also hang it on the wall and chart your route onward" – he'll mark it from Dover to Begbroke with the same meticulousness with which the route to Lhasa had been marked on the map that Tenzin's father had prepared, but what a vast difference there is between those two courses. At the end of the first was a great victory, and at the end of the second? No, he thinks before completing the sentence, that's not quite right. There was also defeat in the first: Tenzin's father, the map draughtsman, had been defeated; and in the second, there's no knowing what will happen. Everything depends on you, Charlie, he tells him and himself, perhaps one day there will be a small victory there as well.

He had not yet hung up the map of the world because it still isn't the time for that, and one way and another he knows it well: most of it is taken up by seas and oceans, they've been there for millions of years and will remain for millions more and won't disappear with the ships that sail them. They contain an abundance of water and quite a number of sunken anchors that will never be recovered. Shells have stuck to them; seaweed is wrapped around them; the sand of the seabed has almost completely covered them. And no gods sail those oceans, not on steamships, not on sailboats, nor any boat whose anchor might resemble a plough in form. At the very most (this thought pops into his head now with steps being heard in the corridor), a god could be seen there clutching onto a piece of an oar with his remaining strength: he's been floating there for thousands of years, emaciated from hunger and the sun and white from the salt, and if he lifts an arm to wave at one of the ships passing in the distance, it's doubtful he would be seen.

For a moment, he can see little Charles standing on the deck of the ship as he himself stood on the way from Brindisi to Bombay; leaning on the stern railing and watching the trail of white foam drawn behind the ship and the gulls flying around it and the entire expanse of the sea, and suddenly he lifts his small hand and waves, there's no knowing at who: at one of the gulls shrieking above him, or at a school of fish passing below, or at the exhausted god who is still clutching the piece of an oar with his remaining strength, or at his father the fool, his father the fraud, the poor, miserable, lonely crook, who it seems will remain here in this sub-continent and in the backwater of backwaters, Leh, even if his crookery is not exposed soon.

"Doctor," a voice calls out from the entrance. As was expected, it was one of those bothersome people who come to complain about some made-up ache (the real ones are left for the Amchi to treat), and instead of his usual rebuke, he invites him in by the arm.

Part Four

1

London – New Delhi, 1994

Through the round window of the plane a clear sky could be seen, at the bottom of which was a layer of off-white clouds, and no birds were visible at that height, and certainly not the stork he had seen for some moments on his previous flight, carrying a small bundle in its beak containing a baby whose facial features were unbearably familiar (the stork was flying straight toward the propeller with it, despite the plane not having a propeller, and in an instant all its tiny organs were sprayed in all directions, so that they wouldn't grow into the ones inside him here, and a mass of feathers whirled around them).

"What would you like?" the air hostess asked, and Amnon hastened to reply, and afterward took only two sips of the orange juice and regretted not having ordered something else. He hadn't drunk alcohol for a long time, and on such a long flight it wouldn't matter if his head became hazy; he was more than enough lucid and sober. In the country he was flying to, India, alcohol would no doubt be hard to find and are the Hindus any different from the Muslims in that? His previous visit had been in Delhi, on a mission for his newspaper, and there wasn't a drink lacking in the hotel bar, from fine Chivas to the lowest liqueur. Not bad at all, and he and the Canadian imbibed a fair amount until the Canadian went up to his room with the two women who agreed to pleasure him on his last night in the city.

The last time he had become blind drunk wasn't hard to remember even on this plane – a British Airways Boeing to Delhi and not a Skyhawk straying from its destination – despite quite some time having passed since then. He was still a young man at the time, and one night after a quarrel with his father during the leave he received from special reserve duty in Lebanon he went to Jerusalem and entered a small pub in the Nachla'ot neighborhood and sat down next to two female students whose faces were swallowed in the darkness, and after the second glass he drank he told them that no alcohol could wipe out what he'd been through the past two weeks in Lebanon, not even ten glasses. The one closest to him, the prettier of the two, was put off by him, and the other perhaps felt sorry for him; he was hoping they wouldn't judge him on his deeds but rather try to understand why they had been done. She was a plump bespectacled girl with a tender voice and a warm laugh. Why she had laughed then was hard to remember; he himself certainly hadn't said anything funny, perhaps he heard her before then laughing with her friend about one of their lecturers. After a while, he was sitting with her in a taxi on the way to the student dormitories; hanging from the rearview mirror a tiny baby shoe swung next to a copper hand-shaped talisman whose shine had dimmed – he noticed them through the haze the alcohol had induced in him. "Just don't throw up on the upholstery," the driver said, "and you, Miss Student, haven't you got anyone better to run around with? You're about my daughter's age; I swear I'd give her a good slap if she went around with drunks in the middle of the night."

"He's not a drunk," she defended him, "he's been through some tough things in Lebanon and he drank a bit."

"Who hasn't been through tough things?" the driver said. "He's been in Lebanon like I've been in Vietnam," he added incredulously.

In her room in the dormitories (there were two beds, hers and her friend's, two cupboards, two posters, two nightlamps with macramé shades) he fell asleep instantly, and when he awoke his head was laid on her lap and she was looking at him and stroking his hair. Her glasses were placed on the cupboard, and without them she appeared more naked. "Sleep," she said, "sleep." And again he sunk into a devouring sleep in which the entire last two weeks whirled.

When he awoke again her pretty friend was in the room and firmly demanded she get rid of him: she'd waited long enough outside, she said, and in that time they could have done it three times, now she wants to go to bed.

"Then go to bed, he's fallen asleep anyway," he heard her tender voice above him and closed his eyes again.

"All we need is for him to throw up here," her friend said, "because if he does, I don't know what I'll do to you."

"He didn't throw up," the soft voice said above him. "He cried."

On his last trip in Delhi, the Canadian said to him that he must be something of a sham journalist if he didn't like taking risks (he had refused to celebrate with him and the two escort girls), and that whoever doesn't take risks doesn't live. About himself he said that even if one of these Indian girls or both of them infect him with something, it's probably his karma and he'll have enough time to think about that in the cave, maybe it will even be of some benefit in the present reincarnation: in that way maybe he'll finally forget the wife he divorced and what she had done with his very best friend in the bedroom of their home.

"Anyone ever done something like that to you?" he asked him, and Amnon shook his head. All his relationships with women until then had been temporary, he hadn't yet lived with any woman for more than a few months. "It hurts," the Canadian said, "her throwing away your life together like that, and maybe even enjoying it." His voice cracked, and the Indian girls, both in bare midriff sarees and high heels, led him gently towards the elevator.

Before the trip to England, Naomi had asked him if he wasn't throwing away all their years together, all they had been through before coming to this house and all they had established in it, she and him and Udi and Albie and Puma and the silly rabbits, as if it was nothing; hasn't he got a heart at all? He once had one and it had died, he thought. Perhaps he had killed it with his own hands and if he hadn't succeeded with the first try, he succeeded well enough with the second. His determination had paid off, he said to himself, pity he had been determined only about that one thing.

"Go," she said after a while and in a completely different tone, "go and don't ever come back. It runs in your family.

At the time Udi shut himself up in his room and turned up the volume of the computer game he was playing, one of those in which the participants receive ten lifetimes and can die a terrible death in each one from a round of bullets or a missile or an electric chainsaw, and instantly come to life armed with the weapon that killed them; and Albie was outside waiting to be let in, and this time he didn't respond to him. Puma was sleeping on one of the shelves between two groups of books and looked like a mound of grey fur that had been designed in the form of the space around it, and the rabbits, owing to the heat of the khamsin, went down the burrow they had dug beneath the cage in the yard.

"Go, go," Naomi said, "go so that I won't see you anymore; only why did I waste all these years on you?" A month later, in telephone calls to the English village, she still tried to persuade him to return, until becoming tired of his refusals.

"One thing you should know, not that you deserve it," she said to him on one of the last calls, as if these words would perhaps have an effect on him, "I really did want to live with you. Not now, now I don't know what I'd do to you if you were here next to me." Long before then, on one of their first meetings, she said that if he tried to leave her she'd nail his hand to the table with a fork. They were sitting in a restaurant on the beach, and under the grains of sand that covered the table, prints of their predecessors' glasses could be seen.

More than once he told her she'd be better off with someone else, someone well-established and responsible, but she completely ignored his words, his age, his past, his failures. "I'm impossible to live with," he would say, but she was sure she could change him. He thought they would tire of each other quickly and wouldn't succeed living together in his apartment or her house for even a month because he had never lived with a woman for a long time, and because she didn't need a lover but a husband and a father to her children, a man with a secure job and a belief in a common future for them, decade after decade to old age. She made no reply but just drew closer for him to see how his body disproves all his declarations.

In moments of anger, she scorned all his little affairs before he met her: a typist from the national or local newspaper who he didn't bother taking out of the building, perhaps also the graphic artist who made the notice about Puma who had gone missing, how pathetic: a man past forty, and that's all he knows about life with a woman, not to mention raising a family, someone whose concept of family life is so screwed up that God only knows why she's risking her and her children's futures like that. At other times, when she told him how she felt about him – especially when her body relaxed and her curves reclined on the bed, limp and accessible – he would recoil from her. He sensed a web being spun around him from which he couldn't be freed, preventing him from doing the things he had dreamed of in his youth, things whose purpose had become hazier from year to year; but nonetheless shouldn't be given up because their renunciation would mean a compromise with all that life has thus far dealt him, and such a compromise would be a living death.

He often had to appease her and did it the only way he knew how, and then her face which could be stern at times of anger, loosened and softened if she acceded to him, and she'd be pleased to discover that the body she so nurtured still reacted to the touch of a male exactly as it had done in her girlhood. When he held down her shoulders with his elbows, she said he was doing it like her cat Puma, that's to say before he was castrated, and if he doesn't wasn't to end up that way he should be careful not to make her angry.

The plane sank into an air pocket, and the hostess asked that seatbelts be fastened, and on one of the seats in the front a boy began to cry.

"Come sit by me," she would say to him when he first started talking about his desire to travel, "it's more interesting here. Besides which, you're no longer twenty." She would seat him with his back to her between her legs and place her chin on his shoulder from the back and hug him, or would say to him in her soft voice, before it became distorted from anger: "Life is here, not overseas," and show him its exact location so he would understand that the only journey in the world of real importance is the one made inside her.

The television opposite them made its sounds: newsflashes showed the alleys of the casbah in Nablus, a wide-eyed boy in a Gaza refugee camp, a coil of smoke rising from a bus that had been blown up with its passengers, the ruins of the house of the family whose son was one of the bombers of the bus. While they were occupied with their own affairs the country was seething. Perhaps throughout time couples had always behaved that way, even during the great wars, but their behavior was of little interest to historians who themselves might have behaved the same way under those circumstances. On the screen, impassioned reporters could be seen broadcasting from the scene of the incident; from the studio, grave commentators delivered gloomy forecasts; doctors with troubled gazes reported from crowded emergency rooms about the state of the injured and the number of the dead; ministers gave reactions from their bureaus with hollow sayings about acts of violence and it seemed that even the folds of the flags behind them with their blue stripes had been arranged by the makeup artist.

"This country's sick," he would then say and no longer tried to fight its sick-
nesses; the time for attempting to do that with his articles had passed; dealing with
matters of life and death, exposing and warning ("getting things moving," they
called it) even at the price of conflict with powerful high-ranking figures of the
establishment, whereas on the local paper to which he had been relegated he only
dealt with trifles and was content to be sucked into them.

"Across the sea, across the sea,"[30] his grandmother used to sing about worlds
beyond the horizon, and from her wrinkled hand, stained with age spots, the
shower head released cold, rusty, spine-tingling arrows at him,

"Will you know the way there, children?

Across the sea, across the sea,"

she continued to sing in a voice quivering like the folds of skin dangling from
her neck,

"Are the golden isles whose name I've forgotten."

The shower gurgled; at the drainage hole a black eye opened and winked; the
sewer monster lay in waiting for the dirt that would be washed from him and for
his toes, the way it eyed his backside seated on the toilet bowl to take a bite from
where it had already nibbled, and like its sister, the floor monster, who hour after
hour gnawed away at the filling between the floor tiles to shake them off and rise
up in the middle of the night and fill the entire room with her body. In the mornings of his childhood he would anxiously peek from his bed to check how she was
progressing: it seemed she would need another few nights before breaking out of
her imprisonment beneath the floor tiles; and in the meantime he was being called
to get up and dress himself, brush his teeth, come and eat, take his satchel, go to
school, study, grow up, enlist in the army, get a profession, marry, father children,
raise a family, establish himself: begin to die.

During the Jewish holidays when his grandmother came to stay in their apartment, much to his mother's discontent, he would hear her at night feeling her
way in worn out squashed slippers to the toilet at the end of the passage holding a pocket light that had been placed on the chair next to her bed so that she
wouldn't have to search for the light switch, and its weak beam would quiver here
and there like one of a pair of feelers, the other having been pulled out or severed.
She would enter the small bathroom with numerous rustlings of the folds of her
rolled up nightgown or the wrinkles of her body, and after what seemed like ages,
long after slamming the toilet seat with a bang that rocked the night and after
which came a silence as if all nocturnal noises had been expended, a thin trickle
could be heard, fragile, intermittent, a feeble strumming over the ripple of the
water in the bowl, a sound that caused Amnon the boy to block his ears yet still
move his pillow away slightly to nevertheless hear it. It was the loneliest sound in

---

30 From a children's poem by Chaim Nachman Bialik, a pioneer of modern Hebrew
    poetry.

the world, the sounds of drops that over eras turn into stalactites and stalagmites, or the sound of the thin drizzle of sand in an emptying hourglass, a sound after which his grandmother would be even smaller than she had been on entering, and he would become small with her instead of growing.

"You have to understand," his father said to him, "she had a hard life in Russia and here as well, that's why she's like that." What exactly his father meant, he wasn't sure, or maybe he did understand and only didn't know it was called bitterness. The smell of it wafted from the bathroom after she left there, and he would hold his breath or breathe through his mouth not to be infected with her bitterness, hoping the toilet bowl wouldn't overflow from the smell of the murky trickle that came out of her body. One night in his sleep he saw the golden isles she had sung about colored with urine and sinking like turds in a toilet bowl.

What was he still expecting from his family, Naomi said during their second year when her patience expired and the period of seeing something in Amnon he himself didn't see had come to an end; someone who with her help could be rescued from the life he had been living and in turn rescue her from her life. When she let herself be angry, there was no telling what her resentment would cause to her to say to him, whether about his grandfather who had destroyed the life of his grandmother in her youth, or his mother who had no doubt caused his father to grow horns years before leaving him, so it's no wonder what the result of all that was in the end – Amnon was the result – but it didn't take long for her resentment to wane. The eternal bachelorhood he swore never to breach didn't weaken her but instead encouraged her, she was like one of those men who are stimulated by the conquest itself rather than the object.

"You fool," she said to him, "is that what you think?" For a moment she was flattered by the male role attributed to her and right away protested; nonetheless, one meeting a week is too little. "Once a week," she would say before they moved in together, "is like a play, it's not life. Once a week I come to you looking my best and making a lot of effort; you've never seen me waking up all bloated in the morning or how I irritable I can be with everyone in the evening or how nasty I can sometimes be."

He saw nastiness in her only when she'd find all sort of faults in women who attracted his gaze even if just for a moment; she would disparage their hairstyles, clothes, shoes, their breasts for being too small or too big, their lips, their empty faces. When he made her angry, she'd threaten to find someone else: not a lover, lovers are ten a penny, just today two men tried to chat her up at a traffic light ("Are you selling?" one of them said to her, "No, not the car, your sweet smile), but a real partner, a friend for life, a man she could live with in one house and have another child with and also grow old with, watching their hair turning grey and white.

He doesn't even know the dishes she cooks, she said to him, and how can one cook anything at his place! Other than the toaster she bought on her own initiative, the kitchen hadn't changed from the years his grandmother lived in the apartment: the same gas stovetop with its oily black sticky covering, and the same yellowish cupboards, and the same washbasin tarnished like the bathtub in his grandmother's first apartment. There, beneath the rusty drizzling of the shower-head, she would shower him on evenings his parents left him with her, placing him on the scarred enamel bottom ("Everything here is full of microbes," she used to say, meaning the entire land of her exile) and clutch him like someone being taken to the gallows – he did not yet know what gallows were nor that his grandfather who wasn't even her husband by law, almost ended his life that way in Russia.

He didn't how old she was then, but each time he crossed the threshold of her apartment her elderliness crammed his nose with sour body odors and the stench of poor digestion and naphthalene, an elderliness that seemingly no youth had preceded, and certainly not childhood and infancy, nor islands across the sea. He hated being left there, but they left him anyway: his parents went to the cinema or to friends or some more reckless recreation. A decade and a half before his mother left home, perhaps they still loved each other, and one summer they even travelled to Italy and sent him postcards which they wrote together; they called him Nonny in them. On this plane to Delhi, a British Airways Boeing 747, he's already older than they were then, and he has no son to send a postcard to, not from England nor from the place to which he is travelling. Despite being fond of each other, Udi isn't his son. It wasn't something he didn't regret; on the contrary, it allowed him freedom.

"Across the sea, across the sea," his grandmother used to sing, and not because she loved that much to sing but for some other reason he wasn't sure of. There was no promise in the song, only bitterness, because not only are the landscapes of those isles concealed, even their names have been forgotten.

She herself hadn't forgotten anything, not names, places or people, not even in her last years; perhaps her entire life had been a constant reminder of the injustice done to her in her youth by the man who had left immediately after making her pregnant. The scoundrel hadn't travelled to lands across the sea (she frequently called him "that scoundrel, that scoundrel," and he still didn't know who she meant), but rather to the mountains of darkness – in her eyes that's how those distant mountains from where his possessions had been sent, appeared – but that first journey of his from the provincial town to the city was enough. "The eight ten train," she would say, as if only yesterday he had fled from her and the fetus growing inside her belly, his father.

Amnon well remembers the time he began to cut himself off from his father. It happened on the single leave he received in Lebanon; his father invited him to a fish restaurant where they argued and quarreled and he exploded at his father and got up and left; and travelled that night to Jerusalem and got drunk in a pub with two female students and went with one of them to her room, and when he opened his eyes in the morning he heard her friend saying: "Very nice, you didn't get to fuck him, but one day you can tell your grandchildren you slept with a killer." A blinding light burst through the window and he wondered if that's what now looks like.

The sign opposite him lit up again: *Fasten Your Seatbelts*.

They were still quite some hours from their destination when the pilot apologized over the loudspeaker for the turbulence they were experiencing. In his seat, whose belt was unfastened as before, he thought: so what if we fall? The thought didn't raise fear but rather indifference and even serenity; he hadn't forgotten the plane in the war diving towards the convoy and how bullets were sprayed from the road and how for those long twenty-four hours it seemed there was nothing worse than the command car having overturned.

Two months later he sailed from Haifa to Piraeus and slept on deck, and in his sleeping bag at night, he dreamed that this "Mano Cruises" ship was making its way between masses of dead fish until it was no longer possible to continue and was condemned to remain in its place like ships around which ice congeals. Not long after he returned from the Greek island, he began to publish testimonies from the war which he gathered from reserve duty friends and their friends and friends of their friends, and only one testimony was missing, his own. In letters to the editor there were readers who praised his articles, and a lot more who said that he was weakening the spirit of the fighters and thereby strengthening Israel's enemies.

Later the matter of the ambassador was raised – he wasn't the first to pay attention to the fact, but was among the first to examine the assassination in detail and even dare pose the question: how could the ambassador in Britain have been left unguarded, after all, the war had broken out on the pretext of his assassination? In a London suburb, through whose streets many dark-skinned women in orange robes walked, he interviewed the Scotland Yard man who had guarded him, someone who looked like a district policeman and not a bodyguard and heard how his little son had suffered ever since the incident, just because his father - Sergeant John O'Brien – hadn't managed to prevent the shooting. "Your father's a coward," children ridiculed his son, "what did they give him a real gun for? A water pistol would have been enough." The sergeant wore a faded T-shirt on which Bart Simpson's face was printed, and a few empty beer bottles stood on the table and among them an ashtray full of cigarette butts and an edition of Vogue magazine in which his son was drawing moustaches on the models. With all due respect to your war, said the sergeant, why should his Geoffrey have to suffer from it, why is he to blame that his father wasn't trained for things like that? "You're not to blame, Geoff, right?" There was no resemblance between his plump son and the boy Ali, but he saw it clearly then, when Geoffrey began to sob on his father's knees. Ali didn't even cry: he was thin and dark, not limp and spineless like Sergeant O'Brien's boy, and was practicality itself.

He had been to Delhi before – four or five years ago – and still remembered the dense air hitting one's face on leaving the airport, and the din of the road and the commotion of the taxi drivers fighting over each client ("Fixed price Mister! Fixed price!") and the murky moist yellowish sky, and the route to the hotel jammed with masses of old motor cars and auto rickshaws and bull-drawn wagons and stray cows and trucks on whose backs was written HORN OK PLEASE. The taxi driver slowed down opposite sacred ficus trees (with funding from the newspaper he allowed himself a taxi, though only a rickety Ambassador) and pointed out their sacredness in order to receive a tip, and in their shade stood puri and samosas and chai sellers who right away were all hidden by passersby and the tumult of cars that scorn all traffic rules, and throughout the whole of his first day, even after lying on his bed in the room – a comfortable bed in a sparkling clean hotel funded by the newspaper – he felt persecuted. When he walked in the streets it seemed to him he was the only white man among millions of dark Indians all wanting something from him, whether a donation, whether to buy their merchandise ("Only come to my shop, Mister") and whether to answer their series of questions ("Where you come from? Where you want to go? Big family at home?"), and more than anything he wanted to shut himself up in his hotel room and not leave until the day of his flight. It was ridiculous; he had been sent to write about the religious riots and only a week had been allotted for that, and more than the riots he was curious about the monks of Northern India, but the whole of the first day he stayed in his room contrary to all he had to do (the fancy hotel itself had been a mistake; the first rule of investigation is to house oneself in a place that facilitates contact with the locals).

Only in the evening he went out of his room and down to the hotel bar, and still hadn't noticed the Canadian, but saw his two night friends sitting there at the bar and chatting with the barman, and at the small tables sat a fifty year old or more Englishwoman tourist with a young Indian in a cream colored suit, a few businessmen drinking beer and three Americans in shirts with prints of palm trees, from looking at them one couldn't tell in in what city the bar was and in what country.

In the coming days he tried to obtain more information about the north, but even then didn't leave the confines of the hotel. For three months and three weeks and three days the monks took retreat in the caves there – the Canadian told him and signaled to the barman to refill his glass – or three years and three months and three weeks and so on, and in the end they were found completely blind and with hair down to their asses and fingernails a meter long. "What do you say about hair down to the ass, honey?" He asked the one on his right and reached out a hand to her after having despaired of the European women who showed little compassion regarding his future seclusion. A moment after he got up and went to the elevator, swaying between the two Indian girls, the barman lay down the washed glass and said if that man reaches the cave, he, Gupta, will hand out free drinks to everyone, including the Corbusier and the Remy-Martin; it wasn't the first time he had heard the Canadian tell about his wife who cheated on him and it certainly wouldn't be the last, it's good to have a story like that to tell each time he wants to get laid. In general, people tell what is nice, he said, to others or to themselves; take that Englishwoman – with a movement of the head he indicated to her table – she probably believes that Rajiv is tired of all the young silly girls and that only an older woman does it for him, but it's only her purse that interests him. "And what do you tell yourself?" he asked Amnon.

"I've got an article to finish before Sunday," Amnon replied.

"People don't come here when they've got an article to finish," the barman said, but soon volunteered to tell him a few things about Bhagalpur he had heard from his cousin who's lived there for a few years. That's always how good research starts: someone tells you something by chance, and that something leads to another something, and from that you reach something else: the son of the owner of the guest house promises to take you to a friend of a friend that maybe heard something, and if not him then one of his cousins must have heard; a driver volunteers to take you to some suburb whose existence you didn't know of before, and there, in a dilapidated old age home, a half-deaf old man tells you some secret no one knows but him; the waiter in the café still remembers the table where the man you are searching for sat as well as all his eating and drinking habits and even the amount of the tips he gave. "He always drank his whiskey with four cubes of ice" – that for example was something he heard in Buenos Aires about the spy Eli Cohen, and also heard about the night he sat there (Kamal Amin Ta'abet he was then called) and got drunk with a Syrian businessman who unknowingly helped him create a cover story. The waiter didn't remember all the details, but remembered the main things, because he had to support Ta'abet on his way out to the taxi and to seat him inside it, and before leaving Ta'abet said to him through the window: "Jorge, you're the only person that I can talk to without using masks, with all the others it's a carnival. Isn't the carnival in Rio?" Far from that quarter in Buenos Aires, where the fabricated past of a businessman had been created, in a housing project in Bat Yam his pregnant wife waited for him without knowing anything of his deeds; with little hesitation he had left her there with the baby growing in her belly, perhaps the way his grandfather had left his grandmother one wintry chilly dark morning, seemingly for a noble cause that would benefit many.

There was one's mission and there was one's life and defining a man only by his mission is labelling him superficially; that's what his father did when he glorified his grandfather, though he wasn't aware for certain what he had got up to, and even had he been aware, no man is just the deed for which he is known, it says more about the one who chooses to represent like that than it does of the man himself. His grandfather might have been a minor revolutionary figure devoid of any glamor like a man in the Mossad administration, he could also have landed up in the East not as an adventurer but rather like any lost soul destined to disappear there.

"About my cousin," the barman said, "I can easily arrange a meeting between him for you, he'll tell you all you want about Bhagalpur. Muslims, Hindis, temples, mosques, girls, whatever you say. You see Rajiv there? Everything he knows about girls is from my cousin."

"I wouldn't call that lady a girl," Amnon said of the Englishwoman.

"But that's the most important thing that he taught him, a woman, no matter what her age, still wants to be thought of as a girl. Even when she's completely wrinkled, she still wants a compliment about her perfume. Don't you have a wife?"

All his relationships up until then had been with temporary typists sent by a personnel company (the last had been fired from a big office and still kept the picture of the boss's son in her purse; "Aunty Shuli," the boy used to call her), or with waitresses at the end of their shift when they return home to a tiny apartment where a sweet potato is blossoming in a jar in the kitchen and on the windowsill there's an adopted street cat called Meir or Shmulik, just so the neighbors will think there's a man in the house.

Puma, Puma, for a while he thought about the cat he had left behind, and on the round windowpane of the airplane his grey fur could be seen for a moment, curled up or spread out in some hidden corner or stretching and responding to a petting from his whiskers to the tip of his tail; and he also saw Naomi combing him the way he liked it, and how the cat would accede not only to the brush that undid knots and frayed ends of his fur and make him soft and fluffy, but also to the broom: he would lie on his back and let her brush his belly with the hard bristles, and purrs of pleasure rose from the floor which would change into moans if Albie came to demand his share of stroking. Then the Persian cat would rise up with a furious face and when it left the room would straighten up its glorious tail in defiance, the complete opposite to the dogs silly tail that had no glory, only wagging foolishly or being folded between his legs when scolded.

"Your son," Naomi used to say every time he reprimanded him over something he had got up to or rewarded him over something else with petting, or she would say "our son", because he had avoided fathering a child with her and for over three years the dog served as a substitute. There were times when he said to her: "I still remember the night we made him," and she was amused by that, until becoming annoyed again over everything that had been passed down to him by his grandfather's genes, and because under no circumstance was he prepared to bind himself to her: not by marriage nor by a child; so there's nothing to bother him – she said already then – about getting up one day and leaving.

She can't depend on his heart, she said, not on his love for her nor the love for her son, she already well understands what happened to a child who once trusted him – wasn't his name Ali? That Ali ended up in the sea, and Amnon, the big hero, didn't lift a finger.

"Neither did his parents," he replied with a mean answer that contained a measure of truth.

The parents indeed couldn't be seen anywhere and only their clothes remained on the beach; it seems that they had drowned when a stray bomb fell in the sea, the one that raised a school of fish to the surface of the water, and that fact did not lessen his guilt by one iota.

But you are on the way to Delhi now, Delhi and not Sidon, he reminded himself, and this time go and visit the red mosque in the old city and see how they play cricket on the plot next to it and the children flying kites (all that was noted in the Lonely Planet guide), and go to Connaught Place and eat ice cream at Nirula's and be swallowed up in the tumult of Paharganj between the stalls and the cows and the auto-rickshaws and ignore everyone there who tries to sell you something. And before you travel to the North perhaps visit the Towers of Silence as well, if those towers are indeed in Delhi; but they aren't in Delhi, they're in Bombay – he remembers that now – and they don't allow foreigners to enter and see the bodies left there for the eagles. And in the place where his grandfather died, if there had been enough wood to burn, it's more likely he was cremated.

But his grandfather's death was determined by a doctor in a hospital in Leh, Dr. McKenzie Sr., and he most probably hadn't been cremated but buried in the small mission cemetery there; and it might still be possible to see the tombstone, if it hadn't been covered by weeds and the engraving hadn't become eroded, provided that a tombstone had been erected and had been engraved and his grandfather had been buried with his real name. Had he himself, Amnon, crossed such a long way, perhaps he too would also have rid himself of his name.

What would you prefer: a sky burial, a cremation, or maggots? Choose. But drowning suits you better, he answered himself, not eagles, not worms, not fire: losing your final strength in the water, not finding a foothold there, struggling to lift the head and the nose and the mouth above water and waving the hands in vain and choking and swallowing water and sinking in the water and seeing the fish floating above you, a ceiling of dead fish that cannot be passed through; exactly the way Ali drowned.

The air hostess continued pushing the drink trolley slowly along the aisle until she reached the stretched-out foot of a passenger who had fallen asleep in his seat, and she waited for the woman with him to wake him.

These are the places one can find further documentation, in addition to cemeteries: hospitals, court houses, police stations, post office branches, churches. Did you forget anything? And no less important is to stay in a central location, not in a large hotel but in a small hostel where it's possible to hear local gossip, and eat your meals in a working class restaurant on the main street, sit among the locals and listen to their conversation, and it's vital to find a contact – the owner of the hostel or the waiter or someone from the hospital who even if he hadn't been born at the time perhaps remembered something from the stories of his father may he rest in peace or his uncle may he rest in peace or whoever may he rest in peace, or however it's said in Hindi, and they would certainly be able to tell him about that Dr. McKenzie, the father of the man he met in England.

And even more important is to be at the scene itself – that's what Kramer who had educated him at the paper explained – because the scene speaks; sometimes very loudly, sometimes softly. The place itself is important, he explained to him during his first year at the paper, more important than all the police leaks; those are a ten a penny. You have to sit there, he said, stand there, check what can be seen from the window, what can be heard, what can be smelled, to lie down where the murdered man had sat or stood or fallen, "Just to try and understand what he heard in his last moments." That's how for many years the crime reporter had checked crime scenes in housing projects and villas and penthouses, he lay down in the silhouette drawn around the body by the forensic guys and tried to under- stand what had happened and if it was possible to shout from there so that some- one in the street or on the other side of the wall would hear ("The very worst," he said, "is to suddenly hear a tap dripping. Then you can be completely certain that there's no one around that can hear you").

He had learned only a little from photographs he had come across about what houses in Leh looked like, and what could be heard and seen inside them and even knew less about what Leh must have looked like at the beginning of the century when the caravans of the Silk Road still stopped there. He had read up quite a bit about that and had been especially helped by Hopkirk's books on Central Asia and the attempts of the British and Russians to raise their flags there. He read as he had used to do in his good days when he still conducted real research and didn't occupy himself with nonsense, but no concrete image was formed in his mind. "I'm not telling you not to read books," Kramer said to him during his first year at the paper. "Read books if it makes you feel good, but only when you touch shit with your hands, you touch life, d'you get me?"

He had touched quite a bit of that in his articles, but perhaps hadn't touched life itself other than in their rented house when living there with her and her small son; there he had been happy and angry and sad and joyful and exploded and was silent and hurled accusations and reconciled, and all the while, they coex- isted every moment, the happiness and the anger and the sadness and the joy and the fury and the reconciliation, and he upped and left it all, and without any mission for the greater good to justify it. Shortly, in a week at the most, he would be wandering around Leh, the so-called scene of the crime, standing and sitting and lying there as if in the silhouette of a body, the body of his grandfather.

What his grandfather had done and why had he gone as far as there, he had learned only a little from McKenzie Jr. His grandfather, a young man from a small Russian village, who Amnon, could now be the father of according to his age, had seemingly become mixed up in something before he crossed half a continent just to get as far away as possible from the place of his birth; and for some reason he had turned eastward and not westward, not to Odessa, not to Warsaw, not to Berlin like other young Jewish men, until his death which had been determined by a British doctor, a veterinarian by profession. And what had he himself, Amnon, done at that age? He had not yet taken risks and become mixed up in anything, there would be more than enough time for that. He had travelled in his van from Utrecht to France and from there through much of Europe and had seen land-scapes changing and his money going up in smoke at gas stations and garages. There was only risk in war, but a few years passed until one broke out, and in his stupidity he then thought an opportunity was presenting itself to him to complete the adventures of his trip; he was still a young man, and it seemed to him that no one becomes a man other than by experiencing war.

There had been a year of wandering before he became a journalist, and the trips he made then were far better than those funded by the newspaper, despite sleeping in a rickety van or in one-star hotels and being sustained mainly by canned food at bargain prices. Throughout his three years in the army, he had waited for this trip, and on one of his holidays in Eilat where he stayed in a youth hostel, a man, not that young, came into the room and unloaded a tattered suitcase tied with rope, and climbed heavily onto one of the vacant beds, covered himself up and began to snore. People came in, people went out, and the Belgian – it trans-pired he was Belgian – snored and slept. He had come to Eilat on a cargo ship, he said when he awoke, perhaps having travelled as a stowaway or perhaps as an aged deckhand, it was hard to understand. It seemed that there wasn't a place in the world the Belgian hadn't been to: he had seen crocodiles devouring a man in the Amazon, a tornado lifting houses into the air in New Orleans, a coconut dropping in Fiji and splitting open the head of someone rocking in a hammock, a stream of lava at night flowing down the slope of a volcano in Chile and setting it aflame for its entire length, and he had also seen the Pacific Ocean on a moonlit tropical night. On such a night, the Belgian said, people think they can walk on the water, and he even once saw someone trying to do just that on the sparkles of the moon. There were quite a number of sharks in the vicinity that smelt the man right away and rose to the surface of the water. Their fins could be seen cutting through the sea by the light of the moon, a giant orange moon not seen anywhere else in the world. It lasted for a second.

God, what a moon at the equator, he said. A kind of giant ball and if by chance you're sleeping in a cabin and not on deck – he still slept in the cabin then, his money had not completely run out yet – it fills the entire porthole like a giant eye. It's scary to wake up like that in the middle of the night, as if that moon is looking into your soul, and especially if you've got something to hide, as he did at the time;

a lot lay on his conscience, never mind now what it was, and the next morning he disappeared with his suitcase and two wallets disappeared from the room as well, but perhaps he wasn't connected to that.

Throughout the three years of Amnon's army service, he had dreamed of the day he could get out of the country, and not because he had become involved in something like his grandfather; at that time, he hadn't yet become involved in anything, not in unnecessary wars and not with a woman. Maggie is what he called the Hanomag van he bought in Holland for a bargain and was pleased about the Dutch plate on the back declaring its owner's nationality. On the way he was joined by two Dutch female hitchhikers who thought he was a fellow countryman, and at night he slept on the bed he installed in the back, and they slept in a tent that they erected next to the van with amazing skill. In a village where they stationed themselves a farmer led them to his barn and showed them a giant peacock spreading its magnificent tail above the hay soiled by cow dung, a sight more spectacular that all the landscapes they had seen; in Bavaria they bumped into a train barrier on a side road when he began to doze off at the wheel, and German policemen in long winter coats like in old war films asked to check their passports and charged him with a large fine equal to a week's budget; in Florence the three of them drank Chianti at every meal and the two giggling girls seemed as close as sisters and every night they zipped up the tent in his presence. For hundreds of kilometers, tiny panties of every conceivable color and pattern were hung out to dry on a washing line that extended across the van, but the ones who hung them rejected all his advances, and after a night when had drunk too much and saw their silhouettes in the tent and tried to join them, their ways parted. Ever since then he's travelled alone, and the sight of the grey road stretched out before him to the horizon and leading him farther onward from city to city and from country to country was no less stirring than the landscapes on either side of it.

From the seat in front of him someone said: "Will you stop that please and let me watch the movie?" The streets of San Francisco could be seen in the film being screened and three police cars were chasing a black Corvette on the upward and downward slopes without leaving it for a moment.

The sign informing them that it was now permitted to unfasten seatbelts was lit.

One evening, not far from Hamburg, he stopped at a gas station where giant trucks were filling up and heard their drivers talking about the prostitutes of Hamburg and the Sankt Pauli quarter and tossed a coin in order to decide whether he would do now what came into his mind or on his way back, and then tossed the coin again, but it gave the same result. Against his will, he boarded a ferry with the van and sailed and travelled onward and boarded another ferry and disembarked from it too and travelled onward farther and crossed Denmark in two days and Sweden in three, and only slowed down in Norway (perhaps his grandfather had decided his destination with the same ease and turned eastward). He stopped beside long narrow inlets whose shores were licked by silent tongues of sea with the clouds reflected in them, they looked like the postcards he bought and didn't send to anyone. He was alone in that vast expanse and didn't miss anyone and didn't want anyone else there but himself; there was freedom in the knowledge that no one in the world knew where he was, and that if the van rolled down into the water of one of the fjords no one would know. But the van didn't roll down, and on inclines it groaned and rattled and devoured oil and water, and the fear arose that all his money would be spent on it and not even one mark would remain for the prostitutes in the Sankt Pauli quarter.

On and on he travelled through the large green country open to the sea from all sides in the great serenity that surrounded him, unbroken other than by a momentary mooing of a cow or chiming of a church bell, only the state of the van bothered him. In the morning the windows were covered by the vapor of his breath and he had difficulty starting the vehicle; the chill seeped into his bones and didn't abate until noon. In a northern city, Trondheim or Tromso, beneath a deceptive sun devoid of any heat, he found a garage that agreed to attend to the van for an exorbitant sum, and around and above seagulls passed in low flight, their shrieks echoing between the buildings, and drunks held empty bottles by their necks and swayed towards some wall for support, and one called out to him: "What you doing here, go back to Holland."

It was also cold during the days, but on the open road where there were no potholes like the roads of his country and the few cars that travelled on it didn't honk their horns or try to overtake, he continued on his way farther north. At Esso and Shell stations at the edge of remote towns he filled up with petrol as well as oil and water that had been exhausted between fillings and travelled on and filled up again with more oil and more water and cursed and travelled on again: not on a dogsled but in this van that was guzzling his money. With an exerted rattling he also passed Lyngen and Hammerfest, until in the distance the sun could be seen slowly descending in the dome of the sky and slowing its movement and stopping above the surface of the sea. Farther on westward its waters were called the Greenland Sea, and farther on eastward the Barents Sea. The sun lingered in its place, orange and round, without descending to the horizon. He was looking at a northern sun and not a tropical moon, but nothing as yet lay on his conscience – it was completely open to all the coming years.

On his way back he stopped in Hamburg and asked a taxi driver about its notorious quarter and was directed there by his hand movements. Far from the masts and cranes of the port, in a place that looked like an underground parking lot, dozens and perhaps hundreds of women were standing between exposed concrete pillars, all of them half-naked, whether in very short minis and whether in tight short pants and black fishnet stockings and deep cleavages, and hordes of men wandered around them and checked them out, and when they tried to bargain with them they were answered with a scornful silence or a curse whose content could be imagined by its tone.

He remembers the hotel that rented rooms by the hour– yes, that's what he's actually remembering now, hotels that rented rooms by the hour, and not the hotels the newspaper funded for him years later – the creaking elevator and a dark corridor into which a door opened that resembled all the others, and inside, apart from the bed he saw an old wooden cupboard and a scratched nightstand on which stood a color photograph in a small carved frame, and the woman approached it and kissed the picture and turned it over carefully.

Afterward, in the reddish light, she bent over him and undid the zipper of his trousers and searched for his organ that had withdrawn and retreated from her fingers. In the end, she took it out and pulled it like a limp rubber band and began to instill life into it with businesslike fingers and she put the condom over it with the skill of a doctor putting surgical gloves over his fingers. Without any pleasantries, not even feigned, like someone filling out a questionnaire she asked him: "You like me?" and he replied: "Yes," and she asked: "Very much?" and he replied: "Yes, yes," and she asked: "Very-very much?" and he replied: "Yes, yes, yes," and after a few minutes she was already peeling the condom off him and holding it between two fingers like the tail of a dead mouse. She then threw it into the small garbage pail opened by a press of the pedal, and before it closed for a moment it was still possible to see its contents. When he got up and bent over the basin and vomited he heard her behind him softly saying "Scheisse," and he vomited more, and in the peeling mirror above the basin he saw her bending over the small nightstand and turning over the photograph toward her and looking at it for a long moment and bringing it to her lips and kissing it and turning it over again, and he then thought if he only knew what was in that small photograph, it would have all been worth it.

A few years later he also thought about his trips to London, Delhi, Buenos Aires, Kiev that way: if he only knew some detail that insisted on evading him, perhaps the picture in its entirety would change; there had to be some detail that would give things a greater meaning than the one that was clear, too obvious, despairing. In the Kiev Theater it was the prompter's box: if he only knew what the prompter had heard and seen on the gala evening when the chief Russian minister had been murdered – a Rimsky-Korsakov opera was being performed – perhaps his entire article would have changed and he wouldn't have gone downhill after that (he entered the prompter's box and sat there and checked what could be seen and heard from his seat. He even found a wrinkled note on the floor with a telephone number on it and he called it as if the voice at the other end of the line would help him understand what happened to Stolypin in the theater eight decades ago, but an angry voice answered him and the receiver was immediately slammed).

After that night in Hamburg he no longer went to prostitutes, not in port cities nor any other cities, nor did he make trips that lasted months, not in a van, not on a ferry, not on a train, but returned to his country and changed jobs, places of residence, women. More than once in his life he had behaved like a scheisse and even worse than that, and there hadn't been anyone to say it to him then, certainly not a giant moon glaring at him through a porthole; there was only the one who shouted it at him from the depths of his mind.

For an entire month he tried to sell the van next to the American Express branch in Paris, not far from the Opera; he would remember that small street often in years to come, even during his successful years at the paper, because it was there, during the long days waiting to be approached by some buyer, that the fate of his first trip was decided. He didn't yet know there would be more trips when hotels and taxis would be funded, even the meals with his interviewees, and certainly didn't yet know that one day there would be this trip on a British Airways Boeing 747 that would be funded by money he received from his grandmother's apartment.

Every morning the red headed guy who parked in front of him declared he had a feeling that today he would sell his Volkswagen, by noon at the very latest; he just had to get to Thailand as soon as possible because there's no sight in the world more lovely than the flowering of the opium fields in the wild region of the golden triangle. Not tulips, not orchids, he said, they're for the bourgeoisie. There's no red redder than the poppies there. He spoke of the meeting of the borders of Thailand and Laos and Burma, and at the sound of those names the small Parisian street faded and Paris suddenly seemed like a dull country town. Years would pass until he would travel to the East, and years would pass until he would discover the resemblance between the buildings of the Paris Opera and the Kiev Theater.

In that small street, images of opium fields in Thailand popped up, jungles of Chang Mai, private armies of drug dealers, helicopters that land in forest clearings in order to transport the opium harvest to secret laboratories in the north. But the red-headed guy was from Brooklyn, and what he said he might have read in some backpacker's tourist guide, and since then he's probably grown a paunch, become a father, perhaps specialized in the selling of used Chevrolets on a giant car lot and lying to the buyers there about the state of the chassis. For a while he found small consolation in that, thinking about people who done something he wouldn't have dared do, and picturing them years later when it all seemed pointless, rather than at the time of their actions. There were years when his consolations were those of a poor man seeing a rich man become impoverished while remaining in his own poverty. Amnon, Amnon, he would say to himself in the mirror, just look at the man you've become.

Later there had been other years, his successful years at the paper: he was sent all over with a generous expense account and returned with four-thousand word articles written in hotel rooms devoid of any character or personal traces, not even a forgotten coin in a drawer, and he knew that if they allotted him another

thousands words, he would have added, for example, those of the chubby policeman who had guarded Ambassador Argov ("Sometimes I think it would have been
better had shot me instead of him, in that way at least my son would have had a
hero for a father"); and in Buenos Aires he would have quoted the woman café
owner surrounded by photographs from her glamor days in movies; and in the
Kiev Theater, while doing his research, suddenly a flap of wings was heard above
him and a small sparrow was discovered. It had repeatedly crashed into the purple
folds of the curtain until becoming exhausted or wounded, and when it fell on to
the stage the daughter of the cleaning woman ran and picked it up and spoke to
it and a moment later burst into inconsolable sobbing; the sobbing couldn't be
quoted, but it was worth taking not of no less than the failure of keeping Stolypin
secure.

There were the major plots and there were the small goings on alongside where
life was also being lived. even if they never won headlines. There were people in
the center of things and others in the background, totally or partially silent, but
living and breathing no less, like that astronaut who waited in the spaceship while
his two colleagues walked on the surface of the moon, or like the man commanded
to carry the cross of Jesus to Golgotha who surely groaned beneath his burden;
what has he to do with the one who claims he's the son of God.

When still a young man, he often recalled the small street next to the American Express branch in Paris and how he had decided there to make use of his open
return ticket and not continue on to another continent. Those trips will be made by
others he thought then: a Belgian with a suitcase tied up with rope, sturdy ex-com-
mando men, red-headed headed men fond of opium. "Are we missing home?" The
counter clerk at the Paris El Al office asked. "We're tired," he answered in the same
plural form, and for quite some time it seemed to him his tiredness refused to
cease and was gradually becoming a part of him: the heaviness of the eyelids, the
eyelashes sticking together, the weakening will. There was a period when he drank
to point of intoxication, and in the apartments he rented he kept the empty wine
bottles as evidence of something unclear, perhaps the lack of satisfaction from his
life. Had it not been for a war and an article written in its wake perhaps he wouldn't
have been promoted at the paper, but the article opened the way for him – that's
what he thought at the time – owing to the penetrating questions it posed (the
editor used those words in the introduction), although the most penetrating question, the one he needed to direct to himself, he didn't ask.

The person sitting in front of him sneezed, causing the seat to shake and the small
table open at the back of it also shook. The glass of juice on it trembled as well and
he reached out his hand to hold onto it.

The supposition he raised in that article was not pleasant to anyone's ears, not
even the bitterest opponents of the Minister of Defense who certainly didn't lack

opponents. The connection between the Lebanon War and the assassination in London was well known; lesser known was the fact that the assassin was not at all a Fatah man, and the Minister of Defence had covered up that fact in order to wage a war that had been planned for months. Two senior journalists had already written about it, and the security arrangements that had been decided on for the ambassador had been briefly covered, but the explicit question hadn't been asked, how come only one Sergeant O'Brien had accompanied Argov to a dinner that was liable to be trouble (eighty-four ambassadors had been invited to the Dorchester Hotel, no less, and at the end of the meal, when everyone left for the adjacent hall, Argov went outside to the lurking assassin) – how come Israel hadn't seen to further security, whether from Scotland Yard or from its own security men? Amnon raised the question, although with a hint, it was clear enough, had it not been convenient for someone in Israel that an assassination attempt be made on the ambassador and in that way giving the Israel Defense Forces a pretext for starting a war? The other supposition, that it was a typical case of Israeli negligence wasn't out of the question, but from the supposition he raised, conspiracies and intrigues were described on which a strong journalistic story was built, both in the details he dug up in his research and in his interviews, though the most penetrating interview of all was the one he should have conducted with himself; after all, in no way was it possible to interview the boy Ali, not in London, not in Sidon, not on land, not at sea, nor any other place.

Afterward he had a few successful years, from which nothing remained: he was sent to Paris and to Brussels to investigate two assassinations of Mossad representatives in the year that preceded the war, and again it transpired how deficient Israeli security arrangements were abroad; he also investigated Begin's depression and total reclusion due to the war (it was far easier to deal with that than his own depression). He had contacts during those years, people revealed classified information to him, whether because they thought it was fitting it become public knowledge or whether they wanted to besmirch their enemies that way ("Let me tell you something about him," they would say). For example, that's how he heard one evening in an almost completely empty beach restaurant, how it had been revealed from the spy Eli Cohen's aptitude tests that he tended to put himself at unnecessary risk and therefore his enlistment had twice been refused, and in his article he wondered who had accepted him in the end and why he had been pushed to the limit. The editor left only a hint of criticism at Cohen's operators, but a quarter page picture of a fancy café in Buenos Aires was published where Cohen had established his cover story (the woman who owned the café was photographed next to the cake refrigerator), and the paragraph describing how in the end he was captured in Damascus appeared in prominent print: how his dispatches were picked up with Russian assistance and how the Syrians located his home and broke in while Cohen was still trying to screw the transmitter into the light socket (only at that moment, almost the very last, could he put himself in the spy's place: half-naked on a chair like someone changing a burned out light bulb, and suddenly the door bursts open opposite him). The article not only aroused public interest but also created Amnon an aura of someone who had dealings with senior intelligence officials, something he made no effort to deny. Those were good years from a professional point of view, and there had also been women, true, only for short periods, but after all he didn't want it any other way. The moment always came when they would turn their gaze, like in Hamburg, to a photograph in which he played no part, they gazed at it or brought it close to their lips; someone hidden from him was being kissed there, a child or an old lover, and that was the moment to leave.

His fall began after the article from Kiev when he compared the Israeli General Security Services to its Russian counterpart and its functioning at the time of Stolypin's assassination at the beginning of the twentieth century. Even close to the end of the century it wasn't clear how that assassination had been made possible: a converted Jew named Bogrov shot Stolypin, and no one yet knows if he did it as a revolutionary or at the behest of the Tsar's secret police (all that information he heard for the first time from his father who for his own reasons took an interest in the beginning of the twentieth century, and afterward he heard and read more at university during the single year he studied there).

Within a week Bogrov was sentenced and executed and left behind him many unsolved questions as to the ease that had made it possible for him to act, despite the secret police having foreknowledge of the assassination from his own mouth. Were the lightening trial and the hasty funeral intended to conceal their involvement in the act? Amnon asked for the funding of a trip to Russia, and he suggested to the editor an investigative article about the Nativ organization[31] that was helping Jews there and about whom all sorts of odd rumors had been spread, and after recurring pleadings the editor gave his approval. Russian oligarchs and covert operations in the Eastern Bloc, immigration visas that were utilized for laundering dubious monies – all that seemed like an excellent basis for a personal interest story in the Saturday supplement, though it wasn't clear who he could interview in Russia: all the Nativ workers had signed declarations of secrecy, no KGB pensioner was waiting for his telephone call, but it was possible that were he to stay in Moscow and Peterburg for a while and visit all the places Jews went to he would hear things he hadn't yet heard. In the end, two days were enough to understand that at the very most he would get to interview the rabbi of the community and perhaps some boy celebrating his Bar Mitzvah and who is an avid fan of the Israel's Maccabi basketball team; while Bogrov's story, though it had already been investigated and told more than once, was worthy of a double page article and more.

It was hard not to think of his grandfather. He and Bogrov had been active during the same period though he had been born to poor people and was a yeshiva student while Bogrov had been born to wealthy people and studied law, which is

---

31 A clandestine underground organization that assisted Jews to immigrate to Israel.

when he joined an anarchist cell and where his fate was decided (only in that did he perhaps resemble his grandfather). After some of his friends were arrested the rumor was spread that he was an agent provocateur, and though the suspicion was examined and he was found innocent, more than a few people continued to suspect him. The summer when the Tsar and his family and government paid a visit to Kiev, Bogrov spoke with the head of the Okhrana in Kiev and informed him that an assassination attempt on prime minister Stolypin had been planned and that he had been asked to shelter the assassins in his home, and as a loyal citizen he saw it his duty to report it to the authorities.

For some reason he received an invitation to the gala performance of the opera at the Kiev Theater in the presence of the Tsar and his entourage, and during the intermission he got up from his seat and walked to the first row and shot Stolypin twice. He was interrogated for eight days and refused the aid of a defense attorney, he also refused to appeal after he was sentenced. He was hung at four in the morning and buried without a tombstone.

Had Bogrov been a double agent and acted on mission of the revolutionaries? And if he had been a revolutionary, had he been sent on the assignment by their trust in him or the contrary, because he had to repent for an old guilt and purify his name? The head of the Okhrana claimed that like Judas Iscariot greed had motivated him, and years later a Russian historian would claim he had acted out of boredom: because he no longer found any meaning in his life he decided to put an end it to with an extravagant act. That historian, Avrech was his name (since it sounded like a Jewish name, Amnon remembered it from the time of his studies), proposed two scenarios: according to the first, the Okhrana planned to murder the prime minister who had fallen out of favor and had used Bogrov for that purpose; and according to the second, their chiefs had used him to stage an attempted murder that they intended to foil with much fanfare in order to win glory – and who the hell could compare a story like that to the stories of a community rabbi, the Nativ organization, and the enthusiasm of a thirteen year old boy for the shooting percentages of the Maccabi Tel Aviv basketball team?

After two days in Moscow he travelled to Kiev without updating anyone on the editorial board. He photographed the secret police headquarters and the theater building from every possible angle, photographed Stolypin's seat in the front row, the giant stage, the magnificent honorary box, the prompter's box, the purple folds of the curtain with the gold tassels, he even photographed the poor bird the cleaner's daughter tried to resuscitate with the breath from her mouth after it had probably entered through the open props storeroom and crashed into the curtain; perhaps a sparrow had also strayed inside on the night of Stolypin's murder, and a little girl had also wept bitterly over it the way no one would weep for the prime minister.

All the rumors he had gathered about the immigration organization and its clandestine activities were compressed into two paragraphs, as if from the start

they had been intended to lead to the deeds of one converted Jew from the beginning of the twentieth century, as if his readers also had a grandfather who had
lived there at the time, of whom it was unclear whether he had been a hero or a
nobody. "How did a Jewish assassin kill the Russian Prime Minister in 1911?" was
the headline, and written below it was the subheading: "And how did the Russian
secret police perhaps assist him?" The pretext he found for the matter was simple:
today the KGB and groups that descended from it are still harassing Russian Jews
who wish to leave their country, but there had been a time when they had perhaps
been assisted by one of them for their own needs on a mission that changed the
face of Russia. He was particularly fascinated by Bogrov, a lost young man who
ended up perpetrating the extreme offence of killing a prime minister and was
also fascinated by the way that deed had been made possible in a place that was
supposed to be under the strict supervision of three security organizations.

It was an excellent article, there was no doubt about it, and had it not been for
the long paragraph that he insisted on adding at the end it would certainly have
won only praise, but he, who a few years before had raised the question of the part
of the General Security Services in the assassination of the ambassador in Britain,
couldn't refrain from the question of whether an act such as Bogrov's, or a security failure such as Russian's, could also be possible in Israel; that's to say whether
someone who isn't favored by the security organizations could be murdered by an
assassin, even if by only turning a blind eye or by negligence in guarding him or
by the arrogant desire to catch the assassin in the act.

After mentioning how members of the Jewish settler's underground movement had been caught in the act just in time, he wrote: "Things like that have
happened, and who can promise they will not happen again?" And not only would
a member of a police bomb disposal unit be liable to be injured – the policeman
injured by an explosive device intended for one of the Arab city mayors – but also
his commanders and his commanders' commanders up to the head of the pyramid. He didn't hesitate to name names and the only thing he deliberated over was
whether there would be a celebratory reception at the president's residence or a
mass rally in the city square, whether it would be President Weizmann or Prime
Minister Rabin.

With that paragraph began his decline: angry letters were sent to the editor,
there were those who protested by telephone, and unlike other articles whose
success was measured by the number or people who responded to them, in this
instance scathing criticism had been levelled. Politicians from the left and the right
responded to his claims, reserve officers and teachers, people from kibbutzim and
people from the city, retired intelligence officials and even an opera singer, greatly
fond of Rimsky-Korsakov. A doctoral student of Professor Konfino, from whose
research much data had been quoted, claimed in the name of his colleagues and
generations of students, that his article as a whole, as well as the parts dealing with
Russia, was a perfect example of things being taken out of context, and it would be

fitting to save Professor Konfino, a dear man by all accounts, this aggravation (only Professor Harsgor, an expert on historical disputes, wrote that one should not reject out of hand the suppositions he had raised, and even backed them up with further evidence). The editor's viewpoint was also published and made it clear that the article did not in any way reflect the policy of the newspaper and expressed only the opinion of its author who is not on the editorial board.

There was also an odd telephone call late in the evening, and the caller, who it seemed presented himself only by the first letter of his private name (there was some disturbance on the line, and perhaps his name was Jay, and he took it as J), suggested in a measured voice that in future he should watch his words. "Libel is easy," his conversation partner said, "there's nothing easier, but I suggest, Poleg, that you don't continue in the direction you started out on. You're entering a mine-field, to put it mildly, and there's no knowing what can happen to someone who takes that step. Deal with Russia at the beginning of the century as much as you want, but leave all the rest, it's out of your jurisdiction, do you understand me?" At the end of the conversation, he was still wondered who it could have been: some-one real or an imposter, perhaps just one of his colleagues trying to prevent him from writing about that subject so that he himself could write about it. Not long after that, a month at the most, he realized that he had been banished from the weekly supplement to the regular newspaper, and it seemed that quite a few of his colleagues were gloating or just giving him sour-faced looks.

"Our supplement isn't intended to make people angry on the weekend," the editor said and no one protested, and in the corridor, as a sort of variation on that telephone call, Kramer said to him: "I warned you, my boy, someone who plays with fire shouldn't complain afterward that he's hot." During the following months he was sent to cover all sorts of dull events such as Knesset sittings and party committees, he was even sent to the Bar Mitzvah of one of the minister's sons to see who had been invited, and one day, when the editor informed him that bear-ing in mind the situation and on the basis of the few events that summer (Barkai liked to say and write "bearing in mind" and "on the basis of") he will stop receiv-ing a regular salary and will be employed only as a freelancer according to need, he understood that they were showing him the way out and he had no doubt as to the reason, though no evidence of it had been found; it was possible that he had simply crossed the line with the concoction he had brewed from the facts that he had gathered.

He seemed to have mentioned everyone possible in that article: the Russian agent provocateur Azef who had simultaneously served the secret police and the terrorists, informing here and assassinating ministers there; "the Lavon affair"[32] in Egypt and the incitement they tried to instigate there, the Nativ members and their subversive actions in Russia; the General Security Services whose men had

---

32 A failed Israeli covert operation carried out in Egypt in 1954 in which civilian targets were blown up in order to create instability.

definitely stirred up the settlers in order to spot the extremists among them as they had apparently done in the seventies to the infamous Dov organization,[33] but as with the Bogrov case there was no knowing how it would end. It's also possible that the series of articles that brought him renown starting with the Lebanon War simply lost their appeal when the voice of his own memories– the thundering of a war plane; the roar of the sea; the silence of the fish – overpowered his judgement.

"I can arrange a half-time position on some local paper in one of the outlying areas," Barkai said to him, "but with your record you probably wouldn't agree to it." He did agree to it. At the time it seemed no other newspaper would want his services, and not because they had all read his article in detail, but because alongside the doubts he had cast on the General Security Services he had, with sound mind, given the settlers an unnecessary boost by questioning the wisdom of controlling agent provocateurs among them and whether it would do more harm than good, and how could one depend (that's what he wrote) on someone who from the start had one foot here and the other there. In the journalist's pub no one came to sit next to him other than when all the other seats were taken, and even then they barely spoke to him; one of his neighbors in the building, a Labor Party man, asked him why he didn't move to the occupied territories, after all, they'd receive him with open arms after the moral support he's given them. One day on the way home, from a distance he saw black graffiti on the wall of his building and wondered if it hadn't been directed at him, until he crossed the road and it transpired it was about the neighbor's teenage daughter, one of whose disappointed suitors had described in brief her acts with half the school. At the end of that month, after too many evenings spent drinking alone, he decided to move far away from it all; the enlightened camp he saw himself an active part of seemed to him then like a rigid party silencing every opinion that slightly deviates from its consensus, and the whole of Tel Aviv appeared to him like a paddock where one herd bellows with one voice. Perhaps they really did talk about his desertion from their camp, and only said he had gone off the rails in Lebanon and it's getting worse from year to year, and he should treat it with professional help and not with the articles for the newspaper – if something traumatic had happened to him there it's very unfortunate, yes, but hundreds of thousands of readers shouldn't have to suffer with all kinds of distorted articles.

A battered truck was enough to move his furniture and possessions to the old house he rented. The loquat tree seen in the window promised fruit in the spring, the mulberry tree at the edge of the yard attracted buzzing bees and at its top was a hideout that children had made from boards, and at the back between two bitter orange trees, he could tie a hammock and sway in it with a bottle of wine and relax; that at least was what he hoped. It seemed to him then, with his moving to the local

---

33 A right-wing extremist organization founded to counter the vociferous left-wing groups on university campuses.

paper, it was better to deal with the sidelines of big events: not with prime ministers but with their drivers, not with the commander of the unit for the protection of personages, but with the son of the English policeman and the names his friends called him, not with a spy in Syria but with an Argentinian woman and her café and what she had told him about Cohen ("An actor can spot an actor"); with the Russian cleaning woman and her daughter ("Tanichka, Tanichka," her mother tried to pacify her, "God will make it fly in the sky again, just close your eyes for a moment and it will go back there," and during the moment her daughter shut her eyes she dropped the bird into the garbage pail).

He lived in that house for a year until the owner sold it to a contractor who planned to build a multi-levelled villa in place of it, and returned to Tel Aviv to his grandmother's apartment but continued to work at the local paper and didn't try to find work in Tel Aviv again. In the corridor on the floor of the editorial staff, he met a woman; perhaps he seemed to her someone ill-fated who had come to terms with his situation and that only she, Naomi, could succeed in putting him on his feet again, or perhaps he seemed as lonely as she was and like her wanted to change his life. In their last quarrels she asked him who he does he think he is that she would wait for him while he wanders the world. She's in her prime, she said, the best period of a woman's life. And true, she had never looked lovelier, that's what he thought when she was calm and carefree, and especially when her little son cuddled up with her and she would pamper him or their two animals who competed for her love; at times like that she was a mighty and beautiful woman, but he never made it known to her.

Never mind her – she said to Amnon – but he's already bonded with her son, Udi, and how can he suddenly get up and leave him as well? She had already thought many bad things about him, yes, even without the war stories, and each time she told herself: he's not like that anymore, he's changed. How mistaken she was. God, how could anyone be so mistaken.

2

Two days after the war broke out, he stood at the side of the freeway trying to hitch a ride, first with an outstretched finger and then with large waves of the entire arm. After some time a small Fiat stopped and at the sight of his uniform the driver said to him: "To the war? Good for you, really, good for you," and the whole way he told him about the wars in which he had participated, especially enjoying talking about the masses of army boots the Egyptians left behind them in the sands of the Sinai. "That's what the Arabs are like," he said, "in the end they lift their legs and run, and d'you think we didn't shoot at them? We also shot when they weren't running. Just give it to them real good this time, because ever since the Katyusha rockets my daughter's started to stammer. Before that she would talk normally and only afterward started to stammer. To do such a thing to a little girl; to be laughed at her whole life?"

Afterward an army truck stopped for him, and he got on at the back and it took a moment for him to adjust to the darkness and find himself a plastic crate to sit on, and from the rear end a soldier sitting on a pile of kitbags called out to him: "Have you come on reserve duty? In your place I would have hopped on to a plane and got out of here." That plane, the imaginary one, was the first of the planes, the one after it, the very next day, was completely real and not meant for passengers.

On the regiment base which was emptied of all its armored personnel carriers, he saw a few soldiers from headquarters wandering about aimlessly, as well as the female soldiers who had remained there; one of them who he remembered from a previous reserve duty said to him: "And good morning to you, now's the time to come?" He tried to recall her name but didn't succeed in doing so. A year before that he had seen her in the war room filling an entire page with red hearts, until the operations officer took notice and reprimanded her. His voice could now be heard on the two-way radio, stern and intense as he gave orders to send extra ammunition to them in Lebanon on one of the emergency trucks as well as equipment from the quartermaster store in a command car, and to dispatch a quartermaster with Amnon and the two drivers.

After the truck was loaded with crates of ammunition which were then covered with a tarpaulin, he saw himself as Yves Montand in the film *The Wages of Fear* (Montand was assigned to transport dynamite or some other explosives in a truck on a never-ending journey): he had never felt so acutely that he had taken his life into his own hands. He offered the red hearts artist, Tali was her name, to have a last cup of coffee with him before leaving. If God forbid something happens to him there, he said, she'd never forgive herself for not having drunk a cup of coffee with him.

In the evening, in the girl's living quarters, in a building totally scarred by shrapnel from previous wars, she also consented to other things, but under no circumstances would she allow him to see her naked. From the adjoining room they heard the female quartermaster store clerk with the ammunition truck driver: with endless patience she was trying to teach the driver one of the Psalms by heart; she promised him that if he learns those few lines, they'll protect him in the war. "Yea, though I walk through the valley of the shadow of death, I will fear no evil," the clerk said for the driver to repeat after her. For a while he tried to memorize the verses until he'd had enough and said: "Come on – leave those psalms alone."

Within a few moments their bed springs could be heard as well as the rhythmic beating of the bed against the wall and Tali contorted her face. "Should I also teach you something?" she asked. They were lying on the bottom bunk, and on the top, through the iron lattice (there was no mattress), Tali's kitbag could be seen with a white woolen squirrel attached to the lock, and when the light was turned off the kitbag looked like a small black cloud floating above them and the squirrel like an angel trying to grasp its rim.

"Teach me what?" he asked. It seemed the female clerk and the driver would be doing it forever and that they had the whole night before them. A convoy of trucks was travelling on the road to the north and as it passed the base, the room was lit up for a moment and right away returned to being swallowed in darkness.

Against the light beams of the trucks, she lifted the sheet up to her neck to cover her small breasts and as they drew away, she pressed close to Amnon again. A tremor passed through her shoulders, and as he tried to embrace her, he once again felt like the hero from some Hollywood movie, until sounds could be heard again from the other side of the wall. In a voice that wasn't his own, he promised that nothing would happen to him; it's just an operation that will last two days – that's what they had been told – and through the thin wall the driver's groans could be heard as well as the voice of the female clerk who had begun to moan beneath him. The driver's voice was animal-like and the clerk's was gentle as her moans followed one after the other.

"She always has to be heard," said Tali. Throughout the act she gave herself completely to him, outstretched beneath him reclining on the bed and completely silent, like someone sacrificing herself for a noble cause, provided that nothing should be seen in the light, the feeble light barely spread by a forty-watt bulb.

Later, when from the next room only faint snoring was heard, she pressed close to him again and asked – but he better not lie - if he had enjoyed it. He said yes, he had enjoyed it very much. Really? Is he telling the truth? Really? And does he – but he mustn't lie – like her just a bit? She has to know, she said, but he mustn't lie, there's nothing she hates more than being lied to because lying's worse than stealing.

Again, he said that he did. Her head lay on his chest, and a hollow false sound rose from there straight to her ear pressed to him, but she lifted her head and peered at him through the dark and said: "I believe you." In a moment she fell asleep like a little girl being told a bedtime story that has come to an end.

In the morning – a hot morning at the beginning of June that one would be better off not imaging how sweltering it will be by noon - they left in a command car and a truck on their way to the nearby border crossing. Next to the gate the two girls stood and waved to them, until they both disappeared from the dusty mirror. Before leaving, the ammunitions truck driver winked at him, a tough well-built guy whose shirtsleeves were rolled up to his biceps; he didn't wink just as someone with a shared secret, but as someone who had shared his bunk on the other side of the wall.

For some minutes the command car driver tried to draw him into a conversation about the war they were travelling to and also about last night ("That one's a nun, how come she agreed?"), but Amnon evaded answering. Something vague stirred inside him and afterward became quiet. The M-16 stood between his knees with the cartridge inserted and its touch was calming; each one of its bullets contained a death with the power to protect his own life, should he insist on holding on to it. And after they cross the border in a short while, they'll put a bullet in the barrel, maybe even travel with the safety catches open and shoot at anything that moves without thinking twice. The thought didn't instill a sense of cowardice in him, and he lifted the M-16 to his eye and looked though the sight. The black rifle that had been taken out of long storage, dripped oil from the bore of the barrel to the bolt, and he began to sponge the oil with a piece of flannel which he took out of the butt. Years before that's how he used to prepare for the commander's roll call when the greatest danger was to be confined to the base for the Sabbath.

"Looks to me like you're glad about all this," said the command car driver slightly adjusting the rear-view mirror from which an orange pacifier hung, and a string of wooden beads swung next to it. "You got bored with civilian life or something?"

In the back of the command car the quartermaster was sitting on a pile of equipment, trying to tune into some station on a large plastic transistor, a gift from the Committee for the Welfare of Soldiers. He turned the dial over and over and all sorts of rustling and crackling could be heard leading to some sound that in a moment will also disappoint.

"Come on, turn it off!" the driver shouted at him. "It's giving us a hole in the head, aren't you tired of it?"

"Soon you'll really get a hole in the head," the quartermaster answered and carried on turning the dial.

"Believe me, Weingarten," said the driver, "I once got ninety days for cocking a M-16 at someone, but in Lebanon who'll do anything about it?" He turned his head to Amnon. "Isn't that right, soldier?" He didn't know his name as yet.

From the movie *The Wages of Fear* a dilapidated truck popped up in his memory, it was transporting a large load of nitroglycerin (nitroglycerin and not dynamite), and Yves Montand and his partner popped up as well; they were travelling on the defective roads of Mexico – Mexico? Suddenly he was also unsure about that detail. He saw the movie years ago with a girl who was a youth movement leader with him, and in the darkness of the cinema when she softly said Montand was attractive he was hurt to the core.

"Come on," said the command car driver after a while, "aren't you gonna tell us even in Lebanon?"

"What do you care how Tali was, Shlomi," said the quartermaster from the back, "aren't you married? Anyway, she wouldn't do it with Yemenites." He had already given up on the radio set and was no longer turning the station dial but instead was spinning his identity chain around his finger, winding it up and unravelling it.

"I should have told her I was going off to the war," the command car driver said, "maybe she would have agreed." He changed gears again and some insect smashed on the windscreen leaving a greenish spray which the wiper spread further.

It was late in the morning, and they continued travelling, the command car in front and the ammunitions truck behind. It was a nice clear day and not too hot, and the surrounding vegetation hadn't yet withered and yellowed. It was green and dense, and the trees were lofty with extensive branching, and birds nested in their tops and flew around them, and the closer their vehicle drew to the border crossing the less they spoke.

Dark skinned soldiers from Fiji were guarding the crossing and let them pass with indifference. One sat reading some magazine while his companion endlessly bounced a football on his knee, not stopping as they passed him, and the third one came out of the entrance of their hut; one cheek was covered in shaving cream which seemed even whiter on his dark face.

"Slackers," the command car driver said, "what did they bring them here for?"

From there onward, Lebanon was spread out as far as the eye could see, but the scenery was unchanged: it was hilly and green, a few cows were grazing in the distance, most probably the same cows that previously had been seen as blurred blots. Their patches were black, and scales of crumbling mud could be seen on their sides; they must have been lying before then in some large puddle to cool their bodies.

"What do they care if there's a war or not?" the quartermaster said from the back.

Amnon turned to him. He was sitting on his pile of work clothes as if on a

throne, and he told him to load a bullet into the chamber right away and to hold
the rifle in a ready position and make sure the safety catch is closed; just don't
shoot some bullet into the ammunitions truck by accident – he warned him – if he
doesn't want to return home in pieces.

"Or shoot at me by accident," said the command car driver. He changed gears
again despite there being no need for it, and right away returned the gear stick to
its previous position.

"Why not? There's nothing you could do about it afterward."

Amnon rested the loaded rifle on his knee and directed its barrel outside.
More gnats smashed onto the front windscreen and in vain the driver tried to
erase their remains with the squeaky wiper whose rubber band was worn down.
Behind them the ammunitions truck travelled at a fixed distance. One of the
tarpaulin flaps that covered the crates of shells had come loose and was waving in
the wind, but it was better not to stop.

In the regimental war room no one had told them if they should beware
of dangers on the way: all the two-way radios were beeping, rustling and emitting brief words; a few lieutenants and a captain were watching the bespectacled
first sergeant sticking colored drawing pins onto a large map; two female soldiers
entered, holding two plastic trays singed by cigarette burns and asked how many
sugars each one wanted. A lanky major began to tell a story he had heard in the
division headquarters, but better the girls don't listen, and the captain said that
these girls could teach everyone here a thing or two. Only one thin second lieutenant insisted on talking about pockets of resistance; about some crazies who
refuse to understand they've already lost the war, and also about ten-year-old
children going around with RPG launchers, children whose mothers and fathers
didn't care at all if they died.

The command car driver again changed gears unnecessarily. "I've got a bad feeling," he said looking at the road ahead of them.

"Have you turned into a prophet, Shlomi?" said the quartermaster from the
back. The large transistor on his knees came to life with a long wailing sound and
the quartermaster silenced it with a blow.

"In our family we feel things," the driver answered and glanced in the rear-
view mirror from which the hanging pacifier was swinging to and fro with the
beads hanging on the other side.

"We know all about you," said the quartermaster, "aren't you guys in compe-
tition with Uri Geller?"

"Laugh all you want Weingarten, why not?" said the driver to the mirror.
"We'll see who laughs in the end." His hand reached out to the little pacifier and
stopped it, and then let go of it.

"If I die, so do you," replied the quartermaster.

On the right, from one of the treetops that passed them by, perhaps oaks, two greyish-black crows flew away, first letting out angry caws and then taking off; the branch on which they had been sitting swayed for a short while until becoming still.

They drove on for some time. The two-way radio was on and every now and then the deputy and the first in command could be heard talking to each other between all sorts of rustling and crackling. There was also a two-way radio in the ammunitions truck behind them, and once in a while Amnon checked to see how the driver was doing. As they were leaving the regiment base the driver answered him: "Great, over"; afterward he answered, "Everything's okay, over"; and after they passed the border and the Fijian soldiers and their hut, the driver was silent before answering: "At least I got laid last night."

Upright in his seat, the rifle lying next to him cocked and loaded, the command car driver turned the windshield wipers on again and tried to remove the remains of the gnats that had stuck to the pane but most of them remained in their places. Between the squeaking of the wiper he said: "I had a cousin who was killed in a road accident. Total loss. The day before he told everyone, I've got a bad feeling. They all said, what do you mean bad feeling, you becoming sensitive or something? Next morning first thing as he's leaving the neighborhood a gasoline tanker went into him from behind, flattened half the car."

"Must have been a Subaru," the quartermaster said from behind and reminded anyone who might have forgotten the thin sheet metal of Japanese cars, everything made in Japan or China from toys to cars is all the same junk.

"Even driving a Volvo, he would've been a goner," the driver answered, "do you know how many tons a gasoline tanker is? Things like that you just feel in your bones, even animals can feel what's gonna happen to them and stay away from people. Who doesn't know that?"

"What animals?" the quartermaster asked from behind, "The horse from your father's wagon?"

"The donkey that screws your mother," the driver replied becoming irritated. "Laugh, laugh, Weingarten, because in a little while you won't be able to laugh anymore."

The squeaking of the wiper on the front windshield could be heard again though it was of not much benefit. "I also had a cousin," Weingarten said from the back, sticking his head between the two backrests of the front seats, "one day he says to everyone, listen, I've a got a feeling this Saturday I'm going to win the big football pool prize. Just give me some money to fill in the columns and I'll split it with all of you afterward, for real, we'll all be millionaires. Everyone chipped in, the whole family, all his friends. And in the end, what?"

"Well?" said the driver.

"In the end a gasoline tanker went into him from behind. Turn off that dumb windscreen wiper."

The wipers were moving to and fro and the worn-out rubber bands weren't wiping anything. Commander codename Cyclamen called Commander Heron on the two-way radio; Deputy Commander Plane Tree called Commander Plane Tree; Commander Heron called Deputy Commander Heron, until his voice was disrupted and swallowed by all the crackling. Some of the voices could be heard very clearly, some were dim; none of them were paying heed to the rules for talking over the communications network.

"Is Heron the regiment or the brigade?" asked the driver, after the rustling had been substituted by crackling and then by silence.

"Heron's a bird," said the quartermaster from the back. "A waterbird, Shlomi. You can see them by the fish pools, haven't you ever seen a heron? I also heard that herons can feel when things are gonna happen them. I swear I saw something move in the bushes over there, didn't you see?" He stuck his hand between their shoulders and pointed ahead with a nail bitten finger.

"Go kid around with your buddies," the driver said to him.

But some vague movement had been seen in the bushes on the slope of the hill: a movement of branches, a shaking of leaves, a form changing its outline. Perhaps an animal passing through them, perhaps someone hiding in the shelter of the foliage with a cocked Kalashnikov in his hand or an RPG launcher: a terrorist bent down in ambush, a man in a spotted uniform with hatred burning in his eyes.

The driver began to slow down, and Amnon shouted at him: "Drive on, drive on, what are you stopping for?" while at the same time he opened the safety catch of his rifle and began to move the barrel over the bushes on the slope. "Shoot!" the quartermaster called out from behind. "Shoot, what are you waiting for, shoot before I do!" The barrel of his rifle was pushed between the tarpaulin panel of the command car and Amnon's shoulder, long and tracking nervously from right to left.

When the rounds were heard – one long and one short – it was unclear from which weapon they had been fired. In the prevailing silence afterward, a complete all-encompassing silence that swallowed the sound of the ammunitions truck behind as well, the bushes could be seen shaking and becoming disentangled, and in the blink of an eye, flickering like a flash, a small animal burst forth from there, perhaps a fox perhaps a jackal pup.

Afterward, without exchanging any words with each other, for a short while they travelled fast down the slope of the road between the bushes on both sides and didn't answer any of the calls coming from the two-way radio, not even the honking of the ammunitions truck, until the driver parted his lips that had dried and said: "If that's the way you're gonna shoot in the war, we're done for," and only then remembered to touch the string of wooden beads that swung beneath the rear view mirror next to the pacifier.

"It's all because of your feeling, Shlomi," said the quartermaster from behind. "Before that we were driving in peace, why did you have to open your mouth?"

Now that they were relieved (the truck driver asked over the two-way radio: "Deputy Spanner from deputy Screwdriver, do you all need glasses, over?") each one sat comfortably in his place: Amnon and the driver in their seats and the quartermaster at the back on the pile of his work clothes, their rifles on their knees with the safety catches open and with a bullet in the barrel; the length of the barrel was hot and the bore was sooty. The three of them were sweating and the quartermaster wiped his face with a piece of flannel.

"Those UN guys," he said after a moment.

"What UN guys?" asked the driver.

"How many UN guys did you see today?" Weingarten said. "The Fiji ones. They come all the way here to see a war, how crazy. What are they short of there? Over there there's nothing but coconuts and pineapples and naked girls, they can take it easy the whole day long on the beach."

When the shot was heard – the whole time Weingarten was sitting on a pile of work clothes and the rifle lying on his knees – at first they didn't know where it had come from or where it was aimed; for a moment longer it echoed on the sides of the way, and only when the ammunition truck began to zigzag from behind did they realize that it or the driver had been hit. It was an old Rio that had been taken out from the emergency truck shed and painted with a thick layer of khaki. The black front bumper with two headlights above it swerved to the right and left over and over and all the while the truck continued to draw close to them. It seemed that even if it wouldn't veer off the road, it would crash into them at an accelerated speed, it and all the ammunition it was carrying.

Amnon called out on the two-way radio and the driver didn't answer; and even when Weingarten and Shlomi shouted together, no answer came from the truck. It's speed accelerated, and suddenly it veered off to the side, raising dust, and somehow returned to the road, all of it swaying, and continued to move forward with the same franticness, until a black M16 burst from its window and began to shoot a long round at the side of the road and another round higher than the previous one, and another long round straight ahead above the canvas roofing of the command car, a round whose bullets ran on the asphalt in front of them.

By then the truck was very close to them and its front bumper and the back of the command car were separated by just two or three meters; its front left wheel could be heard clearly, perforated by a bullet or punctured when it veered off the road, and the drivers face could be seen clearly in the half circle that his wiper vacated in the dust of the windshield, with his features contorted as he anxiously tried to replace a cartridge while at the same time holding on to the steering wheel.

"Stop it!" Amnon shouted at him into the two-way radio, not saying the customary: "Hold fire." Unintentionally, he continued to press the button of the mouthpiece without letting go of it.

"Stop shooting!" the quartermaster shouted from the rear end of the command car, waving both his arms at the truck driver who was still busy with the cartridge he was trying to replace. "Stop it, it was me who fired," he shouted at him again, no longer sitting on the pile of work clothes but standing at the opening at the back of the command car and pointing to himself, "it was by accident, stop!"

When they eventually found a place to stop slowly so the ammunitions truck behind wouldn't crash into them, the truck stopped as well, veering slightly to the right due to the right wheel that had been shot; only a small amount of air was left in it. Over the two-way radio Deputy Cyclamen called again to Commander Cyclamen and Amnon turned their voices down. A few small, agitated birds were flying above the bushes on the right of the road, perhaps Lebanese sparrows, and another bird whistled unfamiliar sounds, and the three of them got down from the vehicle.

The truck driver also got down with his rifle. His face was constricted, and he said nothing. Instead of approaching them he grasped his rifle and shook the strap off from his shoulder and made certain the cartridge that he put in while driving was held firmly in its place. Afterward he rattled the rifle in his hand for a moment to gauge its weight with a full cartridge and placed it on the square wing of the front left wheel. Without uttering a word and without as much as glancing at them he approached the punctured wheel and examined it all around and afterward went to the tool box of the truck and took out the necessary tools, and in the silence broken only by the rustling of the two-way radio he began to change the wheel, a job that definitely required two people for a truck but he was very well built and sturdy.

One after another he loosened the screws of the wheel, and for each one he had to place his leg on the shaft of the spanner and jump on it. Afterward he lifted the wheel from the ground and removed it and in its place lifted the spare wheel up by himself and screwed in the nuts, and with every one he again had to get on to the spanner shaft and jump on it with all his weight until the nut was fastened. Only after finishing the job did he turn to them, who all the watched him from afar. That was what his face indicated: don't come even one step closer.

He then took the M16 from the wing of the wheel and hung it on his shoulder and approached Weingarten and stood opposite him, and without saying a word, in the encompassing silence when all the calls of the two-way radio had disappeared from their ears, he punched him in the face and Weingarten was flung backward and shouted and tottered and collapsed and sat covering his face with the palms of his hands.

On removing them the harm done by the punch was revealed: his left eye was shut, and an ugly cut could be seen above the eyebrow. He slowly turned a blurry gaze to the right and to the left, and then, with a kind of complete acceptance of his new situation, peered at them from the height of their knees.

Not moving from his place he inserted his hand into the pocket of the work clothes and took out a small roll of flannel, opened it and brought the flannel close to the cut above his eye and pressed it there, and when it was removed a moment later it could be seen soaked in blood. He looked at it for a moment and returned it to his eyebrow, and this time fastened the small roll with the base of his palm for some time and gave a sort of smile which didn't so much resemble a smile as the stretching of the lips to the sides and the baring of teeth and said: "Never mind, every dog has its day."

"Who you calling a dog?" the truck driver asked quietly.

"I was talking about myself," Weingarten answered. He removed the small roll again and examined the soaked blood stain and returned it to his eye.

"Are you kidding me?"

"No, why would I kid you, I shot a bullet at you by accident, you punched me. Now we're even." Weingarten opened and rolled the flannel so that the clean side faced outwards.

"Do you want us to really get even?"

Weingarten looked at the truck driver with his good eye.

"Because with all the bumps on the road," said the driver, "I might just shoot by accident, you never know."

When they returned to the vehicles the quartermaster forced his way to the far rear end of the command car and piled a few kitbags around himself, possibly putting them in order, possibly making a barricade for himself, and over the two-way radio Commander Cyclamen and Commander Heron and their deputies could again be heard: some action was taking place not far from them, and according to known code words it was impossible to decipher what it was. New voices were speaking, and all sorts of crackling rose above them and disrupted them and a Middle Eastern musical motif also crept on to the communication network and disappeared. For a while they travelled in silence through the foreign country into which their army was advancing far ahead of them, and on their right and on their left were green hills lapped by white clouds. The enemy was not yet seen around them, nor the cedars of Lebanon, nor cherry trees, and the silence which enveloped them – the silence of the hills and the clouds – ignored the noise of the two-way radio like a giant unperturbed by a gnat.

"Tell me, Amnon," the command car driver suddenly said, "haven't you really got anything better to do with your life than coming here like this?"

A few sparrows flew away from a bush at the side of the road and immediately disappeared, and a donkey hidden from sight brayed irritably, its affront directed at the sky itself.

"I myself have got better things to do," the driver continued. "Married for a year already, would you believe it? I'm not saying its paradise, it's only paradise in the movies. Sometimes me and Etti really have it out with each other, shouting like you wouldn't believe, but afterward? Like nothing happened, all's forgotten. Once when I'd really had it, I said to her, Etti, I can't stay here anymore. If you make me mad one more time, on my mother's life I'm out of here, the only thing you'll see is my back. Do you think that's what I did? One time, right after my birthday, I really had one foot out the door. I thought to myself, Shlomi, you're still young, what do you need all this for, a wife and children and all that, get out before it's really too late, and in the end what?

More sparrows flew away from the bushes at the side of the road.

"But I went back like a good little boy. All in all, I stayed out in the street for a few minutes and had a smoke, it was the middle of the night with no one outdoors other than me, there wasn't even a dog in the street, and when I finished the cigarette I did an about-turn and went back up. And do you think she was mad at me? Not at all, took me as I am, that's why I love her."

The quartermaster put back in place a kitbag that had fallen off the heap he had piled around himself and looked at the driver through the rear-view mirror; perhaps wondering whether to say something or remain silent.

"Commander Cyclamen from Screwdriver Cyclamen," an irritable voice suddenly said from the two-way radio.

"Commander hears you," came the reply. The commander's voice for some reason sounded boyish, perhaps his signal operator answered instead of him.

"Your location, over."

"On Bukito.[34] Your situation, over."

Before the answer was given the dreadful noise of a plane diving was clearly heard and they didn't know if it was thundering from the two-way radio or from the sky itself, until it suddenly burst forth over the curve of the hill, huge in size and shining in the sun like a whale breaking through the ocean. They didn't manage to identify it as it passed above them, as fast and as decisive as a thrust of a sword. Within a few seconds it disappeared in the east, and when it returned north of them, slightly higher and still huge in size, more so than is fitting for planes to be when they're in the sky, they heard its small cannons rattling a short round with no interval between each shell, but they didn't yet see the shells themselves: perhaps they had been aimed at a convoy over the hills, a convoy advancing or retreating, of their army or of their enemy's.

"Drive on," Amnon said when the driver's foot hesitated on the accelerator.

"Shouldn't I stop at the side?"

"Drive on, drive on!" he shouted at him, and the ammunition truck kept a fixed distance behind them, a distance which now seemed minimal and too dangerous, but when he called the driver on the two-way radio, no reply was heard; no doubt the driver's voice was also swallowed by the roar of the plane.

When the plane returned again, this time from a point north-easterly to them, between two curly rimmed clouds, its wings no longer glistened in the sun but it still wasn't possible to identify its type or the insignia of its army, not even when it began to dive in their direction and rattle its rapid cannons in the deafening din, a sharp continuous rattling like the needle of a sewing machine. This time the

---

34 Codename for the coastal highway to Beirut.

small shells could be seen unravelling the ground of the hill and advancing to the road and bouncing on it and unravelling the asphalt stitch by stitch in a straight line drawn toward them, but by then the command car had already swerved into a ditch at the side of the road and all at once the vehicle was at an incline. Amnon was thrown towards the driver and two large pieces of metal shrapnel were hurled at the chassis and were stopped by it and for a long moment the reverberations could be heard. For a while each one of them froze in the place where they had been flung, until Amnon's head slid towards the driver's stomach and from there to under the steering wheel, and from his new position the floor of the command car could be seen, the khaki paint completely eroded next to the pedals and a lump of chewing gum stuck to the accelerator, and close to Amnon's head was the driver's stomach, sweaty and panting rapidly.

Someone swore; perhaps Amnon and perhaps the driver and perhaps both of them together. There was a slight smell of gasoline in the air.

"Why did you have to go there?" Naomi asked him in the bedroom when he told her about it, and he had no answer, and now in this British Airways plane he still doesn't have one. At the time her little son was sleeping in the next room and the entire building was silent: the sound of the pipes, the slamming of doors, the coughing of old people, the squeaking of young people's beds. "Was your life that boring?" she continued, and he didn't reply.

"You'll never be bored with me," she promised him, and he felt the warmth of her soft body pressed close to him for its entire length and saw her eyes glowing in the dark and the extinguished fan and the clothes she had thrown on the floor. He didn't as yet know how particular she usually was about keeping them tidy; only when they moved in together were their habits revealed, the most peculiar of them too, and there was a time when they also took it as a sign of their closeness, since they were no longer embarrassed in front of each other. On the evening of his departure, she said to him: "One day you'll miss it all, but it'll be too late then."

The two-way radio came to life and spoke, perhaps to them perhaps to someone else, and when it fell silent the front wheel of the command car could be heard spinning in the air and sounding a metallic creak with each turn, and the silence between each creak gradually lengthened until the wheel stopped. Close to them a quiet and rhythmic dripping previously unheard began, perhaps water from the damaged radiator or gasoline.

Only afterward the quartermaster was heard from the back. He was struggling to disengage himself from the pile of equipment that had collapsed on top of him, and from time to time let out a faint groan. He didn't call out to them and they didn't call out to him; for that long moment of the plane diving, none of them spoke, as if had they spoken the pilot would be liable to hear them and this time be accurate in his strike. Afterward, Weingarten spat out bloody phlegm with one of his teeth in it.

When the plane returned once more, the driver of the ammunition truck could also already be heard, not by his voice but by the sound of his weapon. He got out of the truck and went down into the ditch at the side of the road and stood a distance of a few meters away from the command car with his M-16 and aimed it at the sky, towards the dot that was growing there, and he shot as if a rifle could hit a plane like in stories about downing helicopters with a round aimed at the base of the propeller. The cannons of the regiment's armored carriers were intended for firing at planes, but the regiment and its armored carriers were still very far off, and he had only an M-16 in his hand.

"Come, you son of a bitch, come," he shouted, "let me whip your ass."

It took a while before they understood what he was doing there, but the round lasted long and they couldn't shout anything; and even when the shooting stopped, they still waited a moment.

"Come and I'll fuck you up real good," the truck driver shouted again to the sky, "come, you shithead, come!" Well-built and sturdy as he was, he looked as small as a midget beneath the diving plane.

Amnon began to extricate himself from the bottom of the command car. One leg was asleep or wounded, it seemed as if ants were crawling in it, he glanced at his trousers but only a small tear in the right trouser could be seen.

"Stop shooting!" he shouted, and the command car driver shouted back. "Because of you, he'll dive down on us again!" And at the back, as the plane drew away and its sound dimmed, the quartermaster again let out a faint, crushed groan.

Another round was heard, as long as the previous one, and was then silenced.

"Come on, you asshole, come and get it, you bastard," the ammunitions truck driver shouted to the ends of the heavens and again pressed the trigger of his weapon for a long while until the cartridge was emptied of all its bullets, and the plane had already drawn away and its roar was silenced.

"Come, you son of a bitch, come," the truck driver shouted again and inserted a new cartridge into his weapon, "come and get it, come baby, come," and shot a long round again to the blue skies between the curly rimmed clouds, and afterward sprayed his bullets on the bushes of the slope on the other side of the road in a circular motion whose starting point was above the ammunitions truck and its continuation the slope and its end just beyond the tip of the command car.

"Come out, you bastards," the truck driver shouted, "come out and I'll stuff your asses!" and between each sentence he shot a short round whose purpose, for a moment, seemed to be to pace his cursing and not to spray the thicket of bushes. "Come and get it from Motti," he shouted, "Motti will show you who's in charge here."

When that cartridge too was emptied and he opened the pouch to take out an new one – and all the while the plane could not be heard, not even in the distance

– they went out toward him: first Amnon who climbed from the bottom of the command car back to the inclined seat and from there put his legs outside and placed them carefully down on the ground, and after him the driver did the same and began to draw close to the truck driver with a careful and moderate step; he was formidable even without his weapon. "What's got into you?" he called out to him, but the truck driver didn't answer. He was still trying to take out a new cartridge from the pouch.

"Buddy, what's got into you?" said the command car driver coming nearer. "The plane's already gone, the pilot's on his way home," but the truck driver didn't answer.

"Motti, my buddy," the command car driver called out to him again.

Before the truck driver could extricate the cartridge with a wrest stronger than the previous ones, the two of them overpowered him: Amnon seized his weapon, and the command car driver enfolded his arms firmly around him and held him for a while until he acceded. When he was completely calm and all his muscles were limp, a shiver passed through him from his broad shoulders to the palms of his large hands, and his crying burst out in rising and shattering sobs like the that of a child, and the command car driver said, without loosening his grip: "Enough Motti, enough," like a mother calming her son.

Behind them, from the rear end of the command car where all the loaded equipment had overturned and was strewn here and there, the quartermaster rose slowly and began to put his feet on the ground, and afterward stood in front of the rear door: hunched and dusty, his mouth reddened by blood which he wiped away with the back of his hand, and then spat a globule of red phlegm and wiped his lips again. He looked at them for a moment and then walked to the side view mirror which had cracked and opened his mouth wide opposite it and saw the gap between his teeth and cursed.

"Who's the nutcase who gave you a license?" he said to the driver and wiped his mouth again with the back of his hand, leaving two bloody smears spread from the wrist to the knuckles.

The driver looked at his hand which had turned red and at his lips which had begun to bleed again. "I saved you, asshole," he said to him, "if it wasn't for me you would have been full of holes long ago."

He had already loosened his grip on the truck driver who after being freed from his arms began slowly, and without his weapon, to go down the side of the ditch, one of his pouches still open and empty of its cartridges. For a moment he looked ahead at the curves of the ground and its bushes and at the sky above them and murmured something. He then undid his flak jacket as well as the belt of the trousers and its buttons in order to piss and said in his regular voice: "I swear this almost as good as a fuck," and carried on pissing with shut eyes and a face gradually becoming relaxed, and they joined him. The four of them stood in a row and pissed, and the piss fizzed on the dry ground, foamed, seeped down, and was swallowed into it.

"Come, you sons of bitches, come," the quartermaster, battered and bleeding, called out to the expanse in front of them, and lifted his organ and pissed on the nearby bushes in a continuous arced motion and the spray glistened in the air. "Come and I'll stuff your asses," he called out to the foreign country through which their army was advancing towards its capital, until the flow of the piss lessened, and he shook his organ and they asked him if that's the size it usually is, or has it shrunk from fear; maybe the hairs have turned grey there? The four of them sweated and dark stains spread in their armpits and their backs.

A few minutes later, after they pushed the inclined command car together until it was stabilized on its wheels, the four of them sat in the ditch and ate; they enjoyed the canned corn, canned beef and canned grapefruit segments all of which at the time was a delicacy to their palates. It seemed to them for a moment, on the edge of that ditch, that all the great dangers were behind them – a bullet accidentally fired, a diving plane, a semi flip – and that there would be no others.

Toward evening the deputy battalion commander stood before half the soldiers of the battalion – the others had already advanced northwards toward Beirut – and he personally read them the guard duty orders point by point in order to instill them into their heads. He then spoke of the dangers still lurking; he mentioned terrorist nests, Syrian commando soldiers, children who instead of slingshots have RPG launchers, he mentioned the rotten villagers who help the sons of bitches for a few dinars, because what wouldn't they do for money; and how everything in this crazy country was mixed up with drugs and politics and religion.

Their battalion, he said, has a very important role in the operation, the most important it's ever had. Their artillery that had originally been designed for shooting at planes, can also hit the high floors of buildings and penetrate them: Tyre, Sidon, maybe even Beirut. No fifty-caliber machinegun can compete with their rate of fire or the damage they can do; the army needs them now and they should be very proud of their weapon.

Behind his back the sun began to sink like a white-hot pupil of an eye, and the long summer twilight was still at its start. On the right, armored carriers were parked with their multi-barreled artillery turrets and on their left the headquarter vehicles. The tent of the deputy battalion commander and the operations officer was erected at the pinnacle of a horseshoe formation, and opposite it, in the center, the soldiers of the battalion sat and listened, paragraph by paragraph, what they could expect during the coming days, should they be fortunate enough to get through them.

With legs apart, two thumbs inserted into the trouser belt and his fingers dangling on either side of his privates, the deputy commander explained exactly what a Sagger missile does to the side of an armored carrier – it might be better not to know, but he wants them to know – what a mine does to the underbelly of an armored carrier, what a grenade does to a man, and what any Abdul can do he doesn't have to be a Syrian commando soldier, to someone who falls asleep on guard duty or even just dozes off. Next morning everyone finds him with his own cock in his mouth.

"Have you ever felt a cock in your mouth?" asked the deputy commander. Maybe some of you already have, he said, and might even want to feel it again, but let it be clear to everyone: he's talking about their own cocks now, not someone else's. For a moment he examined the impression his words had made on the soldiers: there wasn't one who wasn't listening to him. "You won't even choke on it, and you know why?" he asked. "Because by then you'll simply have died of heartache. When you see Abdul with your poor cock in his hand you won't want to live anymore."

The quartermaster bent over to the side with a sudden motion and began to throw up, and someone sitting behind him recoiled and said to him: "Why here, you asshole, is that what you came here for?" And another said: "It's not from fear, it's from disappointment. He was hoping to really feel someone's cock in his mouth."

It was a long night: every rustling woke them up, every snore, every fart. After that night they travelled though the ruins of Tyre and in all directions the remains of buildings could be seen and there was no knowing when they had collapsed, if during this war or the previous one, had it not been for the stench of bodies buried beneath them. That stench permeated the body through the nostrils and the mouth and the ears as well as through the pores of the skin, it and the death it contained. It slowly lodged beneath the skin and the entire abdominal cavity and the internal organs, and seemed it would kill them off like that; not with gunpowder but with that smell which filled the entire body and began to kill you the moment you got used to it as to any smell, and its origin was forgotten: the ruins there where pink porcelain shower tiles can still be seen, or the ruins with a few pale squares left by pictures that were hung on walls; and with all that one could discern, through the heavy stench, the smell of cigarette smoke, the fart someone let out, the smells of slices of canned beef frying, the smell of tinned sardines.

For a period of time, the duration of which it's better not to recall, that stench enveloped them, and only after a very long journey, when they reached the promenade of Sidon and the stench of masses of fish floating on the sea sprawling out from there wafted towards them – a stray bomb had raised them from the depths - were they slightly relieved, because it was like a fragrant smell in comparison to the previous one. It was the smell of the blue expanse, and it merged with its dim roar and its waves and its flickering and the smells of the salt and the seaweed and the iodine before it. And even the fish themselves, all the masses that floated and were cradled here and there on the ripples and sparkled with their silvery scales, brought a calmness to the eye with their slow motion, and for a while they all watched them from their armored carriers. Each time a wave began to curve, a mass of dead fish would surge up with it and the entire swarm would undulate, and when the wave broke, they all disappeared together and a moment later returned and floated in their masses.

A soldier who was looking at the wide strip of sand at the foot of the promenade and surveying the beach from north to south, asked where all the girls they had been promised were – his cousin in the Golani brigade had told how in Jounieh the beach was full of girls, as if there wasn't a war on at all – and another, who stuck his curly head out of the turret of the cannon, was sorry he hadn't brought his surfboard with him: the sea was calm now, but you never know what waves could be soaring tomorrow. This is the season, he said, when the waves are at their highest, five-meter waves, six-meter waves; someone who's never surfed doesn't know what he's missing.

The asked him how he'd surf with the dead fish, and he answered: "What do you mean how? Together with them."

In the darkness of the bedroom – her son had fallen asleep on the couch in the living room again – she asked him once more what it was he was looking for there, what had he gone for, why had he enlisted as a reservist, and still he didn't answer her, although he continued to talk; and even the things he did tell, he wouldn't have told had it not been for what happened between him and her small son.

For a long while she listened to him in silence and asked only those questions, until she added a few to them and then asked no more during the following months and the following two years, until the night when he informed her of his intention to travel. Then she hurled all the details of that incident at him detail by detail, and her conclusion was one: he was a louse, then and now, someone who takes off. And how in the name of God had she been mistaken to think she had succeeded in changing him.

"Someone who surfs," said the soldier from the turret of the cannon, "surfs in all conditions."

From his left they asked him if he would also surf here if instead of these fish – after all what are fish, you can ignore fish – there were some dead Abduls, and right away a soldier whose cousin had returned from a trip to the East interrupted the conversation and said that that's what it's like in India, corpses float on the water of the Ganges, which is their holy river, and those screwy Indians wash themselves between them like it was nothing: men, women, old people, children, all of them half-naked in all that filth that you can catch a disease from just by looking at it. It's enough to stop anyone from passing fifty, and someone forty years old already looks like an old man, and the way people here find a burial plot for themselves here, there they find wood and a bonfire, that's if they haven't been sent floating down the Ganges.

A short argument started about whether in India they burn all the dead or just some of them. Maybe they only burn the ones who've got enough money for wood? That cousin, who lived in India on a dollar a day, said that there are some who they leave for the eagles, that's their burial, in the belly of eagles in the sky. In Bombay there's even a special tower for them where they can eat pieces of flesh taken from the bodies. Believe it or not, but that's what it's like there: instead of the Jewish Burial Society, they've got eagles.

From a nearby armored car whose camouflage netting was rolled up sloppily on its side and whose ends dangled down almost to the caterpillar tracks, a soldier with a hoarse voice said that anyone who wants to see birds of prey doesn't have to go to India He's never seen anything like the fat crows here in Lebanon, he said. The crows here don't look like birds at all, each crow's the size of a dog, and you better not mess with them.

And all the while, a distance of a hundred meters from them, the ripples continued to cradle their silvery loot. One moment the dead fish sparkled and a moment later turned dim on their other sides, and the strip of wet sand on the edge of the beach glistened each time the waves receded, leaving a rim of foam and salt.

The boy – perhaps four years old, perhaps a little more – was only noticed by them when he got up from the foot of the promenade and went to fill the small orange plastic bucket in his hand with water. Perhaps before that the promenade was blocking the view of him, and perhaps he had been concealed by a high mound of sand that had piled up at its foot. He was dressed in white underpants with dinosaurs on them, and in his left hand he held a small plastic rake – they noticed that now as well – orange like the bucket. When he reached the strip of wet sand he squatted on his haunches and waited for a lick of the water to fill his little bucket, but until he managed to tilt it towards the water it had already receded, and he got up and took another step and squatted again and waited for the next lick of the water.

For the entire length of the beach, from south to north, only the boy could be seen in his underpants with wet sand stuck to them; him and his orange bucket and orange rake, and they watched him from their armored car when he got up again and advanced another step toward the sea. His underpants were pressed closely to his little behind and the small plastic bucket swung in his hand, and sea sprawled out in front of him, sparkling and turning grey with its masses of dead fish.

From the turret of the left armored car the curly headed soldier spoke again about the joys of surfing. Pleasure like that, he said, is sometimes even better that a fuck, between us, let's be honest, how long does a fuck last, a quarter of an hour? And another said that on his first furlough he and his girlfriend didn't get out of bed for three days, he had been so starved. In front of them the sea moved its waves and ripples back and forth, and its expanse seemed even vaster than it had previously seemed.

The two-way radio suddenly boomed and turned silent, perhaps they were trying to call someone and gave up. "Lucky the sea's relatively calm," someone said from one of the armored carriers, a soldier who had a little brother waiting for him at home who had sent him a drawing he kept as a good luck charm in his shirt pocket, "who leaves a child alone on a beach that way?" Again, in the distance a small wave arched and crashed, and the water continued to move forward.

From the armored car on the left, the one whose rolled up nets were dangling almost to the caterpillar tracks, someone asked if no one here had anything better to do other than worry about that little Abdul. Are we a welfare department here? If he wants to dig in the sand let him dig, if he wants water let him go to the water, let Allah look after him.

The armored carriers were parked in a straight row on the promenade and from their small turrets the sooty barrels of the cannons stuck out (the cannon was called a Vulcan, like the name of the god of the blacksmiths), and next to the armored carriers, dusty as them, trucks and jeeps were parked, and in between them stood the command car, battered on its left side. The driver, after having cleaned the front windshield with a rag aided by his fingernails and spit, spread out the rag and hung it from the side view mirror. Afterward he lit a cigarette, taking deep drags and keeping his eye on the boy trying to fill his orange bucket with sea water. "How come his parents let him?" he said and took another drag on the cigarette.

From behind, the quartermaster and the ammunitions truck driver were looking for a tin can opener, and around them, from right to left, field rations were already being opened here and there: there were those who dipped crackers in the thick sardine oil, others fished out grapefruit segments from a tin and lifted them dripping to their mouths, some gluttons first took bites of the halva.

"A child, nevertheless," said the one whose brother had sent him a drawing – a house with a red tiled roof and a smoking chimney – and continued looking at the beach.

Then a light breeze began to blow and they all relaxed in their seats and opened their flak jackets and shirts and let the wind cool their bodies, and the smell of dead fish rose again and was carried from the sea and became stronger but didn't bother anyone, on the contrary, there was relief in it. being many times better than the smell of the corpses. And from close by the smell of brewing coffee also rose, and someone shouted: "Who's the son of a bitch making coffee and not offering? He who drinks alone dies alone."

The wind also passed over the sea and wrinkled its surface making white abrasions that instantly mend and open again, but the boy took another step into it. The orange bucket he was holding swung less than before, perhaps it was half filled, and the boy advanced further. Perhaps he saw something in the water that caught his eye, perhaps one of the fish being carried on the ripples to the beach, cradled on its surface. The vast swarm of carcasses, dense and sparkling to a dazzle, now seemed closer than before, but a few dozen meters still separated it from the beach.

"Would you let your brother do that?" the soldier in whose pocket a house with a tiled roof was folded said from the right armored car but stayed where he was.

The command car driver, the ammunition truck driver, the quartermaster and Amnon also stayed where they were: they waited for the captain to return from the command group meeting that was being held in the building behind them, an unfinished structure that had been planned to be a hotel, and the battalion head-quarters had taken over its top floor, the sixth. There were no steps in the build-ing, only concrete ramps between each floor, and Amnon had already gone up and down them twice during the last hour, and was now hoping to be called up again, and that when he returns here the problem will already have been somehow solved.

Opposite them the boy advanced another step farther into the sea and stretched out his left hand with the orange plastic rake, perhaps he was trying to catch a fish floating alongside him with it and put in into his bucket. The water already covered his waistline and only the upper part of his body could be seen, and farther on from him, in the distance, it seemed that the swarm of dead fish was drawing closer to the beach, a threatening army whose objective was that strip of sand at the foot of the promenade and the row of hotels beyond of it.

Again, the boy stretched out his orange rake, this time to his left, and again he missed, perhaps the fish had been diverted from its place. A few dozen meters still separated him from the large swarm, and the boy lifted his head and for a moment looked at the flickering of the sun on the scales of the fish.

"Hasn't he got a mother and a father?" said the command car driver and explored the beach with his eyes from his right to his left, but the beach was as empty as before; nobody could be seen standing or sitting or lying down.

"They don't give a damn about their children," someone answered, "that's why they even send them off with an RPG," and one of them with long arms bent forward from the deck of the armored car and reached his hand downward to the tip of the left net in order to lift it up.

From the right someone firmly demanded they pass him the grapefruit segments: if they don't leave him any one more time, he doesn't know what he'll do to them; he who eats alone dies alone, and that's especially true when it comes to grapefruit segments.

In the sea, twenty or thirty meters from them, the boy could be seen hitting the surface of the water with his orange rake; in that way apparently trying to draw the nearby floating fish to him, and because he didn't succeed, he took another small hesitant step farther in, and the water instantly rose almost to his shoulders.

Perhaps there was a pit in the place where he stood, and perhaps the bottom of the sea began to slope downward to the depth where even a man couldn't stand. The water was already licking his little shoulders, and when it arched again it reached his neck and his mouth. And onward from there, in the distance, the sea had already changed its shade and turned grey; it seemed metallic despite the perpetual motion.

"And what did you do then?" Naomi asked in the darkness of the bedroom.

She insisted on knowing everything; she said that's how it is when you love, you know everything about each other, even the worst things, and nevertheless carry on loving; it doesn't take much to love someone for all the virtues they have or seemingly have, that's just kid's love; it takes a whole lot more to love someone with their worst weaknesses. And besides, people change, love changes them. In point of fact, she noticed how well he had taken care of her son tonight.

"Commander from first in command, over. Commander, commander, do you hear me, over."

When they called over the two-way radio the boy was still trying to rake the dead fish into his orange bucket, he beat b the surface of the water with his rake over and over without a stop, until he suddenly slipped and in the blink of an eye his small head disappeared, the orange rake and orange bucket disappeared as well, and only the sea and the swarm of dead fish could be seen.

A long moment passed until the small head sprouted again from the water: it had black hair and around it the vast grey sea in whose water white abrasions were made and mended and immediately reappeared. For a moment the boy remained where he was and no one tried to call him, certainly not by his name – was it Ali, perhaps? Ali, Ali! Suddenly there was no doubt as to his name being Ali; come out of the water, Ali, what are you waiting for, Ali – perhaps he spat up water from his little lungs, coughed, gathered his breath that the water had choked. Perhaps his eyes teared, and from his small nostrils a watery discharge ran to his lips. He must have been alarmed by the grip of the water and wished, as anyone in his place would have, to place his feet on stable ground again and not be swept away into the depths of the sea.

"Such a bunch of dickheads," she said in the darkness of the bedroom.

For a moment the boy's dark face was turned backward and it seemed that he was looking up at the beach, at the promenade or at the row of hotels; and when he found a foothold for his small feet again, he returned his gaze forward, towards the expanse of the sea. A moment later, in front of their eyes watching him from the row of vehicles, he reached out his orange rake, insistent as before, and again tried to draw the fish carcass floating alongside toward him. At first, he raked some water, afterward beat it repeatedly with all his meager strength in order to stir it up, and it then seemed that some kind of battle was being waged there in the water between the boy and his fish, although the distance between them hadn't narrowed, a battle from which he wouldn't desist until either he or the fish was victorious.

It was a ludicrous battle: not Captain Ahab and his whale, not old Santiago and his swordfish, just a boy with the carcass of a fish that wasn't even a carp; but he too was surrounded by an expanse of water, and oceans and ships weren't required for death or defeat that also waited here for their moment. The sea had now become greyish-green, and on its surface the white abrasions increased and no longer mended themselves.

In the building behind them, the hotel whose construction hadn't been completed ("They've taken over the Hilton," they said about the battalion head-quarters, as if all the exposed concrete surfaces had been covered with porcelain tiles, and a doorman in uniform was stationed at the entrance), the sounds of the two-way radios reverberated and were intermingled: first in command Daffo-dil called deputy Daffodil, officer Heron called first in command Heron, and all Orchid stations were called to return hastily to the compounds.

It was a hot day, but a breeze blew from the west as Amnon ascended to the top floor of the building, and from each floor the expanse of water could be seen from a place where there was no window or even the wall of a window. But the armored carriers and their cannons couldn't be seen from there, nor the section of the sea in front of them; only concrete floors could be seen, filthy with remnants of food and cigarette stubs and empty tin cans and field ration cartons, and at the edge of the concrete a blue strip turning grey and green, vast in size.

On the third floor, two soldiers were standing legs apart and pissing outside, they must have been looking at the large swarm of fish when one of them said: "Sometimes they catch them that way in Jaffa, by throwing a hand grenade into the sea and straight away they come to the top, no two ways about it." On the fourth floor, on a burner blackened by soot, a pot stood filled with white eggs floating in bubbling water, and on a small gas cooker at the side oil sizzled in a black pan, and an unshaven sergeant threw onion rings into it and waited for them to brown. On the fifth floor the sounds of the two-way radios became clearer, and two operations sergeants were sticking colored drawing pins into a board map covered in nylon, and through it and the red and black lines on it, twists of elevation lines could be seen, grid squares, and here and there names that weren't possible to read from far.

"With whom do we have the pleasure?" someone asked Amnon on noticing him and wasn't impressed when he answered the captain had called him over the two-way radio to come up and that he had already been here before.

"Who hasn't been here?" said the thin operations sergeant. "It's turned into a train station here. Even someone who doesn't have to be here has already been here but isn't here anymore."

Before pointing to the concrete ceiling, indicating to Amnon the group orders meeting taking place above it, they told him briefly about someone who had been caught in the building next to them – a real hotel, not a fake like this one – someone who must have come to steal arms or ammunition, maybe even to spy, but the guys from the Golani Brigade beat up him real good; when someone makes them mad there's no stopping them. And when those crazy Golani guys finally came to their senses and called the Security Services to come and interrogate him properly, he just vanished into thin air. That's what they thought, until they discovered him spread on the courtyard. If he just looks down there – they suggested to Amnon – he can see what's left of him.

Amnon looked down: on the concrete surface that must have been meant for the cars of future hotel guests, only a thick rough white outline could be seen, somewhat resembling the ones outlined around murdered bodies in television police series; but the one here wasn't outlined in chalk. "They just poured lime over him afterward," the thin operations sergeant explained. "In this heat, that's all we need, more of a stink. A tractor from the construction department came and took him, and that's what was left afterward. The guy didn't even bleed, except from being beaten up."

The tractor, it turned out, carried the dead man in its large bucket to the beach, and it buried him there with two others who were killed by the bomb that missed the row of hotels and hit the fish. At the time, the tractor didn't have much work – apart from the one who fell from the building there were only the other two, a man and a woman, quite young, and even in their swimsuits, God knows what they were doing at the sea in the middle of this fucking war; and taking a swim. Maybe they decided not to give a damn about it all, and maybe they had been there long before the plane, not that it makes any difference now. Besides which, there must be jellyfish in water like this.

It didn't take the tractor driver more than a few moments, it's nothing for a tractor to dig in the sand. And there was also a little boy there who stood and watched, three or four years old, five at the most, that's how it is with boys: what boy in the world wouldn't watch tractors?

"Also cranes," said the second operations sergeant, the freckled one. When he was a boy, he said, he was crazy about cranes, he could watch them for hours. "I was so jealous of the guy who sat there at the top," he said, "you wouldn't believe it."

The boy, they said, had dinosaurs on his underpants ("Dinosaurs in the middle of the war! Those two go off swimming and he with his dinosaurs and bucket"), and he was so taken by the tractor that even after it finished working he couldn't take his eyes of it. Right after that, he tried to do the same thing with his plastic rake; I mean, digging in the sand, flinging it in all directions until they got him to leave. Little as he was, he screamed and made a big fuss, but they did it with kindness, tractor drivers aren't mean, they're good people, peasants at heart. The tractor driver said to him: "What's your name little boy?" He didn't want to say. "Is it Mohamed?" He didn't answer. He said, "Mustafa?" He didn't answer. He said to him, you seem like an Ali, are you Ali? He didn't answer. He said to him, okay little guy, you want a ride? He still didn't answer. In the end he lifted him onto the tractor and took him to the other end of the beach, some two kilometers from here; near the breakwater. The tractor driver also had work there.

When Amnon came down from the hotel, he didn't see the boy. The command car driver was still smoking his cigarette, and maybe already another; he was still watching the sea.

"Where's the boy?" Amnon asked, and with his hand the driver indicated to him far out in front on the blue-greyish expanse in which the white abrasions were multiplying from moment to moment.

It took a while for him to discern the small head wavering in the distance on the surface of the water, perhaps advancing perhaps floating perhaps being swept away. Only one thing was clear: it was no distance for a child to be in the sea, and certainly not without an adult. It was difficult to know whether the swarm of dead fish was drawing close to him or if the boy was drawing close to the swarm; the fish scales weren't sparkling any more but turning grey like the sky above them.

When Amnon clumsily jumped down to the beach the driver didn't say anything, not even when he stood on the sand and examined the light blue towel spread there with some men's and women's beachwear haphazardly folded on it. Only when he began to take off his shoes did the driver get out of the command car and watch him. First, he had to undo the laces and loosen the uppers of the army boots, while at the same time gazing at the sea in front of him – the small head continued to waver here and there with its black curls – and after taking off his shoes he also removed the socks that had hardened at their edges from sweat and dirt.

"Be careful of whirlpools," said the driver. "It looks calm from here but go figure what it's like in there. Sometimes things happen."

Far in the distance in front of them, the swarm of dead fish bobbed here and there on the water whose glisten had dimmed, too vast to know whether the swarm had enlarged or maybe diminished due to some hidden whirlpool, and the head of black hair wavered to its rhythm, although they were still far from each other: the dead fish and the boy, Ali.

Only then, when he began to undo the buttons of his shirt, did he notice the orange bucket floating upside down next to the head of the boy and cradled on the surface of the water. The orange rake couldn't be seen nearby or anywhere else.

"The sea's the biggest liar there is," he heard the driver say from the promenade which was a meter and a half above the sand, and the armored carriers parked there were another two meters higher above it and the cannon turrets another meter and a half, "I once had a neighbor -"

But then he took off his shirt and dropped it on to the sand not far from the carcass of a fish that had been swept up and undid the belt of his trousers and let them fall to his feet, and from one of the armored carriers on the left, someone whistled with two fingers the way girls are whistled at passing by on the street.

Now the hotels at the back grew tall and with them the one whose construction had been halted, and without a front wall that hadn't managed to be built, all the floors could be seen open on all sides to their rear, and the two soldiers who had pissed from there stood and watched him. From the row of vehicles, the quartermaster's voice could be heard, slightly faint from hoarseness or from the wind. It wasn't a long sentence, six or seven words, no more, but the driver silenced him before he finished. They were both leaning against the command car, the driver and the quartermaster, the one smoking and the other holding a battered tin can he had taken out of the field rations, and they both watched the water and what was floating on it.

"It's better for a child not to have a father and a mother-" said the quartermaster and didn't finish, and again his words were blurred by the wind. He examined the can of corn he was holding: it had apparently been squashed when they overturned.

"What, are you nuts?" said the driver.

"I'm talking from experience," the quartermaster answered and inserted the spoon into the can. For a moment he left it in there and stirred it a little and raised it to his mouth brimming with grains of corn and filled it and began to grind them with his teeth. "It's better, Shlomi, believe me, it's better. It's enough they throw you out of home and put you in some boarding school and take off, and every weekend you wait for them to come." He wiped transparent skins of corn from his lower lip with the back of his hand the way he had previously wiped his blood from them. "Everything's been decided for us, even right now," he said with a mouth chockfull of corn, "a mortar bomb could fall here and finish us off, and is there anything you could do about it?" With the tip of his tongue, he tried to remove the skin that had stuck between his teeth.

"Weingarten, you've gone completely off the rails," said the driver.

The water was warm and pleasant when he entered it, but its clarity turned murky. Then the boy, Ali, could be seen clearly: the lean nape of his neck, his moist black curls, his large ears sticking out. Opposite the setting sun that still hesitated whether to complete its descent or to linger in its place, his ear lobes appeared to be almost completely transparent.

Ali, Ali! He wanted to shout out the name he'd given him but didn't shout it or anything else. Come out, Ali, or stay where you are, Ali, and I'll come to you, Ali, he wanted to shout to him, but the roar of the sea was disrupted only by the calling of the two-way radios from the vehicles on the promenade.

Someone shouted to him from one of the armored carriers, perhaps the same tall, long armed soldier who had attached the camouflage net to the side, and also waved his two long arms at him to return to the shore. He was standing on the deck of the armored carrier in front of the turret, and the gunner was sitting inside and must have been watching the sea through the sight. "Have you lost it completely?" he shouted and turned his finger around next to his temple.

Farther and farther, he waded into the greying water, and its scars, many in number, opened wide again turning whiter each time, and the force that was causing them to open wide from every direction also affected his body on his way towards the head floating in front of him. "Ali, Ali!" he now shouted loudly to the boy and the boy didn't turn his head. "Ali, Ali!" he shouted again, and the boy's large earlobes, which were no longer turned toward the sun, became dimmer right there before his eyes and turned blue. "Stay where you are, Ali," he shouted at him, "don't move," as if the boy could understand his language and as if his small feet were stranding on solid ground and were not being swept onward toward the horizon and toward the swarm of dead fish, some of which were already very close to him, and their stench filled the nostrils. Twenty or more fish were floating nearby, and not far from them hundreds more could be seen and perhaps thousands, the entire vast swarm that the stray bomb had raised from the depths.

When he was close enough, he reached out his hand to the boy between some reeking fish and grasped him by his limp upper arm and was amazed how lean and light the arm was and the body to which it was attached, and how light the head was floating behind with its black curls. In this manner, he dragged him by the slender arm for a while towards the beach without looking directly at him: not at his chest to see if it was rising and falling, not at his throat to see signs of swallowing and certainly not at his black eyes – in no way were they to be looked at, those black eyes – until the seabed below drew nearer and a foothold was found and he stood there until his breathing calmed. For the first time in all those minutes, he pulled the boy towards his body and lifted him up in his arms; he lifted all the lightness of its weight and its limpness and its chill, the meager thighs in this left arm and the bony shoulders in his right and the small head falling slightly backward; and still, he didn't look directly at him.

"But, why?" she asked in the darkness of the bedroom, and he didn't answer.

For a moment he stood there facing the beach, opposite the promenade and the row of armored carriers and jeeps and trucks and the command car, and above them the hotels, those that were whole and those with open sides, and they could have all watched him from there as if from a gallery, but from one end of the row of armored carriers to the other only that same long armed tall soldier could be seen, the camouflage net lifter, and if he shouted something out to him it swallowed by the wind.

I pulled you out of the water, Ali, he thought, and I'll bring you to the beach, Ali, and I'll resuscitate you the way the medic taught us in artificial respiration classes: two breaths mouth to mouth, fifteen thrusts of the chest, two breaths, fifteen thrusts; and not only did he intend to resuscitate Ali that way, because it seemed that if he'll take him out of the sea and revive his breath and Ali will open his eyes and say something, perhaps his own breath will be revived, and his own eyes will be opened.

Two breaths mouth to mouth, fifteen thrusts of the chest, he repeated to himself in the water, two breaths mouth to mouth, fifteen thrusts of the chest, and they still had to cross all the water between themselves and the beach. But you won't need so many thrusts, Ali, he said to the boy, and for the first time dared to look at his small dark face: it was swollen, and the eyes were almost completely shut except for a narrow and very white slit between the lids, and his thin pale lips were slightly apart and the gap of two missing milk teeth could be seen, as if proof of his childhood had been necessary. On his underpants with their decorative dinosaurs that hadn't yet faded in the wash, a small tear could be seen on their side, and pressed close to his behind was green seaweed that had stuck there, vivid in color and as fleshy as a living creature, and when he tried to remove it – it was suddenly extremely important to remove it – he almost lost his balance.

From the promenade, at the end of the row of armored carriers, the command car driver shouted to him to beware of whirlpools: the sea's no laughing matter.

He then clutched Ali with double the force and again sensed how light and cold he was. And in the distance, from the direction of the breakwater that delimited the southern section of the beach, the large armor protected tractor could be seen turning around and starting to return; having finished its job there its large bucket was raised up as if in a gesture of victory and grains of sand flowed between its teeth.

"No, I don't understand," Naomi said, though she understood more than he wished her to understand; that was made clear a few years later. "What's the connection between my child and that Arab boy and why are you telling me all this?"

"Everything's connected," he said to her. It was their first night together in the flat in Tel Aviv and her son was sleeping on the couch in the living room and his anxiety had been calmed (for a long scary moment when the boy was nowhere to be seen, he feared he'd gone out to the balcony and leaned over the railings and lost his balance and fallen).

Afterward the two of them listened carefully: her son was rearranging the cushions and the blanket and changed his position. From the neighboring apartment water from the toilet tank roared, a door was slammed; from a passing car dim bass electronic drumming sounds were beating, a Vespa rattled along the avenue; those were sounds of the city, completely different from the those of the country town where they had met for the first time and the those of the place where they would rent a house.

"But how's it connected?" she insisted, and he began to explain to her in a very soft voice, so as not to wake her son again.

In a beachfront hotel whose construction was unfinished, something sparkled, perhaps one of the sergeants' spectacles or perhaps a female soldier's small mirror. The sun was behind Amnon's back and its white-hot light hadn't yet changed to the orange of sunset.

"Just watch where you're going," the command car driver shouted at him from the promenade, "it's full of rocks, you can even see from here," and the quartermaster also shouted something to him from the other side of the command car; perhaps he had finished eating his corn.

With each step, he came closer to the beach, but didn't draw away from the swarm of dead fish, on the contrary, it seemed they were advancing forward faster than he was. Not just a few were floating around him but dozens, a hundred or more, their scales a dull grey and their eyes round and wide open, and their stench carried above them like a cloud they were sailing towards the shore.

When the sound of the plane was heard – possibly the one that had dived over their small convoy or maybe a different one – a moment passed until he saw it northward of him: it burst from there small and silver with its roar following it. In the blink of an eye, it split the dome of the sky and disappeared at its southern edge, and another moment passed until the water responded to its sound with its dead fleet. No waves rose up and crashed, but some agitated motion passed through it. By then many hundreds of fish surrounded Amnon and the boy, Ali, like an unbroken grey solid scaly mass.

It seemed as if the boy was trembling in his arms, whether from the plane or the fish surrounding them, and in his palm he felt the boniness of his small shoulder blades and their coldness. Again, he refrained from looking directly into his eyes.

When the tractor drew nearer and the silhouette of the driver in the armor protected cabin could be seen, he was still telling himself what exactly he would do on reaching the beach and placing the boy on the strip of sand at the foot of the promenade. The mound of the uniform he had stripped himself of could be seen with his pair of army boots, and farther on from there was the large heap of sand that had been piled up by the bucket of the tractor. He advanced towards the beach, and above the small cold body whose skin had softened and wrinkled in the water like the skin of an old man he repeated to himself: two breaths, fifteen thrusts, two breaths, fifteen thrusts, but for you, Ali, fewer would be needed. Definitely fewer, after all in a moment or two you'll already start to cough and spit up everything that you swallowed, Ali, and you'll open your eyes of which only a little white could be seen without the pupil, where are your pupils, Ali, and where are your breaths, Ali, and where is the thing that led you to the middle of the sea, Ali, you fool, Ali, didn't you have anything better to do?

"Come out," they shouted to Amnon from the row of vehicles standing on the promenade in uniform spacing, "tell the boy the tractor driver will give him a ride."

When the plane burst through again, this time from the east, he saw it right away and at once the masses of fish reacted to its roar and its lunging through the sky, they might have been responding to the wind blowing from the rear; it seemed they were crowding together even more and all their scales were unifying and their hundreds of eyes closed for a moment and immediately opened again.

Perhaps his foot slipped into a pit on the seabed, possibly from the motion of the water; and as if he had been waiting for just such a moment, the boy dropped from his arms and began to sink. Only his hand could be still seen above the water, sticking its fingers out, and it promptly vanished as well. When he dived into the water after him everything became dark: sand rose from the seabed and clouded the water, and above was the ceiling of dead fish casting its shadow downward; and for a while his hands groped about here and there and caught nothing other than a small piece of seaweed, perhaps the one that had previously stuck to the boy's underpants or another, as fleshy as a living creature.

When he rose to the surface of the water, cracking open the scaly ceiling with his head, the fish in their masses floated around him, not hundreds but thousands, touching his shoulders, his neck, his chin, his cheeks, his ears, and all their eyes wide open, and in the sky above the white trail left behind by the plane unraveled into fluffy spirals.

"Hey, come out already!" they shouted at him from the promenade. "Haven't you got anything better to do?" and afterward something else was shouted, but he had already dived down again.

Ali, Ali, he called out to him voicelessly beneath the water as if it would have been possible for the boy to answer from the place he had been swept to. There was salt in his eyes and mouth as well as the stench of the fish as his hands groped about in the murky darkness and a few sunbeams infiltrated between the fish and grains of sand rising from the seabed sand could be seen in them.

Onward and onward he moved beneath the ceiling of dead fish until his breath had been completely exhausted and once again he was pulled from the water like a cork.

"We thought you were a goner," someone shouted at him from the promenade.

"Come out," the command car driver called out to him, "so that we don't have go looking for you too in the end," but he dived again and drew farther away from the beach beneath the ceiling of dead fish that moved with him everywhere he swam. It was unbroken and seemed to cover the entire sea from horizon to horizon.

"Leave him!" the quartermaster shouted at him from the promenade. "Didn't you see his color? He was completely blue, not even an adult could last like that."

He must have been swept away by a wave, he thought. And he blindly groped around in the water and for a moment thought he touched material and for a moment a hand, but it was only a fish, a live fish which slipped away from him.

"My God," she said.

In the darkness of the bedroom and its silence – her son had already sunk into a dream in the next room – the scents of their bodies could be smelled and beneath them lay a moist sweaty sheet and opposite them a fan placed on a chair stirred the air and occasionally something hummed inside it; perhaps the blade rubbing against the shield.

"What made you go there?" she said. By no means could she understand what had driven him to enlist in the first place and also couldn't understand his present trip, or the one after it; all unnecessary in her eyes.

In a weary voice he replied that he was young and foolish at the time and apparently hasn't become much wiser if this is what his life looks like now, at forty.

When he rose from the water again, he was completely spent and dizzy from the lack of air or from the stench of the dead fish, in which it seemed one couldn't move other than by their tacit agreement. He then turned his face towards the promenade and in the water halfway to the shore saw the orange plastic bucket floating and wavering here and there, even smaller and more orange in the light of the setting sun. Never had he experienced such difficulty crossing a distance like that; it seemed the entire sea was tightening around his body to hold him back, and when he reached the bucket, having left the fish behind, the water was translucent and through it the seabed could be seen with its rocks and seaweed and shells and with the orange rake that had fallen there; only the boy, Ali, was nowhere to be seen.

He then gave up. Giving up was at once difficult and simple. His legs decided for him and led him back to the shore, and on his right, from the direction of the breakwater, the tractor continued to advance with its raised bucket.

"The sea gives and the sea takes," someone said from the row of vehicles and the command car driver silenced him, and someone else cursed the Skyhawks in case they let loose some stray bomb here again: aren't enough people dying here without accidents?

For a moment he still turned his gaze backward and saw the swarm of dead fish spread out in the distance concealing all beneath it as before, and beyond it were the white abrasions opening wide again in the water and mending, and above, the white trail of the plane continued to gradually unravel as gently as the spinning of clouds.

"Come out already," the command car driver shouted from the promenade, "we don't want to have to go looking for you," and hurried him up with the agitated honking of the command car's horn. When he responded and came out of the water he first stepped onto the strip of wet sand, the one the breaking waves reach with their fish, and from there advanced further and passed the twisting line of salt and continued towards the sand where a light blue towel had been left, and on the way pulled his wet underpants up towards his navel since they had begun to slip down, and this time nobody whistled at him from the promenade. With the same readiness not guided by will but rather by a series of actions that had to be completed, he passed the towel and approached the heap of his uniform and put it on over his wet underpants and wet skin, first the trousers stained with rifle oil and then the sweaty shirt.

Only then, while doing up the buttons, his gaze fell on the little mounds at the foot of the promenade, firm sand mounds heaped there, row by row, not by the giant bucket of a tractor but rather by the small palm of a hand, and he had no difficulty identifying the stench emitted from them; fish whose graves were too shallow. He sat down on the sand, put his socks and army boots on and tied the laces and got to his feet and stood upright just as the tractor stopped in front of him and from its window the driver, wearing red earphones against the noise, put his head out. The giant metal bucket was raised above the two of them and grains of sand were still being shed between its teeth with no smell or sound, just that motion of theirs.

"How's the water?" he asked, and Amnon replied.

3

He passed a long night in the hotel in Delhi. The smallness of his room wasn't surprising, neither were the grey walls and the damp stains and the smell, nor the standard of the toilet (a bucket full of water placed next to the spot for squatting down), but the noise coming from the street was almost solid in its assault on the ears, and during the rare moments when it quietened slightly, the rattling of the ceiling fan became clearer, tossing with each turn as if any moment it would become detached. The unbearable heat was mixed and blended with the stink of the toilet and the smells that rose from the hotel kitchen and the sourness of his sweat and after pushing his backpack under the bed so that it wouldn't be stolen, the thin mattress became curved and he was too tired to get up and check what had been squashed beneath him. People passed through the corridor incessantly: English, German, Indian, Japanese, French – at least he didn't hear Hebrew – they were all young, and afterward the smell of marijuana and hashish seeped in and blended into the stirred air as well.

You deserve it, he said to himself, you could have rented a good room in a good hotel. There was nothing more contrasting to the home he had left, and that was why he was staying here. It would be fitting to make sure each step of the way, especially at nighttime, that he stick to his decision to leave and not back down from it.

An exposed electric light bulb cast the fan's shadow onto the wall opposite the bed and flattened its blades to the point where they resembled the wings of a giant dragonfly fixed to its spot with a pin like some kind of prank played by a cruel child, and next to the bed, on a Formica table with cigarette burns, stood a stainless steel jug empty of water, and when he looked in it his reflection became round with the room curving there: his nose swelled, his eyes bulged from their sockets like the eyes of a lunatic (the eyes of a murderer, he thought for a moment). At a very late hour he heard Hebrew in the corridor; had a different language been spoken there perhaps he wouldn't have awoken, but the familiar sounds uprooted him from his sleep. A young man's voice said: "The main thing is that there's a bed, Tami, what do we need besides a bed?"

He was hoping they wouldn't be staying in the room next to his and that he wouldn't have to hear all their talking and goings on, and a while passed before he went back to sleep, perhaps for an hour or perhaps just a few moments. There was a banging on a door down the corridor and the Indian bellboy could be heard shouting: "Wake up, Mister, wake up, your train, your train!" until a drowsy voice answered angrily: "Go away, you dumb Indian, you got the wrong room." Again, he sank into a disturbed sweaty sleep, and when he awoke the sheet was saturated with his sweat and the ceiling fan above continued to stir the heat and the commotion rising from the street.

In the morning, in the restaurant on the roof of the hotel, all of Delhi seemed to be steeped in a murky haze, thick as soup, and the sun rose in its sky like an opaque blind eyeball, and around him he saw and heard English and French and Danish and German people and was glad the Israeli couple who had arrived during the night weren't among them. On one of the nearby rooftops a boy was trying to fly an improvised kite: it swayed here and there in the air and for a while was colored by the faint light of the sun and for a while turned grey. On another roof most of which was filled with all sorts of junk, an extremely stooped old woman was walking and feeling her way with a stick, and at the sight of her the thought rose what would happen the moment she reaches the edge of the roof, and just then the Israeli couple blocked his view of her.

"Look how nice it is here," the boy said.

"It's disgusting to eat here," the girl replied.

"But everything that's got a peel is okay, just peel it and it's fine," the boy said, "and you said you felt like a mango." He, on the other hand, needed to eat real food now: a three-egg omelet and lassi.

"Just don't let them put anything in the lassi," said the girl, and the boy reassured her: they don't do that in Delhi nor in the Israeli guest houses.

He had seen some of those guest houses the previous day while wandering through one of the alleys that emerge from the main bazaar and also saw restaurants that offered shakshuka and bourekas in curly Hebrew letters, and from their entrances waiters called out in street Hebrew to backpackers with abundant Rasta braids: "Howsitgoing my buddy?" He also saw a travel agent who called himself Danny Tours in Hebrew letters, and a rickshaw on the back of which some Israeli had scribbled "Ghandi's limousine" with a red felt tipped pen. Piles of garbage emitted a pungent rotting smell, sewage flowed in open ditches, roaming cows searched for food and the smells of urine and excrement and oil frying filled his nose.

"I really could do with a mango," the girl acceded.

She went back to reading the menu and tried to pronounce the names of the Indian deserts aloud: Burfi? Ladoo? Jalebi? Gulab jamun? Kulfi? And the boy explained to her what each one was, until she tired of his explanations: a mango would be enough for her. "No matter how much I ate when I was in Nahal,"[35] she said, "it was never enough. Everyone said to me, Tami, in the end you'll turn

---

35 An Israel Defenses Forces program that combines military service with the establishment of agricultural settlements.

orange like from carrots, and when I little, I really did turn orange from carrots, didn't I ever tell you? They took me to a pediatrician and the minute she saw me she said, the girl's eating too many carrots."

"It makes we want to say something obscene," the boy said, "but I won't."

On the left roof the old woman could no longer be seen, and on the right roof the boy continued to fly his kite, struggling to make it rise through the haze. A memory rose of reed kites he and his friends used to make on the banks of the Yarkon, running on and on until it responded and took off from the ground strewn with pine needles, and the hand-held wooden reel with the string rolled around it extending out and rising and tightening; and without wishing it, the sight of the son of the woman he left also rose in his memory; they hadn't flown a kite together nor would they ever.

The old city of Delhi was in walking distance and all along the way merchants called out to him from the entrances of their shops, "Which country, Mister? Which country?" And only because he was older than the rest of the Israelis, they didn't perceive his nationality. "Which country, which country?" they repeatedly asked him, until he tired of them and replied without thinking: "Spain," and was surprised by the ease with which he lied; there was a certain enjoyment in changing his identity.

The alleys of the old city were no less crowded than the alleys of the bazaar, and again he felt as if the masses around him were encircling and besieging him, brushing up against him and glaring at him, exactly as he had felt on his first trip, but then he had secluded himself in his hotel, while now (he still had a few hours before him until the night train to Pathankot) he mixed in with the crowd that swept him in its motion and tumult. On giant posters Bollywood stars shed sparkling tears or showered white-toothed smiles, as was the case on covers of second-hand magazines sold alongside heaps of pipes and worn-down bicycle tires and rusty screws and nuts and squashed plastic lampshades and tattered shoes and spectacle frames and defective watches. Each bit of merchandise had its vendor, and each one took shelter in the shade of a large umbrella whose black color had long faded and whose patches had turned grey.

In a dark alcove a shoemaker placed a piece of tire on a worn-out sole, an aged amputee was supported by a bamboo reed, and another, both his legs amputated, moved himself with the help of his fists that were swathed in rags until he reached out his begging hand with the rags on it. The moment Amnon put his hand in his pocket, street urchins that previously hadn't been seen popped up, all of them ragged and all reaching out a small hand or pointing with it to their mouths with a motion unbearable to behold, and right away more street urchins came from all directions, and then more, and held on to him by his shirt and by his hands until they saw a group of American tourists and let go of him.

A heap of battered aluminum water bottles was piled up in front of an old vendor, while his neighbor peddled leg warmers from the days of the British Raj, and a third, black dusty jerry-cans, and a surprised hoarse voice said in Hebrew, "Look, an army issue jerry-can," and he hastened his step until the Hebrew was swallowed in the tumult of the street. Rickshaws travelled here and there, their drivers straining the muscles of their thin legs, and horns honked from all directions. On the sidewalk barbers sat and shaved their clients with an old-fashioned razor blade, dentists planed down used false teeth with what looked like a carpenter's file, and street dogs lay between them as if unconsciousness until the smell of something edible reached their noses and right away they rose and fought over it until blood was shed, a sight he found difficult to watch.

He needed to get away from there and did so, until stopping opposite a street cook who rolled out a ball of dough over his fists and flung it into the air and stretched it into a large round sheet the size of the scalding tin dome next to him. People lay on the sidewalks, sunk in sleep, undisturbed by the commotion around them, vendors of cheap plastic toys were selling trucks without wheels and helicopters without propellers, and an old Indian holding a kind of skewering needle with cotton wool wrapped at its tip, inserted it into the ear of his client so deep as if any moment it would burst through the other side ("I swear it's like cleaning a rifle," another voice in said in Hebrew).

Above, in a sky whose azure was turbid and whose heat blazed even through the covering of dust, black shiny crows circled, and a woman with a giant stack of hay on her head was making her way through the road. At the side of the road two brown goats bent their heads down to some rotten vegetables, and on the sidewalk a man carried a tower of sooty pots the height of a person in his hands and only by chance missed the entanglement of electrical wires above him ("He's aced it," the same voice that spoke previously said in Hebrew, "not like the guy from the train"). A girl lifted up a naked baby in front of the passengers of a tuk tuk, her brother or her son, and sadhus sought out gullible tourists with their made-up eyes – they left him alone when they saw the expression on his face. The street urchins then popped up again, the same ones who had approached him before or their twins, they stared at him from all directions and asked him in English for ten rupee, ten rupee, ten rupee, as if they knew that in the end he would accede.

"If you tell them chalo, they won't leave you," one of the Israelis standing alongside advised him in Hebrew. Apparently, he had sworn out loud and they had heard him, the tall one or his friend or one of the two girls. The girl from the hotel also stopped next to them, short and freckled with her brown hair gathered in a small ponytail, and in vain her boyfriend tried to pull her by the arm before the children harass them as well. "He's my nephew's age," she said and pointed to the urchin whose nose was running and opened her purse, and right away all the beggars were driven away by a roaring "chalo" – it was the tall Israeli who shouted and also lifted his hand in a threatening gesture. He was slender and almost fragile in appearance, but the children immediately retreated.

From the sidewalk opposite, the urchin fixed his large sparkling eyes at her and waited.

Children are children, the tall Israeli said, but the Indians not only send the children into the street, they sometimes also actually break some bones of theirs at birth just so that they'll bring home more money. "Did someone do that to your nephew?" he asked, and the curly headed one again tried to pull his girlfriend away from there, and again she insisted on staying. "Look what sad eyes he's got," she said.

The urchin still gazed at her and waited. There was hope in his gaze, and expectation as well as a sad awareness, because he already knew what was about to happen: the moment she reached out her hand to him others preceded him and grabbed the note from between her fingers and his little hand dropped empty to his side.

"You see?" said the tall boy. "That's what it's like here." Not that he had come to India naïve, he said, he wished he was naïve, but he had overcome that completely in the army. "Where did you serve?" he asked the girl, and when she answered him – at first, she was hesitant and exchanged glances with her boyfriend – he giggled, and two dimples appeared in his cheeks. "Did you milk cows all through your army service?" he asked.

"We picked mangos," her boyfriend answered, "and turned orange from them."

The girl turned her eyes again to the little boy, and from within his dusty face two eyes sparkled, black and blazing and sparkling even more than before. One of the goats ran toward them – a small stone was thrown at it and it burst out bleating – and the plump Israeli whose body's outline was blurred by an Indian shirt, asked if the goat doesn't remind him of something: the very same long ears; only that one was black and this one was brown.

Right away he gave an explanation: for a whole month they had been on alert and feared booby-trapped donkeys at the roadblock because one had blown up in the zone next to them, and Ido – he indicated to the tall one with his eyebrow – raised an alert regarding booby-trapped goats as well. "That old woman cried so much over it," he said, "she wouldn't leave it until evening. One would think her daughter had died."

The girl looked at him and didn't say anything, though it was clear she wanted to say something to him, to make some harsh accusations or the opposite, to persuade him gently that he and his tall friend had made a terrible mistake, bigger than all the mistakes of the Indians, but when her boyfriend pulled her arm again, she complied and went with him. Only then did they pay him any attention, standing not far off and watching the stages of naan being prepared in a nearby alcove, from its kneading until the circles of its dough turned brown and were peeled from the sides of the tandoori and others were stuck in their places as a cloud of sparks flew.

"Are you looking for your son here?" the tall one asked all ready to help. He could have answered telling him he's a journalist sent here for the purpose of an article, for example about young people who go missing in India, but the answer already came from his mouth, and again he was surprised by the ease with which he lied and from the enjoyment he derived from it. One false word was enough to change two decades of his life, as if he really had got married at their start with one of the women he met and fathered a son who was now the age of these young people. Before that he had declared himself a Spaniard, and now, with the same ease, had turned himself into a father; and after all, each time that possibility had been raised before him – as a request, a plea, in insult, in anger, in bitterness – it was rebuffed and he never regretted it.

"Go to Goa," the tall one suggested to him, "he wouldn't be here, Pops. Go to Goa or Manali or Kasol, especially Kasol. Delhi's not the place for hanging out. In Kasol they'll probably be able to tell you something about him." He was so full of good will for all his height, from his enormous sandals to his ruffled hair, that it seemed any moment he would offer to accompany him on his search, go north with him should he go north, go south with him should he go south; but for Amnon it was not a son he was searching for here but a grandfather; if indeed he had made the trip for that purpose.

He went to the train station to buy a ticket to Pathankot for the evening train, and on the steps of the station an Indian stood lurking there exactly as was written in the Lonely Planet in the chapter designated for all sorts of frauds. He was dressed in a fairly clean kurta with shiny black hair and turned to him as he passed him and stopped him with a beaming smile and with a nimble hand reaching out to his elbow. "Please, Mister," he said in a fawning voice, "are you searching dee office? Office closed today because of Indian holiday, let me show you where to buy a ticket."

"Chalo," he said and shook off his grip, and just for a moment the thought crossed his mind that perhaps he had offended a well-meaning man for nothing.

When he returned to the hotel his room seemed familiar and comfortable in its dreariness, and he lay on the sunken bed as the fan above him turned its blades and again their shadow on the wall looked like the transparent wings of an insect, and when their rotations were accelerated they became detached from their axis and flew off, drawing away farther and farther, and suddenly he saw the son of the woman he had left holding a dragonfly by its trail and observing it, and from the armrest of the sofa – an Ikea sofa they had bought together – Puma the cat watched and lay in waiting for the appropriate moment; the slow movement of its tail was witness to that, it moved to and fro as if its entire body was set for action, and the moment Udi let go of the dragonfly, the cat pounced with claws unsheathed, not onto the insect nor the boy but onto him, dreaming of them.

He awoke in dread and looked at his watch and hurriedly rose to his feet.

He had already paid for the room, but still had to reach the corner of the

street and stop a tuk tuk and bargain with the stubborn driver ("Good driver more
security, more money also"), and afterward they got caught in traffic jams over
and over and children in tatters pressed their faces to the pane and pointed to
their mouths, and the moment he put his hand into his pocket the driver shouted
at them "Chalo! Chalo!" to chase them away, and when they arrived at the train
station, he waited shamelessly for the donation he had saved him to be added to
his wage.

"Chalo!" he said to the driver, and said it afterward to the porters who offered
to carry his rucksack and to the vendors who tried to sell him all sorts of baked
goods and confections, and in the station, when he entered into a crowded mass of
people moving and encircling and rubbing up against him and pushing, it seemed
there wasn't one centimeter in which some action wasn't taking place: suitcases
and metal boxes were being carried on the backs and the heads of porters in piles
and in towers, sacks were being transported by trolleys and unloaded on the platforms, soldiers were strolling here and there and on their shoulders old rifles from
the days of the Raj, bearded Sikhs wearing turbans were conferring in secret as if it
would be possible to hear their conversations in the tumult, vendors of soft drinks
shouted colacola and vendors of tea shouted chaichai and vendors of baked good
shouted puripuri. Giant ceiling fans shook violently with each rotation of their
blades, and in places where tiles were missing in the ceiling cooing pigeons nested,
and the light of dusk mixed with the light of neon clutched the wings of masses of
small flies. Dozens of people assembled at the food stalls and others slept on the
platforms, and opposite a woman in a shiny sari whose children were kneading in
their little hands fistfuls of rice she had given them, a thin boy stopped and waited
for a donation, and a compressed medley of sounds crammed the air: the din of
trains entering and leaving and the horns of train engines and whistles blowing
and the tumult of conversations in dozens of languages and dialects.

Mice scuttled between the tracks – he saw them when he drew near to the
platform – and a black crow pecked the remains of a rat that had been run over
by the wheels of a train, and when another approached with its dozens of coaches,
the crow rushed off with its bounty. Crowds massed at the entrances of the coaches
and crowds tried to exit from them and both pushed and shoved and made their
way out and in, and immediately after the train left on its way a thin man dressed
in a dirty lungi descended from the platform to the tracks and approached the fire
extinguisher between the tracks and turned it on and began to wash himself: he
soaped his protruding ribs, his armpits, his sunken stomach, his boney legs.

"They've got no shame," a voice in Hebrew was heard from behind. It was one
of the Israelis he met in the old city and hoped they wouldn't be travelling with
him on the same train, but right away they offered to help him in the tumult of
the station; he must have looked lost to them. He, who in his heyday at the newspaper had travelled from Buenos Aires to Kiev and hadn't hesitated to confront
senior Mossad and Secret Service officials and at their age had crossed thousands

of kilometers alone in his van, appeared in their eyes as an old man waiting for a boy scout to help him across the road. He had to make an effort for the insult not to be seen on his face.

They were also travelling to Pathankot, they said, and from there they'll continue by bus, but for him, whose destination was Manali ("A good place to look for him, Pops," they had said not knowing he'd be going onward to the north from there), it actually would be better to travel by bus from the start; but never mind, they said, this way everyone would travel together. That's how he waited with them on the platform, a forty-four-year-old man with these young people who could be his children. Only the two girls showed little interest in him: they probably saw him as an annoying father, helpless, though that's not how he looked at them when they showed each other the rings they had bought, stretching their fingers out for them to sparkle in the neon light – when the curly headed one lifted her arm the side of a clear skinned soft breast was revealed in the opening of the wide sleeve.

Without him having asked them, the tall one and the plump one went to look for his name on the passenger list, and when they returned, they notified him joyously that they would all be sitting together in the same coach, yes, that's how it turned out; and a moment later, unabashedly, they again asked him about his son who had disappeared. Once that falsehood had been fabricated it was no longer possible to renounce it, and in the unbearable commotion of the Delhi train station, among all those waiting and hurrying and eating and sleeping, and opposite two girls one of whom aroused his desire, he consented to being a father. For a moment, he recalled the Tel Aviv taxi driver who thought the rucksack he had bought was meant for his son and he didn't deny it; it seemed this fraudulent fatherhood had been outlined already then.

How old is your son, they asked him, twenty-one or twenty-two? Did he come to clear his head after the army? And the tall one, in the way he would have heartened the father of a close friend, said that it happens here even to the best: one strong bhang lassi would be enough to throw you. And not that they want to make him worried, he said, on the contrary, the boy was probably a bit confused and forgot to phone and in India there's not always somewhere to call from.

As a matter of fact, what's his name? They asked; how can they talk about him without knowing his name at all?

The farce had gone on too long and when he turned his head away, he saw a woman checking the red dot in the center of her forehead in a small mirror with the same exactitude as a western woman checks her lipstick – the way Naomi used to check hers in the powder compact mirror – and since they thought he hadn't heard them they again asked what his son's name was, and before considering what he would answer, he heard his voice replying to them through the tumult in which hundreds of voices were mixed, and when they asked where Nonny had served in the army, he hesitated a moment before saying the name of the unit in which he himself had served more than two decades ago.

"He was in Lebanon," he heard himself saying too loudly, and didn't know whether he was reproaching him about that or for some reason defending the military service of the young man he had then been, when it still seemed in the coming years he could do whatever entered his mind. His whole life was still before him – that's what everyone had said, and only his father pressed him to start studying – and now that he's past half of it, its direction is certain, whether he travels here or whether he travels there.

A train arrived at the platform and hordes of people pushed towards the entrances of the coaches and hordes of people tried to get down from them, and a young man held on to the bars of the coach window and climbed on them in order to overtake those pushing in front of him, and someone pushed him forward by the backside and another pulled his leg backward, and a policeman with an Australian helmet and a club in his hand was hitting here and there, and somehow the commotion abated and those getting off found their way out and those getting on their way in.

"Here at least they don't sit on the roof of the coach," said the plump one, "and the electricity here's okay." Above them, from the sooty ceiling, a dusty neon light shone.

"Electricity?" he pondered.

It transpired that while waiting in some small train station in Rajasthan, an Indian stood on the roof of a coach in order to wave at someone on the platform, and by mistake touched the cable that was less than thirty centimeters from his head and was turned into charcoal. "And after that they'll say it's karma," the tall one let slip derisively. People, he said, should blame themselves and not previous reincarnations. "The man died," said the girl whose hair was plaited into a mass of tiny braids, "what difference does it make now who's to blame?" With his long arms the tall one pulled her toward him and hugged her, he pressed her head close to his narrow chest and lowered his face to her braids and inhaled their scent.

The matter of electricity reminded the plump one what had happened at a roadblock to the soldiers who had served there before them; a bunch of nice guys, Nahal soldiers. They had sent someone to take down the PLO or Hamas flag from the pole and simply hadn't thought it through properly.

"Haven't they got anything else to talk about other than what happened to them in the occupied territories?" asked the girl with the braids, and the tall one, whose nose was still sunk in her braids, replied that it didn't happen to them; and in the same voice that was swallowed in her hair said that he's crazy for the smell of her. "Apple shampoo?" He guessed, and she nodded on his chest.

He didn't ask exactly what had happened at the roadblock, it wasn't hard to guess, and also knew that if he has to give up his ticket and buy another in its place, even postpone his journey and return to the hotel, he'll do it, though it wasn't them that he shrank from but what was reflected in their eyes; it was intolerably familiar. "Are you okay, Pops?" the tall one stretched his long arm out to him to support his shoulder, and his narrow face seemed to be concerned, well-meaning. Had he fainted in front of them, they would certainly have carried him back to the hotel and taken him up to his room and laid him on his bed and covered him; and for the time being they suggested he drink some water, the congestion here really does make one dizzy, even for those who are used to it. Maybe he wants a pill? The curly haired girl reached out a packet of Dexamol Cold and also opened it to make it easier for him.

When he lifted his rucksack on to his shoulder and turned towards the exit, the train to Pathankot was already entering the station with all its dozens of coaches, and they watched him from the platform for a moment longer, before making their way to the coach.

A few minutes before closing time, he went into that same travel agency in the main bazaar whose name had been Hebraized, and since there was no one else there other than him, he said to the man nicknamed Danny Tours that he would like to fly to Leh, and that he knows the flights are full, but there are also cancellations. While speaking he reached out his passport to Danny Tours, and with nimble fingers the Indian paged through the passport to the place where the money note was inserted.

Afterward he returned to his hotel and again had to take his rucksack up to the room, because when he returned from the train station the reception clerk told him it was being cleaned and that he'd have to pay for the room again, because if you check out, Sir, and they clean and tidy up, Sir, then you have to check in, the hotel isn't to blame, Sir, if you missed the train and changed your mind, the hotel has rules, Sir, and rules are very important, for the hotel's good name.

"Tea, Sir?" asked the air hostess.

"Yes, please," he replied. It was a small Air India plane whose destination was Leh, and he was glad not to be hearing Hebrew around him. It took a while for him to discover the Israeli couple on the other side of the aisle (before that, the air hostess had blocked his view; and after her they were blocked by someone trying to push his rucksack into the storage compartment), and an hour later during which he had dozed off the moment he leaned his head back and awoke only towards the landing, he heard them again when the first peaks were revealed in the round window, and the girl said: I just hope it won't be like in that movie where the plane crashed in the Andes and in the end they ate each other."

"I give you permission to eat me, Tami," the boy answered and bent over her toward the round window.

The peaks filled the window, amazingly large and near. Snow covered them though their slopes were arid and the shadow of the plane gradually grew over their surface from its tip to its tail, and below the valley of Leh could be seen, green and cultivated, surrounded by those slopes on whose summits white domes glistened, and the shadow of the giant wings gradually grew down below as well.

Here and there cultivated plots could be seen and around them a thick foliage of trees, and the irrigation tunnels leading thawed snow water to them sparkled criss-crossed in the sun, and on one of the paths a small caravan moved sluggishly, its animals, perhaps donkeys, were laden with sheaves, perhaps of wheat.

"I think we're gonna be happy here," the girl said, and all her youth was heard in her voice; innocent, pure, and blind.

4

A few guests were sitting in the courtyard of the small hotel, and he watched them from his window. It was a nice large window and in it the mountain slope seemed close to the point of being tangible, arid and wild as opposed to the white of the peak and the green of the vegetation at its foot. In the twenty-four hours that passed he saw the light change on the mountain and the valley from hour to hour and even at moments when the clouds hid the sun, and it then seemed that not only were the hues of the landscape transforming but its very essence as well, as if it was being kneaded over and over in order to satisfy some divine desire, and a great calm came upon him from this observation.

He drew the wooden chair close to the window and could stretch his legs out to the low windowsill and stare in front or look sideward at the corner of the courtyard where a few tables were placed and every now and then bits of conversation rose in a few languages, and even the little that reached his ears was quickly blurred by the silence of the valley surrounding the mountains. The world's highest mountains were north of it, and here only the very lowest parts - also immeasurably high - and their peaks, when not glistening, appeared like shreds of clouds, and the clouds themselves at times resemble peaks above the peaks whose slopes have been blurred by the blue of the sky. Far below them were fields of wheat and oats, and these grounds containing beds of radishes and turnips and in its corners lofty poplar trees, creating a pleasing contrast between the wide fleshy leaves of the vegetables and the delicate poplar leaves, and when the wind blew through their treetops their silvery side was revealed as if they had been undressed by the breeze. Toward nightfall the leaves darkened and joined each other and with their branches and trunks, becoming black silhouettes. The previous day at that hour he had gone out of his room, but not to begin his inquiries; they, he thought, could wait a while. They had waited for so many decades and these days wouldn't change anything, for better or for worse.

"Lucky we escaped all those Israelis," the curly haired boy said below.

"They're all so screwed up," said his girlfriend, "it's all because of the army, isn't that so, Ido?"

In another hour or two, should he suffer from end of the day hunger pains, he'll eat here in the hotel, And if a serving of chow mein isn't enough, he'll walk two kilometers from Changspa to what the locals call "the city" and even "the capital," despite that in effect it's just an oversized village and at the most a small town to which even the king's palace overlooking it from the slope doesn't add any royal splendor, nor do its monasteries add any holiness, and all the while it's crowned by the mountains it has little need for either.

"They were screwed up even before that," the boy said.

Perhaps that's how domestication begins: by observing the changing light on the leaves, by following the development of the line of snow on the peak – in the afternoon it seemed it had retreated a little from the place it had been in the morning, and if his stay here lengthens, the slopes would be further revealed day by day until the end of the summer, and afterward they'll again be wrapped in whiteness and every morning the line of snow will be closer than it had been. It will no doubt be a beautiful sight when everything turns white here, he thought, and the season changes, and for nine months all the access roads will be blocked, no one leaves and no one enters. The beds of radishes and turnips will be covered in white; the poplar trunks will turn white; the courtyard will become white up to knee height or up to the height of the tables, and the Israeli couple will no doubt have left here long before then.

"Are you all of a sudden defending the army?"

"I'm the last one to defend the army," the boy answered.

The Austrian couple also sat with them, and the thin Canadian girl with her drawing block, and the short Italian girl who skillfully cut her hair the day before, the way she does in her salon in Milan. They all, it transpired, had come here for a long period, and at least from that point of view it seemed he had come to the right place; like him they were looking for a place as far away as possible from the commotion of the bazaar and from chance tourists. He already knew the Austrian couple were fostering a young monk here and every month transferred money to him for his livelihood ("For us its pennies, and for them it's a fortune") and they had even once hosted him in their home. The Canadian girl was planning a trip to Lake Tsomoriri to draw the nomads who live on its shores, and the Italian hairdresser said that her big dream is to become a nun. He heard all that at one evening dinner, and when they waited for him to tell them why he had come as far as to here, he exempted himself with an evasive answer.

Did they slightly resemble those who had lived here a hundred years ago? To that he had no answer. People who travel so far from their homeland for a long period must certainly have something in common, but their predecessors lived here for years and not months, and there were those who ended their lives here. At that time, the beginning of the twentieth century, there lived here a commissioner, a doctor, a missionary and certainly officials, also British, and the married among them must have come with their wives. All that could have been assumed even without an in-depth investigation, and as to how they had all treated a Russian refugee who had landed up here, he had no answer; it was hard enough even to know about them themselves. For example, what had driven a respectable doctor, the director of the Moravian mission hospital, to become mixed up in an affair causing him to send his son to England and not see him to the end of his days ("He was actually particular about sending me letters," McKenzie Jr. had said in England, "but continued to write to me as if to a little boy").

In fact, it was possible to find out quite a lot by the usual methods: an affair like that must made the newspapers, and he could have rummaged through newspaper archives in London, and if not there, in Delhi, and read everything that had been published during those years of the beginning of the twentieth century, until the doctor's name would pop up in one of those editions, but he preferred to travel and discover everything on the spot itself and not on disintegrating paper.

He also knew where he would start: in the cemetery. There perhaps he would find the tombstones of all those concerned in the matter, if they hadn't been covered in weeds or become worn down. From there he would continue on to the mission hospital and ask not only about the man who had been one of its first directors, but also about someone who had died there a hundred years ago (my grandfather, he thought, but knew that he wouldn't say that), if indeed he had died there and if documentation had been kept of that; and from the hospital he'd go to the Moravian church, records of deaths had probably been kept there, although not of those who weren't Christian; and from the church he'd go to the police station, despite it being hard to pin much hope on that institution (apparently British efficiency had taken root only in the train system and hadn't reached the police). Nevertheless, he hoped that some of the people he would talk with would refer him to other people, and those to others, and one out of all those – after all, one is enough – would in the end give him some useful information. That's what he used to do in his glory years and always achieved his goal. Always? Was that indeed the case? After all, he had persevered with all that for but a few years.

From the corner of his eye, he saw the hotel owner's daughter down below bringing a tray with cups of tea on it to those sitting there, and the Austrian saying something about her to the others; perhaps he was comparing her to her mother who is completely devoid of gentility and rules domineeringly over all matters concerning the hotel, while her husband tries to amuse his guests with the few words he's learned in their languages. He called the Austrian Herr Steffman, and his wife Frau Beate, and the Italian Donna Ornella and the Canadian Miss Rose, and he knew how to count in almost all the European languages. The first time he heard the word "abba"[36] it seemed as if some Israeli family from far away had landed up here, until he learned that that's how Ladakhi children also call their fathers, by those two syllables that he himself had not uttered for a very long time – when was the last time he had spoken to his aged father? He had learned the word from one of the conversation manuals he found in the reception room with maps of the area.

In the manual he also found the Ladakhi greeting – joolay! – And how you ask

---

36 "Father" in Hebrew.

someone how he is – khamsang – and how you invite him to sit down – skyoot-ley; and also how you say soup – thukpa – and how every difficulty can be solved with naychichuan. The word for cemetery wasn't written there, nor for tombstone, but he had no doubt he'd find the cemetery next to the church, and it was there he decided to begin, with the dead.

You're a great fan of cemeteries, he said to himself with derision. When was the last time you went to visit your mother's grave?

The following day, on his way to the city, the fields again could be seen on both sides of the path and one could try to imagine a row of men or women harvesters advancing and scythes or sickles in their hands, but no living soul could be seen there other than a dzo of tremendous proportions reclining regally close to the path and chewing on sheaves, and when he passed by it didn't stop chewing nor granted him a look. Some time elapsed until the army base was revealed around the bend, and in the white booth in front of it a sentry stood in his ironed uniform and stared at the expanse of the fields and the bottom of the mountains, and when he passed him his eyes accompanied Amnon without him moving from his spot. On a small hill across from the barracks the number of the regiment, 798, was written with whitewashed stones, and whitewashed stones also marked the paths of the base, clearly the legacy of British rule. Poplars grew at the sides of the way and their silhouettes spread over it with such slender trunks it seemed the path had been striped with a paint bush, and he already knew that on the way back their directions would be reversed. He found a certain comforting consolation in that knowledge.

Shortly the first houses of Leh could be seen and a moderate din could be heard: the peddlers didn't shout their wares out loud but just sat behind them on the sidewalks of the bazaar street and waited for passersby to stop opposite them. The air was filled with a mixture of bits of conversations and the rattling of old motor car engines and here and there a bleating or a chiming of bells, and after the noises of Delhi it seemed that here, even in the midst of Leh itself and certainly in his hotel outside the town, he would perhaps at long last find rest. Hell, doesn't he deserve some rest? No, he answered himself, no; but nonetheless wanted it.

He found the small Moravian Church easily according to the map, and also the nearby graveyard, but its gate was locked and he had to return to the church and ask the priest if he could pay it a visit. It took a while for the priest to come out toward him – a thickset Ladakh man whose hair was black and shiny – and when a boy's voice was heard from an inner room the priest turned his head there and made some calming remark in Ladakhi. Afterward they both stood on the threshold of the church from where the gravestones could be seen: a few dozen with weeds between them.

He's simply interested in local history, he said to the priest (the voice of the boy could be heard again from behind together with the rhythmic sound of a bouncing ball) and deliberated whether to say he was a journalist, fearing it may intimidate him.

"Exactly whose history?" the priest asked. He must have been one of the few here who had converted from their religion and had he not been suspicious by nature this request might have aroused his suspicion: many tourists came to Leh, there were more than enough temples for them to visit here, but none of them saw fit to visit the small, neglected graveyard.

"Dr. Edward McKenzie's," he answered, and from the look on the priest's face, he added that he – the Dr. McKenzie he's looking for – ran the mission hospital here at the beginning of the century; had by any chance the priest heard something about him?

"And what's your connection to him? Stop that, Andoni!" The priest called out suddenly to the inner room. "We agreed that you play only outside!" And the ball bounced once more and fell silent.

He then answered by saying he had met with McKenzie's son in England and had promised him to visit his father's grave; it was a complete lie, nothing interested McKenzie's son less than his father's grave, but the answer fell effortlessly from his lips, and he already knew he would find no difficulty adding more falsehoods to it, from those he had prepared in advance, should he be asked unnecessary questions, and others he would make up on the spot; he didn't always succeed in that, least of all when not confronted with a defined purpose, but now there was one.

"And how are you connected to his son?" the priest asked.

"We became friendly."

The priest turned his gaze backward; perhaps he was waiting for his son to come outside with the ball. "Where did you say you come from?"

"I came from Delhi."

"And from where to Delhi?"

He hesitated and decided to make do with the name of the city from where he flew to Delhi; that would surely be enough for the priest, not even the border police had asked for more.

"And from where to London?"

Again he hesitated for a moment: he had no desire to tell him where he was born and had lived most of his years, and certainly not to become involved in a theological discussion with a priest about Judaism and Christianity, but even if that were not the case he would certainly lie; a lie once told is easier to repeat than fabricating a new one, and even if he hadn't been persuasive in Delhi, perhaps he would be so here. "From Spain," he replied as he had replied in Delhi, and for a moment there arose in him the amusing notion that he would have to apologize before the priest and the entire Indian nation – more than a billion people – for the despicable treatment of his fellow countrymen toward bulls, if indeed the news of bullfighting had reached the ears of the priest, and if after renouncing the local faith he still believed in the holiness of cows.

"And from where in Spain?"

"Barcelona." He answered without giving it any thought; he could have said Madrid, but his lips had already chosen for him.

"Bar-ce-lo-na," the priest said, rolling the syllables in his mouth syllable by syllable. "Barcelona. I've actually heard a lot about Barcelona, I've even been shown Gaudi's church – I'm not saying it's not beautiful, it is, but I prefer my own. What do you need so many adornments for?" He turned his head backward when a bouncing ball was again heard from there. "You've got good football there," he said, "no question about that," and for a moment it was impossible to know whether he was mocking the second wonder of the Catalonian capital or speaking seriously, or perhaps that was how he found a way to the hearts of the youth who attended his church.

"Is Cruyff still coaching?" The priest asked and behind him his son could be seen kneeling down on the floor to tie his bootlaces, the ball at his side.

The name Cruyff sounded familiar to him: wasn't there a Dutch football player with that name? For a moment, it seemed that even the name of his team was stored in his memory from childhood, Ajax, and as much time had passed since then, more than three decades, maybe the same Cruyff had become a coach? He gestured with his head to the priest a noncommittal motion which he could interpret as he wished.

"Andoni says he's about to retire," the priest said.

It turned out that in Leh it was possible to pick up the matches being broadcast in neighboring Kashmir, and the giant satellite dish that the priest has in his home allowed him and his son to keep up to date not only with the news from CNN but also with what was happening in the Mondial; not at the expense of his community, on the contrary, there's no better way to reach the youth here, and without them the church has no future. Besides – the priest said – a person also needs hours in which to amuse his soul and there's nothing improper about football provided it's played with fairness and mutual respect. What's more, sport even appears in the Bible, its written "Let the young men, I pray thee, arise and play before us," although there, it has to be said, it ended badly. "Come on, Andoni," he called to his son, "we've got a guest from Spain," and the boy, heavy set like his father, got up and stood by his side.

"Cruyff also made mistakes," the priest remarked, "that has to be said. For a long time Andoni thought he should have left. Four consecutive championships are all very well, a really exceptional achievement, but it would have been better for him to go back to Holland if he let Laudrup leave like that when Romario arrived. You don't do a thing like that! Andoni was very angry with him, right, Andoni?"

His son lifted his head on hearing the names mentioned, and Amnon, having no other response - none of those names were familiar to him – nodded to the priest.

"Even if he didn't score the winning goal in the championship match," the priest said, "without Laudrup Barca is definitely not the dream team it was; Andoni would tell you that with harsher language. Either way, it has to be said."

"Without a doubt," he answered.

"But that's not what you came here for."

"No."

"Still, it's a long way from Spain to here," the priest said.

He mentioned that on the way he stopped in England – that's where he met McKenzie's son.

"There's also good football in England," the priest said, and again he didn't know whether he was making fun of him or speaking seriously. "Andoni is also a fan of Manchester United, right, Andoni?" But on the other hand – he said as the boy pulled the edge of his gym pants above his navel – for a long time English football hasn't been what it used to be. Yes, he said, as far as he and Andoni know, there was only one Englishman who played for Barcelona, Gary Lineker. Although Gary didn't play badly at all, it has to be said.

"Gary was okay," Amnon said; it seemed to him he wasn't risking himself with that statement; after all, Barcelona wouldn't have bought that Gary Lineker had it not been for his capabilities.

The priest's son said something to his father which he right away translated into English; this Lineker had once scored three goals against Real in a decisive league match. "Three goals!" the priest said with genuine amazement, if not excessively so for his son's sake; but after all the goals he scored Lineker was sold not long after for half the price and went back to England together with the English coach who had brought him over; yes, there's quite a turnover in the dream team.

The priest and his son also had some criticism concerning Popescu and Stoichkov (the priest mainly translated), who also left the squad, the first name sounded Romanian and the second one Russian, and in an attempt to hang onto the second one in order to change the topic of their conversation – who would have imagined that he would find himself talking to a Ladakh priest about the Barcelona team – he said to the priest it was a pity they had also let Stoichkov go back to Russia with such ease, that's also something you don't do. Right away the priest's son corrected him and said that Stoichkov came from Bulgaria, not Russia, and that a fortune of money had also been paid for him: four hundred million pesetas. "Four hundred million!" the priest repeated his son's words with amazement and his eyes turned towards the mountains as if they had all turned into enormous piles of pesetas, but only arid slopes could be seen with the shadows the cliffs and rocks cast upon them.

The church at whose head he stood was altogether simple: a wooden structure devoid of adornments, the complete opposite of the multi-turreted and curved

Gaudi cathedral, and its interior was similarly modest when his eyes adapted to the duskiness beyond the priest. Without hesitation he joined in the double amazement: at the enormous sum and at the boy who remembered it. Yes, that's how it is, the priest explained with a sort of apologetic pleasure, there's nothing about Barca his son doesn't remember; even if you wake Andoni in the middle of the night, he could recite it all.

"But that's not what you came here for," he said again and waited for him to answer; perhaps he had just been testing him before that.

"No," he admitted again, and the priest waited for him to continue.

He could have spoken directly about the matter for which he had come, and he could have wrapped it in some fictitious package, an article about the mysteries of Ladakh or a series of articles concerning the representatives of empires that had collapsed and the remnants of their grip on India, the Portuguese in Goa, the French in Pondicherry, the Russians in Ladakh, he could also have chosen the disappearance of foreigners here since the beginning of the century, and in the end his lips chose for him. In actual fact – he heard himself say – he's looking for a certain Russian, yes, a Russian, who at the beginning of the century worked with Dr. McKenzie, no, not in the hospital. Perhaps he had been admitted there for a while, perhaps even died there in the doctor's arms and was buried here in the graveyard, more than that he doesn't know.

"There's no Russian here," with a quick glance the priest surveyed all the gravestones before them (from the entrance of the church they could be seen to the last row, mostly plain in their appearance, slanting sideways or backward and the grass between them swaying in the wind) and he went into detail: one German, one Belgian, one Frenchman, and many Englishmen – but no Russian. That's to say no one other than the Russian boy, but he's not looking for a boy.

"So your dream team also isn't complete," the inept quip suddenly came out of his mouth, and the priest didn't approve of his remark at all: his love for football was one thing and his role in the community quite another, and under no circumstance were the two to be mixed; and moreover if he succeeds in bringing the youth closer to him by his love of sport and especially through football, there's only good in it, only good! Besides which, he said, his son Andoni has both these loves in common with him, the church and sport, and show him another father and son as close as they were. His son lifted his gaze, got up and stood by his side and the priest put his arm around his shoulder; the resemblance between them was noticeable.

He had no intention of insulting the dead – Amnon said – may they rest in peace, the German and the Belgian and the Frenchman and all the Englishmen, really, may they rest in peace, nevertheless, even if the Russian who he is looking for isn't buried here, hadn't any Russian visited here in Leh during the years of the beginning of the century?

"Visited maybe yes, but died no," the priest replied. His former chattiness had disappeared and again he gave him a long suspicious look, "that's to say besides the boy. And what's your connection to Russia?"

Only then, after all the time that had passed since the beginning of their conversation, did he tell the priest that he was a journalist doing research for an article concerning foreigners who had come to the area at the beginning of the century and had disappeared without a trace, and that the Russian was one of them ("I write for *El Pais*," he lied to the priest on remembering the name of the Spanish daily, "you must have heard of *El Pais*?"). In recent years, he said, it was a case of backpackers who had trouble recovering from some drug hallucination, in Manali or Kasol for example – perhaps the priest has heard of Kasol? – And in previous years people had disappeared for different reasons. "There's no shortage of reasons for people to disappear," he said and didn't like the critical look the priest gave him, as if he had spoken of himself as well. Had he not spoken of himself as well?

It was a cover-up with many holes in it: assuming the Russian he was looking for had disappeared, how could he know if it had been in Leh or in some other place? And what had a Spanish newspaper to do with this Russian who no one had heard of? And if he does decide to remain here in the coming months, why become entangled in lies at all? But when he thought of all that before, he hadn't been expecting the graveyard to be locked and barred. "Maybe I could just walk around a bit and look at the gravestones," he said to the priest in order to exempt himself from further explanations, "if it's of no bother to you, of course."

It's possible that the priest would have made things more difficult for him, but his son pulled his hand; this was the hour for him to coach him kicking at the goal – an improvised goal, marked by two whitewashed stones in front of the graveyard wall.

"Come on, Andoni," the priest said and skillfully grabbed the ball the boy kicked to him, a new looking leather ball, "show this man what you've learned. The two of us don't want to disappear, we want to stay here together forever and play. Do you know which Andoni this is?" He turned to Amnon who hesitated before making a noncommittal motion with his head, since he did not know who he was speaking about.

"Zubizarreta," the priest said. "Andoni Zubizarreta. There's never been a goal-keeper like Zubizarreta, nor will there ever be. Ask Andoni how many times he kept goal. The best goalie of all time."

"A great goalkeeper," Amnon said and pondered for a moment whether to pat the boy on his back, the way he certainly would have to an Israeli boy, but decided not to take a chance with a gesture not customary here. "You can tell that just from his name, Zubizarreta."

Again the priest cast him a suspicious look, but his son pulled him by the arm again and led him to the improvised goal and remained there another moment or two in order to compliment the boy on his dives for the ball that had been kicked

to one corner and then to the other with surprising skill, and the boy, despite being
heavy-set, hadn't hesitated to dive for the ball.

"Just be sure to honor the dead," the priest said when he saw him turn toward
the graveyard gate with the key he gave him. It was a fitting remark. The last graveyard he visited was in England where he searched in vain for McKenzie senior's
grave, and before that the Kiryat Shaul cemetery which he seldom visited, and had
it not been for his father he wouldn't have frequented it at all. In the British graveyard he only succeeded in finding out the name of the builder Franklin, whose
name he remembered from the church pamphlet ("He who built our abodes" was
engraved on his gravestone, "May heaven be now his abode"), and in the Kiryat
Shaul cemetery on each anniversary of Ada's death his father would find the graves
of his colleagues and acquaintances who had reached there before him, and for the
most part was happy to see them as if he had met them by chance on the street.
There were colleagues from the Brigade, survivors of that unnecessary battle in the
hills of northern Italy, and colleagues from the university who had been granted
tenure and among them the professor who had brought about his retirement, and
colleagues from the *Davar* newspaper and among them the journalist Carmeli,
who in his childhood when accompanying his father, had explained to him what a
prostitute was and why he, Carmeli, was worse than a prostitute.

Only a few people came to his mother's funeral, less than the required quorum
of ten in the Jewish tradition. Her second husband's sons were absent, they had
boycotted her ever since his death owing to him bequeathing most of his property
to her, and he vaguely recognized a few of her friends who had greatly aged; two
were helped by Filipina caregivers and one called him by his father's name. A few
of their neighbors from his childhood home also came, and in the absence of her
second husband who died two years before her, they all treated his father as if he
was still her husband, and for a while, when they all stood in the entrance at the
start of the route to the grave, he looked like a groom, until his shoulders shook
and hunched and standing in front of the pit he covered his face with his hands.

Standing next to his father opposite his mother's grave, he felt almost nothing. He met with once a year her during the time before the stroke, always in the
middle of winter on the date between both their birthdays, and in the first years
she seemed to be blossoming and didn't try to hide it: she wore expensive clothes,
used makeup, spoke in great detail about her trips abroad with her new husband,
brought him small gifts she no doubt bought at the airport. That period lasted
for four years, until her husband suffered from heart failure, and she, who always
feared she would be forced to care for Nachman in his old age, was required to
care for a man her own age who had a pacemaker implanted in his chest and had
to be careful with every action: the trips abroad came to an end, the meals in fancy
restaurants came to an end, other recreations they had enjoyed came to an end.
At first she still hoped he would return to his former strength and it seemed her

caring was solely to enable her to once again enjoy all the pleasures of life he had afforded her (he was grateful for her help in the small company that had encountered difficulties, and for listening to all his troubles with a sympathetic ear; and for having seen in him what others hadn't, least of all his family), but even when it became clear his state wasn't going to improve, she continued to care for him with dedication, and only in her last years was she helped by a sturdy Russian woman who also became a friend to her. "I can't tell you it's easy because it's not," she said to him in their annual meeting, and he wondered if she regretted the choice she had made – his father was still healthy and completely lucid – and as if she read his thoughts she hastened to say: "But that's my life now, and one has to accept it," and for a brief moment he felt sorry for her.

Opposite her grave that moment was already forgotten, and through her shroud and the tiles placed upon her and the soil heaped on them he saw only the one he had been asked to identify in the room where she had been laid immediately after they entered the cemetery ("You go," said his father, despite that only two hours before he had arrived from Athens): a corpse whose temple had sunk in the place where the cranium had been sawed, her head resembling a ball from which all the air has been deflated and with it the facial features, and that was how she appeared to him through the marble slab when he came to visit on all the anniversaries of her death, devoid of defined features – perhaps he hadn't enough love or longing to blot out that last image of her.

He began to pass between the gravestones row by row with the large key in his pocket. Some were a hundred years old and more, cracked and slanted and covered in lichen, some were from the middle of the century with the marks of time evident on them, only a few looked new; apparently the Moravian mission had not had much success here or most of its converts had been saved from death.

Slowly the sound of the beating ball slackened, either because he had drawn away from the graveyard gate or because his attention was focused on the gravestones around him. On the one that stood on the grave of the botanist Schmidt (a flowering plant was engraved above his name) the years of his birth and death were engraved with two short lines: "All his life he longed to breathe the scent of flowers, and in the end was overpowered by the air of the heights," and on a gravestone taller than all its neighbors, all the postings held by a certain colonel were listed: Gujarat, Punjab, Himachal Pradesh, and in Leh. "This stone was erected by his loving wife Mary-Louise," was engraved there, "And not long is the day when the two shall be united forever in eternity," but her gravestone could not be seen there, perhaps she had decided to return to England with her family.

A small stone angel stood on the gravestone of the infant James Bridges, who lived between 12.8.1889 – 11.11.1889 – just three months – and near to it stood a larger angel sheltering him with its wings from the grave of his loving mother Virginia who died one week after her son. Engraved there was: "This monument was erected by his father and her husband who awaits the resurrection of the dead," and he lingered opposite that grave; for a moment he reflected upon the one who almost reached boyhood and died not in the mountains but in the sea, and swiftly banished him from his mind. He also did not see the gravestone of the Russian boy the priest spoke of, owing to its size it was perhaps covered by weeds.

Only on one of the next paths, beyond some cracked and worn-down gravestones and already thinking he wouldn't find it, the gravestone of McKenzie Sr. came into sight: it transpired that he died at the beginning of February 1922 and written in Gothic letters on the gravestone were four lines of praise: "The dedicated director of the Moravian Mission Hospital in his first years, many are those who owe him their lives. For them, local inhabitants and foreigners alike, he acted untiringly all his days, and even when malicious minds attempted to denigrate him, he never ceased healing his patients." He paused for a while opposite that gravestone, as if it would be possible to find some similarity between the death of the father here and the anticipated death of his son in England; for a moment he recalled the ship of the dead which the son had seen in his nightmares, the ship waiting for him alone opposite the dock; and that thought too he banished from his mind and walked on.

Alongside the gravestone of McKenzie Sr. stood the gravestone of his wife Dianne, nee Barnes, who died sixteen years before him, and the inscription engraved there extolled her incomparable dedication and purity of soul, pure as the paints with which she so well portrayed the landscapes of Ladakh. What kind of a woman was she really, and how had the doctor lived out his years of widowhood? On this the stones gave no answer, nor on the loneliness of his son who had been sent to England.

Not far from there the gravestone could be seen of the commissioner Henry Loudon who served seventeen years in Ladakh, "He gave his all for its inhabitants and made his home among them, out of his love for them he prolonged his sojourn here more than all the commissioners who preceded him." He also saw the gravestone nearby of one of the predecessors of the Barcelona fan priest, "The missionary Robert Harper, faithful servant of the Lord and modest shepherd of his believers, who gave of his best years here in order to illuminate faith in the hearts of all." Alongside his gravestone stood the gravestone of his wife Margaret, "Exemplary among women, loved by all, young and old alike, her glory shall be carried to the heavens by a bird of the sky and we shall all lift up our eyes to accompany her on her path to Paradise."

The inscriptions were not easily read, some were worn down and blurred and others covered with lichen, but with a little patience it was possible to read the words engraved by the hand of an anonymous stonecutter who has long ago also passed on from the world. Afterward he sat down on a stone bench and his gaze strayed to the weeds swaying in the breeze between the gravestones; they moved with life in them, while beneath them were just white bones. Thousands of kilometers from there lay his mother in her grave, her legs and arms pressed closely together like a modest schoolgirl, and maggots having already stripped most of her bones. Compassion suddenly rose in him for his old father who in not a long while will lie there too, white haired and scarred from abandonment, and the men of the Jewish Burial Society for whom he had such distaste, will do with him as they please and owing to the shortage of space won't bury him alongside his wife, but above her, and for a moment he wondered how they would have managed had his father died before her and lay beneath her; it was a despicable thought, sick, and thoroughly mistaken (in fact, his mother was buried with her second husband), and by contrast the burial customs carried out here – cremation or sky burial – were far better and more logical. Rather be burned, he thought, and turn to ashes, and rather the birds eat the body than worms. And what about fish, a previous thought came to mind as if it had not been repelled.

Then not far from him the ball fell and he heard the priest shout, "Kick it to us, El Pais!" he called to him in a joyous voice from the other side of the wall, and when he rose unwillingly and drew near to the ball and touched it with his foot, the silly indecision from his boyhood days arose: should he kick the ball with the instep of the shoe or with the its tip? He settled in favor of the instep and lifted his foot and kicked and was glad that he didn't miss and that he was capable of passing the ball over the wall.

"Bravo, El Pais!" the priest called out, and the simple compliment pleased him, much to his surprise, as if it approved not only of this kick but also of all the kicks of his childhood that came before it and even his childhood itself, verifying that there had been a period of his life when he played soccer and catch and hide and seek and ball tag, games all of which Udi replaced with computer games in his room, without a neighborhood to run around in.

When he returned to the stone bench, a game from his childhood years rose in his memory – they were playing a kind of football with the ball rebounding again and again the fence of the synagogue, and all of a sudden Mahlal, a footballer from the Bnei Yehuda team, stopped next to them and began to bounce the ball on his head, on his knee, on his shoulders, he bounced and bounced and bounced and didn't stop even when evening fell and their mothers started calling for them to come home, all except his mother who wasn't home at the time. He remembered the synagogue itself as well, not from the Jewish holidays but from the Bar Mitzvah ceremony his parents decided to celebrate for him in order to demonstrate their family togetherness and thereby disprove all the rumors that his mother was intending to leave his father, and also remembered how he struggled with the singing of the biblical text and how the entire congregation waited for the damn ceremony to end: not because of his off-key singing but because of the pretense that had been imposed upon everyone.

"Bravo, Andoni," he said to the boy when he came out from the cemetery and stopped to watch the two of them play: the priest was good at both kinds of kicking and made no concessions to the boy, so that he'd learn to dive with agility in all directions. "Like a tight spring," he said to his son, "the moment I kick, you unwind. And don't look anywhere else, Andoni, just keep your eye on the ball!"

A moment later he tried to draw the priest back to his matter and asked if he could take a quick look at the church registry, but the priest, taking a step backward in order to gain momentum for the kick and panting slightly, said that he knows all those registries very well and no Russian adult was recorded in them, only that boy. "But why not come on Sunday," he said, "and after the sermon you can search together with me." Until he finishes preparing his sermon, he said, he simply has no spare time, there are some very important things he intends to tell the youth here who've become so dazzled by all sorts of electrical appliances that until a year ago they didn't know existed; to the point where they're prepared to do everything to obtain them, even stealing. Yes, he's sure to hear about it from Tendon – if he's going to him with all these questions of his – because the inspector is no less worried.

"Are you looking at me or at the ball, Andoni?" he said to his son and at the same moment kicked toward the right corner, and the boy, though looking clumsy and distracted a moment before, flew there like one of the angels.

5

He had a negative opinion of the Indian police ever since his previous visit. He well remembered the part a police inspector had played in the riots of Bhagalpur – not only did he not restrain the mob of Hindu rioters, but he incited and led them in apparently unthinkable atrocities carried out with incomprehensible cruelty. Their beginnings were the false rumors about the killing of Hindus by Muslims, and afterward, under police cover, the rioters had no easier prey than the helpless.

The editor was so surprised by those facts which laid the blame mainly on the Hindus that he decided to strike a balance by attaching a note to his article, seemingly as an integral part of the comparison that had been made between the religious conflicts of both countries; in that way the newspaper readers came to know that the Hebron massacre[37] had also been preceded by false rumors, in that case the killing of Muslims by Jews, and there too the police chief had done more harm than good, and if comparisons are to be made, what is Hindi incitement in contrast to the declaration of the Mufti: "Everyone who kills a Jew is promised a place in the next world." The editor also recalled the Mufti's support for the Nazis and ignored Gandhi, who had behaved in a similar fashion.

"Is that what I sent you to India for, Poleg?" he said to him on his return from there a couple of kilos thinner and didn't know that he had barely left the hotel in Delhi, not in order to interview that inspector, nor all the others he quoted in his articles as ones who had seen the horrors firsthand.

He pinned no hopes on his visit to the police station here, if only for the simple reason that in Western police stations information from a hundred years ago is also not kept. In fact, only after he heard that the station was located halfway on the route to the hospital, his next destination, he decided nevertheless to go there, and he had not forgotten what he had learned during his first year at the paper: one thing leads to another. "You start with one thing and cannot know where it will lead to," Kramer explained to him at the time, "sometimes it's good, sometimes it's bad, only by then there's no turning back." Kramer wasn't talking about policemen, but about all the neighbors around – the tenants in the building, the shopkeepers,

---

37 On the 24th August 1929, sixty-seven Jews were killed by Arabs due to rumors that Jews were planning to seize the Temple Mount in Jerusalem.

the greengrocer, the lottery stall owner – each one of them could add some small detail, apparently inconsequential, about the one who had been murdered, but when all the details were joined together you received a complete picture. "D'you understand that sonny?" Kramer asked and he nodded his head and was prepared to learn everything he could teach him, and at the time still saw his profession as a vocation and thought that through his articles he had the power to change the face of society, if he would only place a mirror in front of it from which nothing escapes. Kramer only spoke about policemen afterward and said to be careful of the sorts who leak information: and of those who would use him manipulatively in some investigation and those who would use him to glorify themselves – he would get no benefit from either. "It's actually from the junior ones that you can learn something," he said and detailed it in the rhythm of a dictation: what was the first thing they noticed when entering a crime scene, even before everything that had been documented in the file; it could even be a smell, but of what? Bleach or something that was trying to conceal evidence? Expensive perfume or cheap deodorant? The smell of sweat? Had someone farted a moment before that? It could be a station heard on the radio or a television channel – a pop or classical music station or the army radio, the sport or shopping channel.

"And also, what was in the fridge," Kramer said, "beer cans or half liter bottles of Coke or Milky dairy pudding? And are the bedclothes clean or not? And if not, from what, from sweat or from something else? And does the toilet stink of shit or perfume or cigarettes? What are you making that face for, where did you think you've come to work? It's all petty nonsense, yes, but a person is composed of that nonsense." Kramer-Kramer, he thought two years later when going around his small apartment to bring a few possessions to him in hospital, after the attack; he opened the fridge, peeked into his bedroom, the toilet, even checked what could be seen from his window (a chair stood there next to the window overlooking the next-door apartment, and it was on that chair that Kramer had collapsed).

He was also buried in the Kiryat Shaul cemetery, and on the last anniversary of Ada's death, on which his father seemed more hunched than ever and closer to her with his body shrinking toward her, they stopped as usual opposite his grandmother's grave and there too his father was silent, and only when they lingered opposite the grave of Kramer, who his father knew only from his articles about Africa and from what he had been accused of due to them, he suddenly said with resentment and in a cracked voice: "This Kramer's got one, and he, Amnon, hasn't -" meaning his grandfather of whom there was no knowing where he was buried, and what had been blocked inside him opposite the two previous graves burst out opposite the stranger's grave.

On a large map hung in Kramer's bedroom, the places where he had been were highlighted with a felt tipped pen, and during one of the seven days of mourning, when he stood opposite it, he was reminded with what joy Kramer used to pronounce all those names: Kampala, Kinshasa, Kasese, Tanganyika,

Kakabara, Rwenzori Mountains. More than all of them, he was captivated by the
full name of President Mobutu: Mobutu Sese Seko Kuku Ngbendu Wa Za Banga,
the-brave-and-intrepid-warrior-thanks-to-whose-perserverence-and-uncom-
promising-determination-he-will-go-from-strength-to-strength-leaving-behind-
-him-a-trail-of-fire; there was no greater contradiction than that to Kramer or
perhaps even to the real Mobutu. The names of Ladakhi kings were somewhat
plain in comparison, all Namgyals, But who could compete with the mountain
passes here, them and the sound of them: Khardung-La, Lachulung-La, Tang-
lang-La, Marsimik-La, Zoji-La, Shingo-La; one can repeat them, La and sing
them, La, and if one day, La, he returns to his country, he could perhaps impress
young journalists with them and hang a map of India in his room and mark all
those passes, but where would he be returning to? A year before the end Kramer
said of himself; "This guy's finished," when he discovered his face in one of the
photographs shot at the scene of some crime, a defeated face like one whose time
the doctors have already marked (at the time they hadn't done that yet), and he
now wondered if his own face also looked like that, defeated.

A battered and rusty tin signpost was hung in the entrance of the police station
and the Indian flag unravelling at its edges waved above it, and a policeman in
khaki stood at the rim of the sidewalk and threw apricot pits at an electric pole on
the other side of the road and didn't notice him when he entered. Inside, a small
corridor could be seen that hadn't been whitewashed for a long time, and there
were two rooms: on the right, the office of inspector Jawaharlal Tendon, and on
the left, the large room used by his subordinates – three of them watching a cricket
match broadcast in black and white from a small television set, and a ceiling fan
leafed through the pages on their table. With each successful stroke of the batsman
on the field they cheered and with each miss they all groaned together.

He turned right toward the inspector's door and found him trying to clear
a blockage in the small sink in the corner of the office: murky water stood in the
basin and a few swollen cigarette butts floated on its surface, and the inspector,
kneeling down and his thick glasses on his forehead, took the siphon apart and
a moment later the surface of the water began to lower and the drizzle could be
heard hitting the bottom of the bucket that had been placed below.

"Only that way," the inspector said while bent down, "the old methods, not
with all those fancy tools from America. That" – he pointed to a small can with
something drawn on it that looked like a motorized mole – "only makes it worse!"
For a moment longer he paid attention to the drizzle falling to the bucket like
someone listening to a gurgling brook.

In this room a ceiling fan turned above as well, and added to it was a tiny fan
attached to the edge of the table with a clamp, and after reinstalling the siphon the
inspector rose and stood opposite the fan, first to dry the palms of his hands and

afterward to dry his sweaty forehead; then he bent towards the fan and drew his head close to it almost touching, as if he wanted to kiss it.

From the next room a dim cheering of thousands of people was suddenly heard, and the three policemen sitting there joined in with it. "It looks like we're on the way to victory," the inspector said and returned his glasses to his eyes. "What can I do for you?"

He hesitated. It would have been ridiculous to say that he was looking for a person who had disappeared a hundred years ago, even if that man was his grand-father and even if his father would not rest until he knew how and why he had died. It would be better to inquire about some act of fraud committed during the same period, an act that even if not documented in police annals, had perhaps been perpetuated by local lore, but he didn't know exactly what and how to ask, and while deliberating and the silence becoming longer (the cheer in the next room had died down), he heard himself complimenting the inspector on his nice small fan and also asked where he could buy one like it.

"I didn't buy it," the inspector replied, "a tourist gave it to me." It seemed that he was as proud of his gift as of a decoration awarded him for his war on crime, but when he tried to direct the conversation to that matter, the inspector dismissed his supposition with the wave of a hand. "He simply wouldn't need it in his country" – he indicated to the fan with his eyebrow – "it's cold there the whole time."

"Did he come from Alaska?" he asked the inspector and right away was sorry he didn't ask about Siberia; that way he perhaps could have steered the conversa-tion toward his Russian.

"From Northern Canada," the inspector answered, "from Baffin Island. Snow is always falling on Baffin Island, even when it stops here." He had already sat down in his chair and directed the fan to the wall because it had blown one of the pages piled up there off the table. "Have you been to Baffin Island?"

The Canadian he met in Delhi years ago popped up in his mind, and he asked about him, despite the minimal chances of him being known here. Maybe the inspector had heard about a Canadian who came here to seclude himself in a cave? It was a clumsy opening, but that's how the words came out of his mouth, and often it's best to follow them.

No, the inspector hadn't heard. Not that there's a lack of people here who would do that, he said, foreigners as well, but someone who secludes himself in a cave is simply not heard of again; and that Canadian, according to what he hears now, maybe didn't leave Delhi at all. "Did you come for him?" he asked, and Amnon shook his head.

Only now did he notice the empty cage on the windowsill: a cage whose dimensions were suited to a large parrot, perhaps even a talking one, and in its corner were two small bowls, one for water and one for seeds.

"Yes, he also disappeared," the inspector said. "I had him for fourteen years, and one day he vanished. He's not in a cave."

"A talking parrot?" That was also a way to engage him in conversation: their common love of pets or pet birds.

"Talk, sing, the lot," the inspector replied, proud of his parrot and also mourning his loss. "He imitated me so well that I could have left him here alone to shout at them in my place." He was speaking of those subordinates on the other side of the corridor: the gazes of the three of them were fixed at the set, and on the field one of the players was waiting to bat.

"Those idiots," the inspector said. "They forgot to close his door when they changed the water in the dish. That's what they said, that they forgot." Apparently, not a long time had passed since then and he therefore spoke that way and didn't hesitate to share the facts with him, whether because he saw in him the love for animals or whether being a white man he was still seen here as a source of authority and at least an arbitrator of disputes. On his last trip he was surprised when they called him "Master" and not "Mister" as if with the change of one letter he had been endowed with complete mastery.

"Have you ever had something stolen from you?" the inspector asked. "Not now, but at all, did you ever enter your room and discover something precious had been taken from you?"

He nodded. It happened in the house he rented in a small town in his youth, he had brought only a few belongings to that house, and the disappointed thief had stolen the rucksack with which he had travelled to northern Norway, and when he phoned the police to report the robbery and told them what had been stolen, the policeman on duty thought he was joking. Afterward, he traced the steps of the burglar to the deserted orchard at the side of the garden and found only what had been removed from the pouches of the rucksack: wrinkled maps of European capital cities, used Metro tickets, a program from the Munch Museum in Oslo, receipts from Norwegian garages. He gathered them one by one and continued to walk between the trees whose oranges had shriveled and blackened and on the ground were pieces of torn newspaper and toilet paper stained with feces, until he found the rucksack discarded at the edge of the orchard – apparently the thief had looked for money hidden in its compartments and had no interest in it itself (how pleased he was to see the rucksack; as if it held great promise, not only of further trips but of the very freedom to travel or not to travel).

"It really is unpleasant," he said to the inspector.

"Unpleasant?" the inspector said. He looked at the cage. There was still water in the bowls, and if it had not evaporated, it had all taken place recently, unless the inspector had stuck to his old habits and continued to change the water in the dish or had ordered his subordinates to do so, even if just to teach them a lesson.

"What country are you from?" he asked suddenly, remembering his professional obligation.

He wanted to answer Spain, but lying to a priest is one thing and lying to a police officer, who might still ask to see his passport, is something else entirely.

"There are masses of Israelis in India," the inspector said, "especially young people, not like you. How old are you?" Through the thick glasses that he wore, glasses with an old-fashioned frame, he examined the lines on the skin of his face and the grey in his hair; he also had lines on his skin and his hair had greyed – perhaps they were the same age.

He said his age and the inspector nodded his head.

"Married? Children?"

"I left a woman with two children at home," he gave an answer that wasn't a complete lie, and for a moment he saw the three of them, in the rabbit enclosure, trying to catch the kits with all sorts of tricks – when they multiplied they began to move them to a nearby kibbutz.

"One is fourteen years old and one is nine," he said, despite not being asked, and went on to note how much time had passed since their parting. He had also left his old father in his country, and also the pets they had before the rabbits; they had no parrot, but a flock of parakeets used to come in the afternoon hours to steal loquats and lychees from the trees.

"And don't you miss them?" the inspector wondered. It seemed he had forgotten his professional role; perhaps he was bored or tired of those treacherous subordinates and had at last found someone to talk to. He – he said – had once been sent on a course to Delhi, he didn't see his family for a whole month then, and it was terrible. The guys on the course said to him, come have a drink Jawaharlal, when will you have another opportunity like this, after all, you'll have a family your whole life long, and he replied to them, that's my life, not Delhi. "I couldn't understand how people could live there," he said, "a person could die in the middle of the street and no one would come to his aid. But with you, people are getting killed all the time, is that not so?"

"Yes," he answered.

"And because of that you're travelling all the time?"

"Yes."

"Still, what can I do for you?" More than wanting to help him, he must have longed for conversation; no one came into the station, and his subordinates were absorbed in the game.

"I'm a journalist," Amnon said, and the inspector didn't seem impressed by his profession – for a moment he paid attention to the nearby room where the enthused voice of the broadcaster could be heard – not even when he told him the subject of his article was foreigners who had disappeared in India, mainly in the north. Israelis had and others had disappeared, mainly in the Manali and Kasol areas but possibly here as well.

"Your Canadian isn't here," the inspector said. Something like that, he said, he would have heard about, Leh is a small place.

In the next room his subordinates let out a sigh of disappointment and he looked there. "Such fools," he said. "They've only got that nonsense in their heads.

Look how much they care about a few crazies running around a field, but about Dipankar – no."

"Who is Dipankar?" he asked.

"Who is he really?" the inspector said. "Really, who is Dipankar? A little fool with wings who believed that they wanted to do him good when they released him." He instantly fell silent. Perhaps he thought that it was nevertheless not fitting for a police inspector to make speeches in his station about lost parrots, not even in front of an animal lover like him.

Both their gazes were turned to the cage: the water in the bowl quivered in the breeze of the fan. "Maybe in the end he got along okay," he dredged up an encouraging statement for the inspector. With them in Israel – he said and pondered the plural form that came out of his mouth – a pair of green parrots, parakeets the species is called, had also been released and got along so well outside and multiplied to such an extent that they can't be got rid of; I pity all those with fruit trees in their gardens.

"But how did their owners feel?" the inspector said, despite having decided not to add a word on the subject. "The owners of the first pair, how did they feel when they escaped from him, did you think about that?" He moved the pile of forms on his desk and straightened it, and since he wasn't satisfied, he stood the bundle of pages up and also straightened its bottom and replaced it in the corner of the desk far from the fan.

Dipankar – the inspector said, and now it seemed he would continue to talk, if only to put matters straight – wasn't a gift from a tourist, he bought him in Delhi for quite a sum of money, most probably a tiny amount in Western terms, but very large in his terms. "I thought I would make my children happy with it when I returned," he said, "so that they'd forgive me for not having seen me for such a long time. If you have children, you no doubt understand me." Again, he held the bundle of papers and moved it a little further so that it would be parallel to the edge of the desk.

"And weren't they happy?" It was very easy to be dragged into conversation; there's nothing like expressing empathy at suitable moments to draw someone out and make him inclined towards your needs.

"Yes they were," the inspector said, "but my wife said that he makes a big mess and that he swears at them and uses vulgarities, things one doesn't hear in these parts, only in Delhi." His wife had an idea; she said that if he's so attached to the parrot, let him keep it at the station instead of at home, let his policemen clean after it and not her. "And at the beginning I was angry," the inspector continued. "Why should it be moved here if I had paid so much money for it? But afterward it seemed like an excellent solution. Every time I came here, there was someone waiting for me, not those idiots there."

"I had dogs," Amnon said. "And I've also left one at home now." With that the closeness between them ended: he, unlike the inspector, in the end had decided to part with his pet.

"A dog doesn't talk," Tendon said. A trace of scorn could be heard in his voice and seen in his eyes through the thick lenses of his glasses.

"Maybe not with words," he replied and could have gone into detail how it does: with its tail, its eyes, its nose, by rubbing up affectionately, by skipping, by a rolled back lip (that's how Albie used to express his dissatisfaction when he wasn't let into the house: he would stand on two paws and gaze at them through the window with an expression of insult).

The inspector wasn't impressed. Once more he moved the pile of forms on his desk and straightened its edges. It seemed that he had decided to end this silly conversation, and not only because it wasn't worthy of a police inspector, but also because an inferior creature like a dog was being compared to a talking parrot.

Only when the policeman entered, the one who had been standing at the gateway throwing apricot pits at a pole, did he continue. "They could have sold Dipankar and earned a lot of money off him," he said, "but they'd know I'd find out about something like that right away. You can't keep things like that secret here. Leh is a small place, I would know if he was still around here." Perhaps he was waiting for another word of encouragement, even if false, solely that another person – even one whose love was given to dogs – would recognize the sorrow he cannot share with anyone, not in this whole building and not even at home.

But again, no word of encouragement for the inspector rose from within him. He looked around him. "It seems that you don't have too much work here," he said, and didn't add: if you're occupied with things like that.

"We do what we have to," the inspector replied and shot him a look of suspicion from the other side of the desk, wondering if there was criticism in his words. "And before all of you people came here, we had even less work, everything's gone downhill ever since you came." He aimed his words at foreigners in general, and not just Israelis. Yes, he said, ever since the young people of Leh discovered all the modern appliances, they'll do anything to obtain them, and anything means anything, legal or illegal. Before, when they didn't know all of that existed – he said – they had it good, they lacked for nothing, and now suddenly it seems to them that without a Walkman and a satellite dish one can't be happy; who knew there was such a things like a Walkman and a satellite dish?

"Your priest also has a satellite dish."

"The priest?" the inspector said, "That priest's not mine at all." He must have belonged to the Buddhist majority that hadn't converted to Christianity. "Not more than twenty people come to his church," he said, "and even then they still keep a statue of the Buddha at home and a picture of Avalokiteśvara. The priest doesn't know that."

"He also likes sport, the same as your policemen."

"He thinks he'll get close to the young people that way," the inspector said.

"So they come to him to watch matches, they also eat and drink at his place, why not, and the moment they leave there, they're already saying what an idiot he is." And again, he criticized their running after modern appliances and all they're prepared to do to get hold of some fake Sony or Adidas or Nike. "There's no lack of fake products here," he said, "just tell them what you need and right away they'll arrange it for you."

His interest was now awakened and he asked to know more about that.

"What for example?" The inspector repeated Amnon's question. "Whatever you want. If you want a new identity card they'll arrange it for you, if you want an ancient statue they'll arrange it for you, just ask for a hair from Milarepa and they'll arrange that too. Not to mention passes and army petrol coupons – that's what most popular at the moment, army petrol coupons. Once there were hardly any cars here and now you can hardly breathe because of their smoke. And that too, you all brought with you."

Remnants of holy ones sounded more interesting to him than army petrol coupons and he asked the inspector about them, though his grandfather had no connection to Milarepa and his holiness.

"A hair of theirs or some tooth," the inspector said. "And not even that; it's enough to say some ordinary feather moved a rock, and right away it would look different. Not so?"

From the next room an exclamation of disappointment could be heard: apparently someone on the field has missed hitting the ball.

"Wouldn't it look completely different to you?" the inspector asked again. "Or seashells that you hear the sea with -"

Here he interrupted his words and said what was required to be said on the matter.

"Maybe the sea, yes," the inspector replied, "but not the ships of the gods. Have you ever heard the ships of the gods?"

No, he had never heard that, not with shells nor any other way.

"Then someone who sells them here would tell you that if you cannot hear, you're hard of hearing. The same way with the feather, they'll say to you - how can't you see that it moved a rock?"

And what does the inspector do about the matter?

"Me?" the inspector answered. "Why should I ruin people's faith? I wish that I myself could believe that way."

His subordinates cheered from the other side of the passage and again he turned his head there. "On the day that Dipankar escaped, it was a Tuesday morning, I searched for him in the room for over an hour. Only a feather of his remained here, and do you know what those idiots said? They said that maybe Dipankar will still come back here to take it, because he was such a dandy, and he really was a dandy, busy with his feathers all the time. And I, silly me, believed it for a moment.

That's how it is when people want very much to believe in something." He again looked at the nearby room; his lips were moving, perhaps he was cursing.

"And do people still buy all that," Amnon asked, "the fake documents and the coupons and the holy objects in the bazaar?"

It transpired that only a few things were sold in the bazaar, and certainly not the precious ones. "Someone who knows," the inspector said, "comes to a merchant and says to him, I hear you're selling such and such and I'm interested. Or the merchant comes to someone and says to him, I heard to buy such and such. And the older it is, the more it costs." And no – he replied again to his previous question – the police don't do anything against it, and why should they, if it does people good. "Would you say to someone in hospital who has a week left to live and believes he has another ten years - you don't have?"

He was intending to go to the hospital from the police station and told the inspector so. "That's my next stop," he said to him, "the government hospital. To ask about Dr. Edward McKenzie, perhaps you've heard of him?"

"Dr. Tashi works there. And also Dr. Kapoor and Dr. Chatterjee – no McKenzie."

He clarified: McKenzie worked there a hundred years ago.

"Did the doctor also disappear?" the inspector conjectured. "Like your Canadian?"

He clarified the matter for him: the doctor remained here, he was even buried here in the cemetery, and his wife is buried here as well; he saw their graves with his own eyes. Only the Russian who had been hospitalized under his care a hundred years ago disappeared.

"And you think they'll tell you something about him at the hospital? Things like that even Dr. Tashi doesn't know!"

He then quoted him things he had learned from Kramer two decades ago that hadn't been forgotten even during his years at the local newspaper: people simply talk, and one thing leads to another. Sometimes by complete chance something is discovered, even the most important things can be discovered that way, if you only know how to listen properly.

The inspector gazed at him through the thick lenses of his glasses. He looked pensive. "And what did you discover from me?"

"That you're a good man," he replied as if his white skin authorized him to award marks. "There's no way that someone who loves pets that way can be a bad person." And almost thought simultaneously: no, after all, I loved mine the same way.

With his foot he inspector shifted the bucket of water that had been emptied from the sink and with it a few swollen cigarette butts swayed on the surface. "Even if I had good policemen," he said apologetically and glanced at the next room, "no police force would occupy themselves with things from a hundred years ago, because what would they do, who would they investigate and who would they punish? They're all already dead," as if saying: whoever disappears completely evaporates, not even an empty cage remains after him, and the one who caused its disappearance also disappears. "But I'll tell you someone who maybe could help you."

It turned out – just as he had previously hoped; at least in this matter it seemed that his hopes were materializing – there's a high school teacher here by the name of Gargan, who has appointed himself the local historian; mathematics is his subject but that wasn't enough for this Gargan and his endless plans. "He dreams of establishing a museum here," the inspector said, "and had even calculated how much time it would take for the investment to be returned, if he only had an investor. I could lend you one of those loafers there to show you where the school is," – he indicated to the next room, in which the sounds of the cricket match were still rising – "but it would be better not to."

Perhaps he feared his policemen might disobey him and refuse to go, or perhaps the one who would be sent to accompany him wouldn't be in any hurry to return, or perhaps under his guidance he would get lost like Dipankar the parrot.

6

About a kilometer before the hospital gate stood a battered and rusty tin signpost like the the one above the police station but twice its size and written in its head-line in stained letters was: A Few Facts About Leprosy, and though there wasn't any logic to it, a primordial fear of that terrible disease instantly rose up in him. Eight facts were noted beneath the headline, each one on a separate line, and white bird droppings joined their letters together:

1. Leprosy is a disease caused... germs (the word "by" had turned white).
2. The majority of people have a natural resistance to leprosy germs.
3. Leprosy is not passed on by... (the last word had turned white: perhaps the word "heredity" or perhaps a different word whose aim was to calm.)
4. Leprosy is curable at any stage.
5. Early diagnosis and regular treatment prevent defects.
6. Modern treatment for leprosy is provided without payment in all health centers.
7. Those affected by leprosy can live at home and lead ...mal lives while they are being treated.
8. Leprosy diagnosis is simple.

South of the signpost, within the empty plain – the last houses of Leh stood at the rear, and in front was the arid expanse like the slopes that demarcated it – Amnon could see the low buildings of the government hospital that for some reason had been erected outside the town. No motorcar travelled on the road, and no sound was heard around. A sudden desire to urinate rose in him and he searched for some hidden place, and the best was behind the signpost, but it seemed that if the stream of urine would touch the ground where the signpost had been planted, the person from whose organ it flowed would immediately be infected. There had been a time when he feared venereal diseases that way, he was an almost complete ignoramus at the time, and after his visit to the prostitute in Hamburg, when he fell asleep he saw his organ turning yellow and rotting in his hand and falling off into the toilet bowl while urinating, floating there a moment longer like a turd and sinking.

For the first time he walked from the center of Leh southward, and the way lasted longer than he had imagined. Before that, an old man on his way passed him leading a donkey laden with hay; and two women, not young, also passed by in their traditional garb and greeted him with a joolay to which he replied, and now he walked alone. It wasn't either too hot or too cold and the way was level, but he became short of breath and didn't know whether it was due to the thinning air or some other physical reason. Perhaps he wasn't meant to reach these heights, but he knew it was necessary to continue on his way.

The Sonam Norbu Memorial government hospital was comprised of three single floored buildings joined to each other. At its entrance was a folding lattice whose two parts were drawn to the sides, and a few people waited on a concrete bench in front of it and a few more stood opposite the entrance – perhaps relatives of the those hospitalized or perhaps waiting for a diagnosis or a vacant bed. He already knew that there were only twenty-five beds in the place; it was written in the Lonely Planet: "The local hospital will provide you with preliminary treatment should you suffer from altitude sickness, but you would do well to allow your body to gradually adjust to the altitude and not need its services."

The floor was dirty, and at the edges of the walls traces of murky water could be seen, perhaps from having been washed some time ago. Twenty or more people were assembled inside, and the moderate din resembled that of the post office branch he passed on his way to the police station, but in the silence of this distant place, a silence that the landscape itself apparently inspired on all its surroundings like the shade the mountains cast, the voices were enough to sound like noise.

On the right-hand wall were instructions to visitors – according to the heading – and he stood and read them:

1. It is forbidden to assemble or crowd together in the hospital.

2. Please do not spit, please do not throw chukti pan masala and juice at the walls and on the floor.

3. Please use spittoons and garbage tins for that purpose.

4. Smoking or visiting the hospital in a state of intoxication is strictly forbidden.

5. It is forbidden to donate gifts or money to hospital staff in the event of the birth of a male son, or the recovery from a serious illness, or in order to bypass those waiting in line.

Some of those instructions were being breached right in front of his eyes, and no one rebuked the culprits: they assembled, smoked, and someone spat in a corner. In vain, his eyes sought after anyone who might be able to help him: no one was standing at the information desk, and two nurses passed him by without stopping. An old woman squatted on her heels and a bundle next to her emitted the smell of cooked food, two young children ran after each other and were swallowed in the corridor on his right (there was another corridor, on his left, dark and empty), a fat man was being supported by a stick made from a branch whose shape could still be made out, and a woman in a festive perak held an x-ray of a pelvis close to her body, and it seemed as if her belly was wide open for all to see. Three men were arguing with each other, and every now and then they turned their heads towards the right-hand corridor, and when the children burst out from there boisterously no one hushed them. The tumult abated slightly only when the doctor come out, a stethoscope hanging from his neck, a blue face towel sprouting from his white coat, his walk was brisk despite the redness in his eyes and no group of interns trailed after him. A tag with his name was affixed to his coat – Dr. Tashi Angchok – and when he noticed Amnon, the only foreigner in the place, he turned to him and in a businesslike tone asked in English how he could be of help to him, and no one protested that he had been approached before all the others.

He was hoping that the conversation would develop by itself as had happened in the church and the police station – if he had engaged in conversation with a football loving priest and with an inspector whose subordinates had caused his parrot to disappear, why shouldn't he succeed with a government hospital doctor? "I wanted to ask you, Doctor," he said, and the doctor inclined his head slightly in order to look at him, the dark sacks beneath his eyes stood out; he must not have slept enough for more than one night. When he heard Amnon's question he frowned with annoyance. "You've come at the busiest time of the day," he said to him, "where are you from?"

He almost lied, as in the conversation with the priest, but decided a conversation with a doctor should be without any falsehoods. Who knows, maybe one day he would need to be treated by him?

"You're also from Israel?" Doctor Tashi glanced sideways at the northern window. "There are already two here, a boy and a girl, why don't you wait with them? It's pleasant outside." He indicated to the window that faced north where a tree spotted with orange fruit could be seen, perhaps an apricot tree, and it seemed that the doctor would be only too glad to send him on his way, together with all the rest of the Israelis who had come here.

When he went out to the grounds, he saw the Israeli couple from the window: the girl was sitting in the shade of the tree, leaning on the trunk, and the curly headed boy stretched out his hand and picked her an apricot from a branch sloping down and split it in two and reached it out to her. "Look how orange they are, Tami," he said, and when he noticed him, the girl also turned her head toward him.

"Are you also waiting for the doctor?" he asked them, despite having no will talk to anyone other than the doctor – they could have been his children had he raised a family in time – he asked if something had happened to them.

No, nothing had happened to them, the boy replied, they've simply come here to volunteer their help in the hospital, and Dr. Tashi has to give them an answer. "There's also Dr. Chaterjee," the boy said, "but he isn't authorized for that, only Tashi."

"You're volunteering?"

"Yes, to help out a bit," the boy answered. "I was a combat medic, and she was also -"

"The most bandaging I did was someone scratched by a branch," the girl said from the foot of the tree.

He observed the two of them afterward from the window: they seemed like Adam and Eve in their garden, as the boy reached out the second half of the apricot to his girlfriend, and he watched them like a pervert whose satisfaction is in the pleasures of others, until suddenly an urge rose within him, to call out to them from the window and warn them about eating too many apricots, so that heaven forbid they don't get stomach aches; and right after that, with the same decisiveness, he thought: let them both choke, the two of them together; they looked so young and healthy.

"When we were little," the boy said and in the open palm of his hand an apricot pit could be seen, "we used to collect them like marbles, I had whole packets of them."

From behind someone turned to Amnon, it was one of the waiting patients who had gathered in the entrance.

"You wait Dr. Tashi?" he asked, and he nodded to him. "Waiting long?" He nodded again.

"I used to collect matches," the girl said, "like those from hotels, the thin cardboard ones. And also erasers with a scent, and napkins, and perfume bottles, everything my mother passed on to me, and sometimes a little perfume even remained in it."

"Quite a collector," the boy said. "Did you collect boys that way?"

"Dr. Tashi very good," said the Ladakhi and he nodded to him again.

"Dr. Tashi cure almost everyone," the Ladakhi said. "He cure my mother and my father. Only not my brother. Almost everyone here love Dr. Tashi."

The two Israelis were talking again outside, and the Ladakhi, after listening to them for a moment, asked what language they were speaking, and he answered, and afterward also told him where it's spoken.

"Lot of Israelis come here," the Ladakhi said, "I only go Manali one time, bad place Manali. You come from Manali?"

"I came from Delhi." Amnon replied. "Bad place, Delhi."

"My children their age," the Ladakhi said, "and go no place ever." His gaze passed from the boy to the girl and back and lingered a while on both of them, on his face and her face and on the boy's hand that again reached out to her another apricot on his palm. "They in love, no?" he said and continued to look at them. "People in love is beautiful."

A noise was then heard behind them: a stretcher was being wheeled into the corridor, and until they turned around, they saw only the tip of the stretcher and a male nurse pushing it and the two young children hurriedly following. A few of those gathered in the entrance went into the hall, the folding lattice was drawn further apart, and one of the nurses previously seen there or another who looked a lot like her pushed a service trolley and on it was a small stainless-steel tray and bowl with surgical instruments in something that perhaps was disinfectant fluid. A dusty dog also entered limping, seeking with his nose the thread of a scent that attracted him, until a raised hand and afterward a foot caused it to flee whimpering, its tail between its legs.

A moment or two later a wail could be heard again, not from outside but from the depths of the corridor, from one of the wards. A piercing pain could be heard in it despite that it wasn't loud, the pain of someone already exhausted by his suffering and the wail no longer addressed to a doctor or a nurse. A moment later an old lama entered the hall rolling prayer beads between his fingers and immediately after him another monk, swinging his small drum and rattling the tassels attached to it. In the hospital where his mother had been admitted, all sorts of Chabad[38] emissaries went around ready to break out into song opposite every invalid, and his father repeatedly banished them from her bedside, though she didn't hear or see them.

"Dr. Chaterjee," they mumbled, "Dr. Chaterjee."

Outside, from the foot of the tree, the girl said: "I was worried about you, Ido, not about me. I thought to myself, even if he meets someone there, let's say some easy female regimental clerk, in the end when he comes back to me, he'll know what I'm worth."

"And you were a hundred percent right!"

"But before that, I dreamed of you getting lost in the occupied territories and some masked men catching you. I dreamed of them putting you into a car or stopping your car, and all of a sudden I was with you there inside the car and they began to rock it up and down, they almost turned it over completely and were cursing the whole time, it was so frightening! I was sure they would lynch us."

"And in the end the opposite happened," the boy said.

"Better the opposite, no?"

The boy fell silent for a moment. "No," he replied softly and with all his might flung the pit he was holding.

After a while, Dr. Tashi came of out the corridor with his brisk walk, and after hastily shaking off those gathering around him, he turned to him and asked how he could help him. Perhaps he was thinking of the advantages of a conversation with a foreign journalist, albeit not from a large nation, but one fostered by America and its good friend. Beads of sweat sprouted on his forehead, and he took the blue face towel out of his coat pocket and wiped it.

From the grounds they noticed him, and the curly headed boy reached out his hand to his girlfriend and helped her up.

---

38 An Orthodox Jewish Hasidic movement one of whose missions is the spreading of joy.

"I have some interest in the history of the hospital," he said to the doctor; it seemed a good way to engage him in conversation, not too defined, not threatening, one that could develop in any direction. He also could have asked him who Sonam Norbu was, in whose name the hospital had been called, although he didn't know where Ichilov Hospital in Tel Aviv got its name from and never sought to know.

"Our history?" Dr. Tashi said. "But we're still stuck in history. Just look at the conditions we're working in."

"I mean the distant history," he clarified. His newspaper is especially interested in what took place here a hundred years ago, yes, a long time before the British left.

"A hundred years?" Dr. Tashi asked. "Who the hell cares what was here a hundred years ago? In medicine sometimes what was just ten years ago already doesn't interest anyone. Haven't they heard that at your newspaper?" Again, he wiped his forehead with the blue face towel and returned it to the coat pocket.

There was no point asking about documents that had been kept from that period, and certainly not x-rays, but he was happy for the doctor to be leading him to his office and ignoring all those addressing him on the way; he even shook off the two monks without much ado. They saw the Israeli couple a moment before they entered the corridor leading to the doctors' rooms: the boy patted the girls behind in order to shake off grains of earth from her pants.

The door of the room opened with difficulty and Dr. Tashi had to push it slightly with his shoulder, and a small room without any windows was revealed (or perhaps a window was hidden by a cupboard), in which there was no space other than for a small desk and two plastic chairs and a grey office cupboard whose door wasn't properly closed and dozens of squashed cardboard files could be seen inside it. A pile of papers was growing high in the right corner of the desk and a candle stood in the left one attached to a small plate by its wax with a few matches alongside. A large blue Thermos flask stood on the ground next to the leg of the desk and the doctor leaned over to pick it up, and while doing so, as if seeking to calm him, said that it's not the salty Tibetan tea that he himself doesn't like, not personally nor as a doctor, but sweet Indian chai. Without waiting, he poured the tea into two cups that he took out of one of the desk drawers, plastic disposable cups that had been washed carelessly.

"It's not the only disposable thing that we have to wash a thousand times here," Dr. Tashi said, "and do you think we're pleased about that?"

"I'm sure you're not," Amnon replied.

"It would be good if you wrote about that in the paper," Dr. Tashi said, "at least that way someone will hear about it, the Americans are your friends, aren't they? All my letters on the matter don't help." He began to count on his fingers all those in authority he had turned to, from the regional inspector to the provincial inspector and the head of the department in the ministry of health, and when he lifted up his fourth and fifth finger a dry bloodstain could be seen on the palm of his hand – it seemed that disposable gloves were also lacking in the hospital.

"But we did not come here for that," Dr. Tashi said, "what have our troubles here to do with you?"

It was necessary to set things straight: to tell him that wasn't the purpose of the article he was intending to write, but nevertheless he promised the doctor he would highlight all matters the doctor felt important, from the lack of equipment to the lack of medicines and human resources.

"Yes?" Dr. Tashi said. His gazed was turned to the door; he apparently heard someone drawing close from the corridor and stopping outside it, and a moment later it was opened and the head of the Israeli boy could be seen, his curls flowing and a ring in his ear. "I haven't forgotten you," Dr. Tashi said.

The door was shut, and he told the doctor the name of the man who had worked here at the beginning of the century and who wasn't only the sole doctor but also the director of the hospital – maybe Dr. Tashi had heard something about him?

No, he hadn't heard anything about Dr. McKenzie, not about his abilities as a doctor nor as a director; Dr. Chaterjee also hadn't heard, nor anyone else. He was no less decisive than the head of the department in Ichilov, who explained his mother's condition to him: he didn't give her any chance of waking from her coma and recovering, and with that, it was as if he had given him permission to travel to the Greek island ("I tried to explain to your father, but he refuses to understand," he said in his office).

"There also was a Russian with him," Amnon said. "In the end, the two of them got themselves into trouble with something."

Were they selling medicines privately? Doctor Tashi didn't appear at all surprised by that possibility.

"Perhaps antiques."

This time Dr. Tashi was surprised: what has a doctor to do with antiques? As for him, he said, the farthest he digs here is in order to take out a gall bladder or gallstones; there's no shortage of people here with that problem, and no wonder, after all what makes the stones is all the butter and salt found in Tibetan tea; yes, there's no other place in India that has so many people with gallstones, he's already filled an entire drawer with them. Perhaps he would have opened the drawer and shown them to him, had Amnon not hastened to return the conversation to the matter for which he had come.

"Antiques," he said to him, "are worth a lot more money than medicines."

But Dr. Tashi, even after letting go the matter of gallstones, didn't remember hearing anything connected to antiques or some incident involving a Russian. "I've yet to see a Russian here," he said, "what reasons would Russians have to come here?" He's seen Israelis, no lack of Israelis here. "These two," he indicated to the door, "have travelled thousands of kilometers just to volunteer here at the hospital, doesn't that seem odd to you?"

He nodded his head.

Dr. Tashi swiveled around in his chair, toward the dozens of cardboard files in the cupboard. "Do you see all this?" he said. "Not one of these people here has ever been out of Ladakh, or even tried to. They barely knew where Ladakh starts and where it ends. In the year I was born there was no road here yet, can you imagine that? And when I wanted to study in Delhi my parents feared they wouldn't see me anymore, they did a puja for me every day – do you know what a puja is? They used to pray that I wouldn't vanish there and thought that only because of their prayers I returned. Was your Russian Jewish?"

He nodded.

"I thought so," Dr. Tashi said. "And why didn't he go to Israel?"

"There was no Israel then."

He had to explain to the doctor that it was established approximately at the time India received independence from the British, and for a moment he sounded like he was quoting his editor when he was sent to cover the riots in Bhagalpur.

"The British," Dr. Tashi said, "hardly come here, we see your people a lot more. It seems they are happy in their own country. Are your people not happy?"

Since he did not hasten to reply – it was too complicated to reply about that – the doctor asked him again about the Russian: why did he come here, surely not only because of the landscape; did he perhaps turn into a Buddhist here? That possibility greatly amused Dr. Tashi, and when again he took out the blue face towel from his pocket and wiped his sweat with it, the smile that rose on his face was still not wiped off.

"That's a definite possibility," Amnon answered.

"Those friends of yours," the doctor said and gestured to the door, "it could maybe happen to them. In the beginning they'll volunteer and afterward they'll learn a few words in Ladakhi and begin to take an interest in Buddhism and say: why not? Maybe those Ladakhis are not as stupid as we thought." At that very moment the light went out, and since the room was a small interior room without curtains, the darkness was almost complete.

A curse in Ladakhi was heard, and afterward a drawer being pulled out and fingers searching in it, perhaps among the gallstones placed there, and a moment later the flame of a lighter was ignited and moved toward the candle that stood in the corner of the table, ready for such an occurrence. After it was lit, the doctor got up and went out the room with the flame of the lighter carried in front of him like a sort of miniature torch, and the two Israelis made way for him and withdrew to the wall behind them. "Shortcut, shortcut," Dr. Tashi explained to them, and when he drew away so did his shadow the lighter cast behind him, and the girl said: "I've never heard of a hospital without a generator, what if there's an operation now?"

Since the door remained open and the candle lit the corner of the corridor, he suggested to the two to come into the room, but they preferred to stay where they were.

"Have you found your son yet?" the girl asked.

A moment passed until he pulled himself together and improvised an answer and said that was exactly the reason for him coming to Dr. Tashi, to find out whether in the past months he had treated a young Israeli who looked like his son.

"Did he remember him?" It seemed that the girl would really be happy if he answered yes. "You'll find him," she said, "I'm sure of it, I really feel it here in my heart, I also told that to Ido before."

When she placed her hand on her chest, he tried to smile at her, and it come out pitifully as if his falsehood had already become fact, and that he really did have a son whose trace had been lost in the mountains or in one of the chasms.

"Maybe right now he's looking for you," she said to hearten him, "is your wife at home in case he calls?"

Then a tumult could be heard from the direction of the entrance hall, and they turned their heads towards it: perhaps a stretcher was being wheeled in and the worried family hurrying behind it and Dr. Tashi running in front of them. The rattle of the generator being started could also be heard, and a moment later the bulbs in the small room and the corridor were lit again with a yellowish quivering light. A few more moments passed and Dr. Tashi still didn't return, and when they went out to the entrance hall it seemed that nothing had changed and that the same people who previously waited there were still waiting now. The dog that had been banished before could also be seen again; perhaps it was waiting for its master who was hospitalized or perhaps just for scraps of food.

Dr. Tashi was seen coming from the other corridor, the one leading to the wards, and his steps were brisk and his face angry.

"Write about that!" he said when he stopped opposite them, "How it takes ten minutes for a generator to start working, and in the meantime, what supposed to happen in the operating room? Write about that in your paper, not about some Russian," and before the two could ponder over the meaning of his words he turned to them and asked how exactly they saw themselves fitting in here. Had they perhaps brought a generator with them, or diesel fuel? He was extremely irritated.

"We want to help," the boy replied, "as much as we can. That's what we came for. We've already had some experience treating tough cases."

"Experience?" Doctor Tashi said. "Where do you have experience from?"

"From the army," the boy answered.

"From the army," Dr. Tashi said. He looked at those waiting in the hall and his eyes seemed even more tired that they had seemed before.

"I was a combat medic," said the boy, "I did that for three years, three hundred and sixty days a year, in all sorts of difficult situations I wouldn't wish on anyone."

"A combat medic?" Dr. Tashi said.

"Treating the wounded under fire, even when there's shooting and shelling all around. We even did surgery under those conditions, some really complicated things, because the helicopter couldn't land."

Dr. Tashi gave him a weary look. "Nobody's shooting here," he said quietly. His eyes were turned to the window and lingered over what he saw there, "and there aren't any helicopters." Riding on one of the branches, one of the children stretched out his hand toward two ripe apricots, and it seemed he wouldn't give up his intention of reaching them.

"It's completely peaceful here," Dr. Tashi said, "don't you see? No noise is heard here other than the faulty generator." It's rattling was intermittently strong and weak, the flow of fuel wasn't uniform, or perhaps the tank was about to empty.

"Once," the boy said, determined to prove to the doctor the experience he had accumulated, "there was a situation when in the middle of the night and in the freezing cold, I had to push the intestines of someone back into his stomach. That was the worst; I'll never forget it, that feeling of holding them like that in my hands in the dark and shivering from cold."

"You pushed the intestines back into his stomach," Dr. Tashi said slowly.

"One doesn't forget that."

"Certainly not," Dr. Tashi said. How could one?" He asked the girl if she also happened to push intestines back into somebody's stomach. "It's just that we don't have things like that here, you see; I've been in the profession for twenty-six years and haven't yet pushed anyone's intestines back into his stomach. Do you understand, my young friend, death here is not grandiose, without any fireworks, no helicopter comes to help, sometimes there isn't even an ambulance. A banal, ugly, disgusting death. One simply cannot come to the rescue; the intestines remain inside but the appendix bursts. There are gallstones and it's too complicated to remove them, or the electricity of the respirator suddenly stops just like that." Again, he turned his gaze to the window.

"Not to mention the lack of disinfectant," Dr. Tashi continued, "disinfectant! And disposable equipment, and bedding, even that's lacking here, quite often a patient is put into a bed with the dirty bedding of the previous patient, did you also have that in the army?"

On the fork of the branch, the boy held the fruit that he picked, a large and orange apricot, and split it in two.

"And if there's no electricity stoppage," Dr. Tashi said, "there's a loose connection or half the isolation has been peeled away, it's an absolute wonder that I haven't been electrocuted yet together with the patient. Have you ever seen a person being electrocuted?"

The girl, who had been listening to both of them, reached her hand out to the boy, a small hand whose fingernails had been bitten like the nails of a child. He nodded his curly head.

"By the shooting?" Dr. Tashi asked. "By the shooting or by the helicopter, what the hell was he electrocuted by?"

"Electricity," the boy replied, and the girl intertwined her fingers with his.

"Electrocuted by electricity," Dr. Tashi said.

"By electrical wires," the boy said. "Not that there wasn't isolation, there was, but he… he climbed up the electric pole and was electrocuted." His voice cracked, and when he swallowed his saliva it could be seen going down his throat.

"Why the hell did he climb up an electric pole?"

"To take something down from there," the boy replied and again the swallowing motion could be seen in his throat. "A flag. Their flag."

"Their flag," Dr. Tashi said. "In order to take a flag down from there."

He repeated each word as if to ensure that his ears had not misled him.

"He was forced to do it," the boy said, "he never would have done it by himself. At the very most he would have climbed up some tree like this boy here."

This time Dr. Tashi didn't say anything, but it seemed that the bags under his eyes were growing darker and his eyelids were being pulled down by their weight.

"He was threatened at gunpoint," the boy said. "The weapons convinced him that it would be better for him to begin climbing, even though it wasn't him who had hung up the flag, it was someone else, a long time before then."

"The weapons convinced him," Dr. Tashi said.

"Yes," said the boy, very quietly, and the girl who was holding his hand between her two palms strengthened her grip. "I don't know how old he was," he said, "he was forced to climb and he climbed, he climbed to the top there like a monkey, it barely took two minutes, maybe three, even in a circus they don't climb like that. He wanted to show us that he wasn't afraid."

"Us," Dr. Tashi said.

7

In the evening, the treetops darkened again. It was a hypnotic sight: how the light is gathered from the leaves, first from the low ones and then from the highest at the very top, and they all cohere into one entity that makes discerning the details impossible, and the foliage consolidates with the branches and the trunk into a unified black silhouette.

Had it not been for the hunger, he would have continued sitting opposite the window and waiting for the first stars to sprout in the black of the sky: it was one of the two hours of the day during which the movement of time could be seen, and in his eyes the evening twilight was preferable to that of the morning, but he was hungry, and though he tended not to join the guests sitting in the courtyard whose conversation he heard from his room, in the end he went down there.

In the afternoon, on his way to the hospital, he saw only a little of the town, not the peddlers, not the shops beyond them, not the convoy of yaks, not the man who carried a rolled-up carpet on his shoulder – who he almost bumped into – nor the dusty dogs that lay at the side of the road. Other dogs came to mind, those who fed off what they found between the rabble, they and the crows, and again that stench rose up into his nostrils, and it wasn't not a reminder of what he himself can expect in some distant future but is already the start of that future; and what a relief he had felt at the time, when it was substituted by a different stench, and how momentary that relief had been. A decade and a half had passed, and what had he done during those years? He had become a journalist, stopped being a journalist, met the occasional woman until he stuck to one of them for four years and lived with her in a house they rented and even raised her small son together who with the insight of adults learned to adjust to his new place as well as to his mother's new partner, but when instead of a bicycle for his birthday (Daddy's buying me that!) the boy asked for an aquarium like the one they saw in a restaurant, he firmly refused, despite there being no pet easier to look after than fish. He suddenly found an excuse from his childhood: how fish in his aquarium were found floating on the surface of the water in the morning, and how his father would fish them out with a small net and throw them into the toilet; how cruel the noise of the toilet tank sounded then. "Rabbits are better," he said to him, "you can hold a rabbit in your arms, and if you take a fish out of water do you know what will happen?"

In the parking lot of a local shopping center stood a boy from one of the small towns in the area and in front of him a cardboard box with rabbit pups, and one Saturday morning he brought Udi both Bugs and Bunny, the parents of the dynasty. Udi-Udi, a voice inside him said now, what a good kid you were, what a good kid you are, and what a screwed-up boyfriend your mother found for herself.

From the front section of the courtyard, the group of people sitting there could be heard, and he already identified the voice of the Italian girl who was a hairdresser in her country. In her singsong English she told how lots of actresses and singers and models only wanted her to take care of their hair, and not only their hair, she was like a psychologist to them, and while that's all very nice when business is booming, it's not satisfying. You look at their heads in the washbasin, completely in your hands, from the hair to the neck, and you think to yourself: what's all this beauty for, did we come into the world just for that?

He stopped listening. His thoughts were distracted. There was a salon in Tel Aviv he frequented for a year of his life, one of the dejected ones, just to feel the touch of the hairdresser's thigh as she moved around him with the scissors, he had yearned so much for the touch of a woman. That was his nadir: dandruff could be seen in his hair, hair sprouted from his ears, he sent his clothes to the laundry when they were pungent from sweat. During the months after his firing, it seemed his future was blocked, not only in the world of journalism but in the world in general, and after years of abstention from alcohol he returned to drink, true, only wine, but more and more empty bottles stood on the shelf in the kitchen as testament to his situation.

"Ornella, honey," the Canadian woman said, "what you've only been through! You don't have to tell us all of it, you're a new person now. You've got golden hands, that's what important, not the scars, and with the bracelets no one sees them!"

Then the Israeli girl joined them, and in answer to their questions said that her boyfriend went to sleep early, he was tired from their walk to the hospital; yes, even though he's been here once before, the altitude isn't good for him.

"You can learn from him, Stefan," the Austrian woman said, "those who are tired stay in the room and sleep, and don't come down here to listen to all sorts of melodramas."

"Perhaps you should pay heed to what comes out of your own mouth, Beate," the Canadian woman said.

When he drew near to their tables all eyes were turned on him, and the Canadian woman asked how his search was going and if she could be of help in some way; the lie of his fatherhood he had spread in Delhi had been dragged after him to here, and it was no longer possible to be rid of it.

As if identifying with his worry over his son, they began to speak about the troubles of raising children: the small son of the Canadian woman made her summer hellish until he discovered what a nice person Joy is, and Ornella also has trouble with her son: he drives away every new boyfriend she brings home which is why she found herself alone at the age of forty-five with her depression beginning to return; she had grown and so had her depression, as if it was saying to her: Ornella, honey, did you think you had got rid of me? Did you think Jesus or Mary would help you? Well, see here, they aren't helping.

The Austrian couple kept silent. They didn't have children; their absence was understood before that when they spoke about the monk they had fostered in their home.

"And are you two planning anything?" The Canadian woman suddenly turned to the Israeli girl who was very embarrassed.

"We're still too young," she answered after a moment, and her freckles turned redder.

They asked what her and her boyfriend's ages were, and to that she replied he was a year older than her. With them, she explained, the boys are released from the army a year after the girls.

"Had Stefan been born where you're from, I'm not sure it would have been worth your while enlisting him," the Austrian woman said, "but on the other hand, he could have drawn maps for you, so that you'd know where to drop your bombs and not keep wounding innocent civilians the whole time."

"I think maybe that's enough, Beate," the Canadian woman said.

"Although I wouldn't depend even on that with Stefan," the Austrian woman continued, "because there are things that interest Stefan a lot more than maps? Dirty movies for example. That's what I get to see if suddenly I wake up in the middle of the night at home. Does your wife also get to see that?" She suddenly turned to Amnon, "Girls with silicon breasts."

"What's got into you today, Beate?" the Canadian woman said. "We were sitting here so peacefully, what suddenly got you so annoyed?"

An evening bird called in the distance, though it still had not become completely dark, but the twilight had long lost it ruddiness and had turned blue in the west as well, and no trace remained of the maelstrom of sunset hues. The sky became silent, preparing to be wrapped in its black sheet like the cage of Dipankar the parrot – for a moment that popped into his head.

Then the Israeli girl turned to him and asked if by chance he was going into the town; to her, this overgrown village had become a town.

He still hadn't decided whether to go there to look for one of the restaurants recommended in the guide, and the girl asked if he could bring them something if he goes – not food, but a toy, they want to catch the first bus to Choglamsar tomorrow, and it wouldn't be fitting to arrive there emptyhanded. It transpired that Dr. Tashi thought that they would be of no use to him in the hospital and instead suggested they travel to Choglamsar, just seven kilometers from Leh, where the children of Tibetan refugees are looked after; not only are there teachers there, but social workers and doctors and nurses as well, and in a place like that help is always needed; it also seemed to Dr. Tashi that it would do Ido good to help children, and in that way perhaps slightly alleviate whatever was weighing on his heart. Yes, Dr. Tashi spoke about the heart and not about karma. She'll give him the money, he's likely to find something to buy, after all, he's a father, no? And leaving Ido alone in the room isn't something she wants to do.

He gazed at her: the freckles darkened on her cheeks, an unruly strand of hair fell to her forehead, and she pushed it aside with her small hand whose fingernails were bitten. She lifted her gaze towards the window of their room; the curtain waved in the wind and billowed like a sail.

The path was empty, no one came toward him; no one passed him by. On his left and on his right the fields spread out to the foot of the mountains, and the silence that enveloped him was soft and kind and swallowed the sound of his footsteps, and he could have gone down from the path to one of those fields and walked a long way through it and lain down between the sheaves, like someone entering a sea and lying on its bed; that thought entered his head and lingered for a moment until it was banished. A few lights were lit in the army base farther on the way, and the spotlight whose task was to illuminate the whitewashed stones on which the number of the regiment was written flickered as if hesitant whether to remain lit or be extinguished. The same guard stood at the gate erect and rigid, or possibly someone else, his predecessor's twin. From the next bend of the path, the shadows of the poplars and the fields darkened and the only shades in the sky were between blue and black, and the silence was breached only for a few moments by a distant barking. When had he ever spread himself out on the ground of a field like this and not on his own? And when had he seen an ant climbing over the curve of a body shining with sweat? And when were the ants and the bites and the entire field forgotten and all that remained was the other body receiving him into its depths (only afterward the ants returned to bite; and the small stones to prick; and the straw stems to irritate), never. He only remembered their dog bounding into a field like that and being swallowed until bursting forth from it, excited from some wonder he had sniffed in the heart of it.

When the first lights of Leh were revealed, the sight gladdened him, and within a few minutes, since the capital city was so small, he was already walking along the main road and diners were already sitting in the restaurants and eating: suppertime had arrived. Only a few vehicles travelled on the road, most of them from previous decades, and every once in a while, they frightened the dusty dogs lying at the side of the road, with an irritable horn honked or with black exhaust smoke.

He deliberated whether to first fulfill the mission he had taken upon himself, to search for a toy shop here, but since all the shops were still open, he thought he would first eat. He turned right into one of the alleys and walked through it, despite no restaurant being seen on either side: in small alcoves, weavers sat wrapping fibers of raw wool onto large wooden spinning tops, tailors pedaled sewing machines and ironed the clothes they sewed with charcoal irons, and as he passed by, they shot him a glance and right away returned to their work. In the next alley he entered, jewelers sat fanning a fire with bellows, and one, opposite whose shop he stopped, held tongs clasping a thin ingot whose tip had been seared white-hot and had softened and in a moment the tip was transformed into the head of a cobra; there was a dark magic in that deed of copper turning into a snake.

He turned right again and discovered that he had entered into an alley of butchers: the decapitated heads of goats were displayed in small butcher shop windows with puddles of blood around them, and behind hung the headless skinned bodies, To get out of there he turned left into another alley, the baker's alley, who like their Delhi counterparts bent towards clay ovens whose flames lit their sides with the circles of dough that were stuck to them. The aroma of baking rose up, filling and flooding his nostrils, and he stopped to buy a pastry that had just been taken out, puffy brown and steaming, and after taking a few bites he bought another one and thought it might be enough to satisfy his hunger and from here he would return to the main street and look for a toy store. The chance of finding one in this remote place with plastic cars and dolls and Lego blocks and balloons seemed totally unrealistic, but he wanted to keep his word.

It wasn't difficult to remember all the turns he had taken: twice to the right, once to the left, and right again, but he made one of the turns too soon or too late, and one mistake led to another. He succeeded in returning to the jeweler's alley, but there was no trace of the snake maker, as if he had been swallowed by one of his snakes. He also didn't find the alley before it, and when he decided to continue on solely by instinct, he entered a dark alley where no artisan could be seen and all the houses seemed to have been abandoned. When he turned into another alley, it also seemed dark and empty, and only his footsteps could be heard, rhythmic and heavy as if his body weight had increased in the thin mountain air.

The alleys were so narrow that above the low roofs it wasn't possible to see the mountain slope with its dowdy palace which could have helped him find his direction, and this Leh which had previously seemed to him a small village built around the bazaar street, revealed more and more alleys out of which even more alleys branched, one leading to others, and all with the same darkness flowing through them. For a moment he panicked: what if the smiths were to suddenly pounce upon him with their white-hot ingots, the bakers with their rolling-pins, the butchers with their knives? No one in the world would hear, no one would see, no one would know he had ended his life here.

Almost out of nowhere, the signpost of a hotel illuminated by a flickering light sprung up over the dark roofs like a mirage, and he began to walk towards it: it was impossible to gauge the distance and how much time would be needed to reach it, and he couldn't be sure he wouldn't stray again though the intricacy of the alleys when the sign would vanish from sight; for a while it grew large and then became diminished, for a while it flickered and then became stable, and he still couldn't read the letters written on it. Not a living soul could be seen around him, and the houses were shut and barred, and if people were sitting inside them, not a sound came out of their rooms. That silence was so strange he thought perhaps his ears had become blocked from the thinness of the air at that altitude or from the atmospheric pressure, and he inserted two fingers into his ears and shook them, together with his head, but the silence remained unchanged. A moment passed until all at once it was broken and suddenly bits of conversation in a few languages could be heard and sounds of music, and he still had to cross a small arched wooden bridge over a shallow canal to reach the other bank, and there, under the neon sign whose light had finally stabilized, the garden restaurant of a hotel could be seen, more pleasant than the one he was staying at, but fairly basic by Western standards.

The diners were seated at low tables and were busy with their chow mein and chop suey or some Western dish that the cook had learned to prepare, and he walked on farther toward the last table, the corner one, and sat down. Right then, a short waiter popped up opposite him and tried to explain something to him in Ladakhi, and when he saw that he didn't understand he shook a dwarfish finger at him and in an angry voice said: "No possible, no possible!" and didn't stop until a tall woman dressed in bright cotton clothing drew near them from the hotel.

"Is something wrong, Jigmet?" She asked the waiter, and Amnon hastened to apologize to both of them; he said he that he simply saw the vacant corner table and sat down and that he would get up right away and find another place. "You're not the only one who likes corners," she said, and hung the cotton bag she was carrying on her shoulder on the armrest of the chair, and he didn't know whether it was a reproach or an invitation to sit down. She was taller than him by half a head and appeared to be at least his own age, despite a childish ponytail that swung on her neck. Tiny wrinkles spread from the corners of her eyes, and it was already possible to see how they would spread from her mouth as well, and that like him she too was alone.

"Jigmet has already decided for us," she said when the waiter placed two menus on the table, and in a slight German accent – by now he already identified it – she explained to him the difference between tin tuk, a noodle soup with onion, garlic, ginger and potatoes, and thukpa, a noodle soup with meat; and why the Ladakhi momo is superior to the Italian ravioli, and the Chinese dumpling too, and all because of its simplicity. Generally speaking, she said, simplicity is what most characterizes this fond nation, until the tourists came and spoiled it.

"I also have some part in that," she said, "but I'm trying to put it right."

When she asked if he was also staying here, he replied that he preferred to stay outside of Leh, it's quieter there. "It's also quiet here," she said; she was volunteering in an organization here for Ladakhi women and returning to Changspa alone at night isn't something recommended for a woman – not long ago a soldier from the military base raped an American tourist. True, she's already no longer the suitable age ("And when I forget that for a moment, the mirror reminds me right away"), but in the dark it's impossible to know what passes through the head of some starved soldier.

"Not only a soldier," he heard himself saying, and right away a blush bloomed over her face: over the two cheeks that had already lost their suppleness, over the small wrinkles of the eyes, over the skin of the neck as well. In embarrassment she raised her hand to her neck, to the small ponytail, and tightened its knot.

The waiter returned and she again suggested he try the Ladakhi dishes: what's the point of travelling all the way here and eating European dishes? And instead of going into detail about how they tasted here, she distorted her face the way children do when somebody mentions food that arouses disgust to them.

It's not only the food, she said indignantly, everything is only for tourists now, but the first time she and her husband came here, there were barely any vehicles, only yaks. Her ex-husband, she corrected herself and waited for him to perhaps ask something about that but he chose not to. By the way, she said, her name's Angela and she doesn't have wings – she must have uttered that sentence more than once – and she's from Berlin.

They began to engage in conversation. In the pub in the English village, he had stared nightly at the waitresses eyes, but all other the men had been doing likewise, while here they were both sitting alone in the corner of the restaurant, a man and a woman whose partners were in a different country, thousands of kilometers away, and for a moment he wondered how Naomi would have looked upon them had she come here, but she won't be coming.

Every year when August begins – Angela said – she forgets Berlin completely as well as her job: she's a landscape architect, and here, at the most she worries about her plants being watered. She can't ask Rudy; no, Rudy's not her husband, he's her nephew.

"At first I still used to come to Ladakh with Herman," she said, "he also fell in love with the place, at least that's what he said, and I believed him." And now she comes alone and it's even better, there are advantages to being alone too, doesn't he think so?

He made a noncommittal gesture with his head.

Her husband – she continued, as if she had long waited for a sympathetic ear – wasn't interested in the Ladakhis the third time they came; he met a young girl backpacker and fell in love. And if that's not enough – her voice trembled slightly – he suddenly understood that until then he had never really loved anyone, not her either; he said all that to her one night in their apartment in Berlin.

"And what can you reply to something like that? You can only water the plants with what you suddenly have in your eyes."

The waiter arrived with small bowls of soup, and it seemed she was embarrassed by this confession, but after a short while she sat upright in her place and suggested he taste from her bowl as well, a suggestion that sounded bother humorous and seductive: "Do you want to taste my tin tuk?" How long had it been since she had reached out a bowl of steaming soup to a man with such encouragement, both motherly and wooingly. Her loneliness was clearly apparent; to the point where he could imagine her in her apartment in Berlin tending her plants, perhaps Bonsai trees, according to the rules of landscape architecture, and how every year she would wait for the summer, so that she could return to Leh again and help the women of Ladakh in the changes that their society was undergoing.

After their bowls were emptied, she showed him a few photographs she took out of her purse: gardens she had designed in Berlin as well as the rooms of her apartment where plants decorated the windowsills, equally as many as those Naomi brought with her when they moved in together, and another photograph where she could be seen on the banks of a frozen lake, veiled in a scarf that left only a narrow slit for the eyes between it and the fur cap that she wore, and her gaze, warm and glowing toward the one photographing her.

"That was still in our good years," she said and right away showed him another picture that had been taken in Leh. "This is the shop we opened for the women here, isn't it charming?" Materials and carpets and clothes that had been woven by loom could be seen with other handmade decorative objects of which the most beautiful, she said, would be exhibited in a museum that will open here next summer – they already have a plan as well as the financing! "But I'm making speeches to you," she said, "I knew it would happen in the end, why didn't you stop me?"

Only then did she ask him where he was from and fell silent for a moment and wondered if he didn't mind sitting with a German woman, and he told her he had visited Berlin as a young man and had been through all Europe in his van. "A lovely city," he said, "nice people," and her question brought to memory the policemen who stopped him after he his van had got stuck at a railway crossing on a side road; they wore long coats like the soldiers Second World War films and he feared any moment they would shout "Schnell! Schnell!" at him, the way they had shouted at all his mother's uncles and their sons and daughters, but they made do with a fine.

"You must have had a lot of girlfriends along the way," she said, and when he denied it, she seemed pleased. It crossed his mind that were he to make one small step she would consent, but still didn't know what that step might be and if he indeed wanted it. When she heard what his profession was (an investigative reporter, he said) she again looked worried – did he have a girl in every place he went to investigate? – until he said in earnest that it's been years since his newspaper has sent him anywhere and he had come here completely privately, for family reasons, one could say.

And his wife, she asked hesitantly, doesn't mind him roaming around the world like a free spirit?

Then the lie that had been made up in Delhi came out of his mouth, as if the moment it had been uttered there it had to be adhered to and given further validity each time it was revisited. No, he doesn't roam around the world, he replied, he came here to search for his son; and to that purpose he had already visited the police station.

At once her facial features seemed to unravel: has he been drinking soup with her so calmly at a time when it isn't clear where his son is? The shock exposed the roots of wrinkles on her face he had not previously discerned, and in the depths of her soft brown eyes there was fear, even anxiety: had she been so very mistaken about him? A kind of childish purity was still evident in her face, the purity that forced her to return here every year in order to help the women of Ladakh despite her personal sorrow, and he placed his arm on her arm. She didn't pull it away, but he still felt that he had to calm her.

Many young Israelis come here, he said, and quite often contact is lost with them, but in the end it all turns out okay. If he didn't think that, he wouldn't be sitting here with her and enjoying himself so much – not from the soup, nor from her company; it's been ages since he's enjoyed a conversation with a woman!

He was precise in that detail: his last conversations were telephone conversations from the English village, and he hasn't forgotten, even for a moment, the things Naomi hurled at him when it became clear she wouldn't succeed in persuading him to come back. As for young girl backpackers – he said in order to differentiate himself from someone who chooses to chat with them instead of with a woman like her – what could one talk to them about, what do they know at that age? And concerning my son, he said, the inspector at the police station told him explicitly there was no cause for worry. Things like this happen and, in the end, everything turns out alright.

"So you met Inspector Tendon," she said, and again something softened in her face as well as in the hand beneath his hand. "A dear man, Tendon, so unsuited to be a policeman –"

She asked from whom else did he try to get assistance, and he mentioned the priest for whom she had some criticism, even if he had proved himself a devoted father after his wife died. He also mentioned Dr. Tashi who she praised – if everyone here were like Dr. Tashi, she said, she would be less worried about the exposure to the West; but what is she going on about while his son is missing. She really feels bad now, she said, the way she pestered him before with her talk about tin tuk and thukpa.

"I haven't got any children; you've probably already understood that?" At the very most, she said, she sometimes watched over her nephew Rudi, that naughty kid! His head once got stuck between the bars of the balcony and she feared that they'd have to saw the railing and cause irreparable damage to Rudy. What would she say to her sister? What would she say to herself? "I was never so scared in my whole life, not even when Herman left me," she said and placed her hand on her chest.

"They're at their most worrisome when they're small," he replied, despite never having raised a child from infancy; he had once refused to become a father and had even demanded a choice between pregnancy and him. Yes, he had been quite some bastard, and it doesn't make any difference whether his being a bastard had been determined by genetics.

He'll never forget – he continued with total naturalness, and now didn't need any lie – the night he thought Udi had fallen from the balcony; she has Rudy and he has Udi. There isn't a child that doesn't put his head between the bars, but he thought Udi had fallen to the yard from the height of three floors. He was so scared he hardly could breathe when he went to the railing to look down. "It lasted a second or a year," he said, "it's a wonder my hair didn't turn grey on the spot."

She looked at his temples, causing him to look at her hair: a few white roots could be seen on both sides of the parting in the middle of her head.

"But the very worst," he heard himself say, "was when he almost drowned." She fixed her bright brown eyes on him in total sympathy and without any hesitation he heard himself continue his story, as if from the moment one begins a lie there's no other way, nor is there a need for one when it yields such a large gain. "It happened in the sea," he said, "it was just the two of us at the time: me, him, and the fish." And he didn't tell her they were floating on the surface of the water, completely dead and shining in the sun.

She insisted on hearing the happy end, and he acceded. Of course, he caught hold of Udi, he said; after all, had he not, he wouldn't be looking for him here now.

She then reached out her hand and covered his hand with it and left it like that; he found her touch pleasant. In her eyes he must have seemed a model father, a man who had come thousands of kilometers to save his son again: had had found him in the sea and now he'll find him in these mountains.

"I lifted him up with my hands," he continued and showed her how he had carried the boy in his arms, his head wobbling and his eyes shut, and beneath him the waves from which he had to be distanced, and the rocks he had to be careful not to stumble on. "There were moments when I didn't know if he was dead or alive," he said, "there's nothing worse than that, holding a small body in your hands and not knowing whether it was still alive. I'd never been so scared in my entire life." In that he was precise: he had never been so scared and never would be that scared again.

She strengthened her grip on his hand; in her mind's eye, she must have seen him reach the shore with his son and place him down gently on the sand and bend over him and administer mouth to mouth resuscitation until the boy opened his eyes. There were tears in her eyes, hesitating whether to spill or be swallowed in her eyelashes, and for a moment he felt pangs of conscience; but he had not been with a woman for a long time, and after all there was no cheating here, not for her nor for him; and even if there had been, what difference does it make?

During one of his annual conversations with his mother in one of the new cafés that had opened on the beach promenade, she explained to him why she had left his father and gone off with another man. "Children think that their parents are just parents," she said after tasting the cheesecake that he ordered, "but firstly they're man and woman. It's a pity your father didn't understand that concerning his own parents." The café was almost empty, and the rain washed the large windowpane, and through it the sea could be seen vast and dark, the foam whitening and dispersing and renewing itself and becoming blurred in the rain. "Long before we thought of becoming a father and a mother," she said, "that's just what we were, a man and a woman. And it was good then, it really was. And there was war on, and sometimes I felt like I was in a movie, with all that love that we had in the middle of it all. Why are you looking at me like that?"

"I'll never understand how you could cheat on him," he replied, "a good man like that."

"Those are harsh words, Nonny," she said, "but your mother simply fell in love again. It happens to many couples. I fell in love because my love with your father was over and it's nothing to be ashamed of, maybe it will happen to you once." The rain continued to flow over the windowpane, and beyond it a ridge of foam stormed toward the shore and collapsed. "One can also stop living," she said, "that's also a solution, like your grandmother who gave up on everything and screwed her whole life up. But I wasn't prepared for that to happen to me, why give up on everything? Must you hate me for that?"

"I don't hate you," he said, inferring what he couldn't say to her and she lifted her hand to call the waiter.

When they got up and went into the hotel (Jigmet turned his eyes away so as not to embarrass her), it seemed that had it not been for the alcohol, Angela would never have conceived of inviting him to her room: it would be a sin to behave in such a way with a man whose son is missing and whose wife must be up all night worrying about him, that's what she said. And up in her room, she said, she'll just show him the photographs that she took all over Ladakh – maybe he'll reach there in his search? But her buttocks were already swaying in front of him as they ascended the stairs, and for a very long time he hadn't walked behind a woman to her room for the first time, while still studying the movement of her buttocks. There was great charm in that sight after which there's no knowing what will follow.

"I'm staying here," she said as she opened the door, "this is my second home." And the room really didn't look like a hotel room: she had her carpet there and her embroidered tablecloths and her checkered bedspread and her pillows that the hotel staff prepared every year for her arrival, and flowers in vases; there was almost a vase in every place, perhaps a substitute for her plants in Berlin. And again, the sight of petunias came to mind, the violets, the sage, the lavender of the woman he left; their pot plants had almost filled half a truck when they moved to their rented house, and how upset she was about the one that broke on the way and how annoyed she was with the movers.

There was only one chair in the room, and when she sat down on the wide bed with the small photograph album in her hands, he sat down too and didn't wait for her invitation. "There's no shortage of places to disappear in," she said about his son, "what kind of person is he?" And she tried to find out if his son had adventurous tendencies, the kind that would cause him to disappear on some journey in the mountains, or spiritual tendencies that would make him want to seclude himself in an isolated monastery (while doing so, she showed him photographs of snow-capped mountains with arid slopes and white monasteries with faded prayer flags waving in the wind), or does he make do with simple pleasures, drugs and sex – for that there are better places in India. "Does he have a girlfriend?" she asked, and he replied: "He did have, but they split up," and said that they could have got married, but it didn't happen. "He wanted to travel far away," he said. "I don't think he felt good with her."

"And who does feel good?" she said and immediately regretted the tone of her voice, but he had already taken the album from her hand, and she already knew what his intention was. "What we're doing isn't good," she said even before he had made any move, and for a moment he wondered if she was troubled now, as some Westerners who come here are by their karma and its punishment, and to that she replied: "Not karma, that's for the next reincarnation and I'm talking about now!" But only during the first moments did she still try to object to his hand that reached out to her, and afterward acceded to his fingers in all their paths over her body; she hadn't been with a man for a long time, and her body yearned to be touched. Only when she was completely naked, large and very white, did she stop him again and he was surprised by her force. "This way at least you won't be really cheating on her," she said to him and with a firm hand indicated what would be permissible for both of them and what wouldn't be, with the same firmness his first girlfriend a thousand years ago had done: this no, and that yes, is it good like this? It is good, it's really good, she showed him and stopped him, it's good, it is, it's good for both of them like that, yes like that.

One night on the bank of the Sea of Galilee, after he and the girl who was his co-leader drew away from the youth group members they were in charge of, they put their unzipped sleeping bags close together and felt around each other with blind hot curious hands, and for an immeasurable amount of time that learning continued with great delight, a delight he remembered much more than many other nights. And what remained of it?

When he fell asleep on the hotel bed, drained and depleted opposite the statuettes staring at him from the night table, he dreamed of their rented house – it must have been the plants that led him there in his sleep: something was happening at the back of the bedroom, he heard it from the entrance the moment he opened the front door, and the closer he came, the stronger the sounds were until it was impossible to mistake their nature, and when he reached the bedroom he saw Naomi's clothes strewn on the floor, he also saw the black bra and black panties, and not far from them a man's underpants or bathing suit, with black with white cords and wet through and through, and right outside the room a baby lay on its stomach waving a toy in its hand to the rhythm coming from inside – the door was slightly ajar, and only the night lamp was lit and the shadows it cast swayed over and over, and the scent of two of the bodies emanated from here with their sounds. He woke up startled in a strange room.

The German woman was lying on her stomach next to him, covered by a sheet up to her shoulder blades, and for an hour or more he waited to see light in the window and didn't get up. Her small ponytail was dispersed, an on her neck, under the golden down, a beauty spot could be seen, but he found little beauty in it. The room had a large window, unlike the window of their bedroom, of which Naomi said had it been their house and not just rented, she would have enlarged it at least twice the size for them to be able to see the pines up to their treetops. "Who designs a house like that?" she complained and said the same about the narrow kitchen window and the bathroom and the attic that the previous tenants had used as a storeroom and that she dreamed of turning into a workroom and save her travelling every morning to the studio in the city (in the end she said: "What luck that I kept the studio in the city").

On the day they moved there she instructed the porters where to place each piece of furniture, each crate, each plant, and did so firmly, the way she handled contractors and workers in her job, but after the truck departed and she looked all around, her gaze encountered a doorpost on which the owners of the house had marked the height of their children with pencil lines, and he saw her wipe her eyes with the back of her hand: she had left behind a doorpost exactly like that, and only one of her sons whose height had been measured there agreed to move with her; a long time passed until the eldest forgave her for breaking up their family and became accustomed to Amnon's existence in her life. He was a reserved and wise child, and still is, very reserved and very wise; and how could he, Amnon, not understand his anger – after all, in his own childhood and later, he himself had been angry with his mother in the same way.

The poplars grew from year to year as did the plane tree and Judas tree saplings they had planted together, and in vain she tried to persuade him to sell his grandmother's apartment and invest the money in this house ("Maybe something good would come out of her bitterness?"); and that way they would get to see their trees in their full height, when the treetops would surpass the roof. There were also trees whose growth stopped: the thin trunk of the lemon tree broke in the first winter wind, the quince had odd stains, and the two apple trees died the same year when the rabbits nibbled on their roots from the burrows they dug, and to that she said: "Why didn't you but Udi what he asked for?" He replied by saying that there's no way Udi would give up Bugs and Bunny and all their whole dynasty now.

"He wouldn't or you wouldn't?" she said, because it was he who took the trouble to fill their bowls with food and water, and she claimed he was wasting his abilities on inferior creatures who aren't capable of returning love and could have made not a bad father at all had he only wanted that; that's to say, had he been born into a different family.

8

He did not learn much from the teacher, despite his appointing himself local historian and conceiving the idea of the museum of Ladakhi history and culture. He hadn't even heard of Dr. McKenzie. What could a teacher in a tiny school in this backwater of backwaters know about what took place here at the beginning of the century? But it would have been fitting for Amnon to also ask himself if he really wanted to find out all the details of his grandfather's life and death, and if he had indeed travelled here for that purpose. Yes, ask yourself, he said, ask and reply.

It's better to know, he replied to himself. Know from where you came, you putrid drop.[39]

In the schoolyard, when he mentioned to the teacher that Inspector Tendon had recommended him, he turned his eyes toward his colleagues to make sure they heard him being praised, and afterward, when they sat on the stone bench and he asked him about the first decade of the century, it transpired that the teacher remembered not only the name of the kings that had ruled (it wasn't especially complicated in the Namgyal dynasty), but also the names of the British commissioners who had governed here. When he began to recite them, he had to interrupt him and direct the conversation towards the government hospital – does the teacher by chance remember the names of its directors?

Opposite them, a boy rolled a hoop and another bounced a soccer ball on his foot.

No, the teacher hadn't prepared such a list, a roster of the commissioners and kings was enough for the museum. Yes, the Ladakh historical museum – his youthful face then adopted a serious aspect – half a wall would be taken up with those names and that would certainly be enough; people don't come to a museum to read rosters, and in that matter his friend Nawang was correct.

"One of the former hospital's directors," he said to the teacher, "got himself into some trouble. Dr. Edward McKenzie. Perhaps you've heard something about him?" But the name didn't ring a bell with the teacher.

"He got into trouble with medicines or antiquities," he said to him but no antiquities made a connection in his head with the director of a hospital. There

---

39 A paraphrase from the ancient Hebrew text, *Ethics of the Fathers*, a compilation of ethics and maxims passed down through the ages.

would be antiquities in the museum, naturally: the anchor that was discovered in the desert would be exhibited, but what has a doctor to do with anchors?

His friend Nawang, he said as one of the children came to take the ball out from the bushes, manages a travel agency here, and his grandfather had been very involved in the business of antiquities at the time. All in all that grandfather of his was quite a character, he also spent some time in jail, and before and after that he led caravans along the Silk Road with dozens of horses and camels with dozens of people. And instead of that, Nawang has two jeeps for tourists, a Tata Sumo and a Mahindra, and he's already on the way to another one, an import. If only I, the teacher said, earned in a month what Nawang makes in a day.

It seemed that if he doesn't stop him, he'd be hearing more and more in the matter of jeeps and money, and that Inspector Tendon's recommendation to speak with him about what happened here a hundred years ago was just an empty statement from someone who couldn't even discover who caused his parrot to disappear a month ago. But when he asked the teacher if he had heard about any Russians coming to the region, to his surprise he was answered immediately. With the delight of a well-informed pupil demonstrating his knowledge, and in that English-Indian intonation, the teacher didn't leave out even one of the names specified by Hopkirk in his books, from the nature loving Colonel Przhevalsky to Grombachevsky the spy, he even mentioned Notovich the crook, who claimed he found a document in Hemis Monastery that proves, no more and no less, that Jesus visited here ("If I only earned what he made from his forgeries," the teacher said). They won't be exhibiting that document in the museum, but some of the flowers and butterflies that the colonel discovered will be exhibited there, dried of course, in special glass boxes, and his friend Nawang has already promised to pay for them. Then the teacher fell silent and seemed pensive – perhaps he thought he had spoken too much – and only the ball that landed close to them brought him back to his senses.

A small museum like the one the teacher described, he had seen on the Greek island of Skiathos during the winter his mother died, and its owner was one of the inhabitants of the islands who was looking for way to make money off bored tourists. He hadn't been bored, or even worried, and nevertheless bought a ticket and went in; it was something of a distraction. That same unusual winter ("There hasn't been a winter like it for forty years," they said in the tavern), when the water froze in the pipes and the snow fell on the wharf and on the nets spread on it and on the boats and on the foam of the waves, he was one of the gullible few who paid to enter the small homely museum: a wooden threshing implement studded with small stones was exhibited there together with a wooden plough, and a fisherman's net was spread over one of the walls and with a rusty anchor. While they had some sort of relevance also exhibited were a sooty charcoal iron and large iron pans and a gramophone with a giant horn and a tube radio; cuts could be seen in the material of the speaker, the kind cats make when sharpening their claws on woven material – perhaps everything that the owner inherited from his parents or grandparents – and at the same time Amnon's mother lay unconscious in hospital and the helium balloon that floated above her with the wishes worded on it began to expire together with her.

The teacher began to detail the names of the exhibits he intended to display in the museum with his friend Nawang: vajras, mandalas, ritual bells, ritual masks, prayer rolls and prayer flags and prayer beads, and there'll certainly be a fitting display of Ashtamangala – does he know what an Ashtamangala is? He immediately began to note all the names of the symbols heralding good fortune, from the white shell to the dagger, a dagger called a Phurba.

"Weren't there any other Russians that came here?" he interrupted him.

"There was a Russian woman," the teacher replied – he was slightly annoyed at being disturbed – and again appeared pensive. With the tip of his finger, he raised his glasses up his nose, and around the tiny crack in the center of them the remnants of unremoved glue could be seen, either due to carelessness or because he couldn't see the remnants without glasses. That Russian woman, he said, arrived here at the beginning of the century with her son, and a tragedy happened and he died. Afterward he added details, despite Amnon not asking him; what did his grandfather and his demise have to do with a Russian child here?

It occurred in the first decade of the century, the teacher continued and said there were still people here who remembered the little Russian. When he began to explain that some church festival was the cause of the death, Amnon stopped listening; more than enough dead children had cropped up from the past lately. The saying of Dr. McKenzie Jr. in England also crossed his mind – "leave the dead alone" – before he spoke about the gigantic ship waiting for him and only for him.

"In the end, she recovered from it," he said about the mother of the boy that was killed, "and Nawang's grandfather helped a bit with that," and a sound of irony could be heard in his voice, despite that no derision was evident in his boyish face with its old-fashioned glasses, a serious face, devoid of malice; only the sound of jealousy that emerged when he spoke of his friend somewhat tainted his voice. His grandfather simply befriended her afterward, he said, and from their friendship – that's the term teacher used, "friendship" – Nawang derived his blue eyes, and there were no lack of tourists who fall in love with him due to that ("If I had only half of them," he thought the teacher would say, but this time he was silent and appeared pensive).

The tumult of the children in the schoolyard died down, and for a moment there rose in his memory, from one of its dustiest corners, the sight of his own schoolyard with a basketball pole at one end and a sandbox at the other and he's waiting for his mother to come and take him home at the end of a school day, and the yard that had been bustling, is emptying from the last children and there's no longer anyone but him, not a child nor an adult; and how long that wait was in the sandbox and how threatening the way home seemed, but many times worse was the moment when he realized that his mother wasn't going to arrive, not in the coming minutes, not in the coming hour, perhaps never ("Something came up at work," she said afterward to his father).

The teacher told Amnon - trusting him, a white man older than himself and a Westerner - that the moment Nawang heard about the idea of the museum from him, he called him a genius. You're wasted on little children in the school, Nawang said, your imagination doesn't go far enough. Exhibits are good, Gargan, but it's better to see people. Thangkas and tormas are great, and vajras and mandalas, and also shells from the desert and anchors, but why don't you bring a few monks here – that's what Nawang suggested, and at the time the teacher still thought that Nawang just wanted to help him – with enough colored sand for even for a thousand mandalas, and why make do with examples of handicrafts if you can seat a few women in the museum who will make them right in front of the tourists' eyes? There will be such a long queue here, that he, the teacher, will barely manage to tear one ticket while another fifty tourists approach. That's how Nawang already sees the teacher, as a ticket-seller standing at the entrance, even in uniform, and all the while Nawang manages the museum from his office and takes all the money for himself and leaves something small for the teacher, but who's idea was it, who's, and now he's turning him into a ticket-seller, isn't that insulting?

"You have some nice friend," Amnon said to him, and already knew he would go to Nawang from here. Know from where you came, he said to himself, and to where you are going, to a place of maggots and worms; other than if they cremate you like they perhaps did with your grandfather, if they hadn't left him for the crows.

A large tin signpost hung above the entrance of the travel agency, and under its name – "Explorer Agency" – was a Ford Explorer jeep drawn with reasonable accuracy, despite only Indian jeeps being parked in front of it. A small cardboard sign on the door of the entrance also proclaimed "telephone-fax-document copying services," and stuck around it were faded photographs in which Nawang was seen with all sorts of eminent figures: some senior Indian, perhaps a minister, a glamorous Indian beauty, no doubt an actress or a singer, and someone who looked like Richard Gere's double. The dusty display window was mostly covered by yellowish pages in which trip routes were detailed: to Zanskar, to Lamayuru, to the Nubra Valley, to Lake Tsomoriri, to Manali, to Srinagar, and inside the office two young Europeans were standing and perusing the notes stuck to a crumbling cork board, among them the usual notices of someone looking for travel partners, or offering camping equipment, a motorbike, love ("Almost a year has passed and you're still in my heart"). The Ladakhi who sat at the small desk in the corner, solidly built, dark and blue-eyed, was speaking into two telephones at the same time, and it took a while for him to become free, and when Amnon asked him about the museum that was about to open here, the Ladakhi gave him a suspicious look.

By that time, he was already tired of waiting and of the lie he had been in need of during the past days, whether in the matter of his nationality or of his father-hood, and he decided to speak frankly. He had heard from the teacher – he said – about a museum of the history of Ladakh and also that Nawang's grandfather had been a very famous figure here, and surely must have known all the foreigners who came to Leh: for example, the director of the Moravian mission hospital.

"Gargan talks too much," Nawang answered.

In order to soften him, he backed down and asked, as if it was his chief inter-est in life, about the differences between the jeeps the agency hires out, the Tata and the Mahindra, and the differences between both of them and the Ford jeep, the Explorer that was drawn on the signpost: how much horsepower each one had, and what the engine capacity of the motors were, and how many liters each tank held. He, who for years only travelled by public transport and bought a car only after he had established a small family and, even then, was accused of stinginess – why hadn't he taken into consideration the eldest son as a passenger, after all, he might live with them in the future? – was now busy with this.

Maybe the Ladakhi saw him as someone close to the motor industry by virtue of his being Western, and certainly more so that those living at the bottom of the Himalayas, and therefore his suspicion subsided, and he replied. His knowledge was apparently drawn from some magazine one of the tourists had left here, and the Ford Explorer on the signpost (rust stains had been transferred from the tin to the illustrated jeep) must have been copied from there. The Ladakhi spoke of the six-cylinder German engine that was manufactured in Koln, about the Swedish chassis, about the body of the vehicle that was manufactured in the United States in various places: Chicago, Illinois and also in Hazelwood, Missouri – once there was even an American girl here who came from Hazelwood, Missouri, where her father worked in the Ford factory. When he spoke about that, his voice changed, and it seemed that there was also a change in the shade of his eyes.

"Do all of you in the family have blue eyes?" he suddenly asked, not in accor-dance with his plan.

"Who's all of you?" Nawang replied.

Both phones rang at once, and Nawang lifted the two mouthpieces together, and until he finished talking Amnon's gaze surveyed the small office: more faded photographs were on the right-hand wall, and in all of them Nawang could be seen in the company of Western tourists inside one jeep or another, and on the photo-graphs that all showed the snowy peaks above the clouds ("The distant mountains of darkness" returned and echoed in his head; their name according to his grand-mother), dedications were written, almost all with the same wording: "To Nawang, thanking you for a marvelous trip!" or "The charming!" or "The wonderful!" and one of the writers took more trouble than the others and wrote: "To Nawang, who is familiar with the paths of Ladakh like the paths on the palm of his hand." On another photograph, smaller than all the others and dark, which had apparently been photographed inside a jeep at evening time, written in cursive handwriting was "To Nawang, who knows the paths of Ladakh like the paths on the palm of his hand, Betsy."

In order to return the conversation to its path, he asked the Ladakhi what he thought about Toyota's Landcruiser and Mitsubishi's Pajero, and a vague memory rose in his mind about one of the car reviews in his newspaper that had praised one of those jeeps and found fault with the other, and when it turned out the reporter had done so in exchange for an invitation to visit the factory in Japan, a small scandal took place which ended in the man being fired, a year before he himself was fired due to a scandal many times larger.

"The Japanese still have a lot to learn from the Americans," Nawang answered. "But you haven't come here for that."

Amnon then told him about his grandfather; how he arrived in Leh at the beginning of the century, a young man that only God knows what he was looking for here and for what purpose he had crossed such a distance – perhaps his grandfather knew him?

"And why should he know him?"

"Leh is a small place, and at that time it was even smaller."

Nawang looked at him a moment longer before he turned to the tourists that were still standing opposite the cork board and reading the notices pinned to it. "Have you already decided where you're travelling to?"

No, they haven't decided yet.

Why don't you think about it in the restaurant on the corner? Tell them Nawang sent you."

"And will they lower the price?"

"I'll take it off your price."

"People bargain over everything now," he said when they left. "Until all of you came here no one bargained that way. We would name a price, and it was either yes or no, and all with a smile, without getting angry. Today one has to bargain over everything."

"You're a businessman yourself," Amnon reminded him.

"If my business was run like that, I wouldn't have come to all this," the Ladakhi indicated to the space around him, and the two jeeps were certainly also included in his statement and all the tourists he had driven throughout Ladakh as well as outside of Leh. It seemed like a suitable moment to ask him about the caravans his grandfather had led here at the beginning of the century ("Times have changed," he uttered the saying, hackneyed like all others concerning time; only more hackneyed was the saying of its ability to heal), to inquire for example how many yaks and camels and horses were on it, There were also donkeys and mules and dozens of beasts of burden on every caravan, sometimes even hundreds; but they were not his grandfather's, his grandfather was just a paid employee – not like Nawang who owned all this himself.

It must have been a thrilling sight, a caravan of hundreds of beasts of burden making its way over the dunes or up those mountains, their feet plodding in the sand or the snow and their shadows trailing behind them or preceding them, and the one guiding it possibly resembled this Ladakhi, also in his wariness towards a white man who landed up in a place that is not his own and whose motivation is unclear, perhaps to himself as well.

He couldn't tell the Ladakhi in what way their grandfathers were meant to be connected to each other, but he remembered what he had heard from the teacher in the schoolyard about that grandfather and his Russian girlfriend. Maybe she also had a Russian boyfriend?

"The Russian woman," Nawang said briefly, "had many boyfriends."

He opened his large diary that was laid on his desk and began to write in it until his pen stopped and refused to continue even after it had been shaken in the air. He then replaced it with another he took out of the drawer – a fancy Parker pen with an inscription, perhaps a gift he received from one of the lady tourists.

In order to carry on a conversation that isn't just questions and answers (his profession didn't impress Nawang; perhaps he only placed importance on journalists who wrote in car magazines) to fish any information out of him about his grandfather, at the very least an admission that he had indeed passed through here, he began to tell him about the tourists staying in his hotel, and it transpired that Nawang knew all of them – Leh really is a small place – the irritating Austrian couple, the Canadian woman, and the wacky Italian hairdresser; and Angela as well, yes, he still remembers her husband who used to come with her until some young French girl turned his head around – that's how it is, people are always searching for their happiness elsewhere. He suddenly said, "Why did your grandfather come all the way from Russia if after a year he already gave up on everything?"

For the first time in all this journey on which he had travelled thousands of kilometers from his country, someone was speaking to him who knew his grandfather had lived here at the beginning of the century, and it would have been fitting for him to be excited, to shout for joy or wipe away a tear, but he didn't shout for joy and didn't wipe away a tear, not even deep inside himself. After all, he had not traversed all this distance only for his grandfather.

It had almost happened to him himself, Nawang said, he had almost forgotten where to look for happiness, that's to say, right under his nose. Something softened in his face and his speech; mutual candor wasn't needed for that; it was enough the Ladakhi knew things about his grandfather that were unknown to him himself. "Money is important," he said, "but family more so, and family isn't with all those female tourists that are here today and gone tomorrow." He looked at the name engraved on the pen in his hand and turned the pen around as if to banish it from his eyes. "Have you got a family?"

He had lied more than enough in that matter lately, and this time didn't hasten to reply.

"Gargan doesn't understand that," Nawang said, "he thinks the museum will put everything right for him, and he's depending on all the tourists that will come; but they're here today and gone tomorrow, and what will he be left with?" Since the coming and going of tourists had been raised again, he again spoke about Angela, who returns here every summer and stays a whole month. "She tells everyone that when she's old she'll stay here for good, but your grandfather," he said, "came here to stay from the beginning." They sat in a meager travel agency and discussed their grandfathers as if the details concerning them could change something in a world they've haven't been a part of for very many decades, but still they continued to speak of them.

"Did your grandfather know my grandfather?" For the first time, he asked the question explicitly.

"He had a Russian friend at the time," Nawang said, "he spoke a lot about his Russian friend."

It still wasn't possible to conclude that Russian was indeed his grandfather. Maybe there were a few Russians here at the time? And after all, there was also that Russian woman.

"She's another matter," Nawang answered, and a shadow passed over his face.

She had come with her son (Amnon was again forced to hear about the two of them) on the same train on which his grandfather had travelled to the last station on the Trans-Caspian railway line, but they only had become friendly in Kashgar, and it was there that Tenzin, Nawang's grandfather, also met them.

"Do you know where Kashgar is?" he asked.

He didn't know.

"And where Osh is?"

He again shook his head.

"And Andijan? And the Trans-Caspian? What do you know?"

He knew very little, had he known, he wouldn't have come all this way to Ladakh; that's what he replied, despite it not being the whole truth. Afterward he continued to listen to the Ladakhi, and it transpired that his grandfather, Tenzin, had got into some trouble in Kashgar, and the Russian had saved him there.

"My grandfather saved your grandfather?" That was a surprising fact, and he wondered if indeed his grandfather had been endowed with some of the qualities his father had attributed to him throughout his life and especially in his old age, qualities that neither of them, not his father nor him, had been endowed with: not bravery, not determination, not daring.

"Yes," Nawang replied, "why are you surprised?"

When his father told him how he had rescued his friend from a mine field in Italy, he said with honesty how his main fear was the reaction of his friends in the company if he left their comrade behind, and Amnon found it hard to see in that wrinkle-faced flabby-bellied man, someone who in the fourth decade of his life had enlisted into the British army, left the university and volunteered to fight the Fascists, and at the end of an unnecessary battle had carried a bleeding body over his shoulder up and down the slopes of hills that were pulverized by shells; when he himself drove past those hills in his van, only grazing cows could be seen.

"They almost all arrived together," Nawang said, "and the Russian woman had a room here in the inn with her child. She had many friends, not only my grandfather, if you understand my meaning. And through the window of that room, she saw her child fall from the roof; do you know what it is to see your child fall from a roof like that?"

He shook his head; he had at least been spared that sight.

"Just terrible," Nawang said. "I don't have children yet, but just thinking -"

In the dusty display window of the travel agency for a moment it seemed some falling body was fluttering, but it was only a crow that landed on the ground and started to hop on its way to some remnant it saw in his flight.

"Maybe next year I'll have one," Nawang said.

In order to steer the conversation back to the matter for which he had come and not that Russian boy, he told the Ladakhi that he had already heard quite a lot about that from the teacher, but the tactic produced the opposite result: right away he began the odd story about the little Russian who had taken part in some pageant in the church and had actually tried to fly off the roof of the inn. It was a strange and cruel story, no less terrible than the story about the one who climbed up an electric pole to take a flag down or about the one who went into the sea to gather dead fish and bury them.

He showed no interest in the continuation, but the Ladakhi related what the elders said about that small child and his death: until the road was paved, they could still see his face and the wings there.

He didn't understand and asked for a clarification. It seems that before the ground was levelled and tarred, the imprint of the little Russian boy's face could be seen together with the outline of the wings that had been prepared for that church pageant – at least according to the elders – and from all the villages of the region people came to touch the imprint he had left for luck. On that detail, unlike the previous one, Nawang cast no doubt, not even by means of a mocking tone of voice.

"They said whoever touched it would start to walk if they weren't able to walk, would begin to see if they weren't able to see, to hear if they weren't able to hear. That's what people are like, the more troubles they have the more they'll believe. Every winter it was covered in snow, and every spring they would see it again." He himself, he said, was born many years after that, but had heard the stories.

One could visualize that sight: the tens or hundreds coming to touch the imprint of the small body, a large crowd congregating around it or a queue extending in front of it, and each one in turn kissing the imprint of his mouth or his wing;

as well as the ground revealed beneath the thawing snow, muddy at first with many puddles and later slowing drying out, until hardening in the mold of the face and wings of the little Russian boy. Owing to his lingering gaze and his thoughts turning back, he saw an imprint like that whose features were chillingly familiar: Udi's features.

"Your grandfather," Nawang said, "left Leh afterward, he didn't want to stay here anymore. He left without saying goodbye to anyone, until they suddenly heard he had died. And when my grandfather returned with his caravan, he said, what do you mean died, impossible, he was sure they were all lying. He never believed stories that came out of monasteries." He got up from where he was and pointed at some spot on the map, despite that nothing could be seen there, not a settlement nor a topographical marking. "Khaspang," he said, "even if your grandfather wanted to go into the cave, they wouldn't have let him, there's a waiting line, and also he was a Jew, no?"

"Yes," Amnon replied.

"The monks think everyone's stupid, they said the Russian had suddenly become like one of them, and who benefits from that, the monastery benefits, people tell one another about it and in that way more pupils will come there and bring more money with them. Do you think in Lamayuru they don't benefit from all the tours I bring there? They're certainly do, and also did then." And his grandfather, he said, hated things like that, the moment he could smell a lie he'd become angry.

"Not now," he said to the telephone mouthpiece that he lifted on the first ring, "later. I promised you a jeep and you'll get a jeep." He slammed down the receiver. "People think you can't see this country without a jeep. Don't you need a jeep?"

He shook his head; he didn't yet know if he would be travelling onward from here. He had crossed a very long way until reaching here, and in comparison, the part that remained seemed miniscule, but he still didn't know if he would make that journey.

"My grandfather didn't want anyone to go with him, he said that with the caravans he had to take care of the people all the time, so he didn't want anyone alongside him there. And not that he didn't like his work on the caravan, he liked it a lot, he was always telling us stories about the desert. Here, right away you have mountains, he would say to us, and mountains are like a wall, while there you can go for months without anything around, and when there are sandstorms a person can't even see the tip of his own hand. Your grandfather was with him there once. My grandfather said, the Russian who came here was only used to snow, and in the end got along not at all badly in the desert. The karaburan didn't kill him, only the monks did. Do you know what the karaburan is?"

"The monks killed him?"

The thought of a group of monks in robes attacking an old man – for a moment his grandfather looked old, despite that he was twenty years younger than he is now – brought to mind a scene from some bad movie with waving robes, orange or red, and a glinting knife blade, and blood flowing.

"They didn't kill him with their hands, but they allowed him to die. He rolled down a chasm with his pony, and they then must have thought that if he's already dead, why not make some profit from it? We'll say that he died in the cave like our monks, we'll say he was learning how to pray; we'll say that his shot can still be heard even a month after that, they went down to him just to take his pistol and sell it, but they left him there. He had rolled down from the path; it would have been enough for his pony to suddenly twist a leg."

The picture that rose to mind flickered like the previous ones and like them immediately vanished, it must also have been taken from some movie he had seen: a beast of burden slips on a slope with its load, rolling over again and again on its way to the depths; when in fact it was only motorcars that rolled over like that, motorcars and lorries and buses, whereas how could animals whose legs are not in line with their bodies roll over?

Was his grandfather still alive when he reached the bottom of the chasm, had he shot himself in order to shorten his suffering there? He also found no difficulty picturing that sight: the paralyzed man trying to reach his fingers out to a pistol that had fallen a certain distance from him, stretching them out with enormous effort and still not touching it, and trying to roll over on his side to draw near the pistol with his body and groaning with pain, and above a crow is already circling and cawing. Or perhaps someone else shot him, someone who saw him there and had his eye on his pistol. If a nomad spotted him from the path and went down to him, maybe for a moment, in his heart of hearts, he presumed he was coming to save him and was glad of that, or the opposite, he tried to signal to him to leave him be and was glad only when the stranger lifted up his pistol and pointed it at him.

"The monks," Nawang said, "found him according to the crows, and he hadn't even entered the cave, if he wanted to enter it at all. All in all, he wanted to see if the man who had lived there before was still alive. He and my grandfather got the paper from him."

"Paper?" he asked. He already knew that his grandfather was involved in an act of fraud and that antiquities were connected to it, but he hadn't yet heard about the paper.

It turned out that together with the ancient paper other objects had been hidden in the desert, not only antiquities but shells, mother-of-pearl and salt. "Stupid people," Nawang said, "will believe anything, put an anchor in the desert and they'll think there was once a sea there, put mother-of-pearl and shells there too and they'll be absolutely sure." Some of those objects that were hidden in the sands they intended to exhibit in the museum: one of the anchors that had been discovered there (the rest were taken to Europe) as well as some of the shells, despite that in their appearance they didn't differ from any other shell of their kind.

He asked what was written on the paper; for a moment it seemed that it was of great importance, that everything might become clear by that.

Outside someone pressed his rotund face to the windowpane and Nawang ignored him.

"They wrote about the sea that had been there, and you could hear it in the shells. It was the doctor's idea, my grandfather only helped. They wrote that the people had done something bad and the gods were so furious that they boarded their boats and sailed away together with the sea." Nawang lifted his left hand towards the windowpane, in that way indicating with his watch to the one standing there that the break hadn't ended. "And that every year the people still waited for them to return."

That sight could also be pictured hazily on the background of the dusty windowpane of the travel agency: the boats or the ships drawing away with beating oars or billowing sails, and the sea gathered behind them with all its waves like an enormous trail. And the masses standing and waiting on the dry shore, waiting from morning to night, waiting that whole week, that whole month, and afterward returning there once a year led by that same anticipation. Did not masses many times greater anticipate the return of Jesus and Buddha and Ben David and the Mahdi, and kill each other in the meantime?

"Only ten years later they discovered it was a fraud," Nawang continued. A French researcher exposed the swindle, and until then everyone had been arguing over its revealed and hidden details, and even tried to imagine the ending of the fake tale of which only a piece had been preserved. The Ladakhi was well versed in the details, and not because they excited him but because his grandfather used to joke about them.

There was one who believed the ships of the gods ascended to heaven by the power of the sails, and from the foam of the waves that ascended with them clouds were formed; and another claimed that it was more reasonable to suppose that the gods and their ships and the sea had seeped into the sand. "All together," Nawang said, "as if the lakes seen on the caravans come from that, and people think that is why there's water to drink there. As if in that way the gods continue to punish the people. Do you believe in such things?"

"No," he replied.

"No?"

"One doesn't need gods for punishment. Everyone can manage that very well by himself."

"And for hope?" The Ladakhi looked at him with his blue eyes whose clarity was highlighted by his skin, and he seemed hesitant whether to say anything more.

"Why your grandfather came here," he said a moment later, "I don't know. But when it was found out that it was all a lie, he hadn't been here for a long time. They still had enough wood to cremate the monk from the cave, but not for your grand-father. They left him to the eagles, I'm sorry to have to tell you that."

The picture flickered in his mind for a moment: A deep chasm and a skeleton turning white at its bottom.

"Don't be sorry," he replied. "That's what I came here for."

"It took you some time."

"It's a long way."

"But you people travel the whole time, here today, there tomorrow. See this pen here," – Nawang showed him his pen again – "I got it from Mabel who comes from Liverpool, she's already been here five times. And the chain," – he pointed to a necklace hung on a nail on the wall – "is from Jane, an Australian, she's already come three times, she even invited me to Melbourne, have you ever been to Melbourne?"

"No," he replied.

And before the Australian there had also been an American, Betsy – the Lada-khi was struck by a sudden urge to talk, perhaps brought on by what he had said about the long way he had crossed, or perhaps he would have spoken the same way with any chance stranger, even someone who came just from Srinagar or Chandi-garh. Betsy had been here one summer three years ago and had even given him her address in Hazelwood, Missouri, with her telephone number. "Nawang, I'll never forget this trip and you!" she wrote him on a note, but what good is there in longing for someone?

Indeed what, the thought crossed his mind, but wasn't uttered aloud.

Once, Nawang decided to call her, and when he finally was answered, there was so much shouting he was sorry he had called at all. "Are you crazy?" she yelled at him, "Do you know what time it is here?" All of a sudden, she couldn't remem-ber anything they had done together here, it had all been wiped from her memory. And so he began to understand, before it would be too late, those things are only good for the summer, because those female tourists are like birds, they come before July-August and after that they have another life. Say the name Nawang to them on the phone and they'll say what Nawang, they don't know any Nawang, what kind of a name is Nawang.

"What's your name?" he asked, and Amnon replied.

"What kind of name is Nonny?" Nawang said.

The two tourists he had sent to the restaurant could be seen squashing their noses on the windowpane and peering in, and Nawang signaled to them it was still closed.

"My grandfather," he said, "was fond of your grandfather. He once said, I don't know why that Russian came here but he helped me, and so I'll help him. Take heed children, never forget someone who helps you, only forget those who do you wrong otherwise it will make it worse for you. Not that he himself behaved that way. In the end, they put the blame on him and he was so angry with the doctor that he never forget his wrong doing. The blame fell on him because they didn't believe a doctor would do such a thing! They said it must have been an Indian, and afterward said that even if the doctor had been responsible for some nonsense, he had treated everyone here so well that he should be forgiven; after all, he even treated the Italian."

"The Italian?"

A strange story began, whose connection to the matter wasn't clear, and at its heart was the doctor's ex-wife who had married the Italian, and more than he heard about her part in this affair he heard about McKenzie's collar. It transpired that in the commissioner's house someone who had come from Italy related what had happened in Rome when the swindle was exposed (the servants also heard, and from them things were passed onward): a scandal arose, and Magnani – that was the Italian's name – resigned from all his posts, and one afternoon when his wife returned home and saw only his twitching legs, she who no one in Rome believed would be capable of such a deed, hugged his legs and held him like that for hours until their son returned and helped to bring him down.

The day after it had been spoken about in the commissioner's house, or a week later, it makes no difference, everyone saw the doctor with his face and hands battered and injured, and what did he say? He had been trying to hang a picture and fell from the chair, he even mentioned which picture, of the mountains, and when he was asked why he was wearing a high collar in the peak of summer he explained that he had a rash on his neck.

"And they believed him," Nawang said, "about the picture and also about the collar! And what better proof is there that he was guilty? After all, everyone can manage punishment very well by himself, you said so yourself."

"And what about hope?" Amnon asked.

"People simply want to live," Nawang replied, "who doesn't want that?" And he also went into detail, mentioning in the same breath the priest who recovered after his wife's death and Inspector Tendon who recovered after his parrot disappeared. "And me too," he said, "after being shouted at that way on the phone," – he was speaking again of the American girl from Hazelwood, Missouri – "in the end I said to myself, Nawang, take a look outside and see what a beautiful day it is and how many worthy girls there are here, it's all in your own hands. Did all this help you with anything?"

He hesitated and the silence lengthened.

"Was it worth coming all the way? Leaving home, your wife and children? To long for something so much?"

The movement of his head could be explained this or that way, and he already knew that he would continue to travel.

9

This long way – long in terms of this region and very short in terms of the Indian subcontinent – he preferred to make alone; he didn't want to hire a jeep, nor for Nawang to drive him, and when the Ladakhi expressed surprise at that, since he wouldn't even have to pay for petrol since the army vouchers he'd give him would suffice, he gave an evasive answer. Unlike the usual Indian buses, it wasn't laden, squashed or noisy. There weren't dozens of people sitting on the roof, no goat was bleating in the aisle, there was only one chicken that crowed but the sound was deafened by the growl of the motor and the rattling of the seats and the windows.

Only at the beginning of the journey was there anyone who showed any interest in him, but they didn't barrage him with questions: what country is he from, how old is he, what is his work, how many children does he have, and how is he enjoying India. He had another hope when he boarded, that no young Israelis would be travelling with him and that he wouldn't have to use the same lie he had made up in Delhi, and that hope was also not disappointed. No Israeli had boarded, and the only tourists on the bus other than him were a French couple who attempted to befriend their neighbors in front and behind. With the French that he remembered from high school, he understood the woman was hoping one of the passengers would invite them to their home and in that way they would experience a real Ladakhi evening, because they had had enough of all the play-acting for tourists.

In the rattling window, the peaks moved backward, and his gaze lowered to the sides of the road and to the slopes below, and not infrequently it seemed that one tiny deviation from the flawed asphalt curb would be enough for the bus to roll down into the chasm where it wouldn't be stopped by any rock or any tree. He did not for a moment regret his decision not to be helped by Nawang and one of his jeeps; he wanted to make this journey alone, without being bothered with any mechanical problems. More than twenty years had passed since he travelled on the winding roads of northern Norway in his rickety van, and he didn't want to replace it with a jeep: not a Tata, not a Mahindra, not a Ford.

The day before, when he returned from the travel agency to the hotel, the regular group was sitting in the yard, and before they noticed him, he stopped in his tracks; he didn't want to be asked again about his son who had apparently disappeared here. The Italian hairdresser – he heard her voice clearly – told of how she had sent her son to England to learn English, yes, he's in England and she's here, because only here with the Lamas can she become cleansed. "Can I tell you something, honey?" the Austrian woman said to her. "It's not that I don't respect them, but you shouldn't paint too rosy a picture of them." She certainly had something to say about the monk who stayed with them in April and one night found the cassettes Stefan hides in the cupboard.

"Don't listen to her," the Canadian woman turned to the Israeli girl and asked about her boyfriend: they're like a couple of lovebirds, where is he now? "He's resting," the girl answered. They simply had a terribly tiring day, the trip to Choglamsar didn't do him much good, and after that Ido just wanted to sleep.

"I heard they're doing wonders in that Mahabodhi Center," the Canadian woman said, and a while passed until the girl replied. "It's true," she said, "it's just that seeing so many refugee children can also be terribly sad." Yes, it was wasn't at all easy for them, but they'll go back, they've already decided that.

"As far as I know," the Austrian woman said, "there's no shortage of refugees where you come from, so of all places he comes here to volunteer? Don't you think it's's kind of funny?"

"No," the girl replied, "it's not at all funny."

He turned his eyes to the second floor and looked for the window of their room: it was shut, unlike the past time that he had looked there.

"Do you know what would make Alain and Juliette happy?" said the Frenchwoman who was sitting on one of the two seats in front of him.

"No," replied her husband.

"If something were to happen to us, afterward they could tell how they warned us not to travel here and how we didn't listen to them; who doesn't know that Indians drive like maniacs?"

The same thought that had previously entered his mind returned, and details were added to it: if he himself were to roll down this slope, it would be better with a backpack that would pad him and save his spine from being injured. And if his face would be injured, even beyond recognition, it might be better that way: beyond recognition It was, of course, an immature thought: a man can escape from everyone he knows, sometimes even from the police who could identify him, but not from his own eyes.

He glanced at the aisle to make sure his backpack was still there, and the Ladakhi sitting next to him looked there too and said: "Good bag, very good," and he also said: "Good bag, very good," and he remembered how in the shop where it was bought, a bearded man lectured a group of youngsters sitting around him about the wonders and dangers of India, and with the same seriousness emphasized the importance of a backpack and sleeping bag zipper, and at the time he wondered if those youngsters saw him as an adventurer who had already crossed five continents and whose life experience they could never compete with.

"Where you go?" asked the Ladakhi, and when he said the name of the place, Khaspang, and the French couple fell silent, for a moment he feared they might decide to join him, but right away they renewed their conversation.

"I would also speak about them that way," the man said, "if some lion devoured them in Africa."

"The worst," said his wife, "are actually the hippopotamuses." In a program she had seen on National Geographic they were said to be most lethal, even more so than lions and crocodiles – who would have believed it! That funny animal that children are mad about; Jean had a hippo that he wouldn't part with, he slept with him in bed at night.

"Well, now he has something else to sleep with," her husband said.

There were a few stops on the bus's route, and he was hoping the French couple would get off before him; apart from them, there were no other tourists. His neighbor on the seat had apparently come to Leh to shop, or perhaps had sold something in Leh; or perhaps was in need of some bureaucratic matter or had been hospitalized in the mission hospital like his grandfather in his time.

Why had his grandfather been hospitalized? It was possible he had lost fluids in the desert and become dehydrated, or before that had been frostbitten in the mountains; travel diaries from that period mention many lost their toes that way, there were also those whose lower legs had to be amputated to stop the gangrene. But he rolled down the slope whole – again it was pictured in his eyes when the bus drew nearer to the curb of the road – he rolled down and perhaps tried to hold onto some shrub, and the shrub was uprooted and remained in his hand far down below, and he turned over together with it, being hit and continued downward, crushing ants with his body, causing lizards to flee and one to shed its tail, and must have needed the final blow at the bottom. Had his pony really stumbled, or had he decided to roll off its back far down below? Who could know about that, and what difference would the answer make?

"In that orange robe of his," the Frenchman said, "that young monk was mainly interested how well he would come out in the photograph." He was speaking about some Buddhist ceremony that had taken place for tourists, but he was even more disappointed in the priest of Ladakh: one would have expected, he said, that they would have sent a more esteemed man to such a remote place, a man who would know how to deal with the local beliefs; after all, Lamaism is filled with much nonsense, and instead what do they find, someone more interested in Barca than the Sagrada Familia. If they were to tell that to Alain and Juliette, they simply wouldn't believe them!

"As for them, only if we rolled down there" – the Frenchwoman looked outside to the chasm that opened wide beneath them and her husband turned his gaze there as well – "would they be happy."

His grandfather must have rolled down from a height of dozens or hundreds of meters, and the thought of that in a bus whose wheels were too close to the battered curb of the road was made more and more real as it continued to ascend the incline of the mountain. Whether the pony had remained at the top or whether it had slipped until it was blocked by some rock, his grandfather must certainly have rolled down: his face struck by small stones, scratched and cut, his skull beaten and injured, his forehead bleeding, his chin bleeding, his teeth stuck into his lips if they hadn't been crushed before that, his ribs broken, his testicles squashed (his fucked-up balls from which his father had come and in fact he too). For a moment, since he had never seen him, not even in a photograph, his face was substituted by the face of his other grandfather, his mother's father, a religious Jew who had managed to get his family out of Poland in time, and now his yellowish-white beard was being dirtied here with earth and with blood.

When that grandfather died, his parents didn't take him to the funeral because they thought he was too young, and he still remembered how his mother returned from there with her clothing rent and said to him: "Come Nonny, come to me," and he was surprised because she didn't often embrace him, and when she pulled him toward her he smelt through the perfume the scent of the place to which his grandfather had gone, a dark appealing scent, like that of flowers that cast a spell on bees and lock their petals over them.

And now his mother was also rolling down there, on her way far down below into the distance on the hospital bed and the mattress against bedsores together with the monitors watching her breathing and the beats of her heart and his father after her, his father who came to visit her daily despite her not recognizing him or anything else, and after his father he himself will also roll down with the backpack which at the moment is placed in the aisle: yes, their whole failed, disloyal, lying dynasty would roll down: his grandfather had lied to antiquity buyers, he himself is lying here, his mother lied to his father for most of their married years, and his father, even if he hadn't lied to anyone in the world, lied to himself all his life. Know from where you have come, he said to himself, know from where and from whom.

The ascent did not lessen, and it was a wonder the rattling motor of the bus could make it and that its noise didn't disturb any of the passengers: there were those who slept, those whose voices overpowered it, and those who listened to the driver's large transistor and the rhythm that was mainly coming from it. When had he crossed distances such as these by bus, perhaps on annual school trips, and how far away they now seemed, the boy he had been was also far away; in the youth movement they had crossed distances like this in a small truck, and in the army they had also travelled in trucks (no, he thought, no: you travelled in a command car, have you forgotten? And the command car overturned, have you forgotten? And afterward you reached the sea, you surely remember that).

"Almost two tons," the Frenchwoman said, "and when a thing like that runs after you at the speed of forty kilometers an hour, what would you do?"

She had been amazed by female hippopotamuses: their pregnancies went on for eight months, almost like humans! One in the Indiana Zoo lived to the age of sixty – Donna was her name, and in the end poor Donna died of arthritis. "Sixty," she said, "can you imagine that, Robert?"

"But we've still got our health," her husband said.

Perhaps his grandfather's head hit a rock and he reached the bottom unconscious, bleeding, and there at the bottom of the chasm, lay motionless and waited for his death, perhaps he didn't even remember he had taken his pistol with him. The more he thought of that picture, the more details were added to it: the paralyzed back on the ground, the gaze lifted up to the edge of the slope and the bend in the path from where he had rolled down – accidentally or purposely and exactly at the spot he chose – and perhaps he lifted up his weary gaze to the sky above him, a light blue clear sky like the one seen from the bus window, or to the clouds floating in it or to someone making his way toward him, buoyant and heavy at once, in order to take his life.

But death doesn't come that way, nor equipped with a sickle, but rises up from within when the great relinquishment occurs; and how easy it is to accede to it when the spice of life has run out. Had his grandfather intended to seclude himself in the cave unto the death? At first, he thought he might have come to look for more paper for another fraud since the first had succeeded so well, at least at its start, but Nawang didn't think so. "He didn't come to take anything," he said, "and in the end he didn't reach there at all. Does all this make any difference to you?"

"No," he replied.

Today there are those who make do with a closed building in the monastery courtyard – so it was written in the Lonely Planet – and only a few still fulfill the oath of seclusion in all its severity, they see no one and no one sees them: all the rest probably chat with whoever brings them food and water, listen to the bustle of the monastery; perhaps also answer all those who ask their advice on some matter or other, perhaps even about the next match between Barca and Real. Their seclusion is comfortable, it needs no walls; that's how he himself had felt for one month in his youth. and that whole month he didn't talk to anyone except the owner of a garage in Trondheim or in Hammerfest when he stopped to fix an oil leak and outside the gulls were shrieking and flying at the height of his head as if urging him to speak, and at the sides of streets drunks swayed and called out to him in Norwegian and he didn't answer, and onward in the distance, the North Sea awaited him, and no ship could be seen in it, not a sail not a mast not an oar, and he had no reason yet for that isolation.

And in the house he rented in the small town he stayed in after the war, he also lived in total solitude for quite some time, and in the evenings he lay opposite the small television screen whose height was that of the bottles of white wine he emptied while staring at the changing programs, and one evening a woman came to him to persuade him to return with her to the city and the company of people, and tried over and over to find out why he was living like that; surely he can't be enjoying it? As to the war, well, she has friends who took part in the toughest battles, with people being killed a meter away from them and now you can hardly see anything of that in them, so what happened to him?

"Nothing happened," he replied, and indeed he had not taken part in any bloody battle, on the contrary, everything had been washed away in the water.

Were they travelling to the Golan Heights or to Mt. Hermon then? The road continued to ascend up and up, and the Indian bus groaned. No, the Golan Heights and Mt. Hermon hadn't been conquered at the time; they may have been travelling to Jerusalem to see the snow, despite that it was melting quickly and only remained on the ground for a few hours, not like these peaks here. This snow is everlasting; eternity is granted here to what is temporary by nature.

"A yak in Ladakh," they said in front of him.

Before that, the French couple were recalling their first trip to the east: a beach in Ceylon, Hikkaduwa or Hikkabua (it was difficult to hear), of which it's said is the most beautiful in the world; and Pushkar in Rajasthan, where they met a camel owner who promised them one of his camels if they'd invest a little money in his business, and they were almost tempted.

"A yak in Ladakh," the Frenchman said, "it even sounds better than a camel in Rajasthan."

"Forty years have passed," the woman said, "can you imagine, Robert?"

"And we've still got our health," the husband said again.

On that trip to Jerusalem, he couldn't take his eyes off one of the girls who sat in front of him; she wasn't the classroom queen but her deputy who had also come for youth movement activities, and in one of them, at the end of winter, when they took their sweaters off and placed them on the barred windowsill before going inside, he wrapped the sleeve of his sweater around her sweater so that she'd see them embracing that way when she came out – he, Amnon, was that boy. And in the stairwell of a building on Ibn Gvirol street he stood in the dark with a girl, soft and warm and breathing heavily, and they both stopped what they were doing each time the light went on and one of the neighbors went out or came back – he, Amnon, was that boy; and on a narrow bed in the student dorms he fell asleep in his clothes, stunned by white wine, and heard the owner of the bed telling her roommate what he had said in his drunkenness and how terrible and sad it was – he, Amnon was that young man ("a murderer," her friend said); and in a Berlin hotel renting rooms by the hour, a woman said scheisse about him and was completely right; and in their rented home, Naomi said the same thing in Hebrew, actually in Arabic – he, Amnon, was that man.

"In Kathmandu," the man said, "they used to light fires in front of the shops so that one could see something, do you remember that?"

"I still remember how one morning we went out of the hotel and suddenly saw four strands of wool each of a different color, pulled from the edge of the street and an old man sitting and weaving."

"He wasn't that old," her husband said, "he just seemed like that to us. We were kids."

Then they both fell silent, and from the other end of the bus, the driver's large transistor was playing some frenetic Indian song: a man was singing in a nasal voice and three women answered him, perhaps dancing at the same time, or so it sounded from the rhythm. From bend to bend, the bus continued to climb the slope of the mountain, and for a while it seemed they would surmount the clouds with that strenuous perpetual rattling, if the engine didn't die out on the way and if the wheels didn't veer to the side for some reason; a puncture would also be enough. The driver changed gear again, but the engine strained as before with all its pistons and valves, it groaned and gurgled and exhaled, and it appeared that no one other than him was worried; all those seated in front of him seemed to be immersed in their own affairs.

Then from the depths of his mind, from some remote corner like the place to where he was travelling, he recalled the song they used to sing to the bus driver in his childhood, their tender united voices becoming hoarse; the melody was borrowed from a French children's song addressed to a monk ("Brother Jacques, Brother Jacques, are you sleeping? Are you sleeping?") and was completely distorted by them into: "Our brother the driver, our brother the driver, drive fast, drive fast"); they were seated in pairs, at the head sat the teacher with the good girl pupils, while on the bench at the back the naughty boys of the class huddled and threw peeled peanuts at the those sitting in front of them, and he too added his voice to the singing in which all the voices united as one, gentle and violent at the same time:

"If you speed, you'll be stopped by a cop

If you're slow, you'll be dead with one blow

That song left no escape between detention and death, but they sang it with enormous joy.

10

And this is how the gods will return: at first the tips of the masts will be seen on the horizon, no larger than dots, than stakes, than poles, no eye could ascertain what they are until the sails would be revealed, from the upper to the lower, three to each mast and all of them billowed. The roar of the sea would not be heard yet, but in a short while it would be spread in front of the ships like a rug. In a moment their bows would be visible above the horizon and at their ends statues of women whose bodies lean forward, and around them gulls whose cries echo those of the masses who have been waiting thousands of years for their gods. Hordes would gather on the salt line, men and women and children, their shells pressed closely to their ears to hear the rumble of the sea and the word of God – it would be inconceivable that they not return, having been so long awaited.

No, he thought. They will not return, and they did not sail, and they had never existed.

A long way down below him there was only a small spring water pool, and rings spread over it when the monk scrabbled around the mud with the tip of a rod he held in his hand, and for a while the large black dzo standing on the other side of the spring seemed to be trying to swallow his reflection by lapping the water.

Even from this place at the height of the slope – some tens of meters above the spring – the sound of the lapping, the swishing, the trickling, could be well heard, because apart from them everything was silent from the bottom of the chasm to the peak behind it, and the moment the monk completed his actions with the mud dam, one could hear the water flowing to the canal that led to the small grazing pasture. It flowed on and on, joyous as a small herd whose fenced enclosure has suddenly been opened.

Two more animals stood in the middle of the way to the spring frozen as statues, and another pair could be seen on the opposite slope, and further down from there, the monk continued to scrabble around in the mud with his rod: he filled up one opening of the canal and cleared the entrance to another, blocked this one's water and released another's. Over an hour had passed since he led him to the isolated building at the top of the slope, opened the door for him and made certain he had no misgivings. Only afterward he returned to his work. That was the way in his childhood they had once upon a time played in puddles, trailing canals from them with the edge of a branch, damming them up with mud or a stone, sailing empty matchboxes on them with alarmed ants inside – were not all the pairs of animals in the ark alarmed the same way? They also made canals with a shoe heel and trailed them from the edge of the puddle (not with toe of the shoe; it would get wet that way, and the sock as well). Here the monks were doing just that, like everyone else who worked a plot of land in this region and trailed spring or snow water to it. There was certainly no lack of snow here, in the winter this slope must have been covered with snow down to the bottom.

He also remembered this sight: how he would dig in the sand on the beach, delving farther and farther until the bottom would become damp and water would be discovered in it, and that formless and charmless pit had far more magic to it than castles studded with seashells or stalactite towers – in that way he, little Amnon, was helping the sea to expand its boundaries; he could have been swallowed by the pit up to his navel, his shoulders, the top of his head, and his mother, spread out on a large towel, wouldn't have noticed he had disappeared.

The monk opened another irrigation canal down below: clods of earth were enough to block some canals and others were blocked with large stones, and in that silence, from the place where he stood tens of meters above, the sound of the spade digging could be heard (the monk was now holding a spade in his hand). The sound of water flowing was soon heard: a trickle, a flow, a running stream.

Mounds of sheaves could be seen here and there in the harvested part of the field, and on the fence of unchiseled stones, flattened clods of yak and dzo dung had been stuck and were drying in the sun, and not far from them, at the sides of the path, pieces of turnips placed on sack sheeting to dry could be seen. Pieces like that could also be seen when he went up to this building in which he would either pass this night or not, and since they resembled pieces of apple, he tasted one of them and right way spat it out. Spit, he thought, why not. Spit and spit and spit until you are completely emptied.

On the next slope a large dzo rubbed its neck against a rock and then its shoulders as well; it surrendered itself to the scratching and it seemed any moment it would lie on its back and wriggle self-indulgently, the way Albi used to do on the carpet in their home, but it would be better if he banished that sight from his head immediately. The two pairs of animals perhaps weighed as much as one hippopotamus, but it bothered him to think of even one chasing after you, though they certainly wouldn't reach this isolated building at the top of the slope ("You'll have as much quiet as you want," the monk said, "that's to say except for what you have here," and with the tips of his fingers he patted himself on his shaven temples signaling what lay between them). At first, he had intended to reach the cave, until he was told he would only see the wall of mud bricks at its entrance; and anyway, his grandfather also hadn't reached it.

From one of the hidden crevices the sounds of partridges could be heard, and

some time passed until they became visible to him, and he remembered what he
had heard about them: how they would come every morning and knock on the
window with their beaks in order that the monk, during the period of his seclusion, would open it and throw them crumbs. The monk had other stories from
that period: one about a family of rabbits that used to play not far from his window
and on the small tail of each one was a white spot which he learned to identify
and then gave them names; there was joy in the foreign becoming the familiar ("I
used to wait for them," he said). It was a comfortable seclusion, close to the gompa
and with a window overlooking the entire expanse below him, but the monk took
pride in the months that he lived here, as if he had been one of the holy men from
the past who secluded themselves their whole lives in a dark cave.

Enlightenment was something the monk hadn't achieved, he hadn't gone that
far, but he hadn't forgotten the day he saw Lake Tsomoriri frozen over – it was only
afterward that he chose monkhood. He slept for a whole week on the bank of the
lake and every morning thin pieces of ice could be seen on the surface of the water,
at first only near the banks and afterward farther on as well, and the snow that fell
at night was heaped up on the scales of ice and turned them white, and one morning when he awoke, no motion could be seen from bank to bank, because a transparent cloak of ice covered the entire surface of the lake, and it seemed to him that
not only had the water frozen but he himself, and that if he tried to move his hands
and feet and eyelids he wouldn't succeed. And within that paralysis not only was
the power of nature then revealed to him ("What are we, by comparison?" he said)
but also the workings of time that did not stop, on the contrary, it replaced season
with season as it had done a million times in the past and will do another million
times in the future – without him.

"I became more humble," the monk said. "But why have you come here?"

In a severed Gillette deodorant can in his room, incense sticks were burning and dispersing their scent, and on a rough wooden shelf, probably a board
that had been dismantled from a crate, stood three butter statuettes that had been
sculpted by an unskilled hand, most probably that of the monk, their eyes decorated by a curved red line around them and their gazes blank, but they had an
innocent charm, and he already knew what they were and what their purpose was.

"They're called tormas," the German woman said to him on their first night, when
he saw some like them on the nightstand in her hotel room, and she explained to
him that on the Buddhist New Year those statuettes are thrown into a fire with all
the sins of their owners. And after she pushed him off her once more – again and
again he had tried to do what she had forbidden him – he had a concrete suggestion: why doesn't she consent to him and repent for everything with the aid of the
butter statuettes?

Quietly but adamantly, she repeated her refusal the following night, despite
her body expressing something else entirely; she said under no circumstance

would she do to another woman what had been done to her, under no circumstance! How could he do such a thing? He had seemed to her before – so she said
– a good person. They lay reclined on the bed, a man and woman who were not
young and behaving like a boy and a girl still being stopped by a prohibition that
is not to be breached.

"Well, I'm not," he replied to her, and made some stupid joke concerning her
name, Angela, and in order not to leave any doubt he said that she could stop
worrying about the wholeness of his family: he has no family, he once did but it fell
apart, he caused it to fall apart; and he doesn't have any children nor will he have,
and therefore none of them had disappeared.

The expression on her face changed and her long body recoiled from his, and
in vain he tried to explain to her how he had encountered a group of bothersome
young Israelis in the old quarter of Delhi who wouldn't leave him alone, and how
that lie was born only to be rid of them and their questions and how it had unintentionally stuck to him and again escaped from his lips before he managed to
reflect on it, and even here in Leh it was hard to get rid of; with her as well.

She moved further away from him on the bed and addressed her question to
the low ceiling because she could no longer bear the sight of his face. "And what
you told me about Udi" – she still remembered his name whose sound so resembled that of her nephew – "did that happen?" He nodded his head and the flame
of the scented candle caused shadows to move in the room; after all, what he told
her really had happened.

"And how he almost drowned in the sea?" he nodded again, but this time his
nodding was hesitant; true, he had carried a small boy in his hands to the shore
and had been careful to avoid the rocks and the pits on the seabed, but the ending
had been completely different.

"What kind of person are you?" she said, and for a moment he thought he
might be complimented for his attempt to arouse her interest and that finally
she would allow herself what she had had previously denied herself, but her face
showed all her years and bitter disappointments. She pulled the sheet up slowly
with both hands, first to her hips that had never broadened from giving birth,
afterward to her breasts that had never nursed a baby, and from there to her neck
whose skin had already begun to wrinkle. "Go now," she said, "I don't want to see
you anymore," and from the nightstand, the butter statuettes watched him like a
silent audience, ridiculous and accusatory at once.

An improper thought passed through his mind as he left, indecent and
arousing; for a moment he pictured what Brando did to Maria Schneider in *Last
Tango in Paris*, and another passed, completely different to the previous one; what
Brando did to himself from the high balcony, and he banished both of them from
his head. He walked back to his hotel in the middle of the night and lay down on
his bed without turning on the light, and instead of his conscience weighing upon
him about the lies he had told her, he saw a different nakedness in the dark. He

saw those full curves and their softness and their warmth and their movement
as she breathes heavily and completely surrenders herself on the bed, not to him
but to pleasure itself until she is satisfied; the sight was arousing and hopeless and
incurably painful, and he then surrendered to the darkness of the hotel room and
the sunken mattress and the palm of his hand like when he was a boy, and the bed
groaned along with him.

You're no Brando, he said to himself. No-no, far from it. But perhaps you'll
yet be.

Naomi was much bolder than him, and not only because she had broken up a
family; what did he have to break up? She once stopped the elevator between two
floors of a tower block whose penthouse she designed; there were two large packages of gigantic ceramic tiles there (Pau Santo 80x80) and she said: "Pau Santo can
wait a while," and sat on one of them in her slight dress and pulled him toward
her, and when they entered the apartment he feared the building contractor from
Sakhnin[40] would smell her scent on his tiles. She enjoyed displaying her femininity
in front of his workers: she went into the bathroom where they were busy with the
tiles, and to show them what happens when someone showers in the place designated in the original plan, she stood there and lifted her hands to her hair as if she
was washing it and stayed like that for a while and then rubbed her shoulder slowly
as if soaping herself – the whole street could see that! – and he saw their eyes and
how much pleasure their looks gave her.

During her telephone conversations to the English village, she tried to remind
him something of that: she spoke about the shortage of Pau Santo 80x80 tiles
and about the contractor in Ramallah who can get them from someone who also
imports marble for kitchens and gravestones ("I'll order one for us," she said, "for
the life we had"); about Albi who doesn't have to leave their room at night, because
he used to leave every time they made love; about the neighbor opposite who has
just built a magnificent treehouse for the grandchildren in the mulberry tree in his
yard, nothing like what he, Amnon, had built for Udi.

Even from the distance of tens of meters, the lapping of the dzo from the spring
could be heard in the silence (the monk was no longer to be seen; perhaps he had
returned to the monastery), and the sound was so clear it seemed if the other dzo
would lift his tail that too would be heard. But it only moved a little and right away
became calm and froze again in a royal pose among the leaves and the silence
returned, whole and absolute, the kind that if a wind arose and caused a ripple in
the water of the canals, not only would the rustling of a dry leaf be heard but also
the sigh of relief of an ant sailing on it. Had not billions of people believed in one
who had the power to hear even an ant from the heavens? (Those that had been
sailed in matchboxes were must have been seasick; he and his friends stirred up

the water around them in order to study just how much they clung to their miniscule lives.)

There were other living creatures in the building; he discovered that a short
while after entering. Owing to the absence of retreaters it apparently was serving
as a temporary storage room for surplus foods, or perhaps the contrary, there were
so many retreaters here, the provisions were meant for them. On the food shelves
he could see small heaps of flour, rice, salt and sugar mixed with mice droppings,
possibly caused by the period of time during which no one had stayed here or the
negligence of the tenants, maybe tourists who had stayed here for a night or two.
What are mouse droppings to someone facing eternity or total nothingness?

The flour was stored in a square tin container, and when he moved it to make
room for his backpack, the curved lid of the tin moved as well and from inside
a little mouse visiting there returned him a startled gaze, and its floury whiskers
quivered. At the sight of it he wondered for a moment, perhaps the way prisoners
in solitary confinement wonder, if that tiny creature will prove to be company for
him throughout the coming hours and if he'll open his heart to it, a heart with guilt
("You've got nothing there, nothing!" she said to him before he left and afterward
as well), not for the death of the ants he had drowned, to hell with the ants. There
was a small burner in the corner of the room and on it was a sooty pot and alongside it a small gas balloon, and when he tried to move it, he realized it was empty,
and so even had he wanted to turn the tap on and let the gas flow, perhaps even
disconnect the rubber tube leading from it or put the end into his mouth – but why
should he do such a thing, why should he put the end into his mouth and suckle
from it? – he would have failed miserably.

Brando took the gum he was chewing out his mouth and stuck it to the railing
of the balcony before he jumped.

Had his grandfather come here – had he not rolled down the slope – he
certainly wouldn't have behaved like the Italian. If indeed he had been a terrorist, as his father thought, he wouldn't have chosen the same death he would have
been sentenced to in Russia, he definitely would have substituted the hanging with
a different death. And had Amnon himself found a suitable rope and a hook and
a chair as well as the courage, and had Naomi found him, would she hug his legs
and hold him for hours until one of her sons returned? No, he thought: she would
have hung onto him as the hangmen in Russia did when the sentenced men's
bodyweight was insufficient for breaking their necks. And while pondering that,
instead of being horrified he felt her breasts pressing against him and his erection
rubbing up against her, the final erection that hanged men are said to have.

The ceiling was low enough to hang from and grey from soot like the walls,
and the floor looked filthy as if it had never been washed, and perhaps it never had
been, though in winter a fire from yak and dzo droppings must have been lit there.
In the corner that was designated for sleeping, on a hairy rug whose color was the
color of the floor, rough blankets were spread out and on them was the fur of a yak

that emitted a pungent animal smell, and when his gaze fell on these bedclothes he wondered if he would sleep here and answered himself: of course here, where else if not here, and he didn't know yet how cold it would be at night.

Two dirty tin plates were in the alcove of the window, and he wondered who had eaten there and in what condition they had left here: erect or hunched, on their feet or on a stretcher. Or perhaps there had not been a stretcher and they had been wrapped in one of these blankets and carried outside? His old father ("My father," a voice said inside him), more than death, had been daunted by the thought of the moment when the body, his body, would be unloaded from the black stretcher into the pit like a heap of garbage,[41] and at Ada's funeral he turned his eyes away; in the pit, two men from the Jewish Burial Society stood and placed large concrete tiles on top of Ada, and suddenly from the pocket of one of them a joyful tune played from his cell phone, and he hoped that his father, whose hearing had become poor, hadn't heard it. "Do you remember how we used to dig in the sand together?" he suddenly asked as if he had been struck by dementia, and Amnon couldn't understand why he was reminded of that digging at the seashore; what had that to do with this pit into which his mother had been unloaded?

The door, like the window, was small, the windowpane was murky and probably had never been cleaned – when he stood outside he tried to peer in through it and almost couldn't see a thing – and the wooden shutter was closed with a wooden beam attached by a nail, and in a short while he would have to shut it as well as the door from the cold since he hasn't any warm clothing with him, and the sleeping bag isn't made for temperatures like these. At an altitude of over four thousand meters above sea level, they can plunge below zero at night, and even four or five degrees are enough to freeze the blood if you aren't bundled up as is necessary or if you've chosen to surrender to the cold.

Far away from there, in a rented house in a small sleepy town, they must be sitting and watching television with the dog and the cat, and if her eldest son is there he's probably stretched out on the Ikea couch they bought together, and her little son is sitting on the large armchair that had once been his armchair, and when she looks at the two of them, he, Amnon, isn't missed, and why should be missed? For a moment he saw his father sitting in an armchair, and the carpet threadbare in the place where he puts his feet and getting up is already hard for him; and if he stumbles on the edge of the carpet and falls there'll be no chasm there, but the fall will have the same result.

What kind of person are you, he said to himself, to get up and leave everyone? And not for some European capital, but for this backwater of backwaters, and what did you think would happen to you here, enlightenment? The only thing revealed to you here is a little mouse peering at you from a tin of flour, hello little mouse. What's it like living in your food and also shitting in it, what's it like turning white from flour, doesn't it make you sneeze, little mouse? Actually, perhaps there's not

---

41 In Israel it is customary for the dead to be buried shrouded but without a coffin.

such a big difference between your tin and this room and between this room and the world.

In his youth he had slept in all sorts of places and if he falls asleep in this cold perhaps the soles of his feet will freeze, he almost can't feel them already. And in the house he left they'll carry on watching some trivia quiz, and the two boys will compete with each other with the answers, and she'll be impressed by them both. They came to him preprepared and with time they got to know each other and to respect what was fitting to be respected and also to adapt to each other's weaknesses and like each other nonetheless, and he got up and left them all without even informing them of his intention, but rather let her do that. "He won't be here anymore to help you," she said to her son when she saw him helping Udi with his lessons, and he mumbled something about an article he had to prepare for the newspaper, a long article about all sorts of things that happened abroad and in order to write it he had to make inquiries abroad and they simply take time.

"A while?" she said from the passage.

She also told the eldest, and when he tried again to cling to the journalistic explanation she interrupted him, and he was left with only a garbled answer about a motorcar that would be left for the eldest and driving lessons that would be paid from the money meant for soundproofing. It was, of course, a silly statement – if the soundproofing designed to dull the sounds of his electric guitar would not be done, it meant he wasn't intending to return. Afterward there were a few evenings when the subject wasn't raised and for a while it seemed that the previous routine was continuing, and he wondered what she said to her sons in his absence and what they said. Perhaps they were unified in their opinion of him.

"You two stop arguing the whole time," she would say to them, "it's not nice, you're brothers," but for the most part she was very proud of them both and liked to walk in the street with them, one on her right and one on her left, and Albie running in front and every now and then turning his head towards them to make sure they were behind him, ignoring the cat sticking its glorious tail up like a scepter. How redundant Amnon was in that picture.

In the early morning hour when he left, she pretended to be asleep, and beneath the blanket the curve of her familiar pelvis was rounded, and also familiar were the cascading of her hair over the pillow and the smell of sleep that had not yet dissipated, despite that they had slept only a little, and at the foot of the bed was the jumble of clothing she had taken off as if in the excitement of desire, though the only desire in her was to be swallowed beneath the blanket. For a very long time they listened to each other's breathing until they fell asleep, and an hour before the time he was supposed to awaken, the neighbor's rooster woke him with its crowing. "One day he'll swim in my soup," she often said about it, but that morning said nothing.

On one of the previous evenings, she asked what he would do without them – "You're already used to us, no?" – and also asked whether he could picture himself going back to his miserable apartment in Tel Aviv: the dirty, neglected apartment on whose mattress their dalliance had been imprinted and in whose kitchen they had eaten on the Formica table burnt by cigarettes.

In contrast to this room on the slope of the mountain, that apartment was a king's palace, but no rocky ground or hairy animals could be seen from its window, but rather a small street whose ficus leaves were gilded in the afternoon hours, and the elderly couple in the building opposite would sit on their balcony and take small sips of tea before the husband went out for his evening stroll, and if he lingered the old woman would lean on the railing and call to him like a mother to her child.

How different that couple was to his parents of whom he has no such memory, and the only picture of them when they weren't immersed in some argument is so distant it seems completely imaginary: the three of them sitting on the beach and his father digging in the sand for him after he had become tired. They were sitting far from the din of the bathers and his father's arm was swallowed in the sand almost up to his shoulder on its way to the other side of the earth – so he explained. "Now we only have to decide where in China we want to go," he said, "to Peking or to Shanghai."

"Not to Russia?" his mother asked, and his father replied: "To China, Ada. Don't you want a little panda, Ada?" And his mother turned over on the white towel and rested her chin on her hands. "Your father and his nonsense," she said, and he, Amnon the boy, thought that this time she meant well.

When he shut the door earlier than he had planned because of the cold, the room turned dark and the sounds that had risen from the bottom of the slope were muted: the lapping of the dzo, the trickling of the water in the canal. Caves have no door or window, there's only a wall of mud bricks to stop them up, but this building will meet his needs.

They equipped him with candles and matches, but the time for lighting a candle had not yet arrived, and he waited for his eyes to adjust to the darkness. For a while the room seemed like a vague block in which only the square of the dirty window shed light, until signs of the shelves, the bedclothes, the gas container and the burner began to appear – outside the night had not yet completely fallen – and he then approached the backpack that was no longer new as it had been a month before, but in the darkness the dirt that had stuck to it couldn't be seen.

In vain, Nawang had recommended that he at least take a good sleeping bag with him. "Just don't end up like your grandfather," he warned him, but he didn't want to take anything with him he would have to return, from a bag to a packet, and he still remembered how the salesperson had praised the sleeping bag he was selling as opposed to an army sleeping bag and how he extolled its zipper. "You have no idea how depressing a torn zipper is," he said, probably never having experienced anything worse than that.

From one of the outer pockets of the backpack he took out a bag of toiletries and placed it on the upper shelf and again saw the filth there, and only for a moment deliberated whether to move the bag to the window alcove but decided to leave it on the shelf.

These stages of domesticity he remembered well from his travels on missions for the newspaper; when he entered an ordinary room that had been booked for him and spread out a few of his belongings, hanging his jacket up and placing a towel over the back of the chair, perhaps a scarf on the handle of a window, so that when he'd return to the hotel room it would no longer look like a stranger's room. In Kiev he had more than one scarf, and added to them a brown fur hat his father had called a papakha during the winters when he wore one – perhaps his father imagined his own father in a hat like that on his way to some daring operation to bring down the Tsar, disguised as a wagoner or the master urging him on, as he himself dozens of years later would urge the command car driver on; and perhaps his grandfather also reached the sea – after all, St. Petersburg had a big port – and saw masses of fish floating on the water.

Did he resemble him in appearance? The dirty windowpane did not return any reflection, and no puddle had been formed outside in whose water it would be possible to be mirrored – the water continued to flow in the canals down below – and a thought entered his mind that if he went outside to urinate perhaps he would see his reflection in the yellow of the urine, and perhaps that was a fitting way to observe himself, only in the yellow of the urine; and should his organ freeze outside and turn blue and black and fall off, he had, after all, no use for it now.

"Hold me," Naomi said a few months before his trip. She was lost in an enormous railway station with many platforms, a station from which they were supposed to travel together to some city, she was late and realized that he hadn't waited for her; and in front of the ticketing office (in the dream she was standing in a long queue, despite not knowing where she had to travel to) everyone is dressed in long winter coats while she is completely naked, but at ease in her nakedness and places the palms of her hands in pockets of skin on her stomach as if in a garment, and the looks of the men are pleasing to her, and that feeling continues until the sound of a train's horn leaving the station is suddenly heard, and at once the pleasure dissipates and she knows she'll freeze to death there. "You didn't wait for me!" she said with the insult that remained from the dream, but he still was hearing with what ease she walked around naked and how pleasurable the looks of the men were to her.

Down below perhaps the monk had opened another irrigation canal – even through the closed door it seemed to him he could hear the sound of the water being released – either because it was the best time for watering or because a canal too shallow was liable to freeze over. And what will you do in the cold, dive into your sleeping bag? In the army you practiced doing push-ups and could do dozens at the time, and perhaps also could now. You had muscles then, true, not like a bodybuilder but not flabby either, and even in the years of reserve service they were kept in fair condition, and it wasn't owing to them that the boy Ali fell from your hands. Your legs stumbled in the water and everything you had whispered before then, above the small silent body you carried, was of no use, and who did you turn to then, you know very well who you suddenly turned to with all your heart and all your might, and who didn't respond.

Only once in his life he had turned to that god in the synagogue, and the argument that preceded it he hasn't forgotten, nor will he forget: his parents were sitting in the kitchen and must have thought he was asleep. "It's all a sham anyway," said his mother, despite her wanting the ceremony, and in his room he tried not to make any noise. "Don't do that to him!" his father said, and to that she replied she's only prepared to continue with this sham for her father, because it would kill him if the boy doesn't have a Bar Mitzvah; he Amnon, was that boy.

He blocked his ears with his hands in order not to hear the rest and began to hum a long piercing continuous sound like a siren to drown out their voices ("If your father," his father said, "only knew how righteous you -"), and a week later, when in the synagogue he had to read "Fear thou not, for I am with thee, be not dismayed, for I am thy God; I strengthen thee," the words were swallowed in his mouth, and when candy was thrown[42] at him he felt as if he was being stoned.

The darkness in the window now thickened, and no sound could be heard from outside. The dzo in the valley must have lain down to sleep, and the movement of the water in the canals ensured it wouldn't freeze over, and movement will help you as well if you haven't come here to freeze, sit-ups for example, bending the joints for example, jumping on the spot, running on the spot, rubbing the arms, rubbing the thighs, the calves, the cock, or thoughts of another place on another continent, across the sea, across the sea, where there are islands whose names I have forgotten. Ali, Ali, he thought, you were only five and the entire sea came to drown you.

For a moment, because he turned his head to the window, it seemed to him that sounds of prayer were rising from the monastery, vague and monotonous, but it was only the sound of the wind; perhaps it was moving the water in the canals, making small waves in it if a thin covering had not yet frozen on the surface, sailing a few dry leaves on it and swallowing their rustling with its sound.

Even through all that, the calls made to the yak during its lifetime while being spurred on could surely be heard; its back was burdened with loads, and its wool was sheared and its milk was drunk, and in its death its fur was skinned as if it had been created only for you to lie down on it now and for that fur to act as a partition between the cold of the floor and your body. And as to the chill in the air, what will act as a partition between that and you, only this thin sleeping bag with its

---

42 Customary in Israel at a Bar Mitzvah ceremony.

frozen zipper, a flimsy bag like that in which your mother was wrapped, and how to prevent the trembling of the shoulders and the arms, not from fear, from cold, and the chattering of teeth against each other, not from fear, from cold.

She had been wrapped for sending off, and at her funeral his father was dressed in clothing that had been taken from the back of the cupboard from another era, and asked the way one would ask a child and not a man of Amnon's age: "Won't she be cold like that?" And eras before that, when the three of them went to the beach during the summer and he was just a tot with a giant straw hat that shaded his entire body, he was determined to dig in the sand until water would rise from the bottom and cover the plastic blade, his hand, his elbow, and make waves there. They were sitting close to the sea, and his father went into the water wearing a loose black bathing suit that any wave could seemingly disrobe him of, and when he remained with his mother she asked him to rub suntan lotion on her back, and was already spread out on her stomach on the purple towel, the one she used to take with her when just the two of them went to the beach, and pushed the shoulder straps aside, and he, little Amnon, poured a small amount of lotion and rubbed it over her back in a circular motion as she had requested, and poured again and rubbed again and felt how warm her soft skin was, until a shadow was cast over the two of them. A stranger began to talk to her, and in order to answer him she lifted her chin from the towel and then lifted her neck as well and then raised herself a little more and still a little more and at that moment he saw some movement in the stranger's bathing suit, a blue bathing suit that began to change its form, and not only did he see that, his mother did too, and when his father came out of the water – from the corner of his eye he saw him pulling his bathing suit above his navel – the two of them were still laughing, his mother and the stranger, and only when his father drew near the stranger shot him a glance and went on his way with the swelling that had grown which was not only his but also his mother's. Amnon was certain of that even if he didn't understand what he had seen.

Is that what he remembers now, decades later, when his mother is already in the ground and his father not far from that place? And he himself is also not far from there, if he'll freeze here tonight, but he won't freeze. See, he's warmed himself from that memory, not because it was good, no, but rather because it caused the cold to be forgotten. And perhaps he'll even succeed to fall asleep here on these filthy bedclothes, enveloped by the smell of a yak; hadn't he read about a torture such as that in one of Hopkirk's books? The way they used to wrap a sentenced man in the damp skin of an animal and sew the skin tightly to his body and leave him out under the scorching sun, and when the skin dried and shrunk the sentenced man gradually suffocated in it with his cries and pleas and prayers.

But you haven't been punished, and you can rest peacefully lying down in this cold and in this silence. Listen, a trickling sound can be heard again from the spring down below, as gentle and as loud as the dripping of a tap in an apartment empty of furniture. A few dozen meters separate him and the spring and the closed door, and nevertheless the sound can be heard, at once piercing and gentle. "That's my job," the monk explained, and it was he who diverted the canals here or there, opened them or dammed them up like a child amusing himself with a puddle of water or like a god who changes the channeling of rivers.

Is he standing there now in the dark and opening the stone dams? The sound of water intensified, perhaps the wind stirred it and caused it to rise over the narrow banks; the sound of the wind could now be heard with the sound of the water, water which seemed to be rising from the canals up the slope, climbing and gradually covering its stony ground and its rocks and its few shrubs, but to do that it would have to fill the entire vast space between this slope and the opposite slope, and for that all the water of the snow, should it thaw, would not suffice. An entire sea would be necessary for it to rise farther and farther towards this isolated building.

It will rise up the slope and surge towards his door and towards his window, and will not stop there but penetrate inside through the cracks and cover the floor and the bedclothes and the body lying there, his body – in vain he'll try to wrestle with its waves when they flood this entire dark space and carry him up to the height of this shut window and to the lintel of this shut door and toward this low ceiling that will draw closer and closer to him until it will be hit by his head, his forehead, his nose, and still he'll struggle to exhale and inhale air to the lungs that are imploring for even one last iota of air, but only stinking scales penetrate the nostrils, and from some shore at a greater distance than the opposite slope they are yelling out to him now, a loud hollering, then fading, shouting in an ebbing choir, forever shouting to him: get out before it's too late.

Thanks

This work could not have been undertaken without the help of many books, especially the books and diaries of Reeve and Kathleen Heber, Peter Hopkirk, Kalam Rasul, James Herriot, Sven Hedin, Aurel Stein, Helene Norberg-Hodge, Alexandra David-Néel, Peretz Hirshbein, Michael Confino, Ze'ev Iviansky, Menachem Mendel Rosenboim, Boris Savinkov, Vera Figner, Leonid Andreyev, Yitzhak Sadeh, Ruth Baki Kolodny, Abba Ahimeir, Shmaryahu Levin, Hayim Nahman Bialik, Isaiah Bershadsky, and Eliyahu Meidanik.

It would have been lacking and much longer without out the useful comments I received during its writing from Yaron Sanderovich, Michal Arbel, Ilana Hammerman, Eli Shaltiel, Dror Burstein, Nadav Arnon, Nissim Kalderon, Liviu Carmeli, A. B. Yehoshua, and my two work colleagues Tirza Biron-Fried and Moshe Ron. A heartfelt thanks to the editor Avraham Yavin, who took the assignment upon himself, to Naomi Rivlin and Irit Lourie for their keen eyes and to everyone at the Am Oved publishing house for the heavy task I placed upon them to which they responded with their usual dedication and professionalism.

A special thanks to one who carried the load of this book with me throughout the years of my writing it, reading all the versions in development, my life partner Ayelet Shamir.

About the Author and Translator

Youval Shimoni was born in Jerusalem in 1955. He studied cinema at Tel Aviv University and first began publishing in 1990. Shimoni is a senior editor at the Am Oved Publishing House and has taught creative writing at Tel Aviv, Haifa and Bar Ilan University. He has been awarded the Bernstein Prize (2001), the Prime Minister's Prize (2005) and both the Brenner Prize (2015) and the Newman Prize (2016) for *The Salt Line*.

South African born **Michael Sharp** lives in Israel where for many years he produced music programs for Israel Radio. He has translated a non-fiction work and four novels including Youval Shimoni's *A Room*.